THE WOMAN IN WHITE
THE MOONSTONE
THE LAW AND THE LADY

WILKIE COLLINS was born in London in 1824, the elder son of a successful painter, William Collins. He left school at 17, and after an unhappy spell as a clerk in a tea broker's office, during which he wrote his first, unpublished novel, he entered Lincoln's Inn as a law student in 1846. He considered a career as a painter, but after the publication, in 1848, of his life of his father, and a novel, *Antonina*, in 1850, his future as a writer was assured. His meeting with Dickens in 1851 was perhaps the turning-point of his career. The two became collaborators, and lifelong friends. Collins contributed to Dickens's magazines *Household Words* and *All the Year Round*, and his two best-known novels, *The Woman in White* and *The Moonstone*, were first published in *All the Year Round*. Collins's private life was as complex and turbulent as his novels. He never married, but lived with a widow, Mrs Caroline Graves, from 1858 until his death. He also had three children by a younger woman, Martha Rudd, whom he kept in a separate establishment. Collins suffered from 'rheumatic gout', a form of arthritis which made him an invalid in his later years, and he became addicted to the laudanum he took to ease the pain of the illness. He died in 1889.

WILKIE COLLINS

The Woman in White

❧❦☙

The Moonstone

❧❦☙

The Law and the Lady

❧❦☙

Oxford   New York

OXFORD UNIVERSITY PRESS

1994

Oxford University Press, Walton Street, Oxford OX2 6DP

Oxford New York Toronto
Delhi Bombay Calcutta Madras Karachi
Kuala Lumpur Singapore Hong Kong Tokyo
Nairobi Dar es Salaam Cape Town
Melbourne Auckland Madrid

and associated companies in
Berlin Ibadan

Oxford is a trade mark of Oxford University Press

British Library Cataloguing in Publication Data

Data available

Library of Congress Cataloging in Publication Data
Collins, Wilkie, 1824–1889.
[Selections]
The woman in white. The moonstone. The law and the lady / Wilkie Collins.
p. cm.
1. Detective and mystery stories, English.
823'.8—dc20 PR4492 1994 93-37406
ISBN 0-19-282333-7

1 3 5 7 9 10 8 6 4 2

Typeset by Pure Tech Corporation, Pondicherry, India
Printed in Great Britain by
Clays Ltd, St Ives plc

CONTENTS

A CHRONOLOGY OF WILKIE COLLINS

1856 (Feb.) *After Dark*, a collection of short stories, published.   32
      (Mar.) *A Rogue's Life* serialized in *Household Words*.
      (Oct.) Joins staff of *Household Words* and begins collaboration with
      Dickens in *The Wreck of the Golden Mary* (Dec.).

1857 (Jan.–June) *The Dead Secret* serialized in *Household Words*, published in   33
      volume form (June).
      (6 Jan.) *The Frozen Deep* performed by Dickens's theatrical company at
      Tavistock House.
      (Aug.) *The Lighthouse* performed at the Olympic Theatre.
      (Sept.) Tours Cumberland, Lancashire, and Yorkshire with Dickens,
      their account appearing as *The Lazy Tour of Two Idle Apprentices* in
      Household Words (Oct.).
      Collaborates with Dickens on *The Perils of Certain English Prisoners*.

1858 (Oct.) *The Red Vial* produced at the Olympic Theatre; a failure.   34

1859 From this year no longer living with his mother; lives for the rest of his   35
      life (with one interlude) with Mrs Caroline Graves. (Jan.–Feb.) living
      at 124 Albany Street; (May–Dec.) Living at 2a Cavendish Street.
      (Oct.) *The Queen of Hearts*, a collection of short stories, published.
      (26 Nov.–25 Aug. 1860) *The Woman in White* serialized in *All the Year
      Round*.
      (Dec.) Moves to 12 Harley Street.

1860 (Aug.) *The Woman in White* published in volume form: a best-seller in   36
      Britain and the United States, and rapidly translated into most Euro-
      pean languages.

1861 (Jan.) Resigns from *All the Year Round*.   37

1862 (15 Mar.–17 Jan. 1863) *No Name* serialized in *All the Year Round*, published   38
      in volume form (31 Dec.).

1863 *My Miscellanies*, a collection of journalism from *Household Words* and *All   39
      the Year Round* published.

1864 (Nov.–June 1866) *Armadale* serialized in *The Cornhill*.   40
      (Dec.) Moves to 9 Melcombe Place, Dorset Square.

1866 (May) *Armadale* published in two volumes.   42
      (Oct.) *The Frozen Deep* produced at the Olympic Theatre.

1867 (Sept.) Moves to 90 Gloucester Place, Portman Square.   43
      Collaborates with Dickens on *No Thoroughfare*, published as Christmas
      Number of *All the Year Round*; dramatic version performed at the
      Adelphi Theatre (Christmas Eve).

1868 (4 Jan.–8 Aug.) *The Moonstone* serialized in *All the Year Round*; published   44
      in three volumes (July).
      (19 Mar.) Mother, Harriet Collins, dies.
      Collins forms liaison with Martha Rudd ('Mrs Dawson').
      (4 Oct.) Caroline Graves marries Joseph Charles Clow.

1869 (Mar.) *Black and White*, written in collaboration with Charles Fechter,   45
      produced at the Adelphi Theatre.
      (4 July) Daughter, Marian Dawson, born to Collins and Martha Rudd,
      at 33 Bolsover Street, Portland Place.

1870 (June) *Man and Wife* published in volume form.   46

The Woman in White

PREFACE [1860]

AN experiment is attempted in this novel, which has not (so far as I know) been hitherto tried in fiction. The story of the book is told throughout by the characters of the book. They are all placed in different positions along the chain of events; and they all take the chain up in turn, and carry it on to the end.

If the execution of this idea had led to nothing more than the attainment of mere novelty of form, I should not have claimed a moment's attention for it in this place. But the substance of the book, as well as the form, has profited by it. It has forced me to keep the story constantly moving forward; and it has afforded my characters a new opportunity of expressing themselves, through the medium of the written contributions which they are supposed to make to the progress of the narrative.

In writing these prefatory lines, I cannot prevail on myself to pass over in silence the warm welcome which my story has met with, in its periodical form, among English and American readers. In the first place, that welcome has, I hope, justified me for having accepted the serious literary responsibility of appearing in the columns of 'All The Year Round,' immediately after Mr Charles Dickens had occupied them with the most perfect work of constructive art that has ever proceeded from his pen. In the second place, by frankly acknowledging the recognition that I have obtained thus far, I provide for myself an opportunity of thanking many correspondents (to whom I am personally unknown) for the hearty encouragement I received from them while my work was in progress. Now, while the visionary men and women, among whom I have been living so long, are all leaving me, I remember very gratefully that 'Marian' and 'Laura' made such warm friends in many quarters, that I was peremptorily cautioned at a serious crisis in the story, to be careful how I treated them—that Mr Fairlie found sympathetic fellow-sufferers, who remonstrated with me for not making Christian allowance for the state of his nerves—that Sir Percival's 'secret' became sufficiently exasperating, in course of time, to be made the subject of bets (all of which I hereby declare to be 'off')—and that Count Fosco suggested metaphysical considerations to the learned in such matters (which I don't quite understand to this day), besides provoking numerous inquiries as to the living model, from which he had been really taken. I can only answer these last by confessing that many models, some living, and some dead, have 'sat' for him; and by hinting that the Count would not have been as true to nature as I have tried to make him, if the range of my search for materials had not extended, in his case as well as in others, beyond the narrow human limit which is represented by one man.

In presenting my book to a new class of readers, in its complete form, I have only to say that it has been carefully revised; and that the divisions of the chapters, and other minor matters of the same sort, have been altered here and there, with a view to smoothing and consolidating the story in its course through these volumes. If the readers who have waited until it was done, only prove to be as kind an audience as the readers who followed it through its weekly progress, 'The Woman in White' will be the most precious impersonal Woman on the list of my acquaintance.

Before I conclude, I am desirous of addressing one or two questions, of the most harmless and innocent kind, to the Critics.

In the event of this book being reviewed, I venture to ask whether it is possible to praise the writer, or to blame him, without opening the proceedings by telling his story at second-hand? As that story is written by me—with the inevitable suppressions which the periodical system of publication forces on the novelist—the telling it fills more than a thousand closely printed pages. No small portion of this space is occupied by hundreds of little 'connecting links,' of trifling value in themselves, but of the utmost importance in maintaining the smoothness, the reality, and the probability of the entire narrative. If the critic tells the story *with* these, can he do it in his allotted page, or column, as the case may be? If he tells it *without* these, is he doing a fellow-labourer in another form of Art, the justice which writers owe to one another? And lastly, if he tells it at all, in any way whatever, is he doing a service to the reader, by destroying, beforehand, two main elements in the attraction of all stories—the interest of curiosity, and the excitement of surprise?

Harley Street, London,
August 3, 1860.

PREFACE TO THE PRESENT EDITION [1861]

'THE WOMAN IN WHITE' has been received with such marked favour by a very large circle of readers, that this volume scarcely stands in need of any prefatory introduction on my part. All that it is necessary for me to say on the subject of the present edition—the first issued in a portable and popular form—may be summed up in few words.

I have endeavoured, by careful correction and revision, to make my story as worthy as I could of a continuance of the public approval. Certain technical errors which had escaped me while I was writing the book are here rectified. None of these little blemishes in the slightest degree interfered with the interest of the narrative—but it was as well to remove them at the first opportunity, out of respect to my readers; and in this edition, accordingly, they exist no more.

Some doubts having been expressed, in certain captious quarters, about the correct presentation of the legal 'points' incidental to the story, I may be permitted to mention that I spared no pains—in this instance, as in all others—to preserve myself from unintentionally misleading my readers. A solicitor of great experience in his profession most kindly and carefully guided my steps, whenever the course of the narrative led me into the labyrinth of the Law. Every doubtful question was submitted to this gentleman, before I ventured on putting pen to paper; and all the proof-sheets which referred to legal matters were corrected by his hand before the story was published. I can add, on high judicial authority, that these precautions were not taken in vain. The 'law' in this book has been discussed, since its publication, by more than one competent tribunal, and has been decided to be sound.

One word more, before I conclude, in acknowledgment of the heavy debt of gratitude which I owe to the reading public.

It is no affectation on my part to say that the success of this book has been especially welcome to me, because it implied the recognition of a literary principle which has guided me since I first addressed my readers in the character of a novelist.

I have always held the old-fashioned opinion that the primary object of a work of fiction should be to tell a story; and I have never believed that the novelist who properly performed this first condition of his art, was in danger, on that account, of neglecting the delineation of character—for this plain reason, that the effect produced by any narrative of events is essentially dependent, not on the events themselves, but on the human interest which is directly connected with them. It may be possible, in novel-writing, to present characters successfully without telling a story; but it is not possible to tell a story successfully without presenting characters: their existence, as recognisable realities, being the sole condition on which the story can be effectively told. The only narrative which can hope to lay a strong hold on the attention of readers is a narrative which interests them about men and women—for the perfectly-obvious reason that they are men and women themselves.

The reception accorded to 'The Woman in White' has practically confirmed these opinions, and has satisfied me that I may trust to them in the future. Here is a novel which has met with a very kind reception, because it is a Story; and here is a story, the interest of which—as I know by the testimony, voluntarily addressed to me, of the readers themselves—is never disconnected from the interest of character. 'Laura,' 'Miss Halcombe,' and 'Anne Catherick;' 'Count Fosco,' 'Mr Fairlie,' and 'Walter Hartright;' have made friends for me wherever they have made themselves known. I hope the time is not far distant when I may meet those friends again, and when I may try, through the medium of new characters, to awaken their interest in another story.

Harley Street, London,
February, 1861.

THE WOMAN IN WHITE

THIS is the story of what a Woman's patience can endure, and of what a Man's resolution can achieve.

If the machinery of the Law could be depended on to fathom every case of suspicion, and to conduct every process of inquiry, with moderate assistance only from the lubricating influences of oil of gold, the events which fill these pages might have claimed their share of the public attention in a Court of Justice.

But the Law is still, in certain inevitable cases, the pre-engaged servant of the long purse; and the story is left to be told, for the first time, in this place. As the Judge might once have heard it, so the Reader shall hear it now. No circumstance of importance, from the beginning to the end of the disclosure, shall be related on hearsay evidence. When the writer of these introductory lines (Walter Hartright, by name) happens to be more closely connected than others with the incidents to be recorded, he will describe them in his own person. When his experience fails, he will retire from the position of narrator; and his task will be continued, from the point at which he has left it off, by other persons who can speak to the circumstances under notice from their own knowledge, just as clearly and positively as he has spoken before them.

Thus, the story here presented will be told by more than one pen, as the story of an offence against the laws is told in Court by more than one witness—with the same object, in both cases, to present the truth always in its most direct and most intelligible aspect; and to trace the course of one complete series of events, by making the persons who have been most closely connected with them, at each successive stage, relate their own experience, word for word.

Let Walter Hartright, teacher of drawing, aged twenty-eight years, be heard first.

THE NARRATIVE OF WALTER HARTRIGHT, OF CLEMENT'S INN, LONDON

I

IT was the last day of July. The long hot summer was drawing to a close; and we, the weary pilgrims of the London pavement, were beginning to think of the cloud-shadows on the corn-fields, and the autumn breezes on the sea-shore.

For my own poor part, the fading summer left me out of health, out of spirits, and, if the truth must be told, out of money as well. During the past year, I had not managed my professional resources as carefully as usual; and my extravagance now limited me to the prospect of spending the autumn economically between my mother's cottage at Hampstead, and my own chambers in town.

The evening, I remember, was still and cloudy; the London air was at its heaviest; the distant hum of the street-traffic was at its faintest; the small pulse of the life within me and the great heart of the city around me seemed to be sinking in unison, languidly and more languidly, with the sinking sun. I roused myself from the book which I was dreaming over rather than reading, and left my chambers to meet the cool night air in the suburbs. It was one of the two evenings in every week which I was accustomed to spend with my mother and my sister. So I turned my steps northward, in the direction of Hampstead.

Events which I have yet to relate make it necessary to mention in this place that my father had been dead some years at the period of which I am now writing; and that my sister Sarah, and I, were the sole survivors of a family of five children. My father was a drawing-master before me. His exertions had made him highly successful in his profession; and his affectionate anxiety to provide for the future of those who were dependent on his labours, had impelled him, from the time of his marriage, to devote to the insuring of his life a much larger portion of his income than most men consider it necessary to set aside for that purpose. Thanks to his admirable prudence and self-denial, my mother and sister were left, after his death, as independent of the world as they had been during his lifetime. I succeeded to his connexion, and had every reason to feel grateful for the prospect that awaited me at my starting in life.

The quiet twilight was still trembling on the topmost ridges of the heath; and the view of London below me had sunk into a black gulf in the shadow of the cloudy night, when I stood before the gate of my mother's cottage. I had hardly rung the bell, before the house-door was opened violently; my worthy Italian friend, Professor Pesca, appeared in the servant's place; and darted out joyously to receive me, with a shrill foreign parody on an English cheer.

On his own account, and, I must be allowed to add, on mine also, the Professor merits the honour of a formal introduction. Accident has made him the starting-point of the strange family story which it is the purpose of these pages to unfold.

I had first become acquainted with my Italian friend by meeting him at certain great houses, where he taught his own language and I taught drawing. All I then knew of the history of his life was, that he had once held a situation in the University of Padua; that he had left Italy for political reasons (the nature of which he uniformly declined to mention to anyone); and that he had been for many years respectably established in London as a teacher of languages.

Without being actually a dwarf—for he was perfectly well-proportioned from head to foot—Pesca was, I think, the smallest human being I ever saw, out of a show-room. Remarkable anywhere, by his personal appearance, he was still further distinguished among the rank and file of mankind, by the harmless eccentricity of his character. The ruling idea of his life appeared to be, that he was bound to show his gratitude to the country which had afforded him an asylum and a means of subsistence, by doing his utmost to turn himself into an Englishman. Not content with paying the nation in general the compliment of invariably carrying an umbrella, and invariably wearing gaiters and a white hat, the Professor further aspired to become an Englishman in his habits and amusements, as well as in his personal appearance. Finding us distinguished, as a nation, by our love of athletic exercises, the little man, in the innocence of his heart, devoted himself impromptu to all our English sports and pastimes, whenever he had the opportunity of joining them; firmly persuaded that he could adopt our national amusements of the field, by an effort of will, precisely as he had adopted our national gaiters and our national white hat.

I had seen him risk his limbs blindly at a fox-hunt and in a cricket-field; and, soon afterwards, I saw him risk his life, just as blindly, in the sea at Brighton.

We had met there accidentally, and were bathing together. If we had been engaged in any exercise peculiar to my own nation, I should, of course, have looked after Pesca carefully; but, as foreigners are generally quite as well able to take care of themselves in the water as Englishmen, it never occurred to me that the art of swimming might merely add one more to the list of manly exercises which the Professor believed that he could learn impromptu. Soon after we had both struck out from shore, I stopped, finding my friend did not gain on me, and turned round to look for him. To my horror and amazement, I saw nothing between me and the beach but two little white arms, which struggled for an instant above the surface of the water, and then disappeared from view. When I dived for him, the poor little man was lying quietly coiled up at the bottom, in a hollow of shingle, looking by many degrees smaller than I had ever seen him look before. During the few minutes that elapsed while I was taking him in, the air revived him, and he ascended the steps of the machine with my assistance. With the partial recovery of his animation came the return of his wonderful delusion on the subject of swimming. As soon as his chattering teeth would let him speak, he smiled vacantly, and said he thought it must have been the Cramp.

When he had thoroughly recovered himself and had joined me on the beach, his warm Southern nature broke through all artificial English restraints, in a moment. He overwhelmed me with the wildest expressions of affection—exclaimed passionately, in his exaggerated Italian way, that he would hold his life, henceforth, at my disposal—and declared that he should never be happy again, until he had found an opportunity of proving his gratitude by rendering me some service which I might remember, on my side, to the end of my days.

I did my best to stop the torrent of his tears and protestations, by persisting in treating the whole adventure as a good subject for a joke; and succeeded at last, as I imagined, in lessening Pesca's overwhelming sense of obligation to me. Little did I think then—little did I think afterwards when our pleasant holiday had drawn to an end—that the opportunity of serving me for which my grateful companion so ardently longed, was soon to come; that he was eagerly to seize it on the instant; and that, by so doing, he was to turn the whole current of my existence into a new channel, and to alter me to myself almost past recognition.

Yet, so it was. If I had not dived for Professor Pesca, when he lay under water on his shingle bed, I should, in all human probability, never have been connected with the story which these pages will relate—I should never, perhaps, have heard even the name of the woman, who has lived in all my thoughts, who has possessed herself of all my energies, who has become the one guiding influence that now directs the purpose of my life.

II

PESCA'S face and manner, on the evening when we confronted each other at my mother's gate, were more than sufficient to inform me that something extraordinary had happened. It was quite useless, however, to ask him for an immediate explanation. I could only conjecture, while he was dragging me in by both hands, that (knowing my habits) he had come to the cottage to make sure of meeting me that night, and that he had some news to tell of an unusually agreeable kind.

We both bounced into the parlour in a highly abrupt and undignified manner. My mother sat by the open window, laughing and fanning herself. Pesca was one of her especial favourites; and his wildest eccentricities were always pardonable in her eyes. Poor dear soul! from the first moment when she found out that the little Professor was deeply and gratefully attached to her son, she opened her heart to him unreservedly, and took all his puzzling foreign peculiarities for granted, without so much as attempting to understand any one of them.

My sister Sarah, with all the advantages of youth, was, strangely enough, less pliable. She did full justice to Pesca's excellent qualities of heart; but she could not accept him implicitly, as my mother accepted him, for my sake. Her insular notions of propriety rose in perpetual revolt against Pesca's constitutional contempt for appearances; and she was always more or less undisguisedly astonished at her mother's familiarity with the eccentric little foreigner. I have observed, not only in my sister's case, but in the instances of others, that we of the young generation are nothing like so hearty and so impulsive as some of our elders. I constantly see old people flushed and excited by the prospect of some anticipated pleasure which altogether fails to ruffle the tranquillity of their serene grandchildren. Are we, I wonder, quite such genuine boys and girls now as our seniors were, in their time? Has the great advance in education taken rather too long a stride; and are we, in these modern days, just the least trifle in the world too well brought up?

Without attempting to answer those questions decisively, I may at least record that I never saw my mother and my sister together in Pesca's society, without finding my mother much the younger woman of the two. On this occasion, for example, while the old lady was laughing heartily over the boyish manner in which we tumbled into the parlour, Sarah was perturbedly picking up the broken pieces of a teacup, which the Professor had knocked off the table in his precipitate advance to meet me at the door.

'I don't know what would have happened, Walter,' said my mother, 'if you had delayed much longer. Pesca has been half-mad with impatience; and I have been half-mad with curiosity. The Professor has brought some wonderful news with him, in which he says you are concerned; and he has cruelly refused to give us the smallest hint of it till his friend Walter appeared.'

'Very provoking: it spoils the Set,' murmured Sarah to herself, mournfully absorbed over the ruins of the broken cup.

While these words were being spoken, Pesca, happily and fussily unconscious of the irreparable wrong which the crockery had suffered at his hands, was dragging a large arm-chair to the opposite end of the room, so as to command us all three, in the character of a public speaker addressing an audience. Having turned the chair with its back towards us, he jumped into it on his knees, and excitedly addressed his small congregation of three from an impromptu pulpit.

'Now, my good dears,' began Pesca (who always said 'good dears,' when he meant 'worthy friends'), 'listen to me. The time has come—I recite my good news—I speak at last.'

'Hear, hear!' said my mother, humouring the joke.

'The next thing he will break, mamma,' whispered Sarah, 'will be the back of the best arm-chair.'

'I go back into my life, and I address myself to the noblest of created beings,' continued Pesca, vehemently apostrophising my unworthy self, over the top rail of the chair. 'Who found me dead at the bottom of the sea (through Cramp); and who pulled me up to the top; and what did I say when I got into my own life and my own clothes again?'

'Much more than was at all necessary,' I answered, as doggedly as possible; for the least encouragement in connexion with this subject invariably let loose the Professor's emotions in a flood of tears.

'I said,' persisted Pesca, 'that my life belonged to my dear friend, Walter, for the rest of my days—and so it does. I said that I should never be happy again till I had found the opportunity of doing a good Something for Walter—and I have never been contented with myself till this most blessed day. Now,' cried the enthusiastic little man at the top of his voice, 'the overflowing happiness bursts out of me at every pore of my skin, like a perspiration; for on my faith, and soul, and honour, the Something is done at last, and the only word to say now, is—Right-all-right!'

It may be necessary to explain, here, that Pesca prided himself on being a perfect Englishman in his language, as well as in his dress, manners, and amusements. Having picked up a few of our most familiar colloquial expressions, he scattered them about over his conversation whenever they happened to occur to him, turning them, in his high relish for their sound and his general ignorance of their sense, into compound words and repetitions of his own, and always running them into each other, as if they consisted of one long syllable.

'Among the fine London houses where I teach the language of my native country,' said the Professor, rushing into his long-deferred explanation without another word of preface, 'there is one, mighty fine, in the big place called Portland. You all know where that is? Yes, yes—course-of-course. The fine house, my good dears, has got inside it a fine family. A Mamma, fair and fat; three young Misses, fair and fat; two young Misters, fair and fat; and a Papa, the fairest and the fattest of all, who is a mighty merchant, up to his eyes in gold—a fine man once, but seeing that he has got a naked head and two chins, fine no longer at the present time. Now mind! I teach the sublime Dante to the young Misses, and ah!—my-soul-bless-my-soul!—it is not in human language to say how the sublime Dante puzzles the pretty heads of all three! No matter—all in good time—and the more lessons the better for me. Now mind! Imagine to yourselves that I am teaching the young Misses to-day, as usual. We are all four of us down together in the Hell of Dante. At the Seventh Circle—but no matter for that: all the Circles are alike to the three young Misses, fair and fat,—at the Seventh Circle, nevertheless, my pupils are sticking fast; and I to set them going again, recite, explain, and blow myself up red-hot with useless enthusiasm, when— a creak of boots in the passage outside, and in comes the golden Papa, the mighty merchant with the naked head and the two chins.—Ha! my good dears, I am closer than you think for to the business, now. Have you been patient, so far? or have you said to yourselves, "Deuce-what-the-deuce! Pesca is long-winded to-night?"'

We declared that we were deeply interested. The Professor went on:

'In his hand, the golden Papa has a letter; and after he has made his excuse for disturbing us in our Infernal Region with the common mortal business of the house, he addresses himself to the three young Misses, and begins, as you English begin everything in this blessed world that you have to say, with a great O. "O, my dears," says the mighty merchant, "I have got here a letter from my friend, Mr——" (the name has slipped out of my mind; but no matter; we shall come back to that: yes, yes—right-all-right). So the Papa says, "I have got a letter from my friend, the Mister; and he wants a recommend from me, of a drawing-master, to go down to his house in the country." My-soul-bless-my-soul! when I heard the golden papa say those words, if I had been big enough to reach up to him, I should have put my arms round his neck, and pressed him to my bosom in a long and grateful hug! As it was, I only bounced upon my chair. My seat was on thorns, and my soul was on fire to speak; but I held my tongue, and let Papa go on. "Perhaps you know," says this good man of money, twiddling his friend's letter this way and that, in his golden fingers and thumbs, "perhaps you know, my dears, of a drawing-master that I can recommend?" The three young Misses all look at each other, and then say (with the indispensable great O to begin) "O, dear no, Papa! But here is Mr Pesca——" At the mention of myself I can hold no longer—the thought of you, my good dears, mounts like blood to my head—I start from my seat, as if a spike had grown up from the ground through the bottom of my chair—I address myself to the mighty merchant, and I say (English phrase), "Dear sir, I have the man! The first and foremost drawing-master of the world! Recommend him by the post to-night, and send him off, bag and baggage (English phrase again—ha?), send him off, bag and baggage, by the train to-morrow!" "Stop, stop," says the Papa, "is he a foreigner or an Englishman?" "English to the bone of his back," I answer. "Respectable?" says Papa. "Sir," I say (for this last question of his outrages me, and I have done being familiar with him), "Sir! the immortal fire of genius burns in this Englishman's bosom, and, what is more, his father had it before him!" "Never mind," says the golden barbarian of a Papa, "never mind about his genius, Mr Pesca. We don't want genius in this country, unless it is accompanied by respect-ability—and then we are very glad to have it, very glad indeed. Can your friend produce testimonials—letters that speak to his character?" I wave my hand negligently. "Letters?" I say. "Ha! my-soul-bless-my-soul! I should think so, indeed! Volumes of letters and portfolios of testimonials, if you like?" "One or two will do," says this man of phlegm and money. "Let him send them to me, with his name and address. And—stop, stop, Mr Pesca—before you go to your friend, you had better take a note." "Bank-note!" I say, indignantly. "No bank-note, if you please, till my brave Englishman has earned it first." "Bank-note?" says Papa, in a great surprise, "who talked of bank-note? I mean a note of the terms—a memorandum of what he is expected to do. Go on with your lesson, Mr Pesca, and I will give you the necessary extract from my friend's letter." Down sits the man of merchandise and money to his pen, ink, and paper; and down I go once again into the Hell of Dante, with my three young Misses after me. In ten minutes' time the note is written, and the boots of Papa are creaking themselves away in the passage outside. From that moment, on my faith, and soul, and honour, I know nothing more! The glorious thought that I have caught my opportunity at last, and that my grateful service for my dearest friend in the world is as good as done already, flies up into my head and makes me drunk. How I pull my young Misses and myself out of our Infernal Region again, how my other business is done afterwards, how my little bit of dinner slides itself down my throat, I know no more than a man in the moon. Enough for me, that here I am, with the mighty merchant's note in my hand, as large as life, as hot as fire, and as happy as a king! Ha! ha! ha! right-right-right-all-right!' Here the Professor waved the memorandum of terms over his head, and ended his long and voluble narrative with his shrill Italian parody on an English cheer.

My mother rose the moment he had done, with flushed cheeks and brightened eyes. She caught the little man warmly by both hands.

'My dear, good Pesca,' she said, 'I never doubted your true affection for Walter—but I am more than ever persuaded of it now!'

'I am sure we are very much obliged to Professor Pesca, for Walter's sake,' added Sarah. She half rose, while she spoke, as if to approach the arm-chair, in her turn; but, observing that Pesca was rapturously kissing my mother's hands, looked serious, and resumed her seat. 'If the familiar little man treats my mother in that way, how will he treat *me*?' Faces sometimes tell truth; and that was unquestionably the thought in Sarah's mind, as she sat down again.

Although I was myself gratefully sensible of the kindness of Pesca's motives, my spirits were hardly so much elevated as they ought to have been by the prospect of future employment now placed before me. When the Professor had quite done with my mother's hands, and when I had warmly thanked him for his interference on my behalf, I asked to be allowed to look at the note of terms which his respectable patron had drawn up for my inspection.

Pesca handed me the paper, with a triumphant flourish of the hand.

'Read!' said the little man, majestically. 'I promise you, my friend, the writing of the golden Papa speaks with a tongue of trumpets for itself.'

The note of terms was plain, straightforward, and comprehensive, at any rate. It informed me,

First, That Frederick Fairlie, Esquire, of Limmeridge House, Cumberland, wanted to engage the services of a thoroughly competent drawing-master, for a period of four months certain.

Secondly, That the duties which the master was expected to perform would be of a twofold kind. He was to superintend the instruction of two young ladies in the art of painting in water-colours; and he was to devote his leisure time, afterwards, to the business of arranging and mounting a valuable collection of drawings, which had been suffered to fall into a condition of total neglect.

Thirdly, That the terms offered to the person who should undertake and properly perform these duties, were four guineas a week; that he was to reside at Limmeridge House; and that he was to be treated there on the footing of a gentleman.

Fourthly, and lastly, That no person need think of applying for this situation, unless he could furnish the most unexceptionable references to character and abilities. The references were to be sent to Mr Fairlie's friend in London, who was empowered to conclude all necessary arrangements. These instructions were followed by the name and address of Pesca's employer in Portland-place—and there the note, or memorandum, ended.

The prospect which this offer of an engagement held out was certainly an attractive one. The employment was likely to be both easy and agreeable; it was proposed to me at the autumn time of year when I was least occupied; and the terms, judging by my personal experience in my profession, were surprisingly liberal. I knew this; I knew that I ought to consider myself very fortunate if I succeeded in securing the offered employment—and yet, no sooner had I read the memorandum than I felt an inexplicable unwillingness within me to stir in the matter. I had never in the whole of my previous experience found my duty and my inclination so painfully and so unaccountably at variance as I found them now.

'Oh, Walter, your father never had such a chance as this!' said my mother, when she had read the note of terms and had handed it back to me.

'Such distinguished people to know,' remarked Sarah, straightening herself in her chair; 'and on such gratifying terms of equality, too!'

'Yes, yes; the terms, in every sense, are tempting enough,' I replied, impatiently. 'But, before I send in my testimonials, I should like a little time to consider——'

'Consider!' exclaimed my mother. 'Why, Walter, what is the matter with you!'

'Consider!' echoed my sister. 'What a very extraordinary thing to say, under the circumstances!'

'Consider!' chimed in the Professor. 'What is there to consider about? Answer me this! Have you not been complaining of your health, and have you not been longing for what you call a smack of the country breeze? Well! there in your hand is the paper that offers you perpetual choking mouthfuls of country breeze, for four months' time. Is it not so? Ha? Again—you want money. Well! Is four golden guineas a week nothing? My-soul-bless-my-soul!

only give it to *me*—and my boots shall creak like the golden Papa's, with a sense of the overpowering richness of the man who walks in them! Four guineas a week, and, more than that, the charming society of two young Misses; and, more than that, your bed, your breakfast, your dinner, your gorging English teas and lunches and drinks of foaming beer, all for nothing—why, Walter, my dear good friend—deuce-what-the-deuce!—for the first time in my life I have not eyes enough in my head to look, and wonder at you!'

Neither my mother's evident astonishment at my behaviour, nor Pesca's fervid enumeration of the advantages offered to me by the new employment, had any effect in shaking my unreasonable disinclination to go to Limmeridge House. After stating all the petty objections that I could think of to going to Cumberland; and after hearing them answered, one after another, to my own complete discomfiture, I tried to set up a last obstacle by asking what was to become of my pupils in London, while I was teaching Mr Fairlie's young ladies to sketch from nature. The obvious answer to this was that the greater part of them would be away on their autumn travels, and that the few who remained at home might be confided to the care of one of my brother drawing-masters, whose pupils I had once taken off his hands under similar circumstances. My sister reminded me that this gentleman had expressly placed his services at my disposal, during the present season, in case I wished to leave town; my mother seriously appealed to me not to let an idle caprice stand in the way of my own interests and my own health; and Pesca piteously entreated that I would not wound him to the heart, by rejecting the first grateful offer of service that he had been able to make to the friend who had saved his life.

The evident sincerity and affection which inspired these remonstrances would have influenced any man with an atom of good feeling in his composition. Though I could not conquer my own unaccountable perversity, I had at least virtue enough to be heartily ashamed of it, and to end the discussion pleasantly by giving way and promising to do all that was wanted of me.

The rest of the evening passed merrily enough in humorous anticipations of my coming life with the two young ladies in Cumberland. Pesca, inspired by our national grog, which appeared to get into his head, in the most marvellous manner, five minutes after it had gone down his throat, asserted his claims to be considered a complete Englishman by making a series of speeches in rapid succession; proposing my mother's health, my sister's health, my health, and the healths, in mass, of Mr Fairlie and the two young Misses; pathetically returning thanks himself, immediately afterwards, for the whole party. 'A secret, Walter,' said my little friend, confidentially, as we walked home together. 'I am flushed by the recollection of my own eloquence. My soul bursts itself with ambition. One of these days, I go into your noble Parliament. It is the dream of my whole life to be Honourable Pesca, M.P.!'

The next morning I sent my testimonials to the Professor's employer in Portland-place. Three days passed; and I concluded, with secret satisfaction, that my papers had not been found sufficiently explicit. On the fourth day, however, an answer came. It announced that Mr Fairlie accepted my services, and requested me to start for Cumberland immediately. All the necessary instructions for my journey were carefully and clearly added in a postscript.

I made my arrangements, unwillingly enough, for leaving London early the next day. Towards evening Pesca looked in, on his way to a dinner-party, to bid me good-by.

'I shall dry my tears in your absence,' said the Professor, gaily, 'with this glorious thought. It is my auspicious hand that has given the first push to your fortune in the world. Go, my friend! When your sun shines in Cumberland (English proverb), in the name of Heaven, make your hay. Marry one of the two young Misses; become Honourable Hartright, M.P.; and when you are on the top of the ladder, remember that Pesca, at the bottom, has done it all!'

I tried to laugh with my little friend over his parting jest, but my spirits were not to be commanded. Something jarred in me almost painfully, while he was speaking his light farewell words.

When I was left alone again, nothing remained to be done but to walk to the Hampstead Cottage and bid my mother and Sarah good-by.

III

THE heat had been painfully oppressive all day; and it was now a close and sultry night.

My mother and sister had spoken so many last words, and had begged me to wait another five minutes so many times, that it was nearly midnight when the servant locked the garden-gate behind me. I walked forward a few paces on the shortest way back to London; then stopped, and hesitated.

The moon was full and broad in the dark blue starless sky; and the broken ground of the heath looked wild enough in the mysterious light to be hundreds of miles away from the great city that lay beneath it. The idea of descending any sooner than I could help into the heat and gloom of London repelled me. The prospect of going to bed in my airless chambers, and the prospect of gradual suffocation, seemed, in my present restless frame of mind and body, to be one and the same thing. I determined to stroll home in the purer air, by the most roundabout way I could take; to follow the white winding paths across the lonely heath; and to approach London through its most open suburb by striking into the Finchley-road, and so getting back, in the cool of the new morning, by the western side of the Regent's Park.

I wound my way down slowly over the Heath, enjoying the divine stillness of the scene, and admiring the soft alternations of light and shade as they followed each other over the broken ground on every side of me. So long as I was proceeding through this first and prettiest part of my night-walk, my mind remained passively open to the impressions produced by the view; and I thought but little on any subject—indeed, so far as my own sensations were concerned, I can hardly say that I thought at all.

But when I had left the Heath, and had turned into the by-road, where there was less to see, the ideas naturally engendered by the approaching change in my habits and occupations, gradually drew more and more of my attention exclusively to themselves. By the time I had arrived at the end of the road, I had become completely absorbed in my own fanciful visions of Limmeridge House, of Mr Fairlie, and of the two ladies whose practice in the art of water-colour painting I was so soon to superintend.

I had now arrived at that particular point of my walk where four roads met—the road to Hampstead, along which I had returned; the road to Finchley; the road to West End; and the road back to London. I had mechanically turned in this latter direction, and was strolling along the lonely high-road—idly wondering, I remember, what the Cumberland young ladies would look like—when, in one moment, every drop of blood in my body was brought to a stop by the touch of a hand laid lightly and suddenly on my shoulder from behind me.

I turned on the instant, with my fingers tightening round the handle of my stick.

There, in the middle of the broad, bright high-road—there, as if it had that moment sprung out of the earth or dropped from the heaven—stood the figure of a solitary Woman, dressed from head to foot in white garments; her face bent in grave inquiry on mine, her hand pointing to the dark cloud over London, as I faced her.

I was far too seriously startled by the suddenness with which this extraordinary apparition stood before me, in the dead of night and in that lonely place, to ask what she wanted. The strange woman spoke first.

'Is that the road to London?' she said.

I looked attentively at her, as she put that singular question to me. It was then nearly one o'clock. All I could discern distinctly by the moonlight, was a colourless, youthful face, meagre and sharp to look at, about the cheeks and chin; large, grave, wistfully-attentive eyes; nervous, uncertain lips; and light hair of a pale, brownish-yellow hue. There was nothing wild, nothing immodest in her manner: it was quiet and self-controlled, a little melancholy and a little touched by suspicion; not exactly the manner of a lady, and, at the same time, not the manner of a woman in the humblest rank of life. The voice, little as I had yet heard of it, had something curiously still and mechanical in its tones, and the utterance was remarkably rapid. She held a small bag in her hand: and her dress—bonnet, shawl, and gown all of white—was, so far as I could guess, certainly not composed of very delicate or very expensive materials. Her figure was slight, and rather above the average height—her gait and actions free from the slightest approach to extravagance. This was all that I could observe of her, in the dim light and under the perplexingly-strange circumstances of our meeting. What sort of a woman she was, and how she came to be out alone in the high-road, an hour after midnight, I altogether failed to guess. The one thing of which I felt certain was, that the grossest of mankind could not have misconstrued her motive in speaking, even at that suspiciously late hour and in that suspiciously lonely place.

'Did you hear me?' she said, still quietly and rapidly, and without the least fretfulness or impatience. 'I asked if that was the way to London.'

'Yes,' I replied, 'that is the way: it leads to St John's Wood and the Regent's Park. You must excuse my not answering you before. I was rather startled by your sudden appearance in the road; and I am, even now, quite unable to account for it.'

'You don't suspect me of doing anything wrong, do you? I have done nothing wrong. I have met with an accident—I am very unfortunate in being here alone so late. Why do you suspect me of doing wrong?'

She spoke with unnecessary earnestness and agitation, and shrank back from me several paces. I did my best to reassure her.

'Pray don't suppose that I have any idea of suspecting you,' I said, 'or any other wish than to be of assistance to you, if I can. I only wondered at your appearance in the road, because it seemed to me to be empty the instant before I saw you.'

She turned, and pointed back to a place at the junction of the road to London and the road to Hampstead, where there was a gap in the hedge.

'I heard you coming,' she said, 'and hid there to see what sort of man you were, before I risked speaking. I doubted and feared about it till you passed; and then I was obliged to steal after you, and touch you.'

Steal after me, and touch me? Why not call to me? Strange, to say the least of it.

'May I trust you?' she asked. 'You don't think the worse of me because I have met with an accident?' She stopped in confusion; shifted her bag from one hand to the other; and sighed bitterly.

The loneliness and helplessness of the woman touched me. The natural impulse to assist her and to spare her, got the better of the judgment, the caution, the worldly tact, which an older, wiser, and colder man might have summoned to help him in this strange emergency.

'You may trust me for any harmless purpose,' I said. 'If it troubles you to explain your strange situation to me, don't think of returning to the subject

again. I have no right to ask you for any explanations. Tell me how I can
help you; and if I can, I will.'

'You are very kind, and I am very, very thankful to have met you.' The
first touch of womanly tenderness that I had heard from her, trembled in
her voice as she said the words; but no tears glistened in those large,
wistfully-attentive eyes of hers, which were still fixed on me. 'I have only
been in London once before,' she went on, more and more rapidly; 'and I
know nothing about that side of it, yonder. Can I get a fly, or a carriage
of any kind? Is it too late? I don't know. If you could show me where to get
a fly—and if you will only promise not to interfere with me, and to let me
leave you, when and how I please—I have a friend in London who will be
glad to receive me—I want nothing else—will you promise?'

She looked anxiously up and down the road; shifted her bag again from
one hand to the other; repeated the words, 'Will you promise?' and looked
hard in my face, with a pleading fear and confusion that it troubled me to
see.

What could I do? Here was a stranger utterly and helplessly at my
mercy—and that stranger a forlorn woman. No house was near; no one was
passing whom I could consult; and no earthly right existed on my part to
give me a power of control over her, even if I had known how to exercise
it. I trace these lines, self-distrustfully, with the shadows of after-events
darkening the very paper I write on; and still I say, what could I do?

What I did do, was to try and gain time by questioning her.

'Are you sure that your friend in London will receive you at such a late
hour as this?' I said.

'Quite sure. Only say you will let me leave you when and how I
please—only say you won't interfere with me. Will you promise?'

As she repeated the words for the third time, she came close to me, and
laid her hand, with a sudden gentle stealthiness, on my bosom—a thin hand;
a cold hand (when I removed it with mine) even on that sultry night.
Remember that I was young; remember that the hand which touched me
was a woman's.

'Will you promise?'

'Yes.'

One word! The little familiar word that is on everybody's lips, every hour
in the day. Oh me! and I tremble, now, when I write it.

We set our faces towards London, and walked on together in the first still
hour of the new day—I, and this woman, whose name, whose character,
whose story, whose objects in life, whose very presence by my side, at that
moment, were fathomless mysteries to me. It was like a dream. Was I Walter
Hartright? Was this the well-known, uneventful road, where holiday people
strolled on Sundays? Had I really left, little more than an hour since, the
quiet, decent, conventionally-domestic atmosphere of my mother's cottage?

I was too bewildered—too conscious also of a vague sense of something like self-reproach—to speak to my strange companion for some minutes. It was her voice again that first broke the silence between us.

'I want to ask you something,' she said, suddenly. 'Do you know many people in London?'

'Yes, a great many.'

'Many men of rank and title?' There was an unmistakable tone of suspicion in the strange question. I hesitated about answering it.

'Some,' I said, after a moment's silence.

'Many'—she came to a full stop, and looked me searchingly in the face—'many men of the rank of Baronet?'

Too much astonished to reply, I questioned her in my turn.

'Why do you ask?'

'Because I hope, for my own sake, there is one Baronet that you don't know.'

'Will you tell me his name?'

'I can't—I daren't—I forget myself, when I mention it.' She spoke loudly and almost fiercely, raised her clenched hand in the air, and shook it passionately; then, on a sudden, controlled herself again, and added, in tones lowered to a whisper: 'Tell me which of them *you* know.'

I could hardly refuse to humour her in such a trifle, and I mentioned three names. Two, the names of fathers of families whose daughters I taught; one, the name of a bachelor who had once taken me a cruise in his yacht, to make sketches for him.

'Ah! you *don't* know him,' she said, with a sigh of relief. 'Are you a man of rank and title yourself?'

'Far from it. I am only a drawing-master.'

As the reply passed my lips—a little bitterly, perhaps—she took my arm with the abruptness which characterised all her actions.

'Not a man of rank and title,' she repeated to herself. 'Thank God! I may trust *him*.'

I had hitherto contrived to master my curiosity out of consideration for my companion; but it got the better of me, now.

'I am afraid you have serious reason to complain of some man of rank and title?' I said. 'I am afraid the Baronet, whose name you are unwilling to mention to me, has done you some grievous wrong? Is he the cause of your being out here at this strange time of night?'

'Don't ask me; don't make me talk of it,' she answered. 'I'm not fit, now. I have been cruelly used and cruelly wronged. You will be kinder than ever, if you will walk on fast, and not speak to me. I sadly want to quiet myself, if I can.'

We moved forward again at a quick pace; and for half an hour, at least, not a word passed on either side. From time to time, being forbidden to make any more inquiries, I stole a look at her face. It was always the same, the lips close shut, the brow frowning, the eyes looking straight forward, eagerly and yet absently. We had reached the first houses, and were close on the new Wesleyan College, before her set features relaxed, and she spoke once more.

'Do you live in London?' she said.

'Yes.' As I answered, it struck me that she might have formed some intention of appealing to me for assistance or advice, and that I ought to spare her a possible disappointment by warning her of my approaching absence from home. So I added: 'But tomorrow I shall be away from London for some time. I am going into the country.'

'Where?' she asked. 'North, or south?'

'North—to Cumberland.'

'Cumberland!' she repeated the word tenderly. 'Ah! I wish I was going there, too. I was once happy in Cumberland.'

I tried again to lift the veil that hung between this woman and me.

'Perhaps you were born,' I said, 'in the beautiful Lake country.'

'No,' she answered. 'I was born in Hampshire; but I once went to school for a little while in Cumberland. Lakes? I don't remember any lakes. It's Limmeridge village, and Limmeridge House, I should like to see again.'

It was my turn, now, to stop suddenly. In the excited state of my curiosity, at that moment, the chance reference to Mr Fairlie's place of residence, on the lips of my strange companion, staggered me with astonishment.

'Did you hear anybody calling after us?' she asked, looking up and down the road affrightedly, the instant I stopped.

'No, no. I was only struck by the name of Limmeridge House—I heard it mentioned by some Cumberland people a few days since.'

'Ah! not *my* people. Mrs Fairlie is dead; and her husband is dead; and their little girl may be married and gone away by this time. I can't say who lives at Limmeridge now. If any more are left there of that name, I only know I love them for Mrs Fairlie's sake.'

She seemed about to say more; but while she was speaking, we came within view of the turnpike, at the top of the Avenue-road. Her hand tightened round my arm, and she looked anxiously at the gate before us.

'Is the turnpike man looking out?' she asked.

He was not looking out; no one else was near the place when we passed through the gate. The sight of the gas-lamps and houses seemed to agitate her, and to make her impatient.

'This is London,' she said. 'Do you see any carriage I can get? I am tired and frightened. I want to shut myself in, and be driven away.'

I explained to her that we must walk a little further to get to a cab-stand, unless we were fortunate enough to meet with an empty vehicle; and then tried to resume the subject of Cumberland. It was useless. That idea of shutting herself in, and being driven away, had now got full possession of her mind. She could think and talk of nothing else.

We had hardly proceeded a third of the way down the Avenue-road, when I saw a cab draw up at a house a few doors below us, on the opposite side of the way. A gentleman got out and let himself in at the garden door. I hailed the cab, as the driver mounted the box again. When we crossed the road, my companion's impatience increased to such an extent that she almost forced me to run.

'It's so late,' she said. 'I am only in a hurry because it's so late.'

'I can't take you, sir, if you're not going towards Tottenham-court-road,' said the driver, civilly, when I opened the cab door. 'My horse is dead beat, and I can't get him no further than the stable.'

'Yes, yes. That will do for me. I'm going that way—I'm going that way.' She spoke with breathless eagerness, and pressed by me into the cab.

I had assured myself that the man was sober as well as civil, before I let her enter the vehicle. And now, when she was seated inside, I entreated her to let me see her set down safely at her destination.

'No, no, no,' she said, vehemently. 'I'm quite safe and quite happy now. If you are a gentleman, remember your promise. Let him drive on, till I stop him. Thank you—oh! thank you, thank you!'

My hand was on the cab door. She caught it in hers, kissed it, and pushed it away. The cab drove off at the same moment—I started into the road, with some vague idea of stopping it again, I hardly knew why—hesitated from dread of frightening and distressing her—called, at last, but not loudly enough to attract the driver's attention. The sound of the wheels grew fainter in the distance—the cab melted into the black shadows on the road—the woman in white was gone.

Ten minutes, or more, had passed. I was still on the same side of the way; now mechanically walking forward a few paces; now stopping again absently. At one moment, I found myself doubting the reality of my own adventure; at another, I was perplexed and distressed by an uneasy sense of having done wrong, which yet left me confusedly ignorant of how I could have done right. I hardly knew where I was going, or what I meant to do next; I was conscious of nothing but the confusion of my own thoughts, when I was abruptly recalled to myself—awakened I might almost say—by the sound of rapidly approaching wheels close behind me.

I was on the dark side of the road, in the thick shadow of some garden trees, when I stopped to look round. On the opposite, and lighter, side of the way, a short distance below me, a policeman was strolling along in the direction of the Regent's Park.

The carriage passed me—an open chaise driven by two men.

'Stop!' cried one. 'There's a policeman. Let's ask him.'

The horse was instantly pulled up, a few yards beyond the dark place where I stood.

'Policeman!' cried the first speaker. 'Have you seen a woman pass this way?'

'What sort of woman, sir?'

'A woman in a lavender-coloured gown——'

'No, no,' interposed the second man. 'The clothes we gave her were found on her bed. She must have gone away in the clothes she wore when she came to us. In white, policeman. A woman in white.'

'I haven't seen her, sir.'

'If you, or any of your men meet with the woman, stop her, and send her in careful keeping to that address. I'll pay all expenses, and a fair reward into the bargain.'

The policeman looked at the card that was handed down to him.

'Why are we to stop her, sir? What has she done?'

'Done! She has escaped from my Asylum. Don't forget: a woman in white. Drive on.'

IV

'SHE has escaped from my Asylum.'

I cannot say with truth that the terrible inference which those words suggested flashed upon me like a new revelation. Some of the strange questions put to me by the woman in white, after my ill-considered promise to leave her free to act as she pleased, had suggested the conclusion, either that she was naturally flighty and unsettled, or that some recent shock of terror had disturbed the balance of her faculties. But the idea of absolute insanity which we all associate with the very name of an Asylum, had, I can honestly declare, never occurred to me, in connexion with her. I had seen nothing, in her language or her actions, to justify it at the time; and, even with the new light thrown on her by the words which the stranger had addressed to the policeman, I could see nothing to justify it now.

What had I done? Assisted the victim of the most horrible of all false imprisonments to escape; or cast loose on the wide world of London an unfortunate creature whose actions it was my duty, and every man's duty, mercifully to control? I turned sick at heart when the question occurred to me, and when I felt self-reproachfully that it was asked too late.

In the disturbed state of my mind, it was useless to think of going to bed, when I at last got back to my chambers in Clement's Inn. Before many hours elapsed it would be necessary to start on my journey to Cumberland. I sat down and tried, first to sketch, then to read—but the woman in white got between me and my pencil, between me and my book. Had the forlorn creature come to any harm? That was my first thought, though I shrank

selfishly from confronting it. Other thoughts followed, on which it was less
harrowing to dwell. Where had she stopped the cab? What had become of
her now? Had she been traced and captured by the men in the chaise? Or
was she still capable of controlling her own actions; and were we two
following our widely-parted roads towards one point in the mysterious
future, at which we were to meet once more?

It was a relief when the hour came to lock my door, to bid farewell to
London pursuits, London pupils, and London friends, and to be in movement again towards new interests and a new life. Even the bustle and
confusion at the railway terminus, so wearisome and bewildering at other
times, roused me and did me good.

My travelling instructions directed me to go to Carlisle, and then to
diverge by a branch railway which ran in the direction of the coast. As a
misfortune to begin with, our engine broke down between Lancaster and
Carlisle. The delay occasioned by this accident caused me to be too late for
the branch train, by which I was to have gone on immediately. I had to wait
some hours; and when a later train finally deposited me at the nearest
station to Limmeridge House, it was past ten, and the night was so dark that
I could hardly see my way to the pony-chaise which Mr Fairlie had ordered
to be in waiting for me.

The driver was evidently discomposed by the lateness of my arrival. He
was in that state of highly-respectful sulkiness which is peculiar to English
servants. We drove away slowly through the darkness in perfect silence. The
roads were bad, and the dense obscurity of the night increased the difficulty
of getting over the ground quickly. It was, by my watch, nearly an hour and
an half from the time of our leaving the station, before I heard the sound of
the sea in the distance, and the crunch of our wheels on a smooth gravel
drive. We had passed one gate before entering the drive, and we passed
another before we drew up at the house. I was received by a solemn
man-servant out of livery, was informed that the family had retired for the
night, and was then led into a large and lofty room where my supper was
awaiting me, in a forlorn manner, at one extremity of a lonesome mahogany
wilderness of dining-table.

I was too tired and out of spirits to eat or drink much, especially with the
solemn servant waiting on me as elaborately as if a small dinner-party had
arrived at the house instead of a solitary man. In a quarter of an hour I was
ready to be taken up to my bedchamber. The solemn servant conducted me
into a prettily-furnished room—said: 'Breakfast at nine o'clock, sir'—looked
all round him to see that everything was in its proper place—and noiselessly
withdrew.

'What shall I see in my dreams to-night?' I thought to myself, as I put out
the candle; 'the woman in white? or the unknown inhabitants of this

Cumberland mansion?' It was a strange sensation to be sleeping in the house, like a friend of the family, and yet not to know one of the inmates, even by sight!

V

WHEN I rose the next morning and drew up my blind, the sea opened before me joyously under the broad August sunlight, and the distant coast of Scotland fringed the horizon with its lines of melting blue.

The view was such a surprise, and such a change to me, after my weary London experience of brick and mortar landscape, that I seemed to burst into a new life and a new set of thoughts the moment I looked at it. A confused sensation of having suddenly lost my familiarity with the past, without acquiring any additional clearness of idea in reference to the present or the future, took possession of my mind. Circumstances that were but a few days old, faded back in my memory, as if they had happened months and months since. Pesca's quaint announcement of the means by which he had procured me my present employment; the farewell evening I had passed with my mother and sister; even my mysterious adventure on the way home from Hampstead, had all become like events which might have occurred at some former epoch of my existence. Although the woman in white was still in my mind, the image of her seemed to have grown dull and faint already.

A little before nine o'clock, I descended to the ground-floor of the house. The solemn man-servant of the night before met me wandering among the passages, and compassionately showed me the way to the breakfast-room.

My first glance round me, as the man opened the door, disclosed a well-furnished breakfast-table, standing in the middle of a long room, with many windows in it. I looked from the table to the window farthest from me, and saw a lady standing at it, with her back turned towards me. The instant my eyes rested on her, I was struck by the rare beauty of her form, and by the unaffected grace of her attitude. Her figure was tall, yet not too tall; comely and well-developed, yet not fat; her head set on her shoulders with an easy, pliant firmness; her waist, perfection in the eyes of a man, for it occupied its natural place, it filled out its natural circle, it was visibly and delightfully undeformed by stays. She had not heard my entrance into the room; and I allowed myself the luxury of admiring her for a few moments, before I moved one of the chairs near me, as the least embarassing means of attracting her attention. She turned towards me immediately. The easy elegance of every movement of her limbs and body as soon as she began to advance from the far end of the room, set me in a flutter of expectation to see her face clearly. She left the window—and I said to myself, The lady is dark. She moved forward a few steps—and I said to myself, The lady is young.

She approached nearer—and I said to myself (with a sense of surprise which words fail me to express), The lady is ugly!

Never was the old conventional maxim, that Nature cannot err, more flatly contradicted—never was the fair promise of a lovely figure more strangely and startlingly belied by the face and head that crowned it. The lady's complexion was almost swarthy, and the dark down on her upper lip was almost a moustache. She had a large, firm, masculine mouth and jaw; prominent, piercing, resolute brown eyes; and thick, coal-black hair, growing unusually low down on her forehead. Her expression—bright, frank, and intelligent—appeared, while she was silent, to be altogether wanting in those feminine attractions of gentleness and pliability, without which the beauty of the handsomest woman alive is beauty incomplete. To see such a face as this set on shoulders that a sculptor would have longed to model—to be charmed by the modest graces of action through which the symmetrical limbs betrayed their beauty when they moved, and then to be almost repelled by the masculine form and masculine look of the features in which the perfectly-shaped figure ended—was to feel a sensation oddly akin to the helpless discomfort familiar to us all in sleep, when we recognise yet cannot reconcile the anomalies and contradictions of a dream.

'Mr Hartright?' said the lady, interrogatively; her dark face lighting up with a smile, and softening and growing womanly the moment she began to speak. 'We resigned all hope of you last night, and went to bed as usual. Accept my apologies for our apparent want of attention; and allow me to introduce myself as one of your pupils. Shall we shake hands? I suppose we must come to it sooner or later—and why not sooner?'

These odd words of welcome were spoken in a clear, ringing, pleasant voice. The offered hand—rather large, but beautifully formed—was given to me with the easy, unaffected self-reliance of a highly-bred woman. We sat down together at the breakfast-table in as cordial and customary a manner as if we had known each other for years, and had met at Limmeridge House to talk over old times by previous appointment.

'I hope you come here good-humouredly determined to make the best of your position,' continued the lady. 'You will have to begin this morning by putting up with no other company at breakfast than mine. My sister is in her own room, nursing that essentially feminine malady, a slight headache; and her old governess, Mrs Vesey, is charitably attending on her with restorative tea. My uncle, Mr Fairlie, never joins us at any of our meals: he is an invalid, and keeps bachelor state in his own apartments. There is nobody else in the house but me. Two young ladies have been staying here, but they went away yesterday, in despair; and no wonder. All through their visit (in consequence of Mr Fairlie's invalid condition) we produced no such convenience in the house as a flirtable, danceable, small-talkable creature of the male sex; and the consequence was, we did nothing but quarrel, especially at dinner-time.

How can you expect four women to dine together alone every day, and not quarrel? We are such fools, we can't entertain each other at table. You see I don't think much of my own sex, Mr Hartright—which will you have, tea or coffee?—no woman does think much of her own sex, although few of them confess it as freely as I do. Dear me, you look puzzled. Why? Are you wondering what you will have for breakfast? or are you surprised at my careless way of talking? In the first case, I advise you, as a friend, to have nothing to do with that cold ham at your elbow, and to wait till the omelette comes in. In the second case, I will give you some tea to compose your spirits, and do all a woman can (which is very little, by-the-by) to hold my tongue.'

She handed me my cup of tea, laughing gaily. Her light flow of talk, and her lively familiarity of manner with a total stranger, were accompanied by an unaffected naturalness and an easy inborn confidence in herself and her position, which would have secured her the respect of the most audacious man breathing. While it was impossible to be formal and reserved in her company, it was more than impossible to take the faintest vestige of a liberty with her, even in thought. I felt this instinctively, even while I caught the infection of her own bright gaiety of spirits—even while I did my best to answer her in her own frank, lively way.

'Yes, yes,' she said, when I had suggested the only explanation I could offer, to account for my perplexed looks, 'I understand. You are such a perfect stranger in the house, that you are puzzled by my familiar references to the worthy inhabitants. Natural enough: I ought to have thought of it before. At any rate, I can set it right now. Suppose I begin with myself, so as to get done with that part of the subject as soon as possible? My name is Marian Halcombe; and I am as inaccurate, as women usually are, in calling Mr Fairlie my uncle, and Miss Fairlie my sister. My mother was twice married: the first time to Mr Halcombe, my father; the second time to Mr Fairlie, my half-sister's father. Except that we are both orphans, we are in every respect as unlike each other as possible. My father was a poor man, and Miss Fairlie's father was a rich man. I have got nothing, and she is an heiress. I am dark and ugly, and she is fair and pretty. Everybody thinks me crabbed and odd (with perfect justice); and everybody thinks her sweet-tempered and charming (with more justice still). In short, she is an angel; and I am——Try some of that marmalade, Mr Hartright, and finish the sentence, in the name of female propriety, for yourself. What am I to tell you about Mr Fairlie? Upon my honour, I hardly know. He is sure to send for you after breakfast, and you can study him for yourself. In the mean time, I may inform you, first, that he is the late Mr Fairlie's younger brother; secondly, that he is a single man; and, thirdly, that he is Miss Fairlie's guardian. I won't live without her, and she can't live without me; and that is how I come to be at Limmeridge House. My sister and I are honestly fond of each other; which, you will say, is perfectly unaccountable, under the circumstances, and I quite agree with you—but so it is. You must please both of us, Mr Hartright, or please neither of us; and, what is still more trying, you will be thrown entirely upon our society. Mrs Vesey is an excellent person, who possesses all the cardinal virtues, and counts for nothing; and Mr Fairlie is too great an invalid to be a companion for anybody. I don't know what is the matter with him, and the doctors don't know what is the matter with him, and he doesn't know himself what is the matter with him. We all say it's on the nerves, and we none of us know what we mean when we say it. However, I advise you to humour his little peculiarities, when you see him to-day. Admire his collection of coins, prints, and water-colour drawings, and you will win his heart. Upon my word, if you can be contented with a quiet country life, I don't see why you should not get on very well here. From breakfast to lunch, Mr Fairlie's drawings will occupy you. After lunch, Miss Fairlie and I shoulder our sketch-books, and go out to misrepresent nature, under your directions. Drawing is *her* favourite whim, mind, not mine. Women can't draw—their minds are too flighty, and their eyes are too inattentive. No matter—my sister likes it; so I waste paint and spoil paper, for her sake, as composedly as any woman in England. As for the evenings, I think we can help you through them. Miss Fairlie plays delightfully. For my own poor part, I don't know one note of music from the other; but I can match you at chess, backgammon, écarté, and (with the inevitable female drawbacks) even at billiards as well. What do you think of the programme? Can you reconcile yourself to our quiet, regular life? or do you mean to be restless, and secretly thirst for change and adventure, in the humdrum atmosphere of Limmeridge House?'

She had run on thus far, in her gracefully bantering way, with no other interruptions on my part than the unimportant replies which politeness required of me. The turn of the expression, however, in her last question, or rather the one chance word, 'adventure,' lightly as it fell from her lips, recalled my thoughts to my meeting with the woman in white, and urged me to discover the connexion which the stranger's own reference to Mrs Fairlie informed me must once have existed between the nameless fugitive from the Asylum, and the former mistress of Limmeridge House.

'Even if I were the most restless of mankind,' I said, 'I should be in no danger of thirsting after adventures for some time to come. The very night before I arrived at this house, I met with an adventure; and the wonder and excitement of it, I can assure you, Miss Halcombe, will last me for the whole term of my stay in Cumberland, if not for a much longer period.'

'You don't say so, Mr Hartright! May I hear it?'

'You have a claim to hear it. The chief person in the adventure was a total stranger to me, and may perhaps be a total stranger to you; but she certainly mentioned the name of the late Mrs Fairlie in terms of the sincerest gratitude and regard.'

'Mentioned my mother's name! You interest me indescribably. Pray go on.'

I at once related the circumstances under which I had met the woman in white, exactly as they had occurred; and I repeated what she had said to me about Mrs Fairlie and Limmeridge House, word for word.

Miss Halcombe's bright resolute eyes looked eagerly into mine, from the beginning of the narrative to the end. Her face expressed vivid interest and astonishment, but nothing more. She was evidently as far from knowing of any clue to the mystery as I was myself.

'Are you quite sure of those words referring to my mother?' she asked.

'Quite sure,' I replied. 'Whoever she may be, the woman was once at school in the village of Limmeridge, was treated with especial kindness by Mrs Fairlie, and, in grateful remembrance of that kindness, feels an affectionate interest in all surviving members of the family. She knew that Mrs Fairlie and her husband were both dead; and she spoke of Miss Fairlie as if they had known each other when they were children.'

'You said, I think, that she denied belonging to this place?'

'Yes, she told me she came from Hampshire.'

'And you entirely failed to find out her name?'

'Entirely.'

'Very strange. I think you were quite justified, Mr Hartright, in giving the poor creature her liberty, for she seems to have done nothing in your presence to show herself unfit to enjoy it. But I wish you had been a little more resolute about finding out her name. We must really clear up this mystery, in some way. You had better not speak of it yet to Mr Fairlie, or to my sister. They are both of them, I am certain, quite as ignorant of who the woman is, and of what her past history in connexion with us can be, as I am myself. But they are also, in widely different ways, rather nervous and sensitive, and you would only fidget one and alarm the other to no purpose. As for myself, I am all aflame with curiosity, and I devote my whole energies to the business of discovery from this moment. When my mother came here, after her second marriage, she certainly established the village school just as it exists at the present time. But the old teachers are all dead, or gone elsewhere; and no enlightenment is to be hoped for from that quarter. The only other alternative I can think of——'

At this point we were interrupted by the entrance of the servant, with a message from Mr Fairlie, intimating that he would be glad to see me, as soon as I had done breakfast.

'Wait in the hall,' said Miss Halcombe, answering the servant for me, in her quick, ready way. 'Mr Hartright will come out directly. I was about to say,' she went on, addressing me again, 'that my sister and I have a large collection of my mother's letters, addressed to my father and to hers. In the absence of any other means of getting information, I will pass the morning in looking over my mother's correspondence with Mr Fairlie. He was fond of London, and was constantly away from his country home; and she was accustomed, at such times, to write and report to him how things went on at Limmeridge. Her letters are full of references to the school in which she took so strong an interest; and I think it more than likely that I may have discovered something when we meet again. The luncheon hour is two, Mr Hartright. I shall have the pleasure of introducing you to my sister by that time, and we will occupy the afternoon in driving round the neighbourhood and showing you all our pet points of view. Till two o'clock, then, farewell.'

She nodded to me with the lively grace, the delightful refinement of familiarity, which characterised all that she did and all that she said; and disappeared by a door at the lower end of the room. As soon as she had left me, I turned my steps towards the hall, and followed the servant on my way, for the first time, to the presence of Mr Fairlie.

VI

MY conductor led me up-stairs into a passage which took us back to the bedchamber in which I had slept during the past night; and opening the door next to it, begged me to look in.

'I have my master's orders to show you your own sitting room, sir,' said the man, 'and to inquire if you approve of the situation and the light.'

I must have been hard to please, indeed, if I had not approved of the room, and of everything about it. The bow-window looked out on the same lovely view which I had admired, in the morning, from my bedroom. The furniture was the perfection of luxury and beauty; the table in the centre was bright with gaily-bound books, elegant conveniences for writing, and beautiful flowers; the second table, near the window, was covered with all the necessary materials for mounting water-colour drawings, and had a little easel attached to it, which I could expand or fold up at will; the walls were hung with gaily-tinted chintz; and the floor was spread with Indian matting in maize-colour and red. It was the prettiest and most luxurious little sitting-room I had ever seen; and I admired it with the warmest enthusiasm.

The solemn servant was far too highly trained to betray the slightest satisfaction. He bowed with icy deference when my terms of eulogy were all exhausted, and silently opened the door for me to go out into the passage again.

We turned a corner, and entered a long second passage, ascended a short flight of stairs at the end, crossed a small circular upper hall, and stopped in front of a door covered with dark baize. The servant opened this door, and led me on a few yards to a second; opened that also, and disclosed two curtains of pale sea-green silk hanging before us; raised one of them noiselessly; softly uttered the words, 'Mr Hartright,' and left me.

I found myself in a large, lofty room, with a magnificent carved ceiling, and with a carpet over the floor, so thick and soft that it felt like piles of velvet under my feet. One side of the room was occupied by a long bookcase of some rare inlaid wood that was quite new to me. It was not more than six feet high, and the top was adorned with statuettes in marble, ranged at regular distances one from the other. On the opposite side stood two antique cabinets; and between them, and above them, hung a picture of the Virgin and Child, protected by glass, and bearing Raphael's name on the gilt tablet at the bottom of the frame. On my right hand and on my left, as I stood inside the door, were chiffoniers and little stands in buhl and marquetterie, loaded with figures in Dresden china, with rare vases, ivory ornaments, and toys and curiosities that sparkled at all points with gold, silver, and precious stones. At the lower end of the room, opposite to me, the windows were concealed and the sunlight was tempered by large blinds of the same pale sea-green colour as the curtains over the door. The light thus produced was deliciously soft, mysterious, and subdued; it fell equally upon all the objects in the room; it helped to intensify the deep silence, and the air of profound seclusion that possessed the place; and it surrounded, with an appropriate halo of repose, the solitary figure of the master of the house, leaning back, listlessly composed, in a large easy-chair, with a reading-easel fastened on one of its arms, and a little table on the other.

If a man's personal appearance, when he is out of his dressing-room, and when he has passed forty, can be accepted as a safe guide to his time of life—which is more than doubtful—Mr Fairlie's age, when I saw him, might have been reasonably computed at over fifty and under sixty years. His beardless face was thin, worn, and transparently pale, but not wrinkled; his nose was high and hooked; his eyes were of a dim greyish blue, large, prominent, and rather red round the rims of the eyelids; his hair was scanty, soft to look at, and of that light sandy colour which is the last to disclose its own changes towards grey. He was dressed in a dark frock-coat, of some substance much thinner than cloth, and in waistcoat and trousers of spotless white. His feet were effeminately small, and were clad in buff-coloured silk stockings, and little womanish bronze-leather slippers. Two rings adorned his white delicate hands, the value of which even my inexperienced observation detected to be all but priceless. Upon the whole, he had a frail, languidly-fretful, over-refined look—something singularly and unpleasantly delicate in its association with a man, and, at the same time, something which could by no possibility have looked natural and appropriate if it had been transferred to the personal appearance of a woman. My morning's experience of Miss Halcombe had predisposed me to be pleased with everybody in the house; but my sympathies shut themselves up resolutely at the first sight of Mr Fairlie.

On approaching nearer to him, I discovered that he was not so entirely without occupation as I had at first supposed. Placed amid the other rare and beautiful objects on a large round table near him, was a dwarf cabinet in ebony and silver, containing coins of all shapes and sizes, set out in little drawers lined with dark purple velvet. One of these drawers lay on the small table attached to his chair; and near it were some tiny jewellers' brushes, a washleather 'stump,' and a little bottle of liquid, all waiting to be used in various ways for the removal of any accidental impurities which might be discovered on the coins. His frail white fingers were listlessly toying with something which looked, to my uninstructed eyes, like a dirty pewter medal with ragged edges, when I advanced within a respectful distance of his chair, and stopped to make my bow.

'So glad to possess you at Limmeridge, Mr Hartright,' he said, in a querulous, croaking voice, which combined, in anything but an agreeable manner, a discordantly high tone with a drowsily languid utterance. 'Pray sit down. And don't trouble yourself to move the chair, please. In the wretched state of my nerves, movement of any kind is exquisitely painful to me. Have you seen your studio? Will it do?'

'I have just come from seeing the room, Mr Fairlie; and I assure you——'

He stopped me in the middle of the sentence, by closing his eyes, and holding up one of his white hands imploringly. I paused in astonishment; and the croaking voice honoured me with this explanation:

'Pray excuse me. But *could* you contrive to speak in a lower key? In the wretched state of my nerves, loud sound of any kind is indescribable torture to me. You will pardon an invalid? I only say to you what the lamentable state of my health obliges me to say to everybody. Yes. And you really like the room?'

'I could wish for nothing prettier and nothing more comfortable,' I answered, dropping my voice, and beginning to discover already that Mr Fairlie's selfish affectation and Mr Fairlie's wretched nerves meant one and the same thing.

'So glad. You will find your position here, Mr Hartright, properly recognised. There is none of the horrid English barbarity of feeling about the social position of an artist, in this house. So much of my early life has been passed abroad, that I have quite cast my insular skin in that respect. I wish I could say the same of the gentry—detestable word, but I suppose I must use it—of the gentry in the neighbourhood. They are sad Goths in Art, Mr Hartright. People, I do assure you, who would have opened their eyes in astonishment, if they had seen Charles the Fifth pick up Titian's brush for him. Do you mind putting this tray of coins back in the cabinet, and giving me the next one to it? In the wretched state of my nerves, exertion of any kind is unspeakably disagreeable to me. Yes. Thank you.' As a practical commentary on the liberal social theory which he had just favoured me by illustrating, Mr Fairlie's cool request rather amused me. I put back one drawer and gave him the other, with all possible politeness.

He began trifling with the new set of coins and the little brushes immediately; languidly looking at them and admiring them all the time he was
speaking to me.

'A thousand thanks and a thousand excuses. Do you like coins? Yes. So
glad we have another taste in common besides our taste for Art. Now, about
the pecuniary arrangements between us—do tell me—are they satisfactory?'

'Most satisfactory, Mr Fairlie.'

'So glad. And—what next? Ah! I remember. Yes? In reference to the
consideration which you are good enough to accept for giving me the benefit
of your accomplishments in Art, my steward will wait on you at the end of
the first week, to ascertain your wishes. And—what next? Curious, is it not?
I had a great deal more to say; and I appear to have quite forgotten it. Do
you mind touching the bell? In that corner. Yes. Thank you.'

I rang; and a new servant noiselessly made his appearance—a foreigner,
with a set smile and perfectly brushed hair—a valet every inch of him.

'Louis,' said Mr Fairlie, dreamily dusting the tips of his fingers with one
of the tiny brushes for the coins, 'I made some entries in my tablettes this
morning. Find my tablettes. A thousand pardons, Mr Hartright. I'm afraid
I bore you.'

As he wearily closed his eyes again, before I could answer, and as he did
most assuredly bore me, I sat silent, and looked up at the Madonna and
Child by Raphael. In the mean time, the valet left the room, and returned
shortly with a little ivory book. Mr Fairlie, after first relieving himself by a
gentle sigh, let the book drop open with one hand, and held up the tiny
brush with the other, as a sign to the servant to wait for further orders.

'Yes. Just so!' said Mr Fairlie, consulting the tablettes. 'Louis, take down
that portfolio.' He pointed, as he spoke, to several portfolios placed near the
window, on mahogany stands. 'No. Not the one with the green back—that
contains my Rembrandt etchings, Mr Hartright. Do you like etchings? Yes?
So glad we have another taste in common. The portfolio with the red back,
Louis. Don't drop it! You have no idea of the tortures I should suffer,
Mr Hartright, if Louis dropped that portfolio. Is it safe on the chair? Do *you*
think it safe, Mr Hartright? Yes? So glad. Will you oblige me by looking at
the drawings, if you really think they're quite safe. Louis, go away. What an
ass you are. Don't you see me holding the tablettes? Do you suppose I want
to hold them? Then why not relieve me of the tablettes without being told?
A thousand pardons, Mr Hartright; servants are such asses, are they not?
Do tell me—what do you think of the drawings? They have come from a
sale in a shocking state—I thought they smelt of horrid dealers' and brokers'
fingers when I looked at them last. *Can* you undertake them?'

Although my nerves were not delicate enough to detect the odour of
plebeian fingers which had offended Mr Fairlie's nostrils, my taste was
sufficiently educated to enable me to appreciate the value of the drawings,

while I turned them over. They were, for the most part, really fine specimens of English water-colour Art; and they had deserved much better treatment at the hands of their former possessor than they appeared to have received.

'The drawings,' I answered, 'require careful straining and mounting; and, in my opinion, they are well worth——'

'I beg your pardon,' interposed Mr Fairlie. 'Do you mind my closing my eyes while you speak? Even this light is too much for them. Yes?'

'I was about to say that the drawings are well worth all the time and trouble——'

Mr Fairlie suddenly opened his eyes again, and rolled them with an expression of helpless alarm in the direction of the window.

'I entreat you to excuse me, Mr Hartright,' he said, in a feeble flutter. 'But surely I hear some horrid children in the garden—my private garden—below?'

'I can't say, Mr Fairlie. I heard nothing myself.'

'Oblige me—you have been so very good in humouring my poor nerves—oblige me by lifting up a corner of the blind. Don't let the sun in on me, Mr Hartright! Have you got the blind up? Yes? Then will you be so very kind as to look into the garden and make quite sure?'

I complied with this new request. The garden was carefully walled in, all round. Not a human creature, large or small, appeared in any part of the sacred seclusion. I reported that gratifying fact to Mr Fairlie.

'A thousand thanks. My fancy, I suppose. There are no children, thank Heaven, in the house; but the servants (persons born without nerves) will encourage the children from the village. Such brats—oh, dear me, such brats! Shall I confess it, Mr Hartright?—I sadly want a reform in the construction of children. Nature's only idea seems to be to make them machines for the production of incessant noise. Surely our delightful Raffaello's conception is infinitely preferable?'

He pointed to the picture of the Madonna, the upper part of which represented the conventional cherubs of Italian Art, celestially provided with sitting accommodation for their chins, on balloons of buff-coloured cloud.

'Quite a model family!' said Mr Fairlie, leering at the cherubs. 'Such nice round faces, and such nice soft wings, and—nothing else. No dirty little legs to run about on, and no noisy little lungs to scream with. How immeasurably superior to the existing construction! I will close my eyes again, if you will allow me. And you really can manage the drawings? So glad. Is there anything else to settle? If there is, I think I have forgotten it. Shall we ring for Louis again?'

Being, by this time, quite as anxious, on my side, as Mr Fairlie evidently was on his, to bring the interview to a speedy conclusion, I thought I would try to render the summoning of the servant unnecessary, by offering the requisite suggestion on my own responsibility.

'The only point, Mr Fairlie, that remains to be discussed,' I said, 'refers, I think, to the instruction in sketching which I am engaged to communicate to the two young ladies.'

'Ah! just so,' said Mr Fairlie. 'I wish I felt strong enough to go into that part of the arrangement—but I don't. The ladies, who profit by your kind services, Mr Hartright, must settle, and decide, and so on, for themselves. My niece is fond of your charming art. She knows just enough about it to be conscious of her own sad defects. Please take pains with her. Yes. Is there anything else? No. We quite understand each other—don't we? I have no right to detain you any longer from your delightful pursuit—have I? So pleasant to have settled everything—such a sensible relief to have done business. Do you mind ringing for Louis to carry the portfolio to your own room?'

'I will carry it there, myself, Mr Fairlie, if you will allow me.'

'Will you really? Are you strong enough? How nice to be so strong! Are you sure you won't drop it? So glad to possess you at Limmeridge, Mr Hartright. I am such a sufferer that I hardly dare hope to enjoy much of your society. Would you mind taking great pains not to let the doors bang, and not to drop the portfolio? Thank you. Gently with the curtains, please—the slightest noise from them goes through me like a knife. Yes. *Good* morning!'

When the sea-green curtains were closed, and when the two baize doors were shut behind me, I stopped for a moment in the little circular hall beyond, and drew a long, luxurious breath of relief. It was like coming to the surface of the water, after deep diving, to find myself once more on the outside of Mr Fairlie's room.

As soon as I was comfortably established for the morning in my pretty little studio, the first resolution at which I arrived was to turn my steps no more in the direction of the apartments occupied by the master of the house, except in the very improbable event of his honouring me with a special invitation to pay him another visit. Having settled this satisfactory plan of future conduct, in reference to Mr Fairlie, I soon recovered the serenity of temper of which my employer's haughty familiarity and impudent politeness had, for the moment, deprived me. The remaining hours of the morning passed away pleasantly enough, in looking over the drawings, arranging them in sets, trimming their ragged edges, and accomplishing the other necessary preparations in anticipation of the business of mounting them. I ought, perhaps, to have made more progress than this; but, as the luncheon-time drew near, I grew restless and unsettled, and felt unable to fix my attention on work, even though that work was only of the humble manual kind.

At two o'clock, I descended again to the breakfast-room, a little anxiously. Expectations of some interest were connected with my approaching re-appearance in that part of the house. My introduction to Miss Fairlie was now close at hand; and, if Miss Halcombe's search through her mother's letters had produced the result which she anticipated, the time had come for clearing up the mystery of the woman in white.

VII

WHEN I entered the room, I found Miss Halcombe and an elderly lady seated at the luncheon-table.

The elderly lady, when I was presented to her, proved to be Miss Fairlie's former governess, Mrs Vesey, who had been briefly described to me by my lively companion at the breakfast-table, as possessed of 'all the cardinal virtues, and counting for nothing.' I can do little more than offer my humble testimony to the truthfulness of Miss Halcombe's sketch of the old lady's character. Mrs Vesey looked the personification of human composure and female amiability. A calm enjoyment of a calm existence beamed in drowsy smiles on her plump, placid face. Some of us rush through life; and some of us saunter through life. Mrs Vesey *sat* through life. Sat in the house, early and late; sat in the garden; sat in unexpected window-seats in passages; sat (on a camp-stool) when her friends tried to take her out walking; sat before she looked at anything, before she talked of anything, before she answered, Yes, or No, to the commonest question—always with the same serene smile on her lips, the same vacantly-attentive turn of her head, the same snugly-comfortable position of her hands and arms, under every possible change of domestic circumstances. A mild, a compliant, an unutterably tranquil and harmless old lady, who never by any chance suggested the idea that she had been actually alive since the hour of her birth. Nature has so much to do in this world, and is engaged in generating such a vast variety of co-existent productions, that she must surely be now and then too flurried and confused to distinguish between the different processes that she is carrying on at the same time. Starting from this point of view, it will always remain my private persuasion that Nature was absorbed in making cabbages when Mrs Vesey was born, and that the good lady suffered the consequences of a vegetable preoccupation in the mind of the Mother of us all.

'Now, Mrs Vesey,' said Miss Halcombe, looking brighter, sharper, and readier than ever, by contrast with the undemonstrative old lady at her side, 'what will you have? A cutlet?'

Mrs Vesey crossed her dimpled hands on the edge of the table; smiled placidly; and said, 'Yes, dear.'

'What is that, opposite Mr Hartright? Boiled chicken, is it not? I thought you like boiled chicken better than cutlet, Mrs Vesey?'

Mrs Vesey took her dimpled hands off the edge of the table and crossed them on her lap instead; nodded contemplatively at the boiled chicken; and said 'Yes, dear.'

'Well, but which will you have, to-day? Shall Mr Hartright give you some chicken? or shall I give you some cutlet?'

Mrs Vesey put one of her dimpled hands back again on the edge of the table; hesitated drowsily; and said, 'Which you please, dear.'

'Mercy on me! it's a question for your taste, my good lady, not for mine. Suppose you have a little of both? and suppose you begin with the chicken, because Mr Hartright looks devoured by anxiety to carve for you?'

Mrs Vesey put the other dimpled hand back on the edge of the table; brightened dimly, one moment; went out again, the next; bowed obediently; and said, 'If you please, sir.'

Surely a mild, a compliant, an unutterably tranquil and harmless old lady? But enough, perhaps, for the present, of Mrs Vesey.

All this time, there were no signs of Miss Fairlie. We finished our luncheon; and still she never appeared. Miss Halcombe, whose quick eye nothing escaped, noticed the looks that I cast, from time to time, in the direction of the door.

'I understand you, Mr Hartright,' she said; 'you are wondering what has become of your other pupil. She has been down stairs, and has got over her headache; but has not sufficiently recovered her appetite to join us at lunch. If you will put yourself under my charge, I think I can undertake to find her somewhere in the garden.'

She took up a parasol, lying on a chair near her, and led the way out, by a long window at the bottom of the room, which opened on to the lawn. It is almost unnecessary to say that we left Mrs Vesey still seated at the table, with her dimpled hands still crossed on the edge of it; apparently settled in that position for the rest of the afternoon.

As we crossed the lawn, Miss Halcombe looked at me significantly, and shook her head.

'That mysterious adventure of yours,' she said, 'still remains involved in its own appropriate midnight darkness. I have been all the morning looking over my mother's letters; and I have made no discoveries yet. However, don't despair, Mr Hartright. This is a matter of curiosity; and you have got a woman for your ally. Under such conditions, success is certain, sooner or later. The letters are not exhausted. I have three packets still left, and you may confidently rely on my spending the whole evening over them.'

Here, then, was one of my anticipations of the morning still unfulfilled. I began to wonder, next, whether my introduction to Miss Fairlie would disappoint the expectations that I had been forming of her since breakfast-time.

'And how did you get on with Mr Fairlie?' inquired Miss Halcombe, as we left the lawn and turned into a shrubbery. 'Was he particularly nervous this morning? Never mind considering about your answer, Mr Hartright. The mere fact of your being obliged to consider is enough for me. I see in your face that he *was* particularly nervous; and, as I am amiably unwilling to throw you into the same condition, I ask no more.'

We turned off into a winding path while she was speaking, and approached a pretty summer-house, built of wood, in the form of a miniature Swiss châlet. The one room of the summer-house, as we ascended the steps at the door, was occupied by a young lady. She was standing near a rustic table, looking out at the inland view of moor and hill presented by a gap in the trees, and absently turning over the leaves of a little sketch-book that lay at her side. This was Miss Fairlie.

How can I describe her? How can I separate her from my own sensations, and from all that has happened in the later time? How can I see her again as she looked when my eyes first rested on her—as she should look, now, to the eyes that are about to see her in these pages?

The water-colour drawing that I made of Laura Fairlie, at an after period, in the place and attitude in which I first saw her, lies on my desk while I write. I look at it, and there dawns upon me brightly, from the dark greenish-brown background of the summer-house, a light, youthful figure, clothed in a simple muslin dress, the pattern of it formed by broad alternate stripes of delicate blue and white. A scarf of the same material sits crisply and closely round her shoulders, and a little straw hat, of the natural colour, plainly and sparingly trimmed with ribbon to match the gown, covers her head, and throws its soft pearly shadow over the upper part of her face. Her hair is of so faint and pale a brown—not flaxen, and yet almost as light; not golden, and yet almost as glossy—that it nearly melts, here and there, into the shadow of the hat. It is plainly parted and drawn back over her ears, and the line of it ripples naturally as it crosses her forehead. The eyebrows are rather darker than the hair; and the eyes are of that soft, limpid, turquoise blue, so often sung by the poets, so seldom seen in real life. Lovely eyes in colour, lovely eyes in form—large and tender and quietly thoughtful—but beautiful above all things in the clear truthfulness of look that dwells in their inmost depths, and shines through all their changes of expression with the light of a purer and a better world. The charm—most gently and yet most distinctly expressed—which they shed over the whole face, so covers and transforms its little natural human blemishes elsewhere, that it is difficult to estimate the relative merits and defects of the other features. It is hard to see that the lower part of the face is too delicately refined away towards the chin to be in full and fair proportion with the upper part; that the nose, in escaping the aquiline bend (always hard and cruel in a woman, no matter how abstractedly perfect it may be), has erred a little in the other extreme, and has missed the ideal straightness of line; and that the sweet, sensitive lips are subject to a slight nervous contraction, when she smiles, which draws them upward a little at one corner, towards the cheek. It might be possible to note these blemishes in another woman's face, but it is not easy to dwell on them in hers, so subtly are they connected with all that is individual and characteristic in her expression, and so closely does the expression depend for its full play and life, in every other feature, on the moving impulse of the eyes.

Does my poor portrait of her, my fond, patient labour of long and happy days, show me these things? Ah, how few of them are in the dim mechanical drawing, and how many in the mind with which I regard it! A fair, delicate girl, in a pretty light dress, trifling with the leaves of a sketch-book, while she looks up from it with truthful innocent blue eyes—that is all the drawing can say, all, perhaps, that even the deeper reach of thought and pen can say in their language, either. The woman who first gives life, light, and form to our shadowy conceptions of beauty, fills a void in our spiritual nature that has remained unknown to us till she appeared. Sympathies that lie too deep for words, too deep almost for thoughts, are touched, at such times, by other charms than those which the senses feel and which the resources of expression can realise. The mystery which underlies the beauty of women is never raised above the reach of all expression until it has claimed kindred with the deeper mystery in our own souls. Then, and then only, has it passed beyond the narrow region on which light falls, in this world, from the pencil and the pen.

Think of her, as you thought of the first woman who quickened the pulses within you that the rest of her sex had no art to stir. Let the kind, candid blue eyes meet yours, as they met mine, with the one matchless look which we both remember so well. Let her voice speak the music that you once loved best, attuned as sweetly to your ear as to mine. Let her footstep, as she comes and goes, in these pages, be like that other footstep to whose airy fall your own heart once beat time. Take her as the visionary nursling of your own fancy; and she will grow upon you, all the more clearly, as the living woman who dwells in mine.

Among the sensations that crowded on me, when my eyes first looked upon her—familiar sensations which we all know, which spring to life in most of our hearts, die again in so many, and renew their bright existence in so few—there was one that troubled and perplexed me; one that seemed strangely inconsistent and unaccountably out of place in Miss Fairlie's presence.

Mingling with the vivid impression produced by the charm of her fair face and head, her sweet expression, and her winning simplicity of manner, was another impression, which, in a shadowy way, suggested to me the idea of something wanting. At one time it seemed like something wanting in *her*; at another, like something wanting in myself, which hindered me from under-standing her as I ought. The impression was always strongest, in the most contradictory manner, when she looked at me; or, in other words, when I was most conscious of the harmony and charm of her face, and yet, at the same time, most troubled by the sense of an incompleteness which it was impossible to discover. Something wanting, something wanting—and where it was, and what it was, I could not say.

The effect of this curious caprice of fancy (as I thought it then) was not of a nature to set me at my ease, during a first interview with Miss Fairlie. The few kind words of welcome which she spoke found me hardly self-possessed enough to thank her in the customary phrases of reply. Observing my hesitation, and no doubt attributing it, naturally enough, to some momentary shyness, on my part, Miss Halcombe took the business of talking, as easily and readily as usual, into her own hands.

'Look there, Mr Hartright,' she said, pointing to the sketch-book on the table, and to the little delicate wandering hand that was still trifling with it. 'Surely you will acknowledge that your model pupil is found at last? The moment she hears that you are in the house, she seizes her inestimable sketch-book, looks universal Nature straight in the face, and longs to begin!'

Miss Fairlie laughed with a ready good humour, which broke out, as brightly as if it had been part of the sunshine above us, over her lovely face.

'I must not take credit to myself where no credit is due,' she said; her clear, truthful blue eyes looking alternately at Miss Halcombe and at me. 'Fond as I am of drawing, I am so conscious of my own ignorance that I am more afraid than anxious to begin. Now I know you are here, Mr Hartright, I find myself looking over my sketches, as I used to look over my lessons when I was a little girl, and when I was sadly afraid that I should turn out not fit to be heard.'

She made the confession very prettily and simply, and, with quaint, childish earnestness, drew the sketch-book away close to her own side of the table. Miss Halcombe cut the knot of the little embarrassment forthwith, in her resolute, downright way.

'Good, bad, or indifferent,' she said, 'the pupil's sketches must pass through the fiery ordeal of the master's judgment—and there's an end of it. Suppose we take them with us in the carriage, Laura, and let Mr Hartright see them, for the first time, under circumstances of perpetual jolting and interruption? If we can only confuse him all through the drive, between Nature as it is, when he looks up at the view, and Nature as it is not, when he looks down again at our sketch-books, we shall drive him into the last desperate refuge of paying us compliments, and shall slip through his professional fingers with our pet feathers of vanity all unruffled.'

'I hope Mr Hartright will pay *me* no compliments,' said Miss Fairlie, as we all left the summer-house.

'May I venture to inquire why you express that hope?' I asked.

'Because I shall believe all that you say to me,' she answered, simply.

In those few words she unconsciously gave me the key to her whole character; to that generous trust in others which, in her nature, grew innocently out of the sense of her own truth. I only knew it intuitively, then. I know it by experience, now.

We merely waited to rouse good Mrs Vesey from the place which she still occupied at the deserted luncheon-table, before we entered the open carriage for our promised drive. The old lady and Miss Halcombe occupied the back seat; and Miss Fairlie and I sat together in front, with the sketch-book open between us, fairly exhibited at last to my professional eyes. All serious criticism on the drawings, even if I had been disposed to volunteer it, was rendered impossible by Miss Halcombe's lively resolution to see nothing but the ridiculous side of the Fine Arts, as practised by herself, her sister, and ladies in general. I can remember the conversation that passed, far more easily than the sketches that I mechanically looked over. That part of the talk, especially, in which Miss Fairlie took any share, is still as vividly impressed on my memory as if I had heard it only a few hours ago.

Yes! let me acknowledge that, on this first day, I let the charm of her presence lure me from the recollection of myself and my position. The most trifling of the questions that she put to me, on the subject of using her pencil and mixing her colours; the slightest alterations of expression in the lovely eyes that looked into mine, with such an earnest desire to learn all that I could teach and to discover all that I could show, attracted more of my attention than the finest view we passed through, or the grandest changes of light and shade, as they flowed into each other over the waving moorland and the level beach. At any time, and under any circumstances of human interest, is it not strange to see how little real hold the objects of the natural world amid which we live can gain on our hearts and minds? We go to Nature for comfort in trouble, and sympathy in joy, only in books. Admiration of those beauties of the inanimate world, which modern poetry so largely and so eloquently describes, is not, even in the best of us, one of the original instincts of our nature. As children, we none of us possess it. No uninstructed man or woman possesses it. Those whose lives are most exclusively passed amid the ever-changing wonders of sea and land are also those who are most universally insensible to every aspect of Nature not directly associated with the human interest of their calling. Our capacity of appreciating the beauties of the earth we live on is, in truth, one of the civilised accomplishments which we all learn, as an Art; and, more, that very capacity is rarely practised by any of us except when our minds are most indolent and most unoccupied. How much share have the attractions of Nature ever had in the pleasurable or painful interests and emotions of ourselves or our friends? What space do they ever occupy in the thousand little narratives of personal experience which pass every day by word of mouth from one of us to the other? All that our minds can compass, all that our hearts can learn, can be accomplished with equal certainty, equal profit, and equal satisfaction to ourselves, in the poorest as in the richest prospect that the face of the earth can show. There is surely a reason for this want of inborn sympathy between the creature and the creation around it, a reason which may perhaps be found in the widely differing destinies of man and his earthly sphere. The grandest mountain prospect that the eye can range over is appointed to annihilation. The smallest human interest that the pure heart can feel is appointed to immortality.

We had been out nearly three hours, when the carriage again passed through the gates of Limmeridge House.

On our way back, I had let the ladies settle for themselves the first point of view which they were to sketch, under my instructions, on the afternoon of the next day. When they withdrew to dress for dinner, and when I was alone again in my little sitting-room, my spirits seemed to leave me on a sudden. I felt ill at ease and dissatisfied with myself, I hardly knew why. Perhaps I was now conscious, for the first time, of having enjoyed our drive too much in the character of a guest, and too little in the character of a drawing-master. Perhaps that strange sense of something wanting, either in Miss Fairlie or in myself, which had perplexed me when I was first introduced to her, haunted me still. Anyhow, it was a relief to my spirits when the dinner-hour called me out of my solitude, and took me back to the society of the ladies of the house.

I was struck, on entering the drawing-room, by the curious contrast, rather in material than in colour, of the dresses which they now wore. While Mrs Vesey and Miss Halcombe were richly clad (each in the manner most becoming to her age), the first in silver-grey, and the second in that delicate primrose-yellow colour, which matches so well with a dark complexion and black hair, Miss Fairlie was unpretendingly and almost poorly dressed in plain white muslin. It was spotlessly pure; it was beautifully put on; but still it was the sort of dress which the wife or daughter of a poor man might have worn; and it made her, so far as externals went, look less affluent in circumstances than her own governess. At a later period, when I learnt to know more of Miss Fairlie's character, I discovered that this curious contrast, on the wrong side, was due to her natural delicacy of feeling and natural intensity of aversion to the slightest personal display of her own wealth. Neither Mrs Vesey nor Miss Halcombe could ever induce her to let the advantage in dress desert the two ladies who were poor, to lean to the side of the one lady who was rich.

When dinner was over, we returned together to the drawing-room. Although Mr Fairlie (emulating the magnificent condescension of the monarch who had picked up Titian's brush for him) had instructed his butler to consult my wishes in relation to the wine that I might prefer after dinner, I was resolute enough to resist the temptation of sitting in solitary grandeur among bottles of my own choosing, and sensible enough to ask the ladies' permission to leave the table with them habitually, on the civilised foreign plan, during the period of my residence at Limmeridge House.

The drawing-room, to which we had now withdrawn for the rest of the evening, was on the ground-floor, and was of the same shape and size as the breakfast-room. Large glass doors at the lower end opened on to a terrace, beautifully ornamented along its whole length with a profusion of flowers. The soft, hazy twilight was just shading leaf and blossom alike into harmony with its own sober hues, as we entered the room; and the sweet evening scent of the flowers met us with its fragrant welcome through the open glass doors. Good Mrs Vesey (always the first of the party to sit down) took possession of an arm-chair in a corner, and dozed off comfortably to sleep. At my request, Miss Fairlie placed herself at the piano. As I followed her to a seat near the instrument, I saw Miss Halcombe retire into a recess of one of the side windows, to proceed with the search through her mother's letters by the last quiet rays of the evening light.

How vividly that peaceful home-picture of the drawing-room comes back to me while I write! From the place where I sat, I could see Miss Halcombe's graceful figure, half of it in soft light, half in mysterious shadow, bending intently over the letters in her lap; while, nearer to me, the fair profile of the player at the piano was just delicately defined against the faintly deepening background of the inner wall of the room. Outside, on the terrace, the clustering flowers and long grasses and creepers waved so gently in the light evening air, that the sound of their rustling never reached us. The sky was without a cloud; and the dawning mystery of moonlight began to tremble already in the region of the eastern heaven. The sense of peace and seclusion soothed all thought and feeling into a rapt, unearthly repose; and the balmy quiet that deepened ever with the deepening light, seemed to hover over us with a gentler influence still, when there stole upon it from the piano the heavenly tenderness of the music of Mozart. It was an evening of sights and sounds never to forget.

We all sat silent in the places we had chosen—Mrs Vesey still sleeping, Miss Fairlie still playing, Miss Halcombe still reading—till the light failed us. By this time the moon had stolen round to the terrace, and soft, mysterious rays of light were slanting already across the lower end of the room. The change from the twilight obscurity was so beautiful, that we banished the lamps, by common consent, when the servant brought them in; and kept the large room unlighted, except by the glimmer of the two candles at the piano.

For half an hour more, the music still went on. After that, the beauty of the moonlight view on the terrace tempted Miss Fairlie out to look at it; and I followed her. When the candles at the piano had been lighted, Miss Halcombe had changed her place, so as to continue her examination of the letters by their assistance. We left her, on a low chair, at one side of the instrument, so absorbed over her reading that she did not seem to notice when we moved.

We had been out on the terrace together, just in front of the glass doors, hardly so long as five minutes, I should think; and Miss Fairlie was, by my advice, just tying her white handkerchief over her head as a precaution against the night air—when I heard Miss Halcombe's voice—low, eager, and altered from its natural lively tone—pronounce my name.

'Mr Hartright,' she said, 'will you come here for a minute? I want to speak to you.'

I entered the room again immediately. The piano stood about half way down along the inner wall. On the side of the instrument farthest from the terrace, Miss Halcombe was sitting with the letters scattered on her lap, and with one in her hand selected from them, and held close to the candle. On the side nearest to the terrace there stood a low ottoman, on which I took my place. In this position, I was not far from the glass doors; and I could see Miss Fairlie plainly, as she passed and repassed the opening on to the terrace; walking slowly from end to end of it in the full radiance of the moon.

'I want you to listen while I read the concluding passages in this letter,' said Miss Halcombe. 'Tell me if you think they throw any light upon your strange adventure on the road to London. The letter is addressed by my mother to her second husband, Mr Fairlie; and the date refers to a period of between eleven and twelve years since. At that time, Mr and Mrs Fairlie, and my half-sister Laura, had been living for years in this house; and I was away from them, completing my education at a school in Paris.'

She looked and spoke earnestly, and, as I thought, a little uneasily, as well. At the moment when she raised the letter to the candle before beginning to read it, Miss Fairlie passed us on the terrace, looked in for a moment, and, seeing that we were engaged, slowly walked on.

Miss Halcombe began to read, as follows:

' "You will be tired, my dear Philip, of hearing perpetually about my schools and my scholars. Lay the blame, pray, on the dull uniformity of life at Limmeridge, and not on me. Besides, this time, I have something really interesting to tell you about a new scholar.

' "You know old Mrs Kempe, at the village shop. Well, after years of ailing, the doctor has at last given her up, and she is dying slowly, day by day. Her only living relation, a sister, arrived last week to take care of her. This sister comes all the way from Hampshire—her name is Mrs Catherick. Four days ago Mrs Catherick came here to see me, and brought her only child with her, a sweet little girl about a year older than our darling Laura——" '

As the last sentence fell from the reader's lips, Miss Fairlie passed us on the terrace once more. She was softly singing to herself one of the melodies which she had been playing earlier in the evening. Miss Halcombe waited till she had passed out of sight again; and then went on with the letter:

' "Mrs Catherick is a decent, well-behaved, respectable woman; middle aged, and with the remains of having been moderately, only moderately, nice-looking. There is something in her manner and in her appearance, however, which I can't make out. She is reserved about herself to the point of downright secrecy; and there is a look in her face—I can't describe it—which suggests to me that she has something on her mind. She is altogether what you would call a walking mystery. Her errand at Limme-ridge House, however, was simple enough. When she left Hampshire to nurse her sister, Mrs Kempe, through her last illness, she had been obliged to bring her daughter with her, through having no one at home to take care of the little girl. Mrs Kempe may die in a week's time, or may linger on for months; and Mrs Catherick's object was to ask me to let her daughter, Anne, have the benefit of attending my school; subject to the condition of her being removed from it to go home again with her mother, after Mrs Kempe's death. I consented at once; and when Laura and I went out for our walk, we took the little girl (who is just eleven years old) to the school, that very day." '

Once more, Miss Fairlie's figure, bright and soft in its snowy muslin dress—her face prettily framed by the white folds of the handkerchief which she had tied under her chin—passed by us in the moonlight. Once more, Miss Halcombe waited till she was out of sight; and then went on:

' "I have taken a violent fancy, Philip, to my new scholar, for a reason which I mean to keep till the last for the sake of surprising you. Her mother having told me as little about the child as she told me of herself, I was left to discover (which I did on the first day when we tried her at lessons) that the poor little thing's intellect is not developed as it ought to be at her age. Seeing this, I had her up to the house the next day, and privately arranged with the doctor to come and watch her and question her, and tell me what he thought. His opinion is that she will grow out of it. But he says her careful bringing-up at school is a matter of great importance just now, because her unusual slowness in acquiring ideas implies an unusual tenacity in keeping them, when they are once received into her mind. Now, my love, you must not imagine, in your off-hand way, that I have been attaching myself to an idiot. This poor little Anne Catherick is a sweet, affectionate, grateful girl; and says the quaintest, prettiest things (as you shall judge by an instance), in the most oddly-sudden, surprised, half-frightened way. Although she is dressed very neatly, her clothes show a sad want of taste in colour and pattern. So I arranged, yesterday, that some of our darling Laura's old white frocks and white hats should be altered for Anne Catherick; explaining to her that little girls of her complexion looked neater and better in all white than in anything else. She hesitated and seemed puzzled for a minute; then flushed up, and appeared to understand. Her little hand clasped mine, suddenly. She kissed it, Philip; and said (oh, so earnestly!), 'I will always wear white as long as I live. It will help me to remember you, ma'am, and to think that I am pleasing you still, when I go away and see you no more.' This is only one specimen of the quaint things she says so prettily. Poor little soul! She shall have a stock of white frocks, made with good deep tucks, to let out for her as she grows——" '

Miss Halcombe paused, and looked at me across the piano.

'Did the forlorn woman whom you met in the high-road seem young?' she asked. 'Young enough to be two or three-and-twenty?'

'Yes, Miss Halcombe, as young as that.'

'And she was strangely dressed, from head to foot, all in white?'

'All in white.'

While the answer was passing my lips, Miss Fairlie glided into view on the terrace, for the third time. Instead of proceeding on her walk, she stopped, with her back turned towards us; and, leaning on the balustrade of the terrace, looked down into the garden beyond. My eyes fixed upon the white gleam of her muslin gown and head-dress in the moonlight, and a sensation, for which I can find no name—a sensation that quickened my pulse, and raised a fluttering at my heart—began to steal over me.

'All in white?' Miss Halcombe repeated. 'The most important sentences in the letter, Mr Hartright, are those at the end, which I will read to you immediately. But I can't help dwelling a little upon the coincidence of the white costume of the woman you met, and the white frocks which produced that strange answer from my mother's little scholar. The doctor may have been wrong when he discovered the child's defects of intellect, and predicted that she would "grow out of them." She may never have grown out of them; and the old grateful fancy about dressing in white, which was a serious feeling to the girl, may be a serious feeling to the woman still.'

I said a few words in answer—I hardly know what. All my attention was concentrated on the white gleam of Miss Fairlie's muslin dress.

'Listen to the last sentences of the letter,' said Miss Halcombe. 'I think they will surprise you.'

As she raised the letter to the light of the candle, Miss Fairlie turned from the balustrade, looked doubtfully up and down the terrace, advanced a step towards the glass doors, and then stopped, facing us.

Meanwhile, Miss Halcombe read me the last sentences to which she had referred:

' "And now, my love, seeing that I am at the end of my paper, now for the real reason, the surprising reason, for my fondness for little Anne Catherick. My dear Philip, although she is not half so pretty, she is, nevertheless, by one of those extraordinary caprices of accidental resemblance which one sometimes sees, the living likeness, in her hair, her complexion, the colour of her eyes, and the shape of her face——" '

I started up from the ottoman, before Miss Halcombe could pronounce the next words. A thrill of the same feeling which ran through me when the touch was laid upon my shoulder on the lonely high-road, chilled me again.

There stood Miss Fairlie, a white figure, alone in the moonlight; in her attitude, in the turn of her head, in her complexion, in the shape of her face, the living image, at that distance and under those circumstances, of the woman in white! The doubt which had troubled my mind for hours and hours past, flashed into conviction in an instant. That 'something wanting' was my own recognition of the ominous likeness between the fugitive from the asylum and my pupil at Limmeridge House.

'You see it!' said Miss Halcombe. She dropped the useless letter, and her eyes flashed as they met mine. 'You see it now, as my mother saw it eleven years since!'

'I see it—more unwillingly than I can say. To associate that forlorn, friendless, lost woman, even by an accidental likeness only, with Miss Fairlie, seems like casting a shadow on the future of the bright creature who stands looking at us now. Let me lose the impression again, as soon as possible. Call her in, out of the dreary moonlight—pray call her in!'

'Mr Hartright, you surprise me. Whatever women may be, I thought that men, in the nineteenth century, were above superstition.'

'Pray call her in!'

'Hush, hush! She is coming of her own accord. Say nothing in her presence. Let this discovery of the likeness be kept a secret between you and me. Come in, Laura; come in, and wake Mrs Vesey with the piano. Mr Hartright is petitioning for some more music, and he wants it, this time, of the lightest and liveliest kind.'

VIII

So ended my eventful first day at Limmeridge House.

Miss Halcombe and I kept our secret. After the discovery of the likeness no fresh light seemed destined to break over the mystery of the woman in white. At the first safe opportunity Miss Halcombe cautiously led her half-sister to speak of their mother, of old times, and of Anne Catherick. Miss Fairlie's recollections of the little scholar at Limmeridge were, however, only of the most vague and general kind. She remembered the likeness between herself and her mother's favourite pupil, as something which had been supposed to exist in past times; but she did not refer to the gift of the white dresses, or to the singular form of words in which the child had artlessly expressed her gratitude for them. She remembered that Anne had remained at Limmeridge for a few months only, and had then left it to go back to her home in Hampshire; but she could not say whether the mother and daughter had ever returned, or had ever been heard of afterwards.

No further search, on Miss Halcombe's part, through the few letters of Mrs Fairlie's writing which she had left unread, assisted in clearing up the uncertainties still left to perplex us. We had identified the unhappy woman whom I had met in the night-time, with Anne Catherick—we had made some advance, at least, towards connecting the probably defective condition of the poor creature's intellect with the peculiarity of her being dressed all in white, and with the continuance, in her maturer years, of her childish gratitude towards Mrs Fairlie—and there, so far as we knew at that time, our discoveries had ended.

The days passed on, the weeks passed on; and the track of the golden autumn wound its bright way visibly through the green summer of the trees. Peaceful, fast-flowing, happy time! my story glides by you now, as swiftly as you once glided by me. Of all the treasures of enjoyment that you poured so freely into my heart, how much is left me that has purpose and value enough to be written on this page? Nothing but the saddest of all confessions that a man can make—the confession of his own folly.

The secret which that confession discloses should be told with little effort, for it has indirectly escaped me already. The poor weak words which have failed to describe Miss Fairlie, have succeeded in betraying the sensations she awakened in me. It is so with us all. Our words are giants when they do us an injury, and dwarfs when they do us a service.

I loved her.

Ah! how well I know all the sadness and all the mockery that is contained in those three words. I can sigh over my mournful confession with the tenderest woman who reads it and pities me. I can laugh at it as bitterly as the hardest man who tosses it from him in contempt. I loved her! Feel for me, or despise me, I confess it with the same immovable resolution to own the truth.

Was there no excuse for me? There was some excuse to be found, surely, in the conditions under which my term of hired service was passed at Limmeridge House.

My morning hours succeeded each other calmly in the quiet and seclusion of my own room. I had just work enough to do, in mounting my employer's drawings, to keep my hands and eyes pleasurably employed, while my mind was left free to enjoy the dangerous luxury of its own unbridled thoughts. A perilous solitude, for it lasted long enough to enervate, not long enough to fortify me. A perilous solitude, for it was followed by afternoons and evenings spent, day after day and week after week, alone in the society of two women, one of whom possessed all the accomplishments of grace, wit, and high-breeding, the other all the charms of beauty, gentleness, and simple truth, that can purify and subdue the heart of man. Not a day passed, in that dangerous intimacy of teacher and pupil, in which my hand was not close to Miss Fairlie's; my cheek, as we bent together over her sketchbook, almost touching hers. The more attentively she watched every movement of my brush, the more closely I was breathing the perfume of her hair, and the warm fragrance of her breath. It was part of my service, to live in the very light of her eyes—at one time to be bending over her, so close to her bosom as to tremble at the thought of touching it; at another, to feel her bending over me, bending so close to see what I was about, that her voice sank low when she spoke to me, and her ribbons brushed my cheek in the wind before she could draw them back.

The evenings which followed the sketching excursions of the afternoon, varied, rather than checked, these innocent, these inevitable familiarities. My natural fondness for the music which she played with such tender feeling, such delicate womanly taste, and her natural enjoyment of giving me back, by the practice of her art, the pleasure which I had offered to her by the practice of mine, only wove another tie which drew us closer and closer to one another. The accidents of conversation; the simple habits which regulated even such a little thing as the position of our places at table; the play of Miss Halcombe's ever-ready raillery, always directed against my anxiety, as teacher, while it sparkled over her enthusiasm as pupil; the harmless expression of poor Mrs Vesey's drowsy approval which connected Miss Fairlie and me as two model young people who never disturbed her—every one of these trifles, and many more, combined to fold us together in the same domestic atmosphere, and to lead us both insensibly to the same hopeless end.

I should have remembered my position, and have put myself secretly on my guard. I did so; but not till it was too late. All the discretion, all the experience, which had availed me with other women, and secured me against other temptations, failed me with her. It had been my profession, for years past, to be in this close contact with young girls of all ages, and of all orders of beauty. I had accepted the position as part of my calling in life; I had trained myself to leave all the sympathies natural to my age in my employer's outer hall, as coolly as I left my umbrella there before I went up-stairs. I had long since learnt to understand, composedly and as a matter of course, that my situation in life was considered a guarantee against any of my female pupils feeling more than the most ordinary interest in me, and that I was admitted among beautiful and captivating women, much as a harmless domestic animal is admitted among them. This guardian experience I had gained early; this guardian experience had sternly and strictly guided me straight along my own poor narrow path, without once letting me stray aside, to the right hand or to the left. And now, I and my trusty talisman were parted for the first time. Yes, my hardly-earned self-control was as completely lost to me as if I had never possessed it; lost to me, as it is lost every day to other men, in other critical situations, where women are concerned. I know, now, that I should have questioned myself from the first.

I should have asked why any room in the house was better than home to me when she entered it, and barren as a desert when she went out again—why I always noticed and remembered the little changes in her dress that I had noticed and remembered in no other woman's before—why I saw her, heard her, and touched her (when we shook hands at night and morning) as I had never seen, heard, and touched any other woman in my life? I should have looked into my own heart, and found this new growth springing up there, and plucked it out while it was young. Why was this easiest, simplest work of self-culture always too much for me? The explanation has been written already in the three words that were many enough, and plain enough, for my confession. I loved her.

The days passed, the weeks passed; it was approaching the third month of my stay in Cumberland. The delicious monotony of life in our calm seclusion, flowed on with me like a smooth stream with a swimmer who glides down the current. All memory of the past, all thought of the future, all sense of the falseness and hopelessness of my own position, lay hushed within me into deceitful rest. Lulled by the Syren-song that my own heart sung to me, with eyes shut to all sight, and ears closed to all sound of danger, I drifted nearer and nearer to the fatal rocks. The warning that aroused me at last, and startled me into sudden, self-accusing consciousness of my own weakness, was the plainest, the truest, the kindest of all warnings, for it came silently from *her*.

We had parted one night, as usual. No word had fallen from my lips, at that time or at any time before it, that could betray me, or startle her into sudden knowledge of the truth. But, when we met again in the morning, a change had come over her—a change that told me all.

I shrank then—I shrink still—from invading the innermost sanctuary of her heart, and laying it open to others, as I have laid open my own. Let it be enough to say that the time when she first surprised my secret, was, I firmly believe, the time when she first surprised her own, and the time, also, when she changed towards me in the interval of one night. Her nature, too truthful to deceive others, was too noble to deceive itself. When the doubt that I had hushed asleep, first laid its weary weight on her heart, the true face owned all, and said, in its own frank simple language—I am sorry for him; I am sorry for myself.

It said this, and more, which I could not then interpret. I understood but too well the change in her manner, to greater kindness and quicker readiness in interpreting all my wishes, before others—to constraint and sadness, and nervous anxiety to absorb herself in the first occupation she could seize on, whenever we happened to be left together alone. I understood why the sweet sensitive lips smiled so rarely and so restrainedly now; and why the clear blue eyes looked at me, sometimes with the pity of an angel, sometimes with the innocent perplexity of a child. But the change meant more than this.

There was a coldness in her hand, there was an unnatural immobility in her
face, there was in all her movements the mute expression of constant fear
and clinging self-reproach. The sensations that I could trace to herself and
to me, the unacknowledged sensations that we were feeling in common,
were not these. There were certain elements of the change in her that were
still secretly drawing us together, and others that were, as secretly, beginning
to drive us apart.

In my doubt and perplexity, in my vague suspicion of something hidden
which I was left to find by my own unaided efforts, I examined Miss
Halcombe's looks and manner for enlightenment. Living in such intimacy as
ours, no serious alteration could take place in any one of us which did not
sympathetically affect the others. The change in Miss Fairlie was reflected
in her half-sister. Although not a word escaped Miss Halcombe which
hinted at an altered state of feeling towards myself, her penetrating eyes had
contracted a new habit of always watching me. Sometimes, the look was
like suppressed anger; sometimes, like suppressed dread; sometimes, like
neither—like nothing, in short, which I could understand. A week elapsed,
leaving us all three still in this position of secret constraint towards one
another. My situation, aggravated by the sense of my own miserable weakness and forgetfulness of myself, now too late awakened in me, was becoming intolerable. I felt that I must cast off the oppression under which I was
living, at once and for ever—yet how to act for the best, or what to say first,
was more than I could tell.

From this position of helplessness and humiliation, I was rescued by Miss
Halcombe. Her lips told me the bitter, the necessary, the unexpected truth;
her hearty kindness sustained me under the shock of hearing it; her sense
and courage turned to its right use an event which threatened the worst that
could happen, to me and to others, in Limmeridge House.

IX

It was on a Thursday in the week, and nearly at the end of the third month
of my sojourn in Cumberland.

In the morning, when I went down into the breakfast-room, at the usual
hour, Miss Halcombe, for the first time since I had known her, was absent
from her customary place at the table.

Miss Fairlie was out on the lawn. She bowed to me, but did not come in.
Not a word had dropped from my lips or from hers that could unsettle either
of us—and yet the same unacknowledged sense of embarrassment made us
shrink alike from meeting one another alone. She waited on the lawn; and
I waited in the breakfast-room, till Mrs Vesey or Miss Halcombe came in.
How quickly I should have joined her; how readily we should have shaken
hands, and glided into our customary talk, only a fortnight ago!

In a few minutes, Miss Halcombe entered. She had a preoccupied look, and she made her apologies for being late, rather absently.

'I have been detained,' she said, 'by a consultation with Mr Fairlie on a domestic matter which he wished to speak to me about.'

Miss Fairlie came in from the garden; and the usual morning greeting passed between us. Her hand struck colder to mine than ever. She did not look at me; and she was very pale. Even Mrs Vesey noticed it, when she entered the room a moment after.

'I suppose it's the change in the wind,' said the old lady. 'The winter is coming—ah, my love, the winter is coming soon!'

In her heart and in mine it had come already!

Our morning meal—once so full of pleasant good-humoured discussions of the plans for the day—was short and silent. Miss Fairlie seemed to feel the oppression of the long pauses in the conversation; and looked appealingly to her sister to fill them up. Miss Halcombe, after once or twice hesitating and checking herself, in a most uncharacteristic manner, spoke at last.

'I have seen your uncle this morning, Laura,' she said. 'He thinks the purple room is the one that ought to be got ready; and he confirms what I told you. Monday is the day—not Tuesday.'

While these words were being spoken, Miss Fairlie looked down at the table beneath her. Her fingers moved nervously among the crumbs that were scattered on the cloth. The paleness on her cheeks spread to her lips, and the lips themselves trembled visibly. I was not the only person present who noticed this. Miss Halcombe saw it, too; and at once set us the example of rising from table.

Mrs Vesey and Miss Fairlie left the room together. The kind sorrowful blue eyes looked at me, for a moment, with the prescient sadness of a coming and a long farewell. I felt the answering pang in my own heart—the pang that told me I must lose her soon, and love her the more unchangeably for the loss.

I turned towards the garden, when the door had closed on her. Miss Halcombe was standing with her hat in her hand, and her shawl over her arm, by the large window that led out to the lawn, and was looking at me attentively.

'Have you any leisure time to spare,' she asked, 'before you begin to work in your own room?'

'Certainly, Miss Halcombe. I have always time at your service.'

'I want to say a word to you in private, Mr Hartright. Get your hat, and come out into the garden. We are not likely to be disturbed there at this hour in the morning.'

As we stepped out on to the lawn, one of the under-gardeners—a mere lad—passed us on his way to the house, with a letter in his hand. Miss Halcombe stopped him.

'Is that letter for me?' she asked.

'Nay, miss; it's just said to be for Miss Fairlie,' answered the lad, holding out the letter as he spoke.

Miss Halcombe took it from him, and looked at the address.

'A strange handwriting,' she said to herself. 'Who can Laura's correspondent be? Where did you get this?' she continued, addressing the gardener.

'Well, miss,' said the lad, 'I just got it from a woman.'

'What woman?'

'A woman well stricken in age.'

'Oh, an old woman. Any one you knew?'

'I canna' tak' it on mysel' to say that she was other than a stranger to me.'

'Which way did she go?'

'That gate,' said the under-gardener, turning with great deliberation towards the south, and embracing the whole of that part of England with one comprehensive sweep of his arm.

'Curious,' said Miss Halcombe; 'I suppose it must be a begging-letter. There,' she added, handing the letter back to the lad, 'take it to the house, and give it one of the servants. And now, Mr Hartright, if you have no objection, let us walk this way.'

She led me across the lawn, along the same path by which I had followed her on the day after my arrival at Limmeridge. At the little summer-house in which Laura Fairlie and I had first seen each other, she stopped, and broke the silence which she had steadily maintained while we were walking together.

'What I have to say to you, I can say here.'

With those words, she entered the summer-house, took one of the chairs at the little round table inside, and signed to me take the other. I suspected what was coming when she spoke to me in the breakfast-room; I felt certain of it now.

'Mr Hartright,' she said, 'I am going to begin by making a frank avowal to you. I am going to say—without phrase-making, which I detest; or paying compliments, which I heartily despise—that I have come, in the course of your residence with us, to feel a strong friendly regard for you. I was predisposed in your favour when you first told me of your conduct towards that unhappy woman whom you met under such remarkable circumstances. Your management of the affair might not have been prudent; but it showed the self-control, the delicacy, and the compassion of a man who was naturally a gentleman. It made me expect good things from you; and you have not disappointed my expectations.'

She paused—but held up her hand at the same time, as a sign that she awaited no answer from me before she proceeded. When I entered the summer-house, no thought was in me of the woman in white. But, now, Miss Halcombe's own words had put the memory of my adventure back in my mind. It remained there, throughout the interview—remained, and not without a result.

'As your friend,' she proceeded, 'I am going to tell you, at once, in my own plain, blunt, downright language, that I have discovered your secret—without help or hint, mind, from any one else. Mr Hartright, you have thoughtlessly allowed yourself to form an attachment—a serious and devoted attachment, I am afraid—to my sister, Laura. I don't put you to the pain of confessing it, in so many words, because I see and know that you are too honest to deny it. I don't even blame you—I pity you for opening your heart to a hopeless affection. You have not attempted to take any underhand advantage—you have not spoken to my sister in secret. You are guilty of weakness and want of attention to your own best interests, but of nothing worse. If you had acted, in any single respect, less delicately and less modestly, I should have told you to leave the house, without an instant's notice, or an instant's consultation of anybody. As it is, I blame the misfortune of your years and your position—I don't blame *you*. Shake hands—I have given you pain; I am going to give you more; but there is no help for it—shake hands with your friend, Marian Halcombe, first.'

The sudden kindness—the warm, high-minded, fearless sympathy which met me on such mercifully-equal terms, which appealed with such delicate and generous abruptness straight to my heart, my honour, and my courage, overcame me in an instant. I tried to look at her, when she took my hand, but my eyes were dim. I tried to thank her, but my voice failed me.

'Listen to me,' she said, considerately avoiding all notice of my loss of self-control. 'Listen to me, and let us get it over at once. It is a real, true relief to me that I am not obliged, in what I have now to say, to enter into the question—the hard and cruel question as I think it—of social inequalities. Circumstances which will try *you* to the quick, spare *me* the ungracious necessity of paining a man who has lived in friendly intimacy under the same roof with myself by any humiliating reference to matters of rank and station. You must leave Limmeridge House, Mr Hartright, before more harm is done. It is my duty to say that to you; and it would be equally my duty to say it, under precisely the same serious necessity, if you were the representative of the oldest and wealthiest family in England. You must leave us, not because you are a teacher of drawing——'

She waited a moment; turned her face full on me; and, reaching across the table, laid her hand firmly on my arm.

'Not because you are a teacher of drawing,' she repeated, 'but because Laura Fairlie is engaged to be married.'

The last word went like a bullet to my heart. My arm lost all sensation of the hand that grasped it. I never moved, and never spoke. The sharp autumn breeze that scattered the dead leaves at our feet, came as cold to me, on a sudden, as if my own mad hopes were dead leaves, too, whirled

away by the wind like the rest. Hopes! Betrothed, or not betrothed, she was
equally far from *me*. Would other men have remembered that in my place?
Not if they had loved her as I did.

The pang passed; and nothing but the dull numbing pain of it remained.
I felt Miss Halcombe's hand again, tightening its hold on my arm—I raised
my head, and looked at her. Her large black eyes were rooted on me,
watching the white change on my face, which I felt, and which she saw.

'Crush it!' she said. 'Here, where you first saw her, crush it! Don't shrink
under it like a woman. Tear it out; trample it under foot like a man.'

The suppressed vehemence with which she spoke; the strength which her
will—concentrated in the look she fixed on me, and in the hold on my arm
that she had not yet relinquished—communicated to mine, steadied me. We
both waited for a minute, in silence. At the end of that time, I had justified
her generous faith in my manhood; I had, outwardly at least, recovered my
self-control.

'Are you yourself again?'

'Enough myself, Miss Halcombe, to ask your pardon and hers. Enough
myself, to be guided by your advice, and to prove my gratitude in that way,
if I can prove it in no other.'

'You have proved it already,' she answered, 'by those words. Mr Hartright, concealment is at an end between us. I cannot affect to hide from *you*,
what my sister has unconsciously shown to *me*. You must leave us for her
sake, as well as for your own. Your presence here, your necessary intimacy
with us, harmless as it has been, God knows, in all other respects, has
unsteadied her and made her wretched. I, who love her better than my own
life—I, who have learnt to believe in that pure, noble, innocent nature as I
believe in my religion—know but too well the secret misery of self-reproach
that she has been suffering, since the first shadow of a feeling disloyal to her
marriage engagement entered her heart in spite of her. I don't say—it would
be useless to attempt to say it, after what has happened—that her engagement has ever had a strong hold on her affections. It is an engagement of
honour, not of love—her father sanctioned it on his death-bed, two years
since—she herself neither welcomed it, nor shrank from it—she was content
to make it. Till you came here, she was in the position of hundreds of other
women, who marry men without being greatly attracted to them or greatly
repelled by them, and who learn to love them (when they don't learn to hate!)
after marriage, instead of before. I hope more earnestly than words can
say—and you should have the self-sacrificing courage to hope too—that the
new thoughts and feelings which have disturbed the old calmness and the old
content, have not taken root too deeply to be ever removed. Your absence
(if I had less belief in your honour, and your courage, and your sense, I
should not trust to them as I am trusting now)—your absence will help my
efforts; and time will help us all three. It is something to know that my first

confidence in you was not all misplaced. It is something to know that you will not be less honest, less manly, less considerate towards the pupil whose relation to yourself you have had the misfortune to forget, than towards the stranger and the outcast whose appeal to you was not made in vain.'

Again the chance reference to the woman in white! Was there no possibility of speaking of Miss Fairlie and of me without raising the memory of Anne Catherick, and setting her between us like a fatality that it was hopeless to avoid?

'Tell me what apology I can make to Mr Fairlie for breaking my engagement,' I said. 'Tell me when to go after that apology is accepted. I promise implicit obedience to you and to your advice.'

'Time is, every way, of importance,' she answered. 'You heard me refer this morning to Monday next, and to the necessity of setting the purple room in order. The visitor whom we expect on Monday——'

I could not wait for her to be more explicit. Knowing what I knew now, the memory of Miss Fairlie's look and manner at the breakfast-table told me that the expected visitor at Limmeridge House was her future husband. I tried to force it back; but something rose within me at that moment stronger than my own will; and I interrupted Miss Halcombe.

'Let me go to-day,' I said, bitterly. 'The sooner the better.'

'No; not to-day,' she replied. 'The only reason you can assign to Mr Fairlie for your departure, before the end of your engagement, must be that an unforeseen necessity compels you to ask his permission to return at once to London. You must wait till to-morrow to tell him that, at the time when the post comes in, because he will then understand the sudden change in your plans, by associating it with the arrival of a letter from London. It is miserable and sickening to descend to deceit, even of the most harmless kind—but I know Mr Fairlie, and if you once excite his suspicions that you are trifling with him, he will refuse to release you. Speak to him on Friday morning; occupy yourself afterwards (for the sake of your own interests with your employer), in leaving your unfinished work in as little confusion as possible; and quit this place on Saturday. It will be time enough, then, Mr Hartright, for you, and for all of us.'

Before I could assure her that she might depend on my acting in the strictest accordance with her wishes, we were both startled by advancing footsteps in the shrubbery. Some one was coming from the house to seek for us! I felt the blood rush into my cheeks, and then leave them again. Could the third person who was fast approaching us, at such a time and under such circumstances, be Miss Fairlie?

It was a relief—so sadly, so hopelessly was my position towards her changed already—it was absolutely a relief to me, when the person who had disturbed us appeared at the entrance of the summer-house, and proved to be only Miss Fairlie's maid.

'Could I speak to you for a moment, miss?' said the girl, in rather a flurried, unsettled manner.

Miss Halcombe descended the steps into the shrubbery, and walked aside a few paces with the maid.

Left by myself, my mind reverted, with a sense of forlorn wretchedness which it is not in any words that I can find to describe, to my approaching return to the solitude and the despair of my lonely London home. Thoughts of my kind old mother, and of my sister, who had rejoiced with her so innocently over my prospects in Cumberland—thoughts whose long banishment from my heart it was now my shame and my reproach to realise for the first time—came back to me with the loving mournfulness of old, neglected friends. My mother and my sister, what would they feel when I returned to them from my broken engagement, with the confession of my miserable secret—they who had parted from me so hopefully on that last happy night in the Hampstead cottage!

Anne Catherick again! Even the memory of the farewell evening with my mother and my sister could not return to me now, unconnected with that other memory of the moonlight walk back to London. What did it mean? Were that woman and I to meet once more? It was possible, at the least. Did she know that I lived in London? Yes; I had told her so, either before or after that strange question of hers, when she had asked me so distrustfully if I knew many men of the rank of Baronet. Either before or after—my mind was not calm enough, then, to remember which.

A few minutes elapsed before Miss Halcombe dismissed the maid and came back to me. She, too, looked flurried and unsettled, now.

'We have arranged all that is necessary, Mr Hartright,' she said. 'We have understood each other, as friends should; and we may go back at once to the house. To tell you the truth, I am uneasy about Laura. She has sent to say she wants to see me directly; and the maid reports that her mistress is apparently very much agitated by a letter that she has received this morning—the same letter, no doubt, which I sent to the house before we came here.'

We retraced our steps together hastily along the shrubbery path. Although Miss Halcombe had ended all that she thought it necessary to say, on her side, I had not ended all that I wanted to say on mine. From the moment when I had discovered that the expected visitor at Limmeridge was Miss Fairlie's future husband, I had felt a bitter curiosity, a burning envious eagerness, to know who he was. It was possible that a future opportunity of putting the question might not easily offer; so I risked asking it on our way back to the house.

'Now that you are kind enough to tell me we have understood each other, Miss Halcombe,' I said; 'now that you are sure of my gratitude for your forbearance and my obedience to your wishes, may I venture to ask who'—(I hesitated; I had forced myself to think of him, but it was harder still to speak of him, as her promised husband) 'who the gentleman engaged to Miss Fairlie is?'

Her mind was evidently occupied with the message she had received from her sister. She answered, in a hasty, absent way:

'A gentleman of large property, in Hampshire.'

Hampshire! Anne Catherick's native place. Again, and yet again, the woman in white. There *was* a fatality in it.

'And his name?' I said, as quietly and indifferently as I could.

'Sir Percival Glyde.'

Sir—Sir Percival! Anne Catherick's question—that suspicious question about the men of the rank of Baronet whom I might happen to know—had hardly been dismissed from my mind by Miss Halcombe's return to me in the summer-house, before it was recalled again by her own answer. I stopped suddenly, and looked at her.

'Sir Percival Glyde,' she repeated, imagining that I had not heard her former reply.

'Knight, or Baronet?' I asked, with an agitation that I could hide no longer.

She paused for a moment, and then answered, rather coldly:

'Baronet, of course.'

X

NOT a word more was said, on either side, as we walked back to the house. Miss Halcombe hastened immediately to her sister's room; and I withdrew to my studio to set in order all of Mr Fairlie's drawings that I had not yet mounted and restored before I resigned them to the care of other hands. Thoughts that I had hitherto restrained, thoughts that made my position harder than ever to endure, crowded on me now that I was alone.

She was engaged to be married; and her future husband was Sir Percival Glyde. A man of the rank of Baronet, and the owner of property in Hampshire.

There were hundreds of baronets in England, and dozens of landowners in Hampshire. Judging by the ordinary rules of evidence, I had not the shadow of a reason, thus far, for connecting Sir Percival Glyde with the suspicious words of inquiry that had been spoken to me by the woman in white. And yet, I did connect him with them. Was it because he had now become associated in my mind with Miss Fairlie; Miss Fairlie being, in her turn, associated with Anne Catherick, since the night when I had discovered the ominous likeness between them? Had the events of the morning so unnerved me already that I was at the mercy of any delusion which common chances and common coincidences might suggest to my imagination?

Impossible to say. I could only feel that what had passed between Miss Halcombe and myself, on our way from the summer-house, had affected me very strangely. The foreboding of some undiscoverable danger lying hid from us all in the darkness of the future, was strong on me. The doubt whether I was not linked already to a chain of events which even my approaching departure from Cumberland would be powerless to snap asunder—the doubt whether we any of us saw the end as the end would really be—gathered more and more darkly over my mind. Poignant as it was, the sense of suffering caused by the miserable end of my brief, presumptuous love, seemed to be blunted and deadened by the still stronger sense of something obscurely impending, something invisibly threatening, that Time was holding over our heads.

I had been engaged with the drawings little more than half an hour, when there was a knock at the door. It opened, on my answering; and, to my surprise, Miss Halcombe entered the room.

Her manner was angry and agitated. She caught up a chair for herself, before I could give her one; and sat down in it, close at my side.

'Mr Hartright,' she said, 'I had hoped that all painful subjects of conversation were exhausted between us, for to-day at least. But it is not to be so. There is some underhand villany at work to frighten my sister about her approaching marriage. You saw me send the gardener on to the house, with a letter addressed, in a strange handwriting, to Miss Fairlie?'

'Certainly.'

'The letter is an anonymous letter—a vile attempt to injure Sir Percival Glyde in my sister's estimation. It has so agitated and alarmed her that I have had the greatest possible difficulty in composing her spirits sufficiently to allow me to leave her room and come here. I know this is a family matter on which I ought not to consult you, and in which you can feel no concern or interest——'

'I beg your pardon, Miss Halcombe. I feel the strongest possible concern and interest in anything that affects Miss Fairlie's happiness or yours.'

'I am glad to hear you say so. You are the only person in the house, or out of it, who can advise me. Mr Fairlie, in his state of health and with his horror of difficulties and mysteries of all kinds, is not to be thought of. The clergyman is a good, weak man, who knows nothing out of the routine of his duties; and our neighbours are just the sort of comfortable, jog-trot acquaintances whom one cannot disturb in times of trouble and danger. What I want to know is this: ought I, at once, to take such steps as I can to discover the writer of the letter? or ought I to wait, and apply to Mr Fairlie's legal adviser to-morrow? It is a question—perhaps a very important one—of gaining or losing a day. Tell me what you think, Mr Hartright. If necessity had not already obliged me to take you into my confidence under very delicate circumstances, even my helpless situation would, perhaps, be no excuse for me. But, as things are, I cannot surely be wrong, after all that has passed between us, in forgetting that you are a friend of only three months' standing.'

She gave me the letter. It began abruptly, without any preliminary form of address, as follows:

'Do you believe in dreams? I hope, for your own sake, that you do. See what Scripture says about dreams and their fulfilment (Genesis xl. 8, xli. 25; Daniel iv. 18–25); and take the warning I send you before it is too late.

'Last night, I dreamed about you, Miss Fairlie. I dreamed that I was standing inside the communion rails of a church: I on one side of the altar-table, and the clergyman, with his surplice and his prayer-book, on the other.

'After a time, there walked towards us, down the aisle of the church, a man and a woman, coming to be married. You were the woman. You looked so pretty and innocent in your beautiful white silk dress, and your long white lace veil, that my heart felt for you and the tears came into my eyes.

'They were tears of pity, young lady, that Heaven blesses; and, instead of falling from my eyes like the every-day tears that we all of us shed, they turned into two rays of light which slanted nearer and nearer to the man standing at the altar with you, till they touched his breast. The two rays sprang in arches like two rainbows, between me and him. I looked along them; and I saw down into his inmost heart.

'The outside of the man you were marrying was fair enough to see. He was neither tall, nor short—he was a little below the middle size. A light, active, high-spirited man—about five-and-forty years old, to look at. He had a pale face, and was bald over the forehead, but had dark hair on the rest of his head. His beard was shaven on his chin, but was let to grow, of a fine rich brown, on his cheeks and his upper lip. His eyes were brown too, and very bright; his nose straight and handsome and delicate enough to have done for a woman's. His hands the same. He was troubled from time to time with a dry hacking cough; and when he put up his white right hand to his mouth, he showed the red scar of an old wound across the back of it. Have I dreamt of the right man? You know best, Miss Fairlie; and you can say if I was deceived or not. Read, next, what I saw beneath the outside—I entreat you, read, and profit.

'I looked along the two rays of light; and I saw down into his inmost heart. It was black as night; and on it was written, in the red flaming letters which are the handwriting of the fallen angel: "Without pity and without remorse. He has strewn with misery the paths of others, and he will live to strew with misery the path of this woman by his side." I read that; and then the rays of light shifted and pointed over his shoulder; and there, behind him, stood a fiend, laughing. And the rays of light shifted once more, and pointed over your shoulder; and there, behind you, stood an angel weeping. And the rays of light shifted for the third time, and pointed straight between you and that man. They widened and widened, thrusting you both asunder, one from the other. And the clergyman looked for the marriage-service in vain: it was gone out of the book, and he shut up the leaves, and put it from him in despair. And I woke with my eyes full of tears and my heart beating—for *I* believe in dreams.

'Believe, too, Miss Fairlie—I beg of you, for your own sake, believe as I do. Joseph and Daniel, and others in Scripture, believed in dreams. Inquire into the past life of that man with the scar on his hand, before you say the words that make you his miserable wife. I don't give you this warning on my account, but on yours. I have an interest in your well-being that will live as long as I draw breath. Your mother's daughter has a tender place in my heart—for your mother was my first, my best, my only friend.'

There, the extraordinary letter ended, without signature of any sort.

The handwriting afforded no prospect of a clue. It was traced on ruled lines, in the cramped, conventional, copybook character, technically termed 'small hand.' It was feeble and faint, and defaced by blots, but had otherwise nothing to distinguish it.

'That is not an illiterate letter,' said Miss Halcombe, 'and, at the same time, it is surely too incoherent to be the letter of an educated person in the higher ranks of life. The reference to the bridal dress and veil, and other little expressions, seem to point to it as the production of some woman. What do you think, Mr Hartright?'

'I think so too. It seems to me to be not only the letter of a woman, but of a woman whose mind must be——'

'Deranged?' suggested Miss Halcombe. 'It struck me in that light, too.'

I did not answer. While I was speaking, my eyes rested on the last sentence of the letter: 'Your mother's daughter has a tender place in my heart—for your mother was my first, my best, my only friend.' Those words and the doubt which had just escaped me as to the sanity of the writer of the letter, acting together on my mind, suggested an idea, which I was literally afraid to express openly, or even to encourage secretly. I began to doubt whether my own faculties were not in danger of losing their balance. It seemed almost like a monomania to be tracing back everything strange that happened, everything unexpected that was said, always to the same hidden source and the same sinister influence. I resolved, this time, in defence of my own courage and my own sense, to come to no decision that plain fact did not warrant, and to turn my back resolutely on everything that tempted me in the shape of surmise.

'If we have any chance of tracing the person who has written this,' I said, returning the letter to Miss Halcombe, 'there can be no harm in seizing our opportunity the moment it offers. I think we ought to speak to the gardener again about the elderly woman who gave him the letter, and then to continue our inquiries in the village. But first let me ask a question. You mentioned just now the alternative of consulting Mr Fairlie's legal adviser to-morrow. Is there no possibility of communicating with him earlier? Why not to-day?'

'I can only explain,' replied Miss Halcombe, 'by entering into certain particulars, connected with my sister's marriage engagement, which I did not think it necessary or desirable to mention to you this morning. One of Sir Percival Glyde's objects in coming here, on Monday, is to fix the period of his marriage, which has hitherto been left quite unsettled. He is anxious that the event should take place before the end of the year.'

'Does Miss Fairlie know of that wish?' I asked, eagerly.

'She has no suspicion of it; and, after what has happened, I shall not take the responsibility upon myself of enlightening her. Sir Percival has only mentioned his views to Mr Fairlie, who has told me himself that he is ready and anxious, as Laura's guardian, to forward them. He has written to London, to the family solicitor, Mr Gilmore. Mr Gilmore happens to be away in Glasgow on business; and he has replied by proposing to stop at Limmeridge House, on his way back to town. He will arrive to-morrow, and will stay with us a few days, so as to allow Sir Percival time to plead his own cause. If he succeeds, Mr Gilmore will then return to London, taking with him his instructions for my sister's marriage-settlement. You understand now, Mr Hartright, why I speak of waiting to take legal advice until to-morrow? Mr Gilmore is the old and tried friend of two generations of Fairlies; and we can trust him, as we could trust no one else.'

The marriage-settlement! The mere hearing of those two words stung me with a jealous despair that was poison to my higher and better instincts. I began to think—it is hard to confess this, but I must suppress nothing from beginning to end of the terrible story that I now stand committed to reveal—I began to think, with a hateful eagerness of hope, of the vague charges against Sir Percival Glyde which the anonymous letter contained. What if those wild accusations rested on a foundation of truth? What if their truth could be proved before the fatal words of consent were spoken, and the marriage-settlement was drawn? I have tried to think, since, that the feeling which then animated me began and ended in pure devotion to Miss Fairlie's interests. But I have never succeeded in deceiving myself into believing it; and I must not now attempt to deceive others. The feeling began and ended in reckless, vindictive, hopeless hatred of the man who was to marry her.

'If we are to find out anything,' I said, speaking under the new influence which was now directing me, 'we had better not let another minute slip by us unemployed. I can only suggest, once more, the propriety of questioning the gardener a second time, and of inquiring in the village immediately afterwards.'

'I think I may be of help to you in both cases,' said Miss Halcombe, rising. 'Let us go, Mr Hartright, at once, and do the best we can together.'

I had the door in my hand to open it for her—but I stopped, on a sudden, to ask an important question before we set forth.

'One of the paragraphs of the anonymous letter,' I said, 'contains some sentences of minute personal description. Sir Percival Glyde's name is not mentioned, I know—but does that description at all resemble him?'

'Accurately; even in stating his age to be forty-five——'

Forty-five; and she was not yet twenty-one! Men of his age married wives of her age every day; and experience had shown those marriages to be often the happiest ones. I knew that—and yet even the mention of his age, when I contrasted it with hers, added to my blind hatred and distrust of him.

'Accurately,' Miss Halcombe continued, 'even to the scar on his right hand, which is the scar of a wound that he received years since when he was travelling in Italy. There can be no doubt that every peculiarity of his personal appearance is thoroughly well known to the writer of the letter.'

'Even a cough that he is troubled with is mentioned, if I remember right?'

'Yes, and mentioned correctly. He treats it lightly himself, though it sometimes makes his friends anxious about him.'

'I suppose no whispers have ever been heard against his character?'

'Mr Hartright! I hope you are not unjust enough to let that infamous letter influence you?'

I felt the blood rush into my cheeks, for I knew that it *had* influenced me.

'I hope not,' I answered, confusedly. 'Perhaps I had no right to ask the question.'

'I am not sorry you asked it,' she said, 'for it enables me to do justice to Sir Percival's reputation. Not a whisper, Mr Hartright, has ever reached me, or my family, against him. He has fought successfully two contested elections; and has come out of the ordeal unscathed. A man who can do that, in England, is a man whose character is established.'

I opened the door for her in silence, and followed her out. She had not convinced me. If the recording angel had come down from heaven to confirm her, and had opened his book to my mortal eyes, the recording angel would not have convinced me.

We found the gardener at work as usual. No amount of questioning could extract a single answer of any importance from the lad's impenetrable stupidity. The woman who had given him the letter was an elderly woman; she had not spoken a word to him; and she had gone away towards the south in a great hurry. That was all the gardener could tell us.

The village lay southward of the house. So to the village we went next.

XI

OUR inquiries at Limmeridge were patiently pursued in all directions, and among all sorts and conditions of people. But nothing came of them. Three of the villagers did certainly assure us that they had seen the woman; but as they were quite unable to describe her, and quite incapable of agreeing about the exact direction in which she was proceeding when they last saw her, these three bright exceptions to the general rule of total ignorance afforded no more real assistance to us than the mass of their unhelpful and unobservant neighbours.

The course of our useless investigations brought us, in time, to the end of the village, at which the schools established by Mrs Fairlie were situated. As we passed the side of the building appropriated to the use of the boys, I suggested the propriety of making a last inquiry of the schoolmaster, whom we might presume to be, in virtue of his office, the most intelligent man in the place.

'I am afraid the schoolmaster must have been occupied with his scholars,' said Miss Halcombe, 'just at the time when the woman passed through the village, and returned again. However, we can but try.'

We entered the playground enclosure, and walked by the schoolroom window, to get round to the door, which was situated at the back of the building. I stopped for a moment at the window and looked in.

The schoolmaster was sitting at his high desk, with his back to me, apparently haranguing the pupils, who were all gathered together in front of him, with one exception. The one exception was a sturdy white-headed boy, standing apart from all the rest on a stool in a corner—a forlorn little Crusoe, isolated in his own desert island of solitary penal disgrace.

The door, when we got round to it, was ajar; and the schoolmaster's voice reached us plainly, as we both stopped for a minute under the porch.

'Now, boys,' said the voice, 'mind what I tell you. If I hear another word spoken about ghosts in this school, it will be the worst for all of you. There are no such things as ghosts; and, therefore, any boy who believes in ghosts believes in what can't possibly be; and a boy who belongs to Limmeridge School, and believes in what can't possibly be, sets up his back against reason and discipline, and must be punished accordingly. You all see Jacob Postlethwaite standing up on the stool there in disgrace. He has been punished, not because he said he saw a ghost last night, but because he is too impudent and too obstinate to listen to reason; and because he persists in saying he saw the ghost after I have told him that no such thing can possibly be. If nothing else will do, I mean to cane the ghost out of Jacob Postlethwaite; and if the thing spreads among any of the rest of you, I mean to go a step farther, and cane the ghost out of the whole school.'

'We seem to have chosen an awkward moment for our visit,' said Miss Halcombe, pushing open the door, at the end of the schoolmaster's address, and leading the way in.

Our appearance produced a strong sensation among the boys. They appeared to think that we had arrived for the express purpose of seeing Jacob Postlethwaite caned.

'Go home all of you to dinner,' said the schoolmaster, 'except Jacob. Jacob must stop where he is; and the ghost may bring him his dinner, if the ghost pleases.'

Jacob's fortitude deserted him at the double disappearance of his school-fellows and his prospect of dinner. He took his hands out of his pockets, looked hard at his knuckles, raised them with great deliberation to his eyes, and, when they got there, ground them round and round slowly, accompanying the action by short spasms of sniffing, which followed each other at regular intervals—the nasal minute guns of juvenile distress.

'We came here to ask you a question, Mr Dempster,' said Miss Halcombe, addressing the schoolmaster; 'and we little expected to find you occupied in exorcising a ghost. What does it all mean? What has really happened?'

'That wicked boy has been frightening the whole school, Miss Halcombe, by declaring that he saw a ghost yesterday evening,' answered the master. 'And he still persists in his absurd story, in spite of all that I can say to him.'

'Most extraordinary,' said Miss Halcombe. 'I should not have thought it possible that any of the boys had imagination enough to see a ghost. This is a new accession indeed to the hard labour of forming the youthful mind at Limmeridge—and I heartily wish you well through it, Mr Dempster. In the mean time, let me explain why you see me here, and what it is I want.'

She then put the same question to the schoolmaster, which we had asked already of almost every one else in the village. It was met by the same discouraging answer. Mr Dempster had not set eyes on the stranger of whom we were in search.

'We may as well return to the house, Mr Hartright,' said Miss Halcombe; 'the information we want is evidently not to be found.'

She had bowed to Mr Dempster, and was about to leave the schoolroom, when the forlorn position of Jacob Postlethwaite, piteously sniffing on the stool of penitence, attracted her attention as she passed him, and made her stop good-humouredly to speak a word to the little prisoner before she opened the door.

'You foolish boy,' she said, 'why don't you beg Mr Dempster's pardon, and hold your tongue about the ghost?'

'Eh!—but I saw t' ghaist,' persisted Jacob Postlethwaite, with a stare of terror and a burst of tears.

'Stuff and nonsense! You saw nothing of the kind. Ghost indeed! What ghost——'

'I beg your pardon, Miss Halcombe,' interposed the schoolmaster, a little uneasily—'but I think you had better not question the boy. The obstinate folly of his story is beyond all belief; and you might lead him into ignorantly——'

'Ignorantly, what?' inquired Miss Halcombe, sharply.

'Ignorantly shocking your feelings,' said Mr Dempster, looking very much discomposed.

'Upon my word, Mr Dempster, you pay my feelings a great compliment in thinking them weak enough to be shocked by such an urchin as that!' She turned with an air of satirical defiance to little Jacob, and began to question him directly. 'Come!' she said; 'I mean to know all about this. You naughty boy, when did you see the ghost!'

'Yester'een, at the gloaming,' replied Jacob.

'Oh! you saw it yesterday evening, in the twilight? And what was it like?'

'Arl in white—as a ghaist should be,' answered the ghost-seer, with a confidence beyond his years.

'And where was it?'

'Away yander, in t' kirkyard—where a ghaist ought to be.'

'As a "ghaist" should be—where a "ghaist" ought to be—why, you little fool, you talk as if the manners and customs of ghosts had been familiar to you from your infancy! You have got your story at your fingers' ends, at any rate. I suppose I shall hear next that you can actually tell me whose ghost it was?'

'Eh! but I just can,' replied Jacob, nodding his head with an air of gloomy triumph.

Mr Dempster had already tried several times to speak, while Miss Halcombe was examining his pupil; and he now interposed resolutely enough to make himself heard.

'Excuse me, Miss Halcombe,' he said, 'if I venture to say that you are only encouraging the boy by asking him these questions.'

'I will merely ask one more, Mr Dempster, and then I shall be quite satisfied. Well,' she continued, turning to the boy, 'and whose ghost was it?'

'T' ghaist of Mistress Fairlie,' answered Jacob, in a whisper.

The effect which this extraordinary reply produced on Miss Halcombe, fully justified the anxiety which the schoolmaster had shown to prevent her from hearing it. Her face crimsoned with indignation—she turned upon little Jacob with an angry suddenness which terrified him into a fresh burst of tears—opened her lips to speak to him—then controlled herself—and addressed the master instead of the boy.

'It is useless,' she said, 'to hold such a child as that responsible for what he says. I have little doubt that the idea has been put into his head by others. If there are people in this village, Mr Dempster, who have forgotten the respect and gratitude due from every soul in it to my mother's memory, I will find them out; and, if I have any influence with Mr Fairlie, they shall suffer for it.'

'I hope—indeed, I am sure, Miss Halcombe—that you are mistaken,' said the schoolmaster. 'The matter begins and ends with the boy's own perversity and folly. He saw, or thought he saw, a woman in white, yesterday evening, as he was passing the churchyard; and the figure, real or fancied, was standing by the marble cross, which he and everyone else in Limmeridge knows to be the monument over Mrs Fairlie's grave. These two circumstances are surely sufficient to have suggested to the boy himself the answer which has so naturally shocked you?'

Although Miss Halcombe did not seem to be convinced, she evidently felt that the schoolmaster's statement of the case was too sensible to be openly combated. She merely replied by thanking him for his attention, and by promising to see him again when her doubts were satisfied. This said, she bowed, and led the way out of the schoolroom.

Throughout the whole of this strange scene, I had stood apart, listening attentively, and drawing my own conclusions. As soon as we were alone again, Miss Halcombe asked me if I had formed any opinion on what I had heard.

'A very strong opinion,' I answered; 'the boy's story, as I believe, has a foundation in fact. I confess I am anxious to see the monument over Mrs Fairlie's grave, and to examine the ground about it.'

'You shall see the grave.'

She paused after making that reply, and reflected a little as we walked on. 'What has happened in the schoolroom,' she resumed, 'has so completely distracted my attention from the subject of the letter, that I feel a little bewildered when I try to return to it. Must we give up all idea of making any further inquiries, and wait to place the thing in Mr Gilmore's hands, to-morrow?'

'By no means, Miss Halcombe. What has happened in the schoolroom encourages me to persevere in the investigation.'

'Why does it encourage you?'

'Because it strengthens a suspicion I felt, when you gave me the letter to read.'

'I suppose you had your reasons, Mr Hartright, for concealing that suspicion from me till this moment?'

'I was afraid to encourage it in myself. I thought it was utterly preposterous—I distrusted it as the result of some perversity in my own imagination. But I can do so no longer. Not only the boy's own answers to your questions, but even a chance expression that dropped from the schoolmaster's lips in explaining his story, have forced the idea back into my mind. Events may yet prove that idea to be a delusion, Miss Halcombe; but the belief is strong in me, at this moment, that the fancied ghost in the churchyard, and the writer of the anonymous letter, are one and the same person.'

She stopped, turned pale, and looked me eagerly in the face.

'What person?'

'The schoolmaster unconsciously told you. When he spoke of the figure that the boy saw in the churchyard, he called it "a woman in white." '

'Not Anne Catherick!'

'Yes, Anne Catherick.'

She put her hand through my arm, and leaned on it heavily.

'I don't know why,' she said, in low tones, 'but there is something in this suspicion of yours that seems to startle and unnerve me. I feel——' She stopped, and tried to laugh it off. 'Mr Hartright,' she went on, 'I will show you the grave, and then go back at once to the house. I had better not leave Laura too long alone. I had better go back, and sit with her.'

We were close to the churchyard when she spoke. The church, a dreary building of grey stone, was situated in a little valley, so as to be sheltered from the bleak winds blowing over the moorland all round it. The burial-ground advanced, from the side of the church, a little way up the slope of the hill. It was surrounded by a rough, low stone wall, and was bare and open to the sky, except at one extremity, where a brook trickled down the stony hill side, and a clump of dwarf trees threw their narrow shadows over the short, meagre grass. Just beyond the brook and the trees, and not far from one of the three stone stiles which afforded entrance, at various points, to the churchyard, rose the white marble cross that distinguished Mrs Fairlie's grave from the humbler monuments scattered about it.

'I need go no farther with you,' said Miss Halcombe, pointing to the grave. 'You will let me know if you find anything to confirm the idea you have just mentioned to me. Let us meet again at the house.'

She left me. I descended at once to the churchyard, and crossed the stile which led directly to Mrs Fairlie's grave.

The grass about it was too short, and the ground too hard, to show any marks of footsteps. Disappointed thus far, I next looked attentively at the cross, and at the square block of marble below it, on which the inscription was cut.

The natural whiteness of the cross was a little clouded, here and there, by weather-stains; and rather more than one half of the square block beneath it, on the side which bore the inscription, was in the same condition. The other half, however, attracted my attention at once by its singular freedom from stain or impurity of any kind. I looked closer, and saw that it had been cleaned—recently cleaned, in a downward direction from top to bottom. The boundary line between the part that had been cleaned and the part that had not, was traceable wherever the inscription left a blank space of marble—sharply traceable as a line that had been produced by artificial means. Who had begun the cleansing of the marble, and who had left it unfinished?

I looked about me, wondering how the question was to be solved. No sign of a habitation could be discerned from the point at which I was standing: the burial-ground was left in the lonely possession of the dead. I returned to the church, and walked round it till I came to the back of the building; then crossed the boundary wall beyond, by another of the stone stiles; and found myself at the head of a path leading down into a deserted stone quarry. Against one side of the quarry a little two-room cottage was built; and just outside the door an old woman was engaged in washing.

I walked up to her, and entered into conversation about the church and burial-ground. She was ready enough to talk; and almost the first words she said informed me that her husband filled the two offices of clerk and sexton. I said a few words next in praise of Mrs Fairlie's monument. The old woman shook her head, and told me I had not seen it at its best. It was her husband's business to look after it; but he had been so ailing and weak, for months and months past, that he had hardly been able to crawl into church on Sundays to do his duty; and the monument had been neglected in consequence. He was getting a little better now; and, in a week or ten days' time, he hoped to be strong enough to set to work and clean it.

This information—extracted from a long rambling answer, in the broadest Cumberland dialect—told me all that I most wanted to know. I gave the poor woman a trifle, and returned at once to Limmeridge House.

The partial cleansing of the monument had evidently been accomplished by a strange hand. Connecting what I had discovered, thus far, with what I had suspected after hearing the story of the ghost seen at twilight, I wanted nothing more to confirm my resolution to watch Mrs Fairlie's grave, in secret, that evening; returning to it at sunset, and waiting within sight of it till the night fell. The work of cleansing the monument had been left unfinished; and the person by whom it had been begun might return to complete it.

On getting back to the house, I informed Miss Halcombe of what I intended to do. She looked surprised and uneasy, while I was explaining my purpose; but she made no positive objection to the execution of it. She only said, 'I hope it may end well.' Just as she was leaving me again, I stopped her to inquire, as calmly as I could, after Miss Fairlie's health. She was in better spirits; and Miss Halcombe hoped she might be induced to take a little walking exercise while the afternoon sun lasted.

I returned to my own room, to resume setting the drawings in order. It was necessary to do this, and doubly necessary to keep my mind employed on anything that would help to distract my attention from myself, and from the hopeless future that lay before me. From time to time, I paused in my work to look out of window and watch the sky as the sun sank nearer and nearer to the horizon. On one of those occasions I saw a figure on the broad gravel walk under my window. It was Miss Fairlie.

I had not seen her since the morning; and I had hardly spoken to her then. Another day at Limmeridge was all that remained to me; and after that day my eyes might never look on her again. This thought was enough to hold me at the window. I had sufficient consideration for her, to arrange the blind so that she might not see me if she looked up; but I had no strength to resist the temptation of letting my eyes, at least, follow her as far as they could on her walk.

She was dressed in a brown cloak, with a plain black silk gown under it. On her head was the same simple straw hat which she had worn on the morning when we first met. A veil was attached to it now, which hid her face from me. By her side, trotted a little Italian greyhound, the pet companion of all her walks, smartly dressed in a scarlet cloth wrapper, to keep the sharp air from his delicate skin. She did not seem to notice the dog. She walked straight forward, with her head drooping a little, and her arms folded in her cloak. The dead leaves which had whirled in the wind before me, when I had heard of her marriage engagement in the morning, whirled in the wind before her, and rose and fell and scattered themselves at her feet, as she walked on in the pale waning sunlight. The dog shivered and trembled, and pressed against her dress impatiently for notice and encouragement. But she never heeded him. She walked on, farther and farther away from me, with the dead leaves whirling about her on the path—walked on, till my aching eyes could see her no more, and I was left alone again with my own heavy heart.

In another hour's time, I had done my work, and the sunset was at hand. I got my hat and coat in the hall, and slipped out of the house without meeting anyone.

The clouds were wild in the western heaven, and the wind blew chill from the sea. Far as the shore was, the sound of the surf swept over the intervening moorland, and beat drearily in my ears, when I entered the churchyard. Not a living creature was in sight. The place looked lonelier than ever, as I chose my position, and waited and watched, with my eyes on the white cross that rose over Mrs Fairlie's grave.

XII

THE exposed situation of the churchyard had obliged me to be cautious in choosing the position that I was to occupy.

The main entrance to the church was on the side next to the burial-ground; and the door was screened by a porch walled in on either side. After some little hesitation, caused by a natural reluctance to conceal myself, indispensable as that concealment was to the object in view, I had resolved on entering the porch. A loophole window was pierced in each of its side walls. Through one of these windows I could see Mrs Fairlie's grave. The other looked towards the stone quarry in which the sexton's cottage was built. Before me, fronting the porch entrance, was a patch of bare burial-ground, a line of low stone wall, and a strip of lonely brown hill, with the sunset clouds sailing heavily over it before the strong, steady wind. No living creature was visible or audible—no bird flew by me; no dog barked from the sexton's cottage. The pauses in the dull beating of the surf were filled up by the dreary rustling of the dwarf trees near the grave, and the cold, faint bubble of the brook over its stony bed. A dreary scene and a dreary hour. My spirits sank fast as I counted out the minutes of the evening in my hiding-place under the church porch.

It was not twilight yet—the light of the setting sun still lingered in the heavens, and little more than the first half-hour of my solitary watch had elapsed—when I heard footsteps, and a voice. The footsteps were approaching from the other side of the church; and the voice was a woman's.

'Don't you fret, my dear, about the letter,' said the voice. 'I gave it to the lad quite safe, and the lad he took it from me without a word. He went his way and I went mine; and not a living soul followed me, afterwards—that I'll warrant.'

These words strung up my attention to a pitch of expectation that was almost painful. There was a pause of silence, but the footsteps still advanced. In another moment, two persons, both women, passed within my range of view from the porch window. They were walking straight towards the grave; and therefore they had their backs turned towards me.

One of the women was dressed in a bonnet and shawl. The other wore a long travelling-cloak of a dark blue colour, with the hood drawn over her head. A few inches of her gown were visible below the cloak. My heart beat fast as I noted the colour—it was white.

After advancing about half-way between the church and the grave, they stopped; and the woman in the cloak turned her head towards her companion. But her side face, which a bonnet might now have allowed me to see, was hidden by the heavy, projecting edge of the hood.

'Mind you keep that comfortable warm cloak on,' said the same voice which I had already heard—the voice of the woman in the shawl. 'Mrs Todd is right about your looking too particular, yesterday, all in white. I'll walk about a little, while you're here; churchyards being not at all in my way, whatever they may be in yours. Finish what you want to do, before I come back; and let us be sure and get home again before night.'

With those words, she turned about, and, retracing her steps, advanced with her face towards me. It was the face of an elderly woman, brown, rugged, and healthy, with nothing dishonest or suspicious in the look of it. Close to the church, she stopped to pull her shawl closer round her.

'Queer,' she said to herself, 'always queer, with her whims and her ways, ever since I can remember her. Harmless, though—as harmless, poor soul, as a little child.'

She sighed; looked about the burial-ground nervously; shook her head as if the dreary prospect by no means pleased her; and disappeared round the corner of the church.

I doubted for a moment whether I ought to follow and speak to her, or not. My intense anxiety to find myself face to face with her companion helped me to decide in the negative. I could ensure seeing the woman in the shawl by waiting near the churchyard until she came back—although it seemed more than doubtful whether she could give me the information of which I was in search. The person who had delivered the letter was of little consequence. The person who had written it was the one centre of interest, and the one source of information; and that person I now felt convinced was before me in the churchyard.

While these ideas were passing through my mind, I saw the woman in the cloak approach close to the grave, and stand looking at it for a little while. She then glanced all round her, and, taking a white linen cloth or handkerchief from under her cloak, turned aside towards the brook. The little stream ran into the churchyard under a tiny archway in the bottom of the wall, and ran out again, after a winding course of a few dozen yards, under a similar opening. She dipped the cloth in the water, and returned to the grave. I saw her kiss the white cross; then kneel down before the inscription, and apply her wet cloth to the cleansing of it.

After considering how I could show myself with the least possible chance of frightening her, I resolved to cross the wall before me, to skirt round it outside, and to enter the churchyard again by the stile near the grave, in order that she might see me as I approached. She was so absorbed over her employment that she did not hear me coming until I had stepped over the stile. Then, she looked up, started to her feet with a faint cry, and stood facing me in speechless and motionless terror.

'Don't be frightened,' I said. 'Surely, you remember me?'

I stopped while I spoke—then advanced a few steps gently—then stopped again—and so approached by little and little, till I was close to her. If there had been any doubt still left in my mind, it must have been now set at rest. There, speaking affrightedly for itself—there was the same face confronting me over Mrs Fairlie's grave, which had first looked into mine on the high-road by night.

'You remember me?' I said. 'We met very late, and I helped you to find the way to London. Surely you have not forgotten that?'

Her features relaxed, and she drew a heavy breath of relief. I saw the new life of recognition stirring slowly under the death-like stillness which fear had set on her face.

'Don't attempt to speak to me, just yet,' I went on. 'Take time to recover yourself—take time to feel quite certain that I am a friend.'

'You are very kind to me,' she murmured. 'As kind now, as you were then.'

She stopped, and I kept silence on my side. I was not granting time for composure to her only, I was gaining time also for myself. Under the wan, wild evening light, that woman and I were met together again; a grave between us, the dead about us, the lonesome hills closing us round on every side. The time, the place, the circumstances under which we now stood face to face in the evening stillness of that dreary valley; the life-long interests which might hang suspended on the next chance words that passed between us; the sense that, for aught I knew to the contrary, the whole future of Laura Fairlie's life might be determined, for good or for evil, by my winning or losing the confidence of the forlorn creature who stood trembling by her mother's grave—all threatened to shake the steadiness and the self-control on which every inch of the progress I might yet make now depended. I tried hard, as I felt this, to possess myself of all my resources; I did my utmost to turn the few moments for reflection to the best account.

'Are you calmer, now?' I said, as soon as I thought it time to speak again. 'Can you talk to me, without feeling frightened, and without forgetting that I am a friend?'

'How did you come here?' she asked, without noticing what I had just said to her.

'Don't you remember my telling you, when we last met, that I was going to Cumberland? I have been in Cumberland ever since; I have been staying all the time at Limmeridge House.'

'At Limmeridge House!' Her pale face brightened as she repeated the words; her wandering eyes fixed on me with a sudden interest. 'Ah, how happy you must have been!' she said, looking at me eagerly, without a shadow of its former distrust left in her expression.

I took advantage of her newly-aroused confidence in me, to observe her face, with an attention and a curiosity which I had hitherto restrained myself from showing, for caution's sake. I looked at her, with my mind full of that other lovely face which had so ominously recalled her to my memory on the terrace by moonlight. I had seen Anne Catherick's likeness in Miss Fairlie. I now saw Miss Fairlie's likeness in Anne Catherick—saw it all the more clearly because the points of dissimilarity between the two were presented to me as well as the points of resemblance. In the general outline of the countenance and general proportion of the features; in the colour of the hair and in the little nervous uncertainty about the lips; in the height and size of the figure, and the carriage of the head and body, the likeness appeared even more startling than I had ever felt it to be yet. But there the resemblance ended, and the dissimilarity, in details, began. The delicate beauty of Miss Fairlie's complexion, the transparent clearness of her eyes, the smooth purity of her skin, the tender bloom of colour on her lips, were all missing from the worn, weary face that was now turned towards mine. Although I hated myself even for thinking such a thing, still, while I looked at the woman before me, the idea would force itself into my mind that one sad change, in the future, was all that was wanting to make the likeness complete, which I now saw to be so imperfect in detail. If ever sorrow and suffering set their profaning marks on the youth and beauty of Miss Fairlie's face, then, and then only, Anne Catherick and she would be the twin-sisters of chance resemblance, the living reflexions of one another.

I shuddered at the thought. There was something horrible in the blind, unreasoning distrust of the future which the mere passage of it through my mind seemed to imply. It was a welcome interruption to be roused by feeling Anne Catherick's hand laid on my shoulder. The touch was as stealthy and as sudden as that other touch, which had petrified me from head to foot on the night when we first met.

'You are looking at me; and you are thinking of something,' she said, with her strange, breathless rapidity of utterance. 'What is it?'

'Nothing extraordinary,' I answered. 'I was only wondering how you came here.'

'I came with a friend who is very good to me. I have only been here two days.'

'And you found your way to this place, yesterday?'

'How do you know that?'

'I only guessed it.'

She turned from me, and knelt down before the inscription once more.

'Where should I go, if not here?' she said. 'The friend who was better than a mother to me, is the only friend I have to visit at Limmeridge. Oh, it makes my heart ache to see a stain on her tomb! It ought to be kept white as snow, for her sake. I was tempted to begin cleaning it yesterday; and I can't help coming back to go on with it to-day. Is there anything wrong in that? I hope not. Surely nothing can be wrong that I do for Mrs Fairlie's sake?'

The old grateful sense of her benefactress's kindness was evidently the ruling idea still in the poor creature's mind—the narrow mind which had but too plainly opened to no other lasting impression since that first impression of her younger and happier days. I saw that my best chance of winning her confidence lay in encouraging her to proceed with the artless employment which she had come into the burial-ground to pursue. She resumed it at once, on my telling her she might do so; touching the hard marble as tenderly as if it had been a sentient thing, and whispering the words of the inscription to herself, over and over again, as if the lost days of her girlhood had returned and she was patiently learning her lesson once more at Mrs Fairlie's knees.

'Should you wonder very much,' I said, preparing the way as cautiously as I could for the questions that were to come, 'if I owned that it is a satisfaction to me, as well as a surprise, to see you here? I felt very uneasy about you after you left me in the cab.'

She looked up quickly and suspiciously.

'Uneasy,' she repeated. 'Why?'

'A strange thing happened, after we parted, that night. Two men overtook me in a chaise. They did not see where I was standing; but they stopped near me, and spoke to a policeman, on the other side of the way.'

She instantly suspended her employment. The hand holding the damp cloth with which she had been cleaning the inscription, dropped to her side. The other hand grasped the marble cross at the head of the grave. Her face turned towards me slowly, with the blank look of terror set rigidly on it once more. I went on at all hazards; it was too late now to draw back.

'The two men spoke to the policeman,' I said, 'and asked him if he had seen you. He had not seen you; and then one of the men spoke again, and said you had escaped from his Asylum.'

She sprang to her feet, as if my last words had set the pursuers on her track.

'Stop! and hear the end,' I cried. 'Stop! and you shall know how I befriended you. A word from me would have told the men which way you had gone—and I never spoke that word. I helped your escape—I made it safe and certain. Think, try to think. Try to understand what I tell you.'

My manner seemed to influence her more than my words. She made an effort to grasp the new idea. Her hands shifted the damp cloth hesitatingly from one to the other, exactly as they had shifted the little travelling bag on the night when I first saw her. Slowly, the purpose of my words seemed to force its way through the confusion and agitation of her mind. Slowly, her features relaxed, and her eyes looked at me with their expression gaining in curiosity what it was fast losing in fear.

'*You* don't think I ought to be back in the Asylum, do you?' she said.

'Certainly not. I am glad you escaped from it; I am glad I helped you.'

'Yes, yes; you did help me, indeed; you helped me at the hard part,' she went on, a little vacantly. 'It was easy to escape, or I should not have got away. They never suspected me as they suspected the others. I was so quiet, and so obedient, and so easily frightened. The finding London was the hard part; and there you helped me. Did I thank you at the time? I thank you now, very kindly.'

'Was the Asylum far from where you met me? Come! show that you believe me to be your friend, and tell me where it was.'

She mentioned the place—a private Asylum, as its situation informed me; a private Asylum not very far from the spot where I had seen her—and then, with evident suspicion of the use to which I might put her answer, anxiously repeated her former inquiry. '*You* don't think I ought to be taken back, do you?'

'Once again, I am glad you escaped; I am glad you prospered well, after you left me,' I answered. 'You said you had a friend in London to go to. Did you find the friend?'

'Yes. It was very late; but there was a girl up at needlework in the house, and she helped me to rouse Mrs Clements. Mrs Clements is my friend. A good, kind woman, but not like Mrs Fairlie. Ah, no, nobody is like Mrs Fairlie!'

'Is Mrs Clements an old friend of yours? Have you known her a long time?'

'Yes; she was a neighbour of ours once, at home, in Hampshire; and liked me, and took care of me when I was a little girl. Years ago, when she went away from us, she wrote down in my prayer-book for me, where she was going to live in London, and she said, "If you are ever in trouble, Anne, come to me. I have no husband alive to say me nay, and no children to look after; and I will take care of you." Kind words, were they not? I suppose I remember them because they were kind. It's little enough I remember besides—little enough, little enough!'

'Had you no father or mother to take care of you?'

'Father? I never saw him; I never heard mother speak of him. Father? Ah, dear! he is dead, I suppose.'

'And your mother?'

'I don't get on well with her. We are a trouble and a fear to each other.'

A trouble and a fear to each other! At those words, the suspicion crossed my mind for the first time, that her mother might be the person who had placed her under restraint.

'Don't ask me about mother,' she went on. 'I'd rather talk of Mrs Clements. Mrs Clements is like you, she doesn't think that I ought to be back in the Asylum; and she is as glad as you are that I escaped from it. She cried over my misfortune, and said it must be kept secret from everybody.'

Her 'misfortune.' In what sense was she using that word? In a sense which might explain her motive in writing the anonymous letter? In a sense which might show it to be the too common and too customary motive that has led many a woman to interpose anonymous hindrances to the marriage of the man who has ruined her? I resolved to attempt the clearing up of this doubt, before more words passed between us on either side.

'What misfortune?' I asked.

'The misfortune of my being shut up,' she answered, with every appearance of feeling surprised at my question. 'What other misfortune could there be?'

I determined to persist, as delicately and forbearingly as possible. It was of very great importance that I should be absolutely sure of every step in the investigation that I now gained in advance.

'There is another misfortune,' I said, 'to which a woman may be liable, and by which she may suffer life-long sorrow and shame.'

'What is it?' she asked, eagerly.

'The misfortune of believing too innocently in her own virtue, and in the faith and honour of the man she loves,' I answered.

She looked up at me, with the artless bewilderment of a child. Not the slightest confusion or change of colour; not the faintest trace of any secret consciousness of shame struggling to the surface, appeared in her face—that face which betrayed every other emotion with such transparent clearness. No words that ever were spoken could have assured me, as her look and manner now assured me, that the motive which I had assigned for her writing the letter and sending it to Miss Fairlie was plainly and distinctly the wrong one. That doubt, at any rate, was now set at rest; but the very removal of it opened a new prospect of uncertainty. The letter, as I knew from positive testimony, pointed at Sir Percival Glyde, though it did not name him. She must have had some strong motive, originating in some deep sense of injury, for secretly denouncing him to Miss Fairlie, in such terms as she had employed—and that motive was unquestionably not to be traced to the loss of her innocence and her character. Whatever wrong he might have inflicted on her was not of that nature. Of what nature could it be?

'I don't understand you,' she said, after evidently trying hard, and trying in vain to discover the meaning of the words I had last said to her.

'Never mind,' I answered. 'Let us go on with what we were talking about. Tell me how long you stayed with Mrs Clements in London, and how you came here.'

'How long?' she repeated. 'I stayed with Mrs Clements till we both came to this place, two days ago.'

'You are living in the village, then?' I said. 'It is strange I should not have heard of you, though you have only been here two days.'

'No, no; not in the village. Three miles away at a farm. Do you know the farm? They call it Todd's Corner.'

I remembered the place perfectly; we had often passed by it in our drives. It was one of the oldest farms in the neighbourhood, situated in a solitary, sheltered spot, inland, at the junction of two hills.

'They are relations of Mrs Clements at Todd's Corner,' she went on, 'and they had often asked her to go and see them. She said she would go, and take me with her, for the quiet and the fresh air. It was very kind, was it not? I would have gone anywhere to be quiet, and safe, and out of the way. But when I heard that Todd's Corner was near Limmeridge—oh! I was so happy I would have walked all the way barefoot to get there, and see the schools and the village and Limmeridge House again. They are very good people at Todd's Corner. I hope I shall stay there a long time. There is only one thing I don't like about them, and don't like about Mrs Clements——'

'What is it?'

'They will tease me about dressing all in white—they say it looks so particular. How do they know? Mrs Fairlie knew best. Mrs Fairlie would never have made me wear this ugly blue cloak. Ah! she was fond of white in her lifetime; and here is white stone about her grave—and I am making it whiter for her sake. She often wore white herself; and she always dressed her little daughter in white. Is Miss Fairlie well and happy? Does she wear white now, as she used when she was a girl?'

Her voice sank when she put the questions about Miss Fairlie; and she turned her head farther and farther away from me. I thought I detected, in the alteration in her manner, an uneasy consciousness of the risk she had run in sending the anonymous letter; and I instantly determined so to frame my answer as to surprise her into owning it.

'Miss Fairlie is not very well or very happy this morning,' I said.

She murmured a few words; but they were spoken so confusedly, and in such a low tone, that I could not even guess at what they meant.

'Did you ask me why Miss Fairlie was neither well nor happy this morning?' I continued.

'No,' she said, quickly and eagerly—'oh, no, I never asked that.'

'I will tell you without your asking,' I went on. 'Miss Fairlie has received your letter.'

She had been down on her knees for some little time past, carefully removing the last weather-stains left about the inscription, while we were speaking together. The first sentence of the words I had just addressed to her made her pause in her occupation, and turn slowly, without rising from her knees, so as to face me. The second sentence literally petrified her. The cloth she had been holding dropped from her hands; her lips fell apart; all the little colour that there was naturally in her face left it in an instant.

'How do you know?' she said, faintly. 'Who showed it to you?' The blood rushed back into her face—rushed overwhelmingly, as the sense rushed upon her mind that her own words had betrayed her. She struck her hands together in despair. 'I never wrote it,' she gasped, affrightedly; 'I know nothing about it!'

'Yes,' I said, 'you wrote it, and you know about it. It was wrong to send such a letter; it was wrong to frighten Miss Fairlie. If you had anything to say that it was right and necessary for her to hear, you should have gone yourself to Limmeridge House; you should have spoken to the young lady with your own lips.'

She crouched down over the flat stone of the grave, till her face was hidden on it; and made no reply.

'Miss Fairlie will be as good and kind to you as her mother was, if you mean well,' I went on. 'Miss Fairlie will keep your secret, and not let you come to any harm. Will you see her to-morrow at the farm? Will you meet her in the garden at Limmeridge House?'

'Oh, if I could die, and be hidden and at rest with *you!*' Her lips murmured the words close on the grave-stone; murmured them in tones of passionate endearment, to the dead remains beneath. '*You* know how I love your child, for your sake! Oh, Mrs Fairlie! Mrs Fairlie! tell me how to save

her. Be my darling and my mother once more, and tell me what to do for
the best!'

I heard her lips kissing the stone: I saw her hands beating on it
passionately. The sound and the sight deeply affected me. I stooped
down, and took the poor helpless hands tenderly in mine, and tried to
soothe her.

It was useless. She snatched her hands from me, and never moved her
face from the stone. Seeing the urgent necessity of quieting her at any
hazard and by any means, I appealed to the only anxiety that she appeared
to feel, in connexion with me and with my opinion of her—the anxiety to
convince me of her fitness to be mistress of her own actions.

'Come, come,' I said, gently. 'Try to compose yourself, or you will make
me alter my opinion of you. Don't let me think that the person who put you
in the Asylum might have had some excuse——'

The next words died away on my lips. The instant I risked that chance
reference to the person who had put her in the Asylum, she sprang up on
her knees. A most extraordinary and startling change passed over her. Her
face, at all ordinary times so touching to look at, in its nervous sensitiveness,
weakness, and uncertainty, became suddenly darkened by an expression of
maniacally-intense hatred and fear, which communicated a wild, unnatural
force to every feature. Her eyes dilated in the dim evening light, like the eyes
of a wild animal. She caught up the cloth that had fallen at her side, as if it
had been a living creature that she could kill, and crushed it in both her
hands with such convulsive strength that the few drops of moisture left in it
trickled down on the stone beneath her.

'Talk of something else,' she said, whispering through her teeth. 'I shall
lose myself if you talk of that.'

Every vestige of the gentler thoughts which had filled her mind hardly a
minute since seemed to be swept from it now. It was evident that the
impression left by Mrs Fairlie's kindness was not, as I had supposed, the only
strong impression on her memory. With the grateful remembrance of her
school-days at Limmeridge, there existed the vindictive remembrance of the
wrong inflicted on her by her confinement in the Asylum. Who had done
that wrong? Could it really be her mother?

It was hard to give up pursuing the inquiry to that final point; but I forced
myself to abandon all idea of continuing it. Seeing her as I saw her now, it
would have been cruel to think of anything but the necessity and the
humanity of restoring her composure.

'I will talk of nothing to distress you,' I said soothingly.

'You want something,' she answered, sharply and suspiciously. 'Don't look
at me, like that. Speak to me; tell me what you want.'

'I only want you to quiet yourself, and, when you are calmer, to think over
what I have said.'

'Said?' She paused; twisted the cloth in her hands, backwards and forwards; and whispered to herself, 'What is it he said?' She turned again towards me, and shook her head impatiently. 'Why don't you help me?' she asked, with angry suddenness.

'Yes, yes,' I said; 'I will help you; and you will soon remember. I asked you to see Miss Fairlie to-morrow, and to tell her the truth about the letter.'

'Ah! Miss Fairlie—Fairlie—Fairlie——'

The mere utterance of the loved, familiar name seemed to quiet her. Her face softened and grew like itself again.

'You need have no fear of Miss Fairlie,' I continued; 'and no fear of getting into trouble through the letter. She knows so much about it already, that you will have no difficulty in telling her all. There can be little necessity for concealment where there is hardly anything left to conceal. You mention no names in the letter; but Miss Fairlie knows that the person you write of is Sir Percival Glyde——'

The instant I pronounced that name, she started to her feet; and a scream burst from her that rang through the churchyard and made my heart leap in me with the terror of it. The dark deformity of the expression which had just left her face, lowered on it once more, with doubled and trebled intensity. The shriek at the name, the reiterated look of hatred and fear that instantly followed, told all. Not even a last doubt now remained. Her mother was guiltless of imprisoning her in the Asylum. A man had shut her up—and that man was Sir Percival Glyde.

The scream had reached other ears than mine. On one side, I heard the door of the sexton's cottage open; on the other, I heard the voice of her companion, the woman in the shawl, the woman whom she had spoken of as Mrs Clements.

'I'm coming! I'm coming!' cried the voice, from behind the clump of dwarf trees.

In a moment more, Mrs Clements hurried into view.

'Who are you?' She cried, facing me resolutely, as she set her foot on the stile. 'How dare you frighten a poor helpless woman like that?'

She was at Anne Catherick's side, and had put one arm around her, before I could answer. 'What is it, my dear?' she said. 'What has he done to you?'

'Nothing,' the poor creature answered. 'Nothing. I'm only frightened.'

Mrs Clements turned on me with a fearless indignation, for which I respected her.

'I should be heartily ashamed of myself if I deserved that angry look,' I said. 'But I do not deserve it. I have unfortunately startled her, without intending it. This is not the first time she has seen me. Ask her yourself, and she will tell you that I am incapable of willingly harming her or any woman.'

I spoke distinctly, so that Anne Catherick might hear and understand me: and I saw that the words and their meaning had reached her.

'Yes, yes,' she said; 'he was good to me once; he helped me——' She whispered the rest into her friend's ear.

'Strange, indeed!' said Mrs Clements, with a look of perplexity. 'It makes all the difference, though. I'm sorry I spoke so rough to you, sir; but you must own that appearances looked suspicious to a stranger. It's more my fault than yours, for humouring her whims, and letting her be alone in such a place as this. Come, my dear—come home, now.'

I thought the good woman looked a little uneasy at the prospect of the walk back, and I offered to go with them until they were both within sight of home. Mrs Clements thanked me civilly, and declined. She said they were sure to meet some of the farm-labourers, as soon as they got to the moor.

'Try to forgive me,' I said, when Anne Catherick took her friend's arm to go away. Innocent as I had been of any intention to terrify and agitate her, my heart smote me as I looked at the poor, pale, frightened face.

'I will try,' she answered. 'But you know too much; I'm afraid you'll always frighten me now.'

Mrs Clements glanced at me, and shook her head pityingly.

'Good night, sir,' she said. 'You couldn't help it, I know; but I wish it was me you had frightened, and not her.'

They moved away a few steps. I thought they had left me; but Anne suddenly stopped, and separated herself from her friend.

'Wait a little,' she said. 'I must say good-by.'

She returned to the grave, rested both hands tenderly on the marble cross, and kissed it.

'I'm better, now,' she sighed, looking up at me quietly. 'I forgive you.'

She joined her companion again, and they left the burial-ground. I saw them stop near the church, and speak to the sexton's wife, who had come from the cottage, and had waited, watching us from a distance. Then they went on again up the path that led to the moor. I looked after Anne Catherick as she disappeared, till all trace of her had faded in the twilight—looked, as anxiously and sorrowfully, as if that was the last I was to see in this weary world of the woman in white.

XIII

HALF an hour later, I was back at the house, and was informing Miss Halcombe of all that had happened.

She listened to me from beginning to end, with a steady, silent attention, which, in a woman of her temperament and disposition, was the strongest proof that could be offered of the serious manner in which my narrative affected her.

'My mind misgives me,' was all she said when I had done. 'My mind misgives me sadly about the future.'

'The future may depend,' I suggested, 'on the use we make of the present. It is not improbable that Anne Catherick may speak more readily and unreservedly to a woman than she has spoken to me. If Miss Fairlie——'

'Not to be thought of for a moment,' interposed Miss Halcombe, in her most decided manner.

'Let me suggest, then,' I continued, 'that you should see Anne Catherick yourself, and do all you can to win her confidence. For my own part, I shrink from the idea of alarming the poor creature a second time, as I have most unhappily alarmed her already. Do you see any objection to accompanying me to the farm-house to-morrow?'

'None whatever. I will go anywhere and do anything to serve Laura's interests. What did you say the place was called?'

'You must know it well. It is called Todd's Corner.'

'Certainly. Todd's Corner is one of Mr Fairlie's farms. Our dairy-maid here is the farmer's second daughter. She goes backwards and forwards constantly, between this house and her father's farm; and she may have heard or seen something which it may be useful to us to know. Shall I ascertain, at once, if the girl is down stairs?'

She rang the bell, and sent the servant with his message. He returned, and announced that the dairy-maid was then at the farm. She had not been there for the last three days; and the housekeeper had given her leave to go home, for an hour or two, that evening.

'I can speak to her to-morrow,' said Miss Halcombe, when the servant had left the room again. 'In the mean time, let me thoroughly understand the object to be gained by my interview with Anne Catherick. Is there no doubt in your own mind that the person who confined her in the Asylum was Sir Percival Glyde?'

'There is not the shadow of a doubt. The only mystery that remains, is the mystery of his *motive*. Looking to the great difference between his station in life and hers, which seems to preclude all idea of the most distant relationship between them, it is of the last importance—even assuming that she really required to be placed under restraint—to know why *he* should have been the person to assume the serious responsibility of shutting her up——'

'In a private Asylum, I think you said?'

'Yes, in a private Asylum, where a sum of money which no poor person could afford to give, must have been paid for her maintenance as a patient.'

'I see where the doubt lies, Mr Hartright; and I promise you that it shall be set at rest, whether Anne Catherick assists us to-morrow or not. Sir Percival Glyde shall not be long in this house without satisfying Mr Gilmore, and satisfying me. My sister's future is my dearest care in life; and I have influence enough over her to give me some power, where her marriage is concerned, in the disposal of it.'

We parted for the night.

After breakfast, the next morning, an obstacle, which the events of the evening before had put out of my memory, interposed to prevent our proceeding immediately to the farm. This was my last day at Limmeridge House; and it was necessary, as soon as the post came in, to follow Miss Halcombe's advice, and to ask Mr Fairlie's permission to shorten my engagement by a month, in consideration of an unforeseen necessity for my return to London.

Fortunately for the probability of this excuse, so far as appearances were concerned, the post brought me two letters from London friends, that morning. I took them away at once to my own room; and sent the servant with a message to Mr Fairlie, requesting to know when I could see him on a matter of business.

I awaited the man's return, free from the slightest feeling of anxiety about the manner in which his master might receive my application. With Mr Fairlie's leave or without it, I must go. The consciousness of having now taken the first step on the dreary journey which was henceforth to separate my life from Miss Fairlie's seemed to have blunted my sensibility to every consideration connected with myself. I had done with my poor man's touchy pride; I had done with all my little artist vanities. No insolence of Mr Fairlie's, if he chose to be insolent, could wound me now.

The servant returned with a message for which I was not unprepared. Mr Fairlie regretted that the state of his health, on that particular morning, was such as to preclude all hope of his having the pleasure of receiving me. He begged, therefore, that I would accept his apologies, and kindly communicate what I had to say, in the form of a letter. Similar messages to this had reached me, at various intervals, during my three months' residence in the house. Throughout the whole of that period, Mr Fairlie had been rejoiced to 'possess' me, but had never been well enough to see me for a second time. The servant took every fresh batch of drawings, that I mounted and restored, back to his master, with my 'respects;' and returned empty-handed with Mr Fairlie's 'kind compliments,' 'best thanks,' and 'sincere regrets' that the state of his health still obliged him to remain a solitary prisoner in his own room. A more satisfactory arrangement to both sides could not possibly have been adopted. It would be hard to say which of us, under the circumstances, felt the most grateful sense of obligation to Mr Fairlie's accommodating nerves.

I sat down at once to write the letter, expressing myself in it as civilly, as clearly, and as briefly as possible. Mr Fairlie did not hurry his reply. Nearly an hour elapsed before the answer was placed in my hands. It was written with beautiful regularity and neatness of character, in violet-coloured ink, on note-paper as smooth as ivory and almost as thick as cardboard; and it addressed me in these terms:—

'Mr Fairlie's compliments to Mr Hartright. Mr Fairlie is more surprised and disappointed than he can say (in the present state of his health) by

Mr Hartright's application. Mr Fairlie is not a man of business, but he has consulted his steward, who is, and that person confirms Mr Fairlie's opinion that Mr Hartright's request to be allowed to break his engagement cannot be justified by any necessity whatever, excepting perhaps a case of life and death. If the highly-appreciative feeling towards Art and its professors, which it is the consolation and happiness of Mr Fairlie's suffering existence to cultivate, could be easily shaken, Mr Hartright's present proceeding would have shaken it. It has not done so—except in the instance of Mr Hartright himself.

'Having stated his opinion—so far, that is to say, as acute nervous suffering will allow him to state anything—Mr Fairlie has nothing to add but the expression of his decision, in reference to the highly irregular application that has been made to him. Perfect repose of body and mind being to the last degree important in his case, Mr Fairlie will not suffer Mr Hartright to disturb that repose by remaining in the house under circumstances of an essentially irritating nature to both sides. Accordingly, Mr Fairlie waives his right of refusal, purely with a view to the preservation of his own tranquillity—and informs Mr Hartright that he may go.'

I folded the letter up, and put it away with my other papers. The time had been when I should have resented it as an insult: I accepted it, now, as a written release from my engagement. It was off my mind, it was almost out of my memory, when I went down stairs to the breakfast-room, and informed Miss Halcombe that I was ready to walk with her to the farm.

'Has Mr Fairlie given you a satisfactory answer?' she asked, as we left the house.

'He has allowed me to go, Miss Halcombe.'

She looked up at me quickly; and then, for the first time since I had known her, took my arm of her own accord. No words could have expressed so delicately that she understood how the permission to leave my employment had been granted, and that she gave me her sympathy, not as my superior, but as my friend. I had not felt the man's insolent letter; but I felt deeply the woman's atoning kindness.

On our way to the farm we arranged that Miss Halcombe was to enter the house alone, and that I was to wait outside, within call. We adopted this mode of proceeding from an apprehension that my presence, after what had happened in the churchyard the evening before, might have the effect of renewing Anne Catherick's nervous dread, and of rendering her additionally distrustful of the advances of a lady who was a stranger to her. Miss Halcombe left me, with the intention of speaking, in the first instance, to the farmer's wife (of whose friendly readiness to help her in any way she was well assured), while I waited for her in the near neighbourhood of the house.

I had fully expected to be left alone, for some time. To my surprise, however, little more than five minutes had elapsed, before Miss Halcombe returned.

'Does Anne Catherick refuse to see you?' I asked, in astonishment.

'Anne Catherick is gone,' replied Miss Halcombe.

'Gone!'

'Gone, with Mrs Clements. They both left the farm at eight o'clock this morning.'

I could say nothing—I could only feel that our last chance of discovery had gone with them.

'All that Mrs Todd knows about her guests, I know,' Miss Halcombe went on; 'and it leaves me, as it leaves her, in the dark. They both came back safe, last night, after they left you, and they passed the first part of the evening with Mr Todd's family, as usual. Just before supper-time, however, Anne Catherick startled them all by being suddenly seized with faintness. She had had a similar attack, of a less alarming kind, on the day she arrived at the farm; and Mrs Todd had connected it, on that occasion, with something she was reading at the time in our local newspaper, which lay on the farm table, and which she had taken up only a minute or two before.'

'Does Mrs Todd know what particular passage in the newspaper affected her in that way?' I inquired.

'No,' replied Miss Halcombe. 'She had looked it over, and had seen nothing in it to agitate any one. I asked leave, however, to look it over in my turn; and at the very first page I opened, I found that the editor had enriched his small stock of news by drawing upon our family affairs, and had published my sister's marriage engagement, among his other announcements, copied from the London papers, of Marriages in High Life. I concluded at once that this was the paragraph which had so strangely affected Anne Catherick; and I thought I saw in it, also, the origin of the letter which she sent to our house the next day.'

'There can be no doubt in either case. But what did you hear about her second attack of faintness yesterday evening?'

'Nothing. The cause of it is a complete mystery. There was no stranger in the room. The only visitor was our dairy-maid, who, as I told you, is one of Mr Todd's daughters; and the only conversation was the usual gossip about local affairs. They heard her cry out, and saw her turn deadly pale, without the slightest apparent reason. Mrs Todd and Mrs Clements took her up-stairs; and Mrs Clements remained with her. They were heard talking together until long after the usual bedtime; and, early this morning, Mrs Clements took Mrs Todd aside, and amazed her beyond all power of expression, by saying that they must go. The only explanation Mrs Todd could extract from her guest was, that something had happened, which was not the fault of any one at the farm-house, but which was serious enough to make Anne Catherick resolve to leave Limmeridge immediately. It was quite useless to press Mrs Clements to be more explicit. She only shook her head, and said that, for Anne's sake, she must beg and pray that no one would question her. All she could repeat, with every appearance of being seriously agitated herself, was that Anne must go, that she must go with her, and that the destination to which they might both betake themselves must be kept a secret from everybody. I spare you the recital of Mrs Todd's hospitable remonstrances and refusals. It ended in her driving them both to the nearest station, more than three hours since. She tried hard, on the way, to get them to speak more plainly; but without success. And she set them down outside the station-door, so hurt and offended by the unceremonious abruptness of their departure and their unfriendly reluctance to place the least confidence in her, that she drove away in anger, without so much as stopping to bid them good-by. That is exactly what has taken place. Search your own memory, Mr Hartright, and tell me if anything happened in the burial-ground yesterday evening which can at all account for the extraordinary departure of those two women this morning.'

'I should like to account first, Miss Halcombe, for the sudden change in Anne Catherick which alarmed them at the farm-house, hours after she and I had parted, and when time enough had elapsed to quiet any violent agitation that I might have been unfortunate enough to cause. Did you inquire particularly about the gossip which was going on in the room when she turned faint?'

'Yes. But Mrs Todd's household affairs seem to have divided her attention, that evening, with the talk in the farm-house parlour. She could only tell me that it was "just the news"—meaning, I suppose, that they all talked as usual about each other.'

'The dairy-maid's memory may be better than her mother's,' I said. 'It may be as well for you to speak to the girl, Miss Halcombe, as soon as we get back.'

My suggestion was acted on the moment we returned to the house. Miss Halcombe led me round to the servants' offices, and we found the girl in the dairy, with her sleeves tucked up to her shoulders, cleaning a large milk-pan, and singing blithely over her work.

'I have brought this gentleman to see your dairy, Hannah,' said Miss Halcombe. 'It is one of the sights of the house, and it always does you credit.'

The girl blushed and curtseyed, and said, shyly, that she hoped she always did her best to keep things neat and clean.

'We have just come from your father's,' Miss Halcombe continued. 'You were there yesterday evening, I hear; and you found visitors at the house?'

'Yes, miss.'

'One of them was taken faint and ill, I am told? I suppose nothing was said or done to frighten her? You were not talking of anything very terrible, were you?'

'Oh, no, miss!' said the girl, laughing. 'We were only talking of the news.'

'Your sisters told you the news at Todd's Corner, I suppose?'

'Yes, miss.'

'And you told them the news at Limmeridge House?'

'Yes, miss. And I'm quite sure nothing was said to frighten the poor thing, for I was talking when she was taken ill. It gave me quite a turn, miss, to see it, never having been taken faint myself.'

Before any more questions could be put to her, she was called away to receive a basket of eggs at the dairy door. As she left us, I whispered to Miss Halcombe:

'Ask her if she happened to mention, last night, that visitors were expected at Limmeridge House.'

Miss Halcombe showed me, by a look, that she understood, and put the question as soon as the dairy-maid returned to us.

'Oh, yes, miss; I mentioned that,' said the girl, simply. 'The company coming, and the accident to the brindled cow, was all the news I had to take to the farm.'

'Did you mention names? Did you tell them that Sir Percival Glyde was expected on Monday?'

'Yes, miss—I told them Sir Percival Glyde was coming. I hope there was no harm in it; I hope I didn't do wrong.'

'Oh no, no harm. Come, Mr Hartright; Hannah will begin to think us in the way, if we interrupt her any longer over her work.'

We stopped and looked at one another, the moment we were alone again.

'Is there any doubt in your mind, *now*, Miss Halcombe?'

'Sir Percival Glyde shall remove that doubt, Mr Hartright—or, Laura Fairlie shall never be his wife.'

XIV

As we walked round to the front of the house, a fly from the railway approached us along the drive. Miss Halcombe waited on the door-steps until the fly drew up; and then advanced to shake hands with an old gentleman, who got out briskly the moment the steps were let down. Mr Gilmore had arrived.

I looked at him, when we were introduced to each other, with an interest and a curiosity which I could hardly conceal. This old man was to remain at Limmeridge House after I had left it; he was to hear Sir Percival Glyde's explanation, and was to give Miss Halcombe the assistance of his experience in forming her judgment; he was to wait until the question of the marriage was set at rest; and his hand, if that question were decided in the affirmative, was to draw the settlement which bound Miss Fairlie irrevocably to her engagement. Even then, when I knew nothing by comparison with what I know now, I looked at the family lawyer with an interest which I had never felt before in the presence of any man breathing who was a total stranger to me.

In external appearance, Mr Gilmore was the exact opposite of the conventional idea of an old lawyer. His complexion was florid; his white hair was worn rather long and kept carefully brushed; his black coat, waistcoat, and trousers, fitted him with perfect neatness; his white cravat was carefully tied; and his lavender-coloured kid gloves might have adorned the hands of a fashionable clergyman, without fear and without reproach. His manners were pleasantly marked by the formal grace and refinement of the old school of politeness, quickened by the invigorating sharpness and readiness of a man whose business in life obliges him always to keep his faculties in good working order. A sanguine constitution and fair prospects to begin with; a long subsequent career of creditable and comfortable prosperity; a cheerful, diligent, widely-respected old age—such were the general impressions I derived from my introduction to Mr Gilmore; and it is but fair to him to add, that the knowledge I gained by later and better experience only tended to confirm them.

I left the old gentleman and Miss Halcombe to enter the house together, and to talk of family matters undisturbed by the restraint of a stranger's presence. They crossed the hall on their way to the drawing-room; and I descended the steps again, to wander about the garden alone.

My hours were numbered at Limmeridge House; my departure the next morning was irrevocably settled; my share in the investigation which the anonymous letter had rendered necessary, was at an end. No harm could be done to any one but myself, if I let my heart loose again, for the little time that was left me, from the cold cruelty of restraint which necessity had forced me to inflict upon it, and took my farewell of the scenes which were associated with the brief dream-time of my happiness and my love.

I turned instinctively to the walk beneath my study-window, where I had seen her the evening before with her little dog; and followed the path which her dear feet had trodden so often, till I came to the wicket gate that led into her rose garden. The winter bareness spread drearily over it, now. The flowers that she had taught me to distinguish by their names, the flowers that I had taught her to paint from, were gone; and the tiny white paths that led between the beds, were damp and green already. I went on to the avenue of trees, where we had breathed together the warm fragrance of August evenings; where we had admired together the myriad combinations of shade and sunlight that dappled the ground at our feet. The leaves fell about me from the groaning branches, and the earthy decay in the atmosphere chilled me to the bones. A little farther on, and I was out of the grounds, and following the lane that wound gently upward to the nearest hills. The old felled tree by the wayside, on which we had sat to rest, was sodden with rain;

and the tuft of ferns and grasses which I had drawn for her, nestling under the rough stone wall in front of us, had turned to a pool of water, stagnating round an island of draggled weeds. I gained the summit of the hill; and looked at the view which we had so often admired in the happier time. It was cold and barren—it was no longer the view that I remembered. The sunshine of her presence was far from me; the charm of her voice no longer murmured in my ear. She had talked to me, on the spot from which I now looked down, of her father, who was her last surviving parent; had told me how fond of each other they had been, and how sadly she missed him still, when she entered certain rooms in the house, and when she took up forgotten occupations and amusements with which he had been associated. Was the view that I had seen, while listening to those words, the view that I saw now, standing on the hill-top by myself? I turned, and left it; I wound my way back again, over the moor, and round the sandhills, down to the beach. There was the white rage of the surf, and the multitudinous glory of the leaping waves—but where was the place on which she had once drawn idle figures with her parasol in the sand; the place where we had sat together, while she talked to me about myself and my home, while she asked me a woman's minutely observant questions about my mother and my sister, and innocently wondered whether I should ever leave my lonely chambers and have a wife and a house of my own? Wind and wave had long since smoothed out the trace of her which she had left in those marks on the sand. I looked over the wide monotony of the sea-side prospect, and the place in which we two had idled away the sunny hours, was as lost to me as if I had never known it, as strange to me as if I stood already on a foreign shore.

The empty silence of the beach struck cold to my heart. I returned to the house and the garden, where traces were left to speak of her at every turn.

On the west terrace walk, I met Mr Gilmore. He was evidently in search of me, for he quickened his pace when we caught sight of each other. The state of my spirits little fitted me for the society of a stranger. But the meeting was inevitable; and I resigned myself to make the best of it.

'You are the very person I wanted to see,' said the old gentleman. 'I had two words to say to you, my dear sir; and, if you have no objection, I will avail myself of the present opportunity. To put it plainly, Miss Halcombe and I have been talking over family affairs—affairs which are the cause of my being here—and, in the course of our conversation, she was naturally led to tell me of this unpleasant matter connected with the anonymous letter, and of the share which you have most creditably and properly taken in the proceedings so far. That share, I quite understand, gives you an interest which you might not otherwise have felt, in knowing that the future management of the investigation, which you have begun, will be placed in safe hands. My dear sir, make yourself quite easy on that point—it will be placed in *my* hands.'

'You are, in every way, Mr Gilmore, much fitter to advise and to act in the matter than I am. Is it an indiscretion, on my part, to ask if you have decided yet on a course of proceeding?'

'So far as it is possible to decide, Mr Hartright, I have decided. I mean to send a copy of the letter, accompanied by a statement of the circumstances, to Sir Percival Glyde's solicitor in London, with whom I have some acquaintance. The letter itself, I shall keep here, to show to Sir Percival as soon as he arrives. The tracing of the two women, I have already provided for, by sending one of Mr Fairlie's servants—a confidential person—to the station to make inquiries: the man has his money and his directions, and he will follow the women in the event of his finding any clue. This is all that can be done until Sir Percival comes on Monday. I have no doubt myself that every explanation which can be expected from a gentleman and a man of honour, he will readily give. Sir Percival stands very high, sir—an eminent position, a reputation above suspicion—I feel quite easy about results; quite easy, I am rejoiced to assure you. Things of this sort happen constantly in my experience. Anonymous letters—unfortunate woman—sad state of society. I don't deny that there are peculiar complications in this case; but the case itself is, most unhappily, common—common.'

'I am afraid, Mr Gilmore, I have the misfortune to differ from you in the view I take of the case.'

'Just so, my dear sir—just so. I am an old man; and I take the practical view. You are a young man; and you take the romantic view. Let us not dispute about our views. I live, professionally, in an atmosphere of disputation, Mr Hartright; and I am only too glad to escape from it, as I am escaping here. We will wait for events—yes, yes, yes; we will wait for events. Charming place, this. Good shooting? Probably not—none of Mr Fairlie's land is preserved, I think. Charming place, though; and delightful people. You draw and paint, I hear, Mr Hartright? Enviable accomplishment. What style?'

We dropped into general conversation—or, rather, Mr Gilmore talked, and I listened. My attention was far from him, and from the topics on which he discoursed so fluently. The solitary walk of the last two hours had wrought its effect on me—it had set the idea in my mind of hastening my departure from Limmeridge House. Why should I prolong the hard trial of saying farewell by one unnecessary minute? What further service was required of me by any one? There was no useful purpose to be served by my stay in Cumberland; there was no restriction of time in the permission to leave which my employer had granted to me. Why not end it, there and then?

I determined to end it. There were some hours of daylight still left—there was no reason why my journey back to London should not begin on that afternoon. I made the first civil excuse that occurred to me for leaving Mr Gilmore; and returned at once to the house.

On my way up to my own room, I met Miss Halcombe on the stairs. She saw, by the hurry of my movements and the change in my manner, that I had some new purpose in view; and asked what had happened.

I told her the reasons which induced me to think of hastening my departure, exactly as I have told them here.

'No, no,' she said, earnestly and kindly, 'leave us like a friend; break bread with us once more. Stay here and dine; stay here and help us to spend our last evening with you as happily, as like our first evenings, as we can. It is my invitation; Mrs Vesey's invitation——' she hesitated a little, and then added, 'Laura's invitation as well.'

I promised to remain. God knows I had no wish to leave even the shadow of a sorrowful impression with any one of them.

My own room was the best place for me till the dinner bell rang. I waited there till it was time to go down stairs.

I had not spoken to Miss Fairlie—I had not even seen her—all that day. The first meeting with her, when I entered the drawing-room, was a hard trial to her self-control and to mine. She, too, had done her best to make our last evening renew the golden bygone time—the time that could never come again. She had put on the dress which I used to admire more than any other that she possessed—a dark blue silk, trimmed quaintly and prettily with old-fashioned lace; she came forward to meet me with her former readiness; she gave me her hand with the frank, innocent good will of happier days. The cold fingers that trembled round mine; the pale cheeks with a bright red spot burning in the midst of them; the faint smile that struggled to live on her lips and died away from them while I looked at it, told me at what sacrifice of herself her outward composure was maintained. My heart could take her no closer to me, or I should have loved her then as I had never loved her yet.

Mr Gilmore was a great assistance to us. He was in high good humour, and he led the conversation with unflagging spirit. Miss Halcombe seconded him resolutely; and I did all I could to follow her example. The kind blue eyes whose slightest changes of expression I had learnt to interpret so well, looked at me appealingly when we first sat down to table. Help my sister—the sweet anxious face seemed to say—help my sister, and you will help *me*.

We got through the dinner, to all outward appearance at least, happily enough. When the ladies had risen from table, and Mr Gilmore and I were left alone in the dining-room, a new interest presented itself to occupy our attention, and to give me an opportunity of quieting myself by a few minutes of needful and welcome silence. The servant who had been despatched to trace Anne Catherick and Mrs Clements returned with his report, and was shown into the dining-room immediately.

'Well,' said Mr Gilmore, 'what have you found out?'

'I have found out, sir,' answered the man, 'that both the women took tickets, at our station here, for Carlisle.'

'You went to Carlisle, of course, when you heard that?'

'I did, sir; but I am sorry to say I could find no further trace of them.'

'You inquired at the railway?'

'Yes, sir.'

'And at the different inns?'

'Yes, sir.'

'And you left the statement I wrote for you, at the police station?'

'I did, sir.'

'Well, my friend, you have done all you could, and I have done all I could; and there the matter must rest till further notice. We have played our trump cards, Mr Hartright,' continued the old gentleman, when the servant had withdrawn. 'For the present, at least, the women have out-manœuvred us; and our only resource, now, is to wait till Sir Percival Glyde comes here on Monday next. Won't you fill your glass again? Good bottle of port, that—sound, substantial, old wine. I have got better in my own cellar, though.'

We returned to the drawing-room—the room in which the happiest evenings of my life had been passed; the room which, after this last night, I was never to see again. Its aspect was altered since the days had shortened and the weather had grown cold. The glass doors on the terrace side were closed, and hidden by thick curtains. Instead of the soft twilight obscurity, in which we used to sit, the bright radiant glow of lamplight now dazzled my eyes. All was changed—in-doors and out, all was changed.

Miss Halcombe and Mr Gilmore sat down together at the card-table; Mrs Vesey took her customary chair. There was no restraint on the disposal of *their* evening; and I felt the restraint on the disposal of mine all the more painfully from observing it. I saw Miss Fairlie lingering near the music stand. The time had been when I might have joined her there. I waited irresolutely—I knew neither where to go nor what to do next. She cast one quick glance at me, took a piece of music suddenly from the stand, and came towards me of her own accord.

'Shall I play some of those little melodies of Mozart's, which you used to like so much?' she asked, opening the music nervously, and looking down at it while she spoke.

Before I could thank her, she hastened to the piano. The chair near it, which I had always been accustomed to occupy, stood empty. She struck a few chords—then glanced round at me—then looked back again at her music.

'Won't you take your old place?' she said, speaking very abruptly, and in very low tones.

'I may take it on the last night,' I answered.

She did not reply: she kept her attention riveted on the music—music which she knew by memory, which she had played over and over again, in former times, without the book. I only knew that she had heard me, I only knew that she was aware of my being close to her, by seeing the red spot on the cheek that was nearest to me, fade out, and the face grow pale all over.

'I am very sorry you are going,' she said, her voice almost sinking to a whisper; her eyes looking more and more intently at the music; her fingers flying over the keys of the piano with a strange feverish energy which I had never noticed in her before.

'I shall remember those kind words, Miss Fairlie, long after to-morrow has come and gone.'

The paleness grew whiter on her face, and she turned it farther away from me.

'Don't speak of to-morrow,' she said. 'Let the music speak to us of to-night, in a happier language than ours.'

Her lips trembled—a faint sigh fluttered from them, which she tried vainly to suppress. Her fingers wavered on the piano; she struck a false note; confused herself in trying to set it right; and dropped her hands angrily on her lap. Miss Halcombe and Mr Gilmore looked up in astonishment from the card-table at which they were playing. Even Mrs Vesey, dozing in her chair, woke at the sudden cessation of the music, and inquired what had happened.

'You play at whist, Mr Hartright?' asked Miss Halcombe, with her eyes directed significantly at the place I occupied.

I knew what she meant; I knew she was right; and I rose at once to go to the card-table. As I left the piano, Miss Fairlie turned a page of the music, and touched the keys again with a surer hand.

'I *will* play it,' she said, striking the notes almost passionately. 'I *will* play it on the last night.'

'Come, Mrs Vesey,' said Miss Halcombe; 'Mr Gilmore and I are tired of écarté—come and be Mr Hartright's partner at whist.'

The old lawyer smiled satirically. His had been the winning hand; and he had just turned up a king. He evidently attributed Miss Halcombe's abrupt change in the card-table arrangements to a lady's inability to play the losing game.

The rest of the evening passed without a word or a look from her. She kept her place at the piano; and I kept mine at the card-table. She played unintermittingly—played as if the music was her only refuge from herself. Sometimes, her fingers touched the notes with a lingering fondness, a soft, plaintive, dying tenderness, unutterably beautiful and mournful to hear—sometimes, they faltered and failed her, or hurried over the instrument mechanically, as if their task was a burden to them. But still, change and waver as they might in the expression they imparted to the music, their resolution to play never faltered. She only rose from the piano when we all rose to say good night.

Mrs Vesey was the nearest to the door, and the first to shake hands with me.

'I shall not see you again, Mr Hartright,' said the old lady. 'I am truly sorry you are going away. You have been very kind and attentive; and an old woman, like me, feels kindness and attention. I wish you happy, sir—I wish you a kind good-by.'

Mr Gilmore came next.

'I hope we shall have a future opportunity of bettering our acquaintance, Mr Hartright. You quite understand about that little matter of business being safe in my hands? Yes, yes, of course. Bless me, how cold it is! Don't let me keep you at the door. Bon voyage, my dear sir—bon voyage, as the French say.'

Miss Halcombe followed.

'Half-past seven to-morrow morning,' she said; then added, in a whisper, 'I have heard and seen more than you think. Your conduct to-night has made me your friend for life.'

Miss Fairlie came last. I could not trust myself to look at her, when I took her hand, and when I thought of the next morning.

'My departure must be a very early one,' I said. 'I shall be gone, Miss Fairlie, before you——'

'No, no,' she interposed, hastily; 'not before I am out of my room. I shall be down to breakfast with Marian. I am not so ungrateful, not so forgetful of the past three months——'

Her voice failed her; her hand closed gently round mine—then dropped it suddenly. Before I could say, 'Good night,' she was gone.

The end comes fast to meet me—comes inevitably, as the light of the last morning came at Limmeridge House.

It was barely half-past seven when I went down stairs—but I found them both at the breakfast-table waiting for me. In the chill air, in the dim light, in the gloomy morning silence of the house, we three sat down together, and tried to eat, tried to talk. The struggle to preserve appearances was hopeless and useless; and I rose to end it.

As I held out my hand, as Miss Halcombe, who was nearest to me, took it, Miss Fairlie turned away suddenly, and hurried from the room.

'Better so,' said Miss Halcombe, when the door had closed—'better so, for you and for her.'

I waited a moment before I could speak—it was hard to lose her, without a parting word, or a parting look. I controlled myself; I tried to take leave of Miss Halcombe in fitting terms; but all the farewell words I would fain have spoken, dwindled to one sentence.

'Have I deserved that you should write to me?' was all I could say.

'You have nobly deserved everything that I can do for you, as long as we both live. Whatever the end is, you shall know it.'

'And if I can ever be of help again, at any future time, long after the memory of my presumption and my folly is forgotten——'

I could add no more. My voice faltered, my eyes moistened, in spite of me.

She caught me by both hands—she pressed them with the strong, steady grasp of a man—her dark eyes glittered—her brown complexion flushed deep—the force and energy of her face glowed and grew beautiful with the pure inner light of her generosity and her pity.

'I will trust you—if ever the time comes, I will trust you as *my* friend and *her* friend; as *my* brother and *her* brother.' She stopped; drew me nearer to her—the fearless, noble creature—touched my forehead, sisterlike, with her lips; and called me by my Christian name. 'God bless you, Walter!' she said. 'Wait here alone, and compose yourself—I had better not stay for both our sakes; I had better see you go, from the balcony upstairs.'

She left the room. I turned away towards the window, where nothing faced me but the lonely autumn landscape—I turned away to master myself, before I, too, left the room in my turn, and left it for ever.

A minute passed—it could hardly have been more—when I heard the door open again softly; and the rustling of a woman's dress on the carpet, moved towards me. My heart beat violently as I turned round. Miss Fairlie was approaching me from the farther end of the room.

She stopped and hesitated, when our eyes met, and when she saw that we were alone. Then, with that courage which women have so often in the small emergency, and so seldom in the great, she came on nearer to me, strangely pale and strangely quiet, drawing one hand after her along the table by which she walked, and holding something at her side, in the other, which was hidden by the folds of her dress.

'I only went into the drawing-room,' she said, 'to look for this. It may remind you of your visit here, and of the friends you leave behind you. You told me I had improved very much when I did it—and I thought you might like——'

She turned her head away, and offered me a little sketch drawn throughout by her own pencil, of the summer-house in which we had first met. The paper trembled in her hand as she held it out to me—trembled in mine, as I took it from her.

I was afraid to say what I felt—I only answered: 'It shall never leave me; all my life long it shall be the treasure that I prize most. I am very grateful for it—very grateful to *you*, for not letting me go away without bidding you good-by.'

'Oh!' she said, innocently, 'how could I let you go, after we have passed so many happy days together!'

'Those days may never return, Miss Fairlie—my way of life and yours are very far apart. But if a time should come, when the devotion of my whole heart and soul and strength will give you a moment's happiness or spare you a moment's sorrow, will you try to remember the poor drawing-master who has taught you? Miss Halcombe has promised to trust me—will you promise, too?'

The farewell sadness in the kind blue eyes shone dimly through her gathering tears.

'I promise it,' she said, in broken tones. 'Oh, don't look at me like that! I promise it with all my heart.'

I ventured a little nearer to her, and held out my hand.

'You have many friends who love you, Miss Fairlie. Your happy future is the dear object of many hopes. May I say, at parting, that it is the dear object of *my* hopes too?'

The tears flowed fast down her cheeks. She rested one trembling hand on the table to steady herself, while she gave me the other. I took it in mine—I held it fast. My head drooped over it, my tears fell on it, my lips pressed it—not in love; oh, not in love, at that last moment, but in the agony and the self-abandonment of despair.

'For God's sake, leave me!' she said, faintly.

The confession of her heart's secret burst from her in those pleading words. I had no right to hear them, no right to answer them: they were the words that banished me, in the name of her sacred weakness, from the room. It was all over. I dropped her hand; I said no more. The blinding tears shut her out from my eyes, and I dashed them away to look at her for the last time. One look, as she sank into a chair, as her arms fell on the table, as her fair head dropped on them wearily. One farewell look; and the door had closed upon her—the great gulf of separation had opened between us—the image of Laura Fairlie was a memory of the past already.

THE NARRATIVE OF VINCENT GILMORE, SOLICITOR, OF CHANCERY-LANE, LONDON

I

I WRITE these lines at the request of my friend, Mr Walter Hartright. They are intended to convey a description of certain events which seriously affected Miss Fairlie's interests, and which took place after the period of Mr Hartright's departure from Limmeridge House.

There is no need for me to say whether my own opinion does or does not sanction the disclosure of the remarkable family story, of which my narrative forms an important component part. Mr Hartright has taken that responsibility on himself; and circumstances yet to be related will show that he has amply earned the right to do so, if he chooses to exercise it. The plan he has adopted for presenting the story to others, in the most truthful and most vivid manner, requires that it should be told, at each successive stage in the march of events at the time of their occurrence. My appearance here, as narrator, is the necessary consequence of this arrangement. I was present during the sojourn of Sir Percival Glyde in Cumberland, and was personally concerned in one important result of his short residence under Mr Fairlie's roof. It is my duty, therefore, to add these new links to the chain of events, and to take up the chain itself at the point where, for the present only, Mr Hartright has dropped it.

I arrived at Limmeridge House, on Friday the second of November.

My object was to remain at Mr Fairlie's until the arrival of Sir Percival Glyde. If that event led to the appointment of any given day for Sir Percival's union with Miss Fairlie, I was to take the necessary instructions back with me to London, and to occupy myself in drawing the lady's marriage-settlement.

On the Friday, I was not favoured by Mr Fairlie with an interview. He had been, or had fancied himself to be, an invalid for years past; and he was not well enough to receive me. Miss Halcombe was the first member of the family whom I saw. She met me at the house door; and introduced me to Mr Hartright, who had been staying at Limmeridge for some time past.

I did not see Miss Fairlie until later in the day, at dinner time. She was not looking well, and I was sorry to observe it. She is a sweet, lovable girl, as amiable and attentive to everyone about her as her excellent mother used to be—though, personally speaking, she takes after her father. Mrs Fairlie had dark eyes and hair; and her elder daughter, Miss Halcombe, strongly reminds me of her. Miss Fairlie played to us in the evening—not so well as usual, I thought. We had a rubber at whist; a mere profanation, so far as play was concerned, of that noble game. I had been favourably impressed by Mr Hartright, on our first introduction to one another; but I soon discovered that he was not free from the social failings incidental to his age. There are three things that none of the young men of the present generation can do. They can't sit over their wine; they can't play at whist; and they can't pay a lady a compliment. Mr Hartright was no exception to the general rule. Otherwise, even in those early days and on that short acquaintance, he struck me as being a modest and gentlemanlike young man.

So the Friday passed. I say nothing about the more serious matters which engaged my attention on that day—the anonymous letter to Miss Fairlie; the measures I thought it right to adopt when the matter was mentioned to me; and the conviction I entertained that every possible explanation of the circumstances would be readily afforded by Sir Percival Glyde, having all been fully noticed, as I understand, in the narrative which precedes this.

On the Saturday, Mr Hartright had left before I got down to breakfast. Miss Fairlie kept her room all day; and Miss Halcombe appeared to me to be out of spirits. The house was not what it used to be in the time of Mr and Mrs Philip Fairlie. I took a walk by myself in the forenoon: and looked about at some of the places which I first saw when I was staying at Limmeridge to transact family business, more than thirty years since. They were not what they used to be, either.

At two o'clock Mr Fairlie sent to say he was well enough to see me. *He* had not altered, at any rate, since I first knew him. His talk was to the same purpose as usual—all about himself and his ailments, his wonderful coins, and his matchless Rembrandt etchings. The moment I tried to speak of the business that had brought me to his house, he shut his eyes and said I 'upset' him. I persisted in upsetting him by returning again and again to the subject. All I could ascertain was that he looked on his niece's marriage as a settled thing, that her father had sanctioned it, that he sanctioned it himself, that it was a desirable marriage, and that he should be personally rejoiced when the worry of it was over. As to the settlement, if I would consult his niece, and afterwards dive as deeply as I pleased into my own knowledge of the family affairs, and get everything ready, and limit his share in the business, as guardian, to saying, Yes, at the right moment—why of course he would meet my views, and everybody else's views, with infinite pleasure. In the mean time, there I saw him, a helpless sufferer, confined to his room. Did I think he looked as if he wanted teasing? No. Then why tease him?

I might, perhaps, have been a little astonished at this extraordinary absence of all self-assertion on Mr Fairlie's part, in the character of guardian, if my knowledge of the family affairs had not been sufficient to remind me that he was a single man, and that he had nothing more than a life-interest in the Limmeridge property. As matters stood, therefore, I was neither surprised nor disappointed at the result of the interview. Mr Fairlie had simply justified my expectations—and there was an end of it.

Sunday was a dull day, out of doors and in. A letter arrived for me from Sir Percival Glyde's solicitor, acknowledging the receipt of my copy of the anonymous letter, and my accompanying statement of the case. Miss Fairlie joined us in the afternoon, looking pale and depressed, and altogether unlike herself. I had some talk with her, and ventured on a delicate allusion to Sir Percival. She listened, and said nothing. All other subjects she pursued willingly; but this subject she allowed to drop. I began to doubt whether she might not be repenting of her engagement—just as young ladies often do, when repentance comes too late.

On Monday Sir Percival Glyde arrived.

I found him to be a most prepossessing man, so far as manners and appearance were concerned. He looked rather older than I had expected; his head being bald over the forehead, and his face somewhat marked and worn. But his movements were as active and his spirits as high as a young man's. His meeting with Miss Halcombe was delightfully hearty and un-affected; and his reception of me, upon my being presented to him, was so easy and pleasant that we got on together like old friends. Miss Fairlie was not with us when he arrived, but she entered the room about ten minutes afterwards. Sir Percival rose and paid his compliments with perfect grace. His evident concern on seeing the change for the worse in the young lady's looks was expressed with a mixture of tenderness and respect, with an unassuming delicacy of tone, voice, and manner, which did equal credit to his good breeding and his good sense. I was rather surprised, under these circumstances, to see that Miss Fairlie continued to be constrained and uneasy in his presence, and that she took the first opportunity of leaving the room again. Sir Percival neither noticed the restraint in her reception of him, nor her sudden withdrawal from our society. He had not obtruded his attentions on her while she was present, and he did not embarrass Miss Halcombe by any allusion to her departure when she was gone. His tact and taste were never at fault on this or on any other occasion while I was in his company at Limmeridge House.

As soon as Miss Fairlie had left the room, he spared us all embarrassment on the subject of the anonymous letter, by adverting to it of his own accord. He had stopped in London on his way from Hampshire; had seen his solicitor; had read the documents forwarded by me; and had travelled on to Cumberland, anxious to satisfy our minds by the speediest and the fullest explanation that words could convey. On hearing him express himself to this effect, I offered him the original letter which I had kept for his inspection. He thanked me, and declined to look at it; saying that he had seen the copy, and that he was quite willing to leave the original in our hands.

The statement itself, on which he immediately entered, was as simple and satisfactory as I had all along anticipated it would be.

Mrs Catherick, he informed us, had, in past years, laid him under some obligations for faithful services rendered to his family connexions and to himself. She had been doubly unfortunate in being married to a husband who had deserted her, and in having an only child whose mental faculties had been in a disturbed condition from a very early age. Although her marriage had removed her to a part of Hampshire far distant from the neighbourhood in which Sir Percival's property was situated, he had taken care not to lose sight of her; his friendly feeling towards the poor woman, in consideration of her past services, having been greatly strengthened by his admiration of the patience and courage with which she supported her calamities. In course of time, the symptoms of mental affliction in her unhappy daughter increased to such a serious extent, as to make it a matter of necessity to place her under proper medical care. Mrs Catherick herself recognised this necessity; but she also felt the prejudice common to persons occupying her respectable station, against allowing her child to be admitted, as a pauper, into a public Asylum. Sir Percival had respected this prejudice, as he respected honest independence of feeling in any rank of life; and had resolved to mark his grateful sense of Mrs Catherick's early attachment to the interests of himself and his family, by defraying the expense of her daughter's maintenance in a trustworthy private Asylum. To her mother's regret, and to his own regret, the unfortunate creature had discovered the share which circumstances had induced him to take in placing her under restraint, and had conceived the most intense hatred and distrust of him in consequence. To that hatred and distrust—which had expressed itself in various ways in the Asylum—the anonymous letter, written after her escape, was plainly attributable. If Miss Halcombe's or Mr Gilmore's recollection of the document did not confirm that view, or if they wished for any additional particulars about the Asylum (the address of which he mentioned, as well as the names and addresses of the two doctors on whose certificates the patient was admitted), he was ready to answer any question and to clear up any uncertainty. He had done his duty to the unhappy young woman, by instructing his solicitor to spare no expense in tracing her, and in restoring her once more to medical care; and he was now only anxious to do his duty towards Miss Fairlie and towards her family, in the same plain, straightforward way.

I was the first to speak in answer to this appeal. My own course was plain to me. It is the great beauty of the Law that it can dispute any human statement, made under any circumstances, and reduced to any form. If I had felt professionally called upon to set up a case against Sir Percival Glyde, on the strength of his own explanation, I could have done so beyond all doubt. But my duty did not lie in this direction: my function was of the purely judicial kind. I was to weigh the explanation we had just heard; to allow all due force to the high reputation of the gentleman who offered it; and to decide honestly whether the probabilities, on Sir Percival's own showing, were plainly with him, or plainly against him. My own conviction was that they were plainly with him; and I accordingly declared that his explanation was, to my mind, unquestionably a satisfactory one.

Miss Halcombe, after looking at me very earnestly, said a few words, on her side, to the same effect—with a certain hesitation of manner, however, which the circumstances did not seem to me to warrant. I am unable to say, positively, whether Sir Percival noticed this or not. My opinion is that he did; seeing that he pointedly resumed the subject, although he might, now, with all propriety, have allowed it to drop.

'If my plain statement of facts had only been addressed to Mr Gilmore,' he said, 'I should consider any further reference to this unhappy matter as unnecessary. I may fairly expect Mr Gilmore, as a gentleman, to believe me on my word; and when he has done me that justice, all discussion of the subject between us has come to an end. But my position with a lady is not the same. I owe to her, what I would concede to no man alive—a *proof* of the truth of my assertion. You cannot ask for that proof, Miss Halcombe; and it is therefore my duty to you, and still more to Miss Fairlie, to offer it. May I beg that you will write at once to the mother of this unfortunate woman—to Mrs Catherick—to ask for her testimony in support of the explanation which I have just offered to you.'

I saw Miss Halcombe change colour, and look a little uneasy. Sir Percival's suggestion, politely as it was expressed, appeared to her, as it appeared to me, to point, very delicately, at the hesitation which her manner had betrayed a moment or two since.

'I hope, Sir Percival, you don't do me the injustice to suppose that I distrust you,' she said, quickly.

'Certainly not, Miss Halcombe. I make my proposal purely as an act of attention to *you*. Will you excuse my obstinacy if I still venture to press it?'

He walked to the writing-table, as he spoke; drew a chair to it; and opened the paper-case.

'Let me beg you to write the note,' he said, 'as a favour to me. It need not occupy you more than a few minutes. You have only to ask Mrs Catherick two questions. First, if her daughter was placed in the Asylum with her knowledge and approval. Secondly, if the share I took in the matter was such as to merit the expression of her gratitude towards myself? Mr Gilmore's mind is at ease on this unpleasant subject; and your mind is at ease—pray set my mind at ease also, by writing the note.'

'You oblige me to grant your request, Sir Percival, when I would much rather refuse it.' With those words Miss Halcombe rose from her place, and went to the writing-table. Sir Percival thanked her, handed her a pen, and then walked away towards the fireplace. Miss Fairlie's little Italian greyhound was lying on the rug. He held out his hand, and called to the dog good-humouredly.

'Come, Nina,' he said; 'we remember each other, don't we?'

The little beast, cowardly and cross-grained as pet-dogs usually are, looked up at him sharply, shrank away from his outstretched hand, whined, shivered, and hid itself under a sofa. It was scarcely possible that he could have been put out by such a trifle as a dog's reception of him—but I observed, nevertheless, that he walked away towards the window very suddenly. Perhaps his temper is irritable at times? If so, I can sympathise with him. My temper is irritable at times, too.

Miss Halcombe was not long in writing the note. When it was done, she rose from the writing-table, and handed the open sheet of paper to Sir Percival. He bowed; took it from her; folded it up immediately, without looking at the contents; sealed it; wrote the address; and handed it back to her in silence. I never saw anything more gracefully and more becomingly done, in my life.

'You insist on my posting this letter, Sir Percival?' said Miss Halcombe.

'I beg you will post it,' he answered. 'And now that it is written and sealed up, allow me to ask one or two last questions about the unhappy woman to whom it refers. I have read the communication which Mr Gilmore kindly addressed to my solicitor, describing the circumstances under which the writer of the anonymous letter was identified. But there are certain points to which that statement does not refer. Did Anne Catherick see Miss Fairlie?'

'Certainly not,' replied Miss Halcombe.

'Did she see you?'

'No.'

'She saw nobody from the house, then, except a certain Mr Hartright, who accidentally met with her in the churchyard here?'

'Nobody else.'

'Mr Hartright was employed at Limmeridge as a drawing-master, I believe? Is he a member of one of the Water-Colour Societies?'

'I believe he is,' answered Miss Halcombe.

He paused for a moment, as if he was thinking over the last answer, and then added:

'Did you find out where Anne Catherick was living, when she was in this neighbourhood?'

'Yes. At a farm on the moor, called Todd's Corner.'

'It is a duty we all owe to the poor creature herself to trace her,' continued Sir Percival. 'She may have said something at Todd's Corner which may help us to find her. I will go there, and make inquiries on the chance. In the mean time, as I cannot prevail on myself to discuss this painful subject with Miss Fairlie, may I beg, Miss Halcombe, that you will kindly undertake to give her the necessary explanation, deferring it of course until you have received the reply to that note.'

Miss Halcombe promised to comply with his request. He thanked her— nodded pleasantly—and left us, to go and establish himself in his own room. As he opened the door, the cross-grained greyhound poked out her sharp muzzle from under the sofa, and barked and snapped at him.

'A good morning's work, Miss Halcombe,' I said, as soon as we were alone. 'Here is an anxious day well ended already.'

'Yes,' she answered; 'no doubt. I am very glad your mind is satisfied.'

'*My* mind! Surely, with that note in your hand, your mind is at ease too?'

'Oh, yes—how can it be otherwise? I know the thing could not be,' she went on, speaking more to herself than to me; 'but I almost wish Walter Hartright had stayed here long enough to be present at the explanation, and to hear the proposal to me to write this note.'

I was a little surprised—perhaps a little piqued, also, by these last words.

'Events, it is true, connected Mr Hartright very remarkably with the affair of the letter,' I said: 'and I readily admit that he conducted himself, all things considered, with great delicacy and discretion. But I am quite at a loss to understand what useful influence his presence could have exercised in relation to the effect of Sir Percival's statement on your mind or mine.'

'It was only a fancy,' she said, absently. 'There is no need to discuss it, Mr Gilmore. Your experience ought to be, and is, the best guide I can desire.'

I did not altogether like her thrusting the whole responsibility, in this marked manner, on my shoulders. If Mr Fairlie had done it, I should not have been surprised. But resolute, clear-minded Miss Halcombe, was the very last person in the world whom I should have expected to find shrinking from the expression of an opinion of her own.

'If any doubts still trouble you,' I said, 'why not mention them to me at once? Tell me plainly, have you any reason to distrust Sir Percival Glyde?'

'None whatever.'

'Do you see anything improbable, or contradictory, in his explanation?'

'How can I say I do, after the proof he has offered me of the truth of it? Can there be better testimony in his favour, Mr Gilmore, than the testimony of the woman's mother?'

'None better. If the answer to your note of inquiry proves to be satisfactory, I, for one, cannot see what more any friend of Sir Percival's can possibly expect from him.'

'Then we will post the note,' she said, rising to leave the room, 'and dismiss all further reference to the subject, until the answer arrives. Don't attach any weight to my hesitation. I can give no better reason for it than that I have been over-anxious about Laura lately; and anxiety, Mr Gilmore, unsettles the strongest of us.'

She left me abruptly; her naturally firm voice faltering as she spoke those last words. A sensitive, vehement, passionate nature—a woman of ten thousand in these trivial, superficial times. I had known her from her earliest years; I had seen her tested, as she grew up, in more than one trying family crisis, and my long experience made me attach an importance to her hesitation under the circumstances here detailed, which I should certainly not have felt in the case of another woman. I could see no cause for any uneasiness or any doubt; but she had made me a little uneasy, and a little doubtful, nevertheless. In my youth, I should have chafed and fretted under the irritation of my own unreasonable state of mind. In my age, I knew better; and went out philosophically to walk it off.

II

WE all met again at dinner-time.

Sir Percival was in such boisterous high spirits that I hardly recognised him as the same man whose quiet tact, refinement, and good sense had impressed me so strongly at the interview of the morning. The only trace of his former self that I could detect, reappeared, every now and then, in his manner towards Miss Fairlie. A look or a word from her, suspended his loudest laugh, checked his gayest flow of talk, and rendered him all attention to her, and to no one else at table, in an instant. Although he never openly tried to draw her into the conversation, he never lost the slightest chance she gave him of letting her drift into it by accident, and of saying the words to her, under those favourable circumstances, which a man with less tact and delicacy would have pointedly addressed to her the moment they occurred to him. Rather to my surprise, Miss Fairlie appeared to be sensible of his attentions, without being moved by them. She was a little confused from time to time, when he looked at her, or spoke to her; but she never warmed towards him. Rank, fortune, good breeding, good looks, the respect of a gentleman, and the devotion of a lover, were all humbly placed at her feet, and, so far as appearances went, were all offered in vain.

On the next day, the Tuesday, Sir Percival went in the morning (taking one of the servants with him as a guide) to Todd's Corner. His inquiries, as I afterwards heard, led to no results. On his return, he had an interview with Mr Fairlie; and in the afternoon he and Miss Halcombe rode out together. Nothing else happened worthy of record. The evening passed as usual. There was no change in Sir Percival and no change in Miss Fairlie.

The Wednesday's post brought with it an event—the reply from Mrs Catherick. I took a copy of the document, which I have preserved, and which I may as well present in this place. It ran as follows:

'MADAM,—I beg to acknowledge the receipt of your letter, inquiring whether my daughter, Anne, was placed under medical superintendence with my knowledge and approval, and whether the share taken in the matter by Sir Percival Glyde was such as to merit the expression of my gratitude towards that gentleman. Be pleased to accept my answer in the affirmative to both those questions, and believe me to remain, your obedient servant,

JANE ANNE CATHERICK.'

Short, sharp, and to the point: in form, rather a business-like letter for a woman to write; in substance, as plain a confirmation as could be desired of Sir Percival Glyde's statement. This was my opinion, and with certain minor reservations, Miss Halcombe's opinion also. Sir Percival, when the letter was shown to him, did not appear to be struck by the sharp, short tone of it. He told us that Mrs Catherick was a woman of few words, a clear-headed, straightforward, unimaginative person, who wrote briefly and plainly, just as she spoke.

The next duty to be accomplished, now that the answer had been received, was to acquaint Miss Fairlie with Sir Percival's explanation. Miss Halcombe had undertaken to do this, and had left the room to go to her sister, when she suddenly returned again, and sat down by the easy-chair in which I was reading the newspaper. Sir Percival had gone out a minute before, to look at the stables, and no one was in the room but ourselves.

'I suppose we have really and truly done all we can?' she said, turning and twisting Mrs Catherick's letter in her hand.

'If we are friends of Sir Percival's, who know him and trust him, we have done all, and more than all, that is necessary,' I answered, a little annoyed by this return of her hesitation. 'But if we are enemies who suspect him——'

'That alternative is not even to be thought of,' she interposed. 'We are Sir Percival's friends; and, if generosity and forbearance can add to our regard for him, we ought to be Sir Percival's admirers as well. You know that he saw Mr Fairlie yesterday, and that he afterwards went out with me?'

'Yes. I saw you riding away together.'

'We began the ride by talking about Anne Catherick, and about the singular manner in which Mr Hartright met with her. But we soon dropped that subject; and Sir Percival spoke next, in the most unselfish terms, of his engagement with Laura. He said he had observed that she was out of spirits, and he was willing, if not informed to the contrary, to attribute to that cause the alteration in her manner towards him during his present visit. If, however, there was any other more serious reason for the change, he would entreat that no constraint might be placed on her inclinations either by Mr Fairlie or by me. All he asked, in that case, was that she would recal to mind, for the last time, what the circumstances were under which the engagement between them was made, and what his conduct had been from the beginning of the courtship to the present time. If, after due reflection on those two subjects, she seriously desired that he should withdraw his pretensions to the honour of becoming her husband—and if she would tell him so plainly, with her own lips—he would sacrifice himself by leaving her perfectly free to withdraw from the engagement.'

'No man could say more than that, Miss Halcombe. As to my experience, few men in his situation would have said as much.'

She paused after I had spoken those words, and looked at me with a singular expression of perplexity and distress.

'I accuse nobody and I suspect nothing,' she broke out, abruptly. 'But I cannot and will not accept the responsibility of persuading Laura to this marriage.'

'That is exactly the course which Sir Percival Glyde has himself requested you to take,' I replied, in astonishment. 'He has begged you not to force her inclinations.'

'And he indirectly obliges me to force them, if I give her his message.'

'How can that possibly be?'

'Consult your own knowledge of Laura, Mr Gilmore. If I tell her to reflect on the circumstances of her engagement, I at once appeal to two of the strongest feelings in her nature—to her love for her father's memory, and to her strict regard for truth. You know that she never broke a promise in her life; you know that she entered on this engagement at the beginning of her father's fatal illness, and that he spoke hopefully and happily of her marriage to Sir Percival Glyde on his death-bed.'

I own that I was a little shocked at this view of the case.

'Surely,' I said, 'you don't mean to infer that when Sir Percival spoke to you yesterday, he speculated on such a result as you have just mentioned?'

Her frank, fearless face answered for her before she spoke.

'Do you think I would remain an instant in the company of any man whom I suspected of such baseness as that?' she asked, angrily.

I liked to feel her hearty indignation flash out on me in that way. We see so much malice and so little indignation in my profession.

'In that case,' I said, 'excuse me if I tell you, in our legal phrase, that you are travelling out of the record. Whatever the consequences may be, Sir Percival has a right to expect that your sister should carefully consider her engagement from every reasonable point of view before she claims her release from it. If that unlucky letter has prejudiced her against him, go at once, and tell her that he has cleared himself in your eyes and in mine. What objection can she urge against him after that? What excuse can she possibly have for changing her mind about a man whom she had virtually accepted for her husband more than two years ago?'

'In the eyes of law and reason, Mr Gilmore, no excuse, I dare say. If she still hesitates, and if I still hesitate, you must attribute our strange conduct, if you like, to caprice in both cases, and we must bear the imputation as well as we can.'

With those words, she suddenly rose, and left me. When a sensible woman has a serious question put to her, and evades it by a flippant answer, it is a sure sign, in ninety-nine cases out of a hundred, that she has something to conceal. I returned to the perusal of the newspaper, strongly suspecting that Miss Halcombe and Miss Fairlie had a secret between them which they were keeping from Sir Percival and keeping from me. I thought this hard on both of us—especially on Sir Percival.

My doubts—or, to speak more correctly, my convictions—were confirmed by Miss Halcombe's language and manner, when I saw her again, later in the day. She was suspiciously brief and reserved in telling me the result of her interview with her sister. Miss Fairlie, it appeared, had listened quietly while the affair of the letter was placed before her in the right point of view; but when Miss Halcombe next proceeded to say that the object of Sir Percival's visit at Limmeridge was to prevail on her to let a day be fixed for the marriage, she checked all further reference to the subject by begging for time. If Sir Percival would consent to spare her for the present, she would undertake to give him his final answer, before the end of the year. She pleaded for this delay with such anxiety and agitation, that Miss Halcombe had promised to use her influence, if necessary, to obtain it; and there, at Miss Fairlie's earnest entreaty, all further discussion of the marriage question had ended.

The purely temporary arrangement thus proposed might have been convenient enough to the young lady; but it proved somewhat embarrassing to the writer of these lines. That morning's post had brought a letter from my partner, which obliged me to return to town the next day, by the afternoon train. It was extremely probable that I should find no second opportunity of presenting myself at Limmeridge House during the remainder of the year. In that case, supposing Miss Fairlie ultimately decided on holding to her engagement, my necessary personal communication with her, before I drew her settlement, would become something like a downright impossibility; and we should be obliged to commit to writing questions which ought always to be discussed on both sides by word of mouth. I said nothing about this difficulty, until Sir Percival had been consulted on the subject of the desired delay. He was too gallant a gentleman not to grant the request immediately. When Miss Halcombe informed me of this, I told her that I must absolutely speak to her sister, before I left Limmeridge; and it was, therefore, arranged that I should see Miss Fairlie in her own sitting-room, the next morning. She did not come down to dinner, or join us in the evening. Indisposition was the excuse; and I thought Sir Percival looked, as well he might, a little annoyed when he heard of it.

The next morning, as soon as breakfast was over, I went up to Miss Fairlie's sitting-room. The poor girl looked so pale and sad, and came forward to welcome me so readily and prettily, that the resolution to lecture her on her caprice and indecision, which I had been forming all the way up-stairs, failed me on the spot. I led her back to the chair from which she had risen, and placed myself opposite to her. Her cross-grained pet greyhound was in the room, and I fully expected a barking and snapping reception. Strange to say, the whimsical little brute falsified my expectations by jumping into my lap, and poking its sharp muzzle familiarly into my hand the moment I sat down.

'You used often to sit on my knee when you were a child, my dear,' I said, 'and now your little dog seems determined to succeed you in the vacant throne. Is that pretty drawing your doing?'

I pointed to a little album, which lay on the table by her side, and which she had evidently been looking over when I came in. The page that lay open had a small water-colour landscape very neatly mounted on it. This was the drawing which had suggested my question: an idle question enough—but how could I begin to talk of business to her the moment I opened my lips?

'No,' she said, looking away from the drawing rather confusedly; 'it is not my doing.'

Her fingers had a restless habit, which I remembered in her, as a child, of always playing with the first thing that came to hand, whenever any one was talking to her. On this occasion they wandered to the album, and toyed absently about the margin of the little water-colour drawing. The expression of melancholy deepened on her face. She did not look at the drawing, or look at me. Her eyes moved uneasily from object to object in the room; betraying plainly that she suspected what my purpose was in coming to speak to her. Seeing that, I thought it best to get to the purpose with as little delay as possible.

'One of the errands, my dear, which brings me here is to bid you good-by,' I began. 'I must get back to London to-day; and, before I leave, I want to have a word with you on the subject of your own affairs.'

'I am very sorry you are going, Mr Gilmore,' she said, looking at me kindly. 'It is like the happy old times to have you here.'

'I hope I may be able to come back, and recal those pleasant memories once more,' I continued; 'but as there is some uncertainty about the future, I must take my opportunity when I can get it, and speak to you now. I am your old lawyer and your old friend; and I may remind you, I am sure, without offence of the possibility of your marrying Sir Percival Glyde.'

She took her hand off the little album as suddenly as if it had turned hot and burnt her. Her fingers twined together nervously in her lap; her eyes looked down again at the floor; and an expression of constraint settled on her face which looked almost like an expression of pain.

'Is it absolutely necessary to speak of my marriage engagement?' she asked, in low tones.

'It is necessary to refer to it,' I answered; 'but not to dwell on it. Let us merely say that you may marry, or that you may not marry. In the first case, I must be prepared, beforehand, to draw your settlement; and I ought not to do that without, as a matter of politeness, first consulting you. This may be my only chance of hearing what your wishes are. Let us, therefore, suppose the case of your marrying, and let me inform you, in as few words as possible, what your position is now, and what you may make it, if you please, in the future.'

I explained to her the object of a marriage-settlement; and then told her exactly what her prospects were—in the first place, on her coming of age, and, in the second place, on the decease of her uncle—marking the distinction between the property in which she had a life interest only, and the property which was left at her own control. She listened attentively, with the constrained expression still on her face, and her hands still nervously clasped together in her lap.

'And, now,' I said, in conclusion, 'tell me if you can think of any condition which, in the case we have supposed, you would wish me to make for you—subject, of course, to your guardian's approval, as you are not yet of age.'

She moved uneasily in her chair—then looked in my face, on a sudden, very earnestly.

'If it does happen,' she began, faintly; 'if I am——'

'If you are married,' I added, helping her out.

'Don't let him part me from Marian,' she cried, with a sudden outbreak of energy. 'Oh, Mr Gilmore, pray make it law that Marian is to live with me!'

Under other circumstances, I might perhaps have been amused at this essentially feminine interpretation of my question, and of the long explanation which had preceded it. But her looks and tones, when she spoke, were of a kind to make me more than serious—they distressed me. Her words, few as they were, betrayed a desperate clinging to the past which boded ill for the future.

'Your having Marian Halcombe to live with you, can easily be settled by private arrangement,' I said. 'You hardly understood my question, I think. It referred to your own property—to the disposal of your money. Supposing you were to make a will, when you come of age, who would you like the money to go to?'

'Marian has been mother and sister both to me,' said the good, affectionate girl, her pretty blue eyes glistening while she spoke. 'May I leave it to Marian, Mr Gilmore?'

'Certainly, my love,' I answered. 'But remember what a large sum it is. Would you like it all to go to Miss Halcombe?'

She hesitated; her colour came and went; and her hand stole back again to the little album.

'Not all of it,' she said. 'There is some one else, besides Marian——'

She stopped; her colour heightened; and the fingers of the hand that rested upon the album beat gently on the margin of the drawing, as if her memory had set them going mechanically with the remembrance of a favourite tune.

'You mean some other member of the family besides Miss Halcombe?' I suggested, seeing her at a loss to proceed.

The heightening colour spread to her forehead and her neck, and the nervous fingers suddenly clasped themselves fast round the edge of the book.

'There is some one else,' she said, not noticing my last words, though she had evidently heard them; 'there is some one else who might like a little keepsake, if—if I might leave it. There would be no harm, if I should die first——'

She paused again. The colour that had spread over her cheeks suddenly, as suddenly left them. The hand on the album resigned its hold, trembled a little, and moved the book away from her. She looked at me for an instant—then turned her head aside in the chair. Her handkerchief fell to the floor as she changed her position, and she hurriedly hid her face from me in her hands.

Sad! To remember her, as I did, the liveliest, happiest child that ever laughed the day through; and to see her now, in the flower of her age and her beauty, so broken and so brought down as this!

In the distress that she caused me, I forgot the years that had passed, and the change they had made in our position towards one another. I moved my chair close to her, and picked up her handkerchief from the carpet, and drew her hands from her face gently. 'Don't cry, my love,' I said, and dried the tears that were gathering in her eyes, with my own hand, as if she had been the little Laura Fairlie of ten long years ago.

It was the best way I could have taken to compose her. She laid her head on my shoulder, and smiled faintly through her tears.

'I am very sorry for forgetting myself,' she said, artlessly. 'I have not been well—I have felt sadly weak and nervous lately; and I often cry without reason when I am alone. I am better now; I can answer you as I ought, Mr Gilmore, I can indeed.'

'No, no, my dear,' I replied; 'we will consider the subject as done with, for the present. You have said enough to sanction my taking the best possible care of your interests; and we can settle details at another opportunity. Let us have done with business, now, and talk of something else.'

I led her at once into speaking on other topics. In ten minutes' time, she was in better spirits; and I rose to take my leave.

'Come here again,' she said, earnestly. 'I will try to be worthier of your kind feeling for me and for my interests if you will only come again.'

Still clinging to the past—that past which I represented to her, in my way, as Miss Halcombe did in hers! It troubled me sorely to see her looking back, at the beginning of her career, just as I look back, at the end of mine.

'If I do come again, I hope I shall find you better,' I said—'better and happier. God bless you, my dear!'

She only answered by putting up her cheek to me to be kissed. Even lawyers have hearts; and mine ached a little as I took leave of her.

The whole interview between us had hardly lasted more than half an hour—she had not breathed a word, in my presence, to explain the mystery of her evident distress and dismay at the prospect of her marriage—and yet she had contrived to win me over to her side of the question, I neither knew how nor why. I had entered the room, feeling that Sir Percival Glyde had fair reason to complain of the manner in which she was treating him. I left it, secretly hoping that matters might end in her taking him at his word and claiming her release. A man of my age and experience ought to have known better than to vacillate in this unreasonable manner. I can make no excuse for myself; I can only tell the truth, and say—so it was.

The hour for my departure was now drawing near. I sent to Mr Fairlie to say that I would wait on him to take leave if he liked, but that he must excuse my being rather in a hurry. He sent a message back, written in pencil on a slip of paper: 'Kind love and best wishes, dear Gilmore. Hurry of any kind is inexpressibly injurious to me. Pray take care of yourself. Good-by.'

Just before I left, I saw Miss Halcombe, for a moment, alone.

'Have you said all you wanted to Laura?' she asked.

'Yes,' I replied. 'She is very weak and nervous—I am glad she has you to take care of her.'

Miss Halcombe's sharp eyes studied my face attentively.

'You are altering your opinion about Laura,' she said. 'You are readier to make allowances for her than you were yesterday.'

No sensible man ever engages, unprepared, in a fencing match of words with a woman. I only answered:

'Let me know what happens. I will do nothing till I hear from you.'

She still looked hard in my face. 'I wish it was all over, and well over, Mr Gilmore—and so do you.' With those words she left me.

Sir Percival most politely insisted on seeing me to the carriage door.

'If you are ever in my neighbourhood,' he said, 'pray don't forget that I am sincerely anxious to improve our acquaintance. The tried and trusted old friend of this family will be always a welcome visitor in any house of mine.'

A really irresistible man—courteous, considerate, delightfully free from pride—a gentleman, every inch of him. As I drove away to the station, I felt as if I could cheerfully do anything to promote the interests of Sir Percival Glyde—anything in the world, except drawing the marriage-settlement of his wife.

III

A WEEK passed, after my return to London, without the receipt of any communication from Miss Halcombe.

On the eighth day, a letter in her handwriting was placed among the other letters on my table.

It announced that Sir Percival Glyde had been definitely accepted, and that the marriage was to take place, as he had originally desired, before the end of the year. In all probability the ceremony would be performed during the last fortnight in December. Miss Fairlie's twenty-first birthday was late in March. She would, therefore, by this arrangement, become Sir Percival's wife about three months before she was of age.

I ought not to have been surprised, I ought not to have been sorry; but I was surprised and sorry, nevertheless. Some little disappointment, caused by the unsatisfactory shortness of Miss Halcombe's letter, mingled itself with these feelings, and contributed its share towards upsetting my serenity for the day. In six lines my correspondent announced the proposed marriage; in three more, she told me that Sir Percival had left Cumberland to return to his house in Hampshire; and in two concluding sentences she informed me, first, that Laura was sadly in want of change and cheerful society; secondly, that she had resolved to try the effect of some such change forthwith, by taking her sister away with her on a visit to certain old friends in Yorkshire. There the letter ended, without a word to explain what the circumstances were which had decided Miss Fairlie to accept Sir Percival Glyde in one short week from the time when I had last seen her.

At a later period, the cause of this sudden determination was fully explained to me. It is not my business to relate it imperfectly, on hearsay evidence. The circumstances came within the personal experience of Miss Halcombe; and, when her narrative succeeds mine, she will describe them in every particular, exactly as they happened. In the mean time, the plain duty for me to perform—before I, in my turn, lay down my pen and withdraw from the story—is to relate the one remaining event connected with Miss Fairlie's proposed marriage in which I was concerned, namely, the drawing of the settlement.

It is impossible to refer intelligibly to this document, without first entering into certain particulars, in relation to the bride's pecuniary affairs. I will try to make my explanation briefly and plainly, and to keep it free from professional obscurities and technicalities. The matter is of the utmost importance. I warn all readers of these lines that Miss Fairlie's inheritance is a very serious part of Miss Fairlie's story; and that Mr Gilmore's experience, in this particular, must be their experience also, if they wish to understand the narratives which are yet to come.

Miss Fairlie's expectations, then, were of a twofold kind; comprising her possible inheritance of real property, or land, when her uncle died, and her absolute inheritance of personal property, or money, when she came of age.

Let us take the land first.

In the time of Miss Fairlie's paternal grandfather (whom we will call Mr Fairlie, the elder) the entailed succession to the Limmeridge estate stood thus:

Mr Fairlie, the elder, died and left three sons, Philip, Frederick, and Arthur. As eldest son, Philip succeeded to the estate. If he died without leaving a son, the property went to the second brother, Frederick. And if Frederick died also without leaving a son, the property went to the third brother, Arthur.

As events turned out, Mr Philip Fairlie died leaving an only daughter, the Laura of this story; and the estate, in consequence, went, in course of law, to the second brother, Frederick, a single man. The third brother, Arthur, had died many years before the decease of Philip, leaving a son and a daughter. The son, at the age of eighteen, was drowned at Oxford. His death left Laura, the daughter of Mr Philip Fairlie, presumptive heiress to the estate; with every chance of succeeding to it, in the ordinary course of nature, on her uncle Frederick's death, if the said Frederick died without leaving male issue.

Except in the event, then, of Mr Frederick Fairlie's marrying and leaving an heir (the two very last things in the world that he was likely to do), his niece, Laura, would have the property on his death; possessing, it must be remembered, nothing more than a life-interest in it. If she died single, or died childless, the estate would revert to her cousin Magdalen, the daughter of Mr Arthur Fairlie. If she married, with a proper settlement—or, in other words, with the settlement I meant to make for her—the income from the estate (a good three thousand a year) would, during her lifetime, be at her own disposal. If she died before her husband, he would naturally expect to be left in the enjoyment of the income, for *his* lifetime. If she had a son, that son would be the heir, to the exclusion of her cousin Magdalen. Thus, Sir Percival's prospects in marrying Miss Fairlie (so far as his wife's expectations from real property were concerned) promised him these two advantages, on Mr Frederick Fairlie's death: First, the use of three thousand a year (by his wife's permission, while she lived, and, in his own right, on her death, if he survived her); and, secondly, the inheritance of Limmeridge for his son, if he had one.

So much for the landed property, and for the disposal of the income from it, on the occasion of Miss Fairlie's marriage. Thus far, no difficulty or difference of opinion on the lady's settlement was at all likely to arise between Sir Percival's lawyer and myself.

The personal estate, or, in other words, the money to which Miss Fairlie would become entitled on reaching the age of twenty-one years, is the next point to consider.

This part of her inheritance was, in itself, a comfortable little fortune. It was derived under her father's will, and it amounted to the sum of twenty thousand pounds. Besides this, she had a life-interest in ten thousand pounds more; which latter amount was to go, on her decease, to her aunt Eleanor, her father's only sister. It will greatly assist in setting the family affairs before the reader in the clearest possible light, if I stop here for a moment, to explain why the aunt had been kept waiting for her legacy until the death of the niece.

Mr Philip Fairlie had lived on excellent terms with his sister Eleanor, as long as she remained a single woman. But when her marriage took place, somewhat late in life, and when that marriage united her to an Italian gentleman, named Fosco—or, rather, to an Italian nobleman, seeing that he rejoiced in the title of Count—Mr Fairlie disapproved of her conduct so strongly that he ceased to hold any communication with her, and even went the length of striking her name out of his will. The other members of the family all thought this serious manifestation of resentment at his sister's marriage more or less unreasonable. Count Fosco, though not a rich man, was not a penniless adventurer either. He had a small, but sufficient income of his own; he had lived many years in England; and he held an excellent position in society. These recommendations, however, availed nothing with Mr Fairlie. In many of his opinions he was an Englishman of the old school; and he hated a foreigner, simply and solely because he was a foreigner. The utmost that he could be prevailed on to do, in after years, mainly at Miss Fairlie's intercession, was to restore his sister's name to its former place in his will, but to keep her waiting for her legacy by giving the income of the money to his daughter for life, and the money itself, if her aunt died before her, to her cousin Magdalen. Considering the relative ages of the two ladies, the aunt's chance, in the ordinary course of nature, of receiving the ten thousand pounds, was thus rendered doubtful in the extreme; and Madam Fosco resented her brother's treatment of her, as unjustly as usual in such cases, by refusing to see her niece, and declining to believe that Miss Fairlie's intercession had ever been exerted to restore her name to Mr Fairlie's will.

Such was the history of the ten thousand pounds. Here again no difficulty could arise with Sir Percival's legal adviser. The income would be at the wife's disposal, and the principal would go to her aunt, or her cousin, on her death.

All preliminary explanations being now cleared out of the way, I come, at last, to the real knot of the case—to the twenty thousand pounds.

This sum was absolutely Miss Fairlie's own, on her completing her twenty-first year; and the whole future disposition of it depended, in the first instance, on the conditions I could obtain for her in her marriage-settlement. The other clauses contained in that document were of a formal kind, and need not be recited here. But the clause relating to the money is too important to be passed over. A few lines will be sufficient to give the necessary abstract of it.

My stipulation, in regard to the twenty thousand pounds, was simply this: The whole amount was to be settled so as to give the income to the lady for her life; afterwards to Sir Percival for his life; and the principal to the children of the marriage. In default of issue, the principal was to be disposed of as the lady might by her will direct, for which purpose I reserved to her the right of making a will. The effect of these conditions may be thus summed up. If Lady Glyde died without leaving children, her half-sister, Miss Halcombe, and any other relatives or friends whom she might be anxious to benefit, would, on her husband's death, divide among them such shares of her money as she desired them to have. If, on the other hand, she died, leaving children, then their interest, naturally and necessarily, superseded all other interests whatsoever. This was the clause; and no one who reads it, can fail, I think, to agree with me that it meted out equal justice to all parties.

We shall see how my proposals were met on the husband's side.

At the time when Miss Halcombe's letter reached me, I was even more busily occupied than usual. But I contrived to make leisure for the settlement. I had drawn it, and had sent it for approval to Sir Percival's solicitor, in less than a week from the time when Miss Halcombe had informed me of the proposed marriage.

After a lapse of two days, the document was returned to me, with the notes and remarks of the baronet's lawyer. His objections, in general, proved to be of the most trifling and technical kind, until he came to the clause relating to the twenty thousand pounds. Against this, there were double lines drawn in red ink, and the following note was appended to them:

'Not admissible. The *principal* to go to Sir Percival Glyde, in the event of his surviving Lady Glyde, and there being no issue.'

That is to say, not one farthing of the twenty thousand pounds was to go to Miss Halcombe, or to any other relative or friend of Lady Glyde's. The whole sum, if she left no children, was to slip into the pockets of her husband.

The answer I wrote to this audacious proposal was as short and sharp as I could make it. 'My dear sir. Miss Fairlie's settlement. I maintain the clause to which you object, exactly as it stands. Yours truly.' The rejoinder came back in a quarter of an hour. 'My dear sir. Miss Fairlie's settlement. I maintain the red ink to which you object, exactly as it stands. Yours truly.' In the detestable slang of the day, we were now both 'at a dead-lock,' and nothing was left for it but to refer to our clients on either side.

As matters stood, my client—Miss Fairlie not having yet completed her twenty-first year—was her guardian, Mr Frederick Fairlie. I wrote by that day's post, and put the case before him exactly as it stood; not only urging every argument I could think of to induce him to maintain the clause as I had drawn it, but stating to him plainly the mercenary motive which was at the bottom of the opposition to my settlement of the twenty thousand pounds. The knowledge of Sir Percival's affairs which I necessarily gained when the provisions of the deed on *his* side were submitted in due course to my examination, had but too plainly informed me that the debts on his estate were enormous, and that his income, though nominally a large one, was, virtually, for a man in his position, next to nothing. The want of ready money was the practical necessity of Sir Percival's existence; and his lawyer's note on the clause in the settlement was nothing but the frankly selfish expression of it.

Mr Fairlie's answer reached me by return of post, and proved to be wandering and irrelevant in the extreme. Turned into plain English, it practically expressed itself to this effect: 'Would dear Gilmore be so very obliging as not to worry his friend and client about such a trifle as a remote contingency? Was it likely that a young woman of twenty-one would die before a man of forty- five, and die without children? On the other hand, in such a miserable world as this, was it possible to over-estimate the value of peace and quietness? If those two heavenly blessings were offered in exchange for such an earthly trifle as a remote chance of twenty thousand pounds, was it not a fair bargain? Surely, yes. Then why not make it?'

I threw the letter away in disgust. Just as it had fluttered to the ground, there was a knock at my door; and Sir Percival's solicitor, Mr Merriman, was shown in. There are many varieties of sharp practitioners in this world, but, I think, the hardest of all to deal with are the men who overreach you under the disguise of inveterate good humour. A fat, well-fed, smiling, friendly man of business is of all parties to a bargain the most hopeless to deal with. Mr Merriman was one of this class.

'And how is good Mr Gilmore?' he began, all in a glow with the warmth of his own amiability. 'Glad to see you, sir, in such excellent health. I was passing your door; and I thought I would look in, in case you might have something to say to me. Do—now pray do let us settle this little difference of ours by word of mouth, if we can! Have you heard from your client yet?'

'Yes. Have you heard from yours?'

'My dear, good sir! I wish I had heard from him to any purpose—I wish, with all my heart, the responsibility was off my shoulders; but he is obstinate,—or, let me rather say, resolute—and he won't take it off. "Merriman, I leave details to you. Do what you think right for my interests; and consider me as having personally withdrawn from the business until it is all over." Those were Sir Percival's words a fortnight ago; and all I can get him to do now is to repeat them. I am not a hard man, Mr Gilmore, as you know. Personally and privately, I do assure you, I should like to sponge out that note of mine at this very moment. But if Sir Percival won't go into the matter, if Sir Percival will blindly leave all his interests in my sole care, what course can I possibly take except the course of asserting them? My hands are bound—don't you see, my dear sir?—my hands are bound.'

'You maintain your note on the clause, then, to the letter?' I said.

'Yes—deuce take it! I have no other alternative.' He walked to the fireplace, and warmed himself, humming the fag end of a tune in a rich, convivial bass voice. 'What does your side say?' he went on; 'now pray tell me—what does your side say?'

I was ashamed to tell him. I attempted to gain time—nay, I did worse. My legal instincts got the better of me; and I even tried to bargain.

'Twenty thousand pounds is rather a large sum to be given up by the lady's friends at two days' notice,' I said.

'Very true,' replied Mr Merriman, looking down thoughtfully at his boots. 'Properly put, sir—most properly put!'

'A compromise, recognising the interests of the lady's family as well as the interests of the husband might not, perhaps, have frightened my client quite so much,' I went on. 'Come! come! this contingency resolves itself into a matter of bargaining after all. What is the least you will take?'

'The least we will take,' said Mr Merriman, 'is nineteen-thousand-nine-hundred-and-ninety-nine-pounds-nineteen-shillings-and-eleven-pence-three-farthings. Ha! ha! ha! Excuse me, Mr Gilmore. I must have my little joke.'

'Little enough!' I remarked. 'The joke is just worth the odd farthing it was made for.'

Mr Merriman was delighted. He laughed over my retort till the room rang again. I was not half so good-humoured, on my side: I came back to business, and closed the interview.

'This is Friday,' I said. 'Give us till Tuesday next for our final answer.'

'By all means,' replied Mr Merriman. 'Longer, my dear sir, if you like.' He took up his hat to go; and then addressed me again. 'By the way,' he said, 'your clients in Cumberland have not heard anything more of the woman who wrote the anonymous letter, have they?'

'Nothing more,' I answered. 'Have you found no trace of her?'

'Not yet,' said my legal friend. 'But we don't despair. Sir Percival has his suspicions that Somebody is keeping her in hiding; and we are having that Somebody watched.'

'You mean the old woman who was with her in Cumberland?' I said.

'Quite another party, sir,' answered Mr Merriman. 'We don't happen to have laid hands on the old woman yet. Our Somebody is a man. We have got him close under our eye here in London; and we strongly suspect he had something to do with helping her in the first instance to escape from the Asylum. Sir Percival wanted to question him, at once; but I said, "No. Questioning him will only put him on his guard: watch him, and wait." We shall see what happens. A dangerous woman to be at large, Mr Gilmore; nobody knows what she may do next. I wish you good morning, sir. On Tuesday next I shall hope for the pleasure of hearing from you.' He smiled amiably, and went out.

My mind had been rather absent during the latter part of the conversation with my legal friend. I was so anxious about the matter of the settlement, that I had little attention to give to any other subject; and, the moment I was left alone again, I began to think over what my next proceeding ought to be.

In the case of any other client, I should have acted on my instructions, however personally distasteful to me, and have given up the point about the twenty thousand pounds on the spot. But I could not act with this business-like indifference towards Miss Fairlie. I had an honest feeling of affection and admiration for her; I remembered gratefully that her father had been the kindest patron and friend to me that ever man had; I had felt towards her, while I was drawing the settlement, as I might have felt, if I had not been an old bachelor, towards a daughter of my own; and I was determined to spare no personal sacrifice in her service and where her interests were concerned. Writing a second time to Mr Fairlie was not to be thought of; it would only be giving him a second opportunity of slipping through my fingers. Seeing him and personally remonstrating with him, might possibly be of more use. The next day was Saturday. I determined to take a return ticket, and jolt my old bones down to Cumberland, on the chance of persuading him to adopt the just, the independent, and the honourable course. It was a poor chance enough, no doubt; but, when I had tried it, my conscience would be at ease. I should then have done all that a man in my position could do to serve the interests of my old friend's only child.

The weather on Saturday was beautiful, a west wind and a bright sun. Having felt latterly a return of that fulness and oppression of the head, against which my doctor warned me so seriously more than two years since, I resolved to take the opportunity of getting a little extra exercise, by sending my bag on before me, and walking to the terminus in Euston-square. As I came out into Holborn, a gentleman, walking by rapidly, stopped and spoke to me. It was Mr Walter Hartright.

If he had not been the first to greet me, I should certainly have passed him. He was so changed that I hardly knew him again. His face looked pale and haggard—his manner was hurried and uncertain—and his dress, which I remembered as neat and gentlemanlike when I saw him at Limmeridge, was so slovenly, now, that I should really have been ashamed of the appearance of it on one of my own clerks.

'Have you been long back from Cumberland?' he asked. 'I heard from Miss Halcombe lately. I am aware that Sir Percival Glyde's explanation has been considered satisfactory. Will the marriage take place soon? Do you happen to know, Mr Gilmore?'

He spoke so fast, and crowded his questions together so strangely and confusedly, that I could hardly follow him. However accidentally intimate he might have been with the family at Limmeridge, I could not see that he had any right to expect information on their private affairs; and I determined to drop him, as easily as might be, on the subject of Miss Fairlie's marriage.

'Time will show, Mr Hartright,' I said—'time will show. I dare say if we look out for the marriage in the papers we shall not be far wrong. Excuse my noticing it—but I am sorry to see you not looking so well as you were when we last met.'

A momentary nervous contraction quivered about his lips and eyes, and made me half reproach myself for having answered him in such a significantly guarded manner.

'I had no right to ask about her marriage,' he said, bitterly. 'I must wait to see it in the newspapers like other people. Yes,' he went on, before I could make any apologies, 'I have not been well lately. I am going to another country, to try a change of scene and occupation. Miss Halcombe has kindly assisted me with her influence, and my testimonials have been found satisfactory. It is a long distance off—but I don't care where I go, what the climate is, or how long I am away.' He looked about him, while he said this, at the throng of strangers passing us by on either side, in a strange, suspicious manner, as if he thought that some of them might be watching us.

'I wish you well through it, and safe back again,' I said; and then added, so as not to keep him altogether at arm's length on the subject of the Fairlies, 'I am going down to Limmeridge, to-day, on business. Miss Halcombe and Miss Fairlie are away, just now, on a visit to some friends in Yorkshire.'

His eyes brightened, and he seemed about to say something in answer; but the same momentary nervous spasm crossed his face again. He took my hand, pressed it hard, and disappeared among the crowd, without saying another word. Though he was little more than a stranger to me, I waited for a moment, looking after him almost with a feeling of regret. I had gained, in my profession, sufficient experience of young men, to know what the outward signs and tokens were of their beginning to go wrong; and, when I resumed my walk to the railway, I am sorry to say I felt more than doubtful about Mr Hartright's future.

IV

LEAVING by an early train, I got to Limmeridge in time for dinner. The house was oppressively empty and dull. I had expected that good Mrs Vesey would have been company for me in the absence of the young ladies; but she was confined to her room by a cold. The servants were so surprised at seeing me that they hurried and bustled absurdly, and made all sorts of annoying mistakes. Even the butler, who was old enough to have known better, brought me a bottle of port that was chilled. The reports of Mr Fairlie's health were just as usual; and when I sent up a message to announce my arrival, I was told that he would be delighted to see me the next morning, but that the sudden news of my appearance had prostrated him with palpitations for the rest of the evening. The wind howled dismally, all night, and strange cracking and groaning noises sounded here, there, and everywhere in the empty house. I slept as wretchedly as possible; and got up, in a mighty bad humour, to breakfast by myself the next morning.

At ten o'clock I was conducted to Mr Fairlie's apartments. He was in his usual room, his usual chair, and his usual aggravating state of mind and body. When I went in, his valet was standing before him, holding up for inspection a heavy volume of etchings, as long and as broad as my office writing-desk. The miserable foreigner grinned in the most abject manner, and looked ready to drop with fatigue, while his master composedly turned over the etchings, and brought their hidden beauties to light with the help of a magnifying glass.

'You very best of good old friends,' said Mr Fairlie, leaning back lazily before he could look at me, 'are you *quite* well? How nice of you to come here and see me in my solitude. Dear Gilmore!'

I had expected that the valet would be dismissed when I appeared; but nothing of the sort happened. There he stood, in front of his master's chair, trembling under the weight of the etchings; and there Mr Fairlie sat, serenely twirling the magnifying glass between his white fingers and thumbs.

'I have come to speak to you on a very important matter,' I said; 'and you will therefore excuse me, if I suggest that we had better be alone.'

The unfortunate valet looked at me gratefully. Mr Fairlie faintly repeated my last three words, 'better be alone,' with every appearance of the utmost possible astonishment.

I was in no humour for trifling; and I resolved to make him understand what I meant.

'Oblige me by giving that man permission to withdraw,' I said, pointing to the valet.

Mr Fairlie arched his eyebrows, and pursed up his lips, in sarcastic surprise.

'Man?' he repeated. 'You provoking old Gilmore, what can you possibly mean by calling him a man? He's nothing of the sort. He might have been a man half an hour ago, before I wanted my etchings; and he may be a man half an hour hence, when I don't want them any longer. At present, he is simply a portfolio stand. Why object, Gilmore, to a portfolio stand?'

'I *do* object. For the third time, Mr Fairlie, I beg that we may be alone.'

My tone and manner left him no alternative but to comply with my request. He looked at the servant, and pointed peevishly to a chair at his side.

'Put down the etchings and go away,' he said. 'Don't upset me by losing my place. Have you, or have you not, lost my place? Are you sure you have *not*? And have you put my hand-bell quite within my reach? Yes? Then, why the devil don't you go?'

The valet went out. Mr Fairlie twisted himself round in his chair, polished the magnifying glass with his delicate cambric handkerchief, and indulged himself in a sidelong inspection of the open volume of etchings. It was not easy to keep my temper, under these circumstances; but I did keep it.

'I have come here at great personal inconvenience,' I said, 'to serve the interests of your niece and your family; and I think I have established some slight claim to be favoured with your attention, in return.'

'Don't bully me!' exclaimed Mr Fairlie, falling back helplessly in the chair, and closing his eyes. 'Please don't bully me. I'm not strong enough.'

I was determined not to let him provoke me, for Laura Fairlie's sake.

'My object,' I went on, 'is to entreat you to reconsider your letter, and not to force me to abandon the just rights of your niece, and of all who belong to her. Let me state the case to you once more, and for the last time.'

Mr Fairlie shook his head, and sighed piteously.

'This is heartless of you, Gilmore—very heartless,' he said. 'Never mind; go on.'

I put all the points to him carefully; I set the matter before him in every conceivable light. He lay back in the chair, the whole time I was speaking, with his eyes closed. When I had done, he opened them indolently, took his silver smelling-bottle from the table, and sniffed at it with an air of gentle relish.

'Good Gilmore!' he said, between the sniffs, 'how very nice this is of you! How you reconcile one to human nature!'

'Give me a plain answer to a plain question, Mr Fairlie. I tell you again, Sir Percival Glyde has no shadow of a claim to expect more than the income of the money. The money itself, if your niece has no children, ought to be under her control, and to return to her family. If you stand firm, Sir Percival must give way—he must give way, I tell you, or he exposes himself to the base imputation of marrying Miss Fairlie entirely from mercenary motives.'

Mr Fairlie shook the silver smelling-bottle at me playfully.

'You dear old Gilmore; how you do hate rank and family, don't you? How you detest Glyde, because he happens to be a Baronet. What a Radical you are—oh, dear me, what a Radical you are!'

A Radical!!! I could put up with a great deal of provocation, but, after holding the soundest Conservative principles all my life, I could *not* put up with being called a Radical. My blood boiled at it—I started out of my chair—I was speechless with indignation.

'Don't shake the room!' cried Mr Fairlie—'for Heaven's sake, don't shake the room! Worthiest of all possible Gilmores, I meant no offence. My own views are so extremely liberal that I think I am a Radical myself. Yes. We are a pair of Radicals. Please don't be angry. I can't quarrel—I haven't stamina enough. Shall we drop the subject? Yes. Come and look at these sweet etchings. Do let me teach you to understand the heavenly pearliness of these lines. Do, now, there's a good Gilmore!'

While he was maundering on in this way, I was, fortunately for my own self-respect, returning to my senses. When I spoke again, I was composed enough to treat his impertinence with the silent contempt that it deserved.

'You are entirely wrong, sir,' I said, 'in supposing that I speak from any prejudice against Sir Percival Glyde. I may regret that he has so unreservedly resigned himself, in this matter, to his lawyer's direction, as to make any appeal to himself impossible; but I am not prejudiced against him. What I have said would equally apply to any other man, in his situation, high or low. The principle I maintain is a recognised principle. If you were to apply, at the nearest town here, to the first respectable solicitor you could find, he would tell you, as a stranger, what I tell you, as a friend. He would inform you that it is against all rule to abandon the lady's money entirely to the man she marries. He would decline, on grounds of common legal caution, to give the husband, under any circumstances whatever, an interest of twenty thousand pounds in his wife's death.'

'Would he really, Gilmore?' said Mr Fairlie. 'If he said anything half so horrid I do assure you I should tinkle my bell for Louis, and have him sent out of the house immediately.'

'You shall not irritate me, Mr Fairlie—for your niece's sake and for her father's sake, you shall not irritate me. You shall take the whole responsibility of this discreditable settlement on your own shoulders, before I leave the room.'

'Don't!—now please don't!' said Mr Fairlie. 'Think how precious your time is, Gilmore; and don't throw it away. I would dispute with you, if I could, but I can't—I haven't stamina enough. You want to upset me, to upset yourself, to upset Glyde, and to upset Laura; and—oh, dear me!—all for the sake of the very last thing in the world that is likely to happen. No, dear friend—in the interests of peace and quietness, positively No!'

'I am to understand, then, that you hold by the determination expressed in your letter?'

'Yes, please. So glad we understand each other at last. Sit down again—do!'

I walked at once to the door; and Mr Fairlie resignedly 'tinkled' his hand-bell. Before I left the room, I turned round, and addressed him, for the last time.

'Whatever happens in the future, sir,' I said, 'remember that my plain duty of warning you has been performed. As the faithful friend and servant of your family, I tell you, at parting, that no daughter of mine should be married to any man alive under such a settlement as you are forcing me to make for Miss Fairlie.'

The door opened behind me, and the valet stood waiting on the threshold.

'Louis,' said Mr Fairlie, 'show Mr Gilmore out, and then come back and hold up my etchings for me again. Make them give you a good lunch down stairs. Do, Gilmore, make my idle beasts of servants give you a good lunch!'

I was too much disgusted to reply; I turned on my heel, and left him in silence. There was an up train, at two o'clock in the afternoon; and by that train I returned to London.

On the Tuesday, I sent in the altered settlement, which practically disinherited the very persons whom Miss Fairlie's own lips had informed me she was most anxious to benefit. I had no choice. Another lawyer would have drawn up the deed if I had refused to undertake it.

My task is done. My personal share in the events of the family story extends no farther than the point which I have just reached. Other pens than mine will describe the strange circumstances which are now shortly to follow. Seriously and sorrowfully, I close this brief record. Seriously and sorrowfully, I repeat here the parting words that I spoke at Limmeridge House:—No daughter of mine should have been married to any man alive under such a settlement as I was compelled to make for Laura Fairlie.

THE NARRATIVE OF MARIAN HALCOMBE TAKEN FROM HER DIARY

* * * * *†

Limmeridge House, November 8th

THIS morning, Mr Gilmore left us.

His interview with Laura had evidently grieved and surprised him more than he liked to confess. I felt afraid, from his look and manner when we parted, that she might have inadvertently betrayed to him the real secret of her depression and my anxiety. This doubt grew on me so, after he had gone, that I declined riding out with Sir Percival, and went up to Laura's room instead.

I have been sadly distrustful of myself, in this difficult and lamentable matter, ever since I found out my own ignorance of the strength of Laura's unhappy attachment. I ought to have known that the delicacy and forbearance and sense of honour which drew me to poor Hartright, and made me so sincerely admire and respect him, were just the qualities to appeal most irresistibly to Laura's natural sensitiveness and natural generosity of nature. And yet, until she opened her heart to me of her own accord, I had no suspicion that this new feeling had taken root so deeply. I once thought time and care might remove it. I now fear that it will remain with her and alter her for life. The discovery that I have committed such an error in judgment as this, makes me hesitate about everything else. I hesitate about Sir Percival, in the face of the plainest proofs. I hesitate even in speaking to Laura. On this very morning, I doubted, with my hand on the door, whether I should ask her the questions I had come to put, or not.

When I went into her room, I found her walking up and down in great impatience. She looked flushed and excited; and she came forward at once, and spoke to me before I could open my lips.

† The passages omitted, here and elsewhere, in Miss Halcombe's Diary, are only those which bear no reference to Miss Fairlie or to any of the persons with whom she is associated in these pages.

'I wanted you,' she said. 'Come and sit down on the sofa with me. Marian! I can bear this no longer—I must and will end it.'

There was too much colour in her cheeks, too much energy in her manner, too much firmness in her voice. The little book of Hartright's drawings—the fatal book that she will dream over whenever she is alone—was in one of her hands. I began by gently and firmly taking it from her, and putting it out of sight on a side-table.

'Tell me quietly, my darling, what you wish to do,' I said. 'Has Mr Gilmore been advising you?'

She shook her head. 'No, not in what I am thinking of now. He was very kind and good to me, Marian,—and I am ashamed to say I distressed him by crying. I am miserably helpless; I can't control myself. For my own sake and for all our sakes, I must have courage enough to end it.'

'Do you mean courage enough to claim your release?' I asked.

'No,' she said, simply. 'Courage, dear, to tell the truth.'

She put her arms round my neck, and rested her head quietly on my bosom. On the opposite wall hung the miniature portrait of her father. I bent over her, and saw that she was looking at it while her head lay on my breast.

'I can never claim my release from my engagement,' she went on. 'Whatever way it ends, it must end wretchedly for *me*. All I can do, Marian, is not to add the remembrance that I have broken my promise and forgotten my father's dying words, to make that wretchedness worse.'

'What is it you propose, then?' I asked.

'To tell Sir Percival Glyde the truth, with my own lips,' she answered, 'and to let him release me, if he will, not because I ask him, but because he knows all.'

'What do you mean, Laura, by "all?" Sir Percival will know enough (he has told me so himself) if he knows that the engagement is opposed to your own wishes.'

'Can I tell him that, when the engagement was made for me by my father, with my own consent? I should have kept my promise; not happily, I am afraid; but still contentedly'—she stopped, turned her face to me, and laid her cheek close against mine—'I should have kept my engagement, Marian, if another love had not grown up in my heart, which was not there when I first promised to be Sir Percival's wife.'

'Laura! you will never lower yourself by making a confession to him?'

'I shall lower myself indeed, if I gain my release by hiding from him what he has a right to know.'

'He has not the shadow of a right to know it!'

'Wrong, Marian, wrong! I ought to deceive no one—least of all, the man to whom my father gave me and to whom I gave myself.' She put her lips to mine, and kissed me. 'My own love,' she said, softly, 'you are so much too fond of me and so much too proud of me, that you forget in my case, what you would remember in your own. Better that Sir Percival should doubt my motives and misjudge my conduct, if he will, than that I should be first false to him in thought, and then mean enough to serve my own interests by hiding the falsehood.'

I held her away from me in astonishment. For the first time in our lives, we had changed places; the resolution was all on her side, the hesitation all on mine. I looked into the pale, quiet, resigned young face; I saw the pure, innocent heart, in the loving eyes that looked back at me—and the poor, worldly cautions and objections that rose to my lips, dwindled and died away in their own emptiness. I hung my head in silence. In her place, the despicably-small pride which makes so many women deceitful, would have been my pride, and would have made me deceitful, too.

'Don't be angry with me, Marian,' she said, mistaking my silence.

I only answered by drawing her close to me again. I was afraid of crying if I spoke. My tears do not flow so easily as they ought—they come, almost like men's tears, with sobs that seem to tear me in pieces, and that frighten every one about me.

'I have thought of this, love, for many days,' she went on, twining and twisting my hair, with that childish restlessness in her fingers, which poor Mrs Vesey still tries so patiently and so vainly to cure her of—'I have thought of it very seriously, and I can be sure of my courage, when my own conscience tells me I am right. Let me speak to him to-morrow—in your presence, Marian. I will say nothing that is wrong, nothing that you or I need be ashamed of—but, oh, it will ease my heart so to end this miserable concealment! Only let me know and feel that I have no deception to answer for on my side; and then, when he has heard what I have to say, let him act towards me as he will.'

She sighed, and put her head back in its old position on my bosom. Sad misgivings about what the end would be, weighed on my mind; but, still distrusting myself, I told her that I would do as she wished. She thanked me, and we passed gradually into talking of other things.

At dinner she joined us again, and was more easy and more herself with Sir Percival, than I have seen her yet. In the evening she went to the piano, choosing new music of the dexterous, tuneless, florid kind. The lovely old melodies of Mozart, which poor Hartright was so fond of, she has never played since he left. The book is no longer in the music-stand. She took the volume away herself, so that nobody might find it out and ask her to play from it.

I had no opportunity of discovering whether her purpose of the morning had changed or not, until she wished Sir Percival good night—and then her own words informed me that it was unaltered. She said, very quietly, that she wished to speak to him, after breakfast, and that he would find her in her sitting-room with me. He changed colour at those words, and I felt his hand trembling a little when it came to my turn to take it. The event of the next morning would decide his future life; and he evidently knew it.

I went in, as usual, through the door between our two bedrooms, to bid Laura good night before she went to sleep. In stooping over her to kiss her, I saw the little book of Hartright's drawings half hidden under her pillow, just in the place where she used to hide her favourite toys when she was a child. I could not find it in my heart to say anything; but I pointed to the book and shook my head. She reached both hands up to my cheeks, and drew my face down to hers till our lips met.

'Leave it there, to-night,' she whispered; 'to-morrow may be cruel, and may make me say good-by to it for ever.'

9th.—The first event of the morning was not of a kind to raise my spirits; a letter arrived for me, from poor Walter Hartright. It is the answer to mine, describing the manner in which Sir Percival cleared himself of the suspicions raised by Anne Catherick's letter. He writes shortly and bitterly about Sir Percival's explanations; only saying that he has no right to offer an opinion on the conduct of those who are above him. This is sad; but his occasional references to himself grieve me still more. He says that the effort to return to his old habits and pursuits, grows harder instead of easier to him, every day; and he implores me, if I have any interest, to exert it to get him employment that will necessitate his absence from England, and take him among new scenes and new people. I have been made all the readier to comply with this request, by a passage at the end of his letter, which has almost alarmed me.

After mentioning that he has neither seen nor heard anything of Anne Catherick, he suddenly breaks off, and hints in the most abrupt, mysterious manner, that he has been perpetually watched and followed by strange men, ever since he returned to London. He acknowledges that he cannot prove this extraordinary suspicion by fixing on any particular persons; but he declares that the suspicion itself is present to him night and day. This has frightened me, because it looks as if his one fixed idea about Laura was becoming too much for his mind. I will write immediately to some of my mother's influential old friends in London, and press his claims on their notice. Change of scene and change of occupation may really be the salvation of him at this crisis in his life.

Greatly to my relief, Sir Percival sent an apology for not joining us at breakfast. He had taken an early cup of coffee in his own room, and he was still engaged there in writing letters. At eleven o'clock, if that hour was convenient, he would do himself the honour of waiting on Miss Fairlie and Miss Halcombe.

My eyes were on Laura's face while the message was being delivered. I had found her unaccountably quiet and composed on going into her room in the morning; and so she remained all through breakfast. Even when we were sitting together on the sofa in her room, waiting for Sir Percival, she still preserved her self-control.

'Don't be afraid of me, Marian,' was all she said: 'I may forget myself with an old friend like Mr Gilmore, or with a dear sister like you; but I will not forget myself with Sir Percival Glyde.'

I looked at her, and listened to her in silent surprise. Through all the years of our close intimacy, this passive force in her character had been hidden from me—hidden even from herself, till love found it, and suffering called it forth.

As the clock on the mantelpiece struck eleven, Sir Percival knocked at the door, and came in. There was suppressed anxiety and agitation in every line of his face. The dry, sharp cough, which teases him at most times, seemed to be troubling him more incessantly than ever. He sat down opposite to us at the table; and Laura remained by me. I looked attentively at them both, and he was the palest of the two.

He said a few unimportant words, with a visible effort to preserve his customary ease of manner. But his voice was not to be steadied, and the restless uneasiness in his eyes was not to be concealed. He must have felt this himself; for he stopped in the middle of a sentence, and gave up even the attempt to hide his embarrassment any longer.

There was just one moment of dead silence before Laura addressed him.

'I wish to speak to you, Sir Percival,' she said, 'on a subject that is very important to us both. My sister is here, because her presence helps me, and gives me confidence. She has not suggested one word of what I am going to say: I speak from my own thoughts, not from hers. I am sure you will be kind enough to understand that, before I go any farther?'

Sir Percival bowed. She had proceeded thus far, with perfect outward tranquillity, and perfect propriety of manner. She looked at him, and he looked at her. They seemed, at the outset at least, resolved to understand one another plainly.

'I have heard from Marian,' she went on, 'that I have only to claim my release from our engagement, to obtain that release from you. It was forbearing and generous on your part, Sir Percival, to send me such a message. It is only doing you justice to say that I am grateful for the offer; and I hope and believe that it is only doing myself justice to tell you that I decline to accept it.'

His attentive face relaxed a little. But I saw one of his feet, softly, quietly, incessantly beating on the carpet under the table; and I felt that he was secretly as anxious as ever.

'I have not forgotten,' she said, 'that you asked my father's permission before you honoured me with a proposal of marriage. Perhaps, you have not forgotten, either, what I said when I consented to our engagement? I ventured to tell you that my father's influence and advice had mainly decided me to give you my promise. I was guided by my father, because I had always found him the truest of all advisers, the best and fondest of all protectors and friends. I have lost him now; I have only his memory to love; but my faith in that dear dead friend has never been shaken. I believe, at this moment, as truly as I ever believed, that he knew what was best, and that his hopes and wishes ought to be my hopes and wishes too.'

Her voice trembled, for the first time. Her restless fingers stole their way into my lap, and held fast by one of my hands. There was another moment of silence; and then Sir Percival spoke.

'May I ask,' he said, 'if I have ever proved myself unworthy of the trust, which it has been hitherto my greatest honour and greatest happiness to possess?'

'I have found nothing in your conduct to blame,' she answered. 'You have always treated me with the same delicacy and the same forbearance. You have deserved my trust; and, what is of far more importance in my estimation, you have deserved my father's trust, out of which mine grew. You have given me no excuse, even if I had wanted to find one, for asking to be released from my pledge. What I have said so far, has been spoken with the wish to acknowledge my whole obligation to you. My regard for that obligation, my regard for my father's memory, and my regard for my own promise, all forbid me to set the example, on *my* side, of withdrawing from our present position. The breaking of our engagement must be entirely your wish and your act, Sir Percival—not mine.'

The uneasy beating of his foot suddenly stopped; and he leaned forward eagerly across the table.

'My act?' he said. 'What reason can there be, on *my* side, for withdrawing?'

I heard her breath quickening; I felt her hand growing cold. In spite of what she had said to me, when we were alone, I began to be afraid of her. I was wrong.

'A reason that it is very hard to tell you,' she answered. 'There is a change in me, Sir Percival—a change which is serious enough to justify you, to yourself and to me, in breaking off our engagement.'

His face turned so pale again, that even his lips lost their colour. He raised the arm which lay on the table; turned a little away in his chair; and supported his head on his hand, so that his profile only was presented to us.

'What change?' he asked. The tone in which he put the question jarred on me—there was something painfully suppressed in it.

She sighed heavily, and leaned towards me a little, so as to rest her shoulder against mine. I felt her trembling, and tried to spare her by speaking myself. She stopped me by a warning pressure of her hand, and then addressed Sir Percival once more; but, this time, without looking at him.

'I have heard,' she said, 'and I believe it, that the fondest and truest of all affections is the affection which a woman ought to bear to her husband. When our engagement began, that affection was mine to give, if I could, and yours to win, if you could. Will you pardon me, and spare me, Sir Percival, if I acknowledge that it is not so any longer?'

A few tears gathered in her eyes, and dropped over her cheeks slowly, as she paused and waited for his answer. He did not utter a word. At the beginning of her reply, he had moved the hand on which his head rested, so that it hid his face. I saw nothing but the upper part of his figure at the table. Not a muscle of him moved. The fingers of the hand which supported his head were dented deep in his hair. They might have expressed hidden anger, or hidden grief—it was hard to say which—there was no significant trembling in them. There was nothing, absolutely nothing, to tell the secret of his thoughts at that moment—the moment which was the crisis of his life and the crisis of hers.

I was determined to make him declare himself, for Laura's sake.

'Sir Percival!' I interposed, sharply; 'have you nothing to say, when my sister has said so much? More, in my opinion,' I added, my unlucky temper getting the better of me, 'than any man alive, in your position, has a right to hear from her.'

That last rash sentence opened a way for him by which to escape me if he chose; and he instantly took advantage of it.

'Pardon me, Miss Halcombe,' he said, still keeping his hand over his face—'pardon me, if I remind you that I have claimed no such right.'

The few plain words which would have brought him back to the point from which he had wandered, were just on my lips, when Laura checked me by speaking again.

'I hope I have not made my painful acknowledgment in vain,' she continued. 'I hope it has secured me your entire confidence in what I have still to say?'

'Pray be assured of it.' He made that brief reply, warmly; dropping his hand on the table, while he spoke, and turning towards us again. Whatever outward change had passed over him, was gone now. His face was eager and expectant—it expressed nothing but the most intense anxiety to hear her next words.

'I wish you to understand that I have not spoken from any selfish motive,' she said. 'If you leave me, Sir Percival, after what you have just heard, you do not leave me to marry another man—you only allow me to remain a single woman for the rest of my life. My fault towards you has begun and ended in my own thoughts. It can never go any farther. No word has passed——' She hesitated, in doubt about the expression she should use next; hesitated, in a momentary confusion which it was very sad and very painful to see. 'No word has passed,' she patiently and resolutely resumed, 'between myself and the person to whom I am now referring for the first and last time in your presence, of my feelings towards him, or of his feelings towards me—no word ever can pass—neither he nor I are likely, in this world, to meet again. I earnestly beg you to spare me from saying any more, and to believe me, on my word, in what I have just told you. It is the truth, Sir Percival—the truth which *I* think my promised husband has a claim to hear, at any sacrifice of my own feelings. I trust to his generosity to pardon me, and to his honour to keep my secret.'

'Both those trusts are sacred to me,' he said, 'and both shall be sacredly kept.'

After answering in those terms, he paused, and looked at her, as if he was waiting to hear more.

'I have said all I wished to say,' she added, quietly—'I have said more than enough to justify you in withdrawing from your engagement.'

'You have said more than enough,' he answered, 'to make it the dearest object of my life to *keep* the engagement.' With those words he rose from his chair, and advanced a few steps towards the place where she was sitting.

She started violently, and a faint cry of surprise escaped her. Every word she had spoken had innocently betrayed her purity and truth to a man who thoroughly understood the priceless value of a pure and true woman. Her own noble conduct had been the hidden enemy, throughout, of all the hopes she had trusted to it. I had dreaded this from the first. I would have prevented it, if she had allowed me the smallest chance of doing so. I even waited and watched, now, when the harm was done, for a word from Sir Percival that would give me the opportunity of putting him in the wrong.

'You have left it to *me*, Miss Fairlie, to resign you,' he continued. 'I am not heartless enough to resign a woman who has just shown herself to be the noblest of her sex.'

He spoke with such warmth and feeling, with such passionate enthusiasm and yet with such perfect delicacy, that she raised her head, flushed up a little, and looked at him with sudden animation and spirit.

'No!' she said, firmly. 'The most wretched of her sex, if she must give herself in marriage when she cannot give her love.'

'May she not give it in the future,' he asked, 'if the one object of her husband's life is to deserve it?'

'Never!' she answered. 'If you still persist in maintaining our engagement, I may be your true and faithful wife, Sir Percival—your loving wife, if I know my own heart, never!'

She looked so irresistibly beautiful as she said those brave words that no man alive could have steeled his heart against her. I tried hard to feel that Sir Percival was to blame, and to say so; but my womanhood would pity him, in spite of myself.

'I gratefully accept your faith and truth,' he said. 'The least that *you* can offer is more to me than the utmost that I could hope for from any other woman in the world.'

Her left hand still held mine; but her right hand hung listlessly at her side. He raised it gently to his lips—touched it with them, rather than kissed it—bowed to me—and then, with perfect delicacy and discretion, silently quitted the room.

She neither moved, nor said a word, when he was gone—she sat by me, cold and still, with her eyes fixed on the ground. I saw it was hopeless and useless to speak; and I only put my arm round her, and held her to me in silence. We remained together so, for what seemed a long and weary time—so long and so weary, that I grew uneasy and spoke to her softly, in the hope of producing a change.

The sound of my voice seemed to startle her into consciousness. She suddenly drew herself away from me, and rose to her feet.

'I must submit, Marian, as well as I can,' she said. 'My new life has its hard duties; and one of them begins to-day.'

As she spoke, she went to a side-table near the window, on which her sketching materials were placed; gathered them together carefully; and put them in a drawer of her cabinet. She locked the drawer, and brought the key to me.

'I must part from everything that reminds me of him,' she said. 'Keep the key wherever you please—I shall never want it again.'

Before I could say a word, she had turned away to her bookcase, and had taken from it the album that contained Walter Hartright's drawings. She hesitated for a moment, holding the little volume fondly in her hands—then lifted it to her lips and kissed it.

'Oh, Laura! Laura!' I said, not angrily, not reprovingly—with nothing but sorrow in my voice, and nothing but sorrow in my heart.

'It is the last time, Marian,' she pleaded. 'I am bidding it good-by for ever.'

She laid the book on the table, and drew out the comb that fastened her hair. It fell, in its matchless beauty, over her back and shoulders, and dropped round her, far below her waist. She separated one long, thin lock from the rest, cut it off, and pinned it carefully, in the form of a circle, on the first blank page of the album. The moment it was fastened, she closed the volume hurriedly, and placed it in my hands.

'You write to him, and he writes to you,' she said. 'While I am alive, if he asks after me, always tell him I am well, and never say I am unhappy. Don't distress him, Marian—for *my* sake, don't distress him. If I die first, promise you will give him this little book of his drawings, with my hair in it. There can be no harm, when I am gone, in telling him that I put it there with my own hands. And say—oh, Marian, say for me, then, what I can never say for myself—say I loved him!'

She flung her arms round my neck, and whispered the last words in my ear with a passionate delight in uttering them which it almost broke my heart to hear. All the long restraint she had imposed on herself, gave way in that first last outburst of tenderness. She broke from me with hysterical vehemence, and threw herself on the sofa, in a paroxysm of sobs and tears that shook her from head to foot.

I tried vainly to soothe her and reason with her: she was past being soothed, and past being reasoned with. It was the sad, sudden end, for us two, of this memorable day. When the fit had worn itself out, she was too exhausted to speak. She slumbered towards the afternoon; and I put away the book of drawings so that she might not see it when she woke. My face was calm, whatever my heart might be, when she opened her eyes again and looked at me. We said no more to each other about the distressing interview of the morning. Sir Percival's name was not mentioned, Walter Hartright was not alluded to again by either of us for the remainder of the day.

10th.—Finding that she was composed and like herself, this morning, I returned to the painful subject of yesterday, for the sole purpose of imploring her to let me speak to Sir Percival and Mr Fairlie, more plainly and strongly than she could speak to either of them herself, about this lamentable marriage. She interposed, gently but firmly, in the middle of my remonstrances.

'I left yesterday to decide,' she said; 'and yesterday *has* decided. It is too late to go back.'

Sir Percival spoke to me this afternoon, about what had passed in Laura's room. He assured me that the unparalleled trust she had placed in him had awakened such an answering conviction of her innocence and integrity in his mind, that he was guiltless of having felt even a moment's unworthy jealousy, either at the time when he was in her presence, or afterwards when he had withdrawn from it. Deeply as he lamented the unfortunate attachment which had hindered the progress he might otherwise have made in her esteem and regard, he firmly believed that it had remained unacknowledged in the past, and that it would remain, under all changes of circumstance which it was possible to contemplate, unacknowledged in the future. This was his absolute conviction; and the strongest proof he could give of it was the assurance, which he now offered, that he felt no curiosity to know whether the attachment was of recent date or not, or who had been the object of it. His implicit confidence in Miss Fairlie made him satisfied with what she had thought fit to say to him, and he was honestly innocent of the slightest feeling of anxiety to hear more.

He waited, after saying those words, and looked at me. I was so conscious of my unreasonable prejudice against him—so conscious of an unworthy suspicion, that he might be speculating on my impulsively answering the very questions which he had just described himself as resolved not to ask—that I evaded all reference to this part of the subject with something like a feeling of confusion on my own part. At the same time, I was resolved not to lose even the smallest opportunity of trying to plead Laura's cause; and I told him boldly that I regretted his generosity had not carried him one step farther, and induced him to withdraw from the engagement altogether.

Here, again, he disarmed me by not attempting to defend himself. He would merely beg me to remember the difference there was between his allowing Miss Fairlie to give him up, which was a matter of submission only, and his forcing himself to give up Miss Fairlie, which was, in other words, asking him to be the suicide of his own hopes. Her conduct of the day before had so strengthened the unchangeable love and admiration of two long years, that all active contention against those feelings, on his part, was henceforth entirely out of his power. I must think him weak, selfish, unfeeling towards the very woman whom he idolised, and he must bow to my opinion as resignedly as he could; only putting it to me, at the same time, whether her future as a single woman, pining under an unhappily-placed attachment which she could never acknowledge, could be said to promise her a much brighter prospect than her future as the wife of a man who worshipped the very ground she walked on? In the last case there was hope from time, however slight it might be—in the first case, on her own showing, there was no hope at all.

I answered him—more because my tongue is a woman's, and must answer, than because I had anything convincing to say. It was only too plain that the course Laura had adopted the day before, had offered him the advantage if he chose to take it—and that he *had* chosen to take it. I felt this at the time, and I feel it just as strongly now, while I write these lines, in my own room. The one hope left, is that his motives really spring, as he says they do, from the irresistible strength of his attachment to Laura.

Before I close my diary for to-night, I must record that I wrote to-day, in poor Hartright's interests, to two of my mother's old friends in London—both men of influence and position. If they can do anything for him, I am quite sure they will. Except Laura, I never was more anxious about any one than I am now about Walter. All that has happened since he left us has only increased my strong regard and sympathy for him. I hope I am doing right in trying to help him to employment abroad—I hope, most earnestly and anxiously, that it will end well.

11th.—Sir Percival had an interview with Mr Fairlie; and I was sent for to join them.

I found Mr Fairlie greatly relieved at the prospect of the 'family worry' (as he was pleased to describe his niece's marriage) being settled at last. So far, I did not feel called on to say anything to him about my own opinion; but when he proceeded, in his most aggravatingly-languid manner, to suggest that the time for the marriage had better be settled next, in accordance with Sir Percival's wishes, I enjoyed the satisfaction of assailing Mr Fairlie's nerves with as strong a protest against hurrying Laura's decision as I could put into words. Sir Percival immediately assured me that he felt the force of my objection, and begged me to believe that the proposal had not been made in consequence of any interference on his part. Mr Fairlie leaned back in his chair, closed his eyes, said we both of us did honour to human nature, and then repeated his suggestion, as coolly as if neither Sir Percival nor I had said a word in opposition to it. It ended in my flatly declining to mention the subject to Laura, unless she first approached it of her own accord. I left the room at once after making that declaration. Sir Percival looked seriously embarrassed and distressed. Mr Fairlie stretched out his lazy legs on his velvet footstool; and said: 'Dear Marian! how I envy you your robust nervous system! Don't bang the door!'

On going to Laura's room, I found that she had asked for me, and that Mrs Vesey had informed her that I was with Mr Fairlie. She inquired at once what I had been wanted for; and I told her all that had passed, without attempting to conceal the vexation and annoyance that I really felt. Her answer surprised and distressed me inexpressibly; it was the very last reply that I should have expected her to make.

'My uncle is right,' she said. 'I have caused trouble and anxiety enough to you, and to all about me. Let me cause no more, Marian—let Sir Percival decide.'

I remonstrated warmly; but nothing that I could say moved her.

'I am held to my engagement,' she replied; 'I have broken with my old life. The evil day will not come the less surely because I put it off. No, Marian! once again, my uncle is right. I have caused trouble enough and anxiety enough; and I will cause no more.'

She used to be pliability itself; but she was now inflexibly passive in her resignation—I might almost say in her despair. Dearly as I love her, I should have been less pained if she had been violently agitated; it was so shockingly unlike her natural character to see her as cold and insensible as I saw her now.

12th.—Sir Percival put some questions to me, at breakfast, about Laura, which left me no choice but to tell him what she had said.

While we were talking, she herself came down and joined us. She was just as unnaturally composed in Sir Percival's presence as she had been in mine. When breakfast was over, he had an opportunity of saying a few words to her privately, in a recess of one of the windows. They were not more than two or three minutes together; and, on their separating, she left the room with Mrs Vesey, while Sir Percival came to me. He said he had entreated her to favour him by maintaining her privilege of fixing the time for the marriage at her own will and pleasure. In reply, she had merely expressed her acknowledgements, and had desired him to mention what his wishes were to Miss Halcombe.

I have no patience to write more. In this instance, as in every other, Sir Percival has carried his point, with the utmost possible credit to himself, in spite of everything that I can say or do. His wishes are now, what they were, of course, when he first came here; and Laura having resigned herself to the one inevitable sacrifice of the marriage, remains as coldly hopeless and enduring as ever. In parting with the little occupations and relics that reminded her of Hartright, she seems to have parted with all her tenderness and all her impressibility. It is only three o'clock in the afternoon while I write these lines, and Sir Percival has left us already, in the happy hurry of a bridegroom, to prepare for the bride's reception at his house in Hampshire. Unless some extraordinary event happens to prevent it, they will be married exactly at the time when he wished to be married—before the end of the year. My very fingers burn as I write it!

13th.—A sleepless night, through uneasiness about Laura. Towards the morning, I came to a resolution to try what change of scene would do to rouse her. She cannot surely remain in her present torpor of insensibility, if I take her away from Limmeridge and surround her with the pleasant faces of old friends? After some consideration, I decided on writing to the Arnolds, in Yorkshire. They are simple, kind-hearted, hospitable people; and she has known them from her childhood. When I had put the letter in the post-bag, I told her what I had done. It would have been a relief to me if she had shown the spirit to resist and object. But no—she only said, 'I will go anywhere with *you*, Marian. I dare say you are right—I dare say the change will do me good.'

14th.—I wrote to Mr Gilmore, informing him that there was really a prospect of this miserable marriage taking place, and also mentioning my idea of trying what change of scene would do for Laura. I had no heart to go into particulars. Time enough for them, when we get nearer to the end of the year.

15th.—Three letters for me. The first, from the Arnolds, full of delight at the prospect of seeing Laura and me. The second, from one of the gentlemen to whom I wrote on Walter Hartright's behalf, informing me that he has been fortunate enough to find an opportunity of complying with my request. The third, from Walter himself; thanking me, poor fellow, in the warmest terms, for giving him an opportunity of leaving his home, his country, and his friends. A private expedition to make excavations among the ruined cities of Central America is, it seems, about to sail from Liverpool. The draughtsman who had been already appointed to accompany it, has lost heart, and withdrawn at the eleventh hour; and Walter is to fill his place. He is to be engaged for six months certain, from the time of the landing in Honduras, and for a year afterwards, if the excavations are successful, and if the funds hold out. His letter ends with a promise to write me a farewell line, when they are all on board ship, and when the pilot leaves them. I can only hope and pray earnestly that he and I are both acting in this matter for the best. It seems such a serious step for him to take, that the mere contemplation of it startles me. And yet, in his unhappy position, how can I expect him, or wish him, to remain at home?

16th.—The carriage is at the door. Laura and I set out on our visit to the Arnolds to-day.

*　　*　　*　　*　　*

Polesdean Lodge, Yorkshire.

23rd.—A week in these new scenes, and among these kind-hearted people, has done her some good, though not so much as I had hoped. I have resolved to prolong our stay for another week at least. It is useless to go back to Limmeridge, till there is an absolute necessity for our return.

24th.—Sad news by this morning's post. The expedition to Central America sailed on the twenty-first. We have parted with a true man; we have lost a faithful friend. Walter Hartright has left England.

25th.—Sad news yesterday: ominous news to-day. Sir Percival Glyde has written to Mr Fairlie; and Mr Fairlie has written to Laura and me, to recal us to Limmeridge immediately.

What can this mean? Has the day for the marriage been fixed in our absence?

Limmeridge House.

NOVEMBER 27TH.—My forebodings are realised. The marriage is fixed for the twenty-second of December.

The day after we left for Polesdean Lodge, Sir Percival wrote, it seems, to Mr Fairlie, to say that the necessary repairs and alterations in his house in Hampshire would occupy a much longer time in completion than he had originally anticipated. The proper estimates were to be submitted to him as soon as possible; and it would greatly facilitate his entering into definite arrangements with the workpeople, if he could be informed of the exact period at which the wedding ceremony might be expected to take place. He could then make all his calculations in reference to time, besides writing the necessary apologies to friends who had been engaged to visit him that winter, and who could not, of course, be received when the house was in the hands of the workmen.

To this letter Mr Fairlie had replied by requesting Sir Percival himself to suggest a day for the marriage, subject to Miss Fairlie's approval, which her guardian willingly undertook to do his best to obtain. Sir Percival wrote back by the next post, and proposed (in accordance with his own views and wishes, from the first) the latter part of December—perhaps the twenty-second, or twenty-fourth, or any other day that the lady and her guardian might prefer. The lady not being at hand to speak for herself, her guardian had decided, in her absence, on the earliest day mentioned—the twenty-second of December—and had written to recal us to Limmeridge in consequence.

After explaining these particulars to me at a private interview, yesterday, Mr Fairlie suggested, in his most amiable manner, that I should open the necessary negotiations to-day. Feeling that resistance was useless, unless I could first obtain Laura's authority to make it, I consented to speak to her, but declared, at the same time, that I could on no consideration undertake to gain her consent to Sir Percival's wishes. Mr Fairlie complimented me on my 'excellent conscience,' much as he would have complimented me, if we had been out walking, on my 'excellent constitution,' and seemed perfectly satisfied, so far, with having simply shifted one more family responsibility from his own shoulders to mine.

This morning, I spoke to Laura as I had promised. The composure—I may almost say, the insensibility—which she has so strangely and so resolutely maintained ever since Sir Percival left us, was not proof against the shock of the news I had to tell her. She turned pale, and trembled violently.

'Not so soon!' she pleaded. 'Oh, Marian, not so soon!'

The slightest hint she could give was enough for me. I rose to leave the room, and fight her battle for her at once with Mr Fairlie.

Just as my hand was on the door, she caught fast hold of my dress, and stopped me.

'Let me go!' I said. 'My tongue burns to tell your uncle that he and Sir Percival are not to have it all their own way.'

She sighed bitterly, and still held my dress.

'No!' she said, faintly. 'Too late, Marian—too late!'

'Not a minute too late,' I retorted. 'The question of time is *our* question—and trust me, Laura, to take a woman's full advantage of it.'

I unclasped her hand from my gown while I spoke; but she slipped both her arms round my waist at the same moment, and held me more effectually than ever.

'It will only involve us in more trouble and more confusion,' she said. 'It will set you and my uncle at variance, and bring Sir Percival here again with fresh causes of complaint——'

'So much the better!' I cried out, passionately. 'Who cares for his causes of complaint? Are you to break your heart to set his mind at ease? No man under heaven deserves these sacrifices from us women. Men! They are the enemies of our innocence and our peace—they drag us away from our parents' love and our sisters' friendship—they take us body and soul to themselves, and fasten our helpless lives to theirs as they chain up a dog to his kennel. And what does the best of them give us in return? Let me go, Laura—I'm mad when I think of it!'

The tears—miserable, weak, women's tears of vexation and rage—started to my eyes. She smiled sadly, and put her handkerchief over my face, to hide for me the betrayal of my own weakness—the weakness of all others which she knew that I most despised.

'Oh, Marian!' she said. '*You* crying! Think what you would say to me, if the places were changed, and if those tears were mine. All your love and courage and devotion will not alter what *must* happen, sooner or later. Let my uncle have his way. Let us have no more troubles and heart-burnings that any sacrifice of mine can prevent. Say you will live with me, Marian, when I am married—and say no more.'

But I did say more. I forced back the contemptible tears that were no relief to *me*, and that only distressed *her*; and reasoned and pleaded as calmly as I could. It was of no avail. She made me twice repeat the promise to live with her when she was married, and then suddenly asked a question which turned my sorrow and my sympathy for her into a new direction.

'While we were at Polesdean,' she said, 'you had a letter, Marian——'

Her altered tone; the abrupt manner in which she looked away from me, and hid her face on my shoulder; the hesitation which silenced her before she had completed her question, all told me, but too plainly, to whom the half-expressed inquiry pointed.

'I thought, Laura, that you and I were never to refer to him again,' I said gently.

'You had a letter from him?' she persisted.

'Yes,' I replied, 'if you must know it.'

'Do you mean to write to him again?'

I hesitated. I had been afraid to tell her of his absence from England, or of the manner in which my exertions to serve his new hopes and projects had connected me with his departure. What answer could I make? He was gone where no letters could reach him for months, perhaps for years, to come.

'Suppose I do mean to write to him again,' I said at last. 'What, then, Laura?'

Her cheek grew burning hot against my neck; and her arms trembled and tightened round me.

'Don't tell him about *the twenty-second*,' she whispered. 'Promise, Marian—pray promise you will not even mention my name to him when you write next.'

I gave the promise. No words can say how sorrowfully I gave it. She instantly took her arm from my waist, walked away to the window, and stood looking out, with her back to me. After a moment she spoke once more, but without turning round, without allowing me to catch the smallest glimpse of her face.

'Are you going to my uncle's room?' she asked. 'Will you say that I consent to whatever arrangement he may think best? Never mind leaving me, Marian. I shall be better alone for a little while.'

I went out. If, as soon as I got into the passage, I could have transported Mr Fairlie and Sir Percival Glyde to the uttermost ends of the earth, by lifting one of my fingers, that finger would have been raised without an instant's hesitation. For once, my unhappy temper now stood my friend. I should have broken down altogether and burst into a violent fit of crying, if my tears had not been all burnt up in the heat of my anger. As it was, I dashed into Mr Fairlie's room—called to him as harshly as possible, 'Laura consents to the twenty-second'—and dashed out again without waiting for a word of answer. I banged the door after me; and I hope I shattered Mr Fairlie's nervous system for the rest of the day.

28th.—This morning, I read poor Hartright's farewell letter over again; a doubt having crossed my mind, since yesterday, whether I am acting wisely in concealing the fact of his departure from Laura.

On reflection, I still think I am right. The allusions in his letter to the preparations made for the expedition to Central America, all show that the leaders of it know it to be dangerous. If the discovery of this makes *me* uneasy, what would it make *her*? It is bad enough to feel that his departure has deprived us of the friend of all others to whose devotion we could trust, in the hour of need, if ever that hour comes and finds us helpless. But it is far worse to know that he has gone from us to face the perils of a bad climate, a wild country, and a disturbed population. Surely it would be a cruel candour to tell Laura this, without a pressing and a positive necessity for it?

I almost doubt whether I ought not to go a step farther, and burn the letter at once, for fear of its one day falling into wrong hands. It not only refers to Laura in terms which ought to remain a secret for ever between the writer and me; but it reiterates his suspicion—so obstinate, so unaccountable, and so alarming—that he has been secretly watched since he left Limmeridge. He declares that he saw the faces of the two strange men, who followed him about the streets of London, watching him among the crowd which gathered at Liverpool to see the expedition embark; and he positively asserts that he heard the name of Anne Catherick pronounced behind him, as he got into the boat. His own words are, 'These events have a meaning, these events must lead to a result. The mystery of Anne Catherick is *not* cleared up yet. She may never cross my path again; but if ever she crosses yours, make better use of the opportunity, Miss Halcombe, than I made of it. I speak on strong conviction; I entreat you to remember what I say.' These are his own expressions. There is no danger of my forgetting them—my memory is only too ready to dwell on any words of Hartright's that refer to Anne Catherick. But there is danger in my keeping the letter. The merest accident might place it at the mercy of strangers. I may fall ill; I may die—better to burn it at once, and have one anxiety the less.

It is burnt! The ashes of his farewell letter—the last he may ever write to me—lie in a few black fragments on the hearth. Is this the sad end to all that sad story? Oh, not the end—surely, surely, not the end already!

29th.—The preparations for the marriage have begun. The dressmaker has come to receive her orders. Laura is perfectly impassive, perfectly careless about the question of all others in which a woman's personal interests are most closely bound up. She has left it all to the dressmaker and to me. If poor Hartright had been the Baronet, and the husband of her father's choice, how differently she would have behaved! How anxious and capricious she would have been; and what a hard task the best of dress-makers would have found it to please her!

30th.—We hear every day from Sir Percival. The last news is, that the alterations in his house will occupy from four to six months, before they can be properly completed. If painters, paper-hangers, and upholsterers could make happiness as well as splendour, I should be interested about their proceedings in Laura's future home. As it is, the only part of Sir Percival's last letter which does not leave me as it found me, perfectly indifferent to all his plans and projects, is the part which refers to the wedding tour. He proposes, as Laura is delicate, and as the winter threatens to be unusually severe, to take her to Rome, and to remain in Italy until the early part of next summer. If this plan should not be approved, he is equally ready, although he has no establishment of his own in town, to spend the season in London, in the most suitable furnished house that can be obtained for the purpose.

Putting myself and my own feelings entirely out of the question (which it is my duty to do, and which I have done), I, for one, have no doubt of the propriety of adopting the first of these proposals. In either case, a separation between Laura and me is inevitable. It will be a longer separation, in the event of their going abroad, than it would be in the event of their remaining in London—but we must set against this disadvantage, the benefit to Laura on the other side, of passing the winter in a mild climate; and, more than that, the immense assistance in raising her spirits, and reconciling her to her new existence, which the mere wonder and excitement of travelling for the first time in her life in the most interesting country in the world, must surely afford. She is not of a disposition to find resources in the conventional gaieties and excitements of London. They would only make the first oppression of this lamentable marriage fall the heavier on her. I dread the beginning of her new life more than words can tell; but I see some hope for her if she travels—none if she remains at home.

It is strange to look back at this latest entry in my journal, and to find that I am writing of the marriage and the parting with Laura, as people write of a settled thing. It seems so cold and so unfeeling to be looking at the future already in this cruelly composed way. But what other way is possible, now that the time is drawing so near? Before another month is over our heads, she will be *his* Laura instead of mine! *His* Laura! I am as little able to realise the idea which those two words convey—my mind feels almost as dulled and stunned by it, as if writing of her marriage were like writing of her death.

December 1st.—A sad, sad day; a day that I have no heart to describe at any length. After weakly putting it off, last night, I was obliged to speak to her this morning of Sir Percival's proposal about the wedding tour.

In the full conviction, that I should be with her, wherever she went, the poor child—for a child she is still in many things—was almost happy at the prospect of seeing the wonders of Florence and Rome and Naples. It nearly broke my heart to dispel her delusion, and to bring her face to face with the hard truth. I was obliged to tell her that no man tolerates a rival—not even a woman-rival—in his wife's affections, when he first marries, whatever he may do afterwards. I was obliged to warn her, that my chance of living with her permanently under her own roof, depended entirely on my not arousing Sir Percival's jealousy and distrust by standing between them at the beginning of their marriage, in the position of the chosen depositary of his wife's closest secrets. Drop by drop, I poured the profaning bitterness of this world's wisdom into that pure heart and that innocent mind, while every higher and better feeling within me recoiled from my miserable task. It is over now. She has learnt her hard, her inevitable lesson. The simple illusions of her girlhood are gone; and my hand has stripped them off. Better mine than his—that is all my consolation—better mine than his.

So the first proposal is the proposal accepted. They are to go to Italy; and I am to arrange, with Sir Percival's permission, for meeting them and staying with them, when they return to England. In other words, I am to ask a personal favour, for the first time in my life, and to ask it of the man of all others to whom I least desire to owe a serious obligation of any kind. Well! I think I could do even more than that, for Laura's sake.

2nd.—On looking back, I find myself always referring to Sir Percival in disparaging terms. In the turn affairs have now taken, I must and will root out my prejudice against him. I cannot think how it first got into my mind. It certainly never existed in former times.

Is it Laura's reluctance to become his wife that has set me against him? Have Hartright's perfectly intelligible prejudices infected me without my suspecting their influence? Does that letter of Anne Catherick's still leave a lurking distrust in my mind, in spite of Sir Percival's explanation, and of the proof in my possession of the truth of it? I cannot account for the state of my own feelings: the one thing I am certain of is, that it is my duty—doubly my duty, now—not to wrong Sir Percival by unjustly distrusting him. If it has got to be a habit with me always to write of him in the same unfavourable manner, I must and will break myself of this unworthy tendency, even though the effort should force me to close the pages of my journal till the marriage is over! I am seriously dissatisfied with myself—I will write no more to-day.

*　　*　　*　　*　　*

December 16th.—A whole fortnight has passed; and I have not once opened these pages. I have been long enough away from my journal, to come back to it, with a healthier and better mind, I hope, so far as Sir Percival is concerned.

There is not much to record of the past two weeks. The dresses are almost all finished; and the new travelling-trunks have been sent here from London. Poor dear Laura hardly leaves me for a moment, all day; and, last night, when neither of us could sleep, she came and crept into my bed to talk to me there. 'I shall lose you so soon, Marian,' she said; 'I must make the most of you while I can.'

They are to be married at Limmeridge Church; and, thank Heaven, not one of the neighbours is to be invited to the ceremony. The only visitor will be our old friend, Mr Arnold, who is to come from Polesdean, to give Laura away; her uncle being far too delicate to trust himself outside the door in such inclement weather as we now have. If I were not determined, from this day forth, to see nothing but the bright side of our prospects, the melancholy absence of any male relative of Laura's, at the most important moment of her life, would make me very gloomy and very distrustful of the future. But I have done with gloom and distrust—that is to say, I have done with writing about either the one or the other in this journal.

Sir Percival is to arrive to-morrow. He offered, in case we wished to treat him on terms of rigid etiquette, to write and ask our clergyman to grant him the hospitality of the rectory, during the short period of his sojourn at Limmeridge before the marriage. Under the circumstances, neither Mr Fairlie nor I thought it at all necessary for us to trouble ourselves about attending to trifling forms and ceremonies. In our wild moorland country, and in this great lonely house, we may well claim to be beyond the reach of the trivial conventionalities which hamper people in other places. I wrote to

Sir Percival to thank him for his polite offer, and to beg that he would occupy his old rooms, just as usual, at Limmeridge House.

17th.—He arrived to-day, looking, as I thought, a little worn and anxious, but still talking and laughing like a man in the best possible spirits. He brought with him some really beautiful presents, in jewellery, which Laura received with her best grace, and, outwardly at least, with perfect self-possession. The only sign I can detect of the struggle it must cost her to preserve appearances at this trying time, expresses itself in a sudden unwillingness, on her part, ever to be left alone. Instead of retreating to her own room, as usual, she seems to dread going there. When I went up-stairs to-day, after lunch, to put on my bonnet for a walk, she volunteered to join me; and, again, before dinner, she threw the door open between our two rooms, so that we might talk to each other while we were dressing. 'Keep me always doing something,' she said; 'keep me always in company with somebody. Don't let me think—that is all I ask now, Marian—don't let me think.'

This sad change in her only increases her attractions for Sir Percival. He interprets it, I can see, to his own advantage. There is a feverish flush in her cheeks, a feverish brightness in her eyes, which he welcomes as the return of her beauty and the recovery of her spirits. She talked to-day at dinner with a gaiety and carelessness so false, so shockingly out of her character, that I secretly longed to silence her and take her away. Sir Percival's delight and surprise appeared to be beyond all expression. The anxiety which I had noticed on his face when he arrived, totally disappeared from it; and he looked, even to my eyes, a good ten years younger than he really is.

There can be no doubt—though some strange perversity prevents me from seeing it myself—there can be no doubt that Laura's future husband is a very handsome man. Regular features form a personal advantage to begin with—and he has them. Bright brown eyes, either in man or woman, are a great attraction—and he has them. Even baldness, when it is only baldness over the forehead (as in his case), is rather becoming, than not, in a man, for it heightens the head and adds to the intelligence of the face. Grace and ease of movement; untiring animation of manner; ready, pliant, conversational powers—all these are unquestionable merits, and all these he certainly possesses. Surely, Mr Gilmore, ignorant as he is of Laura's secret, was not to blame for feeling surprised that she should repent of her marriage engagement? Any one else in his place, would have shared our good old friend's opinion. If I were asked, at this moment, to say plainly what defects I have discovered in Sir Percival, I could only point out two. One, his incessant restlessness and excitability—which may be caused, naturally enough, by unusual energy of character. The other, his short, sharp, ill-tempered manner of speaking to the servants—which may be only a bad habit, after all. No: I cannot dispute it, and I will not dispute it—Sir Percival is a very handsome and a very agreeable man. There! I have written it down, at last, and I am glad it's over.

18th.—Feeling weary and depressed, this morning, I left Laura with Mrs Vesey, and went out alone for one of my brisk mid-day walks, which I have discontinued too much of late. I took the dry airy road, over the moor, that leads to Todd's Corner. After having been out half an hour, I was excessively surprised to see Sir Percival approaching me from the direction of the farm. He was walking rapidly, swinging his stick; his head erect as usual, and his shooting jacket flying open in the wind. When we met, he did not wait for me to ask any questions—he told me, at once, that he had been to the farm to inquire if Mr or Mrs Todd had received any tidings, since his last visit to Limmeridge, of Anne Catherick.

'You found, of course, that they had heard nothing?' I said.

'Nothing whatever,' he replied. 'I begin to be seriously afraid that we have lost her. Do you happen to know,' he continued, looking me in the face very attentively, 'if the artist—Mr Hartright—is in a position to give us any further information?'

'He has neither heard of her, nor seen her, since he left Cumberland,' I answered.

'Very sad,' said Sir Percival, speaking like a man who was disappointed, and yet, oddly enough, looking, at the same time, like a man who was relieved. 'It is impossible to say what misfortunes may not have happened to the miserable creature. I am inexpressibly annoyed at the failure of all my efforts to restore her to the care and protection which she so urgently needs.'

This time he really looked annoyed. I said a few sympathising words; and we then talked of other subjects, on our way back to the house. Surely, my chance meeting with him on the moor has disclosed another favourable trait in his character? Surely, it was singularly considerate and unselfish of him to think of Anne Catherick on the eve of his marriage, and to go all the way to Todd's Corner to make inquiries about her, when he might have passed the time so much more agreeably in Laura's society? Considering that he can only have acted from motives of pure charity, his conduct, under the circumstances, shows unusual good feeling, and deserves extraordinary praise. Well! I give him extraordinary praise—and there's an end of it.

19th.—More discoveries in the inexhaustible mine of Sir Percival's virtues.

To-day, I approached the subject of my proposed sojourn under his wife's roof, when he brings her back to England. I had hardly dropped my first hint in this direction, before he caught me warmly by the hand, and said I had made the very offer to him, which he had been, on his side, most anxious to make to me. I was the companion of all others whom he most sincerely longed to secure for his wife; and he begged me to believe that I had conferred a lasting favour on him by making the proposal to live with Laura after her marriage, exactly as I had always lived with her before it.

When I had thanked him, in her name and mine, for his considerate kindness to both of us, we passed next to the subject of his wedding tour, and began to talk of the English society in Rome to which Laura was to be introduced. He ran over the names of several friends whom he expected to meet abroad this winter. They were all English, as well as I can remember, with one exception. The one exception was Count Fosco.

The mention of the Count's name, and the discovery that he and his wife are likely to meet the bride and bridegroom on the continent, puts Laura's marriage, for the first time, in a distinctly favourable light. It is likely to be the means of healing a family feud. Hitherto, Madame Fosco has chosen to forget her obligations as Laura's aunt, out of sheer spite against the late Mr Fairlie for his conduct in the affair of the legacy. Now, however, she can persist in this course of conduct no longer. Sir Percival and Count Fosco are old and fast friends, and their wives will have no choice but to meet on civil terms. Madame Fosco, in her maiden days, was one of the most impertinent women I ever met with—capricious, exacting, and vain to the last degree of absurdity. If her husband has succeeded in bringing her to her senses, he deserves the gratitude of every member of the family—and he may have mine to begin with.

I am becoming anxious to know the Count. He is the most intimate friend of Laura's husband; and, in that capacity, he excites my strongest interest. Neither Laura nor I have ever seen him. All I know of him is that his accidental presence, years ago, on the steps of the Trinità del Monte at Rome, assisted Sir Percival's escape from robbery and assassination, at the critical moment when he was wounded in the hand, and might, the next instant, have been wounded in the heart. I remember also that, at the time of the late Mr Fairlie's absurd objections to his sister's marriage, the Count wrote him a very temperate and sensible letter on the subject, which, I am ashamed to say, remained unanswered. This is all I know of Sir Percival's friend. I wonder if he will ever come to England? I wonder if I shall like him?

My pen is running away into mere speculation. Let me return to sober matter of fact. It is certain that Sir Percival's reception of my venturesome proposal to live with his wife, was more than kind, it was almost affectionate. I am sure Laura's husband will have no reason to complain of me, if I can only go on as I have begun. I have already declared him to be handsome, agreeable, full of good feeling towards the unfortunate, and full of affectionate kindness towards me. Really, I hardly know myself again, in my new character of Sir Percival's warmest friend.

20th.—I hate Sir Percival! I flatly deny his good looks. I consider him to be eminently ill-tempered and disagreeable, and totally wanting in kindness and good feeling. Last night, the cards for the married couple were sent home. Laura opened the packet, and saw her future name in print, for the first time. Sir Percival looked over her shoulder familiarly at the new card which had already transformed Miss Fairlie into Lady Glyde—smiled with the most odious self-complacency—and whispered something in her ear. I don't know what it was—Laura has refused to tell me—but I saw her face turn to such a deadly whiteness that I thought she would have fainted. He took no notice of the change: he seemed to be barbarously unconscious that he had said anything to pain her. All my old feelings of hostility towards him revived on the instant; and all the hours that have passed, since, have done nothing to dissipate them. I am more unreasonable and more unjust than ever. In three words—how glibly my pen writes them!—in three words, I hate him.

21st.—Have the anxieties of this anxious time shaken me a little, at last? I have been writing, for the last few days, in a tone of levity which, Heaven knows, is far enough from my heart, and which it has rather shocked me to discover on looking back at the entries in my journal.

Perhaps I may have caught the feverish excitement of Laura's spirits, for the last week. If so, the fit has already passed away from me, and has left me in a very strange state of mind. A persistent idea has been forcing itself on my attention, ever since last night, that something will yet happen to prevent the marriage. What has produced this singular fancy? Is it the indirect result of my apprehensions for Laura's future? Or has it been unconsciously suggested to me by the increasing restlessness and irritability which I have certainly observed in Sir Percival's manner, as the wedding-day draws nearer and nearer? Impossible to say. I know that I have the idea—surely the wildest idea, under the circumstances, that ever entered a woman's head?—but try as I may, I cannot trace it back to its source.

This last day has been all confusion and wretchedness. How can I write about it?—and yet, I must write. Anything is better than brooding over my own gloomy thoughts.

Kind Mrs Vesey, whom we have all too much overlooked and forgotten of late, innocently caused us a sad morning to begin with. She has been, for months past, secretly making a warm Shetland shawl for her dear pupil—a most beautiful and surprising piece of work to be done by a woman at her age and with her habits. The gift was presented this morning; and poor warm-hearted Laura completely broke down when the shawl was put proudly on her shoulders by the loving old friend and guardian of her motherless childhood. I was hardly allowed time to quiet them both, or even to dry my own eyes, when I was sent for by Mr Fairlie, to be favoured with a long recital of his arrangements for the preservation of his own tranquillity on the wedding-day.

'Dear Laura' was to receive his present—a shabby ring, with her affectionate uncle's hair for an ornament, instead of a precious stone, and with a heartless French inscription, inside, about congenial sentiments and eternal friendship—'dear Laura' was to receive this tender tribute from my hands immediately, so that she might have plenty of time to recover from the agitation produced by the gift, before she appeared in Mr Fairlie's presence. 'Dear Laura' was to pay him a little visit that evening, and to be kind enough not to make a scene. 'Dear Laura' was to pay him another little visit in her wedding dress, the next morning, and to be kind enough, again, not to make a scene. 'Dear Laura' was to look in once more, for the third time, before going away, but without harrowing his feelings by saying *when* she was going away, and without tears—'in the name of pity, in the name of everything, dear Marian, that is most affectionate and most domestic and most delightfully and charmingly self-composed, *without tears!*' I was so exasperated by this miserable selfish trifling, at such a time, that I should certainly have shocked Mr Fairlie by some of the hardest and rudest truths he has ever heard in his life, if the arrival of Mr Arnold from Polesdean had not called me away to new duties down stairs.

The rest of the day is indescribable. I believe no one in the house really knew how it passed. The confusion of small events, all huddled together one on the other, bewildered everybody. There were dresses sent home, that had been forgotten; there were trunks to be packed and unpacked and packed again; there were presents from friends far and near, friends high and low. We were all needlessly hurried; all nervously expectant of the morrow. Sir Percival, especially, was too restless, now, to remain five minutes together in the same place. That short, sharp cough of his troubled him more than ever. He was in and out of doors all day long; and he seemed to grow so inquisitive, on a sudden, that he questioned the very strangers who came on small errands to the house. Add to all this, the one perpetual thought, in Laura's mind and mine, that we were to part the next day, and the haunting dread, unexpressed by either of us, and yet ever present to both, that this deplorable marriage might prove to be the one fatal error of her life and the one hopeless sorrow of mine. For the first time in all the years of our close and happy intercourse we almost avoided looking each other in the face; and we refrained, by common consent, from speaking together in private, through the whole evening. I can dwell on it no longer. Whatever future sorrows may be in store for me, I shall always look back on this twenty-first of December as the most comfortless and most miserable day of my life.

I am writing these lines in the solitude of my own room, long after midnight; having just come back from a stolen look at Laura in her pretty little white bed—the bed she has occupied since the days of her girlhood.

There she lay, unconscious that I was looking at her—quiet, more quiet than I had dared to hope, but not sleeping. The glimmer of the night-light showed me that her eyes were only partially closed: the traces of tears glistened between her eyelids. My little keepsake—only a brooch—lay on the table at her bedside, with her prayer-book, and the miniature portrait of her father which she takes with her wherever she goes. I waited a moment, looking at her from behind her pillow, as she lay beneath me, with one arm and hand resting on the white coverlid, so still, so quietly breathing, that the frill on her night-dress never moved—I waited looking at her, as I have seen her thousands of times, as I shall never see her again—and then stole back to my room. My own love! with all your wealth, and all your beauty, how friendless you are! The one man who would give his heart's life to serve you, is far away, tossing, this stormy night, on the awful sea. Who else is left to you? No father, no brother—no living creature but the helpless, useless woman who writes these sad lines, and watches by you for the morning, in sorrow that she cannot compose, in doubt that she cannot conquer. Oh, what a trust is to be placed in that man's hands to-morrow! If ever he forgets it; if ever he injures a hair of her head!——

THE TWENTY-SECOND OF DECEMBER. *Seven o'clock.* A wild unsettled morning. She has just risen—better and calmer, now that the time has come, than she was yesterday.

Ten o'clock. She is dressed. We have kissed each other; we have promised each other not to lose courage. I am away for a moment in my own room. In the whirl and confusion of my thoughts, I can detect that strange fancy of some hindrance happening to stop the marriage, still hanging about my mind. Is it hanging about *his* mind, too? I see him from the window, moving hither and thither uneasily among the carriages at the door.—How can I write such folly! The marriage is a certainty. In less than half an hour we start for the church.

Eleven o'clock. It is all over. They are married.

Three o'clock. They are gone! I am blind with crying—I can write no more——

* * * * *

Blackwater Park, Hampshire.

JUNE 11TH, 1850.—Six months to look back on—six long, lonely months, since Laura and I last saw each other!

How many days have I still to wait? Only one! To-morrow, the twelfth, the travellers return to England. I can hardly realise my own happiness; I can hardly believe that the next four-and-twenty hours will complete the last day of separation between Laura and me.

She and her husband have been in Italy all the winter, and afterwards in the Tyrol. They come back, accompanied by Count Fosco and his wife, who propose to settle somewhere in the neighbourhood of London, and who have engaged to stay at Blackwater Park for the summer months before deciding on a place of residence. So long as Laura returns, no matter who returns with her. Sir Percival may fill the house from floor to ceiling, if he likes, on condition that his wife and I inhabit it together.

Meanwhile, here I am, established at Blackwater Park; 'the ancient and interesting seat' (as the county history obligingly informs me) 'of Sir Percival Glyde, Bart.'—and the future abiding-place (as I may now venture to add, on my own account) of plain Marian Halcombe, spinster, now settled in a snug little sitting-room, with a cup of tea by her side, and all her earthly possessions ranged round her in three boxes and a bag.

I left Limmeridge yesterday; having received Laura's delightful letter from Paris, the day before. I had been previously uncertain whether I was to meet them in London, or in Hampshire; but this last letter informed me, that Sir Percival proposed to land at Southampton, and to travel straight on to his country-house. He has spent so much money abroad, that he has none left to defray the expenses of living in London, for the remainder of the season; and he is economically resolved to pass the summer and autumn quietly at Blackwater. Laura has had more than enough of excitement and change of scene; and is pleased at the prospect of country tranquillity and retirement which her husband's prudence provides for her. As for me, I am ready to be happy anywhere in her society. We are all, therefore, well contented in our various ways, to begin with.

Last night, I slept in London, and was delayed there so long, to-day, by various calls and commissions, that I did not reach Blackwater, this evening, till after dusk.

Judging by my vague impressions of the place, thus far, it is the exact opposite of Limmeridge.

The house is situated on a dead flat, and seems to be shut in—almost suffocated, to my north-country notions—by trees. I have seen nobody, but the man-servant who opened the door to me, and the housekeeper, a very civil person who showed me the way to my own room, and got me my tea. I have a nice little boudoir and bedroom, at the end of a long passage on the first floor. The servants' and some of the spare rooms are on the second floor; and all the living rooms are on the ground floor. I have not seen one of them yet, and I know nothing about the house, except that one wing of it is said to be five hundred years old, that it had a moat round it once, and that it gets its name of Blackwater from a lake in the park.

Eleven o'clock has just struck, in a ghostly and solemn manner, from a turret over the centre of the house, which I saw when I came in. A large dog has been woke, apparently by the sound of the bell, and is howling and yawning drearily, somewhere round a corner. I hear echoing footsteps in the passages below, and the iron thumping of bolts and bars at the house door. The servants are evidently going to bed. Shall I follow their example?

No: I am not half sleepy enough. Sleepy, did I say? I feel as if I should never close my eyes again. The bare anticipation of seeing that dear face and hearing that well-known voice to-morrow, keeps me in a perpetual fever of excitement. If I only had the privileges of a man, I would order out Sir Percival's best horse instantly, and tear away on a night-gallop, eastward, to meet the rising sun—a long, hard, heavy, ceaseless gallop of hours and hours, like the famous highwayman's ride to York. Being, however, nothing but a woman, condemned to patience, propriety, and petticoats, for life, I must respect the housekeeper's opinions, and try to compose myself in some feeble and feminine way.

Reading is out of the question—I can't fix my attention on books. Let me try if I can write myself into sleepiness and fatigue. My journal has been very much neglected of late. What can I recal—standing, as I now do, on the threshold of a new life—of persons and events, of chances and changes, during the past six months—the long, weary, empty interval since Laura's wedding-day?

Walter Hartright is uppermost in my memory; and he passes first in the shadowy procession of my absent friends. I received a few lines from him, after the landing of the expedition in Honduras, written more cheerfully and hopefully than he has written yet. A month or six weeks later, I saw an extract from an American newspaper, describing the departure of the adventurers on their inland journey. They were last seen entering a wild primeval forest, each man with his rifle on his shoulder and his baggage at his back. Since that time, civilisation has lost all trace of them. Not a line more have I received from Walter; not a fragment of news from the expedition has appeared in any of the public journals.

The same dense, disheartening obscurity hangs over the fate and fortunes of Anne Catherick, and her companion, Mrs Clements. Nothing whatever has been heard of either of them. Whether they are in the country or out of it, whether they are living or dead, no one knows. Even Sir Percival's solicitor has lost all hope, and has ordered the useless search after the fugitives to be finally given up.

Our good old friend Mr Gilmore has met with a sad check in his active professional career. Early in the spring, we were alarmed by hearing that he had been found insensible at his desk, and that the seizure was pronounced to be an apoplectic fit. He had been long complaining of fulness and oppression in the head; and his doctor had warned him of the consequences that would follow his persistency in continuing to work, early and late, as if he was still a young man. The result now is that he has been positively ordered to keep out of his office for a year to come, at least, and to seek repose of body and relief of mind by altogether changing his usual mode of life. The business is left, accordingly, to be carried on by his partner; and he is, himself, at this moment, away in Germany, visiting some relations who are settled there in mercantile persuits. Thus, another true friend, and trustworthy adviser, is lost to us—lost, I earnestly hope and trust, for a time only.

Poor Mrs Vesey travelled with me, as far as London. It was impossible to abandon her to solitude at Limmeridge, after Laura and I had both left the house; and we have arranged that she is to live with an unmarried younger sister of hers, who keeps a school at Clapham. She is to come here this autumn to visit her pupil—I might almost say, her adopted child. I saw the good old lady safe to her destination; and left her in the care of her relative, quietly happy at the prospect of seeing Laura again, in a few months' time.

As for Mr Fairlie, I believe I am guilty of no injustice if I describe him as being unutterably relieved by having the house clear of us women. The idea of his missing his niece is simply preposterous—he used to let months pass, in the old times, without attempting to see her—and, in my case and Mrs Vesey's, I take leave to consider his telling us both that he was half heart-broken at our departure, to be equivalent to a confession that he was secretly rejoiced to get rid of us. His last caprice has led him to keep two photographers incessantly employed in producing sun-pictures of all the treasures and curiosities in his possession. One complete copy of the collection of photographs is to be presented to the Mechanics' Institution of Carlisle, mounted on the finest cardboard, with ostentatious red-letter inscriptions underneath. 'Madonna and Child by Raphael. In the possession of Frederick Fairlie, Esquire.' 'Copper coin of the period of Tiglath Pileser. In the possession of Frederick Fairlie, Esquire.' 'Unique Rembrandt etching. Known all over Europe, as *The Smudge*, from a printer's blot in the corner which exists in no other copy. Valued at three hundred guineas. In the possession of Frederick Fairlie, Esquire.' Dozens of photographs of this sort, and all inscribed in this manner, were completed before I left Cumberland; and hundreds more remain to be done. With this new interest to occupy him, Mr Fairlie will be a happy man for months and months to come; and the two unfortunate photographers will share the social martyrdom which he has hitherto inflicted on his valet alone.

So much for the persons and events which hold the foremost place in my memory. What, next, of the one person who holds the foremost place in my heart? Laura has been present to my thoughts, all the while I have been writing these lines. What can I recal of her, during the past six months, before I close my journal for the night?

I have only her letters to guide me; and, on the most important of all the questions which our correspondence can discuss, every one of those letters leaves me in the dark.

Does he treat her kindly? Is she happier now than she was when I parted with her on the wedding-day? All my letters have contained these two inquiries, put more or less directly, now in one form, and now in another; and all, on that one point only, have remained without reply, or have been answered as if my questions merely related to the state of her health. She informs me, over and over again, that she is perfectly well; that travelling agrees with her; that she is getting through the winter, for the first time in her life, without catching cold—but not a word can I find anywhere which tells me plainly that she is reconciled to her marriage, and that she can now look back to the twenty-second of December without any bitter feelings of repentance and regret. The name of her husband is only mentioned in her letters, as she might mention the name of a friend who was travelling with them, and who had undertaken to make all the arrangements for the journey. 'Sir Percival' has settled that we leave on such a day; 'Sir Percival' has decided that we travel by such a road. Sometimes she writes, 'Percival' only, but very seldom—in nine cases out of ten, she gives him his title.

I cannot find that his habits and opinions have changed and coloured hers in any single particular. The usual moral transformation which is insensibly wrought in a young, fresh, sensitive woman by her marriage, seems never to have taken place in Laura. She writes of her own thoughts and impressions, amid all the wonders she has seen, exactly as she might have written to some one else, if I had been travelling with her instead of her husband. I see no betrayal anywhere, of sympathy of any kind existing between them. Even when she wanders from the subject of her travels, and occupies herself with the prospects that await her in England, her speculations are busied with her future as my sister, and persistently neglect to notice her future as Sir Percival's wife. In all this, there is no under tone of complaint, to warn me that she is absolutely unhappy in her married life. The impression I have derived from our correspondence does not, thank God, lead me to any such distressing conclusion as that. I only see a sad torpor, an unchangeable indifference, when I turn my mind from her in the old character of a sister, and look at her, through the medium of her letters, in the new character of a wife. In other words, it is always Laura Fairlie who has been writing to me for the last six months, and never Lady Glyde.

The strange silence which she maintains on the subject of her husband's character and conduct, she preserves with almost equal resolution in the few references which her later letters contain to the name of her husband's bosom friend, Count Fosco.

For some unexplained reason, the Count and his wife appear to have changed their plans abruptly, at the end of last autumn, and to have gone to Vienna, instead of going to Rome, at which latter place Sir Percival had expected to find them when he left England. They only quitted Vienna in the spring, and travelled as far as the Tyrol to meet the bride and bridegroom on their homeward journey. Laura writes readily enough about the meeting with Madame Fosco, and assures me that she has found her aunt so much changed for the better—so much quieter and so much more sensible as a wife than she was as a single woman—that I shall hardly know her again when I see her here. But, on the subject of Count Fosco (who interests me infinitely more than his wife), Laura is provokingly circumspect and silent. She only says that he puzzles her, and that she will not tell me what her impression of him is, until I have seen him, and formed my own opinion first. This, to my mind, looks ill for the Count. Laura has preserved, far more perfectly than most people do in later life, the child's subtle faculty of knowing a friend by instinct; and, if I am right in assuming that her first impression of Count Fosco has not been favourable, I, for one, am in some danger of doubting and distrusting that illustrious foreigner before I have so much as set eyes on him. But, patience, patience; this uncertainty, and many uncertainties more, cannot last much longer. To-morrow will see all my doubts in a fair way of being cleared up, sooner or later.

Twelve o'clock has struck; and I have just come back to close these pages, after looking out at my open window.

It is a still, sultry, moonless night. The stars are dull and few. The trees that shut out the view on all sides look dimly black and solid in the distance, like a great wall of rock. I hear the croaking of frogs, faint and far off; and the echoes of the great clock hum in the airless calm, long after the strokes have ceased. I wonder how Blackwater Park will look in the daytime? I don't altogether like it by night.

12th.—A day of investigations and discoveries—a more interesting day, for many reasons, than I had ventured to anticipate.

I began my sight-seeing, of course, with the house.

The main body of the building is of the time of that highly-overrated woman, Queen Elizabeth. On the ground floor, there are two hugely-long galleries, with low ceilings, lying parallel with each other, and rendered additionally dark and dismal by hideous family portraits—every one of which I should like to burn. The rooms on the floor above the two galleries, are kept in tolerable repair, but are very seldom used. The civil housekeeper, who acted as my guide, offered to show me over them; but considerately added that she feared I should find them rather out of order. My respect for the integrity of my own petticoats and stockings, infinitely exceeds my respect for all the Elizabethan bedrooms in the kingdom; so I positively declined exploring the upper regions of dust and dirt at the risk of soiling my nice clean clothes. The housekeeper said, 'I am quite of your opinion, miss;' and appeared to think me the most sensible woman she had met with for a long time past.

So much, then, for the main building. Two wings are added, at either end of it. The half-ruined wing on the left (as you approach the house) was once a place of residence standing by itself, and was built in the fourteenth century. One of Sir Percival's maternal ancestors—I don't remember, and don't care, which—tacked on the main building, at right angles to it, in the aforesaid Queen Elizabeth's time. The housekeeper told me that the architecture of 'the old wing,' both outside and inside, was considered remarkably fine by good judges. On further investigation, I discovered that good judges could only exercise their abilities on Sir Percival's piece of antiquity by previously dismissing from their minds all fear of damp, darkness, and rats. Under these circumstances, I unhesitatingly acknowledged myself to be no judge at all; and suggested that we should treat 'the old wing' precisely as we had previously treated the Elizabethan bedrooms. Once more, the housekeeper said, 'I am quite of your opinion, miss;' and once more she looked at me, with undisguised admiration of my extraordinary common sense.

We went, next, to the wing on the right, which was built, by way of completing the wonderful architectural jumble at Blackwater Park, in the time of George the Second.

This is the habitable part of the house, which has been repaired and redecorated, inside, on Laura's account. My two rooms, and all the good bedrooms besides, are on the first floor; and the basement contains a drawing-room, a dining-room, a morning-room, a library, and a pretty little boudoir for Laura—all very nicely ornamented in the bright modern way, and all very elegantly furnished with the delightful modern luxuries. None of the rooms are anything like so large and airy as our rooms at Limmeridge; but they all look pleasant to live in. I was terribly afraid, from what I had heard of Blackwater Park, of fatiguing antique chairs, and dismal stained glass, and musty, frouzy hangings, and all the barbarous lumber which people born without a sense of comfort accumulate about them, in defiance of the consideration due to the convenience of their friends. It is an inexpressible relief to find that the nineteenth century has invaded this strange future home of mine, and has swept the dirty 'good old times' out of the way of our daily life.

I dawdled away the morning—part of the time in the rooms down stairs; and part, out of doors, in the great square which is formed by the three sides of the house, and by the lofty iron railings and gates which protect it in front. A large circular fishpond, with stone sides and an allegorical leaden monster in the middle, occupies the centre of the square. The pond itself is full of gold and silver fish, and is encircled by a broad belt of the softest turf I ever walked on. I loitered here, on the shady side, pleasantly enough, till luncheon time; and, after that, took my broad straw hat, and wandered out alone, in the warm lovely sunlight, to explore the grounds.

Daylight confirmed the impression which I had felt the night before, of there being too many trees at Blackwater. The house is stifled by them. They are, for the most part, young, and planted far too thickly. I suspect there must have been a ruinous cutting down of timber, all over the estate, before Sir Percival's time, and an angry anxiety, on the part of the next possessor, to fill up all the gaps as thickly and rapidly as possible. After looking about me, in front of the house, I observed a flower-garden on my left hand, and walked towards it, to see what I could discover in that direction.

On a nearer view, the garden proved to be small and poor and ill-kept. I left it behind me, opened a little gate in a ring fence, and found myself in a plantation of fir-trees.

A pretty, winding path, artificially made, led me on among the trees; and my north-country experience soon informed me that I was approaching sandy, heathy ground. After a walk of more than half a mile, I should think, among the firs, the path took a sharp turn; the trees abruptly ceased to appear on either side of me; and I found myself standing suddenly on the margin of a vast open space, and looking down at the Blackwater lake from which the house takes its name.

The ground, shelving away below me, was all sand, with a few little heathy hillocks to break the monotony of it in certain places. The lake itself had evidently once flowed to the spot on which I stood, and had been gradually wasted and dried up to less than a third of its former size. I saw its still, stagnant waters, a quarter of a mile away from me in the hollow, separated into pools and ponds, by twining reeds and rushes, and little knolls of earth. On the farther bank from me, the trees rose thickly again, and shut out the view, and cast their black shadows on the sluggish, shallow water. As I walked down to the lake, I saw that the ground on its farther side was damp and marshy, overgrown with rank grass and dismal willows. The water, which was clear enough on the open sandy side, where the sun shone, looked black and poisonous opposite to me, where it lay deeper under the shade of the spongy banks and the rank overhanging thickets and tangled trees. The frogs were croaking, and the rats were slipping in and out of the shadowy water, like live shadows themselves, as I got nearer to the marshy side of the lake. I saw here, lying half in and half out of the water, the rotten wreck of an old overturned boat, with a sickly spot of sunlight glimmering through a gap in the trees on its dry surface, and a snake basking in the midst of the spot, fantastically coiled, and treacherously still. Far and near, the view suggested the same dreary impressions of solitude and decay; and the glorious brightness of the summer sky overhead, seemed only to deepen and harden the gloom and barrenness of the wilderness on which it shone. I turned and retraced my steps to the high, heathy ground; directing them a little aside from my former path, towards a shabby old wooden shed, which stood on the outer skirt of the fir plantation, and which had hitherto been too unimportant to share my notice with the wide, wild prospect of the lake.

On approaching the shed, I found that it had once been a boat-house, and that an attempt had apparently been made to convert it afterwards into a sort of rude arbour, by placing inside it a fir-wood seat, a few stools, and a table. I entered the place, and sat down for a little while, to rest and get my breath again.

I had not been in the boat-house more than a minute, when it struck me that the sound of my own quick breathing was very strangely echoed by something beneath me. I listened intently for a moment, and heard a low, thick, sobbing breath that seemed to come from the ground under the seat which I was occupying. My nerves are not easily shaken by trifles; but, on this occasion, I started to my feet in a fright—called out—received no answer—summoned back my recreant courage—and looked under the seat.

There, crouched up in the farthest corner, lay the forlorn cause of my terror, in the shape of a poor little dog—a black and white spaniel. The creature moaned feebly when I looked at it and called to it, but never stirred. I moved away the seat and looked closer. The poor little dog's eyes were glazing fast, and there were spots of blood on its glossy white side. The misery of a weak, helpless, dumb creature is surely one of the saddest of all the mournful sights which this world can show. I lifted the poor dog in my arms as gently as I could, and contrived a sort of make-shift hammock for him to lie in, by gathering up the front of my dress all round him. In this way, I took the creature, as painlessly as possible, and as fast as possible, back to the house.

Finding no one in the hall, I went up at once to my own sitting-room, made a bed for the dog with one of my old shawls, and rang the bell. The largest and fattest of all possible housemaids answered it, in a state of cheerful stupidity which would have provoked the patience of a saint. The girl's fat, shapeless face actually stretched into a broad grin, at the sight of the wounded creature on the floor.

'What do you see there to laugh at?' I asked, as angrily as if she had been a servant of my own. 'Do you know whose dog it is?'

'No, miss, that I certainly don't.' She stopped, and looked down at the spaniel's injured side—brightened suddenly with the irradiation of a new idea—and, pointing to the wound with a chuckle of satisfaction, said, 'That's Baxter's doings, that is.'

I was so exasperated that I could have boxed her ears. 'Baxter?' I said. 'Who is the brute you call Baxter?'

The girl grinned again, more cheerfully than ever. 'Bless you, miss! Baxter's the keeper; and when he finds strange dogs hunting about, he takes and shoots 'em. It's keeper's dooty, miss. I think that dog will die. Here's where he's been shot, ain't it? That's Baxter's doings, that is. Baxter's doings, miss, and Baxter's dooty.'

I was almost wicked enough to wish that Baxter had shot the housemaid instead of the dog. Seeing that it was quite useless to expect this densely-impenetrable personage to give me any help in relieving the suffering creature at our feet, I told her to request the housekeeper's attendance, with my compliments. She went out exactly as she had come in, grinning from ear to ear. As the door closed on her, she said to herself, softly, 'It's Baxter's doings and Baxter's dooty—that's what it is.'

The housekeeper, a person of some education and intelligence, thoughtfully brought up-stairs with her some milk and some warm water. The instant she saw the dog on the floor, she started and changed colour.

'Why, Lord bless me,' cried the housekeeper, 'that must be Mrs Catherick's dog!'

'Whose?' I asked, in the utmost astonishment.

'Mrs Catherick's. You seem to know Mrs Catherick, Miss Halcombe?'

'Not personally. But I have heard of her. Does she live here? Has she had any news of her daughter?'

'No, Miss Halcombe. She came here to ask for news.'

'When?'

'Only yesterday. She said some one had reported that a stranger answering to the description of her daughter had been seen in our neighbourhood. No such report has reached us here; and no such report was known in the village, when I sent to make inquiries there on Mrs Catherick's account. She certainly brought this poor little dog with her when she came; and I saw it trot out after her when she went away. I suppose the creature strayed into the plantations, and got shot. Where did you find it, Miss Halcombe?'

'In the old shed that looks out on the lake.'

'Ah, yes, that is the plantation side, and the poor thing dragged itself, I suppose, to the nearest shelter, as dogs will, to die. If you can moisten its lips with the milk, Miss Halcombe, I will wash the clotted hair from the wound. I am very much afraid it is too late to do any good. However, we can but try.'

Mrs Catherick! The name still rang in my ears, as if the housekeeper had only that moment surprised me by uttering it. While we were attending to the dog, the words of Walter Hartright's caution to me returned to my memory. 'If ever Anne Catherick crosses your path, make better use of the opportunity, Miss Halcombe, than I made of it.' The finding of the wounded spaniel had led me already to the discovery of Mrs Catherick's visit to Blackwater Park; and that even might lead, in its turn, to something more.

I determined to make the most of the chance which was now offered to me, and to gain as much information as I could.

'Did you say that Mrs Catherick lived anywhere in this neighbourhood?' I asked.

'Oh, dear no,' said the housekeeper. 'She lives at Welmingham; quite at the other end of the county—five-and-twenty miles off at least.'

'I suppose you have known Mrs Catherick for some years?'

'On the contrary, Miss Halcombe; I never saw her before she came here, yesterday. I had heard of her, of course, because I had heard of Sir Percival's kindness in putting her daughter under medical care. Mrs Catherick is rather a strange person in her manners, but extremely respectable-looking. She seemed sorely put out, when she found that there was no foundation— none, at least, that any of *us* could discover—for the report of her daughter having been seen in this neighbourhood.'

'I am rather interested about Mrs Catherick,' I went on, continuing the conversation as long as possible. 'I wish I had arrived here soon enough to see her yesterday. Did she stay for any length of time?'

'Yes,' said the housekeeper, 'she stayed for some time. And I think she would have remained longer, if I had not been called away to speak to a strange gentleman—a gentleman who came to ask when Sir Percival was expected back. Mrs Catherick got up and left at once, when she heard the maid tell me what the visitor's errand was. She said to me, at parting, that there was no need to tell Sir Percival of her coming here. I thought that rather an odd remark to make, especially to a person in my responsible situation.'

I thought it an odd remark, too. Sir Percival had certainly led me to believe, at Limmeridge, that the most perfect confidence existed between himself and Mrs Catherick. If that was the case, why should she be anxious to have her visit at Blackwater Park kept a secret from him?

'Probably,' I said, seeing that the housekeeper expected me to give my opinion on Mrs Catherick's parting words; 'probably, she thought the announcement of her visit might vex Sir Percival to no purpose, by reminding him that her lost daughter was not found yet. Did she talk much on that subject?'

'Very little,' replied the housekeeper. 'She talked principally of Sir Percival, and asked a great many questions about where he had been travelling, and what sort of lady his new wife was. She seemed to be more soured and put out than distressed, by failing to find any traces of her daughter in these parts. "I give her up," were the last words she said that I can remember; "I give her up, ma'am, for lost." And from that, she passed at once to her questions about Lady Glyde; wanting to know if she was a handsome, amiable lady, comely and healthy and young——Ah, dear! I thought how it would end. Look, Miss Halcombe! the poor thing is out of its misery at last!'

The dog was dead. It had given a faint, sobbing cry, it had suffered an instant's convulsion of the limbs, just as those last words, 'comely and healthy and young,' dropped from the housekeeper's lips. The change had happened with startling suddenness—in one moment, the creature lay lifeless under our hands.

Eight o'clock. I have just returned from dining down stairs, in solitary state. The sunset is burning redly on the wilderness of trees that I see from my window; and I am poring over my journal again, to calm my impatience for the return of the travellers. They ought to have arrived, by my calculations, before this. How still and lonely the house is in the drowsy evening quiet! Oh, me! how many minutes more before I hear the carriage-wheels and run down stairs to find myself in Laura's arms?

The poor little dog! I wish my first day at Blackwater Park had not been associated with death—though it is only the death of a stray animal.

Welmingham—I see, on looking back through these private pages of mine, that Welmingham is the name of the place where Mrs Catherick lives. Her note is still in my possession, the note in answer to that letter about her unhappy daughter which Sir Percival obliged me to write. One of these days, when I can find a safe opportunity, I will take the note with me by way of introduction, and try what I can make of Mrs Catherick at a personal interview. I don't understand her wishing to conceal her visit to this place from Sir Percival's knowledge; and I don't feel half so sure, as the housekeeper seems to do, that her daughter Anne is not in the neighbour-hood, after all. What would Walter Hartright have said in this emergency? Poor, dear Hartright! I am beginning to feel the want of his honest advice and his willing help, already.

Surely, I heard something? Was it a bustle of footsteps below stairs? Yes! I hear the horses' feet; I hear the rolling of wheels. Away with my journal and my pen and ink! The travellers have returned—my darling Laura is home again at last!

JUNE 15TH.—The confusion of their arrival has had time to subside. Two days have elapsed since the return of the travellers; and that interval has sufficed to put the new machinery of our lives at Blackwater Park in fair working order. I may now return to my journal, with some little chance of being able to continue the entries in it as collectedly as usual.

I think I must begin by putting down an odd remark, which has suggested itself to me since Laura came back.

When two members of a family, or two intimate friends, are separated, and one goes abroad and one remains at home, the return of the relative or friend who has been travelling, always seems to place the relative or friend who has been staying at home at a painful disadvantage, when the two first meet. The sudden encounter of the new thoughts and new habits eagerly gained in the one case, with the old thoughts and old habits passively preserved in the other, seems, at first, to part the sympathies of the most loving relatives and the fondest friends, and to set a sudden strangeness, unexpected by both and uncontrollable by both, between them on either side. After the first happiness of my meeting with Laura was over, after we had sat down together, hand in hand, to recover breath enough and calmness enough to talk, I felt this strangeness instantly, and I could see that she felt it too. It has partially worn away, now that we have fallen back into most of our old habits; and it will probably disappear before long. But it has certainly had an influence over the first impressions that I have formed of her, now that we are living together again—for which reason only I have thought fit to mention it here.

She has found me unaltered; but I have found her changed.

Changed in person, and, in one respect, changed in character. I cannot absolutely say that she is less beautiful than she used to be: I can only say that she is less beautiful to *me*. Others, who do not look at her with my eyes and my recollections, would probably think her improved. There is more colour, and more decision and roundness of outline in her face than there used to be; and her figure seems more firmly set, and more sure and easy in all its movements than it was in her maiden days. But I miss something when I look at her—something that once belonged to the happy, innocent life of Laura Fairlie, and that I cannot find in Lady Glyde. There was, in the old times, a freshness, a softness, an ever-varying and yet ever-remaining tenderness of beauty in her face, the charm of which it is not possible to express in words—or, as poor Hartright used often to say, in painting, either. This is gone. I thought I saw the faint reflexion of it, for a moment, when she turned pale under the agitation of our sudden meeting, on the evening of her return; but it has never reappeared since. None of her letters had prepared me for a personal change in her. On the contrary, they had led me to expect that her marriage had left her, in appearance at least, quite unaltered. Perhaps, I read her letters wrongly, in the past, and am now reading her face wrongly, in the present? No matter! Whether her beauty has gained, or whether it has lost, in the last six months, the separation, either way, has made her own dear self more precious to me than ever—and that is one good result of her marriage, at any rate!

The second change, the change that I have observed in her character, has not surprised me, because I was prepared for it, in this case, by the tone of her letters. Now that she is at home again, I find her just as unwilling to enter into any details on the subject of her married life, as I had previously found her, all through the time of our separation, when we could only communicate with each other by writing. At the first approach I made to the forbidden topic, she put her hand on my lips, with a look and gesture which touchingly, almost painfully, recalled to my memory the days of her girlhood and the happy bygone time when there were no secrets between us.

'Whenever you and I are together, Marian,' she said, 'we shall both be happier and easier with one another, if we accept my married life for what it is, and say and think as little about it as possible. I would tell you everything, darling, about myself,' she went on, nervously buckling and unbuckling the ribbon round my waist, 'if my confidences could only end there. But they could not—they would lead me into confidences about my husband, too; and, now I am married, I think I had better avoid them, for his sake, and for your sake, and for mine. I don't say that they would distress you, or distress me—I wouldn't have you think that for the world. But—I want to be so happy, now I have got you back again; and I want you to be so happy too——' She broke off abruptly, and looked round the room, my own sitting-room, in which we were talking. 'Ah!' she cried, clapping her hands with a bright smile of recognition, 'another old friend found already! Your bookcase, Marian—your dear-little-shabby-old-satin-wood bookcase—how glad I am you brought it with you from Limmeridge! And the horrid, heavy, man's umbrella, that you always would walk out with when it rained! And, first and foremost of all, your own dear, dark, clever, gipsy-face, looking at me just as usual! It is so like home again to be here. How can we make it more like home still? I will put my father's portrait in your room instead of in mine—and I will keep all my little treasures from Limmeridge here—and we will pass hours and hours every day with these four friendly walls round us. Oh, Marian!' she said, suddenly seating herself on a footstool at my knees, and looking up earnestly in my face, 'promise you will never marry, and leave me. It is selfish to say so, but you are so much better off as a single woman—unless—unless you are very fond of your husband—but you won't be very fond of anybody but me, will you?' She stopped again; crossed my hands on my lap; and laid her face on them. 'Have you been writing many letters, and receiving many letters, lately?' she asked, in low, suddenly-altered tones. I understood what the question meant; but I thought it my duty not to encourage her by meeting her half way. 'Have you heard from him?' she went on, coaxing me to forgive the more direct appeal on which she now ventured, by kissing my hands, upon which her face still rested. 'Is he well and happy, and getting on in his profession? Has he recovered himself—and forgotten *me*?'

She should not have asked those questions. She should have remembered her own resolution, on the morning when Sir Percival held her to her marriage engagement, and when she resigned the book of Hartright's drawings into my hands for ever. But, ah me! where is the faultless human creature who can persevere in a good resolution, without sometimes failing and falling back? Where is the woman who has ever really torn from her heart the image that has been once fixed in it by a true love? Books tell us that such unearthly creatures have existed—but what does our own experience say in answer to books?

I made no attempt to remonstrate with her: perhaps, because I sincerely appreciated the fearless candour which let me see, what other women in her position might have had reasons for concealing even from their dearest friends—perhaps, because I felt, in my own heart and conscience, that, in her place I should have asked the same questions and had the same thoughts. All I could honestly do was to reply that I had not written to him or heard from him lately, and then to turn the conversation to less dangerous topics.

There had been much to sadden me in our interview—my first confidential interview with her since her return. The change which her marriage has produced in our relations towards each other, by placing a forbidden subject between us, for the first time in our lives; the melancholy conviction of the dearth of all warmth of feeling, of all close sympathy, between her husband and herself, which her own unwilling words now force on my mind; the distressing discovery that the influence of that ill-fated attachment still remains (no matter how innocently, how harmlessly) rooted as deeply as ever in her heart—all these are disclosures to sadden any woman who loves her as dearly, and feels for her as acutely, as I do.

There is only one consolation to set against them—a consolation that ought to comfort me, and that does comfort me. All the graces and gentlenesses of her character; all the frank affection of her nature; all the sweet, simple, womanly charms which used to make her the darling and the delight of every one who approached her, have come back to me with herself. Of my other impressions I am sometimes a little inclined to doubt. Of this last, best, happiest of all impressions, I grow more and more certain, every hour in the day.

Let me turn, now, from her to her travelling companions. Her husband must engage my attention first. What have I observed in Sir Percival, since his return, to improve my opinion of him?

I can hardly say. Small vexations and annoyances seem to have beset him since he came back; and no man, under those circumstances, is ever presented at his best. He looks, as I think, thinner than he was when he left England. His wearisome cough and his comfortless restlessness have certainly increased. His manner—at least, his manner towards me—is much more abrupt than it used to be. He greeted me, on the evening of his return, with little or nothing of the ceremony and civility of former times—no polite speeches of welcome—no appearance of extraordinary gratification at seeing me—nothing but a short shake of the hand, and a sharp 'How-d'ye-do, Miss Halcombe—glad to see you again.' He seemed to accept me as one of the necessary fixtures of Blackwater Park; to be satisfied at finding me established in my proper place; and then to pass me over altogether.

Most men show something of their dispositions in their own houses, which they have concealed elsewhere; and Sir Percival has already displayed a mania for order and regularity, which is quite a new revelation of him, so far as my previous knowledge of his character is concerned. If I take a book from the library and leave it on the table, he follows me, and puts it back again. If I rise from a chair, and let it remain where I have been sitting, he carefully restores it to its proper place against the wall. He picks up stray flower-blossoms from the carpet, and mutters to himself as discontentedly as if they were hot cinders burning holes in it; and he storms at the servants, if there is a crease in the tablecloth, or a knife missing from its place at the dinner-table, as fiercely as if they had personally insulted him.

I have already referred to the small annoyances which appear to have troubled him since his return. Much of the alteration for the worse which I have noticed in him, may be due to these. I try to persuade myself that it is so, because I am anxious not to be disheartened already about the future. It is certainly trying to any man's temper to be met by a vexation the moment he sets foot in his own house again, after a long absence; and this annoying circumstance did really happen to Sir Percival in my presence.

On the evening of their arrival, the housekeeper followed me into the hall to receive her master and mistress and their guests. The instant he saw her, Sir Percival asked if any one had called lately. The housekeeper mentioned to him, in reply, what she had previously mentioned to me, the visit of the strange gentleman to make inquiries about the time of her master's return. He asked immediately for the gentleman's name. No name had been left. The gentleman's business? No business had been mentioned. What was the gentleman like? The housekeeper tried to describe him; but failed to distinguish the nameless visitor by any personal peculiarity which her master could recognise. Sir Percival frowned, stamped angrily on the floor, and walked on into the house, taking no notice of anybody. Why he should have been so discomposed by a trifle I cannot say—but he was seriously discomposed, beyond all doubt.

Upon the whole, it will be best, perhaps, if I abstain from forming a decisive opinion of his manners, language, and conduct in his own house, until time has enabled him to shake off the anxieties, whatever they may be, which now evidently trouble his mind in secret. I will turn over to a new page; and my pen shall let Laura's husband alone for the present.

The two guests—the Count and Countess Fosco—come next in my catalogue. I will dispose of the Countess first, so as to have done with the woman as soon as possible.

Laura was certainly not chargeable with any exaggeration, in writing me word that I should hardly recognise her aunt again, when we met. Never before have I beheld such a change produced in a woman by her marriage as has been produced in Madame Fosco.

As Eleanor Fairlie (aged seven-and-thirty), she was always talking pretentious nonsense, and always worrying the unfortunate men with every small exaction which a vain and foolish woman can impose on long-suffering male humanity. As Madame Fosco (aged three-and-forty), she sits for hours together without saying a word, frozen up in the strangest manner in herself. The hideously ridiculous love-locks which used to hang on either side of her face, are now replaced by stiff little rows of very short curls, of the sort that one sees in old-fashioned wigs. A plain, matronly cap covers her head, and makes her look, for the first time in her life, since I remember her, like a decent woman. Nobody (putting her husband out of the question, of course) now sees in her, what everybody once saw—I mean the structure of the female skeleton, in the upper regions of the collar-bones and the shoulder-blades. Clad in quiet black or grey gowns, made high round the throat—dresses that she would have laughed at, or screamed at, as the whim of the moment inclined her, in her maiden days—she sits speechless in corners; her dry white hands (so dry that the pores of her skin look chalky) incessantly engaged, either in monotonous embroidery work, or in rolling up endless little cigarettes for the Count's own particular smoking. On the few occasions, when her cold blue eyes are off her work, they are generally turned on her husband, with the look of mute submissive inquiry which we are all familiar with in the eyes of a faithful dog. The only approach to an inward thaw which I have yet detected under her outer covering of icy constraint, has betrayed itself, once or twice, in the form of a suppressed tigerish jealousy of any woman in the house (the maids included) to whom the Count speaks, or on whom he looks, with anything approaching to special interest or attention. Except in this one particular, she is always, morning, noon, and night, indoors and out, fair weather or foul, as cold as a statue, and as impenetrable as the stone out of which it is cut. For the common purposes of society the extraordinary change thus produced in her, is, beyond all doubt, a change for the better, seeing that it has transformed her into a civil, silent, unobtrusive woman, who is never in the way. How far she is really reformed or deteriorated in her secret self, is another question. I have once or twice seen sudden changes of expression on her pinched lips, and heard sudden inflexions of tone in her calm voice, which have led me to suspect that her present state of suppression may have sealed up something dangerous in her nature, which used to evaporate harmlessly in the freedom of her former life. It is quite possible that I may be altogether wrong in this idea. My own impression, however, is, that I am right. Time will show.

And the magician who has wrought this wonderful transformation—the foreign husband who has tamed this once wayward Englishwoman till her own relations hardly know her again—the Count himself? What of the Count?

This, in two words: He looks like a man who could tame anything. If he had married a tigress, instead of a woman, he would have tamed the tigress. If he had married *me*, I should have made his cigarettes as his wife does—I should have held my tongue when he looked at me, as she holds hers.

I am almost afraid to confess it, even to these secret pages. The man has interested me, has attracted me, has forced me to like him. In two short days, he has made his way straight into my favourable estimation—and how he has worked the miracle, is more than I can tell.

It absolutely startles me, now he is in my mind, to find how plainly I see him!—how much more plainly than I see Sir Percival, or Mr Fairlie, or Walter Hartright, or any other absent person of whom I think, with the one exception of Laura herself! I can hear his voice, as if he was speaking at this moment. I know what his conversation was yesterday, as well as if I was hearing it now. How am I to describe him? There are peculiarities in his personal appearance, his habits, and his amusements, which I should blame in the boldest terms, or ridicule in the most merciless manner, if I had seen them in another man. What is it that makes me unable to blame them, or to ridicule them, in *him*?

For example, he is immensely fat. Before this time, I have always especially disliked corpulent humanity. I have always maintained that the popular notion of connecting excessive grossness of size and excessive good-humour as inseparable allies, was equivalent to declaring, either that no people but amiable people ever get fat, or that the accidental addition of so many pounds of flesh has a directly-favourable influence over the disposition of the person on whose body they accumulate. I have invariably combated both these absurd assertions by quoting examples of fat people who were as mean, vicious, and cruel, as the leanest and the worst of their neighbours. I have asked whether Henry the Eighth was an amiable character? whether Pope Alexander the Sixth was a good man? Whether Mr Murderer and Mrs Murderess Manning were not both unusually stout people? Whether hired nurses, proverbially as cruel a set of women as are to be found in all England, were not, for the most part, also as fat a set of women as are to be found in all England?—and so on, through dozens of other examples, modern and ancient, native and foreign, high and low. Holding these strong opinions on the subject with might and main, as I do at this moment, here, nevertheless, is Count Fosco, as fat as Henry the Eighth himself, established in my favour, at one day's notice, without let or hindrance from his own odious corpulence. Marvellous indeed!

Is it his face that has recommended him?

It may be his face. He is a most remarkable likeness, on a large scale, of the Great Napoleon. His features have Napoleon's magnificent regularity: his expression recals the grandly calm, immovable power of the Great

Soldier's face. This striking resemblance certainly impressed me, to begin with; but there is something in him besides the resemblance, which has impressed me more. I think the influence I am now trying to find, is in his eyes. They are the most unfathomable grey eyes I ever saw; and they have at times a cold, clear, beautiful, irresistible glitter in them, which forces me to look at him, and yet causes me sensations, when I do look, which I would rather not feel. Other parts of his face and head have their strange peculiarities. His complexion, for instance, has a singular sallow-fairness, so much at variance with the dark brown colour of his hair, that I suspect the hair of being a wig; and his face, closely shaven all over, is smoother and freer from all marks and wrinkles than mine, though (according to Sir Percival's account of him) he is close on sixty years of age. But these are not the prominent personal characteristics which distinguish him, to my mind, from all the other men I have ever seen. The marked peculiarity which singles him out from the rank and file of humanity, lies entirely, so far as I can tell at present, in the extraordinary expression and extraordinary power of his eyes.

His manner, and his command of our language, may also have assisted him, in some degree, to establish himself in my good opinion. He has that quiet deference, that look of pleased, attentive interest, in listening to a woman, and that secret gentleness in his voice, in speaking to a woman, which, say what we may, we can none of us resist. Here, too, his unusual command of the English language necessarily helps him. I had often heard of the extraordinary aptitude which many Italians show in mastering our strong, hard Northern speech; but, until I saw Count Fosco, I had never supposed it possible that any foreigner could have spoken English as he speaks it. There are times when it is almost impossible to detect, by his accent, that he is not a countryman of our own; and, as for fluency, there are very few born Englishmen who can talk with as few stoppages and repetitions as the Count. He may construct his sentences, more or less, in the foreign way; but I have never yet heard him use a wrong expression, or hesitate for a moment in his choice of a word.

All the smallest characteristics of this strange man have something strikingly original and perplexingly contradictory in them. Fat as he is, and old as he is, his movements are astonishingly light and easy. He is as noiseless in a room as any of us women; and, more than that, with all his look of unmistakable mental firmness and power, he is as nervously sensitive as the weakest of us. He starts at chance noises as inveterately as Laura herself. He winced and shuddered yesterday, when Sir Percival beat one of the spaniels, so that I felt ashamed of my own want of tenderness and sensibility by comparison with the Count.

The relation of this last incident reminds me of one of his most curious peculiarities, which I have not yet mentioned—his extraordinary fondness for pet animals.

Some of these he has left on the Continent, but he has brought with him to this house a cockatoo, two canary-birds, and a whole family of white mice. He attends to all the necessities of these strange favourites himself, and he has taught the creatures to be surprisingly fond of him, and familiar with him. The cockatoo, a most vicious and treacherous bird towards every one else, absolutely seems to love him. When he lets it out of its cage, it hops on to his knee, and claws its way up his great big body, and rubs its top-knot against his sallow double chin in the most caressing manner imaginable. He has only to set the doors of the canaries' cages open, and to call them; and the pretty little cleverly-trained creatures perch fearlessly on his hand, mount his fat outstretched fingers one by one, when he tells them to 'go up-stairs,' and sing together as if they would burst their throats with delight, when they get to the top finger. His white mice live in a little pagoda of gaily-painted wirework, designed and made by himself. They are almost as tame as the canaries, and they are perpetually let out, like the canaries. They crawl all over him, popping in and out of his waistcoat, and sitting in couples, white as snow, on his capacious shoulders. He seems to be even fonder of his mice than of his other pets, smiles at them, and kisses them, and calls them by all sorts of endearing names. If it be possible to suppose an Englishman with any taste for such childish interests and amusements as these, that Englishman would certainly feel rather ashamed of them, and would be anxious to apologise for them, in the company of grown-up people. But the Count, apparently, sees nothing ridiculous in the amazing contrast between his colossal self and his frail little pets. He would blandly kiss his white mice, and twitter to his canary-birds amid an assembly of English fox-hunters, and would only pity them as barbarians when they were all laughing their loudest at him.

It seems hardly credible, while I am writing it down, but it is certainly true, that this same man, who has all the fondness of an old maid for his cockatoo, and all the small dexterities of an organ-boy in managing his white mice, can talk, when anything happens to rouse him, with a daring independence of thought, a knowledge of books in every language, and an experience of society in half the capitals of Europe, which would make him the prominent personage of any assembly in the civilised world. This trainer of canary-birds, this architect of a pagoda for white mice, is (as Sir Percival himself has told me) one of the first experimental chemists living, and has discovered, among other wonderful inventions, a means of petrifying the body after death, so as to preserve it, as hard as marble, to the end of time. This fat, indolent, elderly man, whose nerves are so finely strung that he starts at chance noises, and winces when he sees a house-spaniel get a whipping, went into the stable-yard, on the morning after his arrival, and put his hand on the head of a chained bloodhound—a beast so savage that the very groom who feeds him keeps out of his reach. His wife and I were present, and I shall not soon forget the scene that followed, short as it was.

'Mind that dog, sir,' said the groom; 'he flies at everybody!' 'He does that, my friend,' replied the Count, quietly, 'because everybody is afraid of him. Let us see if he flies at *me*.' And he laid his plump, yellow-white fingers, on which the canary-birds had been perching ten minutes before, upon the formidable brute's head; and looked him straight in the eyes. 'You big dogs are all cowards,' he said, addressing the animal contemptuously, with his face and the dog's within an inch of each other. 'You would kill a poor cat, you infernal coward. You would fly at a starving beggar, you infernal coward. Anything that you can surprise unawares—anything that is afraid of your big body, and your wicked white teeth, and your slobbering, bloodthirsty mouth, is the thing you like to fly at. You could throttle me at this moment, you mean, miserable bully; and you daren't so much as look me in the face, because I'm not afraid of you. Will you think better of it, and try your teeth in my fat neck? Bah! not you!' He turned away, laughing at the astonishment of the men in the yard; and the dog crept back meekly to his kennel. 'Ah! my nice waistcoat!' he said, pathetically. 'I am sorry I came here. Some of that brute's slobber has got on my pretty clean waistcoat.' Those words express another of his incomprehensible oddities. He is as fond of fine clothes as the veriest fool in existence; and has appeared in four magnificent waistcoats, already—all of light garish colours, and all immensely large even for him—in the two days of his residence at Black-water Park.

His tact and cleverness in small things are quite as noticeable as the singular inconsistencies in his character, and the childish triviality of his ordinary tastes and pursuits.

I can see already that he means to live on excellent terms with all of us, during the period of his sojourn in this place. He has evidently discovered that Laura secretly dislikes him (she confessed as much to me, when I pressed her on the subject)—but he has also found out that she is extravagantly fond of flowers. Whenever she wants a nosegay, he has got one to give her, gathered and arranged by himself; and, greatly to my amusement, he is always cunningly provided with a duplicate, composed of exactly the same flowers, grouped in exactly the same way, to appease his icily jealous wife, before she can so much as think herself aggrieved. His management of the Countess (in public) is a sight to see. He bows to her; he habitually addresses her as 'my angel;' he carries his canaries to pay her little visits on his fingers, and to sing to her; he kisses her hand, when she gives him his cigarettes; he presents her with sugar-plums, in return, which he puts into her mouth playfully, from a box in his pocket. The rod of iron with which he rules her never appears in company—it is a private rod, and is always kept up-stairs.

His method of recommending himself to *me*, is entirely different. He flatters my vanity, by talking to me as seriously and sensibly as if I was a man. Yes! I can find him out when I am away from him; I know he flatters my vanity, when I think of him up here, in my own room—and yet, when I go down stairs, and get into his company again, he will blind me again, and I shall be flattered again, just as if I had never found him out at all! He can manage me, as he manages his wife and Laura, as he managed the blood-hound in the stable-yard, as he manages Sir Percival himself, every hour in the day. 'My good Percival! how I like your rough English humour!'—'My good Percival! how I enjoy your solid English sense!' He puts the rudest remarks Sir Percival can make on his effeminate tastes and amusements quietly away from him in that manner—always calling the Baronet by his Christian name; smiling at him with the calmest superiority; patting him on the shoulder; and bearing with him benignantly, as a good-humoured father bears with a wayward son.

The interest which I really cannot help feeling in this strangely original man, has led me to question Sir Percival about his past life.

Sir Percival either knows little, or will tell me little, about it. He and the Count first met, many years ago, at Rome, under the dangerous circumstances to which I have alluded elsewhere. Since that time, they have been perpetually together in London, in Paris, and in Vienna—but never in Italy again; the Count having, oddly enough, not crossed the frontiers of his native country for years past. Perhaps, he has been made the victim of some political persecution? At all events, he seems to be patriotically anxious not to lose sight of any of his own countrymen who may happen to be in England. On the evening of his arrival, he asked how far we were from the nearest town, and whether we knew of any Italian gentlemen who might happen to be settled there. He is certainly in correspondence with people on the Continent, for his letters have all sorts of odd stamps on them; and I saw one for him, this morning, waiting in his place at the breakfast-table, with a huge official-looking seal on it. Perhaps he is in correspondence with his government? And yet, that is hardly to be reconciled, either, with my other idea that he may be a political exile.

How much I seem to have written about Count Fosco! And what does it all amount to?—as poor, dear Mr Gilmore would ask, in his impenetrable business-like way. I can only repeat that I do assuredly feel, even on this short acquaintance, a strange, half-willing, half-unwilling liking for the Count. He seems to have established over me the same sort of ascendancy which he has evidently gained over Sir Percival. Free, and even rude, as he may occasionally be in his manner towards his fat friend, Sir Percival is nevertheless afraid, as I can plainly see, of giving any serious offence to the Count. I wonder whether I am afraid, too? I certainly never saw a man, in all my experience, whom I should be so sorry to have for an enemy. Is this because I like him, or because I am afraid of him? *Chi sa?*—as Count Fosco might say in his own language. Who knows?

16th.—Something to chronicle, to-day, besides my own ideas and impressions. A visitor has arrived—quite unknown to Laura and to me; and, apparently, quite unexpected by Sir Percival.

We were all at lunch, in the room with the new French windows that open into the verandah; and the Count (who devours pastry as I have never yet seen it devoured by any human beings but girls at boarding-schools) had just amused us by asking gravely for his fourth tart—when the servant entered, to announce the visitor.

'Mr Merriman has just come, Sir Percival, and wishes to see you immediately.'

Sir Percival started, and looked at the man, with an expression of angry alarm.

'Mr Merriman?' he repeated, as if he thought his own ears must have deceived him.

'Yes, Sir Percival: Mr Merriman, from London.'

'Where is he?'

'In the library, Sir Percival.'

He left the table the instant the last answer was given; and hurried out of the room without saying a word to any of us.

'Who is Mr Merriman?' asked Laura, appealing to me.

'I have not the least idea,' was all I could say in reply.

The Count had finished his fourth tart, and had gone to a side-table to look after his vicious cockatoo. He turned round to us, with the bird perched on his shoulder.

'Mr Merriman is Sir Percival's solicitor,' he said, quietly.

Sir Percival's solicitor. It was a perfectly straightforward answer to Laura's question; and yet, under the circumstances, it was not satisfactory. If Mr Merriman had been specially sent for by his client, there would have been nothing very wonderful in his leaving town to obey the summons. But when a lawyer travels from London to Hampshire, without being sent for, and when his arrival at a gentleman's house seriously startles the gentleman himself, it may be safely taken for granted that the legal visitor is the bearer of some very important and very unexpected news—news which may be either very good or very bad, but which cannot, in either case, be of the common, every-day kind.

Laura and I sat silent at the table, for a quarter of an hour or more, wondering uneasily what had happened, and waiting for the chance of Sir Percival's speedy return. There were no signs of his return; and we rose to leave the room.

The Count, attentive as usual, advanced from the corner in which he had been feeding his cockatoo, with the bird still perched on his shoulder, and opened the door for us. Laura and Madame Fosco went out first. Just as I was on the point of following them, he made a sign with his hand, and spoke to me, before I passed him, in the oddest manner.

'Yes,' he said; quietly answering the unexpressed idea at that moment in my mind, as if I had plainly confided it to him in so many words—'yes, Miss Halcombe; something *has* happened.'

I was on the point of answering, 'I never said so.' But the vicious cockatoo ruffled his clipped wings, and gave a screech that set all my nerves on edge in an instant, and made me only too glad to get out of the room.

I joined Laura at the foot of the stairs. The thought in her mind was the same as the thought in mine, which Count Fosco had surprised—and, when she spoke, her words were almost the echo of his. She, too, said to me, secretly, that she was afraid something had happened.

I HAVE a few lines more to add to this day's entry before I go to bed to-night.

About two hours after Sir Percival rose from the luncheon-table to receive his solicitor, Mr Merriman, in the library, I left my room, alone, to take a walk in the plantations. Just as I was at the end of the landing, the library door opened, and the two gentlemen came out. Thinking it best not to disturb them by appearing on the stairs, I resolved to defer going down till they had crossed the hall. Although they spoke to each other in guarded tones, their words were pronounced with sufficient distinctness of utterance to reach my ears.

'Make your mind easy, Sir Percival,' I heard the lawyer say. 'It all rests with Lady Glyde.'

I had turned to go back to my own room, for a minute or two; but the sound of Laura's name, on the lips of a stranger, stopped me instantly. I dare say it was very wrong and very discreditable to listen—but where is the woman, in the whole range of our sex, who can regulate her actions by the abstract principles of honour, when those principles point one way, and when her affections, and the interests which grow out of them, point the other?

I listened; and, under similar circumstances, I would listen again—yes! with my ear at the keyhole, if I could not possible manage it in any other way.

'You quite understand, Sir Percival?' the lawyer went on. 'Lady Glyde is to sign her name in the presence of a witness—or of two witnesses, if you wish to be particularly careful—and is then to put her finger on the seal, and say, "I deliver this as my act and deed." If that is done in a week's time, the arrangement will be perfectly successful, and the anxiety will be all over. If not——'

'What do you mean by "if not?"' asked Sir Percival, angrily. 'If the thing *must* be done, it *shall* be done. I promise you that, Merriman.'

'Just so, Sir Percival—just so; but there are two alternatives in all transactions; and we lawyers like to look both of them in the face boldly. If through any extraordinary circumstance the arrangement should *not* be made, I think I may be able to get the parties to accept bills at three months. But how the money is to be raised when the bills fall due——'

'Damn the bills! The money is only to be got in one way; and in that way, I tell you again, it *shall* be got. Take a glass of wine, Merriman, before you go.'

'Much obliged, Sir Percival; I have not a moment to lose if I am to catch the up train. You will let me know as soon as the arrangement is complete? and you will not forget the caution I recommended——'

'Of course I won't. There's the dog-cart at the door for you. My groom will get you to the station in no time. Benjamin, drive like mad! Jump in. If Mr Merriman misses the train, you lose your place. Hold fast, Merriman, and if you are upset, trust to the devil to save his own.' With that parting benediction, the Baronet turned about, and walked back to the library.

I had not heard much; but the little that had reached my ears was enough to make me feel uneasy. The 'something' that 'had happened,' was but too plainly a serious money-embarrassment; and Sir Percival's relief from it depended upon Laura. The prospect of seeing her involved in her husband's secret difficulties filled me with dismay, exaggerated, no doubt, by my ignorance of business and my settled distrust of Sir Percival. Instead of going out, as I proposed, I went back immediately to Laura's room to tell her what I had heard.

She received my bad news so composedly as to surprise me. She evidently knows more of her husband's character and her husband's embarrassments than I have suspected up to this time.

'I feared as much,' she said, 'when I heard of that strange gentleman who called, and declined to leave his name.'

'Who do you think the gentleman was, then?' I asked.

'Some person who has heavy claims on Sir Percival,' she answered; 'and who has been the cause of Mr Merriman's visit here to-day.'

'Do you know anything about those claims?'

'No; I know no particulars.'

'You will sign nothing, Laura, without first looking at it?'

'Certainly not, Marian. Whatever I can harmlessly and honestly do to help him I will do—for the sake of making your life and mine, love, as easy and as happy as possible. But I will do nothing, ignorantly, which we might, one day, have reason to feel ashamed of. Let us say no more about it, now. You have got your hat on—suppose we go and dream away the afternoon in the grounds?'

On leaving the house, we directed our steps to the nearest shade.

As we passed an open space among the trees in front of the house, there was Count Fosco, slowly walking backwards and forwards on the grass, sunning himself in the full blaze of the hot June afternoon. He had a broad straw hat on, with a violet-coloured ribbon round it. A blue blouse, with profuse white fancy-work over the bosom, covered his prodigious body, and was girt about the place where his waist might once have been, with a broad scarlet leather belt. Nankeen trousers, displaying more white fancy-work over the ankles, and purple morocco slippers adorned his lower extremities. He was singing Figaro's famous song in the Barber of Seville, with that crisply-fluent vocalisation which is never heard from any other than an Italian throat; accompanying himself on the concertina, which he played with ecstatic throwings-up of his arms, and graceful twistings, and turnings of his head, like a fat St Cecilia masquerading in male attire. 'Figaro quà! Figaro là! Figaro sù! Figaro giù!' sang the Count, jauntily tossing up the concertina at arms' length, and bowing to us, on one side of the instrument, with the airy grace and elegance of Figaro himself at twenty years of age.

'Take my word for it, Laura, that man knows something of Sir Percival's embarrassments,' I said, as we returned the Count's salutation from a safe distance.

'What makes you think that?' she asked.

'How should he have known, otherwise, that Mr Merriman was Sir Percival's solicitor?' I rejoined. 'Besides, when I followed you out of the luncheon-room, he told me, without a single word of inquiry on my part, that something had happened. Depend upon it, he knows more than we do.'

'Don't ask him any questions, if he does. Don't take him into our confidence!'

'You seem to dislike him, Laura, in a very determined manner. What has he said or done to justify you?'

'Nothing, Marian. On the contrary, he was all kindness and attention on our journey home, and he several times checked Sir Percival's outbreaks of temper, in the most considerate manner towards *me*. Perhaps, I dislike him because he has so much more power over my husband than I have. Perhaps it hurts my pride to be under any obligations to his interference. All I know is that I *do* dislike him.'

The rest of the day and the evening passed quietly enough. The Count and I played at chess. For the first two games he politely allowed me to conquer him; and then, when he saw that I had found him out, begged my pardon, and, at the third game, checkmated me in ten minutes. Sir Percival never once referred, all through the evening, to the lawyer's visit. But either that event, or something else, had produced a singular alteration for the better in him. He was as polite and agreeable to all of us, as he used to be in the days of his probation at Limmeridge; and he was so amazingly attentive and kind to his wife, that even icy Madame Fosco was roused into looking at him with a grave surprise. What does this mean? I think I can guess; I am afraid Laura can guess; and I am sure Count Fosco knows. I caught Sir Percival looking at him for approval more than once in the course of the evening.

17th.—A day of events. I most fervently hope I may not have to add, a day of disasters as well.

Sir Percival was as silent at breakfast as he had been the evening before, on the subject of the mysterious 'arrangement' (as the lawyer called it), which is hanging over our heads. An hour afterwards, however, he suddenly entered the morning-room, where his wife and I were waiting, with our hats on, for Madame Fosco to join us; and inquired for the Count.

'We expect to see him here directly,' I said.

'The fact is,' Sir Percival went on, walking nervously about the room, 'I want Fosco and his wife in the library, for a mere business formality; and I want you there, Laura, for a minute, too.' He stopped, and appeared to notice, for the first time, that we were in our walking costume. 'Have you just come in?' he asked, 'or were you just going out?'

'We were all thinking of going to the lake this morning,' said Laura. 'But if you have any other arrangement to propose——'

'No, no,' he answered, hastily. 'My arrangement can wait. After lunch will do as well for it, as after breakfast. All going to the lake, eh? A good idea. Let's have an idle morning; I'll be one of the party.'

There was no mistaking his manner, even if it had been possible to mistake the uncharacteristic readiness which his words expressed, to submit his own plans and projects to the convenience of others. He was evidently relieved at finding any excuse for delaying the business formality in the library, to which his own words had referred. My heart sank within me, as I drew the inevitable inference.

The Count and his wife joined us, at that moment. The lady had her husband's embroidered tobacco-pouch, and her store of paper in her hand, for the manufacture of the eternal cigarettes. The gentleman, dressed, as usual, in his blouse and straw hat, carried the gay little pagoda-cage, with his darling white mice in it, and smiled on them, and on us, with a bland amiability which it was impossible to resist.

'With your kind permission,' said the Count, 'I will take my small family, here—my poor-little-harmless-pretty-Mouseys, out for an airing along with us. There are dogs about the house, and shall I leave my forlorn white children at the mercies of the dogs? Ah, never!'

He chirruped paternally at his small white children through the bars of the pagoda; and we all left the house for the lake.

In the plantation, Sir Percival strayed away from us. It seems to be part of his restless disposition always to separate himself from his companions on these occasions, and always to occupy himself, when he is alone, in cutting new walking-sticks for his own use. The mere act of cutting and lopping, at hazard, appears to please him. He has filled the house with walking-sticks of his own making, not one of which he ever takes up for a second time. When they have been once used, his interest in them is all exhausted, and he thinks of nothing but going on, and making more.

At the old boat-house, he joined us again. I will put down the conversation that ensued, when we were all settled in our places, exactly as it passed. It is an important conversation, so far as I am concerned, for it has seriously disposed me to distrust the influence which Count Fosco has exercised over my thoughts and feelings, and to resist it, for the future, as resolutely as I can.

The boat-house was large enough to hold us all; but Sir Percival remained outside, trimming the last new stick with his pocket-axe. We three women found plenty of room on the large seat. Laura took her work, and Madame Fosco began her cigarettes. I, as usual, had nothing to do. My hands always were, and always will be, as awkward as a man's. The Count good-humouredly took a stool, many sizes too small for him, and balanced himself on it with his back against the side of the shed, which creaked and groaned under his weight. He put the pagoda-cage on his lap, and let out the mice to crawl over him as usual. They are pretty, innocent-looking little creatures; but the sight of them creeping about a man's body is, for some reason, not pleasant to me. It excites a strange, responsive creeping in my own nerves; and suggests hideous ideas of men dying in prison, with the crawling creatures of the dungeon preying on them undisturbed.

The morning was windy and cloudy; and the rapid alternations of shadow and sunlight over the waste of the lake, made the view look doubly wild, weird, and gloomy.

'Some people call that picturesque,' said Sir Percival, pointing over the wide prospect with his half-finished walking-stick. 'I call it a blot on a gentleman's property. In my great- grandfather's time, the lake flowed to this place. Look at it now! It is not four feet deep anywhere, and it is all puddles and pools. I wish I could afford to drain it, and plant it all over. My bailiff (a superstitious idiot) says he is quite sure the lake has a curse on it, like the Dead Sea. What do you think, Fosco? It looks just the place for a murder, doesn't it?'

'My good Percival!' remonstrated the Count. 'What is your solid English sense thinking of? The water is too shallow to hide the body; and there is sand everywhere to print off the murderer's footsteps. It is, upon the whole, the very worst place for a murder that I ever set my eyes on.'

'Humbug!' said Sir Percival, cutting away fiercely at his stick. 'You know what I mean. The dreary scenery—the lonely situation. If you choose to understand me, you can—if you don't choose, I am not going to trouble myself to explain my meaning.'

'And why not,' asked the Count, 'when your meaning can be explained by anybody in two words? If a fool was going to commit a murder, your lake is the first place he would choose for it. If a wise man was going to commit a murder, your lake is the last place he would choose for it. Is that your meaning? If it is, there is your explanation for you, ready made. Take it, Percival, with your good Fosco's blessing.'

Laura looked at the Count, with her dislike for him appearing a little too plainly in her face. He was so busy with his mice that he did not notice her.

'I am sorry to hear the lake-view connected with anything so horrible as the idea of murder,' she said. 'And if Count Fosco must divide murderers into classes, I think he has been very unfortunate in his choice of expressions. To describe them as fools only, seems like treating them with an indulgence to which they have no claim. And to describe them as wise men, sounds to me like a downright contradiction in terms. I have always heard that truly wise men are truly good men, and have a horror of crime.'

'My dear lady,' said the Count, 'those are admirable sentiments; and I have seen them stated at the tops of copy-books.' He lifted one of the white mice in the palm of his hand, and spoke to it in his whimsical way. 'My pretty little smooth white rascal,' he said, 'here is a moral lesson for you. A truly wise Mouse is a truly good Mouse. Mention that, if you please, to your companions, and never gnaw at the bars of your cage again as long as you live.'

'It is easy to turn everything into ridicule,' said Laura, resolutely; 'but you will not find it quite so easy, Count Fosco, to give me an instance of a wise man who has been a great criminal.'

The Count shrugged his huge shoulders, and smiled on Laura in the friendliest manner.

'Most true!' he said. 'The fool's crime is the crime that is found out; and the wise man's crime is the crime that is *not* found out. If I could give you an instance, it would not be the instance of a wise man. Dear Lady Glyde, your sound English common sense has been too much for me. It is checkmate for *me* this time, Miss Halcombe—ha?'

'Stand to your guns, Laura,' sneered Sir Percival, who had been listening in his place at the door. 'Tell him, next, that crimes cause their own detection. There's another bit of copy-book morality for you, Fosco. Crimes cause their own detection. What infernal humbug!'

'I believe it to be true,' said Laura, quietly.

Sir Percival burst out laughing; so violently, so outrageously, that he quite startled us all—the Count more than any of us.

'I believe it, too,' I said, coming to Laura's rescue.

Sir Percival, who had been unaccountably amused at his wife's remark, was, just as unaccountably, irritated by mine. He struck the new stick savagely on the sand, and walked away from us.

'Poor, dear Percival!' cried Count Fosco, looking after him gaily; 'he is the victim of English spleen. But, my dear Miss Halcombe, my dear Lady

Glyde, do you really believe that crimes cause their own detection? And you, my angel,' he continued, turning to his wife, who had not uttered a word yet, 'do you think so too?'

'I wait to be instructed,' replied the Countess, in tones of freezing reproof, intended for Laura and me, 'before I venture on giving my opinion in the presence of well-informed men.'

'Do you, indeed?' I said. 'I remember the time, Countess, when you advocated the Rights of Women—and freedom of female opinion was one of them.'

'What is your view of the subject, Count?' asked Madame Fosco, calmly proceeding with her cigarettes, and not taking the least notice of me.

The Count stroked one of his white mice reflectively with his chubby little-finger before he answered.

'It is truly wonderful,' he said, 'how easily Society can console itself for the worst of its short-comings with a little bit of claptrap. The machinery it has set up for the detection of crime is miserably ineffective—and yet only invent a moral epigram, saying that it works well, and you blind everybody to its blunders, from that moment. Crimes cause their own detection, do they? And murder will out (another moral epigram), will it? Ask Coroners who sit at inquests in large towns if that is true, Lady Glyde. Ask secretaries of life-assurance companies if that is true, Miss Halcombe. Read your own public journals. In the few cases that get into the newspapers, are there not instances of slain bodies found, and no murderers ever discovered? Multiply the cases that are reported by the cases that are *not* reported, and the bodies that are found by the bodies that are *not* found; and what conclusion do you come to? This. That there are foolish criminals who are discovered, and wise criminals who escape. The hiding of a crime, or the detection of a crime, what is it? A trial of skill between the police on one side, and the individual on the other. When the criminal is a brutal, ignorant fool, the police, in nine cases out of ten, win. When the criminal is a resolute, educated, highly-intelligent man, the police, in nine cases out of ten, lose. If the police win, you generally hear all about it. If the police lose, you generally hear nothing. And on this tottering foundation you build up your comfortable moral maxim that Crime causes its own detection! Yes—all the crime *you* know of. And, what of the rest?'

'Devilish true, and very well put,' cried a voice at the entrance of the boat-house. Sir Percival had recovered his equanimity, and had come back while we were listening to the Count.

'Some of it may be true,' I said; 'and all of it may be very well put. But I don't see why Count Fosco should celebrate the victory of the criminal over society with so much exultation, or why you, Sir Percival, should applaud him so loudly for doing it.'

'Do you hear that, Fosco?' asked Sir Percival. 'Take my advice, and make your peace with your audience. Tell them Virtue's a fine thing—they like that, I can promise you.'

The Count laughed inwardly and silently; and two of the white mice in his waistcoat, alarmed by the internal convulsion going on beneath them, darted out in a violent hurry, and scrambled into their cage again.

'The ladies, my good Percival, shall tell *me* about virtue,' he said. 'They are better authorities than I am; for they know what virtue is, and I don't.'

'You hear him?' said Sir Percival. 'Isn't it awful?'

'It is true,' said the Count, quietly. 'I am a citizen of the world, and I have met, in my time, with so many different sorts of virtue, that I am puzzled, in my old age, to say which is the right sort and which is the wrong. Here, in England, there is one virtue. And there, in China, there is another virtue. And John Englishman says my virtue is the genuine virtue. And John Chinaman says my virtue is the genuine virtue. And I say Yes to one, or No to the other, and am just as much bewildered about it in the case of John with the top-boots as I am in the case of John with the pigtail. Ah, nice little Mousey! come, kiss me. What is your own private notion of a virtuous man, my pret-pret-pretty? A man who keeps you warm, and gives you plenty to eat. And a good notion, too, for it is intelligible, at the least.'

'Stay a minute, Count,' I interposed. 'Accepting your illustration, surely we have one unquestionable virtue in England, which is wanting in China. The Chinese authorities kill thousands of innocent people, on the most horribly frivolous pretexts. We, in England, are free from all guilt of that kind—we commit no such dreadful crime—we abhor reckless bloodshed, with all our hearts.'

'Quite right, Marian,' said Laura. 'Well thought of, and well expressed.'

'Pray allow the Count to proceed,' said Madame Fosco, with stern civility. 'You will find, young ladies, that *he* never speaks without having excellent reasons for all that he says.'

'Thank you, my angel,' replied the Count. 'Have a bonbon?' He took out of his pocket a pretty little inlaid box, and placed it open on the table. 'Chocolat à la Vanille,' cried the impenetrable man, cheerfully rattling the sweetmeats in the box, and bowing all round. 'Offered by Fosco as an act of homage to the charming society.'

'Be good enough to go on, Count,' said his wife, with a spiteful reference to myself. 'Oblige me by answering Miss Halcombe.'

'Miss Halcombe is unanswerable,' replied the polite Italian—'that is to say, so far as she goes. Yes! I agree with her. John Bull does abhor the crimes of John Chinaman. He is the quickest old gentleman at finding out the faults that are his neighbours', and the slowest old gentleman at finding out the faults that are his own, who exists on the face of creation. Is he so very much better in his way, than the people whom he condemns in their way? English society, Miss Halcombe, is as often the accomplice, as it is the enemy of crime. Yes! yes! Crime is in this country what crime is in other countries—a good friend to a man and to those about him, as often as it is an enemy. A great rascal provides for his wife and family. The worse he is, the more he makes them the objects for your sympathy. He often provides, also, for himself. A profligate spendthrift who is always borrowing money, will get more from his friends than the rigidly-honest man who only borrows of them once, under pressure of the direst want. In the one case, the friends will not be at all surprised, and they will give. In the other case, they will be very much surprised, and they will hesitate. Is the prison that Mr Scoundrel lives in, at the end of his career, a more uncomfortable place than the workhouse that Mr Honesty lives in, at the end of *his* career? When John-Howard-Philanthropist wants to relieve misery, he goes to find it in prisons, where crime is wretched—not in huts and hovels, where virtue is wretched too. Who is the English poet who has won the most universal sympathy—who makes the easiest of all subjects for pathetic writing and pathetic painting? That nice young person who began life with a forgery, and ended it by a suicide—your dear, romantic, interesting Chatterton. Which gets on best, do you think, of two poor starving dressmakers—the woman who resists temptation, and is honest, or the woman who falls under temptation, and steals? You all know that the stealing is the making of that second woman's fortune—it advertises her from length to breadth of good-humoured, charitable England—and she is relieved, as the breaker of a commandment, when she would have been left to starve, as the keeper of it. Come here, my jolly little Mouse! Hey! presto! pass! I transform you, for the time being, into a respectable lady. Stop there, in the palm of my great big hand, my dear, and listen. You marry the poor man whom you love, Mouse; and one half your friends pity, and the other half blame you. And, now, on the contrary, you sell yourself for gold to a man you don't care for; and all your friends rejoice over you; and a minister of public worship sanctions the base horror of the vilest of all human bargains; and smiles and smirks afterwards at your table, if you are polite enough to ask him to breakfast. Hey! presto! pass! Be a mouse again, and squeak. If you continue to be a lady much longer, I shall have you telling me that Society abhors crime—and then, Mouse, I shall doubt if your own eyes and ears are really of any use to you. Ah! I am a bad man, Lady Glyde, am I not? I say what other people only think; and when all the rest of the world is in a conspiracy to accept the mask for the true face, mine is the rash hand that tears off the plump pasteboard, and shows the bare bones beneath. I will get up on my big, elephant's legs, before I do myself any more harm in your amiable estimations—I will get up, and take a little airy walk of my own. Dear ladies, as your excellent Sheridan said, I go—and leave my character behind me.'

He got up; put the cage on the table; and paused, for a moment, to count the mice in it. 'One, two, three, four——Ha!' he cried, with a look of horror, 'where, in the name of Heaven, is the fifth—the youngest, the whitest, the most amiable of all—my Benjamin of mice!'

Neither Laura nor I were in any favourable disposition to be amused. The Count's glib cynicism had revealed a new aspect of his nature from which we both recoiled. But it was impossible to resist the comical distress of so very large a man at the loss of so very small a mouse. We laughed, in spite of ourselves; and when Madame Fosco rose to set the example of leaving the boat-house empty, so that her husband might search it to its remotest corners, we rose also to follow her out.

Before we had taken three steps, the Count's quick eye discovered the lost mouse under the seat that we had been occupying. He pulled aside the bench; took the little animal up in his hand; and then suddenly stopped, on his knees, looking intently at a particular place on the ground just beneath him.

When he rose to his feet again, his hand shook so that he could hardly put the mouse back in the cage, and his face was of a faint livid yellow hue all over.

'Percival!' he said, in a whisper. 'Percival! come here.'

Sir Percival had paid no attention to any of us, for the last ten minutes. He had been entirely absorbed in writing figures on the sand, and then rubbing them out again, with the point of his stick.

'What's the matter, now?' he asked, lounging carelessly into the boat-house.

'Do you see nothing, there?' said the Count, catching him nervously by the collar with one hand, and pointing with the other to the place near which he had found the mouse.

'I see plenty of dry sand,' answered Sir Percival; 'and a spot of dirt in the middle of it.'

'Not dirt,' whispered the Count, fastening the other hand suddenly on Sir Percival's collar, and shaking it in his agitation. 'Blood.'

Laura was near enough to hear the last word, softly as he whispered it. She turned to me with a look of terror.

'Nonsense, my dear,' I said. 'There is no need to be alarmed. It is only the blood of a poor little stray dog.'

Everybody was astonished, and everybody's eyes were fixed on me inquiringly.

'How do you know that?' asked Sir Percival, speaking first.

'I found the dog here, dying, on the day when you all returned from abroad,' I replied. 'The poor creature had strayed into the plantation, and had been shot by your keeper.'

'Whose dog was it?' inquired Sir Percival. 'Not one of mine?'

'Did you try to save the poor thing?' asked Laura, earnestly. 'Surely you tried to save it, Marian?'

'Yes,' I said; 'the housekeeper and I both did our best—but the dog was mortally wounded, and he died under our hands.'

'Whose dog was it?' persisted Sir Percival, repeating his question a little irritably. 'One of mine?'

'No; not one of yours.'

'Whose then? Did the housekeeper know?'

The housekeeper's report of Mrs Catherick's desire to conceal her visit to Blackwater Park from Sir Percival's knowledge, recurred to my memory the moment he put that last question; and I half doubted the discretion of answering it. But, in my anxiety to quiet the general alarm, I had thoughtlessly advanced too far to draw back, except at the risk of exciting suspicion which might only make matters worse. There was nothing for it but to answer at once, without reference to results.

'Yes,' I said. 'The housekeeper knew. She told me it was Mrs Catherick's dog.'

Sir Percival had hitherto remained at the inner end of the boat-house with Count Fosco, while I spoke to him from the door. But the instant Mrs Catherick's name passed my lips, he pushed by the Count roughly, and placed himself face to face with me, under the open daylight.

'How came the housekeeper to know it was Mrs Catherick's dog?' he asked, fixing his eyes on mine with a frowning interest and attention, which half angered, half startled me.

'She knew it,' I said, quietly, 'because Mrs Catherick brought the dog with her.'

'Brought it with her? Where did she bring it with her?'

'To this house.'

'What the devil did Mrs Catherick want at this house?'

The manner in which he put the question was even more offensive than the language in which he expressed it. I marked my sense of his want of common politeness, by silently turning away from him.

Just as I moved, the Count's persuasive hand was laid on his shoulder, and the Count's mellifluous voice interposed to quiet him.

'My dear Percival!—gently—gently.'

Sir Percival looked round in his angriest manner. The Count only smiled, and repeated the soothing application.

'Gently, my good friend—gently!'

Sir Percival hesitated—followed me a few steps—and, to my great surprise, offered me an apology.

'I beg your pardon, Miss Halcombe,' he said. 'I have been out of order lately; and I am afraid I am a little irritable. But I should like to know what Mrs Catherick could possibly want here. When did she come? Was the housekeeper the only person who saw her?'

'The only person,' I answered, 'so far as I know.'

The Count interposed again.

'In that case, why not question the housekeeper?' he said. 'Why not go, Percival, to the fountain-head of information at once?'

'Quite right!' said Sir Percival. 'Of course the housekeeper is the first person to question. Excessively stupid of me not to see it myself.' With those words, he instantly left us to return to the house.

The motive of the Count's interference, which had puzzled me at first, betrayed itself when Sir Percival's back was turned. He had a host of questions to put to me about Mrs Catherick, and the cause of her visit to Blackwater Park, which he could scarcely have asked in his friend's presence. I made my answers as short as I civilly could—for I had already determined to check the least approach to any exchanging of confidences between Count Fosco and myself. Laura, however, unconsciously helped him to extract all my information, by making inquiries herself, which left me no alternative but to reply to her, or to appear in the very unenviable and very false character of a depository of Sir Percival's secrets. The end of it was, that, in about ten minutes' time, the Count knew as much as I know of Mrs Catherick, and of the events which have so strangely connected us with her daughter, Anne, from the time when Hartright met with her, to this day.

The effect of my information on him was, in one respect, curious enough.

Intimately as he knows Sir Percival, and closely as he appears to be associated with Sir Percival's private affairs in general, he is certainly as far as I am from knowing anything of the true story of Anne Catherick. The unsolved mystery in connexion with this unhappy woman is now rendered doubly suspicious, in my eyes, by the absolute conviction which I feel, that the clue to it has been hidden by Sir Percival from the most intimate friend he has in the world. It was impossible to mistake the eager curiosity of the Count's look and manner while he drank in greedily every word that fell from my lips. There are many kinds of curiosity, I know—but there is no misinterpreting the curiosity of blank surprise: if I ever saw it in my life, I saw it in the Count's face.

While the questions and answers were going on, we had all been strolling quietly back, through the plantation. As soon as we reached the house, the first object that we saw in front of it was Sir Percival's dog-cart, with the horse put to and the groom waiting by it in his stable-jacket. If these unexpected appearances were to be trusted, the examination of the house-keeper had produced important results already.

'A fine horse, my friend,' said the Count, addressing the groom with the most engaging familiarity of manner. 'You are going to drive out?'

'*I* am not going, sir,' replied the man, looking at his stable-jacket, and evidently wondering whether the foreign gentleman took it for his livery. 'My master drives himself.'

'Aha!' said the Count, 'does he indeed? I wonder he gives himself the trouble when he has got you to drive for him. Is he going to fatigue that nice, shining, pretty horse by taking him very far, to-day?'

'I don't know, sir,' answered the man. 'The horse is a mare, if you please, sir. She's the highest-couraged thing we've got in the stables. Her name's Brown Molly, sir; and she'll go till she drops. Sir Percival usually takes Isaac of York for the short distances.'

'And your shining courageous Brown Molly for the long?'

'Yes, sir.'

'Logical inference, Miss Halcombe,' continued the Count, wheeling round briskly, and addressing me: 'Sir Percival is going a long distance to-day.'

I made no reply. I had my own inferences to draw, from what I knew through the housekeeper and from what I saw before me; and I did not choose to share them with Count Fosco.

When Sir Percival was in Cumberland (I thought to myself), he walked away a long distance, on Anne's account, to question the family at Todd's Corner. Now he is in Hampshire, is he going to drive away a long distance, on Anne's account again, to question Mrs Catherick at Welmingham?

We all entered the house. As we crossed the hall, Sir Percival came out from the library to meet us. He looked hurried and pale and anxious—but, for all that, he was in his most polite mood, when he spoke to us.

'I am sorry to say, I am obliged to leave you,' he began—'a long drive—a matter that I can't very well put off. I shall be back in good time to-morrow—but, before I go, I should like that little business-formality, which I spoke of this morning, to be settled. Laura, will you come into the library? It won't take a minute—a mere formality. Countess, may I trouble you also? I want you and the Countess, Fosco, to be witnesses to a signature—nothing more. Come in at once, and get it over.'

He held the library door open until they had passed in, followed them, and shut it softly.

I remained, for a moment afterwards, standing alone in the hall, with my heart beating fast, and my mind misgiving me sadly. Then, I went on to the staircase, and ascended slowly to my own room.

JUST as my hand was on the door of my room, I heard Sir Percival's voice calling to me from below.

'I must beg you to come down stairs again,' he said. 'It is Fosco's fault, Miss Halcombe, not mine. He has started some nonsensical objection to his wife being one of the witnesses, and has obliged me to ask you to join us in the library.'

I entered the room immediately with Sir Percival. Laura was waiting by the writing-table, twisting and turning her garden hat uneasily in her hands. Madame Fosco sat near her, in an armchair, imperturbably admiring her husband, who stood by himself at the other end of the library, picking off the dead leaves from the flowers in the window.

The moment I appeared, the Count advanced to meet me, and to offer his explanations.

'A thousand pardons, Miss Halcombe,' he said. 'You know the character which is given to my countrymen by the English? We Italians are all wily and suspicious by nature, in the estimation of the good John Bull. Set me down, if you please, as being no better than the rest of my race. I am a wily Italian and a suspicious Italian. You have thought so yourself, dear lady, have you not? Well! it is part of my wiliness and part of my suspicion to object to Madame Fosco being a witness to Lady Glyde's signature, when I am also a witness myself.'

'There is not the shadow of a reason for his objection,' interposed Sir Percival. 'I have explained to him that the law of England allows Madame Fosco to witness a signature as well as her husband.'

'I admit it,' resumed the Count. 'The law of England says, Yes—but the conscience of Fosco says, No.' He spread out his fat fingers on the bosom of his blouse, and bowed solemnly, as if he wished to introduce his conscience to us all, in the character of an illustrious addition to the society. 'What this document which Lady Glyde is about to sign, may be,' he continued, 'I neither know nor desire to know. I only say this: circumstances may happen in the future which may oblige Percival, or his representatives, to appeal to the two witnesses; in which case it is certainly desirable that those witnesses should represent two opinions which are perfectly independent the one of the other. This cannot be if my wife signs as well as myself, because we have but one opinion between us, and that opinion is mine. I will not have it cast in my teeth, at some future day, that Madame Fosco acted under my coercion, and was, in plain fact, no witness at all. I speak in Percival's interest when I propose that my name shall appear (as the nearest friend of the husband), and your name, Miss Halcombe (as the nearest friend of the wife). I am a Jesuit, if you please to think so—a splitter of straws—a man of trifles and crotchets and scruples—but you will humour me, I hope, in merciful consideration for my suspicious Italian character, and my uneasy Italian conscience.' He bowed again, stepped back a few paces, and withdrew his conscience from our society as politely as he had introduced it.

The Count's scruples might have been honourable and reasonable enough, but there was something in his manner of expressing them which increased my unwillingness to be concerned in the business of the signature. No consideration of less importance than my consideration for Laura, would have induced me to consent to be a witness at all. One look, however, at her anxious face, decided me to risk anything rather than desert her.

'I will readily remain in the room,' I said. 'And if I find no reason for starting any small scruples, on my side, you may rely on me as a witness.'

Sir Percival looked at me sharply, as if he was about to say something. But, at the same moment, Madame Fosco attracted his attention by rising from her chair. She had caught her husband's eye, and had evidently received her orders to leave the room.

'You needn't go,' said Sir Percival.

Madame Fosco looked for her orders again, got them again, said she would prefer leaving us to our business, and resolutely walked out. The Count lit a cigarette, went back to the flowers in the window, and puffed little jets of smoke at the leaves, in a state of the deepest anxiety about killing the insects.

Meanwhile, Sir Percival unlocked a cupboard beneath one of the bookcases, and produced from it a piece of parchment folded, longwise, many times over. He placed it on the table, opened the last fold only, and kept his hand on the rest. The last fold displayed a strip of blank parchment with little wafers stuck on it at certain places. Every line of the writing was hidden in the part which he still held folded up under his hand. Laura and I looked at each other. Her face was pale—but it showed no indecision and no fear.

Sir Percival dipped a pen in ink, and handed it to his wife.

'Sign your name, there,' he said, pointing to the place. 'You and Fosco are to sign afterwards, Miss Halcombe, opposite those two wafers. Come here, Fosco! witnessing a signature is not to be done by mooning out of the window and smoking into the flowers.'

The Count threw away his cigarette, and joined us at the table, with his hands carelessly thrust into the scarlet belt of his blouse, and his eyes steadily fixed on Sir Percival's face. Laura, who was on the other side of her husband, with the pen in her hand, looked at him, too. He stood between them, holding the folded parchment down firmly on the table, and glancing across at me, as I sat opposite to him, with such a sinister mixture of suspicion and embarrassment in his face, that he looked more like a prisoner at the bar than a gentleman in his own house.

'Sign there,' he repeated, turning suddenly on Laura, and pointing once more to the place on the parchment.

'What is it I am to sign?' she asked, quietly.

'I have no time to explain,' he answered. 'The dog-cart is at the door; and I must go directly. Besides, if I had time, you wouldn't understand. It is a purely formal document—full of legal technicalities, and all that sort of thing. Come! come! sign your name, and let us have done as soon as possible.'

'I ought surely to know what I am signing, Sir Percival, before I write my name?'

'Nonsense! What have women to do with business? I tell you again, you can't understand it.'

'At any rate, let me try to understand it. Whenever Mr Gilmore had any business for me to do, he always explained it, first; and I always understood him.'

'I dare say he did. He was your servant, and was obliged to explain. I am your husband, and am *not* obliged. How much longer do you mean to keep me here? I tell you again, there is no time for reading anything: the dog-cart is waiting at the door. Once for all, will you sign, or will you not?'

She still had the pen in her hand; but she made no approach to signing her name with it.

'If my signature pledges me to anything,' she said, 'surely, I have some claim to know what that pledge is?'

He lifted up the parchment, and struck it angrily on the table.

'Speak out!' he said. 'You were always famous for telling the truth. Never mind Miss Halcombe; never mind Fosco—say, in plain terms, you distrust me.'

The Count took one of his hands out of his belt, and laid it on Sir Percival's shoulder. Sir Percival shook it off irritably. The Count put it on again with unruffled composure.

'Control your unfortunate temper, Percival,' he said. 'Lady Glyde is right.'

'Right!' cried Sir Percival. 'A wife right in distrusting her husband!'

'It is unjust and cruel to accuse me of distrusting you,' said Laura. 'Ask Marian if I am not justified in wanting to know what this writing requires of me, before I sign it.'

'I won't have any appeals made to Miss Halcombe,' retorted Sir Percival. 'Miss Halcombe has nothing to do with the matter.'

I had not spoken hitherto, and I would much rather not have spoken now. But the expression of distress in Laura's face when she turned it towards me, and the insolent injustice of her husband's conduct, left me no other alternative than to give my opinion, for her sake, as soon as I was asked for it.

'Excuse me, Sir Percival,' I said—'but, as one of the witnesses to the signature, I venture to think that I *have* something to do with the matter. Laura's objection seems to me a perfectly fair one; and, speaking for myself only, I cannot assume the responsibility of witnessing her signature, unless she first understands what the writing is which you wish her to sign.'

'A cool declaration, upon my soul!' cried Sir Percival. 'The next time you invite yourself to a man's house, Miss Halcombe, I recommend you not to repay his hospitality by taking his wife's side against him in a matter that doesn't concern you.'

I started to my feet as suddenly as if he had struck me. If I had been a man, I would have knocked him down on the threshold of his own door, and have left his house, never, on any earthly consideration, to enter it again. But I was only a woman—and I loved his wife so dearly!

Thank God, that faithful love helped me, and I sat down again, without saying a word. *She* knew what I had suffered and what I had suppressed. She ran round to me, with the tears streaming from her eyes. 'Oh, Marian!' she whispered softly. 'If my mother had been alive, she could have done no more for me!'

'Come back and sign!' cried Sir Percival, from the other side of the table.

'Shall I?' she asked in my ear; 'I will, if you tell me.'

'No,' I answered. 'The right and the truth are with you—sign nothing, unless you have read it first.'

'Come back and sign!' he reiterated, in his loudest and angriest tones.

The Count, who had watched Laura and me with a close and silent attention, interposed for the second time.

'Percival!' he said. '*I* remember that I am in the presence of ladies. Be good enough, if you please, to remember it, too.'

Sir Percival turned on him, speechless with passion. The Count's firm hand slowly tightened its grasp on his shoulder, and the Count's steady voice quietly repeated, 'Be good enough, if you please, to remember it, too.'

They both looked at each other. Sir Percival slowly drew his shoulder from under the Count's hand; slowly turned his face away from the Count's eyes; doggedly looked down for a little while at the parchment on the table; and then spoke, with the sullen submission of a tamed animal, rather than the becoming resignation of a convinced man.

'I don't want to offend anybody,' he said, 'but my wife's obstinacy is enough to try the patience of a saint. I have told her this is merely a formal document—and what more can she want? You may say what you please; but it is no part of a woman's duty to set her husband at defiance. Once more, Lady Glyde, and for the last time, will you sign or will you not?'

Laura returned to his side of the table, and took up the pen again.

'I will sign with pleasure,' she said, 'if you will only treat me as a responsible being. I care little what sacrifice is required of me, if it will affect no one else, and lead to no ill results——'

'Who talked of a sacrifice being required of you?' he broke in, with a half-suppressed return of his former violence.

'I only meant,' she resumed, 'that I would refuse no concession which I could honourably make. If I have a scruple about signing my name to an engagement of which I know nothing, why should you visit it on me so severely? It is rather hard, I think, to treat Count Fosco's scruples so much more indulgently than you have treated mine.'

This unfortunate, yet most natural, reference to the Count's extraordinary power over her husband, indirect as it was, set Sir Percival's smouldering temper on fire again in an instant.

'Scruples!' he repeated. '*Your* scruples! It is rather late in the day for you to be scrupulous. I should have thought you had got over all weakness of that sort, when you made a virtue of necessity by marrying *me*.'

The instant he spoke those words, Laura threw down the pen—looked at him with an expression in her eyes, which, throughout all my experience of her, I had never seen in them before—and turned her back on him in dead silence.

This strong expression of the most open and the most bitter contempt, was so entirely unlike herself, so utterly out of her character, that it silenced us all. There was something hidden, beyond a doubt, under the mere surface-brutality of the words which her husband had just addressed to her. There was some lurking insult beneath them, of which I was wholly ignorant, but which had left the mark of its profanation so plainly on her face that even a stranger might have seen it.

The Count, who was no stranger, saw it as distinctly as I did. When I left my chair to join Laura, I heard him whisper under his breath to Sir Percival: 'You idiot!'

Laura walked before me to the door as I advanced; and, at the same time, her husband spoke to her once more.

'You positively refuse, then, to give me your signature?' he said, in the altered tone of a man who was conscious that he had let his own licence of language seriously injure him.

'After what you have said to me,' she replied, firmly, 'I refuse my signature until I have read every line in that parchment from the first word to the last. Come away, Marian, we have remained here long enough.'

'One moment!' interposed the Count, before Sir Percival could speak again—'one moment, Lady Glyde, I implore you!'

Laura would have left the room without noticing him; but I stopped her.

'Don't make an enemy of the Count!' I whispered. 'Whatever you do, don't make an enemy of the Count!'

She yielded to me. I closed the door again; and we stood near it, waiting. Sir Percival sat down at the table, with his elbow on the folded parchment, and his head resting on his clenched fist. The Count stood between us—master of the dreadful position in which we were placed, as he was master of everything else.

'Lady Glyde,' he said, with a gentleness which seemed to address itself to our forlorn situation instead of to ourselves, 'pray pardon me, if I venture to offer one suggestion; and pray believe that I speak out of my profound respect and my friendly regard for the mistress of this house.' He turned sharply towards Sir Percival. 'Is it absolutely necessary,' he asked, 'that this thing here, under your elbow, should be signed to-day?'

'It is necessary to my plans and wishes,' replied the other, sulkily. 'But that consideration, as you may have noticed, has no influence with Lady Glyde.'

'Answer my plain question, plainly. Can the business of the signature be put off till to-morrow—Yes, or No?'

'Yes—if you will have it so.'

'Then, what are you wasting your time for, here? Let the signature wait till to-morrow—let it wait till you come back.'

Sir Percival looked up with a frown and an oath.

'You are taking a tone with me that I don't like,' he said. 'A tone I won't bear from any man.'

'I am advising you for your good,' returned the Count, with a smile of quiet contempt. 'Give yourself time; give Lady Glyde time. Have you forgotten that your dog-cart is waiting at the door? My tone surprises you—ha? I dare say it does—it is the tone of a man who can keep his temper. How many doses of good advice have I given you in my time? More than you can count. Have I ever been wrong? I defy you to quote me an instance of it. Go! take your drive. The matter of the signature can wait till to-morrow. Let it wait—and renew it when you come back.'

Sir Percival hesitated, and looked at his watch. His anxiety about the secret journey which he was to take that day, revived by the Count's words, was now evidently disputing possession of his mind with his anxiety to obtain Laura's signature. He considered for a little while; and then got up from his chair.

'It is easy to argue me down,' he said, 'when I have no time to answer you. I will take your advice, Fosco—not because I want it, or believe in it, but because I can't stop here any longer.' He paused, and looked round darkly at his wife. 'If you don't give me your signature when I come back to-morrow——!' The rest was lost in the noise of his opening the bookcase cupboard again, and locking up the parchment once more. He took his hat and gloves off the table, and made for the door. Laura and I drew back to let him pass. 'Remember to-morrow!' he said to his wife; and went out.

We waited to give him time to cross the hall, and drive away. The Count approached us while we were standing near the door.

'You have just seen Percival at his worst, Miss Halcombe,' he said. 'As his old friend, I am sorry for him and ashamed of him. As his old friend, I promise you that he shall not break out to-morrow in the same disgraceful manner in which he has broken out to-day.'

Laura had taken my arm while he was speaking, and she pressed it significantly when he had done. It would have been a hard trial to any woman to stand by and see the office of apologist for her husband's misconduct quietly assumed by his male friend in her own house—and it was a hard trial to *her*. I thanked the Count civilly, and led her out. Yes! I thanked him: for I felt already, with a sense of inexpressible helplessness and humiliation, that it was either his interest or his caprice to make sure of my continuing to reside at Blackwater Park; and I knew, after Sir Percival's conduct to me, that without the support of the Count's influence, I could not hope to remain there. His influence, the influence of all others that I dreaded most, was actually the one tie which now held me to Laura in the hour of her utmost need!

We heard the wheels of the dog-cart crashing on the gravel of the drive, as we came into the hall. Sir Percival had started on his journey.

'Where is he going to, Marian?' Laura whispered. 'Every fresh thing he does, seems to terrify me about the future. Have you any suspicions?'

After what she had undergone that morning, I was unwilling to tell her my suspicions.

'How should I know his secrets,' I said, evasively.

'I wonder if the housekeeper knows?' she persisted.

'Certainly not,' I replied. 'She must be quite as ignorant as we are.'

Laura shook her head doubtfully.

'Did you not hear from the housekeeper that there was a report of Anne Catherick having been seen in this neighbourhood? Don't you think he may have gone away to look for her?'

'I would rather compose myself, Laura, by not thinking about it, at all; and, after what has happened, you had better follow my example. Come into my room, and rest and quiet yourself a little.'

We sat down together close to the window, and let the fragrant summer air breathe over our faces.

'I am ashamed to look at you, Marian,' she said, 'after what you submitted to down stairs, for my sake. Oh, my own love, I am almost heart-broken, when I think of it! But I will try to make it up to you—I will indeed!'

'Hush! hush!' I replied; 'don't talk so. What is the trifling mortification of my pride compared to the dreadful sacrifice of your happiness?'

'You heard what he said to me?' she went on, quickly and vehemently. 'You heard the words—but you don't know what they meant—you don't know why I threw down the pen and turned my back on him.' She rose in sudden agitation, and walked about the room. 'I have kept many things from your knowledge, Marian, for fear of distressing you, and making you unhappy at the outset of our new lives. You don't know how he has used me. And yet, you ought to know, for you saw how he used me to-day. You heard him sneer at my presuming to be scrupulous; you heard him say I had made a virtue of necessity in marrying him.' She sat down again; her face flushed deeply, and her hands twisted and twined together in her lap. 'I can't tell you about it, now,' she said; 'I shall burst out crying if I tell you now—later, Marian, when I am more sure of myself. My poor head aches, darling—aches, aches, aches. Where is your smelling-bottle? Let me talk to you about yourself. I wish I had given him my signature, for your sake. Shall I give it to him, to-morrow? I would rather compromise myself than compromise you. After your taking my part against him, he will lay all the blame on you, if I refuse again. What shall we do? Oh, for a friend to help us and advise us!—a friend we could really trust!'

She sighed bitterly. I saw in her face that she was thinking of Hartright— saw it the more plainly because her last words set me thinking of him, too. In six months only from her marriage, we wanted the faithful service he had offered to us in his farewell words. How little I once thought that we should ever want it at all!

'We must do what we can to help ourselves,' I said. 'Let us try to talk it over calmly, Laura—let us do all in our power to decide for the best.'

Putting what she knew of her husband's embarrassments, and what I had heard of his conversation with the lawyer, together, we arrived necessarily at the conclusion that the parchment in the library had been drawn up for the purpose of borrowing money, and that Laura's signature was absolutely necessary to fit it for the attainment of Sir Percival's object.

The second question, concerning the nature of the legal contract by which the money was to be obtained, and the degree of personal responsibility to which Laura might subject herself if she signed it in the dark, involved considerations which lay far beyond any knowledge and experience that either of us possessed. My own convictions led me to believe that the hidden contents of the parchment concealed a transaction of the meanest and the most fraudulent kind.

I had not formed this conclusion in consequence of Sir Percival's refusal to show the writing, or to explain it; for that refusal might well have proceeded from his obstinate disposition and his domineering temper alone. My sole motive for distrusting his honesty, sprang from the change which I had observed in his language and his manners at Blackwater Park, a change which convinced me that he had been acting a part throughout the whole period of his probation at Limmeridge House. His elaborate delicacy; his ceremonious politeness, which harmonised so agreeably with Mr Gilmore's old-fashioned notions, his modesty with Laura, his candour with me, his moderation with Mr Fairlie—all these were the artifices of a mean, cunning, and brutal man, who had dropped his disguise when his practised duplicity had gained its end, and had openly shown himself in the library, on that very day. I say nothing of the grief which this discovery caused me on Laura's account, for it is not to be expressed by any words of mine. I only refer to it at all, because it decided me to oppose her signing the parchment, whatever the consequences might be, unless she was first made acquainted with the contents.

Under these circumstances, the one chance for us, when tomorrow came, was to be provided with an objection to giving the signature, which might rest on sufficiently firm commercial or legal grounds to shake Sir Percival's resolution, and to make him suspect that we two women understood the laws and obligations of business as well as himself.

After some pondering, I determined to write to the only honest man within reach whom we could trust to help us discreetly, in our forlorn situation. That man was Mr Gilmore's partner—Mr Kyrle—who conducted the business, now that our old friend had been obliged to withdraw from it, and to leave London on account of his health. I explained to Laura that I had Mr Gilmore's own authority for placing implicit confidence in his partner's integrity, discretion, and accurate knowledge of all her affairs; and, with her full approval, I sat down at once to write the letter.

I began by stating our position to Mr Kyrle exactly as it was; and then asked for his advice in return, expressed in plain, downright terms which we could comprehend without any danger of misinterpretations and mistakes. My letter was as short as I could possibly make it, and was, I hope, unencumbered by needless apologies and needless details.

Just as I was about to put the address on the envelope, an obstacle was discovered by Laura, which, in the effort and preoccupation of writing, had escaped my mind altogether.

'How are we to get the answer in time?' she asked. 'Your letter will not be delivered in London before to-morrow morning; and the post will not bring the reply here till the morning after.'

The only way of overcoming this difficulty was to have the answer brought to us from the lawyer's office by a special messenger. I wrote a postscript to that effect, begging that the messenger might be despatched with the reply by the eleven o'clock morning train, which would bring him to our station at twenty minutes past one, and so enable him to reach Blackwater Park by two o'clock at the latest. He was to be directed to ask for me, to answer no questions addressed to him by any one else, and to deliver his letter into no hands but mine.

'In case Sir Percival should come back to-morrow before two o'clock,' I said to Laura, 'the wisest plan for you to adopt is to be out in the grounds, all the morning, with your book or your work, and not to appear at the house till the messenger has had time to arrive with the letter. I will wait here for him, all the morning, to guard against any misadventures or mistakes. By following this arrangement I hope and believe we shall avoid being taken by surprise. Let us go down to the drawing-room now. We may excite suspicion if we remain shut up together too long.'

'Suspicion?' she repeated. 'Whose suspicion can we excite, now that Sir Percival has left the house? Do you mean Count Fosco?'

'Perhaps I do, Laura.'

'You are beginning to dislike him as much as I do, Marian.'

'No; not to dislike him. Dislike is always, more or less, associated with contempt—I can see nothing in the Count to despise.'

'You are not afraid of him, are you?'

'Perhaps I am—a little.'

'Afraid of him, after his interference in our favour to-day!'

'Yes. I am more afraid of his interference, than I am of Sir Percival's violence. Remember what I said to you in the library. Whatever you do, Laura, don't make an enemy of the Count!'

We went down stairs. Laura entered the drawing-room; while I proceeded across the hall, with my letter in my hand, to put it into the post-bag, which hung against the wall opposite to me.

The house door was open; and, as I crossed past it, I saw Count Fosco and his wife standing talking together on the steps outside, with their faces turned towards me.

The Countess came into the hall, rather hastily, and asked if I had leisure enough for five minutes' private conversation. Feeling a little surprised by such an appeal from such a person, I put my letter into the bag, and replied that I was quite at her disposal. She took my arm with unaccustomed friendliness and familiarity; and instead of leading me into an empty room, drew me out with her to the belt of turf which surrounded the large fish-pond.

As we passed the Count on the steps, he bowed and smiled, and then went at once into the house; pushing the hall-door to after him, but not actually closing it.

The Countess walked me gently round the fish-pond. I expected to be made the depositary of some extraordinary confidence; and I was astonished to find that Madame Fosco's communication for my private ear was nothing more than a polite assurance of her sympathy for me, after what had happened in the library. Her husband had told her of all that had passed, and of the insolent manner in which Sir Percival had spoken to me. This information had so shocked and distressed her, on my account and on Laura's, that she had made up her mind, if anything of the sort happened again, to mark her sense of Sir Percival's outrageous conduct by leaving the house. The Count had approved of her idea, and she now hoped that I approved of it, too.

I thought this a very strange proceeding on the part of such a remarkably reserved woman as Madame Fosco—especially after the interchange of sharp speeches which had passed between us during the conversation in the boat-house, on that very morning. However, it was my plain duty to meet a polite and friendly advance, on the part of one of my elders, with a polite and friendly reply. I answered the Countess, accordingly, in her own tone; and then, thinking we had said all that was necessary on either side, made an attempt to get back to the house.

But Madame Fosco seemed resolved not to part with me, and, to my unspeakable amazement, resolved also to talk. Hitherto, the most silent of women, she now persecuted me with fluent conventionalities on the subject of married life, on the subject of Sir Percival and Laura, on the subject of her own happiness, on the subject of the late Mr Fairlie's conduct to her in the matter of her legacy, and on half a dozen other subjects besides, until she had detained me, walking round and round the fish-pond for more than half an hour, and had quite wearied me out. Whether she discovered this, or not, I cannot say, but she stopped as abruptly as she had begun—looked towards the house door—resumed her icy manner in a moment—and dropped my arm of her own accord, before I could think of an excuse for accomplishing my own release from her.

As I pushed open the door, and entered the hall, I found myself suddenly face to face with the Count again. He was just putting a letter into the post-bag.

After he had dropped it in, and had closed the bag, he asked me where I had left Madame Fosco. I told him; and he went out at the hall door, immediately, to join his wife. His manner, when he spoke to me, was so unusually quiet and subdued that I turned and looked after him, wondering if he were ill or out of spirits.

Why my next proceeding was to go straight up to the post-bag, and take out my own letter, and look at it again, with a vague distrust on me; and why the looking at it for the second time instantly suggested the idea to my mind of sealing the envelope for its greater security—are mysteries which are either too deep or too shallow for me to fathom. Women, as everybody knows, constantly act on impulses which they cannot explain even to themselves; and I can only suppose that one of those impulses was the hidden cause of my unaccountable conduct on this occasion.

Whatever influence animated me, I found cause to congratulate myself on having obeyed it, as soon as I prepared to seal the letter in my own room. I had originally closed the envelope, in the usual way, by moistening the adhesive point and pressing it on the paper beneath; and, when I now tried it with my finger, after a lapse of full three-quarters of an hour, the envelope opened on the instant, without sticking or tearing. Perhaps I had fastened it insufficiently? Perhaps there might have been some defect in the adhesive gum?

Or, perhaps——No! it is quite revolting enough to feel that third conjecture stirring in my mind. I would rather not see it confronting me, in plain black and white.

I almost dread to-morrow—so much depends on my discretion and self-control. There are two precautions, at all events, which I am sure not to forget. I must be careful to keep up friendly appearances with the Count; and I must be well on my guard, when the messenger from the office comes here with the answer to my letter.

WHEN the dinner hour brought us together again, Count Fosco was in his usual excellent spirits. He exerted himself to interest and amuse us, as if he was determined to efface from our memories all recollection of what had passed in the library that afternoon. Lively descriptions of his adventures in travelling; amusing anecdotes of remarkable people whom he had met with abroad; quaint comparisons between the social customs of various nations, illustrated by examples drawn from men and women indiscriminately all over Europe; humorous confessions of the innocent follies of his own early life, when he ruled the fashions of a second-rate Italian town, and wrote preposterous romances, on the French model, for a second-rate Italian newspaper—all flowed in succession so easily and so gaily from his lips, and all addressed our various curiosities and various interests so directly and so delicately, that Laura and I listened to him with as much attention, and, inconsistent as it may seem, with as much admiration also, as Madame Fosco herself. Women can resist a man's love, a man's fame, a man's personal appearance, and a man's money; but they cannot resist a man's tongue, when he knows how to talk to them.

After dinner, while the favourable impression which he had produced on us was still vivid in our minds, the Count modestly withdrew to read in the library.

Laura proposed a stroll in the grounds to enjoy the close of the long evening. It was necessary, in common politeness, to ask Madame Fosco to join us; but, this time, she had apparently received her orders beforehand, and she begged we would kindly excuse her. 'The Count will probably want a fresh supply of cigarettes,' she remarked, by way of apology; 'and nobody can make them to his satisfaction, but myself.' Her cold blue eyes almost warmed as she spoke the words—she looked actually proud of being the officiating medium through which her lord and master composed himself with tobacco-smoke!

Laura and I went out together alone.

It was a misty, heavy evening. There was a sense of blight in the air; the flowers were drooping in the garden, and the ground was parched and dewless. The western heaven, as we saw it over the quiet trees, was of a pale yellow hue, and the sun was setting faintly in a haze. Coming rain seemed near: it would fall probably with the fall of night.

'Which way shall we go?' I asked.

'Towards the lake, Marian, if you like,' she answered.

'You seem unaccountably fond, Laura, of that dismal lake.'

'No; not of the lake, but of the scenery about it. The sand and heath, and the fir-trees, are the only objects I can discover, in all this large place, to remind me of Limmeridge. But we will walk in some other direction, if you prefer it.'

'I have no favourite walks at Blackwater Park, my love. One is the same as another to me. Let us go to the lake—we may find it cooler in the open space than we find it here.'

We walked through the shadowy plantation in silence. The heaviness in the evening air oppressed us both; and, when we reached the boat-house, we were glad to sit down and rest, inside.

A white fog hung low over the lake. The dense brown line of the trees on the opposite bank, appeared above it, like a dwarf forest floating in the sky. The sandy ground, shelving downward from where we sat, was lost mysteriously in the outward layers of the fog. The silence was horrible. No rustling of the leaves—no bird's note in the wood—no cry of water-fowl from the pools of the hidden lake. Even the croaking of the frogs had ceased to-night.

'It is very desolate and gloomy,' said Laura. 'But we can be more alone here than anywhere else.'

She spoke quietly, and looked at the wilderness of sand and mist with steady, thoughtful eyes. I could see that her mind was too much occupied to feel the dreary impressions from without, which had fastened themselves already on mine.

'I promised, Marian, to tell you the truth about my married life, instead of leaving you any longer to guess it for yourself,' she began. 'That secret is the first I have ever had from you, love, and I am determined it shall be the last. I was silent, as you know, for your sake—and perhaps a little for my own sake as well. It is very hard for a woman to confess that the man to whom she has given her whole life, is the man of all others who cares least for the gift. If you were married yourself, Marian—and especially if you were happily married—you would feel for me as no single woman *can* feel, however kind and true she may be.'

What answer could I make? I could only take her hand, and look at her with my whole heart, as well as my eyes would let me.

'How often,' she went on, 'I have heard you laughing over what you used to call your "poverty!" how often you have made me mock-speeches of congratulation on my wealth! Oh, Marian, never laugh again. Thank God for your poverty—it has made you your own mistress, and has saved you from the lot that has fallen on *me*.'

A sad beginning on the lips of a young wife!—sad, in its quiet, plain-spoken truth. The few days we had all passed together at Blackwater Park, had been many enough to show me—to show any one—what her husband had married her for.

'You shall not be distressed,' she said, 'by hearing how soon my disappointments and my trials began—or, even by knowing what they were. It is bad enough to have them on *my* memory. If I tell you how he received the first, and last, attempt at remonstrance that I ever made, you will know how he has always treated me, as well as if I had described it in so many words. It was one day at Rome, when we had ridden out together to the tomb of Cecilia Metella. The sky was calm and lovely—and the grand old ruin looked beautiful—and the remembrance that a husband's love had raised it in the old time to a wife's memory, made me feel more tenderly and more anxiously towards *my* husband than I had ever felt yet. "Would you build such a tomb for *me*, Percival?" I asked him. "You said you loved me dearly, before we were married; and yet, since that time——" I could get no farther. Marian! he was not even looking at me! I pulled down my veil, thinking it best not to let him see that the tears were in my eyes. I fancied he had not paid any attention to me; but he had. He said, "Come away," and laughed to himself, as he helped me on to my horse. He mounted his own horse; and laughed again, as we rode away. "If I do build you a tomb," he said, "it will be done with your own money. I wonder whether Cecilia Metella had a fortune, and paid for hers." I made no reply—how could I, when I was crying behind my veil? "Ah, you light-complexioned women are all sulky," he said. "What do you want? compliments and soft speeches? Well! I'm in a good humour this morning. Consider the compliments paid, and the speeches said." Men little know, when they say hard things to us, how well we remember them, and how much harm they do us. It would have been better for me if I had gone on crying; but his contempt dried up my tears, and hardened my heart. From that time, Marian, I never checked myself again in thinking of Walter Hartright. I let the memory of those happy days, when we were so fond of each other in secret, come back, and comfort me. What else had I to look to for consolation? If we had been together, you would have helped me to better things. I know it was wrong, darling—but tell me if I was wrong, without any excuse.'

I was obliged to turn my face from her. 'Don't ask me!' I said. 'Have I suffered as you have suffered? What right have I to decide?'

'I used to think of him,' she pursued, dropping her voice, and moving closer to me—'I used to think of him, when Percival left me alone at night, to go among the Opera people. I used to fancy what I might have been, if it had pleased God to bless me with poverty, and if I had been his wife. I used to see myself in my neat cheap gown, sitting at home and waiting for him, while he was earning our bread—sitting at home and working for him, and loving him all the better because I *had* to work for him—seeing him come in tired, and taking off his hat and coat for him—and, Marian, pleasing him with little dishes at dinner that I had learnt to make for his sake.—Oh! I hope he is never lonely enough and sad enough to think of me, and see me, as I have thought of *him* and seen *him*!'

As she said those melancholy words, all the lost tenderness returned to her voice, and all the lost beauty trembled back into her face. Her eyes rested as lovingly on the blighted, solitary, ill-omened view before us, as if they saw the friendly hills of Cumberland in the dim and threatening sky.

'Don't speak of Walter any more,' I said, as soon as I could control myself. 'Oh, Laura, spare us both the wretchedness of talking of him, now!'

She roused herself, and looked at me tenderly.

'I would rather be silent about him for ever,' she answered, 'than cause you a moment's pain.'

'It is in your interests,' I pleaded; 'it is for your sake that I speak. If your husband heard you——'

'It would not surprise him, if he did hear me.'

She made that strange reply with a weary calmness and coldness. The change in her manner, when she gave the answer, startled me almost as much as the answer itself.

'Not surprise him!' I repeated. 'Laura! remember what you are saying—you frighten me!'

'It is true,' she said—'it is what I wanted to tell you to-day, when we were talking in your room. My only secret when I opened my heart to him at Limmeridge, was a harmless secret, Marian—you said so yourself. The name was all I kept from him—and he has discovered it.'

I heard her; but I could say nothing. Her last words had killed the little hope that still lived in me.

'It happened at Rome,' she went on, as wearily calm and cold as ever. 'We were at a little party, given to the English by some friends of Sir Percival's—Mr and Mrs Markland. Mrs Markland had the reputation of sketching very beautifully; and some of the guests prevailed on her to show us her drawings. We all admired them—but something I said attracted her attention particularly to me. "Surely you draw yourself?" she asked. "I used to draw a little once," I answered, "but I have given it up." "If you have once drawn," she said, "you may take to it again one of these days; and, if you do, I wish you would let me recommend you a master." I said nothing—you know why, Marian—and tried to change the conversation. But Mrs Markland persisted. "I have had all sorts of teachers," she went on; "but the best of all, the most intelligent and the most attentive, was a Mr Hartright. If you ever take up your drawing again, do try him as a master. He is a young man—modest and gentleman-like—I am sure you will like him." Think of those words being spoken to me publicly, in the presence of strangers—strangers who had been invited to meet the bride and bride-groom! I did all I could to control myself—I said nothing, and looked down close at the drawings. When I ventured to raise my head again, my eyes and my husband's eyes met; and I knew, by his look, that my face had betrayed me. "We will see about Mr Hartright," he said, looking at me all the time, "when we get back to England. I agree with you, Mrs Markland—I think Lady Glyde is sure to like him." He laid an emphasis on the last words which made my cheeks burn, and set my heart beating as if it would stifle me. Nothing more was said—we came away early. He was silent in the carriage, driving back to the hotel. He helped me out, and followed me up-stairs as usual. But the moment we were in the drawing-room, he locked the door, pushed me down into a chair, and stood over me with his hands on my shoulders. "Ever since that morning when you made your audacious confession to me at Limmeridge," he said, "I have wanted to find out the man; and I found him in your face, to-night. Your drawing-master was the man; and his name is Hartright. You shall repent it, and he shall repent it, to the last hour of your lives. Now go to bed, and dream of him, if you like—with the marks of my horsewhip on his shoulders." Whenever he is angry with me now, he refers to what I acknowledged to him in your presence, with a sneer or a threat. I have no power to prevent him from putting his own horrible construction on the confidence I placed in him. I have no influence to make him believe me, or to keep him silent. You looked surprised, to-day, when you heard him tell me that I had made a virtue of necessity in marrying him. You will not be surprised again, when you hear him repeat it, the next time he is out of temper—Oh, Marian! don't! don't! you hurt me!'

I had caught her in my arms; and the sting and torment of my remorse had closed them round her like a vice. Yes! my remorse. The white despair of Walter's face, when my cruel words struck him to the heart in the summer-house at Limmeridge, rose before me in mute, unendurable reproach. My hand had pointed the way which led the man my sister loved, step by step, far from his country and his friends. Between those two young hearts I had stood, to sunder them for ever, the one from the other—and his life and her life lay wasted before me, alike, in witness of the deed. I had done this; and done it for Sir Percival Glyde.

For Sir Percival Glyde.

I heard her speaking, and I knew by the tone of her voice that she was comforting me—*I*, who deserved nothing but the reproach of her silence! How long it was before I mastered the absorbing misery of my own thoughts, I cannot tell. I was first conscious that she was kissing me; and then my eyes seemed to wake on a sudden to their sense of outward things, and I knew that I was looking mechanically straight before me at the prospect of the lake.

'It is late,' I heard her whisper. 'It will be dark in the plantation.' She shook my arm, and repeated, 'Marian! it will be dark in the plantation.'

'Give me a minute longer,' I said—'a minute, to get better in.'

I was afraid to trust myself to look at her yet; and I kept my eyes fixed on the view.

It *was* late. The dense brown line of trees in the sky had faded in the gathering darkness, to the faint resemblance of a long wreath of smoke. The mist over the lake below had stealthily enlarged, and advanced on us. The silence was as breathless as ever—but the horror of it had gone, and the solemn mystery of its stillness was all that remained.

'We are far from the house,' she whispered. 'Let us go back.'

She stopped suddenly and turned her face from me towards the entrance of the boat-house.

'Marian!' she said, trembling violently. 'Do you see nothing? Look!'

'Where?'

'Down there, below us.'

She pointed. My eyes followed her hand; and I saw it, too.

A living figure was moving over the waste of heath in the distance. It crossed our range of view from the boat-house, and passed darkly along the outer edge of the mist. It stopped, far off, in front of us—waited—and passed on; moving slowly, with the white cloud of mist behind it and above it—slowly, slowly, till it glided by the edge of the boat-house, and we saw it no more.

We were both unnerved by what had passed between us that evening. Some minutes elapsed before Laura would venture into the plantation, and before I could make up my mind to lead her back to the house.

'Was it a man, or a woman?' she asked, in a whisper, as we moved, at last, into the dark dampness of the outer air.

'I am not certain.'

'Which do you think?'

'It looked like a woman.'

'I was afraid it was a man in a long cloak.'

'It may be a man. In this dim light it is not possible to be certain.'

'Wait, Marian! I'm frightened—I don't see the path. Suppose the figure should follow us?'

'Not at all likely, Laura. There is really nothing to be alarmed about. The shores of the lake are not far from the village, and they are free to any one to walk on, by day or night. It is only wonderful we have seen no living creature there before.'

We were now in the plantation. It was very dark—so dark, that we found some difficulty in keeping the path. I gave Laura my arm, and we walked as fast as we could on our way back.

Before we were half way through, she stopped, and forced me to stop with her. She was listening.

'Hush!' she whispered. 'I hear something behind us.'

'Dead leaves,' I said, to cheer her, 'or a twig blown off the trees.'

'It is summer time, Marian; and there is not a breath of wind. Listen!'

I heard the sound, too—a sound like a light footstep following us.

'No matter who it is, or what it is,' I said; 'let us walk on. In another minute, if there is anything to alarm us, we shall be near enough to the house to be heard.'

We went on quickly—so quickly, that Laura was breathless by the time we were nearly through the plantation, and within sight of the lighted windows.

I waited a moment, to give her breathing-time. Just as we were about to proceed, she stopped me again, and signed to me with her hand to listen once more. We both heard distinctly a long, heavy sigh, behind us, in the black depths of the trees.

'Who's there?' I called out.

There was no answer.

'Who's there?' I repeated.

An instant of silence followed; and then we heard the light fall of the footsteps again, fainter and fainter—sinking away into the darkness—sinking, sinking, sinking—till they were lost in the silence.

We hurried out from the trees to the open lawn beyond; crossed it rapidly; and without another word passing between us, reached the house.

In the light of the hall-lamp, Laura looked at me, with white cheeks and startled eyes.

'I am half dead with fear,' she said. 'Who could it have been?'

'We will try to guess to-morrow,' I replied. 'In the mean time, say nothing to any one of what we have heard and seen.'

'Why not?'

'Because silence is safe—and we have need of safety in this house.'

I sent Laura up-stairs immediately—waited a minute to take off my hat, and put my hair smooth—and then went at once to make my first investigations in the library, on pretence of searching for a book.

There sat the Count, filling out the largest easy-chair in the house; smoking and reading calmly, with his feet on an ottoman, his cravat across his knees, and his shirt collar wide open. And there sat Madame Fosco, like a quiet child, on a stool by his side, making cigarettes. Neither husband nor wife could, by any possibility, have been out late that evening, and have just got back to the house in a hurry. I felt that my object in visiting the library was answered the moment I set eyes on them.

Count Fosco rose in polite confusion, and tied his cravat on, when I entered the room.

'Pray don't let me disturb you,' I said. 'I have only come here to get a book.'

'All unfortunate men of my size suffer from the heat,' said the Count, refreshing himself gravely with a large green fan. 'I wish I could change places with my excellent wife. She is as cool, at this moment, as a fish in the pond outside.'

The Countess allowed herself to thaw under the influence of her husband's quaint comparison. 'I am never warm, Miss Halcombe,' she remarked, with the modest air of a woman who was confessing to one of her own merits.

'Have you and Lady Glyde been out this evening?' asked the Count, while I was taking a book from the shelves, to preserve appearances.

'Yes; we went out to get a little air.'

'May I ask in what direction?'

'In the direction of the lake—as far as the boat-house.'

'Aha? As far as the boat-house?'

Under other circumstances, I might have resented his curiosity. But, to-night I hailed it as another proof that neither he nor his wife were connected with the mysterious appearance at the lake.

'No more adventures, I suppose, this evening?' he went on. 'No more discoveries, like your discovery of the wounded dog?'

He fixed his unfathomable grey eyes on me, with that cold, clear, irresistible glitter in them, which always forces me to look at him, and always makes me uneasy, while I do look. An unutterable suspicion that his mind is prying into mine, overcomes me at these times; and it overcame me now.

'No,' I said, shortly; 'no adventures—no discoveries.'

I tried to look away from him, and leave the room. Strange as it seems, I hardly think I should have succeeded in the attempt, if Madame Fosco had not helped me by causing him to move and look away first.

'Count, you are keeping Miss Halcombe standing,' she said.

The moment he turned round to get me a chair, I seized my opportunity—thanked him—made my excuses—and slipped out.

An hour later, when Laura's maid happened to be in her mistress's room, I took occasion to refer to the closeness of the night, with a view to ascertaining next how the servants had been passing their time.

'Have you been suffering much from the heat, down stairs?' I asked.

'No, miss,' said the girl; 'we have not felt it to speak of.'

'You have been out in the woods, then, I suppose?'

'Some of us thought of going, miss. But cook said she should take her chair into the cool court-yard, outside the kitchen door; and, on second thoughts, all the rest of us took our chairs out there, too.'

The housekeeper was now the only person who remained to be accounted for.

'Is Mrs Michelson gone to bed yet?' I inquired.

'I should think not, miss,' said the girl, smiling. 'Mrs Michelson is more likely to be getting up, just now, than going to bed.'

'Why? What do you mean? Has Mrs Michelson been taking to her bed in the daytime?'

'No, miss; not exactly, but the next thing to it. She's been asleep all the evening, on the sofa in her own room.'

Putting together what I observed for myself in the library and what I have just heard from Laura's maid, one conclusion seems inevitable. The figure we saw at the lake, was not the figure of Madame Fosco, of her husband, or of any of the servants. The footsteps we heard behind us were not the footsteps of any one belonging to the house.

Who could it have been?

It seems useless to inquire. I cannot even decide whether the figure was a man's or a woman's. I can only say that I think it was a woman's.

JUNE 18TH.—The misery of self-reproach which I suffered, yesterday evening, on hearing what Laura told me in the boat-house, returned in the loneliness of the night, and kept me waking and wretched for hours.

I lighted the candle at last, and searched through my old journals to see what my share in the fatal error of her marriage had really been, and what I might have once done to save her from it. The result soothed me a little—for it showed that, however blindly and ignorantly I acted, I acted for the best. Crying generally does me harm; but it was not so last night—I think it relieved me. I rose this morning with a settled resolution and a quiet mind. Nothing Sir Percival can say or do shall ever irritate me again, or make me forget, for one moment, that I am staying here, in defiance of mortifications, insults, and threats, for Laura's service and for Laura's sake.

The speculations in which we might have indulged, this morning, on the subject of the figure at the lake and the footsteps in the plantation, have been all suspended by a trifling accident which has caused Laura great regret. She has lost the little brooch I gave her for a keepsake, on the day before her marriage. As she wore it when we went out yesterday evening, we can only suppose that it must have dropped from her dress, either in the boat-house, or on our way back. The servants have been sent to search, and have returned unsuccessful. And now Laura herself has gone to look for it. Whether she finds it, or not, the loss will help to excuse her absence from the house, if Sir Percival returns before the letter from Mr Gilmore's partner is placed in my hands.

One o'clock has just struck. I am considering whether I had better wait here for the arrival of the messenger from London, or slip away quietly, and watch for him outside the lodge gate.

My suspicion of everybody and everything in this house inclines me to think that the second plan may be the best. The Count is safe in the breakfast-room. I heard him, through the door, as I ran up-stairs, ten minutes since, exercising his canary-birds at their tricks:—'Come out on my little finger, my pret-pret-pretties! Come out, and hop up-stairs! One, two, three—and up! Three, two, one—and down! One, two, three—twit-twit-twit-tweet!' The birds burst into their usual ecstasy of singing, and the Count chirruped and whistled at them in return, as if he was a bird himself. My room door is open, and I can hear the shrill singing and whistling at this moment. If I am really to slip out, without being observed—now is my time.

Four o'clock. The three hours that have passed since I made my last entry, have turned the whole march of events at Blackwater Park in a new direction. Whether for good or for evil, I cannot and dare not decide.

Let me get back first to the place at which I left off—or I shall lose myself in the confusion of my own thoughts.

I went out, as I had proposed, to meet the messenger with my letter from London, at the lodge gate. On the stairs I saw no one. In the hall I heard the Count still exercising his birds. But on crossing the quadrangle outside, I passed Madame Fosco, walking by herself in her favourite circle, round and round the great fish-pond. I at once slackened my pace, so as to avoid all appearance of being in a hurry; and even went the length, for caution's sake, of inquiring if she thought of going out before lunch. She smiled at me in the friendliest manner—said she preferred remaining near the house—nodded pleasantly—and re-entered the hall. I looked back, and saw that she had closed the door before I had opened the wicket by the side of the carriage gates.

In less than a quarter of an hour, I reached the lodge.

The lane outside took a sudden turn to the left, ran on straight for a hundred yards or so, and then took another sharp turn to the right to join the high-road. Between these two turns, hidden from the lodge on one side and from the way to the station on the other, I waited, walking backwards and forwards. High hedges were on either side of me; and, for twenty minutes by my watch, I neither saw nor heard anything. At the end of that time, the sound of a carriage caught my ear; and I was met, as I advanced towards the second turning, by a fly from the railway. I made a sign to the driver to stop. As he obeyed me, a respectable-looking man put his head out of the window to see what was the matter.

'I beg your pardon.' I said; 'but am I right in supposing that you are going to Blackwater Park?'

'Yes, ma'am.'

'With a letter for any one?'

'With a letter for Miss Halcombe, ma'am.'

'You may give me the letter. I am Miss Halcombe.'

The man touched his hat, got out of the fly immediately, and gave me the letter.

I opened it at once; and read these lines. I copy them here, thinking it best to destroy the original for caution's sake.

'DEAR MADAM. Your letter, received this morning, has caused me very great anxiety. I will reply to it as briefly and plainly as possible.

'My careful consideration of the statement made by yourself, and my knowledge of Lady Glyde's position, as defined in the settlement, lead me, I regret to say, to the conclusion that a loan of the trust money to Sir Percival (or, in other words, a loan of some portion of the twenty thousand pounds of Lady Glyde's fortune), is in contemplation, and that she is made a party to the deed, in order to secure her approval of a flagrant breach of trust, and to have her signature produced against her, if she should complain hereafter. It is impossible, on any other supposition, to account, situated as she is, for her execution to a deed of any kind being wanted at all.

'In the event of Lady Glyde's signing such a document as I am compelled to suppose the deed in question to be, her trustees would be at liberty to advance money to Sir Percival out of her twenty thousand pounds. If the amount so lent should not be paid back, and if Lady Glyde should have children, their fortune would then be diminished by the sum, large or small, so advanced. In plainer terms still, the transaction, for anything that Lady Glyde knows to the contrary, may be a fraud upon her unborn children.

'Under these serious circumstances, I would recommend Lady Glyde to assign as a reason for withholding her signature, that she wishes the deed to be first submitted to myself, as her family solicitor (in the absence of my partner, Mr Gilmore). No reasonable objection can be made to taking this course—for, if the transaction is an honourable one, there will necessarily be no difficulty in my giving my approval.

'Sincerely assuring you of my readiness to afford any additional help or advice that may be wanted, I beg to remain, Madam, your faithful servant,
WILLIAM KYRLE.'

I read this kind and sensible letter very thankfully. It supplied Laura with a reason for objecting to the signature which was unanswerable, and which we could both of us understand. The messenger waited near me while I was reading, to receive his directions when I had done.

'Will you be good enough to say that I understand the letter, and that I am very much obliged?' I said. 'There is no other reply necessary at present.'

Exactly at the moment when I was speaking those words, holding the letter open in my hand, Count Fosco turned the corner of the lane from the high-road, and stood before me as if he had sprung up out of the earth.

The suddenness of his appearance, in the very last place under heaven in which I should have expected to see him, took me completely by surprise. The messenger wished me good morning, and got into the fly again. I could not say a word to him—I was not even able to return his bow. The conviction that I was discovered—and by that man, of all others—absolutely petrified me.

'Are you going back to the house, Miss Halcombe?' he inquired, without showing the least surprise on his side, and without even looking after the fly, which drove off while he was speaking to me.

I collected myself sufficiently to make a sign in the affirmative.

'I am going back, too,' he said. 'Pray allow me the pleasure of accompanying you. Will you take my arm? You look surprised at seeing me!'

I took his arm. The first of my scattered senses that came back was the sense that warned me to sacrifice anything rather than make an enemy of him.

'You look surprised at seeing me!' he repeated, in his quietly pertinacious way.

'I thought, Count, I heard you with your birds in the breakfast-room,' I answered, as quietly and firmly as I could.

'Surely. But my little feathered children, dear lady, are only too like other children. They have their days of perversity; and this morning was one of them. My wife came in, as I was putting them back in their cage, and said she had left you going out alone for a walk. You told her so, did you not?'

'Certainly.'

'Well, Miss Halcombe, the pleasure of accompanying you was too great a temptation for me to resist. At my age there is no harm in confessing so much as that, is there? I seized my hat, and set off to offer myself as your escort. Even so fat an old man as Fosco is surely better than no escort at all? I took the wrong path—I came back, in despair—and here I am, arrived (may I say it?) at the height of my wishes.'

He talked on, in this complimentary strain, with a fluency which left me no exertion to make beyond the effort of maintaining my composure. He never referred in the most distant manner to what he had seen in the lane, or to the letter which I still had in my hand. This ominous discretion helped to convince me that he must have surprised, by the most dishonourable means, the secret of my application in Laura's interests, to the lawyer; and that, having now assured himself of the private manner in which I had received the answer, he had discovered enough to suit his purposes, and was only bent on trying to quiet the suspicions which he knew he must have aroused in my mind. I was wise enough, under these circumstances, not to attempt to deceive him by plausible explanations—and woman enough, notwithstanding my dread of him, to feel as if my hand was tainted by resting on his arm.

On the drive in front of the house we met the dog-cart being taken round to the stables. Sir Percival had just returned. He came out to meet us at the house-door. Whatever other results his journey might have had, it had not ended in softening his savage temper.

'Oh! here are two of you come back,' he said, with a lowering face. 'What is the meaning of the house being deserted in this way? Where is Lady Glyde?'

I told him of the loss of the brooch, and said that Laura had gone into the plantation to look for it.

'Brooch or no brooch,' he growled, sulkily, 'I recommend her not to forget her appointment in the library, this afternoon. I shall expect to see her in half an hour.'

I took my hand from the Count's arm, and slowly ascended the steps. He honoured me with one of his magnificent bows; and then addressed himself gaily to the scowling master of the house.

'Tell me, Percival,' he said, 'have you had a pleasant drive? And has your pretty shining Brown Molly come back at all tired?'

'Brown Molly be hanged—and the drive, too! I want my lunch.'

'And I want five minutes' talk with you, Percival, first,' returned the Count. 'Five minutes' talk, my friend, here on the grass.'

'What about?'

'About business that very much concerns you.'

I lingered long enough, in passing through the hall-door, to hear this question and answer, and to see Sir Percival thrust his hands into his pockets, in sullen hesitation.

'If you want to badger me with any more of your infernal scruples,' he said, 'I, for one, won't hear them. I want my lunch!'

'Come out here, and speak to me,' repeated the Count, still perfectly uninfluenced by the rudest speech that his friend could make to him.

Sir Percival descended the steps. The Count took him by the arm, and walked him away gently. The 'business,' I was sure, referred to the question of the signature. They were speaking of Laura and of me, beyond a doubt. I felt heart-sick and faint with anxiety. It might be of the last importance to both of us to know what they were saying to each other at that moment—and not one word of it could, by any possibility, reach my ears.

I walked about the house, from room to room, with the lawyer's letter in my bosom (I was afraid, by this time, even to trust it under lock and key), till the oppression of my suspense half maddened me. There were no signs of Laura's return; and I thought of going out to look for her. But my strength was so exhausted by the trials and anxieties of the morning, that the heat of the day quite overpowered me; and, after an attempt to get to the door, I was obliged to return to the drawing-room, and lie down on the nearest sofa to recover.

I was just composing myself, when the door opened softly, and the Count looked in.

'A thousand pardons, Miss Halcombe,' he said; 'I only venture to disturb you because I am the bearer of good news. Percival—who is capricious in everything, as you know—has seen fit to alter his mind, at the last moment; and the business of the signature is put off for the present. A great relief to all of us, Miss Halcombe, as I see with pleasure in your face. Pray present my best respects and felicitations, when you mention this pleasant change of circumstances to Lady Glyde.'

He left me before I had recovered my astonishment. There could be no doubt that this extraordinary alteration of purpose in the matter of the signature, was due to his influence; and that his discovery of my application to London yesterday, and of my having received an answer to it to-day, had offered him the means of interfering with certain success.

I felt these impressions; but my mind seemed to share the exhaustion of my body, and I was in no condition to dwell on them, with any useful reference to the doubtful present, or the threatening future. I tried a second time to run out, and find Laura; but my head was giddy, and my knees trembled under me. There was no choice but to give it up again, and return to the sofa, sorely against my will.

The quiet in the house, and the low murmuring hum of summer insects outside the open window, soothed me. My eyes closed of themselves; and I passed gradually into a strange condition, which was not waking—for I knew nothing of what was going on about me; and not sleeping—for I was conscious of my own repose. In this state, my fevered mind broke loose from me, while my weary body was at rest; and, in a trance, or day-dream of my fancy—I know not what to call it—I saw Walter Hartright. I had not thought of him, since I rose that morning; Laura had not said one word to me either directly or indirectly referring to him—and yet, I saw him now, as plainly as if the past time had returned, and we were both together again at Limmeridge House.

He appeared to me as one among many other men, none of whose faces I could plainly discern. They were all lying on the steps of an immense ruined temple. Colossal tropical trees—with rank creepers twining endlessly about their trunks, and hideous stone idols glimmering and grinning at intervals behind leaves and stalks and branches—surrounded the temple, and shut out the sky, and threw a dismal shadow over the forlorn band of men on the steps. White exhalations twisted and curled up stealthily from the ground; approached the men in wreaths, like smoke; touched them; and stretched them out dead, one by one, in the places where they lay. An agony of pity and fear for Walter loosened my tongue, and I implored him to escape. 'Come back! come back!' I said. 'Remember your promise to *her* and to *me*. Come back to us, before the Pestilence reaches you, and lays you dead like the rest!'

He looked at me, with an unearthly quiet in his face. 'Wait,' he said. 'I shall come back. The night, when I met the lost Woman on the highway, was the night which set my life apart to be the instrument of a Design that is yet unseen. Here, lost in the wilderness, or there, welcomed back in the land of my birth, I am still walking on the dark road which leads me, and you, and the sister of your love and mine, to the unknown Retribution and the inevitable End. Wait and look. The Pestilence which touches the rest will pass *me*.'

I saw him again. He was still in the forest; and the numbers of his lost companions had dwindled to very few. The temple was gone, and the idols were gone—and, in their place, the figures of dark, dwarfish men lurked murderously among the trees, with bows in their hands, and arrows fitted to the string. Once more, I feared for Walter, and cried out to warn him. Once more, he turned to me, with the immovable quiet in his face. 'Another step,' he said, 'on the dark road. Wait and look. The arrows that strike the rest will spare *me*.'

I saw him for the third time, in a wrecked ship, stranded on a wild, sandy shore. The overloaded boats were making away from him for the land, and he alone was left, to sink with the ship. I cried to him to hail the hindmost boat, and to make a last effort for his life. The quiet face looked at me in return, and the unmoved voice gave me back the changeless reply. 'Another step on the journey. Wait and look. The Sea which drowns the rest will spare *me*.'

I saw him for the last time. He was kneeling by a tomb of white marble; and the shadow of a veiled woman rose out of the grave beneath, and waited by his side. The unearthly quiet of his face had changed to an unearthly sorrow. But the terrible certainty of his words remained the same. 'Darker and darker,' he said; 'farther and farther yet. Death takes the good, the beautiful, and the young—and spares *me*. The Pestilence that wastes, the Arrow that strikes, the Sea that drowns, the Grave that closes over Love and Hope, are steps of my journey, and take me nearer and nearer to the End.'

My heart sank under a dread beyond words, under a grief beyond tears. The darkness closed round the pilgrim at the marble tomb; closed round the veiled woman from the grave; closed round the dreamer who looked on them. I saw and heard no more.

I was aroused by a hand laid on my shoulder. It was Laura's.

She had dropped on her knees by the side of the sofa. Her face was flushed and agitated; and her eyes met mine in a wild bewildered manner. I started up the instant I saw her.

'What has happened?' I asked. 'What has frightened you?'

She looked round at the half-open door—put her lips close to my ear—and answered in a whisper:

'Marian!—the figure at the lake—the footsteps last night—I've just seen her! I've just spoken to her!'

'Who, for Heaven's sake?'

'Anne Catherick.'

I WAS so startled by the disturbance in Laura's face and manner, and so dismayed by the first waking impressions of my dream, that I was not fit to bear the revelation which burst upon me, when the name of Anne Catherick passed her lips. I could only stand rooted to the floor, looking at her in breathless silence.

She was too much absorbed by what had happened to notice the effect which her reply had produced on me. 'I have seen Anne Catherick! I have spoken to Anne Catherick!' she repeated, as if I had not heard her. 'Oh, Marian, I have such things to tell you! Come away—we may be interrupted here—come at once into my room!'

With those eager words, she caught me by the hand, and led me through the library, to the end room on the ground floor, which had been fitted up for her own especial use. No third person, except her maid, could have any excuse for surprising us here. She pushed me in before her, locked the door, and drew the chintz curtains that hung over the inside.

The strange, stunned feeling which had taken possession of me still remained. But a growing conviction that the complications which had long threatened to gather about her, and to gather about me, had suddenly closed fast round us both, was now beginning to penetrate my mind. I could not express it in words—I could hardly even realise it dimly in my own thoughts. 'Anne Catherick!' I whispered to myself, with useless, helpless reiteration—'Anne Catherick!'

Laura drew me to the nearest seat, an ottoman in the middle of the room. 'Look!' she said; 'look here!'—and pointed to the bosom of her dress.

I saw, for the first time, that the lost brooch was pinned in its place again. There was something real in the sight of it, something real in the touching of it afterwards, which seemed to steady the whirl and confusion in my thoughts, and to help me to compose myself.

'Where did you find your brooch?' The first words I could say to her were the words which put that trivial question at that important moment.

'*She* found it, Marian.'

'Where?'

'On the floor of the boat-house. Oh, how shall I begin—how shall I tell you about it! She talked to me so strangely—she looked so fearfully ill—she left me so suddenly——!'

Her voice rose as the tumult of her recollections pressed upon her mind. The inveterate distrust which weighs, night and day, on my spirits in this house, instantly roused me to warn her—just as the sight of the brooch had roused me to question her, the moment before.

'Speak low,' I said. 'The window is open, and the garden path runs beneath it. Begin at the beginning, Laura. Tell me, word for word, what passed between that woman and you.'

'Shall I close the window first?'

'No; only speak low: only remember that Anne Catherick is a dangerous subject under your husband's roof. Where did you first see her?'

'At the boat-house, Marian. I went out, as you know, to find my brooch; and I walked along the path through the plantation, looking down on the ground carefully at every step. In that way I got on, after a long time, to the boat-house; and, as soon as I was inside it, I went on my knees to hunt over the floor. I was still searching, with my back to the doorway, when I heard a soft, strange voice, behind me, say, "Miss Fairlie."'

'Miss Fairlie!'

'Yes—my old name—the dear, familiar name that I thought I had parted from for ever. I started up—not frightened, the voice was too kind and gentle to frighten anybody—but very much surprised. There, looking at me from the doorway, stood a woman, whose face I never remembered to have seen before——'

'How was she dressed?'

'She had a neat, pretty white gown on, and over it a poor worn thin dark shawl. Her bonnet was of brown straw, as poor and worn as the shawl. I was struck by the difference between her gown and the rest of her dress, and she saw that I noticed it. "Don't look at my bonnet and shawl," she said, speaking in a quick, breathless, sudden way; "if I mustn't wear white, I don't care what I wear. Look at my gown, as much as you please; I'm not ashamed of that." Very strange, was it not? Before I could say anything to soothe her, she held out one of her hands, and I saw my brooch in it. I was so pleased and so grateful, that I went quite close to her to say what I really felt. "Are you thankful enough to do me one little kindness?" she asked. "Yes, indeed," I answered; "any kindness in my power I shall be glad to show you." "Then let me pin your brooch on for you, now I have found it." Her request was so unexpected, Marian, and she made it with such extraordinary eagerness, that I drew back a step or two, not well knowing what to do. "Ah!" she said, "your mother would have let me pin on the brooch." There was something in her voice and her look, as well as in her mentioning my mother in that reproachful manner, which made me ashamed of my distrust. I took her hand with the brooch in it, and put it up gently on the bosom of my dress. "You knew my mother?" I said. "Was it very long ago? have I ever seen you before?" Her hands were busy fastening the brooch: she stopped and pressed them against my breast. "You don't remember a fine spring day at Limmeridge," she said, "and your mother walking down the path that led to the school, with a little girl on each side of her? I have had nothing else to think of since; and *I* remember it. You were one of the little girls, and I was the other. Pretty, clever Miss Fairlie, and poor dazed Anne Catherick were nearer to each other, then, than they are now!"——'

'Did you remember her, Laura, when she told you her name?'

'Yes—I remembered your asking me about Anne Catherick at Limmeridge, and your saying that she had once been considered like me.'

'What reminded you of that, Laura?'

'*She* reminded me. While I was looking at her, while she was very close to me, it came over my mind suddenly that we were like each other! Her face was pale and thin and weary—but the sight of it startled me, as if it had been the sight of my own face in the glass after a long illness. The discovery—I don't know why—gave me such a shock, that I was perfectly incapable of speaking to her, for the moment.'

'Did she seem hurt by your silence?'

'I am afraid she was hurt by it. "You have not got your mother's face," she said, "or your mother's heart. Your mother's face was dark; and your mother's heart, Miss Fairlie, was the heart of an angel." "I am sure I feel kindly towards you," I said, "though I may not be able to express it as I ought. Why do you call me Miss Fairlie——?" "Because I love the name of

Fairlie and hate the name of Glyde," she broke out, violently. I had seen nothing like madness in her before this; but I fancied I saw it now in her eyes. "I only thought you might not know I was married," I said, remembering the wild letter she wrote to me at Limmeridge, and trying to quiet her. She sighed bitterly, and turned away from me. "Not know you were married!" she repeated. "I am here *because* you are married. I am here to make atonement to you, before I meet your mother in the world beyond the grave." She drew farther and farther away from me, till she was out of the boat-house—and, then, she watched and listened for a little while. When she turned round to speak again, instead of coming back, she stopped where she was, looking in at me, with a hand on each side of the entrance. "Did you see me at the lake last night?" she said. "Did you hear me following you in the wood? I have been waiting for days together to speak to you alone—I have left the only friend I have in the world, anxious and frightened about me—I have risked being shut up again in the madhouse—and all for your sake, Miss Fairlie, all for your sake." Her words alarmed me, Marian; and yet, there was something in the way she spoke, that made me pity her with all my heart. I am sure my pity must have been sincere, for it made me bold enough to ask the poor creature to come in, and sit down in the boat-house, by my side.'

'Did she do so?'

'No. She shook her head, and told me she must stop where she was, to watch and listen, and see that no third person surprised us. And from first to last, there she waited at the entrance, with a hand on each side of it; sometimes bending in suddenly to speak to me; sometimes drawing back suddenly to look about her. "I was here yesterday," she said, "before it came dark; and I heard you, and the lady with you, talking together. I heard you tell her about your husband. I heard you say you had no influence to make him believe you, and no influence to keep him silent. Ah! I knew what those words meant; my conscience told me while I was listening. Why did I ever let you marry him! Oh, my fear—my mad, miserable, wicked fear!——" She covered up her face in her poor worn shawl, and moaned and murmured to herself behind it. I began to be afraid she might break out into some terrible despair which neither she nor I could master. "Try to quiet yourself," I said; "try to tell me how you might have prevented my marriage." She took the shawl from her face, and looked at me vacantly. "I ought to have had heart enough to stop at Limmeridge," she answered. "I ought never to have let the news of his coming there frighten me away. I ought to have warned you and saved you before it was too late. Why did I only have courage enough to write you that letter? Why did I only do harm, when I wanted and meant to do good? Oh, my fear—my mad, miserable, wicked fear!" She repeated those words again, and hid her face again in the end of her poor worn shawl. It was dreadful to see her, and dreadful to hear her.'

'Surely, Laura, you asked what the fear was which she dwelt on so earnestly?'

'Yes; I asked that.'

'And what did she say?'

'She asked me, in return, if *I* should not be afraid of a man who had shut me up in a madhouse, and who would shut me up again, if he could? I said, "Are you afraid still? Surely you would not be here, if you were afraid now?" "No," she said, "I am not afraid now." I asked why not. She suddenly bent forward into the boat-house, and said, "Can't you guess why?" I shook my head. "Look at me," she went on. I told her I was grieved to see that she looked very sorrowful and very ill. She smiled, for the first time. "Ill?" she repeated; "I'm dying. You know why I'm not afraid of him now. Do you think I shall meet your mother in heaven? Will she forgive me, if I do?" I was so shocked and so startled, that I could make no reply. "I have been thinking of it," she went on, "all the time I have been in hiding from your husband, all the time I lay ill. My thoughts have driven me here—I want to make atonement—I want to undo all I can of the harm I once did." I begged her as earnestly as I could to tell me what she meant. She still looked at me with fixed, vacant eyes. "*Shall* I undo the harm?" she said to herself, doubtfully. "You have friends to take your part. If *you* know his Secret, he will be afraid of you; he won't dare use you as he used me. He must treat you mercifully for his own sake, if he is afraid of you and your friends. And if he treats you mercifully, and if I can say it was my doing——" I listened eagerly for more; but she stopped at those words.'

'You tried to make her go on?'

'I tried; but she only drew herself away from me again, and leaned her face and arms against the side of the boat-house. "Oh!" I heard her say, with a dreadful, distracted tenderness in her voice, "oh! if I could only be buried with your mother! If I could only wake at her side, when the angel's trumpet sounds, and the graves give up their dead at the resurrection!"—Marian! I trembled from head to foot—it was horrible to hear her. "But there is no hope of that," she said, moving a little, so as to look at me again; "no hope for a poor stranger like me. *I* shall not rest under the marble cross that I washed with my own hands, and made so white and pure for her sake. Oh no! oh no! God's mercy, not man's, will take me to her, where the wicked cease from troubling and the weary are at rest." She spoke those words quietly and sorrowfully, with a heavy, hopeless sigh; and then waited a little. Her face was confused and troubled; she seemed to be thinking, or trying to think. "What was it I said just now?" she asked, after a while. "When your mother is in my mind, everything else goes out of it. What was I saying? what was I saying?" I reminded the poor creature, as kindly and delicately as I could. "Ah, yes, yes," she said, still in a vacant, perplexed manner. "You are helpless with your wicked husband. Yes. And I must do what I have

come to do here—I must make it up to you for having been afraid to speak
out at a better time." "What *is* it you have to tell me?" I asked. "The Secret
that your cruel husband is afraid of," she answered. "I once threatened him
with the Secret, and frightened him. You shall threaten him with the Secret,
and frighten him, too." Her face darkened; and a hard, angry stare fixed
itself in her eyes. She began waving her hand at me in a vacant, unmeaning
manner. "My mother knows the Secret," she said. "My mother has wasted
under the Secret half her lifetime. One day, when I was grown up, she said
something to *me*. And, the next day, your husband——" '

'Yes! yes! Go on. What did she tell you about your husband?'

'She stopped again, Marian, at that point——'

'And said no more?'

'And listened eagerly. "Hush!" she whispered, still waving her hand at me.
"Hush!" She moved aside out of the doorway, moved slowly and stealthily,
step by step, till I lost her past the edge of the boat-house.'

'Surely, you followed her?'

'Yes; my anxiety made me bold enough to rise and follow her. Just as I
reached the entrance, she appeared again, suddenly, round the side of the
boat-house. "The secret," I whispered to her—"wait and tell me the secret!"
She caught hold of my arm, and looked at me, with wild, frightened eyes.
"Not now," she said; "we are not alone—we are watched. Come here
to-morrow at this time—by yourself—mind—by yourself." She pushed me
roughly into the boat-house again; and I saw her no more.'

'Oh, Laura, Laura, another chance lost! If I had only been near you, she
should not have escaped us. On which side did you lose sight of her?'

'On the left side, where the ground sinks and the wood is thickest.'

'Did you run out again? did you call after her?'

'How could I? I was too terrified to move or speak.'

'But when you *did* move—when you came out——?'

'I ran back here, to tell you what had happened.'

'Did you see any one, or hear any one in the plantation?'

'No—it seemed to be all still and quiet, when I passed through it.'

I waited for a moment, to consider. Was this third person, supposed to
have been secretly present at the interview, a reality, or the creature of Anne
Catherick's excited fancy? It was impossible to determine. The one thing
certain was that we had failed again on the very brink of discovery—failed
utterly and irretrievably, unless Anne Catherick kept her appointment at the
boat-house, for the next day.

'Are you quite sure you have told me everything that passed? Every word
that was said?' I inquired.

'I think so,' she answered. 'My powers of memory, Marian, are not like
yours. But I was so strongly impressed, so deeply interested, that nothing of
any importance can possibly have escaped me.'

'My dear Laura, the merest trifles are of importance where Anne Catherick is concerned. Think again. Did no chance reference escape her as to the place in which she is living at the present time?'

'None that I can remember.'

'Did she not mention a companion and friend—a woman named Mrs Clements?'

'Oh, yes! yes! I forgot that. She told me Mrs Clements wanted sadly to go with her to the lake, and take care of her, and begged and prayed that she would not venture into this neighbourhood alone.'

'Was that all she said about Mrs Clements?'

'Yes, that was all.'

'She told you nothing about the place in which she took refuge after leaving Todd's Corner?'

'Nothing—I am quite sure.'

'Nor where she has lived since? Nor what her illness had been?'

'No, Marian; not a word. Tell me, pray tell me, what you think about it. I don't know what to think, or what to do next.'

'You must do this, my love: You must carefully keep the appointment at the boat-house, to-morrow. It is impossible to say what interests may not depend on your seeing that woman again. You shall not be left to yourself a second time. I will follow you, at a safe distance. Nobody shall see me; but I will keep within hearing of your voice, if anything happens. Anne Catherick has escaped Walter Hartright, and has escaped *you*. Whatever happens, she shall not escape *me*.'

Laura's eyes read mine attentively.

'You believe,' she said, 'in this secret that my husband is afraid of? Suppose, Marian, it should only exist, after all, in Anne Catherick's fancy? Suppose she only wanted to see me and to speak to me, for the sake of old remembrances? Her manner was so strange, I almost doubted her. Would you trust her in other things?'

'I trust nothing, Laura, but my own observation of your husband's conduct. I judge Anne Catherick's words by his actions—and I believe there *is* a secret.

I said no more, and got up to leave the room. Thoughts were troubling me, which I might have told her if we had spoken together longer, and which it might have been dangerous for her to know. The influence of the terrible dream from which she had awakened me, hung darkly and heavily over every fresh impression which the progress of her narrative produced on my mind. I felt the ominous Future, coming close; chilling me, with an unutterable awe; forcing on me the conviction of an unseen Design in the long series of complications which had now fastened round us. I thought of Hartright—as I saw him, in the body, when he said farewell; as I saw him, in the spirit, in my dream—and I, too, began to doubt now whether we were not advancing, blindfold, to an appointed and an inevitable End.

Leaving Laura to go up-stairs alone, I went out to look about me in the walks near the house. The circumstances under which Anne Catherick had parted from her, had made me secretly anxious to know how Count Fosco was passing the afternoon; and had rendered me secretly distrustful of the results of the solitary journey from which Sir Percival had returned but a few hours since.

After looking for them in every direction, and discovering nothing, I returned to the house, and entered the different rooms on the ground floor, one after another. They were all empty. I came out again into the hall, and went up-stairs to return to Laura. Madame Fosco opened her door, as I passed it in my way along the passage; and I stopped to see if she could inform me of the whereabouts of her husband and Sir Percival. Yes; she had seen them both from her window more than an hour since. The Count had looked up, with his customary kindness, and had mentioned, with his habitual attention to her in the smallest trifles, that he and his friend were going out together for a long walk.

For a long walk! They had never yet been in each other's company with that object in my experience of them. Sir Percival cared for no exercise but riding: and the Count (except when he was polite enough to be my escort) cared for no exercise at all.

When I joined Laura again, I found that she had called to mind, in my absence, the impending question of the signature to the deed, which, in the interest of discussing her interview with Anne Catherick, we had hitherto overlooked. Her first words when I saw her, expressed her surprise at the absence of the expected summons to attend Sir Percival in the library.

'You may make your mind easy on that subject,' I said. 'For the present, at least, neither your resolution nor mine will be exposed to any further trial. Sir Percival has altered his plans: the business of the signature is put off.'

'Put off?' Laura repeated, amazedly. 'Who told you so?'

'My authority is Count Fosco. I believe it is to his interference that we are indebted for your husband's sudden change of purpose.'

'It seems impossible, Marian. If the object of my signing was, as we suppose, to obtain money for Sir Percival that he urgently wanted, how can the matter be put off?'

'I think, Laura, we have the means at hand of setting that doubt at rest. Have you forgotten the conversation that I heard between Sir Percival and the lawyer, as they were crossing the hall?'

'No; but I don't remember——'

'I do. There were two alternatives proposed. One, was to obtain your signature to the parchment. The other, was to gain time by giving bills at three months. The last resource is evidently the resource now adopted—and we may fairly hope to be relieved from our share in Sir Percival's embarrassments for some time to come.'

'Oh, Marian, it sounds too good to be true!'

'Does it, my love? You complimented me on my ready memory not long since—but you seem to doubt it now. I will get my journal, and you shall see if I am right or wrong.'

I went away and got the book at once.

On looking back to the entry referring to the lawyer's visit, we found that my recollection of the two alternatives presented was accurately correct. It was almost as great a relief to my mind as to Laura's, to find that my memory had served me, on this occasion, as faithfully as usual. In the perilous uncertainty of our present situation, it is hard to say what future interests may not depend upon the regularity of the entries in my journal, and upon the reliability of my recollection at the time when I make them.

Laura's face and manner suggested to me that this last consideration had occurred to her as well as to myself. Any way, it is only a trifling matter; and I am almost ashamed to put it down here in writing—it seems to set the forlornness of our situation in such a miserably vivid light. We must have little indeed to depend on, when the discovery that my memory can still be trusted to serve us, is hailed as if it was the discovery of a new friend!

The first bell for dinner separated us. Just as it had done ringing, Sir Percival and the Count returned from their walk. We heard the master of the house storming at the servants for being five minutes late; and the master's guest interposing, as usual, in the interests of propriety, patience, and peace.

    *   *   *   *   *

The evening has come and gone. No extraordinary event has happened. But I have noticed certain peculiarities in the conduct of Sir Percival and the Count, which have sent me to my bed, feeling very anxious and uneasy about Anne Catherick, and about the results which to-morrow may produce.

I know enough by this time, to be sure that the aspect of Sir Percival which is the most false, and which, therefore, means the worst, is his polite aspect. That long walk with his friend had ended in improving his manners, especially towards his wife. To Laura's secret surprise and to my secret alarm, he called her by her Christian name, asked if she had heard lately from her uncle, inquired when Mrs Vesey was to receive her invitation to Blackwater, and showed her so many other little attentions, that he almost recalled the days of his hateful courtship at Limmeridge House. This was a bad sign, to begin with; and I thought it more ominous still, that he should pretend, after dinner, to fall asleep in the drawing-room, and that his eyes should cunningly follow Laura and me, when he thought we neither of us suspected him. I have never had any doubt that his sudden journey by himself took him to Welmingham to question Mrs Catherick—but the experience of to-night has made me fear that the expedition was not

undertaken in vain, and that he has got the information which he unquestionably left us to collect. If I knew where Anne Catherick was to be found,
I would be up to-morrow with sunrise, and warn her.

While the aspect under which Sir Percival presented himself, to-night, was
unhappily but too familiar to me, the aspect under which the Count
appeared was, on the other hand, entirely new in my experience of him. He
permitted me, this evening, to make his acquaintance, for the first time, in
the character of a Man of Sentiment—of sentiment, as I believe, really felt,
not assumed for the occasion.

For instance, he was quiet and subdued; his eyes and his voice expressed
a restrained sensibility. He wore (as if there was some hidden connexion
between his showiest finery and his deepest feeling) the most magnificent
waistcoat he had yet appeared in—it was made of pale sea-green silk, and
delicately trimmed with fine silver braid. His voice sank into the tenderest
inflections, his smile expressed a thoughtful, fatherly admiration, whenever
he spoke to Laura or to me. He pressed his wife's hand under the table,
when she thanked him for trifling little attentions at dinner. He took wine
with her. 'Your health and happiness, my angel! he said, with fond,
glistening eyes. He ate little or nothing; and sighed, and said 'Good
Percival!' when his friend laughed at him. After dinner, he took Laura by
the hand, and asked her if she would be 'so sweet as to play to him.' She
complied, through sheer astonishment. He sat by the piano, with his
watch-chain resting in folds, like a golden serpent, on the sea-green
protuberance of his waistcoat. His immense head lay languidly on one side;
and he gently beat time with two of his yellow-white fingers. He highly
approved of the music, and tenderly admired Laura's manner of playing—
not as poor Hartright used to praise it, with an innocent enjoyment of the
sweet sounds, but with a clear, cultivated, practical knowledge of the merits
of the composition, in the first place, and of the merits of the player's touch,
in the second. As the evening closed in, he begged that the lovely dying light
might not be profaned, just yet, by the appearance of the lamps. He came,
with his horribly silent tread, to the distant window at which I was standing,
to be out of his way and to avoid the very sight of him—he came to ask me
to support his protest against the lamps. If any one of them could only have
burnt him up, at that moment, I would have gone down to the kitchen, and
fetched it myself.

'Surely you like this modest, trembling English twilight?' he said, softly.
'Ah! I love it. I feel my inborn admiration of all that is noble and great and
good, purified by the breath of Heaven, on an evening like this. Nature has
such imperishable charms, such inextinguishable tendernesses for me!—I am
an old, fat man: talk which would become your lips, Miss Halcombe, sounds
like a derision and a mockery on mine. It is hard to be laughed at in my
moments of sentiment, as if my soul was like myself, old and overgrown.

Observe, dear lady, what a light is dying on the trees! Does it penetrate your heart, as it penetrates mine?'

He paused—looked at me—and repeated the famous lines of Dante on the Evening-time, with a melody and tenderness which added a charm of their own to the matchless beauty of the poetry itself.

'Bah!' he cried suddenly, as the last cadence of those noble Italian words died away on his lips; 'I make an old fool of myself, and only weary you all! Let us shut up the window in our bosoms and get back to the matter-of-fact world. Percival! I sanction the admission of the lamps. Lady Glyde—Miss Halcombe—Eleanor, my good wife—which of you will indulge me with a game at dominoes?'

He addressed us all; but he looked especially at Laura.

She had learnt to feel my dread of offending him, and she accepted his proposal. It was more than I could have done, at that moment. I could not have sat down at the same table with him, for any consideration. His eyes seemed to reach my inmost soul through the thickening obscurity of the twilight. His voice trembled along every nerve in my body, and turned me hot and cold alternately. The mystery and terror of my dream, which had haunted me, at intervals, all through the evening, now oppressed my mind with an unendurable foreboding and an unutterable awe. I saw the white tomb again, and the veiled woman rising out of it, by Hartright's side. The thought of Laura welled up like a spring in the depths of my heart, and filled it with waters of bitterness, never, never known to it before. I caught her by the hand, as she passed me on her way to the table, and kissed her as if that night was to part us for ever. While they were all gazing at me in astonishment, I ran out through the low window which was open before me to the ground—ran out to hide from them in the darkness; to hide even from myself.

We separated, that evening, later than usual. Towards midnight, the summer silence was broken by the shuddering of a low, melancholy wind among the trees. We all felt the sudden chill in the atmosphere; but the Count was the first to notice the stealthy rising of the wind. He stopped while he was lighting my candle for me, and held up his hand warningly:

'Listen!' he said. 'There will be a change to-morrow.'

JUNE 19TH.—The events of yesterday warned me to be ready, sooner or later, to meet the worst. To-day is not yet at an end; and the worst has come.

Judging by the closest calculation of time that Laura and I could make, we arrived at the conclusion that Anne Catherick must have appeared at the boat-house at half-past two o'clock, on the afternoon of yesterday. I accordingly arranged that Laura should just show herself at the luncheon table, to-day, and should then slip out at the first opportunity; leaving me behind to preserve appearances, and to follow her as soon as I could safely do so. This mode of proceeding, if no obstacles occurred to thwart us, would enable her to be at the boat-house before half-past two; and (when I left the table, in my turn) would take me to a safe position in the plantation, before three.

The change in the weather, which last night's wind warned us to expect, came with the morning. It was raining heavily, when I got up; and it continued to rain until twelve o'clock—when the clouds dispersed, the blue sky appeared, and the sun shone again with the bright promise of a fine afternoon.

My anxiety to know how Sir Percival and the Count would occupy the early part of the day, was by no means set at rest, so far as Sir Percival was concerned, by his leaving us immediately after breakfast, and going out by himself, in spite of the rain. He neither told us where he was going, nor when we might expect him back. We saw him pass the breakfast-room window, hastily, with his high boots and his waterproof coat on—and that was all.

The Count passed the morning quietly, in-doors; some part of it, in the library; some part, in the drawing-room, playing odds and ends of music on the piano, and humming to himself. Judging by appearances, the senti-mental side of his character was persistently inclined to betray itself still. He was silent and sensitive, and ready to sigh and languish ponderously (as only fat men *can* sigh and languish), on the smallest provocation.

Luncheon-time came; and Sir Percival did not return. The Count took his friend's place at the table—plaintively devoured the greater part of a fruit tart, submerged under a whole jugful of cream—and explained the full merit of the achievement to us, as soon as he had done. 'A taste for sweets,' he said, in his softest tones and his tenderest manner, 'is the innocent taste of women and children. I love to share it with them—it is another bond, dear ladies, between you and me.'

Laura left the table in ten minutes' time. I was sorely tempted to accompany her. But if we had both gone out together, we must have excited suspicion; and, worse still, if we allowed Anne Catherick to see Laura accompanied by a second person who was a stranger to her, we should in all probability forfeit her confidence, from that moment, never to regain it again.

I waited, therefore, as patiently as I could, until the servant came in to clear the table. When I quitted the room, there were no signs, in the house or out of it, of Sir Percival's return. I left the Count with a piece of sugar between his lips, and the vicious cockatoo scrambling up his waistcoat to get at it; while Madame Fosco, sitting opposite to her husband, watched the proceedings of his bird and himself, as attentively as if she had never seen anything of the sort before in her life. On my way to the plantation I kept carefully beyond the range of view from the luncheon-room window. Nobody saw me and nobody followed me. It was then a quarter to three o'clock by my watch.

Once among the trees, I walked rapidly, until I had advanced more than half way through the plantation. At that point, I slackened my pace, and proceeded cautiously—but I saw no one, and heard no voices. By little and little, I came within view of the back of the boat-house—stopped and listened—then went on, till I was close behind it, and must have heard any persons who were talking inside. Still the silence was unbroken: still, far and near, no sign of a living creature appeared anywhere.

After skirting round by the back of the building, first on one side, and then on the other, and making no discoveries, I ventured in front of it, and fairly looked in. The place was empty.

I called, 'Laura!'—at first, softly—then louder and louder. No one answered, and no one appeared. For all that I could see and hear, the only human creature in the neighbourhood of the lake and the plantation, was myself.

My heart began to beat violently; but I kept my resolution, and searched, first the boat-house, and then the ground in front of it, for any signs which might show me whether Laura had really reached the place or not. No mark of her presence appeared inside the building; but I found traces of her outside it, in footsteps on the sand.

I detected the footsteps of two persons—large footsteps, like a man's, and small footsteps, which, by putting my own feet into them and testing their size in that manner, I felt certain were Laura's. The ground was confusedly marked in this way, just before the boat-house. Close against one side of it, under shelter of the projecting roof, I discovered a little hole in the sand—a hole artificially made, beyond a doubt. I just noticed it, and then turned away immediately to trace the footsteps as far as I could, and to follow the direction in which they might lead me.

They led me, starting from the left-hand side of the boat-house, along the edge of the trees, a distance, I should think, of between two and three hundred yards—and then, the sandy ground showed no further trace of them. Feeling that the persons whose course I was tracking, must necessarily have entered the plantation at this point, I entered it, too. At first, I could find no path—but I discovered one, afterwards, just faintly traced among the trees; and followed it. It took me, for some distance, in the direction of the village, until I stopped at a point where another foot-track crossed it. The brambles grew thickly on either side of this second path. I stood, looking down it, uncertain which way to take next; and, while I looked, I saw on one thorny branch, some fragments of fringe from a woman's shawl. A closer examination of the fringe satisfied me that it had been torn from a shawl of Laura's; and I instantly followed the second path. It brought me out, at last, to my great relief, at the back of the house. I say to my great relief, because I inferred that Laura must, for some unknown reason, have returned before me by this roundabout way. I went in by the court-yard and the offices. The first person whom I met in crossing the servants'-hall, was Mrs Michelson, the housekeeper.

'Do you know,' I asked, 'whether Lady Glyde has come in from her walk or not?'

'My lady came in, a little while ago, with Sir Percival,' answered the housekeeper. 'I am afraid, Miss Halcombe, something very distressing has happened.'

My heart sank within me. 'You don't mean an accident!' I said, faintly.

'No, no—thank God, no accident. But my lady ran up-stairs to her own room in tears; and Sir Percival has ordered me to give Fanny warning to leave in an hour's time.'

Fanny was Laura's maid; a good, affectionate girl who had been with her for years—the only person in the house, whose fidelity and devotion we could both depend upon.

'Where is Fanny?' I inquired.

'In my room, Miss Halcombe. The young woman is quite overcome; and I told her to sit down, and try to recover herself.'

I went to Mrs Michelson's room, and found Fanny in a corner, with her box by her side, crying bitterly.

She could give me no explanation whatever of her sudden dismissal. Sir Percival had ordered that she should have a month's wages, in place of a month's warning, and go. No reason had been assigned; no objection had been made to her conduct. She had been forbidden to appeal to her mistress, forbidden even to see her for a moment to say good-by. She was to go without explanations or farewells—and to go at once.

After soothing the poor girl by a few friendly words, I asked where she proposed to sleep that night. She replied that she thought of going to the little inn in the village, the landlady of which was a respectable woman, known to the servants at Blackwater Park. The next morning, by leaving early, she might get back to her friends in Cumberland, without stopping in London, where she was a total stranger.

I felt directly that Fanny's departure offered us a safe means of communication with London and with Limmeridge House, of which it might be very important to avail ourselves. Accordingly, I told her that she might expect to hear from her mistress or from me in the course of the evening, and that she might depend on our both doing all that lay in our power to help her, under the trial of leaving us for the present. Those words said, I shook hands with her, and went up-stairs.

The door which led to Laura's room, was the door of an antechamber, opening on to the passage. When I tried it, it was bolted on the inside.

I knocked, and the door was opened by the same heavy, overgrown housemaid, whose lumpish insensibility had tried my patience so severely, on the day when I found the wounded dog. I had, since that time, discovered that her name was Margaret Porcher, and that she was the most awkward, slatternly, and obstinate servant in the house.

On opening the door, she instantly stepped out to the threshold, and stood grinning at me in stolid silence.

'Why do you stand there?' I said. 'Don't you see that I want to come in?'

'Ah, but you mustn't come in,' was the answer, with another and a broader grin still.

'How dare you talk to me in that way? Stand back instantly!'

She stretched out a great red hand and arm on each side of her, so as to bar the doorway, and slowly nodded her addle head at me.

'Master's orders,' she said; and nodded again.

I had need of all my self-control to warn me against contesting the matter with *her*, and to remind me that the next words I had to say must be addressed to her master. I turned my back on her, and instantly went down stairs to find him. My resolution to keep my temper under all the irritations that Sir Percival could offer, was, by this time, as completely forgotten—I say so to my shame—as if I had never made it. It did me good—after all I had sufered and suppressed in that house—it actually did me good to feel how angry I was.

The drawing-room and the breakfast-room were both empty. I went on to the library; and there I found Sir Percival, the Count, and Madame Fosco. They were all three standing up, close together, and Sir Percival had a little slip of paper in his hand. As I opened the door, I heard the Count say to him, 'No—a thousand times over, No.'

I walked straight up to him, and looked him full in the face.

'Am I to understand, Sir Percival, that your wife's room is a prison, and that your housemaid is the gaoler who keeps it?' I asked.

'Yes; that *is* what you are to understand,' he answered. 'Take care my gaoler hasn't got double duty to do—take care your room is not a prison, too.'

'Take *you* care how you treat your wife, and how you threaten *me*,' I broke out, in the heat of my anger. 'There are laws in England to protect women from cruelty and outrage. If you hurt a hair of Laura's head, if you dare to interfere with my freedom, come what come may, to those laws I will appeal.'

Instead of answering me, he turned round to the Count.

'What did I tell you?' he asked. 'What do you say now?'

'What I said before,' replied the Count—'No.'

Even in the vehemence of my anger, I felt his calm, cold, grey eyes on my face. They turned away from me, as soon as he had spoken, and looked significantly at his wife. Madame Fosco immediately moved close to my side, and, in that position, addressed Sir Percival before either of us could speak again.

'Favour me with your attention, for one moment,' she said, in her clear, icily-suppressed tones. 'I have to thank you, Sir Percival, for your hospitality; and to decline taking advantage of it any longer. I remain in no house in which ladies are treated as your wife and Miss Halcombe have been treated here to-day!'

Sir Percival drew back a step, and stared at her in dead silence. The declaration he had just heard—a declaration which he well knew, as I well knew, Madame Fosco would not have ventured to make without her husband's permission—seemed to petrify him with surprise. The Count stood by, and looked at his wife with the most enthusiastic admiration.

'She is sublime!' he said to himself. He approached her, while he spoke, and drew her hand through his arm. 'I am at your service, Eleanor,' he went on, with a quiet dignity that I had never noticed in him before. 'And at Miss Halcombe's service, if she will honour me by accepting all the assistance I can offer her.'

'Damn it! what do you mean?' cried Sir Percival, as the Count quietly moved away, with his wife, to the door.

'At other times I mean what I say; but, at this time, I mean what my wife says,' replied the impenetrable Italian. 'We have changed places, Percival, for once; and Madame Fosco's opinion is—mine.'

Sir Percival crumpled up the paper in his hand; and, pushing past the Count, with another oath, stood between him and the door.

'Have your own way,' he said, with baffled rage in his low, half-whispering tones. 'Have your own way—and see what comes of it.' With those words, he left the room.

Madame Fosco glanced inquiringly at her husband. 'He has gone away very suddenly,' she said. 'What does it mean?'

'It means that you and I together have brought the worst-tempered man in all England to his senses,' answered the Count. 'It means, Miss Halcombe, that Lady Glyde is relieved from a gross indignity, and you from the repetition of an unpardonable insult. Suffer me to express my admiration of your conduct and your courage at a very trying moment.'

'Sincere admiration,' suggested Madame Fosco.

'Sincere admiration,' echoed the Count.

I had no longer the strength of my first angry resistance to outrage and injury to support me. My heart-sick anxiety to see Laura; my sense of my own helpless ignorance of what had happened at the boat-house, pressed on me with an intolerable weight. I tried to keep up appearances, by speaking to the Count and his wife in the tone which they had chosen to adopt in speaking to me. But the words failed on my lips—my breath came short and thick—my eyes looked longingly, in silence, at the door. The Count, understanding my anxiety, opened it, went out, and pulled it to after him. At the same time Sir Percival's heavy step descended the stairs, I heard them whispering together, outside, while Madame Fosco was assuring me in her calmest and most conventional manner, that she rejoiced, for all our sakes, that Sir Percival's conduct had not obliged her husband and herself to leave Blackwater Park. Before she had done speaking, the whispering ceased, the door opened, and the Count looked in.

'Miss Halcombe,' he said, 'I am happy to inform you that Lady Glyde is mistress again in her own house. I thought it might be more agreeable to you to hear of this change for the better from *me*, than from Sir Percival— and I have, therefore, expressly returned to mention it.'

'Admirable delicacy!' said Madame Fosco, paying back her husband's tribute of admiration, with the Count's own coin, in the Count's own manner. He smiled and bowed as if he had received a formal compliment from a polite stranger, and drew back to let me pass out first.

Sir Percival was standing in the hall. As I hurried to the stairs I heard him call impatiently to the Count, to come out of the library.

'What are you waiting there for?' he said; 'I want to speak to you.'

'And I want to think a little by myself,' replied the other. 'Wait till later, Percival—wait till later.'

Neither he nor his friend said any more. I gained the top of the stairs, and ran along the passage. In my haste and my agitation, I left the door of the ante-chamber open—but I closed the door of the bedroom the moment I was inside it.

Laura was sitting alone at the far end of the room; her arms resting wearily on a table, and her face hidden in her hands. She started up, with a cry of delight, when she saw me.

'How did you get here?' she asked. 'Who gave you leave? Not Sir Percival?'

In my overpowering anxiety to hear what she had to tell me, I could not answer her—I could only put questions, on my side. Laura's eagerness to know what had passed down stairs proved, however, too strong to be resisted. She persistently repeated her inquiries.

'The Count, of course,' I answered, impatiently. 'Whose influence in the house——?'

She stopped me, with a gesture of disgust.

'Don't speak of him,' she cried. 'The Count is the vilest creature breathing! The Count is a miserable Spy——!'

Before we could either of us say another word, we were alarmed by a soft knocking at the door of the bedroom.

I had not yet sat down; and I went first to see who it was. When I opened the door, Madame Fosco confronted me, with my handkerchief in her hand.

'You dropped this down stairs, Miss Halcombe,' she said; 'and I thought I could bring it to you, as I was passing by to my own room.'

Her face, naturally pale, had turned to such a ghastly whiteness, that I started at the sight of it. Her hands, so sure and steady at all other times, trembled violently; and her eyes looked wolfishly past me through the open door, and fixed on Laura.

She had been listening before she knocked! I saw it in her white face; I saw it in her trembling hands; I saw it in her look at Laura.

After waiting an instant, she turned from me in silence, and slowly walked away.

I closed the door again. 'Oh, Laura! Laura! We shall both rue the day when you called the Count a Spy!'

'You would have called him so yourself, Marian, if you had known what I know. Anne Catherick was right. There *was* a third person watching us in the plantation, yesterday; and that third person——'

'Are you sure it was the Count?'

'I am absolutely certain. He was Sir Percival's spy—he was Sir Percival's informer—he set Sir Percival watching and waiting, all the morning through, for Anne Catherick and for me.'

'Is Anne found? Did you see her at the lake?'

'No. She has saved herself by keeping away from the place. When I got to the boat-house, no one was there.'

'Yes? yes?'

'I went in, and sat waiting for a few minutes. But my restlessness made me get up again, to walk about a little. As I passed out, I saw some marks on the sand, close under the front of the boat-house. I stooped down to examine them, and discovered a word written in large letters, on the sand. The word was—LOOK.'

'And you scraped away the sand, and dug a hollow place in it?'

'How do you know that, Marian?'

'I saw the hollow place myself, when I followed you to the boat-house. Go on—go on!'

'Yes; I scraped away the sand on the surface; and in a little while, I came to a strip of paper hidden beneath, which had writing on it. The writing was signed with Anne Catherick's initials.'

'Where is it?'

'Sir Percival has taken it from me.'

'Can you remember what the writing was? Do you think you can repeat it to me?'

'In substance I can, Marian. It was very short. You would have remembered it, word for word.'

'Try to tell me what the substance was, before we go any further.'

She complied. I write the lines down here, exactly as she repeated them to me. They ran thus:

'I was seen with you, yesterday, by a tall stout old man, and had to run to save myself. He was not quick enough on his feet to follow me, and he lost me among the trees. I dare not risk coming back here to-day, at the same time. I write this, and hide it in the sand, at six in the morning, to tell you so. When we speak next of your wicked husband's Secret we must speak safely, or not at all. Try to have patience. I promise you shall see me again; and that soon.—A.C.'

The reference to the 'tall stout old man' (the terms of which Laura was certain that she had repeated to me correctly), left no doubt as to who the intruder had been. I called to mind that I had told Sir Percival, in the Count's presence, the day before, that Laura had gone to the boat-house to look for her brooch. In all probability he had followed her there, in his officious way, to relieve her mind about the matter of the signature, immediately after he had mentioned the change in Sir Percival's plans to me in the drawing-room. In this case, he could only have got to the neighbourhood of the boat-house, at the very moment when Anne Catherick discovered him. The suspiciously hurried manner in which she parted from Laura, had no doubt prompted his useless attempt to follow her. Of the conversation which had previously taken place between them, he could have heard nothing. The distance between the house and the lake, and the time at which he left me in the drawing-room, as compared with the time at which Laura and Anne Catherick had been speaking together, proved that fact to us, at any rate, beyond a doubt.

Having arrived at something like a conclusion, so far, my next great interest was to know what discoveries Sir Percival had made, after Count Fosco had given him his information.

'How came you to lose possession of the letter?' I asked. 'What did you do with it, when you found it in the sand?'

'After reading it once through,' she replied, 'I took it into the boat-house with me, to sit down, and look over it a second time. While I was reading, a shadow fell across the paper. I looked up; and saw Sir Percival standing in the doorway watching me.'

'Did you try to hide the letter?'

'I tried—but he stopped me. "You needn't trouble to hide that," he said. "I happen to have read it." I could only look at him, helplessly—I could say nothing. "You understand?" he went on; "I have read it. I dug it up out of the sand two hours since, and buried it again, and wrote the word above it again, and left it ready to your hands. You can't lie yourself out of the scrape now. You saw Anne Catherick in secret yesterday; and you have got her letter in your hand at this moment. I have not caught *her* yet; but I have caught *you*. Give me the letter." He stepped close up to me—I was alone with him, Marian—what could I do?—I gave him the letter.'

'What did he say, when you gave it to him?'

'At first, he said nothing. He took me by the arm, and led me out of the boat-house, and looked about him, on all sides, as if he was afraid of our being seen or heard. Then, he clasped his hand fast round my arm, and whispered to me—"What did Anne Catherick say to you yesterday?—I insist on hearing every word, from first to last." '

'Did you tell him?'

'I was alone with him, Marian—his cruel hand was bruising my arm—what could I do?'

'Is the mark on your arm still? Let me see it?'

'Why do you want to see it?'

'I want to see it, Laura, because our endurance must end, and our resistance must begin, to-day. That mark is a weapon to strike him with. Let me see it now—I may have to swear to it, at some future time.'

'Oh, Marian, don't look so! don't talk so! It doesn't hurt me, now!'

'Let me see it!'

She showed me the marks. I was past grieving over them, past crying over them, past shuddering over them. They say we are either better than men, or worse. If the temptation that has fallen in some women's way, and made them worse, had fallen in mine, at that moment——Thank God! my face betrayed nothing that his wife could read. The gentle, innocent, affectionate creature thought I was frightened for her and sorry for her—and thought no more.

'Don't think too seriously of it, Marian,' she said, simply, as she pulled her sleeve down again. 'It doesn't hurt me, now.'

'I will try to think quietly of it, my love, for your sake.—Well! well! And you told him all that Anne Catherick had said to you—all that you told me?'

'Yes; all. He insisted on it—I was alone with him—I could conceal nothing.'

'Did he say anything when you had done?'

'He looked at me, and laughed to himself, in a mocking, bitter way. "I mean to have the rest out of you," he said; "do you hear?—the rest." I declared to him solemnly that I had told him everything I knew. "Not you!" he answered; "you know more than you choose to tell. Won't you tell it? You shall! I'll wring it out of you at home, if I can't wring it out of you, here." He led me away by a strange path through the plantation—a path where there was no hope of our meeting *you*—and he spoke no more, till we came within sight of the house. Then he stopped again, and said, "Will you take a second chance, if I give it to you? Will you think better of it, and tell me the rest?" I could only repeat the same words I had spoken before. He cursed my obstinacy, and went on, and took me with him to the house. "You can't deceive me," he said; "you know more than you choose to tell. I'll have your secret out of you; and I'll have it out of that sister of yours, as well. There shall be no more plotting and whispering between you. Neither you nor she shall see each other again till you have confessed the truth. I'll have you watched morning, noon, and night, till you confess the truth." He was deaf to everything I could say. He took me straight up-stairs into my own room. Fanny was sitting there, doing some work for me; and he instantly ordered her out. "I'll take good care *you're* not mixed up in the conspiracy," he said. "You shall leave this house to-day. If your mistress wants a maid, she shall have one of my choosing." He pushed me into the room, and locked the door on me—he set that senseless woman to watch me outside—Marian! he looked and spoke like a madman. You may hardly understand it—he did indeed.'

'I do understand it, Laura. He *is* mad—mad with the terrors of a guilty conscience. Every word you have said makes me positively certain that when Anne Catherick left you yesterday, you were on the eve of discovering a secret, which might have been your vile husband's ruin—and he thinks you *have* discovered it. Nothing you can say or do, will quiet that guilty distrust, and convince his false nature of your truth. I don't say this, my love, to alarm you I say it to open your eyes to your position, and to convince you of the urgent necessity of letting me act, as I best can, for your protection, while the chance is our own. Count Fosco's interference has secured me access to you to-day; but he may withdraw that interference to-morrow. Sir Percival has already dismissed Fanny, because she is a quick-witted girl, and devotedly attached to you; and has chosen a woman to take her place, who cares nothing for your interests, and whose dull intelligence lowers her to the level of the watch-dog in the yard. It is impossible to say what violent measures he may take next, unless we make the most of our opportunities while we have them.'

'What can we do, Marian? Oh, if we could only leave this house, never to see it again!'

'Listen to me, my love—and try to think that you are not quite helpless so long as I am here with you.'

'I will think so—I do think so. Don't altogether forget poor Fanny, in thinking of me. She wants help and comfort, too.'

'I will not forget her. I saw her before I came up here; and I have arranged to communicate with her to-night. Letters are not safe in the post-bag at Blackwater Park—and I shall have two to write to-day, in your interests, which must pass through no hands but Fanny's.'

'What letters?'

'I mean to write first, Laura, to Mr Gilmore's partner, who has offered to help us in any fresh emergency. Little as I know of the law, I am certain that it can protect a woman from such treatment as that ruffian has inflicted on you to-day. I will go into no details about Anne Catherick, because I have no certain information to give. But the lawyer shall know of those bruises on your arm, and of the violence offered to you in this room—he shall, before I rest to-night!'

'But, think of the exposure, Marian!'

'I am calculating on the exposure. Sir Percival has more to dread from it than you have. The prospect of an exposure may bring him to terms, when nothing else will.'

I rose, as I spoke; but Laura entreated me not to leave her.

'You will drive him to desperation,' she said, 'and increase our dangers tenfold.'

I felt the truth—the disheartening truth—of those words. But I could not bring myself plainly to acknowledge it to her. In our dreadful position, there was no help and no hope for us, but in risking the worst. I said so, in guarded terms. She sighed bitterly—but did not contest the matter. She only asked about the second letter that I had proposed writing. To whom was it to be addressed?

'To Mr Fairlie,' I said. 'Your uncle is your nearest male relative, and the head of the family. He must and shall interfere.'

Laura shook her head sorrowfully.

'Yes, yes,' I went on; 'your uncle is a weak, selfish, worldly man, I know. But he is not Sir Percival Glyde; and he has no such friend about him as Count Fosco. I expect nothing from his kindness, or his tenderness of feeling towards you, or towards me. But he will do anything to pamper his own indolence, and to secure his own quiet. Let me only persuade him that his interference, at this moment, will save him inevitable trouble, and wretchedness, and responsibility hereafter, and he will bestir himself for his own sake. I know how to deal with him, Laura—I have had some practice.'

'If you could only prevail on him to let me go back to Limmeridge for a little while, and stay there quietly with you, Marian, I could be almost as happy again as I was before I was married!'

Those words set me thinking in a new direction. Would it be possible to place Sir Percival between the two alternatives of either exposing himself to the scandal of legal interference on his wife's behalf, or of allowing her to be quietly separated from him for a time, under pretext of a visit to her uncle's house? And could he, in that case, be reckoned on as likely to accept the last resource? It was doubtful—more than doubtful. And yet, hopeless as the experiment seemed, surely it was worth trying? I resolved to try it, in sheer despair of knowing what better to do.

'Your uncle shall know the wish you have just expressed,' I said; 'and I will ask the lawyer's advice on the subject, as well. Good may come of it—and will come of it, I hope.'

Saying that, I rose again; and again Laura tried to make me resume my seat.

'Don't leave me,' she said, uneasily. 'My desk is on that table. You can write here.'

It tried me to the quick to refuse her, even in her own interests. But we had been too long shut up alone together already. Our chance of seeing each other again might entirely depend on our not exciting any fresh suspicions. It was full time to show myself, quietly and unconcernedly, among the wretches who were, at that very moment, perhaps, thinking of us and talking of us down stairs. I explained the miserable necessity to Laura; and prevailed on her to recognise it, as I did.

'I will come back again, love, in an hour or less,' I said. 'The worst is over for to-day. Keep yourself quiet, and fear nothing.'

'Is the key in the door, Marian? Can I lock it on the inside?'

'Yes; here is the key. Lock the door; and open it to nobody, until I come up-stairs again.'

I kissed her, and left her. It was a relief to me, as I walked away, to hear the key turned in the lock, and to know that the door was at her own command.

I HAD only got as far as the top of the stairs, when the locking of Laura's door suggested to me the precaution of also locking my own door, and keeping the key safely about me while I was out of the room. My journal was already secured, with other papers, in the table-drawer, but my writing materials were left out. These included a seal, bearing the common device of two doves drinking out of the same cup; and some sheets of blotting-paper, which had the impression on them of the closing lines of my writing in these pages, traced during the past night. Distorted by the suspicion which had now become a part of myself, even such trifles as these looked too dangerous to be trusted without a guard—even the locked table-drawer seemed to be not sufficiently protected, in my absence, until the means of access to it had been carefully secured as well.

I found no appearance of any one having entered the room while I had been talking with Laura. My writing materials (which I had given the servant instructions never to meddle with) were scattered over the table much as usual. The only circumstance in connexion with them that at all struck me was, that the seal lay tidily in the tray with the pencils and the wax. It was not in my careless habits (I am sorry to say) to put it there; neither did I remember putting it there. But, as I could not call to mind, on the other hand, where else I had thrown it down, and as I was also doubtful whether I might not, for once, have laid it mechanically in the right place, I abstained from adding to the perplexity with which the day's events had filled my mind, by troubling it afresh about a trifle. I locked the door; put the key in my pocket; and went down stairs.

Madame Fosco was alone in the hall, looking at the weather-glass.

'Still falling,' she said. 'I am afraid we must expect more rain.'

Her face was composed again to its customary expression and its customary colour. But the hand with which she pointed to the dial of the weather-glass still trembled.

Could she have told her husband already, that she had overheard Laura reviling him, in my company, as a 'Spy?' My strong suspicion that she must have told him; my irresistible dread (all the more overpowering from its very vagueness) of the consequences which might follow; my fixed conviction, derived from various little self-betrayals which women notice in each other, that Madame Fosco, in spite of her well-assumed external civility, had not forgiven her niece for innocently standing between her and the legacy of ten thousand pounds—all rushed upon my mind together; all impelled me to speak, in the vain hope of using my own influence and my own powers of persuasion for the atonement of Laura's offence.

'May I trust to your kindness to excuse me, Madame Fosco, if I venture to speak to you on an exceedingly-painful subject?'

She crossed her hands in front of her, and bowed her head solemnly, without uttering a word, and without taking her eyes off mine for a moment.

'When you were so good as to bring me back my handkerchief,' I went on, 'I am very, very much afraid you must have accidentally heard Laura say something which I am unwilling to repeat, and which I will not attempt to defend. I will only venture to hope that you have not thought it of sufficient importance to be mentioned to the Count?'

'I think it of no importance whatever,' said Madame Fosco, sharply and suddenly. 'But,' she added, resuming her icy manner in a moment, 'I have no secrets from my husband, even in trifles. When he noticed, just now, that I looked distressed, it was my painful duty to tell him why I was distressed; and I frankly acknowledge to you, Miss Halcombe, that I *have* told him.'

I was prepared to hear it, and yet she turned me cold all over when she said those words.

'Let me earnestly entreat you, Madame Fosco—let me earnestly entreat the Count—to make some allowances for the sad position in which my sister is placed. She spoke while she was smarting under the insult and injustice inflicted on her by her husband—and she was not herself when she said those rash words. May I hope that they will be considerately and generously forgiven?'

'Most assuredly,' said the Count's quiet voice, behind me. He had stolen on us, with his noiseless tread, and his book in his hand, from the library.

'When Lady Glyde said those hasty words,' he went on, 'she did me an injustice, which I lament—and forgive. Let us never return to the subject,

Miss Halcombe; let us all comfortably combine to forget it, from this moment.'

'You are very kind,' I said; 'you relieve me inexpressibly——'

I tried to continue—but his eyes were on me; his deadly smile, that hides everything, was set, hard and unwavering, on his broad, smooth face. My distrust of his unfathomable falseness, my sense of my own degradation in stooping to conciliate his wife and himself, so disturbed and confused me, that the next words failed on my lips, and I stood there in silence.

'I beg you on my knees to say no more, Miss Halcombe—I am truly shocked that you should have thought it necessary to say so much.' With that polite speech, he took my hand—oh, how I despise myself! oh, how little comfort there is, even in knowing that I submitted to it for Laura's sake!—he took my hand, and put it to his poisonous lips. Never did I know all my horror of him till then. That innocent familiarity turned my blood, as if it had been the vilest insult that a man could offer me. Yet I hid my disgust from him—I tried to smile—I, who once mercilessly despised deceit in other women, was as false as the worst of them, as false as the Judas whose lips had touched my hand.

I could not have maintained my degrading self-control—it is all that redeems me in my own estimation to know that I could not—if he had still continued to keep his eyes on my face. His wife's tigerish jealousy came to my rescue, and forced his attention away from me, the moment he possessed himself of my hand. Her cold blue eyes caught light; her dull white cheeks flushed into bright colour; she looked years younger than her age, in an instant.

'Count!' she said. 'Your foreign forms of politeness are not understood by Englishwomen.'

'Pardon me, my angel! The best and dearest Englishwoman in the world understands them.' With those words, he dropped my hand, and quietly raised his wife's hand to his lips, in place of it.

I ran back up the stairs, to take refuge in my own room. If there had been time to think, my thoughts, when I was alone again, would have caused me bitter suffering. But there was no time to think. Happily for the preservation of my calmness and my courage, there was time for nothing but action.

The letters to the lawyer and to Mr Fairlie, were still to be written; and I sat down at once, without a moment's hesitation, to devote myself to them.

There was no multitude of resources to perplex me—there was absolutely no one to depend on, in the first instance, but myself. Sir Percival had neither friends nor relatives in the neighbourhood whose intercession I could attempt to employ. He was on the coldest terms—in some cases, on the worst terms—with the families of his own rank and station who lived near him. We two women had neither father, nor brother, to come to the house, and take our parts. There was no choice, but to write those two doubtful letters—or to put Laura in the wrong and myself in the wrong, and to make all peaceable negotiation in the future impossible, by secretly escaping from Blackwater Park. Nothing but the most imminent personal peril could justify our taking that second course. The letters must be tried first; and I wrote them.

I said nothing to the lawyer about Anne Catherick; because (as I had already hinted to Laura) that topic was connected with a mystery which we could not yet explain, and which it would therefore be useless to write about to a professional man. I left my correspondent to attribute Sir Percival's disgraceful conduct, if he pleased, to fresh disputes about money matters; and simply consulted him on the possibility of taking legal proceedings for Laura's protection, in the event of her husband's refusal to allow her to leave Blackwater Park for a time, and return with me to Limmeridge. I referred him to Mr Fairlie for the details of this last arrangement—I assured him that I wrote with Laura's authority—and I ended by entreating him to act in her name, to the utmost extent of his power, and with the least possible loss of time.

The letter to Mr Fairlie occupied me next. I appealed to him on the terms which I had mentioned to Laura as the most likely to make him bestir himself; I enclosed a copy of my letter to the lawyer, to show him how serious the case was; and I represented our removal to Limmeridge as the only compromise which would prevent the danger and distress of Laura's present position from inevitably affecting her uncle as well as herself, at no very distant time.

When I had done, and had sealed and directed the two envelopes, I went back with the letters to Laura's room, to show her that they were written.

'Has anybody disturbed you?' I asked, when she opened the door to me.

'Nobody has knocked,' she replied. 'But I heard some one in the outer room.'

'Was it a man or a woman?'

'A woman. I heard the rustling of her gown.'

'A rustling like silk?'

'Yes; like silk.'

Madame Fosco had evidently been watching outside. The mischief she might do by herself, was little to be feared. But the mischief she might do, as a willing instrument in her husband's hands, was too formidable to be overlooked.

'What became of the rustling of the gown when you no longer heard it in the ante-room?' I inquired. 'Did you hear it go past your wall, along the passage?'

'Yes. I kept still, and listened; and just heard it.'

'Which way did it go?'

'Towards your room.'

I considered again. The sound had not caught my ears. But I was then deeply absorbed in my letters; and I write with a heavy hand, and a quill pen, scraping and scratching noisily over the paper. It was more likely that Madame Fosco would hear the scraping of my pen than that I should hear the rustling of her dress. Another reason (if I had wanted one) for not trusting my letters to the post-bag in the hall.

Laura saw me thinking. 'More difficulties!' she said, wearily; 'more difficulties and more dangers!'

'No dangers,' I replied. 'Some little difficulty, perhaps. I am thinking of the safest way of putting my two letters into Fanny's hands.'

'You have really written them, then? Oh, Marian, run no risks—pray, pray run no risks!'

'No, no—no fear. Let me see—what o'clock is it now?'

It was a quarter to six. There would be time for me to get to the village inn, and to come back again, before dinner. If I waited till the evening, I might find no second opportunity of safely leaving the house.

'Keep the key turned in the lock, Laura,' I said, 'and don't be afraid about me. If you hear any inquiries made, call through the door, and say that I am gone out for a walk.'

'When shall you be back?'

'Before dinner, without fail. Courage, my love. By this time to-morrow, you will have a clear-headed, trustworthy man acting for your good. Mr Gilmore's partner is our next best friend to Mr Gilmore himself.'

A moment's reflection, as soon as I was alone, convinced me that I had better not appear in my walking-dress, until I had first discovered what was going on in the lower part of the house. I had not ascertained yet whether Sir Percival was in-doors or out.

The singing of the canaries in the library, and the smell of tobacco-smoke that came through the door, which was not closed, told me at once where the Count was. I looked over my shoulder, as I passed the doorway; and saw, to my surprise, that he was exhibiting the docility of the birds, in his most engagingly-polite manner, to the housekeeper. He must have specially invited her to see them—for she would never have thought of going into the library of her own accord. The man's slightest actions had a purpose of some kind at the bottom of every one of them. What could be his purpose here?

It was no time then to inquire into his motives. I looked about for Madame Fosco, next; and found her following her favourite circle, round and round the fish-pond.

I was a little doubtful how she would meet me, after the outbreak of jealousy, of which I had been the cause so short a time since. But her husband had tamed her in the interval; and she now spoke to me with the same civility as usual. My only object in addressing myself to her was to ascertain if she knew what had become of Sir Percival. I contrived to refer to him indirectly; and, after a little fencing on either side, she at last mentioned that he had gone out.

'Which of the horses has he taken?' I asked, carelessly.

'None of them,' she replied. 'He went away, two hours since, on foot. As I understood it, his object was to make fresh inquiries about the woman named Anne Catherick. He appears to be unreasonably anxious about tracing her. Do you happen to know if she is dangerously mad, Miss Halcombe?'

'I do not, Countess.'

'Are you going in?'

'Yes, I think so. I suppose it will soon be time to dress for dinner.'

We entered the house together. Madame Fosco strolled into the library, and closed the door. I went at once to fetch my hat and shawl. Every moment was of importance, if I was to get to Fanny at the inn and be back before dinner.

When I crossed the hall again, no one was there; and the singing of the birds in the library had ceased. I could not stop to make any fresh investigations. I could only assure myself that the way was clear, and then leave the house, with the two letters safe in my pocket.

On my way to the village, I prepared myself for the possibility of meeting Sir Percival. As long as I had him to deal with alone, I felt certain of not losing my presence of mind. Any woman who is sure of her own wits, is a match, at any time, for a man who is not sure of his own temper. I had no such fear of Sir Percival as I had of the Count. Instead of fluttering, it had composed me, to hear of the errand on which he had gone out. While the tracing of Anne Catherick was the great anxiety that occupied him, Laura and I might hope for some cessation of any active persecution at his hands. For our sakes now, as well as for Anne's, I hoped and prayed fervently that she might still escape him.

I walked on as briskly as the heat would let me, till I reached the cross-road which led to the village; looking back, from time to time, to make sure that I was not followed by any one. Nothing was behind me, all the way, but an empty country waggon. The noise made by the lumbering wheels annoyed me; and when I found that the waggon took the road to the village, as well as myself, I stopped to let it go by, and pass out of hearing. As I looked towards it, more attentively than before, I thought I detected, at intervals, the feet of a man walking close behind it; the carter being in front, by the side of his horses. The part of the cross-road which I had just passed over was so narrow, that the waggon coming after me brushed the trees and thickets on either side; and I had to wait until it went by, before I could test the correctness of my impression. Apparently, that impression was wrong, for when the waggon had passed me, the road behind it was quite clear.

I reached the inn without meeting Sir Percival, and without noticing anything more; and was glad to find that the landlady had received Fanny with all possible kindness. The girl had a little parlour to sit in, away from the noise of the tap-room, and a clean bed-chamber at the top of the house. She began crying again, at the sight of me; and said, poor soul, truly enough, that it was dreadful to feel herself turned out into the world, as if she had committed some unpardonable fault, when no blame could be laid at her door by anybody—not even by her master who had sent her away.

'Try to make the best of it, Fanny,' I said. 'Your mistress and I will stand your friends, and will take care that your character shall not suffer. Now, listen to me. I have very little time to spare, and I am going to put a great trust in your hands. I wish you to take care of these two letters. The one with the stamp on it you are to put into the post, when you reach London, to-morrow. The other, directed to Mr Fairlie, you are to deliver to him yourself, as soon as you get home. Keep both the letters about you, and give them up to no one. They are of the last importance to your mistress's interests.'

Fanny put the letters into the bosom of her dress. 'There they shall stop, miss,' she said, 'till I have done what you tell me.'

'Mind you are at the station in good time to-morrow morning,' I continued. 'And, when you see the housekeeper at Limmeridge, give her my compliments, and say that you are in my service, until Lady Glyde is able to take you back. We may meet again sooner than you think. So keep a good heart, and don't miss the seven o'clock train.'

'Thank you, miss—thank you kindly. It gives one courage to hear your voice again. Please to offer my duty to my lady; and say I left all the things as tidy as I could in the time. Oh, dear! dear! who will dress her for dinner to-day? It really breaks my heart, miss, to think of it.'

When I got back to the house, I had only a quarter of an hour to spare, to put myself in order for dinner, and to say two words to Laura before I went down stairs.

'The letters are in Fanny's hands,' I whispered to her, at the door. 'Do you mean to join us at dinner?'

'Oh, no, no—not for the world!'

'Has anything happened? Has any one disturbed you?'

'Yes—just now—Sir Percival——'

'Did he come in?'

'No: he frightened me by a thump on the door, outside. I said, "Who's there?" "You know," he answered. "Will you alter your mind, and tell me the rest? You shall! Sooner or later, I'll wring it out of you. You know where Anne Catherick is, at this moment!" "Indeed, indeed," I said, "I don't." "You do!" he called back. "I'll crush your obstinacy—mind that!—I'll wring it out of you!" He went away, with those words—went away, Marian, hardly five minutes ago.'

He had not found Anne! We were safe for that night—he had not found her yet.

'You are going down stairs, Marian? Come up again in the evening.'

'Yes, yes. Don't be uneasy, if I am a little late—I must be careful not to give offence by leaving them too soon.'

The dinner-bell rang; and I hastened away.

Sir Percival took Madame Fosco into the dining-room; and the Count gave me his arm. He was hot and flushed, and was not dressed with his customary care and completeness. Had he, too, been out before dinner, and been late in getting back? or was he only suffering from the heat a little more severely than usual?

However this might be, he was unquestionably troubled by some secret annoyance or anxiety, which, with all his powers of deception, he was not able entirely to conceal. Through the whole of dinner, he was almost as silent as Sir Percival himself; and he, every now and then, looked at his wife with an expression of furtive uneasiness, which was quite new in my experience of him. The one social obligation which he seemed to be self-possessed enough to perform as carefully as ever, was the obligation of being persistently civil and attentive to me. What vile object he has in view, I cannot still discover; but, be the design what it may, invariable politeness towards myself, invariable humility towards Laura, and invariable suppression (at any cost) of Sir Percival's clumsy violence, have been the means he has resolutely and impenetrably used to get to his end, ever since he set foot in this house. I suspected it, when he first interfered in our favour, on the day when the deed was produced in the library, and I feel certain of it, now.

When Madame Fosco and I rose to leave the table, the Count rose also to accompany us back to the drawing-room.

'What are you going away for?' asked Sir Percival—'I mean *you*, Fosco.'

'I am going away, because I have had dinner enough, and wine enough,' answered the Count. 'Be so kind, Percival, as to make allowances for my foreign habit of going out with the ladies, as well as coming in with them.'

'Nonsense! Another glass of claret won't hurt you. Sit down again like an Englishman. I want half an hour's quiet talk with you over our wine.'

'A quiet talk, Percival, with all my heart, but not now, and not over the wine. Later in the evening, if you please—later in the evening.'

'Civil!' said Sir Percival, savagely. 'Civil behaviour, upon my soul, to a man in his own house!'

I had more than once seen him look at the Count uneasily during dinner-time, and had observed that the Count carefully abstained from looking at him in return. This circumstance, coupled with the host's anxiety for a little quiet talk over the wine and the guest's obstinate resolution not to sit down again at the table, revived in my memory the request which Sir Percival had vainly addressed to his friend, earlier in the day, to come out of the library and speak to him. The Count had deferred granting that private interview, when it was first asked for in the afternoon, and had again deferred granting it, when it was a second time asked for at the dinner-table. Whatever the coming subject of discussion between them might be, it was clearly an important subject in Sir Percival's estimation—and perhaps (judging from his evident reluctance to approach it), a dangerous subject as well, in the estimation of the Count.

These considerations occurred to me while we were passing from the dining-room to the drawing-room. Sir Percival's angry commentary on his friend's desertion of him had not produced the slightest effect. The Count obstinately accompanied us to the tea-table—waited a minute or two in the room—went out into the hall—and returned with the post-bag in his hands. It was then eight o'clock—the hour at which the letters were always despatched from Blackwater Park.

'Have you any letter for the post, Miss Halcombe?' he asked, approaching me, with the bag.

I saw Madame Fosco, who was making the tea, pause, with the sugar-tongs in her hand, to listen for my answer.

'No, Count, thank you. No letters to-day.'

He gave the bag to the servant, who was then in the room; sat down at the piano; and played the air of the lively Neapolitan street-song, 'La mia Carolina,' twice over. His wife, who was usually the most deliberate of women in all her movements, made the tea as quickly as I could have made it myself—finished her own cup in two minutes—and quietly glided out of the room.

I rose to follow her example—partly because I suspected her of attempting some treachery up-stairs with Laura; partly, because I was resolved not to remain alone in the same room with her husband.

Before I could get to the door, the Count stopped me, by a request for a cup of tea. I gave him the cup of tea; and tried a second time to get away. He stopped me again—this time, by going back to the piano, and suddenly appealing to me on a musical question in which he declared that the honour of his country was concerned.

I vainly pleaded my own total ignorance of music, and total want of taste in that direction. He only appealed to me again with a vehemence which set all further protest on my part at defiance. 'The English and the Germans (he indignantly declared) were always reviling the Italians for their inability to cultivate the higher kinds of music. We were perpetually talking of our Oratorios; and they were perpetually talking of their Symphonies. Did we forget and did they forget his immortal friend and countryman, Rossini? What was "Moses in Egypt," but a sublime oratorio, which was acted on the stage, instead of being coldly sung in a concert-room? What was the overture to Guillaume Tell, but a symphony under another name? Had I heard Moses in Egypt? Would I listen to this, and this, and this, and say if anything more sublimely sacred and grand had ever been composed by mortal man?'—And, without waiting for a word of assent or dissent on my part, looking me hard in the face all the time, he began thundering on the piano, and singing to it with loud and lofty enthusiasm; only interrupting himself, at intervals, to announce to me fiercely the titles of the different pieces of music: 'Chorus of Egyptians, in the Plague of Darkness, Miss Halcombe!'—'Recitativo of Moses, with the tables of the Law.'—'Prayer of Israelites, at the passage of the Red Sea. Aha! Aha! Is that sacred? is that sublime?' The piano trembled under his powerful hands; and the teacups on the table rattled, as his big bass voice thundered out the notes, and his heavy foot beat time on the floor.

There was something horrible—something fierce and devilish, in the outburst of his delight at his own singing and playing, and in the triumph with which he watched its effect upon me, as I shrank nearer and nearer to the door. I was released, at last, not by my own efforts, but by Sir Percival's interposition. He opened the dining-room door, and called out angrily to know what 'that infernal noise' meant. The Count instantly got up from the piano. 'Ah! if Percival is coming,' he said, 'harmony and melody are both at an end. The Muse of Music, Miss Halcombe, deserts us in dismay; and I, the fat old minstrel, exhale the rest of my enthusiasm in the open air!' He stalked out into the verandah, put his hands in his pockets, and resumed the 'recitativo of Moses,' sotto voce, in the garden.

I heard Sir Percival call after him, from the dining-room window. But he took no notice: he seemed determined not to hear. That long-deferred quiet talk between them was still to be put off, was still to wait for the Count's absolute will and pleasure.

He had detained me in the drawing-room nearly half an hour from the time when his wife left us. Where had she been, and what had she been doing in that interval?

I went up-stairs to ascertain, but I made no discoveries; and when I questioned Laura, I found that she had not heard anything. Nobody had disturbed her—no faint rustling of the silk dress had been audible, either in the ante-room or in the passage.

It was, then, twenty minutes to nine. After going to my room to get my journal, I returned, and sat with Laura; sometimes writing, sometimes stopping to talk with her. Nobody came near us, and nothing happened. We remained together till ten o'clock. I then rose; said my last cheering words; and wished her good night. She locked her door again, after we had arranged that I should come in and see her the first thing in the morning.

I had a few sentences more to add to my diary, before going to bed myself; and, as I went down again to the drawing-room, after leaving Laura, for the last time that weary day, I resolved merely to show myself there, to make my excuses, and then to retire an hour earlier than usual, for the night.

Sir Percival, and the Count and his wife, were sitting together. Sir Percival was yawning in an easy-chair; the Count was reading; Madame Fosco was fanning herself. Strange to say, *her* face was flushed, now. She, who never suffered from the heat, was most undoubtedly suffering from it to-night.

'I am afraid, Countess, you are not quite so well as usual?' I said.

'The very remark I was about to make to *you*,' she replied. 'You are looking pale, my dear.'

My dear! It was the first time she had ever addressed me with that familiarity! There was an insolent smile, too, on her face when she said the words.

'I am suffering from one of my bad headaches,' I answered, coldly.

'Ah, indeed? Want of exercise, I suppose? A walk before dinner would have been just the thing for you.' She referred to the 'walk' with a strange emphasis. Had she seen me go out? No matter if she had. The letters were safe, now, in Fanny's hands.

'Come, and have a smoke, Fosco,' said Sir Percival, rising, with another uneasy look at his friend.

'With pleasure, Percival, when the ladies have gone to bed,' replied the Count.

'Excuse me, Countess, if I set you the example of retiring,' I said. 'The only remedy for such a headache as mine is going to bed.'

I took my leave. There was the same insolent smile on the woman's face when I shook hands with her. Sir Percival paid no attention to me. He was looking impatiently at Madame Fosco, who showed no signs of leaving the room with me. The Count smiled to himself behind his book. There was yet another delay to that quiet talk with Sir Percival—and the Countess was the impediment, this time.

Once safely shut into my own room, I opened these pages, and prepared to go on with that part of the day's record which was still left to write.

For ten minutes or more, I sat idle, with the pen in my hand, thinking over the events of the last twelve hours. When I at last addressed myself to my task, I found a difficulty in proceeding with it which I had never experienced before. In spite of my efforts to fix my thoughts on the matter in hand, they wandered away, with the strangest persistency, in the one direction of Sir Percival and the Count; and all the interest which I tried to concentrate on my journal, centred, instead, in that private interview between them, which had been put off all through the day, and which was now to take place in the silence and solitude of the night.

In this perverse state of my mind, the recollection of what had passed since the morning would not come back to me; and there was no resource but to close my journal and to get away from it for a little while.

I opened the door which led from my bedroom into my sitting-room, and, having passed through, pulled it to again, to prevent any accident, in case of draught, with the candle left on the dressing-table. My sitting-room window was wide open; and I leaned out, listlessly, to look at the night.

It was dark and quiet. Neither moon nor stars were visible. There was a smell like rain in the still, heavy air; and I put my hand out of the window. No. The rain was only threatening; it had not come yet.

I REMAINED leaning on the window-sill for nearly a quarter of an hour, looking out absently into the black darkness, and hearing nothing, except, now and then, the voices of the servants, or the distant sound of a closing door, in the lower part of the house.

Just as I was turning away wearily from the window, to go back to the bedroom, and make a second attempt to complete the unfinished entry in my journal, I smelt the odour of tobacco-smoke, stealing towards me on the heavy night air. The next moment I saw a tiny red spark advancing from the farther end of the house in the pitch darkness. I heard no footsteps, and I could see nothing but the spark. It travelled along in the night; passed the window at which I was standing; and stopped opposite my bedroom window, inside which I had left the light burning on the dressing-table.

The spark remained stationary, for a moment, then moved back again in the direction from which it had advanced. As I followed its progress, I saw a second red spark, larger than the first, approaching from the distance. The two met together in the darkness. Remembering who smoked cigarettes, and who smoked cigars, I inferred, immediately, that the Count had come out first to look and listen, under my window, and that Sir Percival had afterwards joined him. They must both have been walking on the lawn—or I should certainly have heard Sir Percival's heavy footfall, though the Count's soft step might have escaped me, even on the gravel walk.

I waited quietly at the window, certain that they could neither of them see me, in the darkness of the room.

'What's the matter?' I heard Sir Percival say, in a low voice. 'Why don't you come in and sit down?'

'I want to see the light out of that window,' replied the Count, softly.

'What harm does the light do?'

'It shows she is not in bed yet. She is sharp enough to suspect something, and bold enough to come down stairs and listen, if she can get the chance. Patience, Percival—patience.'

'Humbug! You're always talking of patience.'

'I shall talk of something else presently. My good friend, you are on the edge of your domestic precipice; and if I let you give the women one other chance, on my sacred word of honour, they will push you over it!'

'What the devil do you mean?'

'We will come to our explanations, Percival, when the light is out of that window, and when I have had one little look at the rooms on each side of the library, and a peep at the staircase as well.'

They slowly moved away; and the rest of the conversation between them (which had been conducted, throughout, in the same low tones) ceased to be audible. It was no matter. I had heard enough to determine me on justifying the Count's opinion of my sharpness and my courage. Before the red sparks were out of sight in the darkness, I had made up my mind that there should be a listener when those two men sat down to their talk—and that the listener, in spite of all the Count's precautions to the contrary, should be myself. I wanted but one motive to sanction the act to my own conscience, and to give me courage enough for performing it; and that motive I had. Laura's honour, Laura's happiness—Laura's life itself—might depend on my quick ears, and my faithful memory, to-night.

I had heard the Count say that he meant to examine the rooms on each side of the library, and the staircase as well, before he entered on any explanations with Sir Percival. This expression of his intentions was neces- sarily sufficient to inform me that the library was the room in which he proposed that the conversation should take place. The one moment of time which was long enough to bring me to that conclusion, was also the moment which showed me a means of baffling his precautions—or, in other words, of hearing what he and Sir Percival said to each other, without the risk of descending at all into the lower regions of the house.

In speaking of the rooms on the ground floor, I have mentioned incident- ally the verandah outside them, on which they all opened by means of French windows, extending from the cornice to the floor. The top of this verandah was flat; the rain-water being carried off from it, by pipes, into tanks which helped to supply the house. On the narrow leaden roof, which ran along past the bedrooms, and which was rather less, I should think, than three feet below the sills of the windows, a row of flower-pots was ranged, with wide intervals between each pot; the whole being protected from falling, in high winds, by an ornamental iron railing along the edge of the roof.

The plan which had now occurred to me was to get out, at my sitting-room window, on to this roof; to creep along noiselessly, till I reached that part of it which was immediately over the library window; and to crouch down between the flower-pots, with my ear against the outer railing. If Sir Percival and the Count sat and smoked to-night, as I had seen them sitting and smoking many nights before, with their chairs close at the open window, and their feet stretched on the zinc garden seats which were placed under the verandah, every word they said to each other above a whisper (and no long conversation, as we all know by experience, can be carried on *in* a whisper) must inevitably reach my ears. If, on the other hand, they chose, to-night, to sit far back inside the room, then, the chances were, that I should hear little or nothing; and, in that case, I must run the far more serious risk of trying to outwit them down stairs.

Strongly as I was fortified in my resolution by the desperate nature of our situation, I hoped most fervently that I might escape this last emergency. My courage was only a woman's courage, after all; and it was very near to failing me, when I thought of trusting myself on the ground floor, at the dead of night, within reach of Sir Percival and the Count.

I went softly back to my bedroom, to try the safer experiment of the verandah roof, first.

A complete change in my dress was imperatively necessary, for many reasons. I took off my silk gown to begin with, because the slightest noise from it, on that still night, might have betrayed me. I next removed the white and cumbersome parts of my underclothing, and replaced them by a petticoat of dark flannel. Over this, I put my black travelling cloak, and pulled the hood on to my head. In my ordinary evening costume, I took up the room of three men at least. In my present dress, when it was held close about me, no man could have passed through the narrowest spaces more easily than I. The little breadth left on the roof of the verandah, between the flower-pots on one side, and the wall and the windows of the house on the other, made this a serious consideration. If I knocked anything down, if I made the least noise, who could say what the consequences might be?

I only waited to put the matches near the candle, before I extinguished it, and groped my way back into the sitting-room. I locked that door, as I had locked my bedroom door—then quietly got out of the window, and cautiously set my feet on the leaden roof of the verandah.

My two rooms were at the inner extremity of the new wing of the house in which we all lived; and I had five windows to pass, before I could reach the position it was necessary to take up immediately over the library. The first window belonged to a spare room, which was empty. The second and third windows belonged to Laura's room. The fourth window belonged to Sir Percival's room. The fifth, belonged to the Countess's room. The others, by which it was not necessary for me to pass, were the windows of the Count's dressing-room, of the bath-room, and of the second empty spare-room.

No sound reached my ears—the black blinding darkness of the night was all round me when I first stood on the verandah, except at that part of it which Madame Fosco's window overlooked. There, at the very place above the library, to which my course was directed—there, I saw a gleam of light! The Countess was not yet in bed.

It was too late to draw back; it was no time to wait. I determined to go on at all hazards, and trust for security to my own caution and to the darkness of the night. 'For Laura's sake!' I thought to myself, as I took the first step forward on the roof, with one hand holding my cloak close round me, and the other groping against the wall of the house. It was better to brush close by the wall, than to risk striking my feet against the flower-pots within a few inches of me, on the other side.

I passed the dark window of the spare-room, trying the leaden roof, at each step, with my foot, before I risked resting my weight on it. I passed the dark windows of Laura's room ('God bless her and keep her to-night!'). I passed the dark window of Sir Percival's room. Then, I waited a moment, knelt down, with my hands to support me; and so crept to my position, under the protection of the low wall between the bottom of the lighted window and the verandah roof.

When I ventured to look up at the window itself, I found that the top of it only was open, and that the blind inside was drawn down. While I was looking, I saw the shadow of Madame Fosco pass across the white field of the blind—then pass slowly back again. Thus far, she could not have heard me—or the shadow would surely have stopped at the blind, even if she had wanted courage enough to open the window, and look out?

I placed myself sideways against the railing of the verandah; first ascertaining, by touching them, the position of the flower-pots on either side of me. There was room enough for me to sit between them, and no more. The sweet-scented leaves of the flower on my left hand, just brushed my cheek as I lightly rested my head against the railing.

The first sounds that reached me from below were caused by the opening or closing (most probably the latter) of three doors in succession—the doors, no doubt, leading into the hall, and into the rooms on each side of the library, which the Count had pledged himself to examine. The first object that I saw was the red spark again travelling out into the night, from under the verandah; moving away towards my window; waiting a moment; and then returning to the place from which it had set out.

'The devil take your restlessness! When do you mean to sit down?' growled Sir Percival's voice beneath me.

'Ouf! how hot it is!' said the Count, sighing and puffing wearily.

His exclamation was followed by the scraping of the garden chairs on the tiled pavement under the verandah—the welcome sound which told me they were going to sit close at the window as usual. So far, the chance was mine. The clock in the turret struck the quarter to twelve as they settled themselves in their chairs. I heard Madame Fosco through the open window, yawning; and saw her shadow pass once more across the white field of the blind.

Meanwhile, Sir Percival and the Count began talking together below; now and then dropping their voices a little lower than usual, but never sinking them to a whisper. The strangeness and peril of my situation, the dread, which I could not master, of Madame Fosco's lighted window, made it difficult, almost impossible for me, at first, to keep my presence of mind, and to fix my attention solely on the conversation beneath. For some minutes, I could only succeed in gathering the general substance of it. I understood the Count to say that the one window alight was his wife's; that the ground floor of the house was quite clear; and that they might now speak to each other, without fear of accidents. Sir Percival merely answered by upbraiding his friend with having unjustifiably slighted his wishes and neglected his interests, all through the day. The Count, thereupon, defended himself by declaring that he had been beset by certain troubles and anxieties which had absorbed all his attention, and that the only safe time to come to an explanation, was a time when they could feel certain of being neither interrupted nor overheard. 'We are at a serious crisis in our affairs, Percival,' he said; 'and if we are to decide on the future at all, we must decide secretly to-night.'

That sentence of the Count's was the first which my attention was ready enough to master, exactly as it was spoken. From this point, with certain breaks and interruptions, my whole interest fixed breathlessly on the conversation; and I followed it word for word.

'Crisis?' repeated Sir Percival. 'It's a worse crisis than you think for, I can tell you!'

'So I should suppose, from your behaviour for the last day or two,' returned the other, coolly. 'But, wait a little. Before we advance to what I do *not* know, let us be quite certain of what I *do* know. Let us first see if I am right about the time that is past, before I make any proposal to you for the time that is to come.'

'Stop till I get the brandy and water. Have some yourself.'

'Thank you, Percival. The cold water with pleasure, a spoon, and the basin of sugar. Eau sucrée, my friend—nothing more.'

'Sugar and water, for a man of your age!—There! mix your sickly mess. You foreigners are all alike.'

'Now, listen, Percival. I will put our position plainly before you, as I understand it; and you shall say if I am right or wrong. You and I both came back to this house from the Continent, with our affairs very seriously embarrassed——'

'Cut it short! I wanted some thousands, and you some hundreds—and, without the money, we were both in a fair way to go to the dogs together. There's the situation. Make what you can of it. Go on.'

'Well, Percival, in your own solid English words, you wanted some thousands and I wanted some hundreds; and the only way of getting them was for you to raise the money for your own necessity (with a small margin, beyond, for my poor little hundreds), by the help of your wife. What did I tell you about your wife on our way to England? and what did I tell you again, when we had come here, and when I had seen for myself the sort of woman Miss Halcombe was?'

'How should I know? You talked nineteen to the dozen, I suppose, just as usual.'

'I said this: Human ingenuity, my friend, has hitherto only discovered two ways in which a man can manage a woman. One way is to knock her down—a method largely adopted by the brutal lower orders of the people, but utterly abhorrent to the refined and educated classes above them. The other way (much longer, much more difficult, but, in the end, not less certain) is never to accept a provocation at a woman's hands. It holds with animals, it holds with children, and it holds with women, who are nothing but children grown up. Quiet resolution is the one quality the animals, the children, and the women all fail in. If they can once shake this superior quality in their master, they get the better of *him*. If they can never succeed in disturbing it, he gets the better of *them*. I said to you, Remember that plain truth, when you want your wife to help you to the money. I said, Remember it doubly and trebly, in the presence of your wife's sister, Miss Halcombe. Have you remembered it? Not once, in all the complications that have twisted themselves about us in this house. Every provocation that your wife, and her sister, could offer to you, you instantly accepted from them. Your mad temper lost the signature to the deed, lost the ready money, set Miss Halcombe writing to the lawyer, for the first time——'

'First time? Has she written again?'

'Yes; she has written again to-day.'

A chair fell on the pavement of the verandah—fell with a crash, as if it had been kicked down.

It was well for me that the Count's revelation roused Sir Percival's anger, as it did. On hearing that I had been once more discovered, I started so that the railing, against which I leaned, cracked again. Had he followed me to the inn? Did he infer that I must have given my letters to Fanny, when I told him I had none for the post-bag? Even if it was so, how could he have examined the letters, when they had gone straight from my hand to the bosom of the girl's dress?

'Thank your lucky star,' I heard the Count say next, 'that you have me in the house, to undo the harm, as fast as you do it. Thank your lucky star that I said, No, when you were mad enough to talk of turning the key to-day on Miss Halcombe, as you turned it, in your mischievous folly, on your wife. Where are your eyes? Can you look at Miss Halcombe, and not see that she has the foresight and the resolution of a man? With that woman for my friend, I would snap these fingers of mine at the world. With that woman for my enemy, I, with all my brains and experience—I, Fosco, cunning as the devil himself, as you have told me a hundred times—I walk, in your English phrase, upon egg-shells! And this grand creature—I drink her health in my sugar and water—this grand creature, who stands in the strength of her love and her courage, firm as a rock between us two, and that poor flimsy pretty blonde wife of yours—this magnificent woman, whom I admire with all my soul, though I oppose her in your interests and in mine, you drive to extremities, as if she was no sharper and no bolder than the rest of her sex. Percival! Percival! you deserve to fail, and you *have* failed.'

There was a pause. I write the villain's words about myself, because I mean to remember them, because I hope yet for the day when I may speak out, once for all in his presence, and cast them back, one by one, in his teeth.

Sir Percival was the first to break the silence again.

'Yes, yes; bully and bluster as much as you like,' he said, sulkily; the difficulty about the money is not the only difficulty. You would be for taking strong measures with the women, yourself—if you knew as much as I do.'

'We will come to that second difficulty, all in good time,' rejoined the Count. 'You may confuse yourself, Percival, as much as you please, but you shall not confuse me. Let the question of the money be settled first. Have I convinced your obstinacy? have I shown you that your temper will not let you help yourself?—Or must I go back, and (as you put it in your dear straightforward English) bully and bluster a little more?'

'Pooh! It's easy enough to grumble at *me*. Say what is to be done—that's a little harder.'

'Is it? Bah! This is what is to be done: You give up all direction in the business from to-night; you leave it, for the future, in my hands only. I am talking to a Practical British Man—ha? Well, Practical, will that do for you?'

'What do you propose, if I leave it all to you?'

'Answer me first. Is it to be in my hands or not?'

'Say it is in your hands—what then?'

'A few questions, Percival, to begin with. I must wait a little, yet, to let circumstances guide me; and I must know, in every possible way, what those circumstances are likely to be. There is no time to lose. I have told you already that Miss Halcombe has written to the lawyer to-day, for the second time.'

'How did you find it out? What did she say?'

'If I told you, Percival, we should only come back at the end to where we are now. Enough that I have found out—and the finding has caused that trouble and anxiety which made me so inaccessible to you all through to-day. Now, to refresh my memory about your affairs—it is some time since I talked them over with you. The money has been raised, in the absence of your wife's signature, by means of bills at three months—raised at a cost that makes my poverty-stricken foreign hair stand on end to think of it! When the bills are due, is there really and truly no earthly way of paying them but by the help of your wife?'

'None.'

'What! You have no money at the banker's!'

'A few hundreds, when I want as many thousands.'

'Have you no other security to borrow upon?'

'Not a shred.'

'What have you actually got with your wife, at the present moment?'

'Nothing, but the interest of her twenty thousand pounds—barely enough to pay our daily expenses.'

'What do you expect from your wife?'

'Three thousand a year, when her uncle dies.'

'A fine fortune, Percival. What sort of a man is this uncle? Old?'

'No—neither old nor young.'

'A good-tempered, freely-living man? Married? No—I think my wife told me, not married.'

'Of course not. If he was married, and had a son, Lady Glyde would not be next heir to the property. I'll tell you what he is. He's a maudlin, twaddling, selfish fool, and bores everybody who comes near him about the state of his health.'

'Men of that sort, Percival, live long, and marry malevolently when you least expect it. I don't give you much, my friend, for your chance of the three thousand a year. Is there nothing more that comes to you from your wife?'

'Nothing.'

'Absolutely nothing?'

'Absolutely nothing—except in the case of her death.'

'Aha? in the case of her death.'

There was another pause. The Count moved from the verandah to the gravel walk outside. I knew that he had moved, by his voice. 'The rain has come at last,' I heard him say. It *had* come. The state of my cloak showed that it had been falling thickly for some little time.

The Count went back under the verandah—I heard the chair creak beneath his weight as he sat down in it again.

'Well, Percival,' he said; 'and, in the case of Lady Glyde's death, what do you get then?'

'If she leaves no children——'

'Which she is likely to do?'

'Which she is not in the least likely to do——'

'Yes?'

'Why, then I get her twenty thousand pounds.'

'Paid down?'

'Paid down.'

They were silent once more. As their voices ceased, Madame Fosco's shadow darkened the blind again. Instead of passing this time, it remained, for a moment, quite still. I saw her fingers steal round the corner of the blind, and draw it on one side. The dim white outline of her face, looking out straight over me, appeared behind the window. I kept still, shrouded from head to foot in my black cloak. The rain, which was fast wetting me, dripped over the glass, blurred it, and prevented her from seeing anything. 'More rain!' I heard her say to herself. She dropped the blind—and I breathed again freely.

The talk went on below me; the Count resuming it, this time.

'Percival! do you care about your wife?'

'Fosco! that's rather a downright question.'

'I am a downright man; and I repeat it.'

'Why the devil do you look at me in that way?'

'You won't answer me? Well, then; let us say your wife dies before the summer is out——'

'Drop it, Fosco!'

'Let us say your wife dies——'

'Drop it, I tell you!'

'In that case, you would gain twenty thousand pounds; and you would lose——'

'I should lose the chance of three thousand a year.'

'The *remote* chance, Percival—the remote chance only. And you want money, at once. In your position, the gain is certain—the loss doubtful.'

'Speak for yourself as well as for me. Some of the money I want has been borrowed for *you*. And if you come to gain, *my* wife's death would be ten thousand pounds in *your* wife's pocket. Sharp as you are, you seem to have conveniently forgotten Madame Fosco's legacy. Don't look at me in that way! I won't have it! What with your looks and your questions, upon my soul, you make my flesh creep!'

'Your flesh? Does flesh mean conscience in English? I speak of your wife's death, as I speak of a possibility. Why not? The respectable lawyers who scribble-scrabble your deeds and your wills, look the deaths of living people in the face. Do lawyers make your flesh creep? Why should I? It is my business to-night, to clear up your position beyond the possibility of mistake—and I have now done it. Here is your position. If your wife lives, you pay those bills with her signature to the parchment. If your wife dies, you pay them with her death.'

As he spoke, the light in Madame Fosco's room was extinguished; and the whole second floor of the house was now sunk in darkness.

'Talk! talk!' grumbled Sir Percival. 'One would think, to hear you, that my wife's signature to the deed was got already.'

'You have left the matter in my hands,' retorted the Count; 'and I have more than two months before me to turn round in. Say no more about it, if you please, for the present. When the bills are due, you will see for yourself if my "talk! talk!" is worth something, or if it is not. And now, Percival, having done with the money-matters, for to-night, I can place my attention at your disposal, if you wish to consult me on that second difficulty, which has mixed itself up with our little embarrassments, and which has so altered you for the worse, that I hardly know you again. Speak, my friend—and pardon me if I shock your fiery national tastes by mixing myself a second glass of sugar-and-water.'

'It's very well to say speak,' replied Sir Percival, in a far more quiet and more polite tone than he had yet adopted; 'but it's not so easy to know how to begin.'

'Shall I help you?' suggested the Count. 'Shall I give this private difficulty of yours a name? What, if I call it—Anne Catherick?'

'Look here, Fosco, you and I have known each other for a long time; and, if you have helped me out of one or two scrapes before this, I have done the best I could to help you in return, as far as money would go. We have made as many friendly sacrifices, on both sides, as men could; but we have had our secrets from each other, of course—haven't we?'

'You have had a secret from *me*, Percival. There is a skeleton in your cupboard here at Blackwater Park, that has peeped out, in these last few days, at other people besides yourself.'

'Well, suppose it has. If it doesn't concern you, you needn't be curious about it, need you?'

'Do I look curious about it?'

'Yes, you do.'

'So! so! my face speaks the truth, then? What an immense foundation of good there must be in the nature of a man who arrives at my age, and whose face has not yet lost the habit of speaking the truth!—Come, Glyde! let us be candid one with the other. This secret of yours has sought *me*: I have not sought *it*. Let us say I am curious—do you ask me, as your old friend, to respect your secret, and to leave it, once for all, in your own keeping?'

'Yes—that's just what I do ask.'

'Then my curiosity is at an end. It dies in me, from this moment.'

'Do you really mean that?'

'What makes you doubt me?'

'I have had some experience, Fosco, of your roundabout ways; and I am not so sure that you won't worm it out of me, after all.'

The chair below suddenly creaked again—I felt the trelliswork pillar under me shake from top to bottom. The Count had started to his feet and had struck it with his hand, in indignation.

'Percival! Percival!' he cried, passionately, 'do you know me no better than that? Has all your experience shown you nothing of my character yet? I am a man of the antique type! I am capable of the most exalted acts of virtue—when I have the chance of performing them. It has been the misfortune of my life that I have had few chances. My conception of friendship is sublime! Is it my fault that your skeleton has peeped out at me? Why do I confess my curiosity? You poor superficial Englishman, it is to magnify my own self-control. I could draw your secret out of you, if I liked, as I draw this finger out of the palm of my hand—you know I could! But you have appealed to my friendship; and the duties of friendship are sacred to me. See! I trample my base curiosity under my feet. My exalted sentiments lift me above it. Recognise them, Percival! imitate them, Percival! Shake hands—I forgive you.'

His voice faltered over the last words—faltered, as if he was actually shedding tears!

Sir Percival confusedly attempted to excuse himself. But the Count was too magnanimous to listen to him.

'No!' he said. 'When my friend has wounded me, I can pardon him without apologies. Tell me, in plain words, do you want my help?'

'Yes, badly enough.'

'And you can ask for it without compromising yourself?'

'I can try, at any rate.'

'Try, then.'

'Well, this is how it stands:—I told you, to-day, that I had done my best to find Anne Catherick, and failed.'

'Yes; you did.'

'Fosco! I'm a lost man, if I *don't* find her.'

'Ha! Is it so serious as that?'

A little stream of light travelled out under the verandah, and fell over the gravel-walk. The Count had taken the lamp from the inner part of the room, to see his friend clearly by the light of it.

'Yes!' he said. '*Your* face speaks the truth this time. Serious, indeed—as serious as the money matters themselves.'

'More serious. As true as I sit here, more serious!'

The light disappeared again, and the talk went on.

'I showed you the letter to my wife that Anne Catherick hid in the sand,' Sir Percival continued. 'There's no boasting in that letter, Fosco—she *does* know the Secret.'

'Say as little as possible, Percival, in my presence, of the Secret. Does she know it from you?'

'No; from her mother.'

'Two women in possession of your private mind—bad, bad, bad, my friend! One question here, before we go any farther. The motive of your shutting up the daughter in the asylum, is now plain enough to me—but the manner of her escape is not quite so clear. Do you suspect the people in charge of her of closing their eyes purposely, at the instance of some enemy, who could afford to make it worth their while?'

'No; she was the best-behaved patient they had—and, like fools, they trusted her. She's just mad enough to be shut up, and just sane enough to ruin me when she's at large—if you understand that?'

'I do understand it. Now, Percival, come at once to the point; and then I shall know what to do. Where is the danger of your position at the present moment?'

'Anne Catherick is in this neighbourhood, and in communication with Lady Glyde—there's the danger, plain enough. Who can read the letter she hid in the sand, and not see that my wife is in possession of the secret, deny it as she may?'

'One moment, Percival. If Lady Glyde does know the secret, she must know also that it is a compromising secret for *you*. As your wife, surely it is her interest to keep it?'

'Is it? I'm coming to that. It might be her interest if she cared two straws about me. But I happen to be an encumbrance in the way of another man. She was in love with him, before she married me—she's in love with him now—an infernal vagabond of a drawing-master, named Hartright.'

'My dear friend! what is there extraordinary in that? They are all in love with some other man. Who gets the first of a woman's heart? In all my experience I have never yet met with the man who was Number One. Number Two, sometimes. Number Three, Four, Five, often. Number One, never! He exists, of course—but, I have not met with him.'

'Wait! I haven't done yet. Who do you think helped Anne Catherick to get the start, when the people from the madhouse were after her? Hartright. Who do you think saw her again in Cumberland? Hartright. Both times, he spoke to her alone. Stop! don't interrupt me. The scoundrel's as sweet on my wife, as she is on him. He knows the secret, and she knows the secret. Once let them both get together again, and it's her interest and his interest to turn their information against me.'

'Gently, Percival—gently! Are you insensible to the virtue of Lady Glyde?'

'That for the virtue of Lady Glyde! I believe in nothing about her but her money. Don't you see how the case stands? She might be harmless enough by herself; but if she and that vagabond Hartright——'

'Yes, yes, I see. Where is Mr Hartright?'

'Out of the country. If he means to keep a whole skin on his bones, I recommend him not to come back in a hurry.'

'Are you sure he is out of the country?'

'Certain. I had him watched from the time he left Cumberland to the time he sailed. Oh, I've been careful, I can tell you! Anne Catherick lived with some people at a farm-house near Limmeridge. I went there, myself, after she had given me the slip, and made sure that they knew nothing. I gave her mother a form of letter to write to Miss Halcombe, exonerating me from any bad motive in putting her under restraint. I've spent, I'm afraid to say how much, in trying to trace her. And, in spite of it all, she turns up here, and escapes me on my own property! How do I know who else may see her, who else may speak to her? That prying scoundrel, Hartright, may come back without my knowing it, and may make use of her to-morrow——'

'Not he, Percival! While I am on the spot, and while that woman is in the neighbourhood, I will answer for our laying hands on her, before Mr Hartright—even if he does come back. I see! yes, yes, I see! The finding of Anne Catherick is the first necessity: make your mind easy about the rest. Your wife is here, under your thumb; Miss Halcombe is inseparable from her, and is, therefore, under your thumb also; and Mr Hartright is out of the country. This invisible Anne of yours, is all we have to think of for the present. You have made your inquiries?'

'Yes. I have been to her mother; I have ransacked the village—and all to no purpose.'

'Is her mother to be depended on?'

'Yes.'

'She has told your secret once.'

'She won't tell it again.'

'Why not? Are her own interests concerned in keeping it, as well as yours?'

'Yes—deeply concerned.'

'I am glad to hear it, Percival, for your sake. Don't be discouraged, my friend. Our money matters, as I told you, leave me plenty of time to turn round in; and I may search for Anne Catherick to-morrow to better purpose than you. One last question, before we go to bed.'

'What is it?'

'It is this. When I went to the boat-house to tell Lady Glyde that the little difficulty of her signature was put off, accident took me there in time to see a strange woman parting in a very suspicious manner from your wife. But accident did not bring me near enough to see this same woman's face plainly. I must know how to recognise our invisible Anne. What is she like?'

'Like? Come! I'll tell you in two words. She's a sickly likeness of my wife.'

The chair creaked, and the pillar shook once more. The Count was on his feet again—this time in astonishment.

'What!!!' he exclaimed, eagerly.

'Fancy my wife, after a bad illness, with a touch of something wrong in her head—and there is Anne Catherick for you,' answered Sir Percival.

'Are they related to each other?'

'Not a bit of it.'

'And yet, so like?'

'Yes, so like. What are you laughing about?'

There was no answer, and no sound of any kind. The Count was laughing in his smooth, silent, internal way.

'What are you laughing about?' reiterated Sir Percival.

'Perhaps, at my own fancies, my good friend. Allow me my Italian humour—do I not come of the illustrious nation which invented the exhibition of Punch? Well, well, well, I shall know Anne Catherick when I see her—and so enough for to-night. Make your mind easy, Percival. Sleep, my son, the sleep of the just; and see what I will do for you, when daylight comes to help us both. I have my projects and my plans, here in my big head. You shall pay those bills and find Anne Catherick—my sacred word of honour on it, but you shall! Am I a friend to be treasured in the best corner of your heart, or am I not? Am I worth those loans of money which you so delicately reminded me of a little while since? Whatever you do, never wound me in my sentiments any more. Recognise them, Percival! imitate them, Percival! I forgive you again; I shake hands again. Good night!'

Not another word was spoken. I heard the Count close the library door. I heard Sir Percival barring up the window-shutters. It had been raining, raining all the time. I was cramped by my position, and chilled to the bones. When I first tried to move, the effort was so painful to me, that I was obliged to desist. I tried a second time, and succeeded in rising to my knees on the wet roof.

As I crept to the wall, and raised myself against it, I looked back, and saw the window of the Count's dressing-room gleam into light. My sinking courage flickered up in me again, and kept my eyes fixed on his window, as I stole my way back, step by step, past the wall of the house.

The clock struck the quarter after one, when I laid my hands on the window-sill of my own room. I had seen nothing and heard nothing which could lead me to suppose that my retreat had been discovered.

*   *   *   *   *

JUNE 20TH.—Eight o'clock. The sun is shining in a clear sky. I have not been near my bed—I have not once closed my weary, wakeful eyes. From the same window at which I looked out into the darkness of last night, I look out, now, at the bright stillness of the morning.

I count the hours that have passed since I escaped to the shelter of this room, by my own sensations—and those hours seem like weeks.

How short a time, and yet how long to *me*—since I sank down in the darkness, here, on the floor, drenched to the skin, cramped in every limb, cold to the bones, a useless, helpless, panic-stricken creature.

I hardly know when I roused myself. I hardly know when I groped my way back to the bedroom, and lighted the candle, and searched (with a strange ignorance, at first, of where to look for them) for dry clothes to warm me. The doing of these things is in my mind, but not the time when they were done.

Can I even remember when the chilled, cramped feeling left me, and the throbbing heat came in its place?

Surely it was before the sun rose? Yes; I heard the clock strike three. I remember the time by the sudden brightness and clearness, the feverish strain and excitement of all my faculties which came with it. I remember my resolution to control myself, to wait patiently hour after hour, till the chance offered of removing Laura from this horrible place, without the danger of immediate discovery and pursuit. I remember the persuasion settling itself in my mind that the words those two men had said to each other, would furnish us, not only with our justification for leaving the house, but with our weapons of defence against them as well. I recal the impulse that awakened in me to preserve those words in writing, exactly as they were spoken, while the time was my own, and while my memory vividly retained them. All this I remember plainly: there is no confusion in my head yet. The coming in here, from the bedroom, with my pen and ink and paper, before sunrise—the sitting down at the widely-opened window to get all the air I could to cool me—the ceaseless writing, faster and faster, hotter and hotter, driving on, more and more wakefully, all through the dreadful interval before the house was astir again—how clearly I recal it, from the beginning by candle-light, to the end on the page before this, in the sunshine of the new day!

Why do I sit here still? Why do I weary my hot eyes and my burning head by writing more? Why not lie down and rest myself, and try to quench the fever that consumes me, in sleep?

I dare not attempt it. A fear beyond all other fears has got possession of me. I am afraid of this heat that parches my skin. I am afraid of the creeping and throbbing that I feel in my head. If I lie down now, how do I know that I may have the sense and the strength to rise again?

Oh, the rain, the rain—the cruel rain that chilled me last night!

*   *   *   *   *

Nine o'clock. Was it nine struck, or eight? Nine, surely? I am shivering again—shivering, from head to foot, in the summer air. Have I been sitting here asleep? I don't know what I have been doing.

Oh, my God! am I going to be ill?

Ill, at such a time as this!

My head—I am sadly afraid of my head. I can write, but the lines all run together. I see the words. Laura—I can write Laura, and see I write it. Eight or nine—which was it?

So cold, so cold—oh, that rain last night!—and the strokes of the clock, the strokes I can't count, keep striking in my head—

*   *   *   *   *

NOTE

[At this place the entry in the Diary ceases to be legible. The two or three lines which follow, contain fragments of words only, mingled with blots and scratches of the pen. The last marks on the paper bear some resemblance to the first two letters (L. and A.) of the name of Lady Glyde.

On the next page of the Diary, another entry appears. It is in a man's handwriting, large, bold, and firmly regular; and the date is 'June the 21st.' It contains these lines:]

[POSTSCRIPT BY A SINCERE FRIEND]

The illness of our excellent Miss Halcombe has afforded me the opportunity of enjoying an unexpected intellectual pleasure.

I refer to the perusal (which I have just completed) of this interesting Diary.

There are many hundred pages here. I can lay my hand on my heart, and declare that every page has charmed, refreshed, delighted me.

To a man of my sentiments, it is unspeakably gratifying to be able to say this.

Admirable woman!

I allude to Miss Halcombe.

Stupendous effort!

I refer to the Diary.

Yes! these pages are amazing. The tact which I find here, the discretion, the rare courage, the wonderful power of memory, the accurate observation of character, the easy grace of style, the charming outbursts of womanly feeling, have all inexpressibly increased my admiration of this sublime creature, of this magnificent Marian. The presentation of my own character is masterly in the extreme. I certify, with my whole heart, to the fidelity of the portrait. I feel how vivid an impression I must have produced to have been painted in such strong, such rich, such massive colours as these. I lament afresh the cruel necessity which sets our interests at variance, and opposes us to each other. Under happier circumstances how worthy I should have been of Miss Halcombe—how worthy Miss Halcombe would have been of ME.

The sentiments which animate my heart assure me that the lines I have just written express a Profound Truth.

Those sentiments exalt me above all merely personal considerations. I bear witness, in the most disinterested manner, to the excellence of the stratagem by which this unparalleled woman surprised the private interview between Percival and myself. Also to the marvellous accuracy of her report of the whole conversation from its beginning to its end.

Those sentiments have induced me to offer to the unimpressionable doctor who attends on her, my vast knowledge of chemistry, and my luminous experience of the more subtle resources which medical and magnetic science have placed at the disposal of mankind. He has hitherto declined to avail himself of my assistance. Miserable man!

Finally, those sentiments dictate the lines—grateful, sympathetic, paternal lines—which appear in this place. I close the book. My strict sense of propriety restores it (by the hands of my wife) to its place on the writer's table. Events are hurrying me away. Circumstances are guiding me to serious issues. Vast perspectives of success unrol themselves before my eyes. I accomplish my destiny with a calmness which is terrible to myself. Nothing but the homage of my admiration is my own. I deposit it, with respectful tenderness, at the feet of Miss Halcombe.

I breathe my wishes for her recovery.

I condole with her on the inevitable failure of every plan that she has formed for her sister's benefit. At the same time, I entreat her to believe that the information which I have derived from her diary will in no respect help me to contribute to that failure. It simply confirms the plan of conduct which I had previously arranged. I have to thank these pages for awakening the finest sensibilities in my nature—nothing more.

To a person of similar sensibility, this simple assertion will explain and excuse everything.

Miss Halcombe is a person of similar sensibility.

In that persuasion, I sign myself,

FOSCO.

THE NARRATIVE OF FREDERICK FAIRLIE, ESQUIRE, OF LIMMERIDGE HOUSE[1]

IT is the grand misfortune of my life that nobody will let me alone. Why—I ask everybody—why worry me? Nobody answers that question; and nobody lets me alone. Relatives, friends, and strangers all combine to annoy me. What have I done? I ask myself, I ask my servant, Louis, fifty times a day—what have I done? Neither of us can tell. Most extraordinary!

The last annoyance that has assailed me is the annoyance of being called upon to write this Narrative. Is a man in my state of nervous wretchedness capable of writing narratives? When I put this extremely reasonable objection, I am told that certain very serious events, relating to my niece, have happened within my experience; and that I am the fit person to describe them on that account. I am threatened, if I fail to exert myself in the manner required, with consequences which I cannot so much as think of, without perfect prostration. There is really no need to threaten me. Shattered by my miserable health and my family troubles, I am incapable of resistance. If you insist, you take your unjust advantage of me; and I give way immediately. I

---

[1] The manner in which Mr Fairlie's Narrative, and other Narratives that are shortly to follow it, were originally obtained, forms the subject of an explanation which will appear at a later period.

will endeavour to remember what I can (under protest), and to write what I can (also under protest); and what I can't remember and can't write, Louis must remember, and write for me. He is an ass, and I am an invalid; and we are likely to make all sorts of mistakes between us. How humiliating!

I am told to remember dates. Good Heavens! I never did such a thing in my life—how am I to begin now?

I have asked Louis. He is not quite such an ass as I have hitherto supposed. He remembers the date of the event, within a week or two—and I remember the name of the person. The date was towards the end of June, or the beginning of July; and the name (in my opinion a remarkably vulgar one) was Fanny.

At the end of June, or the beginning of July, then, I was reclining, in my customary state, surrounded by the various objects of Art which I have collected about me to improve the taste of the barbarous people in my neighbourhood. That is to say, I had the photographs of my pictures, and prints, and coins, and so forth, all about me, which I intend, one of these days, to present (the photographs, I mean, if the clumsy English language will let me mean anything)—to present to the Institution at Carlisle (horrid place!), with a view to improving the tastes of the Members (Goths and Vandals to a man). It might be supposed that a gentleman who was in course of conferring a great national benefit on his countrymen, was the last gentleman in the world to be unfeelingly worried about private difficulties and family affairs. Quite a mistake, I assure you, in my case.

However, there I was, reclining, with my art-treasures about me, and wanting a quiet morning. Because I wanted a quiet morning, of course Louis came in. It was perfectly natural that I should inquire what the deuce he meant by making his appearance, when I had not rung my bell. I seldom swear—it is such an ungentleman-like habit—but when Louis answered by a grin, I think it was also perfectly natural that I should damn him for grinning. At any rate, I did.

This rigorous mode of treatment, I have observed, invariably brings persons in the lower class of life to their senses. It brought Louis to *his* senses. He was so obliging as to leave off grinning, and inform me that a Young Person was outside, wanting to see me. He added (with the odious talkativeness of servants), that her name was Fanny.

'Who is Fanny?'

'Lady Glyde's maid, sir.'

'What does Lady Glyde's maid want with *me*?'

'A letter, sir——'

'Take it.'

'She refuses to give it to anybody but you, sir.'

'Who sends the letter?'

'Miss Halcombe, sir.'

The moment I heard Miss Halcombe's name, I gave up. It is a habit of mine always to give up to Miss Halcombe. I find, by experience, that it saves noise. I gave up on this occasion. Dear Marian!

'Let Lady Glyde's maid come in, Louis. Stop! Do her shoes creak?'

I was obliged to ask the question. Creaking shoes invariably upset me for the day. I was resigned to see the Young Person, but I was *not* resigned to let the Young Person's shoes upset me. There is a limit even to my endurance.

Louis affirmed distinctly that her shoes were to be depended upon. I waved my hand. He introduced her. Is it necessary to say that she expressed her sense of embarrassment by shutting up her mouth and breathing through her nose? To the student of female human nature in the lower orders, surely not.

Let me do the girl justice. Her shoes did *not* creak. But why do Young Persons in service all perspire at the hands? Why have they all got fat noses, and hard cheeks? And why are their faces so sadly unfinished, especially about the corners of the eyelids? I am not strong enough to think deeply myself, on any subject; but I appeal to professional men who are. Why have we no variety in our breed of Young Persons?

'You have a letter for me, from Miss Halcombe? Put it down on the table, please; and don't upset anything. How is Miss Halcombe?'

'Very well, thank you, sir.'

'And Lady Glyde?'

I received no answer. The Young Person's face became more unfinished than ever; and, I think she began to cry. I certainly saw something moist about her eyes. Tears or perspiration? Louis (whom I have just consulted) is inclined to think, tears. He is in her class of life; and he ought to know best. Let us say, tears.

Except when the refining process of Art judiciously removes from them all resemblance to Nature, I distinctly object to tears. Tears are scientifically described as a Secretion. I can understand that a secretion may be healthy or unhealthy, but I cannot see the interest of a secretion from a sentimental point of view. Perhaps, my own secretions being all wrong together, I am a little prejudiced on the subject. No matter. I behaved, on this occasion, with all possible propriety and feeling. I closed my eyes, and said to Louis,

'Endeavour to ascertain what she means.'

Louis endeavoured, and the Young Person endeavoured. They succeeded in confusing each other to such an extent that, I am bound in common gratitude to say, they really amused me. I think I shall send for them again, when I am in low spirits. I have just mentioned this idea to Louis. Strange to say, it seems to make him uncomfortable. Poor devil!

Surely, I am not expected to repeat my niece's maid's explanation of her tears, interpreted in the English of my Swiss valet? The thing is manifestly impossible. I can give my own impressions and feelings perhaps. Will that do as well? Please say, Yes.

My idea is that she began by telling me (through Louis) that her master had dismissed her from her mistress's service. (Observe, throughout, the strange irrelevancy of the Young Person. Was it my fault that she had lost her place?) On her dismissal, she had gone to the inn to sleep. (*I* don't keep the inn—why mention it to *me*?) Between six o'clock and seven, Miss Halcombe had come to say good-by, and had given her two letters, one for me, and one for a gentleman in London. (*I* am not a gentleman in London—hang the gentleman in London!) She had carefully put the two letters into her bosom (what have I to do with her bosom?); she had been very unhappy, when Miss Halcombe had gone away again; she had not had the heart to put bit or drop between her lips till it was near bedtime; and then, when it was close on nine o'clock, she had thought she should like a cup of tea. (Am I responsible for any of these vulgar fluctuations, which begin with unhappiness and end with tea?) Just as she was *warming the pot* (I give the words on the authority of Louis, who says he knows what they mean, and wishes to explain, but I snub him on principle)—just as she was warming the pot, the door opened, and she was *struck of a heap* (her own words again, and perfectly unintelligible, this time, to Louis, as well as to myself) by the appearance, in the inn parlour, of her ladyship, the Countess. I give my niece's maid's description of my sister's title with a sense of the highest relish. My poor dear sister is a tiresome woman who married a foreigner. To resume: the door opened; her ladyship, the Countess, appeared in the parlour; and the Young Person was struck of a heap. Most remarkable!

I must really rest a little before I can get on any farther. When I have reclined for a few minutes, with my eyes closed, and when Louis has refreshed my poor aching temples with a little eau-de-Cologne, I may be able to proceed.

Her ladyship, the Countess——

No. I am able to proceed, but not to sit up. I will recline, and dictate. Louis has a horrid accent; but he knows the language, and can write. How very convenient!

Her ladyship, the Countess, explained her unexpected appearance at the inn by telling Fanny that she had come to bring one or two little messages which Miss Halcombe, in her hurry, had forgotten. The Young Person thereupon waited anxiously to hear what the messages were; but the Countess seemed disinclined to mention them (so like my sister's tiresome way!), until Fanny had had her tea. Her ladyship was surprisingly kind and thoughtful about it (extremely unlike my sister), and said, 'I am sure, my poor girl, you must want your tea. We can let the messages wait till afterwards. Come, come, if nothing else will put you at your ease, I'll make the tea, and have a cup with you.' I think those were the words, as reported excitably, in my presence, by the Young Person. At any rate, the Countess insisted on making the tea, and carried her ridiculous ostentation of humility so far as to take one cup herself, and to insist on the girl's taking the other. The girl drank the tea; and, according to her own account, solemnised the extraordinary occasion, five minutes afterwards, by fainting dead away, for the first time in her life. Here, again, I use her own words. Louis thinks they were accompanied by an increased secretion of tears. I can't say, myself. The effort of listening being quite as much as I could manage, my eyes were closed.

Where did I leave off? Ah, yes—she fainted, after drinking a cup of tea with the Countess: a proceeding which might have interested me, if I had been her medical man; but, being nothing of the sort, I felt bored by hearing of it, nothing more. When she came to herself, in half an hour's time, she was on the sofa, and nobody was with her but the landlady. The Countess, finding it too late to remain any longer at the inn, had gone away as soon as the girl showed signs of recovering; and the landlady had been good enough to help her up-stairs to bed. Left by herself, she had felt in her bosom (I regret the necessity of referring to this part of the subject a second time), and had found the two letters there, quite safe, but strangely crumpled. She had been giddy in the night; but had got up well enough to travel in the morning. She had put the letter addressed to that obtrusive stranger, the gentleman in London, into the post; and had now delivered the other letter into my hands, as she was told. This was the plain truth; and, though she could not blame herself for any intentional neglect, she was sadly troubled in her mind, and sadly in want of a word of advice. At this point, Louis thinks the secretions appeared again. Perhaps they did; but it is of infinitely-greater importance to mention that, at this point also, I lost my patience, opened my eyes, and interfered.

'What is the purport of all this?' I inquired.

My niece's irrelevant maid stared, and stood speechless.

'Endeavour to explain,' I said to my servant. 'Translate me, Louis.'

Louis endeavoured, and translated. In other words, he descended immediately into a bottomless pit of confusion; and the Young Person followed him down. I really don't know when I have been so amused. I left them at the bottom of the pit, as long as they diverted me. When they ceased to divert me, I exerted my intelligence, and pulled them up again.

It is unnecessary to say that my interference enabled me, in due course of time, to ascertain the purport of the Young Person's remarks. I discovered that she was uneasy in her mind, because the train of events that she had just described to me, had prevented her from receiving those supplementary messages which Miss Halcombe had entrusted to the Countess to deliver. She was afraid the messages might have been of great importance to her mistress's interests. Her dread of Sir Percival had deterred her from going to Blackwater Park late at night to inquire about them; and Miss Halcombe's own directions to her, on no account to miss the train in the morning, had prevented her from waiting at the inn the next day. She was most anxious that the misfortune of her fainting-fit should not lead to the second misfortune of making her mistress think her neglectful, and she would humbly beg to ask me whether I would advise her to write her explanations and excuses to Miss Halcombe, requesting to receive the messages by letter, if it was not too late. I make no apologies for this extremely prosy paragraph. I have been ordered to write it. There are people, unaccountable as it may appear, who actually take more interest in what my niece's maid said to me on this occasion, than in what I said to my niece's maid. Amusing perversity!

'I should feel very much obliged to you, sir, if you would kindly tell me what I had better do,' remarked the Young Person.

'Let things stop as they are,' I said, adapting my language to my listener. '*I* invariably let things stop as they are. Yes. Is that all?'

'If you think it would be a liberty in me, sir, to write, of course I wouldn't venture to do so. But I am so very anxious to do all I can to serve my mistress faithfully——'

People in the lower class of life never know when or how to go out of a room. They invariably require to be helped out by their betters. I thought it high time to help the Young Person out. I did it with two judicious words:

'Good morning!'

Something, outside or inside this singular girl, suddenly creaked. Louis, who was looking at her (which I was not) says she creaked when she curtseyed. Curious. Was it her shoes, her stays, or her bones? Louis thinks it was her stays. Most extraordinary!

As soon as I was left by myself, I had a little nap—I really wanted it. When I awoke again, I noticed dear Marian's letter. If I had had the least idea of what it contained, I should certainly not have attempted to open it. Being, unfortunately for myself, quite innocent of all suspicion, I read the letter. It immediately upset me for the day.

I am, by nature, one of the most easy-tempered creatures that ever lived—I make allowances for everybody, and I take offence at nothing. But, as I have before remarked, there are limits to my endurance. I laid down Marian's letter, and felt myself—justly felt myself—an injured man.

I am about to make a remark. It is, of course, applicable to the very serious matter now under notice—or I should not allow it to appear in this place.

Nothing, in my opinion, sets the odious selfishness of mankind in such a repulsively-vivid light, as the treatment, in all classes of society, which the Single people receive at the hands of the Married people. When you have once shown yourself too considerate and self-denying to add a family of your own to an already overcrowded population, you are vindictively marked out, by your married friends, who have no similar consideration and no similar self-denial, as the recipient of half their conjugal troubles, and the born friend of all their children. Husbands and wives *talk* of the cares of matrimony; and bachelors and spinsters *bear* them. Take my own case. I considerately remain single; and my poor dear brother, Philip, inconsiderately marries. What does he do when he dies? He leaves his daughter to *me*. She is a sweet girl. She is also a dreadful responsibility. Why lay her on my shoulders? Because I am bound, in the harmless character of a single man, to relieve my married connexions of all their own troubles. I do my best with my brother's responsibility; I marry my niece, with infinite fuss and difficulty, to the man her father wanted her to marry. She and her husband disagree, and unpleasant consequences follow. What does she do with those consequences? She transfers them to *me*. Why transfer them to *me*? Because I am bound, in the harmless character of a single man, to relieve my married connexions of all their own troubles. Poor single people! Poor human nature!

It is quite unnecessary to say that Marian's letter threatened me. Everybody threatens me. All sorts of horrors were to fall on my devoted head, if I hesitated to turn Limmeridge House into an asylum for my niece and her misfortunes. I did hesitate, nevertheless.

I have mentioned that my usual course, hitherto, had been to submit to dear Marian, and save noise. But, on this occasion, the consequences involved in her extremely inconsiderate proposal, were of a nature to make me pause. If I opened Limmeridge House as an asylum to Lady Glyde, what security had I against Sir Percival Glyde's following her here, in a state of violent resentment against *me* for harbouring his wife? I saw such a perfect labyrinth of troubles involved in this proceeding, that I determined to feel my ground, as it were. I wrote, therefore, to dear Marian, to beg (as she had no husband to lay claim to her) that she would come here by herself, first, and talk the matter over with me. If she could answer my objections to my own perfect satisfaction, then I assured her that I would receive our sweet Laura with the greatest pleasure—but not otherwise.

I felt, of course, at the time, that this temporising, on my part, would probably end in bringing Marian here in a state of virtuous indignation, banging doors. But, then, the other course of proceeding might end in bringing Sir Percival here in a state of virtuous indignation, banging doors also; and, of the two indignations and bangings, I preferred Marian's— because I was used to her. Accordingly, I despatched the letter by return of post. It gained me time, at all events—and, oh dear me! what a point that was to begin with.

When I am totally prostrated (did I mention that I was totally prostrated by Marian's letter?), it always takes me three days to get up again. I was very unreasonable—I expected three days of quiet. Of course, I didn't get them.

The third day's post brought me a most impertinent letter from a person with whom I was totally unacquainted. He described himself, as the acting partner of our man of business—our dear, pig-headed old Gilmore—and he informed me that he had lately received, by the post, a letter addressed to him in Miss Halcombe's handwriting. On opening the envelope, he had discovered, to his astonishment, that it contained nothing but a blank sheet of note paper. This circumstance appeared to him so suspicious (as suggesting to his restless legal mind that the letter had been tampered with) that he had at once written to Miss Halcombe, and had received no answer by return of post. In this difficulty, instead of acting like a sensible man and letting things take their proper course, his next absurd proceeding, on his own showing, was to pester *me*, by writing to inquire if I knew anything about it. What the deuce should I know about it? Why alarm *me* as well as himself? I wrote back to that effect. It was one of my keenest letters. I have produced nothing with a sharper epistolary edge to it, since I tendered his dismissal in writing to that extremely troublesome person, Mr Walter Hartright.

My letter produced its effect. I heard nothing more from the lawyer.

This, perhaps, was not altogether surprising. But it was certainly a remarkable circumstance that no second letter reached me from Marian, and that no warning signs appeared of her arrival. Her unexpected absence did me amazing good. It was so very soothing and pleasant to infer (as I did of course) that my married connexions had made it up again. Five days of undisturbed tranquillity, of delicious single blessedness, quite restored me. On the sixth day, I felt strong enough to send for my photographer, and to set him at work again on the presentation copies of my art-treasures, with a view, as I have already mentioned, to the improvement of taste in this barbarous neighbourhood. I had just dismissed him to his workshop, and had just begun coquetting with my coins, when Louis suddenly made his appearance with a card in his hand.

'Another Young Person?' I said. 'I won't see her. In my state of health, Young Persons disagree with me. Not at home.'

'It is a gentleman this time, sir.'

A gentleman of course made a difference. I looked at the card.

Gracious Heaven! my tiresome sister's foreign husband. Count Fosco.

Is it necessary to say what my first impression was, when I looked at my visitor's card? Surely not? My sister having married a foreigner, there was but one impression that any man in his senses could possibly feel. Of course the Count had come to borrow money of me.

'Louis,' I said, 'do you think he would go away, if you gave him five shillings?'

Louis looked quite shocked. He surprised me inexpressibly, by declaring that my sister's foreign husband was dressed superbly, and looked the picture of prosperity. Under these circumstances, my first impression altered to a certain extent. I now took it for granted, that the Count had matrimonial difficulties of his own to contend with, and that he had come, like the rest of the family, to cast them all on my shoulders.

'Did he mention his business?' I asked.

'Count Fosco said he had come here, sir, because Miss Halcombe was unable to leave Blackwater Park.'

Fresh troubles, apparently. Not exactly his own, as I had supposed, but dear Marian's. Troubles, any way. Oh dear!

'Show him in,' I said, resignedly.

The Count's first appearance really startled me. He was such an alarmingly-large person, that I quite trembled. I felt certain that he would shake the floor, and knock down my art-treasures. He did neither the one nor the other. He was refreshingly dressed in summer costume; his manner was delightfully self-possessed and quiet—he had a charming smile. My first impression of him was highly favourable. It is not creditable to my penetration—as the sequel will show—to acknowledge this; but I am a naturally candid man, and I *do* acknowledge it, notwithstanding.

'Allow me to present myself, Mr Fairlie,' he said. 'I come from Blackwater Park, and I have the honour and the happiness of being Madame Fosco's husband. Let me take my first, and last, advantage of that circumstance, by entreating you not to make a stranger of me. I beg you will not disturb yourself—I beg you will not move.'

'You are very good,' I replied. 'I wish I was strong enough to get up. Charmed to see you at Limmeridge. Please take a chair.'

'I am afraid you are suffering to-day,' said the Count.

'As usual,' I said. 'I am nothing but a bundle of nerves dressed up to look like a man.'

'I have studied many subjects in my time,' remarked this sympathetic person. 'Among others, the inexhaustible subject of nerves. May I make a suggestion, at once the simplest and the most profound? Will you let me alter the light in your room?'

'Certainly—if you will be so very kind as not to let any of it in on me.'

He walked to the window. Such a contrast to dear Marian! so extremely considerate in all his movements!

'Light,' he said, in that delightfully confidential tone which is so soothing to an invalid, 'is the first essential. Light stimulates, nourishes, preserves.

You can no more do without it, Mr Fairlie, than if you were a flower. Observe. Here, where you sit, I close the shutters, to compose you. There, where you do *not* sit, I draw up the blind and let in the invigorating sun. Admit the light into your room, if you cannot bear it on yourself. Light, sir, is the grand decree of Providence. You accept Providence with your own restrictions. Accept Light—on the same terms.'

I thought this very convincing and attentive. He had taken me in—up to that point about the light, he had certainly taken me in.

'You see me confused,' he said, returning to his place—'on my word of honour, Mr Fairlie, you see me confused in your presence.'

'Shocked to hear it, I am sure. May I inquire why?'

'Sir, can I enter this room (where you sit a sufferer), and see you surrounded by these admirable objects of Art, without discovering that you are a man whose feelings are acutely impressionable, whose sympathies are perpetually alive? Tell me, can I do this?'

If I had been strong enough to sit up in my chair, I should of course have bowed. Not being strong enough, I smiled my acknowledgments instead. It did just as well; we both understood one another.

'Pray follow my train of thought,' continued the Count. 'I sit here, a man of refined sympathies myself, in the presence of another man of refined sympathies also. I am conscious of a terrible necessity for lacerating those sympathies, by referring to domestic events of a very melancholy kind. What is the inevitable consequence? I have done myself the honour of pointing it out to you, already. I sit confused.'

Was it at this point that I began to suspect he was going to bore me? I rather think it was.

'Is it absolutely necessary to refer to these unpleasant matters?' I inquired. 'In our homely English phrase, Count Fosco, won't they keep?'

The Count, with the most alarming solemnity, sighed and shook his head.

'Must I really hear them?'

He shrugged his shoulders (it was the first foreign thing he had done, since he had been in the room); and looked at me in an unpleasantly penetrating manner. My instincts told me that I had better close my eyes. I obeyed my instincts.

'Please, break it gently,' I pleaded. 'Anybody dead?'

'Dead!' cried the Count, with unnecessary foreign fierceness. 'Mr Fairlie!' your national composure terrifies me. In the name of Heaven, what have I said, or done, to make you think me the messenger of death?'

'Pray accept my apologies,' I answered. 'You have said and done nothing. I make it a rule, in these distressing cases, always to anticipate the worst. It breaks the blow, by meeting it half way, and so on. Inexpressibly relieved, I am sure, to hear that nobody is dead. Anybody ill?'

I opened my eyes, and looked at him. Was he very yellow, when he came in? or had he turned very yellow, in the last minute or two? I really can't say; and I can't ask Louis, because he was not in the room at the time.

'Anybody ill?' I repeated; observing that my national composure still appeared to affect him.

'That is part of my bad news, Mr Fairlie. Yes. Somebody is ill.'

'Grieved, I am sure. Which of them is it?'

'To my profound sorrow, Miss Halcombe. Perhaps you were in some degree prepared to hear this? Perhaps, when you found that Miss Halcombe did not come here by herself, as you proposed, and did not write a second time, your affectionate anxiety may have made you fear that she was ill?'

I have no doubt my affectionate anxiety had led to that melancholy apprehension, at some time or other; but, at the moment, my wretched memory entirely failed to remind me of the circumstance. However, I said, Yes, in justice to myself. I was much shocked. It was so very uncharacteristic of such a robust person as dear Marian to be ill, that I could only suppose she had met with an accident. A horse, or a false step on the stairs, or something of that sort.

'Is it serious?' I asked.

'Serious—beyond a doubt,' he replied. 'Dangerous—I hope and trust not. Miss Halcombe unhappily exposed herself to be wetted through by a heavy rain. The cold that followed was of an aggravated kind; and it has now brought with it the worst consequence—Fever.'

When I heard the word, Fever, and when I remembered, at the same moment, that the unscrupulous person who was now addressing me had just come from Blackwater Park, I thought I should have fainted on the spot.

'Good God!' I said. 'Is it infectious?'

'Not at present,' he answered, with detestable composure. 'It may turn to infection—but no such deplorable complication had taken place when I left Blackwater Park. I have felt the deepest interest in the case, Mr Fairlie—I have endeavoured to assist the regular medical attendant in watching it—accept my personal assurances of the uninfectious nature of the fever, when I last saw it.'

Accept his assurances! I never was farther from accepting anything in my life. I would not have believed him on his oath. He was too yellow to be believed. He looked like a walking-West-Indian-epidemic. He was big enough to carry typhus by the ton, and to dye the very carpet he walked on with scarlet fever. In certain emergencies, my mind is remarkably soon made up. I instantly determined to get rid of him.

'You will kindly excuse an invalid,' I said—'but long conferences of any kind invariably upset me. May I beg to know exactly what the object is to which I am indebted for the honour of your visit?'

I fervently hoped that this remarkably-broad hint would throw him off his balance—confuse him—reduce him to polite apologies—in short, get him out of the room. On the contrary, it only settled him in his chair. He became additionally solemn and dignified and confidential. He held up two of his horrid fingers, and gave me another of his unpleasantly-penetrating looks. What was I to do? I was not strong enough to quarrel with him. Conceive my situation, if you please. Is language adequate to describe it? I think not.

'The objects of my visit,' he went on, quite irrepressibly, 'are numbered on my fingers. They are two. First, I come to bear my testimony, with profound sorrow, to the lamentable disagreements between Sir Percival and Lady Glyde. I am Sir Percival's oldest friend; I am related to Lady Glyde by marriage; I am an eyewitness of all that has happened at Blackwater Park. In those three capacities I speak with authority, with confidence, with honourable regret. Sir! I inform you, as the head of Lady Glyde's family, that Miss Halcombe has exaggerated nothing in the letter which she wrote to your address. I affirm that the remedy which that admirable lady has proposed, is the only remedy that will spare you the horrors of public scandal. A temporary separation between husband and wife is the one peaceable solution of this difficulty. Part them for the present; and when all causes of irritation are removed, I, who have now the honour of addressing you—I will undertake to bring Sir Percival to reason. Lady Glyde is innocent, Lady Glyde is injured; but—follow my thought here!—she is, on that very account (I say it with shame), the cause of irritation while she remains under her husband's roof. No other house can receive her with propriety, but yours. I invite you to open it!'

Cool. Here was a matrimonial hailstorm pouring in the South of England; and I was invited, by a man with fever in every fold of his coat, to come out from the North of England, and take my share of the pelting. I tried to put the point forcibly, just as I have put it here. The Count deliberately lowered one of his horrid fingers; kept the other up; and went on—rode over me, as it were, without even the common coachmanlike attention of crying 'Hi!' before he knocked me down.

'Follow my thought once more, if you please,' he resumed. 'My first object you have heard. My second object in coming to this house is to do what Miss Halcombe's illness has prevented her from doing for herself. My large experience is consulted on all difficult matters at Blackwater Park; and my friendly advice was requested on the interesting subject of your letter to Miss Halcombe. I understood at once—for my sympathies are your sympathies—why you wished to see her here, before you pledged yourself to inviting Lady Glyde. You are most right, sir, in hesitating to receive the wife, until you are quite certain that the husband will not exert his authority to reclaim her. I agree to that. I also agree that such delicate explanations as this difficulty involves, are not explanations which can be properly disposed of by writing only. My presence here (to my own great inconvenience) is the proof that I speak sincerely. As for the explanations themselves, I—Fosco—I who know

Sir Percival much better than Miss Halcombe knows him, affirm to you, on my honour and my word, that he will not come near this house, or attempt to communicate with this house, while his wife is living in it. His affairs are embarrassed. Offer him his freedom, by means of the absence of Lady Glyde. I promise you he will take his freedom, and go back to the Continent, at the earliest moment when he can get away. Is this clear to you as crystal? Yes, it is. Have you questions to address to me? Be it so; I am here to answer. Ask, Mr Fairlie—oblige me by asking, to your heart's content.'

He had said so much already in spite of me; and he looked so dreadfully capable of saying a great deal more, also in spite of me, that I declined his amiable invitation, in pure self-defence.

'Many thanks,' I replied. 'I am sinking fast. In my state of health, I must take things for granted. Allow me to do so, on this occasion. We quite understand each other. Yes. Much obliged, I am sure, for your kind interference. If I ever get better, and ever have a second opportunity of improving our acquaintance——'

He got up. I thought he was going. No. More talk; more time for the development of infectious influences—in *my* room, too; remember that, in *my* room!

'One moment, yet,' he said; 'one moment, before I take my leave. I ask permission, at parting, to impress on you an urgent necessity. It is this, sir! You must not think of waiting till Miss Halcombe recovers, before you receive Lady Glyde. Miss Halcombe has the attendance of the doctor, of the housekeeper at Blackwater Park, and of an experienced nurse as well—three persons for whose capacity and devotion I answer with my life. I tell you that. I tell you, also, that the anxiety and alarm of her sister's illness has already affected the health and spirits of Lady Glyde, and has made her totally unfit to be of use in the sick-room. Her position with her husband grows more and more deplorable and dangerous, every day. If you leave her any longer at Blackwater Park, you do nothing whatever to hasten her sister's recovery, and, at the same time, you risk the public scandal, which you, and I, and all of us, are bound, in the sacred interests of the Family, to avoid. With all my soul, I advise you to remove the serious responsibility of delay from your own shoulders, by writing to Lady Glyde to come here at once. Do your affectionate, your honourable, your inevitable duty; and, whatever happens in the future, no one can lay the blame on *you*. I speak from my large experience; I offer my friendly advice. Is it accepted—Yes, or No?'

I looked at him—merely looked at him—with my sense of his amazing assurance, and my dawning resolution to ring for Louis, and have him shown out of the room, expressed in every line of my face. It is perfectly incredible, but quite true, that my face did not appear to produce the slightest impression on him. Born without nerves—evidently, born without nerves!

'You hesitate?' he said. 'Mr Fairlie! I understand that hesitation. You object—see, sir, how my sympathies look straight down into your thoughts!—you object that Lady Glyde is not in health and not in spirits to take the long journey, from Hampshire to this place, by herself. Her own maid is removed from her, as you know; and, of other servants fit to travel with her, from one end of England to another, there are none at Blackwater Park. You object, again, that she cannot comfortably stop and rest in London, on her way here, because she cannot comfortably go alone to a public hotel where she is a total stranger. In one breath, I grant both objections—in another breath, I remove them. Follow me, if you please, for the last time. It was my intention, when I returned to England with Sir Percival, to settle myself in the neighbourhood of London. That purpose has just been happily accomplished. I have taken, for six months, a little furnished house, in the quarter called St John's Wood. Be so obliging as to keep this fact in your mind; and observe the programme I now propose. Lady Glyde travels to London (a short journey)—I myself meet her at the station—I take her to rest and sleep at my house, which is also the house of her aunt—when she is restored, I escort her to the station again—she travels to this place, and her own maid (who is now under your roof) receives her at the carriage-door. Here is comfort consulted; here are the interests of propriety consulted; here is your own duty—duty of hospitality, sympathy, protection, to an unhappy Lady in need of all three—smoothed and made easy, from the beginning to the end. I cordially invite you, sir, to second my efforts in the sacred interests of the Family. I seriously advise you to write, by my hands, offering the hospitality of your house (and heart), and the hospitality of my house (and heart), to that injured and unfortunate lady whose cause I plead to-day.'

He waved his horrid hand at me; he struck his infectious breast; he addressed me oratorically—as if I was laid up in the House of Commons. It was high time to take a desperate course of some sort. It was also high time to send for Louis, and adopt the precaution of fumigating the room.

In this trying emergency, an idea occurred to me—an inestimable idea which, so to speak, killed two intrusive birds with one stone. I determined to get rid of the Count's tiresome eloquence, and of Lady Glyde's tiresome troubles, by complying with this odious foreigner's request, and writing the letter at once. There was not the least danger of the invitation being accepted, for there was not the least chance that Laura would consent to leave Blackwater Park, while Marian was lying there ill. How this charmingly-convenient obstacle could have escaped the officious penetration of the Count, it was impossible to conceive—but it *had* escaped him. My dread that he might yet discover it, if I allowed him any more time to think, stimulated me to such an amazing degree, that I struggled into a sitting position; seized, really seized, the writing materials by my side; and produced the letter as rapidly as if I had been a common clerk in an office. 'Dearest Laura, Please come, whenever you like. Break the journey by sleeping in London at your aunt's house. Grieved to hear of dear Marian's illness. Ever affectionately yours.' I handed these lines, at arm's length, to the Count—I sank back in my chair—I said, 'Excuse me; I am entirely prostrated; I can do no more. Will you rest and lunch down stairs? Love to all, and sympathy, and so on. *Good* morning.'

He made another speech—the man was absolutely inexhaustible. I closed my eyes; I endeavoured to hear as little as possible. In spite of my endeavours, I was obliged to hear a great deal. My sister's endless husband congratulated himself and congratulated me, on the result of our interview; he mentioned a great deal more about his sympathies and mine; he deplored my miserable health; he offered to write me a prescription; he impressed on me the necessity of not forgetting what he had said about the importance of light; he accepted my obliging invitation to rest and lunch; he recommended me to expect Lady Glyde in two or three days' time; he begged my permission to look forward to our next meeting, instead of paining himself and paining me, by saying farewell; he added a great deal more, which, I rejoice to think, I did not attend to at the time, and do not remember now. I heard his sympathetic voice travelling away from me by degrees—but, large as he was, I never heard *him*. He had the negative merit of being absolutely noiseless. I don't know when he opened the door, or when he shut it. I ventured to make use of my eyes again, after an interval of silence—and he was gone.

I rang for Louis, and retired to my bath-room. Tepid water, strengthened with aromatic vinegar, for myself, and copious fumigation, for my study, were the obvious precautions to take; and of course I adopted them. I rejoice to say, they proved successful. I enjoyed my customary siesta. I awoke moist and cool.

My first inquiries were for the Count. Had we really got rid of him? Yes—he had gone away by the afternoon train. Had he lunched; and, if so, upon what? Entirely upon fruit-tart and cream. What a man! What a digestion!

Am I expected to say anything more? I believe not. I believe I have reached the limits assigned to me. The shocking circumstances which happened at a later period, did not, I am thankful to say, happen in my presence. I do beg and entreat that nobody will be so very unfeeling as to lay any part of the blame of those circumstances on *me*. I did everything for the best. I am not answerable for a deplorable calamity, which it was quite impossible to foresee. I am shattered by it; I have suffered under it, as nobody else has suffered. My servant, Louis (who is really attached to me, in his unintelligent way), thinks I shall never get over it. He sees me dictating at this moment, with my handkerchief to my eyes. I wish to mention, in justice to myself, that it was not my fault, and that I am quite exhausted and heartbroken. Need I say more?

THE NARRATIVE OF ELIZA MICHELSON, HOUSEKEEPER AT BLACKWATER PARK

I AM asked to state plainly what I know of the progress of Miss Halcombe's illness, and of the circumstances under which Lady Glyde left Blackwater Park for London.

The reason given for making this demand on me is, that my testimony is wanted in the interests of truth. As the widow of a clergyman of the Church of England (reduced by misfortune to the necessity of accepting a situation), I have been taught to place the claims of truth above all other considerations. I therefore comply with a request which I might otherwise, through reluctance to connect myself with distressing family affairs, have hesitated to grant.

I made no memorandum at the time, and I cannot therefore be sure to a day, of the date; but I believe I am correct in stating that Miss Halcombe's serious illness began during the last fortnight or ten days in June. The breakfast hour was late at Blackwater Park—sometimes as late as ten, never earlier than half-past nine. On the morning to which I am now referring, Miss Halcombe (who was usually the first to come down) did not make her appearance at the table. After the family had waited a quarter of an hour, the upper housemaid was sent to see after her, and came running out of the room, dreadfully frightened. I met the servant on the stairs, and went at once to Miss Halcombe to see what was the matter. The poor lady was incapable of telling me. She was walking about her room with a pen in her hand, quite light-headed, in a state of burning fever.

Lady Glyde (being no longer in Sir Percival's service, I may, without impropriety, mention my former mistress by her name, instead of calling her My Lady) was the first to come in, from her own bedroom. She was so dreadfully alarmed and distressed, that she was quite useless. The Count Fosco, and his lady, who came up-stairs immediately afterwards, were both most serviceable and kind. Her ladyship assisted me to get Miss Halcombe to her bed. His lordship the Count, remained in the sitting-room, and, having sent for my medicine-chest, made a mixture for Miss Halcombe, and a cooling lotion to be applied to her head, so as to lose no time before the doctor came. We applied the lotion; but we could not get her to take the mixture. Sir Percival undertook to send for the doctor. He despatched a groom, on horseback, for the nearest medical man, Mr Dawson, of Oak Lodge.

Mr Dawson arrived in less than an hour's time. He was a respectable elderly man, well known, all round the country; and we were much alarmed when we found that he considered the case to be a very serious one.

His lordship the Count affably entered into conversation with Mr Dawson, and gave his opinions with a judicious freedom. Mr Dawson, not over-courteously, inquired if his lordship's advice was the advice of a doctor; and being informed that it was the advice of one who had studied medicine, unprofessionally, replied that he was not accustomed to consult with amateur-physicians. The Count, with truly Christian meekness of temper, smiled, and left the room. Before he went out, he told me that he might be found, in case he was wanted in the course of the day, at the boat-house on the banks of the lake. Why he should have gone there, I cannot say. But he did go; remaining away the whole day till seven o'clock, which was dinner-time. Perhaps, he wished to set the example of keeping the house as quiet as possible. It was entirely in his character to do so. He was a most considerate nobleman.

Miss Halcombe passed a very bad night; the fever coming and going, and getting worse towards the morning, instead of better. No nurse fit to wait on her being at hand in the neighbourhood, her ladyship the Countess, and myself, undertook the duty, relieving each other. Lady Glyde, most unwisely, insisted on sitting up with us. She was much too nervous and too delicate in health to bear the anxiety of Miss Halcombe's illness calmly. She only did herself harm, without being of the least real assistance. A more gentle and affectionate lady never lived; but she cried, and she was frightened—two weaknesses which made her entirely unfit to be present in a sick-room.

Sir Percival and the Count came in the morning to make their inquiries. Sir Percival (from distress, I presume, at his lady's affliction, and at Miss Halcombe's illness) appeared much confused and unsettled in his mind. His lordship testified, on the contrary, a becoming composure and interest. He had his straw hat in one hand, and his book in the other; and he mentioned to Sir Percival, in my hearing, that he would go out again, and study at the lake. 'Let us keep the house quiet,' he said. 'Let us not smoke in-doors, my friend, now Miss Halcombe is ill. You go your way, and I will go mine. When I study, I like to be alone. Good morning, Mrs Michelson.'

Sir Percival was not civil enough—perhaps, I ought, in justice to say, not composed enough—to take leave of me with the same polite attention. The only person in the house, indeed, who treated me, at that time or at any other, on the footing of a lady in distressed circumstances, was the Count. He had the manners of a true nobleman; he was considerate towards every one. Even the young person (Fanny, by name) who attended on Lady Glyde, was not beneath his notice. When she was sent away by Sir Percival, his lordship (showing me his sweet little birds at the time) was most kindly anxious to know what had become of her, where she was to go the day she left Blackwater Park, and so on. It is in such little delicate attentions that the advantages of aristocratic birth always show themselves. I make no apology for introducing these particulars; they are brought forward in justice to his lordship, whose character, I have reason to know, is viewed rather harshly in certain quarters. A nobleman who can respect a lady in distressed circumstances, and can take a fatherly interest in the fortunes of an humble servant girl, shows principles and feelings of too high an order to be lightly called in question. I advance no opinions—I offer facts only. My endeavour through life is to judge not, that I be not judged. One of my beloved husband's finest sermons was on that text. I read it constantly—in my own copy of the edition printed by subscription, in the first days of my widowhood—and, at every fresh perusal, I derive an increase of spiritual benefit and edification.

There was no improvement in Miss Halcombe; and the second night was even worse than the first. Mr Dawson was constant in his attendance. The practical duties of nursing were still divided between the Countess and myself; Lady Glyde persisting in sitting up with us, though we both entreated her to take some rest. 'My place is by Marian's bedside,' was her only answer. 'Whether I am ill, or well, nothing will induce me to lose sight of her.'

Towards mid-day, I went down stairs to attend to some of my regular duties. An hour afterwards, on my way back to the sick-room, I saw the Count (who had gone out again early, for the third time), entering the hall, to all appearance in the highest good spirits. Sir Percival, at the same moment, put his head out of the library-door, and addressed his noble friend, with extreme eagerness, in these words:

'Have you found her?'

His lordship's large face became dimpled all over with placid smiles; but he made no reply in words. At the same time, Sir Percival turned his head, observed that I was approaching the stairs, and looked at me in the most rudely-angry manner possible.

'Come in here and tell me about it,' he said, to the Count. 'Whenever there are women in a house, they're always sure to be going up or down stairs.'

'My dear Percival,' observed his lordship, kindly, 'Mrs Michelson has duties. Pray recognise her admirable performance of them as sincerely as I do! How is the sufferer, Mrs Michelson?'

'No better, my lord, I regret to say.'

'Sad—most sad!' remarked the Count. 'You look fatigued, Mrs Michelson. It is certainly time you and my wife had some help in nursing. I think I may be the means of offering you that help. Circumstances have happened which will oblige Madame Fosco to travel to London, either to-morrow or the day after. She will go away in the morning, and return at night; and she will bring back with her, to relieve you, a nurse of excellent conduct and capacity, who is now disengaged. The woman is known to my wife as a person to be trusted. Before she comes here, say nothing about her, if you please, to the doctor, because he will look with an evil eye on any nurse of my providing. When she appears in this house, she will speak for herself; and Mr Dawson will be obliged to acknowledge that there is no excuse for not employing her. Lady Glyde will say the same. Pray present my best respects and sympathies to Lady Glyde.'

I expressed my grateful acknowledgments for his lordship's kind considerations. Sir Percival cut them short by calling to his noble friend (using, I regret to say, a profane expression) to come into the library, and not to keep him waiting there any longer.

I proceeded up-stairs. We are poor erring creatures; and however well established a woman's principles may be, she cannot always keep on her guard against the temptation to exercise an idle curiosity. I am ashamed to say that an idle curiosity, on this occasion, got the better of *my* principles, and made me unduly inquisitive about the question which Sir Percival had addressed to his noble friend, at the library door. Who was the Count expected to find, in the course of his studious morning rambles at Blackwater Park? A woman, it was to be presumed, from the terms of Sir Percival's inquiry. I did not suspect the Count of any impropriety—I knew his moral character too well. The only question I asked myself was—Had he found her?

To resume. The night passed as usual, without producing any change for the better in Miss Halcombe. The next day, she seemed to improve a little. The day after that, her ladyship the Countess, without mentioning the object of her journey to any one in my hearing, proceeded by the morning train to London; her noble husband, with his customary attention, accompanying her to the station.

I was now left in sole charge of Miss Halcombe, with every apparent chance, in consequence of her sister's resolution not to leave the bedside, of having Lady Glyde herself to nurse next.

The only circumstance of any importance that happened in the course of the day, was the occurrence of another unpleasant meeting between the doctor and the Count.

His lordship, on returning from the station, stepped up into Miss Halcombe's sitting-room to make his inquiries. I went out from the bedroom to speak to him; Mr Dawson and Lady Glyde being both with the patient at the time. The Count asked me many questions about the treatment and the symptoms. I informed him that the treatment was of the kind described as 'saline;' and that the symptoms, between the attacks of fever, were certainly those of increasing weakness and exhaustion. Just as I was mentioning these last particulars, Mr Dawson came out from the bedroom.

'Good morning, sir,' said his lordship, stepping forward in the most urbane manner, and stopping the doctor, with a high-bred resolution impossible to resist, 'I greatly fear you find no improvement in the symptoms to-day?'

'I find decided improvement,' answered Mr Dawson.

'You still persist in your lowering treatment of this case of fever?' continued his lordship.

'I persist in the treatment which is justified by my own professional experience,' said Mr Dawson.

'Permit me to put one question to you on the vast subject of professional experience,' observed the Count. 'I presume to offer no more advice—I only presume to make an inquiry. You live at some distance, sir, from the gigantic centres of scientific activity—London and Paris. Have you ever heard of the wasting effects of fever being reasonably and intelligibly repaired by fortifying the exhausted patient with brandy, wine, ammonia, and quinine? Has that new heresy of the highest medical authorities ever reached your ears—Yes, or No?'

'When a professional man puts that question to me, I shall be glad to answer him,' said the doctor, opening the door to go out. 'You are not a professional man; and I beg to decline answering *you*.'

Buffeted in this inexcusably-uncivil way, on one cheek, the Count, like a practical Christian, immediately turned the other, and said, in the sweetest manner, 'Good morning, Mr Dawson.'

If my late beloved husband had been so fortunate as to know his lordship, how highly he and the Count would have esteemed each other!

Her ladyship the Countess returned by the last train that night, and brought with her the nurse from London. I was instructed that this person's name was Mrs Rubelle. Her personal appearance, and her imperfect English, when she spoke, informed me that she was a foreigner.

I have always cultivated a feeling of humane indulgence for foreigners. They do not possess our blessings and advantages; and they are, for the most part, brought up in the blind errors of popery. It has also always been my precept and practice, as it was my dear husband's precept and practice before me (see Sermon XXIX, in the Collection by the late Rev. Samuel Michelson, M.A.), to do as I would be done by. On both these accounts, I will not say that Mrs Rubelle struck me as being a small, wiry, sly person, of fifty or thereabouts, with a dark brown, or Creole complexion, and watchful light grey eyes. Nor will I mention, for the reasons just alleged, that I thought her dress, though it was of the plainest black silk, inappropriately costly in texture and unnecessarily refined in trimming and finish, for a person in her position in life. I should not like these things to be said of me, and therefore it is my duty not to say them of Mrs Rubelle. I will merely mention that her manners were—not perhaps unpleasantly reserved—but only remarkably quiet and retiring; that she looked about her a great deal, and said very little, which might have arisen quite as much from her own modesty, as from distrust of her position at Blackwater Park; and that she declined to partake of supper (which was curious, perhaps, but surely not suspicious?), although I myself politely invited her to that meal, in my own room.

At the Count's particular suggestion (so like his lordship's forgiving kindness!), it was arranged that Mrs Rubelle should not enter on her duties, until she had been seen and approved by the doctor the next morning. I sat up that night. Lady Glyde appeared to be very unwilling that the new nurse should be employed to attend on Miss Halcombe. Such want of liberality towards a foreigner on the part of a lady of her education and refinement surprised me. I ventured to say, 'My lady, we must all remember not to be hasty in our judgments on our inferiors—especially when they come from foreign parts.' Lady Glyde did not appear to attend to me. She only sighed, and kissed Miss Halcombe's hand as it lay on the counterpane. Scarcely a judicious proceeding in a sick-room, with a patient whom it was highly desirable not to excite. But poor Lady Glyde knew nothing of nursing— nothing whatever, I am sorry to say.

The next morning, Mrs Rubelle was sent to the sitting-room, to be approved by the doctor, on his way through to the bedroom.

I left Lady Glyde with Miss Halcombe, who was slumbering at the time, and joined Mrs Rubelle, with the object of kindly preventing her from feeling strange and nervous in consequence of the uncertainty of her situation. She did not appear to see it in that light. She seemed to be quite satisfied, beforehand, that Mr Dawson would approve of her; and she sat calmly looking out of window, with every appearance of enjoying the country air. Some people might have thought such conduct suggestive of brazen assurance. I beg to say that I more liberally set it down to extraordinary strength of mind.

Instead of the doctor coming up to us, I was sent for to see the doctor. I thought this change of affairs rather odd, but Mrs Rubelle did not appear to be affected by it in any way. I left her still calmly looking out of window, and still silently enjoying the country air.

Mr Dawson was waiting for me, by himself, in the breakfast-room.

'About this new nurse, Mrs Michelson,' said the doctor.

'Yes, sir?'

'I find that she has been brought here from London by the wife of that fat old foreigner, who is always trying to interfere with me. Mrs Michelson, the fat old foreigner is a Quack.'

This was very rude, I was naturally shocked at it.

'Are you aware, sir,' I said, 'that you are talking of a nobleman?'

'Pooh! He isn't the first Quack with a handle to his name. They're all Counts—hang 'em!'

'He would not be a friend of Sir Percival Glyde's, sir, if he was not a member of the highest aristocracy—excepting the English aristocracy, of course.'

'Very well, Mrs Michelson, call him what you like; and let us get back to the nurse. I have been objecting to her already.'

'Without having seen her, sir?'

'Yes; without having seen her. She may be the best nurse in existence; but she is not a nurse of my providing. I have put that objection to Sir Percival, as the master of the house. He doesn't support me. He says a nurse of my providing would have been a stranger from London also; and he thinks the woman ought to have a trial, after his wife's aunt has taken the trouble to fetch her from London. There is some justice in that; and I can't decently say No. But I have made it a condition that she is to go at once, if I find reason to complain of her. This proposal being one which I have some right to make, as medical attendant, Sir Percival has consented to it. Now, Mrs Michelson, I know I can depend on you; and I want you to keep a sharp eye on the nurse, for the first day or two, and to see that she gives Miss Halcombe no medicines but mine. This foreign nobleman of yours is dying to try his quack remedies (mesmerism included) on my patient; and a nurse who is brought here by his wife may be a little too willing to help him. You understand? Very well, then, we may go up-stairs. Is the nurse there? I'll say a word to her, before she goes into the sick-room.'

We found Mrs Rubelle still enjoying herself at the window. When I introduced her to Mr Dawson, neither the doctor's doubtful looks nor the doctor's searching questions appeared to confuse her in the least. She answered him quietly in her broken English; and, though he tried hard to puzzle her, she never betrayed the least ignorance, so far, about any part of her duties. This was doubtless the result of strength of mind, as I said before, and not of brazen assurance by any means.

We all went into the bedroom.

Mrs Rubelle looked, very attentively, at the patient; curtseyed to Lady Glyde; set one or two little things right in the room; and sat down quietly in a corner to wait until she was wanted. Her ladyship seemed startled and annoyed by the appearance of the strange nurse. No one said anything, for fear of rousing Miss Halcombe, who was still slumbering—except the doctor, who whispered a question about the night. I softly answered, 'Much as usual;' and then Mr Dawson went out. Lady Glyde followed him, I suppose to speak about Mrs Rubelle. For my own part, I had made up my mind already that this quiet foreign person would keep her situation. She had all her wits about her; and she certainly understood her business. So far, I could hardly have done much better, by the bedside, myself.

Remembering Mr Dawson's caution to me, I subjected Mrs Rubelle to a severe scrutiny, at certain intervals, for the next three or four days. I over and over again entered the room softly and suddenly, but I never found her out in any suspicious action. Lady Glyde, who watched her as attentively as I did, discovered nothing either. I never detected a sign of the medicine bottles being tampered with; I never saw Mrs Rubelle say a word to the Count, or the Count to her. She managed Miss Halcombe with unquestionable care and discretion. The poor lady wavered backwards and forwards between a sort of sleepy exhaustion which was half faintness and half slumbering, and attacks of fever which brought with them more or less of wandering in her mind. Mrs Rubelle never disturbed her in the first case, and never startled her in the second, by appearing too suddenly at the bedside in the character of a stranger. Honour to whom honour is due (whether foreign or English)—and I give her privilege impartially to Mrs Rubelle. She was remarkably uncommunicative about herself, and she was too quietly independent of all advice from experienced persons who understood the duties of a sick-room—but, with these drawbacks, she was a good nurse; and she never gave either Lady Glyde or Mr Dawson the shadow of a reason for complaining of her.

The next circumstance of importance that occurred in the house was the temporary absence of the Count, occasioned by business which took him to London. He went away (I think) on the morning of the fourth day after the arrival of Mrs Rubelle; and, at parting, he spoke to Lady Glyde, very seriously, in my presence, on the subject of Miss Halcombe.

'Trust Mr Dawson,' he said, 'for a few days more, if you please. But, if there is not some change for the better, in that time, send for advice from London, which this mule of a doctor must accept in spite of himself. Offend Mr Dawson, and save Miss Halcombe. I say those words seriously, on my word of honour and from the bottom of my heart.'

His lordship spoke with extreme feeling and kindness. But poor Lady Glyde's nerves were so completely broken down that she seemed quite frightened at him. She trembled from head to foot; and allowed him to take his leave, without uttering a word on her side. She turned to me, when he had gone, and said, 'Oh, Mrs Michelson, I am heart-broken about my sister, and I have no friend to advise me! Do *you* think Mr Dawson is wrong? He told me himself, this morning, that there was no fear, and no need to send for another doctor.'

'With all respect to Mr Dawson,' I answered, 'in your ladyship's place, I should remember the Count's advice.'

Lady Glyde turned away from me suddenly, with an appearance of despair, for which I was quite unable to account.

'*His* advice!' she said to herself. 'God help us—*his* advice!'

The Count was away from Blackwater Park, as nearly as I remember, a week.

Sir Percival seemed to feel the loss of his lordship in various ways, and appeared also, I thought, much depressed and altered by the sickness and sorrow in the house. Occasionally, he was so very restless, that I could not help noticing it; coming and going, and wandering here and there and everywhere in the grounds. His inquiries about Miss Halcombe, and about his lady (whose failing health seemed to cost him sincere anxiety), were most attentive. I think his heart was much softened. If some kind clerical friend—some such friend as he might have found in my late excellent husband—had been near him at this time, cheering moral progress might have been made with Sir Percival. I seldom find myself mistaken on a point of this sort; having had experience to guide me in my happy married days.

Her ladyship, the Countess, who was now the only company for Sir Percival down stairs, rather neglected him, as I considered. Or, perhaps, it might have been that he neglected her. A stranger might almost have supposed that they were bent, now they were left together alone, on actually avoiding one another. This, of course, could not be. But it did so happen, nevertheless, that the Countess made her dinner at luncheon-time, and that she always came up-stairs towards evening, although Mrs Rubelle had taken the nursing duties entirely off her hands. Sir Percival dined by himself; and William (the man out of livery) made the remark, in my hearing, that his master had put himself on half rations of food and on a double allowance of drink. I attach no importance to such an insolent observation as this, on the part of a servant. I reprobated it at the time, and I wish to be understood as reprobating it once more, on this occasion.

In the course of the next few days, Miss Halcombe did certainly seem to all of us to be mending a little. Our faith in Mr Dawson revived. He appeared to be very confident about the case, and he assured Lady Glyde, when she spoke to him on the subject, that he would himself propose to send for a physician, the moment he felt so much as the shadow of a doubt crossing his own mind.

The only person among us who did not appear to be relieved by these words was the Countess. She said to me privately that she could not feel easy about Miss Halcombe, on Mr Dawson's authority, and that she should wait anxiously for her husband's opinion, on his return. That return, his letters informed her, would take place in three days' time. The Count and Countess corresponded regularly every morning, during his lordship's absence. They were in that respect, as in all others, a pattern to married people.

On the evening of the third day, I noticed a change in Miss Halcombe, which caused me serious apprehension. Mrs Rubelle noticed it too. We said nothing on the subject to Lady Glyde, who was then lying asleep, completely overpowered by exhaustion, on the sofa in the sitting-room.

Mr Dawson did not pay his evening visit till later than usual. As soon as he set eyes on his patient, I saw his face alter. He tried to hide it; but he looked both confused and alarmed. A messenger was sent to his residence for his medicine-chest, disinfecting preparations were used in the room, and a bed was made up for him in the house by his own directions. 'Has the fever turned to infection?' I whispered to him. 'I am afraid it has,' he answered; 'we shall know better to-morrow morning.'

By Mr Dawson's own directions Lady Glyde was kept in ignorance of this change for the worse. He himself absolutely forbade her, on account of her health, to join us in the bedroom that night. She tried to resist—there was a sad scene—but he had his medical authority to support him; and he carried his point.

The next morning, one of the men servants was sent to London, at eleven o'clock, with a letter to a physician in town, and with orders to bring the new doctor back with him by the earliest possible train. Half an hour after the messenger had gone, the Count returned to Blackwater Park.

The Countess, on her own responsibility, immediately brought him in to see the patient. There was no impropriety that I could discover in her taking this course. His lordship was a married man; he was old enough to be Miss Halcombe's father; and he saw her in the presence of a female relative, Lady Glyde's aunt. Mr Dawson nevertheless protested against his presence in the room; but, I could plainly remark the doctor was too much alarmed to make any serious resistance on this occasion.

The poor suffering lady was past knowing any one about her. She seemed to take her friends for enemies. When the Count approached her bedside, her eyes, which had been wandering incessantly round and round the room before, settled on his face, with a dreadful stare of terror, which I shall remember to my dying day. The Count sat down by her; felt her pulse, and her temples; looked at her very attentively; and then turned round upon the doctor with such an expression of indignation and contempt in his face, that the words failed on Mr Dawson's lips, and he stood, for a moment, pale with anger and alarm—pale and perfectly speechless.

His lordship looked next at me.

'When did the change happen?' he asked.

I told him the time.

'Has Lady Glyde been in the room since?'

I replied that she had not. The doctor had absolutely forbidden her to come into the room, on the evening before, and had repeated the order again in the morning.

'Have you and Mrs Rubelle been made aware of the full extent of the mischief?'—was his next question.

We were aware, I answered, that the malady was considered infectious. He stopped me, before I could add anything more.

'It is Typhus Fever,' he said.

In the minute that passed, while these questions and answers were going on, Mr Dawson recovered himself, and addressed the Count, with his customary firmness.

'It is *not* typhus fever,' he said, sharply. 'I protest against this intrusion, sir. No one has a right to put questions here, but me. I have done my duty to the best of my ability——'

The Count interrupted him—not by words, but only by pointing to the bed. Mr Dawson seemed to feel that silent contradiction to his assertion of his own ability, and to grow only the more angry under it.

'I say I have done my duty,' he reiterated. 'A physician has been sent for from London. I will consult on the nature of the fever with him, and with no one else. I insist on your leaving the room.'

'I entered this room, sir, in the sacred interests of humanity,' said the Count. 'And in the same interests, if the coming of the physician is delayed, I will enter it again. I warn you once more that the fever has turned to Typhus, and that your treatment is responsible for this lamentable change. If that unhappy lady dies, I will give my testimony in a court of justice that your ignorance and obstinacy have been the cause of her death.'

Before Mr Dawson could answer, before the Count could leave us, the door was opened from the sitting-room, and we saw Lady Glyde on the threshold.

'I *must*, and *will* come in,' she said, with extraordinary firmness. Instead of stopping her, the Count moved into the sitting-room, and made way for her to go in. On all other occasions, he was the last man in the world to forget anything; but, in the surprise of the moment, he apparently forgot the danger of infection from typhus, and the urgent necessity of forcing Lady Glyde to take proper care of herself.

To my astonishment, Mr Dawson showed more presence of mind. He stopped her ladyship at the first step she took towards the bedside.

'I am sincerely sorry, I am sincerely grieved,' he said. 'The fever may, I fear, be infectious. Until I am certain that it is not, I entreat you to keep out of the room.'

She struggled for a moment; then suddenly dropped her arms, and sank forward. She had fainted. The Countess and I took her from the doctor, and carried her into her own room. The Count preceded us, and waited in the passage, till I came out, and told him that we had recovered her from the swoon.

I went back to the doctor to tell him, by Lady Glyde's desire, that she insisted on speaking to him immediately. He withdrew at once to quiet her ladyship's agitation, and to assure her of the physician's arrival in the course of a few hours. Those hours passed very slowly. Sir Percival and the Count were together down stairs, and sent up, from time to time, to make their inquiries. At last, between five and six o'clock, to our great relief, the physician came.

He was a younger man than Mr Dawson; very serious, and very decided. What he thought of the previous treatment, I cannot say; but it struck me as curious that he put many more questions to myself and to Mrs Rubelle than he put to the doctor, and that he did not appear to listen with much interest to what Mr Dawson said, while he was examining Mr Dawson's patient. I began to suspect, from what I observed in this way, that the Count had been right about the illness all the way through; and I was naturally confirmed in that idea, when Mr Dawson, after some little delay, asked the one important question which the London doctor had been sent for to set at rest.

'What is your opinion of the fever?' he inquired.

'Typhus,' replied the physician. 'Typhus fever beyond all doubt.'

That quiet foreign person, Mrs Rubelle, crossed her thin, brown hands in front of her, and looked at me with a very significant smile. The Count himself could hardly have appeared more gratified, if he had been present in the room, and had heard the confirmation of his own opinion.

After giving us some useful directions about the management of the patient, and mentioning that he would come again in five day's time, the physician withdrew to consult in private with Mr Dawson. He would offer no opinion on Miss Halcombe's chances of recovery: he said it was impossible at that stage of the illness to pronounce, one way or the other.

The five days passed anxiously.

Countess Fosco and myself took it by turns to relieve Mrs Rubelle; Miss Halcombe's condition growing worse and worse, and requiring our utmost care and attention. It was a terribly trying time. Lady Glyde (supported, as Mr Dawson said, by the constant strain of her suspense on her sister's account) rallied in the most extraordinary manner, and showed a firmness and determination for which I should myself never have given her credit. She insisted on coming into the sick-room, two or three times every day, to look at Miss Halcombe with her own eyes; promising not to go too close to the bed, if the doctor would consent to her wishes, so far. Mr Dawson very unwillingly made the concession required of him: I think he saw that it was hopeless to dispute with her. She came in every day; and she self-denyingly kept her promise. I felt it personally so distressing (as reminding me of my own affliction during my husband's last illness) to see how she suffered under these circumstances, that I must beg not to dwell on this part of the subject any longer. It is more agreeable to me to mention that no fresh disputes took place between Mr Dawson and the Count. His lordship made all his inquiries by deputy; and remained continually in company with Sir Percival, down stairs.

On the fifth day, the physician came again, and gave us a little hope. He said the tenth day from the first appearance of the typhus would probably decide the result of the illness, and he arranged for his third visit to take place on that date. The interval passed as before—except that the Count went to London again, one morning, and returned at night.

On the tenth day, it pleased a merciful Providence to relieve our household from all further anxiety and alarm. The physician positively assured us that Miss Halcombe was out of danger. 'She wants no doctor, now—all she requires is careful watching and nursing, for some time to come; and that I see she has.' Those were his own words. That evening I read my husband's touching sermon on Recovery from Sickness, with more happiness and advantage (in a spiritual point of view) than I ever remember to have derived from it before.

The effect of the good news on poor Lady Glyde was, I grieve to say, quite overpowering. She was too weak to bear the violent reaction; and, in another day or two, she sank into a state of debility and depression, which obliged her to keep her room. Rest and quiet, and change of air afterwards, were the best remedies which Mr Dawson could suggest for her benefit. It was fortunate that matters were no worse, for, on the very day after she took to her room, the Count and the doctor had another disagreement; and, this time, the dispute between them was of so serious a nature, that Mr Dawson left the house.

I was not present at the time; but I understood that the subject of the dispute was the amount of nourishment which it was necessary to give to assist Miss Halcombe's convalescence, after the exhaustion of the fever. Mr Dawson, now that his patient was safe, was less inclined than ever to submit to unprofessional interference; and the Count (I cannot imagine why) lost all the self-control which he had so judiciously preserved on former occasions, and taunted the doctor, over and over again, with his mistake about the fever, when it changed to typhus. The unfortunate affair ended in Mr Dawson's appealing to Sir Percival, and threatening (now that he could leave without absolute danger to Miss Halcombe) to withdraw from his attendance at Blackwater Park, if the Count's interference was not peremptorily suppressed from that moment. Sir Percival's reply (though not designedly uncivil) had only resulted in making matters worse; and Mr Dawson had thereupon withdrawn from the house, in a state of extreme indignation at Count Fosco's usage of him, and had sent in his bill the next morning.

We were now, therefore, left without the attendance of a medical man. Although there was no actual necessity for another doctor—nursing and watching being, as the physician had observed, all that Miss Halcombe required—I should still, if my authority had been consulted, have obtained professional assistance, from some other quarter, for form's sake.

The matter did not seem to strike Sir Percival in that light. He said it would be time enough to send for another doctor, if Miss Halcombe showed any signs of a relapse. In the mean while, we had the Count to consult in any minor difficulty; and we need not unnecessarily disturb our patient, in her present weak and nervous condition, by the presence of a stranger at her bedside. There was much that was reasonable, no doubt, in these considerations; but they left me a little anxious, nevertheless. Nor was I quite satisfied, in my own mind, of the propriety of our concealing the doctor's absence, as we did, from Lady Glyde. It was a merciful deception, I admit—for she was in no state to bear any fresh anxieties. But still it was a deception; and, as such, to a person of my principles, at best a doubtful proceeding.

A second perplexing circumstance which happened on the same day, and which took me completely by surprise, added greatly to the sense of uneasiness that was now weighing on my mind.

I was sent for to see Sir Percival in the library. The Count, who was with him when I went in, immediately rose and left us alone together. Sir Percival civilly asked me to take a seat; and then, to my great astonishment, addressed me in these terms:

'I want to speak to you, Mrs Michelson, about a matter which I decided on some time ago, and which I should have mentioned before, but for the sickness and trouble in the house. In plain words, I have reasons for wishing to break up my establishment immediately at this place—leaving you in charge, of course, as usual. As soon as Lady Glyde and Miss Halcombe can travel, they must both have change of air. My friends, Count Fosco and the Countess, will leave us, before that time, to live in the neighbourhood of London. And I have reasons for not opening the house to any more company, with a view to economising as carefully as I can. I don't blame you—but my expenses here are a great deal too heavy. In short, I shall sell the horses, and get rid of all the servants at once. I never do things by halves, as you know; and I mean to have the house clear of a pack of useless people by this time to-morrow.'

I listened to him, perfectly aghast with astonishment.

'Do you mean, Sir Percival, that I am to dismiss the in-door servants, under my charge, without the usual month's warning?' I asked.

'Certainly, I do. We may all be out of the house before another month; and I am not going to leave the servants here in idleness, with no master to wait on.'

'Who is to do the cooking, Sir Percival, while you are still staying here?'

'Margaret Porcher can roast and boil—keep her. What do I want with a cook, if I don't mean to give any dinner-parties?'

'The servant you have mentioned is the most unintelligent servant in the house, Sir Percival——'

'Keep her, I tell you; and have a woman in from the village to do the cleaning, and go away again. My weekly expenses must and shall be lowered immediately. I don't send for you to make objections, Mrs Michelson—I send for you to carry out my plans of economy. Dismiss the whole lazy pack of in-door servants to-morrow, except Porcher. She is as strong as a horse—and we'll make her work like a horse.'

'You will excuse me for reminding you, Sir Percival, that if the servants go to-morrow, they must have a month's wages in lieu of a month's warning.'

'Let them! A month's wages saves a month's waste and gluttony in the servants'-hall.'

This last remark conveyed an aspersion of the most offensive kind on my management. I had too much self-respect to defend myself under so gross an imputation. Christian consideration for the helpless position of Miss Halcombe and Lady Glyde, and for the serious inconvenience which my sudden absence might inflict on them, alone prevented me from resigning my situation on the spot. I rose immediately. It would have lowered me in my own estimation to have permitted the interview to continue a moment longer.

'After that last remark, Sir Percival, I have nothing more to say. Your directions shall be attended to.' Pronouncing those words, I bowed my head with the most distant respect, and went out of the room.

The next day, the servants left in a body. Sir Percival himself dismissed the grooms and stablemen; sending them, with all the horses but one, to London. Of the whole domestic establishment, in-doors and out, there now remained only myself, Margaret Porcher, and the gardener; this last living in his own cottage, and being wanted to take care of the one horse that remained in the stables.

With the house left in this strange and lonely condition; with the mistress of it ill in her room; with Miss Halcombe still as helpless as a child; and with the doctor's attendance withdrawn from us in enmity—it was surely not unnatural that my spirits should sink, and my customary composure be very hard to maintain. My mind was ill at ease. I wished the poor ladies both well again; and I wished myself away from Blackwater Park.

THE next event that occurred was of so singular a nature, that it might have caused me a feeling of superstitious surprise, if my mind had not been fortified by principle against any pagan weakness of that sort. The uneasy sense of something wrong in the family which had made me wish myself away from Blackwater Park, was actually followed, strange to say, by my departure from the house. It is true that my absence was for a temporary period only: but the coincidence was, in my opinion, not the less remarkable on that account.

My departure took place under the following circumstances:

A day or two after the servants all left, I was again sent for to see Sir Percival. The undeserved slur which he had cast on my management of the household did not, I am happy to say, prevent me from returning good for evil to the best of my ability, by complying with his request as readily and respectfully as ever. It cost me a struggle with that fallen nature which we all share in common, before I could suppress my feelings. Being accustomed to self-discipline, I accomplished the sacrifice.

I found Sir Percival and Count Fosco sitting together, again. On this occasion his lordship remained present at the interview, and assisted in the development of Sir Percival's views.

The subject to which they now requested my attention, related to the healthy change of air by which we all hoped that Miss Halcombe and Lady Glyde might soon be enabled to profit. Sir Percival mentioned that both the ladies would probably pass the autumn (by invitation of Frederick Fairlie, Esquire) at Limmeridge House, Cumberland. But before they went there, it was his opinion, confirmed by Count Fosco (who here took up the conversation, and continued it to the end), that they would benefit by a short residence first in the genial climate of Torquay. The great object, therefore, was to engage lodgings at that place, affording all the comforts and advantages of which they stood in need; and the great difficulty was to find an experienced person capable of choosing the sort of residence which they wanted. In this emergency, the Count begged to inquire, on Sir Percival's behalf, whether I would object to give the ladies the benefit of my assistance, by proceeding myself to Torquay in their interests.

It was impossible, for a person in my situation, to meet any proposal, made in these terms, with a positive objection.

I could only venture to represent the serious inconvenience of my leaving Blackwater Park, in the extraordinary absence of all the in-door servants, with the one exception of Margaret Porcher. But Sir Percival and his lordship declared that they were both willing to put up with inconvenience for the sake of the invalids. I next respectfully suggested writing to an agent at Torquay; but I was met here by being reminded of the imprudence of taking lodgings without first seeing them. I was also informed that the Countess (who would otherwise have gone to Devonshire herself) could not, in Lady Glyde's present condition, leave her niece; and that Sir Percival and the Count had business to transact together, which would oblige them to remain at Blackwater Park. In short, it was clearly shown me, that if I did not undertake the errand, no one else could be trusted with it. Under these circumstances, I could only inform Sir Percival that my services were at the disposal of Miss Halcombe and Lady Glyde.

It was thereupon arranged that I should leave the next morning; that I should occupy one or two days in examining all the most convenient houses in Torquay; and that I should return, with my report, as soon as I conveniently could. A memorandum was written for me by his lordship, stating the various requisites which the place I was sent to take must be found to possess; and a note of the pecuniary limit assigned to me was added by Sir Percival.

My own idea, on reading over these instructions, was, that no such residence as I saw described could be found at any watering-place in England; and that, even if it could by chance be discovered, it would certainly not be parted with for any period, on such terms as I was permitted to offer. I hinted at these difficulties to both the gentlemen; but Sir Percival (who undertook to answer me) did not appear to feel them. It was not for me to dispute the question. I said no more; but I felt a very strong conviction that the business on which I was sent away was so beset by difficulties that my errand was almost hopeless at starting.

Before I left, I took care to satisfy myself that Miss Halcombe was going on favourably.

There was a painful expression of anxiety in her face, which made me fear that her mind, on first recovering itself, was not at ease. But she was certainly strengthening more rapidly than I could have ventured to anticipate; and she was able to send kind messages to Lady Glyde, saying that she was fast getting well, and entreating her ladyship not to exert herself again too soon. I left her in charge of Mrs Rubelle, who was still as quietly independent of every one else in the house as ever. When I knocked at Lady Glyde's door, before going away, I was told that she was still sadly weak and depressed; my informant being the Countess, who was then keeping her company in her room. Sir Percival and the Count were walking on the road to the lodge, as I was driven by in the chaise. I bowed to them, and quitted the house, with not a living soul left in the servants' offices but Margaret Porcher.

Every one must feel, what I have felt myself since that time, that these circumstances were more than unusual—they were almost suspicious. Let me, however, say again, that it was impossible for me, in my dependent position, to act otherwise than I did.

The result of my errand at Torquay was exactly what I had foreseen. No such lodgings as I was instructed to take could be found in the whole place; and the terms I was permitted to give were much too low for the purpose, even if I had been able to discover what I wanted. I accordingly returned to Blackwater Park; and informed Sir Percival, who met me at the door, that my journey had been taken in vain. He seemed too much occupied with some other subject to care about the failure of my errand, and his first words informed me that even in the short time of my absence, another remarkable change had taken place in the house.

The Count and Countess Fosco had left Blackwater Park for their new residence in St John's Wood.

I was not made aware of the motive for this sudden departure—I was only told that the Count had been very particular in leaving his kind compliments to me. When I ventured on asking Sir Percival whether Lady Glyde had any one to attend to her comforts in the absence of the Countess, he replied that she had Margaret Porcher to wait on her; and he added that a woman from the village had been sent for to do the work down stairs.

The answer really shocked me—there was such a glaring impropriety in permitting an under-housemaid to fill the place of confidential attendant on Lady Glyde. I went up-stairs at once, and met Margaret on the bedroom landing. Her services had not been required (naturally enough); her mistress having sufficiently recovered, that morning, to be able to leave her bed. I asked, next, after Miss Halcombe; but I was answered in a slouching, sulky way, which left me no wiser than I was before. I did not choose to repeat the question, and perhaps provoke an impertinent reply. It was in every respect more becoming, to a person in my position, to present myself immediately in Lady Glyde's room.

I found that her ladyship had certainly gained in health during the last three days. Although still sadly weak and nervous, she was able to get up without assistance, and to walk slowly about her room, feeling no worse effect from the exertion than a slight sensation of fatigue. She had been made a little anxious that morning about Miss Halcombe, through having received no news of her from any one. I thought this seemed to imply a blamable want of attention on the part of Mrs Rubelle; but I said nothing, and remained with Lady Glyde, to assist her to dress. When she was ready, we both left the room together to go to Miss Halcombe.

We were stopped in the passage by the appearance of Sir Percival. He looked as if he had been purposely waiting there to see us.

'Where are you going?' he said to Lady Glyde.

'To Marian's room,' she answered.

'It may spare you a disappointment,' remarked Sir Percival, 'if I tell you at once that you will not find her there.'

'Not find her there!'

'No. She left the house yesterday morning with Fosco and his wife.'

Lady Glyde was not strong enough to bear the surprise of this extraordinary statement. She turned fearfully pale; and leaned back against the wall, looking at her husband in dead silence.

I was so astonished myself, that I hardly knew what to say. I asked Sir Percival if he really meant that Miss Halcombe had left Blackwater Park.

'I certainly mean it,' he answered.

'In her state, Sir Percival! Without mentioning her intentions to Lady Glyde!'

Before he could reply, her ladyship recovered herself a little, and spoke.

'Impossible!' she cried out, in a loud, frightened manner; taking a step or two forward from the wall. 'Where was the doctor? where was Mr Dawson when Marian went away?'

'Mr Dawson wasn't wanted, and wasn't here,' said Sir Percival. 'He left of his own accord, which is enough of itself to show that she was strong enough to travel. How you stare! If you don't believe she has gone, look for yourself. Open her room door, and all the other room doors, if you like.'

She took him at his word, and I followed her. There was no one in Miss Halcombe's room but Margaret Porcher, who was busy setting it to rights. There was no one in the spare rooms, or the dressing-rooms, when we looked into them afterwards. Sir Percival still waited for us in the passage. As we were leaving the last room that we had examined, Lady Glyde whispered, 'Don't go, Mrs Michelson! don't leave me, for God's sake!' Before I could say anything in return, she was out again in the passage, speaking to her husband.

'What does it mean, Sir Percival? I insist—I beg and pray you will tell me what it means!'

'It means,' he answered, 'that Miss Halcombe was strong enough yesterday morning to sit up, and be dressed; and that she insisted on taking advantage of Fosco's going to London, to go there too.'

'To London!'

'Yes—on her way to Limmeridge.'

Lady Glyde turned, and appealed to me.

'You saw Miss Halcombe last,' she said. 'Tell me plainly, Mrs Michelson, did you think she looked fit to travel?'

'Not in *my* opinion, your ladyship.'

Sir Percival, on his side, instantly turned, and appealed to me also.

'Before you went away,' he said, 'did you, or did you not, tell the nurse that Miss Halcombe looked much stronger and better?'

'I certainly made the remark, Sir Percival.'

He addressed her ladyship again, the moment I offered that reply.

'Set one of Mrs Michelson's opinions fairly against the other,' he said, 'and try to be reasonable about a perfectly-plain matter. If she had not been well enough to be moved, do you think we should any of us have risked letting her go? She has got three competent people to look after her—Fosco and your aunt, and Mrs Rubelle, who went away with them expressly for that purpose. They took a whole carriage yesterday, and made a bed for her on the seat, in case she felt tired. To-day, Fosco and Mrs Rubelle go on with her themselves to Cumberland——'

'Why does Marian go to Limmeridge, and leave me here by myself?' said her ladyship, interrupting Sir Percival.

'Because your uncle won't receive you till he has seen your sister first,' he replied. 'Have you forgotten the letter he wrote to her, at the beginning of her illness? It was shown to you; you read it yourself; and you ought to remember it.'

'I do remember it.'

'If you do, why should you be surprised at her leaving you? You want to be back at Limmeridge; and she has gone there to get your uncle's leave for you, on his own terms.'

Poor Lady Glyde's eyes filled with tears.

'Marian never left me before,' she said, 'without bidding me good-by.'

'She would have bid you good-by this time,' returned Sir Percival, 'if she had not been afraid of herself and of you. She knew you would try to stop her; she knew you would distress her by crying. Do you want to make any more objections? If you do, you must come down stairs and ask questions in the dining-room. These worries upset me. I want a glass of wine.'

He left us suddenly.

His manner all through this strange conversation had been very unlike what it usually was. He seemed to be almost as nervous and fluttered, every now and then, as his lady herself. I should never have supposed that his health had been so delicate, or his composure so easy to upset.

I tried to prevail on Lady Glyde to go back to her room; but it was useless. She stopped in the passage, with the look of a woman whose mind was panic-stricken:

'Something has happened to my sister!' she said.

'Remember, my lady, what surprising energy there is in Miss Halcombe,' I suggested. 'She might well make an effort which other ladies, in her situation, would be unfit for. I hope and believe there is nothing wrong—I do indeed.'

'I must follow Marian!' said her ladyship, with the same panic-stricken look. 'I must go where she has gone; I must see that she is alive and well with my own eyes. Come! come down with me to Sir Percival.'

I hesitated; fearing that my presence might be considered an intrusion. I attempted to represent this to her ladyship; but she was deaf to me. She held my arm fast enough to force me to go down stairs with her; and she still clung to me with all the little strength she had, at the moment when I opened the dining-room door.

Sir Percival was sitting at the table with a decanter of wine before him. He raised the glass to his lips, as we went in, and drained it at a draught. Seeing that he looked at me angrily when he put it down again, I attempted to make some apology for my accidental presence in the room.

'Do you suppose there are any secrets going on here?' he broke out, suddenly; 'there are none—there is nothing underhand; nothing kept from you or from any one.' After speaking those strange words, loudly and sternly, he filled himself another glass of wine, and asked Lady Glyde what she wanted of him.

'If my sister is fit to travel, I am fit to travel,' said her ladyship, with more firmness than she had yet shown. 'I come to beg you will make allowances for my anxiety about Marian, and let me follow her at once, by the afternoon train.'

'You must wait till to-morrow,' replied Sir Percival; 'and then, if you don't hear to the contrary, you can go. I don't suppose you are at all likely to hear to the contrary—so I shall write to Fosco by to-night's post.'

He said those last words, holding his glass up to the light, and looking at the wine in it, instead of at Lady Glyde. Indeed, he never once looked at her throughout the conversation. Such a singular want of good breeding in a gentleman of his rank impressed me, I own, very painfully.

'Why should you write to Count Fosco?' she asked, in extreme surprise.

'To tell him to expect you by the mid-day train,' said Sir Percival. 'He will meet you at the station, when you get to London, and take you on to sleep at your aunt's, in St John's Wood.'

Lady Glyde's hand began to tremble violently round my arm—why, I could not imagine.

'There is no necessity for Count Fosco to meet me,' she said. 'I would rather not stay in London to sleep.'

'You must. You can't take the whole journey to Cumberland in one day. You must rest a night in London—and I don't choose you to go by yourself to an hotel. Fosco made the offer to your uncle to give you house-room on the way down; and your uncle has accepted it. Here! here is a letter from him, addressed to yourself. I ought to have sent it up this morning; but I forgot. Read it, and see what Mr Fairlie himself says to you.'

Lady Glyde looked at the letter for a moment; and then placed it in my hands.

'Read it,' she said, faintly. 'I don't know what is the matter with me. I can't read it, myself.'

It was a note of only four lines—so short and so careless, that it quite struck me. If I remember correctly, it contained no more than these words:

'Dearest Laura, Please come, whenever you like. Break the journey by sleeping at your aunt's house. Grieved to hear of dear Marian's illness. Affectionately yours, Frederick Fairlie.'

'I would rather not go there—I would rather not stay a night in London,' said her ladyship, breaking out eagerly with those words, before I had quite done reading the note, short at it was. 'Don't write to Count Fosco! Pray, pray don't write to him!'

Sir Percival filled another glass from the decanter, so awkwardly that he upset it, and spilt all the wine over the table. 'My sight seems to be failing me,' he muttered to himself, in an odd, muffled voice. He slowly set the glass up again, refilled it, and drained it once more at a draught. I began to fear, from his look and manner, that the wine was getting into his head.

'Pray don't write to Count Fosco!' persisted Lady Glyde, more earnestly than ever.

'Why not, I should like to know?' cried Sir Percival, with a sudden burst of anger that startled us both. 'Where can you stay more properly in London, than at the place your uncle himself chooses for you—at your aunt's house? Ask Mrs Michelson.'

The arrangement proposed was so unquestionably the right and the proper one, that I could make no possible objection to it. Much as I sympathised with Lady Glyde in other respects, I could not sympathise with her in her unjust prejudices against Count Fosco. I never before met with any lady, of her rank and station, who was so lamentably narrow-minded on the subject of foreigners. Neither her uncle's note, nor Sir Percival's increasing impatience, seemed to have the least effect on her. She still objected to staying a night in London; she still implored her husband not to write to the Count.

'Drop it!' said Sir Percival, rudely turning his back on us. 'If you haven't sense enough to know what is best for yourself, other people must know for you. The arrangement is made; and there is an end of it. You are only wanted to do what Miss Halcombe has done before you——'

'Marian?' repeated her ladyship, in a bewildered manner; 'Marian sleeping in Count Fosco's house!'

'Yes, in Count Fosco's house. She slept there, last night, to break the journey. And you are to follow her example, and do what your uncle tells you. You are to sleep at Fosco's, to-morrow night, as your sister did, to break the journey. Don't throw too many obstacles in my way! don't make me repent of letting you go at all!'

He started to his feet; and suddenly walked out into the verandah, through the open glass doors.

'Will your ladyship excuse me,' I whispered, 'if I suggest that we had better not wait here till Sir Percival comes back? I am very much afraid he is over-excited with wine.'

She consented to leave the room, in a weary, absent manner.

As soon as we were safe up-stairs again, I did all I could to compose her ladyship's spirits. I reminded her that Mr Fairlie's letters to Miss Halcombe and to herself did certainly sanction, and even render necessary, sooner or later, the course that had been taken. She agreed to this, and even admitted, of her own accord, that both letters were strictly in character with her uncle's peculiar disposition—but her fears about Miss Halcombe, and her unaccountable dread of sleeping at the Count's house in London, still remained unshaken in spite of every consideration that I could urge. I thought it my duty to protest against Lady Glyde's unfavourable opinion of his lordship; and I did so, with becoming forbearance and respect.

'Your ladyship will pardon my freedom,' I remarked, in conclusion; 'but it is said, "by their fruits ye shall know them." I am sure the Count's constant kindness and constant attention from the very beginning of Miss Halcombe's illness, merit our best confidence and esteem. Even his lordship's serious misunderstanding with Mr Dawson was entirely attributable to his anxiety of Miss Halcombe's account.'

'What misunderstanding?' inquired her ladyship, with a look of sudden interest.

I related the unhappy circumstances under which Mr Dawson had withdrawn his attendance—mentioning them all the more readily, because I disapproved of Sir Percival's continuing to conceal what had happened (as he had done in my presence) from the knowledge of Lady Glyde.

Her ladyship started up, with every appearance of being additionally agitated and alarmed by what I had told her.

'Worse! worse than I thought!' she said, walking about the room, in a bewildered manner. 'The Count knew Mr Dawson would never consent to Marian's taking a journey—he purposely insulted the doctor to get him out of the house.'

'Oh, my lady! my lady!' I remonstrated.

'Mrs Michelson!' she went on, vehemently; 'no words that ever were spoken will persuade me that my sister is in that man's power and in that man's house, with her own consent. My horror of him is such, that nothing Sir Percival could say, and no letters my uncle could write, would induce me, if I had only my own feelings to consult, to eat, drink, or sleep under his roof. But my misery of suspense about Marian gives me the courage to follow her anywhere—to follow her even into Count Fosco's house.'

I thought it right, at this point, to mention that Miss Halcombe had already gone on to Cumberland, according to Sir Percival's account of the matter.

'I am afraid to believe it!' answered her ladyship. 'I am afraid she is still in that man's house. If I am wrong—if she has really gone on to Limmeridge—I am resolved I will not sleep to-morrow night under Count Fosco's roof. My dearest friend in the world, next to my sister, lives near London. You have heard me, you have heard Miss Halcombe, speak of Mrs Vesey? I mean to write, and propose to sleep at her house. I don't know how I shall get there—I don't know how I shall avoid the Count—but to that refuge I will escape in some way, if my sister has gone to Cumberland. All I ask of you to do, is to see yourself that my letter to Mrs Vesey goes to London to-night, as certainly as Sir Percival's letter goes to Count Fosco. I have reasons for not trusting the post-bag down stairs. Will you keep my secret, and help me in this? it is the last favour, perhaps, that I shall ever ask of you.'

I hesitated—I thought it all very strange—I almost feared that her ladyship's mind had been a little affected by recent anxiety and suffering. At my own risk, however, I ended by giving my consent. If the letter had been addressed to a stranger, or to any one but a lady so well known to me by report as Mrs Vesey, I might have refused. I thank God—looking to what happened afterwards—I thank God I never thwarted that wish, or any other, which Lady Glyde expressed to me, on the last day of her residence at Blackwater Park.

The letter was written, and given into my hands. I myself put it into the post-box in the village, that evening.

We saw nothing more of Sir Percival for the rest of the day.

I slept, by Lady Glyde's own desire, in the next room to hers, with the door open between us. There was something so strange and dreadful in the loneliness and emptiness of the house, that I was glad, on my side, to have a companion near me. Her ladyship sat up late, reading letters and burning them, and emptying her drawers and cabinets of little things she prized, as if she never expected to return to Blackwater Park. Her sleep was sadly disturbed when she at last went to bed: she cried out in it, several times—once, so loud that she woke herself. Whatever her dreams were, she did not think fit to communicate them to me. Perhaps, in my situation, I had no right to expect that she should do so. It matters little, now. I was sorry for her—I was indeed heartily sorry for her all the same.

The next day was fine and sunny. Sir Percival came up, after breakfast, to tell us that the chaise would be at the door at a quarter to twelve; the train to London stopping at our station, at twenty minutes after. He informed Lady Glyde that he was obliged to go out, but added that he hoped to be back before she left. If any unforeseen accident delayed him, I was to accompany her to the station, and to take special care that she was in time for the train. Sir Percival communicated these directions very hastily; walking, here and there, about the room all the time. Her ladyship looked attentively after him, wherever he went. He never once looked at her in return.

She only spoke when he had done; and then she stopped him as he approached the door, by holding out her hand.

'I shall see you no more,' she said, in a very marked manner. 'This is our parting—our parting, it may be for ever. Will you try to forgive me, Percival, as heartily as I forgive *you*?'

His face turned of an awful whiteness all over; and great beads of perspiration broke out on his bald forehead. 'I shall come back,' he said—and made for the door, as hastily as if his wife's farewell words had frightened him out of the room.

I had never liked Sir Percival—but the manner in which he left Lady Glyde made me feel ashamed of having eaten his bread and lived in his service. I thought of saying a few comforting and Christian words to the poor lady; but there was something in her face, as she looked after her husband when the door closed on him, that made me alter my mind and keep silence.

At the time named, the chaise drew up at the gates. Her ladyship was right—Sir Percival never came back. I waited for him till the last moment—and waited in vain.

No positive responsibility lay on my shoulders; and yet, I did not feel easy in my mind. 'It is of your own free will,' I said, as the chaise drove through the lodge-gates, 'that your ladyship goes to London?'

'I will go anywhere,' she answered, 'to end the dreadful suspense that I am suffering at this moment.'

She had made me feel almost as anxious and as uncertain about Miss Halcombe as she felt herself. I presumed to ask her to write me a line, if all went well in London. She answered, 'Most willingly, Mrs Michelson.' 'We all have our crosses to bear, my lady,' I said, seeing her silent and thoughtful, after she had promised to write. She made no reply: she seemed to be too much wrapped up in her own thoughts to attend to me. 'I fear your ladyship rested badly last night,' I remarked, after waiting a little. 'Yes,' she said; 'I was terribly disturbed by dreams.' 'Indeed, my lady?' I thought she was going to tell me her dreams; but no, when she spoke next it was only to ask a question. 'You posted the letter to Mrs Vesey with your own hands?' 'Yes, my lady.'

'Did Sir Percival say, yesterday, that Count Fosco was to meet me at the terminus in London?' 'He did, my lady.'

She sighed heavily when I answered that last question, and said no more.

We arrived at the station, with hardly two minutes to spare. The gardener (who had driven us) managed about the luggage, while I took the ticket. The whistle of the train was sounding, when I joined her ladyship on the platform. She looked very strangely, and pressed her hand over her heart, as if some sudden pain or fright had overcome her at that moment.

'I wish you were going with me!' she said, catching eagerly at my arm, when I gave her the ticket.

If there had been time; if I had felt the day before, as I felt then, I would have made my arrangements to accompany her—even though the doing so had obliged me to give Sir Percival warning on the spot. As it was, her wishes expressed at the last moment only, were expressed too late for me to comply with them. She seemed to understand this herself before I could explain it, and did not repeat her desire to have me for a travelling companion. The train drew up at the platform. She gave the gardener a present for his children, and took my hand, in her simple, hearty manner, before she got into the carriage.

'You have been very kind to me and to my sister,' she said—'kind when we were both friendless. I shall remember you gratefully, as long as I live to remember any one. Good-by—and God bless you!'

She spoke those words, with a tone and a look which brought the tears into my eyes—she spoke them as if she was bidding me farewell for ever.

'Good-by, my lady,' I said, putting her into the carriage, and trying to cheer her; 'good-by, for the present only; good-by, with my best and kindest wishes for happier times!'

She shook her head, and shuddered as she settled herself in the carriage. The guard closed the door. 'Do you believe in dreams?' she whispered to me, at the window. '*My* dreams, last night, were dreams I have never had before. The terror of them is hanging over me still.' The whistle sounded before I could answer, and the train moved. Her pale quiet face looked at me, for the last time, looked sorrowfully and solemnly from the window— she waved her hand—and I saw her no more.

Towards five o'clock on the afternoon of that same day, having a little time to myself in the midst of the household duties which now pressed upon me, I sat down alone in my own room, to try and compose my mind with the volume of my husband's Sermons. For the first time in my life, I found my attention wandering over those pious and cheering words. Concluding that Lady Glyde's departure must have disturbed me far more seriously than I had myself supposed, I put the book aside, and went out to take a turn in the garden. Sir Percival had not yet returned, to my knowledge, so I could feel no hesitation about showing myself in the grounds.

On turning the corner of the house, and gaining a view of the garden, I was startled by seeing a stranger walking in it. The stranger was a woman—she was lounging along the path, with her back to me, and was gathering the flowers.

As I approached, she heard me, and turned round.

My blood curdled in my veins. The strange woman in the garden was Mrs Rubelle!

I could neither move, nor speak. She came up to me, as composedly as ever, with her flowers in her hand.

'What is the matter, ma'am?' she said, quietly.

'*You* here!' I gasped out. 'Not gone to London! Not gone to Cumberland!'

Mrs Rubelle smelt at her flowers with a smile of malicious pity.

'Certainly not,' she said. 'I have never left Blackwater Park.'

I summoned breath enough and courage enough for another question.

'Where is Miss Halcombe?'

Mrs Rubelle fairly laughed at me, this time; and answered in these words: 'Miss Halcombe, ma'am, has not left Blackwater Park, either.'

MISS HALCOMBE had never left Blackwater Park!

When I heard those words, all my thoughts were startled back on the instant to my parting with Lady Glyde. I can hardly say I reproached myself—but, at that moment, I think I would have given many a year's hard savings to have known four hours earlier what I knew now.

Mrs Rubelle waited, quietly arranging her nosegay, as if she expected me to say something.

I could say nothing. I thought of Lady Glyde's worn-out energies and weakly health; and I trembled for the time when the shock of the discovery that I had made would fall on her. For a minute, or more, my fears for the poor ladies silenced me. At the end of that time, Mrs Rubelle looked up sideways from her flowers, and said, 'Here is Sir Percival, ma'am, returned from his ride.'

I saw him as soon as she did. He came towards us, slashing viciously at the flowers with his riding-whip. When he was near enough to see my face, he stopped, struck at his boot with the whip, and burst out laughing, so harshly and so violently, that the birds flew away, startled, from the tree by which he stood.

'Well, Mrs Michelson,' he said; 'you have found it out at last—have you?'

I made no reply. He turned to Mrs Rubelle.

'When did you show yourself in the garden?'

'I showed myself about half an hour ago, sir. You said I might take my liberty again, as soon as Lady Glyde had gone away to London.'

'Quite right. I don't blame you—I only asked the question.' He waited a moment, and then addressed himself once more to me. 'You can't believe it, can you?' he said, mockingly. 'Here! come along and see for yourself.'

He led the way round to the front of the house. I followed him; and Mrs Rubelle followed me. After passing through the iron gates, he stopped, and pointed with his whip to the disused middle wing of the building.

'There!' he said. 'Look up at the first floor. You know the old Elizabethan bedrooms? Miss Halcombe is snug and safe in one of the best of them, at this moment. Take her in, Mrs Rubelle (you have got your key?); take Mrs Michelson in, and let her own eyes satisfy her that there is no deception, this time.'

The tone in which he spoke to me, and the minute or two that had passed since we left the garden, helped me to recover my spirits a little. What I might have done, at this critical moment, if all my life had been passed in service, I cannot say. As it was, possessing the feelings, the principles, and the bringing-up of a lady, I could not hesitate about the right course to pursue. My duty to myself, and my duty to Lady Glyde, alike forbade me to remain in the employment of a man who had shamefully deceived us both by a series of atrocious falsehoods.

'I must beg permission, Sir Percival, to speak a few words to you in private,' I said. 'Having done so, I shall be ready to proceed with this person to Miss Halcombe's room.'

Mrs Rubelle, whom I had indicated by a slight turn of my head, insolently sniffed at her nosegay, and walked away, with great deliberation, towards the house door.

'Well,' said Sir Percival, sharply; 'what is it now?'

'I wish to mention, sir, that I am desirous of resigning the situation I now hold at Blackwater Park.' That was literally how I put it. I was resolved that the first words spoken in his presence should be words which expressed my intention to leave his service.

He eyed me with one of his blackest looks, and thrust his hands savagely into the pockets of his riding-coat.

'Why?' he said; 'why, I should like to know?'

'It is not for me, Sir Percival, to express an opinion on what has taken place in this house. I desire to give no offence. I merely wish to say that I do not feel it consistent with my duty to Lady Glyde and to myself to remain any longer in your service.'

'Is it consistent with your duty to *me* to stand there, casting suspicion on me to my face?' he broke out, in his most violent manner. 'I see what you're driving at. You have taken your own mean, underhand view of an innocent deception practised on Lady Glyde, for her own good. It was essential to her health that she should have a change of air immediately—and, you know as well as I do, she would never have gone away, if she had been told Miss Halcombe was still left here. She has been deceived in her own interests—and I don't care who knows it. Go, if you like—there are plenty of housekeepers as good as you, to be had for the asking. Go, when you please—but take care how you spread scandals about me and my affairs, when you're out of my service. Tell the truth, and nothing but the truth, or it will be the worse for you! See Miss Halcombe for yourself; see if she hasn't been as well taken care of in one part of the house as in the other. Remember the doctor's own orders that Lady Glyde was to have a change of air at the earliest possible opportunity. Bear all that well in mind—and then say anything against me and my proceedings if you dare!'

He poured out these words fiercely, all in a breath, walking backwards and forwards, and striking about him in the air with his whip.

Nothing that he said or did shook my opinion of the disgraceful series of falsehoods that he had told, in my presence, the day before, or of the cruel deception by which he had separated Lady Glyde from her sister, and had sent her uselessly to London, when she was half distracted with anxiety on Miss Halcombe's account. I naturally kept these thoughts to myself, and said nothing more to irritate him; but I was not the less resolved to persist in my purpose. A soft answer turneth away wrath; and I suppressed my own feelings, accordingly, when it was my turn to reply.

'While I am in your service, Sir Percival,' I said, 'I hope I know my duty well enough not to inquire into your motives. When I am out of your service, I hope I know my own place well enough not to speak of matters which don't concern me——'

'When do you want to go?' he asked, interrupting me without ceremony. 'Don't suppose I am anxious to keep you—don't suppose I care about your leaving the house. I am perfectly fair and open in this matter, from first to last. When do you want to go?'

'I should wish to leave at your earliest convenience, Sir Percival.'

'My convenience has nothing to do with it. I shall be out of the house, for good and all, to-morrow morning; and I can settle your accounts to-night. If you want to study anybody's convenience, it had better be Miss Halcombe's. Mrs Rubelle's time is up to-day, and she has reasons for wishing to be in London to-night. If you go at once, Miss Halcombe won't have a soul left here to look after her.'

I hope it is unnecessary for me to say that I was quite incapable of deserting Miss Halcombe in such an emergency as had now befallen Lady Glyde and herself. After first distinctly ascertaining from Sir Percival that Mrs Rubelle was certain to leave at once if I took her place, and after also obtaining permission to arrange for Mr Dawson's resuming his attendance on his patient, I willingly consented to remain at Blackwater Park, until Miss Halcombe no longer required my services. It was settled that I should give Sir Percival's solicitor a week's notice before I left, and that he was to undertake the necessary arrangements for appointing my successor. The matter was discussed in very few words. At its conclusion, Sir Percival abruptly turned on his heel, and left me free to join Mrs Rubelle. That singular foreign person had been sitting composedly on the door-step, all this time, waiting till I could follow her to Miss Halcombe's room.

I had hardly walked half way towards the house, when Sir Percival, who had withdrawn in the opposite direction, suddenly stopped, and called me back.

'Why are you leaving my service?' he asked.

The question was so extraordinary, after what had just passed between us, that I hardly knew what to say in answer to it.

'Mind! *I* don't know why you are going,' he went on. 'You must give a reason for leaving me, I suppose, when you get another situation. What reason? The breaking-up of the family? Is that it?'

'There can be no positive objection, Sir Percival, to that reason——'

'Very well! That's all I want to know. If people apply for your character, that's your reason, stated by yourself. You go in consequence of the breaking-up of the family.'

He turned away again, before I could say another word, and walked out rapidly into the grounds. His manner was as strange as his language. I acknowledge he alarmed me.

Even the patience of Mrs Rubelle was getting exhausted, when I joined her at the house door.

'At last!' she said, with a shrug of her lean foreign shoulders. She led the way into the inhabited side of the house, ascended the stairs, and opened with her key the door at the end of the passage, which communicated with the old Elizabethan rooms—a door never previously used, in my time, at Blackwater Park. The rooms themselves I knew well, having entered them myself, on various occasions, from the other side of the house. Mrs Rubelle stopped at the third door along the old gallery, handed me the key of it, with the key of the door of communication, and told me I should find Miss Halcombe in that room. Before I went in, I thought it desirable to make her understand that her attendance had ceased. Accordingly, I told her in plain words that the charge of the sick lady henceforth devolved entirely on myself.

'I am glad to hear it, ma'am,' said Mrs Rubelle. 'I want to go very much.'

'Do you leave to-day?' I asked, to make sure of her.

'Now, that you have taken charge, ma'am, I leave in half an hour's time. Sir Percival has kindly placed at my disposition the gardener, and the chaise, whenever I want them. I shall want them in half an hour's time, to go to the station. I am packed up, in anticipation, already. I wish you good day, ma'am.'

She dropped a brisk curtsey, and walked back along the gallery, humming a little tune, and keeping time to it cheerfully with the nosegay in her hand. I am sincerely thankful to say, that was the last I saw of Mrs Rubelle.

When I went into the room, Miss Halcombe was asleep. I looked at her anxiously, as she lay in the dismal, high, old-fashioned bed. She was certainly not in any respect altered for the worse, since I had seen her last. She had not been neglected, I am bound to admit, in any way that I could perceive. The room was dreary, and dusty, and dark; but the window (looking on a solitary courtyard at the back of the house) was opened to let in the fresh air, and all that could be done to make the place comfortable had been done. The whole cruelty of Sir Percival's deception had fallen on poor Lady Glyde. The only ill-usage which either he or Mrs Rubelle had inflicted on Miss Halcombe, consisted, so far as I could see, in the first offence of hiding her away.

I stole back, leaving the sick lady still peacefully asleep, to give the gardener instructions about bringing the doctor. I begged the man, after he had taken Mrs Rubelle to the station, to drive round by Mr Dawson's, and leave a message, in my name, asking him to call and see me. I knew he would come on my account, and I knew he would remain when he found Count Fosco had left the house.

In due course of time, the gardener returned, and said that he had driven round by Mr Dawson's residence, after leaving Mrs Rubelle at the station. The doctor sent me word that he was poorly in health himself, but that he would call, if possible, the next morning.

Having delivered his message, the gardener was about to withdraw, but I stopped him to request that he would come back before dark, and sit up, that night, in one of the empty bedrooms, so as to be within call, in case I wanted him. He understood readily enough my unwillingness to be left alone all night, in the most desolate part of that desolate house, and we arranged that he should come in between eight and nine.

He came punctually, and I found cause to be thankful that I had adopted the precaution of calling him in. Before midnight, Sir Percival's strange temper broke out in the most violent and most alarming manner; and if the gardener had not been on the spot to pacify him on the instant, I am afraid to think what might have happened.

Almost all the afternoon and evening, he had been walking about the house and grounds in an unsettled, excitable manner; having, in all probability, as I thought, taken an excessive quantity of wine at his solitary dinner. However that may be, I heard his voice calling loudly and angrily, in the new wing of the house, as I was taking a turn backwards and forwards along the gallery, the last thing at night. The gardener immediately ran down to him; and I closed the door of communication, to keep the alarm, if possible, from reaching Miss Halcombe's ears. It was full half an hour before the gardener came back. He declared that his master was quite out of his senses—not through the excitement of drink, as I had supposed, but through a kind of panic or frenzy of mind, for which it was impossible to account. He had found Sir Percival walking backwards and forwards by himself in the hall; swearing, with every appearance of the most violent passion, that he would not stop another minute alone in such a dungeon as his own house, and that he would take the first stage of his journey immediately, in the middle of the night. The gardener, on approaching him, had been hunted out, with oaths and threats, to get the horse and chaise ready instantly. In a quarter of an hour Sir Percival had joined him in the yard, had jumped into the chaise, and, lashing the horse into a gallop, had driven himself away, with his face as pale as ashes in the moonlight. The gardener had heard him shouting and cursing at the lodge-keeper to get up and open the gate—had heard the wheels roll furiously on again, in the still night, when the gate was unlocked—and knew no more.

The next day, or a day or two after, I forget which, the chaise was brought back from Knowlesbury, our nearest town, by the ostler at the old inn. Sir Percival had stopped there, and had afterwards left by the train—for what destination the man could not tell. I never received any further information, either from himself, or from any one else, of Sir Percival's proceedings; and I am not even aware, at this moment, whether he is in England or out of it. He and I have not met, since he drove away, like an escaped criminal, from his own house; and it is my fervent hope and prayer that we may never meet again.

My own part of this sad family story is now drawing to an end.

I have been informed that the particulars of Miss Halcombe's waking, and of what passed between us when she found me sitting by her bedside, are not material to the purpose which is to be answered by the present narrative. It will be sufficient for me to say, in this place, that she was not herself conscious of the means adopted to remove her from the inhabited to the uninhabited part of the house. She was in a deep sleep at the time, whether naturally or artificially produced she could not say. In my absence at Torquay, and in the absence of all the resident servants, except Margaret Porcher (who was perpetually eating, drinking, or sleeping when she was not at work), the secret transfer of Miss Halcombe from one part of the house to the other was no doubt easily performed. Mrs Rubelle (as I discovered for myself, in looking about the room) had provisions, and all other necessaries, together with the means of heating water, broth, and so on, without kindling a fire, placed at her disposal during the few days of her imprisonment with the sick lady. She had declined to answer the questions which Miss Halcombe naturally put; but had not, in other respects, treated her with unkindness or neglect. The disgrace of lending herself to a vile deception is the only disgrace with which I can conscientiously charge Mrs Rubelle.

I need write no particulars (and I am relieved to know it) of the effect produced on Miss Halcombe by the news of Lady Glyde's departure, or by the far more melancholy tidings which reached us only too soon afterwards at Blackwater Park. In both cases, I prepared her mind beforehand as gently and as carefully as possible; having the doctor's advice to guide me, in the last case only, through Mr Dawson's being too unwell to come to the house for some days after I had sent for him. It was a sad time, a time which it afflicts me to think of, or to write of, now. The precious blessings of religious consolation which I endeavoured to convey, were long in reaching Miss Halcombe's heart; but I hope and believe they came home to her at last. I never left her till her strength was restored. The train which took me away from that miserable house was the train which took her away also. We parted very mournfully in London. I remained with a relative at Islington; and she went on to Mr Fairlie's house in Cumberland.

I have only a few lines more to write, before I close this painful statement. They are dictated by a sense of duty.

In the first place, I wish to record my own personal conviction that no blame whatever, in connexion with the events which I have now related, attaches to Count Fosco. I am informed that a dreadful suspicion has been raised, and that some very serious constructions are placed upon his lordship's conduct. My persuasion of the Count's innocence remains, however, quite unshaken. If he assisted Sir Percival in sending me to Torquay, he assisted under a delusion, for which, as a foreigner and a stranger, he was not to blame. If he was concerned in bringing Mrs Rubelle to Blackwater Park, it was his misfortune and not his fault, when that foreign person was base enough to assist a deception planned and carried out by the master of the house. I protest, in the interests of morality, against blame being gratuitously and wantonly attached to the proceedings of the Count.

In the second place, I desire to express my regret at my own inability to remember the precise day on which Lady Glyde left Blackwater Park for London. I am told that it is of the last importance to ascertain the exact date of that lamentable journey; and I have anxiously taxed my memory to recal it. The effort has been in vain. I can only remember now that it was towards the latter part of July. We all know the difficulty, after a lapse of time, of fixing precisely on a past date, unless it has been previously written down. That difficulty is greatly increased, in my case, by the alarming and confusing events which took place about the period of Lady Glyde's departure. I heartily wish I had made a memorandum at the time. I heartily wish my memory of the date was as vivid as my memory of that poor lady's face, when it looked at me sorrowfully for the last time from the carriage window.

THE NARRATIVE OF HESTER PINHORN, COOK IN THE SERVICE OF COUNT FOSCO [TAKEN DOWN FROM HER OWN STATEMENT]

I AM sorry to say that I have never learnt to read or write. I have been a hard-working woman all my life, and have kept a good character. I know that it is a sin and wickedness to say the thing which is not; and I will truly beware of doing so on this occasion. All that I know, I will tell; and I humbly beg the gentleman who takes this down to put my language right as he goes on, and to make allowances for my being no scholar.

In this last summer, I happened to be out of place (through no fault of my own); and I heard of a situation, as plain cook, at Number Five, Forest-road, St John's Wood. I took the place, on trial. My master's name was Fosco. My mistress was an English lady. He was Count and she was Countess. There was a girl to do housemaid's work, when I got there. She was not over clean or tidy—but there was no harm in her. I and she were the only servants in the house.

Our master and mistress came after we got in. And, as soon as they did come, we were told, down stairs, that company was expected from the country.

The company was my mistress's niece, and the back bedroom on the first floor was got ready for her. My mistress mentioned to me that Lady Glyde (that was her name) was in poor health, and that I must be particular in my cooking accordingly. She was to come that day, as well as I can remember— but, whatever you do, don't trust *my* memory in the matter. I am sorry to say it's no use asking me about days of the month, and such-like. Except

Sundays, half my time I take no heed of them; being a hard-working woman and no scholar. All I know is, Lady Glyde came; and, when she did come, a fine fright she gave us all, surely. I don't know how master brought her to the house, being at work at the time. But he did bring her, in the afternoon, I think; and the housemaid opened the door to them, and showed them into the parlour. Before she had been long down in the kitchen again with me, we heard a hurry-skurry, up-stairs, and the parlour bell ringing like mad, and my mistress's voice calling out for help.

We both ran up; and there we saw the lady laid on the sofa, with her face ghastly white, and her hands fast clenched, and her head drawn down to one side. She had been taken with a sudden fright, my mistress said; and master he told us she was in a fit of convulsions. I ran out, knowing the neighbourhood a little better than the rest of them, to fetch the nearest doctor's help. The nearest help was at Goodricke's and Garth's, who worked together as partners, and had a good name and connexion, as I have heard, all round St John's Wood. Mr Goodricke was in; and he came back with me directly.

It was some time before he could make himself of much use. The poor unfortunate lady fell out of one fit into another—and went on so, till she was quite wearied out, and as helpless as a new-born babe. We then got her to bed. Mr Goodricke went away to his house for medicine, and came back again in a quarter of an hour or less. Besides the medicine he brought a bit of hollow mahogany wood with him, shaped like a kind of trumpet; and, after waiting a little while, he put one end over the lady's heart and the other to his ear, and listened carefully.

When he had done, he says to my mistress, who was in the room, 'This is a very serious case,' he says; 'I recommend you to write to Lady Glyde's friends directly.' My mistress, says to him, 'Is it heart-disease?' And he says 'Yes; heart-disease of a most dangerous kind.' He told her exactly what he thought was the matter, which I was not clever enough to understand. But I know this, he ended by saying that he was afraid neither his help nor any other doctor's help was likely to be of much service.

My mistress took this ill news more quietly than my master. He was a big, fat, odd sort of elderly man, who kept birds and white mice, and spoke to them as if they were so many Christian children. He seemed terribly cut up by what had happened. 'Ah! poor Lady Glyde! poor dear Lady Glyde!' he says—and went stalking about, wringing his fat hands more like a play-actor than a gentleman. For one question my mistress asked the doctor about the lady's chances of getting round, he asked a good fifty at least. I declare he quite tormented us all—and, when he was quiet at last, out he went into the bit of back garden, picking trumpery little nosegays, and asking me to take them up-stairs and make the sick-room look pretty with them. As if *that* did any good! I think he must have been, at times, a little soft in his head. But he was not a bad master: he had a monstrous civil tongue of his own; and a jolly, easy, coaxing way with him. I liked him a deal better than my mistress. She was a hard one, if ever there was a hard one yet.

Towards night-time, the lady roused up a little. She had been so wearied out, before that, by the convulsions, that she never stirred hand or foot, or spoke a word to anybody. She moved in the bed now; and stared about her at the room and us in it. She must have been a nice-looking lady, when well, with light hair, and blue eyes, and all that. Her rest was troubled at night—at least so I heard from my mistress, who sat up alone with her. I only went in once before going to bed, to see if I could be of any use; and then she was talking to herself, in a confused, rambling manner. She seemed to want sadly to speak to somebody, who was absent from her somewhere. I couldn't catch the name, the first time; and the second time master knocked at the door, with his regular mouthful of questions, and another of his trumpery nosegays. When I went in, early the next morning, the lady was clean worn out again, and lay in a kind of faint sleep. Mr Goodricke brought his partner, Mr Garth, with him to advise. They said she must not be disturbed out of her rest, on any account. They asked my mistress a many questions, at the other end of the room, about what the lady's health had been in past times, and who had attended her, and whether she had ever suffered much and long together under distress of mind. I remember my mistress said, 'Yes,' to that last question. And Mr Goodricke looked at Mr Garth, and shook his head; and Mr Garth looked at Mr Goodricke, and shook his head. They seemed to think that the distress might have something to do with the mischief at the lady's heart. She was but a frail thing to look at, poor creature! Very little strength, at any time, I should say—very little strength.

Later on the same morning, when she woke, the lady took a sudden turn, and got seemingly a great deal better. I was not let in again to see her, no more was the housemaid, for the reason that she was not to be disturbed by strangers. What I heard of her being better was through my master. He was in wonderful good spirits about the change, and looked in at the kitchen window from the garden, with his great big curly-brimmed white hat on, to go out.

'Good Mrs Cook,' says he, 'Lady Glyde is better. My mind is more easy than it was; and I am going out to stretch my big legs with a sunny little summer walk. Shall I order for you, shall I market for you, Mrs Cook? What are you making there? A nice tart for dinner? Much crust, if you please—much crisp crust, my dear, that melts and crumbles delicious in the mouth.' That was his way. He was past sixty, and fond of pastry. Just think of that!

The doctor came again in the forenoon, and saw for himself that Lady Glyde had woke up better. He forbid us to talk to her, or to let her talk to us, in case she was that way disposed; saying she must be kept quiet before all things, and encouraged to sleep as much as possible. She did not seem to want to talk whenever I saw her—except overnight, when I couldn't make out what she was saying—she seemed too much worn down. Mr Goodricke was not nearly in such good spirits about her as master. He said nothing when he came down stairs, except that he would call again at five o'clock. About that time (which was before master came home again), the bell rang hard from the bedroom, and my mistress ran out into the landing, and called to me to go for Mr Goodricke, and tell him the lady had fainted. I got on my bonnet and shawl, when, as good luck would have it, the doctor himself came to the house for his promised visit.

I let him in, and went up-stairs along with him. 'Lady Glyde was just as usual,' says my mistress to him at the door; 'she was awake, and looking about her, in a strange, forlorn manner, when I heard her give a sort of half cry, and she fainted in a moment.' The doctor went up to the bed, and stooped down over the sick lady. He looked very serious, all on a sudden, at the sight of her; and put his hand on her heart.

My mistress stared hard in Mr Goodricke's face. 'Not dead!' says she, whispering, and turning all of a tremble from head to foot.

'Yes,' says the doctor, very quiet and grave. 'Dead. I was afraid it would happen suddenly, when I examined her heart yesterday.' My mistress stepped back from the bedside, while he was speaking, and trembled and trembled again. 'Dead!' she whispers to herself; 'dead so suddenly! dead so soon! What will the Count say?' Mr Goodricke advised her to go down stairs, and quiet herself a little. 'You have been sitting up all night,' says he; 'and your nerves are shaken. This person,' says he, meaning me, 'this person will stay in the room, till I can send for the necessary assistance.' My mistress did as he told her. 'I must prepare the Count,' she says. 'I must carefully prepare the Count.' And so she left us, shaking from head to foot, and went out.

'Your master is a foreigner,' says Mr Goodricke, when my mistress had left us. 'Does he understand about registering the death?' 'I can't rightly tell, sir,' says I; 'but I should think not.' The doctor considered a minute; and then, says he, 'I don't usually do such things,' says he, 'but it may save the family trouble in this case, if I register the death myself. I shall pass the district office in half an hour's time; and I can easily look in. Mention, if you please, that I will do so.' 'Yes, sir,' says I, 'with thanks, I'm sure, for your kindness in thinking of it.' 'You don't mind staying here, till I can send you the proper person?' says he. 'No, sir,' says I; 'I'll stay with the poor lady, till then. I suppose nothing more could be done, sir, than was done?' says I. 'No,' says he; 'nothing; she must have suffered sadly before ever I saw her: the case was hopeless when I was called in.' 'Ah, dear me! we all come to it, sooner or later, don't we, sir?' says I. He gave no answer to that; he didn't seem to care about talking. He said, 'Good day,' and went out.

I stopped by the bedside from that time, till the time when Mr Goodricke sent the person in, as he had promised. She was, by name, Jane Gould. I considered her to be a respectable-looking woman. She made no remark, except to say that she understood what was wanted of her, and that she had winded a many of them in her time.

How master bore the news, when he first heard it, is more than I can tell; not having been present. When I did see him, he looked awfully overcome by it, to be sure. He sat quiet in a corner, with his fat hands hanging over his thick knees, and his head down, and his eyes looking at nothing. He seemed not so much sorry, as scared and dazed like, by what had happened. My mistress managed all that was to be done about the funeral. It must have cost a sight of money: the coffin, in particular, being most beautiful. The dead lady's husband was away, as we heard, in foreign parts. But my mistress (being her aunt) settled it with her friends in the country (Cumberland, I think) that she should be buried there, in the same grave along with her mother. Everything was done handsomely, in respect of the funeral, I say again; and master went down to attend the burying in the country himself. He looked grand in his deep mourning, with his big solemn face, and his slow walk, and his broad hatband—that he did!

In conclusion, I have to say, in answer to questions put to me,

(1) That neither I nor my fellow-servant ever saw my master give Lady Glyde any medicine himself.

(2) That he was never, to my knowledge and belief, left alone in the room with Lady Glyde.

(3) That I am not able to say what caused the sudden fright, which my mistress informed me had seized the lady on her first coming into the house. The cause was never explained, either to me or to my fellow-servant.

The above statement has been read over in my presence. I have nothing to add to it, or to take away from it. I say, on my oath as a Christian woman, This is the truth.

(Signed) Hester Pinhorn, Her + Mark

THE NARRATIVE OF THE DOCTOR

To The Registrar of the Sub-District in which the undermentioned Death took place.—I hereby certify that I attended *Lady Glyde*, aged *Twenty-one* last Birthday; that I last saw her, on *the 25th July*, 1850; that she died *on the same day* at *No. 5, Forest-road, St John's Wood*; and that the cause of her death was

CAUSE OF DEATH	DURATION OF DISEASE
Aneurism	*Not known*

Signed,
Alfred Goodricke

Prof. Title *M.R.C.S. Eng. L.S.A.*
Address. 12, *Croydon Gardens, St John's Wood.*

THE NARRATIVE OF JANE GOULD

I WAS the person sent in by Mr Goodricke, to do what was right and needful by the remains of a lady, who had died at the house named in the certificate which precedes this. I found the body in charge of the servant, Hester Pinhorn. I remained with it, and prepared it, at the proper time, for the grave. It was laid in the coffin, in my presence; and I afterwards saw the coffin screwed down, previous to its removal. When that had been done, and not before, I received what was due to me, and left the house. I refer persons who may wish to investigate my character to Mr Goodricke. He will bear witness that I can be trusted to tell the truth.

(Signed) *Jane Gould*

THE NARRATIVE OF THE TOMBSTONE

> #### 𝔖acred
> ## TO THE MEMORY OF
> # LAURA,
> ### LADY GLYDE,
> ### WIFE OF SIR PERCIVAL GLYDE, BART.,
> ### OF BLACKWATER PARK, HAMPSHIRE;
> ### AND
> ### DAUGHTER OF THE LATE PHILIP FAIRLIE ESQ.,
> ### OF LIMMERIDGE HOUSE, IN THIS PARISH.
> ### BORN, MARCH 27TH, 1829.
> ### MARRIED, DECEMBER 22ND, 1849
> ### DIED, JULY 25TH, 1850.

THE NARRATIVE OF WALTER HARTRIGHT, RESUMED

I

EARLY in the summer of 1850, I, and my surviving companions, left the wilds and forests of Central America for home. Arrived at the coast, we took ship there for England. The vessel was wrecked in the Gulf of Mexico; I was among the few saved from the sea. It was my third escape from peril of death. Death by disease, death by the Indians, death by drowning—all three had approached me; all three had passed me by.

The survivors of the wreck were rescued by an American vessel, bound for Liverpool. The ship reached her port on the thirteenth day of October, 1850. We landed late in the afternoon; and I arrived in London the same night.

These pages are not the record of my wanderings and my dangers away from home. The motives which led me from my country and my friends to a new world of adventure and peril are known. From that self-imposed exile I came back, as I had hoped, prayed, believed I should come back—a changed man. In the waters of a new life I had tempered my nature afresh. In the stern school of extremity and danger my will had learnt to be strong, my heart to be resolute, my mind to rely on itself. I had gone out to fly from my own future. I came back to face it, as a man should.

To face it with that inevitable suppression of myself which I knew it would demand from me. I had parted with the worst bitterness of the past, but not with my heart's remembrance of the sorrow and the tenderness of that memorable time. I had not ceased to feel the one irreparable disappointment of my life—I had only learnt to bear it. Laura Fairlie was in all my thoughts when the ship bore me away, and I looked my last at England. Laura Fairlie was in all my thoughts when the ship brought me back, and the morning light showed the friendly shore in view.

My pen traces the old letters as my heart goes back to the old love. I write of her as Laura Fairlie still. It is hard to think of her, it is hard to speak of her, by her husband's name.

There are no more words of explanation to add, on my appearing for the second time in these pages. This final narrative, if I have the strength and the courage to write it, may now go on.

My first anxieties and first hopes, when the morning came, centred in my mother and my sister. I felt the necessity of preparing them for the joy and surprise of my return, after an absence, during which it had been impossible for them to receive any tidings of me for months past. Early in the morning, I sent a letter to the Hampstead Cottage; and followed it myself, in an hour's time.

When the first meeting was over, when our quiet and composure of other days began gradually to return to us, I saw something in my mother's face which told me that a secret oppression lay heavy on her heart. There was more than love—there was sorrow in the anxious eyes that looked on me so tenderly; there was pity in the kind hand that slowly and fondly strengthened its hold on mine. We had no concealments from each other. She knew how the hope of my life had been wrecked—she knew why I had left her. It was on my lips to ask as composedly as I could, if any letter had come for me from Miss Halcombe—if there was any news of her sister that I might hear. But, when I looked in my mother's face, I lost courage to put the question even in that guarded form. I could only say, doubtingly and restrainedly,

'You have something to tell me.'

My sister, who had been sitting opposite to us, rose suddenly, without a word of explanation—rose, and left the room.

My mother moved closer to me on the sofa, and put her arms round my neck. Those fond arms trembled; the tears flowed fast over the faithful, loving face.

'Walter!' she whispered—'my own darling! my heart is heavy for you. Oh, my son! my son! try to remember that I am still left!'

My head sank on her bosom. She had said all, in saying those words.

II

IT was the morning of the third day since my return—the morning of the sixteenth of October.

I had remained with them at the Cottage; I had tried hard not to embitter the happiness of my return, to *them*, as it was embittered to *me*. I had done all man could to rise after the shock, and accept my life resignedly—to let my great sorrow come in tenderness to my heart, and not in despair. It was useless and hopeless. No tears soothed my aching eyes; no relief came to me from my sister's sympathy or my mother's love.

On that third morning, I opened my heart to them. At last the words passed my lips which I had longed to speak on the day when my mother told me of her death.

'Let me go away alone, for a little while,' I said. 'I shall bear it better when I have looked once more at the place where I first saw her—when I have knelt and prayed by the grave where they have laid her to rest.'

I departed on my journey—my journey to the grave of Laura Fairlie.

It was a quiet autumn afternoon, when I stopped at the solitary station, and set forth alone, on foot, by the well-remembered road. The waning sun was shining faintly through thin white clouds; the air was warm and still; the peacefulness of the lonely country was over-shadowed and saddened by the influence of the falling year.

I reached the moor; I stood again on the brow of the hill; I looked on, along the path—and there were the familiar garden trees in the distance, the clear sweeping semicircle of the drive, the high white walls of Limme-ridge House. The chances and changes, the wanderings and dangers of months and months past, all shrank and shrivelled to nothing in my mind. It was like yesterday, since my feet had last trodden the fragrant heathy ground! I thought I should see her coming to meet me, with her little straw hat shading her face, her simple dress fluttering in the air, and her well-filled sketch-book ready in her hand.

Oh, Death, thou hast thy sting! oh, Grave, thou hast thy victory!

I turned aside; and there below me, in the glen, was the lonesome grey church; the porch where I had waited for the coming of the woman in white; the hills encircling the quiet burial-ground; the brook bubbling cold over its stony bed. There was the marble cross, fair and white, at the head of the tomb—the tomb that now rose over mother and daughter alike.

I approached the grave. I crossed once more the low stone stile, and bared my head as I touched the sacred ground. Sacred to gentleness and goodness; sacred to reverence and grief.

I stopped before the pedestal from which the cross rose. On one side of it, on the side nearest to me, the newly-cut inscription met my eyes—the hard, clear, cruel black letters which told the story of her life and death. I tried to read them. I did read, as far as the name. 'Sacred to the Memory of Laura——' The kind blue eyes dim with tears; the fair head drooping wearily; the innocent, parting words which implored me to leave her—oh, for a happier last memory of her than this; the memory I took away with me, the memory I bring back with me to her grave!

A second time, I tried to read the inscription. I saw, at the end, the date of her death; and, above it——

Above it, there were lines on the marble, there was a name among them, which disturbed my thoughts of her. I went round to the other side of the grave, where there was nothing to read—nothing of earthly vileness to force its way between her spirit and mine.

I knelt down by the tomb. I laid my hands, I laid my head, on the broad white stone, and closed my weary eyes on the earth around, on the light above. I let her come back to me. Oh, my love! my love! my heart may speak to you *now*! It is yesterday again, since we parted—yesterday, since your dear hand lay in mine—yesterday, since my eyes looked their last on you. My love! my love!

*   *   *   *   *

Time had flowed on; and Silence had fallen, like thick night, over its course. The first sound that came, after the heavenly peace, rustled faintly, like a passing breath of air, over the grass of the burial-ground. I heard it nearing me slowly, until it came changed to my ear—came like footsteps moving onward—then stopped.

I looked up.

The sunset was near at hand. The clouds had parted; the slanting light fell mellow over the hills. The last of the day was cold and clear and still in the quiet valley of the dead.

Beyond me, in the burial-ground, standing together in the cold clearness of the lower light, I saw two women. They were looking towards the tomb; looking towards *me*.

Two.

They came a little on; and stopped again. Their veils were down, and hid their faces from me. When they stopped, one of them raised her veil. In the still evening light, I saw the face of Marian Halcombe.

Changed, changed as if years had passed over it! The eyes large and wild, and looking at me with a strange terror in them. The face worn and wasted piteously. Pain and fear and grief written on her as with a brand.

I took one step towards her from the grave. She never moved—she never spoke. The veiled woman with her cried out faintly. I stopped. The springs of my life fell low; and the shuddering of an unutterable dread crept over me from head to foot.

The woman with the veiled face moved away from her companion, and came towards me slowly. Left by herself, standing by herself, Marian Halcombe spoke. It was the voice that I remembered—the voice not changed, like the frightened eyes and the wasted face.

'My dream! my dream!' I heard her say those words softly, in the awful silence. She sank on her knees, and raised her clasped hands to the heaven. 'Father! strengthen him. Father! help him, in his hour of need.'

The woman came on; slowly and silently came on. I looked at her—at her, and at none other, from that moment.

The voice that was praying for me, faltered and sank low—then rose on a sudden, and called affrightedly, called despairingly to me to come away.

But the veiled woman had possession of me, body and soul. She stopped on one side of the grave. We stood face to face, with the tombstone between us. She was close to the inscription on the side of the pedestal. Her gown touched the black letters.

The voice came nearer, and rose and rose more passionately still. 'Hide your face! don't look at her! Oh, for God's sake, spare him!——'

The woman lifted her veil.

𝔖acred

TO THE MEMORY OF

LAURA,

LADY GLYDE,——

Laura, Lady Glyde, was standing by the inscription, and was looking at me over the grave.

THE END OF THE FIRST PART

PART THE SECOND

===

I

I OPEN a new page. I advance my narrative by one week.

The history of the interval which I thus pass over must remain un-recorded. My heart turns faint, my mind sinks in darkness and confusion when I think of it. This must not be, if I, who write, am to guide, as I ought, you who read. This must not be, if the clue that leads through the windings of the Story is to remain, from end to end, untangled in my hands.

A life suddenly changed—its whole purpose created afresh; its hopes and fears, its struggles, its interests, and its sacrifices, all turned at once and for ever into a new direction—this is the prospect which now opens before me, like the burst of view from a mountain's top. I left my narrative in the quiet shadow of Limmeridge church: I resume it, one week later, in the stir and turmoil of a London street.

The street is in a populous and a poor neighbourhood. The ground floor of one of the houses in it is occupied by a small news-vendor's shop; and the first floor and the second are let as furnished lodgings of the humblest kind.

I have taken those two floors, in an assumed name. On the upper floor I live, with a room to work in, a room to sleep in. On the lower floor, under the same assumed name, two women live, who are described as my sisters. I get my bread by drawing and engraving on wood for the cheap periodicals. My sisters are supposed to help me by taking in a little needlework. Our poor place of abode, our humble calling, our assumed relationship, and our assumed name, are all used alike as a means of hiding us in the house-forest of London. We are numbered no longer with the people whose lives are open and known. I am an obscure, unnoticed man, without patron or friend to help me. Marian Hal-combe is nothing now, but my eldest sister, who provides for our household wants by the toil of her own hands. We two, in the estimation of others, are at once the dupes and the agents of a daring imposture. We are supposed to be the accomplices of mad Anne Catherick, who claims the name, the place, and the living personality of dead Lady Glyde.

That is our situation. That is the changed aspect in which we three must appear, henceforth, in this narrative, for many and many a page to come.

In the eye of reason and of law, in the estimation of relatives and friends, according to every received formality of civilised society, 'Laura, Lady Glyde,' lay buried with her mother in Limmeridge churchyard. Torn in her own lifetime from the list of the living, the daughter of Philip Fairlie and the wife of Percival Glyde might still exist for her sister, might still exist for me, but to all the world besides she was dead. Dead to her uncle who had renounced her; dead to the servants of the house, who had failed to recognise her; dead to the persons in authority who had transmitted her fortune to her husband and her aunt; dead to my mother and my sister, who believed me to be the dupe of an adventuress and the victim of a fraud; socially, morally, legally—dead.

And yet alive! Alive in poverty and in hiding. Alive, with the poor drawing-master to fight her battle, and to win the way back for her to her place in the world of living beings.

Did no suspicion, excited by my own knowledge of Anne Catherick's resemblance to her, cross my mind, when her face was first revealed to me? Not the shadow of a suspicion, from the moment when she lifted the veil by the side of the inscription which recorded her death.

Before the sun of that day had set, before the last glimpse of the home which was closed against her had passed from our view, the farewell words I spoke, when we parted at Limmeridge House, had been recalled by both of us; repeated by me, recognised by her. 'If ever the time comes, when the devotion of my whole heart and soul and strength will give you a moment's happiness, or spare you a moment's sorrow, will you try to remember the poor drawing-master who has taught you?' She, who now remembered so little of the trouble and terror of a later time, remembered those words, and laid her poor head innocently and trustingly on the bosom of the man who had spoken them. In that moment, when she called me by my name, when she said, 'They have tried to make me forget everything, Walter; but I remember Marian, and I remember *you*'—in that moment, I, who had long since given her my love, gave her my life, and thanked God that it was mine to bestow on her. Yes! the time had come. From thousands on thousands of miles away; through forest and wilderness, where companions stronger than I had fallen by my side; through peril of death thrice renewed, and thrice escaped, the Hand that leads men on the dark road to the future, had led me to meet that time. Forlorn and disowned, sorely tried and sadly changed; her beauty faded, her mind clouded; robbed of her station in the world, of her place among living creatures—the devotion I had promised, the devotion of my whole heart and soul and strength might be laid blamelessly, now, at those dear feet. In the right of her calamity, in the right of her friendlessness, she was mine at last! Mine to support, to protect, to cherish, to restore. Mine to love and honour as father and brother both. Mine to vindicate through all risks and all sacrifices—through the hopeless struggle against Rank and Power, through the long fight with armed Deceit and fortified Success, through the waste of my reputation, through the loss of my friends, through the hazard of my life.

II

MY position is defined; my motives are acknowledged. The story of Marian and the story of Laura must come next.

I shall relate both narratives, not in the words (often interrupted, often inevitably confused) of the speakers themselves, but in the words of the brief, plain, studiously-simple abstract which I committed to writing for my own guidance, and for the guidance of my legal adviser. So the tangled web will be most speedily and most intelligibly unrolled.

The story of Marian begins, where the narrative of the house-keeper at Blackwater Park left off.

On Lady Glyde's departure from her husband's house, the fact of that departure, and the necessary statement of the circumstances under which it had taken place, were communicated to Miss Halcombe by the housekeeper. It was not till some days afterwards (how many days exactly, Mrs Michelson, in the absence of any written memorandum on the subject, could not undertake to say) that a letter arrived from Madame Fosco announcing Lady Glyde's sudden death in Count Fosco's house. The letter avoided mentioning dates, and left it to Mrs Michelson's discretion to break the news at once to Miss Halcombe, or to defer doing so until that lady's health should be more firmly established.

Having consulted Mr Dawson (who had been himself delayed, by ill health, in resuming his attendance at Blackwater Park), Mrs Michelson, by the doctor's advice and in the doctor's presence, communicated the news, either on the day when the letter was received, or on the day after. It is not necessary to dwell here upon the effect which the intelligence of Lady Glyde's sudden death produced on her sister. It is only useful to the present purpose to say that she was not able to travel for more than three weeks afterwards. At the end of that time she proceeded to London, accompanied by the housekeeper. They parted there; Mrs Michelson previously informing Miss Halcombe of her address, in case they might wish to communicate at a future period.

On parting with the housekeeper, Miss Halcombe went at once to the office of Messrs. Gilmore and Kyrle, to consult with the latter gentleman, in Mr Gilmore's absence. She mentioned to Mr Kyrle, what she had thought it desirable to conceal from every one else (Mrs Michelson included)—her suspicion of the circumstances under which Lady Glyde was said to have met her death. Mr Kyrle, who had previously given friendly proof of his anxiety to serve Miss Halcombe, at once undertook to make such inquiries as the delicate and dangerous nature of the investigation proposed to him would permit.

To exhaust this part of the subject before going farther, it may be here mentioned that Count Fosco offered every facility to Mr Kyrle, on that gentleman's stating that he was sent by Miss Halcombe to collect such particulars as had not yet reached her of Lady Glyde's decease. Mr Kyrle was placed in communication with the medical man, Mr Goodricke, and with the two servants. In the absence of any means of ascertaining the exact date of Lady Glyde's departure from Blackwater Park, the result of the doctor's and the servants' evidence, and of the volunteered statements of Count Fosco and his wife, was conclusive to the mind of Mr Kyrle. He could only assume that the intensity of Miss Halcombe's suffering under the loss of her sister, had misled her judgment in a most deplorable manner; and he wrote her word that the shocking suspicion to which she had alluded in his presence, was, in his opinion, destitute of the smallest fragment of foundation in truth. Thus the investigation by Mr Gilmore's partner began and ended.

Meanwhile, Miss Halcombe had returned to Limmeridge House; and had there collected all the additional information which she was able to obtain.

Mr Fairlie had received his first intimation of his niece's death from his sister, Madame Fosco; this letter also not containing any exact reference to dates. He had sanctioned his sister's proposal that the deceased lady should be laid in her mother's grave in Limmeridge churchyard. Count Fosco had accompanied the remains to Cumberland, and had attended the funeral at Limmeridge, which took place on the 30th of July. It was followed, as a mark of respect, by all the inhabitants of the village and the neighbourhood. On the next day, the inscription (originally drawn out, it was said, by the aunt of the deceased lady, and submitted for approval to her brother, Mr Fairlie) was engraved on one side of the monument over the tomb.

On the day of the funeral, and for one day after it, Count Fosco had been received as a guest at Limmeridge House; but no interview had taken place between Mr Fairlie and himself, by the former gentleman's desire. They had communicated by writing; and, through this medium, Count Fosco had made Mr Fairlie acquainted with the details of his niece's last illness and death. The letter presenting this information added no new facts to the facts already known; but one very remarkable paragraph was contained in the postscript. It referred to Anne Catherick.

The substance of the paragraph in question was as follows:

It first informed Mr Fairlie that Anne Catherick (of whom he might hear full particulars from Miss Halcombe when she reached Limmeridge) had been traced and recovered in the neighbourhood of Blackwater Park, and had been, for the second time, placed under the charge of the medical man from whose custody she had once escaped.

This was the first part of the postscript. The second part warned Mr Fairlie that Anne Catherick's mental malady had been aggravated by her long freedom from control; and that the insane hatred and distrust of Sir Percival Glyde, which had been one of her most marked delusions in former times, still existed, under a newly-acquired form. The unfortunate woman's last idea in connexion with Sir Percival, was the idea of annoying and distressing him, and of elevating herself, as she supposed, in the estimation of the patients and nurses, by assuming the character of his deceased wife; the scheme of this personation having evidently occurred to her, after a stolen interview which she had succeeded in obtaining with Lady Glyde, and at which she had observed the extraordinary accidental likeness between the deceased lady and herself. It was to the last degree improbable that she would succeed a second time in escaping from the Asylum; but it was just possible she might find some means of annoying the late Lady Glyde's relatives with letters; and, in that case, Mr Fairlie was warned beforehand how to receive them.

The postscript, expressed in these terms, was shown to Miss Halcombe, when she arrived at Limmeridge. There were also placed in her possession the clothes Lady Glyde had worn, and the other effects she had brought with her to her aunt's house. They had been carefully collected and sent to Cumberland by Madame Fosco.

Such was the posture of affairs when Miss Halcombe reached Limmeridge, in the early part of September.

Shortly afterwards, she was confined to her room by a relapse; her weakened physical energies giving way under the severe mental affliction from which she was now suffering. On getting stronger again, in a month's time, her suspicion of the circumstances described as attending her sister's death, still remained unshaken. She had heard nothing, in the interim, of Sir Percival Glyde; but letters had reached her from Madame Fosco, making the most affectionate inquiries on the part of her husband and herself. Instead of answering these letters, Miss Halcombe caused the house in St John's Wood, and the proceedings of its inmates, to be privately watched.

Nothing doubtful was discovered. The same result attended the next investigations, which were secretly instituted on the subject of Mrs Rubelle. She had arrived in London, about six months before, with her husband. They had come from Lyons; and they had taken a house in the neighbourhood of Leicester-square, to be fitted up as a boarding-house for foreigners, who were expected to visit England in large numbers to see the Exhibition of 1851. Nothing was known against husband or wife, in the neighbourhood. They were quiet people; and they had paid their way honestly up to the present time. The final inquiries related to Sir Percival Glyde. He was settled in Paris; and living there quietly in a small circle of English and French friends.

Foiled at all points, but still not able to rest, Miss Halcombe next determined to visit the Asylum in which she then supposed Anne Catherick to be for the second time confined. She had felt a strong curiosity about the woman in former days; and she was now doubly interested—first, in ascertaining whether the report of Anne Catherick's attempted personation of Lady Glyde was true, and, secondly (if it proved to be true), in discovering for herself what the poor creature's real motives were for attempting the deceit.

Although Count Fosco's letter to Mr Fairlie did not mention the address of the Asylum, that important omission cast no difficulties in Miss Halcombe's way. When Mr Hartright had met Anne Catherick at Limmeridge, she had informed him of the locality in which the house was situated; and Miss Halcombe had noted down the direction in her diary, with all the other particulars of the interview, exactly as she heard them from Mr Hartright's own lips. Accordingly, she looked back at the entry, and extracted the address, furnished herself with the Count's letter to Mr Fairlie, as a species of credential which might be useful to her, and started by herself for the Asylum, on the eleventh of October.

She passed the night of the eleventh in London. It had been her intention to sleep at the house inhabited by Lady Glyde's old governess; but Mrs Vesey's agitation at the sight of her lost pupil's nearest and dearest friend was so distressing, that Miss Halcombe considerately refrained from remaining in her presence, and removed to a respectable boarding-house in the neighbourhood, recommended by Mrs Vesey's married sister. The next day, she proceeded to the Asylum, which was situated, not far from London, on the northern side of the metropolis.

She was immediately admitted to see the proprietor.

At first, he appeared to be decidedly unwilling to let her communicate with his patient. But, on her showing him the postscript to Count Fosco's letter—on her reminding him that she was the 'Miss Halcombe' there referred to, that she was a near relative of the deceased Lady Glyde, and that she was therefore naturally interested, for family reasons, in observing for herself the extent of Anne Catherick's delusion, in relation to her late sister—the tone and manner of the owner of the Asylum altered, and he withdrew his objections. He probably felt that a continued refusal, under these circumstances, would not only be an act of discourtesy in itself, but would also imply that the proceedings in his establishment were not of a nature to bear investigation by respectable strangers.

Miss Halcombe's own impression was that the owner of the Asylum had not been received into the confidence of Sir Percival and the Count. His consenting at all to let her visit his patient seemed to afford one proof of this, and his readiness in making admissions which could scarcely have escaped the lips of an accomplice, certainly appeared to furnish another.

For example, in the course of the introductory conversation which took place, he informed Miss Halcombe that Anne Catherick had been brought back to him, with the necessary order and certificates, by Count Fosco, on the twenty-seventh of July; the Count also producing a letter of explanations and instructions, signed by Sir Percival Glyde. On receiving his inmate again, the proprietor of the Asylum acknowledged that he had observed some curious personal changes in her. Such changes, no doubt, were not without precedent in his experience of persons mentally afflicted. Insane people were often, at one time, outwardly as well as inwardly, unlike what they were at another; the change from better to worse, or from worse to better, in the madness, having a necessary tendency to produce alterations of appearance externally. He allowed for these; and he allowed also for the modification in the form of Anne Catherick's delusion, which was reflected, no doubt, in her manner and expression. But he was still perplexed, at times, by certain differences between his patient before she had escaped, and his patient since she had been brought back. Those differences were too minute to be described. He could not say, of course, that she was absolutely altered in height or shape or complexion, or in the colour of her hair and eyes, or in the general form of her face: the change was something that he felt, more than something that he saw. In short, the case had been a puzzle from the first, and one more perplexity was added to it now.

It cannot be said that this conversation led to the result of even partially preparing Miss Halcombe's mind for what was to come. But it produced, nevertheless, a very serious effect upon her. She was so completely unnerved by it, that some little time elapsed before she could summon composure enough to follow the proprietor of the Asylum to that part of the house in which the inmates were confined.

On inquiry, it turned out that the supposed Anne Catherick was then taking exercise in the grounds attached to the establishment. One of the nurses volunteered to conduct Miss Halcombe to the place; the proprietor of the Asylum remaining in the house for a few minutes to attend to a case which required his services, and then engaging to join his visitor in the grounds.

The nurse led Miss Halcombe to a distant part of the property, which was prettily laid out; and, after looking about her a little, turned into a turf walk, shaded by a shrubbery on either side. About half way down this walk, two women were slowly approaching. The nurse pointed to them, and said, 'There is Anne Catherick, ma'am, with the attendant who waits on her. The attendant will answer any questions you wish to put.' With those words the nurse left her, to return to the duties of the house.

Miss Halcombe advanced on her side, and the women advanced on theirs. When they were within a dozen paces of each other, one of the women stopped for an instant, looked eagerly at the strange lady, shook off the nurse's grasp on her, and, the next moment, rushed into Miss Halcombe's arms. In that moment Miss Halcombe recognised her sister—recognised the dead-alive.

Fortunately for the success of the measures taken subsequently, no one was present, at that moment, but the nurse. She was a young woman; and she was so startled that she was at first quite incapable of interfering. When she was able to do so, her whole services were required by Miss Halcombe, who had for the moment sunk altogether in the effort to keep her own senses under the shock of the discovery. After waiting a few minutes in the fresh air and the cool shade, her natural energy and courage helped her a little, and she became sufficiently mistress of herself to feel the necessity of recalling her presence of mind for her unfortunate sister's sake.

She obtained permission to speak alone with the patient, on condition that they both remained well within the nurse's view. There was no time for questions—there was only time for Miss Halcombe to impress on the unhappy lady the necessity of controlling herself, and to assure her of immediate help and rescue if she did so. The prospect of escaping from the Asylum by obedience to her sister's directions, was sufficient to quiet Lady Glyde, and to make her understand what was required of her. Miss Halcombe next returned to the nurse, placed all the gold she then had in her pocket (three sovereigns) in the nurse's hands, and asked when and where she could speak to her alone.

The woman was at first surprised and distrustful. But, on Miss Halcombe's declaring that she only wanted to put some questions which she was too much agitated to ask at that moment, and that she had no intention of misleading the nurse into any dereliction of duty, the woman took the money, and proposed three o'clock on the next day as the time for the interview. She might then slip out for half an hour, after the patients had dined; and she would meet the lady in a retired place, outside the high north wall which screened the grounds of the house. Miss Halcombe had only time to assent, and to whisper to her sister that she should hear from her on the next day, when the proprietor of the Asylum joined them. He noticed his visitor's agitation, which Miss Halcombe accounted for by saying that her interview with Anne Catherick had a little startled her, at first. She took her leave as soon after as possible—that is to say, as soon as she could summon courage to force herself from the presence of her unfortunate sister.

A very little reflection, when the capacity to reflect returned, convinced her that any attempt to identify Lady Glyde and to rescue her by legal means, would, even if successful, involve a delay that might be fatal to her sister's intellects, which were shaken already by the horror of the situation to which she had been consigned. By the time Miss Halcombe had got back to London, she had determined to effect Lady Glyde's escape privately, by means of the nurse.

She went at once to her stockbroker; and sold out of the funds all the little property she possessed, amounting to rather less than seven hundred pounds. Determined, if necessary, to pay the price of her sister's liberty with every farthing she had in the world, she repaired the next day, having the whole sum about her, in banknotes, to her appointment outside the Asylum wall.

The nurse was there. Miss Halcombe approached the subject cautiously by many preliminary questions. She discovered, among other particulars, that the nurse who had, in former times, attended on the true Anne Catherick, had been held responsible (although she was not to blame for it) for the patient's escape, and had lost her place in consequence. The same penalty, it was added, would attach to the person then speaking to her, if the supposed Anne Catherick was missing a second time; and, moreover, the nurse, in this case, had an especial interest in keeping her place. She was engaged to be married; and she and her future husband were waiting till they could save, together, between two and three hundred pounds to start in business. The nurse's wages were good; and she might succeed, by strict economy, in contributing her small share towards the sum required in two years' time.

On this hint, Miss Halcombe spoke. She declared that the supposed Anne Catherick was nearly related to her; that she had been placed in the Asylum, under a fatal mistake; and that the nurse would be doing a good and a Christian action in being the means of restoring them to one another. Before there was time to start a single objection, Miss Halcombe took four bank-notes of a hundred pounds each from her pocket-book, and offered them to the woman, as a compensation for the risk she was to run, and for the loss of her place.

The nurse hesitated, through sheer incredulity and surprise. Miss Halcombe pressed the point on her firmly.

'You will be doing a good action,' she repeated; 'you will be helping the most injured and unhappy woman alive. There is your marriage-portion for a reward. Bring her safely to me, here; and I will put these four bank-notes into your hand, before I claim her.'

'Will you give me a letter saying those words, which I can show to my sweetheart, when he asks how I got the money?' inquired the woman.

'I will bring the letter with me, ready written and signed,' answered Miss Halcombe.

'Then I'll risk it,' said the nurse.

'When?'

'To-morrow.'

It was hastily agreed between them that Miss Halcombe should return early the next morning, and wait out of sight, among the trees—always, however, keeping near the quiet spot of ground under the north wall. The nurse could fix no time for her appearance; caution requiring that she should wait, and be guided by circumstances. On that understanding, they separated.

Miss Halcombe was at her place, with the promised letter, and the promised bank-notes, before ten the next morning. She waited more than an hour and a half. At the end of that time, the nurse came quickly round the corner of the wall, holding Lady Glyde by the arm. The moment they met, Miss Halcombe put the bank-notes and the letter into her hand—and the sisters were united again.

The nurse had dressed Lady Glyde, with excellent forethought, in a bonnet, veil, and shawl of her own. Miss Halcombe only detained her to suggest a means of turning the pursuit in a false direction, when the escape was discovered at the Asylum. She was to go back to the house; to mention in the hearing of the other nurses that Anne Catherick had been inquiring, latterly, about the distance from London to Hampshire; to wait till the last moment, before discovery was inevitable; and then to give the alarm that Anne was missing. The supposed inquiries about Hampshire, when communicated to the owner of the Asylum, would lead him to imagine that his patient had returned to Blackwater Park, under the influence of the delusion which made her persist in asserting herself to be Lady Glyde; and the first pursuit would, in all probability, be turned in that direction.

The nurse consented to follow these suggestions—the more readily, as they offered her the means of securing herself against any worse consequences than the loss of her place, by remaining in the Asylum, and so maintaining the appearance of innocence, at least. She at once returned to the house; and Miss Halcombe lost no time in taking her sister back with her to London. They caught the afternoon train to Carlisle the same afternoon, and arrived at Limmeridge, without accident or difficulty of any kind, that night.

During the latter part of their journey, they were alone in the carriage, and Miss Halcombe was able to collect such remembrances of the past as her sister's confused and weakened memory was able to recal. The terrible story of the conspiracy so obtained, was presented in fragments, sadly incoherent in themselves, and widely detached from each other. Imperfect as the revelation was, it must nevertheless be recorded here before this explanatory narrative closes with the events of the next day at Limmeridge House.

The following particulars comprise all that Miss Halcombe was able to discover.

LADY GLYDE's recollection of the events which followed her departure from Blackwater Park began with her arrival at the London terminus of the

South Western Railway. She had omitted to make a memorandum before-hand of the day on which she took the journey. All hope of fixing that important date, by any evidence of hers, or of Mrs Michelson's, must be given up for lost.

On the arrival of the train at the platform, Lady Glyde found Count Fosco waiting for her. He was at the carriage-door as soon as the porter could open it. The train was unusually crowded, and there was great confusion in getting the luggage. Some person whom Count Fosco brought with him procured the luggage which belonged to Lady Glyde. It was marked with her name. She drove away alone with the Count, in a vehicle which she did not particularly notice at the time.

Her first question, on leaving the terminus, referred to Miss Halcombe. The Count informed her that Miss Halcombe had not yet gone to Cumber-land; after-consideration having caused him to doubt the prudence of her taking so long a journey without some days' previous rest.

Lady Glyde next inquired whether her sister was then staying in the Count's house. Her recollection of the answer was confused, her only distinct impression in relation to it being that the Count declared he was then taking her to see Miss Halcombe. Lady Glyde's experience of London was so limited, that she could not tell, at the time, through what streets they were driving. But they never left the streets, and they never passed any gardens or trees. When the carriage stopped, it stopped in a small street, behind a square—a square in which there were shops, and public buildings, and many people. From these recollections (of which Lady Glyde was certain) it seems quite clear that Count Fosco did not take her to his own residence in the suburb of St John's Wood.

They entered the house, and went up-stairs to a back-room, either on the first or second floor. The luggage was carefully brought in. A female servant opened the door; and a man with a dark beard, apparently a foreigner, met them in the hall, and with great politeness showed them the way up-stairs. In answer to Lady Glyde's inquiries, the Count assured her that Miss Halcombe was in the house, and that she should be immediately informed of her sister's arrival. He and the foreigner then went away, and left her by herself in the room. It was poorly furnished as a sitting-room, and it looked out on the backs of houses.

The place was remarkably quiet; no footsteps went up or down the stairs—she only heard in the room beneath her a dull, rumbling sound of men's voices talking. Before she had been long left alone, the Count returned, to explain that Miss Halcombe was then taking rest, and could not be disturbed for a little while. He was accompanied into the room by a gentleman (an Englishman) whom he begged to present as a friend of his.

After this singular introduction—in the course of which no names, to the best of Lady Glyde's recollection, had been mentioned—she was left alone with the stranger. He was perfectly civil; but he startled and confused her by some odd questions about herself, and by looking at her, while he asked them, in a strange manner. After remaining a short time, he went out; and a minute or two afterwards a second stranger—also an Englishman—came in. This person introduced himself as another friend of Count Fosco's; and he, in his turn, looked at her very oddly, and asked some curious questions— never, as well as she could remember, addressing her by name; and going out again, after a little while, like the first man. By this time, she was so frightened about herself, and so uneasy about her sister, that she had thoughts of venturing down stairs again, and claiming the protection and assistance of the only woman she had seen in the house—the servant who answered the door.

Just as she had risen from her chair, the Count came back into the room. The moment he appeared, she asked anxiously how long the meeting between her sister and herself was to be still delayed. At first, he returned an evasive answer; but, on being pressed, he acknowledged, with great apparent reluctance, that Miss Halcombe was by no means so well as he had hitherto represented her to be. His tone and manner, in making this reply, so alarmed Lady Glyde, or rather so painfully increased the uneasiness which she had felt in the company of the two strangers, that a sudden faintness overcame her, and she was obliged to ask for a glass of water. The Count called from the door for water, and for a bottle of smelling-salts. Both were brought in by the foreign-looking man with the beard. The water, when Lady Glyde attempted to drink it, had so strange a taste that it increased her faintness; and she hastily took the bottle of salts from Count Fosco, and smelt at it. Her head became giddy on the instant. The Count caught the bottle as it dropped out of her hand; and the last impression of which she was conscious was that he held it to her nostrils again.

From this point, her recollections were found to be confused, fragmentary, and difficult to reconcile with any reasonable probability.

Her own impression was that she recovered her senses later in the evening; that she then left the house; that she went (as she had previously arranged to go, at Blackwater Park) to Mrs Vesey's; that she drank tea there; and that she passed the night under Mrs Vesey's roof. She was totally unable to say how, or when, or in what company, she left the house to which Count Fosco had brought her. But she persisted in asserting that she had been to Mrs Vesey's; and, still more extraordinary, that she had been helped to undress and get to bed by Mrs Rubelle! She could not remember what the conversation was at Mrs Vesey's, or whom she saw there besides that lady, or why Mrs Rubelle should have been present in the house to help her.

Her recollection of what happened to her the next morning, was still more vague and unreliable.

She had some dim idea of driving out (at what hour she could not say) with Count Fosco—and with Mrs Rubelle, again, for a female attendant. But when, and why, she left Mrs Vesey she could not tell; neither did she know what direction the carriage drove in, or where it set her down, or whether the Count and Mrs Rubelle did or did not remain with her all the time she was out. At this point in her sad story there was a total blank. She had no impressions of the faintest kind to communicate—no idea whether one day, or more than one day, had passed—until she came to herself suddenly in a strange place, surrounded by women who were all unknown to her.

This was the Asylum. Here she first heard herself called by Anne Catherick's name; and here, as a last remarkable circumstance in the story of the conspiracy, her own eyes informed her that she had Anne Catherick's clothes on. The nurse, on the first night in the Asylum, had shown her the marks on each article of her underclothing as it was taken off, and had said, not at all irritably or unkindly, 'Look at your own name on your own clothes, and don't worry us all any more about being Lady Glyde. She's dead and buried; and you're alive and hearty. Do look at your clothes now! There it is, in good marking-ink; and there you will find it on all your old things, which we have kept in the house—Anne Catherick, as plain as print!' And there it was, when Miss Halcombe examined the linen her sister wore, on the night of their arrival at Limmeridge House.

These were the only recollections—all of them uncertain, and some of them contradictory—which could be extracted from Lady Glyde, by careful questioning, on the journey to Cumberland. Miss Halcombe abstained from pressing her with any inquiries relating to events in the Asylum: her mind being but too evidently unfit to bear the trial of reverting to them. It was known, by the voluntary admission of the owner of the madhouse, that she was received there on the twenty-seventh of July. From that date, until the fifteenth of October (the day of her rescue), she had been under restraint; her identity with Anne Catherick systematically asserted, and her sanity, from first to last, practically denied. Faculties less delicately balanced, constitutions less tenderly organised, must have suffered under such an ordeal as this. No man could have gone through it, and come out of it unchanged.

Arriving at Limmeridge late on the evening of the fifteenth, Miss Halcombe wisely resolved not to attempt the assertion of Lady Glyde's identity, until the next day.

The first thing in the morning, she went to Mr Fairlie's room; and, using all possible cautions and preparations beforehand, at last told him, in so many words, what had happened. As soon as his first astonishment and alarm had subsided, he angrily declared that Miss Halcombe had allowed herself to be duped by Anne Catherick. He referred her to Count Fosco's letter, and to what she had herself told him of the personal resemblance between Anne and his deceased niece; and he positively declined to admit to his presence, even for one minute only, a madwoman whom it was an insult and an outrage to have brought into his house at all.

Miss Halcombe left the room; waited till the first heat of her indignation had passed away; decided, on reflection, that Mr Fairlie should see his niece, in the interests of common humanity, before he closed his doors on her as a stranger; and, thereupon, without a word of previous warning, took Lady Glyde with her to his room. The servant was posted at the door to prevent their entrance; but Miss Halcombe insisted on passing him, and made her way into Mr Fairlie's presence, leading her sister by the hand.

The scene that followed, though it only lasted for a few minutes, was too painful to be described—Miss Halcombe herself shrank from referring to it. Let it be enough to say that Mr Fairlie declared, in the most positive terms, that he did not recognise the woman who had been brought into his room; that he saw nothing in her face and manner to make him doubt for a moment that his niece lay buried in Limmeridge churchyard; and that he would call on the law to protect him if before the day was over she was not removed from the house.

Taking the very worst view of Mr Fairlie's selfishness, indolence, and habitual want of feeling, it was manifestly impossible to suppose that he was capable of such infamy as secretly recognising and openly disowning his brother's child. Miss Halcombe humanely and sensibly allowed all due force to the influence of prejudice and alarm in preventing him from fairly exercising his perceptions; and accounted for what had happened, in that way. But when she next put the servants to the test, and found that they too were, in every case, uncertain, to say the least of it, whether the lady presented to them was their young mistress, or Anne Catherick, of whose resemblance to her they had all heard, the sad conclusion was inevitable, that the change produced in Lady Glyde's face and manner by her imprisonment in the Asylum, was far more serious than Miss Halcombe had at first supposed. The vile deception which had asserted her death, defied exposure even in the house where she was born, and among the people with whom she had lived.

In a less critical situation, the effort need not have been given up as hopeless, even yet.

For example, the maid, Fanny, who happened to be then absent from Limmeridge, was expected back in two days; and there would be a chance of gaining her recognition to start with, seeing that she had been in much more constant communication with her mistress, and had been much more heartily attached to her than the other servants. Again, Lady Glyde might have been privately kept in the house, or in the village, to wait until her health was a little recovered, and her mind was a little steadied again. When her memory could be once more trusted to serve her, she would naturally refer to persons and events, in the past, with a certainty and a familiarity which no impostor could simulate; and so the fact of her identity, which her own appearance had failed to establish, might subsequently be proved, with time to help her, by the surer test of her own words.

But the circumstances under which she had regained her freedom, rendered all recourse to such means as these simply impracticable. The pursuit from the Asylum, diverted to Hampshire for the time only, would infallibly next take the direction of Cumberland. The persons appointed to seek the fugitive, might arrive at Limmeridge House at a few hours' notice; and in Mr Fairlie's present temper of mind, they might count on the immediate exertion of his local influence and authority to assist them. The commonest consideration for Lady Glyde's safety, forced on Miss Halcombe the necessity of resigning the struggle to do her justice, and of removing her at once from the place of all others that was now most dangerous to her—the neighbourhood of her own home.

An immediate return to London was the first and wisest measure of security which suggested itself. In the great city all traces of them might be most speedily and most surely effaced. There were no preparations to make—no farewell words of kindness to exchange with any one. On the afternoon of that memorable day of the sixteenth, Miss Halcombe roused her sister to a last exertion of courage; and, without a living soul to wish them well at parting, the two took their way into the world alone, and turned their backs for ever on Limmeridge House.

They had passed the hill above the churchyard, when Lady Glyde insisted on turning back to look her last at her mother's grave. Miss Halcombe tried to shake her resolution; but, in this one instance, tried in vain. She was immovable. Her dim eyes lit with a sudden fire, and flashed through the veil that hung over them; her wasted fingers strengthened, moment by moment, round the friendly arm, by which they had held so listlessly till this time. I believe in my soul that the Hand of God was pointing their way back to them; and that the most innocent and the most afflicted of His creatures was chosen, in that dread moment, to see it.

They retraced their steps to the burial-ground; and by that act sealed the future of our three lives.

III

THIS was the story of the past—the story, so far as we knew it then.

Two obvious conclusions presented themselves to my mind, after hearing it. In the first place, I saw darkly what the nature of the conspiracy had been; how chances had been watched, and how circumstances had been handled to ensure impunity to a daring and an intricate crime. While all details were still a mystery to me, the vile manner in which the personal resemblance between the woman in white and Lady Glyde had been turned to account, was clear beyond a doubt. It was plain that Anne Catherick had been introduced into Count Fosco's house as Lady Glyde; it was plain that Lady Glyde had taken the dead woman's place in the Asylum—the substitution having been so managed as to make innocent people (the doctor and the two servants certainly; and the owner of the madhouse in all probability) accomplices in the crime.

The second conclusion came as the necessary consequence of the first. We three had no mercy to expect from Count Fosco and Sir Percival Glyde. The success of the conspiracy had brought with it a clear gain to those two men of thirty thousand pounds—twenty thousand to one: ten thousand to the other, through his wife. They had that interest, as well as other interests, in ensuring their impunity from exposure; and they would leave no stone unturned, no sacrifice unattempted, no treachery untried, to discover the place in which their victim was concealed, and to part her from the only friends she had in the world—Marian Halcombe and myself.

The sense of this serious peril—a peril which every day and every hour might bring nearer and nearer to us—was the one influence that guided me in fixing the place of our retreat. I chose it in the far East of London, where there were fewest idle people to lounge and look about them in the streets. I chose it in a poor and a populous neighbourhood—because the harder the struggle for existence among the men and women about us, the less the risk of their having the time or taking the pains to notice chance strangers who came among them. These were the great advantages I looked to; but our locality was a gain to us also, in another and a hardly less important respect. We could live cheaply by the daily work of my hands; and could save every farthing we possessed to forward the purpose—the righteous purpose of redressing an infamous wrong, which, from first to last, I now kept steadily in view.

In a week's time, Marian Halcombe and I had settled how the course of our new lives should be directed.

There were no other lodgers in the house; and we had the means of going in and out without passing through the shop. I arranged, for the present at least, that neither Marian nor Laura should stir outside the door without my being with them; and that, in my absence from home, they should let no one into their rooms on any pretence whatever. This rule established, I went to a friend whom I had known in former days—a wood engraver, in large practice—to seek for employment; telling him, at the same time, that I had reasons for wishing to remain unknown.

He at once concluded that I was in debt; expressed his regret in the usual forms; and then promised to do what he could to assist me. I left his false impression undisturbed; and accepted the work he had to give. He knew that he could trust my experience and my industry. I had, what he wanted, steadiness and facility; and though my earnings were but small, they sufficed for our necessities. As soon as we could feel certain of this, Marian Halcombe and I put together what we possessed. She had between two and three hundred pounds left of her own property; and I had nearly as much remaining from the purchase-money obtained by the sale of my drawing-master's practice before I left England. Together we made up between us more than four hundred pounds. I deposited this little fortune in a bank, to be kept for the expense of those secret inquiries and investigations which I was determined to set on foot, and to carry on by myself if I could find no one to help me. We calculated our weekly expenditure to the last farthing; and we never touched our little fund, except in Laura's interests and for Laura's sake.

The house-work, which, if we had dared trust a stranger near us, would have been done by a servant, was taken on the first day, taken as her own right, by Marian Halcombe. 'What a woman's hands *are* fit for,' she said, 'early and late, these hands of mine shall do.' They trembled as she held them out. The wasted arms told their sad story of the past, as she turned up the sleeves of the poor plain dress that she wore for safety's sake; but the unquenchable spirit of the woman burnt bright in her even yet. I saw the big tears rise thick in her eyes, and fall slowly over her cheeks as she looked at me. She dashed them away with a touch of her old energy, and smiled with a faint reflexion of her old good spirits. 'Don't doubt my courage, Walter,' she pleaded, 'it's my weakness that cries, not *me*. The house-work shall conquer it, if *I* can't.' And she kept her word—the victory was won when we met in the evening, and she sat down to rest. Her large steady black eyes looked at me with a flash of their bright firmness of bygone days. 'I am not quite broken down yet,' she said; 'I am worth trusting with my share of the work.' Before I could answer, she added in a whisper, 'And worth trusting with my share in the risk and the danger, too. Remember that, if the time comes!'

I did remember it, when the time came.

As early as the end of October, the daily course of our lives had assumed its settled direction; and we three were as completely isolated in our place of concealment, as if the house we lived in had been a desert island, and the great network of streets and the thousands of our fellow-creatures all round us the waters of an illimitable sea. I could now reckon on some leisure time for considering what my future plan of action should be, and how I might arm myself most securely, at the outset, for the coming struggle with Sir Percival and the Count.

I gave up all hope of appealing to my recognition of Laura, or to Marian's recognition of her, in proof of her identity. If we had loved her less dearly,

if the instinct implanted in us by that love had not been far more certain
than any exercise of reasoning, far keener than any process of observation,
even we might have hesitated, on first seeing her.

The outward changes wrought by the suffering and the terror of the past
had fearfully, almost hopelessly, strengthened the fatal resemblance between
Anne Catherick and herself. In my narrative of events at the time of my
residence in Limmeridge House, I have recorded, from my own observation
of the two, how the likeness, striking as it was when viewed generally, failed
in many important points of similarity when tested in detail. In those former
days, if they had both been seen together, side by side, no person could for
a moment have mistaken them one for the other—as has happened often in
the instances of twins. I could not say this now. The sorrow and suffering
which I had once blamed myself for associating even by a passing thought
with the future of Laura Fairlie, *had* set their profaning marks on the youth
and beauty of her face; and the fatal resemblance which I had once seen
and shuddered at seeing, in idea only, was now a real and living resemblance
which asserted itself before my own eyes. Strangers, acquaintances, friends
even who could not look at her as we looked, if she had been shown to them
in the first days of her rescue from the Asylum, might have doubted if she
were the Laura Fairlie they had once seen, and doubted without blame.

The one remaining chance, which I had at first thought might be trusted
to serve us—the chance of appealing to her recollection of persons and
events with which no impostor could be familiar, was proved, by the sad test
of our later experience, to be hopeless. Every little caution that Marian and
I practised towards her; every little remedy we tried to strengthen and steady
slowly the weakened, shaken faculties, was a fresh protest in itself against the
risk of turning her mind back on the troubled and the terrible past.

The only events of former days which we ventured on encouraging her to
recal, were the little trivial domestic events of that happy time at Limmeridge, when I first went there, and taught her to draw. The day when I
roused those remembrances by showing her the sketch of the summer-house
which she had given me on the morning of our farewell, and which had
never been separated from me since, was the birthday of our first hope.
Tenderly and gradually, the memory of the old walks and drives dawned
upon her; and the poor weary pining eyes, looked at Marian and at me with
a new interest, with a faltering thoughtfulness in them, which, from that
moment, we cherished and kept alive. I bought her a little box of colours,
and a sketch-book like the old sketch-book which I had seen in her hands
on the morning when we first met. Once again—oh me, once again!—at
spare hours saved from my work, in the dull London light, in the poor
London room, I sat by her side, to guide the faltering touch, to help the
feeble hand. Day by day, I raised and raised the new interest till its place in
the blank of her existence was at last assured—till she could think of her

drawing, and talk of it, and patiently practise it by herself, with some faint reflexion of the innocent pleasure in my encouragement, the growing enjoyment in her own progress which belonged to the lost life and the lost happiness of past days.

We helped her mind slowly by this simple means; we took her out between us to walk, on fine days, in a quiet old City square, near at hand, where there was nothing to confuse or alarm her; we spared a few pounds from the fund at the banker's to get her wine, and the delicate strengthening food that she required; we amused her in the evenings with children's games at cards, with scrap-books full of prints which I borrowed from the engraver who employed me—by these, and other trifling attentions like them, we composed her and steadied her, and hoped all things, as cheerfully as we could, from time and care, and love that never neglected and never despaired of her. But to take her mercilessly from seclusion and repose; to confront her with strangers, or with acquaintances who were little better than strangers; to rouse the painful impressions of her past life which we had so carefully hushed to rest—this, even in her own interests, we dared not do. Whatever sacrifices it cost, whatever long, weary, heart-breaking delays it involved, the wrong that had been inflicted on her, if mortal means could grapple it, must be redressed without her knowledge and without her help.

This resolution settled, it was next necessary to decide how the first risk should be ventured, and what the first proceedings should be.

After consulting with Marian, I resolved to begin by gathering together as many facts as could be collected—then, to ask the advice of Mr Kyrle (whom we knew we could trust); and to ascertain from him, in the first instance, if the legal remedy lay fairly within our reach. I owed it to Laura's interests not to stake her whole future on my own unaided exertions, so long as there was the faintest prospect of strengthening our position by obtaining reliable assistance of any kind.

The first source of information to which I applied, was the journal kept at Blackwater Park by Marian Halcombe. There were passages in this diary, relating to myself, which she thought it best that I should not see. Accordingly, she read to me from the manuscript, and I took the notes I wanted as she went on. We could only find time to pursue this occupation by sitting up late at night. Three nights were devoted to the purpose, and were enough to put me in possession of all that Marian could tell.

My next proceeding was to gain as much additional evidence as I could procure from other people, without exciting suspicion. I went myself to Mrs Vesey to ascertain if Laura's impression of having slept there, was correct or not. In this case, from consideration for Mrs Vesey's age and infirmity, and in all subsequent cases of the same kind from considerations of caution, I kept our real position a secret, and was always careful to speak of Laura as 'the late Lady Glyde.'

Mrs Vesey's answer to my inquiries only confirmed the apprehensions which I had previously felt. Laura had certainly written to say she would pass the night under the roof of her old friend—but she had never been near the house.

Her mind, in this instance, and, as I feared, in other instances besides, confusedly presented to her something which she had only intended to do in the false light of something which she had really done. The unconscious contradiction of herself was easy to account for in this way—but it was likely to lead to serious results. It was a stumble on the threshold at starting; it was a flaw in the evidence which told fatally against us.

When I next asked for the letter which Laura had written to Mrs Vesey from Blackwater Park, it was given to me without the envelope, which had been thrown into the waste-paper basket, and long since destroyed. In the letter itself, no date was mentioned—not even the day of the week. It only contained these lines:—'Dearest Mrs Vesey, I am in sad distress and anxiety, and I may come to your house to-morrow night, and ask for a bed. I can't tell you what is the matter in this letter—I write it in such fear of being found out that I can fix my mind on nothing. Pray be at home to see me. I will give you a thousand kisses, and tell you everything. Your affectionate Laura.' What help was there in those lines? None.

On returning from Mrs Vesey's, I instructed Marian to write (observing the same caution which I practised myself) to Mrs Michelson. She was to express, if she pleased, some general suspicion of Count Fosco's conduct; and she was to ask the house-keeper to supply us with a plain statement of events, in the interests of truth. While we were waiting for the answer, which reached us in a week's time, I went to the doctor in St John's Wood; introducing myself as sent by Miss Halcombe to collect, if possible, more particulars of her sister's last illness than Mr Kyrle had found the time to procure. By Mr Goodricke's assistance, I obtained a copy of the certificate of death, and an interview with the woman (Jane Gould) who had been employed to prepare the body for the grave. Through this person, I also discovered a means of communicating with the servant, Hester Pinhorn. She had recently left her place, in consequence of a disagreement with her mistress; and she was lodging with some people in the neighbourhood whom Mrs Gould knew. In the manner here indicated, I obtained the Narratives of the housekeeper, of the doctor, of Jane Gould, and of Hester Pinhorn, exactly as they are presented in these pages.

Furnished with such additional evidence as these documents afforded, I considered myself to be sufficiently prepared for a consultation with Mr Kyrle; and Marian wrote accordingly to mention my name to him, and to specify the day and hour at which I requested to see him on private business.

There was time enough, in the morning, for me to take Laura out for her walk as usual, and to see her quietly settled at her drawing afterwards. She looked up at me with a new anxiety in her face, as I rose to leave the room; and her fingers began to toy doubtfully, in the old way, with the brushes and pencils on the table.

'You are not tired of me yet?' she said. 'You are not going away because you are tired of me? I will try to do better—I will try to get well. Are you as fond of me, Walter, as you used to be, now I am so pale and thin, and so slow in learning to draw?'

She spoke as a child might have spoken; she showed me her thoughts as a child might have shown them. I waited a few minutes longer—waited to tell her that she was dearer to me now than she had ever been in the past times. 'Try to get well again,' I said, encouraging the new hope in the future which I saw dawning in her mind; 'try to get well again, for Marian's sake and for mine.'

'Yes,' she said to herself, returning to her drawing. 'I must try, because they are both so fond of me.' She suddenly looked up again. 'Don't be gone long! I can't get on with my drawing, Walter, when you are not here to help me.'

'I shall soon be back, my darling—soon be back to see how you are getting on.'

My voice faltered a little in spite of me. I forced myself from the room. It was no time, then, for parting with the self-control which might yet serve me in my need before the day was out.

As I opened the door, I beckoned to Marian to follow me to the stairs. It was necessary to prepare her for a result which I felt might sooner or later follow my showing myself openly in the streets.

'I shall, in all probability, be back in a few hours,' I said; 'and you will take care, as usual, to let no one inside the doors in my absence. But if anything happens——'

'What can happen?' she interposed, quickly. 'Tell me plainly, Walter, if there is any danger—and I shall know how to meet it.'

'The only danger,' I replied, 'is that Sir Percival Glyde may have been recalled to London by the news of Laura's escape. You are aware that he had me watched before I left England; and that he probably knows me by sight, although I don't know him?'

She laid her hand on my shoulder, and looked at me in anxious silence. I saw she understood the serious risk that threatened us.

'It is not likely,' I said, 'that I shall be seen in London again so soon, either by Sir Percival himself or by the persons in his employ. But it is barely possible that an accident may happen. In that case, you will not be alarmed if I fail to return to-night; and you will satisfy any inquiries of Laura's with the best excuse that you can make for me? If I find the least reason to suspect that I am watched, I will take good care that no spy follows me back to this house. Don't doubt my return, Marian, however it may be delayed—and fear nothing.'

'Nothing!' she answered, firmly. 'You shall not regret, Walter, that you have only a woman to help you.' She paused, and detained me for a moment longer. 'Take care!' she said, pressing my hand anxiously—'take care!'

I left her; and set forth to pave the way for discovery—the dark and doubtful way, which began at the lawyer's door.

IV

No circumstance of the slightest importance happened on my way to the offices of Messrs. Gilmore and Kyrle, in Chancery-lane.

While my card was being taken in to Mr Kyrle, a consideration occurred to me which I deeply regretted not having thought of before. The information derived from Marian's diary made it a matter of certainty that Count Fosco had opened her first letter from Blackwater Park to Mr Kyrle, and had, by means of his wife, intercepted the second. He was therefore well aware of the address of the office; and he would naturally infer that if Marian wanted advice and assistance, after Laura's escape from the Asylum, she would apply once more to the experience of Mr Kyrle. In this case, the office in Chancery-lane was the very first place which he and Sir Percival would cause to be watched; and, if the same persons were chosen for the purpose who had been employed to follow me, before my departure from England, the fact of my return would in all probability be ascertained on that very day. I had thought, generally, of the chances of my being recognised in the streets; but the special risk connected with the office had never occurred to me until the present moment. It was too late now to repair this unfortunate error in judgment—too late to wish that I had made arrangements for meeting the lawyer in some place privately appointed beforehand. I could only resolve to be cautious on leaving Chancery-lane, and not to go straight home again under any circumstances whatever.

After waiting a few minutes, I was shown into Mr Kyrle's private room. He was a pale, thin, quiet, self-possessed man, with a very attentive eye, a very low voice, and a very undemonstrative manner; not (as I judged) ready with his sympathy, where strangers were concerned; and not at all easy to disturb in his professional composure. A better man for my purpose could hardly have been found. If he committed himself to a decision at all, and if the decision was favourable, the strength of our case was as good as proved from that moment.

'Before I enter on the business which brings me here,' I said, 'I ought to warn you, Mr Kyrle, that the shortest statement I can make of it may occupy some little time.'

'My time is at Miss Halcombe's disposal,' he replied. 'Where any interests of hers are concerned. I represent my partner personally as well as professionally. It was his request that I should do so, when he ceased to take an active part in business.'

'May I inquire whether Mr Gilmore is in England?'

'He is not: he is living with his relatives in Germany. His health has improved, but the period of his return is still uncertain.'

While we were exchanging these few preliminary words, he had been searching among the papers before him, and he now produced from them a sealed letter. I thought he was about to hand the letter to me; but, apparently changing his mind, he placed it by itself on the table, settled himself in his chair, and silently waited to hear what I had to say.

Without wasting a moment in prefatory words of any sort, I entered on my narrative, and put him in full possession of the events which have already been related in these pages.

Lawyer as he was to the very marrow of his bones, I startled him out of his professional composure. Expressions of incredulity and surprise, which he could not repress, interrupted me several times, before I had done. I persevered, however, to the end, and as soon as I reached it, boldly asked the one important question:

'What is your opinion, Mr Kyrle?'

He was too cautious to commit himself to an answer, without taking time to recover his self-possession first.

'Before I give my opinion,' he said, 'I must beg permission to clear the ground by a few questions.'

He put the questions—sharp, suspicious, unbelieving questions, which clearly showed me, as they proceeded, that he thought I was the victim of a delusion; and that he might even have doubted, but for my introduction to him by Miss Halcombe, whether I was not attempting the perpetration of a cunningly-designed fraud.

'Do you believe that I have spoken the truth, Mr Kyrle?' I asked, when he had done examining me.

'So far as your own convictions are concerned, I am certain you have spoken the truth,' he replied. 'I have the highest esteem for Miss Halcombe, and I have therefore every reason to respect a gentleman whose mediation she trusts in a matter of this kind. I will even go farther, if you like, and admit, for courtesy's sake and for argument's sake, that the identity of Lady Glyde, as a living person, is a proved fact to Miss Halcombe and yourself. But you come to me for a legal opinion. As a lawyer, and as a lawyer only, it is my duty to tell you, Mr Hartright, that you have not the shadow of a case.'

'You put it strongly, Mr Kyrle.'

'I will try to put it plainly as well. The evidence of Lady Glyde's death is, on the face of it, clear and satisfactory. There is her aunt's testimony to prove that she came to Count Fosco's house, that she fell ill, and that she died. There is the testimony of the medical certificate to prove the death, and to show that it took place under natural circumstances. There is the fact of the funeral at Limmeridge, and there is the assertion of the inscription on the tomb. That is the case you want to overthrow. What evidence have you to support the declaration on your side that the person who died and was buried was not Lady Glyde? Let us run through the main points of your statement and see what they are worth. Miss Halcombe goes to a certain private Asylum, and there sees a certain female patient. It is known that a woman named Anne Catherick, and bearing an extraordinary personal resemblance to Lady Glyde, escaped from the Asylum; it is known that the person received there last July, was received as Anne Catherick brought back; it is known that the gentleman who brought her back warned Mr Fairlie that it was part of her insanity to be bent on personating his dead niece; and it is known that she did repeatedly declare herself, in the Asylum (where no one believed her), to be Lady Glyde. These are all facts. What have you to set against them? Miss Halcombe's recognition of the woman, which recognition after-events invalidate or contradict. Does Miss Halcombe assert her supposed sister's identity to the owner of the Asylum, and take legal means for rescuing her? No: she secretly bribes a nurse to let her escape. When the patient has been released in this doubtful manner, and is taken to Mr Fairlie, does he recognise her? is he staggered for one instant in his belief of his niece's death? No. Do the servants recognise her? No. Is she kept in the neighbourhood to assert her own identity, and to stand the test of further proceedings? No: she is privately taken to London. In the mean time, you have recognised her also—but you are not a relative; you are not even an old friend of the family. The servants contradict you; and Mr Fairlie contradicts Miss Halcombe; and the supposed Lady Glyde contradicts herself. She declares she passed the night in London at a certain house. Your own evidence shows that she has never been near that house; and your own admission is, that her condition of mind prevents you from producing her anywhere to submit to investigation, and to speak for herself. I pass over minor points of evidence, on both sides, to save time; and I ask you, if this case were to go now into a court of law—to go before a jury, bound to take facts as they reasonably appear—where are your proofs?'

I was obliged to wait and collect myself before I could answer him. It was the first time the story of Laura and the story of Marian had been presented to me from a stranger's point of view—the first time the terrible obstacles that lay across our path had been made to show themselves in their true character.

'There can be no doubt,' I said, 'that the facts, as you have stated them, appear to tell against us; but——'

'But you think those facts can be explained away,' interposed Mr Kyrle. 'Let me tell you the result of my experience on that point. When an English jury has to choose between a plain fact, *on* the surface, and a long explanation *under* the surface, it always takes the fact, in preference to the explanation. For example, Lady Glyde (I call the lady you represent by that name for argument's sake) declares she has slept at a certain house, and it is proved that she has not slept at that house. You explain this circumstance by entering into the state of her mind, and deducing from it a metaphysical conclusion. I don't say the conclusion is wrong—I only say that the jury will take the fact of her contradicting herself, in preference to any reason for the contradiction that you can offer.'

'But is it not possible,' I urged, 'by dint of patience and exertion, to discover additional evidence? Miss Halcombe and I have a few hundred pounds——'

He looked at me with a half-suppressed pity, and shook his head.

'Consider the subject, Mr Hartright, from your own point of view,' he said. 'If you are right about Sir Percival Glyde and Count Fosco (which I don't admit, mind), every imaginable difficulty would be thrown in the way of your getting fresh evidence. Every obstacle of litigation would be raised; every point in the case would be systematically contested—and by the time we had spent our thousands, instead of our hundreds, the final result would, in all probability, be against us. Questions of identity, where instances of personal resemblance are concerned, are, in themselves, the hardest of all questions to settle—the hardest, even when they are free from the complications which beset the case we are now discussing. I really see no prospect of throwing any light whatever on this extraordinary affair. Even if the person buried in Limmeridge churchyard be not Lady Glyde, she was, in life, on your own showing, so like her, that we should gain nothing, if we applied for the necessary authority to have the body exhumed. In short, there is no case, Mr Hartright—there is really no case.'

I was determined to believe that there *was* a case; and, in that determination, shifted my ground, and appealed to him once more.

'Are there not other proofs that we might produce, besides the proof of identity?' I asked.

'Not as you are situated,' he replied. 'The simplest and surest of all proofs, the proof by comparison of dates, is, as I understand, altogether out of your reach. If you could show a discrepancy between the date of the doctor's certificate and the date of Lady Glyde's journey to London, the matter would wear a totally different aspect; and I should be the first to say, Let us go on.'

'That date may yet be recovered, Mr Kyrle.'

'On the day when it *is* recovered, Mr Hartright, you will have a case. If you have any prospect, at this moment, of getting at it—tell me, and we shall see if I can advise you.'

I considered. The housekeeper could not help us; Laura could not help us; Marian could not help us. In all probability, the only persons in existence who knew the date were Sir Percival and the Count.

'I can think of no means of ascertaining the date at present,' I said, 'because I can think of no persons who are sure to know it, but Count Fosco and Sir Percival Glyde.'

Mr Kyrle's calmly-attentive face relaxed, for the first time, into a smile.

'With your opinion of the conduct of those two gentlemen,' he said, 'you don't expect help in that quarter, I presume? If they have combined to gain large sums of money by a conspiracy, they are not likely to confess it, at any rate.'

'They may be forced to confess it, Mr Kyrle.'

'By whom?'

'By me.'

We both rose. He looked me attentively in the face with more appearance of interest than he had shown yet. I could see that I had perplexed him a little.

'You are very determined,' he said. 'You have, no doubt, a personal motive for proceeding, into which it is not my business to inquire. If a case can be produced in the future, I can only say, my best assistance is at your service. At the same time, I must warn you, as the money question always enters into the law question, that I see little hope, even if you ultimately established the fact of Lady Glyde's being alive, of recovering her fortune. The foreigner would probably leave the country, before proceedings were commenced; and Sir Percival's embarrassments are numerous enough and pressing enough to transfer almost any sum of money he may possess from himself to his creditors. You are, of course, aware——'

I stopped him at that point.

'Let me beg that we may not discuss Lady Glyde's affairs,' I said. 'I have never known anything about them, in former times; and I know nothing of them now—except that her fortune is lost. You are right in assuming that I have personal motives for stirring in this matter. I wish those motives to be always as disinterested as they are at the present moment——'

He tried to interpose and explain. I was a little heated, I suppose, by feeling that he had doubted me; and I went on bluntly, without waiting to hear him.

'There shall be no money-motive,' I said, 'no idea of personal advantage, in the service I mean to render to Lady Glyde. She has been cast out as a stranger from the house in which she was born—a lie which records her death has been written on her mother's tomb—and there are two men, alive and unpunished, who are responsible for it. That house shall open again to receive her, in the presence of every soul who followed the false funeral to the grave; that lie shall be publicly erased from the tombstone, by the authority of the head of the family; and those two men shall answer for their crime to ME, though the justice that sits in tribunals is powerless to pursue them. I have given my life to that purpose; and, alone as I stand, if God spares me, I will accomplish it.'

He drew back towards his table, and said nothing. His face showed plainly that he thought my delusion had got the better of my reason, and that he considered it totally useless to give me any more advice.

'We each keep our opinion, Mr Kyrle,' I said; 'and we must wait till the events of the future decide between us. In the mean time, I am much obliged to you for the attention you have given to my statement. You have shown me that the legal remedy lies, in every sense of the word, beyond our means. We cannot produce the law-proof; and we are not rich enough to pay the law-expenses. It is something gained to know that.'

I bowed, and walked to the door. He called me back, and gave me the letter which I had seen him place on the table by itself at the beginning of our interview.

'This came by post, a few days ago,' he said. 'Perhaps you will not mind delivering it? Pray tell Miss Halcombe, at the same time, that I sincerely regret being, thus far, unable to help her—except by advice, which will not be more welcome, I am afraid, to her than to you.'

I looked at the letter while he was speaking. It was addressed to 'Miss Halcombe. Care of Messrs. Gilmore and Kyrle, Chancery-lane.' The hand-writing was quite unknown to me.

On leaving the room, I asked one last question.

'Do you happen to know,' I said, 'if Sir Percival Glyde is still in Paris?'

'He has returned to London,' replied Mr Kyrle. 'At least, I heard so from his solicitor, whom I met yesterday.'

After that answer I went out.

On leaving the office, the first precaution to be observed was to abstain from attracting attention by stopping to look about me. I walked towards one of the quietest of the large squares on the north of Holborn—then suddenly stopped, and turned round at a place where a long stretch of pavement was left behind me.

There were two men at the corner of the square who had stopped also, and who were standing talking together. After a moment's reflexion, I turned back, so as to pass them. One moved, as I came near, and turned the corner, leading from the square, into the street. The other remained stationary. I looked at him, as I passed, and instantly recognised one of the men who had watched me before I left England.

If I had been free to follow my own instincts, I should probably have begun by speaking to the man, and have ended by knocking him down. But I was bound to consider consequences. If I once placed myself publicly in the wrong, I put the weapons at once into Sir Percival's hands. There was no choice but to oppose cunning by cunning. I turned into the street down which the second man had disappeared, and passed him, waiting in a doorway. He was a stranger to me; and I was glad to make sure of his personal appearance, in case of future annoyance. Having done this, I again walked northward, till I reached the New-road. There, I turned aside to the west (having the men behind me all the time), and waited at a point where I knew myself to be at some distance from a cab-stand, until a fast two-wheeled cab, empty, should happen to pass me. One passed in a few minutes. I jumped in, and told the man to drive rapidly towards Hyde Park. There was no second fast cab for the spies behind me. I saw them dart across to the other side of the road, to follow me by running, until a cab, or a cab-stand, came in their way. But I had the start of them; and when I stopped the driver, and got out, they were nowhere in sight. I crossed Hyde Park, and made sure, on the open ground, that I was free. When I at last turned my steps homewards, it was not till many hours later—not till after dark.

I found Marian waiting for me, alone in the little sitting-room. She had persuaded Laura to go to rest, after first promising to show me her drawing, the moment I came in. The poor little dim faint sketch—so trifling in itself, so touching in its associations—was propped up carefully on the table with two books, and was placed where the faint light of the one candle we allowed ourselves might fall on it to the best advantage. I sat down to look at the drawing, and to tell Marian, in whispers, what had happened. The partition which divided us from the next room was so thin that we could almost hear Laura's breathing, and we might have disturbed her if we had spoken aloud.

Marian preserved her composure while I described my interview with Mr Kyrle. But her face became troubled when I spoke next of the men who had followed me from the lawyer's office, and when I told her of the discovery of Sir Percival's return.

'Bad news, Walter,' she said; 'the worst news you could bring. Have you nothing more to tell me?'

'I have something to give you,' I replied, handing her the note which Mr Kyrle had confided to my care.

She looked at the address, and recognised the handwriting instantly.

'You know your correspondent?' I said.

'Too well,' she answered. 'My correspondent is Count Fosco.'

With that reply she opened the note. Her face flushed deeply while she read it—her eyes brightened with anger, as she handed it to me to read in my turn.

The note contained these lines:

'Impelled by honourable admiration—honourable to myself, honourable to you—I write, magnificent Marian, in the interests of your tranquillity, to say two consoling words:

'Fear nothing!

'Exercise your fine natural sense, and remain in retirement. Dear and admirable woman! invite no dangerous publicity. Resignation is sublime—adopt it. The modest repose of home is eternally fresh—enjoy it. The Storms of life pass harmless over the valley of Seclusion—dwell, dear lady, in the valley.

'Do this; and I authorise you to fear nothing. No new calamity shall lacerate your sensibilities—sensibilities precious to me as my own. You shall not be molested; the fair companion of your retreat shall not be pursued. She has found a new asylum, in your heart. Priceless asylum!—I envy her, and leave her there.

'One last word of affectionate warning, of paternal caution—and I tear myself from the charm of addressing you; I close these fervent lines.

'Advance no farther than you have gone already; compromise no serious interests; threaten nobody. Do not, I implore you, force me into action—ME, the Man of Action—when it is the cherished object of my ambition to be passive, to restrict the vast reach of my energies and my combinations, for your sake. If you have rash friends, moderate their deplorable ardour. If Mr Hartright returns to England, hold no communication with him. I walk on a path of my own; and Percival follows at my heels. On the day when Mr Hartright crosses that path, he is a lost man.'

The only signature to these lines was the initial letter F, surrounded by a circle of intricate flourishes. I threw the letter on the table, with all the contempt that I felt for it.

'He is trying to frighten you—a sure sign that he is frightened himself,' I said.

She was too genuine a woman to treat the letter as I treated it. The insolent familiarity of the language was too much for her self-control. As she looked at me across the table, her hands clenched themselves in her lap, and the old quick fiery temper flamed out again, brightly, in her cheeks and her eyes.

'Walter!' she said, 'if ever those two men are at your mercy, and if you are obliged to spare one of them—don't let it be the Count.'

'I will keep his letter, Marian, to help my memory when the time comes.'

She looked at me attentively as I put the letter away in my pocket-book.

'When the time comes?' she repeated. 'Can you speak of the future as if you were certain of it?—certain after what you have heard in Mr Kyrle's office, after what has happened to you to-day?'

'I don't count the time from to-day, Marian. All I have done to-day, is to ask another man to act for me. I count from to-morrow——'

'Why from to-morrow?'

'Because to-morrow I mean to act for myself.'

'How?'

'I shall go to Blackwater by the first train; and return, I hope, at night.'

'To Blackwater!'

'Yes. I have had time to think, since I left Mr Kyrle. His opinion, on one point, confirms my own. We must persist, to the last, in hunting down the date of Laura's journey. The one weak point in the conspiracy, and probably the one chance of proving that she is a living woman, centre in the discovery of that date.'

'You mean,' said Marian, 'the discovery that Laura did not leave Blackwater Park till *after* the date of her death on the doctor's certificate?'

'Certainly.'

'What makes you think it might have been *after*? Laura can tell us nothing of the time she was in London.'

'But the owner of the Asylum told you that she was received there on the twenty-seventh of July. I doubt Count Fosco's ability to keep her in London, and to keep her insensible to all that was passing around her, more than one night. In that case, she must have started on the twenty-sixth, and must have come to London one day after the date of her own death on the doctor's certificate. If we can prove that date, we prove our case against Sir Percival and the Count.'

'Yes, yes—I see! But how is the proof to be obtained?'

'Mrs Michelson's narrative has suggested to me two ways of trying to obtain it. One of them is to question the doctor, Mr Dawson—who must know when he resumed his attendance at Blackwater Park, after Laura left the house. The other is to make inquiries at the inn to which Sir Percival drove away by himself, at night. We know that his departure followed Laura's, after the lapse of a few hours; and we may get at the date in that way. The attempt is at least worth making—and, to-morrow, I am determined it shall be made.'

'And suppose it fails—I look at the worst, now, Walter; but I will look at the best, if disappointments come to try us—suppose no one can help you at Blackwater?'

'There are two men who can help me, and shall help me, in London—Sir Percival and the Count. Innocent people may well forget the date—but *they* are guilty, and *they* know it. If I fail everywhere else, I mean to force a confession out of one or both of them, on my own terms.'

All the woman flushed up in Marian's face, as I spoke.

'Begin with the Count!' she whispered, eagerly. 'For my sake, begin with the Count.'

'We must begin, for Laura's sake, where there is the best chance of success,' I replied.

The colour faded from her face again, and she shook her head sadly.

'Yes,' she said, 'you are right—it was mean and miserable of me to say that. I try to be patient, Walter, and succeed better now than I did in happier times. But I have a little of my old temper still left—and it *will* get the better of me when I think of the Count!'

'His turn will come,' I said. 'But, remember, there is no weak place in his life that we know of, yet.' I waited a little to let her recover her self-possession; and then spoke the decisive words:

'Marian! There is a weak place we both know of in Sir Percival's life——'

'You mean the Secret!'

'Yes: the Secret. It is our only sure hold on him. I can force him from his position of security, I can drag him and his villany into the face of day, by no other means. Whatever the Count may have done, Sir Percival has consented to the conspiracy against Laura from another motive besides the motive of gain. You heard him tell the Count that he believed his wife knew enough to ruin him? You heard him say that he was a lost man if the secret of Anne Catherick was known?'

'Yes! yes! I did.'

'Well, Marian, when our other resources have failed us, I mean to know the secret. My old superstition clings to me, even yet. I say again, the woman in white is a living influence in our three lives. The End is appointed; the End is drawing us on—and Anne Catherick, dead in her grave, points the way to it still!'

V

THE story of my first inquiries in Hampshire is soon told.

My early departure from London enabled me to reach Mr Dawson's house in the forenoon. Our interview, so far as the object of my visit was concerned, led to no satisfactory result.

Mr Dawson's books certainly showed when he had resumed his attendance on Miss Halcombe, at Blackwater Park; but it was not possible to calculate back from this date with any exactness, without such help from Mrs Michelson as I knew she was unable to afford. She could not say from memory (who, in similar cases, ever can?) how many days had elapsed between the renewal of the doctor's attendance on his patient and the previous departure of Lady Glyde. She was almost certain of having mentioned the circumstance of the departure to Miss Halcombe, on the day after it happened—but then she was no more able to fix the date of the day on which this disclosure took place, than to fix the date of the day before, when Lady Glyde had left for London. Neither could she calculate, with any nearer approach to exactness, the time that had passed from the departure of her mistress, to the period when the undated letter from Madame Fosco arrived. Lastly, as if to complete the series of difficulties, the doctor himself, having been ill at the time, had omitted to make his usual entry of the day of the week and month when the gardener from Blackwater Park had called on him to deliver Mrs Michelson's message.

Hopeless of obtaining assistance from Mr Dawson, I resolved to try next if I could establish the date of Sir Percival's arrival at Knowlesbury.

It seemed like a fatality! When I reached Knowlesbury the inn was shut up; and bills were posted on the walls. The speculation had been a bad one, as I was informed, ever since the time of the railway. The new hotel at the station had gradually absorbed the business; and the old inn (which we knew to be the inn at which Sir Percival had put up), had been closed about two months since. The proprietor had left the town with all his goods and chattels, and where he had gone I could not positively ascertain from any one. The four people of whom I inquired gave me four different accounts of his plans and projects when he left Knowlesbury.

There were still some hours to spare before the last train left for London; and I drove back again, in a fly from the Knowlesbury station, to Blackwater Park, with the purpose of questioning the gardener and the person who kept the lodge. If they, too, proved unable to assist me, my resources, for the present, were at an end, and I might return to town.

I dismissed the fly a mile distant from the park; and, getting my directions from the driver, proceeded by myself to the house. As I turned into the lane from the high-road, I saw a man, with a carpet-bag, walking before me rapidly on the way to the lodge. He was a little man, dressed in shabby black, and wearing a remarkably-large hat. I set him down (as well as it was possible to judge) for a lawyer's clerk; and stopped at once to widen the distance between us. He had not heard me; and he walked on out of sight, without looking back. When I passed through the gates myself, a little while afterwards, he was not visible—he had evidently gone on to the house.

There were two women in the lodge. One of them was old; the other, I knew at once, by Marian's description of her, to be Margaret Porcher. I asked first if Sir Percival was at the park; and, receiving a reply in the negative, inquired next when he had left it. Neither of the women could tell me more than that he had gone away in the summer. I could extract nothing from Margaret Porcher but vacant smiles and shakings of the head. The old woman was a little more intelligent; and I managed to lead her into speaking of the manner of Sir Percival's departure, and of the alarm that it caused her. She remembered her master calling her out of bed, and remembered his frightening her by swearing—but the date at which the occurrence happened was, as she honestly acknowledged, 'quite beyond her.'

On leaving the lodge, I saw the gardener at work not far off. When I first addressed him, he looked at me rather distrustfully; but, on my using Mrs Michelson's name, with a civil reference to himself, he entered into conversation readily enough. There is no need to describe what passed between us: it ended, as all my other attempts to discover the date had ended. The gardener knew that his master had driven away, at night 'some time in July, the last fortnight or the last ten days in the month'—and knew no more.

While we were speaking together, I saw the man in black, with the large hat, come out from the house, and stand at some little distance observing us.

Certain suspicions of his errand at Blackwater Park had already crossed my mind. They were now increased by the gardener's inability (or unwillingness) to tell me who the man was; and I determined to clear the way before me, if possible, by speaking to him. The plainest question I could put, as a stranger, would be to inquire if the house was allowed to be shown to visitors. I walked up to the man at once, and accosted him in those words.

His look and manner unmistakably betrayed that he knew who I was, and that he wanted to irritate me into quarrelling with him. His reply was insolent enough to have answered the purpose, if I had been less determined to control myself. As it was, I met him with the most resolute politeness; apologised for my involuntary intrusion (which he called a 'trespass'), and left the grounds. It was exactly as I suspected. The recognition of me, when I left Mr Kyrle's office, had been evidently communicated to Sir Percival Glyde; and the man in black had been sent to the park, in anticipation of my making inquiries at the house, or in the neighbourhood. If I had given him the least chance of lodging any sort of legal complaint against me, the interference of the local magistrate would no doubt have been turned to account, as a clog on my proceedings, and a means of separating me from Marian and Laura for some days at least.

I was prepared to be watched on the way from Blackwater Park to the station, exactly as I had been watched, in London, the day before. But I could not discover at the time, and I have never found out since, whether I was really followed on this occasion or not. The man in black might have had means of tracking me at his disposal of which I was not aware—but I certainly saw nothing of him, in his own person, either on the way to the station, or afterwards on my arrival at the London terminus, in the evening. I reached home, on foot; taking the precaution, before I approached our own door, of walking round by the loneliest street in the neighbourhood, and there stopping and looking back more than once over the open space behind me. I had first learnt to use this stratagem against suspected treachery in the wilds of Central America—and now I was practising it again, with the same purpose and with even greater caution, in the heart of civilised London!

Nothing had happened to alarm Marian during my absence. She asked eagerly what success I had met with. When I told her, she could not conceal her surprise at the indifference with which I spoke of the failure of my investigations, thus far.

The truth was that the ill-success of my inquiries had in no sense daunted me. I had pursued them as a matter of duty, and I had expected nothing from them. In the state of my mind, at that time, it was almost a relief to me to know that the struggle was now narrowed to a trial of strength between myself and Sir Percival Glyde. The vindictive motive had mingled itself, all along, with my other and better motives; and I confess it was a satisfaction to me to feel that the surest way—the only way left—of serving Laura's cause, was to fasten my hold firmly on the villain who had married her.

While I acknowledge that I was not strong enough to keep my motives above the reach of this instinct of revenge, I can honestly say something in my own favour, on the other side. No base speculation on the future relations of Laura and myself, and on the private and personal concessions which I might force from Sir Percival if I once had him at my mercy, ever entered my mind. I never said to myself, 'If I do succeed, it shall be one result of my success that I put it out of her husband's power to take her from me again.' I could not look at her and think of the future with such thoughts as those. The sad sight of the change in her from her former self, made the one interest of my love an interest of tenderness and compassion, which her father or her brother might have felt, and which I felt, God knows, in my inmost heart. All my hopes looked no farther on, now, than to the day of her recovery. There, till she was strong again and happy again—there, till she could look at me as she had once looked, and speak to me as she had once spoken—the future of my happiest thoughts and my dearest wishes ended.

These words are written under no prompting of idle self-contemplation. Passages in this narrative are soon to come, which will set the minds of others in judgment on my conduct. It is right that the best and the worst of me should be fairly balanced, before that time.

On the morning after my return from Hampshire, I took Marian up-stairs into my working-room; and there laid before her the plan that I had matured, thus far, for mastering the one assailable point in the life of Sir Percival Glyde.

The way to the Secret lay through the mystery, hitherto impenetrable to all of us, of the woman in white. The approach to that, in its turn, might be gained by obtaining the assistance of Anne Catherick's mother; and the only ascertainable means of prevailing on Mrs Catherick to act or to speak in the matter, depended on the chance of my discovering local particulars and family particulars, first of all, from Mrs Clements. After thinking the subject over carefully, I felt certain that I could only begin the new inquiries by placing myself in communication with the faithful friend and protectress of Anne Catherick.

The first difficulty, then, was to find Mrs Clements.

I was indebted to Marian's quick perception for meeting this necessity at once by the best and simplest means. She proposed to write to the farm near

Limmeridge (Todd's Corner), to inquire whether Mrs Clements had communicated with Mrs Todd during the past few months. How Mrs Clements had been separated from Anne, it was impossible for us to say; but that separation once effected, it would certainly occur to Mrs Clements to inquire after the missing woman in the neighbourhood of all others to which she was known to be most attached—the neighbourhood of Limmeridge. I saw directly that Marian's proposal offered us a prospect of success; and she wrote to Mrs Todd accordingly by that day's post.

While we were waiting for the reply, I made myself master of all the information Marian could afford on the subject of Sir Percival's family, and of his early life. She could only speak on these topics from hearsay; but she was reasonably certain of the truth of what little she had to tell.

Sir Percival was an only child. His father, Sir Felix Glyde, had suffered, from his birth, under a painful and incurable deformity, and had shunned all society from his earliest years. His sole happiness was in the enjoyment of music; and he had married a lady with tastes similar to his own, who was said to be a most accomplished musician. He inherited the Blackwater property while still a young man. Neither he nor his wife, after taking possession, made advances of any sort towards the society of the neighbourhood; and no one endeavoured to tempt them into abandoning their reserve, with the one disastrous exception of the rector of the parish.

The rector was the worst of all innocent mischief-makers—an over-zealous man. He had heard that Sir Felix had left College with the character of being little better than a revolutionist in politics and an infidel in religion; and he arrived conscientiously at the conclusion that it was his bounden duty to summon the lord of the manor to hear sound views enunciated in the parish church. Sir Felix fiercely resented the clergyman's well-meant but ill-directed interference; insulting him so grossly and so publicly, that the families in the neighbourhood sent letters of indignant remonstrance to the park; and even the tenants on the Blackwater property expressed their opinion as strongly as they dared. The Baronet, who had no country tastes of any kind, and no attachment to the estate, or to any one living on it, declared that society at Blackwater should never have a second chance of annoying him; and left the place from that moment. After a short residence in London, he and his wife departed for the Continent; and never returned to England again. They lived part of the time in France, and part in Germany—always keeping themselves in the strict retirement which the morbid sense of his own personal deformity had made a necessity to Sir Felix. Their son, Percival, had been born abroad, and had been educated there by private tutors. His mother was the first of his parents whom he lost. His father had died a few years after her, either in 1825 or 1826. Sir Percival had been in England, as a young man, once or twice before that period; but his acquaintance with the late Mr Fairlie did not begin till after the time of his father's death. They soon became very intimate, although Sir Percival was seldom, or never, at Limmeridge House in those days. Mr Frederick Fairlie might have met him once or twice in Mr Philip Fairlie's company; but he could have known little of him at that or at any other time. Sir Percival's only intimate friend in the Fairlie family had been Laura's father.

These were all the particulars that I could gain from Marian. They suggested nothing which was useful to my present purpose, but I noted them down carefully, in the event of their proving to be of importance at any future period.

Mrs Todd's reply (addressed, by our own wish, to a post-office at some distance from us) had arrived at its destination when I went to apply for it. The chances, which had been all against us, hitherto, turned, from this moment, in our favour. Mrs Todd's letter contained the first item of information of which we were in search.

Mrs Clements, it appeared, had (as we had conjectured) written to Todd's Corner; asking pardon, in the first place, for the abrupt manner in which she and Anne had left their friends at the farm-house (on the morning after I had met the woman in white in Limmeridge churchyard); and then informing Mrs Todd of Anne's disappearance, and entreating that she would cause inquiries to be made in the neighbourhood, on the chance that the lost woman might have strayed back to Limmeridge. In making this request, Mrs Clements had been careful to add to it the address at which she might always be heard of; and that address Mrs Todd now transmitted to Marian. It was in London; and within half an hour's walk of our own lodging.

In the words of the proverb, I was resolved not to let the grass grow under my feet. The next morning, I set forth to seek an interview with Mrs Clements. This was my first step forward in the investigation. The story of the desperate attempt to which I now stood committed begins here.

VI

THE address communicated by Mrs Todd took me to a lodging-house situated in a respectable street near the Gray's Inn-road.

When I knocked, the door was opened by Mrs Clements herself. She did not appear to remember me; and asked what my business was. I recalled to her our meeting in Limmeridge churchyard, at the close of my interview there with the woman in white; taking special care to remind her that I was the person who assisted Anne Catherick (as Anne had herself declared) to escape the pursuit from the Asylum. This was my only claim to the confidence of Mrs Clements. She remembered the circumstance the moment I spoke of it; and asked me into the parlour, in the greatest anxiety to know if I had brought her any news of Anne.

It was impossible for me to tell her the whole truth, without, at the same time, entering into particulars on the subject of the conspiracy, which it would have been dangerous to confide to a stranger. I could only abstain most carefully from raising any false hopes, and then explain that the object of my visit was to discover the persons who were really responsible for Anne's disappearance. I even added, so as to exonerate myself from any after-reproach of my own conscience, that I entertained not the least hope of being able to trace her, that I believed we should never see her alive again; and that my main interest in the affair was to bring to punishment two men whom I suspected to be concerned in luring her away, and at whose hands I and some dear friends of mine had suffered a grievous wrong. With this explanation, I left it to Mrs Clements to say whether our interest in the matter (whatever difference there might be in the motives which actuated us) was not the same; and whether she felt any reluctance to forward my object by giving me such information on the subject of my inquiries as she happened to possess.

The poor woman was, at first, too much confused and agitated to understand thoroughly what I said to her. She could only reply that I was welcome to anything she could tell me in return for the kindness I had shown to Anne. But as she was not very quick and ready, at the best of times, in talking to strangers, she would beg me to put her in the right way, and to say where I wished her to begin.

Knowing by experience that the plainest narrative attainable from persons who are not accustomed to arrange their ideas is the narrative which goes far enough back at the beginning to avoid all impediments of retrospection in its course, I asked Mrs Clements to tell me, first, what had happened after she had left Limmeridge; and so, by watchful questioning, carried her on from point to point till we reached the period of Anne's disappearance.

The substance of the information which I thus obtained, was as follows:

On leaving the farm at Todd's Corner, Mrs Clements and Anne had travelled, that day, as far as Derby; and had remained there a week, on Anne's account. They had then gone on to London, and had lived in the lodging occupied by Mrs Clements, at that time, for a month or more, when circumstances connected with the house and the landlord had obliged them to change their quarters. Anne's terror of being discovered in London or its neighbourhood, whenever they ventured to walk out, had gradually communicated itself to Mrs Clements; and she had determined on removing to one of the most out-of-the-way places in England, to the town of Grimsby in Lincolnshire, where her deceased husband had passed all his early life. His relatives were respectable people settled in the town; they had always treated Mrs Clements with great kindness; and she thought it impossible to do better than go there, and take the advice of her husband's friends. Anne would not hear of returning to her mother at Welmingham, because she had been removed to the Asylum from that place, and because Sir Percival would be certain to go back there and find her again. There was serious weight in this objection, and Mrs Clements felt that it was not to be easily removed.

At Grimsby the first serious symptoms of illness had shown themselves in Anne. They appeared soon after the news of Lady Glyde's marriage had been made public in the newspapers, and had reached her through that medium.

The medical man who was sent for to attend the sick woman, discovered at once that she was suffering from a serious affection of the heart. The illness lasted long, left her very weak, and returned, at intervals, though with mitigated severity, again and again. They remained at Grimsby, in consequence, during the first half of the new year; and there they might probably have stayed much longer, but for the sudden resolution which Anne took, at this time, to venture back to Hampshire, for the purpose of obtaining a private interview with Lady Glyde.

Mrs Clements did all in her power to oppose the execution of this hazardous and unaccountable project. No explanation of her motives was offered by Anne, except that she believed the day of her death was not far off, and that she had something on her mind which must be communicated to Lady Glyde, at any risk, in secret. Her resolution to accomplish this purpose was so firmly settled, that she declared her intention of going to Hampshire by herself, if Mrs Clements felt any unwillingness to go with her. The doctor, on being consulted, was of opinion that serious opposition to her wishes would, in all probability, produce another and perhaps a fatal fit of illness; and Mrs Clements, under this advice, yielded to necessity, and once more, with sad forebodings of trouble and danger to come, allowed Anne Catherick to have her own way.

On the journey from London to Hampshire, Mrs Clements discovered that one of their fellow-passengers was well acquainted with the neighbourhood of Blackwater, and could give her all the information she needed on the subject of localities. In this way, she found out that the only place they could go to which was not dangerously near to Sir Percival's residence, was a large village, called Sandon. The distance, here, from Blackwater Park was between three and four miles—and that distance, and back again, Anne had walked, on each occasion when she had appeared in the neighbourhood of the lake.

For the few days, during which they were at Sandon without being discovered, they had lived a little away from the village, in the cottage of a decent widow-woman, who had a bedroom to let, and whose discreet silence Mrs Clements had done her best to secure, for the first week at least. She had also tried hard to induce Anne to be content with writing to Lady Glyde, in the first instance. But the failure of the warning contained in the anonymous letter sent to Limmeridge had made Anne resolute to speak this time, and obstinate in the determination to go on her errand alone.

Mrs Clements, nevertheless, followed her privately on each occasion when she went to the lake—without, however, venturing near enough to the boat-house to be witness of what took place there. When Anne returned for the last time from the dangerous neighbourhood, the fatigue of walking, day after day, distances which were far too great for her strength, added to the exhausting effect of the agitation from which she had suffered, produced the result which Mrs Clements had dreaded all along. The old pain over the heart and the other symptoms of the illness at Grimsby returned; and Anne was confined to her bed in the cottage.

In this emergency, the first necessity, as Mrs Clements knew by experience, was to endeavour to quiet Anne's anxiety of mind; and, for this purpose, the good woman went herself the next day to the lake, to try if she could find Lady Glyde (who would be sure, as Anne said, to take her daily walk to the boat-house), and prevail on her to come back privately to the cottage near Sandon. On reaching the outskirts of the plantation, Mrs Clements encountered, not Lady Glyde, but a tall, stout, elderly gentleman with a book in his hand—in other words, Count Fosco.

The Count, after looking at her very attentively for a moment, asked if she expected to see any one in that place; and added, before she could reply, that he was waiting there with a message from Lady Glyde, but that he was not quite certain whether the person then before him answered the description of the person with whom he was desired to communicate.

Upon this, Mrs Clements at once confided her errand to him, and entreated that he would help to allay Anne's anxiety by trusting his message to her. The Count most readily and kindly complied with her request. The message, he said, was a most important one. Lady Glyde entreated Anne and her good friend to return immediately to London, as she felt certain that Sir Percival would discover them, if they remained any longer in the neighbourhood of Blackwater. She was herself going to London in a short time; and if Mrs Clements and Anne would go there first, and would let her know what their address was, they should hear from her and see her, in a fortnight or less. The Count added, that he had already attempted to give a friendly warning to Anne herself, but that she had been too much startled by seeing that he was a stranger, to let him approach and speak to her.

To this, Mrs Clements replied, in the greatest alarm and distress, that she asked nothing better than to take Anne safely to London; but that there was no present hope of removing her from the dangerous neighbourhood, as she lay ill in her bed at that moment. The Count inquired if Mrs Clements had sent for medical advice; and, hearing that she had hitherto hesitated to do so, from the fear of making their position publicly known in the village, informed her that he was himself a medical man, and that he would go back with her, if she pleased, and see what could be done for Anne. Mrs Clements (feeling a natural confidence in the Count, as a person trusted with a secret message from Lady Glyde) gratefully accepted the offer; and they went back together to the cottage.

Anne was asleep when they got there. The Count started at the sight of her (evidently from astonishment at her resemblance to Lady Glyde). Poor Mrs Clements supposed that he was only shocked to see how ill she was. He would not allow her to be awakened; he was contented with putting questions to Mrs Clements about her symptoms, with looking at her, and with lightly touching her pulse. Sandon was a large enough place to have a grocer's and druggist's shop in it; and thither the Count went, to write his prescription and to get the medicine made up. He brought it back himself; and told Mrs Clements that the medicine was a powerful stimulant, and that it would certainly give Anne strength to get up and bear the fatigue of a journey to London of only a few hours. The remedy was to be administered at stated times, on that day, and on the day after. On the third day she would be well enough to travel; and he arranged to meet Mrs Clements at the Blackwater station, and to see them off by the mid-day train. If they did not appear, he would assume that Anne was worse, and would proceed at once to the cottage.

As events turned out, no such emergency as this occurred.

The medicine had an extraordinary effect on Anne, and the good results of it were helped by the assurance Mrs Clements could now give her that she would soon see Lady Glyde in London. At the appointed day and time (when they had not been quite so long as a week in Hampshire, altogether), they arrived at the station. The Count was waiting there for them, and was talking to an elderly lady, who appeared to be going to travel by the train to London also. He most kindly assisted them, and put them into the carriage himself; begging Mrs Clements not to forget to send her address to Lady Glyde. The elderly lady did not travel in the same compartment; and they did not notice what became of her on reaching the London terminus. Mrs Clements secured respectable lodgings in a quiet neighbourhood; and then wrote, as she had engaged to do, to inform Lady Glyde of the address.

A little more than a fortnight passed, and no answer came.

At the end of that time, a lady (the same elderly lady whom they had seen at the station) called in a cab, and said that she came from Lady Glyde, who was then at an hotel in London, and who wished to see Mrs Clements for the purpose of arranging a future interview with Anne. Mrs Clements expressed her willingness (Anne being present at the time, and entreating her to do so) to forward the object in view, especially as she was not required to be away from the house for more than half an hour at the most. She and the elderly lady (clearly Madame Fosco) then left in the cab. The lady stopped the cab, after it had driven some distance, at a shop, before they got to the hotel; and begged Mrs Clements to wait for her for a few minutes, while she made a purchase that had been forgotten. She never appeared again.

After waiting some time, Mrs Clements became alarmed, and ordered the cabman to drive back to her lodgings. When she got there, after an absence of rather more than half an hour, Anne was gone.

The only information to be obtained from the people of the house was derived from the servant who waited on the lodgers. She had opened the door to a boy from the street, who had left a letter for 'the young woman who lived on the second floor' (the part of the house which Mrs Clements occupied). The servant had delivered the letter; had then gone down stairs; and, five minutes afterwards, had observed Anne open the front door, and go out, dressed in her bonnet and shawl. She had probably taken the letter with her; for it was not to be found, and it was therefore impossible to tell what inducement had been offered to make her leave the house. It must have been a strong one—for she would never stir out alone in London of her own accord. If Mrs Clements had not known this by experience, nothing would have induced her to go away in the cab, even for so short a time as half an hour only.

As soon as she could collect her thoughts, the first idea that naturally occurred to Mrs Clements, was to go and make inquiries at the Asylum, to which she dreaded that Anne had been taken back.

She went there the next day—having been informed of the locality in which the house was situated by Anne herself. The answer she received (her application having, in all probability, been made a day or two before the false Anne Catherick had really been consigned to safe keeping in the Asylum) was that no such person had been brought back there. She had then written to Mrs Catherick, at Welmingham, to know if she had seen or heard anything of her daughter; and had received an answer in the negative. After that reply had reached her, she was at the end of her resources, and perfectly ignorant where else to inquire, or what else to do. From that time to this, she had remained in total ignorance of the cause of Anne's disappearance, and of the end of Anne's story.

THUS far, the information which I had received from Mrs Clements— though it established facts of which I had not previously been aware— was of a preliminary character only.

It was clear that the series of deceptions which had removed Anne Catherick to London and separated her from Mrs Clements, had been accomplished solely by Count Fosco and the Countess; and the question whether any part of the conduct of husband or wife had been of a kind to place either of them within reach of the law, might be well worthy of future consideration. But the purpose I had now in view led me in another direction than this. The immediate object of my visit to Mrs Clements was to make some approach at least to the discovery of Sir Percival's secret; and she had said nothing, as yet, which advanced me on my way to that important end. I felt the necessity of trying to awaken her recollections of other times, persons, and events, than those on which her memory had hitherto been employed; and, when I next spoke, I spoke with that object indirectly in view.

'I wish I could be of any help to you in this sad calamity,' I said. 'All I can do is to feel heartily for your distress. If Anne had been your own child, Mrs Clements, you could have shown her no truer kindness—you could have made no readier sacrifices for her sake.'

'There's no great merit in that, sir,' said Mrs Clements, simply. 'The poor thing was as good as my own child to me. I nursed her from a baby, sir; bringing her up by hand—and a hard job it was to rear her. It wouldn't go to my heart so to lose her, if I hadn't made her first short-clothes, and taught her to walk. I always said she was sent to console me for never having chick or child of my own. And now she's lost, the old times keep coming back to my mind; and, even at my age, I can't help crying about her—I can't indeed, sir!'

I waited a little to give Mrs Clements time to compose herself. Was the light that I had been looking for so long, glimmering on me—far off, as yet—in the good woman's recollections of Anne's early life?

'Did you know Mrs Catherick before Anne was born?' I asked.

'Not very long, sir—not above four months. We saw a great deal of each other in that time, but we were never very friendly together.'

Her voice was steadier as she made that reply. Painful as many of her recollections might be, I observed that it was, unconsciously, a relief to her mind to revert to the dimly-seen troubles of the past, after dwelling so long on the vivid sorrows of the present.

'Were you and Mrs Catherick neighbours?' I inquired, leading her memory on, as encouragingly as I could.

'Yes, sir—neighbours at Old Welmingham.'

'*Old* Welmingham? There are two places of that name, then, in Hampshire?'

'Well, sir, there used to be in those days—better than three-and-twenty years ago. They built a new town about two miles off, convenient to the river—and Old Welmingham, which was never much more than a village, got in time to be deserted. The new town is the place they call Welmingham, now—but the old parish church is the parish church still. It stands by itself, with the houses pulled down, or gone to ruin, all round it. I've lived to see sad changes. It was a pleasant, pretty place in my time.'

'Did you live there before your marriage, Mrs Clements?'

'No, sir—I'm a Norfolk woman. It wasn't the place my husband belonged to, either. He was from Grimsby, as I told you; and he served his
apprenticeship there. But having friends down south, and hearing of an
opening, he got into business at Southampton. It was in a small way, but he
made enough for a plain man to retire on, and settled at Old Welmingham.
I went there with him, when he married me. We were neither of us young; but
we lived very happy together—happier than our neighbour, Mr Catherick,
lived along with his wife, when they came to Old Welmingham, a year or
two afterwards.'

'Was your husband acquainted with them before that?'

'With Catherick, sir—not with his wife. She was a stranger to both of us.
Some gentlemen had made interest for Catherick; and he got the situation
of clerk at Welmingham church, which was the reason of his coming to settle
in our neighbourhood. He brought his newly-married wife along with him;
and we heard, in course of time, she had been lady's maid in a family that
lived at Varneck Hall, near Southampton. Catherick had found it a hard
matter to get her to marry him—in consequence of her holding herself
uncommonly high. He had asked and asked, and given the thing up at last,
seeing she was so contrary about it. When he *had* given it up, she turned
contrary, just the other way, and came to him of her own accord, without
rhyme or reason seemingly. My poor husband always said that was the time
to have given her a lesson. But Catherick was too fond of her to do anything
of the sort; he never checked her, either before they were married or after.
He was a quick man in his feelings, letting them carry him a deal too far,
now in one way, and now in another; and he would have spoilt a better wife
than Mrs Catherick, if a better had married him. I don't like to speak ill of
any one, sir—but she was a heartless woman, with a terrible will of her own;
fond of foolish admiration and fine clothes, and not caring to show so much
as decent outward respect to Catherick, kindly as he always treated her. My
husband said he thought things would turn out badly, when they first came
to live near us; and his words proved true. Before they had been quite four
months in our neighbourhood, there was a dreadful scandal and a miserable
break-up in their household. Both of them were in fault—I am afraid both
of them were equally in fault.'

'You mean both husband and wife?'

'Oh, no, sir! I don't mean Catherick—he was only to be pitied. I meant
his wife, and the person——'

'And the person who caused the scandal?'

'Yes, sir. A gentleman born and brought up, who ought to have set a
better example. You know him, sir—and my poor, dear Anne knew him,
only too well.'

'Sir Percival Glyde?'

'Yes. Sir Percival Glyde.'

My heart beat fast—I thought I had my hand on the clue. How little I knew, then, of the windings of the labyrinth which were still to mislead me!

'Did Sir Percival live in your neighbourhood at that time?' I asked.

'No, sir. He came among us as a stranger. His father had died, not long before, in foreign parts. I remember he was in mourning. He put up at the little inn on the river (they have pulled it down since that time), where gentlemen used to go to fish. He wasn't much noticed when he first came—it was a common thing enough for gentlemen to travel, from all parts of England, to fish in our river.'

'Did he make his appearance in the village before Anne was born?'

'Yes, sir. Anne was born in the June month of eighteen hundred and twenty-seven—and I think he came at the end of April, or the beginning of May.'

'Came as a stranger to all of you? A stranger to Mrs Catherick, as well as to the rest of the neighbours?'

'So we thought at first, sir. But when the scandal broke out, nobody believed they were strangers. I remember how it happened, as well as if it was yesterday. Catherick came into our garden one night, and woke us by throwing up a handful of gravel from the walk, at our window. I heard him beg my husband, for the Lord's sake, to come down and speak to him. They were a long time together talking in the porch. When my husband came back up-stairs, he was all of a tremble. He sat down on the side of the bed, and he says to me, "Lizzie! I always told you that woman was a bad one; I always said she would end ill—and I'm afraid, in my own mind, that the end has come already. Catherick has found a lot of lace handkerchiefs, and two fine rings, and a new gold watch and chain, hid away in his wife's drawer—things that nobody but a born lady ought ever to have—and his wife won't say how she came by them." "Does he think she stole them?" says I. "No," says he, "stealing would be bad enough. But it's worse than that—she's had no chance of stealing such things as those, and she's not a woman to take them, if she had. They're gifts, Lizzie—there's her own initials engraved inside the watch—and Catherick has seen her, talking privately, and carrying on as no married woman should, with that gentleman in mourning—Sir Percival Glyde. Don't you say anything about it—I've quieted Catherick for tonight. I've told him to keep his tongue to himself, and his eyes and his ears open, and to wait a day or two, till he can be quite certain." "I believe you are both of you wrong," says I. "It's not in nature, comfortable and respectable as she is here, that Mrs Catherick should take up with a chance stranger like Sir Percival Glyde." "Ay, but *is* he a stranger to her?" says my husband. "You forget how Catherick's wife came to marry him. She went to him of her own accord, after saying No, over and over again, when he asked her. There have been wicked women, before her time, Lizzie, who have used honest men who loved them as a means of saving their characters—and I'm sorely afraid this Mrs Catherick is as wicked as the worst of them. We shall see," says my husband, "we shall soon see." And only two days afterwards, we did see.'

Mrs Clements waited for a moment, before she went on. Even in that moment, I began to doubt whether the clue that I thought I had found was really leading me to the central mystery of the labyrinth, after all. Was this common, too common, story of a man's treachery and a woman's frailty the key to a secret which had been the life-long terror of Sir Percival Glyde?

'Well, sir, Catherick took my husband's advice, and waited,' Mrs Clements continued. 'And, as I told you, he hadn't long to wait. On the second day, he found his wife and Sir Percival whispering together, quite familiar, close under the vestry of the church. I suppose they thought the neighbourhood of the vestry was the last place in the world where anybody would think of looking after them—but, however that may be, there they were. Sir Percival, being seemingly surprised and confounded, defended himself in such a guilty way, that poor Catherick (whose quick temper I have told you of already) fell into a kind of frenzy at his own disgrace, and struck Sir Percival. He was no match (and I am sorry to say it) for the man who had wronged him—and he was beaten in the cruelest manner, before the neighbours, who had come to the place on hearing the disturbance, could run in to part them. All this happened towards evening; and, before nightfall, when my husband went to Catherick's house, he was gone, nobody knew where. No living soul in the village ever saw him again. He knew too well, by that time, what his wife's vile reason had been for marrying him; and he felt his misery and disgrace—especially after what had happened to him with Sir Percival—too keenly. The clergyman of the parish put an advertisement in the paper, begging him to come back, and saying that he should not lose his situation or his friends. But Catherick had too much pride and spirit, as some people said—too much feeling, as I think, sir—to face his neighbours again, and try to live down the memory of his disgrace. My husband heard from him, when he had left England; and heard a second time, when he was settled, and doing well, in America. He is alive there now, as far as I know; but none of us in the old country—his wicked wife least of all—are ever likely to set eyes on him again.'

'What became of Sir Percival?' I inquired. 'Did he stay in the neighbourhood?'

'Not he, sir. The place was too hot to hold him. He was heard at high words with Mrs Catherick, the same night when the scandal broke out—and the next morning he took himself off.'

'And Mrs Catherick? Surely she never remained in the village, among the people who knew of her disgrace?'

'She did, sir. She was hard enough and heartless enough to set the opinions of all her neighbours at flat defiance. She declared to everybody, from the clergyman downwards, that she was the victim of a dreadful mistake, and that all the scandal-mongers in the place should not drive her out of it as if she was a guilty woman. All through my time, she lived at Old Welmingham; and, after my time, when the new town was building, and the respectable neighbours began moving to it, she moved too, as if she was determined to live among them and scandalise them to the very last. There she is now, and there she will stop, in defiance of the best of them, to her dying day.'

'But how has she lived, through all these years?' I asked. 'Was her husband able and willing to help her?'

'Both able and willing, sir,' said Mrs Clements. 'In the second letter he wrote to my good man, he said she had borne his name, and lived in his home, and, wicked as she was, she must not starve like a beggar in the street. He could afford to make her some small allowance, and she might draw for it quarterly, at a place in London.'

'Did she accept the allowance?'

'Not a farthing of it, sir. She said she would never be beholden to Catherick for bit or drop, if she lived to be a hundred. And she has kept her word ever since. When my poor dear husband died, and left all to me, Catherick's letter was put in my possession with the other things—and I told her to let me know if she was ever in want. "I'll let all England know I'm in want," she said, "before I tell Catherick, or any friend of Catherick's. Take that for your answer—and give it to *him* for an answer, if he ever writes again."'

'Do you suppose that she had money of her own?'

'Very little, if any, sir. It was said, and said truly, I am afraid, that her means of living came privately from Sir Percival Glyde.'

After that last reply, I waited a little, to reconsider what I had heard. If I unreservedly accepted the story so far, it was now plain that no approach, direct or indirect, to the Secret had yet been revealed to me, and that the pursuit of my object had ended again in leaving me face to face with the most palpable and the most disheartening failure.

But there was one point in the narrative which made me doubt the propriety of accepting it unreservedly, and which suggested the idea of something hidden below the surface.

I could not account to myself for the circumstance of the clerk's guilty wife voluntarily living out all her after-existence on the scene of her disgrace. The woman's own reported statement that she had taken this strange course as a practical assertion of her innocence did not satisfy me. It seemed, to my mind, more natural and more probable to assume that she was not so completely a free agent in this matter as she had herself asserted. In that case, who was the likeliest person to possess the power of compelling her to remain at Welmingham? The person unquestionably from whom she derived the means of living. She had refused assistance from her husband, she had no adequate resources of her own, she was a friendless, degraded woman: from what source should she derive help but from the source at which report pointed—Sir Percival Glyde?

Reasoning on these assumptions, and always bearing in mind the one certain fact to guide me, that Mrs Catherick was in possession of the Secret, I easily understood that it was Sir Percival's interest to keep her at Welmingham, because her character in that place was certain to isolate her from all communication with female neighbours, and to allow her no opportunities of talking incautiously, in moments of free intercourse with inquisitive bosom friends. But what was the mystery to be concealed? Not Sir Percival's infamous connexion with Mrs Catherick's disgrace—for the neighbours were the very people who knew of it. Not the suspicion that he was Anne's father—for Welmingham was the place in which that suspicion must inevitably exist. If I accepted the guilty appearances described to me, as unreservedly as others had accepted them; if I drew from them the same superficial conclusion which Mr Catherick and all his neighbours had drawn—where was the suggestion, in all that I had heard, of a dangerous secret between Sir Percival and Mrs Catherick, which had been kept hidden from that time to this?

And yet, in those stolen meetings, in those familiar whisperings between the clerk's wife and 'the gentleman in mourning,' the clue to discovery existed beyond a doubt.

Was it possible that appearances, in this case, had pointed one way, while the truth lay, all the while, unsuspected, in another direction? Could Mrs Catherick's assertion that she was the victim of a dreadful mistake, by any possibility be true? Or, assuming it to be false, could the conclusion which associated Sir Percival with her guilt have been founded in some inconceivable error? Had Sir Percival, by any chance, courted the suspicion that was wrong, for the sake of diverting from himself some other suspicion that was right? Here, if I could find it—here was the approach to the Secret, hidden deep under the surface of the apparently-unpromising story which I had just heard.

My next questions were now directed to the one object of ascertaining whether Mr Catherick had, or had not, arrived truly at the conviction of his wife's misconduct. The answers I received from Mrs Clements, left me in no doubt whatever on that point. Mrs Catherick had, on the clearest evidence, compromised her reputation, while a single woman, with some person unknown; and had married to save her character. It had been positively ascertained, by calculations of time and place into which I need not enter particularly, that the daughter who bore her husband's name was not her husband's child.

The next object of inquiry, whether it was equally certain that Sir Percival must have been the father of Anne, was beset by far greater difficulties. I was in no position to try the probabilities on one side or on the other, in this instance, by any better test than the test of personal resemblance.

'I suppose you often saw Sir Percival, when he was in your village?' I said.

'Yes, sir—very often,' replied Mrs Clements.

'Did you ever observe that Anne was like him?'

'She was not at all like him, sir.'

'Was she like her mother, then?'

'Not like her mother, either, sir. Mrs Catherick was dark, and full in the face.'

Not like her mother, and not like her (supposed) father. I knew that the test by personal resemblance was not to be implicitly trusted—but, on the other hand, it was not to be altogether rejected on that account. Was it possible to strengthen the evidence, by discovering any conclusive facts in relation to the lives of Mrs Catherick and Sir Percival, before they either of them appeared at Old Welmingham? When I asked my next questions, I put them with this view.

'When Sir Percival first arrived in your neighbourhood,' I said, 'did you hear where he had come from last?'

'No, sir. Some said from Blackwater Park, and some said from Scotland—but nobody knew.'

'Was Mrs Catherick living in service at Varneck Hall, immediately before her marriage?'

'Yes, sir.'

'And had she been long in her place?'

'Three or four years, sir; I am not quite certain which.'

'Did you ever hear the name of the gentleman to whom Varneck Hall belonged at that time?'

'Yes, sir. His name was Major Donthorne.'

'Did Mr Catherick, or did any one else you knew, ever hear that Sir Percival was a friend of Major Donthorne's, or ever see Sir Percival in the neighbourhood of Varneck Hall?'

'Catherick never did, sir, that I can remember—nor any one else, either, that I know of.'

I noted down Major Donthorne's name and address, on the chance that he might still be alive, and that it might be useful, at some future time, to apply to him. Meanwhile, the impression on my mind was now decidedly adverse to the opinion that Sir Percival was Anne's father, and decidedly favourable to the conclusion that the secret of his stolen interviews with Mrs Catherick was entirely unconnected with the disgrace which the woman had inflicted on her husband's good name. I could think of no further inquiries which I might make to strengthen this impression—I could only encourage

Mrs Clements to speak next of Anne's early days, and watch for any chance-suggestion which might in this way offer itself to me.

'I have not heard yet,' I said, 'how the poor child, born in all this sin and misery, came to be trusted, Mrs Clements, to your care.'

'There was nobody else, sir, to take the little helpless creature in hand,' replied Mrs Clements. 'The wicked mother seemed to hate it—as if the poor baby was in fault!—from the day it was born. My heart was heavy for the child; and I made the offer to bring it up as tenderly as if it was my own.'

'Did Anne remain entirely under your care, from that time?'

'Not quite entirely, sir. Mrs Catherick had her whims and fancies about it, at times; and used now and then to lay claim to the child, as if she wanted to spite me for bringing it up. But these fits of hers never lasted for long. Poor little Anne was always returned to me, and was always glad to get back—though she led but a gloomy life in my house, having no playmates, like other children, to brighten her up. Our longest separation was when her mother took her to Limmeridge. Just at that time, I lost my husband; and I felt it was as well, in that miserable affliction, that Anne should not be in the house. She was between ten and eleven year old, then; slow at her lessons, poor soul, and not so cheerful as other children—but as pretty a little girl to look at as you would wish to see. I waited at home till her mother brought her back; and then I made the offer to take her with me to London—the truth being, sir, that I could not find it in my heart to stop at Old Welmingham, after my husband's death, the place was so changed and so dismal to me.'

'And did Mrs Catherick consent to your proposal?'

'No, sir. She came back from the north, harder and bitterer than ever. Folks did say that she had been obliged to ask Sir Percival's leave to go, to begin with; and that she only went to nurse her dying sister at Limmeridge because the poor woman was reported to have saved money—the truth being that she hardly left enough to bury her. These things may have soured Mrs Catherick, likely enough—but, however that may be, she wouldn't hear of my taking the child away. She seemed to like distressing us both by parting us. All I could do was to give Anne my direction, and to tell her, privately, if she was ever in trouble, to come to me. But years passed before she was free to come. I never saw her again, poor soul, till the night she escaped from the madhouse.'

'You know, Mrs Clements, why Sir Percival Glyde shut her up?'

'I only know what Anne herself told me, sir. The poor thing used to ramble and wander about it, sadly. She said her mother had got some secret of Sir Percival's to keep, and had let it out to her, long after I left Hampshire—and when Sir Percival found she knew it, he shut her up. But she never could say what it was, when I asked her. All she could tell me was that her mother might be the ruin and destruction of Sir Percival, if she chose. Mrs Catherick may have let out just as much as that, and no more. I'm next to certain I should have heard the whole truth from Anne, if she had really known it, as she pretended to do—and as she very likely fancied she did, poor soul.'

This idea had more than once occurred to my own mind. I had already told Marian that I doubted whether Laura was really on the point of making any important discovery when she and Anne Catherick were disturbed by Count Fosco at the boat-house. It was perfectly in character with Anne's mental affliction that she should assume an absolute knowledge of the Secret on no better grounds than vague suspicion, derived from hints which her mother had incautiously let drop in her presence. Sir Percival's guilty distrust would, in that case, infallibly inspire him with the false idea that Anne knew all from her mother, just as it had afterwards fixed in his mind the equally false suspicion that his wife knew all from Anne.

The time was passing; the morning was wearing away. It was doubtful, if I stayed longer, whether I should hear anything more from Mrs Clements that would be at all useful to my purpose. I had already discovered those local and family particulars, in relation to Mrs Catherick, of which I had been in search; and I had arrived at certain conclusions, entirely new to me, which might immensely assist in directing the course of my future proceedings. I rose to take my leave, and to thank Mrs Clements for the friendly readiness she had shown in affording me information.

'I am afraid you must have thought me very inquisitive,' I said. 'I have troubled you with more questions than many people would have cared to answer.'

'You are heartily welcome, sir, to anything I can tell you,' answered Mrs Clements. She stopped, and looked at me wistfully. 'But I do wish,' said the poor woman, 'you could have told me a little more about Anne, sir. I thought I saw something in your face, when you came in, which looked as if you could. You can't think how hard it is not even to know whether she is living or dead. I could bear it better, if I was only certain. You said you never expected we should see her alive again. Do you know, sir—do you know for truth—that it has pleased God to take her?'

I was not proof against this appeal: it would have been unspeakably mean and cruel of me if I had resisted it.

'I am afraid there is no doubt of the truth,' I answered, gently; 'I have the certainty, in my own mind, that her troubles in this world are over.'

The poor woman dropped into her chair, and hid her face from me. 'Oh, sir,' she said, 'how do you know it? Who can have told you?'

'No one has told me, Mrs Clements. But I have reasons for feeling sure of it—reasons which I promise you shall know, as soon as I can safely explain them. I am certain she was not neglected in her last moments; I am certain the heart-complaint, from which she suffered so sadly, was the true cause of her death. You shall feel as sure of this as I do, soon—you shall know, before long, that she is buried in a quiet country churchyard; in a pretty, peaceful place, which you might have chosen for her yourself.'

'Dead!' said Mrs Clements; 'dead so young—and I am left to hear it! I made her first short frocks. I taught her to walk. The first time she ever said, Mother, she said it to *me*—and, now, I am left, and Anne is taken! Did you say, sir,' said the poor woman, removing the handkerchief from her face, and looking up at me for the first time—'did you say that she had been nicely buried? Was it the sort of funeral she might have had, if she had really been my own child?'

I assured her that it was. She seemed to take an inexplicable pride in my answer—to find a comfort in it, which no other and higher considerations could afford. 'It would have broken my heart,' she said, simply, 'if Anne had not been nicely buried—but, how do you know it, sir? who told you?' I once more entreated her to wait until I could speak to her unreservedly. 'You are sure to see me again,' I said; 'for I have a favour to ask, when you are a little more composed—perhaps in a day or two.'

'Don't keep it waiting, sir, on my account,' said Mrs Clements. 'Never mind my crying, if I can be of use. If you have anything on your mind to say to me, sir—please to say it now.'

'I only wished to ask you one last question,' I said. 'I only want to know Mrs Catherick's address at Welmingham.'

My request so startled Mrs Clements, that, for the moment, even the tidings of Anne's death seemed to be driven from her mind. Her tears suddenly ceased to flow, and she sat looking at me in blank amazement.

'For the Lord's sake, sir!' she said, 'what do you want with Mrs Catherick?'

'I want this, Mrs Clements,' I replied: 'I want to know the secret of those private meetings of hers with Sir Percival Glyde. There is something more, in what you have told me of that woman's past conduct and of that man's past relations with her, than you, or any of your neighbours, ever suspected. There is a Secret we none of us know of between those two—and I am going to Mrs Catherick, with the resolution to find it out.'

'Think twice about it, sir!' said Mrs Clements, rising, in her earnestness, and laying her hand on my arm. 'She's an awful woman—you don't know her, as I do. Think twice about it.'

'I am sure your warning is kindly meant, Mrs Clements. But I am determined to see the woman, whatever comes of it.'

Mrs Clements looked me anxiously in the face.

'I see your mind is made up, sir,' she said. 'I will give you the address.'

I wrote it down in my pocket-book; and then took the good woman by the hand, to say farewell.

'You shall hear from me, soon,' I said; 'you shall know all that I have promised to tell you.'

Mrs Clements sighed and shook her head doubtfully.

'An old woman's advice is sometimes worth taking, sir,' she said. 'Think twice before you go to Welmingham.'

VII

WHEN I reached home again, after my interview with Mrs Clements, I was struck by the appearance of a change in Laura.

The unvarying gentleness and patience which long misfortune had tried so cruelly and had never conquered yet, seemed now to have suddenly failed her. Insensible to all Marian's attempts to soothe and amuse her, she sat, with her neglected drawing pushed away on the table; her eyes resolutely cast down, her fingers twining and untwining themselves restlessly in her lap. Marian rose when I came in, with a silent distress in her face; waited for a moment, to see if Laura would look up at my approach; whispered to me, 'Try if *you* can rouse her;' and left the room.

I sat down in the vacant chair; gently unclasped the poor, worn, restless fingers; and took both her hands in mine.

'What are you thinking of, Laura? Tell me, my darling—try and tell me what it is.'

She struggled with herself, and raised her eyes to mine. 'I can't feel happy,' she said; 'I can't help thinking——' She stopped, bent forward a little, and laid her head on my shoulder, with a terrible mute helplessness that struck me to the heart.

'Try to tell me,' I repeated, gently; 'try to tell me why you are not happy.'

'I am so useless—I am such a burden on both of you,' she answered, with a weary, hopeless sigh. 'You work and get money, Walter; and Marian helps you. Why is there nothing I can do? You will end in liking Marian better than you like me—you will, because I am so helpless! Oh, don't, don't, don't treat me like a child!'

I raised her head, and smoothed away the tangled hair that fell over her face, and kissed her—my poor, faded flower! my lost, afflicted sister! 'You shall help us, Laura,' I said; 'you shall begin, my darling, to-day.'

She looked at me with a feverish eagerness, with a breathless interest, that made me tremble for the new life of hope which I had called into being by those few words.

I rose, and set her drawing materials in order, and placed them near her again.

'You know that I work and get money by drawing,' I said. 'Now you have taken such pains, now you are so much improved, you shall begin to work and get money, too. Try to finish this little sketch as nicely and prettily as you can. When it is done, I will take it away with me; and the same person will buy it who buys all that I do. You shall keep your own earnings in your own purse; and Marian shall come to you to help us, as often as she comes to me. Think how useful you are going to make yourself to both of us, and you will soon be as happy, Laura, as the day is long.'

Her face grew eager, and brightened into a smile. In the moment while it lasted, in the moment when she again took up the pencils that had been laid aside, she almost looked like the Laura of past days.

I had rightly interpreted the first signs of a new growth and strength in her mind, unconsciously expressing themselves in the notice she had taken of the occupations which filled her sister's life and mine. Marian (when I told her what had passed) saw, as I saw, that she was longing to assume her own little position of importance, to raise herself in her own estimation and in ours—and, from that day, we tenderly helped the new ambition which gave promise of the hopeful, happier future, that might now not be far off. Her drawings, as she finished them, or tried to finish them, were placed in my hands; Marian took them from me and hid them carefully; and I set aside a little weekly tribute from my earnings, to be offered to her as the price paid by strangers for the poor, faint, valueless sketches, of which I was the only purchaser. It was hard sometimes to maintain our innocent deception, when she proudly brought out her purse to contribute her share towards the expenses, and wondered, with serious interest, whether I or she had earned the most that week. I have all those hidden drawings in my possession still: they are my treasures beyond price—the dear remembrances that I love to keep alive—the friends, in past adversity, that my heart will never part from, my tenderness never forget.

Am I trifling, here, with the necessities of my task? am I looking forward to the happier time which my narrative has not yet reached? Yes. Back again—back to the days of doubt and dread, when the spirit within me struggled hard for its life, in the icy stillness of perpetual suspense. I have paused and rested for a while on my forward course. It is not, perhaps, time wasted, if the friends who read these pages have paused and rested too.

I took the first opportunity I could find of speaking to Marian in private, and of communicating to her the result of the inquiries which I had made that morning. She seemed to share the opinion on the subject of my proposed journey to Welmingham, which Mrs Clements had already expressed to me.

'Surely, Walter,' she said, 'you hardly know enough yet to give you any hope of claiming Mrs Catherick's confidence? Is it wise to proceed to these extremities, before you have really exhausted all safer and simpler means of attaining your object? When you told me that Sir Percival and the Count were the only two people in existence who knew the exact date of Laura's journey, you forgot, and I forgot, that there was a third person who must surely know it—I mean Mrs Rubelle. Would it not be far easier, and far less dangerous, to insist on a confession from her, than to force it from Sir Percival?'

'It might be easier,' I replied; 'but we are not aware of the full extent of Mrs Rubelle's connivance and interest in the conspiracy; and we are therefore not certain that the date has been impressed on her mind, as it has been assuredly impressed on the minds of Sir Percival and the Count. It is too late, now, to waste the time on Mrs Rubelle, which may be all-important to the discovery of the one assailable point in Sir Percival's life. Are you thinking a little too seriously, Marian, of the risk I may run in returning to Hampshire? Are you beginning to doubt whether Sir Percival Glyde may not, in the end, be more than a match for me?'

'He will not be more than your match,' she replied, decidedly, 'because he will not be helped in resisting you by the impenetrable wickedness of the Count.'

'What has led you to that conclusion?' I asked, in some surprise.

'My own knowledge of Sir Percival's obstinacy and impatience of the Count's control,' she answered. 'I believe he will insist on meeting you single-handed—just as he insisted, at first, on acting for himself at Black-water Park. The time for suspecting the Count's interference, will be the time when you have Sir Percival at your mercy. His own interests will then be directly threatened—and he will act, Walter, to terrible purpose, in his own defence.'

'We may deprive him of his weapons, beforehand,' I said. 'Some of the particulars I have heard from Mrs Clements may yet be turned to account against him; and other means of strengthening the case may be at our disposal. There are passages in Mrs Michelson's narrative which show that the Count found it necessary to place himself in communication with Mr Fairlie; and there may be circumstances which compromise him in that proceeding. While I am away, Marian, write to Mr Fairlie, and say that you want an answer describing exactly what passed between the Count and himself, and informing you also of any particulars that may have come to his knowledge at the same time, in connexion with his niece. Tell him that the statement you request will, sooner or later, be insisted on, if he shows any reluctance to furnish you with it of his own accord.'

'The letter shall be written, Walter. But, are you really determined to go to Welmingham?'

'Absolutely determined. I will devote the next two days to earning what we want for the week to come; and, on the third day, I go to Hampshire.'

When the third day came, I was ready for my journey.

As it was possible that I might be absent for some little time, I arranged with Marian that we were to correspond every day; of course addressing each other by assumed names, for caution's sake. As long as I heard from her regularly, I should assume that nothing was wrong. But if the morning came and brought me no letter, my return to London would take place, as a matter of course, by the first train. I contrived to reconcile Laura to my departure by telling her that I was going to the country to find new purchasers for her drawings and for mine; and I left her occupied and happy. Marian followed me down stairs to the street door.

'Remember what anxious hearts you leave here,' she whispered, as we stood together in the passage; 'remember all the hopes that hang on your safe return. If strange things happen to you on this journey; if you and Sir Percival meet——'

'What makes you think we shall meet?' I asked.

'I don't know—I have fears and fancies that I can't account for. Laugh at them, Walter, if you like—but, for God's sake, keep your temper, if you come in contact with that man!'

'Never fear, Marian! I answer for my self-control.'

With those words we parted.

I walked briskly to the station. There was a glow of hope in me; there was a growing conviction in my mind that my journey, this time, would not be taken in vain. It was a fine, clear, cold morning; my nerves were firmly strung, and I felt all the strength of my resolution stirring in me vigorously from head to foot.

As I crossed the railway platform, and looked right and left among the people congregated on it, to search for any faces among them that I knew, the doubt occurred to me whether it might not have been to my advantage, if I had adopted a disguise, before setting out for Hampshire. But there was something so repellent to me in the idea—something so meanly like the common herd of spies and informers in the mere act of adopting a disguise—that I dismissed the question from consideration, almost as soon as it had risen in my mind. Even as a mere matter of expediency the proceeding was doubtful in the extreme. If I tried the experiment at home, the landlord of the house would, sooner or later, discover me, and would have his suspicions aroused immediately. If I tried it away from home, the same persons might see me, by the commonest accident, with the disguise and without it; and I should, in that way, be inviting the notice and distrust which it was my most pressing interest to avoid. In my own character I had acted thus far—and in my own character I was resolved to continue to the end.

The train left me at Welmingham, early in the afternoon.

Is there any wilderness of sand in the deserts of Arabia, is there any prospect of desolation among the ruins of Palestine, which can rival the repelling effect on the eye, and the depressing influence on the mind, of an English country town, in the first stage of its existence, and in the transition state of its prosperity? I asked myself that question, as I passed through the clean desolation, the neat ugliness, the prim torpor of the streets of Welmingham. And the tradesmen who stared after me from their lonely shops; the trees that drooped helpless in their arid exile of unfinished crescents and squares; the dead house-carcases that waited in vain for the vivifying human element to animate them with the breath of life; every creature that I saw; every object that I passed—seemed to answer with one accord: The deserts of Arabia are innocent of our civilised desolation; the ruins of Palestine are incapable of our modern gloom!

I inquired my way to the quarter of the town in which Mrs Catherick lived; and on reaching it found myself in a square of small houses, one story high. There was a bare little plot of grass in the middle, protected by a cheap wire fence. An elderly nursemaid and two children were standing in a corner of the enclosure, looking at a lean goat tethered to the grass. Two foot passengers were talking together on one side of the pavement before the houses, and an idle little boy was leading an idle little dog along by a string, on the other. I heard the dull tinkling of a piano at a distance, accompanied by the intermittent knocking of a hammer nearer at hand. These were all the sights and sounds of life that encountered me when I entered the square.

I walked at once to the door of Number Thirteen—the number of Mrs Catherick's house—and knocked, without waiting to consider beforehand how I might best present myself when I got in. The first necessity was to see Mrs Catherick. I could then judge, from my own observation, of the safest and easiest manner of approaching the object of my visit.

The door was opened by a melancholy, middle-aged woman servant. I gave her my card, and asked if I could see Mrs Catherick. The card was taken into the front parlour; and the servant returned with a message requesting me to mention what my business was.

'Say, if you please, that my business relates to Mrs Catherick's daughter,' I replied. This was the best pretext I could think of, on the spur of the moment, to account for my visit.

The servant again retired to the parlour; again returned; and, this time, begged me, with a look of gloomy amazement, to walk in.

I entered a little room, with a flaring paper, of the largest pattern, on the walls. Chairs, tables, chiffonier, and sofa, all gleamed with the glutinous brightness of cheap upholstery. On the largest table, in the middle of the room, stood a smart Bible, placed exactly in the centre, on a red and yellow wollen mat; and at the side of the table nearest to the window, with a little knitting-basket on her lap, and a wheezing, blear-eyed old spaniel crouched at her feet, there sat an elderly woman, wearing a black net cap and a black silk gown, and having slate-coloured mittens on her hands. Her iron-grey hair hung in heavy bands on either side of her face; her dark eyes looked straight forward, with a hard, defiant, implacable stare. She had full, square cheeks; a long, firm chin; and thick, sensual, colourless lips. Her figure was stout and sturdy, and her manner aggressively self-possessed. This was Mrs Catherick.

'You have come to speak to me about my daughter,' she said, before I could utter a word on my side. 'Be so good as to mention what you have to say.'

The tone of her voice was as hard, as defiant, as implacable as the expression of her eyes. She pointed to a chair, and looked me all over attentively, from head to foot, as I sat down in it. I saw that my only chance with this woman was to speak to her in her own tone, and to meet her, at the outset of our interview, on her own ground.

'You are aware,' I said, 'that your daughter has been lost?'

'I am perfectly aware of it.'

'Have you felt any apprehension that the misfortune of her loss might be followed by the misfortune of her death?'

'Yes. Have you come here to tell me she is dead?'

'I have.'

'Why?'

She put that extraordinary question without the slightest change in her voice, her face, or her manner. She could not have appeared more perfectly unconcerned if I had told her of the death of the goat in the enclosure outside.

'Why?' I repeated. 'Do you ask why I come here to tell you of your daughter's death?'

'Yes. What interest have you in me, or in her? How do you come to know anything about my daughter?'

'In this way. I met her on the night when she escaped from the Asylum; and I assisted her in reaching a place of safety.'

'You did very wrong.'

'I am sorry to hear her mother say so.'

'Her mother does say so. How do you know she is dead?'

'I am not at liberty to say how I know it—but I *do* know it.'

'Are you at liberty to say how you found out my address?'

'Certainly. I got your address from Mrs Clements.'

'Mrs Clements is a foolish woman. Did she tell you to come here?'

'She did not.'

'Then, I ask you again, why did you come?'

As she was determined to have the answer, I gave it to her in the plainest possible form.

'I came,' I said, 'because I thought Anne Catherick's mother might have some natural interest in knowing whether she was alive or dead.'

'Just so,' said Mrs Catherick, with additional self-possession. 'Had you no other motive?'

I hesitated. The right answer to that question was not easy to find, at a moment's notice.

'If you have no other motive,' she went on, deliberately taking off her slate-coloured mittens, and rolling them up, 'I have only to thank you for your visit; and to say that I will not detain you here, any longer. Your information would be more satisfactory if you were willing to explain how you became possessed of it. However, it justifies me, I suppose, in going into mourning. There is not much alteration necessary in my dress, as you see. When I have changed my mittens, I shall be all in black.'

She searched in the pocket of her gown; drew out a pair of black-lace mittens; put them on with the stoniest and steadiest composure; and then quietly crossed her hands in her lap.

'I wish you good morning,' she said.

The cool contempt of her manner irritated me into directly avowing that the purpose of my visit had not been answered yet.

'I *have* another motive in coming here,' I said.

'Ah! I thought so,' remarked Mrs Catherick.

'Your daughter's death——'

'What did she die of?'

'Of disease of the heart.'

'Yes? Go on.'

'Your daughter's death has been made the pretext for inflicting serious injury on a person who is very dear to me. Two men have been concerned, to my certain knowledge, in doing that wrong. One of them is Sir Percival Glyde.'

'Indeed?'

I looked attentively to see if she flinched at the sudden mention of that name. Not a muscle of her stirred—the hard, defiant, implacable stare in her eyes never wavered for an instant.

'You may wonder,' I went on, 'how the event of your daughter's death can have been made the means of inflicting injury on another person.'

'No,' said Mrs Catherick; 'I don't wonder at all. This appears to be your affair. You are interested in my affairs. I am not interested in yours.'

'You may ask, then,' I persisted, 'why I mention the matter, in your presence.'

'Yes: I *do* ask that.'

'I mention it because I am determined to bring Sir Percival Glyde to account for the wickedness he has committed.'

'What have I to do with your determination?'

'You shall hear. There are certain events in Sir Percival's past life which it is necessary to my purpose to be fully acquainted with. *You* know them—and for that reason, I come to *you*.'

'What events do you mean?'

'Events that occurred at Old Welmingham, when your husband was parish-clerk at that place, and before the time when your daughter was born.'

I had reached the woman at last, through the barrier of impenetrable reserve that she had tried to set up between us. I saw her temper smouldering in her eyes—as plainly as I saw her hands grow restless, then unclasp themselves, and begin mechanically smoothing her dress over her knees.

'What do you know of those events?' she asked.

'All that Mrs Clements could tell me,' I answered.

There was a momentary flush on her firm, square face, a momentary stillness in her restless hands, which seemed to betoken a coming outburst of anger that might throw her off her guard. But, no—she mastered the rising irritation; leaned back in her chair; crossed her arms on her broad bosom; and, with a smile of grim sarcasm on her thick lips, looked at me as steadily as ever.

'Ah! I begin to understand it all, now,' she said; her tamed and disciplined anger only expressing itself in the elaborate mockery of her tone and manner. 'You have got a grudge of your own against Sir Percival Glyde—and I must help you to wreak it. I must tell you this, that, and the other about Sir Percival and myself, must I? Yes, indeed? You have been prying into my private affairs. You think you have found a lost woman to deal with, who lives here on sufferance; and who will do anything you ask, for fear you may injure her in the opinions of the townspeople. I see through you and your precious speculation—I do! and it amuses me. Ha! ha!'

She stopped for a moment: her arms tightened over her bosom, and she laughed to herself—a hard, harsh, angry laugh.

'You don't know how I have lived in this place, and what I have done in this place, Mr What's-your-name,' she went on. 'I'll tell you, before I ring the bell and have you shown out. I came here a wronged woman. I came here, robbed of my character, and determined to claim it back. I've been years and years about it—and I *have* claimed it back. I have matched the respectable people, fairly and openly, on their own ground. If they say anything against me, now, they must say it in secret: they can't say it, they daren't say it, openly. I stand high enough in this town, to be out of your reach. *The clergyman bows to me.* Aha! you didn't bargain for that, when you came here. Go to the church, and inquire about me—you will find Mrs Catherick has her sitting, like the rest of them, and pays the rent on the day it's due. Go to the town-hall. There's a petition lying there; a petition of the respectable inhabitants against allowing a Circus to come and perform here and corrupt our morals: yes! OUR morals. I signed that petition, this morning. Go to the bookseller's shop. The clergyman's Wednesday evening Lectures on Justification by Faith are publishing there by subscription—I'm down on the list. The doctor's wife only put a shilling in the plate at our last charity sermon—I put half-a-crown. Mr Churchwarden Soward held the plate, and bowed to me. Ten years ago he told Pigrum, the chemist, I ought to be whipped out of the town, at the cart's tail. Is your mother alive? Has she got a better Bible on her table than I have got on mine? Does she stand better with her tradespeople than I do with mine? Has she always lived within her income? I have always lived within mine. —Ah! there *is* the clergyman coming along the square. Look, Mr What's-your-name—look, if you please!'

She started up, with the activity of a young woman; went to the window; waited till the clergyman passed; and bowed to him solemnly. The clergyman ceremoniously raised his hat, and walked on. Mrs Catherick returned to her chair, and looked at me with a grimmer sarcasm than ever.

'There!' she said. 'What do you think of that for a woman with a lost character? How does your speculation look now?'

The singular manner in which she had chosen to assert herself, the extraordinary practical vindication of her position in the town which she had just offered, had so perplexed me, that I listened to her in silent surprise. I was not the less resolved, however, to make another effort to throw her off her guard. If the woman's fierce temper once got beyond her control, and once flamed out on me, she might yet say the words which would put the clue in my hands.

'How does your speculation look now?' she repeated.

'Exactly as it looked when I first came in,' I answered. 'I don't doubt the position you have gained in the town; and I don't wish to assail it, even if I could. I came here because Sir Percival Glyde is, to my certain knowledge, your enemy, as well as mine. If I have a grudge against him, you have a grudge against him, too. You may deny it, if you like; you may distrust me as much as you please; you may be as angry as you will—but, of all the women in England, you, if you have any sense of injury, are the woman who ought to help me to crush that man.'

'Crush him for yourself,' she said—'then come back here, and see what I say to you.'

She spoke those words, as she had not spoken yet—quickly, fiercely, vindictively. I had stirred in its lair the serpent-hatred of years—but only for a moment. Like a lurking reptile, it leapt up at me—as she eagerly bent forward towards the place in which I was sitting. Like a lurking reptile, it dropped out of sight again—as she instantly resumed her former position in the chair.

'You won't trust me?' I said.

'No.'

'You are afraid?'

'Do I look as if I was?'

'You are afraid of Sir Percival Glyde.'

'Am I?'

Her colour was rising, and her hands were at work again, smoothing her gown. I pressed the point farther and farther home—I went on, without allowing her a moment of delay.

'Sir Percival has a high position in the world,' I said; 'it would be no wonder if you were afraid of him. Sir Percival is a powerful man—a Baronet—the possessor of a fine estate—the descendant of a great family——'

She amazed me beyond expression by suddenly bursting out laughing.

'Yes,' she repeated, in tones of the bitterest, steadiest contempt. 'A Baronet—the possessor of a fine estate—the descendant of a great family. Yes, indeed! A great family—especially by the mother's side.'

There was no time to reflect on the words that had just escaped her; there was only time to feel that they were well worth thinking over the moment I left the house.

'I am not here to dispute with you about family questions,' I said. 'I know nothing of Sir Percival's mother——'

'And you know as little of Sir Percival himself,' she interposed, sharply.

'I advise you not to be too sure of that,' I rejoined. 'I know some things about him—and I suspect many more.'

'What do you suspect?'

'I'll tell you what I *don't* suspect. I *don't* suspect him of being Anne's father.'

She started to her feet, and came close up to me with a look of fury.

'How dare you talk to me about Anne's father! How dare you say who was her father, or who wasn't!' she broke out, her face quivering, her voice trembling with passion.

'The secret between you and Sir Percival is not *that* secret,' I persisted. 'The mystery which darkens Sir Percival's life was not born with your daughter's birth, and has not died with your daughter's death.'

She drew back a step. 'Go!' she said, and pointed sternly to the door.

'There was no thought of the child in your heart or in his,' I went on, determined to press her back to her last defences. 'There was no bond of guilty love between you and him, when you held those stolen meetings—when your husband found you whispering together under the vestry of the church.'

Her pointing hand instantly dropped to her side, and the deep flush of anger faded from her face while I spoke. I saw the change pass over her; I saw that hard, firm, fearless, self-possessed woman quail under a terror which her utmost resolution was not strong enough to resist—when I said those five last words, 'the vestry of the church.'

For a minute, or more, we stood looking at each other in silence. I spoke first.

'Do you still refuse to trust me?' I asked.

She could not call the colour that had left it back to her face—but she had steadied her voice, she had recovered the defiant self-possession of her manner, when she answered me.

'I do refuse,' she said.

'Do you still tell me to go?'

'Yes. Go—and never come back.'

I walked to the door, waited a moment before I opened it, and turned round to look at her again.

'I may have news to bring you of Sir Percival, which you don't expect,' I said; 'and, in that case, I shall come back.'

'There is no news of Sir Percival that I don't expect, except——'

She stopped; her pale face darkened; and she stole back, with a quiet, stealthy, cat-like step to her chair.

'Except the news of his death,' she said, sitting down again, with the mockery of a smile just hovering on her cruel lips, and the furtive light of hatred lurking deep in her steady eyes.

As I opened the door of the room, to go out, she looked round at me quickly. The cruel smile slowly widened her lips—she eyed me, with a strange, stealthy interest, from head to foot—an unutterable expectation showed itself wickedly all over her face. Was she speculating, in the secrecy of her own heart, on my youth and strength, on the force of my sense of injury and the limits of my self-control; and was she considering the lengths to which they might carry me, if Sir Percival and I ever chanced to meet? The bare doubt that it might be so, drove me from her presence, and silenced even the common forms of farewell on my lips. Without a word more, on my side or on hers, I left the room.

As I opened the outer door, I saw the same clergyman who had already passed the house once, about to pass it again, on his way back through the square. I waited on the door-step to let him go by, and looked round, as I did so, at the parlour window.

Mrs Catherick had heard his footsteps approaching, in the silence of that lonely place; and she was on her feet at the window again, waiting for him. Not all the strength of all the terrible passions I had roused in that woman's heart, could loosen her desperate hold on the one fragment of social consideration which years of resolute effort had just dragged within her grasp. There she was again, not a minute after I had left her, placed purposely in a position which made it a matter of common courtesy on the part of the clergyman to bow to her for a second time. He raised his hat, once more. I saw the hard, ghastly face behind the window, soften and light up with gratified pride; I saw the head with the grim black cap bend ceremoniously in return. The clergyman had bowed to her—and in my presence—twice in one day!

The new direction which my inquiries must now take was plainly presented to my mind, as I left the house. Mrs Catherick had helped me a step forward, in spite of herself. The next stage to be reached in the investigation was, beyond all doubt, the vestry of Old Welmingham church.

VIII

BEFORE I had reached the turning which led out of the square, my attention was aroused by the sound of a closing door, in the row of houses behind me.

I looked round, and saw an undersized man in black, on the door-step of the house, which, as well as I could judge, stood next to Mrs Catherick's place of abode—next to it, on the side nearest to me. The man did not hesitate a moment about the direction he should take. He advanced rapidly towards the turning at which I had stopped. I recognised him as the lawyer's clerk who had preceded me in my visit to Blackwater Park, and who had tried to pick a quarrel with me, when I asked him if I could see the house.

I waited where I was, to ascertain whether his object was to come to close quarters and speak, on this occasion. To my surprise, he passed on rapidly, without saying a word, without even looking up in my face as he went by. This was such a complete inversion of the course of proceeding which I had every reason to expect on his part, that my curiosity, or rather my suspicion, was aroused, and I determined, on my side, to keep him cautiously in view, and to discover what the business might be on which he was now employed. Without caring whether he saw me or not, I walked after him. He never looked back; and he led me straight through the streets to the railway station.

The train was on the point of starting, and two or three passengers who were late were clustering round the small opening through which the tickets were issued. I joined them, and distinctly heard the lawyer's clerk demand a ticket for the Blackwater station. I satisfied myself that he had actually left by the train, before I came away.

There was only one interpretation that I could place on what I had just seen and heard. I had unquestionably observed the man leaving a house which closely adjoined Mrs Catherick's residence. He had been probably placed there, by Sir Percival's directions, as a lodger, in anticipation of my inquiries leading me, sooner or later, to communicate with Mrs Catherick. He had doubtless seen me go in and come out; and he had hurried away by the first train to make his report at Blackwater Park—to which place Sir Percival would naturally betake himself (knowing what he evidently knew of my movements), in order to be ready on the spot, if I returned to Hampshire. I saw this clearly; and I felt for the first time that the apprehensions which Marian had expressed to me at parting, might be realised. Before many days were over, there seemed every likelihood, now, that he and I might meet.

Whatever result events might be destined to produce, I resolved to pursue my own course, straight to the end in view, without stopping or turning aside, for Sir Percival, or for any one. The great responsibility which weighed on me heavily in London—the responsibility of so guiding my slightest actions as to prevent them from leading accidentally to the discovery of Laura's place of refuge—was removed, now that I was in Hampshire. I could go and come as I pleased, at Welmingham; and if I chanced to fail in observing any necessary precautions, the immediate results, at least, would affect no one but myself.

When I left the station, the winter evening was beginning to close in. There was little hope of continuing my inquiries after dark to any useful purpose, in a neighbourhood that was strange to me. Accordingly, I made my way to the nearest hotel, and ordered my dinner and my bed. This done, I wrote to Marian, to tell her that I was safe and well, and that I had fair prospects of success. I had directed her, on leaving home, to address the first letter she wrote to me (the letter I expected to receive the next morning) to 'The Post-office, Welmingham;' and I now begged her to send her second day's letter to the same address. I could easily receive it, by writing to the postmaster, if I happened to be away from the town when it arrived.

The coffee-room of the hotel, as it grew late in the evening, became a perfect solitude. I was left to reflect on what I had accomplished that afternoon, as uninterruptedly as if the house had been my own. Before I retired to rest, I had attentively thought over my extraordinary interview with Mrs Catherick, from beginning to end; and had verified, at my leisure, the conclusions which I had hastily drawn in the earlier part of the day.

The vestry of Old Welmingham church was the starting-point from which my mind slowly worked its way back through all that I had heard Mrs Catherick say, and through all that I had seen Mrs Catherick do.

At the time when the neighbourhood of the vestry was first referred to in my presence by Mrs Clements, I had thought it the strangest and most unaccountable of all places for Sir Percival to select for a clandestine meeting with the clerk's wife. Influenced by this impression, and by no other, I had mentioned 'the vestry of the church,' before Mrs Catherick, on pure speculation—it represented one of the minor peculiarities of the story, which occurred to me while I was speaking. I was prepared for her answering me confusedly, or angrily; but the blank terror that seized her, when I said the words, took me completely by surprise. I had, long before, associated Sir Percival's Secret with the concealment of a serious crime, which Mrs Catherick knew of—but I had gone no farther than this. Now, the woman's paroxysm of terror associated the crime, either directly or indirectly, with the vestry, and convinced me that she had been more than the mere witness of it—she was also the accomplice, beyond a doubt.

What had been the nature of the crime? Surely there was a contemptible side to it, as well as a dangerous side—or Mrs Catherick would not have repeated my own words, referring to Sir Percival's rank and power, with such marked disdain as she had certainly displayed. It was a contemptible crime, then, and a dangerous crime; and she had shared in it, and it was associated with the vestry of the church.

The next consideration to be disposed of led me a step farther from this point.

Mrs Catherick's undisguised contempt for Sir Percival plainly extended to his mother as well. She had referred, with the bitterest sarcasm, to the great family he had descended from—'especially by the mother's side.' What did this mean? There appeared to be only two explanations of it. Either his mother's birth had been low? or his mother's reputation was damaged by some hidden flaw with which Mrs Catherick and Sir Percival were both privately acquainted? I could only put the first explanation to the test by looking at the register of her marriage, and so ascertaining her maiden name and her parentage, as a preliminary to further inquiries.

On the other hand, if the second case supposed were the true one, what had been the flaw in her reputation? Remembering the account which Marian had given me of Sir Percival's father and mother, and of the suspiciously-unsocial secluded life they had both led, I now asked myself, whether it might not be possible that his mother had never been married at all. Here again, the register might, by offering written evidence of the marriage, prove to me, at any rate, that this doubt had no foundation in truth. But where was the register to be found? At this point, I took up the conclusions which I had previously formed; and the same mental process which had discovered the locality of the concealed crime, now lodged the register, also, in the vestry of Old Welmingham church.

These were the results of my interview with Mrs Catherick—these were the various considerations, all steadily converging to one point, which decided the course of my proceedings on the next day.

The morning was cloudy and lowering, but no rain fell. I left my bag at the hotel, to wait there till I called for it; and, after inquiring the way, set forth on foot for Old Welmingham church.

It was a walk of rather more than two miles, the ground rising slowly all the way.

On the highest point stood the church—an ancient, weather-beaten building, with heavy buttresses at its sides, and a clumsy square tower in front. The vestry, at the back, was built out from the church, and seemed to be of the same age. Round the building, at intervals, appeared the remains of the village which Mrs Clements had described to me as her husband's place of abode in former years, and which the principal inhabitants had long since deserted for the new town. Some of the empty houses had been dismantled to their outer walls; some had been left to decay with time; and some were still inhabited by persons evidently of the poorest class. It was a dreary scene—and yet, in the worst aspect of its ruin, not so dreary as the modern town that I had just left. Here, there was the brown, breezy sweep of surrounding fields for the eye to repose on; here the trees, leafless as they were, still varied the monotony of the prospect, and helped the mind to look forward to summer time and shade.

As I moved away from the back of the church, and passed some of the dismantled cottages in search of a person who might direct me to the clerk, I saw two men saunter out after me, from behind a wall. The tallest of the two—a stout muscular man, in the dress of a gamekeeper—was a stranger to me. The other was one of the men who had followed me in London, on the day when I left Mr Kyrle's office. I had taken particular notice of him, at the time; and I felt sure that I was not mistaken in identifying the fellow on this occasion.

Neither he nor his companion attempted to speak to me, and both kept themselves at a respectful distance—but the motive of their presence in the neighbourhood of the church was plainly apparent. It was exactly as I had supposed—Sir Percival was already prepared for me. My visit to Mrs Catherick had been reported to him the evening before; and those two men had been placed on the look-out, near the church, in anticipation of my appearance at Old Welmingham. If I had wanted any further proof that my investigations had taken the right direction at last, the plan now adopted for watching me would have supplied it.

I walked on, away from the church, till I reached one of the inhabited houses, with a patch of kitchen garden attached to it, on which a labourer was at work. He directed me to the clerk's abode—a cottage, at some little distance off, standing by itself on the outskirts of the forsaken village. The clerk was in-doors, and was just putting on his great-coat. He was a cheerful, familiar, loudly-talkative old man, with a very poor opinion (as I soon discovered) of the place in which he lived, and a happy sense of superiority to his neighbours in virtue of the great distinction of having once been in London.

'It's well you came so early, sir,' said the old man, when I had mentioned the object of my visit. 'I should have been away in ten minutes more. Parish business, sir—and a goodish long trot before it's all done, for a man at my age. But, bless you, I'm strong on my legs still! As long as a man don't give at his legs, there's a deal of work left in him. Don't you think so, yourself, sir?'

He took his keys down, while he was talking, from a hook behind the fireplace, and locked his cottage door behind us.

'Nobody at home to keep house for me,' said the clerk, with a cheerful sense of perfect freedom from all family encumbrances. 'My wife's in the churchyard, there; and my children are all married. A wretched place this, isn't it, sir? But the parish is a large one—every man couldn't get through the business as I do. It's learning does it; and I've had my share, and a little more. I can talk the Queen's English (God bless the Queen!)—and that's more than most of the people about here can do. You're from London, I suppose, sir? I've been in London, a matter of five-and-twenty year ago. What's the news there, now, if you please?'

Chattering on in this way, he led me back to the vestry. I looked about, to see if the two spies were still in sight. They were not visible anywhere. After having discovered my application to the clerk, they had probably concealed themselves where they could watch my next proceedings in perfect freedom.

The vestry door was of stout old oak, studded with strong nails; and the clerk put his large, heavy key into the lock, with the air of a man who knew that he had a difficulty to encounter, and who was not quite certain of creditably conquering it.

'I'm obliged to bring you this way, sir,' he said, 'because the door from the vestry to the church is bolted on the vestry side. We might have got in through the church, otherwise. This is a perverse lock, if ever there was one yet. It's big enough for a prison-door; it's been hampered over and over again; and it ought to be changed for a new one. I've mentioned that to the churchwarden, fifty times over at least: he's always saying "I'll see about it"—and he never does see. Ah, it's a sort of lost corner, this place. Not like London—is it, sir? Bless you, we are all asleep here! *We* don't march with the times.'

After some twisting and turning of the key, the heavy lock yielded; and he opened the door.

The vestry was larger than I should have supposed it to be, judging from the outside only. It was a dim, mouldy, melancholy old room, with a low, raftered ceiling. Round two sides of it, the sides nearest to the interior of the church, ran heavy wooden presses, wormeaten and gaping with age. Hooked to the inner corner of one of these presses hung several surplices, all bulging out at their lower ends in an irreverent-looking bundle of limp drapery. Below the surplices, on the floor, stood three packing-cases, with the lids half off, half on, and the straw profusely bursting out of their cracks and crevices in every direction. Behind them, in a corner, was a litter of dusty papers; some large and rolled up, like architects' plans; some loosely strung together on files, like bills or letters. The room had once been lighted by a small side window; but this had been bricked up, and a lantern skylight was now substituted for it. The atmosphere was heavy and mouldy; being rendered additionally oppressive by the closing of the door which led into the church. This door also was composed of solid oak, and was bolted, at top and bottom, on the vestry side.

'We might be tidier, mightn't we, sir?' said the cheerful clerk. 'But when you're in a lost corner of a place like this, what are you to do? Why, look here, now—just look at these packing-cases. There they've been, for a year or more, ready to go to London—there they are, littering the place—and there they'll stop as long as the nails hold them together. I'll tell you what, sir, as I said before, this is not London. We are all asleep here. Bless you, *we* don't march with the times!'

'What is there in the packing-cases?' I asked.

'Bits of old wood carvings from the pulpit, and panels from the chancel, and images from the organ-loft,' said the clerk. 'Portraits of the twelve apostles in wood—and not a whole nose among 'em. All broken, and wormeaten, and crumbling to dust at the edges—as brittle as crockery, sir, and as old as the church, if not older.'

'And why were they going to London? To be repaired?'

'That's it, sir. To be repaired; and where they were past repair, to be copied in sound wood. But, bless you, the money fell short—and there they are, waiting for new subscriptions, and nobody to subscribe. It was all done a year ago, sir. Six gentlemen dined together about it, at the hotel in the new town. They made speeches, and passed resolutions, and put their names down, and printed off thousands of prospectuses. Beautiful prospectuses, sir, all flourished over with Gothic devices in red ink, saying it was a disgrace not to restore the church and repair the famous carvings, and so on. There are the prospectuses that couldn't be distributed, and the architect's plans and estimates, and the whole correspondence which set everybody at loggerheads and ended in a dispute, all down together in that corner, behind the packing-cases. The money dribbled in a little at first—but what *can* you expect out of London? There was just enough, you know, to pack the broken carvings, and get the estimates, and pay the printer's bill—and after that, there wasn't a halfpenny left. There the things are, as I've said before. We have nowhere else to put them—nobody in the new town cares about accommodating *us*—we're in a lost corner—and this is an untidy vestry— and who's to help it?—that's what I want to know.'

My anxiety to examine the register did not dispose me to offer much encouragement to the old man's talkativeness. I agreed with him that nobody could help the untidiness of the vestry—and then suggested that we should proceed to our business without more delay.

'Ay, ay, the marriage register, to be sure,' said the clerk, taking a little bunch of keys from his pocket. 'How far do you want to look back, sir?'

Marian had informed me of Sir Percival's age, at the time when we had spoken together of his marriage engagement with Laura. She had then described him as being forty-five years old. Calculating back from this, and making due allowance for the year that had passed since I had gained my information, I found that he must have been born in eighteen hundred and four, and that I might safely start on my search through the register from that date.

'I want to begin with the year eighteen hundred and four,' I said.

'Which way after that, sir?' asked the clerk. 'Forwards to our time, or backwards away from us?'

'Backwards from eighteen hundred and four.'

He opened the door of one of the presses—the press from the side of which the surplices were hanging—and produced a large volume bound in greasy brown leather. I was struck by the insecurity of the place in which the register was kept. The door of the press was warped and cracked with age; and the lock was of the smallest and commonest kind. I could have forced it easily with the walking-stick I carried in my hand.

'Is that considered a sufficiently secure place for the register?' I inquired. 'Surely, a book of such importance ought to be protected by a better lock, and kept carefully in an iron safe?'

'Well, now, that's curious!' said the clerk, shutting up the book again, just after he had opened it, and smacking his hand cheerfully on the cover. 'Those were the very words my old master was always saying, years and years ago, when I was a lad. "Why isn't the register" (meaning this register here, under my hand)—"why isn't it kept in an iron safe?" If I've heard him say that once, I've heard him say it a hundred times. He was the solicitor, in those days, sir, who had the appointment of vestry-clerk to this church. A fine hearty old gentleman—and the most particular man breathing. As long as he lived, he kept a copy of this book, in his office at Knowlesbury, and had it posted up regular, from time to time, to correspond with the fresh entries here. You would hardly think it, but he had his own appointed days, once or twice, in every quarter, for riding over to this church on his old white pony to check the copy, by the register, with his own eyes and hands. "How do I know" (he used to say)—"how do I know that the register in this vestry may not be stolen or destroyed? Why isn't it kept in an iron safe? Why can't I make other people as careful as I am myself? Some of these days there will be an accident happen—and when the register's lost, then the parish will find out the value of my copy." He used to take his pinch of snuff after that, and look about him as bold as a lord. Ah! the like of him for doing business isn't easy to find now. You may go to London, and not match him, even *there*. Which year did you say, sir? Eighteen hundred and what?'

'Eighteen hundred and four,' I replied; mentally resolving to give the old man no more opportunities of talking, until my examination of the register was over.

The clerk put on his spectacles, and turned over the leaves of the register, carefully wetting his finger and thumb, at every third page. 'There it is, sir,' he said, with another cheerful smack on the open volume. 'There's the year you want.'

As I was ignorant of the month in which Sir Percival was born, I began my backward search with the early part of the year. The register-book was of the old fashioned kind; the entries being all made on blank pages, in manuscript, and the divisions which separated them being indicated by ink lines drawn across the page, at the close of each entry.

I reached the beginning of the year eighteen hundred and four, without encountering the marriage; and then travelled back through December, eighteen hundred and three; through November, and October; through——

No! not through September also. Under the heading of that month in the year I found the marriage!

I looked carefully at the entry. It was at the bottom of a page, and was, for want of room, compressed into a smaller space than that occupied by the marriages above. The marriage immediately before it was impressed on my attention by the circumstance of the bridegroom's Christian name being the same as my own. The entry immediately following it (on the top of the next page) was noticeable, in another way, from the large space it occupied; the record, in this case, registering the marriages of two brothers at the same time. The register of the marriage of Sir Felix Glyde was in no respect remarkable, except for the narrowness of the space into which it was compressed at the bottom of the page. The information about his wife, was the usual information given in such cases. She was described as 'Cecilia Jane Elster, of Park-View Cottages, Knowlesbury; only daughter of the late Patrick Elster, Esq., formerly of Bath.'

I noted down these particulars in my pocket-book, feeling, as I did so, both doubtful and disheartened about my next proceedings. The Secret, which I had believed, until this moment, to be within my grasp, seemed now farther from my reach than ever.

What suggestions of any mystery unexplained had arisen out of my visit to the vestry? I saw no suggestions anywhere. What progress had I made towards discovering the suspected stain on the reputation of Sir Percival's mother? The one fact I had ascertained, vindicated her reputation. Fresh doubts, fresh difficulties, fresh delays, began to open before me in interminable prospect. What was I to do next? The one immediate resource left to me, appeared to be this: I might institute inquiries about 'Miss Elster, of Knowlesbury,' on the chance of advancing towards the main object of my investigation, by first discovering the secret of Mrs Catherick's contempt for Sir Percival's mother.

'Have you found what you wanted, sir?' said the clerk, as I closed the register-book.

'Yes,' I replied; 'but I have some inquiries still to make. I suppose the clergyman who officiated here in the year eighteen hundred and three is no longer alive?'

'No, no, sir; he was dead three or four years before I came here—and that was as long ago as the year twenty-seven. I got this place, sir,' persisted my talkative old friend, 'through the clerk before me leaving it. They say he was driven out of house and home by his wife—and she's living still, down in the new town there. I don't know the rights of the story, myself; all I know is, I got the place. Mr Wansborough got it for me—the son of my old master that I was telling you of. He's a free, pleasant gentleman as ever lived; rides to the hounds, keeps his pointers, and all that. He's vestry-clerk here now, as his father was before him.'

'Did you not tell me your former master lived at Knowlesbury?' I asked, calling to mind the long story about the precise gentleman of the old school, with which my talkative friend had wearied me before he opened the register-book.

'Yes, to be sure, sir,' replied the clerk. 'Old Mr Wansborough lived at Knowlesbury; and young Mr Wansborough lives there too.'

'You said just now he was vestry-clerk, like his father before him. I am not quite sure that I know what a vestry-clerk is.'

'Don't you indeed, sir?—and you come from London, too! Every parish church, you know, has a vestry-clerk and a parish-clerk. The parish-clerk is a man like me (except that I've got a deal more learning than most of them—though I don't boast of it). The vestry-clerk is a sort of an appointment that the lawyers get; and if there's any business to be done for the vestry, why there they are to do it. It's just the same in London. Every parish church there has got its vestry-clerk—and, you may take my word for it, he's sure to be a lawyer.'

'Then, young Mr Wansborough is a lawyer, I suppose?'

'Of course he is, sir! A lawyer in High-street, Knowlesbury—the old offices that his father had before him. The number of times I've swept those offices out, and seen the old gentleman come trotting in to business on his white pony, looking right and left all down the street, and nodding to everybody! Bless you, he was a popular character!—he'd have done in London!'

'How far is it to Knowlesbury from this place?'

'A long stretch, sir,' said the clerk, with that exaggerated idea of distances and that vivid perception of difficulties in getting from place to place, which is peculiar to all country people. 'Nigh on five mile, I can tell you!'

It was still early in the forenoon. There was plenty of time for a walk to Knowlesbury and back again to Welmingham; and there was no person probably in the town who was fitter to assist my inquiries about the character and position of Sir Percival's mother, before her marriage, than the local solicitor. Resolving to go at once to Knowlesbury on foot, I led the way out of the vestry.

'Thank you kindly, sir,' said the clerk, as I slipped my little present into his hand. 'Are you really going to walk all the way to Knowlesbury and back? Well! you're strong on your legs, too—and what a blessing that is, isn't it? There's the road; you can't miss it. I wish I was going your way—it's pleasant to meet with gentlemen from London, in a lost corner like this. One hears the news. Wish you good morning, sir—and thank you kindly, once more.'

We parted. As I left the church behind me, I looked back—and there were the two men again, on the road below, with a third in their company; that third person being the short man in black, whom I had traced to the railway the evening before.

The three stood talking together for a little while—then separated. The man in black went away by himself towards Welmingham; the other two remained together, evidently waiting to follow me, as soon as I walked on.

I proceeded on my way, without letting the fellows see that I took any special notice of them. They caused me no conscious irritation of feeling at that moment—on the contrary, they rather revived my sinking hopes. In the surprise of discovering the evidence of the marriage, I had forgotten the inference I had drawn, on first perceiving the men in the neighbourhood of the vestry. Their reappearance reminded me that Sir Percival had anticipated my visit to Old Welmingham church, as the next result of my interview with Mrs Catherick—otherwise, he would never have placed his spies there to wait for me. Smoothly and fairly as appearances looked in the vestry, there was something wrong beneath them—there was something in the register-book, for aught I knew, that I had not discovered yet.

'I shall come back,' I thought to myself, as I turned for a farewell look at the tower of the old church. 'I shall trouble the cheerful clerk a second time to conquer the perverse lock, and to open the vestry door.'

IX

ONCE out of sight of the church, I pressed forward briskly on my way to Knowlesbury.

The road was, for the most part, straight and level. Whenever I looked back over it, I saw the two spies, steadily following me. For the greater part of the way, they kept at a safe distance behind. But, once or twice, they quickened their pace, as if with the purpose of overtaking me—then stopped—consulted together—and fell back again to their former position. They had some special object evidently in view; and they seemed to be hesitating, or differing, about the best means of accomplishing it. I could not guess exactly what their design might be; but I felt serious doubts of reaching Knowlesbury without some mischance happening to me on the way. Those doubts were realised.

I had just entered on a lonely part of the road, with a sharp turn at some distance ahead, and had concluded (calculating by time) that I must be getting near to the town, when I suddenly heard the steps of the men close behind me.

Before I could look round, one of them (the man by whom I had been followed in London) passed rapidly on my left side, and hustled me with his shoulder. I had been more irritated by the manner in which he and his companion had dogged my steps all the way from Old Welmingham than I was myself aware of; and I unfortunately pushed the fellow away smartly with my open hand. He instantly shouted for help. His companion, the tall man in the gamekeeper's clothes, sprang to my right side—and the next moment the two scoundrels held me pinioned between them in the middle of the road.

The conviction that a trap had been laid for me, and the vexation of knowing that I had fallen into it, fortunately restrained me from making my position still worse by an unavailing struggle with two men—one of whom would in all probability have been more than a match for me, single handed. I repressed the first natural movement by which I had attempted to shake them off, and looked about to see if there was any person near to whom I could appeal.

A labourer was at work in an adjoining field, who must have witnessed all that had passed. I called to him to follow us to the town. He shook his head with stolid obstinacy, and walked away, in the direction of a cottage which stood back from the high-road. At the same time the men who held me between them declared their intention of charging me with an assault. I was cool enough and wise enough, now, to make no opposition. 'Drop your hold of my arms,' I said, 'and I will go with you to the town.' The man in the gamekeeper's dress roughly refused. But the shorter man was sharp enough to look to consequences, and not to let his companion commit himself by unnecessary violence. He made a sign to the other, and I walked on between them, with my arms free.

We reached the turning in the road; and there, close before us, were the suburbs of Knowlesbury. One of the local policemen was walking along the path by the roadside. The men at once appealed to him. He replied that the magistrate was then sitting at the town-hall; and recommended that we should appear before him immediately.

We went on to the town-hall. The clerk made out a formal summons; and the charge was preferred against me, with the customary exaggeration and the customary perversion of the truth, on such occasions. The magistrate (an ill-tempered man, with a sour enjoyment in the exercise of his own power) inquired if any one on, or near, the road had witnessed the assault; and, greatly to my surprise, the complainant admitted the presence of the labourer in the field. I was enlightened, however, as to the object of the admission, by the magistrate's next words. He remanded me, at once, for the production of the witness; expressing, at the same time, his willingness to take bail for my reappearance, if I could produce one responsible surety to offer it. If I had been known in the town, he would have liberated me on my own recognisances; but, as I was a total stranger, it was necessary that I should find responsible bail.

The whole object of the stratagem was now disclosed to me. It had been so managed as to make a remand necessary in a town where I was a perfect stranger, and where I could not hope to get my liberty on bail. The remand merely extended over three days, until the next sitting of the magistrate. But, in that time, while I was in confinement, Sir Percival might use any means he pleased to embarrass my future proceedings—perhaps to screen himself from detection altogether—without the slightest fear of any hindrance on my part. At the end of the three days, the charge would, no doubt, be withdrawn; and the attendance of the witness would be perfectly useless.

My indignation, I may almost say, my despair, at this mischievous check to all further progress—so base and trifling in itself, and yet so disheartening and so serious in its probable results—quite unfitted me, at first, to reflect on the best means of extricating myself from the dilemma in which I now stood. I had the folly to call for writing materials, and to think of privately communicating my real position to the magistrate. The hopelessness and the imprudence of this proceeding failed to strike me before I had actually written the opening lines of the letter. It was not till I had pushed the paper away—not till, I am ashamed to say, I had almost allowed the vexation of my helpless position to conquer me—that a course of action suddenly occurred to my mind, which Sir Percival had probably not anticipated, and which might set me free again in a few hours. I determined to communicate the situation in which I was placed to Mr Dawson, of Oak Lodge.

I had visited this gentleman's house, it may be remembered, at the time of my first inquiries in the Blackwater Park neighbourhood; and I had presented to him a letter of introduction from Miss Halcombe, in which she recommended me to his friendly attention in the strongest terms. I now wrote, referring to this letter, and to what I had previously told Mr Dawson of the delicate and dangerous nature of my inquiries. I had not revealed to him the truth about Laura; having merely described my errand as being of the utmost importance to private family interests with which Miss Halcombe was concerned. Using the same caution still, I now accounted for my presence at Knowlesbury in the same manner—and I put it to the doctor to say whether the trust reposed in me by a lady whom he well knew, and the hospitality I had myself received in his house, justified me or not in asking him to come to my assistance in a place where I was quite friendless.

I obtained permission to hire a messenger to drive away at once with my letter, in a conveyance which might be used to bring the doctor back immediately. Oak Lodge was on the Knowlesbury side of Blackwater. The man declared he could drive there in forty minutes, and could bring Mr Dawson back in forty more. I directed him to follow the doctor wherever he might happen to be, if he was not at home—and then sat down to wait for the result with all the patience and all the hope that I could summon to help me.

It was not quite half-past one when the messenger departed. Before half-past three, he returned, and brought the doctor with him. Mr Dawson's kindness, and the delicacy with which he treated his prompt assistance quite as a matter of course, almost overpowered me. The bail required was offered, and accepted immediately. Before four o'clock, on that afternoon, I was shaking hands warmly with the good old doctor—a free man again—in the streets of Knowlesbury.

Mr Dawson hospitably invited me to go back with him to Oak Lodge, and take up my quarters there for the night. I could only reply that my time was not my own; and I could only ask him to let me pay my visit in a few days, when I might repeat my thanks, and offer to him all the explanations which I felt to be only his due, but which I was not then in a position to make. We parted with friendly assurances on both sides; and I turned my steps at once to Mr Wansborough's office in the High-street.

Time was now of the last importance.

The news of my being free on bail would reach Sir Percival, to an absolute certainty, before night. If the next few hours did not put me in a position to justify his worst fears, and to hold him helpless at my mercy, I might lose every inch of the ground I had gained, never to recover it again. The unscrupulous nature of the man, the local influence he possessed, the desperate peril of exposure with which my blindfold inquiries threatened him—all warned me to press on to positive discovery, without the useless waste of a single minute. I had found time to think, while I was waiting for Mr Dawson's arrival; and I had well employed it. Certain portions of the conversation of the talkative old clerk, which had wearied me at the time, now recurred to my memory with a new significance; and a suspicion crossed my mind darkly, which had not occurred to me while I was in the vestry. On my way to Knowlesbury, I had only proposed to apply to Mr Wansborough for information on the subject of Sir Percival's mother. My object, now, was to examine the duplicate register of Old Welmingham church.

Mr Wansborough was in his office when I inquired for him.

He was a jovial, red-faced, easy-looking man—more like a country squire than a lawyer—and he seemed to be both surprised and amused by my application. He had heard of his father's copy of the register; but had not even seen it himself. It had never been inquired after—and it was no doubt in the strong-room, among other papers that had not been disturbed since his father's death. It was a pity (Mr Wansborough said) that the old gentleman was not alive to hear his precious copy asked for at last. He would have ridden his favourite hobby harder than ever, now. How had I come to hear of the copy? was it through anybody in the town?

I parried the question as well as I could. It was impossible at this stage of the investigation to be too cautious; and it was just as well not to let Mr Wansborough know prematurely that I had already examined the original register. I described myself, therefore, as pursuing a family inquiry, to the object of which every possible saving of time was of great importance. I was anxious to send certain particulars to London by that day's post; and one look at the duplicate register (paying, of course, the necessary fees) might supply what I required, and save me a further journey to Old Welmingham. I added that, in the event of my subsequently requiring a copy of the original register, I should make application to Mr Wansborough's office to furnish me with the document.

After this explanation, no objection was made to producing the copy. A clerk was sent to the strong-room, and, after some delay, returned with the volume. It was of exactly the same size as the volume in the vestry; the only difference being that the copy was more smartly bound. I took it with me to an unoccupied desk. My hands were trembling—my head was burning hot—I felt the necessity of concealing my agitation as well as I could from the persons about me in the room, before I ventured on opening the book.

On the blank page at the beginning, to which I first turned, were traced some lines, in faded ink. They contained these words:

'Copy of the Marriage Register of Welmingham Parish Church. Executed under my orders; and afterwards compared, entry by entry, with the original, by myself. (Signed) Robert Wansborough, vestry-clerk.' Below this note, there was a line added, in another handwriting, as follows: 'Extending from the first of January, 1800, to the thirtieth of June, 1815.'

I turned to the month of September, eighteen hundred and three. I found the marriage of the man whose Christian name was the same as my own. I found the double register of the marriages of the two brothers. And between these entries at the bottom of the page——?

Nothing! Not a vestige of the entry which recorded the marriage of Sir Felix Glyde and Cecilia Jane Elster, in the register of the church!

My heart gave a great bound, and throbbed as if it would stifle me. I looked again—I was afraid to believe the evidence of my own eyes. No! not a doubt. The marriage was not there. The entries on the copy occupied exactly the same places on the page as the entries in the original. The last entry on one page recorded the marriage of the man with my Christian name. Below it, there was a blank space—a space evidently left because it was too narrow to contain the entry of the marriages of the two brothers, which in the copy, as in the original, occupied the top of the next page. That space told the whole story! There it must have remained, in the church register, from eighteen hundred and three (when the marriages had been solemnised and the copy had been made) to eighteen hundred and twenty-seven, when Sir Percival appeared at Old Welmingham. Here, at Knowlesbury, was the chance of committing the forgery, shown to me in the copy—and there, at Old Welmingham, was the forgery committed, in the register of the church!

My head turned giddy; I held by the desk to keep myself from falling. Of all the suspicions which had struck me, in relation to that desperate man, not one had been near the truth. The idea that he was not Sir Percival Glyde at all, that he had no more claim to the baronetcy and to Blackwater Park than the poorest labourer who worked on the estate, had never once occurred to my mind. At one time, I had thought he might be Anne Catherick's father; at another time, I had thought he might have been Anne Catherick's husband—the offence of which he was really guilty had been, from first to last, beyond the widest reach of my imagination. The paltry means by which the fraud had been effected, the magnitude and daring of the crime that it represented, the horror of the consequences involved in its discovery, overwhelmed me. Who could wonder, now, at the brute-restlessness of the wretch's life; at his desperate alternations between abject duplicity and reckless violence; at the madness of guilty distrust which had made him imprison Anne Catherick in the Asylum, and had given him over to the vile conspiracy against his wife, on the bare suspicion that the one and the other knew his terrible secret? The disclosure of that secret might, in past years, have hanged him—might now transport him for life. The disclosure of that secret, even if the sufferers by his deception spared him the penalties of the law, would deprive him, at one blow, of the name, the rank, the estate, the whole social existence that he had usurped. This was the Secret, and it was mine! A word from me; and house, lands, baronetcy, were gone from him for ever—a word from me, and he was driven out into the world a nameless, penniless, friendless outcast! The man's whole future hung on my lips—and he knew it, by this time, as certainly as I did!

That last thought steadied me. Interests far more precious than my own depended on the caution which must now guide my slightest actions. There was no possible treachery which Sir Percival might not attempt against me. In the danger and desperation of his position, he would be staggered by no risks, he would recoil at no crime—he would, literally, hesitate at nothing to save himself.

I considered for a minute. My first necessity was to secure positive evidence, in writing, of the discovery that I had just made, and, in the event of any personal misadventure happening to me, to place that evidence beyond Sir Percival's reach. The copy of the register was sure to be safe in Mr Wansborough's strong-room. But the position of the original, in the vestry, was, as I had seen with my own eyes, anything but secure.

In this emergency, I resolved to return to the church, to apply again to the clerk, and to take the necessary extract from the register, before I slept that night. I was not then aware that a legally-certified copy was necessary, and that no document merely drawn out by myself could claim the proper importance, as a proof. I was not aware of this; and my determination to keep my present proceedings a secret, prevented me from asking any questions which might have procured the necessary information. My one anxiety was the anxiety to get back to Old Welmingham. I made the best excuses I could for the discomposure in my face and manner, which Mr Wansborough had already noticed; laid the necessary fee on his table; arranged that I should write to him, in a day or two; and left the office, with my head in a whirl, and my blood throbbing through my veins at fever heat.

It was just getting dark. The idea occurred to me that I might be followed again, and attacked on the high-road.

My walking-stick was a light one, of little or no use for purposes of defence. I stopped, before leaving Knowlesbury, and bought a stout country cudgel, short, and heavy at the head. With this homely weapon, if any one man tried to stop me, I was a match for him. If more than one attacked me, I could trust to my heels. In my school-days, I had been a noted runner— and I had not wanted for practice since, in the later time of my experience in Central America.

I started from the town at a brisk pace, and kept the middle of the road.

A small misty rain was falling; and it was impossible, for the first half of the way, to make sure whether I was followed or not. But at the last half of my journey, when I supposed myself to be about two miles from the church, I saw a man run by me in the rain—and then heard the gate of a field by the roadside shut to, sharply. I kept straight on, with my cudgel ready in my hand, my ears on the alert, and my eyes straining to see through the mist and the darkness. Before I had advanced a hundred yards, there was a rustling in the hedge on my right, and three men sprang out into the road.

I drew aside on the instant to the footpath. The two foremost men were carried beyond me, before they could check themselves. The third was as quick as lightning. He stopped—half turned—and struck at me with his stick. The blow was aimed at hazard, and was not a severe one. It fell on my left shoulder. I returned it heavily on his head. He staggered back, and jostled his two companions, just as they were both rushing at me. This circumstance gave me a moment's start. I slipped past them, and took to the middle of the road again, at the top of my speed.

The two unhurt men pursued me. They were both good runners; the road was smooth and level; and, for the first five minutes or more, I was conscious that I did not gain on them. It was perilous work to run for long in the darkness. I could barely see the dim black line of the hedges on either side; and any chance obstacle in the road would have thrown me down to a certainty. Ere long, I felt the ground changing: it descended from the level, at a turn, and then rose again beyond. Down-hill, the men rather gained on me; but, up-hill, I began to distance them. The rapid, regular thump of their feet grew fainter on my ear; and I calculated by the sound that I was far enough in advance to take to the fields, with a good chance of their passing me in the darkness. Diverging to the footpath, I made for the first break that I could guess at, rather than see, in the hedge. It proved to be a closed gate. I vaulted over, and finding myself in a field, kept across it steadily, with my back to the road. I heard the men pass the gate, still running—then, in a minute more, heard one of them call to the other to come back. It was no matter what they did, now; I was out of their sight and out of their hearing. I kept straight across the field, and, when I had reached the further extremity of it, waited there for a minute to recover my breath.

It was impossible to venture back to the road; but I was determined, nevertheless, to get to Old Welmingham that evening.

Neither moon nor stars appeared to guide me. I only knew that I had kept the wind and rain at my back on leaving Knowlesbury—and if I now kept them at my back still, I might at least be certain of not advancing altogether in the wrong direction.

Proceeding on this plan, I crossed the country—meeting with no worse obstacles than hedges, ditches, and thickets, which every now and then obliged me to alter my course for a little while—until I found myself on a hill-side, with the ground sloping away steeply before me. I descended to the bottom of the hollow, squeezed my way through a hedge, and got out into a lane. Having turned to the right on leaving the road, I now turned to the left, on the chance of regaining the line from which I had wandered. After following the muddy windings of the lane for ten minutes or more, I saw a cottage with a light in one of the windows. The garden gate was open to the lane; and I went in at once to inquire my way.

Before I could knock at the door, it was suddenly opened, and a man came running out with a lighted lantern in his hand. He stopped and held it up at the sight of me. We both started as we saw each other. My wanderings had led me round the outskirts of the village, and had brought me out at the lower end of it. I was back at Old Welmingham; and the man with the lantern was no other than my acquaintance of the morning, the parish-clerk.

His manner appeared to have altered strangely, in the interval since I had last seen him. He looked suspicious and confused; his ruddy cheeks were deeply flushed; and his first words, when he spoke, were quite unintelligible to me.

'Where are the keys?' he said. 'Have you taken them?'

'What keys?' I repeated. 'I have this moment come from Knowlesbury. What keys do you mean?'

'The keys of the vestry. Lord save us and help us! what shall I do? The keys are gone! Do you hear?' cried the old man, shaking the lantern at me in his agitation; 'the keys are gone!'

'How? When? Who can have taken them?'

'I don't know,' said the clerk, staring about him wildly in the darkness. 'I've only just got back. I told you I had a long day's work this morning—I locked the door, and shut the window down—it's open now, the window's open. Look! somebody has got in there, and taken the keys.'

He turned to the casement-window to show me that it was wide open. The door of the lantern came loose from its fastening as he swayed it round; and the wind blew the candle out instantly.

'Get another light,' I said; 'and let us both go to the vestry together. Quick! quick!'

I hurried him into the house. The treachery that I had every reason to expect, the treachery that might deprive me of every advantage I had gained, was, at that moment, perhaps, in process of accomplishment. My impatience to reach the church was so great, that I could not remain inactive in the cottage while the clerk lit the lantern again. I walked out, down the garden path, into the lane.

Before I had advanced ten paces, a man approached me from the direction leading to the church. He spoke respectfully as we met. I could not see his face; but, judging by his voice only, he was a perfect stranger to me.

'I beg your pardon, Sir Percival——' he began.

I stopped him before he could say more.

'The darkness misleads you,' I said. 'I am not Sir Percival.'

The man drew back directly.

'I thought it was my master,' he muttered, in a confused, doubtful way.

'You expected to meet your master here?'

'I was told to wait in the lane.'

With that answer, he retraced his steps. I looked back at the cottage, and saw the clerk coming out, with the lantern lighted once more. I took the old man's arm to help him on the more quickly. We hastened along the lane, and passed the person who had accosted me. As well as I could see by the light of the lantern, he was a servant out of livery.

'Who's that?' whispered the clerk. 'Does he know anything about the keys?'

'We won't wait to ask him,' I replied. 'We will go on to the vestry first.'

The church was not visible, even by daytime, until the end of the lane was reached. As we mounted the rising ground which led to the building from that point, one of the village children—a boy—came close up to us, attracted by the light we carried, and recognised the clerk.

'I say, measter,' said the boy, pulling officiously at the clerk's coat, 'there be summun up yander in the church. I heerd un lock the door on hisself—I heerd un strike a loight wi' a match.'

The clerk trembled, and leaned against me heavily.

'Come! come!' I said, encouragingly. 'We are not too late. We will catch the man, whoever he is. Keep the lantern, and follow me as fast as you can.'

I mounted the hill rapidly. The dark mass of the church-tower was the first object I discerned dimly against the night sky. As I turned aside to get round to the vestry, I heard heavy footsteps close to me. The servant had ascended to the church after us. 'I don't mean any harm,' he said, when I turned round on him; 'I'm only looking for my master.' The tone in which he spoke betrayed unmistakable fear. I took no notice of him, and went on.

The instant I turned the corner, and came in view of the vestry, I saw the lantern-skylight on the roof brilliantly lit up from within. It shone out with dazzling brightness against the murky, starless sky.

I hurried through the churchyard to the door.

As I got near, there was a strange smell stealing out on the damp night air. I heard a snapping noise inside—I saw the light above grow brighter and brighter—a pane of the glass cracked—I ran to the door, and put my hands on it. The vestry was on fire!

Before I could move, before I could draw my breath after that discovery, I was horror-struck by a heavy thump against the door, from the inside. I heard the key worked violently in the lock—I heard a man's voice, behind the door, raised to a dreadful shrillness, screaming for help.

The servant, who had followed me, staggered back shuddering, and dropped to his knees. 'Oh, my God!' he said; 'it's Sir Percival!'

As the words passed his lips, the clerk joined us—and, at the same moment, there was another, and a last, grating turn of the key in the lock.

'The Lord have mercy on his soul!' said the old man. 'He is doomed and dead. He has hampered the lock.'

I rushed to the door. The one absorbing purpose that had filled all my thoughts, that had controlled all my actions, for weeks and weeks past, vanished in an instant from my mind. All remembrance of the heartless injury the man's crimes had inflicted; of the love, the innocence, the happiness he had pitilessly laid waste; of the oath I had sworn in my own heart to summon him to the terrible reckoning that he deserved—passed from my memory like a dream. I remembered nothing but the horror of his situation. I felt nothing but the natural human impulse to save him from a frightful death.

'Try the other door!' I shouted. 'Try the door into the church! The lock's hampered. You're a dead man if you waste another moment on it!'

There had been no renewed cry for help, when the key was turned for the last time. There was no sound, now, of any kind, to give token that he was still alive. I heard nothing but the quickening crackle of the flames, and the sharp snap of the glass in the skylight above.

I looked round at my two companions. The servant had risen to his feet: he had taken the lantern, and was holding it up vacantly at the door. Terror seemed to have struck him with downright idiocy—he waited at my heels, he followed me about when I moved, like a dog. The clerk sat crouched up on one of the tombstones, shivering, and moaning to himself. The one moment in which I looked at them was enough to show me that they were both helpless.

Hardly knowing what I did, acting desperately on the first impulse that occurred to me, I seized the servant and pushed him against the vestry wall. 'Stoop!' I said, 'and hold by the stones. I am going to climb over you to the roof—I am going to break the skylight, and give him some air!'

The man trembled from head to foot, but he held firm. I got on his back, with my cudgel in my mouth; seized the parapet with both hands; and was instantly on the roof. In the frantic hurry and agitation of the moment, it never struck me that I might let out the flame instead of letting in the air. I struck at the skylight, and battered in the cracked, loosened glass at a blow. The fire leaped out like a wild beast from its lair. If the wind had not chanced, in the position I occupied, to set it away from me, my exertions might have ended then and there. I crouched on the roof as the smoke poured out above me, with the flame. The gleams and flashes of the light showed me the servant's face staring up vacantly under the wall; the clerk risen to his feet on the tombstone, wringing his hands in despair; and the scanty population of the village, haggard men and terrified women, clustered beyond in the churchyard—all appearing and disappearing, in the red of the dreadful glare, in the black of the choking smoke. And the man beneath my feet!—the man, suffocating, burning, dying so near us all, so utterly beyond our reach!

The thought half maddened me. I lowered myself from the roof by my hands, and dropped to the ground.

'The key of the church!' I shouted to the clerk. 'We must try it that way—we may save him yet if we can burst open the inner door.'

'No, no, no!' cried the old man. 'No hope! the church key and the vestry key are on the same ring—both inside there! Oh, sir, he's past saving—he's dust and ashes by this time!'

'They'll see the fire from the town,' said a voice from among the men behind me. 'There's a ingine in the town. They'll save the church.'

I called to that man—*he* had his wits about him—I called to him to come and speak to me. It would be a quarter of an hour at least before the town engine could reach us. The horror of remaining inactive, all that time, was more than I could face. In defiance of my own reason I persuaded myself that the doomed and lost wretch in the vestry might still be lying senseless on the floor, might not be dead yet. If we broke open the door, might we save him? I knew the strength of the heavy lock—I knew the thickness of the nailed oak—I knew the hopelessness of assailing the one and the other by ordinary means. But surely there were beams still left in the dismantled cottages near the church? What if we got one, and used it as a battering-ram against the door?

The thought leaped through me, like the fire leaping out of the shattered skylight. I appealed to the man who had spoken first of the fire-engine in the town. 'Have you got your pickaxes handy?' Yes; they had. And a hatchet, and a saw, and a bit of rope? Yes! yes! yes! I ran down among the villagers, with the lantern in my hand. 'Five shillings apiece to every man who helps me!' They started into life at the words. That ravenous second hunger of poverty—the hunger for money—roused them into tumult and activity in a moment. 'Two of you for more lanterns if you have them! Two of you for the pickaxes and the tools! The rest after me to find the beam!' They cheered—with shrill starveling voices they cheered. The women and the children fled back on either side. We rushed in a body down the churchyard path to the first empty cottage. Not a man was left behind but the clerk—the poor old clerk standing on the flat tombstone sobbing and wailing over the church. The servant was still at my heels; his white, helpless, panic-stricken face was close over my shoulder as we pushed into the cottage. There were rafters from the torn-down floor above, lying loose on the ground—but they were too light. A beam ran across over our heads, but not out of reach of our arms and our pickaxes—a beam fast at each end in the ruined wall, with ceiling and flooring all ripped away, and a great gap in the roof above, open to the sky. We attacked the beam at both ends at once. God! how it held—how the brick and mortar of the wall resisted us! We struck, and tugged, and tore. The beam gave at one end—it came down with a lump of brickwork after it. There was a scream from the women all huddled in the doorway to look at us—a shout from the men—two of them down, but not hurt. Another tug all together—and the beam was loose at both ends. We raised it, and gave the word to clear the doorway. Now for the work! now for the rush at the door! There is the fire streaming into the sky, streaming brighter than ever to light us! Steady, along the churchyard path—steady with the beam, for a rush at the door. One, two, three—and off. Out rings the cheering again, irrepressibly. We have shaken it already; the hinges must give, if the lock won't. Another run with the beam! One, two, three—and off. It's loose! the stealthy fire darts at us through the crevice all round it. Another, and a last rush! The door falls in with a crash. A great hush of awe, a stillness of breathless expectation, possesses every living soul of us. We look for the body. The scorching heat on our faces drives us back: we see nothing—above, below, all through the room, we see nothing but a sheet of living fire.

'Where is he?' whispered the servant, staring vacantly at the flames.

'He's dust and ashes,' said the clerk. 'And the books are dust and ashes—and oh, sirs! the church will be dust and ashes soon.'

Those were the only two who spoke. When they were silent again, nothing stirred in the stillness but the bubble and the crackle of the flames.

Hark!

A harsh rattling sound in the distance—then, the hollow beat of horses' hoofs at full gallop—then, the low roar, the all-predominant tumult of hundreds of human voices clamouring and shouting together. The engine at last!

The people about me all turned from the fire, and ran eagerly to the brow of the hill. The old clerk tried to go with the rest; but his strength was exhausted. I saw him holding by one of the tombstones. 'Save the church!' he cried out, faintly, as if the firemen could hear him already. 'Save the church!'

The only man who never moved was the servant. There he stood, his eyes still fastened on the flames in a changeless, vacant stare. I spoke to him, I shook him by the arm. He was past rousing. He only whispered once more, 'Where is he?'

In ten minutes, the engine was in position; the well at the back of the church was feeding it; and the hose was carried to the doorway of the vestry. If help had been wanted from me, I could not have afforded it now. My energy of will was gone—my strength was exhausted—the turmoil of my thoughts was fearfully and suddenly stilled, now I knew that he was dead. I stood useless and helpless—looking, looking, looking into the burning room.

I saw the fire slowly conquered. The brightness of the glare faded—the steam rose in white clouds, and the smouldering heaps of embers showed red and black through it on the floor. There was a pause—then, an advance altogether of the firemen and the police, which blocked up the doorway—then a consultation in low voices—and then, two men were detached from the rest, and sent out of the churchyard through the crowd. The crowd drew back on either side, in dead silence, to let them pass.

After a while, a great shudder ran through the people; and the living lane widened slowly. The men came back along it, with a door from one of the empty houses. They carried it to the vestry, and went in. The police closed again round the doorway; and men stole out from among the crowd by twos and threes, and stood behind them, to be the first to see. Others waited near, to be the first to hear. Women and children were among these last.

The tidings from the vestry began to flow out among the crowd—they dropped slowly from mouth to mouth, till they reached the place where I was standing. I heard the questions and answers repeated again and again, in low, eager tones, all round me.

'Have they found him?' 'Yes.'—'Where?' 'Against the door; on his face.'—'Which door?' 'The door that goes into the church. His head was against it; he was down on his face.'—'Is his face burnt?' 'No.' 'Yes, it is.' 'No; scorched, not burnt; he lay on his face, I tell you.'—'Who was he? A lord, they say.' 'No, not a lord. *Sir* Something; Sir means Knight.' 'And Baronight, too.' 'No.' 'Yes, it does.'—'What did he want in there?' 'No good, you may depend on it.'—'Did he do it on purpose?'—'Burn himself on purpose!'—'I don't mean himself; I mean the vestry.'—'Is he dreadful to look at?' 'Dreadful!'—'Not about the face, though?' 'No, no; not so much about the face.'—'Don't anybody know him?' 'There's a man says he does.'—'Who?' 'A servant, they say. But he's struck stupid-like, and the police don't believe him.'—'Don't anybody else know who it is?' 'Hush——!'

The loud, clear voice of a man in authority silenced the low hum of talking all round me, in an instant.

'Where is the gentleman who tried to save him?' said the voice.

'Here, sir—here he is!' Dozens of eager faces pressed about me—dozens of eager arms, parted the crowd. The man in authority came up to me with a lantern in his hand.

'This way, sir, if you please,' he said, quietly.

I was unable to speak to him; I was unable to resist him, when he took my arm. I tried to say that I had never seen the dead man, in his lifetime—that there was no hope of identifying him by means of a stranger like me. But the words failed on my lips. I was faint and silent and helpless.

'Do you know him, sir?'

I was standing inside a circle of men. Three of them, opposite to me, were holding lanterns low down to the ground. Their eyes, and the eyes of all the rest, were fixed silently and expectantly on my face. I knew what was at my feet—I knew why they were holding the lanterns so low to the ground.

'Can you identify him, sir?'

My eyes dropped slowly. At first, I saw nothing under them but a coarse canvas cloth. The dripping of the rain on it was audible in the dreadful silence. I looked up, along the cloth; and there at the end, stark and grim and black, in the yellow light—there, was his dead face.

So, for the first and last time, I saw him. So the Visitation of God ruled it that he and I should meet.

X

THE Inquest was hurried for certain local reasons which weighed with the coroner and the town authorities. It was held on the afternoon of the next day. I was, necessarily, one among the witnesses summoned to assist the objects of the investigation.

My first proceeding, in the morning, was to go to the post-office, and inquire for the letter which I expected from Marian. No change of circumstances, however extraordinary, could affect the one great anxiety which weighed on my mind while I was away from London. The morning's letter, which was the only assurance I could receive that no misfortune had happened in my absence, was still the absorbing interest with which my day began.

To my relief, the letter from Marian was at the office waiting for me.

Nothing had happened—they were both as safe and as well as when I had left them. Laura sent her love, and begged that I would let her know of my return, a day beforehand. Her sister added, in explanation of this message, that she had saved 'nearly a sovereign' out of her own private purse, and that she had claimed the privilege of ordering the dinner and giving the dinner which was to celebrate the day of my return. I read these little domestic confidences, in the bright morning, with the terrible recollection of what had happened the evening before, vivid in my memory. The necessity of sparing Laura any sudden knowledge of the truth was the first consideration which the letter suggested to me. I wrote at once to Marian, to tell her what I have told in these pages; presenting the tidings as gradually and gently as I could, and warning her not to let any such thing as a newspaper fall in Laura's way while I was absent. In the case of any other woman, less courageous and less reliable, I might have hesitated before I ventured on unreservedly disclosing the whole truth. But I owed it to Marian to be faithful to my past experience of her, and to trust her as I trusted myself.

My letter was necessarily a long one. It occupied me until the time for proceeding to the Inquest.

The objects of the legal inquiry were necessarily beset by peculiar complications and difficulties. Besides the investigation into the manner in which the deceased had met his death, there were serious questions to be settled relating to the cause of the fire, to the abstraction of the keys, and to the presence of a stranger in the vestry at the time when the flames broke out. Even the identification of the dead man had not yet been accomplished. The helpless condition of the servant had made the police distrustful of his asserted recognition of his master. They had sent to Knowlesbury over-night to secure the attendance of witnesses who were well acquainted with the personal appearance of Sir Percival Glyde, and they had communicated, the first thing in the morning, with Blackwater Park. These precautions enabled the coroner and jury to settle the question of identity, and to confirm the correctness of the servant's assertion; the evidence offered by competent witnesses, and by the discovery of certain facts, being subsequently strengthened by an examination of the dead man's watch. The crest and the name of Sir Percival Glyde were engraved inside it.

The next inquiries related to the fire.

The servant and I, and the boy who had heard the light struck in the vestry, were the first witnesses called. The boy gave his evidence clearly enough; but the servant's mind had not yet recovered the shock inflicted on it—he was plainly incapable of assisting the objects of the inquiry, and he was desired to stand down.

To my own relief, my examination was not a long one. I had not known the deceased; I had never seen him; I was not aware of his presence at Old

Welmingham; and I had not been in the vestry at the finding of the body. All I could prove was that I had stopped at the clerk's cottage to ask my way; that I had heard from him of the loss of the keys; that I had accompanied him to the church to render what help I could; that I had seen the fire; that I had heard some person unknown, inside the vestry, trying vainly to unlock the door; and that I had done what I could, from motives of humanity, to save the man. Other witnesses, who had been acquainted with the deceased, were asked if they could explain the mystery of his presumed abstraction of the keys, and his presence in the burning room. But the coroner seemed to take it for granted, naturally enough, that I, as a total stranger in the neighbourhood, and a total stranger to Sir Percival Glyde, could not be in a position to offer any evidence on these two points.

The course that I was myself bound to take, when my formal examination had closed, seemed clear to me. I did not feel called on to volunteer any statement of my own private convictions; in the first place, because my doing so could serve no practical purpose, now that all proof in support of any surmises of mine was burnt with the burnt register; in the second place, because I could not have intelligibly stated my opinion—my unsupported opinion—without disclosing the whole story of the conspiracy; and producing beyond a doubt, the same unsatisfactory effect on the minds of the coroner and the jury which I had already produced on the mind of Mr Kyrle.

In these pages, however, and after the time that has now elapsed, no such cautions and restraints as are here described, need fetter the free expression of my opinion. I will state briefly, before my pen occupies itself with other events, how my own convictions lead me to account for the abstraction of the keys, for the outbreak of the fire, and for the death of the man.

The news of my being free on bail drove Sir Percival, as I believe, to his last resources. The attempted attack on the road was one of those resources; and the suppression of all practical proof of his crime, by destroying the page of the register on which the forgery had been committed, was the other, and the surest of the two. If I could produce no extract from the original book, to compare with the certified copy at Knowlesbury, I could produce no positive evidence, and could threaten him with no fatal exposure. All that was necessary to the attainment of his end was, that he should get into the vestry unperceived, that he should tear out the page in the register, and that he should leave the vestry again as privately as he had entered it.

On this supposition, it is easy to understand why he waited until nightfall before he made the attempt, and why he took advantage of the clerk's absence to possess himself of the keys. Necessity would oblige him to strike a light to find his way to the right register; and common caution would suggest his locking the door on the inside, in case of intrusion on the part of any inquisitive stranger, or on my part, if I happened to be in the neighbourhood at the time.

I cannot believe that it was any part of his intention to make the destruction of the register appear to be the result of accident, by purposely setting the vestry on fire. The bare chance that prompt assistance might arrive, and that the books might, by the remotest possibility, be saved, would have been enough, on a moment's consideration, to dismiss any idea of this sort from his mind. Remembering the quantity of combustible objects in the vestry—the straw, the papers, the packing-cases, the dry wood, the old wormeaten presses—all the probabilities, in my estimation, point to the fire as the result of an accident with his matches or his light.

His first impulse, under these circumstances, was doubtless to try to extinguish the flames—and, failing in that, his second impulse (ignorant as he was of the state of the lock) had been to attempt to escape by the door which had given him entrance. When I had called to him, the flames must have reached across the door leading into the church, on either side of which the presses extended, and close to which the other combustible objects were placed. In all probability, the smoke and flame (confined as they were to the room) had been too much for him, when he tried to escape by the inner door. He must have dropped in his death-swoon—he must have sunk in the place where he was found—just as I got on the roof to break the skylight-window. Even if we had been able, afterwards, to get into the church, and to burst open the door from that side, the delay must have been fatal. He would have been past saving, long past saving, by that time. We should only have given the flames free ingress into the church: the church, which was now preserved, but which, in that event, would have shared the fate of the vestry. There is no doubt in my mind—there can be no doubt in the mind of any one—that he was a dead man before ever we got to the empty cottage, and worked with might and main to tear down the beam.

This is the nearest approach that any theory of mine can make towards accounting for a result which was visible matter of fact. As I have described them, so events passed to us outside. As I have related it, so his body was found.

The Inquest was adjourned over one day; no explanation that the eye of the law could recognise having been discovered, thus far, to account for the mysterious circumstances of the case.

It was arranged that more witnesses should be summoned, and that the London solicitor of the deceased should be invited to attend. A medical man was also charged with the duty of reporting on the mental condition of the servant, which appeared at present to debar him from giving any evidence of the least importance. He could only declare, in a dazed way, that he had been ordered, on the night of the fire, to wait in the lane, and that he knew nothing else, except that the deceased was certainly his master.

My own impression was, that he had been first used (without any guilty knowledge on his own part) to ascertain the fact of the clerk's absence from home on the previous day; and that he had been afterwards ordered to wait near the church (but out of sight of the vestry) to assist his master, in the event of my escaping the attack on the road, and of a collision occurring between Sir Percival and myself. It is necessary to add, that the man's own testimony was never obtained to confirm this view. The medical report of him declared that what little mental faculty he possessed was seriously shaken; nothing satisfactory was extracted from him at the adjourned Inquest; and, for aught I know to the contrary, he may never have recovered to this day.

I returned to the hotel at Welmingham, so jaded in body and mind, so weakened and depressed by all that I had gone through, as to be quite unfit to endure the local gossip about the Inquest, and to answer the trivial questions that the talkers addressed to me in the coffee-room. I withdrew from my scanty dinner to my cheap garret-chamber, to secure myself a little quiet, and to think, undisturbed, of Laura and Marian.

If I had been a richer man, I would have gone back to London, and would have comforted myself with a sight of the two dear faces again, that night. But, I was bound to appear, if called on, at the adjourned Inquest, and doubly bound to answer my bail before the magistrate at Knowlesbury. Our slender resources had suffered already; and the doubtful future—more doubtful than ever now—made me dread decreasing our means unnecessarily, by allowing myself an indulgence, even at the small cost of a double railway journey, in the carriages of the second class.

The next day—the day immediately following the Inquest—was left at my own disposal. I began the morning by again applying at the post-office for my regular report from Marian. It was waiting for me, as before, and it was written, throughout, in good spirits. I read the letter thankfully; and then set forth, with my mind at ease for the day, to go to Old Welmingham, and to view the scene of the fire by the morning light.

What changes met me when I got there!

Through all the ways of our unintelligible world, the trivial and the terrible walk hand in hand together. The irony of circumstances holds no mortal catastrophe in respect. When I reached the church, the trampled condition of the burial-ground was the only serious trace left to tell of the fire and the death. A rough hoarding of boards had been knocked up before the vestry doorway. Rude caricatures were scrawled on it already; and the village children were fighting and shouting for the possession of the best peephole to see through. On the spot where I had heard the cry for help from the burning room, on the spot where the panic-stricken servant had dropped on his knees, a fussy flock of poultry was now scrambling for the first choice of worms after the rain—and on the ground at my feet, where the door and its dreadful burden had been laid, a workman's dinner was waiting for him, tied up in a yellow basin, and his faithful cur in charge was yelping at me for coming near the food. The old clerk, looking idly at the slow commencement of the repairs, had only one interest that he could talk about, now—the interest of escaping all blame, for his own part, on account of the accident that had happened. One of the village women, whose white, wild face I remembered, the picture of terror, when we pulled down the beam, was giggling with another woman, the picture of inanity, over an old washing-tub. Nothing serious in mortality! Solomon in all his glory, was Solomon with the elements of the contemptible lurking in every fold of his robes and in every corner of his palace.

As I left the place, my thoughts turned, not for the first time, to the complete overthrow that all present hope of establishing Laura's identity had now suffered through Sir Percival's death. He was gone—and, with him, the chance was gone which had been the one object of all my labours and all my hopes.

Could I look at my failure from no truer point of view than this?

Suppose he had lived—would that change of circumstance have altered the result? Could I have made my discovery a marketable commodity, even for Laura's sake, after I had found out that robbery of the rights of others was the essence of Sir Percival's crime? Could I have offered the price of *my* silence for *his* confession of the conspiracy, when the effect of that silence must have been to keep the right heir from the estates, and the right owner from the name? Impossible! If Sir Percival had lived, the discovery, from which (in my ignorance of the true nature of the Secret) I had hoped so much, could not have been mine to suppress, or to make public, as I thought best, for the vindication of Laura's rights. In common honesty and common honour, I must have gone at once to the stranger whose birthright had been usurped—I must have renounced the victory at the moment when it was mine, by placing my discovery unreservedly in that stranger's hands—and I must have faced afresh all the difficulties which stood between me and the one object of my life, exactly as I was resolved, in my heart of hearts, to face them now!

I returned to Welmingham with my mind composed; feeling more sure of myself and my resolution than I had felt yet.

On my way to the hotel, I passed the end of the square in which Mrs Catherick lived. Should I go back to the house, and make another attempt to see her? No. That news of Sir Percival's death, which was the last news she ever expected to hear, must have reached her, hours since. All the proceedings at the Inquest had been reported in the local paper that morning: there was nothing I could tell her which she did not know already.

My interest in making her speak had slackened. I remembered the furtive hatred in her face, when she said, 'There is no news of Sir Percival that I don't expect—except the news of his death.' I remembered the stealthy interest in her eyes when they settled on me at parting, after she had spoken those words. Some instinct, deep in my heart, which I felt to be a true one, made the prospect of again entering her presence repulsive to me—I turned away from the square, and went straight back to the hotel.

Some hours later, while I was resting in the coffee-room, a letter was placed in my hands by the waiter. It was addressed to me, by name; and I found, on inquiry, that it had been left at the bar by a woman, just as it was near dusk, and just before the gas was lighted. She had said nothing; and she had gone away again before there was time to speak to her, or even to notice who she was.

I opened the letter. It was neither dated, nor signed; and the handwriting was palpably disguised. Before I had read the first sentence, however, I knew who my correspondent was. Mrs Catherick.

The letter ran as follows—I copy it exactly, word for word:

'Sir, you have not come back, as you said you would. No matter; I know the news, and I write to tell you so. Did you see anything particular in my face when you left me? I was wondering, in my own mind, whether the day of his downfal had come at last, and whether you were the chosen instrument for working it. You were—and you *have* worked it. You were weak enough, as I have heard, to try and save his life. If you had succeeded, I should have looked upon you as my enemy. Now you have failed, I hold you as my friend. Your inquiries frightened him into the vestry by night; your inquiries, without your privity, and against your will, have served the hatred and wreaked the vengeance of three-and-twenty years. Thank you, sir, in spite of yourself.

'I owe something to the man who has done this. How can I pay my debt? If I was a young woman still, I might say, "Come! put your arm round my waist, and kiss me, if you like." I should have been fond enough of you, even to go that length; and you would have accepted my invitation—you would, sir, twenty years ago! But I am an old woman, now. Well! I can satisfy your curiosity, and pay my debt in that way. You *had* a great curiosity to know certain private affairs of mine, when you came to see me—private affairs which all your sharpness could not look into without my help—private affairs which you have not discovered, even now. You *shall* discover them; your curiosity shall be satisfied. I will take any trouble to please you, my estimable young friend!

'You were a little boy, I suppose, in the year twenty-seven? I was a handsome young woman, at that time, living at Old Welmingham. I had a contemptible fool for a husband. I had also the honour of being acquainted (never mind how) with a certain gentleman (never mind whom). I shall not call him by his name. Why should I? It was not his own. He never had a name: you know that, by this time, as well as I do.

'It will be more to the purpose to tell you how he worked himself into my good graces. I was born with the tastes of a lady; and he gratified them. In other words, he admired me, and he made me presents. No woman can resist admiration and presents—especially presents, provided they happen to be just the things she wants. He was sharp enough to know that—most men are. Naturally, he wanted something, in return—all men do. And what do you think was the something? The merest trifle. Nothing but the key of the vestry, and the key of the press inside it, when my husband's back was turned. Of course he lied when I asked him why he wished me to get him the keys, in that private way. He might have saved himself the trouble—I didn't believe him. But I liked my presents, and I wanted more. So I got him the keys, without my husband's knowledge; and I watched him, without his own knowledge. Once, twice, four times, I watched him—and the fourth time I found him out.

'I was never over-scrupulous where other people's affairs were concerned; and I was not over-scrupulous about his adding one to the marriages in the register, on his own account.

'Of course, I knew it was wrong; but it did no harm to *me*—which was one good reason for not making a fuss about it. And I had not got a gold watch and chain—which was another, still better. And he had promised me one from London, only the day before—which was a third, best of all. If I had known what the law considered the crime to be, and how the law punished it, I should have taken proper care of myself, and have exposed him then and there. But I knew nothing—and I longed for the gold watch. All the conditions I insisted on were that he should take me into his confidence and tell me everything. I was as curious about his affairs then, as you are about mine now. He granted my conditions—why, you will see presently.

'This, put in short, is what I heard from him. He did not willingly tell me all that I tell you here. I drew some of it from him by persuasion and some of it by questions. I was determined to have all the truth—and I believe I got it.

'He knew no more than any one else of what the state of things really was between his father and mother, till after his mother's death. Then, his father confessed it, and promised to do what he could for his son. He died having done nothing—not having even made a will. The son (who can blame him?) wisely provided for himself. He came to England at once, and took possession of the property. There was no one to suspect him, and no one to say him nay. His father and mother had always lived as man and wife—none of the few people who were acquainted with them ever supposed them to be anything else. The right person to claim the property (if the truth had been known) was a distant relation, who had no idea of ever getting it, and who was away at sea when his father died. He had no difficulty, so far—he took possession, as a matter of course. There were two things wanted of him, before he could do this. One was a certificate of his birth, and the other was a certificate of his parents' marriage. The certificate of his birth was easily got—he was born abroad, and the certificate was there in due form. The other matter was a difficulty—and that difficulty brought him to Old Welmingham.

'But for one consideration, he might have gone to Knowlesbury instead.

'His mother had been living there just before she met with his father—living under her maiden name; the truth being that she was really a married woman, married in Ireland, where her husband had ill-used her and had afterwards gone off with some other person. I give you this fact on good authority: Sir Felix mentioned it to his son, as the reason why he had not married. You may wonder why the son, knowing that his parents had met each other at Knowlesbury, did not play his first tricks with the register of that church, where it might have been fairly presumed his father and mother were married. The reason was that the clergyman who did duty at Knowlesbury church, in the year eighteen hundred and three (when, according to his birth-certificate, his father and mother *ought* to have been married), was alive still, when he took possession of the property in the New Year of eighteen hundred and twenty-seven. This awkward circumstance forced him to extend his inquiries to our neighbourhood. There, no such danger existed: the former clergyman at our church having been dead for some years.

'Old Welmingham suited his purpose, as well as Knowlesbury. His father had removed his mother from Knowlesbury, and had lived with her at a cottage on the river, a little distance from our village. People who had known his solitary ways when he was single, did not wonder at his solitary ways when he was supposed to be married. If he had not been a hideous creature to look at, his retired life with the lady might have raised suspicions: but, as things were, his hiding his ugliness and his deformity in the strictest privacy surprised nobody. He lived in our neighbourhood till he came in possession of the Park. After three or four and twenty years had passed, who was to say (the clergyman being dead) that his marriage had not been as private as the rest of his life, and that it had not taken place at Old Welmingham church?

'So, as I told you, the son found our neighbourhood the surest place he could choose, to set things right secretly in his own interests. It may surprise you to hear that what he really did to the marriage-register was done on the spur of the moment—done on second thoughts.

'His first notion was only to tear the leaf out (in the right year and month), to destroy it privately, to go back to London, and to tell the lawyers to get him the necessary certificate of his father's marriage, innocently referring them of course to the date on the leaf that was gone. Nobody could say his father and mother had *not* been married, after that—and whether, under the circumstances, they would stretch a point or not, about lending him the money (he thought they would), he had his answer ready, at all events, if a question was ever raised about his right to the name and the estate.

'But when he came to look privately at the register for himself, he found at the bottom of one of the pages for the year eighteen hundred and three, a blank space left, seemingly through there being no room to make a long entry there, which was made instead at the top of the next page. The sight of this chance altered all his plans. It was an opportunity he had never hoped for, or thought of—and he took it, you know how. The blank space, to have exactly tallied with his birth-certificate, ought to have occurred in the July part of the register. It occurred in the September part instead. However, in this case, if suspicious questions were asked, the answer was not hard to find. He had only to describe himself as a seven months' child.

'I was fool enough, when he told me his story, to feel some interest and some pity for him—which was just what he calculated on, as you will see. I thought him hardly used. It was not his fault that his father and mother were not married; and it was not his father's and mother's fault, either. A more scrupulous woman than I was—a woman who had not set her heart on a gold watch and chain—would have found some excuses for him. At all events, I held my tongue, and helped to screen what he was about.

'He was some time getting the ink the right colour (mixing it over and over again in pots and bottles of mine), and some time, afterwards, in practising the handwriting. But he succeeded in the end—and made an honest woman of his mother, after she was dead in her grave! So far, I don't deny that he behaved honourably enough to myself. He gave me my watch and chain, and spared no expense in buying them; both were of superior workmanship, and very expensive. I have got them still—the watch goes beautifully.

'You said, the other day, that Mrs Clements had told you everything she knew. In that case, there is no need for me to write about the trumpery scandal by which I was the sufferer—the innocent sufferer, I positively assert. You must know as well as I do what the notion was which my husband took into his head, when he found me and my fine-gentleman acquaintance meeting each other privately, and talking secrets together. But what you don't know, is how it ended between that same gentleman and myself. You shall read, and see how he behaved to me.

'The first words I said to him, when I saw the turn things had taken, were, "Do me justice—clear my character of a stain on it which you know I don't deserve. I don't want you to make a clean breast of it to my husband—only tell him, on your word of honour as a gentleman, that he is wrong, and that

I am not to blame in the way he thinks I am. Do me that justice, at least, after all I have done for you." He flatly refused, in so many words. He told me, plainly, that it was his interest to let my husband and all my neighbours believe the falsehood—because, as long as they did so, they were quite certain never to suspect the truth. I had a spirit of my own; and I told him they should know the truth from my lips. His reply was short, and to the point. If I spoke, I was a lost woman, as certainly as he was a lost man.

'Yes! it had come to that. He had deceived me about the risk I ran in helping him. He had practised on my ignorance; he had tempted me with his gifts; he had interested me with his story—and the result of it was that he had made me his accomplice. He owned this, coolly; and he ended by telling me, for the first time, what the frightful punishment really was for his offence, and for any one who helped him to commit it. In those days, the Law was not so tender-hearted as I hear it is now. Murderers were not the only people liable to be hanged; and women convicts were not treated like ladies in undeserved distress. I confess he frightened me—the mean impostor! the cowardly blackguard! Do you understand, now, how I hated him? Do you understand why I am taking all this trouble—thankfully taking it—to gratify the curiosity of the meritorious young gentleman who hunted him down?

'Well, to go on. He was hardly fool enough to drive me to downright desperation. I was not the sort of woman whom it was quite safe to hunt into a corner—he knew that, and wisely quieted me with proposals for the future.

'I deserved some reward (he was kind enough to say) for the service I had done him, and some compensation (he was so obliging as to add) for what I had suffered. He was quite willing—generous scoundrel!—to make me a handsome yearly allowance, payable quarterly, on two conditions. First, I was to hold my tongue—in my own interests as well as in his. Secondly, I was not to stir away from Welmingham, without first letting him know, and waiting till I had obtained his permission. In my own neighbourhood, no virtuous female friends would tempt me into dangerous gossiping at the tea-table. In my own neighbourhood, he would always know where to find me. A hard condition, that second one—but I accepted it.

'What else was I to do? I was left helpless, with the prospect of a coming incumbrance in the shape of a child. What else was I to do? Cast myself on the mercy of my runaway idiot of a husband who had raised the scandal against me? I would have died first. Besides, the allowance *was* a handsome one. I had a better income, a better house over my head, better carpets on my floors, than half the women who turned up the whites of their eyes at the sight of me. The dress of Virtue, in our parts, was cotton print. I had silk.

'So, I accepted the conditions he offered me, and made the best of them, and fought my battle with my respectable neighbours on their own ground, and won it in course of time—as you saw yourself. How I kept his Secret (and mine) through all the years that have passed from that time to this; and whether my late daughter, Anne, ever really crept into my confidence, and got the keeping of the Secret too—are questions, I dare say, to which you are curious to find an answer. Well! my gratitude refuses you nothing. I will turn to a fresh page, and give you the answer, presently.'

'I MUST begin this fresh page, Mr Hartright, by expressing my surprise at the interest which you appear to have felt in my late daughter. It is quite unaccountable to me. If that interest makes you anxious for any particulars of her early life, I must refer you to Mrs Clements, who knows more of the subject than I do. Pray understand that I do not profess to have been at all over-fond of my late daughter. She was a worry to me from first to last, with the additional disadvantage of being always weak in the head. You like candour, and I hope this satisfies you.

'There is no need to trouble you with many personal particulars relating to those past times. It will be enough to say that I observed the terms of the bargain on my side, and that I enjoyed my comfortable income, in return, paid quarterly.

'Now and then I got away, and changed the scene for a short time; always asking leave of my lord and master first, and generally getting it. He was not, as I have already told you, fool enough to drive me too hard; and he could reasonably rely on my holding my tongue, for my own sake, if not for his. One of my longest trips away from home was the trip I took to Limmeridge, to nurse a half-sister there, who was dying. She was reported to have saved money; and I thought it as well (in case any accident happened to stop my allowance) to look after my own interests in that direction. As things turned out, however, my pains were all thrown away; and I got nothing, because nothing was to be had.

'I had taken Anne to the north with me; having my whims and fancies, occasionally, about my child, and getting, at such times, jealous of Mrs Clements's influence over her. I never liked Mrs Clements. She was a poor, empty-headed, spiritless woman—what you call a born drudge—and I was, now and then, not averse to plaguing her by taking Anne away. Not knowing what else to do with my girl, while I was nursing in Cumberland, I put her to school at Limmeridge. The lady of the manor, Mrs Fairlie (a remarkably plain-looking woman, who had entrapped one of the hand-somest men in England into marrying her), amused me wonderfully, by taking a violent fancy to my girl. The consequence was she learnt nothing at school, and was petted and spoilt at Limmeridge House. Among other whims and fancies which they taught her there, they put some nonsense into her head about always wearing white. Hating white and liking colours myself, I determined to take the nonsense out of her head as soon as we got home again.

'Strange to say, my daughter resolutely resisted me. When she *had* got a notion once fixed in her mind, she was, like other half-witted people, as obstinate as a mule in keeping it. We quarrelled finely; and Mrs Clements, not liking to see it, I suppose, offered to take Anne away to live in London with her. I should have said, Yes, if Mrs Clements had not sided with my daughter about her dressing herself in white. But, being determined she should *not* dress herself in white, and disliking Mrs Clements more than ever for taking part against me, I said No, and meant No, and stuck to No. The consequence was my daughter remained with me; and the consequence of that, in its turn, was the first serious quarrel that happened about the Secret.

'The circumstance took place long after the time I have just been writing of. I had been settled for years in the new town; and was steadily living down my bad character, and slowly gaining ground among the respectable inhabitants. It helped me forward greatly towards this object, to have my daughter with me. Her harmlessness, and her fancy for dressing in white, excited a certain amount of sympathy. I left off opposing her favourite whim, on that account, because some of the sympathy was sure, in course of time, to fall to my share. Some of it did fall. I date my getting a choice of the two best sittings to let in the church, from that time; and I date the clergyman's first bow from my getting the sittings.

'Well, being settled in this way, I received a letter one morning from that highly-born gentleman (now deceased), in answer to one of mine, warning him, according to agreement, of my wishing to leave the town, for a little change of air and scene.

'The ruffianly side of him must have been uppermost, I suppose, when he got my letter—for he wrote back, refusing me, in such abominably-insolent language, that I lost all command over myself; and abused him, in my daughter's presence, as "a low impostor, whom I could ruin for life, if I chose to open my lips and let out his secret." I said no more about him than that; being brought to my senses, as soon as those words had escaped me, by the sight of my daughter's face, looking eagerly and curiously at mine. I instantly ordered her out of the room, until I had composed myself again.

'My sensations were not pleasant, I can tell you, when I came to reflect on my own folly. Anne had been more than usually crazy and queer, that year; and when I thought of the chance there might be of her repeating my words in the town, and mentioning *his* name in connexion with them, if inquisitive people got hold of her, I was finely terrified at the possible consequences. My worst fears for myself, my worst dread of what he might do, led me no farther than this. I was quite unprepared for what really did happen, only the next day.

'On that next day, without any warning to me to expect him, he came to the house.

'His first words, and the tone in which he spoke them, surly as it was, showed me plainly enough that he had repented already of his insolent answer to my application, and that he had come, in a mighty bad temper, to try and set matters right again, before it was too late. Seeing my daughter in the room with me (I had been afraid to let her out of my sight, after what had happened the day before), he ordered her away. They neither of them liked each other; and he vented the ill-temper on *her*, which he was afraid to show to *me*.

' "Leave us," he said, looking at her over his shoulder. She looked back over *her* shoulder, and waited, as if she didn't care to go. "Do you hear?" he roared out; "leave the room." "Speak to me civilly," says she, getting red in the face. "Turn the idiot out," says he, looking my way. She had always had crazy notions of her own about her dignity; and that word, "idiot," upset her in a moment. Before I could interfere, she stepped up to him, in a fine passion. "Beg my pardon, directly," says she, "or I'll make it the worse for you. I'll let out your Secret! I can ruin you for life, if I choose to open my lips." My own words!—repeated exactly from what I had said the day before—repeated, in his presence, as if they had come from herself. He sat speechless, as white as the paper I am writing on, while I pushed her out of the room. When he recovered himself—

'No! I am too respectable a woman to mention what he said when he recovered himself. My pen is the pen of a member of the rector's congregation, and a subscriber to the "Wednesday Lectures on Justification by Faith"—how can you expect me to employ it in writing bad language? Suppose, for yourself, the raging, swearing frenzy of the lowest ruffian in England; and let us get on together, as fast as may be, to the way in which it all ended.

'It ended, as you probably guess, by this time, in his insisting on securing his own safety by shutting her up.

'I tried to set things right. I told him that she had merely repeated, like a parrot, the words she had heard me say, and that she knew no particulars whatever, because I had mentioned none. I explained that she had affected, out of crazy spite against him, to know what she really did *not* know; that she only wanted to threaten him and aggravate him, for speaking to her as he had just spoken; and that my unlucky words gave her just the chance of doing mischief of which she was in search. I referred him to other queer ways of hers, and to his own experience of the vagaries of half-witted people—it was all to no purpose—he would not believe me on my oath—he was absolutely certain I had betrayed the whole Secret. In short, he would hear of nothing but shutting her up.

'Under these circumstances, I did my duty as a mother. "No pauper Asylum," I said; "I won't have her put in a pauper Asylum. A Private

Establishment, if *you* please. I have my feelings, as a mother, and my character to preserve in the town; and I will submit to nothing but a Private Establishment, of the sort which my genteel neighbours would choose for afflicted relatives of their own." Those were my words. It is gratifying to me to reflect that I did my duty. Though never over-fond of my late daughter, I had a proper pride about her. No pauper stain—thanks to my firmness and resolution—ever rested on MY child.

'Having carried my point (which I did the more easily, in consequence of the facilities offered by private Asylums), I could not refuse to admit that there were certain advantages gained by shutting her up. In the first place, she was taken excellent care of—being treated (as I took care to mention in the town) on the footing of a Lady. In the second place, she was kept away from Welmingham, where she might have set people suspecting and inquiring, by repeating my own incautious words.

'The only drawback of putting her under restraint, was a very slight one. We merely turned her empty boast about knowing the Secret into a fixed delusion. Having first spoken in sheer crazy spitefulness against the man who had offended her, she was cunning enough to see that she had seriously frightened him, and sharp enough afterwards to discover that *he* was concerned in shutting her up. The consequence was she flamed out into a perfect frenzy of passion against him, going to the Asylum; and the first words she said to the nurses, after they had quieted her, were, that she was put in confinement for knowing his secret, and that she meant to open her lips and ruin him, when the right time came.

'She may have said the same thing to you, when you thoughtlessly assisted her escape. She certainly said it (as I heard last summer) to the unfortunate woman who married our sweettempered, nameless gentleman, lately deceased. If either you, or that unlucky lady, had questioned my daughter closely, and had insisted on her explaining what she really meant, you would have found her lose all her self-importance suddenly, and get vacant, and restless, and confused—you would have discovered that I am writing nothing here but the plain truth. She knew that there was a Secret—she knew who was connected with it—she knew who would suffer by its being known—and, beyond that, whatever airs of importance she may have given herself, whatever crazy boasting she may have indulged in with strangers, she never to her dying day knew more.

'Have I satisfied your curiosity? I have taken pains enough to satisfy it, at any rate. There is really nothing else I have to tell you about myself, or my daughter. My worst responsibilities, so far as she was concerned, were all over when she was secured in the Asylum. I had a form of letter relating to the circumstances under which she was shut up, given me to write, in answer to one Miss Halcombe, who was curious in the matter, and who must have heard plenty of lies about me from a certain tongue well accustomed to the telling of the same. And I did what I could afterwards to trace my runaway daughter, and prevent her from doing mischief, by making inquiries, myself, in the neighbourhood where she was falsely reported to have been seen. But these and other trifles like them are of little or no interest to you after what you have heard already.

'So far, I have written in the friendliest possible spirit. But I cannot close this letter without adding a word here of serious remonstrance and reproof, addressed to yourself.

'In the course of your personal interview with me, you audaciously referred to my late daughter's parentage, on the father's side, as if that parentage was a matter of doubt. This was highly improper and very ungentlemanlike on your part! If we see each other again, remember, if you please, that I will allow no liberties to be taken with my reputation, and that the moral atmosphere of Welmingham (to use a favourite expression of my friend the rector's) must not be tainted by loose conversation of any kind. If you allow yourself to doubt that my husband was Anne's father, you personally insult me in the grossest manner. If you have felt, and if you still continue to feel, an unhallowed curiosity on this subject, I recommend you, in your own interests, to check it at once and for ever. On this side of the grave, Mr Hartright, whatever may happen on the other, *that* curiosity will never be gratified.

'Perhaps, after what I have just said, you will see the necessity of writing me an apology. Do so; and I will willingly receive it. I will, afterwards, if your wishes point to a second interview with me, go a step farther, and receive *you*. My circumstances only enable me to invite you to tea—not that they are at all altered for the worse by what has happened. I have always lived, as I think I told you, well within my income; and I have saved enough, in the last twenty years, to make me quite comfortable for the rest of my life. It is not my intention to leave Welmingham. There are one or two little advantages which I have still to gain in the town. The clergyman bows to me—as you saw. He is married; and his wife is not quite so civil. I propose to join the Dorcas Society; and I mean to make the clergyman's wife bow to me next.

'If you favour me with your company, pray understand that the conversation must be entirely on general subjects. Any attempted reference to this letter will be quite useless—I am determined not to acknowledge having written it. The evidence has been destroyed in the fire, I know; but I think it desirable to err on the side of caution, nevertheless.

'On this account, no names are mentioned here, nor is any signature attached to these lines: the handwriting is disguised throughout, and I mean to deliver the letter myself, under circumstances which will prevent all fear of its being traced to my house. You can have no possible cause to complain of these precautions; seeing that they do not affect the information I here communicate, in consideration of the special indulgence which you have deserved at my hands. My hour for tea is half-past five, and my buttered toast waits for nobody.'

XI

MY first impulse, after reading Mrs Catherick's extraordinary narrative, was to destroy it. The hardened, shameless depravity of the whole composition, from beginning to end—the atrocious perversity of mind which persistently associated me with a calamity for which I was in no sense answerable, and with a death which I had risked my life in trying to avert—so disgusted me, that I was on the point of tearing the letter, when a consideration suggested itself, which warned me to wait a little before I destroyed it.

This consideration was entirely unconnected with Sir Percival. The information communicated to me, so far as it concerned him, did little more than confirm the conclusions at which I had already arrived.

He had committed his offence as I had supposed him to have committed it; and the absence of all reference, on Mrs Catherick's part, to the duplicate register at Knowlesbury, strengthened my previous conviction that the existence of the book, and the risk of detection which it implied, must have been necessarily unknown to Sir Percival. My interest in the question of the forgery was now at an end; and my only object in keeping the letter was to make it of some future service, in clearing up the last mystery that still remained to baffle me—the parentage of Anne Catherick, on the father's side. There were one or two sentences dropped in her mother's narrative, which it might be useful to refer to again, when matters of more immediate importance allowed me leisure to search for the missing evidence. I did not despair of still finding that evidence; and I had lost none of my anxiety to discover it, for I had lost none of my interest in tracing the father of the poor creature who now lay at rest in Mrs Fairlie's grave.

Accordingly, I sealed up the letter, and put it away carefully in my pocket-book, to be referred to again when the time came.

The next day was my last in Hampshire. When I had appeared again before the magistrate at Knowlesbury, and when I had attended at the adjourned Inquest, I should be free to return to London by the afternoon or the evening train.

My first errand in the morning was, as usual, to the post-office. The letter from Marian was there; but I thought, when it was handed to me, that it felt unusually light. I anxiously opened the envelope. There was nothing inside but a small strip of paper, folded in two. The few blotted, hurriedly-written lines which were traced on it contained these words:

'Come back as soon as you can. I have been obliged to move. Come to Gower's Walk, Fulham, (number five). I will be on the look-out for you. Don't be alarmed about us; we are both safe and well. But come back.— Marian.'

The news which those lines contained—news which I instantly associated with some attempted treachery on the part of Count Fosco—fairly overwhelmed me. I stood breathless, with the paper crumpled up in my hand. What had happened? What subtle wickedness had the Count planned and executed in my absence? A night had passed since Marian's note was written—hours must elapse still, before I could get back to them—some new disaster might have happened already, of which I was ignorant. And here, miles and miles away from them, here I must remain—held, doubly held, at the disposal of the law!

I hardly know to what forgetfulness of my obligations anxiety and alarm might not have tempted me, but for the quieting influence of my faith in Marian. My absolute reliance on her was the one earthly consideration which helped me to restrain myself, and gave me courage to wait. The Inquest was the first of the impediments in the way of my freedom of action. I attended it at the appointed time; the legal formalities requiring my presence in the room, but, as it turned out, not calling on me to repeat my evidence. This useless delay was a hard trial, although I did my best to quiet my impatience by following the course of the proceedings as closely as I could.

The London solicitor of the deceased (Mr Merriman) was among the persons present. But he was quite unable to assist the objects of the inquiry. He could only say that he was inexpressibly shocked and astonished, and that he could throw no light whatever on the mysterious circumstances of the case. At intervals during the adjourned investigation, he suggested questions which the Corner put, but which led to no results. After a patient inquiry, which lasted nearly three hours, and which exhausted every available source of information, the jury pronounced the customary verdict in cases of sudden death by accident. They added to the formal decision a statement that there had been no evidence to show how the keys had been abstracted, how the fire had been caused, or what the purpose was for which the deceased had entered the vestry. This act closed the proceedings. The legal representative of the dead man was left to provide for the necessities of the interment; and the witnesses were free to retire.

Resolved not to lose a minute in getting to Knowlesbury, I paid my bill at the hotel, and hired a fly to take me to the town. A gentleman who heard me give the order, and who saw that I was going alone, informed me that he lived in the neighbourhood of Knowlesbury, and asked if I would have any objection to his getting home by sharing the fly with me. I accepted his proposal as a matter of course.

Our conversation during the drive was naturally occupied by the one absorbing subject of local interest.

My new acquaintance had some knowledge of the late Sir Percival's solicitor; and he and Mr Merriman had been discussing the state of the deceased gentleman's affairs and the succession to the property. Sir Percival's embarrassments were so well known all over the county that his solicitor could only make a virtue of necessity and plainly acknowledge them. He had died without leaving a will, and he had no personal property to bequeath, even if he had made one; the whole fortune which he had derived from his wife having been swallowed up by his creditors. The heir to the estate (Sir Percival having left no issue) was a son of Sir Felix Glyde's first cousin—an officer in command of an East Indiaman. He would find his unexpected inheritance sadly encumbered; but the property would recover with time, and, if 'the captain' was careful, he might be a rich man yet, before he died.

Absorbed as I was in the one idea of getting to London, this information (which events proved to be perfectly correct) had an interest of its own to attract my attention. I thought it justified me in keeping secret my discovery of Sir Percival's fraud. The heir whose rights he had usurped was the heir who would now have the estate. The income from it, for the last three-and-twenty years, which should properly have been his, and which the dead man had squandered to the last farthing, was gone beyond recal. If I spoke, my speaking would confer advantage on no one. If I kept the secret, my silence concealed the character of the man who had cheated Laura into marrying him. For her sake, I wished to conceal it—for her sake, still, I tell this story under feigned names.

I parted with my chance companion at Knowlesbury; and went at once to the town-hall. As I had anticipated, no one was present to prosecute the case against me—the necessary formalities were observed—and I was discharged. On leaving the court, a letter from Mr Dawson was put into my hand. It informed me that he was absent on professional duty, and it reiterated the offer I had already received from him of any assistance which I might require at his hands. I wrote back, warmly acknowledging my obligations to his kindness, and apologising for not expressing my thanks personally, in consequence of my immediate recal, on pressing business, to town.

Half an hour later I was speeding back to London by the express train.

XII

IT was between nine and ten o'clock before I reached Fulham, and found my way to Gower's Walk.

Both Laura and Marian came to the door to let me in. I think we had hardly known how close the tie was which bound us three together, until the evening came which united us again. We met as if we had been parted for months, instead of for a few days only. Marian's face was sadly worn and anxious. I saw who had known all the danger, and borne all the trouble, in my absence, the moment I looked at her. Laura's brighter looks and better spirits told me how carefully she had been spared all knowledge of the dreadful death at Welmingham, and of the true reason for our change of abode.

The stir of the removal seemed to have cheered and interested her. She only spoke of it as a happy thought of Marian's to surprise me, on my return, with a change from the close, noisy street, to the pleasant neighbour-hood of trees and fields and the river. She was full of projects for the future—of the drawings she was to finish; of the purchasers I had found in the country, who were to buy them; of the shillings and sixpences she had saved, till her purse was so heavy that she proudly asked me to weigh it in my own hand. The change for the better which had been wrought in her, during the few days of my absence, was a surprise to me for which I was quite unprepared—and for all the unspeakable happiness of seeing it I was indebted to Marian's courage and to Marian's love.

When Laura had left us, and when we could speak to one another without restraint, I tried to give some expression to the gratitude and the admiration which filled my heart. But the generous creature would not wait to hear me. That sublime self-forgetfulness of women, which yields so much and asks so little, turned all her thoughts from herself to me.

'I had only a moment left before post-time,' she said, 'or I should have written less abruptly. You look worn and weary, Walter—I am afraid my letter must have seriously alarmed you?'

'Only at first,' I replied. 'My mind was quieted, Marian, by my trust in you. Was I right in attributing this sudden change of place to some threatened annoyance on the part of Count Fosco?'

'Perfectly right,' she said. 'I saw him yesterday; and, worse than that, Walter—I spoke to him.'

'Spoke to him? Did he know where we lived? Did he come to the house?'

'He did. To the house—but not up-stairs. Laura never saw him; Laura suspects nothing. I will tell you how it happened: the danger, I believe and hope, is over now. Yesterday, I was in the sitting-room, at our old lodgings. Laura was drawing at the table; and I was walking about and setting things to rights. I passed the window, and, as I passed it, looked out into the street. There, on the opposite side of the way, I saw the Count, with a man talking to him——'

'Did he notice you at the window?'

'No—at least, I thought not. I was too violently startled to be quite sure.'

'Who was the other man? A stranger?'

'Not a stranger, Walter. As soon as I could draw my breath again, I recognised him. He was the owner of the Lunatic Asylum.'

'Was the Count pointing out the house to him?'

'No; they were talking together as if they had accidentally met in the street. I remained at the window looking at them from behind the curtain. If I had turned round, and if Laura had seen my face at that moment——Thank God, she was absorbed over her drawing! They soon parted. The man from the Asylum went one way, and the Count the other. I began to hope they were in the street by chance, till I saw the Count come back, stop opposite to us again, take out his card-case and pencil, write something, and then cross the road to the shop below us. I ran past Laura before she could see me, and said I had forgotten something up-stairs. As soon as I was out of the room, I went down to the first landing, and waited—I was determined to stop him if he tried to come upstairs. He made no such attempt. The girl from the shop came through the door into the passage, with his card in her hand—a large gilt card, with his name, and a coronet above it, and these lines underneath in pencil. 'Dear lady' (yes! the villain could address me in that way still)—'dear lady, one word, I implore you, on a matter serious to us both.' If one can think at all, in serious difficulties, one thinks quick. I felt directly that it might be a fatal mistake to leave myself and to leave you in the dark, where such a man as the Count was concerned. I felt that the doubt of what he might do, in your absence, would be ten times more trying to me if I declined to see him than if I consented. 'Ask the gentleman to wait in the shop.' I said. 'I will be with him in a moment.' I ran up-stairs for my bonnet, being determined not to let him speak to me in-doors. I knew his deep ringing voice; and I was afraid Laura might hear it, even in the shop. In less than a minute I was down again in the passage, and had opened the door into the street. He came round to meet me from the shop. There he was, in deep mourning, with his smooth bow and his deadly smile, and some idle boys and women near him, staring at his great size, his fine black clothes, and his large cane with the gold knob to it. All the horrible time at Blackwater came back to me the moment I set eyes on him. All the old loathing crept and crawled through me, when he took off his hat with a flourish, and spoke to me, as if we had parted on the friendliest terms hardly a day since.'

'You remember what he said?'

'I can't repeat it, Walter. You shall know directly what he said about *you*—but I can't repeat what he said to *me*. It was worse than the polite insolence of his letter. My hands tingled to strike him, as if I had been a man! I only kept them quiet by tearing his card to pieces under my shawl. Without saying a word on my side, I walked away from the house (for fear of Laura seeing us); and he followed, protesting softly all the way. In the first by-street, I turned, and asked him what he wanted with me. He wanted two things. First, if I had no objection, to express his sentiments. I declined to hear them. Secondly, to repeat the warning in his letter. I asked, what occasion there was for repeating it. He bowed and smiled, and said he would explain. The explanation exactly confirmed the fears I expressed before you left us. I told you, if you remember, that Sir Percival would be too headstrong to take his friend's advice where you were concerned; and that there was no danger to be dreaded from the Count till his own interests were threatened, and he was roused into acting for himself?'

'I recollect, Marian.'

'Well; so it has really turned out. The Count offered his advice; but it was refused. Sir Percival would only take counsel of his own violence, his own obstinacy, and his own hatred of *you*. The Count let him have his way; first privately ascertaining, in case of his own interests being threatened next, where we lived. You were followed, Walter, on returning here, after your first journey to Hampshire—by the lawyer's men for some distance from the railway, and by the Count himself to the door of the house. How he contrived to escape being seen by you, he did not tell me; but he found us out on that occasion, and in that way. Having made the discovery, he took no advantage of it till the news reached him of Sir Percival's death—and then, as I told you, he acted for himself, because he believed you would next proceed against the dead man's partner in the conspiracy. He at once made his arrangements to meet the owner of the Asylum in London, and to take him to the place where his runaway patient was hidden; believing that the results, whichever way they ended, would be to involve you in interminable legal disputes and difficulties, and to tie your hands for all purposes of offence, so far as he was concerned. That was his purpose, on his own confession to me. The only consideration which made him hesitate, at the last moment——'

'Yes?'

'It is hard to acknowledge it, Walter—and yet I must! *I* was the only consideration. No words can say how degraded I feel in my own estimation when I think of it—but the one weak point in that man's iron character is the horrible admiration he feels for *me*. I have tried, for the sake of my own self-respect, to disbelieve it as long as I could; but his looks, his actions, force on me the shameful conviction of the truth. The eyes of that monster of wickedness moistened while he was speaking to me—they did, Walter! He declared, that at the moment of pointing out the house to the doctor, he thought of my misery if I was separated from Laura, of my responsibility if I was called on to answer for effecting her escape—and he risked the worst that you could do to him, the second time, for *my* sake. All he asked was that I would remember the sacrifice, and restrain your rashness, in my own interests—interests which he might never be able to consult again. I made no such bargain with him; I would have died first. But believe him, or not—whether it is true or false that he sent the doctor away with an excuse—one thing is certain, I saw the man leave him, without so much as a glance at our window, or even at our side of the way.'

'I believe it, Marian. The best men are not consistent in good—why should the worst men be consistent in evil?' At the same time, I suspect him of merely attempting to frighten you, by threatening what he cannot really do. I doubt his power of annoying us, by means of the owner of the Asylum, now that Sir Percival is dead, and Mrs Catherick is free from all control. But let me hear more. What did the Count say of me?'

'He spoke last of you. His eyes brightened and hardened, and his manner changed to what I remember it, in past times—to that mixture of pitiless resolution and mountebank mockery which makes it so impossible to fathom him. "Warn Mr Hartright!" he said, in his loftiest manner. "He has a man of brains to deal with, a man who snaps his big fingers at the laws and conventions of society, when he measures himself with ME. If my lamented friend had taken my advice, the business of the Inquest would have been with the body of Mr Hartright. But my lamented friend was obstinate. See! I mourn his loss—inwardly in my soul; outwardly on my hat. This trivial crape expresses sensibilities which I summon Mr Hartright to respect. They may be transformed to immeasurable enmities, if he ventures to disturb them! Let him be content with what he has got—with what I leave unmolested, for your sake, to him and to you. Say to him (with my compliments), if he stirs me, he has FOSCO to deal with. In the English of the Popular Tongue, I inform him—FOSCO sticks at nothing! Dear lady, good morning." His cold grey eyes settled on my face—he took off his hat solemnly—bowed, bareheaded—and left me.'

'Without returning? without saying more last words?'

'He turned at the corner of the street, and waved his hand, and then struck it theatrically on his breast. I lost sight of him, after that. He disappeared in the opposite direction to our house; and I ran back to Laura. Before I was in-doors again, I had made up my mind that we must go. The house (especially in your absence) was a place of danger instead of a place of safety, now that the Count had discovered it. If I could have felt certain of your return, I should have risked waiting till you came back. But I was certain of nothing, and I acted at once on my own impulse. You had spoken, before leaving us, of moving into a quieter neighbourhood and purer air, for the sake of Laura's health. I had only to remind her of that, and to suggest surprising you and saving you trouble by managing the move in your absence, to make her quite as anxious for the change as I was. She helped me to pack up your things—and she has arranged them all for you in your new working-room here.'

'What made you think of coming to this place?'

'My ignorance of other localities in the neighbourhood of London. I felt the necessity of getting as far away as possible from our old lodgings; and I knew something of Fulham because I had once been at school there. I despatched a messenger with a note, on the chance that the school might still be in existence. It was in existence: the daughters of my old mistress were carrying it on for her, and they engaged this place from the instructions I had sent. It was just post-time when the messenger returned to me with the address of the house. We moved after dark—we came here quite unobserved. Have I done right, Walter? Have I justified your trust in me?'

I answered her warmly and gratefully, as I really felt. But the anxious look still remained on her face while I was speaking; and the first question she asked, when I had done, related to Count Fosco.

I saw that she was thinking of him now with a changed mind. No fresh outbreak of anger against him, no new appeal to me to hasten the day of reckoning, escaped her. Her conviction that the man's hateful admiration of herself was really sincere, seemed to have increased a hundredfold her distrust of his unfathomable cunning, her inborn dread of the wicked energy and vigilance of all his faculties. Her voice fell low, her manner was hesitating, her eyes searched into mine with an eager fear, when she asked me what I thought of his message, and what I meant to do next, after hearing it.

'Not many weeks have passed, Marian,' I answered, 'since my interview with Mr Kyrle. When he and I parted, the last words I said to him about Laura were these: "Her uncle's house shall open to receive her, in the presence of every soul who followed the false funeral to the grave; the lie that records her death shall be publicly erased from the tombstone by the authority of the head of the family; and the two men who have wronged her shall answer for their crime to ME, though the justice that sits in tribunals is powerless to pursue them." One of those men is beyond mortal reach. The other remains—and my resolution remains.'

Her eyes lit up; her colour rose. She said nothing; but I saw all her sympathies gathering to mine, in her face.

'I don't disguise from myself, or from you,' I went on, 'that the prospect before us is more than doubtful. The risks we have run already are, it may be, trifles, compared with the risks that threaten us in the future—but the venture shall be tried, Marian, for all that. I am not rash enough to measure myself against such a man as the Count before I am well prepared for him. I have learnt patience; I can wait my time. Let him believe that his message has produced its effect; let him know nothing of us, and hear nothing of us; let us give him full time to feel secure—his own boastful nature, unless I seriously mistake him, will hasten that result. This is one reason for waiting; but there is another, more important still. My position, Marian, towards you and towards Laura, ought to be a stronger one than it is now, before I try our last chance.'

She leaned near to me, with a look of surprise.

'How can it be stronger?' she asked.

'I will tell you,' I replied, 'when the time comes. It has not come yet: it may never come at all. I may be silent about it to Laura for ever—I must be silent, now, even to *you*, till I see for myself that I can harmlessly and honourably speak. Let us leave that subject. There is another which has more pressing claims on our attention. You have kept Laura, mercifully kept her, in ignorance of her husband's death——'

'Oh, Walter, surely it must be long yet, before we tell her of it?'

'No, Marian. Better that you should reveal it to her now, than that accident, which no one can guard against, should reveal it to her at some future time. Spare her all the details—break it to her very tenderly—but tell her that he is dead.'

'You have a reason, Walter, for wishing her to know of her husband's death, besides the reason you have just mentioned?'

'I have.'

'A reason connected with that subject which must not be mentioned between us yet?—which may never be mentioned to Laura at all?'

She dwelt on the last words, meaningly. When I answered her, in the affirmative, I dwelt on them too.

Her face grew pale. For a while, she looked at me with a sad, hesitating interest. An unaccustomed tenderness trembled in her dark eyes and softened her firm lips, as she glanced aside at the empty chair in which the dear companion of all our joys and sorrows had been sitting.

'I think I understand,' she said. 'I think I owe it to her and to you, Walter, to tell her of her husband's death.'

She sighed, and held my hand fast for a moment—then dropped it abruptly, and left the room. On the next day, Laura knew that his death had released her, and that the error and the calamity of her life lay buried in his tomb.

His name was mentioned among us no more. Thenceforward, we shrank from the slightest approach to the subject of his death; and, in the same scrupulous manner, Marian and I avoided all further reference to that other subject, which, by her consent and mine, was not to be mentioned between us yet. It was not the less present to our minds—it was rather kept alive in them by the restraint which we had imposed on ourselves. We both watched Laura more anxiously than ever; sometimes waiting and hoping, sometimes waiting and fearing, till the time came.

By degrees, we returned to our accustomed way of life. I resumed the daily work, which had been suspended during my absence in Hampshire. Our new lodgings cost us more than the smaller and less convenient rooms which we had left; and the claim thus implied on my increased exertions was strengthened by the doubtfulness of our future prospects. Emergencies might yet happen which would exhaust our little fund at the banker's; and the work of my hands might be, ultimately, all we had to look to for support. More permanent and more lucrative employment than had yet been offered to me was a necessity of our position—a necessity for which I now diligently set myself to provide.

It must not be supposed that the interval of rest and seclusion of which I am now writing, entirely suspended, on my part, all pursuit of the one absorbing purpose with which my thoughts and actions are associated in these pages. That purpose was, for months and months yet, never to relax its claims on me. The slow ripening of it still left me a measure of precaution to take, an obligation of gratitude to perform, and a doubtful question to solve.

The measure of precaution related, necessarily, to the Count. It was of the last importance to ascertain, if possible, whether his plans committed him to remaining in England—or, in other words, to remaining within my reach. I contrived to set this doubt at rest by very simple means. His address in St John's Wood being known to me, I inquired in the neighbourhood; and having found out the agent who had the disposal of the furnished house in which he lived, I asked if number five, Forest-road, was likely to be let within a reasonable time. The reply was in the negative. I was informed that the foreign gentleman then residing in the house had renewed his term of occupation for another six months, and would remain in possession until the end of June in the following year. We were then at the beginning of December only. I left the agent with my mind relieved from all present fear of the Count's escaping me.

The obligation I had to perform, took me once more into the presence of Mrs Clements. I had promised to return, and to confide to her those particulars relating to the death and burial of Anne Catherick, which I had been obliged to withhold at our first interview. Changed as circumstances now were, there was no hindrance to my trusting the good woman with as much of the story of the conspiracy as it was necessary to tell. I had every reason that sympathy and friendly feeling could suggest to urge on me the speedy performance of my promise—and I did conscientiously and carefully perform it. There is no need to burden these pages with any statement of what passed at the interview. It will be more to the purpose to say that the interview itself necessarily brought to my mind the one doubtful question still remaining to be solved—the question of Anne Catherick's parentage on the father's side.

A multitude of small considerations in connexion with this subject—trifling enough in themselves, but strikingly important, when massed together—had latterly led my mind to a conclusion which I resolved to verify. I obtained Marian's permission to write to Major Donthorne, of Varneck Hall (where Mrs Catherick had lived in service for some years previous to her marriage), to ask him certain questions. I made the inquiries in Marian's name, and described them as relating to matters of personal interest in her family, which might explain and excuse my application. When I wrote the letter, I had no certain knowledge that Major Donthorne was still alive; I despatched it on the chance that he might be living, and able and willing to reply.

After a lapse of two days, proof came, in the shape of a letter, that the Major was living, and that he was ready to help us.

The idea in my mind when I wrote to him, and the nature of my inquiries, will be easily inferred from his reply. His letter answered my questions, by communicating these important facts:

In the first place, 'the late Sir Percival Glyde, of Blackwater Park,' had never set foot in Varneck Hall. The deceased gentleman was a total stranger to Major Donthorne, and to all his family.

In the second place, 'the late Mr Philip Fairlie, of Limmeridge House,' had been, in his younger days, the intimate friend and constant guest of Major Donthorne. Having refreshed his memory by looking back to old letters and other papers, the Major was in a position to say positively, that Mr Philip Fairlie was staying at Varneck Hall in the month of August, eighteen hundred and twenty-six, and that he remained there, for the shooting, during the month of September and part of October following. He then left, to the best of the Major's belief, for Scotland, and did not return to Varneck Hall till after a lapse of time, when he reappeared in the character of a newly-married man.

Taken by itself, this statement was, perhaps, of little positive value—but, taken in connexion with certain facts, every one of which either Marian or I knew to be true, it suggested one plain conclusion that was, to our minds, irresistible.

Knowing, now, that Mr Philip Fairlie had been at Varneck Hall in the autumn of eighteen hundred and twenty-six, and that Mrs Catherick had been living there in service at the same time, we knew also:—first, that Anne had been born in June, eighteen hundred and twenty-seven; secondly, that she had always presented an extraordinary personal resemblance to Laura; and, thirdly, that Laura herself was strikingly like her father. Mr Philip Fairlie had been one of the notoriously-handsome men of his time. In disposition entirely unlike his brother Frederick, he was the spoilt darling of society, especially of the women—an easy, light-hearted, impulsive, affectionate man; generous to a fault; constitutionally lax in his principles, and notoriously thoughtless of moral obligations where women were concerned. Such were the facts we knew; such was the character of the man. Surely, the plain inference that follows needs no pointing out?

Read by the new light which had now broken upon me, even Mrs Catherick's letter, in despite of herself, rendered its mite of assistance towards strengthening the conclusion at which I had arrived. She had described Mrs Fairlie (in writing to me) as 'plain-looking,' and as having 'entrapped the handsomest man in England into marrying her.' Both assertions were gratuitously made, and both were false. Jealous dislike (which, in such a woman as Mrs Catherick, would express itself in petty malice rather than not express itself at all) appeared to me to be the only assignable cause for the peculiar insolence of her reference to Mrs Fairlie, under circumstances which did not necessitate any reference at all.

The mention here of Mrs Fairlie's name naturally suggests one other question. Did she ever suspect whose child the little girl brought to her at Limmeridge might be?

Marian's testimony was positive on this point. Mrs Fairlie's letter to her husband, which had been read to me in former days—the letter describing Anne's resemblance to Laura, and acknowledging her affectionate interest in the little stranger—had been written, beyond all question, in perfect innocence of heart. It even seemed doubtful, on consideration, whether Mr Philip Fairlie himself had been nearer than his wife to any suspicion of the truth. The disgracefully-deceitful circumstances under which Mrs Catherick had married, the purpose of concealment which the marriage was intended to answer, might well keep her silent for caution's sake, perhaps for her own pride's sake also—even assuming that she had the means, in his absence, of communicating with the father of her unborn child.

As this surmise floated through my mind, there rose on my memory the remembrance of the Scripture denunciation which we have all thought of, in our time, with wonder and with awe: 'The sins of the fathers shall be visited on the children.' But for the fatal resemblance between the two daughters of one father, the conspiracy of which Anne had been the innocent instrument and Laura the innocent victim, could never have been planned. With what unerring and terrible directness the long chain of circumstances led down from the thoughtless wrong committed by the father to the heartless injury inflicted on the child!

These thoughts came to me, and others with them, which drew my mind away to the little Cumberland churchyard where Anne Catherick now lay buried. I thought of the bygone days when I had met her by Mrs Fairlie's grave, and met her for the last time. I thought of her poor helpless hands beating on the tombstone, and her weary, yearning words, murmured to the dead remains of her protectress and her friend. 'Oh, if I could die, and be hidden and at rest with *you*!' Little more than a year had passed since she breathed that wish; and how inscrutably, how awfully, it had been fulfilled! The words she had spoken to Laura by the shores of the lake, the very words had now come true. 'Oh, if I could only be buried with your mother! If I could only wake at her side when the angel's trumpet sounds, and the graves give up their dead at the resurrection!' Through what mortal crime and horror, through what darkest windings of the way down to Death, the lost creature had wandered in God's leading to the last home that, living, she never hoped to reach! There (I said in my own heart)—there, if ever I have the power to will it, all that is mortal of her shall remain, and share the grave-bed with the loved friend of her childhood, with the dear remembrance of her life. *That* rest shall be sacred—*that* companionship always undisturbed!

So the ghostly figure which has haunted these pages as it haunted my life, goes down into the impenetrable Gloom. Like a Shadow she first came to me, in the loneliness of the night. Like a Shadow she passes away, in the loneliness of the dead.

*   *   *   *   *

Forward now! Forward on the way that winds through other scenes, and leads to brighter times.

THE END OF THE SECOND PART

PART THE THIRD

===

I

FOUR months elapsed. April came—the month of Spring; the month of change.

The course of Time had flowed through the interval since the winter, peacefully and happily in our new home. I had turned my long leisure to good account; had largely increased my sources of employment; and had placed our means of subsistence on surer grounds. Freed from the suspense and the anxiety which had tried her so sorely, and hung over her so long, Marian's spirits rallied; and her natural energy of character began to assert itself again, with something, if not all, of the freedom and the vigour of former times.

More pliable under change than her sister, Laura showed more plainly the progress made by the healing influences of her new life. The worn and wasted look which had prematurely aged her face, was fast leaving it; and the expression which had been the first of its charms in past days, was the first of its beauties that now returned. My closest observation of her detected but one serious result of the conspiracy which had once threatened her reason and her life. Her memory of events, from the period of her leaving Blackwater Park to the period of our meeting in the burial-ground of Limmeridge church, was lost beyond all hope of recovery. At the slightest reference to that time, she changed and trembled still; her words became confused; her memory wandered and lost itself as helplessly as ever. Here, and here only, the traces of the past lay deep—too deep to be effaced.

In all else, she was now so far on the way to recovery, that, on her best and brightest days, she sometimes looked and spoke like the Laura of old times. The happy change wrought its natural result in us both. From their long slumber, on her side and on mine, those imperishable memories of our past life in Cumberland now awoke, which were one and all alike, the memories of our love.

Gradually and insensibly, our daily relations towards each other became constrained. The fond words which I had spoken to her so naturally, in the days of her sorrow and her suffering, faltered strangely on my lips. In the time when my dread of losing her was most present to my mind, I had always kissed her when she left me at night and when she met me in the morning. The kiss seemed now to have dropped between us—to be lost out of our lives. Our hands began to tremble again when they met. We hardly ever looked long at one another out of Marian's presence. The talk often flagged between us when we were alone. When I touched her by accident, I felt my heart beating fast, as it used to beat at Limmeridge House—I saw the lovely answering flush glowing again in her cheeks, as if we were back among the Cumberland Hills, in our past characters of master and pupil once more. She had long intervals of silence and thoughtfulness; and denied she had been thinking, when Marian asked her the question. I surprised myself, one day, neglecting my work, to dream over the little water-colour portrait of her which I had taken in the summer-house where we first met—just as I used to neglect Mr Fairlie's drawings, to dream over the same likeness, when it was newly finished in the bygone time. Changed as all the circumstances now were, our position towards each other in the golden days of our first companionship, seemed to be revived with the revival of our love. It was as if Time had drifted us back, on the wreck of our early hopes, to the old familiar shore!

To any other woman, I could have spoken the decisive words which I still hesitated to speak to *her*. The utter helplessness of her position, her friendless dependence on all the forbearing gentleness that I could show her, my fear of touching too soon some secret sensitiveness in her, which my instinct, as a man, might not have been fine enough to discover—these considerations, and others like them, kept me self-distrustfully silent. And yet, I knew that the restraint on both sides must be ended; that the relations in which we stood towards one another must be altered, in some settled manner, for the future, and that it rested with me, in the first instance, to recognise the necessity for a change.

The more I thought of our position, the harder the attempt to alter it appeared, while the domestic conditions on which we three had been living together since the winter, remained undisturbed. I cannot account for the capricious state of mind in which this feeling originated—but the idea nevertheless possessed me, that some previous change of place and circumstances, some sudden break in the quiet monotony of our lives, so managed as to vary the home aspect under which we had been accustomed to see each other, might prepare the way for me to speak, and might make it easier and less embarrassing for Laura and Marian to hear.

With this purpose in view, I said, one morning, that I thought we had all earned a little holiday and a change of scene. After some consideration, it was decided that we should go for a fortnight to the sea-side.

On the next day, we left Fulham for a quiet town on the south coast. At that early season of the year, we were the only visitors in the place. The cliffs, the beach, and the walks inland, were all in the solitary condition which was most welcome to us. The air was mild; the prospects over hill and wood and down were beautifully varied by the shifting April light and shade; and the restless sea leapt under our windows, as if it felt, like the land, the glow and freshness of spring.

I owed it to Marian to consult her before I spoke to Laura, and to be guided afterwards by her advice.

On the third day from our arrival, I found a fit opportunity of speaking to her alone. The moment we looked at one another, her quick instinct detected the thought in my mind before I could give it expression. With her customary energy and directness, she spoke at once, and spoke first.

'You are thinking of that subject which was mentioned between us on the evening of your return from Hampshire,' she said. 'I have been expecting you to allude to it, for some time past. There must be a change in our little household, Walter; we cannot go on much longer as we are now. I see it as plainly as you do—as plainly as Laura sees it, though she says nothing. How strangely the old times in Cumberland seem to have come back! You and I are together again; and the one subject of interest between us is Laura once more. I could almost fancy that this room is the summer-house at Limmeridge, and that those waves beyond us are beating on *our* sea-shore.'

'I was guided by your advice in those past days,' I said; 'and now, Marian, with reliance tenfold greater, I will be guided by it again.'

She answered by pressing my hand. I saw that she was deeply touched by my reference to the past. We sat together near the window; and, while I spoke and she listened, we looked at the glory of the sunlight shining on the majesty of the sea.

'Whatever comes of this confidence between us,' I said, 'whether it ends happily or sorrowfully for *me*, Laura's interests will still be the interests of my life. When we leave this place, on whatever terms we leave it, my determination to wrest from Count Fosco the confession which I failed to obtain from his accomplice, goes back with me to London, as certainly as I go back myself. Neither you nor I can tell how that man may turn on me, if I bring him to bay; we only know by his own words and actions, that he is capable of striking at me, through Laura, without a moment's hesitation, or a moment's remorse. In our present position, I have no claim on her, which society sanctions, which the law allows, to strengthen me in resisting *him*, and in protecting *her*. This places me at a serious disadvantage. If I am to fight our cause with the Count, strong in the consciousness of Laura's safety, I must fight it for my Wife. Do you agree to that, Marian, so far?'

'To every word of it,' she answered.

'I will not plead out of my own heart,' I went on; 'I will not appeal to the love which has survived all changes and all shocks—I will rest my only vindication of myself for thinking of her and speaking of her as my wife, on what I have just said. If the chance of forcing a confession from the Count, is, as I believe it to be, the last chance left of publicly establishing the fact of Laura's existence, the least selfish reason that I can advance for our marriage is recognised by us both. But I may be wrong in my conviction; other means of achieving our purpose may be in our power, which are less uncertain and less dangerous. I have searched anxiously, in my own mind, for those means—and I have not found them. Have you?'

'No. I have thought about it, too, and thought in vain.'

'In all likelihood,' I continued, 'the same questions have occurred to you, in considering this difficult subject, which have occurred to me. Ought we to return with her to Limmeridge, now that she is like herself again, and trust to the recognition of her by the people of the village, or by the children at the school? Ought we to appeal to the practical test of her handwriting? Suppose we did so. Suppose the recognition of her obtained, and the identity of the handwriting established. Would success in both those cases do more than supply an excellent foundation for a trial in a court of law? Would the recognition and the handwriting prove her identity to Mr Fairlie and take her back to Limmeridge House, against the evidence of her aunt, against the evidence of the medical certificate, against the fact of the funeral and the fact of the inscription on the tomb? No! We could only hope to succeed in throwing a serious doubt on the assertion of her death—a doubt which nothing short of a legal inquiry can settle. I will assume that we possess (what we have certainly not got) money enough to carry this inquiry on through all its stages. I will assume that Mr Fairlie's prejudices might be reasoned away; that the false testimony of the Count and his wife, and all the rest of the false testimony, might be confuted; that the recognition could not possibly be ascribed to a mistake between Laura and Anne Catherick, or the handwriting be declared by our enemies to be a clever fraud—all these are assumptions which, more or less, set plain probabilities at defiance, but let them pass—and let us ask ourselves what would be the first consequence of the first questions put to Laura herself on the subject of the conspiracy. We know only too well what the consequence would be—for we know that she has never recovered her memory of what happened to her in London. Examine her privately, or examine her publicly, she is utterly incapable of assisting the assertion of her own case. If you don't see this, Marian, as plainly as I see it, we will go to Limmeridge and try the experiment, to-morrow.'

'I *do* see it, Walter. Even if we had the means of paying all the law expenses, even if we succeeded in the end, the delays would be unendurable; the perpetual suspense, after what we have suffered already, would be heart-breaking. You are right about the hopelessness of going to Limmeridge. I wish I could feel sure that you are right also in determining to try that last chance with the Count. *Is* it a chance at all?'

'Beyond a doubt, Yes. It is the chance of recovering the lost date of Laura's journey to London. Without returning to the reasons I gave you some time since, I am still as firmly persuaded as ever, that there is a discrepancy between the date of that journey and the date on the certificate of death. There lies the weak point of the whole conspiracy—it crumbles to pieces if we attack it in that way; and the means of attacking it are in possession of the Count. If I succeed in wresting them from him, the object of your life and mine is fulfilled. If I fail, the wrong that Laura has suffered, will, in this world, never be redressed.'

'Do you fear failure, yourself, Walter?'

'I dare not anticipate success; and, for that very reason, Marian, I speak openly and plainly, as I have spoken now. In my heart and my conscience, I can say it—Laura's hopes for the future are at their lowest ebb. I know that her fortune is gone; I know that the last chance of restoring her to her place in the world lies at the mercy of her worst enemy, of a man who is now absolutely unassailable, and who may remain unassailable to the end. With every worldly advantage gone from her; with all prospect of recovering her rank and station more than doubtful; with no clearer future before her than the future which her husband can provide—the poor drawing-master may harmlessly open his heart at last. In the days of her prosperity, Marian, I was only the teacher who guided her hand—I ask for it, in her adversity, as the hand of my wife!'

Marian's eyes met mine affectionately—I could say no more. My heart was full, my lips were trembling. In spite of myself, I was in danger of appealing to her pity. I got up to leave the room. She rose at the same moment, laid her hand gently on my shoulder, and stopped me.

'Walter!' she said, 'I once parted you both, for your good and for hers. Wait here, my Brother!—wait, my dearest, best friend, till Laura comes, and tells you what I have done now!'

For the first time since the farewell morning at Limmeridge, she touched my forehead with her lips. A tear dropped on my face, as she kissed me. She turned quickly, pointed to the chair from which I had risen, and left the room.

I sat down alone at the window, to wait through the crisis of my life. My mind, in that breathless interval, felt like a total blank. I was conscious of nothing but a painful intensity of all familiar perceptions. The sun grew blinding bright; the white sea birds chasing each other far beyond me, seemed to be flitting before my face, the mellow murmur of the waves on the beach was like thunder in my ears.

The door opened; and Laura came in alone. So she had entered the breakfast-room at Limmeridge House, on the morning when we parted. Slowly and falteringly, in sorrow and in hesitation, she had once approached me. Now, she came with the haste of happiness in her feet, with the light of happiness radiant in her face. Of their own accord, those dear arms clasped themselves round me; of their own accord, the sweet lips came to meet mine.

'My darling!' she whispered, 'we may own we love each other, now!' Her head nestled with a tender contentedness on my bosom. 'Oh,' she said, innocently, 'I am so happy at last!'

Ten days later, we were happier still. We were married.

II

THE course of this narrative, steadily flowing on, bears me away from the morning-time of our married life, and carries me forward to the End.

In a fortnight more we three were back in London; and the shadow was stealing over us of the struggle to come.

Marian and I were careful to keep Laura in ignorance of the cause that had hurried us back—the necessity of making sure of the Count. It was now the beginning of May, and his term of occupation at the house in Forest-road expired in June. If he renewed it (and I had reasons, shortly to be mentioned, for anticipating that he would), I might be certain of his not escaping me. But, if by any chance he disappointed my expectations, and left the country—then, I had no time to lose in arming myself to meet him as I best might.

In the first fulness of my new happiness, there had been moments when my resolution faltered—moments, when I was tempted to be safely content, now that the dearest aspiration of my life was fulfilled in the possession of Laura's love. For the first time, I thought faint-heartedly of the greatness of the risk; of the adverse chances arrayed against me; of the fair promise of our new lives, and of the peril in which I might place the happiness which we had so hardly earned. Yes! let me own it honestly. For a brief time, I wandered, in the sweet guiding of love, far from the purpose to which I had been true, under sterner discipline and in darker days. Innocently, Laura had tempted me aside from the hard path—innocently, she was destined to lead me back again.

At times, dreams of the terrible past still disconnectedly recalled to her, in the mystery of sleep, the events of which her waking memory had lost all trace. One night (barely two weeks after our marriage), when I was watching her at rest, I saw the tears come slowly through her closed eyelids, I heard the faint murmuring words escape her which told me that her spirit was back again on the fatal journey from Blackwater Park. That unconscious appeal, so touching and so awful in the sacredness of her sleep, ran through me like fire. The next day was the day we came back to London—the day when my resolution returned to me with tenfold strength.

The first necessity was to know something of the man. Thus far, the true story of his life was an impenetrable mystery to me.

I began with such scanty sources of information as were at my own disposal. The important narrative written by Mr Frederick Fairlie (which

Marian had obtained by following the directions I had given to her in the winter) proved to be of no service to the special object with which I now looked at it. While reading it, I reconsidered the disclosure revealed to me by Mrs Clements, of the series of deceptions which had brought Anne Catherick to London, and which had there devoted her to the interests of the conspiracy. Here, again, the Count had not openly committed himself; here again, he was, to all practical purpose, out of my reach.

I next returned to Marian's journal at Blackwater Park. At my request she read to me again a passage which referred to her past curiosity about the Count, and to the few particulars which she had discovered relating to him.

The passage to which I allude occurs in that part of her journal which delineates his character and his personal appearance. She describes him as 'not having crossed the frontiers of his native country for years past'—as 'anxious to know if any Italian gentlemen were settled in the nearest town to Blackwater Park'—as 'receiving letters with all sorts of odd stamps on them, and one with a large, official-looking seal on it.' She is inclined to consider that his long absence from his native country may be accounted for by assuming that he is a political exile. But she is, on the other hand, unable to reconcile this idea with the reception of the letter from abroad, bearing 'the large official-looking seal'—letters from the Continent addressed to political exiles being usually the last to court attention from foreign post-offices in that way.

The considerations thus presented to me in the diary, joined to certain surmises of my own that grew out of them, suggested a conclusion which I wondered I had not arrived at before. I now said to myself—what Laura had once said to Marian at Blackwater Park; what Madame Fosco had overheard by listening at the door—the Count is a Spy!

Laura had applied the word to him at hazard, in natural anger at his proceedings towards herself. *I* applied it to him, with the deliberate conviction that his vocation in life was the vocation of a Spy. On this assumption, the reason for his extraordinary stay in England, so long after the objects of the conspiracy had been gained, became, to my mind, quite intelligible.

The year of which I am now writing was the year of the famous Crystal Palace Exhibition in Hyde Park. Foreigners, in unusually large numbers, had arrived already, and were still arriving, in England. Men were among us, by thousands, whom the ceaseless distrustfulness of their governments had followed privately, by means of appointed agents, to our shores. My surmises did not for a moment class a man of the Count's abilities and social position with the ordinary rank and file of foreign spies. I suspected him of holding a position of authority, of being entrusted, by the government which he secretly served, with the organisation and management of agents specially employed in this country, both men and women; and I believed Mrs Rubelle, who had been so opportunely found to act as nurse at Blackwater Park, to be, in all probability, one of the number.

Assuming that this idea of mine had a foundation in truth, the position of the Count might prove to be more assailable than I had hitherto ventured to hope. To whom could I apply to know something more of the man's history, and of the man himself, than I knew now?

In this emergency, it naturally occurred to my mind that a countryman of his own, on whom I could rely, might be the fittest person to help me. The first man whom I thought of, under these circumstances, was also the only Italian with whom I was intimately acquainted—my quaint little friend, Professor Pesca.

The Professor has been so long absent from these pages, that he has run some risk of being forgotten altogether.

It is the necessary law of such a story as mine, that the persons concerned in it only appear when the course of events takes them up—they come and go, not by favour of my personal partiality, but by right of their direct connexion with the circumstances to be detailed. For this reason, not Pesca only, but my mother and sister as well, have been left far in the background of the narrative. My visits to the Hampstead cottage; my mother's belief in the denial of Laura's identity which the conspiracy had accomplished; my vain efforts to overcome the prejudice, on her part and on my sister's, to which, in their jealous affection for me, they both continued to adhere; the painful necessity which that prejudice imposed on me of concealing my marriage from them till they had learnt to do justice to my wife—all these little domestic occurrences have been left unrecorded, because they were not essential to the main interest of the story. It is nothing that they added to my anxieties and embittered my disappointments—the steady march of events has inexorably passed them by.

For the same reason, I have said nothing, here, of the consolation that I found in Pesca's brotherly affection for me, when I saw him again after the sudden cessation of my residence at Limmeridge House. I have not recorded the fidelity with which my warm-hearted little friend followed me to the place of embarkation, when I sailed for Central America, or the noisy transport of joy with which he received me when we next met in London. If I had felt justified in accepting the offers of service which he made to me, on my return, he would have appeared again, long ere this. But, though I knew that his honour and his courage were to be implicitly relied on, I was not so sure that his discretion was to be trusted; and, for that reason only, I followed the course of all my inquiries alone. It will now be sufficiently understood that Pesca was not separated from all connexion with me and my interests, although he has hitherto been separated from all connexion with the progress of this narrative. He was as true and as ready a friend of mine still, as ever he had been in his life.

Before I summoned Pesca to my assistance, it was necessary to see for myself what sort of man I had to deal with. Up to this time, I had never once set eyes on Count Fosco.

Three days after my return with Laura and Marian to London, I set forth alone for Forest-road, St John's Wood, between ten and eleven o'clock in the morning. It was a fine day—I had some hours to spare—and I thought it likely, if I waited a little for him, that the Count might be tempted out. I had no great reason to fear the chance of his recognising me in the day-time, for the only occasion when I had been seen by him was the occasion on which he had followed me home at night.

No one appeared at the windows in the front of the house. I walked down a turning which ran past the side of it, and looked over the low garden wall. One of the back windows on the lower floor was thrown up, and a net was stretched across the opening. I saw nobody; but I heard, in the room, first a shrill whistling and singing of birds—then, the deep ringing voice which Marian's description had made familiar to me. 'Come out on my little finger, my pret-pret-pretties!' cried the voice. 'Come out, and hop upstairs! One, two, three—and up! Three, two, one—and down! One, two, three— twit-twit-twit-tweet!' The Count was exercising his canaries, as he used to exercise them in Marian's time, at Blackwater Park.

I waited a little while, and the singing and the whistling ceased. 'Come, kiss me, my pretties!' said the deep voice. There was a responsive twittering and chirping—a low, oily laugh—a silence of a minute or so—and then I heard the opening of the house door. I turned, and retraced my steps. The magnificent melody of the Prayer in Rossini's 'Moses,' sung in a sonorous bass voice, rose grandly through the suburban silence of the place. The front garden gate opened and closed. The Count had come out.

He crossed the road, and walked towards the western boundary of the Regent's Park. I kept on my own side of the way, a little behind him, and walked in that direction also.

Marian had prepared me for his high stature, his monstrous corpulence, and his ostentatious mourning garments—but not for the horrible freshness and cheerfulness and vitality of the man. He carried his sixty years as if they had been fewer than forty. He sauntered along, wearing his hat a little on one side, with a light jaunty step; swinging his big stick; humming to himself; looking up, from time to time, at the houses and gardens on either side of him, with superb, smiling patronage. If a stranger had been told that the whole neighbourhood belonged to him, that stranger would not have been surprised to hear it. He never looked back: he paid no apparent attention to me, no apparent attention to any one who passed him on his own side of the road—except, now and then, when he smiled and smirked, with an easy, paternal good humour, at the nurserymaids and the children whom he met. In this way, he led me on, till we reached a colony of shops outside the western terraces of the Park.

Here, he stopped at a pastrycook's, went in (probably to give an order), and came out again immediately with a tart in his hand. An Italian was grinding an organ before the shop, and a miserable little shrivelled monkey was sitting on the instrument. The Count stopped; bit a piece for himself out of the tart; and gravely handed the rest to the monkey. 'My poor little man!' he said, with grotesque tenderness; 'you look hungry. In the sacred name of humanity, I offer you some lunch!' The organ-grinder piteously put in his claim to a penny from the benevolent stranger. The Count shrugged his shoulders contemptuously—and passed on.

We reached the streets and the better class of shops, between the New-road and Oxford-street. The Count stopped again, and entered a small optician's shop, with an inscription in the window, announcing that repairs were neatly executed inside. He came out again, with an opera-glass in his hand; walked a few paces on; and stopped to look at a bill of the Opera, placed outside a music-seller's shop. He read the bill attentively, considered a moment, and then hailed an empty cab as it passed him. 'Opera-box-office,' he said to the man—and was driven away.

I crossed the road, and looked at the bill in my turn. The performance announced was 'Lucrezia Borgia,' and it was to take place that evening. The opera-glass in the Count's hand, his careful reading of the bill, and his direction to the cabman, all suggested that he proposed making one of the audience. I had the means of getting an admission for myself and a friend, to the pit, by applying to one of the scene-painters attached to the theatre, with whom I had been well acquainted in past times. There was a chance, at least, that the Count might be easily visible among the audience, to me, and to any one with me; and, in this case, I had the means of ascertaining whether Pesca knew his countryman, or not, that very night.

This consideration at once decided the disposal of my evening. I procured the tickets, leaving a note at the Professor's lodgings on the way. At a quarter to eight, I called to take him with me to the theatre. My little friend was in a state of the highest excitement, with a festive flower in his button-hole, and the largest opera-glass I ever saw hugged up under his arm.

'Are you ready?' I asked.

'Right-all-right,' said Pesca.

We started for the theatre.

III

THE last notes of the introduction to the opera were being played, and the seats in the pit were all filled, when Pesca and I reached the theatre.

There was plenty of room, however, in the passage that ran round the pit—precisely the position best calculated to answer the purpose for which I was attending the performance. I went first to the barrier separating us from the stalls; and looked for the Count in that part of the theatre. He was not there. Returning along the passage, on the left hand side from the stage, and looking about me attentively, I discovered him in the pit. He occupied an excellent place, some twelve or fourteen seats from the end of a bench, within three rows of the stalls. I placed myself exactly on a line with him; Pesca standing by my side. The Professor was not yet aware of the purpose for which I had brought him to the theatre, and he was rather surprised that we did not move nearer to the stage.

The curtain rose, and the opera began.

Throughout the whole of the first act, we remained in our position; the Count, absorbed by the orchestra and the stage, never casting so much as a chance glance at us. Not a note of Donizetti's delicious music was lost on him. There he sat, high above his neighbours, smiling, and nodding his great head enjoyingly, from time to time. When the people near him applauded the close of an air (as an English audience in such circumstances always *will* applaud), without the least consideration for the orchestral movement which immediately followed it, he looked round at them with an expression of compassionate remonstrance, and held up one hand with a gesture of polite entreaty. At the more refined passages of the singing, at the more delicate phrases of the music, which passed unapplauded by others, his fat hands adorned with perfectly-fitting black kid gloves, softly patted each other, in token of the cultivated appreciation of a musical man. At such times, his oily murmur of approval, 'Bravo! Bra-a-a-a!' hummed through the silence, like the purring of a great cat. His immediate neighbours on either side—hearty, ruddy-faced people from the country, basking amazedly in the sunshine of fashionable London—seeing and hearing him, began to follow his lead. Many a burst of applause from the pit, that night, started from the soft, comfortable patting of the black-gloved hands. The man's voracious vanity devoured this implied tribute to his local and critical supremacy, with an appearance of the highest relish. Smiles rippled continuously over his fat face. He looked about him, at the pauses in the music, serenely satisfied with himself and his fellow-creatures. 'Yes! yes! these barbarous English people are learning something from ME. Here, there, and everywhere, I—Fosco—am an Influence that is felt, a Man who sits supreme!' If ever face spoke, his face spoke then—and that was its language.

The curtain fell on the first act; and the audience rose to look about them. This was the time I had waited for—the time to try if Pesca knew him.

He rose with the rest, and surveyed the occupants of the boxes grandly with his opera-glass. At first, his back was towards us; but he turned round, in time, to our side of the theatre, and looked at the boxes above us; using his glass for a few minutes—then removing it, but still continuing to look up. This was the moment I chose, when his full face was in view, for directing Pesca's attention to him.

'Do you know that man?' I asked.

'Which man, my friend?'

'The tall, fat man, standing there, with his face towards us.'

Pesca raised himself on tiptoe, and looked at the Count.

'No,' said the Professor. 'The big fat man is a stranger to me. Is he famous? Why do you point him out?'

'Because I have particular reasons for wishing to know something of him. He is a countryman of yours; his name is Count Fosco. Do you know that name?'

'Not I, Walter. Neither the name nor the man is known to me.'

'Are you quite sure you don't recognise him? Look again; look carefully. I will tell you why I am so anxious about it, when we leave the theatre. Stop! let me help you up here, where you can see him better.'

I helped the little man to perch himself on the edge of the raised dais upon which the pit-seats were all placed. Here, his small stature was no hindrance to him; here, he could see over the heads of the ladies who were seated near the outermost part of the bench.

A slim, light-haired man, standing by us, whom I had not noticed before—a man with a scar on his left cheek—looked attentively at Pesca as I helped him up, and then looked still more attentively, following the direction of Pesca's eyes, at the Count. Our conversation might have reached his ears, and might, as it struck me, have roused his curiosity.

Meanwhile, Pesca fixed his eyes earnestly on the broad, full, smiling face, turned a little upward, exactly opposite to him.

'No,' he said; 'I have never set my two eyes on that big fat man before, in all my life.'

As he spoke, the Count looked downwards towards the boxes behind us on the pit tier.

The eyes of the two Italians met.

The instant before, I had been perfectly satisfied, from his own reiterated assertion, that Pesca did not know the Count. The instant afterwards, I was equally certain that the Count knew Pesca!

Knew him; and—more surprising still—*feared* him as well! There was no mistaking the change that passed over the villain's face. The leaden hue that altered his yellow complexion in a moment, the sudden rigidity of all his features, the furtive scrutiny of his cold grey eyes, the motionless stillness of him from head to foot, told their own tale. A mortal dread had mastered him, body and soul—and his own recognition of Pesca was the cause of it!

The slim man, with the scar on his cheek, was still close by us. He had apparently drawn his inference from the effect produced on the Count by the sight of Pesca, as I had drawn mine. He was a mild gentlemanlike man, looking like a foreigner; and his interest in our proceedings was not expressed in anything approaching to an offensive manner.

For my own part, I was so startled by the change in the Count's face, so astounded at the entirely-unexpected turn which events had taken, that I knew neither what to say or do next. Pesca roused me by stepping back to his former place at my side, and speaking first.

'How the fat man stares!' he exclaimed. 'Is it at *me*? Am *I* famous? How can he know me, when I don't know him?'

I kept my eye still on the Count. I saw him move for the first time when Pesca moved, so as not to lose sight of the little man, in the lower position in which he now stood. I was curious to see what would happen, if Pesca's attention, under these circumstances, was withdrawn from him; and I accordingly asked the Professor if he recognised any of his pupils, that evening, among the ladies in the boxes. Pesca immediately raised the large opera-glass to his eyes, and moved it slowly all round the upper part of the theatre, searching for his pupils with the most conscientious scrutiny.

The moment he showed himself to be thus engaged, the Count turned round; slipped past the persons who occupied seats on the farther side of him from where we stood; and disappeared in the middle passage down the centre of the pit. I caught Pesca by the arm; and, to his inexpressible astonishment, hurried him round with me to the back of the pit, to intercept the Count before he could get to the door. Somewhat to my surprise, the slim man hastened out before us, avoiding a stoppage caused by some people on our side of the pit leaving their places, by which Pesca and myself were delayed. When we reached the lobby the Count had disappeared—and the foreigner with the scar was gone too.

'Come home,' I said; 'come home, Pesca, to your lodgings. I must speak to you in private—I must speak directly.'

'My-soul-bless-my-soul!' cried the Professor, in a state of the extremest bewilderment. 'What on earth is the matter?'

I walked on rapidly, without answering. The circumstances under which the Count had left the theatre suggested to me that his extraordinary anxiety to escape Pesca might carry him to further extremities still. He might escape *me*, too, by leaving London. I doubted the future, if I allowed him so much as a day's freedom to act as he pleased. And I doubted that foreign stranger who had got the start of us, and whom I suspected of intentionally following him out.

With this double distrust in my mind, I was not long in making Pesca understand what I wanted. As soon as we two were alone in his room, I increased his confusion and amazement a hundredfold by telling him what my purpose was, as plainly and unreservedly as I have acknowledged it here.

'My friend, what can I do?' cried the Professor, piteously appealing to me with both hands. 'Deuce-what-the-deuce! how can I help you, Walter, when I don't know the man?'

'*He* knows *you*—he is afraid of you—he has left the theatre to escape you. Pesca! there must be a reason for this. Look back into your own life, before you came to England. You left Italy, as you have told me yourself, for political reasons. You have never mentioned those reasons to me; and I don't inquire into them, now. I only ask you to consult your own recollections, and to say if they suggest no past cause for the terror which the first sight of you produced in that man.'

To my unutterable surprise, these words, harmless as they appeared to *me*, produced the same astounding effect on Pesca which the sight of Pesca had produced on the Count. The rosy face of my little friend whitened in an instant; and he drew back from me slowly, trembling from head to foot.

'Walter!' he said. 'You don't know what you ask.'

He spoke in a whisper—he looked at me as if I had suddenly revealed to him some hidden danger to both of us. In less than one minute of time, he was so altered from the easy, lively, quaint little man of all my past experience, that if I had met him in the street, changed as I saw him now, I should most certainly not have known him again.

'Forgive me, if I have unintentionally pained and shocked you,' I replied. 'Remember the cruel wrong my wife has suffered at Count Fosco's hands. Remember that the wrong can never be redressed, unless the means are in my power of forcing him to do her justice. I spoke in *her* interests, Pesca—I ask you again to forgive me—I can say no more.'

I rose to go. He stopped me before I reached the door.

'Wait,' he said. 'You have shaken me from head to foot. You don't know how I left my country, and why I left my country. Let me compose myself—let me think, if I can.'

I returned to my chair. He walked up and down the room, talking to himself incoherently in his own language. After several turns backwards and forwards, he suddenly came up to me, and laid his little hands with a strange tenderness and solemnity on my breast.

'On your heart and soul, Walter,' he said, 'is there no other way to get to that man but the chance-way through *me*?'

'There is no other way,' I answered.

He left me again; opened the door of the room and looked out cautiously into the passage; closed it once more; and came back.

'You won your right over me, Walter,' he said, 'on the day when you saved my life. It was yours from that moment, when you pleased to take it. Take it now. Yes! I mean what I say. My next words, as true as the good God is above us, will put my life into your hands.'

The trembling earnestness with which he uttered this extraordinary warning carried with it to my mind the conviction that he spoke the truth.

'Mind this!' he went on, shaking his hands at me in the vehemence of his agitation. 'I hold no thread, in my own mind, between that man, FOSCO, and the past time which I call back to me, for your sake. If *you* find the thread, keep it to yourself—tell me nothing—on my knees, I beg and pray, let me be ignorant, let me be innocent, let me be blind to all the future, as I am now!'

He said a few words more, hesitatingly and disconnectedly—then stopped again.

I saw that the effort of expressing himself in English, on an occasion too serious to permit him the use of the quaint turns and phrases of his ordinary vocabulary, was painfully increasing the difficulty he had felt from the first in speaking to me at all. Having learnt to read and understand his native language (though not to speak it), in the earlier days of our intimate companionship, I now suggested to him that he should express himself in Italian, while I used English in putting any questions which might be necessary to my enlightenment. He accepted the proposal. In his own smooth-flowing language—spoken with a vehement agitation which betrayed itself in the perpetual working of his features, in the wildness and the suddenness of his foreign gesticulations, but never in the raising of his voice—I now heard the words which armed me to meet the last struggle that is left for this story to record.[1]

'You know nothing of my motive for leaving Italy,' he began, 'except that it was for political reasons. If I had been driven to this country by the persecution of my government, I should not have kept those reasons a secret from you or from any one. I have concealed them because no government authority has pronounced the sentence of my exile. You have heard, Walter, of the political Societies that are hidden in every great city on the continent of Europe? To one of those Societies I belonged in Italy—and belong still, in England. When I came to this country, I came by the direction of my Chief. I was over-zealous, in my younger time; I ran the risk of compromising myself and others. For those reasons, I was ordered to emigrate to England, and to wait. I emigrated—I have waited—I wait, still. To-morrow, I may be called away: ten years hence, I may be called away. It is all one to me—I am here, I support myself by teaching, and I wait. I violate no oath (you shall hear why presently) in making my confidence complete by telling you the name of the Society to which I belong. All I do is to put my life in your hands. If what I say to you now is ever known by others to have passed my lips, as certainly as we two sit here, I am a dead man.'

He whispered the next words in my ear. I keep the secret which he thus communicated. The Society to which he belonged will be sufficiently individualised for the purpose of these pages, if I call it 'The Brotherhood,'

[1] It is only right to mention, here, that I repeat Pesca's statement to me, with the careful suppressions and alterations which the serious nature of the subject and my own sense of duty to my friend demand. My first and last concealments from the reader are those which caution renders absolutely necessary in this portion of the narrative.

on the few occasions when any reference to the subject will be needed in this place.

'The object of the Brotherhood,' Pesca went on, 'is, briefly, the object of other political Societies of the same sort—the destruction of tyranny, and the assertion of the rights of the people. The principles of the Brotherhood are two. So long as a man's life is useful, or even harmless only, he has the right to enjoy it. But, if his life inflicts injury on the well-being of his fellow-men, from that moment he forfeits the right, and it is not only no crime but a positive merit to deprive him of it. It is not for me to say in what frightful circumstances of oppression and suffering this Society took its rise. It is not for you to say—you Englishmen, who have conquered your freedom so long ago, that you have conveniently forgotten what blood you shed, and what extremities you proceeded to in the conquering—it is not for *you* to say how far the worst of all exasperations may, or may not, carry the maddened men of an enslaved nation. The iron that has entered into our souls has gone too deep for *you* to find it. Leave the refugee alone! Laugh at him, distrust him, open your eyes in wonder at that secret self which smoulders in him, sometimes under the every-day respectability and tranquillity of a man like me; sometimes under the grinding poverty, the fierce squalor, of men less lucky, less pliable, less patient than I am—but judge us not! In the time of your first Charles you might have done us justice; the long luxury of your own freedom has made you incapable of doing us justice now.'

All the deepest feelings of his nature seemed to force themselves to the surface in those words; all his heart was poured out to me, for the first time in our lives—but still, his voice never rose; still his dread of the terrible revelation he was making to me, never left him.

'So far,' he resumed, 'you think the Society like other Societies. Its object (in your English opinion) is anarchy and revolution. It takes the life of a bad King or a bad Minister, as if the one and the other were dangerous wild beasts to be shot at the first opportunity. I grant you this. But the laws of the Brotherhood are the laws of no other political Society on the face of the earth. The members are not known to one another. There is a President in Italy; there are Presidents abroad. Each of these has his Secretary. The Presidents and the Secretaries know the members; but the members, among themselves, are all strangers, until their Chiefs see fit, in the political necessity of the time, or in the private necessity of the Society, to make them known to each other. With such a safeguard as this, there is no oath among us on admittance. We are identified with the Brotherhood by a secret mark, which we all bear, which lasts while our lives last. We are told to go about our ordinary business, and to report ourselves to the President, or the Secretary, four times a year, in the event of our services being required. We are warned, if we betray the Brotherhood, or if we injure it by serving other interests, that we die by the principles of the Brotherhood—die by the hand of a stranger who may be sent from the other end of the world to strike the blow—or by the hand of our own bosom-friend, who may have been a member unknown to us through all the years of our intimacy. Sometimes, the death is delayed; sometimes, it follows close on the treachery. It is our first business to know how to wait—our second business to know how to obey when the word is spoken. Some of us may wait our lives through, and may not be wanted. Some of us may be called to the work, or to the preparation for the work, the very day of our admission. I myself—the little, easy, cheerful man you know, who, of his own accord, would hardly lift up his handkerchief to strike down the fly that buzzes about his face—I, in my younger time, under provocation so dreadful that I will not tell you of it, entered the Brotherhood by an impulse, as I might have killed myself by an impulse. I must remain in it, now—it has got me, whatever I may think of it in my better circumstances and my cooler manhood, to my dying day. While I was still in Italy, I was chosen Secretary; and all the members of that time, who were brought face to face with my President, were brought face to face also with *me*.'

I began to understand him; I saw the end towards which his extraordinary disclosure was now tending. He waited a moment, watching me earnestly—watching, till he had evidently guessed what was passing in my mind, before he resumed.

'You have drawn your own conclusion already,' he said. 'I see it in your face. Tell me nothing; keep me out of the secret of your thoughts. Let me make my one last sacrifice of myself, for your sake—and then have done with this subject, never to return to it again.'

He signed to me not to answer him—rose—removed his coat—and rolled up the shirt-sleeve on his left arm.

'I promised you that this confidence should be complete,' he whispered, speaking close at my ear, with his eyes looking watchfully at the door. 'Whatever comes of it, you shall not reproach me with having hidden anything from you which it was necessary to your interests to know. I have said that the Brotherhood identifies its members by a mark that lasts for life. See the place, and the mark on it, for yourself.'

He raised his bare arm, and showed me, high on the upper part of it and on the inner side, a brand deeply burnt in the flesh and stained of a bright blood-red colour. I abstain from describing the device which the brand represented. It will be sufficient to say that it was circular in form, and so small that it would have been completely covered by a shilling coin.

'A man who has this mark, branded in this place,' he said, covering his arm again, 'is a member of the Brotherhood. A man who has been false to the Brotherhood is discovered, sooner or later, by the Chiefs who know him—Presidents or Secretaries, as the case may be. And a man discovered by the Chiefs is dead. *No human laws can protect him.* Remember what you have seen and heard; draw what conclusions you like; act as you please. But, in the name of God, whatever you discover, whatever you do, tell me nothing! Let me remain free from a responsibility which it horrifies me to think of—which I know, in my conscience, is not *my* responsibility, now. For the last time, I say it—on my honour as a gentleman, on my oath as a Christian, if the man you pointed out at the Opera knows *me*, he is so altered, or so disguised, that I do not know *him*. I am ignorant of his proceedings or his purposes in England—I never saw him, I never heard the name he goes by, to my knowledge, before to-night. I say no more. Leave me a little, Walter: I am overpowered by what has happened; I am shaken by what I have said. Let me try to be like myself again, when we meet next.'

He dropped into a chair; and, turning away from me, hid his face in his hands. I gently opened the door, so as not to disturb him—and spoke my few parting words in low tones, which he might hear or not, as he pleased.

'I will keep the memory of to-night in my heart of hearts,' I said. 'You shall never repent the trust you have reposed in me. May I come to you to-morrow? May I come as early as nine o'clock?'

'Yes, Walter,' he replied, looking up at me kindly, and speaking in English once more, as if his one anxiety, now, was to get back to our former relations towards each other. 'Come to my little bit of breakfast, before I go my ways among the pupils that I teach.'

'Good night, Pesca.'

'Good night, my friend.'

IV

MY first conviction, as soon as I found myself outside the house, was that no alternative was left me but to act at once on the information I had received—to make sure of the Count, that night, or to risk the loss, if I only delayed till the morning, of Laura's last chance. I looked at my watch: it was ten o'clock.

Not the shadow of a doubt crossed my mind of the purpose for which the Count had left the theatre. His escape from us, that evening, was, beyond all question, the preliminary only to his escape from London. The mark of the Brotherhood was on his arm—I felt as certain of it as if he had shown me the brand—and the betrayal of the Brotherhood was on his conscience—I had seen it in his recognition of Pesca.

It was easy to understand why that recognition had not been mutual. A man of the Count's character would never risk the terrible consequences of turning spy without looking to his personal security quite as carefully as he looked to his golden reward. The shaven face, which I had pointed out at the Opera, might have been covered by a beard in Pesca's time; his dark brown hair might be a wig; his name was evidently a false one. The accident of time might have helped him as well—his immense corpulence might have come with his later years. There was every reason why Pesca should not have known him again—every reason, also, why he should have known Pesca, whose singular personal appearance made a marked man of him, go where he might.

I have said that I felt certain of the purpose in the Count's mind when he escaped us at the theatre. How could I doubt it, when I saw, with my own eyes, that he believed himself, in spite of the change in his appearance, to have been recognised by Pesca, and to be therefore in danger of his life? If I could get speech of him that night, if I could show him that I, too, knew of the mortal peril in which he stood, what result would follow? Plainly this. One of us must be master of the situation—one of us must inevitably be at the mercy of the other.

I owed it to myself to consider the chances against me, before I confronted them. I owed it to my wife to do all that lay in my power to lessen the risk.

The chances against me wanted no reckoning up: they were all merged in one. If the Count discovered, by my own avowal, that the direct way to his safety lay through my life, he was probably the last man in existence who would shrink from throwing me off my guard and taking that way, when he had me alone within his reach. The only means of defence against him on which I could at all rely to lessen the risk, presented themselves, after a little careful thinking, clearly enough. Before I made any personal acknowledgment of my discovery in his presence, I must place the discovery itself where it would be ready for instant use against him, and safe from any attempt at suppression on his part. If I laid the mine under his feet before I approached him, and if I left instructions with a third person to fire it, on the expiration of a certain time, unless directions to the contrary were previously received under my own hand, or from my own lips—in that event, the Count's security was absolutely dependent upon mine, and I might hold the vantage ground over him securely, even in his own house.

This idea occurred to me when I was close to the new lodgings which we had taken on returning from the sea-side. I went in, without disturbing any one, by the help of my key. A light was in the hall; and I stole up with it to my workroom, to make my preparations, and absolutely to commit myself to an interview with the Count, before either Laura or Marian could have the slightest suspicion of what I intended to do.

A letter addressed to Pesca represented the surest measure of precaution which it was now possible for me to take. I wrote as follows:

'The man whom I pointed out to you at the Opera is a member of the Brotherhood, and has been false to his trust. Put both these assertions to the test, instantly. You know the name he goes by in England. His address is No. 5, Forest-road, St John's Wood. On the love you once bore me, use the power entrusted to you, without mercy and without delay, against that man. I have risked all and lost all—and the forfeit of my failure has been paid with my life.'

I signed and dated these lines, enclosed them in an envelope, and sealed it up. On the outside, I wrote this direction: 'Keep the enclosure unopened, until nine o'clock to-morrow morning. If you do not hear from me, or see me, before that time, break the seal when the clock strikes, and read the contents.' I added my initials; and protected the whole by enclosing it in a second sealed envelope, addressed to Pesca at his lodgings.

Nothing remained to be done after this, but to find the means of sending my letter to its destination immediately. I should then have accomplished all that lay in my power. If anything happened to me in the Count's house, I had now provided for his answering it with his life.

That the means of preventing his escape under any circumstances whatever, were at Pesca's disposal, if he chose to exert them, I did not for an instant doubt. The extraordinary anxiety which he had expressed to remain unenlightened as to the Count's identity—or, in other words, to be left uncertain enough about facts to justify him to his own conscience in remaining passive—betrayed plainly that the means of exercising the terrible justice of the Brotherhood were ready to his hand, although, as a naturally-humane man, he had shrunk from plainly saying as much in my presence. The deadly certainty with which the vengeance of foreign political Societies can hunt down a traitor to the cause, hide himself where he may, had been too often exemplified, even in my superficial experience, to allow of any doubt. Considering the subject only as a reader of newspapers, cases recurred to my memory, both in London and in Paris, of foreigners found stabbed in the streets, whose assassins could never be traced—of bodies and parts of bodies, thrown into the Thames and the Seine, by hands that could never be discovered—of deaths by secret violence which could only be accounted for in one way. I have disguised nothing relating to myself in these pages—and I do not disguise here—that I believed I had written Count Fosco's death-warrant, if the fatal emergency happened which authorised Pesca to open my enclosure.

I left my room to go down to the ground-floor of the house, and speak to the landlord about finding me a messenger. He happened to be ascending the stairs at the time, and we met on the landing. His son, a quick lad, was the messenger he proposed to me, on hearing what I wanted. We had the boy up-stairs; and I gave him his directions. He was to take the letter in a cab, to put it into Professor Pesca's own hands, and to bring me back a line of acknowledgement from that gentleman; returning in the cab, and keeping it at the door for my use. It was then nearly half-past ten. I calculated that the boy might be back in twenty minutes; and that I might drive to St John's Wood, on his return, in twenty minutes more.

When the lad had departed on his errand, I returned to my own room for a little while, to put certain papers in order, so that they might be easily found, in case of the worst. The key of the old-fashioned bureau in which the papers were kept, I sealed up, and left it on my table, with Marian's name written on the outside of the little packet. This done, I went down stairs to the sitting-room, in which I expected to find Laura and Marian awaiting my return from the Opera. I felt my hand trembling for the first time, when I laid it on the lock of the door.

No one was in the room but Marian. She was reading; and she looked at her watch, in surprise, when I came in.

'How early you are back!' she said. 'You must have come away before the opera was over.'

'Yes,' I replied; 'neither Pesca nor I waited for the end. Where is Laura?'

'She had one of her bad headaches this evening; and I advised her to go to bed, when we had done tea.'

I left the room again, on the pretext of wishing to see whether Laura was asleep. Marian's quick eyes were beginning to look inquiringly at my face; Marian's quick instinct was beginning to discover that I had something weighing on my mind.

When I entered the bed-chamber, and softly approached the bedside by the dim flicker of the night-lamp, my wife was asleep.

We had not been married quite a month yet. If my heart was heavy, if my resolution for a moment faltered again, when I looked at her face turned faithfully to *my* pillow in her sleep—when I saw her hand resting open on the coverlid, as if it was waiting unconsciously for mine—surely there was some excuse for me? I only allowed myself a few minutes to kneel down at the bedside, and to look close at her—so close that her breath, as it came and went, fluttered on my face. I only touched her hand and her cheek with my lips, at parting. She stirred in her sleep, and murmured my name—but without waking. I lingered for an instant at the door to look at her again. 'God bless and keep you, my darling!' I whispered—and left her.

Marian was at the stair-head waiting for me. She had a folded slip of paper in her hand.

'The landlord's son has brought this for you,' she said. 'He has got a cab at the door—he says you ordered him to keep it at your disposal.'

'Quite right, Marian. I want the cab; I am going out again.'

I descended the stairs as I spoke, and looked into the sitting-room to read the slip of paper by the light on the table. It contained these two sentences, in Pesca's handwriting:

'Your letter is received. If I don't see you before the time you mention, I will break the seal when the clock strikes.'

I placed the paper in my pocket-book and made for the door. Marian met me on the threshold, and pushed me back into the room where the candlelight fell full on my face. She held me by both hands, and her eyes fastened searchingly on mine.

'I see' she said, in a low eager whisper. 'You are trying the last chance to-night.'

'Yes—the last chance and the best,' I whispered back.

'Not alone! Oh, Walter, for God's sake, not alone! Let me go with you. Don't refuse me because I'm only a woman. I must go! I will go! I'll wait outside in the cab!'

It was my turn, now, to hold *her*. She tried to break away from me, and get down first to the door.

'If you want to help me,' I said, 'stop here, and sleep in my wife's room to-night. Only let me go away, with my mind easy about Laura, and I answer for everything else. Come, Marian, give me a kiss, and show that you have the courage to wait till I come back.'

I dared not allow her time to say a word more. She tried to hold me again. I unclasped her hands—and was out of the room in a moment. The boy below heard me on the stairs, and opened the hall-door. I jumped into the cab, before the driver could get off the box. 'Forest-road, St John's Wood,' I called to him through the front window. 'Double fare, if you get there in a quarter of an hour.' 'I'll do it, sir.' I looked at my watch. Eleven o'clock—not a minute to lose.

The rapid motion of the cab, the sense that every instant now was bringing me nearer to the Count, the conviction that I was embarked at last, without let or hindrance, on my hazardous enterprise, heated me into such a fever of excitement that I shouted to the man to go faster and faster. As we left the streets, and crossed St John's Wood-road, my impatience so completely overpowered me that I stood up in the cab and stretched my head out of the window, to see the end of the journey before we reached it. Just as a church clock in the distance struck the quarter past, we turned into the Forest-road. I stopped the driver a little away from the Count's house—paid, and dismissed him—and walked on to the door.

As I approached the garden gate, I saw another person advancing towards it also, from the direction opposite to mine. We met under the gas-lamp in the road, and looked at each other. I instantly recognised the light-haired foreigner, with the scar on his cheek; and I thought he recognised *me*. He said nothing; and, instead of stopping at the house, as I did, he slowly walked on. Was he in the Forest-road by accident? Or had he followed the Count home from the Opera?

I did not pursue those questions. After waiting a little, till the foreigner had slowly passed out of sight, I rang the gate bell. It was then twenty minutes past eleven—late enough to make it quite easy for the Count to get rid of me by the excuse that he was in bed.

The only way of providing against this contingency was to send in my name, without asking any preliminary questions, and to let him know, at the same time, that I had a serious motive for wishing to see him at that late hour. Accordingly, while I was waiting, I took out my card, and wrote under my name, 'On important business.' The maid-servant answered the door, while I was writing the last word in pencil; and asked me distrustfully what I 'pleased to want.'

'Be so good as to take that to your master,' I replied, giving her the card.

I saw, by the girl's hesitation of manner, that if I had asked for the Count in the first instance, she would only have followed her instructions by telling me he was not at home. She was staggered by the confidence with which I gave her the card. After staring at me in great perturbation, she went back into the house with my message, closing the door, and leaving me to wait in the garden.

In a minute or so, she reappeared. 'Her master's compliments, and would I be so obliging as to say what my business was?' 'Take my compliments back,' I replied; 'and say that the business cannot be mentioned to any one but your master.' She left me again—again returned—and, this time, asked me to walk in.

I followed her at once. In another moment, I was inside the Count's house.

There was no lamp in the hall; but by the dim light of the kitchen candle which the girl had brought up-stairs with her, I saw an elderly lady steal noiselessly out of a back room on the ground-floor. She cast one viperish look at me as I entered the hall, but said nothing, and went slowly up-stairs, without returning my bow. My familiarity with Marian's journal sufficiently assured me that the elderly lady was Madame Fosco.

The servant led me to the room which the Countess had just left. I entered it; and found myself face to face with the Count.

He was still in his evening dress, except his coat, which he had thrown across a chair. His shirt-sleeves were turned up at the wrists—but no higher. A carpet-bag was on one side of him, and a box on the other. Books, papers, and articles of wearing apparel were scattered about the room. On a table, at one side of the door, stood the cage, so well known to me by description, which contained his white mice. The canaries and the cockatoo were probably in some other room. He was seated before the box, packing it, when I went in, and rose with some papers in his hand to receive me. His face still betrayed plain traces of the shock that had overwhelmed him at the Opera. His fat cheeks hung loose; his cold grey eyes were furtively vigilant; his voice, look, and manner were all sharply suspicious alike, as he advanced a step to meet me, and requested, with distant civility, that I would take a chair.

'You come here on business, sir?' he said. 'I am at a loss to know what that business can possibly be.'

The unconcealed curiosity with which he looked hard in my face while he spoke, convinced me that I had passed unnoticed by him at the Opera. He had seen Pesca first; and from that moment, till he left the theatre, he had evidently seen nothing else. My name would necessarily suggest to him that I had not come into his house with other than a hostile purpose towards himself—but he appeared to be utterly ignorant, thus far, of the real nature of my errand.

'I am fortunate in finding you here to-night,' I said. 'You seem to be on the point of taking a journey?'

'Is your business connected with my journey?'

'In some degree.'

'In what degree? Do you know where I am going to?'

'No. I only know why you are leaving London.'

He slipped by me with the quickness of thought; locked the door of the room; and put the key in his pocket.

'You and I, Mr Hartright, are excellently well acquainted with one another by reputation,' he said. 'Did it, by any chance, occur to you when you came to this house that I was not the sort of man you could trifle with?'

'It did occur to me,' I replied. 'And I have not come to trifle with you. I am here on a matter of life and death—and if that door which you have locked was open at this moment, nothing you could say or do would induce me to pass through it.'

I walked farther into the room and stood opposite to him, on the rug before the fireplace. He drew a chair in front of the door, and sat down on it, with his left arm resting on the table. The cage with the white mice was close to him; and the little creatures scampered out of their sleeping-place, as his heavy arm shook the table, and peered at him through the gaps in the smartly-painted wires.

'On a matter of life and death?' he repeated to himself. 'Those words are more serious, perhaps, than you think. What do you mean?'

'What I say.'

The perspiration broke out thickly on his broad forehead. His left hand stole over the edge of the table. There was a drawer in it, with a lock, and the key was in the lock. His finger and thumb closed over the key, but did not turn it.

'So you know why I am leaving London?' he went on. 'Tell me the reason, if you please.' He turned the key, and unlocked the drawer as he spoke.

'I can do better than that,' I replied; 'I can *show* you the reason, if you like.'

'How can you show it?'

'You have got your coat off,' I said. 'Roll up the shirt-sleeve on your left arm—and you will see it there.'

The same livid, leaden change passed over his face, which I had seen pass over it at the theatre. The deadly glitter in his eyes shone steady and straight into mine. He said nothing. But his left hand slowly opened the table drawer, and softly slipped into it. The harsh grating noise of something heavy that he was moving, unseen to me, sounded for a moment—then ceased. The silence that followed was so intense, that the faint ticking nibble of the white mice at their wires was distinctly audible where I stood.

My life hung by a threat—and I knew it. At that final moment, I thought with *his* mind; I felt with *his* fingers—I was as certain, as if I had seen it, of what he kept hidden from me in the drawer.

'Wait a little,' I said. 'You have got the door locked—you see I don't move—you see my hands are empty. Wait a little. I have something more to say.'

'You have said enough,' he replied, with a sudden composure, so unnatural and so ghastly that it tried my nerves as no outbreak of violence could have tried them. 'I want one moment for my own thoughts, if you please. Do you guess what I am thinking about?'

'Perhaps I do.'

'I am thinking,' he remarked quietly, 'whether I shall add to the disorder in this room, by scattering your brains about the fireplace.'

If I had moved at that moment, I saw in his face that he would have done it.

'I advise you to read two lines of writing which I have about me,' I rejoined, 'before you finally decide that question.'

The proposal appeared to excite his curiosity. He nodded his head. I took Pesca's acknowledgment of the receipt of my letter out of my pocket-book; handed it to him at arm's length; and returned to my former position in front of the fireplace.

He read the lines aloud: ' "Your letter is received. If I don't hear from you before the time you mention, I will break the seal when the clock strikes." '

Another man, in his position, would have needed some explanation of those words—the Count felt no such necessity. One reading of the note showed him the precaution that I had taken, as plainly as if he had been present at the time when I adopted it. The expression of his face changed on the instant; and his hand came out of the drawer, empty.

'I don't lock up my drawer, Mr Hartright,' he said; 'and I don't say that I may not scatter your brains about the fireplace, yet. But I am a just man, even to my enemy—and I will acknowledge, beforehand, that they are cleverer brains than I thought them. Come to the point, sir! You want something of me?'

'I do—and I mean to have it.'

'On conditions?'

'On no conditions.'

His hand dropped into the drawer again.

'Bah! we are travelling in a circle,' he said; 'and those clever brains of yours are in danger again. Your tone is deplorably imprudent, sir—moderate it on the spot! The risk of shooting you on the place where you stand, is less to *me*, than the risk of letting you out of this house, except on conditions that I dictate and approve. You have not got my lamented friend to deal with, now—you are face to face with FOSCO! If the lives of twenty Mr Hartrights were the stepping-stones to my safety, over all those stones I would go, sustained by my sublime indifference, self-balanced by my impenetrable calm. Respect me, if you love your own life! I summon you to answer three questions, before you open your lips again. Hear them—they are necessary to this interview. Answer them—they are necessary to ME.' He held up one finger of his right hand. 'First question!' he said. 'You come here possessed of information, which may be true, or may be false—where did you get it?'

'I decline to tell you.'

'No matter: I shall find out. If that information is true—mind I say, with the whole force of my resolution, *if*—you are making your market of it here, by treachery of your own, or by treachery of some other man. I note that circumstance, for future use, in my memory which forgets nothing, and proceed.' He held up another finger. 'Second question! Those lines you invited me to read, are without signature. Who wrote them?'

'A man whom *I* have every reason to depend on; and whom *you* have every reason to fear.'

My answer reached him to some purpose. His left hand trembled audibly in the drawer.

'How long do you give me,' he asked, putting his third question in a quieter tone, 'before the clock strikes and the seal is broken?'

'Time enough for you to come to my terms,' I replied.

'Give me a plainer answer, Mr Hartright. What hour is the clock to strike?'

'Nine, to-morrow morning.'

'Nine, to-morrow morning? Yes, yes—your trap is laid for me, before I can get my passport regulated, and leave London. It is not earlier, I suppose? We will see about that, presently—I can keep you hostage here, and bargain with you to send for your letter before I let you go. In the mean time, be so good, next, as to mention your terms.'

'You shall hear them. They are simple, and soon stated. You know whose interests I represent in coming here?'

He smiled with the most supreme composure; and carelessly waved his right hand.

'I consent to hazard a guess,' he said, jeeringly. 'A lady's interests, of course!'

'My Wife's interests.'

He looked at me with the first honest expression that had crossed his face in my presence—an expression of blank amazement. I could see that I sank in his estimation, as a dangerous man, from that moment. He shut up the drawer at once, folded his arms over his breast, and listened to me with a smile of satirical attention.

'You are well enough aware,' I went on, 'of the course which my inquiries have taken for many months past, to know that any attempted denial of plain facts will be quite useless in my presence. You are guilty of an infamous conspiracy. And the gain of a fortune of ten thousand pounds was your motive for it.'

He said nothing. But his face became overclouded suddenly by a lowering anxiety.

'Keep your gain,' I said. (His face lightened again immediately, and his eyes opened on me in wider and wider astonishment.) 'I am not here to disgrace myself by bargaining for money which has passed through your hands, and which has been the price of a vile crime——'

'Gently, Mr Hartright. Your moral clap-traps have an excellent effect in England—keep them for yourself and your own countrymen, if you please. The ten thousand pounds was a legacy left to my excellent wife by the late Mr Fairlie. Place the affair on those grounds; and I will discuss it, if you like. To a man of my sentiments, however, the subject is deplorably sordid. I prefer to pass it over. I invite you to resume the discussion of your terms. What do you demand?'

'In the first place, I demand a full confession of the conspiracy, written and signed in my presence, by yourself.'

He raised his finger again. 'One!' he said, checking me off with the steady attention of a practical man.

'In the second place, I demand a plain proof, which does not depend on your personal asseveration, of the date at which my wife left Blackwater Park, and travelled to London.'

'So! so! you can lay your finger, I see, on the weak place,' he remarked, composedly. 'Any more?'

'At present, no more.'

'Good! You have mentioned your terms; now listen to mine. The responsibility to myself of admitting, what you are pleased to call the "conspiracy," is less, perhaps, upon the whole, than the responsibility of laying you dead on that hearth-rug. Let us say that I meet your proposal—on my own conditions. The statement you demand of me shall be written; and the plain proof shall be produced. You call a letter from my late lamented friend, informing me of the day and hour of his wife's arrival in London, written, signed, and dated by himself, a proof, I suppose? I can give you this. I can also send you to the man of whom I hired the carriage to fetch my visitor from the railway, on the day when she arrived—his order-book may help you to your date, even if his coachman who drove me proves to be of no use. These things I can do, and will do, on conditions. I recite them. First condition! Madame Fosco and I leave this house, when and how we please, without interference of any kind, on your part. Second condition! You wait here, in company with me, to see my agent, who is coming at seven o'clock in the morning to regulate my affairs. You give my agent a written order to the man who has got your sealed letter to resign his possession of it. You wait here till my agent places that letter unopened in my hands; and you then allow me one clear half-hour to leave the house—after which you resume your own freedom of action, and go where you please. Third condition! You give me the satisfaction of a gentleman, for your intrusion into my private affairs, and for the language you have allowed yourself to use to me, at this conference. The time and place, abroad, to be fixed in a letter from my hand when I am safe on the Continent; and that letter to contain a strip of paper measuring accurately the length of my sword. Those are *my* terms. Inform me if you accept them—Yes, or No.'

The extraordinary mixture of prompt decision, far-sighted cunning, and mountebank bravado in this speech, staggered me for a moment—and only for a moment. The one question to consider was whether I was justified, or not, in possessing myself of the means of establishing Laura's identity, at the cost of allowing the scoundrel who had robbed her of it to escape me with impunity. I knew that the motive of securing the just recognition of my wife in the birthplace from which she had been driven out as an impostor, and of publicly erasing the lie that still profaned her mother's tombstone, was far purer, in its freedom from all taint of evil passion, than the vindictive motive which had mingled itself with my purpose from the first. And yet I cannot honestly say that my own moral convictions were strong enough to decide the struggle in me, by themselves. They were helped by my remembrance of Sir Percival's death. How awfully, at the last moment, had the working of the retribution, *there*, been snatched from my feeble hands! What right had I to decide, in my poor mortal ignorance of the future, that this man, too, must escape with impunity, because he escaped *me*? I thought of these things—perhaps, with the superstition inherent in my nature; perhaps, with a sense worthier of me than superstition. It was hard, when I had fastened my hold on him, at last, to loosen it again of my own accord—but I forced myself to make the sacrifice. In plainer words, I determined to be guided by the one higher motive of which I was certain, the motive of serving the cause of Laura and the cause of Truth.

'I accept your conditions,' I said. 'With one reservation, on my part.'

'What reservation may that be?' he asked.

'It refers to the sealed letter,' I answered. 'I require you to destroy it, unopened, in my presence, as soon as it is placed in your hands.'

My object in making this stipulation was simply to prevent him from carrying away written evidence of the nature of my communication with Pesca. The *fact* of my communication he would necessarily discover, when I gave the address to his agent, in the morning. But he could make no use of it, on his own unsupported testimony—even if he really ventured to try the experiment—which need excite in me the slightest apprehension on Pesca's account.

'I grant your reservation,' he replied, after considering the question gravely for a minute or two. 'It is not worth dispute—the letter shall be destroyed when it comes into my hands.'

He rose, as he spoke, from the chair in which he had been sitting opposite to me, up to this time. With one effort, he appeared to free his mind from the whole pressure on it of the interview between us, thus far. 'Ouf!' he cried, stretching his arms luxuriously; 'the skirmish was hot while it lasted. Take a seat, Mr Hartright. We meet as mortal enemies hereafter—let us, like gallant gentlemen, exchange polite attentions in the mean time. Permit me to take the liberty of calling for my wife.'

He unlocked and opened the door. 'Eleanor!' he called out, in his deep voice. The lady of the viperish face came in. 'Madame Fosco—Mr Hartright,' said the Count, introducing us with easy dignity. 'My angel,' he went on, addressing his wife; 'will your labours of packing-up allow you time to make me some nice strong coffee? I have writing-business to transact with Mr Hartright—and I require the full possession of my intelligence to do justice to myself.'

Madame Fosco bowed her head twice—once sternly to me; once submissively to her husband—and glided out of the room.

The Count walked to a writing-table near the window; opened his desk, and took from it several quires of paper and a bundle of quill pens. He scattered the pens about the table, so that they might lie ready in all directions to be taken up when wanted, and then cut the paper into a heap of narrow slips, of the form used by professional writers for the press. 'I shall make this a remarkable document,' he said, looking at me over his shoulder. 'Habits of literary composition are perfectly familiar to me. One of the rarest of all the intellectual accomplishments that a man can possess is the grand faculty of arranging his ideas. Immense privilege! I possess it. Do you?'

He marched backwards and forwards in the room, until the coffee appeared, humming to himself, and marking the places at which obstacles occurred in the arrangement of his ideas, by striking his forehead, from time to time, with the palm of his hand. The enormous audacity with which he seized on the situation in which I had placed him, and made it the pedestal on which his vanity mounted for the one cherished purpose of self-display, mastered my astonishment by main force. Sincerely as I loathed the man, the prodigious strength of his character, even in its most trivial aspects, impressed me in spite of myself.

The coffee was brought in by Madame Fosco. He kissed her hand, in grateful acknowledgment, and escorted her to the door; returned, poured out a cup of coffee for himself, and took it to the writing-table.

'May I offer you some coffee, Mr Hartright?' he said, before he sat down. I declined.

'What! you think I shall poison you?' he said, gaily. 'The English intellect is sound, so far as it goes,' he continued, seating himself at the table; 'but it has one grave defect—it is always cautious in the wrong place.'

He dipped his pen in the ink; placed the first slip of paper before him, with a thump of his hand on the desk; cleared his throat; and began. He wrote with great noise and rapidity, in so large and bold a hand, and with such wide spaces between the lines, that he reached the bottom of the slip in not more than two minutes certainly from the time when he started at the top. Each slip as he finished it was paged, and tossed over his shoulder, out of his way, on the floor. When his first pen was worn out, *that* went over his shoulder too; and he pounced on a second from the supply scattered about the table. Slip after slip, by dozens, by fifties, by hundreds, flew over his shoulders on either side of him, till he had snowed himself up in paper all round his chair. Hour after hour passed—and there I sat, watching; there he sat, writing. He never stopped, except to sip his coffee; and when that was exhausted, to smack his forehead, from time to time. One o'clock struck, two, three, four—and still the slips flew about all round him; still the untiring pen scraped its way ceaselessly from top to bottom of the page; still the white chaos of paper rose higher and higher all round his chair. At four o'clock, I heard a sudden splutter of the pen, indicative of the flourish with which he signed his name. 'Bravo!' he cried—springing to his feet with the activity of a young man, and looking me straight in the face with a smile of superb triumph.

'Done, Mr Hartright!' he announced, with a self-renovating thump of his fist on his broad breast. 'Done, to my own profound satisfaction—to *your* profound astonishment, when you read what I have written. The subject is exhausted: the Man—Fosco—is not. I proceed to the arrangement of my slips, to the revision of my slips, to the reading of my slips—addressed, emphatically, to your private ear. Four o'clock has just struck. Good! Arrangement, revision, reading, from four to five. Short snooze of restoration for myself, from five to six. Final preparations, from six to seven. Affair of agent and sealed letter from seven to eight. At eight, *en route*. Behold the programme!'

He sat down cross-legged on the floor, among his papers; strung them together with a bodkin and a piece of string; revised them; wrote all the titles and honours by which he was personally distinguished, at the head of the first page; and then read the manuscript to me, with loud theatrical emphasis and profuse theatrical gesticulation. The reader will have an opportunity, ere long, of forming his own opinion of the document. It will be sufficient to mention here that it answered my purpose.

He next wrote me the address of the person from whom he had hired the fly, and handed me Sir Percival's letter. It was dated from Hampshire, on the 25th of July; and it announced the journey of 'Lady Glyde' to London, on the 26th. Thus, on the very day (the 25th), when the doctor's certificate declared that she had died in St John's Wood, she was alive, by Sir Percival's own showing, at Blackwater—and, on the day after, she was to take a journey! When the proof of that journey was obtained from the flyman, the evidence would be complete.

'A quarter past five,' said the Count, looking at his watch. 'Time for my restorative snooze. I personally resemble Napoleon the Great, as you may have remarked, Mr Hartright—I also resemble that immortal man in my power of commanding sleep at will. Excuse me, one moment. I will summon Madame Fosco, to keep you from feeling dull.'

Knowing as well as he did, that he was summoning Madame Fosco, to ensure my not leaving the house while he was asleep, I made no reply, and occupied myself in tying up the papers which he had placed in my possession.

The lady came in, cool, pale, and venomous as ever. 'Amuse Mr Hartright, my angel,' said the Count. He placed a chair for her, kissed her hand for the second time, withdrew to a sofa, and, in three minutes, was as peacefully and happily asleep as the most virtuous man in existence.

Madame Fosco took a book from the table—sat down—and looked at me, with the steady, vindictive malice of a woman who never forgot and never forgave.

'I have been listening to your conversation with my husband,' she said. 'If I had been in *his* place—*I* would have laid you dead on the hearth-rug.'

With those words, she opened her book; and never looked at me, or spoke to me, from that time till the time when her husband woke.

He opened his eyes and rose from the sofa, accurately to an hour from the time when he had gone to sleep.

'I feel infinitely refreshed,' he remarked. 'Eleanor, my good wife, are you all ready, up-stairs? That is well. My little packing here can be completed in ten minutes—my travelling-dress assumed in ten minutes more. What remains, before the agent comes?' He looked about the room, and noticed the cage with his white mice in it. 'Ah!' he cried, piteously; 'a last laceration of my sympathies still remains. My innocent pets! my little cherished children! what am I to do with them? For the present, we are settled nowhere; for the present, we travel incessantly—the less baggage we carry, the better for ourselves. My cockatoo, my canaries, and my little mice—who will cherish them, when their good Papa is gone?'

He walked about the room, deep in thought. He had not been at all troubled about writing his confession, but he was visibly perplexed and distressed about the far more important question of the disposal of his pets. After long consideration, he suddenly sat down again at the writing-table.

'An idea!' he exclaimed. 'I will offer my canaries and my cockatoo to this vast Metropolis—my agent shall present them, in my name, to the Zoological Gardens of London. The Document that describes them shall be drawn out on the spot.'

He began to write, repeating the words as they flowed from his pen.

'Number One. Cockatoo of transcendent plumage: attraction, of himself, to all visitors of taste. Number Two. Canaries of unrivalled vivacity and intelligence: worthy of the garden of Eden, worthy also of the garden in the Regent's Park. Homage to British Zoology. Offered by FOSCO.'

The pen spluttered again; and the flourish was attached to his signature.

'Count! you have not included the mice,' said Madame Fosco.

He left the table, took her hand, and placed it on his heart.

'All human resolution, Eleanor,' he said, solemnly, 'has its limits. My limits are inscribed on that Document. I cannot part with my white mice. Bear with me, my angel, and remove them to their travelling-cage, up-stairs.'

'Admirable tenderness!' said Madame Fosco, admiring her husband, with a last viperish look in my direction. She took up the cage carefully, and left the room.

The Count looked at his watch. In spite of his resolute assumption of composure, he was getting anxious for the agent's arrival. The candles had long since been extinguished; and the sunlight of the new morning poured into the room. It was not till five minutes past seven that the gate bell rang, and the agent made his appearance. He was a foreigner, with a dark beard.

'Mr Hartright—Monsieur Rubelle,' said the Count, introducing us. He took the agent (a foreign spy, in every line of his face, if ever there was one yet) into a corner of the room; whispered some directions to him; and then left us together. 'Monsieur Rubelle,' as soon as we were alone, suggested, with great politeness, that I should favour him with his instructions. I wrote two lines to Pesca, authorising him to deliver my sealed letter 'to the Bearer;' directed the note; and handed it to Monsieur Rubelle.

The agent waited with me till his employer returned, equipped in travelling costume. The Count examined the address of my letter before he dismissed the agent. 'I thought so!' he said, turning on me, with a dark look, and altering again in his manner from that moment.

He completed his packing; and then sat consulting a travelling map, making entries in his pocket-book, and looking, every now and then, impatiently at his watch. Not another word, addressed to myself, passed his lips. The near approach of the hour for his departure, and the proof he had seen of the communication established between Pesca and myself, had plainly recalled his whole attention to the measures that were necessary for securing his escape.

A little before eight o'clock, Monsieur Rubelle came back with my unopened letter in his hand. The Count looked carefully at the superscription and the seal—lit a candle—and burnt the letter. 'I perform my promise,' he said; 'but this matter, Mr Hartright, shall not end here.'

The agent had kept at the door the cab in which he had returned. He and the maid-servant now busied themselves in removing the luggage. Madame Fosco came down stairs, thickly veiled, with the travelling-cage of the white mice in her hand. She neither spoke to me, nor looked towards me. Her husband escorted her to the cab. 'Follow me, as far as the passage,' he whispered in my ear; 'I may want to speak to you at the last moment.'

I went out to the door; the agent standing below me in the front garden. The Count came back alone, and drew me a few steps inside the passage.

'Remember the Third condition!' he whispered. 'You shall hear from me, Mr Hartright—I may claim from you the satisfaction of a gentleman sooner than you think for.' He caught my hand, before I was aware of him, and wrung it hard—then turned to the door, stopped, and came back to me again.

'One word more,' he said, confidentially. 'When I last saw Miss Halcombe, she looked thin and ill. I am anxious about that admirable woman. Take care of her, sir! With my hand on my heart, I solemnly implore you—take care of Miss Halcombe!'

Those were the last words he said to me, before he squeezed his huge body into the cab, and drove off.

The agent and I waited at the door a few moments, looking after him. While we were standing together, a second cab appeared from a turning a little way down the road. It followed the direction previously taken by the Count's cab; and, as it passed the house and the open garden gate, a person inside looked at us out of the window. The stranger at the Opera again!— the foreigner with the scar on his left cheek!

'You wait here with me, sir, for half an hour more?' said Monsieur Rubelle.

'I do.'

We returned to the sitting-room. I was in no humour to speak to the agent, or to allow him to speak to me. I took out the papers which the Count had placed in my hands; and read the terrible story of the conspiracy told by the man who had planned and perpetrated it.

THE NARRATIVE OF ISIDOR OTTAVIO BALDASSARE
FOSCO. COUNT OF THE HOLY ROMAN EMPIRE.
KNIGHT GRAND CROSS OF THE ORDER OF THE
BRAZEN CROWN. PERPETUAL ARCH-MASTER OF THE
ROSICRUCIAN MASONS OF MESOPOTAMIA. ATTACHED,

IN HONORARY CAPACITIES, TO SOCIETIES MUSICAL,
SOCIETIES MEDICAL, SOCIETIES PHILOSOPHICAL, AND
SOCIETIES GENERAL BENEVOLENT, THROUGHOUT
EUROPE, &c. &c. &c.

IN the summer of eighteen hundred and fifty, I arrived in England, charged with a delicate political mission from abroad. Confidential persons were semi-officially connected with me, whose exertions I was authorised to direct— Monsieur and Madame Rubelle being among the number. Some weeks of spare time were at my disposal, before I entered on my functions by establishing myself in the suburbs of London. Curiosity may stop here, to ask for some explanation of those functions on my part. I entirely sympathise with the request. I also regret that diplomatic reserve forbids me to comply with it.

I arranged to pass the preliminary period of repose, to which I have just referred, in the superb mansion of my late lamented friend, Sir Percival Glyde. *He* arrived from the Continent with *his* wife. *I* arrived from the Continent with *mine*. England is the land of domestic happiness—how appropriately we entered it under these domestic circumstances!

The bond of friendship which united Percival and myself, was strengthened, on this occasion, by a touching similarity in the pecuniary position, on his side and on mine. We both wanted money. Immense necessity! Universal want! Is there a civilised human being who does not feel for us? How insensible must that man be! Or how rich!

I enter into no sordid particulars, in discussing this part of the subject. My mind recoils from them. With a Roman austerity, I show my empty purse and Percival's to the shrinking public gaze. Let us allow the deplorable fact to assert itself, once for all, in that manner—and pass on.

We were received at the mansion by the magnificent creature who is inscribed on my heart as 'Marian'—who is known in the colder atmosphere of Society, as 'Miss Halcombe.'

Just Heaven! with what inconceivable rapidity I learnt to adore that woman. At sixty, I worshipped her with the volcanic ardour of eighteen. All the gold of my rich nature was poured hopelessly at her feet. My wife—poor angel!—my wife, who adores me, got nothing but the shillings and the pennies. Such is the World; such Man; such Love. What are we (I ask) but puppets in a show-box? Oh, omnipotent Destiny, pull our strings gently! Dance us mercifully off our miserable little stage!

The preceding lines, rightly understood, express an entire system of philosophy. It is Mine.

I resume.

The domestic position at the commencement of our residence at Black-water Park has been drawn with amazing accuracy, with profound mental insight, by the hand of Marian herself. (Pass me the intoxicating familiarity of mentioning this sublime creature by her Christian name.) Accurate knowledge of the contents of her journal—to which I obtained access by clandestine means, unspeakably precious to me in the remembrance—warns my eager pen from topics which this essentially-exhaustive woman has already made her own.

The interests—interests, breathless and immense!—with which I am here concerned begin with the deplorable calamity of Marian's illness.

The situation, at this period, was emphatically a serious one. Large sums of money, due at a certain time, were wanted by Percival (I say nothing of the modicum equally necessary to myself); and the one source to look to for supplying them was the fortune of his wife, of which not one farthing was at his disposal until her death. Bad, so far; and worse still farther on. My lamented friend had private troubles of his own, into which the delicacy of my disinterested attachment to him forbade me from inquiring too curiously. I knew nothing but that a woman, named Anne Catherick, was hidden in the neighbourhood; that she was in communication with Lady Glyde; and that the disclosure of a secret, which would be the certain ruin of Percival, might be the result. He had told me himself that he was a lost man, unless his wife was silenced, and unless Anne Catherick was found. If he was a lost man, what would become of our pecuniary interests? Courageous as I am by nature, I absolutely trembled at the idea!

The whole force of my intelligence was now directed to the finding of Anne Catherick. Our money affairs, important as they were, admitted of delay—but the necessity of discovering the woman admitted of none. I only knew her, by description, as presenting an extraordinary personal resemblance to Lady Glyde. The statement of this curious fact—intended merely to assist me in identifying the person of whom we were in search—when coupled with the additional information that Anne Catherick had escaped from a madhouse, started the first immense conception in my mind, which subsequently led to such amazing results. That conception involved nothing less than the complete transformation of two separate identities. Lady Glyde and Anne Catherick were to change names, places, and destinies, the one with the other—the prodigious consequences contemplated by the change, being the gain of thirty thousand pounds, and the eternal preservation of Sir Percival's secret.

My instincts (which seldom err) suggested to me, on reviewing the circumstances, that our invisible Anne would, sooner or later, return to the boat-house at the Blackwater lake. There I posted myself; previously mentioning to Mrs Michelson, the housekeeper, that I might be found when wanted, immersed in study, in that solitary place. It is my rule never to make unnecessary mysteries, and never to set people suspecting me for want of a little seasonable candour, on my part. Mrs Michelson believed in me from first to last. This ladylike person (widow of a Protestant Priest) overflowed with faith. Touched by such superfluity of simple confidence, in a woman of her mature years, I opened the ample reservoirs of my nature, and absorbed it all.

I was rewarded for posting myself sentinel at the lake, by the appearance—not of Anne Catherick herself, but of the person in charge of her. This individual also overflowed with simple faith, which I absorbed in myself, as in the case already mentioned. I leave her to describe the circumstances (if she has not done so already) under which she introduced me to the object of her maternal care. When I first saw Anne Catherick, she was asleep. I was electrified by the likeness between this unhappy woman and Lady Glyde. The details of the grand scheme, which had suggested themselves in outline only, up to that period, occurred to me, in all their masterly combination, at the sight of the sleeping face. At the same time, my heart, always accessible to tender influences, dissolved in tears at the spectacle of suffering before me. I instantly set myself to impart relief. In other words, I provided the necessary stimulant for strengthening Anne Catherick to perform the journey to London.

At this point, I enter a necessary protest, and correct a lamentable error.

The best years of my life have been passed in the ardent study of medical and chemical science. Chemistry, especially, has always had irresistible attractions for me, from the enormous, the illimitable power which the knowledge of it confers. Chemists, I assert it emphatically, might sway, if they pleased, the destinies of humanity. Let me explain this before I go further.

Mind, they say, rules the world. But what rules the mind? The body. The body (follow me closely here) lies at the mercy of the most omnipotent of all potentates—the Chemist. Give me—Fosco—chemistry; and when Shakespeare has conceived Hamlet, and sits down to execute the conception—with a few grains of powder dropped into his daily food, I will reduce his mind, by the action of his body, till his pen pours out the most abject drivel that has ever degraded paper. Under similar circumstances, revive me the illustrious Newton. I guarantee that, when he sees the apple fall, he shall *eat it*, instead of discovering the principle of gravitation. Nero's dinner shall transform Nero into the mildest of men, before he has done digesting it; and the morning draught of Alexander the Great shall make Alexander run for his life, at the first sight of the enemy, the same afternoon. On my sacred word of honour, it is lucky for society that modern chemists are, by incomprehensible good fortune, the most harmless of mankind. The mass are worthy fathers of families, who keep shops. The few are philosophers besotted with admiration for the sound of their own lecturing voices; visionaries who waste their lives on fantastic impossibilities; or quacks whose ambition soars no higher than our corns. Thus Society escapes; and the illimitable power of Chemistry remains the slave of the most superficial and the most insignificant ends.

Why this outburst? Why this withering eloquence?

Because my conduct has been misrepresented; because my motives have been misunderstood. It has been assumed that I used my vast chemical resources against Anne Catherick; and that I would have used them, if I could, against the magnificent Marian herself. Odious insinuations both! All my interests were concerned (as will be seen presently) in the preservation of Anne Catherick's life. All my anxieties were concentrated on Marian's rescue from the hands of the licensed Imbecile who attended her; and who found my advice confirmed, from first to last, by the physician from London. On two occasions only—both equally harmless to the individual on whom I practised—did I summon to myself the assistance of chemical knowledge. On the first of the two, after following Marian to the Inn at Blackwater (studying, behind a convenient waggon which hid me from her, the poetry of motion, as embodied in her walk), I availed myself of the services of my invaluable wife, to copy one and to intercept the other of two letters which my adored enemy had entrusted to a discarded maid. In this case, the letters being in the bosom of the girl's dress, Madame Fosco could only open them, read them, perform her instructions, seal them, and put them back again, by scientific assistance—which assistance I rendered in a half-ounce bottle. The second occasion when the same means were employed was the occasion (to which I shall soon refer) of Lady Glyde's arrival in London. Never, at any other time, was I indebted to my Art, as distinguished from myself. To all other emergencies and complications my natural capacity for grappling, single-handed, with circumstances, was invariably equal. I affirm the all-pervading intelligence of that capacity. At the expense of the Chemist, I vindicate the Man.

Respect this outburst of generous indignation. It has inexpressibly relieved me. *En route!* Let us proceed.

Having suggested to Mrs Clement (or Clements, I am not sure which) that the best method of keeping Anne out of Percival's reach was to remove her to London; having found that my proposal was eagerly received; and having appointed a day to meet the travellers at the station, and to see them leave it—I was at liberty to return to the house, and to confront the difficulties which still remained to be met.

My first proceeding was to avail myself of the sublime devotion of my wife. I had arranged with Mrs Clements that she should communicate her London address, in Anne's interests, to Lady Glyde. But this was not enough. Designing persons, in my absence, might shake the simple confidence of Mrs Clements, and she might not write, after all. Who could I find capable of travelling to London by the train she travelled by, and of privately seeing her home? I asked myself this question. The conjugal part of me immediately answered—Madame Fosco.

After deciding on my wife's mission to London, I arranged that the journey should serve a double purpose. A nurse for the suffering Marian, equally devoted to the patient and to myself, was a necessity of my position. One of the most eminently confidential and capable women in existence was by good fortune at my disposal. I refer to that respectable matron, Madame Rubelle—to whom I addressed a letter, at her residence in London, by the hands of my wife.

On the appointed day, Mrs Clements and Anne Catherick met me at the station. I politely saw them off. I politely saw Madame Fosco off by the same train. The last thing at night, my wife returned to Blackwater, having followed her instructions with the most unimpeachable accuracy. She was accompanied by Madame Rubelle; and she brought me the London address of Mrs Clements. After-events proved this last precaution to have been unnecessary. Mrs Clements punctually informed Lady Glyde of her place of abode. With a wary eye on future emergencies, I kept the letter.

The same day, I had a brief interview with the doctor, at which I protested, in the sacred interests of humanity, against his treatment of Marian's case. He was insolent, as all ignorant people are. I showed no resentment; I deferred quarrelling with him till it was necessary to quarrel to some purpose.

My next proceeding was to leave Blackwater myself. I had my London residence to take, in anticipation of coming events. I had also a little business, of the domestic sort, to transact with Mr Frederick Fairlie. I found the house I wanted, in St John's Wood. I found Mr Fairlie at Limmeridge, Cumberland.

My own private familiarity with the nature of Marian's correspondence had previously informed me that she had written to Mr Fairlie, proposing, as a relief to Lady Glyde's matrimonial embarrassments, to take her on a visit to her uncle in Cumberland. This letter I had wisely allowed to reach its destination; feeling, at the time, that it could do no harm, and might do good. I now presented myself before Mr Fairlie, to support Marian's own proposal—with certain modifications which, happily for the success of my plans, were rendered really inevitable by her illness. It was necessary that Lady Glyde should leave Blackwater alone, by her uncle's invitation, and that she should rest a night on the journey, at her aunt's house (the house I had in St John's Wood), by her uncle's express advice. To achieve these results, and to secure a note of invitation which could be shown to Lady Glyde, were the objects of my visit to Mr Fairlie. When I have mentioned that this gentleman was equally feeble in mind and body, and that I let loose the whole force of my character on him, I have said enough. I came, saw, and conquered Fairlie.

On my return to Blackwater Park (with the letter of invitation) I found that the doctor's imbecile treatment of Marian's case had led to the most alarming results. The fever had turned to Typhus. Lady Glyde, on the day of my return, tried to force herself into the room to nurse her sister. She and I had no affinities of sympathy; she had committed the unpardonable outrage on my sensibilities of calling me a Spy; she was a stumbling-block in my way and in Percival's—but, for all that, my magnanimity forbade me to put her in danger of infection with my own hand. At the same time, I offered no hindrance to her putting herself in danger. If she had succeeded in doing so, the intricate knot which I was slowly and patiently operating on, might perhaps have been cut, by circumstances. As it was, the doctor interfered, and she was kept out of the room.

I had myself previously recommended sending for advice to London. This course had been now taken. The physician, on his arrival, confirmed my view of the case. The crisis was serious. But we had hope of our charming patient on the fifth day from the appearance of the Typhus. I was only once absent from Blackwater at this time—when I went to London by the morning train, to make the final arrangements at my house in St John's Wood; to assure myself, by private inquiry, that Mrs Clements had not moved; and to settle one or two little preliminary matters with the husband of Madame Rubelle. I returned at night. Five days afterwards, the physician pronounced our interesting Marian to be out of all danger, and to be in need of nothing but careful nursing. This was the time I had waited for. Now that medical attendance was no longer indispensable, I played the first move in the game by asserting myself against the doctor. He was one among many witnesses in my way, whom it was necessary to remove. A lively altercation between us (in which Percival, previously instructed by me, refused to interfere) served the purpose in view. I descended on the miserable man in an irresistible avalanche of indignation—and swept him from the house.

The servants were the next encumbrances to get rid of. Again I instructed Percival (whose moral courage required perpetual stimulants), and Mrs Michelson was amazed, one day, by hearing from her master that the establishment was to be broken up. We cleared the house of all the servants but one, who was kept for domestic purposes, and whose lumpish stupidity we could trust to make no embarrassing discoveries. When they were gone, nothing remained but to relieve ourselves of Mrs Michelson—a result which was easily achieved by sending this amiable lady to find lodgings for her mistress at the sea-side.

The circumstances were now—exactly what they were required to be. Lady Glyde was confined to her room by nervous illness; and the lumpish housemaid (I forget her name) was shut up there, at night, in attendance on her mistress. Marian, though fast recovering, still kept her bed, with

Mrs Rubelle for nurse. No other living creatures but my wife, myself, and Percival, were in the house. With all the chances thus in our favour, I confronted the next emergency, and played the second move in the game.

The object of the second move was to induce Lady Glyde to leave Blackwater, unaccompanied by her sister. Unless we could persuade her that Marian had gone on to Cumberland first, there was no chance of removing her, of her own free will, from the house. To produce this necessary operation in her mind, we concealed our interesting invalid in one of the uninhabited bedrooms at Blackwater. At the dead of night, Madame Fosco, Madame Rubelle, and myself (Percival not being cool enough to be trusted), accomplished the concealment. The scene was picturesque, mysterious, dramatic, in the highest degree. By my directions, the bed had been made, in the morning, on a strong movable framework of wood. We had only to lift the framework gently at the head and foot, and to transport our patient where we pleased, without disturbing herself or her bed. No chemical assistance was needed, or used, in this case. Our interesting Marian lay in the deep repose of convalescence. We placed the candles and opened the doors, beforehand. I, in right of my great personal strength, took the head of the framework—my wife and Madame Rubelle took the foot. I bore my share of that inestimably-precious burden with a manly tenderness, with a fatherly care. Where is the modern Rembrandt who could depict our midnight procession? Alas for the Arts! alas for this most pictorial of subjects! the modern Rembrandt is nowhere to be found.

The next morning, my wife and I started for London—leaving Marian secluded, in the uninhabited middle of the house, under care of Madame Rubelle; who kindly consented to imprison herself with her patient for two or three days. Before taking our departure, I gave Percival Mr Fairlie's letter of invitation to his niece (instructing her to sleep on the journey to Cumberland at her aunt's house), with directions to show it to Lady Glyde on hearing from me. I also obtained from him the address of the Asylum in which Anne Catherick had been confined, and a letter to the proprietor, announcing to that gentleman the return of his runaway patient to medical care.

I had arranged, at my last visit to the metropolis, to have our modest domestic establishment ready to receive us when we arrived in London by the early train. In consequence of this wise precaution, we were enabled that same day to play the third move in the game—the getting possession of Anne Catherick.

Dates are of importance here. I combine in myself the opposite characteristics of a Man of Sentiment and a Man of Business. I have all the dates at my fingers' ends.

On Wednesday, the 24th of July, 1850, I sent my wife, in a cab, to clear Mrs Clements out of the way, in the first place. A supposed message from

Lady Glyde in London was sufficient to obtain this result. Mrs Clements was taken away in the cab, and was left in the cab, while my wife (on pretence of purchasing something at a shop) gave her the slip, and returned to receive her expected visitor at our house in St John's Wood. It is hardly necessary to add that the visitor had been described to the servants as 'Lady Glyde.'

In the meanwhile I had followed in another cab, with a note for Anne Catherick, merely mentioning that Lady Glyde intended to keep Mrs Clements to spend the day with her, and that she was to join them, under care of the good gentleman waiting outside, who had already saved her from discovery in Hampshire by Sir Percival. The 'good gentleman' sent in this note by a street boy, and paused for results, a door or two farther on. At the moment when Anne appeared at the house-door and closed it, this excellent man had the cab-door open ready for her—absorbed her into the vehicle—and drove off.

(Pass me, here, one exclamation in parenthesis. How interesting this is!)

On the way to Forest-road, my companion showed no fear. I can be paternal—no man more so—when I please; and I was intensely paternal on this occasion. What titles I had to her confidence! I had compounded the medicine which had done her good; I had warned her of her danger from Sir Percival. Perhaps, I trusted too implicitly to these titles; perhaps, I underrated the keenness of the lower instincts in persons of weak intellect—it is certain that I neglected to prepare her sufficiently for a disappointment on entering my house. When I took her into the drawing-room—when she saw no one present but Madame Fosco, who was a stranger to her—she exhibited the most violent agitation: if she had scented danger in the air, as a dog scents the presence of some creature unseen, her alarm could not have displayed itself more suddenly and more causelessly. I interposed in vain. The fear from which she was suffering, I might have soothed—but the serious heart-disease, under which she laboured, was beyond the reach of all moral palliatives. To my unspeakable horror, she was seized with convulsions—a shock to the system, in her condition, which might have laid her dead at any moment, at our feet.

The nearest doctor was sent for, and was told that 'Lady Glyde' required his immediate services. To my infinite relief, he was a capable man. I represented my visitor to him as a person of weak intellect, and subject to delusions; and I arranged that no nurse but my wife should watch in the sick-room. The unhappy woman was too ill, however, to cause any anxiety about what she might say. The one dread which now oppressed me was the dread that the false Lady Glyde might die, before the true Lady Glyde arrived in London.

I had written a note in the morning to Madame Rubelle, telling her to join me, at her husband's house, on the evening of Friday, the 26th; with another note to Percival, warning him to show his wife her uncle's letter of invitation, to assert that Marian had gone on before her, and to despatch her to town, by the mid-day train, on the 26th, also. On reflection, I had felt the necessity, in Anne Catherick's state of health, of precipitating events, and of having Lady Glyde at my disposal earlier than I had originally contemplated. What fresh directions, in the terrible uncertainty of my position, could I now issue? I could do nothing but trust to chance and the doctor. My emotions expressed themselves in pathetic apostrophes—which I was just self-possessed enough to couple, in the hearing of other people, with the name of 'Lady Glyde.' In all other respects, Fosco, on that memorable day, was Fosco shrouded in total eclipse.

She passed a bad night—she awoke worn out—but, later in the day, she revived amazingly. My elastic spirits revived with her. I could receive no answers from Percival and Madame Rubelle till the morning of the next day—the 26th. In anticipation of their following my directions, which, accident apart, I knew they would do, I went to secure a fly to fetch Lady Glyde from the railway; directing it to be at my house, on the 26th, at two o'clock. After seeing the order entered in the book, I went on to arrange matters with Monsieur Rubelle. I also procured the services of two gentlemen, who could furnish me with the necessary certificates of lunacy. One of them I knew personally: the other was known to Monsieur Rubelle. Both were men whose vigorous minds soared superior to narrow scruples—both were labouring under temporary embarrassments—both believed in ME.

It was past five o'clock in the afternoon before I returned from the performance of these duties. When I got back, Anne Catherick was dead. Dead on the 25th; and Lady Glyde was not to arrive in London till the 26th!

I was stunned. Meditate on that. Fosco stunned!

It was too late to retrace our steps. Before my return, the doctor had officiously undertaken to save me all trouble, by registering the death, on the date when it happened, with his own hand. My grand scheme, unassailable hitherto, had its weak place now—no efforts, on my part, could alter the fatal event of the 25th. I turned manfully to the future. Percival's interests and mine being still at stake, nothing was left but to play the game through to the end. I recalled my impenetrable calm—and played it.

On the morning of the 26th, Percival's letter reached me, announcing his wife's arrival by the mid-day train. Madame Rubelle also wrote to say she would follow in the evening. I started in the fly, leaving the false Lady Glyde dead in the house, to receive the true Lady Glyde, on her arrival by the railway, at three o'clock. Hidden under the seat of the carriage, I carried with me all the clothes Anne Catherick had worn on coming into my house—they were destined to assist the resurrection of the woman who was dead, in the person of the woman who was living. What a situation! I suggest it to the rising romance writers of England. I offer it, as totally new, to the worn-out dramatists of France.

Lady Glyde was at the station. There was great crowding and confusion, and more delay than I liked (in case any of her friends had happened to be on the spot), in reclaiming her luggage. Her first questions, as we drove off, implored me to tell her news of her sister. I invented news of the most pacifying kind; assuring her that she was about to see her sister at my house. My house, on this occasion only, was in the neighbourhood of Leicester-square, and was in the occupation of Monsieur Rubelle, who received us in the hall.

I took my visitor up-stairs into a back room; the two medical gentlemen being there in waiting on the floor beneath, to see the patient, and to give me their certificates. After quieting Lady Glyde by the necessary assurances about her sister, I introduced my friends, separately, to her presence. They performed the formalities of the occasion, briefly, intelligently, conscientiously. I entered the room again, as soon as they had left it; and at once precipitated events by a reference, of the alarming kind, to 'Miss Halcombe's' state of health.

Results followed as I had anticipated. Lady Glyde became frightened, and turned faint. For the second time, and the last, I called Science to my assistance. A medicated glass of water, and a medicated bottle of smelling-salts, relieved her of all further embarrassment and alarm. Additional applications, later in the evening, procured her the inestimable blessing of a good night's rest. Madame Rubelle arrived in time to preside at Lady Glyde's toilet. Her own clothes were taken away from her at night, and Anne Catherick's were put on her in the morning, with the strictest regard to propriety, by the matronly hands of the good Rubelle. Throughout the day, I kept our patient in a state of partially-suspended consciousness, until the dexterous assistance of my medical friends enabled me to procure the necessary order, rather earlier than I had ventured to hope. That evening (the evening of the 27th) Madame Rubelle and I took our revived 'Anne Catherick' to the Asylum. She was received, with great surprise—but without suspicion; thanks to the order and certificates, to Percival's letter, to the likeness, to the clothes, and to the patient's own confused mental condition at the time. I returned at once to assist Madame Fosco in the preparations for the burial of the false 'Lady Glyde,' having the clothes and luggage of the true 'Lady Glyde' in my possession. They were afterwards sent to Cumberland by the conveyance which was used for the funeral. I attended the funeral, with becoming dignity, attired in the deepest mourning.

My narrative of these remarkable events, written under equally-remarkable circumstances, closes here. The minor precautions which I observed, in communicating with Limmeridge House, are already known—so is the magnificent success of my enterprise—so are the solid pecuniary results which followed it. I have to assert, with the whole force of my conviction, that the one weak place in my scheme would never have been found out, if the one weak place in my heart had not been discovered first. Nothing but my fatal admiration for Marian restrained me from stepping in to my own rescue, when she effected her sister's escape. I ran the risk, and trusted in the complete destruction of Lady Glyde's identity. If either Marian or Mr Hartright attempted to assert that identity, they would publicly expose themselves to the imputation of sustaining a rank deception; they would be distrusted and discredited accordingly; and they would, therefore, be powerless to place my interests or Percival's secret in jeopardy. I committed one error in trusting myself to such a blindfold calculation of chances as this. I committed another when Percival had paid the penalty of his own obstinacy and violence, by granting Lady Glyde a second reprieve from the madhouse, and allowing Mr Hartright a second chance of escaping me. In brief, Fosco, at this serious crisis, was untrue to himself. Deplorable and uncharacteristic fault! Behold the cause, in my Heart—behold, in the image of Marian Halcombe, the first and last weakness of Fosco's life!

At the ripe age of sixty, I make this unparalleled confession. Youths! I invoke your sympathy. Maidens! I claim your tears.

A word more—and the attention of the reader (concentrated breathlessly on myself) shall be released.

My own mental insight informs me that three inevitable questions will be asked, here, by persons of inquiring minds. They shall be stated; they shall be answered.

First question. What is the secret of Madame Fosco's unhesitating devotion of herself to the fulfilment of my boldest wishes, to the furtherance of my deepest plans? I might answer this, by simply referring to my own character, and by asking, in my turn:—Where, in the history of the world, has a man of my order ever been found without a woman in the background, self-immolated on the altar of his life? But, I remember that I am writing in England; I remember that I was married in England—and I ask, if a woman's marriage-obligations, in this country, provide for her private opinion of her husband's principles? No! They charge her unreservedly, to love, honour, and obey him. That is exactly what my wife has done. I stand, here, on a supreme moral elevation; and I loftily assert her accurate performance of her conjugal duties. Silence, Calumny! Your sympathy, Wives of England, for Madame Fosco!

Second question. If Anne Catherick had not died when she did, what should I have done? I should, in that case, have assisted worn-out Nature in finding permanent repose. I should have opened the doors of the Prison of Life, and have extended to the captive (incurably afflicted in mind and body both) a happy release.

Third question. On a calm revision of all the circumstances—Is my conduct worthy of any serious blame? Most emphatically, No! Have I not carefully avoided exposing myself to the odium of committing unnecessary crime? With my vast resources in chemistry, I might have taken Lady Glyde's life. At immense personal sacrifice, I followed the dictates of my own ingenuity, my own humanity, my own caution—and took her identity, instead. Judge me by what I might have done. How comparatively innocent! how indirectly virtuous I appear, in what I really did!

I announced, on beginning it, that this narrative would be a remarkable document. It has entirely answered my expectations. Receive these fervid lines—my last legacy to the country I leave for ever. They are worthy of the occasion, and worthy of

FOSCO

HARTRIGHT'S NARRATIVE, CONCLUDED

I

WHEN I closed the last leaf of the Count's manuscript, the half-hour during which I had engaged to remain at Forest-road had expired. Monsieur Rubelle looked at his watch, and bowed. I rose immediately, and left the agent in possession of the empty house. I never saw him again; I never heard more of him or of his wife. Out of the dark byways of villany and deceit, they had crawled across our path—into the same byways they crawled back secretly, and were lost.

In a quarter of an hour after leaving Forest-road, I was at home again.

But few words sufficed to tell Laura and Marian how my desperate venture had ended, and what the next event in our lives was likely to be. I left all details to be described later in the day; and hastened back to St John's Wood, to see the person of whom Count Fosco had ordered the fly, when he went to meet Laura at the station.

The address in my possession led me to some 'livery stables,' about a quarter of a mile distant from Forest-road. The proprietor proved to be a civil and respectable man. When I explained that an important family matter obliged me to ask him to refer to his books, for the purpose of ascertaining a date with which the record of his business transactions might supply me, he offered no objection to granting my request. The book was produced; and there, under the date of 'July 26th, 1850,' the order was entered, in these words:

'Brougham to Count Fosco, 5, Forest-road. Two o'clock. (John Owen).'

I found, on inquiry, that the name of 'John Owen,' attached to the entry, referred to the man who had been employed to drive the fly. He was then at work in the stable-yard, and was sent for to see me, at my request.

'Do you remember driving a gentleman, in the month of July last, from Number Five, Forest-road, to the Waterloo-bridge station?' I asked.

'Well, sir,' said the man; 'I can't exactly say I do.'

'Perhaps you remember the gentleman himself? Can you call to mind driving a foreigner, last summer—a tall gentleman, and remarkably fat?'

The man's face brightened directly. 'I remember him, sir! The fattest gentleman as ever I see—and the heaviest customer as ever I drove. Yes, yes—I call him to mind, sir. We *did* go to the station, and it *was* from Forest-road. There was a parrot, or summut like it, screeching in the window. The gentleman was in a mortal hurry about the lady's luggage; and he give me a handsome present for looking sharp and getting the boxes.'

Getting the boxes! I recollected immediately that Laura's own account of herself, on her arrival in London, described her luggage as being collected for her by some person whom Count Fosco brought with him to the station. This was the man.

'Did you see the lady?' I asked. 'What did she look like? Was she young or old?'

'Well, sir, what with the hurry and the crowd of people pushing about, I can't rightly say what the lady looked like. I can't call nothing to mind about her that I know of—excepting her name.'

'You remember her name!'

'Yes, sir. Her name was Lady Glyde.'

'How do you come to remember that, when you have forgotten what she looked like?'

The man smiled, and shifted his feet in some little embarrassment.

'Why, to tell you the truth, sir,' he said, 'I hadn't been long married at that time; and my wife's name, before she changed it for mine, was the same as the lady's—meaning the name of Glyde, sir. The lady mentioned it herself. "Is your name on your boxes, ma'am?" says I. "Yes," says she, "my name is on my luggage—it is Lady Glyde." "Come!" I says to myself, "I've a bad head for gentlefolks' names in general—but *this* one comes like an old friend, at any rate." I can't say nothing about the time, sir: it might be nigh on a year ago, or it mightn't. But I can swear to the stout gentleman, and swear to the lady's name.'

There was no need that he should remember the time; the date was positively established by his master's order-book. I felt at once that the means were now in my power of striking down the whole conspiracy at a blow with the irresistible weapon of plain fact. Without a moment's hesitation, I took the proprietor of the livery stables aside, and told him what the real importance was of the evidence of his order-book and the evidence of his driver. An arrangement to compensate him for the temporary loss of the man's services was easily made; and a copy of the entry in the book was taken by myself, and certified as true by the master's own signature. I left the livery stables, having settled that John Owen was to hold himself at my disposal for the next three days, or for a longer period, if necessity required it.

I now had in my possession all the papers that I wanted; the district registrar's own copy of the certificate of death, and Sir Percival's dated letter to the Count, being safe in my pocket-book.

With this written evidence about me, and with the coachman's answers fresh in my memory, I next turned my steps, for the first time since the beginning of all my inquiries, in the direction of Mr Kyrle's office. One of my objects, in paying him this second visit, was, necessarily, to tell him what I had done. The other, was to warn him of my resolution to take my wife to Limmeridge the next morning, and to have her publicly received and recognised in her uncle's house. I left it to Mr Kyrle to decide, under these circumstances, and in Mr Gilmore's absence, whether he was or was not bound, as the family solicitor, to be present, on that occasion, in the family interests.

I will say nothing of Mr Kyrle's amazement, or of the terms in which he expressed his opinion of my conduct, from the first stage of the investigation to the last. It is only necessary to mention that he at once decided on accompanying us to Cumberland.

We started, the next morning, by the early train. Laura, Marian, Mr Kyrle, and myself in one carriage; and John Owen, with a clerk from Mr Kyrle's office, occupying places in another. On reaching the Limmeridge station, we went first to the farm-house at Todd's Corner. It was my firm determination that Laura should not enter her uncle's house till she appeared there publicly recognised as his niece: I left Marian to settle the question of accommodation with Mrs Todd, as soon as the good woman had recovered from the bewilderment of hearing what our errand was in Cumberland; and I arranged with her husband that John Owen was to be committed to the ready hospitality of the farm-servants. These preliminaries completed, Mr Kyrle and I set forth together for Limmeridge House.

I cannot write at any length of our interview with Mr Fairlie, for I cannot recal it to mind, without feelings of impatience and contempt, which make the scene, even in remembrance only, utterly repulsive to me. I prefer to record simply that I carried my point. Mr Fairlie attempted to treat us on his customary plan. We passed without notice his polite insolence at the outset of the interview. We heard without sympathy the protestations with which he tried next to persuade us that the disclosure of the conspiracy had overwhelmed him. He absolutely whined and whimpered, at last, like a fretful child. 'How was he to know that his niece was alive, when he was told that she was dead? He would welcome dear Laura, with pleasure, if we would only allow him time to recover. Did we think he looked as if he wanted hurrying into his grave? No. Then, why hurry him?' He reiterated these remonstrances at every available opportunity, until I checked them once for all, by placing him firmly between two inevitable alternatives. I gave him his choice between doing his niece justice, on my terms—or facing the consequences of a public assertion of her identity in a court of law. Mr Kyrle, to whom he turned for help, told him plainly that he must decide the question, then and there. Characteristically choosing the alternative which promised soonest to release him from all personal anxiety, he announced, with a sudden outburst of energy, that he was not strong enough to bear any more bullying, and that we might do as we pleased.

Mr Kyrle and I at once went down stairs, and agreed upon a form of letter which was to be sent round to the tenants who had attended the false funeral, summoning them, in Mr Fairlie's name, to assemble in Limmeridge House, on the next day but one. An order, referring to the same date, was also written, directing a statuary in Carlisle to send a man to Limmeridge churchyard, for the purpose of erasing an inscription—Mr Kyrle, who had arranged to sleep in the house, undertaking that Mr Fairlie should hear these letters read to him, and should sign them with his own hand.

I occupied the interval-day, at the farm, in writing a plain narrative of the conspiracy, and in adding to it a statement of the practical contradiction which facts offered to the assertion of Laura's death. This I submitted to Mr Kyrle, before I read it, the next day, to the assembled tenants. We also arranged the form in which the evidence should be presented at the close of the reading. After these matters were settled, Mr Kyrle endeavoured to turn the conversation, next, to Laura's affairs. Knowing, and desiring to know, nothing of those affairs; and doubting whether he would approve, as a man of business, of my conduct in relation to my wife's life-interest in the legacy left to Madame Fosco, I begged Mr Kyrle to excuse me if I abstained from discussing the subject. It was connected, as I could truly tell him, with those sorrows and troubles of the past, which we never referred to among ourselves, and which we instinctively shrank from discussing with others.

My last labour, as the evening approached, was to obtain 'The Narrative of the Tombstone,' by taking a copy of the false inscription on the grave, before it was erased.

The day came—the day when Laura once more entered the familiar breakfast-room at Limmeridge House. All the persons assembled rose from their seats as Marian and I led her in. A perceptible shock of surprise, an audible murmur of interest, ran through them, at the sight of her face. Mr Fairlie was present (by my express stipulation), with Mr Kyrle by his side. His valet stood behind him with a smelling-bottle ready in one hand, and a white handkerchief, saturated with eau-de-Cologne, in the other.

I opened the proceedings by publicly appealing to Mr Fairlie to say whether I appeared there with his authority and under his express sanction.

He extended an arm, on either side, to Mr Kyrle and to his valet; was by them assisted to stand on his legs; and then expressed himself in these terms: 'Allow me to present Mr Hartright. I am as great an invalid as ever; and he is so very obliging as to speak for me. The subject is dreadfully embarrassing. Please hear him—and don't make a noise!' With those words, he slowly sank back again into the chair, and took refuge in his scented pocket-handkerchief.

The disclosure of the conspiracy followed—after I had offered my preliminary explanation, first of all, in the fewest and the plainest words. I was there present (I informed my hearers) to declare first, that my wife, then sitting by me, was the daughter of the late Mr Philip Fairlie; secondly, to prove, by positive facts, that the funeral which they had attended in Limmeridge churchyard, was the funeral of another woman; thirdly, to give them a plain account of how it had all happened. Without further preface, I at once read the narrative of the conspiracy, describing it in clear outline, and dwelling only upon the pecuniary motive for it, in order to avoid complicating my statement by unnecessary reference to Sir Percival's secret. This done, I reminded my audience of the date on the inscription in the churchyard (the 25th of July), and confirmed its correctness by producing the certificate of death. I then read them Sir Percival's letter of the 25th, announcing his wife's intended journey from Hampshire to London on the 26th. I next showed that she had taken that journey, by the personal testimony of the driver of the fly; and I proved that she had performed it on the appointed day, by the order-book at the livery stables. Marian then added her own statement of the meeting between Laura and herself at the madhouse, and of her sister's escape. After which, I closed the proceedings by informing the persons present of Sir Percival's death, and of my marriage.

Mr Kyrle rose, when I resumed my seat, and declared, as the legal adviser of the family, that my case was proved by the plainest evidence he had ever heard in his life. As he spoke those words, I put my arm round Laura, and raised her so that she was plainly visible to every one in the room. 'Are you all of the same opinion?' I asked, advancing towards them a few steps, and pointing to my wife.

The effect of the question was electrical. Far down at the lower end of the room, one of the oldest tenants on the estate, started to his feet, and led the rest with him in an instant. I see the man now, with his honest brown face and his iron-grey hair, mounted on the window-seat, waving his heavy riding-whip over his head, and leading the cheers. 'There she is alive and hearty—God bless her! Gi' it tongue, lads! Gi' it tongue!' The shout that answered him, reiterated again and again, was the sweetest music I ever heard. The labourers in the village and the boys from the school, assembled on the lawn, caught up the cheering and echoed it back on us. The farmers' wives clustered round Laura, and struggled which should be first to shake hands with her, and to implore her, with the tears pouring over their own cheeks, to bear up bravely and not to cry. She was so completely overwhelmed, that I was obliged to take her from them, and carry her to the door. There I gave her into Marian's care—Marian, who had never failed us yet, whose courageous self-control did not fail us now. Left by myself at the door, I invited all the persons present (after thanking them in Laura's name and mine) to follow me to the churchyard, and see the false inscription struck off the tombstone with their own eyes.

They all left the house, and all joined the throng of villagers collected round the grave, where the statuary's man was waiting for us. In a breathless silence, the first sharp stroke of the steel sounded on the marble. Not a voice was heard; not a soul moved, till those three words, 'Laura, Lady Glyde,' had vanished from sight. Then, there was a great heave of relief among the crowd, as if they felt that the last fetters of the conspiracy had been struck off Laura herself—and the assembly slowly withdrew. It was late in the day before the whole inscription was erased. One line only was afterwards engraved in its place: 'Anne Catherick, July 25th, 1850.'

I returned to Limmeridge House early enough in the evening to take leave of Mr Kyrle. He, and his clerk, and the driver of the fly, went back to London by the night train. On their departure, an insolent message was delivered to me from Mr Fairlie—who had been carried from the room in a shattered condition, when the first outbreak of cheering answered my appeal to the tenantry. The message conveyed to us 'Mr Fairlie's best congratulations,' and requested to know whether 'we contemplated stopping in the house.' I sent back word that the only object for which we had entered his doors was accomplished; that I contemplated stopping in no man's house but my own; and that Mr Fairlie need not entertain the slightest apprehension of ever seeing us, or hearing from us again. We went back to our friends at the farm, to rest that night; and the next morning—escorted to the station, with the heartiest enthusiasm and good will, by the whole village and by all the farmers in the neighbourhood—we returned to London.

As our view of the Cumberland hills faded in the distance, I thought of the first disheartening circumstances under which the long struggle that was now past and over had been pursued. It was strange to look back and to see, now, that the poverty which had denied us all hope of assistance, had been the indirect means of our success, by forcing me to act for myself. If we had been rich enough to find legal help, what would have been the result? The gain (on Mr Kyrle's own showing) would have been more than doubtful; the loss—judging by the plain test of events as they had really happened—certain. The Law would never have obtained me my interview with Mrs Catherick. The Law would never have made Pesca the means of forcing a confession from the Count.

II

Two more events remain to be added to the chain, before it reaches fairly from the outset of the story to the close.

While our new sense of freedom from the long oppression of the past was still strange to us, I was sent for by the friend who had given me my first employment in wood engraving, to receive from him a fresh testimony of his regard for my welfare. He had been commissioned by his employers to go to Paris, and to examine for them a French discovery in the practical application of his Art, the merits of which they were anxious to ascertain. His own engagements had not allowed him leisure time to undertake the errand; and he had most kindly suggested that it should be transferred to me. I could have no hesitation in thankfully accepting the offer; for if I acquitted myself of my commission as I hoped I should, the result would be a permanent engagement on the illustrated newspaper, to which I was now only occasionally attached.

I received my instructions and packed up for the journey the next day. On leaving Laura once more (under what changed circumstances!) in her sister's care, a serious consideration recurred to me, which had more than once crossed my wife's mind, as well as my own, already—I mean the consideration of Marian's future. Had we any right to let our selfish affection accept the devotion of all that generous life? Was it not our duty, our best expression of gratitude, to forget ourselves, and to think only of *her*? I tried to say this, when we were alone for a moment, before I went away. She took my hand, and silenced me, at the first words.

'After all that we three have suffered together,' she said, 'there can be no parting between us, till the last parting of all. My heart and my happiness, Walter, are with Laura and you. Wait a little till there are children's voices at your fireside. I will teach them to speak for me, in *their* language; and the first lesson they say to their father and mother shall be—We can't spare our aunt!'

My journey to Paris was not undertaken alone. At the eleventh hour, Pesca decided that he would accompany me. He had not recovered his customary cheerfulness, since the night at the Opera; and he determined to try what a week's holiday would do to raise his spirits.

I performed the errand entrusted to me, and drew out the necessary report, on the fourth day from our arrival in Paris. The fifth day, I arranged to devote to sight-seeing and amusements in Pesca's company.

Our hotel had been too full to accommodate us both on the same floor. My room was on the second story, and Pesca's was above me, on the third. On the morning of the fifth day, I went up-stairs to see if the Professor was ready to go out. Just before I reached the landing, I saw his door opened from the inside; a long, delicate, nervous hand (not my friend's hand certainly) held it ajar. At the same time, I heard Pesca's voice saying eagerly, in low tones, and in his own language: 'I remember the name, but I don't know the man. You saw at the Opera, he was so changed that I could not recognise him. I will forward the report—I can do no more.' 'No more need be done,' answered a second voice. The door opened wide; and the light-haired man with the scar on his cheek—the man I had seen following Count Fosco's cab a week before—came out. He bowed, as I drew aside to let him pass—his face was fearfully pale—and he held fast by the banisters, as he descended the stairs.

I pushed open the door, and entered Pesca's room. He was crouched up, in the strangest manner, in a corner of the sofa. He seemed to shrink from me, when I approached him.

'Am I disturbing you?' I asked. 'I did not know you had a friend with you till I saw him come out.'

'No friend,' said Pesca, eagerly. 'I see him to-day for the first time, and the last.'

'I am afraid he has brought you bad news?'

'Horrible news, Walter! Let us go back to London—I don't want to stop here—I am sorry I ever came. The misfortunes of my youth are very hard upon me,' he said, turning his face to the wall; 'very hard upon me, in my later time. I try to forget them—and they will not forget *me*!'

'We can't return, I am afraid, before the afternoon,' I replied. 'Would you like to come out with me, in the mean time?'

'No, my friend; I will wait here. But let us go back to-day—pray let us go back.'

I left him, with the assurance that he should leave Paris that afternoon. We had arranged, the evening before, to ascend the Cathedral of Notre-Dame, with Victor Hugo's noble romance for our guide. There was nothing in the French capital that I was more anxious to see—and I departed, by myself, for the church.

Approaching Notre-Dame by the river-side, I passed, on my way, the terrible dead-house of Paris—the Morgue. A great crowd clamoured and heaved round the door. There was evidently something inside which excited the popular curiosity, and fed the popular appetite for horror.

I should have walked on to the church, if the conversation of two men and a woman on the outskirts of the crowd had not caught my ear. They had just come out from seeing the sight in the Morgue; and the account they were giving of the dead body to their neighbours, described it as the corpse of a man—a man of immense size, with a strange mark on his left arm.

The moment those words reached me, I stopped, and took my place with the crowd going in. Some dim foreshadowing of the truth had crossed my mind, when I heard Pesca's voice through the open door, and when I saw the stranger's face as he passed me on the stairs of the hotel. Now, the truth itself was revealed to me—revealed, in the chance words that had just reached my ears. Other vengeance than mine had followed that fated man from the theatre to his own door: from his own door to his refuge in Paris. Other vengeance than mine had called him to the day of reckoning, and had exacted from him the penalty of his life. The moment when I had pointed him out to Pesca, at the theatre, in the hearing of that stranger by our side, who was looking for him, too—was the moment that sealed his doom. I remembered the struggle in my own heart, when he and I stood face to face—the struggle before I could let him escape me—and shuddered as I recalled it.

Slowly, inch by inch, I pressed in with the crowd, moving nearer and nearer to the great glass screen that parts the dead from the living at the Morgue—nearer and nearer, till I was close behind the front row of spectators, and could look in.

There he lay, unowned, unknown; exposed to the flippant curiosity of a French mob! There was the dreadful end of that long life of degraded ability and heartless crime! Hushed in the sublime repose of death, the broad, firm, massive face and head fronted us so grandly, that the chattering French-women about me lifted their hands in admiration, and cried, in shrill chorus, 'Ah, what a handsome man!' The wound that had killed him had been struck with a knife or dagger exactly over his heart. No other traces of violence appeared about the body, except on the left arm; and there, exactly in the place where I had seen the brand on Pesca's arm, were two deep cuts in the shape of the letter T, which entirely obliterated the mark of the Brotherhood. His clothes, hung above him, showed that he had been himself conscious of his danger—they were clothes that had disguised him as a French artisan. For a few moments, but not for longer, I forced myself to see these things through the glass screen. I can write of them at no greater length, for I saw no more.

The few facts, in connexion with his death which I subsequently ascertained (partly from Pesca and partly from other sources), may be stated here, before the subject is dismissed from these pages.

His body was taken out of the Seine, in the disguise which I have described; nothing being found on him which revealed his name, his rank, or his place of abode. The hand that struck him was never traced; and the circumstances under which he was killed were never discovered. I leave others to draw their own conclusions, in reference to the secret of the assassination, as I have drawn mine. When I have intimated that the foreigner with the scar was a Member of the Brotherhood (admitted in Italy, after Pesca's departure from his native country), and when I have further added that the two cuts, in the form of a T, on the left arm of the dead man, signified the Italian word, 'Traditore,' and showed that justice had been done by the Brotherhood on a Traitor, I have contributed all that I know towards elucidating the mystery of Count Fosco's death.

The body was identified, the day after I had seen it, by means of an anonymous letter addressed to his wife. He was buried, by Madame Fosco, in the cemetery of Père la Chaise. Fresh funeral wreaths continue, to this day, to be hung on the ornamental bronze-railings round the tomb, by the Countess's own hand. She lives, in the strictest retirement, at Versailles. Not long since, she published a Biography of her deceased husband. The work throws no light whatever on the name that was really his own, or on the secret history of his life: it is almost entirely devoted to the praise of his domestic virtues, the assertion of his rare abilities, and the enumeration of the honours conferred on him. The circumstances attending his death are very briefly noticed; and are summed up, on the last page, in this sentence:—'His life was one long assertion of the rights of the aristocracy, and the sacred principles of Order—and he died a Martyr to his cause.'

III

THE summer and autumn passed, after my return from Paris, and brought no changes with them which need be noticed here. We lived so simply and quietly, that the income which I was now steadily earning sufficed for all our wants.

In the February of the new year, our first child was born—a son. My mother and sister and Mrs Vesey, were our guests at the little christening party; and Mrs Clements was present, to assist my wife, on the same occasion. Marian was our boy's godmother; and Pesca and Mr Gilmore (the latter acting by proxy) were his godfathers. I may add here, that, when Mr Gilmore returned to us, a year later, he assisted the design of these pages, at my request, by writing the Narrative which appears early in the story under his name, and which, though the first in order of precedence, was thus, in order of time, the last that I received.

The only event in our lives which now remains to be recorded, occurred when our little Walter was six months old.

At that time, I was sent to Ireland, to make sketches for certain forthcoming illustrations in the newspaper to which I was attached. I was away for nearly a fortnight, corresponding regularly with my wife and Marian, except during the last three days of my absence, when my movements were too uncertain to enable me to receive letters. I performed the latter part of my journey back, at night; and when I reached home in the morning, to my utter astonishment, there was no one to receive me. Laura and Marian and the child had left the house on the day before my return.

A note from my wife, which was given to me by the servant, only increased my surprise, by informing me that they had gone to Limmeridge House. Marian had prohibited any attempt at written explanations—I was entreated to follow them the moment I came back—complete enlightenment awaited me on my arrival in Cumberland—and I was forbidden to feel the slightest anxiety, in the mean time. There the note ended.

It was still early enough to catch the morning train. I reached Limmeridge House the same afternoon.

My wife and Marian were both up-stairs. They had established themselves (by way of completing my amazement) in the little room which had once been assigned to me for a studio, when I was employed on Mr Fairlie's drawings. On the very chair which I used to occupy when I was at work, Marian was sitting now, with the child industriously sucking his coral upon her lap—while Laura was standing by the well-remembered drawing-table which I had so often used, with the little album that I had filled for her, in past times, open under her hand.

'What in the name of heaven has brought you here?' I asked. 'Does Mr Fairlie know——?'

Marian suspended the question on my lips, by telling me that Mr Fairlie was dead. He had been struck by paralysis, and had never rallied after the shock. Mr Kyrle had informed them of his death, and had advised them to proceed immediately to Limmeridge House.

Some dim perception of a great change dawned on my mind. Laura spoke before I had quite realised it. She stole close to me, to enjoy the surprise which was still expressed in my face.

'My darling Walter,' she said, 'must we really account for our boldness in coming here? I am afraid, love, I can only explain it by breaking through our rule, and referring to the past.'

'There is not the least necessity for doing anything of the kind,' said Marian. 'We can be just as explicit, and much more interesting, by referring to the future.' She rose; and held up the child, kicking and crowing in her arms. 'Do you know who this is, Walter?' she asked, with bright tears of happiness gathering in her eyes.

'Even *my* bewilderment has its limits,' I replied. 'I think I can still answer for knowing my own child.'

'Child!' she exclaimed, with all her easy gaiety of old times. 'Do you talk in that familiar manner of one of the landed gentry of England? Are you aware, when I present this illustrious baby to your notice, in whose presence you stand? Evidently not! Let me make two eminent personages known to one another: Mr Walter Hartright—*the Heir of Limmeridge*.'

So she spoke. In writing those last words, I have written all. The pen falters in my hand; the long, happy labour of many months is over! Marian was the good angel of our lives—let Marian end our Story.

THE END

The Moonstone

IN MEMORIAM MATRIS

PREFACE

IN some of my former novels, the object proposed has been to trace the influence of circumstances upon character. In the present story I have reversed the process. The attempt made here is to trace the influence of character on circumstances. The conduct pursued, under a sudden emergency, by a young girl, supplies the foundation on which I have built this book.

The same object has been kept in view in the handling of the other characters which appear in these pages. Their course of thought and action under the circumstances which surround them is shown to be (what it would most probably have been in real life) sometimes right and sometimes wrong. Right or wrong, their conduct, in either event, equally directs the course of those portions of the story in which they are concerned.

In the case of the physiological experiment which occupies a prominent place in the closing scenes of *The Moonstone*, the same principle has guided me once more. Having first ascertained, not only from books, but from living authorities as well, what the result of that experiment would really have been, I have declined to avail myself of the novelist's privilege of supposing something which might have happened, and have so shaped the story as to make it grow out of what actually would have happened—which, I beg to inform my readers, is also what actually does happen, in these pages.

With reference to the story of the Diamond, as here set forth, I have to acknowledge that it is founded, in some important particulars, on the stories of two of the royal diamonds of Europe. The magnificent stone which adorns the top of the Russian Imperial Sceptre was once the eye of an Indian idol. The famous Koh-i-Noor is also supposed to have been one of the sacred gems of India; and, more than this, to have been the subject of a prediction, which prophesied certain misfortune to the persons who should divert it from its ancient uses.

Gloucester Place, Portman Square,
June 30th, 1868.

PREFACE TO A NEW EDITION

THE circumstances under which *The Moonstone* was originally written have invested the book—in the author's mind—with an interest peculiarly its own.

While this work was still in course of periodical publication in England and in the United States, and when not more than one-third of it was completed, the bitterest affliction of my life and the severest illness from which I have ever suffered fell on me together. At the time when my mother lay dying in her little cottage in the country, I was struck prostrate, in London—crippled in every limb by the torture of rheumatic gout. Under the weight of this double calamity, I had my duty to the public still to bear in mind. My good readers in England and in America, whom I had never yet disappointed, were expecting their regular weekly instalments of the new story. I held to the story—for my own sake as well as for theirs. In the intervals of grief, in the occasional remissions of pain, I dictated from my bed that portion of *The Moonstone* which has since proved most successful in amusing the public—the 'Narrative of Miss Clack.' Of the physical sacrifice which the effort cost me I shall say nothing. I only look back now at the blessed relief which my occupation (forced as it was) brought to my mind. The Art which had been always the pride and the pleasure of my life became now more than ever 'its own exceeding great reward.' I doubt if I should have lived to write another book, if the responsibility of the weekly publication of this story had not forced me to rally my sinking energies of body and mind—to dry my useless tears, and to conquer my merciless pains.

The novel completed, I awaited its reception by the public with an eagerness of anxiety which I have never felt before or since for the fate of any other writings of mine. If *The Moonstone* had failed, my mortification would have been bitter indeed. As it was, the welcome accorded to the story in England, in America, and on the Continent of Europe was instantly and universally favourable. Never have I had better reason than this work has given me to feel gratefully to novel-readers of all nations. Everywhere my characters made friends, and my story roused interest. Everywhere the public favour looked over my faults—and repaid me a hundredfold for the hard toil which these pages cost me in the dark time of sickness and grief.

I have only to add that the present edition has had the benefit of my careful revision. All that I can do towards making the book worthy of the reader's continued approval has now been done.

W.C.

May, 1871.

THE MOONSTONE

PROLOGUE

THE STORMING OF SERINGAPATAM (1799)

Extracted from a family paper

I

I ADDRESS these lines—written in India—to my relatives in England.

My object is to explain the motive which has induced me to refuse the right hand of friendship to my cousin, John Herncastle. The reserve which I have hitherto maintained in this matter has been misinterpreted by members of my family whose good opinion I cannot consent to forfeit. I request them to suspend their decision until they have read my narrative. And I declare, on my word of honour, that what I am now about to write is, strictly and literally, the truth.

The private difference between my cousin and me took its rise in a great public event in which we were both concerned—the storming of Seringapatam, under General Baird, on the 4th of May, 1799.

In order that the circumstances may be clearly understood, I must revert for a moment to the period before the assault, and to the stories current in our camp of the treasure in jewels and gold stored up in the Palace of Seringapatam.

II

One of the wildest of these stories related to a Yellow Diamond—a famous gem in the native annals of India.

The earliest known traditions describe the stone as having been set in the forehead of the four-handed Indian god who typifies the Moon. Partly from its peculiar colour, partly from a superstition which represented it as feeling the influence of the deity whom it adorned, and growing and lessening in lustre with the waxing and waning of the moon, it first gained the name by which it continues to be known in India to this day—the name of THE MOONSTONE. A similar superstition was once prevalent, as I have heard, in ancient Greece and Rome; not applying, however (as in India), to a diamond devoted to the service of a god, but to a semi-transparent stone of the inferior order of gems, supposed to be affected by the lunar influences—the moon, in this latter case also, giving the name by which the stone is still known to collectors in our own time.

The adventures of the Yellow Diamond begin with the eleventh century of the Christian era.

At that date, the Mohammedan conqueror, Mahmoud of Ghizni, crossed India; seized on the holy city of Somnauth; and stripped of its treasures the famous temple, which had stood for centuries—the shrine of Hindoo pilgrimage, and the wonder of the Eastern world.

Of all the deities worshipped in the temple, the moon-god alone escaped the rapacity of the conquering Mohammedans. Preserved by three Brahmins, the inviolate deity, bearing the Yellow Diamond in its forehead, was removed by night, and was transported to the second of the sacred cities of India—the city of Benares.

Here, in a new shrine—in a hall inlaid with precious stones, under a roof supported by pillars of gold—the moon-god was set up and worshipped. Here, on the night when the shrine was completed, Vishnu the Preserver appeared to the three Brahmins in a dream.

The deity breathed the breath of his divinity on the Diamond in the forehead of the god. And the Brahmins knelt and hid their faces in their robes. The deity commanded that the Moonstone should be watched, from that time forth, by three priests in turn, night and day, to the end of the generations of men. And the Brahmins heard, and bowed before his will. The deity predicted certain disaster to the presumptuous mortal who laid hands on the sacred gem, and to all of his house and name who received it after him. And the Brahmins caused the prophecy to be written over the gates of the shrine in letters of gold.

One age followed another—and still, generation after generation, the successors of the three Brahmins watched their priceless Moonstone, night and day. One age followed another until the first years of the eighteenth Christian century saw the reign of Aurungzebe, Emperor of the Moguls. At his command havoc and rapine were let loose once more among the temples of the worship of Brahmah. The shrine of the four-handed god was polluted by the slaughter of sacred animals; the images of the deities were broken in pieces; and the Moonstone was seized by an officer of rank in the army of Aurungzebe.

Powerless to recover their lost treasure by open force, the three guardian priests followed and watched it in disguise. The generations succeeded each other; the warrior who had committed the sacrilege perished miserably; the Moonstone passed (carrying its curse with it) from one lawless Moham-medan hand to another; and still, through all chances and changes, the successors of the three guardian priests kept their watch, waiting the day when the will of Vishnu the Preserver should restore to them their sacred gem. Time rolled on from the first to the last years of the eighteenth Christian century. The Diamond fell into the possession of Tippoo, Sultan of Seringapatam, who caused it to be placed as an ornament in the handle of a dagger, and who commanded it to be kept among the choicest treasures of his armoury. Even then—in the palace of the Sultan himself—the three guardian priests still kept their watch in secret. There were three officers of Tippoo's household, strangers to the rest, who had won their master's confidence by conforming, or appearing to conform, to the Mussulman faith; and to those three men report pointed as the three priests in disguise.

III

So, as told in our camp, ran the fanciful story of the Moonstone. It made no serious impression on any of us except my cousin—whose love of the marvellous induced him to believe it. On the night before the assault on Seringapatam, he was absurdly angry with me, and with others, for treating the whole thing as a fable. A foolish wrangle followed; and Herncastle's unlucky temper got the better of him. He declared, in his boastful way, that we should see the Diamond on his finger, if the English army took Seringapatam. The sally was saluted by a roar of laughter, and there, as we all thought that night, the thing ended.

Let me now take you on to the day of the assault.

My cousin and I were separated at the outset. I never saw him when we forded the river; when we planted the English flag in the first breach; when we crossed the ditch beyond; and, fighting every inch of our way, entered the town. It was only at dusk, when the place was ours, and after General Baird himself had found the dead body of Tippoo under a heap of the slain, that Herncastle and I met.

We were each attached to a party sent out by the general's orders to prevent the plunder and confusion which followed our conquest. The camp-followers committed deplorable excesses; and, worse still, the soldiers found their way, by an unguarded door, into the treasury of the Palace, and loaded themselves with gold and jewels. It was in the court outside the treasury that my cousin and I met, to enforce the laws of discipline on our own soldiers. Herncastle's fiery temper had been, as I could plainly see, exasperated to a kind of frenzy by the terrible slaughter through which we had passed. He was very unfit, in my opinion, to perform the duty that had been entrusted to him.

There was riot and confusion enough in the treasury, but no violence that I saw. The men (if I may use such an expression) disgraced themselves good-humouredly. All sorts of rough jests and catchwords were bandied about among them; and the story of the Diamond turned up again unexpectedly, in the form of a mischievous joke. 'Who's got the Moonstone?'

was the rallying cry which perpetually caused the plundering, as soon as it was stopped in one place, to break out in another. While I was still vainly trying to establish order, I heard a frightful yelling on the other side of the courtyard, and at once ran towards the cries, in dread of finding some new outbreak of the pillage in that direction.

I got to an open door, and saw the bodies of two Indians (by their dress, as I guessed, officers of the palace) lying across the entrance, dead.

A cry inside hurried me into a room, which appeared to serve as an armoury. A third Indian, mortally wounded, was sinking at the feet of a man whose back was towards me. The man turned at the instant when I came in, and I saw John Herncastle, with a torch in one hand, and a dagger dripping with blood in the other. A stone, set like a pommel, in the end of the dagger's handle, flashed in the torchlight, as he turned on me, like a gleam of fire. The dying Indian sank to his knees, pointed to the dagger in Herncastle's hand, and said, in his native language:—'The Moonstone will have its vengeance yet on you and yours!' He spoke those words, and fell dead on the floor.

Before I could stir in the matter, the men who had followed me across the courtyard crowded in. My cousin rushed to meet them, like a madman. 'Clear the room!' he shouted to me, 'and set a guard on the door!' The men fell back as he threw himself on them with his torch and his dagger. I put two sentinels of my own company, on whom I could rely, to keep the door. Through the remainder of the night, I saw no more of my cousin.

Early in the morning, the plunder still going on, General Baird announced publicly by beat of drum, that any thief detected in the fact, be he whom he might, should be hung. The provost-marshal was in attendance, to prove that the General was in earnest; and in the throng that followed the proclamation, Herncastle and I met again.

He held out his hand, as usual, and said, 'Good morning.'

I waited before I gave him my hand in return.

'Tell me first,' I said, 'how the Indian in the armoury met his death, and what those last words meant, when he pointed to the dagger in your hand.'

'The Indian met his death, as I suppose, by a mortal wound,' said Herncastle. 'What his last words meant I know no more than you do.'

I looked at him narrowly. His frenzy of the previous day had all calmed down. I determined to give him another chance.

'Is that all you have to tell me?' I asked.

He answered, 'That is all.'

I turned my back on him; and we have not spoken since.

IV

I beg it to be understood that what I write here about my cousin (unless some necessity should arise for making it public) is for the information of the family only. Herncastle has said nothing that can justify me in speaking to our commanding officer. He has been taunted more than once about the Diamond, by those who recollect his angry outbreak before the assault; but, as may easily be imagined, his own remembrance of the circumstances under which I surprised him in the armoury has been enough to keep him silent. It is reported that he means to exchange into another regiment, avowedly for the purpose of separating himself from *me*.

Whether this be true or not, I cannot prevail upon myself to become his accuser—and I think with good reason. If I made the matter public, I have no evidence but moral evidence to bring forward. I have not only no proof that he killed the two men at the door; I cannot even declare that he killed the third man inside—for I cannot say that my own eyes saw the deed committed. It is true that I heard the dying Indian's words; but if those words were pronounced to be the ravings of delirium, how could I contradict the assertion from my own knowledge? Let our relatives, on either side, form their own opinion on what I have written, and decide for themselves whether the aversion I now feel towards this man is well or ill founded.

Although I attach no sort of credit to the fantastic Indian legend of the gem, I must acknowledge, before I conclude, that I am influenced by a certain superstition of my own in this matter. It is my conviction, or my delusion, no matter which, that crime brings its own fatality with it. I am not only persuaded of Herncastle's guilt; I am even fanciful enough to believe that he will live to regret it, if he keeps the Diamond; and that others will live to regret taking it from him, if he gives the Diamond away.

THE STORY

FIRST PERIOD
THE LOSS OF THE DIAMOND (1848)

The events related by Gabriel Betteredge, house-steward
in the service of Julia, Lady Verinder

CHAPTER I

IN the first part of *Robinson Crusoe*, at page one hundred and twenty-nine, you will find it thus written:

'Now I saw, though too late, the Folly of beginning a Work before we count the Cost, and before we judge rightly of our own Strength to go through with it.'

Only yesterday, I opened my *Robinson Crusoe* at that place. Only this morning (May twenty-first, Eighteen hundred and fifty), came my lady's nephew, Mr Franklin Blake, and held a short conversation with me, as follows:—

'Betteredge,' says Mr Franklin, 'I have been to the lawyer's about some family matters; and, among other things, we have been talking of the loss of the Indian Diamond, in my aunt's house in Yorkshire, two years since. Mr Bruff thinks as I think, that the whole story ought, in the interests of truth, to be placed on record in writing—and the sooner the better.'

Not perceiving his drift yet, and thinking it always desirable for the sake of peace and quietness to be on the lawyer's side, I said I thought so too. Mr Franklin went on.

'In this matter of the Diamond,' he said, 'the characters of innocent people have suffered under suspicion already—as you know. The memories of innocent people may suffer, hereafter, for want of a record of the facts to which those who come after us can appeal. There can be no doubt that this strange family story of ours ought to be told. And I think, Betteredge, Mr Bruff and I together have hit on the right way of telling it.'

Very satisfactory to both of them, no doubt. But I failed to see what I myself had to do with it, so far.

'We have certain events to relate,' Mr Franklin proceeded; 'and we have certain persons concerned in those events who are capable of relating them. Starting from these plain facts, the idea is that we should all write the story of the Moonstone in turn—as far as our own personal experience extends, and no farther. We must begin by showing how the Diamond first fell into the hands of my uncle Herncastle, when he was serving in India fifty years since. This prefatory narrative I have already got by me in the form of an old family paper, which relates the necessary particulars on the authority of an eye-witness. The next thing to do is to tell how the Diamond found its way into my aunt's house in Yorkshire, two years ago, and how it came to be lost in little more than twelve hours afterwards. Nobody knows as much as you do, Betteredge, about what went on in the house at that time. So you must take the pen in hand, and start the story.'

In those terms I was informed of what my personal concern was with the matter of the Diamond. If you are curious to know what course I took under the circumstances, I beg to inform you that I did what you would probably have done in my place. I modestly declared myself to be quite unequal to the task imposed upon me—and I privately felt, all the time, that I was quite clever enough to perform it, if I only gave my own abilities a fair chance. Mr Franklin, I imagine, must have seen my private sentiments in my face. He declined to believe in my modesty; and he insisted on giving my abilities a fair chance.

Two hours have passed since Mr Franklin left me. As soon as his back was turned, I went to my writing desk to start the story. There I have sat helpless (in spite of my abilities) ever since; seeing what Robinson Crusoe saw, as quoted above—namely, the folly of beginning a work before we count the cost, and before we judge rightly of our own strength to go through with it. Please to remember, I opened the book by accident, at that bit, only the day before I rashly undertook the business now in hand; and, allow me to ask—if *that* isn't prophecy, what is?

I am not superstitious; I have read a heap of books in my time; I am a scholar in my own way. Though turned seventy, I possess an active memory, and legs to correspond. You are not to take it, if you please, as the saying of an ignorant man, when I express my opinion that such a book as *Robinson Crusoe* never was written, and never will be written again. I have tried that book for years—generally in combination with a pipe of tobacco—and I have found it my friend in need in all the necessities of this mortal life. When my spirits are bad—*Robinson Crusoe*. When I want advice—*Robinson Crusoe*. In past times when my wife plagued me; in present times when I have had a drop too much—*Robinson Crusoe*. I have worn out six stout *Robinson Crusoes* with hard work in my service. On my lady's last birthday she gave me a seventh. I took a drop too much on the strength of it; and *Robinson Crusoe* put me right again. Price four shillings and sixpence, bound in blue, with a picture into the bargain.

Still, this don't look much like starting the story of the Diamond—does it? I seem to be wandering off in search of Lord knows what, Lord knows where. We will take a new sheet of paper, if you please, and begin over again, with my best respects to you.

CHAPTER II

I SPOKE of my lady a line or two back. Now the Diamond could never have been in our house, where it was lost, if it had not been made a present of to my lady's daughter; and my lady's daughter would never have been in existence to have the present, if it had not been for my lady who (with pain and travail) produced her into the world. Consequently, if we begin with my lady, we are pretty sure of beginning far enough back. And that, let me tell you, when you have got such a job as mine in hand, is a real comfort at starting.

If you know anything of the fashionable world, you have heard tell of the three beautiful Miss Herncastles. Miss Adelaide; Miss Caroline; and Miss Julia—this last being the youngest and the best of the three sisters, in my opinion; and I had opportunities of judging, as you shall presently see. I went into the service of the old lord, their father (thank God, we have got nothing to do with *him*, in this business of the Diamond; he had the longest tongue and the shortest temper of any man, high or low, I ever met with)—I say, I went into the service of the old lord. as page-boy in waiting on the three honourable young ladies, at the age of fifteen years. There I lived till Miss Julia married the late Sir John Verinder. An excellent man, who only wanted somebody to manage him; and, between ourselves, he found somebody to do it; and what is more, he throve on it, and grew fat on it, and lived happy and died easy on it, dating from the day when my lady took him to church to be married, to the day when she relieved him of his last breath, and closed his eyes for ever.

I have omitted to state that I went with the bride to the bride's husband's house and lands down here. 'Sir John,' she says, 'I can't do without Gabriel Betteredge.' 'My lady,' says Sir John, 'I can't do without him, either.' That was his way with her—and that was how I went into his service. It was all one to me where I went, so long as my mistress and I were together.

Seeing that my lady took an interest in the out-of-door work, and the farms, and such like, I took an interest in them too—with all the more reason that I was a small farmer's seventh son myself. My lady got me put under the bailiff, and I did my best, and gave satisfaction, and got promotion accordingly. Some years later, on the Monday as it might be, my lady says, 'Sir John, your bailiff is a stupid old man. Pension him liberally, and let Gabriel Betteredge have his place.' On the Tuesday as it might be, Sir John says, 'My lady, the bailiff is pensioned liberally; and Gabriel Betteredge has got his place.' You hear more than enough of married people living together miserably. Here is an example to the contrary. Let it be a warning to some of you, and an encouragement to others. In the meantime, I will go on with my story.

Well, there I was in clover, you will say. Placed in a position of trust and honour with a little cottage of my own to live in, with my rounds on the estate to occupy me in the morning, and my accounts in the afternoon, and my pipe and my *Robinson Crusoe* in the evening—what more could I possibly want to make me happy? Remember what Adam wanted when he was alone in the Garden of Eden; and if you don't blame it in Adam, don't blame it in me.

The woman I fixed my eye on, was the woman who kept house for me at my cottage. Her name was Selina Goby. I agree with the late William Cobbett about picking a wife. See that she chews her food well, and sets her foot down firmly on the ground when she walks, and you're all right. Selina Goby was all right in both these respects, which was one reason for marrying her. I had another reason, likewise, entirely of my own discovering. Selina, being a single woman, made me pay so much a week for her board and services. Selina, being my wife, couldn't charge for her board, and would have to give me her services for nothing. That was the point of view I looked at it from. Economy—with a dash of love. I put it to my mistress, as in duty bound, just as I had put it to myself.

'I have been turning Selina Goby over in my mind,' I said, 'and I think, my lady, it will be cheaper to marry her than to keep her.'

My lady burst out laughing, and said she didn't know which to be most shocked at—my language or my principles. Some joke tickled her, I suppose, of the sort that you can't take unless you are a person of quality. Understanding nothing myself but that I was free to put it next to Selina, I went and put it accordingly. And what did Selina say? Lord! how little you must know of women, if you ask that. Of course she said, Yes.

As my time drew nearer, and there got to be talk of my having a new coat for the ceremony, my mind began to misgive me. I have compared notes with other men as to what they felt while they were in my interesting situation; and they have all acknowledged that, about a week before it happened, they privately wished themselves out of it. I went a trifle further than that myself; I actually rose up, as it were, and tried to get out of it. Not for nothing! I was too just a man to expect she would let me off for nothing. Compensation to the woman when the man gets out of it, is one of the laws of England. In obedience to the laws, and after turning it over carefully in my mind, I offered Selina Goby a feather-bed and fifty shillings to be off the bargain. You will hardly believe it, but it is nevertheless true—she was fool enough to refuse.

After that it was all over with me, of course. I got the new coat as cheap as I could, and I went through all the rest of it as cheap as I could. We were not a happy couple, and not a miserable couple. We were six of one and half-a-dozen of the other. How it was I don't understand, but we always seemed to be getting, with the best of motives, in one another's way. When I wanted to go upstairs, there was my wife coming down; or when my wife wanted to go down, there was I coming up. That is married life, according to my experience of it.

After five years of misunderstandings on the stairs, it pleased an all-wise Providence to relieve us of each other by taking my wife. I was left with my little girl Penelope, and with no other child. Shortly afterwards Sir John died, and my lady was left with her little girl, Miss Rachel, and no other child. I have written to very poor purpose of my lady, if you require to be told that my little Penelope was taken care of, under my good mistress's own eye, and was sent to school and taught, and made a sharp girl, and promoted, when old enough, to be Miss Rachel's own maid.

As for me, I went on with my business as bailiff year after year up to Christmas 1847, when there came a change in my life. On that day, my lady invited herself to a cup of tea alone with me in my cottage. She remarked that, reckoning from the year when I started as page-boy in the time of the old lord, I had been more than fifty years in her service, and she put into my hands a beautiful waistcoat of wool that she had worked herself, to keep me warm in the bitter winter weather.

I received this magnificent present quite at a loss to find words to thank my mistress with for the honour she had done me. To my great astonishment, it turned out, however, that the waistcoat was not an honour, but a bribe. My lady had discovered that I was getting old before I had discovered it myself, and she had come to my cottage to wheedle me (if I may use such an expression) into giving up my hard out-of-door work as bailiff, and taking my ease for the rest of my days as steward in the house. I made as good a fight of it against the indignity of taking my ease as I could. But my mistress knew the weak side of me; she put it as a favour to herself. The dispute between us ended, after that, in my wiping my eyes, like an old fool, with my new woollen waistcoat, and saying I would think about it.

The perturbation in my mind, in regard to thinking about it, being truly dreadful after my lady had gone away, I applied the remedy which I have never yet found to fail me in cases of doubt and emergency. I smoked a pipe and took a turn at *Robinson Crusoe*. Before I had occupied myself with that extraordinary book five minutes, I came on a comforting bit (page one hundred and fifty-eight), as follows: 'To-day we love, what to-morrow we hate.' I saw my way clear directly. To-day I was all for continuing to be farm-bailiff; to-morrow, on the authority of *Robinson Crusoe*, I should be all the other way. Take myself to-morrow while in to-morrow's humour, and the thing was done. My mind being relieved in this manner, I went to sleep that night in the character of Lady Verinder's farm-bailiff, and I woke up the next morning in the character of Lady Verinder's house-steward. All quite comfortable, and all through *Robinson Crusoe!*

My daughter Penelope has just looked over my shoulder to see what I have done so far. She remarks that it is beautifully written, and every word of it true. But she points out one objection. She says what I have done so far isn't in the least what I was wanted to do. I am asked to tell the story of the Diamond, and, instead of that, I have been telling the story of my own self. Curious, and quite beyond me to account for. I wonder whether the gentlemen who make a business and a living out of writing books, ever find their own selves getting in the way of their subjects, like me? If they do, I can feel for them. In the meantime, here is another false start, and more waste of good writing-paper. What's to be done now? Nothing that I know of, except for you to keep your temper, and for me to begin it all over again for the third time.

CHAPTER III

THE question of how I am to start the story properly I have tried to settle in two ways. First, by scratching my head, which led to nothing. Second, by consulting my daughter Penelope, which has resulted in an entirely new idea.

Penelope's notion is that I should set down what happened, regularly day by day, beginning with the day when we got the news that Mr Franklin Blake was expected on a visit to the house. When you come to fix your memory with a date in this way, it is wonderful what your memory will pick up for you upon that compulsion. The only difficulty is to fetch out the dates, in the first place. This Penelope offers to do for me by looking into her own diary, which she was taught to keep when she was at school, and which she has gone on keeping ever since. In answer to an improvement on this notion, devised by myself, namely, that she should tell the story instead of me, out of her own diary, Penelope observes, with a fierce look and a red face, that her journal is for her own private eye, and that no living creature shall ever know what is in it but herself. When I inquire what this means, Penelope says, 'Fiddlesticks!' I say, Sweethearts.

Beginning, then, on Penelope's plan, I beg to mention that I was specially called one Wednesday morning into my lady's own sitting-room, the date being the twenty-fourth of May, Eighteen hundred and forty-eight.

'Gabriel,' says my lady, 'here is news that will surprise you. Franklin Blake has come back from abroad. He has been staying with his father in London, and he is coming to us to-morrow to stop till next month, and keep Rachel's birthday.'

If I had had a hat in my hand, nothing but respect would have prevented me from throwing that hat up to the ceiling. I had not seen Mr Franklin since he was a boy, living along with us in this house. He was, out of all sight (as I remembered him), the nicest boy that ever spun a top or broke a window. Miss Rachel, who was present, and to whom I made that remark, observed, in return, that *she* remembered him as the most atrocious tyrant that ever tortured a doll, and the hardest driver of an exhausted little girl in string harness that England could produce. 'I burn with indignation, and I ache with fatigue,' was the way Miss Rachel summed it up, 'when I think of Franklin Blake.'

Hearing what I now tell you, you will naturally ask how it was that Mr Franklin should have passed all the years, from the time when he was a boy to the time when he was a man, out of his own country. I answer, because his father had the misfortune to be next heir to a Dukedom, and not to be able to prove it.

In two words, this was how the thing happened:

My lady's eldest sister married the celebrated Mr Blake—equally famous for his great riches, and his great suit at law. How many years he went on worrying the tribunals of his country to turn out the Duke in possession, and to put himself in the Duke's place—how many lawyers' purses he filled to bursting, and how many otherwise harmless people he set by the ears together disputing whether he was right or wrong—is more by a great deal than I can reckon up. His wife died, and two of his three children died, before the tribunals could make up their minds to show him the door and take no more of his money. When it was all over, and the Duke in possession was left in possession, Mr Blake discovered that the only way of being even with his country for the manner in which it had treated him, was not to let his country have the honour of educating his son. 'How can I trust my native institutions,' was the form in which he put it, 'after the way in which my native institutions have behaved to *me*?' Add to this, that Mr Blake disliked all boys, his own included, and you will admit that it could only end in one way. Master Franklin was taken from us in England, and was sent to institutions which his father *could* trust, in that superior country, Germany; Mr Blake himself, you will observe, remaining snug in England, to improve his fellow-countrymen in the Parliament House, and to publish a statement on the subject of the Duke in possession, which has remained an unfinished statement from that day to this.

There! thank God, that's told! Neither you nor I need trouble our heads any more about Mr Blake, senior. Leave him to the Dukedom; and let you and I stick to the Diamond.

The Diamond takes us back to Mr Franklin, who was the innocent means of bringing that unlucky jewel into the house.

Our nice boy didn't forget us after he went abroad. He wrote every now and then; sometimes to my lady, sometimes to Miss Rachel, and sometimes to me. We had had a transaction together, before he left, which consisted in his borrowing of me a ball of string, a four-bladed knife, and seven-and-six-pence in money—the colour of which last I have not seen, and never expect to see again. His letters to me chiefly related to borrowing more. I heard, however, from my lady, how he got on abroad, as he grew in years and stature. After he had learnt what the institutions of Germany could teach him, he gave the French a turn next, and the Italians a turn after that. They made him among them a sort of universal genius, as well as I could under-stand it. He wrote a little; he painted a little; he sang and played and composed a little—borrowing, as I suspect, in all these cases, just as he had borrowed from me. His mother's fortune (seven hundred a year) fell to him when he came of age, and ran through him, as it might be through a sieve. The more money he had, the more he wanted; there was a hole in Mr Franklin's pocket that nothing would sew up. Wherever he went, the lively, easy way of him made him welcome. He lived here, there, and everywhere; his address (as he used to put it himself) being 'Post Office, Europe—to be left till called for.' Twice over, he made up his mind to come back to England and see us; and twice over (saving your presence), some unmentionable woman stood in the way and stopped him. His third attempt succeeded, as you know already from what my lady told me. On Thursday the twenty-fifth of May, we were to see for the first time what our nice boy had grown to be as a man. He came of good blood; he had a high courage; and he was five-and-twenty years of age, by our reckoning. Now you know as much of Mr Franklin Blake as I did—before Mr Franklin Blake came down to our house.

The Thursday was as fine a summer's day as ever you saw: and my lady and Miss Rachel (not expecting Mr Franklin till dinner-time) drove out to lunch with some friends in the neighbourhood.

When they were gone, I went and had a look at the bedroom which had been got ready for our guest, and saw that all was straight. Then, being butler in my lady's establishment, as well as steward (at my own particular request, mind, and because it vexed me to see anybody but myself in possession of the key of the late Sir John's cellar)—then, I say, I fetched up some of our famous Latour claret, and set it in the warm summer air to take off the chill before dinner. Concluding to set myself in the warm summer air next—seeing that what is good for old claret is equally good for old age—I took up my beehive chair to go out into the back court, when I was stopped by hearing a sound like the soft beating of a drum, on the terrace in front of my lady's residence.

Going round to the terrace, I found three mahogany-coloured Indians, in white linen frocks and trousers, looking up at the house.

The Indians, as I saw on looking closer, had small hand-drums slung in front of them. Behind them stood a little delicate-looking light-haired English boy carrying a bag. I judged the fellows to be strolling conjurors, and the boy with the bag to be carrying the tools of their trade. One of the three, who spoke English and who exhibited, I must own, the most elegant manners, presently informed me that my judgment was right. He requested permission to show his tricks in the presence of the lady of the house.

Now I am not a sour old man. I am generally all for amusement, and the last person in the world to distrust another person because he happens to be a few shades darker than myself. But the best of us have our weaknesses—and my weakness, when I know a family plate-basket to be out on a pantry-table, is to be instantly reminded of that basket by the sight of a strolling stranger whose manners are superior to my own. I accordingly informed the Indian that the lady of the house was out; and I warned him and his party off the premises. He made me a beautiful bow in return; and he and his party went off the premises. On my side, I returned to my beehive chair, and set myself down on the sunny side of the court, and fell (if the truth must be owned), not exactly into a sleep, but into the next best thing to it.

I was roused up by my daughter Penelope running out at me as if the house was on fire. What do you think she wanted? She wanted to have the three Indian jugglers instantly taken up; for this reason, namely, that they knew who was coming from London to visit us, and that they meant some mischief to Mr Franklin Blake.

Mr Franklin's name roused me. I opened my eyes, and made my girl explain herself.

It appeared that Penelope had just come from our lodge, where she had been having a gossip with the lodge-keeper's daughter. The two girls had seen the Indians pass out, after I had warned them off, followed by their little boy. Taking it into their heads that the boy was ill-used by the foreigners—for no reason that I could discover, except that he was pretty and delicate-looking—the two girls had stolen along the inner side of the hedge between us and the road, and had watched the proceedings of the foreigners on the outer side. Those proceedings resulted in the performance of the following extraordinary tricks.

They first looked up the road, and down the road, and made sure that they were alone. Then they all three faced about, and stared hard in the direction of our house. Then they jabbered and disputed in their own language, and looked at each other like men in doubt. Then they all turned to their little English boy, as if they expected *him* to help them. And then the chief Indian, who spoke English, said to the boy, 'Hold out your hand.'

On hearing those dreadful words, my daughter Penelope said she didn't know what prevented her heart from flying straight out of her. I thought privately that it might have been her stays. All I said, however, was, 'You make my flesh creep.' (*Nota bene:* Women like these little compliments.)

Well, when the Indian said, 'Hold out your hand,' the boy shrunk back, and shook his head, and said he didn't like it. The Indian, thereupon, asked him (not at all unkindly), whether he would like to be sent back to London, and left where they had found him, sleeping in an empty basket in a market—a hungry, ragged, and forsaken little boy. This, it seems, ended the difficulty. The little chap unwillingly held out his hand. Upon that, the Indian took a bottle from his bosom, and poured out of it some black stuff, like ink, into the palm of the boy's hand. The Indian—first touching the boy's head, and making signs over it in the air—then said, 'Look.' The boy became quite stiff, and stood like a statue, looking into the ink in the hollow of his hand.

(So far, it seemed to me to be juggling, accompanied by a foolish waste of ink. I was beginning to feel sleepy again, when Penelope's next words stirred me up.)

The Indians looked up the road and down the road once more—and then the chief Indian said these words to the boy: 'See the English gentleman from foreign parts.'

The boy said, 'I see him.'

The Indian said, 'Is it on the road to this house, and on no other, that the English gentleman will travel to-day?'

The boy said, 'It is on the road to this house, and on no other, that the English gentleman will travel to-day.'

The Indian put a second question—after waiting a little first. He said: 'Has the English gentleman got It about him?'

The boy answered—also, after waiting a little first—'Yes.'

The Indian put a third and last question: 'Will the English gentleman come here, as he has promised to come, at the close of day?'

The boy said, 'I can't tell.'

The Indian asked why.

The boy said, 'I am tired. The mist rises in my head, and puzzles me. I can see no more to-day.'

With that, the catechism ended. The chief Indian said something in his own language to the other two, pointing to the boy, and pointing towards the town, in which (as we afterwards discovered) they were lodged. He then, after making more signs on the boy's head, blew on his forehead, and so woke him up with a start. After that, they all went on their way towards the town, and the girls saw them no more.

Most things they say have a moral, if you only look for it. What was the moral of this?

The moral was, as I thought: First, that the chief juggler had heard Mr Franklin's arrival talked of among the servants out-of-doors, and saw his way to making a little money by it. Second, that he and his men and boy (with a view to making the said money) meant to hang about till they saw my lady drive home, and then to come back, and foretell Mr Franklin's arrival by magic. Third, that Penelope had heard them rehearsing their hocus-pocus, like actors rehearsing a play. Fourth, that I should do well to have an eye, that evening, on the plate-basket. Fifth, that Penelope would do well to cool down, and leave me, her father, to doze off again in the sun.

That appeared to me to be the sensible view. If you know anything of the ways of young women, you won't be surprised to hear that Penelope wouldn't take it. The moral of the thing was serious, according to my daughter. She particularly reminded me of the Indian's third question, Has the English gentleman got It about him? 'Oh, father!' says Penelope, clasping her hands, 'don't joke about this. What does "It" mean?'

'We'll ask Mr Franklin, my dear,' I said, 'if you can wait till Mr Franklin comes.' I winked to show I meant that in joke. Penelope took it quite seriously. My girl's earnestness tickled me. 'What on earth should Mr Franklin know about it?' I inquired. 'Ask him,' says Penelope. 'And see whether *he* thinks it a laughing matter, too.' With that parting shot, my daughter left me.

I settled it with myself, when she was gone, that I really would ask Mr Franklin—mainly to set Penelope's mind at rest. What was said between us, when I did ask him, later on that same day, you will find set out fully in its proper place. But as I don't wish to raise your expectations and then disappoint them, I will take leave to warn you here—before we go any further—that you won't find the ghost of a joke in our conversation on the subject of the jugglers. To my great surprise, Mr Franklin, like Penelope, took the thing seriously. How seriously, you will understand, when I tell you that, in his opinion, 'It' meant the Moonstone.

CHAPTER IV

I AM truly sorry to detain you over me and my beehive chair. A sleepy old man, in a sunny back yard, is not an interesting object, I am well aware. But things must be put down in their places, as things actually happened— and you must please to jog on a little while longer with me, in expectation of Mr Franklin Blake's arrival later in the day.

Before I had time to doze off again, after my daughter Penelope had left me, I was disturbed by a rattling of plates and dishes in the servants' hall, which meant that dinner was ready. Taking my own meals in my own sitting-room, I had nothing to do with the servants' dinner, except to wish them a good stomach to it all round, previous to composing myself once more in my chair. I was just stretching my legs, when out bounced another woman on me. Not my daughter again; only Nancy, the kitchen-maid, this time. I was straight in her way out; and I observed, as she asked me to let her by, that she had a sulky face—a thing which, as head of the servants, I never allow, on principle, to pass me without inquiry.

'What are you turning your back on your dinner for?' I asked. 'What's wrong now, Nancy?'

Nancy tried to push by, without answering; upon which I rose up, and took her by the ear. She is a nice plump young lass, and it is customary with me to adopt that manner of showing that I personally approve of a girl.

'What's wrong now?' I said once more.

'Rosanna's late again for dinner,' says Nancy. 'And I'm sent to fetch her in. All the hard work falls on my shoulders in this house. Let me alone, Mr Betteredge!'

The person here mentioned as Rosanna was our second housemaid. Having a kind of pity for our second housemaid (why, you shall presently know), and seeing in Nancy's face that she would fetch her fellow-servant in with more hard words than might be needful under the circumstances, it struck me that I had nothing particular to do, and that I might as well fetch Rosanna myself; giving her a hint to be punctual in future, which I knew she would take kindly from *me*.

'Where is Rosanna?' I inquired.

'At the sands, of course!' says Nancy, with a toss of her head. 'She had another of her fainting fits this morning, and she asked to go out and get a breath of fresh air. I have no patience with her!'

'Go back to your dinner, my girl,' I said. 'I have patience with her, and I'll fetch her in.'

Nancy (who has a fine appetite) looked pleased. When she looks pleased, she looks nice. When she looks nice, I chuck her under the chin. It isn't immorality—it's only habit.

Well, I took my stick, and set off for the sands.

No! it won't do to set off yet. I am sorry again to detain you; but you really must hear the story of the sands, and the story of Rosanna—for this reason, that the matter of the Diamond touches them both nearly. How hard I try to get on with my statement without stopping by the way, and how badly I succeed! But, there!—Persons and Things do turn up so vexatiously in this life, and will in a manner insist on being noticed. Let us take it easy, and let us take it short; we shall be in the thick of the mystery soon, I promise you!

Rosanna (to put the Person before the Thing, which is but common politeness) was the only new servant in our house. About four months before the time I am writing of, my lady had been in London, and had gone over a Reformatory, intended to save forlorn women from drifting back into bad ways, after they had got released from prison. The matron, seeing my lady took an interest in the place, pointed out a girl to her, named Rosanna Spearman, and told her a most miserable story, which I haven't the heart to repeat here; for I don't like to be made wretched without any use, and no more do you. The upshot of it was, that Rosanna Spearman had been a thief, and not being of the sort that get up Companies in the City, and rob from thousands, instead of only robbing from one, the law laid hold of her, and the prison and the reformatory followed the lead of the law. The matron's opinion of Rosanna was (in spite of what she had done) that the girl was one in a thousand, and that she only wanted a chance to prove herself worthy of any Christian woman's interest in her. My lady (being a Christian woman, if ever there was one yet) said to the matron, upon that, 'Rosanna Spearman shall have her chance, in my service.' In a week afterwards, Rosanna Spearman entered this establishment as our second housemaid.

Not a soul was told the girl's story, excepting Miss Rachel and me. My lady, doing me the honour to consult me about most things, consulted me about Rosanna. Having fallen a good deal latterly into the late Sir John's way of always agreeing with my lady, I agreed with her heartily about Rosanna Spearman.

A fairer chance no girl could have had than was given to this poor girl of ours. None of the servants could cast her past life in her teeth, for none of the servants knew what it had been. She had her wages and her privileges, like the rest of them; and every now and then a friendly word from my lady, in private, to encourage her. In return, she showed herself, I am bound to say, well worthy of the kind treatment bestowed upon her. Though far from strong, and troubled occasionally with those fainting-fits already mentioned, she went about her work modestly and uncomplainingly, doing it carefully, and doing it well. But, somehow, she failed to make friends among the other women servants, excepting my daughter Penelope, who was always kind to Rosanna, though never intimate with her.

I hardly know what the girl did to offend them. There was certainly no beauty about her to make the others envious; she was the plainest woman in the house, with the additional misfortune of having one shoulder bigger than the other. What the servants chiefly resented, I think, was her silent tongue and her solitary ways. She read or worked in leisure hours when the rest gossiped. And when it came to her turn to go out, nine times out of ten she quietly put on her bonnet, and had her turn by herself. She never quarrelled, she never took offence; she only kept a certain distance, obstinately and civilly, between the rest of them and herself. Add to this that, plain as she was, there was just a dash of something that wasn't like a housemaid, and that *was* like a lady, about her. It might have been in her voice, or it might have been in her face. All I can say is, that the other women pounced on it like lightning the first day she came into the house, and said (which was most unjust) that Rosanna Spearman gave herself airs.

Having now told the story of Rosanna, I have only to notice one of the many queer ways of this strange girl to get on next to the story of the sands.

Our house is high up on the Yorkshire coast, and close by the sea. We have got beautiful walks all round us, in every direction but one. That one I acknowledge to be a horrid walk. It leads, for a quarter of a mile, through a melancholy plantation of firs, and brings you out between low cliffs on the loneliest and ugliest little bay on all our coast.

The sand-hills here run down to the sea, and end in two spits of rock jutting out opposite each other, till you lose sight of them in the water. One is called the North Spit, and one the South. Between the two, shifting backwards and forwards at certain seasons of the year, lies the most horrible quicksand on the shores of Yorkshire. At the turn of the tide, something goes on in the unknown deeps below, which sets the whole face of the quicksand shivering and trembling in a manner most remarkable to see, and which has given to it, among the people in our parts, the name of the Shivering Sand. A great bank, half a mile out, nigh the mouth of the bay, breaks the force of the main ocean coming in from the offing. Winter and summer, when the tide flows over the quicksand, the sea seems to leave the waves behind it on the bank, and rolls its waters in smoothly with a heave, and covers the sand in silence. A lonesome and a horrid retreat, I can tell you! No boat ever ventures into this bay. No children from our fishing-village, called Cobb's Hole, ever come here to play. The very birds of the air, as it seems to me, give the Shivering Sand a wide berth. That a young woman, with dozens of nice walks to choose from, and company to go with her, if she only said 'Come!' should prefer this place, and should sit and work or read in it, all alone, when it's her turn out, I grant you, passes belief. It's true, nevertheless, account for it as you may, that this was Rosanna Spearman's favourite walk, except when she went once or twice to Cobb's Hole, to see the only friend she had in our neighbourhood, of whom more anon. It's also true that I was now setting out for this same place, to fetch the girl in to dinner, which brings us round happily to our former point, and starts us fair again on our way to the sands.

I saw no sign of the girl in the plantation. When I got out, through the sand-hills, on to the beach, there she was, in her little straw bonnet, and her plain grey cloak that she always wore to hide her deformed shoulder as much as might be—there she was, all alone, looking out on the quicksand and the sea.

She started when I came up with her, and turned her head away from me. Not looking me in the face being another of the proceedings which, as head of the servants, I never allow, on principle, to pass without inquiry—I turned her round my way, and saw that she was crying. My bandanna handkerchief—one of six beauties given to me by my lady—was handy in my pocket. I took it out, and I said to Rosanna, 'Come and sit down, my dear, on the slope of the beach along with me. I'll dry your eyes for you first, and then I'll make so bold as to ask what you have been crying about.'

When you come to my age, you will find sitting down on the slope of a beach a much longer job than you think it now. By the time I was settled, Rosanna had dried her own eyes with a very inferior handkerchief to mine—cheap cambric. She looked very quiet, and very wretched; but she sat down by me like a good girl, when I told her. When you want to comfort a woman by the shortest way, take her on your knee. I thought of this golden rule. But there! Rosanna wasn't Nancy, and that's the truth of it!

'Now, tell me, my dear,' I said, 'what are you crying about?'

'About the years that are gone, Mr Betteredge,' says Rosanna quietly. 'My past life still comes back to me sometimes.'

'Come, come, my girl,' I said, 'your past life is all sponged out. Why can't you forget it?'

She took me by one of the lappets of my coat. I am a slovenly old man, and a good deal of my meat and drink gets splashed about on my clothes. Sometimes one of the women, and sometimes another, cleans me of my grease. The day before, Rosanna had taken out a spot for me on the lappet of my coat, with a new composition, warranted to remove anything. The grease was gone, but there was a little dull place left on the nap of the cloth where the grease had been. The girl pointed to that place, and shook her head.

'The stain is taken off,' she said. 'But the place shows, Mr Betteredge—the place shows!'

A remark which takes a man unawares by means of his own coat is not an easy remark to answer. Something in the girl herself, too, made me particularly sorry for her just then. She had nice brown eyes, plain as she was in other ways—and she looked at me with a sort of respect for my happy old age and my good character, as things for ever out of her own reach, which made my heart heavy for our second housemaid. Not feeling myself able to comfort her, there was only one other thing to do. That thing was—to take her in to dinner.

'Help me up,' I said. 'You're late for dinner, Rosanna—and I have come to fetch you in.'

'You, Mr Betteredge!' says she.

'They told Nancy to fetch you,' I said. 'But I thought you might like your scolding better, my dear, if it came from me.'

Instead of helping me up, the poor thing stole her hand into mine, and gave it a little squeeze. She tried hard to keep from crying again, and succeeded—for which I respected her. 'You're very kind, Mr Betteredge,' she said. 'I don't want any dinner to-day—let me bide a little longer here.'

'What makes you like to be here?' I asked. 'What is it that brings you everlastingly to this miserable place?'

'Something draws me to it,' says the girl, making images with her finger in the sand. 'I try to keep away from it, and I can't. Sometimes,' says she in a low voice, as if she was frightened at her own fancy, 'sometimes, Mr Betteredge, I think that my grave is waiting for me here.'

'There's roast mutton and suet-pudding waiting for you!' says I. 'Go in to dinner directly. This is what comes, Rosanna, of thinking on an empty stomach!' I spoke severely, being naturally indignant (at my time of life) to hear a young woman of five-and-twenty talking about her latter end!

She didn't seem to hear me: she put her hand on my shoulder, and kept me where I was, sitting by her side.

'I think the place has laid a spell on me,' she said. 'I dream of it night after night; I think of it when I sit stitching at my work. You know I am grateful, Mr Betteredge—you know I try to deserve your kindness, and my lady's confidence in me. But I wonder sometimes whether the life here is too quiet and too good for such a woman as I am, after all I have gone through, Mr Betteredge—after all I have gone through. It's more lonely to me to be among the other servants, knowing I am not what they are, than it is to be here. My lady doesn't know, the matron at the reformatory doesn't know, what a dreadful reproach honest people are in themselves to a woman like me. Don't scold me, there's a dear good man. I do my work, don't I? Please not to tell my lady I am discontented—I am not. My mind's unquiet, sometimes, that's all.' She snatched her hand off my shoulder, and suddenly pointed down to the quicksand. 'Look!' she said. 'Isn't it wonderful? isn't it terrible? I have seen it dozens of times, and it's always as new to me as if I had never seen it before!'

I looked where she pointed. The tide was on the turn, and the horrid sand began to shiver. The broad brown face of it heaved slowly, and then dimpled and quivered all over. 'Do you know what it looks like to *me?*' says Rosanna, catching me by the shoulder again. 'It looks as if it had hundreds of suffocating people under it—all struggling to get to the surface, and all sinking lower and lower in the dreadful deeps! Throw a stone in, Mr Betteredge! Throw a stone in, and let's see the sand suck it down!'

Here was unwholesome talk! Here was an empty stomach feeding on an unquiet mind! My answer—a pretty sharp one, in the poor girl's own interests, I promise you!—was at my tongue's end, when it was snapped short off on a sudden by a voice among the sand-hills shouting for me by my name. 'Betteredge!' cries the voice, 'where are you?' 'Here!' I shouted out in return, without a notion in my mind of who it was. Rosanna started to her feet, and stood looking towards the voice. I was just thinking of getting on my own legs next, when I was staggered by a sudden change in the girl's face.

Her complexion turned of a beautiful red, which I had never seen in it before; she brightened all over with a kind of speechless and breathless surprise. 'Who is it?' I asked. Rosanna gave me back my own question. 'Oh! who is it?' she said softly, more to herself than to me. I twisted round on the sand and looked behind me. There, coming out on us from among the hills, was a bright-eyed young gentleman, dressed in a beautiful fawn-coloured suit, with gloves and hat to match, with a rose in his button-hole, and a smile on his face that might have set the Shivering Sand itself smiling at him in return. Before I could get on my legs, he plumped down on the sand by the side of me, put his arm round my neck, foreign fashion, and gave me a hug that fairly squeezed the breath out of my body. 'Dear old Betteredge!' says he. 'I owe you seven-and-sixpence. Now do you know who I am?'

Lord bless us and save us! Here—four good hours before we expected him—was Mr Franklin Blake!

Before I could say a word, I saw Mr Franklin, a little surprised to all appearance, look up from me to Rosanna. Following his lead, I looked at the girl too. She was blushing of a deeper red than ever, seemingly at having caught Mr Franklin's eye; and she turned and left us suddenly, in a confusion quite unaccountable to my mind, without either making her curtsey to the gentleman or saying a word to me. Very unlike her usual self: a civiller and better-behaved servant, in general, you never met with.

'That's an odd girl,' says Mr Franklin. 'I wonder what she sees in me to surprise her?'

'I suppose, sir,' I answered, drolling on our young gentleman's Continental education, 'it's the varnish from foreign parts.'

I set down here Mr Franklin's careless question, and my foolish answer, as a consolation and encouragement to all stupid people—it being, as I have remarked, a great satisfaction to our inferior fellow-creatures to find that their betters are, on occasions, no brighter than they are. Neither Mr Franklin, with his wonderful foreign training, nor I, with my age, experience, and natural mother-wit, had the ghost of an idea of what Rosanna Spearman's unaccountable behaviour really meant. She was out of our thoughts, poor soul, before we had seen the last flutter of her little grey cloak among the sand-hills. And what of that? you will ask, naturally enough. Read on, good friend, as patiently as you can, and perhaps you will be as sorry for Rosanna Spearman as I was, when I found out the truth.

CHAPTER V

THE first thing I did, after we were left together alone, was to make a third attempt to get up from my seat on the sand. Mr Franklin stopped me.

'There is one advantage about this horrid place,' he said; 'we have got it all to ourselves. Stay where you are, Betteredge; I have something to say to you.'

While he was speaking, I was looking at him, and trying to see something of the boy I remembered, in the man before me. The man put me out. Look as I might, I could see no more of his boy's rosy cheeks than of his boy's trim little jacket. His complexion had got pale: his face, at the lower part, was covered, to my great surprise and disappointment, with a curly brown beard and mustachios. He had a lively touch-and-go way with him, very pleasant and engaging, I admit; but nothing to compare with his free-and-easy manners of other times. To make matters worse, he had promised to be tall, and had not kept his promise. He was neat, and slim, and well made; but he wasn't by an inch or two up to the middle height. In short, he baffled me altogether. The years that had passed had left nothing of his old self, except the bright, straightforward look in his eyes. There I found our nice boy again, and there I concluded to stop in my investigation.

'Welcome back to the old place, Mr Franklin,' I said. 'All the more welcome, sir, that you have come some hours before we expected you.'

'I have a reason for coming before you expected me,' answered Mr Franklin. 'I suspect, Betteredge, that I have been followed and watched in London, for the last three or four days; and I have travelled by the morning instead of the afternoon train, because I wanted to give a certain dark-looking stranger the slip.'

Those words did more than surprise me. They brought back to my mind, in a flash, the three jugglers, and Penelope's notion that they meant some mischief to Mr Franklin Blake.

'Who's watching you, sir,—and why?' I inquired.

'Tell me about the three Indians you have had at the house to-day,' says Mr Franklin, without noticing my question. 'It's just possible, Betteredge, that my stranger and your three jugglers may turn out to be pieces of the same puzzle.'

'How do you come to know about the jugglers, sir?' I asked, putting one question on the top of another, which was bad manners, I own. But you don't expect much from poor human nature—so don't expect much from me.

'I saw Penelope at the house,' says Mr Franklin; 'and Penelope told me. Your daughter promised to be a pretty girl, Betteredge, and she has kept her promise. Penelope has got a small ear and a small foot. Did the late Mrs Betteredge possess those inestimable advantages?'

'The late Mrs Betteredge possessed a good many defects, sir,' says I. 'One of them (if you will pardon my mentioning it) was never keeping to the matter in hand. She was more like a fly than a woman: she couldn't settle on anything.'

'She would just have suited me,' says Mr Franklin. 'I never settle on anything either. Betteredge, your edge is better than ever. Your daughter said as much, when I asked for particulars about the jugglers. "Father will tell you, sir. He's a wonderful man for his age; and he expresses himself beautifully." Penelope's own words—blushing divinely. Not even my respect for you prevented me from—never mind; I knew her when she was a child, and she's none the worse for it. Let's be serious. What did the jugglers do?'

I was something dissatisfied with my daughter—not for letting Mr Franklin kiss her; Mr Franklin was welcome to *that*—but for forcing me to tell her foolish story at second hand. However, there was no help for it now but to mention the circumstances. Mr Franklin's merriment all died away as I went on. He sat knitting his eyebrows, and twisting his beard. When I had done, he repeated after me two of the questions which the chief juggler had put to the boy—seemingly for the purpose of fixing them well in his mind.

' "Is it on the road to this house, and on no other, that the English gentleman will travel to-day?" "Has the English gentleman got It about him?" I suspect,' says Mr Franklin, pulling a little sealed paper parcel out of his pocket, 'that "It" means *this*. And "this," Betteredge, means my uncle Herncastle's famous Diamond.'

'Good Lord, sir!' I broke out, 'how do you come to be in charge of the wicked Colonel's Diamond.'

'The wicked Colonel's will has left his Diamond as a birthday present to my cousin Rachel,' says Mr Franklin. 'And my father, as the wicked Colonel's executor, has given it in charge to me to bring down here.'

If the sea, then oozing in smoothly over the Shivering Sand, had been changed into dry land before my own eyes, I doubt if I could have been more surprised than I was when Mr Franklin spoke those words.

'The Colonel's Diamond left to Miss Rachel!' says I. 'And your father, sir, the Colonel's executor! Why, I would have laid any bet you like, Mr Franklin, that your father wouldn't have touched the Colonel with a pair of tongs!'

'Strong language, Betteredge! What was there against the Colonel? He belonged to your time, not to mine. Tell me what you know about him, and I'll tell you how my father came to be his executor, and more besides. I have made some discoveries in London about my uncle Herncastle and his Diamond, which have rather an ugly look to my eyes; and I want you to confirm them. You called him the "wicked Colonel" just now. Search your memory, my old friend, and tell me why.'

I saw he was in earnest, and I told him.

Here follows the substance of what I said, written out entirely for your benefit. Pay attention to it, or you will be all abroad, when we get deeper into the story. Clear your mind of the children, or the dinner, or the new bonnet, or what not. Try if you can't forget politics, horses, prices in the City, and grievances at the club. I hope you won't take this freedom on my part amiss; it's only a way I have of appealing to the gentle reader. Lord! haven't I seen you with the greatest authors in your hands, and don't I know how ready your attention is to wander when it's a book that asks for it, instead of a person?

I spoke, a little way back, of my lady's father, the old lord with the short temper and the long tongue. He had five children in all. Two sons to begin with; then, after a long time, his wife broke out breeding again, and the three young ladies came briskly one after the other, as fast as the nature of things would permit; my mistress, as before mentioned, being the youngest and best of the three. Of the two sons, the eldest, Arthur, inherited the title and estates. The second, the Honourable John, got a fine fortune left him by a relative, and went into the army.

It's an ill bird, they say, that fouls its own nest. I look on the noble family of the Herncastles as being my nest; and I shall take it as a favour if I am not expected to enter into particulars on the subject of the Honourable John. He was, I honestly believe, one of the greatest blackguards that ever lived. I can hardly say more or less for him than that. He went into the army, beginning in the Guards. He had to leave the Guards before he was two-and-twenty— never mind why. They are very strict in the army, and they were too strict for the Honourable John. He went out to India to see whether they were equally strict there, and to try a little active service. In the matter of bravery (to give him his due), he was a mixture of bull-dog and game-cock, with a dash of the savage. He was at the taking of Seringapatam. Soon afterwards he changed into another regiment, and, in course of time, changed into a third. In the third he got his last step as lieutenant-colonel, and, getting that, got also a sunstroke, and came home to England.

He came back with a character that closed the doors of all his family against him, my lady (then just married) taking the lead, and declaring (with Sir John's approval, of course) that her brother should never enter any house of hers. There was more than one slur on the Colonel that made people shy of him; but the blot of the Diamond is all I need mention here.

It was said he had got possession of his Indian jewel by means which, bold as he was, he didn't dare acknowledge. He never attempted to sell it—not being in need of money, and not (to give him his due again) making money an object. He never gave it away; he never even showed it to any living soul. Some said he was afraid of its getting him into a difficulty with the military authorities; others (very ignorant indeed of the real nature of the man) said he was afraid, if he showed it, of its costing him his life.

There was perhaps a grain of truth mixed up with this last report. It was false to say that he was afraid; but it was a fact that his life had been twice threatened in India; and it was firmly believed that the Moonstone was at the bottom of it. When he came back to England, and found himself avoided by everybody, the Moonstone was thought to be at the bottom of it again. The mystery of the Colonel's life got in the Colonel's way, and outlawed him, as you may say, among his own people. The men wouldn't let him into their clubs; the women—more than one—whom he wanted to marry, refused him; friends and relations got too near-sighted to see him in the street.

Some men in this mess would have tried to set themselves right with the world. But to give in, even when he was wrong, and had all society against him, was not the way of the Honourable John. He had kept the Diamond, in flat defiance of assassination, in India. He kept the Diamond, in flat defiance of public opinion, in England. There you have the portrait of the man before you, as in a picture: a character that braved everything; and a face, handsome as it was, that looked possessed by the devil.

We heard different rumours about him from time to time. Sometimes they said he was given up to smoking opium and collecting old books; sometimes he was reported to be trying strange things in chemistry; sometimes he was seen carousing and amusing himself among the lowest people in the lowest slums of London. Anyhow, a solitary, vicious, underground life was the life the Colonel led. Once, and once only, after his return to England, I myself saw him, face to face.

About two years before the time of which I am now writing, and about a year and a half before the time of his death, the Colonel came unexpectedly to my lady's house in London. It was the night of Miss Rachel's birthday, the twenty-first of June; and there was a party in honour of it, as usual. I received a message from the footman to say that a gentleman wanted to see me. Going up into the hall, there I found the Colonel, wasted, and worn, and old, and shabby, and as wild and as wicked as ever.

'Go up to my sister,' says he, 'and say that I have called to wish my niece many happy returns of the day.'

He had made attempts by letter, more than once already, to be reconciled with my lady, for no other purpose, I am firmly persuaded, than to annoy her. But this was the first time he had actually come to the house. I had it on the tip of my tongue to say that my mistress had a party that night. But the devilish look of him daunted me. I went upstairs with his message, and left him, by his own desire, waiting in the hall. The servants stood staring at him, at a distance, as if he was a walking engine of destruction, loaded with powder and shot, and likely to go off among them at a moment's notice.

My lady had a dash—no more—of the family temper. 'Tell Colonel Herncastle,' she said, when I gave her her brother's message, 'that Miss Verinder is engaged, and that *I* decline to see him.' I tried to plead for a civiller answer than that; knowing the Colonel's constitutional superiority to the restraints which govern gentlemen in general. Quite useless! The family temper flashed out at me directly. 'When I want your advice,' says my lady, 'you know that I always ask for it. I don't ask for it now.' I went downstairs with the message, of which I took the liberty of presenting a new and amended edition of my own contriving, as follows: 'My lady and Miss Rachel regret that they are engaged, Colonel; and beg to be excused having the honour of seeing you.'

I expected him to break out, even at that polite way of putting it. To my surprise he did nothing of the sort; he alarmed me by taking the thing with an unnatural quiet. His eyes, of a glittering bright grey, just settled on me for a moment; and he laughed, not *out* of himself, like other people, but *into* himself, in a soft, chuckling, horridly mischievous way. 'Thank you, Betteredge,' he said. 'I shall remember my niece's birthday.' With that, he turned on his heel, and walked out of the house.

The next birthday came round, and we heard he was ill in bed. Six months afterwards—that is to say, six months before the time I am now writing of—there came a letter from a highly respectable clergyman to my lady. It communicated two wonderful things in the way of family news. First, that the Colonel had forgiven his sister on his death-bed. Second, that he had forgiven everybody else, and had made a most edifying end. I have myself (in spite of the bishops and the clergy) an unfeigned respect for the Church; but I am firmly persuaded, at the same time, that the devil remained in undisturbed possession of the Honourable John, and that the last abominable act in the life of that abominable man was (saving your presence) to take the clergyman in!

This was the sum-total of what I had to tell Mr Franklin. I remarked that he listened more and more eagerly the longer I went on. Also, that the story of the Colonel being sent away from his sister's door, on the occasion of his niece's birthday, seemed to strike Mr Franklin like a shot that had hit the mark. Though he didn't acknowledge it, I saw that I had made him uneasy, plainly enough, in his face.

'You have said your say, Betteredge,' he remarked. 'It's my turn now. Before, however, I tell you what discoveries I have made in London, and how I came to be mixed up in this matter of the Diamond, I want to know one thing. You look, my old friend, as if you didn't quite understand the object to be answered by this consultation of ours. Do your looks belie you?'

'No, sir,' I said. 'My looks, on this occasion at any rate, tell the truth.'

'In that case,' says Mr Franklin, 'suppose I put you up to my point of view, before we go any further. I see three very serious questions involved in the Colonel's birthday-gift to my cousin Rachel. Follow me carefully, Betteredge; and count me off on your fingers, if it will help you,' says Mr Franklin, with a certain pleasure in showing how clear-headed he could be, which reminded me wonderfully of old times when he was a boy. 'Question the first: Was the Colonel's Diamond the object of a conspiracy in India? Question the second: Has the conspiracy followed the Colonel's Diamond to England? Question the third: Did the Colonel know the conspiracy followed the Diamond; and has he purposely left a legacy of trouble and danger to his sister, through the innocent medium of his sister's child? *That* is what I am driving at, Betteredge. Don't let me frighten you.'

It was all very well to say that, but he *had* frightened me.

If he was right, here was our quiet English house suddenly invaded by a devilish Indian Diamond—bringing after it a conspiracy of living rogues, set loose on us by the vengeance of a dead man. There was our situation as revealed to me in Mr Franklin's last words! Who ever heard the like of it—in the nineteenth century, mind; in an age of progress, and in a country which rejoices in the blessings of the British constitution? Nobody ever heard the like of it, and, consequently, nobody can be expected to believe it. I shall go on with my story, however, in spite of that.

When you get a sudden alarm, of the sort that I had got now, nine times out of ten the place you feel it in is your stomach. When you feel it in your stomach, your attention wanders, and you begin to fidget. I fidgeted silently in my place on the sand. Mr Franklin noticed me, contending with a perturbed stomach or mind—which you please; they mean the same thing—and, checking himself just as he was starting with his part of the story, said to me sharply, 'What do you want?'

What did I want? I didn't tell *him*; but I'll tell *you*, in confidence. I wanted a whiff of my pipe, and a turn at *Robinson Crusoe*.

CHAPTER VI

KEEPING my private sentiments to myself, I respectfully requested Mr Franklin to go on. Mr Franklin replied, 'Don't fidget, Betteredge,' and went on.

Our young gentleman's first words informed me that his discoveries, concerning the wicked Colonel and the Diamond, had begun with a visit which he had paid (before he came to us) to the family lawyer, at Hampstead. A chance word dropped by Mr Franklin, when the two were alone, one day, after dinner, revealed that he had been charged by his father with a birthday present to be taken to Miss Rachel. One thing led to another; and it ended in the lawyer mentioning what the present really was, and how the friendly connexion between the late Colonel and Mr Blake, senior, had taken its rise. The facts here are really so extraordinary, that I doubt if I can trust my own language to do justice to them. I prefer trying to report Mr Franklin's discoveries, as nearly as may be, in Mr Franklin's own words.

'You remember the time, Betteredge,' he said, 'when my father was trying to prove his title to that unlucky Dukedom? Well! that was also the time when my uncle Herncastle returned from India. My father discovered that his brother-in-law was in possession of certain papers which were likely to be of service to him in his lawsuit. He called on the Colonel, on pretence of welcoming him back to England. The Colonel was not to be deluded in that way. "You want something," he said, "or you would never have compromised your reputation by calling on *me*." My father saw that the one chance for him was to show his hand; he admitted, at once, that he wanted the papers. The Colonel asked for a day to consider his answer. His answer came in the shape of a most extraordinary letter, which my friend the lawyer showed me. The Colonel began by saying that he wanted something of my father, and that he begged to propose an exchange of friendly services between them. The fortune of war (that was the expression he used) had placed him in possession of one of the largest Diamonds in the world; and he had reason to believe that neither he nor his precious jewel was safe in any house, in any quarter of the globe, which they occupied together. Under these alarming circumstances, he had determined to place his Diamond in the keeping of another person. That person was not expected to run any risk. He might deposit the precious stone in any place especially guarded and set apart—like a banker's or jeweller's strong-room—for the safe custody of valuables of high price. His main personal responsibility in the matter was to be of the passive kind. He was to undertake—either by himself, or by a trustworthy representative—to receive at a prearranged address, on certain prearranged days in every year, a note from the Colonel, simply stating the fact that he was a living man at that date. In the event of the date passing over without the note being received, the Colonel's silence might be taken as a sure token of the Colonel's death by murder. In that case, and in no other, certain sealed instructions relating to the disposal of the Diamond, and deposited with it, were to be opened, and followed implicitly. If my father chose to accept this strange charge, the Colonel's papers were at his disposal in return. That was the letter.'

'What did your father do, sir?' I asked.

'Do?' says Mr Franklin. 'I'll tell you what he did. He brought the invaluable faculty, called common sense, to bear on the Colonel's letter. The whole thing, he declared, was simply absurd. Somewhere in his Indian wanderings, the Colonel had picked up with some wretched crystal which he took for a diamond. As for the danger of his being murdered, and the precautions devised to preserve his life and his piece of crystal, this was the nineteenth century, and any man in his senses had only to apply to the police. The Colonel had been a notorious opium-eater for years past; and, if the only way of getting at the valuable papers he possessed was by accepting a matter of opium as a matter of fact, my father was quite willing to take the ridiculous responsibility imposed on him—all the more readily that it involved no trouble to himself. The Diamond and the sealed instructions went into his banker's strong-room, and the Colonel's letters, periodically reporting him a living man, were received and opened by our family lawyer, Mr Bruff, as my father's representative. No sensible person, in a similar position, could have viewed the matter in any other way. Nothing in this world, Betteredge, is probable unless it appeals to our own trumpery experience; and we only believe in a romance when we see it in a newspaper.'

It was plain to me from this, that Mr Franklin thought his father's notion about the Colonel hasty and wrong.

'What is your own private opinion about the matter, sir?' I asked.

'Let's finish the story of the Colonel first,' says Mr Franklin. 'There is a curious want of system, Betteredge, in the English mind; and your question, my old friend, is an instance of it. When we are not occupied in making machinery, we are (mentally speaking) the most slovenly people in the universe.'

'So much,' I thought to myself, 'for a foreign education! He has learned that way of girding at us in France, I suppose.'

Mr Franklin took up the lost thread, and went on.

'My father,' he said, 'got the papers he wanted, and never saw his brother-in-law again from that time. Year after year, on the prearranged days, the prearranged letter came from the Colonel, and was opened by Mr Bruff. I have seen the letters, in a heap, all of them written in the same brief, business-like form of words: 'Sir,—This is to certify that I am still a living man. Let the Diamond be. John Herncastle.' That was all he ever wrote, and that came regularly to the day; until some six or eight months since, when the form of the letter varied for the first time. It ran now: 'Sir,—They tell me I am dying. Come to me, and help me to make my will.' Mr Bruff went, and found him, in the little suburban villa, surrounded by its own grounds, in which he had lived alone, ever since he had left India. He had dogs, cats, and birds to keep him company; but no human being near him, except the person who came daily to do the house-work, and the doctor at the bedside. The will was a very simple matter. The Colonel had dissipated the greater part of his fortune in his chemical investigations. His will began and ended in three clauses, which he dictated from his bed, in perfect possession of his faculties. The first clause provided for the safe keeping and support of his animals. The second founded a professorship of experimental chemistry at a northern university. The third bequeathed the Moonstone as a birthday present to his niece, on condition that my father would act as executor. My father at first refused to act. On second thoughts, however, he

gave way, partly because he was assured that the executorship would involve
him in no trouble; partly because Mr Bruff suggested, in Rachel's interest,
that the Diamond might be worth something, after all.'

'Did the Colonel give any reason, sir,' I inquired, 'why he left the
Diamond to Miss Rachel?'

'He not only gave the reason—he had the reason written in his will,' said
Mr Franklin. 'I have got an extract, which you shall see presently. Don't be
slovenly-minded, Betteredge! One thing at a time. You have heard about the
Colonel's Will; now you must hear what happened after the Colonel's death.
It was formally necessary to have the Diamond valued, before the Will could
be proved. All the jewellers consulted, at once confirmed the Colonel's
assertion that he possessed one of the largest diamonds in the world. The
question of accurately valuing it presented some serious difficulties, Its size
made it a phenomenon in the diamond market; its colour placed it in a
category by itself; and, to add to these elements of uncertainty, there was a
defect, in the shape of a flaw, in the very heart of the stone. Even with this
last serious drawback, however, the lowest of the various estimates given was
twenty thousand pounds. Conceive my father's astonishment! He had been
within a hair's-breadth of refusing to act as executor, and of allowing this
magnificent jewel to be lost to the family. The interest he took in the matter
now, induced him to open the sealed instructions which had been deposited
with the Diamond. Mr Bruff showed this document to me, with the other
papers; and it suggests (to my mind) a clue to the nature of the conspiracy
which threatened the Colonel's life.'

'Then you do believe, sir,' I said, 'that there was a conspiracy?'

'Not possessing my father's excellent common sense,' answered
Mr Franklin, 'I believe the Colonel's life was threatened, exactly as the
Colonel said. The sealed instructions, as I think, explain how it was that he
died, after all, quietly in his bed. In the event of his death by violence (that
is to say, in the absence of the regular letter from him at the appointed date),
my father was then directed to send the Moonstone secretly to Amsterdam.
It was to be deposited in that city with a famous diamond-cutter, and it was
to be cut up into from four to six separate stones. The stones were then to
be sold for what they would fetch, and the proceeds were to be applied
to the founding of that professorship of experimental chemistry, which the
Colonel has since endowed by his Will. Now, Betteredge, exert those sharp
wits of yours, and observe the conclusion to which the Colonel's instructions
point!'

I instantly exerted my wits. They were of the slovenly English sort; and
they consequently muddled it all, until Mr Franklin took them in hand, and
pointed out what they ought to see.

'Remark,' says Mr Franklin, 'that the integrity of the Diamond, as a
whole stone, is here artfully made dependent on the preservation from

violence of the Colonel's life. He is not satisfied with saying to the enemies he dreads, 'Kill me—and you will be no nearer to the Diamond than you are now; it is where you can't get at it—in the guarded strong-room of a bank.' He says instead, "Kill me—and the Diamond will be the Diamond no longer; its identity will be destroyed." What does that mean?'

Here I had (as I thought) a flash of the wonderful foreign brightness.

'I know,' I said. 'It means lowering the value of the stone, and cheating the rogues in that way!'

'Nothing of the sort,' says Mr Franklin. 'I have inquired about that. The flawed Diamond, cut up, would actually fetch more than the Diamond as it now is; for this plain reason—that from four to six perfect brilliants might be cut from it, which would be, collectively, worth more money than the large—but imperfect—single stone. If robbery for the purpose of gain was at the bottom of the conspiracy, the Colonel's instructions absolutely made the Diamond better worth stealing. More money could have been got for it, and the disposal of it in the diamond market would have been infinitely easier, if it had passed through the hands of the workmen of Amsterdam.'

'Lord bless us, sir!' I burst out. 'What was the plot, then?'

'A plot organised among the Indians who orginally owned the jewel,' says Mr Franklin—'a plot with some old Hindoo superstition at the bottom of it. That is my opinion, confirmed by a family paper which I have about me at this moment.'

I saw, now, why the appearance of the three Indian jugglers at our house had presented itself to Mr Franklin in the light of a circumstance worth noting.

'I don't want to force my opinion on you,' Mr Franklin went on. 'The idea of certain chosen servants of an old Hindoo superstition devoting themselves, through all difficulties and dangers, to watching the opportunity of recovering their sacred gem, appears to *me* to be perfectly consistent with everything that we know of the patience of Oriental races, and the influence of Oriental religions. But then I am an imaginative man; and the butcher, the baker, and the tax-gatherer are not the only credible realities in existence to *my* mind. Let the guess I have made at the truth in this matter go for what it is worth, and let us get on to the only practical question that concerns us. Does the conspiracy against the Moonstone survive the Colonel's death? And did the Colonel know it, when he left the birthday gift to his niece?'

I began to see my lady and Miss Rachel at the end of it all, now. Not a word he said escaped me.

'I was not very willing, when I discovered the story of the Moonstone,' said Mr Franklin, 'to be the means of bringing it here. But Mr Bruff reminded me that somebody must put my cousin's legacy into my cousin's hands—and that I might as well do it as anybody else. After taking the Diamond out of the bank, I fancied I was followed in the streets by a shabby, dark-complexioned man. I went to my father's house to pick up my luggage, and found a letter there, which unexpectedly detained me in London. I went back to the bank with the Diamond, and thought I saw the shabby man again. Taking the Diamond once more out of the bank this morning, I saw the man for the third time, gave him the slip, and started (before he recovered the trace of me) by the morning instead of the afternoon train. Here I am, with the Diamond safe and sound—and what is the first news that meets me? I find that three strolling Indians have been at the house, and that my arrival from London, and something which I am expected to have about me, are two special objects of investigation to them when they believe themselves to be alone. I don't waste time and words on their pouring the ink into the boy's hand, and telling him to look in it for a man at a distance, and for something in that man's pocket. The thing (which I have often seen done in the East) is "hocus-pocus" in my opinion, as it is in yours. The present question for us to decide is, whether I am wrongly attaching a meaning to a mere accident? or whether we really have evidence of the Indians being on the track of the Moonstone, the moment it is removed from the safe keeping of the bank?'

Neither he nor I seemed to fancy dealing with this part of the inquiry. We looked at each other, and then we looked at the tide, oozing in smoothly, higher and higher, over the Shivering Sand.

'What are you thinking of?' says Mr Franklin, suddenly.

'I was thinking, sir,' I answered, 'that I should like to shy the Diamond into the quicksand, and settle the question in *that* way.'

'If you have got the value of the stone in your pocket,' answered Mr Franklin, 'say so, Betteredge, and in it goes!'

It's curious to note, when your mind's anxious, how very far in the way of relief a very small joke will go. We found a fund of merriment, at the time, in the notion of making away with Miss Rachel's lawful property, and getting Mr Blake, as executor, into dreadful trouble—though where the merriment was, I am quite at a loss to discover now.

Mr Franklin was the first to bring the talk back to the talk's proper purpose. He took an envelope out of his pocket, opened it, and handed to me the paper inside.

'Betteredge,' he said, 'we must face the question of the Colonel's motive in leaving this legacy to his niece, for my aunt's sake. Bear in mind how Lady Verinder treated her brother from the time when he returned to England, to the time when he told you he should remember his niece's birthday. And read that.'

He gave me the extract from the Colonel's Will. I have got it by me while I write these words; and I copy it, as follows, for your benefit:

'Thirdly, and lastly, I give and bequeath to my niece, Rachel Verinder, daughter and only child of my sister, Julia Verinder, widow—if her mother, the said Julia Verinder, shall be living on the said Rachel Verinder's next Birthday after my death—the yellow Diamond belonging to me, and known in the East by the name of The Moonstone: subject to this condition, that her mother, the said Julia Verinder, shall be living at the time. And I hereby desire my executor to give my Diamond, either by his own hands or by the hands of some trustworthy representative whom he shall appoint, into the personal possession of my said niece Rachel, on her next birthday after my death, and in the presence, if possible, of my sister, the said Julia Verinder. And I desire that my said sister may be informed, by means of a true copy of this, the third and last clause of my Will, that I give the Diamond to her daughter Rachel, in token of my free forgiveness of the injury which her conduct towards me has been the means of inflicting on my reputation in my lifetime; and especially in proof that I pardon, as becomes a dying man, the insult offered to me as an officer and a gentleman, when her servant, by her orders, closed the door of her house against me, on the occasion of her daughter's birthday.'

More words followed these, providing if my lady was dead, or if Miss Rachel was dead, at the time of the testator's decease, for the Diamond being sent to Holland, in accordance with the sealed instructions originally deposited with it. The proceeds of the sale were, in that case, to be added to the money already left by the Will for the professorship of chemistry at the university in the north.

I handed the paper back to Mr Franklin, sorely troubled what to say to him. Up to that moment, my own opinion had been (as you know) that the Colonel had died as wickedly as he had lived. I don't say the copy from his Will actually converted me from that opinion: I only say it staggered me.

'Well,' says Mr Franklin, 'now you have read the Colonel's own statement, what do you say? In bringing the Moonstone to my aunt's house, am I serving his vengeance blindfold, or am I vindicating him in the character of a penitent and Christian man?'

'It seems hard to say, sir,' I answered, 'that he died with a horrid revenge in his heart, and a horrid lie on his lips. God alone knows the truth. Don't ask *me*.'

Mr Franklin sat twisting and turning the extract from the Will in his fingers, as if he expected to squeeze the truth out of it in that manner. He altered quite remarkably, at the same time. From being brisk and bright, he now became, most unaccountably, a slow, solemn, and pondering young man.

'This question has two sides,' he said. 'An Objective side, and a Subjective side. Which are we to take?'

He had had a German education as well as a French. One of the two had been in undisturbed possession of him (as I supposed) up to this time. And now (as well as I could make out) the other was taking its place. It is one of my rules in life, never to notice what I don't understand. I steered a middle course between the Objective side and the Subjective side. In plain English I stared hard, and said nothing.

'Let's extract the inner meaning of this,' says Mr Franklin. 'Why did my uncle leave the Diamond to Rachel? Why didn't he leave it to my aunt?'

'That's not beyond guessing, sir, at any rate,' I said. 'Colonel Herncastle knew my lady well enough to know that she would have refused to accept any legacy that came to her from *him.*'

'How did he know that Rachel might not refuse to accept it, too?'

'Is there any young lady in existence, sir, who could resist the temptation of accepting such a birthday present as The Moonstone?'

'That's the Subjective view,' says Mr Franklin. 'It does you great credit, Betteredge, to be able to take the Subjective view. But there's another mystery about the Colonel's legacy which is not accounted for yet. How are we to explain his only giving Rachel her birthday present conditionally on her mother being alive?'

'I don't want to slander a dead man, sir,' I answered. 'But if he *has* purposely left a legacy of trouble and danger to his sister, by the means of her child, it must be a legacy made conditional on his sister's being alive to feel the vexation of it.'

'Oh! That's your interpretation of his motive, is it? The Subjective interpretation again! Have you ever been in Germany, Betteredge?'

'No, sir. What's your interpretation, if you please?'

'I can see,' says Mr Franklin, 'that the Colonel's object may, quite possibly, have been—not to benefit his niece, whom he had never even seen—but to prove to his sister that he had died forgiving her, and to prove it very prettily by means of a present made to her child. There is a totally different explanation from yours, Betteredge, taking its rise in a Subjective-Objective point of view. From all I can see, one interpretation is just as likely to be right as the other.'

Having brought matters to this pleasant and comforting issue, Mr Franklin appeared to think that he had completed all that was required of him. He laid down flat on his back on the sand, and asked what was to be done next.

He had been so clever, and clear-headed (before he began to talk the foreign gibberish), and had so completely taken the lead in the business up to the present time, that I was quite unprepared for such a sudden change as he now exhibited in this helpless leaning upon *me.* It was not till later that I learned—by assistance of Miss Rachel, who was the first to make the discovery—that these puzzling shifts and transformations in Mr Franklin were due to the effect on him of his foreign training. At the age when we are all of us most apt to take our colouring, in the form of a reflection from the colouring of other people, he had been sent abroad, and had been passed on from one nation to another, before there was time for any one colouring more than another to settle itself on him firmly. As a consequence of this, he had come back with so many different sides to his character, all more or less jarring with each other, that he seemed to pass his life in a state of perpetual contradiction with himself. He could be a busy man, and a lazy man; cloudy in the head, and clear in the head; a model of determination, and a spectacle of helplessness, all together. He had his French side, and his German side, and his Italian side—the original English foundation showing through, every now and then, as much as to say, 'Here I am, sorely transmogrified, as you see, but there's something of me left at the bottom of him still.' Miss Rachel used to remark that the Italian side of him was uppermost, on those occasions when he unexpectedly gave in, and asked you in his nice sweet-tempered way to take his own responsibilities on your shoulders. You will do him no injustice, I think, if you conclude that the Italian side of him was uppermost now.

'Isn't it your business, sir,' I asked, 'to know what to do next? Surely it can't be mine?'

Mr Franklin didn't appear to see the force of my question—not being in a position, at the time, to see anything but the sky over his head.

'I don't want to alarm my aunt without reason,' he said. 'And I don't want to leave her without what may be a needful warning. If you were in my place, Betteredge, tell me, in one word, what would you do?'

In one word, I told him: 'Wait.'

'With all my heart,' says Mr Franklin. 'How long?'

I proceeded to explain myself.

'As I understand it, sir,' I said, 'somebody is bound to put this plaguy Diamond into Miss Rachel's hands on her birthday—and you may as well do it as another. Very good. This is the twenty-fifth of May, and the birthday is on the twenty-first of June. We have got close on four weeks before us. Let's wait and see what happens in that time; and let's warn my lady or not, as the circumstances direct us.'

'Perfect, Betteredge, as far as it goes!' says Mr Franklin. 'But between this and the birthday, what's to be done with the Diamond?'

'What your father did with it, to be sure, sir!' I answered. 'Your father put it in the safe keeping of a bank in London. You put it in the safe keeping of the bank at Frizinghall.' (Frizinghall was our nearest town, and the Bank of England wasn't safer than the bank there.) 'If I were you, sir,' I added, 'I would ride straight away with it to Frizinghall before the ladies come back.'

The prospect of doing something—and, what is more, of doing that something on a horse—brought Mr Franklin up like lightning from the flat of his back. He sprang to his feet, and pulled me up, without ceremony, on to mine. 'Betteredge, you are worth your weight in gold,' he said. 'Come along, and saddle the best horse in the stables directly!'

Here (God bless it!) was the original English foundation of him showing through all the foreign varnish at last! Here was the Master Franklin I remembered, coming out again in the good old way at the prospect of a ride, and reminding me of the good old times! Saddle a horse for him? I would have saddle a dozen horses, if he could only have ridden them all!

We went back to the house in a hurry; we had the fleetest horse in the stables saddled in a hurry; and Mr Franklin rattled off in a hurry, to lodge the cursed Diamond once more in the strong-room of a bank. When I heard the last of his horse's hoofs on the drive, and when I turned about in the yard and found I was alone again, I felt half inclined to ask myself if I hadn't woke up from a dream.

CHAPTER VII

WHILE I was in this bewildered frame of mind, sorely needing a little quiet time by myself to put me right again, my daughter Penelope got in my way (just as her late mother used to get in my way on the stairs), and instantly summoned me to tell her all that had passed at the conference between Mr Franklin and me. Under present circumstances, the one thing to be done was to clap the extinguisher upon Penelope's curiosity on the spot. I accordingly replied that Mr Franklin and I had both talked of foreign politics, till we could talk no longer, and had then mutually fallen asleep in the heat of the sun. Try that sort of answer when your wife or your daughter next worries you with an awkward question at an awkward time, and depend on the natural sweetness of women for kissing and making it up again at the next opportunity.

The afternoon wore on, and my lady and Miss Rachel came back.

Needless to say how astonished they were, when they heard that Mr Franklin Blake had arrived, and had gone off again on horseback. Needless also to say, that *they* asked awkward questions directly, and that the 'foreign politics' and the 'falling asleep in the sun' wouldn't serve a second time over with *them*. Being at the end of my invention, I said Mr Franklin's arrival by the early train was entirely attributable to one of Mr Franklin's freaks. Being asked, upon that, whether his galloping off again on horseback was another of Mr Franklin's freaks, I said, 'Yes, it was'; and slipped out of it—I think very cleverly—in that way.

Having got over my difficulties with the ladies, I found more difficulties waiting for me when I went back to my own room. In came Penelope—with the natural sweetness of women—to kiss and make it up again; and—with the natural curiosity of women—to ask another question. This time she only wanted me to tell her what was the matter with our second housemaid, Rosanna Spearman.

After leaving Mr Franklin and me at the Shivering Sand, Rosanna, it appeared, had returned to the house in a very unaccountable state of mind. She had turned (if Penelope was to be believed) all the colours of the rainbow. She had been merry without reason, and sad without reason. In one breath she asked hundreds of questions about Mr Franklin Blake, and in another breath she had been angry with Penelope for presuming to suppose that a strange gentleman could possess any interest for her. She had been surprised, smiling, and scribbling Mr Franklin's name inside her workbox. She had been surprised again, crying and looking at her deformed shoulder in the glass. Had she and Mr Franklin known anything of each other before to-day? Quite impossible! Had they heard anything of each other? Impossible again! I could speak to Mr Franklin's astonishment as genuine, when he saw how the girl stared at him. Penelope could speak to the girl's inquisitiveness as genuine, when she asked questions about Mr Franklin. The conference between us, conducted in this way, was tiresome enough, until my daughter suddenly ended it by bursting out with what I thought the most monstrous supposition I had ever heard in my life.

'Father!' says Penelope, quite seriously, 'there's only one explanation of it. Rosanna has fallen in love with Mr Franklin Blake at first sight!'

You have heard of beautiful young ladies falling in love at first sight, and have thought it natural enough. But a housemaid out of a reformatory, with a plain face and a deformed shoulder, falling in love, at first sight, with a gentleman who comes on a visit to her mistress's house, match me that, in the way of an absurdity, out of any story-book in Christendom, if you can! I laughed till the tears rolled down my cheeks. Penelope resented my merriment, in rather a strange way. 'I never knew you cruel before, father,' she said, very gently, and went out.

My girl's words fell upon me like a splash of cold water. I was savage with myself, for feeling uneasy in myself the moment she had spoken them—but so it was. We will change the subject, if you please. I am sorry I drifted into writing about it; and not without reason, as you will see when we have gone on together a little longer.

The evening came, and the dressing-bell for dinner rang, before Mr Franklin returned from Frizinghall. I took his hot water up to his room myself, expecting to hear, after this extraordinary delay, that something had happened. To my great disappointment (and no doubt to yours also), nothing had happened. He had not met with the Indians, either going or returning. He had deposited the Moonstone in the bank—describing it merely as a valuable of great price—and he had got the receipt for it safe in his pocket. I went down-stairs, feeling that this was rather a flat ending, after all our excitement about the Diamond earlier in the day.

How the meeting between Mr Franklin and his aunt and cousin went off, is more than I can tell you.

I would have given something to have waited at table that day. But, in my position in the household, waiting at dinner (except on high family festivals) was letting down my dignity in the eyes of the other servants—a thing which my lady considered me quite prone enough to do already, without seeking occasions for it. The news brought to me from the upper regions, that evening, came from Penelope and the footman. Penelope mentioned that she had never known Miss Rachel so particular about the dressing of her hair, and had never seen her look so bright and pretty as she did when she went down to meet Mr Franklin in the drawing-room. The footman's report was, that the preservation of a respectful composure in the presence of his betters, and the waiting on Mr Franklin Blake at dinner, were two of the hardest things to reconcile with each other that had ever tried his training in service. Later in the evening, we heard them singing and playing duets, Mr Franklin piping high, Miss Rachel piping higher, and my lady, on the piano, following them as it were over hedge and ditch, and seeing them safe through it in a manner most wonderful and pleasant to hear through the open windows, on the terrace at night. Later still, I went to Mr Franklin in the smoking-room, with the soda-water and brandy, and found that Miss Rachel had put the Diamond clean out of his head. 'She's the most charming girl I have seen since I came back to England!' was all I could extract from him, when I endeavoured to lead the conversation to more serious things.

Towards midnight, I went round the house to lock up, accompanied by my second in command (Samuel, the footman), as usual. When all the doors were made fast, except the side door that opened on the terrace, I sent Samuel to bed, and stepped out for a breath of fresh air before I too went to bed in my turn.

The night was still and close, and the moon was at the full in the heavens. It was so silent out of doors, that I heard from time to time, very faint and low, the fall of the sea, as the ground-swell heaved it in on the sand-bank near the mouth of our little bay. As the house stood, the terrace side was the dark side; but the broad moonlight showed fair on the gravel walk that ran along the next side to the terrace. Looking this way, after looking up at the sky, I saw the shadow of a person in the moonlight thrown forward from behind the corner of the house.

Being old and sly, I forbore to call out; but being also, unfortunately, old and heavy, my feet betrayed me on the gravel. Before I could steal suddenly round the corner, as I had proposed, I heard lighter feet than mine—and more than one pair of them as I thought—retreating in a hurry. By the time I had got to the corner, the trespassers, whoever they were, had run into the shrubbery at the off side of the walk, and were hidden from sight among the thick trees and bushes in that part of the grounds. From the shrubbery, they could easily make their way, over our fence into the road. If I had been forty years younger, I might have had a chance of catching them before they got clear of our premises. As it was, I went back to set a-going a younger pair of legs than mine. Without disturbing anybody, Samuel and I got a couple of guns, and went all round the house and through the shrubbery. Having made sure that no persons were lurking about anywhere in our grounds, we turned back. Passing over the walk where I had seen the shadow, I now noticed, for the first time, a little bright object, lying on the clean gravel, under the light of the moon. Picking the object up, I discovered it was a small bottle, containing a thick sweet-smelling liquor, as black as ink.

I said nothing to Samuel. But, remembering what Penelope had told me about the jugglers, and the pouring of the little pool of ink into the palm of the boy's hand, I instantly suspected that I had disturbed the three Indians, lurking about the house, and bent, in their heathenish way, on discovering the whereabouts of the Diamond that night.

CHAPTER VIII

HERE, for one moment, I find it necessary to call a halt.

On summoning up my own recollections—and on getting Penelope to help me, by consulting her journal—I find that we may pass pretty rapidly over the interval between Mr Franklin Blake's arrival and Miss Rachel's birthday. For the greater part of that time the days passed, and brought nothing with them worth recording. With your good leave, then, and with Penelope's help, I shall notice certain dates only in this place; reserving to myself to tell the story day by day, once more, as soon as we get to the time when the business of the Moonstone became the chief business of everybody in our house.

This said, we may now go on again—beginning, of course, with the bottle of sweet-smelling ink which I found on the gravel walk at night.

On the next morning (the morning of the twenty-sixth) I showed Mr Franklin this article of jugglery, and told him what I have already told you. His opinion was, not only that the Indians had been lurking about after the Diamond, but also that they were actually foolish enough to believe in their own magic—meaning thereby the making of signs on a boy's head, and the pouring of ink into a boy's hand, and then expecting him to see persons and things beyond the reach of human vision. In our country, as well as in the East, Mr Franklin informed me, there are people who practise this curious hocus-pocus (without the ink, however); and who call it by a French name, signifying something like brightness of sight. 'Depend upon it,' says

Mr Franklin, 'the Indians took it for granted that we should keep the
Diamond here; and they brought their clairvoyant boy to show them the way
to it, if they succeeded in getting into the house last night.'

'Do you think they'll try again, sir?' I asked.

'It depends,' says Mr Franklin, 'on what the boy can really do. If he can
see the Diamond through the iron safe of the bank at Frizinghall, we shall
be troubled with no more visits from the Indians for the present. If he can't,
we shall have another chance of catching them in the shrubbery, before
many more nights are over our heads.'

I waited pretty confidently for that latter chance; but, strange to relate, it
never came.

Whether the jugglers heard, in the town, of Mr Franklin having been seen
at the bank, and drew their conclusions accordingly; or whether the boy
really did see the Diamond where the Diamond was now lodged (which I,
for one, flatly disbelieve); or whether, after all, it was a mere effect of chance,
this at any rate is the plain truth—not the ghost of an Indian came near the
house again, through the weeks that passed before Miss Rachel's birthday.
The jugglers remained in and about the town plying their trade; and
Mr Franklin and I remained waiting to see what might happen, and resolute
not to put the rogues on their guard by showing our suspicions of them too
soon. With this report of the proceedings on either side, ends all that I have
to say about the Indians for the present.

On the twenty-ninth of the month, Miss Rachel and Mr Franklin hit on
a new method of working their way together through the time which might
otherwise have hung heavy on their hands. There are reasons for taking
particular notice here of the occupation that amused them. You will find it
has a bearing on something that is still to come.

Gentlefolks in general have a very awkward rock ahead in life—the rock
ahead of their own idleness. Their lives being, for the most part, passed in
looking about them for something to do, it is curious to see—especially when
their tastes are of what is called the intellectual sort—how often they drift
blindfold into some nasty pursuit. Nine times out of ten they take to
torturing something, or to spoiling something—and they firmly believe they
are improving their minds, when the plain truth is, they are only making a
mess in the house. I have seen them (ladies, I am sorry to say, as well as
gentlemen) go out, day after day, for example, with empty pill-boxes, and
catch newts, and beetles, and spiders, and frogs, and come home and stick
pins through the miserable wretches, or cut them up, without a pang of
remorse, into little pieces. You see my young master, or my young mistress,
poring over one of their spiders' insides with a magnifying-glass; or you meet
one of their frogs walking down-stairs without his head—and when you
wonder what this cruel nastiness means, you are told that it means a taste

in my young master or my young mistress for natural history. Sometimes, again, you see them occupied for hours together in spoiling a pretty flower with pointed instruments, out of a stupid curiosity to know what the flower is made of. Is its colour any prettier, or its scent any sweeter, when you *do* know? But there! the poor souls must get through the time, you see—they must get through the time. You dabbled in nasty mud, and made pies, when you were a child; and you dabble in nasty science, and dissect spiders, and spoil flowers, when you grow up. In the one case and in the other, the secret of it is, that you have got nothing to think of in your poor empty head, and nothing to do with your poor idle hands. And so it ends in your spoiling canvas with paints, and making a smell in the house; or in keeping tadpoles in a glass box full of dirty water, and turning everybody's stomach in the house; or in chipping off bits of stone here, there, and everywhere, and dropping grit into all the victuals in the house; or in staining your fingers in the pursuit of photography, and doing justice without mercy on everybody's face in the house. It often falls heavy enough, no doubt, on people who are really obliged to get their living, to be forced to work for the clothes that cover them, the roof that shelters them, and the food that keeps them going. But compare the hardest day's work you ever did with the idleness that splits flowers and pokes its way into spiders' stomachs, and thank your stars that your head has got something it *must* think of, and your hands something that they *must* do.

As for Mr Franklin and Miss Rachel, they tortured nothing, I am glad to say. They simply confined themselves to making a mess; and all they spoilt, to do them justice, was the panelling of a door.

Mr Franklin's universal genius, dabbling in everything, dabbled in what he called 'decorative painting'. He had invented, he informed us, a new mixture to moisten paint with, which he described as a 'vehicle'. What it was made of, I don't know. What it did, I can tell you in two words—it stank. Miss Rachel being wild to try her hand at the new process, Mr Franklin sent to London for the materials; mixed them up, with accompaniment of a smell which made the very dogs sneeze when they came into the room; put an apron and a bib over Miss Rachel's gown, and set her to work decorating her own little sitting-room—called, for want of English to name it in, her 'boudoir'. They began with the inside of the door. Mr Franklin scraped off all the nice varnish with pumice-stone, and made what he described as a surface to work on. Miss Rachel then covered the surface, under his directions and with his help, with patterns and devices—griffins, birds, flowers, cupids, and such like—copied from designs made by a famous Italian painter, whose name escapes me: the one, I mean, who stocked the world with Virgin Maries, and had a sweetheart at the baker's. Viewed as work, this decoration was slow to do, and dirty to deal with. But our young lady and gentleman never seemed to tire of it. When they were not riding, or seeing company, or taking their meals, or piping their songs, there they were with their heads together, as busy as bees, spoiling the door. Who was the poet who said that Satan finds some mischief still for idle hands to do? If he had occupied my place in the family, and had seen Miss Rachel with her brush, and Mr Franklin with his vehicle, he could have written nothing truer of either of them than that.

The next date worthy of notice is Sunday the fourth of June.

On that evening we, in the servants' hall, debated a domestic question for the first time, which, like the decoration of the door, has its bearing on something that is still to come.

Seeing the pleasure which Mr Franklin and Miss Rachel took in each other's society, and noting what a pretty match they were in all personal respects, we naturally speculated on the chance of their putting their heads together with other objects in view besides the ornamenting of a door. Some of us said there would be a wedding in the house before the summer was over. Others (led by me) admitted it was likely enough Miss Rachel might be married; but we doubted (for reasons which will presently appear) whether her bridegroom would be Mr Franklin Blake.

That Mr Franklin was in love, on his side, nobody who saw and heard him could doubt. The difficulty was to fathom Miss Rachel. Let me do myself the honour of making you acquainted with her; after which, I will leave you to fathom for yourself—if you can.

My young lady's eighteenth birthday was the birthday now coming, on the twenty-first of June. If you happen to like dark women (who, I am informed, have gone out of fashion latterly in the gay world), and if you have no particular prejudice in favour of size, I answer for Miss Rachel as one of the prettiest girls your eyes ever looked on. She was small and slim, but all in fine proportion from top to toe. To see her sit down, to see her get up, and specially to see her walk, was enough to satisfy any man in his senses that the graces of her figure (if you will pardon me the expression) were in her flesh and not in her clothes. Her hair was the blackest I ever saw. Her eyes matched her hair. Her nose was not quite large enough, I admit. Her mouth and chin were (to quote Mr Franklin) morsels for the gods; and her complexion (on the same undeniable authority) was as warm as the sun itself, with this great advantage over the sun, that it was always in nice order to look at. Add to the foregoing that she carried her head as upright as a dart, in a dashing, spirited, thoroughbred way—that she had a clear voice, with a ring of the right metal in it, and a smile that began very prettily in her eyes before it got to her lips—and there behold the portrait of her, to the best of my painting, as large as life!

And what about her disposition next? Had this charming creature no faults? She had just as many faults as you have, ma'am—neither more nor less.

To put it seriously, my dear pretty Miss Rachel, possessing a host of graces and attractions, had one defect, which strict impartiality compels me to acknowledge. She was unlike most other girls of her age, in this—that she had ideas of her own, and was stiff-necked enough to set the fashions themselves at defiance, if the fashions didn't suit her views. In trifles, this independence of hers was all well enough; but in matters of importance, it carried her (as my lady thought, and as I thought) too far. She judged for herself, as few women of twice her age judge in general; never asked your advice; never told you beforehand what she was going to do; never came with secrets and confidences to anybody, from her mother downwards. In little things and great, with people she loved, and people she hated (and she did both with equal heartiness), Miss Rachel always went on a way of her own, sufficient for herself in the joys and sorrows of her life. Over and over again I have heard my lady say, 'Rachel's best friend and Rachel's worst enemy are, one and the other—Rachel herself.'

Add one thing more to this, and I have done.

With all her secrecy, and self-will, there was not so much as the shadow of anything false in her. I never remember her breaking her word; I never remember her saying No, and meaning Yes. I can call to mind, in her childhood, more than one occasion when the good little soul took the blame, and suffered the punishment, for some fault committed by a playfellow whom she loved. Nobody ever knew her to confess to it, when the thing was found out, and she was charged with it afterwards. But nobody ever knew her to lie about it, either. She looked you straight in the face, and shook her little saucy head, and said plainly, 'I won't tell you!' Punished again for this, she would own to being sorry for saying 'won't'; but, bread and water notwithstanding, she never told you. Self-willed—devilish self-willed some-times—I grant; but the finest creature, nevertheless, that ever walked the ways of this lower world. Perhaps you think you see a certain contradiction here? In that case, a word in your ear. Study your wife closely, for the next four-and-twenty hours. If your good lady doesn't exhibit something in the shape of a contradiction in that time, Heaven help you!—you have married a monster.

I have now brought you acquainted with Miss Rachel, which you will find puts us face to face, next, with the question of that young lady's matrimonial views.

On June the twelfth, an invitation from my mistress was sent to a gentleman in London, to come and help to keep Miss Rachel's birthday. This was the fortunate individual on whom I believed her heart to be privately set! Like Mr Franklin, he was a cousin of hers. His name was Mr Godfrey Ablewhite.

My lady's second sister (don't be alarmed; we are not going very deep into family matters this time)—my lady's second sister, I say, had a disappointment in love; and taking a husband afterwards, on the neck or nothing principle, made what they call a misalliance. There was terrible work in the family when the Honourable Caroline insisted on marrying plain Mr Ablewhite, the banker at Frizinghall. He was very rich and very respectable, and he begot a prodigious large family—all in his favour, so far. But he had presumed to raise himself from a low station in the world—and that was against him. However, time and the progress of modern enlightenment put things right; and the misalliance passed muster very well. We are all getting liberal now; and (provided you can scratch me, if I scratch you) what do I care, in or out of Parliament, whether you are a Dustman or a Duke? That's the modern way of looking at it—and I keep up with the modern way. The Ablewhites lived in a fine house and grounds, a little out of Frizinghall. Very worthy people, and greatly respected in the neighbourhood. We shall not be much troubled with them in these pages—excepting Mr Godfrey, who was Mr Ablewhite's second son, and who must take his proper place here, if you please, for Miss Rachel's sake.

With all his brightness and cleverness and general good qualities, Mr Franklin's chance of topping Mr Godfrey in our young lady's estimation was, in my opinion, a very poor chance indeed.

In the first place, Mr Godfrey was, in point of size, the finest man by far of the two. He stood over six feet high; he had a beautiful red and white colour; a smooth round face, shaved as bare as your hand; and a head of lovely long flaxen hair, falling negligently over the poll of his neck. But why do I try to give you this personal description of him? If you ever subscribed to a Ladies' Charity in London, you know Mr Godfrey Ablewhite as well as I do. He was a barrister by profession; a ladies' man by temperament; and a good Samaritan by choice. Female benevolence and female destitution could do nothing without him. Maternal societies for confining poor women; Magdalen societies for rescuing poor women; strong-minded societies for putting poor women into poor men's places, and leaving the men to shift for themselves;—he was vice-president, manager, referee to them all. Wherever there was a table with a committee of ladies sitting round it in council, there was Mr Godfrey at the bottom of the board, keeping the temper of the committee, and leading the dear creatures along the thorny ways of business, hat in hand. I do suppose this was the most accomplished philanthropist (on a small independence) that England ever produced. As a speaker at charitable meetings the like of him for drawing your tears and your money was not easy to find. He was quite a public character. The last time I was in London, my mistress gave me two treats. She sent me to the theatre to see a dancing woman who was all the rage; and she sent me to Exeter Hall to hear Mr Godfrey. The lady did it, with a band of music. The gentleman did it, with a handkerchief and a glass of water. Crowds at the performance with the legs. Ditto at the performance with the tongue.

And with all this, the sweetest-tempered person (I allude to Mr Godfrey)—
the simplest and pleasantest and easiest to please—you ever met with. He
loved everybody. And everybody loved *him*. What chance had Mr Franklin—what chance had anybody of average reputation and capacities—
against such a man as this?

On the fourteenth, came Mr Godfrey's answer.

He accepted my mistress's invitation, from the Wednesday of the birthday
to the evening of Friday—when his duties to the Ladies' Charities would
oblige him to return to town. He also enclosed a copy of verses on what he
elegantly called his cousin's 'natal day'. Miss Rachel, I was informed, joined
Mr Franklin in making fun of the verses at dinner; and Penelope, who was
all on Mr Franklin's side, asked me, in great triumph, what I thought of that.
'Miss Rachel has led *you* off on a false scent, my dear,' I replied; 'but *my* nose
is not so easily mystified. Wait till Mr Ablewhite's verses are followed by Mr
Ablewhite himself.'

My daughter replied, that Mr Franklin might strike in, and try his luck,
before the verses were followed by the poet. In favour of this view, I must
acknowledge that Mr Franklin left no chance untried of winning Miss
Rachel's good graces.

Though one of the most inveterate smokers I ever met with, he gave up his
cigar, because she said, one day, she hated the stale smell of it in his clothes.
He slept so badly, after this effort of self-denial, for want of the composing
effect of the tobacco to which he was used, and came down morning after
morning looking so haggard and worn, that Miss Rachel herself begged him
to take to his cigars again. No! he would take to nothing again that could
cause her a moment's annoyance; he would fight it out resolutely, and get
back his sleep, sooner or later, by main force of patience in waiting for it.
Such devotion as this, you may say (as some of them said downstairs), could
never fail of producing the right effect on Miss Rachel—backed up, too, as it
was, by the decorating work every day on the door. All very well—but she
had a photograph of Mr Godfrey in her bed-room; represented speaking at
a public meeting, with all his hair blown out by the breath of his own
eloquence, and his eyes, most lovely, charming the money out of your
pockets. What do you say to that? Every morning—as Penelope herself
owned to me—there was the man whom the women couldn't do without,
looking on, in effigy, while Miss Rachel was having her hair combed. He
would be looking on, in reality, before long—that was my opinion of it.

June the sixteenth brought an event which made Mr Franklin's chance
look, to my mind, a worse chance than ever.

A strange gentleman, speaking English with a foreign accent, came that
morning to the house, and asked to see Mr Franklin Blake on business. The

business could not possibly have been connected with the Diamond, for these two reasons—first, that Mr Franklin told me nothing about it; secondly, that he communicated it (when the gentleman had gone, as I suppose) to my lady. She probably hinted something about it next to her daughter. At any rate, Miss Rachel was reported to have said some severe things to Mr Franklin, at the piano that evening, about the people he had lived among, and the principles he had adopted in foreign parts. The next day, for the first time, nothing was done towards the decoration of the door. I suspect some imprudence of Mr Franklin's on the Continent—with a woman or a debt at the bottom of it—had followed him to England. But that is all guesswork. In this case, not only Mr Franklin, but my lady too, for a wonder, left me in the dark.

On the seventeenth, to all appearance, the cloud passed away again. They returned to their decorating work on the door, and seemed to be as good friends as ever. If Penelope was to be believed, Mr Franklin had seized the opportunity of the reconciliation to make an offer to Miss Rachel, and had neither been accepted nor refused. My girl was sure (from signs and tokens which I need not trouble you with) that her young mistress had fought Mr Franklin off by declining to believe that he was in earnest, and had then secretly regretted treating him in that way afterwards. Though Penelope was admitted to more familiarity with her young mistress than maids generally are—for the two had been almost brought up together as children—still I knew Miss Rachel's reserved character too well to believe that she would show her mind to anybody in this way. What my daughter told me, on the present occasion, was, as I suspected, more what she wished than what she really knew.

On the nineteenth another event happened. We had the doctor in the house professionally. He was summoned to prescribe for a person whom I have had occasion to present to you in these pages—our second housemaid, Rosanna Spearman.

This poor girl—who had puzzled me, as you know already, at the Shivering Sand—puzzled me more than once again, in the interval time of which I am now writing. Penelope's notion that her fellow-servant was in love with Mr Franklin (which my daughter, by my orders, kept strictly secret) seemed to be just as absurd as ever. But I must own that what I myself saw, and what my daughter saw also, of our second housemaid's conduct, began to look mysterious, to say the least of it.

For example, the girl constantly put herself in Mr Franklin's way—very slyly and quietly, but she did it. He took about as much notice of her as he took of the cat: it never seemed to occur to him to waste a look on Rosanna's plain face. The poor thing's appetite, never much, fell away dreadfully; and her eyes in the morning showed plain signs of waking and crying at night. One day Penelope made an awkward discovery, which we hushed up on the spot. She caught Rosanna at Mr Franklin's dressing-table, secretly removing a rose which Miss Rachel had given him to wear in his button-hole, and putting another rose like it, of her own picking, in its place. She was, after that, once or twice impudent to me, when I gave her a well-meant general hint to be careful in her conduct; and, worse still, she was not over-respectful now, on the few occasions when Miss Rachel accidentally spoke to her.

My lady noticed the change, and asked me what I thought about it. I tried to screen the girl by answering that I thought she was out of health; and it ended in the doctor being sent for, as already mentioned, on the nineteenth. He said it was her nerves, and doubted if she was fit for service. My lady offered to remove her for change of air to one of our farms, inland. She begged and prayed, with the tears in her eyes, to be let to stop; and, in an evil hour, I advised my lady to try her for a little longer. As the event proved, and as you will soon see, this was the worst advice I could have given. If I could only have looked a little way into the future, I would have taken Rosanna Spearman out of the house, then and there, with my own hand.

On the twentieth, there came a note from Mr Godfrey. He had arranged to stop at Frizinghall that night, having occasion to consult his father on business. On the afternoon of the next day, he and his two eldest sisters would ride over to us on horseback, in good time before dinner. An elegant little casket in China accompanied the note, presented to Miss Rachel, with her cousin's love and best wishes. Mr Franklin had only given her a plain locket not worth half the money. My daughter Penelope, nevertheless—such is the obstinacy of women—still backed him to win.

Thanks be to Heaven, we have arrived at the eve of the birthday at last! You will own, I think, that I have got you over the ground this time, without much loitering by the way. Cheer up! I'll ease you with another new chapter here—and, what is more, that chapter shall take you straight into the thick of the story.

CHAPTER IX

JUNE twenty-first, the day of the birthday, was cloudy and unsettled at sunrise, but towards noon it cleared up bravely.

We, in the servants' hall, began this happy anniversary, as usual, by offering our little presents to Miss Rachel, with the regular speech delivered annually by me as the chief. I follow the plan adopted by the Queen in opening

Parliament—namely, the plan of saying much the same thing regularly every year. Before it is delivered, my speech (like the Queen's) is looked for as eagerly as if nothing of the kind had ever been heard before. When it is delivered, and turns out not to be the novelty anticipated, though they grumble a little, they look forward hopefully to something newer next year. An easy people to govern, in the Parliament and in the Kitchen—that's the moral of it.

After breakfast, Mr Franklin and I had a private conference on the subject of the Moonstone—the time having now come for removing it from the bank at Frizinghall, and placing it in Miss Rachel's own hands.

Whether he had been trying to make love to his cousin again, and had got a rebuff—or whether his broken rest, night after night, was aggravating the queer contradictions and uncertainties in his character—I don't know. But certain it is, that Mr Franklin failed to show himself at his best on the morning of the birthday. He was in twenty different minds about the Diamond in as many minutes. For my part, I stuck fast by the plain facts as we knew them. Nothing had happened to justify us in alarming my lady on the subject of the jewel; and nothing could alter the legal obligation that now lay on Mr Franklin to put it in his cousin's possession. That was my view of the matter; and, twist and turn it as he might, he was forced in the end to make it his view too. We arranged that he was to ride over, after lunch, to Frizinghall, and bring the Diamond back, with Mr Godfrey and the two young ladies, in all probability, to keep him company on the way home again.

This settled, our young gentleman went back to Miss Rachel.

They consumed the whole morning, and part of the afternoon, in the everlasting business of decorating the door, Penelope standing by to mix the colours, as directed; and my lady, as luncheon time drew near, going in and out of the room, with her handkerchief to her nose (for they used a deal of Mr Franklin's vehicle that day), and trying vainly to get the two artists away from their work. It was three o'clock before they took off their aprons, and released Penelope (much the worse for the vehicle), and cleaned themselves of their mess. But they had done what they wanted—they had finished the door on the birthday, and proud enough they were of it. The griffins, cupids, and so on, were, I must own, most beautiful to behold; though so many in number, so entangled in flowers and devices, and so topsy-turvy in their actions and attitudes, that you felt them unpleasantly in your head for hours after you had done with the pleasure of looking at them. If I add that Penelope ended her part of the morning's work by being sick in the back-kitchen, it is in no unfriendly spirit towards the vehicle. No! no! It left off stinking when it dried; and if Art requires these sort of sacrifices—though the girl is my own daughter—I say, let Art have them!

Mr Franklin snatched a morsel from the luncheon-table, and rode off to Frizinghall—to escort his cousins, as he told my lady. To fetch the Moonstone, as was privately known to himself and to me.

This being one of the high festivals on which I took my place at the side-board, in command of the attendance at table, I had plenty to occupy my mind while Mr Franklin was away. Having seen to the wine, and reviewed my men and women who were to wait at dinner, I retired to collect myself before the company came. A whiff of—you know what, and a turn at a certain book which I have had occasion to mention in these pages, composed me, body and mind. I was aroused from what I am inclined to think must have been, not a nap, but a reverie, by the clatter of horses' hoofs outside; and, going to the door, received a cavalcade comprising Mr Franklin and his three cousins, escorted by one of old Mr Ablewhite's grooms.

Mr Godfrey struck me, strangely enough, as being like Mr Franklin in this respect—that he did not seem to be in his customary spirits. He kindly shook hands with me as usual, and was most politely glad to see his old friend Betteredge wearing so well. But there was a sort of cloud over him, which I couldn't at all account for; and when I asked how he had found his father in health, he answered rather shortly, 'Much as usual.' However, the two Miss Ablewhites were cheerful enough for twenty, which more than restored the balance. They were nearly as big as their brother; spanking, yellow-haired, rosy lasses, overflowing with superabundant flesh and blood; bursting from head to foot with health and spirits. The legs of the poor horses trembled with carrying them; and when they jumped from their saddles (without waiting to be helped), I declare they bounced on the ground as if they were made of india-rubber. Everything the Miss Ablewhites said began with a large O; everything they did was done with a bang; and they giggled and screamed, in season and out of season, on the smallest provocation. Bouncers—that's what I call them.

Under cover of the noise made by the young ladies, I had an opportunity of saying a private word to Mr Franklin in the hall.

'Have you got the Diamond safe, sir?'

He nodded, and tapped the breast-pocket of his coat.

'Have you seen anything of the Indians?'

'Not a glimpse.' With that answer, he asked for my lady, and, hearing she was in the small drawing-room, went there straight. The bell rang, before he had been a minute in the room, and Penelope was sent to tell Miss Rachel that Mr Franklin Blake wanted to speak to her.

Crossing the hall, about half an hour afterwards, I was brought to a sudden standstill by an outbreak of screams from the small drawing-room. I can't say I was at all alarmed; for I recognised in the screams the favourite large O of the Miss Ablewhites. However, I went in (on pretence of asking for instructions about the dinner) to discover whether anything serious had really happened.

There stood Miss Rachel at the table, like a person fascinated, with the Colonel's unlucky Diamond in her hand. There, on either side of her, knelt the two Bouncers, devouring the jewel with their eyes, and screaming with ecstasy every time it flashed on them in a new light. There, at the opposite side of the table, stood Mr Godfrey, clapping his hands like a large child, and singing out softly, 'Exquisite! exquisite!' There sat Mr Franklin in a chair by the bookcase, tugging at his beard, and looking anxiously towards the window. And there, at the window, stood the object he was contemplating— my lady, having the extract from the Colonel's Will in her hand, and keeping her back turned on the whole of the company.

She faced me, when I asked for my instructions; and I saw the family frown gathering over her eyes, and the family temper twitching at the corners of her mouth.

'Come to my room in half an hour,' she answered. 'I shall have something to say to you then.'

With those words she went out. It was plain enough that she was posed by the same difficulty which had posed Mr Franklin and me in our conference at the Shivering Sand. Was the legacy of the Moonstone a proof that she had treated her brother with cruel injustice? or was it a proof that he was worse than the worst she had ever thought of him? Serious questions those for my lady to determine, while her daughter, innocent of all knowledge of the Colonel's character, stood there with the Colonel's birthday gift in her hand.

Before I could leave the room in my turn, Miss Rachel, always considerate to the old servant who had been in the house when she was born, stopped me. 'Look, Gabriel!' she said, and flashed the jewel before my eyes in a ray of sunlight that poured through the window.

Lord bless us! it *was* a Diamond! As large, or nearly, as a plover's egg! The light that streamed from it was like the light of the harvest moon. When you looked down into the stone, you looked into a yellow deep that drew your eyes into it so that they saw nothing else. It seemed unfathomable; this jewel, that you could hold between your finger and thumb, seemed unfathomable as the heavens themselves. We set it in the sun, and then shut the light out of the room, and it shone awfully out of the depths of its own brightness, with a moony gleam, in the dark. No wonder Miss Rachel was fascinated: no wonder her cousins screamed. The Diamond laid such a hold on *me* that I burst out with as large an 'O' as the Bouncers themselves. The only one of us who kept his senses was Mr Godfrey. He put an arm round each of his sisters' waists, and, looking compassionately backwards and forwards between the Diamond and me, said, 'Carbon, Betteredge! mere carbon, my good friend, after all!'

His object, I suppose, was to instruct me. All he did, however, was to remind me of the dinner. I hobbled off to my army of waiters downstairs. As I went out, Mr Godfrey said, 'Dear old Betteredge, I have the truest regard for him!' He was embracing his sisters, and ogling Miss Rachel, while he honoured me with that testimony of affection. Something like a stock of love to draw on *there!* Mr Franklin was a perfect savage by comparison with him.

At the end of half an hour, I presented myself, as directed, in my lady's room.

What passed between my mistress and me, on this occasion, was, in the main, a repetition of what had passed between Mr Franklin and me at the Shivering Sand—with this difference, that I took care to keep my own counsel about the jugglers, seeing that nothing had happened to justify me in alarming my lady on this head. When I received my dismissal, I could see that she took the blackest view possible of the Colonel's motives, and that she was bent on getting the Moonstone out of her daughter's possession at the first opportunity.

On my way back to my own part of the house, I was encountered by Mr Franklin. He wanted to know if I had seen anything of his cousin Rachel. I had seen nothing of her. Could I tell him where his cousin Godfrey was? I didn't know; but I began to suspect that cousin Godfrey might not be far away from cousin Rachel. Mr Franklin's suspicions apparently took the same turn. He tugged hard at his beard, and went and shut himself up in the library with a bang of the door that had a world of meaning in it.

I was interrupted no more in the business of preparing for the birthday dinner till it was time for me to smarten myself up for receiving the company. Just as I had got my white waistcoat on, Penelope presented herself at my toilet, on pretence of brushing what little hair I have got left, and improving the tie of my white cravat. My girl was in high spirits, and I saw she had something to say to me. She gave me a kiss on the top of my bald head, and whispered, 'News for you, father! Miss Rachel has refused him.'

'Who's "*him*"?' I asked.

'The ladies' committee-man, father,' says Penelope. 'A nasty sly fellow! I hate him for trying to supplant Mr Franklin!'

If I had had breath enough, I should certainly have protested against this indecent way of speaking of an eminent philanthropic character. But my daughter happened to be improving the tie of my cravat at that moment, and the whole strength of her feelings found its way into her fingers. I never was more nearly strangled in my life.

'I saw him take her away alone into the rose-garden,' says Penelope. 'And I waited behind the holly to see how they came back. They had gone out arm-in-arm, both laughing. They came back, walking separate, as grave as grave could be, and looking straight away from each other in a manner which there was no mistaking. I never was more delighted, father, in my life! There's one woman in the world who can resist Mr Godfrey Ablewhite, at any rate; and, if I was a lady, I should be another!'

Here I should have protested again. But my daughter had got the hair-brush by this time, and the whole strength of her feelings had passed into *that*. If you are bald, you will understand how she scarified me. If you are not, skip this bit, and thank God you have got something in the way of a defence between your hair-brush and your head.

'Just on the other side of the holly,' Penelope went on, 'Mr Godfrey came to a standstill. "You prefer," says he, "that I should stop here as if nothing had happened?" Miss Rachel turned on him like lightning. "You have accepted my mother's invitation," she said; "and you are here to meet her guests. Unless you wish to make a scandal in the house, you will remain, of course!" She went on a few steps, and then seemed to relent a little. "Let us forget what has passed, Godfrey," she said, "and let us remain cousins still." She gave him her hand. He kissed it, which *I* should have considered taking a liberty, and then she left him. He waited a little by himself, with his head down, and his heel grinding a hole slowly in the gravel walk; you never saw a man look more put out in your life. "Awkward!" he said between his teeth, when he looked up, and went on to the house—"very awkward!" If that was his opinion of himself, he was quite right. Awkward enough, I'm sure. And the end of it is, father, what I told you all along,' cries Penelope, finishing me off with a last scarification, the hottest of all. 'Mr Franklin's the man!'

I got possession of the hair-brush, and opened my lips to administer the reproof which, you will own, my daughter's language and conduct richly deserved.

Before I could say a word, the crash of carriage-wheels outside struck in, and stopped me. The first of the dinner-company had come. Penelope instantly ran off. I put on my coat, and looked in the glass. My head was as red as a lobster; but, in other respects, I was as nicely dressed for the ceremonies of the evening as a man need be. I got into the hall just in time to announce the two first of the guests. You needn't feel particularly interested about them. Only the philanthropist's father and mother—Mr and Mrs Ablewhite.

CHAPTER X

ONE on the top of the other the rest of the company followed the Ablewhites, till we had the whole tale of them complete. Including the family, they were twenty-four in all. It was a noble sight to see, when they were settled in their places round the dinner-table, and the Rector of Frizinghall (with beautiful elocution) rose and said grace.

There is no need to worry you with a list of the guests. You will meet none of them a second time—in my part of the story, at any rate—with the exception of two.

Those two sat on either side of Miss Rachel, who, as queen of the day, was naturally the great attraction of the party. On this occasion she was more particularly the centre-point towards which everybody's eyes were directed; for (to my lady's secret annoyance) she wore her wonderful birthday present, which eclipsed all the rest—the Moonstone. It was without any setting when it had been placed in her hands; but that universal genius, Mr Franklin, had contrived, with the help of his neat fingers and a little bit of silver wire, to fix it as a brooch in the bosom of her white dress. Everybody wondered at the prodigious size and beauty of the Diamond, as a matter of course. But the only two of the company who said anything out of the common way about it were those two guests I have mentioned, who sat by Miss Rachel on her right hand and her left.

The guest on her left was Mr Candy, our doctor at Frizinghall. This was a pleasant, companionable little man, with the drawback, however, I must own, of being too fond, in season and out of season, of his joke, and of his plunging in rather a headlong manner into talk with strangers, without waiting to feel his way first. In society he was constantly making mistakes, and setting people unintentionally by the ears together. In his medical practice he was a more prudent man; picking up his discretion (as his enemies said) by a kind of instinct, and proving to be generally right where more carefully conducted doctors turned out to be wrong. What *he* said about the Diamond to Miss Rachel was said, as usual, by way of a mystification or joke. He gravely entreated her (in the interests of science) to let him take it home and burn it. 'We will first heat it, Miss Rachel,' says the doctor, 'to such and such a degree; then we will expose it to a current of air; and, little by little—puff!—we evaporate the Diamond, and spare you a world of anxiety about the safe keeping of a valuable precious stone!' My lady, listening with rather a careworn expression on her face, seemed to wish that the doctor had been in earnest, and that he could have found Miss Rachel zealous enough in the cause of science to sacrifice her birthday gift.

The other guest, who sat on my young lady's right hand, was an eminent public character—being no other than the celebrated Indian traveller, Mr Murthwaite, who, at risk of his life, had penetrated in disguise where no European had ever set foot before.

This was a long, lean, wiry, brown, silent man. He had a weary look, and a very steady, attentive eye. It was rumoured that he was tired of the humdrum life among the people in our parts, and longing to go back and wander off on the tramp again in the wild places of the East. Except what he said to Miss Rachel about her jewel, I doubt if he spoke six words or drank so much as a single glass of wine, all through the dinner. The Moonstone was the only object that interested him in the smallest degree. The fame of it seemed to have reached him, in some of those perilous Indian places where his wanderings had lain. After looking at it silently for so long a time that Miss Rachel began to get confused, he said to her in his cool immovable way, 'If you ever go to India, Miss Verinder, don't take your uncle's birthday gift with you. A Hindoo diamond is sometimes part of a Hindoo religion. I know a certain city, and a certain temple in that city, where, dressed as you are now, your life would not be worth five minutes' purchase.' Miss Rachel, safe in England, was quite delighted to hear of her danger in India. The Bouncers were more delighted still; they dropped their knives and forks with a crash, and burst out together vehemently, 'O! how interesting!' My lady fidgeted in her chair, and changed the subject.

As the dinner got on, I became aware, little by little, that this festival was not prospering as other like festivals had prospered before it.

Looking back at the birthday now, by the light of what happened afterwards, I am half inclined to think that the cursed Diamond must have cast a blight on the whole company. I plied them well with wine; and being a privileged character, followed the unpopular dishes round the table, and whispered to the company confidentially, 'Please to change your mind and try it; for I know it will do you good.' Nine times out of ten they changed their minds—out of regard for their old original Betteredge, they were pleased to say—but all to no purpose. There were gaps of silence in the talk, as the dinner got on, that made me feel personally uncomfortable. When they did use their tongues again, they used them innocently, in the most unfortunate manner and to the worst possible purpose. Mr Candy, the doctor, for instance, said more unlucky things than I ever knew him to say before. Take one sample of the way in which he went on, and you will understand what I had to put up with at the sideboard, officiating as I was in the character of a man who had the prosperity of the festival at heart.

One of our ladies present at dinner was worthy Mrs Threadgall, widow of the late Professor of that name. Talking of her deceased husband perpetually, this good lady never mentioned to strangers that he *was* deceased. She thought, I suppose, that every able-bodied adult in England ought to know as much as that. In one of the gaps of silence, somebody mentioned the dry and rather nasty subject of human anatomy; whereupon good Mrs Threadgall straightway brought in her late husband as usual, without mentioning that he was dead. Anatomy she described as the Professor's favourite recreation in his leisure hours. As ill-luck would have it, Mr Candy, sitting opposite (who knew nothing of the deceased gentle-man), heard her. Being the most polite of men, he seized the opportunity of assisting the Professor's anatomical amusements on the spot.

'They have got some remarkably fine skeletons lately at the College of Surgeons,' says Mr Candy, across the table, in a loud cheerful voice. 'I strongly recommend the Professor, ma'am, when he next has an hour to spare, to pay them a visit.'

You might have heard a pin fall. The company (out of respect to the Professor's memory) all sat speechless. I was behind Mrs Threadgall at the time, plying her confidentially with a glass of hock. She dropped her head, and said in a very low voice, 'My beloved husband is no more.'

Unluckily Mr Candy, hearing nothing, and miles away from suspecting the truth, went on across the table louder and politer than ever.

'The Professor may not be aware,' says he, 'that the card of a member of the College will admit him, on any day but Sunday, between the hours of ten and four.'

Mrs Threadgall dropped her head right into her tucker, and, in a lower voice still, repeated the solemn words, 'My beloved husband is no more.'

I winked hard at Mr Candy across the table. Miss Rachel touched his arm. My lady looked unutterable things at him. Quite useless! On he went, with a cordiality that there was no stopping anyhow. 'I shall be delighted,' says he, 'to send the Professor my card, if you will oblige me by mentioning his present address.'

'His present address, sir, is *the grave*,' says Mrs Threadgall, suddenly losing her temper, and speaking with an emphasis and fury that made the glasses ring again. 'The Professor has been dead these ten years.'

'Oh, good heavens!' says Mr Candy. Excepting the Bouncers, who burst out laughing, such a blank now fell on the company, that they might all have been going the way of the Professor, and hailing as he did from the direction of the grave.

So much for Mr Candy. The rest of them were nearly as provoking in their different ways as the doctor himself. When they ought to have spoken, they didn't speak; or when they did speak they were perpetually at cross purposes. Mr Godfrey, though so eloquent in public, declined to exert himself in private. Whether he was sulky, or whether he was bashful, after his discomfiture in the rose-garden, I can't say. He kept all his talk for the private ear of the lady (a member of our family) who sat next to him. She was one of his committee-women—a spiritually-minded person, with a fine show of collar-bone and a pretty taste in champagne; liked it dry, you understand, and plenty of it. Being close behind these two at the sideboard, I can testify, from what I heard pass between them, that the company lost a good deal of very improving conversation, which I caught up while drawing the corks, and carving the mutton, and so forth. What they said about their Charities I didn't hear. When I had time to listen to them, they had got a long way beyond their women to be confined, and their women to be rescued, and were disputing on serious subjects. Religion (I understand Mr Godfrey to say, between the corks and the carving) meant love. And love meant religion. And earth was heaven a little the worse for wear. And heaven was earth, done up again to look like new. Earth had some very objectionable people in it; but, to make amends for that, all the women in heaven would be members of a prodigious committee that never quarrelled, with all the men in attendance on them as ministering angels. Beautiful! beautiful! But why the mischief did Mr Godfrey keep it all to his lady and himself?

Mr Franklin again—surely, you will say, Mr Franklin stirred the company up into making a pleasant evening of it?

Nothing of the sort! He had quite recovered himself, and he was in wonderful force and spirits, Penelope having informed him, I suspect, of Mr Godfrey's reception in the rose-garden. But, talk as he might, nine times out of ten he pitched on the wrong subject, or he addressed himself to the wrong person; the end of it being that he offended some, and puzzled all of them. That foreign training of his—those French and German and Italian sides of him, to which I have already alluded—came out, at my lady's hospitable board, in a most bewildering manner.

What do you think, for instance, of his discussing the lengths to which a married woman might let her admiration go for a man who was not her husband, and putting it in his clear-headed witty French way to the maiden aunt of the Vicar of Frizinghall? What do you think, when he shifted to the German side, of his telling the lord of the manor, while that great authority on cattle was quoting his experience in the breeding of bulls, that experience, properly understood, counted for nothing, and that the proper way to breed bulls was to look deep into your own mind, evolve out of it the idea of a perfect bull, and produce him? What do you say, when our county member, growing hot, at cheese and salad time, about the spread of democracy in England, burst out as follows: 'If we once lose our ancient safeguards, Mr Blake, I beg to ask you, what have we got left?'—what do you say to Mr Franklin answering, from the Italian point of view: 'We have got three things left, sir—Love, Music, and Salad'? He not only terrified the company with such outbreaks as these, but, when the English side of him turned up in due course, he lost his foreign smoothness; and, getting on the subject of the medical profession, said such downright things in ridicule of doctors, that he actually put good-humoured little Mr Candy in a rage.

The dispute between them began in Mr Franklin being led—I forget how—to acknowledge that he had latterly slept very badly at night. Mr Candy thereupon told him that his nerves were all out of order, and that he ought to go through a course of medicine immediately. Mr Franklin replied that a course of medicine, and a course of groping in the dark, meant, in his estimation, one and the same thing. Mr Candy, hitting back smartly, said that Mr Franklin himself was, constitutionally speaking, groping in the dark after sleep, and that nothing but medicine could help him to find it. Mr Franklin, keeping the ball up on his side, said he had often heard of the blind leading the blind, and now, for the first time, he knew what it meant. In this way, they kept it going briskly, cut and thrust, till they both of them got hot—Mr Candy, in particular, so completely losing his self-control, in defence of his profession, that my lady was obliged to interfere, and forbid the dispute to go on. This necessary act of authority put the last extinguisher on the spirits of the company. The talk spurted up again here and there, for a minute or two at a time; but there was a miserable lack of life and sparkle in it. The Devil (or the Diamond) possessed that dinner-party; and it was a relief to everybody when my mistress rose, and gave the ladies the signal to leave the gentlemen over their wine.

I had just ranged the decanters in a row before old Mr Ablewhite (who represented the master of the house), when there came a sound from the terrace which startled me out of my company manners on the instant. Mr Franklin and I looked at each other; it was the sound of the Indian drum. As I live by bread, here were the jugglers returning to us with the return of the Moonstone to the house!

As they rounded the corner of the terrace, and came in sight, I hobbled out to warn them off. But, as ill-luck would have it, the two Bouncers were beforehand with me. They whizzed out on to the terrace like a couple of sky-rockets, wild to see the Indians exhibit their tricks. The other ladies followed; the gentlemen came out on their side. Before you could say, 'Lord bless us!' the rogues were making their salaams; and the Bouncers were kissing the pretty little boy.

Mr Franklin got on one side of Miss Rachel, and I put myself behind her. If our suspicions were right, there she stood, innocent of all knowledge of the truth, showing the Indians the Diamond in the bosom of her dress!

I can't tell you what tricks they performed, or how they did it. What with the vexation about the dinner, and what with the provocation of the rogues coming back just in the nick of time to see the jewel with their own eyes, I own I lost my head. The first thing that I remember noticing was the sudden appearance on the scene of the Indian traveller, Mr Murthwaite. Skirting the half-circle in which the gentlefolks stood or sat, he came quietly behind the jugglers and spoke to them on a sudden in the language of their own country.

If he had pricked them with a bayonet, I doubt if the Indians could have started and turned on him with a more tigerish quickness than they did, on hearing the first words that passed his lips. The next moment they were bowing and salaaming to him in their most polite and snaky way. After a few words in the unknown tongue had passed on either side, Mr Murthwaite withdrew as quietly as he had approached. The chief Indian, who acted as interpreter, thereupon wheeled about again towards the gentlefolks. I noticed that the fellow's coffee-coloured face had turned grey since Mr Murthwaite had spoken to him. He bowed to my lady, and informed her that the exhibition was over. The Bouncers, indescribably disappointed, burst out with a loud 'O!' directed against Mr Murthwaite for stopping the performance. The chief Indian laid his hand humbly on his breast, and said a second time that the juggling was over. The little boy went round with the hat. The ladies withdrew to the drawing-room; and the gentlemen (excepting Mr Franklin and Mr Murthwaite) returned to their wine. I and the footman followed the Indians, and saw them safe off the premises.

Going back by way of the shrubbery, I smelt tobacco, and found Mr Franklin and Mr Murthwaite (the latter smoking a cheroot) walking slowly up and down among the trees. Mr Franklin beckoned to me to join them.

'This,' says Mr Franklin, presenting me to the great traveller, 'is Gabriel Betteredge, the old servant and friend of our family of whom I spoke to you just now. Tell him, if you please, what you have just told me.'

Mr Murthwaite took his cheroot out of his mouth, and leaned, in his weary way, against the trunk of a tree.

'Mr Betteredge,' he began, 'those three Indians are no more jugglers than you and I are.'

Here was a new surprise! I naturally asked the traveller if he had ever met with the Indians before.

'Never,' says Mr Murthwaite; 'but I know what Indian juggling really is. All you have seen to-night is a very bad and clumsy imitation of it. Unless, after long experience, I am utterly mistaken, those men are high-caste Brahmins. I charged them with being disguised, and you saw how it told on them, clever as the Hindoo people are in concealing their feelings. There is a mystery about their conduct that I can't explain. They have doubly sacrificed their caste—first, in crossing the sea; secondly, in disguising themselves as jugglers. In the land they live in that is a tremendous sacrifice to make. There must be some very serious motive at the bottom of it, and some justification of no ordinary kind to plead for them, in recovery of their caste, when they return to their own country.'

I was struck dumb. Mr Murthwaite went on with his cheroot. Mr Franklin, after what looked to me like a little private veering about between the different sides of his character, broke the silence as follows:

'I feel some hesitation, Mr Murthwaite, in troubling you with family affairs, in which you can have no interest and which I am not very willing to speak of out of our own circle. But, after what you have said, I feel bound, in the interests of Lady Verinder and her daughter, to tell you something which may possibly put the clue into your hands. I speak to you in confidence; you will oblige me, I am sure, by not forgetting that?'

With this preface, he told the Indian traveller all that he had told me at the Shivering Sand. Even the immovable Mr Murthwaite was so interested in what he heard, that he let his cheroot go out.

'Now,' says Mr Franklin, when he had done, 'what does your experience say?'

'My experience,' answered the traveller, 'says that you have had more narrow escapes of your life, Mr Franklin Blake, than I have had of mine; and that is saying a great deal.'

It was Mr Franklin's turn to be astonished now.

'Is it really as serious as that?' he asked.

'In my opinion it is,' answered Mr Murthwaite. 'I can't doubt, after what you have told me, that the restoration of the Moonstone to its place on the forehead of the Indian idol, is the motive and the justification of that sacrifice of caste which I alluded to just now. Those men will wait their opportunity with the patience of cats, and will use it with the ferocity of tigers. How you have escaped them I can't imagine,' says the eminent traveller, lighting his cheroot again, and staring hard at Mr Franklin. 'You have been carrying the Diamond backwards and forwards, here and in London, and you are still a living man! Let us try and account for it. It was daylight, both times, I suppose, when you took the jewel out of the bank in London?'

'Broad daylight,' says Mr Franklin.

'And plenty of people in the streets?'

'Plenty.'

'You settled, of course, to arrive at Lady Verinder's house at a certain time? It's a lonely country between this and the station. Did you keep your appointment?'

'No. I arrived four hours earlier than my appointment.'

'I beg to congratulate you on that proceeding! When did you take the Diamond to the bank at the town here?'

'I took it an hour after I had brought it to this house—and three hours before anybody was prepared for seeing me in these parts.'

'I beg to congratulate you again! Did you bring it back here alone?'

'No. I happened to ride back with my cousins and the groom.'

'I beg to congratulate you for the third time! If you ever feel inclined to travel beyond the civilised limits, Mr Blake, let me know, and I will go with you. You are a lucky man.'

Here I struck in. This sort of thing didn't at all square with my English ideas.

'You don't really mean to say, sir,' I asked, 'that they would have taken Mr Franklin's life, to get their Diamond, if he had given them the chance?'

'Do you smoke, Mr Betteredge?' says the traveller.

'Yes, sir.'

'Do you care much for the ashes left in your pipe when you empty it?'

'No, sir.'

'In the country those men came from, they care just as much about killing a man, as you care about emptying the ashes out of your pipe. If a thousand lives stood between them and the getting back of their Diamond—and if they thought they could destroy those lives without discovery—they would take them all. The sacrifice of caste is a serious thing in India, if you like. The sacrifice of life is nothing at all.'

I expressed my opinion upon this, that they were a set of murdering thieves. Mr Murthwaite expressed *his* opinion that they were a wonderful people. Mr Franklin, expressing no opinion at all, brought us back to the matter in hand.

'They have seen the Moonstone on Miss Verinder's dress,' he said. 'What is to be done?'

'What your uncle threatened to do,' answered Mr Murthwaite. 'Colonel Herncastle understood the people he had to deal with. Send the Diamond to-morrow (under guard of more than one man) to be cut up at Amsterdam. Make half a dozen diamonds of it, instead of one. There is an end of its sacred identity as the Moonstone—and there is an end of the conspiracy.'

Mr Franklin turned to me.

'There is no help for it,' he said. 'We must speak to Lady Verinder to-morrow.'

'What about to-night, sir?' I asked. 'Suppose the Indians come back?'

Mr Murthwaite answered me before Mr Franklin could speak.

'The Indians won't risk coming back to-night,' he said. 'The direct way is hardly ever the way they take to anything—let alone a matter like this, in which the slightest mistake might be fatal to their reaching their end.'

'But suppose the rogues are bolder than you think, sir?' I persisted.

'In that case,' says Mr Murthwaite, 'let the dogs loose. Have you got any big dogs in the yard?'

'Two, sir. A mastiff and a bloodhound.'

'They will do. In the present emergency, Mr Betteredge, the mastiff and the bloodhound have one great merit—they are not likely to be troubled with your scruples about the sanctity of human life.'

The strumming of the piano reached us from the drawing-room, as he fired that shot at me. He threw away his cheroot, and took Mr Franklin's arm, to go back to the ladies. I noticed that the sky was clouding over fast, as I followed them to the house. Mr Murthwaite noticed it too. He looked round at me, in his dry, drolling way, and said:

'The Indians will want their umbrellas, Mr Betteredge, to-night!'

It was all very well for *him* to joke. But I was not an eminent traveller—and my way in this world had not led me into playing ducks and drakes with my own life, among thieves and murderers in the outlandish places of the earth. I went into my own little room, and sat down in my chair in a perspiration, and wondered helplessly what was to be done next. In this anxious frame of mind, other men might have ended by working themselves up into a fever; *I* ended in a different way. I lit my pipe, and took a turn at *Robinson Crusoe.*

Before I had been at it five minutes, I came to this amazing bit—page one hundred and sixty-one—as follows:

'Fear of Danger is ten thousand times more terrifying than Danger itself, when apparent to the Eyes; and we find the Burthen of Anxiety greater, by much, than the Evil which we are anxious about.'

The man who doesn't believe in *Robinson Crusoe*, after *that*, is a man with a screw loose in his understanding, or a man lost in the mist of his own self-conceit! Argument is thrown away upon him; and pity is better reserved for some person with a livelier faith.

I was far on with my second pipe, and still lost in admiration of that wonderful book, when Penelope (who had been handing round the tea) came in with her report from the drawing-room. She had left the Bouncers singing a duet—words beginning with a large 'O,' and music to correspond. She had observed that my lady made mistakes in her game of whist for the first time in our experience of her. She had seen the great traveller asleep in a corner. She had overheard Mr Franklin sharpening his wits on Mr Godfrey, at the expense of Ladies' Charities in general; and she had noticed that Mr Godfrey hit him back again rather more smartly than became a gentleman of his benevolent character. She had detected Miss Rachel, apparently engaged in appeasing Mrs Threadgall by showing her some photographs, and really occupied in stealing looks at Mr Franklin, which no intelligent lady's maid could misinterpret for a single instant. Finally, she had missed Mr Candy, the doctor, who had mysteriously disappeared from the drawing-room, and had then mysteriously returned, and entered into conversation with Mr Godfrey. Upon the whole, things were prospering better than the experience of the dinner gave us any right to expect. If we could only hold on for another hour, old Father Time would bring up their carriages, and relieve us of them altogether.

Everything wears off in this world; and even the comforting effect of *Robinson Crusoe* wore off, after Penelope left me. I got fidgety again, and resolved on making a survey of the grounds before the rain came. Instead of taking the footman, whose nose was human, and therefore useless in any emergency, I took the bloodhound with me. *His* nose for a stranger was to be depended on. We went all round the premises, and out into the road—and returned as wise as we went, having discovered no such thing as a lurking human creature anywhere.

The arrival of the carriages was the signal for the arrival of the rain. It poured as if it meant to pour all night. With the exception of the doctor, whose gig was waiting for him, the rest of the company went home snugly, under cover, in close carriages. I told Mr Candy that I was afraid he would get wet through. He told me, in return, that he wondered I had arrived at my time of life, without knowing that a doctor's skin was waterproof. So he drove away in the rain, laughing over his own little joke; and so we got rid of our dinner company.

The next thing to tell is the story of the night.

CHAPTER XI

WHEN the last of the guests had driven away, I went back into the inner hall and found Samuel at the side-table, presiding over the brandy and soda-water. My lady and Miss Rachel came out of the drawing-room, followed by the two gentlemen. Mr Godfrey had some brandy and soda-water. Mr Franklin took nothing. He sat down, looking dead tired; the talking on this birthday occasion had, I suppose, been too much for him.

My lady, turning round to wish them good-night, looked hard at the wicked Colonel's legacy shining in her daughter's dress.

'Rachel,' she asked, 'where are you going to put your Diamond to-night?'

Miss Rachel was in high good spirits, just in that humour for talking nonsense, and perversely persisting in it as if it was sense, which you may sometimes have observed in young girls, when they are highly wrought up, at the end of an exciting day. First, she declared she didn't know where to put the Diamond. Then she said, 'on her dressing-table, of course, along with her other things.' Then she remembered that the Diamond might take to shining of itself, with its awful moony light in the dark—and that would terrify her in the dead of night. Then she bethought herself of an Indian cabinet which stood in her sitting-room; and instantly made up her mind to put the Indian diamond in the Indian cabinet, for the purpose of permitting two beautiful native productions to admire each other. Having let her little flow of nonsense run on as far as that point, her mother interposed and stopped her.

'My dear! your Indian cabinet has no lock to it,' says my lady.

'Good Heavens, mamma!' cried Miss Rachel, 'is this an hotel? Are there thieves in the house?'

Without taking notice of this fantastic way of talking, my lady wished the gentlemen good-night. She next turned to Miss Rachel, and kissed her. 'Why not let *me* keep the Diamond for you to-night?' she asked.

Miss Rachel received that proposal as she might, ten years since, have received a proposal to part her from a new doll. My lady saw there was no reasoning with her that night. 'Come into my room, Rachel, the first thing to-morrow morning,' she said. 'I shall have something to say to you. With those last words she left us slowly; thinking her own thoughts, and, to all appearance, not best pleased with the way by which they were leading her.

Miss Rachel was the next to say good-night. She shook hands first with Mr Godfrey, who was standing at the other end of the hall, looking at a picture. Then she turned back to Mr Franklin, still sitting weary and silent in a corner.

What words passed between them I can't say. But standing near the old oak frame which holds our large looking-glass, I saw her reflected in it, slyly slipping the locket which Mr Franklin had given to her, out of the bosom of her dress, and showing it to him for a moment, with a smile which certainly meant something out of the common, before she tripped off to bed. This incident staggered me a little in the reliance I had previously felt on my own judgment. I began to think that Penelope might be right about the state of her young lady's affections, after all.

As soon as Miss Rachel left him eyes to see with, Mr Franklin noticed me. His variable humour, shifting about everything, had shifted about the Indians already.

'Betteredge,' he said, 'I'm half inclined to think I took Mr Murthwaite too seriously, when we had that talk in the shrubbery. I wonder whether he has been trying any of his traveller's tales on us? Do you really mean to let the dogs loose?'

'I'll relieve them of their collars, sir,' I answered, 'and leave them free to take a turn in the night, if they smell a reason for it.'

'All right,' says Mr Franklin. 'We'll see what is to be done to-morrow. I am not at all disposed to alarm my aunt, Betteredge, without a very pressing reason for it. Good-night.'

He looked so worn and pale as he nodded to me, and took his candle to go upstairs, that I ventured to advise his having a drop of brandy-and-water, by way of night-cap. Mr Godfrey, walking towards us from the other end of the hall, backed me. He pressed Mr Franklin, in the friendliest manner, to take something, before he went to bed.

I only note these trifling circumstances, because, after all I had seen and heard, that day, it pleased me to observe that our two gentlemen were on just as good terms as ever. Their warfare of words (heard by Penelope in the drawing-room), and their rivalry for the best place in Miss Rachel's good graces, seemed to have set no serious difference between them. But there! they were both good-tempered, and both men of the world. And there is certainly this merit in people of station, that they are not nearly so quarrelsome among each other as people of no station at all.

Mr Franklin declined the brandy-and-water, and went upstairs with Mr Godfrey, their rooms being next door to each other. On the landing, however, either his cousin persuaded him, or he veered about and changed his mind as usual. 'Perhaps I may want it in the night,' he called down to me. 'Send up some brandy-and-water into my room.'

I sent up Samuel with the brandy-and-water; and then went out and unbuckled the dogs' collars. They both lost their heads with astonishment on being set loose at that time of night, and jumped upon me like a couple of puppies! However, the rain soon cooled them down again: they lapped a drop of water each, and crept back into their kennels. As I went into the house I noticed signs in the sky which betokened a break in the weather for the better. For the present, it still poured heavily, and the ground was in a perfect sop.

Samuel and I went all over the house, and shut up as usual. I examined everything myself, and trusted nothing to my deputy on this occasion. All was safe and fast when I rested my old bones in bed, between midnight and one in the morning.

The worries of the day had been a little too much for me, I suppose. At any rate, I had a touch of Mr Franklin's malady that night. It was sunrise before I fell off at last into a sleep. All the time I lay awake the house was as quiet as the grave. Not a sound stirred but the splash of the rain, and the sighing of the wind among the trees as a breeze sprang up with the morning.

About half-past seven I woke, and opened my window on a fine sunshiny day. The clock had struck eight, and I was just going out to chain up the dogs again, when I heard a sudden whisking of petticoats on the stairs behind me.

I turned about, and there was Penelope flying down after me like mad. 'Father!' she screamed, 'come upstairs, for God's sake! *The Diamond is gone!*'

'Are you out of your mind?' I asked her.

'Gone!' says Penelope. 'Gone, nobody knows how! Come up and see.'

She dragged me after her into our young lady's sitting-room, which opened into her bed-room. There, on the threshold of her bed-room door, stood Miss Rachel, almost as white in the face as the white dressing-gown that clothed her. There also stood the two doors of the Indian cabinet, wide open. One of the drawers inside was pulled out as far as it would go.

'Look!' says Penelope. 'I myself saw Miss Rachel put the Diamond into that drawer last night.'

I went to the cabinet. The drawer was empty.

'Is this true, miss?' I asked.

With a look that was not like herself, with a voice that was not like her own, Miss Rachel answered as my daughter had answered: 'The Diamond is gone!'

Having said those words, she withdrew into her bed-room, and shut and locked the door.

Before we knew which way to turn next, my lady came in, hearing my voice in her daughter's sitting-room, and wondering what had happened. The news of the loss of the Diamond seemed to petrify her. She went straight to Miss Rachel's bed-room, and insisted on being admitted. Miss Rachel let her in.

The alarm, running through the house like fire, caught the two gentlemen next.

Mr Godfrey was the first to come out of his room. All he did when he heard what had happened was to hold up his hands in a state of bewilderment, which didn't say much for his natural strength of mind. Mr Franklin, whose clear head I had confidently counted on to advise us, seemed to be as helpless as his cousin when he heard the news in his turn. For a wonder, he had had a good night's rest at last; and the unaccustomed luxury of sleep had, as he said himself, apparently stupefied him. However, when he had swallowed his cup of coffee—which he always took, on the foreign plan, some hours before he ate any breakfast—his brains brightened; the clear-headed side of him turned up, and he took the matter in hand, resolutely and cleverly, much as follows:

He first sent for the servants, and told them to leave all the lower doors and windows (with the exception of the front door, which I had opened) exactly as they had been left when we locked up overnight. He next proposed to his cousin and to me to make quite sure, before we took any further steps, that the Diamond had not accidentally dropped somewhere out of sight—say at the back of the cabinet, or down behind the table on which the cabinet stood. Having searched in both places, and found nothing—having also questioned Penelope, and discovered from her no more than the little she had already told me—Mr Franklin suggested next extending our inquiries to Miss Rachel, and sent Penelope to knock at her bed-room door.

My lady answered the knock, and closed the door behind her. The moment after we heard it locked inside by Miss Rachel. My mistress came out among us, looking sorely puzzled and distressed. 'The loss of the Diamond seems to have quite overwhelmed Rachel,' she said, in reply to Mr Franklin. 'She shrinks, in the strangest manner, from speaking of it, even to *me*. It is impossible you can see her for the present.'

Having added to our perplexities by this account of Miss Rachel, my lady, after a little effort, recovered her usual composure, and acted with her usual decision.

'I suppose there is no help for it?' she said, quietly. 'I suppose I have no alternative but to send for the police?'

'And the first thing for the police to do,' added Mr Franklin, catching her up, 'is to lay hands on the Indian jugglers who performed here last night.'

My lady and Mr Godfrey (not knowing what Mr Franklin and I knew) both started, and both looked surprised.

'I can't stop to explain myself now,' Mr Franklin went on. 'I can only tell you that the Indians have certainly stolen the Diamond. Give me a letter of introduction,' says he, addressing my lady, 'to one of the magistrates at Frizinghall—merely telling him that I represent your interests and wishes, and let me ride off with it instantly. Our chance of catching the thieves may depend on our not wasting one unnecessary minute.' (*Nota bene:* Whether it was the French side or the English, the right side of Mr Franklin seemed to be uppermost now. The only question was, How long would it last?)

He put pen, ink, and paper before his aunt, who (as it appeared to me) wrote the letter he wanted a little unwillingly. If it had been possible to overlook such an event as the loss of a jewel worth twenty thousand pounds, I believe—with my lady's opinion of her late brother, and her distrust of his birthday-gift—it would have been privately a relief to her to let the thieves get off with the Moonstone scot free.

I went out with Mr Franklin to the stables, and took the opportunity of asking him how the Indians (whom I suspected, of course, as shrewdly as he did) could possibly have got into the house.

'One of them might have slipped into the hall, in the confusion, when the dinner company were going away,' says Mr Franklin. 'The fellow may have been under the sofa while my aunt and Rachel were talking about where the Diamond was to be put for the night. He would only have to wait till the house was quiet, and there it would be in the cabinet, to be had for the taking.' With those words, he called to the groom to open the gate, and galloped off.

This seemed certainly to be the only rational explanation. But how had the thief contrived to make his escape from the house? I had found the front door locked and bolted, as I had left it at night, when I went to open it, after getting up. As for the other doors and windows, there they were still, all safe and fast, to speak for themselves. The dogs, too? Suppose the thief had got away by dropping from one of the upper windows, how had he escaped the dogs? Had he come provided for them with drugged meat? As the doubt crossed my mind, the dogs themselves came galloping at me round a corner, rolling each other over on the wet grass, in such lively health and spirits that it was with no small difficulty I brought them to reason, and chained them up again. The more I turned it over in my mind, the less satisfactory Mr Franklin's explanation appeared to be.

We had our breakfasts—whatever happens in a house, robbery or murder, it doesn't matter, you must have your breakfast. When we had done, my lady sent for me; and I found myself compelled to tell her all that I had hitherto concealed, relating to the Indians and their plot. Being a woman of a high courage, she soon got over the first startling effect of what I had to communicate. Her mind seemed to be far more perturbed about her daughter than about the heathen rogues and their conspiracy. 'You know how odd Rachel is, and how differently she behaves sometimes from other girls,' my lady said to me. 'But I have never, in all my experience, seen her so strange and so reserved as she is now. The loss of her jewel seems almost to have turned her brain. Who would have thought that horrible Diamond could have laid such a hold on her in so short a time?'

It was certainly strange. Taking toys and trinkets in general, Miss Rachel was nothing like so mad after them as most young girls. Yet there she was, still locked up inconsolably in her bed-room. It is but fair to add that she was not the only one of us in the house who was thrown out of the regular groove. Mr Godfrey, for instance—though professionally a sort of consoler-general—seemed to be at a loss where to look for his own resources. Having no company to amuse him, and getting no chance of trying what his experience of women in distress could do towards comforting Miss Rachel, he wandered hither and thither about the house and gardens in an aimless uneasy way. He was in two different minds about what it became him to do, after the misfortune that had happened to us. Ought he to relieve the family, in their present situation, of the responsibility of him as a guest, or ought he to stay on the chance that even his humble services might be of some use? He decided ultimately that the last course was perhaps the most customary and considerate course to take, in such a very peculiar case of family distress as this was. Circumstances try the metal a man is really made of. Mr Godfrey, tried by circumstances, showed himself of weaker metal than I had thought him to be. As for the women-servants—excepting Rosanna Spearman, who kept by herself—they took to whispering together in corners, and staring at nothing suspiciously, as is the manner of that weaker half of the human family, when anything extraordinary happens in a house. I myself acknowledge to have been fidgety and ill-tempered. The cursed Moonstone had turned us all upside down.

A little before eleven Mr Franklin came back. The resolute side of him had, to all appearance, given way, in the interval since his departure, under the stress that had been laid on it. He had left us at a gallop; he came back to us at a walk. When he went away, he was made of iron. When he returned, he was stuffed with cotton, as limp as limp could be.

'Well,' says my lady, 'are the police coming?'

'Yes,' says Mr Franklin; 'they said they would follow me in a fly. Superintendent Seegrave, of your local police force, and two of his men. A mere form! The case is hopeless.'

'What! have the Indians escaped, sir?' I asked.

'The poor ill-used Indians have been most unjustly put in prison,' says Mr Franklin. 'They are as innocent as the babe unborn. My idea that one of them was hidden in the house has ended, like all the rest of my ideas, in smoke. It's been proved,' says Mr Franklin, dwelling with great relish on his own incapacity, 'to be simply impossible.'

After astonishing us by announcing this totally new turn in the matter of the Moonstone, our young gentleman, at his aunt's request, took a seat, and explained himself.

It appeared that the resolute side of him had held out as far as Frizinghall. He had put the whole case plainly before the magistrate, and the magistrate had at once sent for the police. The first inquiries instituted about the Indians showed that they had not so much as attempted to leave the town. Further questions addressed to the police proved that all three had been seen returning to Frizinghall with their boy, on the previous night between ten and eleven—which (regard being had to hours and distances) also proved that they had walked straight back after performing on our terrace. Later still, at midnight, the police, having occasion to search the common lodging-house where they lived, had seen them all three again, and their little boy with them as usual. Soon after midnight I myself had safely shut up the house. Plainer evidence than this, in favour of the Indians, there could not well be. The magistrate said there was not even a case of suspicion against them so far. But, as it was just possible, when the police came to investigate the matter, that discoveries affecting the jugglers might be made, he would contrive, by committing them as rogues and vagabonds, to keep them at our disposal, under lock and key, for a week. They had ignorantly done something (I forget what) in the town, which barely brought them within the operation of the law. Every human institution (Justice included) will stretch a little, if you only pull it the right way. The worthy magistrate was an old friend of my lady's, and the Indians were 'committed' for a week, as soon as the court opened that morning.

Such was Mr Franklin's narrative of events at Frizinghall. The Indian clue to the mystery of the lost jewel was now, to all appearance, a clue that had broken in our hands. If the jugglers were innocent, who, in the name of wonder, had taken the Moonstone out of Miss Rachel's drawer?

Ten minutes later, to our infinite relief, Superintendent Seegrave arrived at the house. He reported passing Mr Franklin on the terrace, sitting in the sun (I suppose with the Italian side of him uppermost), and warning the police, as they went by, that the investigation was hopeless, before the investigation had begun.

For a family in our situation, the Superintendent of the Frizinghall police was the most comforting officer you could wish to see. Mr Seegrave was tall and portly, and military in his manners. He had a fine commanding voice, and a mighty resolute eye, and a grand frock-coat which buttoned beautifully up to his leather stock. 'I'm the man you want!' was written all over his face; and he ordered his two inferior policemen about with a severity which convinced us all that there was no trifling with *him*.

He began by going round the premises, outside and in; the result of that investigation proving to him that no thieves had broken in upon us from outside, and that the robbery, consequently, must have been committed by some person in the house. I leave you to imagine the state the servants were in when this official announcement first reached their ears. The Superintendent decided to begin by examining the boudoir, and, that done, to examine the servants next. At the same time, he posted one of his men on the staircase which led to the servants' bed-rooms, with instructions to let nobody in the house pass him, till further orders.

At this latter proceeding, the weaker half of the human family went distracted on the spot. They bounced out of their corners, whisked upstairs in a body to Miss Rachel's room (Rosanna Spearman being carried away among them this time), burst in on Superintendent Seegrave, and, all looking equally guilty, summoned him to say which of them he suspected, at once.

Mr Superintendent proved equal to the occasion; he looked at them with his resolute eye, and he cowed them with his military voice.

'Now, then, you women, go downstairs again, every one of you; I won't have you here. Look!' says Mr Superintendent, suddenly pointing to a little smear of the decorative painting on Miss Rachel's door, at the outer edge, just under the lock. 'Look what mischief the petticoats of some of you have done already. Clear out! clear out!' Rosanna Spearman, who was nearest to him, and nearest to the little smear on the door, set the example of obedience, and slipped off instantly to her work. The rest followed her out. The Superintendent finished his examination of the room, and, making nothing of it, asked me who had first discovered the robbery. My daughter had first discovered it. My daughter was sent for.

Mr Superintendent proved to be a little too sharp with Penelope at starting. 'Now, young woman, attend to me, and mind you speak the truth.' Penelope fired up instantly. 'I've never been taught to tell lies, Mr Police-man!—and if father can stand there and hear me accused of falsehood and thieving, and my own bed-room shut against me, and my character taken away, which is all a poor girl has left, he's not the good father I take him for!' A timely word from me put Justice and Penelope on a pleasanter footing together. The questions and answers went swimmingly, and ended in nothing worth mentioning. My daughter had seen Miss Rachel put the Diamond in the drawer of the cabinet the last thing at night. She had gone in with Miss Rachel's cup of tea at eight the next morning, and had found the drawer open and empty. Upon that, she had alarmed the house—and there was an end of Penelope's evidence.

Mr Superintendent next asked to see Miss Rachel herself. Penelope mentioned his request through the door. The answer reached us by the same road: 'I have nothing to tell the policeman—I can't see anybody.' Our experienced officer looked equally surprised and offended when he heard that reply. I told him my young lady was ill, and begged him to wait a little and see her later. We thereupon went downstairs again, and were met by Mr Godfrey and Mr Franklin crossing the hall.

The two gentlemen, being inmates of the house, were summoned to say if they could throw any light on the matter. Neither of them knew anything about it. Had they heard any suspicious noises during the previous night? They had heard nothing but the pattering of the rain. Had I, lying awake longer than either of them, heard nothing either? Nothing! Released from examination, Mr Franklin, still sticking to the helpless view of our difficulty, whispered to me: 'That man will be of no earthly use to us. Superintendent Seegrave is an ass.' Released in his turn, Mr Godfrey whispered to me:—'Evidently a most competent person. Betteredge, I have the greatest faith in him!' Many men, many opinions, as one of the ancients said, before my time.

Mr Superintendent's next proceeding took him back to the 'boudoir' again, with my daughter and me at his heels. His object was to discover whether any of the furniture had been moved, during the night, out of its customary place—his previous investigation in the room having, apparently, not gone quite far enough to satisfy his mind on this point.

While we were still poking about among the chairs and tables, the door of the bed-room was suddenly opened. After having denied herself to everybody, Miss Rachel, to our astonishment, walked into the midst of us of her own accord. She took up her garden hat from a chair, and then went straight to Penelope with this question:—

'Mr Franklin Blake sent you with a message to me this morning?'

'Yes, miss.'

'He wished to speak to me, didn't he?'

'Yes, miss.'

'Where is he now?'

Hearing voices on the terrace below, I looked out of window, and saw the two gentlemen walking up and down together. Answering for my daughter, I said, 'Mr Franklin is on the terrace, miss.'

Without another word, without heeding Mr Superintendent, who tried to speak to her, pale as death, and wrapped up strangely in her own thoughts, she left the room, and went down to her cousins on the terrace.

It showed a want of due respect, it showed a breach of good manners, on my part, but, for the life of me, I couldn't help looking out of window when Miss Rachel met the gentlemen outside. She went up to Mr Franklin without appearing to notice Mr Godfrey, who thereupon drew back and left them by themselves. What she said to Mr Franklin appeared to be spoken vehemently. It lasted but for a short time, and, judging by what I saw of his face from the window, seemed to astonish him beyond all power of expression. While they were still together, my lady appeared on the terrace. Miss Rachel saw her—said a few last words to Mr Franklin—and suddenly went back into the house again, before her mother came up with her. My lady, surprised herself, and noticing Mr Franklin's surprise, spoke to him. Mr Godfrey joined them, and spoke also. Mr Franklin walked away a little, between the two, telling them what had happened I suppose, for they both stopped short, after taking a few steps, like persons struck with amazement. I had just seen as much as this, when the door of the sitting-room was opened violently. Miss Rachel walked swiftly through to her bed-room, wild and angry, with fierce eyes and flaming cheeks. Mr Superintendent once more attempted to question her. She turned round on him at her bed-room door. '*I* have not sent for you!' she cried out vehemently. '*I* don't want you. My Diamond is lost. Neither you nor anybody else will ever find it!' With those words she went in, and locked the door in our faces. Penelope, standing nearest to it, heard her burst out crying the moment she was alone again.

In a rage, one moment; in tears, the next! What did it mean?

I told the Superintendent it meant that Miss Rachel's temper was upset by the loss of her jewel. Being anxious for the honour of the family, it distressed me to see my young lady forget herself—even with a police-officer—and I made the best excuse I could, accordingly. In my own private mind, I was more puzzled by Miss Rachel's extraordinary language and conduct than words can tell. Taking what she had said at her bedroom door as a guide to guess by, I could only conclude that she was mortally offended by our sending for the police, and that Mr Franklin's astonishment on the terrace was caused by her having expressed herself to him (as the person chiefly instrumental in fetching the police) to that effect. If this guess was right, why—having lost her Diamond—should she object to the presence in the house of the very people whose business it was to recover it for her? And how, in Heaven's name, could *she* know that the Moonstone would never be found again?

As things stood, at present, no answer to those questions was to be hoped for from anybody in the house. Mr Franklin appeared to think it a point of honour to forbear repeating to a servant—even to so old a servant as I was—what Miss Rachel had said to him on the terrace. Mr Godfrey, who, as a gentleman and a relative, had been probably admitted into Mr Franklin's confidence, respected that confidence as he was bound to do. My lady, who was also in the secret no doubt, and who alone had access to Miss Rachel, owned openly that she could make nothing of her. 'You madden me when you talk of the Diamond!' All her mother's influence failed to extract from her a word more than that.

Here we were, then, at a dead-lock about Miss Rachel—and at a dead-lock about the Moonstone. In the first case, my lady was powerless to help us. In the second (as you shall presently judge), Mr Seegrave was fast approaching the condition of a superintendent at his wits' end.

Having ferreted about all over the 'boudoir', without making any discoveries among the furniture, our experienced officer applied to me to know, whether the servants in general were or were not acquainted with the place in which the Diamond had been put for the night.

'I knew where it was put, sir,' I said, 'to begin with. Samuel, the footman, knew also—for he was present in the hall, when they were talking about where the Diamond was to be kept that night. My daughter knew, as she has already told you. She or Samuel may have mentioned the thing to the other servants—or the other servants may have heard the talk for themselves, through the side-door of the hall, which might have been open to the back staircase. For all I can tell, everybody in the house may have known where the jewel was, last night.'

My answer presenting rather a wide field for Mr Superintendent's suspicions to range over, he tried to narrow it by asking about the servants' characters next.

I thought directly of Rosanna Spearman. But it was neither my place nor my wish to direct suspicion against a poor girl, whose honesty had been above all doubt as long as I had known her. The matron of the Reformatory had reported her to my lady as a sincerely penitent and thoroughly trustworthy girl. It was the Superintendent's business to discover reason for suspecting her first—and then, and not till then, it would be my duty to tell him how she came into my lady's service. 'All our people have excellent characters,' I said. 'And all have deserved the trust their mistress has placed in them.' After that, there was but one thing left for Mr Seegrave to do—namely, to set to work, and tackle the servants' characters himself.

One after another, they were examined. One after another, they proved to have nothing to say—and said it (so far as the women were concerned) at great length, and with a very angry sense of the embargo laid on their bedrooms. The rest of them being sent back to their places downstairs, Penelope was then summoned, and examined separately a second time.

My daughter's little outbreak of temper in the 'boudoir', and her readiness to think herself suspected, appeared to have produced an unfavourable impression on Superintendent Seegrave. It seemed also to dwell a little on his mind, that she had been the last person who saw the Diamond at night. When the second questioning was over, my girl came back to me in a frenzy. There was no doubt of it any longer—the police-officer had almost as good as told her she was the thief! I could scarcely believe him (taking Mr Franklin's view) to be quite such an ass as that. But, though he said nothing, the eye with which he looked at my daughter was not a very pleasant eye to see. I laughed it off with poor Penelope, as something too ridiculous to be treated seriously—which it certainly was. Secretly, I am afraid I was foolish enough to be angry too. It was a little trying—it was, indeed. My girl sat down in a corner, with her apron over her head, quite broken-hearted. Foolish of her, you will say: she might have waited till he openly accused her. Well, being a man of just and equal temper, I admit that. Still Mr Superintendent might have remembered—never mind what he might have remembered. The devil take him!

The next and last step in the investigation brought matters, as they say, to a crisis. The officer had an interview (at which I was present) with my lady. After informing her that the Diamond *must* have been taken by somebody in the house, he requested permission for himself and his men to search the servants' rooms and boxes on the spot. My good mistress, like the generous high-bred woman she was, refused to let us be treated like thieves. 'I will never consent to make such a return as that,' she said, 'for all I owe to the faithful servants who are employed in my house.'

Mr Superintendent made his bow, with a look in my direction, which said plainly, 'Why employ me, if you are to tie my hands in this way?' As head of the servants, I felt directly that we were bound, in justice to all parties, not to profit by our mistress's generosity. 'We gratefully thank your ladyship,' I said; 'but we ask permission to do what is right in this matter, by giving up our keys. When Gabriel Betteredge sets the example,' says I, stopping Superintendent Seegrave at the door, 'the rest of the servants will follow, I promise you. There are my keys, to begin with!' My lady took me by the hand, and thanked me with the tears in her eyes. Lord! what would I not have given, at that moment, for the privilege of knocking Superintendent Seegrave down!

As I had promised for them, the other servants followed my lead, sorely against the grain, of course, but all taking the view that I took. The women were a sight to see, while the police-officers were rummaging among their things. The cook looked as if she could grill Mr Superintendent alive on a furnace, and the other women looked as if they could eat him when he was done.

The search over, and no Diamond or sign of a Diamond being found, of course, anywhere, Superintendent Seegrave retired to my little room to consider with himself what he was to do next. He and his men had now been hours in the house, and had not advanced us one inch towards a discovery of how the Moonstone had been taken, or of whom we were to suspect as the thief.

While the police-officer was still pondering in solitude, I was sent for to see Mr Franklin in the library. To my unutterable astonishment, just as my hand was on the door, it was suddenly opened from the inside, and out walked Rosanna Spearman!

After the library had been swept and cleaned in the morning, neither first nor second housemaid had any business in that room at any later period of the day. I stopped Rosanna Spearman, and charged her with a breach of domestic discipline on the spot.

'What might you want in the library at this time of day?' I inquired.

'Mr Franklin Blake dropped one of his rings up-stairs,' says Rosanna; 'and I have been into the library to give it to him.' The girl's face was all in a flush as she made me that answer; and she walked away with a toss of her head and a look of self-importance which I was quite at a loss to account for. The proceedings in the house had doubtless upset all the women-servants more or less; but none of them had gone clean out of their natural characters, as Rosanna, to all appearance, had now gone out of hers.

I found Mr Franklin writing at the library-table. He asked for a convey-ance to the railway station the moment I entered the room. The first sound of his voice informed me that we now had the resolute side of him uppermost once more. The man made of cotton had disappeared, and the man made of iron sat before me again.

'Going to London, sir?' I asked.

'Going to telegraph to London,' says Mr Franklin. 'I have convinced my aunt that we must have a cleverer head than Superintendent Seegrave's to help us; and I have got her permission to despatch a telegram to my father. He knows the Chief Commissioner of Police, and the Commissioner can lay his hand on the right man to solve the mystery of the Diamond. Talking of mysteries, by-the-bye,' says Mr Franklin, dropping his voice, 'I have another word to say to you before you go to the stables. Don't breathe a word of it to anybody as yet; but either Rosanna Spearman's head is not quite right, or I am afraid she knows more about the Moonstone than she ought to know.'

I can hardly tell whether I was more startled or distressed at hearing him say that. If I had been younger, I might have confessed as much to Mr Franklin. But when you are old, you acquire one excellent habit. In cases where you don't see your way clearly, you hold your tongue.

'She came in here with a ring I dropped in my bedroom,' Mr Franklin went on. 'When I had thanked her, of course I expected her to go. Instead of that, she stood opposite to me at the table, looking at me in the oddest manner—half frightened, and half familiar—I couldn't make it out. "This is a strange thing about the Diamond, sir," she said, in a curiously sudden, headlong way. I said, "Yes, it was," and wondered what was coming next. Upon my honour, Betteredge, I think she must be wrong in the head! She said, "They will never find the Diamond, sir, will they? No! nor the person who took it—I'll answer for that." She actually nodded and smiled at me! Before I could ask her what she meant, we heard your step outside. I suppose she was afraid of your catching her here. At any rate, she changed colour, and left the room. What on earth does it mean?'

I could not bring myself to tell him the girl's story, even then. It would have been almost as good as telling him that she was the thief. Besides, even if I had made a clean breast of it, and even supposing she was the thief, the reason why she should let out her secret to Mr Franklin, of all the people in the world, would have been still as far to seek as ever.

'I can't bear the idea of getting the poor girl into a scrape, merely because she has a flighty way with her, and talks very strangely,' Mr Franklin went on. 'And yet if she had said to the Superintendent what she said to me, fool as he is, I'm afraid——' He stopped there, and left the rest unspoken.

'The best way, sir,' I said, 'will be for me to say two words privately to my mistress about it at the first opportunity. My lady has a very friendly interest in Rosanna; and the girl may only have been forward and foolish, after all. When there's a mess of any kind in a house, sir, the women-servants like to look at the gloomy side—it gives the poor wretches a kind of importance in their own eyes. If there's anybody ill, trust the women for prophesying that the person will die. If it's a jewel lost, trust them for prophesying that it will never be found again.'

This view (which, I am bound to say, I thought a probable view myself, on reflection) seemed to relieve Mr Franklin mightily: he folded up his telegram, and dismissed the subject. On my way to the stables, to order the pony-chaise, I looked in at the servants' hall, where they were at dinner. Rosanna Spearman was not among them. On inquiry, I found that she had been suddenly taken ill, and had gone upstairs to her own room to lie down.

'Curious! She looked well enough when I saw her last,' I remarked.

Penelope followed me out. 'Don't talk in that way before the rest of them, father,' she said. 'You only make them harder on Rosanna than ever. The poor thing is breaking her heart about Mr Franklin Blake.'

Here was another view of the girl's conduct. If it was possible for Penelope to be right, the explanation of Rosanna's strange language and behaviour might have been all in this—that she didn't care what she said, so long as she could surprise Mr Franklin into speaking to her. Granting that to be the right reading of the riddle, it accounted, perhaps, for her flighty, self-conceited manner when she passed me in the hall. Though he had only said three words, still she had carried her point, and Mr Franklin *had* spoken to her.

I saw the pony harnessed myself. In the infernal network of mysteries and uncertainties that now surrounded us, I declare it was a relief to observe how well the buckles and straps understood each other! When you had seen the pony backed into the shafts of the chaise, you had seen something there was no doubt about. And that, let me tell you, was becoming a treat of the rarest kind in our household.

Going round with the chaise to the front door, I found not only Mr Franklin, but Mr Godfrey and Superintendent Seegrave also waiting for me on the steps.

Mr Superintendent's reflections (after failing to find the Diamond in the servants' rooms or boxes) had led him, it appeared, to an entirely new conclusion. Still sticking to his first text, namely, that somebody in the house had stolen the jewel, our experienced officer was now of opinion that the thief (he was wise enough not to name poor Penelope, whatever he might privately think of her!) had been acting in concert with the Indians; and he accordingly proposed shifting his inquiries to the jugglers in the prison at Frizinghall. Hearing of this new move, Mr Franklin had volunteered to take the Superintendent back to the town, from which he could telegraph to London as easily as from our station. Mr Godfrey, still devoutly believing in Mr Seegrave, and greatly interested in witnessing the examination of the Indians, had begged leave to accompany the officer to Frizinghall. One of the two inferior policemen was to be left at the house, in case anything happened. The other was to go back with the Superintendent to the town. So the four places in the pony-chaise were just filled.

Before he took the reins to drive off, Mr Franklin walked me away a few steps out of hearing of the others.

'I will wait to telegraph to London,' he said, 'till I see what comes of our examination of the Indians. My own conviction is, that this muddle-headed local police-officer is as much in the dark as ever, and is simply trying to gain time. The idea of any of the servants being in league with the Indians is a preposterous absurdity, in my opinion. Keep about the house, Better-edge, till I come back, and try what you can make of Rosanna Spearman. I don't ask you to do anything degrading to your own self-respect, or anything cruel towards the girl. I only ask you to exercise your observation more carefully than usual. We will make as light of it as we can before my aunt—but this is a more important matter than you may suppose.'

'It is a matter of twenty thousand pounds, sir,' I said, thinking of the value of the Diamond.

'It's a matter of quieting Rachel's mind,' answered Mr Franklin gravely. 'I am very uneasy about her.'

He left me suddenly, as if he desired to cut short any further talk between us. I thought I understood why. Further talk might have let me into the secret of what Miss Rachel had said to him on the terrace.

So they drove away to Frizinghall. I was ready enough, in the girl's own interest, to have a little talk with Rosanna in private. But the needful opportunity failed to present itself. She only came down-stairs again at tea-time. When she did appear, she was flighty and excited, had what they call an hysterical attack, took a dose of sal-volatile by my lady's order, and was sent back to her bed.

The day wore on to its end drearily and miserably enough, I can tell you. Miss Rachel still kept her room, declaring that she was too ill to come down to dinner that day. My lady was in such low spirits about her daughter, that I could not bring myself to make her additionally anxious, by reporting what Rosanna Spearman had said to Mr Franklin. Penelope persisted in believing that she was to be forthwith tried, sentenced, and transported for theft. The other women took to their Bibles and hymn-books, and looked as sour as verjuice over their reading—a result, which I have observed, in my sphere of life, to follow generally on the performance of acts of piety at unaccustomed periods of the day. As for me, I hadn't even heart enough to open my *Robinson Crusoe*. I went out into the yard, and, being hard up for a little cheerful society, set my chair by the kennels, and talked to the dogs.

Half an hour before dinner-time, the two gentlemen came back from Frizinghall, having arranged with Superintendent Seegrave that he was to return to us the next day. They had called on Mr Murthwaite, the Indian traveller, at his present residence, near the town. At Mr Franklin's request, he had kindly given them the benefit of his knowledge of the language, in dealing with those two, out of the three Indians, who knew nothing of English. The examination, conducted carefully, and at great length, had ended in nothing; not the shadow of a reason being discovered for suspecting the jugglers of having tampered with any of our servants. On reaching that conclusion, Mr Franklin had sent his telegraphic message to London, and there the matter now rested till to-morrow came.

So much for the history of the day that followed the birthday. Not a glimmer of light had broken in on us, so far. A day or two after, however, the darkness lifted a little. How, and with what result, you shall presently see.

CHAPTER XII

THE Thursday night passed, and nothing happened. With the Friday morning came two pieces of news.

Item the first: the baker's man declared he had met Rosanna Spearman, on the previous afternoon, with a thick veil on, walking towards Frizinghall by the footpath way over the moor. It seemed strange that anybody should be mistaken about Rosanna, whose shoulder marked her out pretty plainly, poor thing—but mistaken the man must have been; for Rosanna, as you know, had been all the Thursday afternoon ill up-stairs in her room.

Item the second came through the postman. Worthy Mr Candy had said one more of his many unlucky things, when he drove off in the rain on the birthday night, and told me that a doctor's skin was waterproof. In spite of his skin, the wet had got through him. He had caught a chill that night, and was now down with a fever. The last accounts, brought by the postman, represented him to be light-headed—talking nonsense as glibly, poor man, in his delirium as he often talked it in his sober senses. We were all sorry for the little doctor; but Mr Franklin appeared to regret his illness, chiefly on Miss Rachel's account. From what he said to my lady, while I was in the room at breakfast-time, he appeared to think that Miss Rachel—if the suspense about the Moonstone was not soon set at rest—might stand in urgent need of the best medical advice at our disposal.

Breakfast had not been long over, when a telegram from Mr Blake, the elder, arrived, in answer to his son. It informed us that he had laid hands (by help of his friend, the Commissioner) on the right man to help us. The name of him was Sergeant Cuff; and the arrival of him from London might be expected by the morning train.

At reading the name of the new police-officer, Mr Franklin gave a start. It seems that he had heard some curious anecdotes about Sergeant Cuff, from his father's lawyer, during his stay in London.

'I begin to hope we are seeing the end of our anxieties already,' he said. 'If half the stories I have heard are true, when it comes to unravelling a mystery, there isn't the equal in England of Sergeant Cuff!'

We all got excited and impatient as the time drew near for the appearance of this renowned and capable character. Superintendent Seegrave, returning to us at his appointed time, and hearing that the Sergeant was expected, instantly shut himself up in a room, with pen, ink, and paper, to make notes of the Report which would be certainly expected from him. I should have liked to have gone to the station myself, to fetch the Sergeant. But my lady's carriage and horses were not to be thought of, even for the celebrated Cuff; and the pony-chaise was required later for Mr Godfrey. He deeply regretted being obliged to leave his aunt at such an anxious time; and he kindly put off the hour of his departure till as late as the last train, for the purpose of hearing what the clever London police-officer thought of the case. But on Friday night he must be in town, having a Ladies' Charity, in difficulties, waiting, to consult him on Saturday morning.

When the time came for the Sergeant's arrival, I went down to the gate to look out for him.

A fly from the railway drove up as I reached the lodge; and out got a grizzled, elderly man, so miserably lean that he looked as if he had not got an ounce of flesh on his bones in any part of him. He was dressed all in decent black, with a white cravat round his neck. His face was as sharp as a hatchet, and the skin of it was as yellow and dry and withered as an autumn leaf. His eyes, of a steely light grey, had a very disconcerting trick, when they encountered your eyes, of looking as if they expected something more from you than you were aware of yourself. His walk was soft; his voice was melancholy; his long lanky fingers were hooked like claws. He might have been a parson, or an undertaker—or anything else you like, except what he really was. A more complete opposite to Superintendent Seegrave than Sergeant Cuff, and a less comforting officer to look at, for a family in distress, I defy you to discover, search where you may.

'Is this Lady Verinder's?' he asked.

'Yes, sir.'

'I am Sergeant Cuff.'

'This way, sir, if you please.'

On our road to the house, I mentioned my name and position in the family, to satisfy him that he might speak to me about the business on which my lady was to employ him. Not a word did he say about the business, however, for all that. He admired the grounds, and remarked that he felt the sea air very brisk and refreshing. I privately wondered, on my side, how the celebrated Cuff had got his reputation. We reached the house, in the temper of two strange dogs, coupled up together for the first time in their lives by the same chain.

Asking for my lady, and hearing that she was in one of the conservatories, we went round to the gardens at the back, and sent a servant to seek her. While we were waiting, Sergeant Cuff looked through the evergreen arch on our left, spied out our rosery, and walked straight in, with the first appearance of anything like interest that he had shown yet. To the gardener's astonishment, and to my disgust, this celebrated policeman proved to be quite a mine of learning on the trumpery subject of rose-gardens.

'Ah, you've got the right exposure here to the south and sou'-west,' says the Sergeant, with a wag of his grizzled head, and a streak of pleasure in his melancholy voice. 'This is the shape for a rosery—nothing like a circle set in a square. Yes, yes; with walks between all the beds. But they oughtn't to be gravel walks like these. Grass, Mr Gardener—grass walks between your roses; gravel's too hard for them. That's a sweet pretty bed of white roses and blush roses. They always mix well together, don't they? Here's the white musk rose, Mr Betteredge—our old English rose holding up its head along with the best and the newest of them. Pretty dear!' says the Sergeant, fondling the Musk Rose with his lanky fingers, and speaking to it as if he was speaking to a child.

This was a nice sort of man to recover Miss Rachel's Diamond, and to find out the thief who stole it!

'You seem to be fond of roses, Sergeant?' I remarked.

'I haven't much time to be fond of anything,' says Sergeant Cuff. 'But when I *have* a moment's fondness to bestow, most times, Mr Betteredge, the roses get it. I began my life among them in my father's nursery garden, and I shall end my life among them, if I can. Yes. One of these days (please God) I shall retire from catching thieves, and try my hand at growing roses. There will be grass walks, Mr Gardener, between my beds,' says the Sergeant, on whose mind the gravel paths of our rosery seemed to dwell unpleasantly.

'It seems an odd taste, sir,' I ventured to say, 'for a man in your line of life.'

'If you will look about you (which most people won't do),' says Sergeant Cuff, 'you will see that the nature of a man's tastes is, most times, as opposite as possible to the nature of a man's business. Show me any two things more opposite one from the other than a rose and a thief; and I'll correct my tastes accordingly—if it isn't too late at my time of life. You find the damask rose a goodish stock for most of the tender sorts, don't you, Mr Gardener? Ah! I thought so. Here's a lady coming. Is it Lady Verinder?'

He had seen her before either I or the gardener had seen her, though we knew which way to look, and he didn't. I began to think him rather a quicker man than he appeared to be at first sight.

The Sergeant's appearance, or the Sergeant's errand—one or both—seemed to cause my lady some little embarrassment. She was, for the first time in all my experience of her, at a loss what to say at an interview with a stranger. Sergeant Cuff put her at ease directly. He asked if any other person had been employed about the robbery before we sent for him; and hearing that another person had been called in, and was now in the house, begged leave to speak to him before anything else was done.

My lady led the way back. Before he followed her, the Sergeant relieved his mind on the subject of the gravel walks by a parting word to the gardener. 'Get her ladyship to try grass,' he said, with a sour look at the paths. 'No gravel! no gravel!'

Why Superintendent Seegrave should have appeared to be several sizes smaller than life, on being presented to Sergeant Cuff, I can't undertake to explain. I can only state the fact. They retired together; and remained a weary long time shut up from all mortal intrusion. When they came out, Mr Superintendent was excited, and Mr Sergeant was yawning.

'The Sergeant wishes to see Miss Verinder's sitting-room,' says Mr Seegrave, addressing me with great pomp and eagerness. 'The Sergeant may have some questions to ask. Attend the Sergeant, if you please!'

While I was being ordered about in this way, I looked at the great Cuff. The great Cuff, on his side, looked at Superintendent Seegrave in that quietly expecting way which I have already noticed. I can't affirm that he was on the watch for his brother officer's speedy appearance in the character of an Ass—I can only say that I strongly suspected it.

I led the way upstairs. The Sergeant went softly all over the Indian cabinet and all round the 'boudoir'; asking questions (occasionally only of Mr Superintendent, and continually of me), the drift of which I believe to have been equally unintelligible to both of us. In due time, his course brought him to the door, and put him face to face with the decorative painting that you know of. He laid one lean inquiring finger on the small smear, just under the lock, which Superintendent Seegrave had already noticed, when he reproved the women-servants for all crowding together into the room.

'That's a pity,' says Sergeant Cuff. 'How did it happen?'

He put the question to me. I answered that the women-servants had crowded into the room on the previous morning, and that some of their petticoats had done the mischief. 'Superintendent Seegrave ordered them out, sir,' I added, 'before they did any more harm.'

'Right!' says Mr Superintendent in his military way. 'I ordered them out. The petticoats did it, Sergeant—the petticoats did it.'

'Did you notice which petticoat did it?' asked Sergeant Cuff, still addressing himself, not to his brother-officer, but to me.

'No, sir.'

He turned to Superintendent Seegrave upon that, and said, '*You* noticed, I suppose?'

Mr Superintendent looked a little taken aback; but he made the best of it. 'I can't charge my memory, Sergeant,' he said, 'a mere trifle—a mere trifle.'

Sergeant Cuff looked at Mr Seegrave as he had looked at the gravel walks in the rosery, and gave us, in his melancholy way, the first taste of his quality which we had had yet.

'I made a private inquiry last week, Mr Superintendent,' he said. 'At one end of the inquiry there was a murder, and at the other end there was a spot of ink on a tablecloth that nobody could account for. In all my experience along the dirtiest ways of this dirty little world, I have never met with such a thing as a trifle yet. Before we go a step further in this business we must see the petticoat that made the smear, and we must know for certain when that paint was wet.'

Mr Superintendent—taking his set-down rather sulkily—asked if he should summon the women. Sergeant Cuff, after considering a minute, sighed, and shook his head.

'No,' he said, 'we'll take the matter of the paint first. It's a question of Yes or No with the paint—which is short. It's a question of petticoats with the women—which is long. What o'clock was it when the servants were in this room yesterday morning? Eleven o'clock—eh? Is there anybody in the house who knows whether that paint was wet or dry, at eleven yesterday morning?'

'Her ladyship's nephew, Mr Franklin Blake, knows,' I said.

'Is the gentleman in the house?'

Mr Franklin was as close at hand as could be—waiting for his first chance of being introduced to the great Cuff. In half a minute he was in the room, and was giving his evidence as follows:

'That door, Sergeant,' he said, 'has been painted by Miss Verinder, under my inspection, with my help, and in a vehicle of my own composition. The vehicle dries whatever colours may be used with it, in twelve hours.'

'Do you remember when the smeared bit was done, sir?' asked the Sergeant.

'Perfectly,' answered Mr Franklin. 'That was the last morsel of the door to be finished. We wanted to get it done, on Wednesday last—and I myself completed it by three in the afternoon, or soon after.'

'To-day is Friday,' said Sergeant Cuff, addressing himself to Superintendent Seegrave. 'Let us reckon back, sir. At three on the Wednesday afternoon, that bit of the painting was completed. The vehicle dried it in twelve hours—that is to say, dried it by three o'clock on Thursday morning. At eleven on Thursday morning you held your inquiry here. Take three from eleven, and eight remains. That paint had been *eight hours dry*, Mr Superintendent, when you supposed that the women-servants' petticoats smeared it.'

First knock-down blow for Mr Seegrave! If he had not suspected poor Penelope, I should have pitied him.

Having settled the question of the paint, Sergeant Cuff, from that moment, gave his brother-officer up as a bad job—and addressed himself to Mr Franklin, as the more promising assistant of the two.

'It's quite on the cards, sir,' he said, 'that you have put the clue into our hands.'

As the words passed his lips, the bedroom door opened, and Miss Rachel came out among us suddenly.

She addressed herself to the Sergeant, without appearing to notice (or to heed) that he was a perfect stranger to her.

'Did you say,' she asked, pointing to Mr Franklin, 'that *he* had put the clue into your hands?'

('This is Miss Verinder,' I whispered, behind the Sergeant.)

'That gentleman, miss,' says the Sergeant—with his steely-grey eyes carefully studying my young lady's face—'has possibly put the clue into our hands.'

She turned for one moment, and tried to look at Mr Franklin. I say, tried, for she suddenly looked away again before their eyes met. There seemed to be some strange disturbance in her mind. She coloured up, and then she turned pale again. With the paleness, there came a new look into her face—a look which it startled me to see.

'Having answered your question, miss,' says the Sergeant, 'I beg leave to make an inquiry in my turn. There is a smear on the painting of your door, here. Do you happen to know when it was done? or who did it?'

Instead of making any reply, Miss Rachel went on with her questions, as if he had not spoken, or as if she had not heard him.

'Are you another police-officer?' she asked.

'I am Sergeant Cuff, miss, of the Detective Police.'

'Do you think a young lady's advice worth having?'

'I shall be glad to hear it, miss.'

'Do your duty by yourself—and don't allow Mr Franklin Blake to help you!'

She said those words so spitefully, so savagely, with such an extraordinary outbreak of ill-will towards Mr Franklin, in her voice and in her look, that—though I had known her from a baby, though I loved and honoured her next to my lady herself—I was ashamed of Miss Rachel for the first time in my life.

Sergeant Cuff's immovable eyes never stirred from off her face. 'Thank you, miss,' he said. 'Do you happen to know anything about the smear? Might you have done it by accident yourself?'

'I know nothing about the smear.'

With that answer, she turned away, and shut herself up again in her bedroom. This time, I heard her—as Penelope had heard her before—burst out crying as soon as she was alone again.

I couldn't bring myself to look at the Sergeant—I looked at Mr Franklin, who stood nearest to me. He seemed to be even more sorely distressed at what had passed than I was.

'I told you I was uneasy about her,' he said. 'And now you see why.'

'Miss Verinder appears to be a little out of temper about the loss of her Diamond,' remarked the Sergeant. 'It's a valuable jewel. Natural enough! natural enough!'

Here was the excuse that I had made for her (when she forgot herself before Superintendent Seegrave, on the previous day) being made for her over again, by a man who couldn't have had *my* interest in making it—for he was a perfect stranger! A kind of cold shudder ran through me, which I couldn't account for at the time. I know, now, that I must have got my first suspicion, at that moment, of a new light (and horrid light) having suddenly fallen on the case, in the mind of Sergeant Cuff—purely and entirely in consequence of what he had seen in Miss Rachel, and heard from Miss Rachel, at that first interview between them.

'A young lady's tongue is a privileged member, sir,' says the Sergeant to Mr Franklin. 'Let us forget what has passed, and go straight on with this business. Thanks to you, we know when the paint was dry. The next thing to discover is when the paint was last seen without that smear. *You* have got a head on your shoulders—and you understand what I mean.'

Mr Franklin composed himself, and came back with an effort from Miss Rachel to the matter in hand.

'I think I do understand,' he said. 'The more we narrow the question of time, the more we also narrow the field of inquiry.'

'That's it, sir,' said the Sergeant. 'Did you notice your work here, on the Wednesday afternoon, after you had done it?'

Mr Franklin shook his head, and answered, 'I can't say I did.'

'Did *you?*' inquired Sergeant Cuff, turning to me.

'I can't say I did either, sir.'

'Who was the last person in the room, the last thing on Wednesday night?'

'Miss Rachel, I suppose, sir.'

Mr Franklin struck in there, 'Or possibly your daughter, Betteredge.' He turned to Sergeant Cuff, and explained that my daughter was Miss Verinder's maid.

'Mr Betteredge, ask your daughter to step up. Stop!' says the Sergeant, taking me away to the window, out of earshot, 'Your Superintendent here,' he went on, in a whisper, 'has made a pretty full report to me of the manner in which he has managed this case. Among other things, he has, by his own confession, set the servants' backs up. It's very important to smooth them down again. Tell your daughter, and tell the rest of them, these two things, with my compliments: First, that I have no evidence before me, yet, that the Diamond has been stolen; I only know that the Diamond has been lost. Second, that *my* business here with the servants is simply to ask them to lay their heads together and help me to find it.'

My experience of the women-servants, when Superintendent Seegrave laid his embargo on their rooms, came in handy here.

'May I make so bold, Sergeant, as to tell the women a third thing?' I asked. 'Are they free (with your compliments) to fidget up and downstairs, and whisk in and out of their bedrooms, if the fit takes them?'

'Perfectly free,' said the Sergeant.

'*That* will smooth them down, sir,' I remarked, 'from the cook to the scullion.'

'Go, and do it at once, Mr Betteredge.'

I did it in less than five minutes. There was only one difficulty when I came to the bit about the bedrooms. It took a pretty stiff exertion of my authority, as chief, to prevent the whole of the female household from following me and Penelope up-stairs, in the character of volunteer witnesses in a burning fever of anxiety to help Sergeant Cuff.

The Sergeant seemed to approve of Penelope. He became a trifle less dreary; and he looked much as he had looked when he noticed the white musk rose in the flower-garden. Here is my daughter's evidence, as drawn off from her by the Sergeant. She gave it, I think, very prettily—but, there! she is my child all over: nothing of her mother in her; Lord bless you, nothing of her mother in her!

Penelope examined: Took a lively interest in the painting on the door, having helped to mix the colours. Noticed the bit of work under the lock, because it was the last bit done. Had seen it, some hours afterwards, without a smear. Had left it, as late as twelve at night, without a smear. Had, at that hour, wished her young lady good night in the bedroom; had heard the clock strike in the 'boudoir'; had her hand at the time on the handle of the painted door; knew the paint was wet (having helped to mix the colours, as aforesaid); took particular pains not to touch it; could swear that she held up the skirts of her dress, and that there was no smear on the paint then; could *not* swear that her dress mightn't have touched it accidentally in going out; remembered the dress she had on, because it was new, a present from Miss Rachel; her father remembered, and could speak to it, too; could, and would, and did fetch it; dress recognised by her father as the dress she wore that night; skirts examined, a long job from the size of them; not the ghost of a paint-stain discovered anywhere. End of Penelope's evidence—and very pretty and convincing, too. Signed, Gabriel Betteredge.

The Sergeant's next proceeding was to question me about any large dogs in the house who might have got into the room, and done the mischief with a whisk of their tails. Hearing that this was impossible, he next sent for a magnifying-glass, and tried how the smear looked, seen that way. No skin-mark (as of a human hand) printed off on the paint. All the signs visible—signs which told that the paint had been smeared by some loose article of somebody's dress touching it in going by. That somebody (putting together Penelope's evidence and Mr Franklin's evidence) must have been in the room, and done the mischief, between midnight and three o'clock on the Thursday morning.

Having brought his investigation to this point, Sergeant Cuff discovered that such a person as Superintendent Seegrave was still left in the room, upon which he summed up the proceedings for his brother-officer's benefit, as follows:

'This trifle of yours, Mr Superintendent,' says the Sergeant, pointing to the place on the door, 'has grown a little in importance since you noticed it last. At the present stage of the inquiry there are, as I take it, three discoveries to make, starting from that smear. Find out (first) whether there is any article of dress in this house with the smear of the paint on it. Find out (second) who that dress belongs to. Find out (third) how the person can account for having been in this room, and smeared the paint, between midnight and three in the morning. If the person can't satisfy you, you haven't far to look for the hand that has got the Diamond. I'll work this by myself, if you please, and detain you no longer from your regular business in the town. You have got one of your men here, I see. Leave him here at my disposal, in case I want him—and allow me to wish you good morning.'

Superintendent Seegrave's respect for the Sergeant was great; but his respect for himself was greater still. Hit hard by the celebrated Cuff, he hit back smartly, to the best of his ability, on leaving the room.

'I have abstained from expressing any opinion, so far,' says Mr Superintendent, with his military voice still in good working order. 'I have now only one remark to offer on leaving this case in your hands. There *is* such a thing, Sergeant, as making a mountain out of a molehill. Good morning.'

'There is also such a thing as making nothing out of a molehill, in consequence of your head being too high to see it.' Having returned his brother-officer's compliments in those terms, Sergeant Cuff wheeled about, and walked away to the window by himself.

Mr Franklin and I waited to see what was coming next. The Sergeant stood at the window with his hands in his pockets, looking out, and whistling the tune of 'The Last Rose of Summer' softly to himself. Later in the proceedings, I discovered that he only forgot his manners so far as to whistle, when his mind was hard at work, seeing its way inch by inch to its own private ends, on which occasions 'The Last Rose of Summer' evidently helped and encouraged him. I suppose it fitted in somehow with his character. It reminded him, you see, of his favourite roses, and, as *he* whistled it, it was the most melancholy tune going.

Turning from the window, after a minute or two, the Sergeant walked into the middle of the room, and stopped there, deep in thought, with his eyes on Miss Rachel's bedroom door. After a little he roused himself, nodded his head, as much as to say, 'That will do,' and, addressing me, asked for ten minutes' conversation with my mistress, at her ladyship's earliest convenience.

Leaving the room with this message, I heard Mr Franklin ask the Sergeant a question, and stopped to hear the answer also at the threshold of the door.

'Can you guess yet,' inquired Mr Franklin, 'who has stolen the Diamond?'

'*Nobody has stolen the Diamond*,' answered Sergeant Cuff.

We both started at that extraordinary view of the case, and both earnestly begged him to tell us what he meant.

'Wait a little,' said the Sergeant. 'The pieces of the puzzle are not all put together yet.'

CHAPTER XIII

I FOUND my lady in her own sitting-room. She started and looked annoyed when I mentioned that Sergeant Cuff wished to speak to her.

'*Must* I see him?' she asked. 'Can't you represent me, Gabriel?'

I felt at a loss to understand this, and showed it plainly, I suppose, in my face. My lady was so good as to explain herself.

'I am afraid my nerves are a little shaken,' she said. 'There is something in that police-officer from London which I recoil from—I don't know why. I have a presentiment that he is bringing trouble and misery with him into the house. Very foolish, and very unlike *me*—but so it is.'

I hardly knew what to say to this. The more *I* saw of Sergeant Cuff, the better I liked him. My lady rallied a little after having opened her heart to me—being, naturally, a woman of a high courage, as I have already told you.

'If I must see him, I must,' she said. 'But I can't prevail on myself to see him alone. Bring him in, Gabriel, and stay here as long as he stays.'

This was the first attack of the megrims that I remembered in my mistress since the time when she was a young girl. I went back to the 'boudoir'. Mr Franklin strolled out into the garden, and joined Mr Godfrey, whose time for departure was now drawing near. Sergeant Cuff and I went straight to my mistress's room.

I declare my lady turned a shade paler at the sight of him! She commanded herself, however, in other respects, and asked the Sergeant if he had any objection to my being present. She was so good as to add, that I was her trusted adviser, as well as her old servant, and that in anything which related to the household I was the person whom it might be most profitable to consult. The Sergeant politely answered that he would take my presence as a favour, having something to say about the servants in general, and having found my experience in that quarter already of some use to him. My lady pointed to two chairs, and we set in for our conference immediately.

'I have already formed an opinion on this case,' says Sergeant Cuff, 'which I beg your ladyship's permission to keep to myself for the present. My business now is to mention what I have discovered up-stairs in Miss Verinder's sitting-room, and what I have decided (with your ladyship's leave) on doing next.'

He then went into the matter of the smear on the paint, and stated the conclusions he drew from it—just as he had stated them (only with greater respect of language) to Superintendent Seegrave. 'One thing,' he said, in conclusion, 'is certain. The Diamond is missing out of the drawer in the cabinet. Another thing is next to certain. The marks from the smear on the door must be on some article of dress belonging to somebody in this house. We must discover that article of dress before we go a step further.'

'And that discovery,' remarked my mistress, 'implies, I presume, the discovery of the thief?'

'I beg your ladyship's pardon—I don't say the Diamond is stolen. I only say, at present, that the Diamond is missing. The discovery of the stained dress may lead the way to finding it.'

Her ladyship looked at me. 'Do you understand this?' she said.

'Sergeant Cuff understands it, my lady,' I answered.

'How do you propose to discover the stained dress?' inquired my mistress, addressing once more to the Sergeant. 'My good servants, who have been with me for years, have, I am ashamed to say, had their boxes and rooms searched already by the other officer. I can't and won't permit them to be insulted in that way a second time!'

(There was a mistress to serve! There was a woman in ten thousand, if you like!)

'That is the very point I was about to put to your ladyship,' said the Sergeant. 'The other officer has done a world of harm to this inquiry, by letting the servants see that he suspected them. If I give them cause to think themselves suspected a second time, there's no knowing what obstacles they may not throw in my way—the women especially. At the same time, their boxes *must* be searched again—for this plain reason, that the first investigation only looked for the Diamond, and that the second investigation must look for the stained dress. I quite agree with you, my lady, that the servants' feelings ought to be consulted. But I am equally clear that the servants' wardrobes ought to be searched.'

This looked very like a dead-lock. My lady said so, in choicer language than mine.

'I have got a plan to meet the difficulty,' said Sergeant Cuff, 'if your ladyship will consent to it. I propose explaining the case to the servants.'

'The women will think themselves suspected directly,' I said, interrupting him.

'The women won't, Mr Betteredge,' answered the Sergeant, 'if I can tell them I am going to examine the wardrobes of *everybody*—from her ladyship downwards—who slept in the house on Wednesday night. It's a mere formality,' he added, with a side look at my mistress; 'but the servants will accept it as even dealing between them and their betters; and, instead of hindering the investigation, they will make a point of honour of assisting it.'

I saw the truth of that. My lady, after her first surprise was over, saw the truth of it also.

'You are certain the investigation is necessary?' she said.

'It's the shortest way that I can see, my lady, to the end we have in view.'

My mistress rose to ring the bell for her maid. 'You shall speak to the servants,' she said, 'with the keys of my wardrobe in your hand.'

Sergeant Cuff stopped her by a very unexpected question.

'Hadn't we better make sure first,' he asked, 'that the other ladies and gentlemen in the house will consent, too?'

'The only other lady in the house is Miss Verinder,' answered my mistress, with a look of surprise. 'The only gentlemen are my nephews, Mr Blake and Mr Ablewhite. There is not the least fear of a refusal from any of the three.'

I reminded my lady here that Mr Godfrey was going away. As I said the words, Mr Godfrey himself knocked at the door to say good-bye, and was followed in by Mr Franklin, who was going with him to the station. My lady explained the difficulty. Mr Godfrey settled it directly. He called to Samuel, through the window, to take his portmanteau up-stairs again, and he then put the key himself into Sergeant Cuff's hand. 'My luggage can follow me to London,' he said, 'when the inquiry is over.' The Sergeant received the key with a becoming apology. 'I am sorry to put you to any inconvenience, sir, for a mere formality; but the example of their betters will do wonders in reconciling the servants to this inquiry.' Mr Godfrey, after taking leave of my lady, in a most sympathising manner, left a farewell message for Miss Rachel, the terms of which made it clear to my mind that he had not taken No for an answer, and that he meant to put the marriage question to her once more, at the next opportunity. Mr Franklin, on following his cousin out, informed the Sergeant that all his clothes were open to examination, and that nothing he possessed was kept under lock and key. Sergeant Cuff made his best acknowledgments. His views, you will observe, had been met with the utmost readiness by my lady, by Mr Godfrey, and by Mr Franklin.

There was only Miss Rachel now wanting to follow their lead, before we called the servants together, and began the search for the stained dress.

My lady's unaccountable objection to the Sergeant seemed to make our conference more distasteful to her than ever, as soon as we were left alone again. 'If I send you down Miss Verinder's keys,' she said to him, 'I presume I shall have done all you want of me for the present?'

'I beg your ladyship's pardon,' said Sergeant Cuff. 'Before we begin, I should like, if convenient, to have the washing-book. The stained article of dress may be an article of linen. If the search leads to nothing, I want to be able to account next for all the linen in the house, and for all the linen sent to the wash. If there is an article missing, there will be at least a presumption that it has got the paint-stain on it, and that it was purposely made away with, yesterday or to-day, by the person owning it. Superintendent Seegrave,' added the Sergeant, turning to me, 'pointed the attention of the women-servants to the smear, when they all crowded into the room on Thursday morning. That *may* turn out, Mr Betteredge, to have been one more of Superintendent Seegrave's many mistakes.'

My lady desired me to ring the bell, and order the washing-book. She remained with us until it was produced, in case Sergeant Cuff had any further request to make of her after looking at it.

The washing-book was brought in by Rosanna Spearman. The girl had come down to breakfast that morning miserably pale and haggard, but sufficiently recovered from her illness of the previous day to do her usual work. Sergeant Cuff looked attentively at our second housemaid—at her face, when she came in; at her crooked shoulder, when she went out.

'Have you anything more to say to me?' asked my lady, still as eager as ever to be out of the Sergeant's society.

The great Cuff opened the washing-book, understood it perfectly in half a minute, and shut it up again. 'I venture to trouble your ladyship with one last question.' he said. 'Has the young woman who brought us this book been in your employment as long as the other servants?'

'Why do you ask?' said my lady.

'The last time I saw her,' answered the Sergeant, 'she was in prison for theft.'

After that, there was no help for it, but to tell him the truth. My mistress dwelt strongly on Rosanna's good conduct in her service, and on the high opinion entertained of her by the matron at the reformatory. 'You don't suspect her, I hope?' my lady added, in conclusion, very earnestly.

'I have already told your ladyship that I don't suspect any person in the house of thieving—up to the present time.'

After that answer, my lady rose to go up-stairs, and ask for Miss Rachel's keys. The Sergeant was beforehand with me in opening the door for her. He made a very low bow. My lady shuddered as she passed him.

We waited, and waited, and no keys appeared. Sergeant Cuff made no remark to me. He turned his melancholy face to the window; he put his lanky hands into his pockets; and he whistled 'The Last Rose of Summer' softly to himself.

At last, Samuel came in, not with the keys, but with a morsel of paper for me. I got at my spectacles, with some fumbling and difficulty, feeling the Sergeant's dismal eyes fixed on me all the time. There were two or three lines on the paper, written in pencil by my lady. They informed me that Miss Rachel flatly refused to have her wardrobe examined. Asked for her reasons, she had burst out crying. Asked again, she had said: 'I won't, because I won't. I must yield to force if you use it, but I will yield to nothing else.' I understood my lady's disinclination to face Sergeant Cuff with such an answer from her daughter as that. If I had not been too old for the amiable weaknesses of youth, I believe I should have blushed at the notion of facing him myself.

'Any news of Miss Verinder's keys?' asked the Sergeant.

'My young lady refuses to have her wardrobe examined.'

'Ah!' said the Sergeant.

His voice was not quite in such a perfect state of discipline as his face. When he said 'Ah!' he said it in the tone of a man who had heard something which he expected to hear. He half angered and half frightened me—why I couldn't tell, but he did it.

'Must the search be given up?' I asked.

'Yes,' said the Sergeant, 'the search must be given up, because your young lady refuses to submit to it like the rest. We must examine all the wardrobes in the house or none. Send Mr Ablewhite's portmanteau to London by the next train, and return the washing-book, with my compliments and thanks, to the young woman who brought it in.'

He laid the washing-book on the table, and, taking out his penknife, began to trim his nails.

'You don't seem to be much disappointed,' I said.

'No,' said Sergeant Cuff; 'I am not much disappointed.'

I tried to make him explain himself.

'Why should Miss Rachel put an obstacle in your way?' I inquired. 'Isn't it her interest to help you?'

'Wait a little, Mr Betteredge—wait a little.'

Cleverer heads than mine might have seen his drift. Or a person less fond of Miss Rachel than I was, might have seen his drift. My lady's horror of him might (as I have since thought) have meant that *she* saw his drift (as the scripture says) 'in a glass darkly.' I didn't see it yet—that's all I know.

'What's to be done next?' I asked.

Sergeant Cuff finished the nail on which he was then at work, looked at it for a moment with a melancholy interest, and put up his penknife.

'Come out into the garden,' he said, 'and let's have a look at the roses.'

CHAPTER XIV

THE nearest way to the garden, on going out of my lady's sitting-room, was by the shrubbery path, which you already know of. For the sake of your better understanding of what is now to come, I may add to this, that the shrubbery path was Mr Franklin's favourite walk. When he was out in the grounds, and when we failed to find him anywhere else, we generally found him here.

I am afraid I must own that I am rather an obstinate old man. The more firmly Sergeant Cuff kept his thoughts shut up from me, the more firmly I persisted in trying to look in at them. As we turned into the shrubbery path, I attempted to circumvent him in another way.

'As things are now,' I said, 'if I was in your place, I should be at my wits' end.'

'If you were in my place,' answered the Sergeant, 'you would have formed an opinion—and, as things are now, any doubt you might previously have felt about your own conclusions would be completely set at rest. Never mind for the present what those conclusions are, Mr Betteredge. I haven't brought you out here to draw me like a badger; I have brought you out here to ask for some information. You might have given it to me no doubt, in the house, instead of out of it. But doors and listeners have a knack of getting together; and, in my line of life, we cultivate a healthy taste for the open air.'

Who was to circumvent *this* man? I gave in—and waited as patiently as I could to hear what was coming next.

'We won't enter into your young lady's motives,' the Sergeant went on; 'we will only say it's a pity she declines to assist me, because, by so doing, she makes this investigation more difficult than it might otherwise have been. We must now try to solve the mystery of the smear on the door— which, you may take my word for it, means the mystery of the Diamond also—in some other way. I have decided to see the servants, and to search their thoughts and actions, Mr Betteredge, instead of searching their wardrobes. Before I begin, however, I want to ask you a question or two. You are an observant man—did you notice anything strange in any of the servants (making due allowance, of course, for fright and fluster), after the loss of the Diamond was found out? Any particular quarrel among them? Any one of them not in his or her usual spirits? Unexpectedly out of temper, for instance? or unexpectedly taken ill?'

I had just time to think of Rosanna Spearman's sudden illness at yesterday's dinner—but not time to make any answer—when I saw Sergeant Cuff's eyes suddenly turn aside towards the shrubbery; and I heard him say softly to himself, 'Hullo!'

'What's the matter?' I asked.

'A touch of the rheumatics in my back,' said the Sergeant, in a loud voice, as if he wanted some third person to hear us. 'We shall have a change in the weather before long.'

A few steps further brought us to the corner of the house. Turning off sharp to the right, we entered on the terrace, and went down, by the steps in the middle, into the garden below. Sergeant Cuff stopped there, in the open space, where we could see round us on every side.

'About that young person, Rosanna Spearman?' he said. 'It isn't very likely, with her personal appearance, that she has got a lover. But, for the girl's own sake, I must ask you at once whether *she* has provided herself with a sweetheart, poor wretch, like the rest of them?'

What on earth did he mean, under present circumstances, by putting such a question to me as that? I stared at him, instead of answering him.

'I saw Rosanna Spearman hiding in the shrubbery as we went by,' said the Sergeant.

'When you said "Hullo"?'

'Yes—when I said "Hullo!" If there's a sweetheart in the case, the hiding doesn't much matter. If there isn't—as things are in this house—the hiding is a highly suspicious circumstance, and it will be my painful duty to act on it accordingly.'

What, in God's name, was I to say to him? I knew the shrubbery was Mr Franklin's favourite walk; I knew he would most likely turn that way when he came back from the station; I knew that Penelope had over and over again caught her fellow-servant hanging about there, and had always declared to me that Rosanna's object was to attract Mr Franklin's attention. If my daughter was right, she might well have been lying in wait for Mr Franklin's return when the Sergeant noticed her. I was put between the two difficulties of mentioning Penelope's fanciful notion as if it was mine, or of leaving an unfortunate creature to suffer the consequences, the very serious consequences, of exciting the suspicion of Sergeant Cuff. Out of pure pity for the girl—on my soul and my character, out of pure pity for the girl—I gave the Sergeant the necessary explanations, and told him that Rosanna had been mad enough to set her heart on Mr Franklin Blake.

Sergeant Cuff never laughed. On the few occasions when anything amused him, he curled up a little at the corners of the lips, nothing more. He curled up now.

'Hadn't you better say she's mad enough to be an ugly girl and only a servant?' he asked. 'The falling in love with a gentleman of Mr Franklin Blake's manners and appearance doesn't seem to *me* to be the maddest part of her conduct by any means. However, I'm glad the thing is cleared up: it relieves one's mind to have things cleared up. Yes, I'll keep it a secret, Mr Betteredge. I like to be tender to human infirmity—though I don't get many chances of exercising that virtue in my line of life. You think Mr Franklin Blake hasn't got a suspicion of the girl's fancy for him? Ah! he would have found it out fast enough if she had been nice-looking. The ugly women have a bad time of it in this world; let's hope it will be made up to them in another. You have got a nice garden here, and a well-kept lawn. See for yourself how much better the flowers look with grass about them instead of gravel. No, thank you. I won't take a rose. It goes to my heart to break them off the stem. Just as it goes to your heart, you know, when there's something wrong in the servants' hall. Did you notice anything you couldn't account for in any of the servants when the loss of the Diamond was first found out?'

I had got on very fairly well with Sergeant Cuff so far. But the slyness with which he slipped in that last question put me on my guard. In plain English, I didn't at all relish the notion of helping his inquiries, when those inquiries took him (in the capacity of snake in the grass) among my fellow-servants.

'I noticed nothing,' I said, 'except that we all lost our heads together, myself included.'

'Oh,' says the Sergeant, 'that's all you have to tell me, is it?'

I answered, with (as I flattered myself) an unmoved countenance, 'That is all.'

Sergeant Cuff's dismal eyes looked me hard in the face.

'Mr Betteredge,' he said, 'have you any objection to oblige me by shaking hands? I have taken an extraordinary liking to you.'

(Why he should have chosen the exact moment when I was deceiving him to give me that proof of his good opinion, is beyond all comprehension! I felt a little proud—I really did feel a little proud of having been one too many at last for the celebrated Cuff!)

We went back to the house; the Sergeant requesting that I would give him a room to himself, and then send in the servants (the indoor servants only), one after another, in the order of their rank, from first to last.

I showed Sergeant Cuff into my own room, and then called the servants together in the hall. Rosanna Spearman appeared among them, much as usual. She was as quick in her way as the Sergeant in his, and I suspect she had heard what he said to me about the servants in general, just before he discovered her. There she was, at any rate, looking as if she had never heard of such a place as the shrubbery in her life.

I sent them in, one by one, as desired. The cook was the first to enter the Court of Justice, otherwise my room. She remained but a short time. Report, on coming out: 'Sergeant Cuff is depressed in his spirits; but Sergeant Cuff is a perfect gentleman.' My lady's own maid followed.

Remained much longer. Report, on coming out: 'If Sergeant Cuff doesn't believe a respectable woman, he might keep his opinion to himself, at any rate!' Penelope went next. Remained only a moment or two. Report, on coming out: 'Sergeant Cuff is much to be pitied. He must have been crossed in love, father, when he was a young man.' The first housemaid followed Penelope. Remained, like my lady's maid, a long time. Report, on coming out: 'I didn't enter her ladyship's service, Mr Betteredge, to be doubted to my face by a low police-officer!' Rosanna Spearman went next. Remained longer than any of them. No report on coming out—dead silence, and lips as pale as ashes. Samuel, the footman, followed Rosanna. Remained a minute or two. Report, on coming out: 'Whoever blacks Sergeant Cuff's boots ought to be ashamed of himself.' Nancy, the kitchenmaid, went last. Remained a minute or two. Report, on coming out: 'Sergeant Cuff has a heart; *he* doesn't cut jokes, Mr Betteredge, with a poor hard-working girl.'

Going into the Court of Justice, when it was all over, to hear if there were any further commands for me, I found the Sergeant at his old trick—looking out of window, and whistling 'The Last Rose of Summer' to himself.

'Any discoveries, sir?' I inquired.

'If Rosanna Spearman asks leave to go out,' said the Sergeant, 'let the poor thing go; but let me know first.'

I might as well have held my tongue about Rosanna and Mr Franklin! It was plain enough; the unfortunate girl had fallen under Sergeant Cuff's suspicions, in spite of all I could do to prevent it.

'I hope you don't think Rosanna is concerned in the loss of the Diamond?' I ventured to say.

The corners of the Sergeant's melancholy mouth curled up, and he looked hard in my face, just as he had looked in the garden.

'I think I had better not tell you, Mr Betteredge,' he said. 'You might lose your head, you know, for the second time.'

I began to doubt whether I had been one too many for the celebrated Cuff, after all! It was rather a relief to me that we were interrupted here by a knock at the door, and a message from the cook. Rosanna Spearman *had* asked to go out, for the usual reason, that her head was bad, and she wanted a breath of fresh air. At a sign from the Sergeant, I said, Yes. 'Which is the servants' way out?' he asked, when the messenger had gone. I showed him the servants' way out. 'Lock the door of your room,' says the Sergeant; 'and if anybody asks for me, say I'm in there, composing my mind.' He curled up again at the corners of the lips, and disappeared.

Left alone, under those circumstances, a devouring curiosity pushed me on to make some discoveries for myself.

It was plain that Sergeant Cuff's suspicions of Rosanna had been roused by something that he had found out at his examination of the servants in my room. Now, the only two servants (excepting Rosanna herself) who had remained under examination for any length of time, were my lady's own maid and the first housemaid, those two being also the women who had taken the lead in persecuting their unfortunate fellow-servant from the first. Reaching these conclusions, I looked in on them, casually as it might be, in the servants' hall, and, finding tea going forward, instantly invited myself to that meal. (For, *nota bene*, a drop of tea is to a woman's tongue what a drop of oil is to a wasting lamp.)

My reliance on the tea-pot, as an ally, did not go unrewarded. In less than half an hour I knew as much as the Sergeant himself.

My lady's maid and the housemaid had, it appeared, neither of them believed in Rosanna's illness of the previous day. These two devils—I ask your pardon; but how else *can* you describe a couple of spiteful women?— had stolen up-stairs, at intervals during the Thursday afternoon; had tried Rosanna's door, and found it locked; had knocked, and not been answered; had listened, and not heard a sound inside. When the girl had come down to tea, and had been sent up, still out of sorts, to bed again, the two devils aforesaid had tried her door once more, and found it locked; had looked at the keyhole, and found it stopped up; had seen a light under the door at midnight, and had heard the crackling of a fire (a fire in a servant's bed-room in the month of June!) at four in the morning. All this they had told Sergeant Cuff, who, in return for their anxiety to enlighten him, had eyed them with sour and suspicious looks, and had shown them plainly that he didn't believe either one or the other. Hence, the unfavourable reports of him which these two women had brought out with them from the examination. Hence, also (without reckoning the influence of the tea-pot), their readiness to let their tongues run to any length on the subject of the Sergeant's ungracious behaviour to them.

Having had some experience of the great Cuff's roundabout ways, and having last seen him evidently bent on following Rosanna privately when she went out for her walk, it seemed clear to me that he had thought it unadvisable to let the lady's maid and the housemaid know how materially they had helped him. They were just the sort of women, if he had treated their evidence as trustworthy, to have been puffed up by it, and to have said or done something which would have put Rosanna Spearman on her guard.

I walked out in the fine summer afternoon, very sorry for the poor girl, and very uneasy in my mind at the turn things had taken. Drifting towards the shrubbery, some time later, there I met Mr Franklin. After returning from seeing his cousin off at the station, he had been with my lady, holding a long conversation with her. She had told him of Miss Rachel's unaccountable refusal to let her wardrobe be examined; and had put him in such low spirits about my young lady, that he seemed to shrink from speaking on the subject. The family temper appeared in his face that evening, for the first time in my experience of him.

'Well, Betteredge,' he said, 'how does the atmosphere of mystery and suspicion in which we are all living now agree with you? Do you remember that morning when I first came here with the Moonstone? I wish to God we had thrown it into the quicksand!'

After breaking out in that way, he abstained from speaking again until he had composed himself. We walked silently, side by side, for a minute or two, and then he asked me what had become of Sergeant Cuff. It was impossible to put Mr Franklin off with the excuse of the Sergeant being in my room, composing his mind. I told him exactly what had happened, mentioning particularly what my lady's maid and the housemaid had said about Rosanna Spearman.

Mr Franklin's clear head saw the turn the Sergeant's suspicions had taken, in the twinkling of an eye.

'Didn't you tell me this morning,' he said, 'that one of the tradespeople declared he had met Rosanna yesterday, on the footway to Frizinghall, when we supposed her to be ill in her room?'

'Yes, sir.'

'If my aunt's maid and the other woman have spoken the truth, you may depend upon it the tradesman *did* meet her. The girl's attack of illness was a blind to deceive us. She had some guilty reason for going to the town secretly. The paint-stained dress is a dress of hers; and the fire heard crackling in her room at four in the morning was a fire lit to destroy it. Rosanna Spearman has stolen the Diamond. I'll go in directly, and tell my aunt the turn things have taken.'

'Not just yet, if you please, sir,' said a melancholy voice behind us.

We both turned about, and found ourselves face to face with Sergeant Cuff.

'Why not just yet?' asked Mr Franklin.

'Because, sir, if you tell her ladyship, her ladyship will tell Miss Verinder.'

'Suppose she does. What then?' Mr Franklin said those words with a sudden heat and vehemence, as if the Sergeant had mortally offended him.

'Do you think it's wise, sir,' said Sergeant Cuff, quietly, 'to put such a question as that to me—at such a time as this?'

There was a moment's silence between them: Mr Franklin walked close up to the Sergeant. The two looked each other straight in the face. Mr Franklin spoke first, dropping his voice as suddenly as he had raised it.

'I suppose you know, Mr Cuff,' he said, 'that you are treading on delicate ground?'

'It isn't the first time, by a good many hundreds, that I find myself treading on delicate ground,' answered the other, as immovable as ever.

'I am to understand that you forbid me to tell my aunt what has happened?'

'You are to understand, if you please, sir, that I throw up the case, if you tell Lady Verinder, or tell anybody, what has happened, until I give you leave.'

That settled it. Mr Franklin had no choice but to submit. He turned away in anger—and left us.

I had stood there listening to them, all in a tremble; not knowing whom to suspect, or what to think next. In the midst of my confusion, two things, however, were plain to me. First, that my young lady was, in some unaccountable manner, at the bottom of the sharp speeches that had passed between them. Second, that they thoroughly understood each other, without having previously exchanged a word of explanation on either side.

'Mr Betteredge,' says the Sergeant, 'you have done a very foolish thing in my absence. You have done a little detective business on your own account. For the future, perhaps you will be so obliging as to do your detective business along with me.'

He took me by the arm, and walked me away with him along the road by which he had come. I dare say I had deserved his reproof—but I was not going to help him to set traps for Rosanna Spearman, for all that. Thief or no thief, legal or not legal, I don't care—I pitied her.

'What do you want of me?' I asked, shaking him off, and stopping short.

'Only a little information about the country round here,' said the Sergeant.

I couldn't well object to improve Sergeant Cuff in his geography.

'Is there any path, in that direction, leading to the sea-beach from this house?' asked the Sergeant. He pointed, as he spoke, to the fir-plantation which led to the Shivering Sand.

'Yes,' I said, 'there is a path.'

'Show it to me.'

Side by side, in the grey of the summer evening, Sergeant Cuff and I set forth for the Shivering Sand.

CHAPTER XV

THE Sergeant remained silent, thinking his own thoughts, till we entered the plantation of firs which led to the quicksand. There he roused himself, like a man whose mind was made up, and spoke to me again.

'Mr Betteredge,' he said, 'as you have honoured me by taking an oar in my boat, and as you may, I think, be of some assistance to me before the evening is out, I see no use in our mystifying one another any longer, and I propose to set you an example of plain speaking on my side. You are determined to give me no information to the prejudice of Rosanna Spearman, because she has been a good girl to *you*, and because you pity her heartily. Those humane considerations do you a world of credit, but they happen in this instance to be humane considerations clean thrown away.

Rosanna Spearman is not in the slightest danger of getting into trouble—no, not if I fix her with being concerned in the disappearance of the Diamond, on evidence which is as plain as the nose on your face!'

'Do you mean that my lady won't prosecute?' I asked.

'I mean that your lady *can't* prosecute,' said the Sergeant. 'Rosanna Spearman is simply an instrument in the hands of another person, and Rosanna Spearman will be held harmless for that other person's sake.'

He spoke like a man in earnest—there was no denying that. Still, I felt something stirring uneasily against him in my mind. 'Can't you give that other person a name?' I said.

'Can't *you*, Mr Betteredge?'

'No.'

Sergeant Cuff stood stock still, and surveyed me with a look of melancholy interest.

'It's always a pleasure to me to be tender towards human infirmity,' he said. 'I feel particularly tender at the present moment, Mr Betteredge, towards you. And you, with the same excellent motive, feel particularly tender towards Rosanna Spearman, don't you? Do you happen to know whether she has had a new outfit of linen lately?'

What he meant by slipping in this extraordinary question unawares, I was at a total loss to imagine. Seeing no possible injury to Rosanna if I owned the truth, I answered that the girl had come to us rather sparely provided with linen, and that my lady, in recompense for her good conduct (I laid a stress on her good conduct), had given her a new outfit not a fortnight since.

'This is a miserable world,' says the Sergeant. 'Human life, Mr Betteredge, is a sort of target—misfortune is always firing at it, and always hitting the mark. But for that outfit, we should have discovered a new nightgown or petticoat among Rosanna's things, and have nailed her in that way. You're not at a loss to follow me, are you? You have examined the servants yourself, and you know what discoveries two of them made outside Rosanna's door. Surely you know what the girl was about yesterday, after she was taken ill? You can't guess? Oh dear me, it's as plain as that strip of light there, at the end of the trees. At eleven, on Thursday morning, Superintendent Seegrave (who is a mass of human infirmity) points out to all the women servants the smear on the door. Rosanna has her own reasons for suspecting her own things; she takes the first opportunity of getting to her room, finds the paint-stain on her night-gown, or petticoat, or what not, shams ill and slips away to the town, gets the materials for making a new petticoat or night-gown, makes it alone in her room on the Thursday night, lights a fire (not to destroy it; two of her fellow-servants are prying outside her door, and she knows better than to make a smell of burning, and to have a lot of tinder to get rid of)—lights a fire, I say, to dry and iron the substitute dress after wringing it out, keeps the stained dress hidden (probably *on* her), and is at this moment occupied in making away with it, in some convenient place, on that lonely bit of beach ahead of us. I have traced her this evening to your fishing village, and to one particular cottage, which we may possibly have to visit, before we go back. She stopped in the cottage for some time, and she came out with (as I believe) something hidden under her cloak. A cloak (on a woman's back) is an emblem of charity—it covers a multitude of sins. I saw her set off northwards along the coast, after leaving the cottage. Is your sea-shore here considered a fine specimen of marine landscape, Mr Betteredge?'

I answered, 'Yes,' as shortly as might be.

'Tastes differ,' says Sergeant Cuff. 'Looking at it from my point of view, I never saw a marine landscape that I admired less. If you happen to be following another person along your sea-coast, and if that person happens to look round, there isn't a scrap of cover to hide you anywhere. I had to choose between taking Rosanna in custody on suspicion, or leaving her, for the time being, with her little game in her own hands. For reasons which I won't trouble you with, I decided on making any sacrifice rather than give the alarm as soon as to-night to a certain person who shall be nameless between us. I came back to the house to ask you to take me to the north end of the beach by another way. Sand—in respect of its printing off people's footsteps—is one of the best detective officers I know. If we don't meet with Rosanna Spearman by coming round on her in this way, the sand may tell us what she has been at, if the light only lasts long enough. Here *is* the sand. If you will excuse my suggesting it—suppose you hold your tongue, and let me go first?'

If there is such a thing known at the doctor's shop as a *detective-fever*, that disease had now got fast hold of your humble servant. Sergeant Cuff went on between the hillocks of sand, down to the beach. I followed him (with my heart in my mouth); and waited at a little distance for what was to happen next.

As it turned out, I found myself standing nearly in the same place where Rosanna Spearman and I had been talking together when Mr Franklin suddenly appeared before us, on arriving at our house from London. While my eyes were watching the Sergeant, my mind wandered away in spite of me to what had passed, on that former occasion, between Rosanna and me. I declare I almost felt the poor thing slip her hand again into mine, and give it a little grateful squeeze to thank me for speaking kindly to her. I declare I almost heard her voice telling me again that the Shivering Sand seemed to draw her to it against her own will, whenever she went out—almost saw her face brighten again, as it brightened when she first set eyes upon Mr Franklin coming briskly out on us from among the hillocks. My spirits fell lower and lower as I thought of these things—and the view of the lonesome little bay, when I looked about to rouse myself, only served to make me feel more uneasy still.

The last of the evening light was fading away; and over all the desolate place there hung a still and awful calm. The heave of the main ocean on the great sand-bank out in the bay, was a heave that made no sound. The inner sea lay lost and dim, without a breath of wind to stir it. Patches of nasty ooze floated, yellow-white, on the dead surface of the water. Scum and slime shone faintly in certain places, where the last of the light still caught them on the two great spits of rock jutting out, north and south, into the sea. It was now the time of the turn of the tide: and even as I stood there waiting, the broad brown face of the quicksand began to dimple and quiver—the only moving thing in all the horrid place.

I saw the Sergeant start as the shiver of the sand caught his eye. After looking at it for a minute or so, he turned and came back to me.

'A treacherous place, Mr Betteredge,' he said; 'and no signs of Rosanna Spearman anywhere on the beach, look where you may.'

He took me down lower on the shore, and I saw for myself that his footsteps and mine were the only footsteps printed off on the sand.

'How does the fishing village bear, standing where we are now?' asked Sergeant Cuff.

'Cobb's Hole,' I answered (that being the name of the place), 'bears as near as may be, due south.'

'I saw the girl this evening, walking northward along the shore, from Cobb's Hole,' said the Sergeant. 'Consequently, she must have been walking towards this place. Is Cobb's Hole on the other side of that point of land there? And can we get to it—now it's low water—by the beach?'

I answered 'Yes,' to both those questions.

'If you'll excuse my suggesting it, we'll step out briskly,' said the Sergeant. 'I want to find the place where she left the shore, before it gets dark.'

We had walked, I should say, a couple of hundred yards towards Cobb's Hole, when Sergeant Cuff suddenly went down on his knees on the beach, to all appearance seized with a sudden frenzy for saying his prayers.

'There's something to be said for your marine landscape here, after all,' remarked the Sergeant. 'Here are a woman's footsteps, Mr Betteredge! Let us call them Rosanna's footsteps, until we find evidence to the contrary that we can't resist. Very confused footsteps, you will please to observe—purposely confused, I should say. Ah, poor soul, she understands the detective virtues of sand as well as I do! But hasn't she been in rather too great a hurry to tread out the marks thoroughly? I think she has. Here's one footstep going *from* Cobb's Hole; and here is another going back to it. Isn't that the toe of her shoe pointing straight to the water's edge? And don't I see two heel-marks further down the beach, close at the water's edge also? I don't want to hurt your feelings, but I'm afraid Rosanna is sly. It looks as if she had determined to get to that place you and I have just come from, without leaving any marks on the sand to trace her by. Shall we say that she walked through the water from this point till she got to that ledge of rocks behind us, and came back the same way, and then took to the beach again where those two heel-marks are still left? Yes, we'll say that. It seems to fit in with my notion that she had something under her cloak, when she left the cottage. No! not something to destroy—for, in that case, where would have been the need of all these precautions to prevent my tracing the place at which her walk ended? Something to hide is, I think, the better guess of the two. Perhaps, if we go on to the cottage, we may find out what that something is?'

At this proposal, my detective-fever suddenly cooled. 'You don't want me,' I said. 'What good can I do?'

'The longer I know you, Mr Betteredge,' said the Sergeant, 'the more virtues I discover. Modesty—oh dear me, how rare modesty is in this world! and how much of that rarity you possess! If I go alone to the cottage, the people's tongues will be tied at the first question I put to them. If I go with you, I go introduced by a justly respected neighbour, and a flow of conversation is the necessary result. It strikes me in that light; how does it strike you?'

Not having an answer of the needful smartness as ready as I could have wished, I tried to gain time by asking him what cottage he wanted to go to.

On the Sergeant describing the place, I recognised it as a cottage inhabited by a fisherman named Yolland, with his wife and two grown-up children, a son and a daughter. If you will look back, you will find that, in first presenting Rosanna Spearman to your notice, I have described her as occasionally varying her walk to the Shivering Sand, by a visit to some friends of hers at Cobb's Hole. Those friends were the Yollands—respectable, worthy people, a credit to the neighbourhood. Rosanna's acquaintance with them had begun by means of the daughter, who was afflicted with a misshapen foot, and who was known in our parts by the name of Limping Lucy. The two deformed girls had, I suppose, a kind of fellow-feeling for each other. Anyway, the Yollands and Rosanna always appeared to get on together, at the few chances they had of meeting, in a pleasant and friendly manner. The fact of Sergeant Cuff having traced the girl to *their* cottage, set the matter of my helping his inquiries in quite a new light. Rosanna had merely gone where she was in the habit of going; and to show that she had been in company with the fisherman and his family was as good as to prove that she had been innocently occupied, so far, at any rate. It would be doing the girl a service, therefore, instead of an injury, if I allowed myself to be convinced by Sergeant Cuff's logic. I professed myself convinced by it accordingly.

We went on to Cobb's Hole, seeing the footsteps on the sand, as long as the light lasted.

On reaching the cottage, the fisherman and his son proved to be out in the boat; and Limping Lucy, always weak and weary, was resting on her bed up-stairs. Good Mrs Yolland received us alone in her kitchen. When she heard that Sergeant Cuff was a celebrated character in London, she clapped a bottle of Dutch gin and a couple of clean pipes on the table, and stared as if she could never see enough of him.

I sat quiet in a corner, waiting to hear how the Sergeant would find his way to the subject of Rosanna Spearman. His usual roundabout manner of going to work proved, on this occasion, to be more roundabout than ever. How he managed it is more than I could tell at the time, and more than I can tell now. But this is certain, he began with the Royal Family, the Primitive Methodists, and the price of fish; and he got from that (in his dismal, underground way) to the loss of the Moonstone, the spitefulness of our first housemaid, and the hard behaviour of the women-servants generally towards Rosanna Spearman. Having reached his subject in this fashion, he described himself as making his inquiries about the lost Diamond, partly with a view to find it, and partly for the purpose of clearing Rosanna from the unjust suspicions of her enemies in the house. In about a quarter of an hour from the time when we entered the kitchen, good Mrs Yolland was persuaded that she was talking to Rosanna's best friend, and was pressing Sergeant Cuff to comfort his stomach and revive his spirits out of the Dutch bottle.

Being firmly persuaded that the Sergeant was wasting his breath to no purpose on Mrs Yolland, I sat enjoying the talk between them, much as I have sat, in my time, enjoying a stage play. The great Cuff showed a wonderful patience; trying his luck drearily this way and that way, and firing shot after shot, as it were, at random, on the chance of hitting the mark. Everything to Rosanna's credit, nothing to Rosanna's prejudice—that was how it ended, try as he might; with Mrs Yolland talking nineteen to the dozen, and placing the most entire confidence in him. His last effort was made, when we had looked at our watches, and had got on our legs previous to taking leave.

'I shall now wish you good-night, ma'am,' says the Sergeant. 'And I shall only say, at parting, that Rosanna Spearman has a sincere well-wisher in myself, your obedient servant. But, oh dear me! she will never get on in her present place; and my advice to her is—leave it.'

'Bless your heart alive! she is *going* to leave it!' cries Mrs Yolland. (*Nota bene*—I translate Mrs Yolland out of the Yorkshire language into the English language. When I tell you that the all-accomplished Cuff was every now and then puzzled to understand her until I helped him, you will draw your own conclusions as to what *your* state of mind would be if I reported her in her native tongue.)

Rosanna Spearman going to leave us! I pricked up my ears at that. It seemed strange, to say the least of it, that she should have given no warning, in the first place, to my lady or to me. A certain doubt came up in my mind whether Sergeant Cuff's last random shot might not have hit the mark. I began to question whether my share in the proceedings was quite as harmless a one as I had thought it. It might be all in the way of the Sergeant's business to mystify an honest woman by wrapping her round in a network of lies; but it was my duty to have remembered, as a good Protestant, that the father of lies is the Devil—and that mischief and the Devil are never far apart. Beginning to smell mischief in the air, I tried to take Sergeant Cuff out. He sat down again instantly, and asked for a little drop of comfort out of the Dutch bottle. Mrs Yolland sat down opposite to him, and gave him his nip. I went on to the door, excessively uncomfortable, and said I thought I must bid them good-night—and yet I didn't go.

'So she means to leave?' says the Sergeant. 'What is she to do when she does leave? Sad, sad! The poor creature has got no friends in the world, except you and me.'

'Ah, but she has though!' says Mrs Yolland. 'She came in here, as I told you, this evening; and, after sitting and talking a little with my girl Lucy and me, she asked to go up-stairs by herself, into Lucy's room. It's the only room in our place where there's pen and ink. "I want to write a letter to a friend," she says, "and I can't do it for the prying and peeping of the servants up at the house." Who the letter was written to I can't tell you: it must have been a mortal long one, judging by the time she stopped upstairs over it. I offered her a postage-stamp when she came down. She hadn't got the letter in her hand, and she didn't accept the stamp. A little close, poor soul (as you know), about herself and her doings. But a friend she has got somewhere, I can tell you; and to that friend, you may depend upon it, she will go.'

'Soon?' asked the Sergeant.

'As soon as she can,' says Mrs Yolland.

Here I stepped in again from the door. As chief of my lady's establishment, I couldn't allow this sort of loose talk about a servant of ours going, or not going, to proceed any longer in my presence, without noticing it.

'You must be mistaken about Rosanna Spearman,' I said. 'If she had been going to leave her present situation, she would have mentioned it, in the first place, to *me*.'

'Mistaken?' cries Mrs Yolland. 'Why, only an hour ago she bought some things she wanted for travelling—of my own self, Mr Betteredge, in this very room. And that reminds me,' says the wearisome woman, suddenly beginning to feel in her pocket, 'of something I have got it on my mind to say about Rosanna and her money. Are you either of you likely to see her when you go back to the house?'

'I'll take a message to the poor thing, with the greatest pleasure,' answered Sergeant Cuff, before I could put in a word edgewise.

Mrs Yolland produced out of her pocket a few shillings and sixpences, and counted them out with a most particular and exasperating carefulness in the palm of her hand. She offered the money to the Sergeant, looking mighty loth to part with it all the while.

'Might I ask you to give this back to Rosanna, with my love and respects?' says Mrs Yolland. 'She insisted on paying me for the one or two things she took a fancy to this evening—and money's welcome enough in our house, I don't deny it. Still, I'm not easy in my mind about taking the poor thing's little savings. And to tell you the truth, I don't think my man would like to hear that I had taken Rosanna Spearman's money, when he comes back to-morrow morning from his work. Please say she's heartily welcome to the things she bought of me—as a gift. And don't leave the money on the table,' says Mrs Yolland, putting it down suddenly before the Sergeant, as if it burnt her fingers—'don't, there's a good man! For times are hard, and flesh is weak; and I *might* feel tempted to put it back in my pocket again.'

'Come along!' I said, 'I can't wait any longer: I must go back to the house.'

'I'll follow you directly,' says Sergeant Cuff.

For the second time, I went to the door; and, for the second time, try as I might, I couldn't cross the threshold.

'It's a delicate matter, ma'am,' I heard the Sergeant say, 'giving money back. You charged her cheap for the things, I'm sure?'

'Cheap!' says Mrs Yolland. 'Come and judge for yourself.'

She took up the candle and led the Sergeant to a corner of the kitchen. For the life of me, I couldn't help following them. Shaken down in the corner was a heap of odds and ends (mostly old metal), which the fisherman had picked up at different times from wrecked ships, and which he hadn't found a market for yet, to his own mind. Mrs Yolland dived into this rubbish, and brought up an old japanned tin case, with a cover to it, and a hasp to hang it up by—the sort of thing they use, on board ship, for keeping their maps and charts, and such-like, from the wet.

'There!' says she. 'When Rosanna came in this evening, she bought the fellow to that. "It will just do," she says, "to put my cuffs and collars in, and keep them from being crumpled in my box." One and ninepence, Mr Cuff. As I live by bread, not a halfpenny more!'

'Dirt cheap!' says the Sergeant, with a heavy sigh.

He weighed the case in his hand. I thought I heard a note or two of 'The Last Rose of Summer' as he looked at it. There was no doubt now! He had made another discovery to the prejudice of Rosanna Spearman, in the place of all others where I thought her character was safest, and all through me! I leave you to imagine what I felt, and how sincerely I repented having been the medium of introduction between Mrs Yolland and Sergeant Cuff.

'That will do,' I said. 'We really must go.'

Without paying the least attention to me, Mrs Yolland took another dive into the rubbish, and came up out of it, this time, with a dog-chain.

'Weigh it in your hand, sir,' she said to the Sergeant. 'We had three of these; and Rosanna has taken two of them. "What can you want, my dear, with a couple of dog's chains?" says I. "If I join them together they'll go round my box nicely," says she. "Rope's cheapest," says I. "Chain's surest," says she. "Who ever heard of a box corded with chain," says I. "Oh, Mrs Yolland, don't make objections!" says she; "let me have my chains!" A strange girl, Mr Cuff—good as gold, and kinder than a sister to my Lucy—but always a little strange. There! I humoured her. Three and sixpence. On the word of an honest woman, three *and* sixpence, Mr Cuff!'

'Each?' says the Sergeant.

'Both together!' says Mrs Yolland. 'Three and sixpence for the two.'

'Given away, ma'am,' says the Sergeant, shaking his head. 'Clean given away!'

'There's the money,' says Mrs Yolland, getting back sideways to the little heap of silver on the table, as if it drew her in spite of herself. 'The tin case and the dog chains were all she bought, and all she took away. One and ninepence and three and sixpence—total, five and three. With my love and respects—and I can't find it in my conscience to take a poor girl's savings, when she may want them herself.'

'I can't find it in *my* conscience, ma'am, to give the money back,' says Sergeant Cuff. 'You have as good as made her a present of the things—you have indeed.'

'Is that your sincere opinion, sir?' says Mrs Yolland, brightening up wonderfully.

'There can't be a doubt about it,' answered the Sergeant. 'Ask Mr Betteredge.'

It was no use asking *me*. All they got out of *me* was, 'Good-night.'

'Bother the money!' says Mrs Yolland. With these words, she appeared to lose all command over herself; and, making a sudden snatch at the heap of silver, put it back, holus-bolus, in her pocket. 'It upsets one's temper, it does, to see it lying there, and nobody taking it,' cries this unreasonable woman, sitting down with a thump, and looking at Sergeant Cuff, as much as to say, 'It's in my pocket again now—get it out if you can!'

This time, I not only went to the door, but went fairly out on the road back. Explain it how you may, I felt as if one or both of them had mortally offended me. Before I had taken three steps down the village, I heard the Sergeant behind me.

'Thank you for your introduction, Mr Betteredge,' he said. 'I am indebted to the fisherman's wife for an entirely new sensation. Mrs Yolland has puzzled me.'

It was on the tip of my tongue to have given him a sharp answer, for no better reason than this—that I was out of temper with him, because I was out of temper with myself. But when he owned to being puzzled, a comforting doubt crossed my mind whether any great harm had been done after all. I waited in discreet silence to hear more.

'Yes,' says the Sergeant, as if he was actually reading my thoughts in the dark. 'Instead of putting me on the scent, it may console you to know, Mr Betteredge (with your interest in Rosanna), that you have been the means of throwing me off. What the girl has done, to-night, is clear enough, of course. She has joined the two chains, and has fastened them to the hasp in the tin case. She has sunk the case, in the water or in the quicksand. She has made the loose end of the chain fast to some place under the rocks, known only to herself. And she will leave the case secure at its anchorage till the present proceedings have come to an end; after which she can privately pull it up again out of its hiding-place, at her own leisure and convenience. All perfectly plain, so far. But,' says the Sergeant, with the first tone of impatience in his voice that I had heard yet, 'the mystery is—what the devil has she hidden in the tin case?'

I thought to myself, 'The Moonstone!' But I only said to Sergeant Cuff, 'Can't you guess?'

'It's not the Diamond,' says the Sergeant. 'The whole experience of my life is at fault, if Rosanna Spearman has got the Diamond.'

On hearing those words, the infernal detective-fever began, I suppose, to burn in me again. At any rate, I forgot myself in the interest of guessing this new riddle. I said rashly, 'The stained dress!'

Sergeant Cuff stopped short in the dark, and laid his hand on my arm.

'Is anything thrown into that quicksand of yours, ever thrown up on the surface again?' he asked.

'Never,' I answered. 'Light or heavy, whatever goes into the Shivering Sand is sucked down, and seen no more.'

'Does Rosanna Spearman know that?'

'She knows it as well as I do.'

'Then,' says the Sergeant, 'what on earth has she got to do but to tie up a bit of stone in the stained dress, and throw it into the quicksand? There isn't the shadow of a reason why she should have hidden it—and yet she *must* have hidden it. Query,' says the Sergeant, walking on again, 'is the paint-stained dress a petticoat or a nightgown? or is it something else which there is a reason for preserving at any risk? Mr Betteredge, if nothing occurs to prevent it, I must go to Frizinghall to-morrow, and discover what she bought in the town, when she privately got the materials for making the substitute dress. It's a risk to leave the house, as things are now—but it's a worse risk still to stir another step in this matter in the dark. Excuse my being a little out of temper; I'm degraded in my own estimation—I have let Rosanna Spearman puzzle me.'

When we got back, the servants were at supper. The first person we saw in the outer yard was the policeman whom Superintendent Seegrave had left at the Sergeant's disposal. The Sergeant asked if Rosanna Spearman had returned. Yes. When? Nearly an hour since. What had she done? She had gone up-stairs to take off her bonnet and cloak—and she was now at supper quietly with the rest.

Without making any remark, Sergeant Cuff walked on, sinking lower and lower in his own estimation, to the back of the house. Missing the entrance in the dark, he went on (in spite of my calling to him) till he was stopped by a wicket-gate which led into the garden. When I joined him to bring him back by the right way, I found that he was looking up attentively at one particular window, on the bed-room floor, at the back of the house.

Looking up, in my turn, I discovered that the object of his contemplation was the window of Miss Rachel's room, and that lights were passing backwards and forwards there as if something unusual was going on.

'Isn't that Miss Verinder's room?' asked Sergeant Cuff.

I replied that it was, and invited him to go in with me to supper. The Sergeant remained in his place, and said something about enjoying the smell of the garden at night. I left him to his enjoyment. Just as I was turning in at the door, I heard 'The Last Rose of Summer' at the wicket-gate. Sergeant Cuff had made another discovery! And my young lady's window was at the bottom of it this time!

The latter reflection took me back again to the Sergeant, with a polite intimation that I could not find it in my heart to leave him by himself. 'Is there anything you don't understand up there?' I added, pointing to Miss Rachel's window.

Judging by his voice, Sergeant Cuff had suddenly risen again to the right place in his own estimation. 'You are great people for betting in Yorkshire, are you not?' he asked.

'Well?' I said. 'Suppose we are?'

'If I was a Yorkshireman,' proceeded the Sergeant, taking my arm, 'I would lay you an even sovereign, Mr Betteredge, that your young lady has suddenly resolved to leave the house. If I won on that event, I should offer to lay another sovereign, that the idea has occurred to her within the last hour.'

The first of the Sergeant's guesses startled me. The second mixed itself up somehow in my head with the report we had heard from the policeman, that Rosanna Spearman had returned from the sands within the last hour. The two together had a curious effect on me as we went in to supper. I shook off Sergeant Cuff's arm, and, forgetting my manners, pushed by him through the door to make my own inquiries for myself.

Samuel, the footman, was the first person I met in the passage.

'Her ladyship is waiting to see you and Sergeant Cuff,' he said, before I could put any questions to him.

'How long has she been waiting?' asked the Sergeant's voice behind me.

'For the last hour, sir.'

There it was again! Rosanna had come back; Miss Rachel had taken some resolution out of the common; and my lady had been waiting to see the Sergeant—all within the last hour! It was not pleasant to find these very different persons and things linking themselves together in this way. I went on up-stairs, without looking at Sergeant Cuff, or speaking to him. My hand took a sudden fit of trembling as I lifted it to knock at my mistress's door.

'I shouldn't be surprised,' whispered the Sergeant over my shoulder, 'if a scandal was to burst up in the house to-night. Don't be alarmed! I have put the muzzle on worse family difficulties than this, in my time.'

As he said the words, I heard my mistress's voice calling to us to come in.

CHAPTER XVI

WE found my lady with no light in the room but the reading-lamp. The shade was screwed down so as to overshadow her face. Instead of looking up at us in her usual straightforward way, she sat close at the table, and kept her eyes fixed obstinately on an open book.

'Officer,' she said, 'is it important to the inquiry you are conducting, to know beforehand if any person now in this house wishes to leave it?'

'Most important, my lady.'

'I have to tell you, then, that Miss Verinder proposes going to stay with her aunt, Mrs Ablewhite, of Frizinghall. She has arranged to leave us the first thing to-morrow morning.'

Sergeant Cuff looked at me. I made a step forward to speak to my mistress—and, feeling my heart fail me (if I must own it), took a step back again, and said nothing.

'May I ask your ladyship *when* Miss Verinder informed you that she was going to her aunt's?' inquired the Sergeant.

'About an hour since,' answered my mistress.

Sergeant Cuff looked at me once more. They say old people's hearts are not very easily moved. *My* heart couldn't have thumped much harder than it did now, if I had been five-and-twenty again!

'I have no claim, my lady,' says the Sergeant, 'to control Miss Verinder's actions. All I can ask you to do is to put off her departure, if possible, till later in the day. I must go to Frizinghall myself to-morrow morning—and I shall be back by two o'clock, if not before. If Miss Verinder can be kept here till that time, I should wish to say two words to her—unexpectedly—before she goes.'

My lady directed me to give the coachman her orders, that the carriage was not to come for Miss Rachel until two o'clock. 'Have you more to say?' she asked of the Sergeant, when this had been done.

'Only one thing, your ladyship. If Miss Verinder is surprised at this change in the arrangements, please not to mention Me as being the cause of putting off her journey.'

My mistress lifted her head suddenly from her book as if she was going to say something—checked herself by a great effort—and, looking back again at the open page, dismissed us with a sign of her hand.

'That's a wonderful woman,' said Sergeant Cuff, when we were out in the hall again. 'But for her self-control, the mystery that puzzles you, Mr Betteredge, would have been at an end to-night.'

At those words, the truth rushed at last into my stupid old head. For the moment, I suppose I must have gone clean out of my senses. I seized the Sergeant by the collar of his coat, and pinned him against the wall.

'Damn you!' I cried out, 'there's something wrong about Miss Rachel—and you have been hiding it from me all this time!'

Sergeant Cuff looked up at me—flat against the wall—without stirring a hand, or moving a muscle of his melancholy face.

'Ah,' he said, 'you've guessed it at last.'

My hand dropped from his collar, and my head sunk on my breast. Please to remember, as some excuse for my breaking out as I did, that I had served the family for fifty years. Miss Rachel had climbed upon my knees, and pulled my whiskers, many and many a time when she was a child. Miss Rachel, with all her faults, had been, to my mind, the dearest and prettiest and best young mistress that ever an old servant waited on, and loved. I begged Sergeant Cuff's pardon, but I am afraid I did it with watery eyes, and not in a very becoming way.

'Don't distress yourself, Mr Betteredge,' says the Sergeant, with more kindness than I had any right to expect from him. 'In my line of life, if we were quick at taking offence, we shouldn't be worth salt to our porridge. If it's any comfort to you, collar me again. You don't in the least know how to do it; but I'll overlook your awkwardness in consideration of your feelings.'

He curled up at the corners of his lips, and, in his own dreary way, seemed to think he had delivered himself of a very good joke.

I led him into my own little sitting-room, and closed the door.

'Tell me the truth, Sergeant,' I said. 'What do you suspect? It's no kindness to hide it from me now.'

'I don't suspect,' said Sergeant Cuff. 'I know.'

My unlucky temper began to get the better of me again.

'Do you mean to tell me, in plain English,' I said, 'that Miss Rachel has stolen her own Diamond?'

'Yes,' says the Sergeant; 'that is what I mean to tell you, in so many words. Miss Verinder has been in secret possession of the Moonstone from first to last; and she has taken Rosanna Spearman into her confidence, because she has calculated on our suspecting Rosanna Spearman of the theft. There is the whole case in a nutshell. Collar me again, Mr Betteredge. If it's any vent to your feelings, collar me again.'

God help me! my feelings were not to be relieved in that way. 'Give me your reasons!' That was all I could say to him.

'You shall hear my reasons to-morrow,' said the Sergeant. 'If Miss Verinder refuses to put off her visit to her aunt (which you will find Miss Verinder will do), I shall be obliged to lay the whole case before your mistress tomorrow. And, as I don't know what may come of it, I shall request you to be present, and to hear what passes on both sides. Let the matter rest for to-night. No, Mr Betteredge, you don't get a word more on the subject of the Moonstone out of me. There is your table spread for supper. That's one of the many human infirmities which I always treat tenderly. If you will ring the bell, I'll say grace. "For what we are going to receive——".'

'I wish you a good appetite to it, Sergeant,' I said. '*My* appetite is gone. I'll wait and see you served, and then I'll ask you to excuse me, if I go away, and try to get the better of this by myself.'

I saw him served with the best of everything—and I shouldn't have been sorry if the best of everything had choked him. The head gardener (Mr Begbie) came in at the same time, with his weekly account. The Sergeant got on the subject of roses and the merits of grass walks and gravel walks immediately. I left the two together, and went out with a heavy heart. This was the first trouble I remember for many a long year which wasn't to be blown off by a whiff of tobacco, and which was even beyond the reach of *Robinson Crusoe.*

Being restless and miserable, and having no particular room to go to, I took a turn on the terrace, and thought it over in peace and quietness by myself. It doesn't much matter what my thoughts were. I felt wretchedly old, and worn out, and unfit for my place—and began to wonder, for the first time in my life, when it would please God to take me. With all this, I held firm, notwithstanding, to my belief in Miss Rachel. If Sergeant Cuff had been Solomon in all his glory, and had told me that my young lady had mixed herself up in a mean and guilty plot, I should have had but one answer for Solomon, wise as he was, 'You don't know her; and I do.'

My meditations were interrupted by Samuel. He brought me a written message from my mistress.

Going into the house to get a light to read it by, Samuel remarked that there seemed a change coming in the weather. My troubled mind had prevented me from noticing it before. But, now my attention was roused, I heard the dogs uneasy, and the wind moaning low. Looking up at the sky, I saw the rack of clouds getting blacker and blacker, and hurrying faster and faster over a watery moon. Wild weather coming—Samuel was right, wild weather coming.

The message from my lady informed me, that the magistrate at Frizinghall had written to remind her about the three Indians. Early in the coming week, the rogues must needs be released, and left free to follow their own devices. If we had any more questions to ask them, there was no time to lose. Having forgotten to mention this, when she had last seen Sergeant Cuff, my mistress now desired me to supply the omission. The Indians had gone clean out of my head (as they have, no doubt, gone clean out of yours). I didn't see much use in stirring that subject again. However, I obeyed my orders on the spot, as a matter of course.

I found Sergeant Cuff and the gardener, with a bottle of Scotch whisky between them, head over ears in an argument on the growing of roses. The Sergeant was so deeply interested that he held up his hand, and signed to me not to interrupt the discussion, when I came in. As far as I could understand it, the question between them was, whether the white moss rose did, or did not, require to be budded on the dog-rose to make it grow well. Mr Begbie said, Yes; and Sergeant Cuff said, No. They appealed to me, as hotly as a couple of boys. Knowing nothing whatever about the growing of roses, I steered a middle course—just as her Majesty's judges do, when the scales of justice bother them by hanging even to a hair. 'Gentlemen,' I remarked, 'there is much to be said on both sides.' In the temporary lull produced by that impartial sentence, I laid my lady's written message on the table, under the eyes of Sergeant Cuff.

I had got by this time, as nearly as might be, to hate the Sergeant. But truth compels me to acknowledge that, in respect of readiness of mind, he was a wonderful man.

In half a minute after he had read the message, he had looked back into his memory for Superintendent Seegrave's report; had picked out that part of it in which the Indians were concerned; and was ready with his answer. A certain great traveller, who understood the Indians and their language, had figured in Mr Seegrave's report, hadn't he? Very well. Did I know the gentleman's name and address? Very well again. Would I write them on the back of my lady's message? Much obliged to me. Sergeant Cuff would look that gentleman up, when he went to Frizinghall in the morning.

'Do you expect anything to come of it?' I asked. 'Superintendent Seegrave found the Indians as innocent as the babe unborn.'

'Superintendent Seegrave has been proved wrong, up to this time, in all his conclusions,' answered the Sergeant. 'It may be worth while to find out to-morrow whether Superintendent Seegrave was wrong about the Indians as well.' With that he turned to Mr Begbie, and took up the argument again exactly at the place where it had left off. 'This question between us is a question of soils and seasons, and patience and pains, Mr Gardener. Now let me put it to you from another point of view. You take your white moss rose—'

By that time, I had closed the door on them, and was out of hearing of the rest of the dispute.

In the passage, I met Penelope hanging about, and asked what she was waiting for.

She was waiting for her young lady's bell, when her young lady chose to call her back to go on with the packing for the next day's journey. Further inquiry revealed to me, that Miss Rachel had given it as a reason for wanting to go to her aunt at Frizinghall, that the house was unendurable to her, and that she could bear the odious presence of a policeman under the same roof with herself no longer. On being informed, half an hour since, that her departure would be delayed till two in the afternoon, she had flown into a violent passion. My lady, present at the time, had severely rebuked her, and then (having apparently something to say, which was reserved for her daughter's private ear) had sent Penelope out of the room. My girl was in wretchedly low spirits about the changed state of things in the house. 'Nothing goes right, father; nothing is like what it used to be. I feel as if some dreadful misfortune was hanging over us all.'

That was my feeling too. But I put a good face on it, before my daughter. Miss Rachel's bell rang while we were talking. Penelope ran up the back stairs to go on with the packing. I went by the other way to the hall, to see what the glass said about the change in the weather.

Just as I approached the swing-door leading into the hall from the servants' offices, it was violently opened from the other side, and Rosanna Spearman ran by me, with a miserable look of pain in her face, and one of her hands pressed hard over her heart, as if the pang was in that quarter. 'What's the matter, my girl?' I asked, stopping her. 'Are you ill?' 'For God's sake, don't speak to me,' she answered, and twisted herself out of my hands, and ran on towards the servants' staircase. I called to the cook (who was within hearing) to look after the poor girl. Two other persons proved to be within hearing, as well as the cook. Sergeant Cuff darted softly out of my room, and asked what was the matter. I answered 'Nothing.' Mr Franklin, on the other side, pulled open the swing-door, and beckoning me into the hall, inquired if I had seen anything of Rosanna Spearman.

'She has just passed me, sir, with a very disturbed face, and in a very odd manner.'

'I am afraid I am innocently the cause of that disturbance, Betteredge.'

'You, sir!'

'I can't explain it,' says Mr Franklin; 'but, if the girl *is* concerned in the loss of the Diamond, I do really believe she was on the point of confessing everything—to me, of all the people in the world—not two minutes since.'

Looking towards the swing-door, as he said those last words, I fancied I saw it opened a little way from the inner side.

Was there anybody listening? The door fell to, before I could get to it. Looking through, the moment after, I thought I saw the tails of Sergeant Cuff's respectable black coat disappearing round the corner of the passage. He knew, as well as I did, that he could expect no more help from me, now that I had discovered the turn which his investigations were really taking. Under those circumstances, it was quite in his character to help himself, and to do it by the underground way.

Not feeling sure that I had really seen the Sergeant—and not desiring to make needless mischief, where, Heaven knows, there was mischief enough going on already—I told Mr Franklin that I thought one of the dogs had got into the house—and then begged him to describe what had happened between Rosanna and himself.

'Were you passing through the hall, sir?' I asked. 'Did you meet her accidentally, when she spoke to you?'

Mr Franklin pointed to the billiard-table.

'I was knocking the balls about,' he said, 'and trying to get this miserable business of the Diamond out of my mind. I happened to look up—and there stood Rosanna Spearman at the side of me, like a ghost! Her stealing on me in that way was so strange, that I hardly knew what to do at first. Seeing a very anxious expression in her face, I asked her if she wished to speak to me. She answered, "Yes, if I dare." Knowing what suspicion attached to her, I could only put one construction on such language as that. I confess it made me uncomfortable. I had no wish to invite the girl's confidence. At the same time, in the difficulties that now beset us, I could hardly feel justified in refusing to listen to her, if she was really bent on speaking to me. It was an awkward position; and I dare say I got out of it awkwardly enough. I said to her, "I don't quite understand you. Is there anything you want me to do?" Mind, Betteredge, I didn't speak unkindly! The poor girl can't help being ugly—I felt that, at the time. The cue was still in my hand, and I went on knocking the balls about, to take off the awkwardness of the thing. As it turned out, I only made matters worse still. I'm afraid I mortified her without meaning it! She suddenly turned away. "He looks at the billiard balls," I heard her say. "Anything rather than look at *me*!" Before I could stop her, she had left the hall. I am not quite easy about it, Betteredge. Would you mind telling Rosanna that I meant no unkindness? I have been a little hard on her, perhaps, in my own thoughts—I have almost hoped that the loss of the Diamond might be traced to *her*. Not from any ill-will to the poor girl: but—' He stopped there, and going back to the billiard-table, began to knock the balls about once more.

After what had passed between the Sergeant and me, I knew what it was that he had left unspoken as well as he knew it himself.

Nothing but the tracing of the Moonstone to our second housemaid could now raise Miss Rachel above the infamous suspicion that rested on her in the mind of Sergeant Cuff. It was no longer a question of quieting my young lady's nervous excitement; it was a question of proving her innocence. If Rosanna had done nothing to compromise herself, the hope which Mr Franklin confessed to having felt would have been hard enough on her in all conscience. But this was not the case. She had pretended to be ill, and had gone secretly to Frizinghall. She had been up all night, making something or destroying something, in private. And she had been at the Shivering Sand, that evening, under circumstances which were highly suspicious, to say the least of them. For all these reasons (sorry as I was for Rosanna) I could not but think that Mr Franklin's way of looking at the matter was neither unnatural nor unreasonable, in Mr Franklin's position. I said a word to him to that effect.

'Yes, yes!' he said in return. 'But there is just a chance—a very poor one, certainly—that Rosanna's conduct may admit of some explanation which we don't see at present. I hate hurting a woman's feelings, Betteredge! Tell the poor creature what I told you to tell her. And if she wants to speak to me—I don't care whether I get into a scrape or not—send her to me in the library.' With those kind words he laid down the cue and left me.

Inquiry at the servants' offices informed me that Rosanna had retired to her own room. She had declined all offers of assistance with thanks, and had only asked to be left to rest in quiet. Here, therefore, was an end of any confession on her part (supposing she really had a confession to make) for that night. I reported the result to Mr Franklin, who, thereupon, left the library, and went up to bed.

I was putting the lights out, and making the windows fast, when Samuel came in with news of the two guests whom I had left in my room.

The argument about the white moss rose had apparently come to an end at last. The gardener had gone home, and Sergeant Cuff was nowhere to be found in the lower regions of the house.

I looked into my room. Quite true—nothing was to be discovered there but a couple of empty tumblers and a strong smell of hot grog. Had the Sergeant gone of his own accord to the bed-chamber that was prepared for him? I went up-stairs to see.

After reaching the second landing, I thought I heard a sound of quiet and regular breathing on my left-hand side. My left-hand side led to the corridor which communicated with Miss Rachel's room. I looked in, and there, coiled up on three chairs placed right across the passage—there, with a red handkerchief tied round his grizzled head, and his respectable black coat rolled up for a pillow, lay and slept Sergeant Cuff!

He woke, instantly and quietly, like a dog, the moment I approached him.

'Good night, Mr Betteredge,' he said. 'And mind, if you ever take to growing roses, the white moss rose is all the better for *not* being budded on the dog-rose, whatever the gardener may say to the contrary!'

'What are you doing here?' I asked. 'Why are you not in your proper bed?'

'I am not in my proper bed,' answered the Sergeant, 'because I am one of the many people in this miserable world who can't earn their money honestly and easily at the same time. There was a coincidence, this evening, between the period of Rosanna Spearman's return from the Sands and the period when Miss Verinder stated her resolution to leave the house. Whatever Rosanna may have hidden, it's clear to my mind that your young lady couldn't go away until she knew that it *was* hidden. The two must have communicated privately once already tonight. If they try to communicate again, when the house is quiet, I want to be in the way, and stop it. Don't blame me for upsetting your sleeping arrangements, Mr Betteredge—blame the Diamond.'

'I wish to God the Diamond had never found its way into this house!' I broke out.

Sergeant Cuff looked with a rueful face at the three chairs on which he had condemned himself to pass the night.

'So do I,' he said, gravely.

CHAPTER XVII

NOTHING happened in the night; and (I am happy to add) no attempt at communication between Miss Rachel and Rosanna rewarded the vigilance of Sergeant Cuff.

I had expected the Sergeant to set off for Frizinghall the first thing in the morning. He waited about, however, as if he had something else to do first. I left him to his own devices; and going into the grounds shortly after, met Mr Franklin on his favourite walk by the shrubbery side.

Before we had exchanged two words, the Sergeant unexpectedly joined us. He made up to Mr Franklin, who received him, I must own, haughtily enough. 'Have you anything to say to me?' was all the return he got for politely wishing Mr Franklin good morning.

'I have something to say to you, sir,' answered the Sergeant, 'on the subject of the inquiry I am conducting here. You detected the turn that inquiry was really taking, yesterday. Naturally enough, in your position, you are shocked and distressed. Naturally enough, also, you visit your own angry sense of your own family scandal upon Me.'

'What do you want?' Mr Franklin broke in, sharply enough.

'I want to remind you, sir, that I have at any rate, thus far, not been *proved* to be wrong. Bearing that in mind, be pleased to remember, at the same time, that I am an officer of the law acting here under the sanction of the mistress of the house. Under these circumstances, is it, or is it not, your duty as a good citizen, to assist me with any special information which you may happen to possess?'

'I possess no special information,' says Mr Franklin.

Sergeant Cuff put that answer by him, as if no answer had been made.

'You may save my time, sir, from being wasted on an inquiry at a distance,' he went on, 'if you choose to understand me and speak out.'

'I don't understand you,' answered Mr Franklin; 'and I have nothing to say.'

'One of the female servants (I won't mention names) spoke to you privately, sir, last night.'

Once more Mr Franklin cut him short; once more Mr Franklin answered, 'I have nothing to say.'

Standing by in silence, I thought of the movement in the swing-door on the previous evening, and of the coat-tails which I had seen disappearing down the passage. Sergeant Cuff had, no doubt, just heard enough, before I interrupted him, to make him suspect that Rosanna had relieved her mind by confessing something to Mr Franklin Blake.

This notion had barely struck me—when who should appear at the end of the shrubbery walk but Rosanna Spearman in her own proper person! She was followed by Penelope, who was evidently trying to make her retrace her steps to the house. Seeing that Mr Franklin was not alone, Rosanna came to a standstill, evidently in great perplexity what to do next. Penelope waited behind her. Mr Franklin saw the girls as soon as I saw them. The Sergeant, with his devilish cunning, took on not to have noticed them at all. All this happened in an instant. Before either Mr Franklin or I could say a word, Sergeant Cuff struck in smoothly, with an appearance of continuing the previous conversation.

'You needn't be afraid of harming the girl, sir,' he said to Mr Franklin, speaking in a loud voice, so that Rosanna might hear him. 'On the contrary, I recommend you to honour me with your confidence, if you feel any interest in Rosanna Spearman.'

Mr Franklin instantly took on not to have noticed the girls either. He answered, speaking loudly on his side:

'I take no interest whatever in Rosanna Spearman.'

I looked towards the end of the walk. All I saw at the distance was that Rosanna suddenly turned round, the moment Mr Franklin had spoken. Instead of resisting Penelope, as she had done the moment before, she now let my daughter take her by the arm and lead her back to the house.

The breakfast-bell rang as the two girls disappeared—and even Sergeant Cuff was now obliged to give it up as a bad job! He said to me quietly, 'I shall go to Frizinghall, Mr Betteredge; and I shall be back before two.' He went his way without a word more—and for some few hours we were well rid of him.

'You must make it right with Rosanna,' Mr Franklin said to me, when we were alone. 'I seem to be fated to say or do something awkward, before that unlucky girl. You must have seen yourself that Sergeant Cuff laid a trap for both of us. If he could confuse *me*, or irritate *her* into breaking out, either she or I might have said something which would answer his purpose. On the spur of the moment, I saw no better way out of it than the way I took. It stopped the girl from saying anything, and it showed the Sergeant that I saw through him. He was evidently listening, Betteredge, when I was speaking to you last night.'

He had done worse than listen, as I privately thought to myself. He had remembered my telling him that the girl was in love with Mr Franklin; and he had calculated on *that*, when he appealed to Mr Franklin's interest in Rosanna—in Rosanna's hearing.

'As to listening, sir,' I remarked (keeping the other point to myself), 'we shall all be rowing in the same boat, if this sort of thing goes on much longer. Prying, and peeping, and listening are the natural occupations of people situated as we are. In another day or two, Mr Franklin, we shall all be struck dumb together—for this reason, that we shall all be listening to surprise each other's secrets, and all know it. Excuse my breaking out, sir. The horrid mystery hanging over us in this house gets into my head like liquor, and makes me wild. I won't forget what you have told me. I'll take the first opportunity of making it right with Rosanna Spearman.'

'You haven't said anything to her yet about last night, have you?' Mr Franklin asked.

'No, sir.'

'Then say nothing now. I had better not invite the girl's confidence, with the Sergeant on the look-out to surprise us together. My conduct is not very consistent, Betteredge—is it? I see no way out of this business, which isn't dreadful to think of, unless the Diamond is traced to Rosanna. And yet I can't, and won't, help Sergeant Cuff to find the girl out.'

Unreasonable enough, no doubt. But it was my state of mind as well. I thoroughly understood him. If you will, for once in your life, remember that you are mortal, perhaps you will thoroughly understand him too.

The state of things, indoors and out, while Sergeant Cuff was on his way to Frizinghall, was briefly this:

Miss Rachel waited for the time when the carriage was to take her to her aunt's, still obstinately shut up in her own room. My lady and Mr Franklin breakfasted together. After breakfast, Mr Franklin took one of his sudden resolutions, and went out precipitately to quiet his mind by a long walk. I was the only person who saw him go; and he told me he should be back before the Sergeant returned. The change in the weather, foreshadowed overnight, had come. Heavy rain had been followed, soon after dawn, by high wind. It was blowing fresh as the day got on. But though the clouds threatened more than once, the rain still held off. It was not a bad day for a walk, if you were young and strong, and could breast the great gusts of wind which came sweeping in from the sea.

I attended my lady after breakfast, and assisted her in the settlement of our household accounts. She only once alluded to the matter of the Moonstone, and that was in the way of forbidding any present mention of it between us. 'Wait till that man comes back,' she said, meaning the Sergeant. 'We *must* speak of it then: we are not obliged to speak of it now.'

After leaving my mistress, I found Penelope waiting for me in my room.

'I wish, father, you would come and speak to Rosanna,' she said. 'I am very uneasy about her.'

I suspected what was the matter readily enough. But it is a maxim of mine that men (being superior creatures) are bound to improve women—if they can. When a woman wants me to do anything (my daughter, or not, it doesn't matter), I always insist on knowing why. The oftener you make them rummage their own minds for a reason, the more manageable you will find them in all the relations of life. It isn't their fault (poor wretches!) that they act first, and think afterwards; it's the fault of the fools who humour them.

Penelope's reason why, on this occasion, may be given in her own words. 'I am afraid, father,' she said, 'Mr Franklin has hurt Rosanna cruelly, without intending it.'

'What took Rosanna into the shrubbery walk?' I asked.

'Her own madness,' says Penelope; 'I can call it nothing else. She was bent on speaking to Mr Franklin, this morning, come what might of it. I did my best to stop her; you saw that. If I could only have got her away before she heard those dreadful words——'

'There! there!' I said, 'don't lose your head. I can't call to mind that anything happened to alarm Rosanna.'

'Nothing to alarm her, father. But Mr Franklin said he took no interest whatever in her—and, oh, he said it in such a cruel voice!'

'He said it to stop the Sergeant's mouth,' I answered.

'I told her that,' says Penelope. 'But you see, father (though Mr Franklin isn't to blame), he's been mortifying and disappointing her for weeks and weeks past; and now this comes on the top of it all! She has no right, of course, to expect him to take any interest in her. It's quite monstrous that she should forget herself and her station in that way. But she seems to have lost pride, and proper feeling, and everything. She frightened me, father, when Mr Franklin said those words. They seemed to turn her into stone. A sudden quiet came over her, and she has gone about her work, ever since, like a woman in a dream.'

I began to feel a little uneasy. There was something in the way Penelope put it which silenced my superior sense. I called to mind, now my thoughts were directed that way, what had passed between Mr Franklin and Rosanna overnight. She looked cut to the heart on that occasion; and now, as ill-luck would have it, she had been unavoidably stung again, poor soul, on the tender place. Sad! sad!—all the more sad because the girl had no reason to justify her, and no right to feel it.

I had promised Mr Franklin to speak to Rosanna, and this seemed the fittest time for keeping my word.

We found the girl sweeping the corridor outside the bedrooms, pale and composed, and neat as ever in her modest print dress. I noticed a curious dimness and dulness in her eyes—not as if she had been crying, but as if she had been looking at something too long. Possibly, it was a misty something raised by her own thoughts. There was certainly no object about her to look at which she had not seen already hundreds on hundreds of times.

'Cheer up, Rosanna!' I said. 'You mustn't fret over your own fancies. I have got something to say to you from Mr Franklin.'

I thereupon put the matter in the right view before her, in the friendliest and most comforting words I could find. My principles, in regard to the other sex, are, as you may have noticed, very severe. But somehow or other, when I come face to face with the women, my practice (I own) is not conformable.

'Mr Franklin is very kind and considerate. Please to thank him.' That was all the answer she made me.

My daughter had already noticed that Rosanna went about her work like a woman in a dream. I now added to this observation, that she also listened and spoke like a woman in a dream. I doubted if her mind was in a fit condition to take in what I had said to her.

'Are you quite sure, Rosanna, that you understand me?' I asked.

'Quite sure.'

She echoed me, not like a living woman, but like a creature moved by machinery. She went on sweeping all the time. I took away the broom as gently and as kindly as I could.

'Come, come, my girl!' I said, 'this is not like yourself. You have got something on your mind. I'm your friend—and I'll stand your friend, even if you have done wrong. Make a clean breast of it, Rosanna—make a clean breast of it!'

The time had been, when my speaking to her in that way would have brought the tears into her eyes. I could see no change in them now.

'Yes,' she said, 'I'll make a clean breast of it.'

'To my lady?' I asked.

'No.'

'To Mr Franklin?'

'Yes; to Mr Franklin.'

I hardly knew what to say to that. She was in no condition to understand the caution against speaking to him in private, which Mr Franklin had directed me to give her. Feeling my way, little by little, I only told her Mr Franklin had gone out for a walk.

'It doesn't matter,' she answered. 'I sha'n't trouble Mr Franklin, to-day.'

'Why not speak to my lady?', I said. 'The way to relieve your mind is to speak to the merciful and Christian mistress who has always been kind to you.'

She looked at me for a moment with a grave and steady attention, as if she was fixing what I said in her mind. Then she took the broom out of my hands; and moved off with it slowly, a little way down the corridor.

'No,' she said, going on with her sweeping, and speaking to herself; 'I know a better way of relieving my mind than that.'

'What is it?'

'Please to let me go on with my work.'

Penelope followed her, and offered to help her.

She answered, 'No. I want to do my work. Thank you, Penelope.' She looked round at me. 'Thank you, Mr Betteredge.'

There was no moving her—there was nothing more to be said. I signed to Penelope to come away with me. We left her, as we had found her, sweeping the corridor, like a woman in a dream.

'This is a matter for the doctor to look into,' I said. 'It's beyond me.'

My daughter reminded me of Mr Candy's illness, owing (as you may remember) to the chill he had caught on the night of the dinner-party. His assistant—a certain Mr Ezra Jennings—was at our disposal, to be sure. But nobody knew much about him in our parts. He had been engaged by Mr Candy, under rather peculiar circumstances; and, right or wrong, we none of us liked him or trusted him. There were other doctors at Frizinghall. But they were strangers to our house; and Penelope doubted, in Rosanna's present state, whether strangers might not do her more harm than good.

I thought of speaking to my lady. But, remembering the heavy weight of anxiety which she already had on her mind, I hesitated to add to all the other vexations this new trouble. Still, there was a necessity for doing something. The girl's state was, to my thinking, downright alarming—and my mistress ought to be informed of it. Unwilling enough, I went to her sitting-room. No one was there. My lady was shut up with Miss Rachel. It was impossible for me to see her till she came out again.

I waited in vain till the clock on the front staircase struck the quarter to two. Five minutes afterwards, I heard my name called, from the drive outside the house. I knew the voice directly. Sergeant Cuff had returned from Frizinghall.

CHAPTER XVIII

GOING down to the front door, I met the Sergeant on the steps.

It went against the grain with me, after what had passed between us, to show him that I felt any sort of interest in his proceedings. In spite of myself, however, I felt an interest that there was no resisting. My sense of dignity sank from under me, and out came the words: 'What news from Frizinghall?'

'I have seen the Indians,' answered Sergeant Cuff. 'And I have found out what Rosanna bought privately in the town, on Thursday last. The Indians will be set free on Wednesday in next week. There isn't a doubt on my mind, and there isn't a doubt on Mr Murthwaite's mind, that they came to this place to steal the Moonstone. Their calculations were all thrown out, of course, by what happened in the house on Wednesday night; and they have no more to do with the actual loss of the jewel than you have. But I can tell you one thing, Mr Betteredge—if *we* don't find the Moonstone, *they* will. You have not heard the last of the three jugglers yet.'

Mr Franklin came back from his walk as the Sergeant said those startling words. Governing his curiosity better than I had governed mine, he passed us without a word, and went on into the house.

As for me, having already dropped my dignity, I determined to have the whole benefit of the sacrifice. 'So much for the Indians,' I said. 'What about Rosanna next?'

Sergeant Cuff shook his head.

'The mystery in that quarter is thicker than ever,' he said. 'I have traced her to a shop at Frizinghall, kept by a linendraper named Maltby. She bought nothing whatever at any of the other drapers' shops, or at any milliners' or tailors' shops; and she bought nothing at Maltby's but a piece of long cloth. She was very particular in choosing a certain quality. As to quantity, she bought enough to make a nightgown.'

'Whose nightgown?' I asked.

'Her own, to be sure. Between twelve and three, on the Thursday morning, she must have slipped down to your young lady's room, to settle the hiding of the Moonstone while all the rest of you were in bed. In going back to her own room, her nightgown must have brushed the wet paint on the door. She couldn't wash out the stain; and she couldn't safely destroy the nightgown without first providing another like it, to make the inventory of her linen complete.'

'What proves that it was Rosanna's nightgown?' I objected.

'The material she bought for making the substitute dress,' answered the Sergeant. 'If it had been Miss Verinder's nightgown, she would have had to buy lace, and frilling, and Lord knows what besides; and she wouldn't have had time to make it in one night. Plain long cloth means a plain servant's nightgown. No, no, Mr Betteredge,—all that is clear enough. The pinch of the question is—why, after having provided the substitute dress, does she hide the smeared nightgown, instead of destroying it? If the girl won't speak out, there is only one way of settling the difficulty. The hiding-place at the Shivering Sand must be searched—and the true state of the case will be discovered there.'

'How are you to find the place?' I inquired.

'I am sorry to disappoint you,' said the Sergeant—'but that's a secret which I mean to keep to myself.'

(Not to irritate your curiosity, as he irritated mine, I may here inform you that he had come back from Frizinghall provided with a search-warrant. His experience in such matters told him that Rosanna was in all probability carrying about her a memorandum of the hiding-place, to guide her, in case she returned to it, under changed circumstances and after a lapse of time. Possessed of this memorandum, the Sergeant would be furnished with all that he could desire.)

'Now, Mr Betteredge,' he went on, 'suppose we drop speculation, and get to business. I told Joyce to have an eye on Rosanna. Where is Joyce?'

Joyce was the Frizinghall policeman, who had been left by Superintendent Seegrave at Sergeant Cuff's disposal. The clock struck two, as he put the question; and, punctual to the moment, the carriage came round to take Miss Rachel to her aunt's.

'One thing at a time,' said the Sergeant, stopping me as I was about to send in search of Joyce. 'I must attend to Miss Verinder first.'

As the rain was still threatening, it was the close carriage that had been appointed to take Miss Rachel to Frizinghall. Sergeant Cuff beckoned Samuel to come down to him from the rumble behind.

'You will see a friend of mine waiting among the trees, on this side of the lodge gate,' he said. 'My friend, without stopping the carriage, will get up into the rumble with you. You have nothing to do but to hold your tongue, and shut your eyes. Otherwise, you will get into trouble.'

With that advice, he sent the footman back to his place. What Samuel thought I don't know. It was plain, to my mind, that Miss Rachel was to be privately kept in view from the time when she left our house—if she did leave it. A watch set on my young lady! A spy behind her in the rumble of her mother's carriage! I could have cut my own tongue out for having forgotten myself so far as to speak to Sergeant Cuff.

The first person to come out of the house was my lady. She stood aside, on the top step, posting herself there to see what happened. Not a word did she say, either to the Sergeant or to me. With her lips closed, and her arms folded in the light garden cloak which she had wrapped round her on coming into the air, there she stood, as still as a statue, waiting for her daughter to appear.

In a minute more, Miss Rachel came downstairs—very nicely dressed in some soft yellow stuff, that set off her dark complexion, and clipped her tight (in the form of a jacket) round the waist. She had a smart little straw hat on her head, with a white veil twisted round it. She had primrose-coloured gloves that fitted her hands like a second skin. Her beautiful black hair looked as smooth as satin under her hat. Her little ears were like rosy shells—they had a pearl dangling from each of them. She came swiftly out to us, as straight as a lily on its stem, and as lithe and supple in every movement she made as a young cat. Nothing that I could discover was altered in her pretty face, but her eyes and her lips. Her eyes were brighter and fiercer than I liked to see; and her lips had so completely lost their colour and their smile that I hardly knew them again. She kissed her mother in a hasty and sudden manner on the cheek. She said, 'Try to forgive me, mamma'—and then pulled down her veil over her face so vehemently that she tore it. In another moment she had run down the steps, and had rushed into the carriage as if it was a hiding-place.

Sergeant Cuff was just as quick on his side. He put Samuel back, and stood before Miss Rachel, with the open carriage-door in his hand, at the instant when she settled herself in her place.

'What do you want?' says Miss Rachel, from behind her veil.

'I want to say one word to you, miss,' answered the Sergeant, 'before you go. I can't presume to stop your paying a visit to your aunt. I can only venture to say that your leaving us, as things are now, puts an obstacle in the way of my recovering your Diamond. Please to understand that; and now decide for yourself whether you go or stay.'

Miss Rachel never even answered him. 'Drive on, James!' she called out to the coachman.

Without another word, the Sergeant shut the carriage-door. Just as he closed it, Mr Franklin came running down the steps. 'Good-bye, Rachel,' he said, holding out his hand.

'Drive on!' cried Miss Rachel, louder than ever, and taking no more notice of Mr Franklin than she had taken of Sergeant Cuff.

Mr Franklin stepped back thunderstruck, as well he might be. The coachman, not knowing what to do, looked towards my lady, still standing immovable on the top step. My lady, with anger and sorrow and shame all struggling together in her face, made him a sign to start the horses, and then turned back hastily into the house. Mr Franklin, recovering the use of his speech, called after her, as the carriage drove off, 'Aunt! you were quite right. Accept my thanks for all your kindness—and let me go.'

My lady turned as though to speak to him. Then, as if distrusting herself, waved her hand kindly. 'Let me see you, before you leave us, Franklin,' she said, in a broken voice—and went on to her own room.

'Do me a last favour, Betteredge,' says Mr Franklin, turning to me, with the tears in his eyes. 'Get me away to the train as soon as you can!'

He too went his way into the house. For the moment, Miss Rachel had completely unmanned him. Judge from that, how fond he must have been of her!

Sergeant Cuff and I were left face to face, at the bottom of the steps. The Sergeant stood with his face set towards a gap in the trees, commanding a view of one of the windings of the drive which led from the house. He had his hands in his pockets, and he was softly whistling 'The Last Rose of Summer' to himself.

'There's a time for everything,' I said, savagely enough. 'This isn't a time for whistling.'

At that moment, the carriage appeared in the distance, through the gap, on its way to the lodge-gate. There was another man, besides Samuel, plainly visible in the rumble behind.

'All right!' said the Sergeant to himself. He turned round to me. 'It's no time for whistling, Mr Betteredge, as you say. It's time to take this business in hand, now, without sparing anybody. We'll begin with Rosanna Spearman. Where is Joyce?'

We both called for Joyce, and received no answer. I sent one of the stable-boys to look for him.

'You heard what I said to Miss Verinder?' remarked the Sergeant, while we were waiting. 'And you saw how she received it? I tell her plainly that her leaving us will be an obstacle in the way of my recovering her Diamond—and she leaves, in the face of that statement! Your young lady has got a travelling companion in her mother's carriage, Mr Betteredge—and the name of it is, the Moonstone.'

I said nothing. I only held on like death to my belief in Miss Rachel.

The stable boy came back, followed—very unwillingly, as it appeared to me—by Joyce.

'Where is Rosanna Spearman?' asked Sergeant Cuff.

'I can't account for it, sir,' Joyce began; 'and I am very sorry. But somehow or other—'

'Before I went to Frizinghall,' said the Sergeant, cutting him short, 'I told you to keep your eyes on Rosanna Spearman, without allowing her to discover that she was being watched. Do you mean to tell me that you have let her give you the slip?'

'I am afraid, sir,' says Joyce, beginning to tremble, 'that I was perhaps a little *too* careful not to let her discover me. There are such a many passages in the lower parts of this house—'

'How long is it since you missed her?'

'Nigh on an hour since, sir.'

'You can go back to your regular business at Frizinghall,' said the Sergeant, speaking just as composedly as ever, in his usual quiet and dreary way. 'I don't think your talents are at all in our line, Mr Joyce. Your present form of employment is a trifle beyond you. Good morning.'

The man slunk off. I find it very difficult to describe how I was affected by the discovery that Rosanna Spearman was missing. I seemed to be in fifty different minds about it, all at the same time. In that state, I stood staring at Sergeant Cuff—and my powers of language quite failed me.

'No, Mr Betteredge,' said the Sergeant, as if he had discovered the uppermost thought in me, and was picking it out to be answered, before all the rest. 'Your young friend, Rosanna, won't slip through my fingers so easy as you think. As long as I know where Miss Verinder is, I have the means at my disposal of tracing Miss Verinder's accomplice. I prevented them from communicating last night. Very good. They will get together at Frizinghall, instead of getting together here. The present inquiry must be simply shifted (rather sooner than I had anticipated) from this house, to the house at which Miss Verinder is visiting. In the meantime, I'm afraid I must trouble you to call the servants together again.'

I went round with him to the servants' hall. It is very disgraceful, but it is not the less true, that I had another attack of the detective-fever, when he said those last words. I forgot that I hated Sergeant Cuff. I seized him confidentially by the arm. I said, 'For goodness' sake, tell us what you are going to do with the servants now?'

The great Cuff stood stock still, and addressed himself in a kind of melancholy rapture to the empty air.

'If this man,' said the Sergeant (apparently meaning me), 'only understood the growing of roses, he would be the most completely perfect character on the face of creation!' After that strong expression of feeling, he sighed, and put his arm through mine. 'This is how it stands,' he said, dropping down again to business. 'Rosanna has done one of two things. She has either gone direct to Frizinghall (before I can get there), or she has gone first to visit her hiding-place at the Shivering Sand. The first thing to find out is, which of the servants saw the last of her before she left the house.'

On instituting this inquiry, it turned out that the last person who had set eyes on Rosanna was Nancy, the kitchen-maid.

Nancy had seen her slip out with a letter in her hand, and stop the butcher's man who had just been delivering some meat at the back door. Nancy had heard her ask the man to post the letter when he got back to Frizinghall. The man had looked at the address, and had said it was a roundabout way of delivering a letter directed to Cobb's Hole, to post it at Frizinghall—and that, moreover, on a Saturday, which would prevent the letter from getting to its destination until Monday morning. Rosanna had answered that the delivery of the letter being delayed till Monday was of no importance. The only thing she wished to be sure of was that the man would do what she told him. The man had promised to do it, and had driven away. Nancy had been called back to her work in the kitchen. And no other person had seen anything afterwards of Rosanna Spearman.

'Well?' I asked, when we were alone again.

'Well,' says the Sergeant. 'I must go to Frizinghall.'

'About the letter, sir?'

'Yes. The memorandum of the hiding-place is in that letter. I must see the address at the post-office. If it is the address I suspect, I shall pay our friend, Mrs Yolland, another visit on Monday next.'

I went with the Sergeant to order the pony-chaise. In the stable-yard we got a new light thrown on the missing girl.

CHAPTER XIX

THE news of Rosanna's disappearance had, as it appeared, spread among the out-of-door servants. They too had made their inquiries; and they had just laid hands on a quick little imp, nicknamed 'Duffy'—who was occasionally employed in weeding the garden, and who had seen Rosanna Spearman as lately as half-an-hour since. Duffy was certain that the girl had passed him in the fir-plantation, not walking, but *running*, in the direction of the sea-shore.

'Does this boy know the coast hereabouts?' asked Sergeant Cuff.

'He has been born and bred on the coast,' I answered.

'Duffy!' says the Sergeant, 'do you want to earn a shilling? If you do, come along with me. Keep the pony-chaise ready, Mr Betteredge, till I come back.'

He started for the Shivering Sand, at a rate that my legs (though well enough preserved for my time of life) had no hope of matching. Little Duffy, as the way is with the young savages in our parts when they are in high spirits, gave a howl, and trotted off at the Sergeant's heels.

Here again, I find it impossible to give anything like a clear account of the state of my mind in the interval after Sergeant Cuff had left us. A curious and stupefying restlessness got possession of me. I did a dozen different needless things in and out of the house, not one of which I can now remember. I don't even know how long it was after the Sergeant had gone to the sands, when Duffy came running back with a message for me. Sergeant Cuff had given the boy a leaf torn out of his pocket-book, on which was written in pencil, 'Send me one of Rosanna Spearman's boots, and be quick about it.'

I despatched the first woman-servant I could find to Rosanna's room; and I sent the boy back to say that I myself would follow him with the boot.

This, I am well aware, was not the quickest way to take of obeying the directions which I had received. But I was resolved to see for myself what new mystification was going on, before I trusted Rosanna's boot in the Sergeant's hands. My old notion of screening the girl, if I could, seemed to have come back on me again, at the eleventh hour. This state of feeling (to say nothing of the detective-fever) hurried me off, as soon as I had got the boot, at the nearest approach to a run which a man turned seventy can reasonably hope to make.

As I got near the shore, the clouds gathered black, and the rain came down, drifting in great white sheets of water before the wind. I heard the thunder of the sea on the sand-bank at the mouth of the bay. A little further on, I passed the boy crouching for shelter under the lee of the sand-hills. Then I saw the raging sea, and the rollers tumbling in on the sand-bank, and the driven rain sweeping over the waters like a flying garment, and the yellow wilderness of the beach with one solitary black figure standing on it—the figure of Sergeant Cuff.

He waved his hand towards the north, when he first saw me. 'Keep on that side!' he shouted. 'And come on down here to me!'

I went down to him, choking for breath, with my heart leaping as if it was like to leap out of me. I was past speaking. I had a hundred questions to put to him; and not one of them would pass my lips. His face frightened me. I saw a look in his eyes which was a look of horror. He snatched the boot out of my hand, and set it in a footmark on the sand, bearing south from us as we stood, and pointing straight towards the rocky ledge called the South Spit. The mark was not yet blurred out by the rain—and the girl's boot fitted it to a hair.

The Sergeant pointed to the boot in the footmark, without saying a word.

I caught at his arm, and tried to speak to him, and failed as I had failed when I tried before. He went on, following the footsteps down and down to where the rocks and the sand joined. The South Spit was just awash with the flowing tide; the waters heaved over the hidden face of the Shivering Sand. Now this way and now that, with an obstinate patience that was dreadful to see, Sergeant Cuff tried the boot in the footsteps, and always found it pointing the same way—straight *to* the rocks. Hunt as he might, no sign could he find anywhere of the footsteps walking *from* them.

He gave it up at last. Still keeping silence, he looked again at me; and then he looked out at the waters before us, heaving in deeper and deeper over the quicksand. I looked where he looked—and I saw his thought in his face. A dreadful dumb trembling crawled all over me on a sudden. I fell upon my knees on the beach.

'She has been back at the hiding-place,' I heard the Sergeant say to himself. 'Some fatal accident has happened to her on those rocks.'

The girl's altered looks, and words, and actions—the numbed, deadened way in which she listened to me, and spoke to me—when I had found her sweeping the corridor but a few hours since, rose up in my mind, and warned me, even as the Sergeant spoke, that his guess was wide of the dreadful truth. I tried to tell him of the fear that had frozen me up. I tried to say, 'The death she has died, Sergeant, was a death of her own seeking.' No! the words wouldn't come. The dumb trembling held me in its grip. I couldn't feel the driving rain. I couldn't see the rising tide. As in the vision of a dream, the poor lost creature came back before me. I saw her again as I had seen her in the past time—on the morning when I went to fetch her into the house. I heard her again, telling me that the Shivering Sand seemed to draw her to it against her will, and wondering whether her grave was waiting for her *there*. The horror of it struck at me, in some unfathomable way, through my own child. My girl was just her age. My girl, tried as Rosanna was tried, might have lived that miserable life, and died this dreadful death.

The Sergeant kindly lifted me up, and turned me away from the sight of the place where she had perished.

With that relief, I began to fetch my breath again, and to see things about me, as things really were. Looking towards the sand-hills, I saw the men-servants from out-of-doors, and the fisherman, named Yolland, all running down to us together; and all, having taken the alarm, calling out to know if the girl had been found. In the fewest words, the Sergeant showed them the evidence of the footmarks, and told them that a fatal accident must have happened to her. He then picked out the fisherman from the rest, and put a question to him, turning about again towards the sea: 'Tell me,' he said. 'Could a boat have taken her off, in such weather as this, from those rocks where her footmarks stop?'

The fisherman pointed to the rollers tumbling in on the sand-bank, and to the great waves leaping up in clouds of foam against the headlands on either side of us.

'No boat that ever was built,' he answered, 'could have got to her through *that*.'

Sergeant Cuff looked for the last time at the foot-marks on the sand, which the rain was now fast blurring out.

'There,' he said, 'is the evidence that she can't have left this place by land. And here,' he went on, looking at the fisherman, 'is the evidence that she can't have got away by sea.' He stopped, and considered for a minute. 'She was seen running towards this place, half an hour before I got here from the house,' he said to Yolland. 'Some time has passed since then. Call it, altogether, an hour ago. How high would the water be, at that time, on this side of the rocks?' He pointed to the south side—otherwise, the side which was not filled up by the quicksand.

'As the tide makes to-day,' said the fisherman, 'there wouldn't have been water enough to drown a kitten on that side of the Spit, an hour since.'

Sergeant Cuff turned about northward, towards the quicksand.

'How much on this side?' he asked.

'Less still,' answered Yolland. 'The Shivering Sand would have been just awash, and no more.'

The Sergeant turned to me, and said that the accident must have happened on the side of the quicksand. My tongue was loosened at that. 'No accident!' I told him. 'When she came to this place, she came, weary of her life, to end it here.'

He started back from me. 'How do you know?' he asked. The rest of them crowded round. The Sergeant recovered himself instantly. He put them back from me; he said I was an old man; he said the discovery had shaken me; he said, 'Let him alone a little.' Then he turned to Yolland, and asked, 'Is there any chance of finding her, when the tide ebbs again?' And Yolland answered. 'None. What the Sand gets, the Sand keeps for ever.' Having said that, the fisherman came a step nearer, and addressed himself to me.

'Mr Betteredge,' he said, 'I have a word to say to you about the young woman's death. Four foot out, broadwise, along the side of the Spit, there's a shelf of rock, about half fathom down under the sand. My question is—why didn't she strike that? If she slipped, by accident, from off the Spit, she fell in where there's foothold at the bottom, at a depth that would barely cover her to the waist. She must have waded out, or jumped out, into the Deeps beyond—or she wouldn't be missing now. No accident, sir! The Deeps of the Quicksand have got her. And they have got her by her own act.'

After that testimony from a man whose knowledge was to be relied on, the Sergeant was silent. The rest of us, like him, held our peace. With one accord, we all turned back up the slope of the beach.

At the sand-hillocks we were met by the under-groom, running to us from the house. The lad is a good lad, and has an honest respect for me. He handed me a little note, with a decent sorrow in his face. 'Penelope sent me with this, Mr Betteredge,' he said. 'She found it in Rosanna's room.'

It was her last farewell word to the old man who had done his best—thank God, always done his best—to befriend her.

'You have often forgiven me, Mr Betteredge, in past times. When you next see the Shivering Sand, try to forgive me once more. I have found my grave where my grave was waiting for me. I have lived, and died, sir, grateful for your kindness.'

There was no more than that. Little as it was, I hadn't manhood enough to hold up against it. Your tears come easy, when you're young, and beginning the world. Your tears come easy, when you're old, and leaving it. I burst out crying.

Sergeant Cuff took a step nearer to me—meaning kindly, I don't doubt. I shrank back from him. 'Don't touch me,' I said. 'It's the dread of you, that has driven her to it.'

'You are wrong, Mr Betteredge,' he answered, quietly. 'But there will be time enough to speak of it when we are indoors again.'

I followed the rest of them, with the help of the groom's arm. Through the driving rain we went back—to meet the trouble and the terror that were waiting for us at the house.

CHAPTER XX

THOSE in front had spread the news before us. We found the servants in a state of panic. As we passed my lady's door, it was thrown open violently from the inner side. My mistress came out among us (with Mr Franklin following, and trying vainly to compose her), quite beside herself with the horror of the thing.

'You are answerable for this!' she cried out, threatening the Sergeant wildly with her hand. 'Gabriel! give that wretch his money—and release me from the sight of him!'

The Sergeant was the only one among us who was fit to cope with her—being the only one among us who was in possession of himself.

'I am no more answerable for this distressing calamity, my lady, than you are,' he said. 'If, in half an hour from this, you still insist on my leaving the house, I will accept your ladyship's dismissal, but not your ladyship's money.'

It was spoken very respectfully, but very firmly at the same time—and it had its effect on my mistress as well as on me. She suffered Mr Franklin to lead her back into the room. As the door closed on the two, the Sergeant, looking about among the women-servants in his observant way, noticed that while all the rest were merely frightened, Penelope was in tears. 'When your father has changed his wet clothes,' he said to her, 'come and speak to us, in your father's room.'

Before the half-hour was out, I had got my dry clothes on, and had lent Sergeant Cuff such change of dress as he required. Penelope came in to us to hear what the Sergeant wanted with her. I don't think I ever felt what a good dutiful daughter I had, so strongly as I felt it at that moment. I took her and sat her on my knee—and I prayed God bless her. She hid her head on my bosom, and put her arms round my neck—and we waited a little while in silence. The poor dead girl must have been at the bottom of it, I think, with my daughter and with me. The Sergeant went to the window, and stood there looking out. I thought it right to thank him for considering us both in this way—and I did.

People in high life have all the luxuries to themselves—among others, the luxury of indulging their feelings. People in low life have no such privilege. Necessity, which spares our betters, has no pity on *us*. We learn to put our feelings back into ourselves, and to jog on with our duties as patiently as may be. I don't complain of this—I only notice it. Penelope and I were ready for the Sergeant, as soon as the Sergeant was ready on his side. Asked if she knew what had led her fellow-servant to destroy herself, my daughter answered (as you will foresee) that it was for love of Mr Franklin Blake. Asked next, if she had mentioned this notion of hers to any other person, Penelope answered, 'I have not mentioned it, for Rosanna's sake.' I felt it necessary to add a word to this. I said, 'And for Mr Franklin's sake, my dear, as well. If Rosanna *has* died for love of him, it is not with his knowledge or by his fault. Let him leave the house to-day, if he does leave it, without the useless pain of knowing the truth.' Sergeant Cuff said, 'Quite right,' and fell silent again; comparing Penelope's notion (as it seemed to me) with some other notion of his own which he kept to himself.

At the end of the half-hour, my mistress's bell rang.

On my way to answer it, I met Mr Franklin coming out of his aunt's sitting-room. He mentioned that her ladyship was ready to see Sergeant Cuff—in my presence as before—and he added that he himself wanted to say two words to the Sergeant first. On our way back to my room, he stopped, and looked at the railway time-table in the hall.

'Are you really going to leave us, sir?' I asked. 'Miss Rachel will surely come right again, if you only give her time?'

'She will come right again,' answered Mr Franklin, 'when she hears that I have gone away, and that she will see me no more.'

I thought he spoke in resentment of my young lady's treatment of him. But it was not so. My mistress had noticed, from the time when the police first came into the house, that the bare mention of him was enough to set Miss Rachel's temper in a flame. He had been too fond of his cousin to like to confess this to himself, until the truth had been forced on him, when she drove off to her aunt's. His eyes once opened in that cruel way which you know of, Mr Franklin had taken his resolution—the one resolution which a man of any spirit *could* take—to leave the house.

What he had to say to the Sergeant was spoken in my presence. He described her ladyship as willing to acknowledge that she had spoken over-hastily. And he asked if Sergeant Cuff would consent—in that case—to accept his fee, and to leave the matter of the Diamond where the matter stood now. The Sergeant answered, 'No, sir. My fee is paid me for doing my duty. I decline to take it, until my duty is done.'

'I don't understand you,' says Mr Franklin.

'I'll explain myself, sir,' says the Sergeant. 'When I came here, I undertook to throw the necessary light on the matter of the missing Diamond. I am now ready, and waiting, to redeem my pledge. When I have stated the case to Lady Verinder as the case now stands, and when I have told her plainly what course of action to take for the recovery of the Moonstone, the responsibility will be off my shoulders. Let her ladyship decide, after that, whether she does, or does not, allow me to go on. I shall then have done what I undertook to do—and I'll take my fee.'

In those words Sergeant Cuff reminded us that, even in the Detective Police, a man may have a reputation to lose.

The view he took was so plainly the right one, that there was no more to be said. As I rose to conduct him to my lady's room, he asked if Mr Franklin wished to be present. Mr Franklin answered, 'Not unless Lady Verinder desires it.' He added, in a whisper to me, as I was following the Sergeant out, 'I know what that man is going to say about Rachel; and I am too fond of her to hear it, and keep my temper. Leave me by myself.'

I left him, miserable enough, leaning on the sill of my window, with his face hidden in his hands—and Penelope peeping through the door, longing to comfort him. In Mr Franklin's place, I should have called her in. When you are ill-used by one woman, there is great comfort in telling it to another—because, nine times out of ten, the other always takes your side. Perhaps, when my back was turned, he did call her in? In that case, it is only doing my daughter justice to declare that she would stick at nothing, in the way of comforting Mr Franklin Blake.

In the meantime, Sergeant Cuff and I proceeded to my lady's room.

At the last conference we had held with her, we had found her not over willing to lift her eyes from the book which she had on the table. On this occasion there was a change for the better. She met the Sergeant's eye with an eye that was as steady as his own. The family spirit showed itself in every line of her face; and I knew that Sergeant Cuff would meet his match, when a woman like my mistress was strung up to hear the worst he could say to her.

CHAPTER XXI

THE first words, when we had taken our seats, were spoken by my lady.

'Sergeant Cuff,' she said, 'there was perhaps some excuse for the inconsiderate manner in which I spoke to you half an hour since. I have no wish, however, to claim that excuse. I say, with perfect sincerity, that I regret it, if I wronged you.'

The grace of voice and manner with which she made him that atonement had its due effect on the Sergeant. He requested permission to justify himself—putting his justification as an act of respect to my mistress. It was impossible, he said, that he could be in any way responsible for the calamity which had shocked us all, for this sufficient reason, that his success in bringing his inquiry to its proper end depended on his neither saying nor doing anything that could alarm Rosanna Spearman. He appealed to me to testify whether he had, or had not, carried that object out. I could, and did, bear witness that he had. And there, as I thought, the matter might have been judiciously left to come to an end.

Sergeant Cuff, however, took it a step further, evidently (as you shall now judge) with the purpose of forcing the most painful of all possible explanations to take place between her ladyship and himself.

'I have heard a motive assigned for the young woman's suicide,' said the Sergeant, 'which may possibly be the right one. It is a motive quite unconnected with the case which I am conducting here. I am bound to add, however, that my own opinion points the other way. Some unbearable anxiety in connexion with the missing Diamond, has, I believe, driven the poor creature to her own destruction. I don't pretend to know what that unbearable anxiety may have been. But I think (with your ladyship's permission) I can lay my hand on a person who is capable of deciding whether I am right or wrong.'

'Is the person now in the house?' my mistress asked, after waiting a little.

'The person has left the house, my lady.'

That answer pointed as straight to Miss Rachel as straight could be. A silence dropped on us which I thought would never come to an end. Lord! how the wind howled, and how the rain drove at the window, as I sat there waiting for one or other of them to speak again!

'Be so good as to express yourself plainly,' said my lady. 'Do you refer to my daughter?'

'I do,' said Sergeant Cuff, in so many words.

My mistress had her cheque-book on the table when we entered the room—no doubt to pay the Sergeant his fee. She now put it back in the drawer. It went to my heart to see how her poor hand trembled—the hand that had loaded her old servant with benefits; the hand that, I pray God, may take mine, when my time comes, and I leave my place for ever!

'I had hoped,' said my lady, very slowly and quietly, 'to have recompensed your services, and to have parted with you without Miss Verinder's name having been openly mentioned between us as it has been mentioned now. My nephew has probably said something of this, before you came into the room?'

'Mr Blake gave his message, my lady. And I gave Mr Blake a reason——'

'It is needless to tell me your reason. After what you have just said, you know as well as I do that you have gone too far to go back. I owe it to myself, and I owe it to my child, to insist on your remaining here, and to insist on your speaking out.'

The Sergeant looked at his watch.

'If there had been time, my lady,' he answered, 'I should have preferred writing my report, instead of communicating it by word of mouth. But, if this inquiry is to go on, time is of too much importance to be wasted in writing. I am ready to go into the matter at once. It is a very painful matter for me to speak of, and for you to hear——'

There my mistress stopped him once more.

'I may possibly make it less painful to you, and to my good servant and friend here,' she said, 'if I set the example of speaking boldly, on my side. You suspect Miss Verinder of deceiving us all, by secreting the Diamond for some purpose of her own? Is that true?'

'Quite true, my lady.'

'Very well. Now, before you begin, I have to tell you, as Miss Verinder's mother, that she is *absolutely incapable* of doing what you suppose her to have done. Your knowledge of her character dates from a day or two since. My knowledge of her character dates from the beginning of her life. State your suspicion of her as strongly as you please—it is impossible that you can offend me by doing so. I am sure, beforehand, that (with all your experience) the circumstances have fatally misled you in this case. Mind! I am in possession of no private information. I am as absolutely shut out of my daughter's confidence as you are. My one reason for speaking positively, is the reason you have heard already. I know my child.'

She turned to me, and gave me her hand. I kissed it in silence. 'You may go on,' she said, facing the Sergeant again as steadily as ever.

Sergeant Cuff bowed. My mistress had produced but one effect on him. His hatchet-face softened for a moment, as if he was sorry for her. As to shaking him in his own conviction, it was plain to see that she had not moved him by a single inch. He settled himself in his chair; and he began his vile attack on Miss Rachel's character in these words:

'I must ask your ladyship,' he said, 'to look this matter in the face, from my point of view as well as from yours. Will you please to suppose yourself coming down here, in my place, and with my experience? and will you allow me to mention very briefly what that experience has been?'

My mistress signed to him that she would do this. The Sergeant went on:

'For the last twenty years,' he said, 'I have been largely employed in cases of family scandal, acting in the capacity of confidential man. The one result of my domestic practice which has any bearing on the matter now in hand, is a result which I may state in two words. It is well within my experience, that young ladies of rank and position do occasionally have private debts which they dare not acknowledge to their nearest relatives and friends. Sometimes, the milliner and the jeweller are at the bottom of it. Sometimes, the money is wanted for purposes which I don't suspect in this case, and which I won't shock you by mentioning. Bear in mind what I have said, my lady—and now let us see how events in this house have forced me back on my own experience, whether I liked it or not!'

He considered with himself for a moment, and went on—with a horrid clearness that obliged you to understand him; with an abominable justice that favoured nobody.

'My first information relating to the loss of the Moonstone,' said the Sergeant, 'came to me from Superintendent Seegrave. He proved to my complete satisfaction that he was perfectly incapable of managing the case. The one thing he said which struck me as worth listening to, was this—that Miss Verinder had declined to be questioned by him, and had spoken to him with a perfectly incomprehensible rudeness and contempt. I thought this curious—but I attributed it mainly to some clumsiness on the Superintendent's part which might have offended the young lady. After that, I put it by in my mind, and applied myself, single-handed, to the case. It ended, as you are aware, in the discovery of the smear on the door, and in Mr Franklin Blake's evidence satisfying me, that this same smear, and the loss of the Diamond, were pieces of the same puzzle. So far, if I suspected anything, I suspected that the Moonstone had been stolen, and that one of the servants might prove to be the thief. Very good. In this state of things, what happens? Miss Verinder suddenly comes out of her room, and speaks to me. I observe three suspicious appearances in that young lady. She is still violently agitated, though more than four-and-twenty hours have passed since the Diamond was lost. She treats me, as she has already treated Superintendent Seegrave. And she is mortally offended with Mr Franklin Blake. Very good again. Here (I say to myself) is a young lady who has lost a valuable jewel—a young lady, also, as my own eyes and ears inform me, who is of an impetuous temperament. Under these circumstances, and with that character, what does she do? She betrays an incomprehensible resentment against Mr Blake, Mr Superintendent, and myself—otherwise, the very three people who have all, in their different ways, been trying to help her to recover her lost jewel. Having brought my inquiry to that point—*then*, my lady, and not till then, I begin to look back into my own mind for my own experience. My own experience explains Miss Verinder's otherwise incomprehensible conduct. It associates her with those other young ladies that I know of. It tells me she has debts she daren't acknowledge, that must be paid. And it sets me asking myself, whether the loss of the Diamond may not mean—that the Diamond must be secretly pledged to pay them. That is the conclusion which my experience draws from plain facts. What does your ladyship's experience say against it?'

'What I have said already,' answered my mistress. 'The circumstances have misled you.'

I said nothing on my side. *Robinson Crusoe*—God knows how—had got into my muddled old head. If Sergeant Cuff had found himself, at that moment, transported to a desert island, without a man Friday to keep him company, or a ship to take him off—he would have found himself exactly where I wished him to be! (*Nota bene:*—I am an average good Christian, when you don't push my Christianity too far. And all the rest of you—which is a great comfort—are, in this respect, much the same as I am.)

Sergeant Cuff went on:

'Right or wrong, my lady,' he said, 'having drawn my conclusion, the next thing to do was to put it to the test. I suggested to your ladyship the examination of all the wardrobes in the house. It was a means of finding the article of dress which had, in all probability, made the smear; and it was a means of putting my conclusion to the test. How did it turn out? Your ladyship consented; Mr Blake consented; Mr Ablewhite consented. Miss Verinder alone stopped the whole proceeding by refusing point-blank. That result satisfied me that my view was the right one. If your ladyship and Mr Betteredge persist in not agreeing with me, you must be blind to what happened before you this very day. In your hearing, I told the young lady that her leaving the house (as things were then) would put an obstacle in the way of my recovering her jewel. You saw yourselves that she drove off in the face of that statement. You saw yourselves that, so far from forgiving Mr Blake for having done more than all the rest of you to put the clue into my hands, she publicly insulted Mr Blake, on the steps of her mother's house. What do these things mean? If Miss Verinder is not privy to the suppression of the Diamond, what do these things mean?'

This time he looked my way. It was downright frightful to hear him piling up proof after proof against Miss Rachel, and to know, while one was longing to defend her, that there was no disputing the truth of what he said. I am (thank God!) constitutionally superior to reason. This enabled me to hold firm to my lady's view, which was my view also. This roused my spirit, and made me put a bold face on it before Sergeant Cuff. Profit, good friends, I beseech you, by my example. It will save you from many troubles of the vexing sort. Cultivate a superiority to reason, and see how you pare the claws of all the sensible people when they try to scratch you for your own good!

Finding that I made no remark, and that my mistress made no remark, Sergeant Cuff proceeded. Lord! how it did enrage me to notice that he was not in the least put out by our silence!

'There is the case, my lady, as it stands against Miss Verinder alone,' he said. 'The next thing is to put the case as it stands against Miss Verinder and the deceased Rosanna Spearman, taken together. We will go back for a moment, if you please, to your daughter's refusal to let her wardrobe be examined. My mind being made up, after that circumstance, I had two questions to consider next. First, as to the right method of conducting my inquiry. Second, as to whether Miss Verinder had an accomplice among the female servants in the house. After carefully thinking it over, I determined to conduct the inquiry in, what we should call at our office, a highly irregular manner. For this reason: I had a family scandal to deal with, which it was my business to keep within the family limits. The less noise made, and the fewer strangers employed to help me, the better. As to the usual course of taking people in custody on suspicion, going before the magistrate, and all the rest of it—nothing of the sort was to be thought of, when your ladyship's daughter was (as I believed) at the bottom of the whole business. In this case, I felt that a person of Mr Betteredge's character and position in the house—knowing the servants as he did, and having the honour of the family at heart—would be safer to take as an assistant than any other person whom I could lay my hand on. I should have tried Mr Blake as well—but for one obstacle in the way. *He* saw the drift of my proceedings at a very early date; and, with his interest in Miss Verinder, any mutual understanding was impossible between him and me. I trouble your ladyship with these particulars to show you that I have kept the family secret within the family circle. I am the only outsider who knows it—and my professional existence depends on holding my tongue.'

Here I felt that *my* professional existence depended on not holding *my* tongue. To be held up before my mistress, in my old age, as a sort of deputy-policeman, was, once again, more than my Christianity was strong enough to bear.

'I beg to inform your ladyship,' I said, 'that I never, to my knowledge, helped this abominable detective business, in any way, from first to last; and I summon Sergeant Cuff to contradict me, if he dares!'

Having given vent in those words, I felt greatly relieved. Her ladyship honoured me by a little friendly pat on the shoulder. I looked with righteous indignation at the Sergeant, to see what he thought of such a testimony as *that*. The Sergeant looked back like a lamb, and seemed to like me better than ever.

My lady informed him that he might continue his statement. 'I understand,' she said, 'that you have honestly done your best, in what you believe to be my interest. I am ready to hear what you have to say next.'

'What I have to say next,' answered Sergeant Cuff, 'relates to Rosanna Spearman. I recognised the young woman, as your ladyship may remember, when she brought the washing-book into this room. Up to that time I was inclined to doubt whether Miss Verinder had trusted her secret to any one. When I saw Rosanna, I altered my mind. I suspected her at once of being privy to the suppression of the Diamond. The poor creature has met her death by a dreadful end, and I don't want your ladyship to think, now she's gone, that I was unduly hard on her. If this had been a common case of thieving, I should have given Rosanna the benefit of the doubt just as freely as I should have given it to any of the other servants in the house. Our experience of the Reformatory women is, that when tried in service—and when kindly and judiciously treated—they prove themselves in the majority of cases to be honestly penitent, and honestly worthy of the pains taken with them. But this was not a common case of thieving. It was a case—in my mind—of a deeply planned fraud, with the owner of the Diamond at the bottom of it. Holding this view, the first consideration which naturally presented itself to me, in connection with Rosanna, was this. Would Miss Verinder be satisfied (begging your ladyship's pardon) with leading us all to think that the Moonstone was merely lost? Or would she go a step further, and delude us into believing that the Moonstone was stolen? In the latter event there was Rosanna Spearman—with the character of a thief—ready to her hand; the person of all others to lead your ladyship off, and to lead me off, on a false scent.'

Was it possible (I asked myself) that he could put his case against Miss Rachel and Rosanna in a more horrid point of view than this? It *was* possible, as you shall now see.

'I had another reason for suspecting the deceased woman,' he said, 'which appears to me to have been stronger still. Who would be the very person to help Miss Verinder in raising money privately on the Diamond? Rosanna Spearman. No young lady in Miss Verinder's position could manage such a risky matter as that by herself. A go-between she must have, and who so fit, I ask again, as Rosanna Spearman? Your ladyship's deceased housemaid was at the top of her profession when she was a thief. She had relations, to my certain knowledge, with one of the few men in London (in the money-lending line) who would advance a large sum on such a notable jewel as the Moonstone, without asking awkward questions, or insisting on awkward conditions. Bear this in mind, my lady; and now let me show you how my suspicions have been justified by Rosanna's own acts, and by the plain inferences to be drawn from them.'

He thereupon passed the whole of Rosanna's proceedings under review. You are already as well acquainted with those proceedings as I am; and you will understand how unanswerably this part of his report fixed the guilt of being concerned in the disappearance of the Moonstone on the memory of the poor dead girl. Even my mistress was daunted by what he said now. She made him no answer when he had done. It didn't seem to matter to the Sergeant whether he was answered or not. On he went (devil take him!), just as steady as ever.

'Having stated the whole case as I understand it,' he said, 'I have only to tell your ladyship, now, what I propose to do next. I see two ways of bringing this inquiry successfully to an end. One of those ways I look upon as a certainty. The other, I admit, is a bold experiment, and nothing more. Your ladyship shall decide. Shall we take the certainty first?'

My mistress made him a sign to take his own way, and choose for himself.

'Thank you,' said the Sergeant. 'We'll begin with the certainty, as your ladyship is so good as to leave it to me. Whether Miss Verinder remains at Frizinghall, or whether she returns here, I propose, in either case, to keep a careful watch on all her proceedings—on the people she sees, on the rides and walks she may take, and on the letters she may write and receive.'

'What next?' asked my mistress.

'I shall next,' answered the Sergeant, 'request your ladyship's leave to introduce into the house, as a servant in the place of Rosanna Spearman, a woman accustomed to private inquiries of this sort, for whose discretion I can answer.'

'What next?' repeated my mistress.

'Next,' proceeded the Sergeant, 'and last, I propose to send one of my brother-officers to make an arrangement with that money-lender in London, whom I mentioned just now as formerly acquainted with Rosanna Spearman—and whose name and address, your ladyship may rely on it, have been communicated by Rosanna to Miss Verinder. I don't deny that the course of action I am now suggesting will cost money, and consume time. But the result is certain. We run a line round the Moonstone, and we draw that line closer and closer till we find it in Miss Verinder's possession, supposing she decides to keep it. If her debts press, and she decides on sending it away, then we have our man ready, and we meet the Moonstone on its arrival in London.'

To hear her own daughter made the subject of such a proposal as this, stung my mistress into speaking angrily for the first time.

'Consider your proposal declined, in every particular,' she said. 'And go on to your other way of bringing the inquiry to an end.'

'My other way,' said the Sergeant, going on as easy as ever, 'is to try that bold experiment to which I have alluded. I think I have formed a pretty correct estimate of Miss Verinder's temperament. She is quite capable (according to my belief) of committing a daring fraud. But she is too hot and impetuous in temper, and too little accustomed to deceit as a habit, to act the hypocrite in small things, and to restrain herself under all provocations. Her feelings, in this case, have repeatedly got beyond her control, at the very time when it was plainly her interest to conceal them. It is on this peculiarity in her character that I now propose to act. I want to give her a great shock suddenly, under circumstances that will touch her to the quick. In plain English, I want to tell Miss Verinder, without a word of warning, of Rosanna's death—on the chance that her own better feelings will hurry her into making a clean breast of it. Does your ladyship accept *that* alternative?'

My mistress astonished me beyond all power of expression. She answered him on the instant:

'Yes; I do.'

'The pony-chaise is ready,' said the Sergeant. 'I wish your ladyship good morning.'

My lady held up her hand, and stopped him at the door.

'My daughter's better feelings shall be appealed to, as you propose,' she said. 'But I claim the right, as her mother, of putting her to the test myself. You will remain here, if you please; and I will go to Frizinghall.'

For once in his life, the great Cuff stood speechless with amazement; like an ordinary man.

My mistress rang the bell, and ordered her waterproof things. It was still pouring with rain; and the close carriage had gone, as you know, with Miss Rachel to Frizinghall. I tried to dissuade her ladyship from facing the severity of the weather. Quite useless! I asked leave to go with her, and hold the umbrella. She wouldn't hear of it. The pony-chaise came round, with the groom in charge. 'You may rely on two things,' she said to Sergeant Cuff, in the hall. 'I will try the experiment on Miss Verinder as boldly as you could try it yourself. And I will inform you of the result, either personally or by letter, before the last train leaves for London to-night.'

With that, she stepped into the chaise, and, taking the reins herself, drove off to Frizinghall.

CHAPTER XXII

MY mistress having left us, I had leisure to think of Sergeant Cuff. I found him sitting in a snug corner of the hall, consulting his memorandum book, and curling up viciously at the corners of the lips.

'Making notes of the case?' I asked.

'No,' said the Sergeant. 'Looking to see what my next professional engagement is.'

'Oh!' I said. 'You think it's all over then, here?'

'I think,' answered Sergeant Cuff, 'that Lady Verinder is one of the cleverest women in England. I also think a rose much better worth looking at than a diamond. Where is the gardener, Mr Betteredge?'

There was no getting a word more out of him on the matter of the Moonstone. He had lost all interest in his own inquiry; and he would persist in looking for the gardener. An hour afterwards, I heard them at high words in the conservatory, with the dog-rose once more at the bottom of the dispute.

In the meantime, it was my business to find out whether Mr Franklin persisted in his resolution to leave us by the afternoon train. After having been informed of the conference in my lady's room, and of how it had ended, he immediately decided on waiting to hear the news from Frizing-hall. This very natural alteration in his plans—which, with ordinary people, would have led to nothing in particular—proved, in Mr Franklin's case, to have one objectionable result. It left him unsettled, with a legacy of idle time on his hands, and, in so doing, it let out all the foreign sides of his character, one on the top of another, like rats out of a bag.

Now as an Italian-Englishman, now as a German-Englishman, and now as a French-Englishman, he drifted in and out of all the sitting-rooms in the house, with nothing to talk of but Miss Rachel's treatment of him; and with nobody to address himself to but me. I found him (for example) in the library, sitting under the map of Modern Italy, and quite unaware of any other method of meeting his troubles, except the method of talking about them. 'I have several worthy aspirations, Betteredge; but what am I to do with them now? I am full of dormant good qualities, if Rachel would only have helped me to bring them out!' He was so eloquent in drawing the picture of his own neglected merits, and so pathetic in lamenting over it when it was done, that I felt quite at my wits' end how to console him, when it suddenly occurred to me that here was a case for the wholesome application of a bit of *Robinson Crusoe*. I hobbled out to my own room, and hobbled back with that immortal book. Nobody in the library! The map of Modern Italy stared at *me*; and *I* stared at the map of Modern Italy.

I tried the drawing-room. There was his handkerchief on the floor, to prove that he had drifted in. And there was the empty room to prove that he had drifted out again.

I tried the dining-room, and discovered Samuel with a biscuit and a glass of sherry, silently investigating the empty air. A minute since, Mr Franklin had rung furiously for a little light refreshment. On its production, in a violent hurry, by Samuel, Mr Franklin had vanished before the bell down-stairs had quite done ringing with the pull he had given to it.

I tried the morning-room, and found him at last. There he was at the window, drawing hieroglyphics with his finger in the damp on the glass.

'Your sherry is waiting for you, sir,' I said to him. I might as well have addressed myself to one of the four walls of the room; he was down in the bottomless deep of his own meditations, past all pulling up. 'How do *you* explain Rachel's conduct, Betteredge?' was the only answer I received. Not being ready with the needful reply, I produced *Robinson Crusoe*, in which I am firmly persuaded some explanation might have been found, if we had only searched long enough for it. Mr Franklin shut up *Robinson Crusoe*, and floundered into his German-English gibberish on the spot. 'Why not look into it?' he said, as if I had personally objected to looking into it. 'Why the devil lose your patience, Betteredge, when patience is all that's wanted to arrive at the truth? Don't interrupt me. Rachel's conduct is perfectly intelligible, if you will only do her the common justice to take the Objective view first, and the Subjective view next, and the Objective-Subjective view to wind up with. What do we know? We know that the loss of the Moonstone, on Thursday morning last, threw her into a state of nervous excitement, from which she has not recovered yet. Do you mean to deny the Objective view, so far? Very well, then—don't interrupt me. Now, being in a state of nervous excitement, how are we to expect that she should behave as she might otherwise have behaved to any of the people about her? Arguing in this way, from within-outwards, what do we reach? We reach the Subjective view. I defy you to controvert the Subjective view. Very well then—what follows! Good Heavens! the Objective-Subjective explanation follows, of course! Rachel, properly speaking, is *not* Rachel, but somebody Else. Do I mind being cruelly treated by Somebody Else? You are unreasonable enough, Betteredge; but you can hardly accuse me of that. Then how does it end? It ends, in spite of your confounded English narrowness and prejudice, in my being perfectly happy and comfortable. Where's the sherry?'

My head was by this time in such a condition, that I was not quite sure whether it was my own head, or Mr Franklin's. In this deplorable state, I contrived to do, what I take to have been, three Objective things. I got Mr Franklin his sherry; I retired to my own room; and I solaced myself with the most composing pipe of tobacco I ever remember to have smoked in my life.

Don't suppose, however, that I was quit of Mr Franklin on such easy terms as these. Drifting again, out of the morning-room into the hall, he found his way to the offices next, smelt my pipe, and was instantly reminded that he had been simple enough to give up smoking for Miss Rachel's sake. In the twinkling of an eye, he burst in on me with his cigar-case, and came out strong on the one everlasting subject, in his neat, witty, unbelieving, French way. 'Give me a light, Betteredge. Is it conceivable that a man can have smoked as long as I have without discovering that there is a complete system for the treatment of women at the bottom of his cigar-case? Follow me carefully, and I will prove it in two words. You choose a cigar, you try it, and it disappoints you. What do you do upon that? You throw it away and try another. Now observe the application! You choose a woman, you try her, and she breaks your heart. Fool! take a lesson from your cigar-case. Throw her away, and try another!'

I shook my head at that. Wonderfully clever, I dare say, but my own experience was dead against it. 'In the time of the late Mrs Betteredge,' I said, 'I felt pretty often inclined to try your philosophy, Mr Franklin. But the law insists on your smoking your cigar, sir, when you have once chosen it.' I pointed that observation with a wink. Mr Franklin burst out laughing— and we were as merry as crickets, until the next new side of his character turned up in due course. So things went on with my young master and me; and so (while the Sergeant and the gardener were wrangling over the roses) we two spent the interval before the news came back from Frizinghall.

The pony-chaise returned a good half hour before I had ventured to expect it. My lady had decided to remain for the present, at her sister's house. The groom brought two letters from his mistress; one addressed to Mr Franklin, and the other to me.

Mr Franklin's letter I sent to him in the library—into which refuge his driftings had now taken him for the second time. My own letter, I read in my own room. A cheque, which dropped out when I opened it, informed me (before I had mastered the contents) that Sergeant Cuff's dismissal from the inquiry after the Moonstone was now a settled thing.

I sent to the conservatory to say that I wished to speak to the Sergeant directly. He appeared, with his mind full of the gardener and the dog-rose, declaring that the equal of Mr Begbie for obstinacy never had existed yet, and never would exist again. I requested him to dismiss such wretched trifling as this from our conversation, and to give his best attention to a really serious matter. Upon that he exerted himself sufficiently to notice the letter in my hand. 'Ah!' he said in a weary way, 'you have heard from her ladyship. Have I anything to do with it, Mr Betteredge?'

'You shall judge for yourself, Sergeant.' I thereupon read him the letter (with my best emphasis and discretion), in the following words:

'My Good Gabriel,—I request that you will inform Sergeant Cuff, that I have performed the promise I made to him; with this result, so far as Rosanna Spearman is concerned. Miss Verinder solemnly declares, that she has never spoken a word in private to Rosanna, since that unhappy woman first entered my house. They never met, even accidentally, on the night when the Diamond was lost; and no communication of any sort whatever took place between them, from the Thursday morning when the alarm was first raised in the house, to this present Saturday afternoon, when Miss Verinder left us. After telling my daughter suddenly, and in so many words, of Rosanna Spearman's suicide—this is what has come of it.'

Having reached that point, I looked up, and asked Sergeant Cuff what he thought of the letter, so far?

'I should only offend you if I expressed *my* opinion,' answered the Sergeant. 'Go on, Mr Betteredge,' he said, with the most exasperating resignation, 'go on.'

When I remembered that this man had had the audacity to complain of our gardener's obstinacy, my tongue itched to 'go on' in other words than my mistress's. This time, however, my Christianity held firm. I proceeded steadily with her ladyship's letter:

'Having appealed to Miss Verinder in the manner which the officer thought most desirable, I spoke to her next in the manner which I myself thought most likely to impress her. On two different occasions, before my daughter left my roof, I privately warned her that she was exposing herself to suspicion of the most unendurable and most degrading kind. I have now told her, in the plainest terms, that my apprehensions have been realised.

'Her answer to this, on her own solemn affirmation, is as plain as words can be. In the first place, she owes no money privately to any living creature. In the second place, the Diamond is not now, and never has been, in her possession, since she put it into her cabinet on Wednesday night.

'The confidence which my daughter has placed in me goes no further than this. She maintains an obstinate silence, when I ask her if she can explain the disappearance of the Diamond. She refuses, with tears, when I appeal to her to speak out for my sake. "The day will come when you will know why I am careless about being suspected, and why I am silent even to *you*. I have done much to make my mother pity me—nothing to make my mother blush for me." Those are my daughter's own words.

'After what has passed between the officer and me, I think—stranger as he is—that he should be made acquainted with what Miss Verinder has said, as well as you. Read my letter to him, and then place in his hands the cheque which I enclose. In resigning all further claim on his services, I have only to say that I am convinced of his honesty and his intelligence; but I am more firmly persuaded than ever, that the circumstances, in this case, have fatally misled him.'

There the letter ended. Before presenting the cheque, I asked Sergeant Cuff if he had any remark to make.

'It's no part of my duty, Mr Betteredge,' he answered, 'to make remarks on a case, when I have done with it.'

I tossed the cheque across the table to him. 'Do you believe in *that* part of her ladyship's letter?' I said, indignantly.

The Sergeant looked at the cheque, and lifted up his dismal eyebrows in acknowledgment of her ladyship's liberality.

'This is such a generous estimate of the value of my time,' he said, 'that I feel bound to make some return for it. I'll bear in mind the amount in this cheque, Mr Betteredge, when the occasion comes round for remembering it.'

'What do you mean?' I asked.

'Her ladyship has smoothed matters over for the present very cleverly,' said the Sergeant. 'But *this* family scandal is of the sort that bursts up again when you least expect it. We shall have more detective-business on our hands, sir, before the Moonstone is many months older.'

If those words meant anything, and if the manner in which he spoke them meant anything—it came to this. My mistress's letter had proved, to his mind, that Miss Rachel was hardened enough to resist the strongest appeal that could be addressed to her, and that she had deceived her own mother (good God, under what circumstances!) by a series of abominable lies. How other people, in my place, might have replied to the Sergeant, I don't know. I answered what he said in these plain terms;

'Sergeant Cuff, I consider your last observation as an insult to my lady and her daughter!'

'Mr Betteredge, consider it as a warning to yourself, and you will be nearer the mark.'

Hot and angry as I was, the infernal confidence with which he gave me that answer closed my lips.

I walked to the window to compose myself. The rain had given over; and, who should I see in the courtyard, but Mr Begbie, the gardener, waiting outside to continue the dog-rose controversy with Sergeant Cuff.

'My compliments to the Sairgent,' said Mr Begbie, the moment he set eyes on me. 'If he's minded to walk to the station, I'm agreeable to go with him.'

'What!' cries the Sergeant, behind me, 'are you not convinced yet?'

'The de'il a bit I'm convinced!' answered Mr Begbie.

'Then I'll walk to the station!' says the Sergeant.

'Then I'll meet you at the gate!' says Mr Begbie.

I was angry enough, as you know—but how was any man's anger to hold out against such an interruption as this? Sergeant Cuff noticed the change in me, and encouraged it by a word in season. 'Come! come!' he said, 'why not treat my view of the case as her ladyship treats it? Why not say, the circumstances have fatally misled me?'

To take anything as her ladyship took it, was a privilege worth enjoying—even with the disadvantage of its having been offered to me by Sergeant Cuff. I cooled slowly down to my customary level. I regarded any other opinion of Miss Rachel, than my lady's opinion or mine, with a lofty contempt. The only thing I could *not* do, was to keep off the subject of the Moonstone! My own good sense ought to have warned me, I know, to let the matter rest—but, there! the virtues which distinguish the present generation were not invented in my time. Sergeant Cuff had hit me on the raw, and, though I did look down upon him with contempt, the tender place still tingled for all that. The end of it was that I perversely led him back to the subject of her ladyship's letter. 'I am quite satisfied myself,' I said. 'But never mind that! Go on, as if I was still open to conviction. You think Miss Rachel is not to be believed on her word; and you say we shall hear of the Moonstone again. Back your opinion, Sergeant,' I concluded, in an airy way. 'Back your opinion.'

Instead of taking offence, Sergeant Cuff seized my hand, and shook it till my fingers ached again.

'I declare to heaven,' says this strange officer solemnly, 'I would take to domestic service to-morrow, Mr Betteredge, if I had a chance of being employed along with You! To say you are as transparent as a child, sir, is to pay the children a compliment which nine out of ten of them don't deserve. There! there! we won't begin to dispute again. You shall have it out of me on easier terms than that. I won't say a word more about her ladyship, or about Miss Verinder—I'll only turn prophet, for once in a way, and for your sake. I have warned you already that you haven't done with the Moonstone yet. Very well. Now I'll tell you, at parting, of three things which will happen in the future, and which, I believe, will force themselves on your attention, whether you like it or not.'

'Go on!' I said, quite unabashed, and just as airy as ever.

'First,' said the Sergeant, 'you will hear something from the Yollands—when the postman delivers Rosanna's letter at Cobb's Hole, on Monday next.'

If he had thrown a bucket of cold water over me, I doubt if I could have felt it much more unpleasantly than I felt those words. Miss Rachel's assertion of her innocence had left Rosanna's conduct—the making the new nightgown, the hiding the smeared nightgown, and all the rest of it—entirely without explanation. And this had never occurred to me, till Sergeant Cuff forced it on my mind all in a moment!

'In the second place,' proceeded the Sergeant, 'you will hear of the three Indians again. You will hear of them in the neighbourhood, if Miss Rachel remains in the neighbourhood. You will hear of them in London, if Miss Rachel goes to London.'

Having lost all interest in the three jugglers, and having thoroughly convinced myself of my young lady's innocence, I took this second prophecy easily enough. 'So much for two of the three things that are going to happen,' I said. 'Now for the third!'

'Third, and last,' said Sergeant Cuff, 'you will, sooner or later, hear something of that money-lender in London, whom I have twice taken the liberty of mentioning already. Give me your pocket-book, and I'll make a note for you of his name and address—so that there may be no mistake about it if the thing really happens.'

He wrote accordingly on a blank leaf:—'Mr Septimus Luker, Middlesex-place, Lambeth, London.'

'There,' he said, pointing to the address, 'are the last words, on the subject of the Moonstone, which I shall trouble you with for the present. Time will show whether I am right or wrong. In the meanwhile, sir, I carry away with me a sincere personal liking for you, which I think does honour to both of us. If we don't meet again before my professional retirement takes place, I hope you will come and see me in a little house near London, which I have got my eye on. There will be grass walks, Mr Betteredge, I promise you, in *my* garden. And as for the white moss rose——'

'The de'il a bit ye'll get the white moss rose to grow, unless ye bud him on the dogue-rose first,' cried a voice a voice at the window.

We both turned round. There was the everlasting Mr Begbie, too eager for the controversy to wait any longer at the gate. The Sergeant wrung my hand, and darted out into the court-yard, hotter still on his side. 'Ask him about the moss rose, when he comes back, and see if I have left him a leg to stand on!' cried the great Cuff, hailing me through the window in his turn. 'Gentlemen both!' I answered, moderating them again as I had moderated them once already. 'In the matter of the moss rose there is a great deal to be said on both sides!' I might as well (as the Irish say) have whistled jigs to a milestone. Away they went together, fighting the battle of the roses without asking or giving quarter on either side. The last I saw of them, Mr Begbie was shaking his obstinate head, and Sergeant Cuff had got him by the arm like a prisoner in charge. Ah, well! well! I own I couldn't help liking the Sergeant—though I hated him all the time.

Explain that state of mind, if you can. You will soon be rid, now, of me and my contradictions. When I have reported Mr Franklin's departure, the history of the Saturday's events will be finished at last. And when I have next described certain strange things that happened in the course of the new week, I shall have done my part of the Story, and shall hand over the pen to the person who is appointed to follow my lead. If you are as tired of reading this narrative as I am of writing it—Lord, how we shall enjoy ourselves on both sides a few pages further on!

CHAPTER XXIII

I HAD kept the pony-chaise ready, in case Mr Franklin persisted in leaving us by the train that night. The appearance of the luggage, followed down-stairs by Mr Franklin himself, informed me plainly enough that he had held firm to a resolution for once in his life.

'So you have really made up your mind, sir?' I said, as we met in the hall. 'Why not wait a day or two longer, and give Miss Rachel another chance?'

The foreign varnish appeared to have all worn off Mr Franklin, now that the time had come for saying good-bye. Instead of replying to me in words, he put the letter which her ladyship had addressed to him into my hand. The greater part of it said over again what had been said already in the other communication received by me. But there was a bit about Miss Rachel added at the end, which will account for the steadiness of Mr Franklin's determination, if it accounts for nothing else.

'You will wonder, I dare say' (her ladyship wrote), 'at my allowing my own daughter to keep me perfectly in the dark. A Diamond worth twenty thousand pounds has been lost—and I am left to infer that the mystery of its disappearance is no mystery to Rachel, and that some incomprehensible obligation of silence has been laid on her, by some person or persons utterly unknown to me, with some object in view at which I cannot even guess. Is it conceivable that I should allow myself to be trifled with in this way? It is quite conceivable, in Rachel's present state. She is in a condition of nervous agitation pitiable to see. I dare not approach the subject of the Moonstone again until time has done something to quiet her. To help this end, I have not hesitated to dismiss the police-officer. The mystery which baffles us, baffles him too. This is not a matter in which any stranger can help us. He adds to what I have to suffer; and he maddens Rachel if she only hears his name.

'My plans for the future are as well settled as they can be. My present idea is to take Rachel to London—partly to relieve her mind by a complete change, partly to try what may be done by consulting the best medical advice. Can I ask you to meet us in town? My dear Franklin, you, in your way, must imitate my patience, and wait, as I do, for a fitter time. The valuable assistance which you rendered to the inquiry after the lost jewel is still an unpardoned offence, in the present dreadful state of Rachel's mind. Moving blindfold in this matter, you have added to the burden of anxiety which she has had to bear, by innocently threatening her secret with discovery, through your exertions. It is impossible for me to excuse the perversity that holds you responsible for consequences which neither you nor I could imagine or foresee. She is not to be reasoned with—she can only be pitied. I am grieved to have to say it, but, for the present, you and Rachel are better apart. The only advice I can offer you is, to give her time.'

I handed the letter back, sincerely sorry for Mr Franklin, for I knew how fond he was of my young lady; and I saw that her mother's account of her had cut him to the heart. 'You know the proverb, sir,' was all I said to him. 'When things are at the worst, they're sure to mend. Things can't be much worse, Mr Franklin, than they are now.'

Mr Franklin folded up his aunt's letter, without appearing to be much comforted by the remark which I had ventured on addressing to him.

'When I came here from London with that horrible Diamond,' he said, 'I don't believe there was a happier household in England than this. Look at the household now! Scattered, disunited—the very air of the place poisoned with mystery and suspicion! Do you remember that morning at the Shivering Sand, when we talked about my uncle Herncastle, and his birthday gift? The Moonstone has served the Colonel's vengeance, Betteredge, by means which the Colonel himself never dreamt of!'

With that he shook me by the hand, and went out to the pony-chaise.

I followed him down the steps. It was very miserable to see him leaving the old place, where he had spent the happiest years of his life, in this way. Penelope (sadly upset by all that had happened in the house) came round crying, to bid him good-bye. Mr Franklin kissed her. I waved my hand as much as to say, 'You're heartily welcome, sir.' Some of the other female servants appeared, peeping after him round the corner. He was one of those men whom the women all like. At the last moment, I stopped the pony-chaise, and begged as a favour that he would let us hear from him by letter. He didn't seem to heed what I said—he was looking round from one thing to another, taking a sort of farewell of the old house and grounds. 'Tell us where you are going to, sir!' I said, holding on by the chaise, and trying to get at his future plans in that way. Mr Franklin pulled his hat down suddenly over his eyes. 'Going?' says he, echoing the word after me. 'I am going to the devil!' The pony started at the word, as if he had felt a Christian horror of it. 'God bless you, sir, go where you may!' was all I had time to say, before he was out of sight and hearing. A sweet and pleasant gentleman! With all his faults and follies, a sweet and pleasant gentleman! He left a sad gap behind him, when he left my lady's house.

It was dull and dreary enough, when the long summer evening closed in, on that Saturday night.

I kept my spirits from sinking by sticking fast to my pipe and my *Robinson Crusoe*. The women (excepting Penelope) beguiled the time by talking of Rosanna's suicide. They were all obstinately of opinion that the poor girl had stolen the Moonstone, and that she had destroyed herself in terror of being found out. My daughter, of course, privately held fast to what she had said all along. Her notion of the motive which was really at the bottom of the suicide failed, oddly enough, just where my young lady's assertion of her innocence failed also. It left Rosanna's secret journey to Frizinghall, and Rosanna's proceedings in the matter of the nightgown entirely unaccounted for. There was no use in pointing this out to Penelope; the objection made about as much impression on her as a shower of rain on a waterproof coat. The truth is, my daughter inherits my superiority to reason—and, in respect to that accomplishment, has got a long way ahead of her own father.

On the next day (Sunday), the close carriage, which had been kept at Mr Ablewhite's, came back to us empty. The coachman brought a message for me, and written instructions for my lady's own maid and for Penelope.

The message informed me that my mistress had determined to take Miss Rachel to her house in London, on the Monday. The written instructions informed the two maids of the clothing that was wanted, and directed them to meet their mistresses in town at a given hour. Most of the other servants were to follow. My lady had found Miss Rachel so unwilling to return to the house, after what had happened in it, that she had decided on going to London direct from Frizinghall. I was to remain in the country, until further orders, to look after things indoors and out. The servants left with me were to be put on board wages.

Being reminded, by all this, of what Mr Franklin had said about our being a scattered and disunited household, my mind was led naturally to Mr Franklin himself. The more I thought of him, the more uneasy I felt about his future proceedings. It ended in my writing, by the Sunday's post, to his father's valet, Mr Jeffco (whom I had known in former years), to beg he would let me know what Mr Franklin had settled to do, on arriving in London.

The Sunday evening was, if possible, duller even than the Saturday evening. We ended the day of rest, as hundreds of thousands of people end it regularly, once a week, in these islands—that is to say, we all anticipated bedtime, and fell asleep in our chairs.

How the Monday affected the rest of the household I don't know. The Monday gave *me* a good shake up. The first of Sergeant Cuff's prophecies of what was to happen—namely, that I should hear from the Yollands—came true on that day.

I had seen Penelope and my lady's maid off in the railway with the luggage for London, and was pottering about the grounds, when I heard my name called. Turning round, I found myself face to face with the fisherman's daughter, Limping Lucy. Bating her lame foot and her leanness (this last a horrid drawback to a woman, in my opinion), the girl had some pleasing qualities in the eye of a man. A dark, keen, clever face, and a nice clear voice, and a beautiful brown head of hair counted among her merits. A crutch appeared in the list of her misfortunes. And a temper reckoned high in the sum total of her defects.

'Well, my dear,' I said, 'what do you want with me?'

'Where's the man you call Franklin Blake?' says the girl, fixing me with a fierce look, as she rested herself on her crutch.

'That's not a respectful way to speak of any gentleman,' I answered. 'If you wish to inquire for my lady's nephew you will please to mention him as Mr Franklin Blake.'

She limped a step nearer to me, and looked as if she could have eaten me alive. '*Mr.* Franklin Blake?' she repeated after me. 'Murderer Franklin Blake would be a fitter name for him.'

My practice with the late Mrs Betteredge came in handy here. Whenever a woman tries to put *you* out of temper, turn the tables, and put *her* out of temper instead. They are generally prepared for every effort you can make in your own defence, but that. One word does it as well as a hundred; and one word did it with Limping Lucy. I looked her pleasantly in the face; and I said—'Pooh!'

The girl's temper flamed out directly. She poised herself on her sound foot, and she took her crutch, and beat it furiously three times on the ground. 'He's a murderer! he's a murderer! he's a murderer! He has been the death of Rosanna Spearman!' She screamed that answer out at the top of her voice. One or two of the people at work in the grounds near us looked up—saw it was Limping Lucy—knew what to expect from that quarter—and looked away again.

'He has been the death of Rosanna Spearman?' I repeated. 'What makes you say that, Lucy?'

'What do you care? What does any man care? Oh! if she had only thought of the men as I think, she might have been living now!'

'She always thought kindly of *me*, poor soul,' I said; 'and, to the best of my ability, I always tried to act kindly by *her*.'

I spoke those words in as comforting a manner as I could. The truth is, I hadn't the heart to irritate the girl by another of my smart replies. I had only noticed her temper at first. I noticed her wretchedness now—and wretchedness is not uncommonly insolent, you will find, in humble life. My answer melted Limping Lucy. She bent her head down, and laid it on the top of her crutch.

'I loved her,' the girl said softly. 'She had lived a miserable life, Mr Betteredge—vile people had ill-treated her and led her wrong—and it hadn't spoiled her sweet temper. She was an angel. She might have been happy with me. I had a plan for our going to London together like sisters, and living by our needles. That man came here, and spoilt it all. He bewitched her. Don't tell me he didn't mean it, and didn't know it. He ought to have known it. He ought to have taken pity on her. "I can't live without him—and, oh, Lucy, he never even looks at me." That's what she said. Cruel, cruel, cruel. I said, "No man is worth fretting for in that way." And she said, "There are men worth dying for, Lucy, and he is one of them." I had saved up a little money. I had settled things with father and mother. I meant to take her away from the mortification she was suffering here. We should have had a little lodging in London, and lived together like sisters. She had a good education, sir, as you know, and she wrote a good hand. She was quick at her needle. I have a good education, and I write a good hand. I am not as quick at my needle as she was—but I could have done. We might have got our living nicely. And, oh! what happens this morning? what happens this morning? Her letter comes and tells me that she has done with the burden of her life. Her letter comes, and bids me good-bye for ever. Where is he?' cries the girl, lifting her head from the crutch, and flaming out again through her tears. 'Where's this gentleman that I mustn't speak of, except with respect? Ha, Mr Betteredge, the day is not far off when the poor will rise against the rich. I pray Heaven they may begin with *him*. I pray Heaven they may begin with *him*.'

Here was another of your average good Christians, and here was the usual break-down, consequent on that same average Christianity being pushed too far! The parson himself (though I own this is saying a great deal) could hardly have lectured the girl in the state she was in now. All I ventured to do was to keep her to the point—in the hope of something turning up which might be worth hearing.

'What do you want with Mr Franklin Blake?' I asked.

'I want to see him.'

'For anything particular?'

'I have got a letter to give him.'

'From Rosanna Spearman?'

'Yes.'

'Sent to you in your own letter?'

'Yes.'

Was the darkness going to lift? Were all the discoveries that I was dying to make, coming and offering themselves to me of their own accord? I was obliged to wait a moment. Sergeant Cuff had left his infection behind him. Certain signs and tokens, personal to myself, warned me that the detective-fever was beginning to set in again.

'You can't see Mr Franklin,' I said.

'I must, and will, see him.'

'He went to London last night.'

Limping Lucy looked me hard in the face, and saw that I was speaking the truth. Without a word more, she turned about again instantly towards Cobb's Hole.

'Stop!' I said. 'I expect news of Mr Franklin Blake to-morrow. Give me your letter, and I'll send it on to him by the post.'

Limping Lucy steadied herself on her crutch and looked back at me over her shoulder.

'I am to give it from my hands into his hands,' she said. 'And I am to give it to him in no other way.'

'Shall I write, and tell him what you have said?'

'Tell him I hate him. And you will tell him the truth.'

'Yes, yes. But about the letter——?'

'If he wants the letter, he must come back here, and get it from Me.'

With those words she limped off on the way to Cobb's Hole. The detective-fever burnt up all my dignity on the spot. I followed her, and tried to make her talk. All in vain. It was my misfortune to be a man—and Limping Lucy enjoyed disappointing me. Later in the day, I tried my luck with her mother. Good Mrs Yolland could only cry, and recommend a drop of comfort out of the Dutch bottle. I found the fisherman on the beach. He said it was 'a bad job,' and went on mending his net. Neither father nor mother knew more than I knew. The one way left to try was the chance, which might come with the morning, of writing to Mr Franklin Blake.

I leave you to imagine how I watched for the postman on Tuesday morning. He brought me two letters. One, from Penelope (which I had hardly patience enough to read), announced that my lady and Miss Rachel were safely established in London. The other, from Mr Jeffco, informed me that his master's son had left England already.

On reaching the metropolis, Mr Franklin had, it appeared, gone straight to his father's residence. He arrived at an awkward time. Mr Blake, the elder, was up to his eyes in the business of the House of Commons, and was amusing himself at home that night with the favourite parliamentary plaything which they call 'a private bill.' Mr Jeffco himself showed Mr Franklin into his father's study. 'My dear Franklin! why do you surprise me in this way? Anything wrong?' 'Yes; something wrong with Rachel; I am dreadfully distressed about it.' 'Grieved to hear it. But I can't listen to you now.' 'When *can* you listen?' 'My dear boy! I won't deceive you. I can listen at the end of the session, not a moment before. Good-night.' 'Thank you, sir. Good-night.'

Such was the conversation, inside the study, as reported to me by Mr Jeffco. The conversation outside the study, was shorter still. 'Jeffco, see what time the tidal train starts to-morrow morning?' 'At six-forty, Mr Franklin.' 'Have me called at five.' 'Going abroad, sir?' 'Going, Jeffco, wherever the railway chooses to take me.' 'Shall I tell your father, sir?' 'Yes; tell him at the end of the session.'

The next morning Mr Franklin had started for foreign parts. To what particular place he was bound, nobody (himself included) could presume to guess. We might hear of him next in Europe, Asia, Africa, or America. The chances were as equally divided as possible, in Mr Jeffco's opinion, among the four quarters of the globe.

This news—by closing up all prospect of my bringing Limping Lucy and Mr Franklin together—at once stopped any further progress of mine on the way to discovery. Penelope's belief that her fellow-servant had destroyed herself through unrequited love for Mr Franklin Blake, was confirmed—and that was all. Whether the letter which Rosanna had left to be given to him after her death did, or did not, contain the confession which Mr Franklin had suspected her of trying to make to him in her life-time, it was impossible to say. It might be only a farewell word, telling nothing but the secret of her unhappy fancy for a person beyond her reach. Or it might own the whole truth about the strange proceedings in which Sergeant Cuff had detected her, from the time when the Moonstone was lost, to the time when she rushed to her own destruction at the Shivering Sand. A sealed letter it had been placed in Limping Lucy's hands, and a sealed letter it remained to me and to every one about the girl, her own parents included. We all suspected her of having been in the dead woman's confidence; we all tried to make her speak; we all failed. Now one, and now another, of the servants—still holding to the belief that Rosanna had stolen the Diamond and had hidden it—peered and poked about the rocks to which she had been traced, and peered and poked in vain. The tide ebbed, and the tide flowed; the summer went on, and the autumn came. And the Quicksand, which hid her body, hid her secret too.

The news of Mr Franklin's departure from England on the Sunday morning, and the news of my lady's arrival in London with Miss Rachel on the Monday afternoon, had reached me, as you are aware, by the Tuesday's post. The Wednesday came, and brought nothing. The Thursday produced a second budget of news from Penelope.

My girl's letter informed me that some great London doctor had been consulted about her young lady, and had earned a guinea by remarking that she had better be amused. Flower-shows, operas, balls—there was a whole round of gaieties in prospect; and Miss Rachel, to her mother's astonishment, eagerly took to it all. Mr Godfrey had called; evidently as sweet as ever on his cousin, in spite of the reception he had met with, when he tried his luck on the occasion of the birthday. To Penelope's great regret, he had been most graciously received, and had added Miss Rachel's name to one of his Ladies' Charities on the spot. My mistress was reported to be out of spirits, and to have held two long interviews with her lawyer. Certain speculations followed, referring to a poor relation of the family—one Miss Clack, whom I have mentioned in my account of the birthday dinner, as sitting next to Mr Godfrey, and having a pretty taste in champagne. Penelope was astonished to find that Miss Clack had not called yet. She would surely not be long before she fastened herself on my lady as usual—and so forth, and so forth, in the way women have of girding at each other, on and off paper. This would not have been worth mentioning, I admit, but for one reason. I hear you are likely to be turned over to Miss Clack, after parting with me. In that case, just do me the favour of not believing a word she says, if she speaks of your humble servant.

On Friday, nothing happened—except that one of the dogs showed signs of a breaking out behind the ears. I gave him a dose of syrup of buckthorn, and put him on a diet of pot-liquor and vegetables till further orders. Excuse my mentioning this. It has slipped in somehow. Pass it over please. I am fast coming to the end of my offences against your cultivated modern taste. Besides, the dog was a good creature, and deserved a good physicking; he did indeed.

Saturday, the last day of the week, is also the last day in my narrative.

The morning's post brought me a surprise in the shape of a London newspaper. The handwriting on the direction puzzled me. I compared it with the money-lender's name and address as recorded in my pocket-book, and identified it at once as the writing of Sergeant Cuff.

Looking through the paper eagerly enough, after this discovery, I found an ink-mark drawn round one of the police reports. Here it is, at your service. Read it as I read it, and you will set the right value on the Sergeant's polite attention in sending me the news of the day:

'LAMBETH—Shortly before the closing of the court, Mr Septimus Luker, the well-known dealer in ancient gems, carvings, intagli, &c., &c., applied to the sitting magistrate for advice. The applicant stated that he had been annoyed, at intervals throughout the day, by the proceedings of some of those strolling Indians who infest the streets. The persons complained of were three in number. After having been sent away by the police, they had returned again and again, and had attempted to enter the house on pretence of asking for charity. Warned off in the front, they had been discovered again at the back of the premises. Besides the annoyance complained of, Mr Luker expressed himself as being under some apprehension that robbery might be contemplated. His collection contained many unique gems, both classical and Oriental, of the highest value. He had only the day before been compelled to dismiss a skilled workman in ivory carving from his employment (a native of India, as we understood), on suspicion of attempted theft; and he felt by no means sure that this man and the street jugglers of whom he complained, might not be acting in concert. It might be their object to collect a crowd, and create a disturbance in the street, and, in the confusion thus caused, to obtain access to the house. In reply to the magistrate, Mr Luker admitted that he had no evidence to produce of any attempt at robbery being in contemplation. He could speak positively to the annoyance and interruption caused by the Indians, but not to anything else. The magistrate remarked that, if the annoyance were repeated, the applicant could summon the Indians to that court, where they might easily be dealt with under the Act. As to the valuables in Mr Luker's possession, Mr Luker himself must take the best measures for their safe custody. He would do well perhaps to communicate with the police, and to adopt such additional precautions as their experience might suggest. The applicant thanked his worship, and withdrew.'

One of the wise ancients is reported (I forget on what occasion) as having recommended his fellow-creatures to 'look to the end.' Looking to the end of these pages of mine, and wondering for some days past how I should manage to write it, I find my plain statement of facts coming to a conclusion, most appropriately, of its own self. We have gone on, in this matter of the Moonstone, from one marvel to another; and here we end with the greatest marvel of all—namely, the accomplishment of Sergeant Cuff's three predictions in less than a week from the time when he had made them.

After hearing from the Yollands on the Monday, I had now heard of the Indians, and heard of the money-lender, in the news from London—Miss Rachel herself, remember, being also in London at the time. You see, I put things at their worst, even when they tell dead against my own view. If you desert me, and side with the Sergeant, on the evidence before you—if the only rational explanation you can see is, that Miss Rachel and Mr Luker must have got together, and that the Moonstone must be now in pledge in the money-lender's house—I own I can't blame you for arriving at that conclusion. In the dark, I have brought you thus far. In the dark I am compelled to leave you, with my best respects.

Why compelled? it may be asked. Why not take the persons who have gone along with me, so far, up into those regions of superior enlightenment in which I sit myself?

In answer to this, I can only state that I am acting under orders, and that those orders have been given to me (as I understand) in the interests of truth. I am forbidden to tell more in this narrative than I knew myself at the time. Or, to put it plainer, I am to keep strictly within the limits of my own experience, and am not to inform you of what other persons told me—for the very sufficient reason that you are to have the information from those other persons themselves, at first hand. In this matter of the Moonstone the plan is, not to present reports, but to produce witnesses. I picture to myself a member of the family reading these pages fifty years hence. Lord! what a compliment he will feel it, to be asked to take nothing on hearsay, and to be treated in all respects like a Judge on the bench.

At this place, then, we part—for the present, at least—after long journeying together, with a companionable feeling, I hope, on both sides. The devil's dance of the Indian Diamond has threaded its way to London; and to London you must go after it, leaving me at the country-house. Please to excuse the faults of this composition—my talking so much of myself, and being too familiar, I am afraid, with you. I mean no harm; and I drink most respectfully (having just done dinner) to your health and prosperity, in a tankard of her ladyship's ale. May you find in these leaves of my writing, what *Robinson Crusoe* found in his experience on the desert island—namely, 'something to comfort yourselves from, and to set in the Description of Good and Evil, on the Credit Side of the Account.'—Farewell.

THE END OF THE FIRST PERIOD

SECOND PERIOD

THE DISCOVERY OF THE TRUTH (1848-1849)

The events related in several narratives

FIRST NARRATIVE

Contributed by Miss Clack; niece of the late Sir John Verinder

CHAPTER I

I AM indebted to my dear parents (both now in heaven) for having had habits of order and regularity instilled into me at a very early age.

In that happy bygone time, I was taught to keep my hair tidy at all hours of the day and night, and to fold up every article of my clothing carefully, in the same order, on the same chair, in the same place at the foot of the bed, before retiring to rest. An entry of the day's events in my little diary invariably preceded the folding up. The 'Evening Hymn' (repeated in bed) invariably followed the folding up. And the sweet sleep of childhood invariably followed the 'Evening Hymn.'

In later life (alas!) the Hymn has been succeeded by sad and bitter meditations; and the sweet sleep has been but ill exchanged for the broken slumbers which haunt the uneasy pillow of care. On the other hand, I have continued to fold my clothes, and to keep my little diary. The former habit links me to my happy childhood—before papa was ruined. The latter habit—hitherto mainly useful in helping me to discipline the fallen nature which we all inherit from Adam—has unexpectedly proved important to my humble interests in quite another way. It has enabled poor Me to serve the caprice of a wealthy member of the family into which my late uncle married. I am fortunate enough to be useful to Mr Franklin Blake.

I have been cut off from all news of my relatives by marriage for some time past. When we are isolated and poor, we are not infrequently forgotten. I am now living, for economy's sake, in a little town in Brittany, inhabited by a select circle of serious English friends, and possessed of the inestimable advantages of a Protestant clergyman and a cheap market.

In this retirement—a Patmos amid the howling ocean of popery that surrounds us—a letter from England has reached me at last. I find my insignificant existence suddenly remembered by Mr Franklin Blake. My wealthy relative—would that I could add my spiritually-wealthy relative!—writes, without even an attempt at disguising that he wants something of me. The whim has seized him to stir up the deplorable scandal of the Moonstone: and I am to help him by writing the account of what I myself witnessed while visiting at Aunt Verinder's house in London. Pecuniary remuneration is offered to me—with the want of feeling peculiar to the rich. I am to re-open wounds that Time has barely closed; I am to recall the most intensely painful remembrances—and this done, I am to feel myself compensated by a new laceration, in the shape of Mr Blake's cheque. My nature is weak. It cost me a hard struggle, before Christian humility conquered sinful pride, and self-denial accepted the cheque.

Without my diary, I doubt—pray let me express it in the grossest terms!—if I could have honestly earned my money. With my diary, the poor labourer (who forgives Mr Blake for insulting her) is worthy of her hire. Nothing escaped me at the time I was visiting dear Aunt Verinder. Everything was entered (thanks to my early training) day by day as it happened; and everything down to the smallest particular, shall be told here. My sacred regard for truth is (thank God) far above my respect for persons. It will be easy for Mr Blake to suppress what may not prove to be sufficiently flattering in these pages to the person chiefly concerned in them. He has purchased my time; but not even *his* wealth can purchase my conscience too.[1]

My diary informs me, that I was accidentally passing Aunt Verinder's house in Montagu Square, on Monday, 3rd July, 1848.

Seeing the shutters opened, and the blinds drawn up, I felt that it would be an act of polite attention to knock, and make inquiries. The person who answered the door, informed me that my aunt and her daughter (I really cannot call her my cousin!) had arrived from the country a week since, and meditated making some stay in London. I sent up a message at once, declining to disturb them, and only begging to know whether I could be of any use.

The person who answered the door, took my message in insolent silence, and left me standing in the hall. She is the daughter of a heathen old man named Betteredge—long, too long, tolerated in my aunt's family. I sat down

---

[1] NOTE. *Added by Franklin Blake.*—Miss Clack may make her mind quite easy on this point. Nothing will be added, altered, or removed, in her manuscript, or in any of the other manuscripts which pass through my hands. Whatever opinions any of the writers may express, whatever peculiarities of treatment may mark, and perhaps, in a literary sense, disfigure, the narratives which I am now collecting, not a line will be tampered with anywhere, from first to last. As genuine documents they are sent to me—and as genuine documents I shall preserve them; endorsed by the attestations of witnesses who can speak to the facts. It only remains to be added, that 'the person chiefly concerned' in Miss Clack's narrative, is happy enough at the present moment, not only to brave the smartest exercise of Miss Clack's pen, but even to recognise its unquestionable value as an instrument for the exhibition of Miss Clack's character.

in the hall to wait for my answer—and, having always a few tracts in my bag, I selected one which proved to be quite providentially applicable to the person who answered the door. The hall was dirty, and the chair was hard; but the blessed consciousness of returning good for evil raised me quite above any trifling considerations of that kind. The tract was one of a series addressed to young women on the sinfulness of dress. In style it was devoutly familiar. Its title was, 'A Word With You On Your Cap-Ribbons.'

'My lady is much obliged, and begs you will come and lunch to-morrow at two.'

I passed over the manner in which she gave her message, and the dreadful boldness of her look. I thanked this young castaway; and I said, in a tone of Christian interest, 'Will you favour me by accepting a tract?'

She looked at the title. 'Is it written by a man or a woman, Miss? If it's written by a woman, I had rather not read it on that account. If it's written by a man, I beg to inform him that he knows nothing about it.' She handed me back the tract, and opened the door. We must sow the good seed somehow. I waited till the door was shut on me, and slipped the tract into the letter-box. When I had dropped another tract through the area railings, I felt relieved, in some small degree, of a heavy responsibility towards others.

We had a meeting that evening of the Select Committee of the Mothers'-Small-Clothes-Conversion-Society. The object of this excellent Charity is—as all serious people know—to rescue unredeemed fathers' trousers from the pawnbroker, and to prevent their resumption, on the part of the irreclaimable parent, by abridging them immediately to suit the proportions of the innocent son. I was a member, at that time, of the select committee; and I mention the Society here, because my precious and admirable friend, Mr Godfrey Ablewhite, was associated with our work of moral and material usefulness. I had expected to see him in the board-room, on the Monday evening of which I am now writing, and had proposed to tell him, when we met, of dear Aunt Verinder's arrival in London. To my great disappointment he never appeared. On my expressing a feeling of surprise at his absence, my sisters of the Committee all looked up together from their trousers (we had a great pressure of business that night), and asked in amazement, if I had not heard the news. I acknowledged my ignorance, and was then told, for the first time, of an event which forms, so to speak, the starting-point of this narrative. On the previous Friday, two gentlemen—occupying widely-different positions in society—had been the victims of an outrage which had startled all London. One of the gentlemen was Mr Septimus Luker, of Lambeth. The other was Mr Godfrey Ablewhite.

Living in my present isolation, I have no means of introducing the newspaper-account of the outrage into my narrative. I was also deprived, at the time, of the inestimable advantage of hearing the events related by the fervid eloquence of Mr Godfrey Ablewhite. All I can do is to state the facts as they were stated, on that Monday evening, to me; proceeding on the plan which I have been taught from infancy to adopt in folding up my clothes. Everything shall be put neatly, and everything shall be put in its place. These lines are written by a poor weak woman. From a poor weak woman who will be cruel enough to expect more?

The date—thanks to my dear parents, no dictionary that ever was written can be more particular than I am about dates—was Friday, June 30th, 1848.

Early on that memorable day, our gifted Mr Godfrey happened to be cashing a cheque at a banking-house in Lombard-street. The name of the firm is accidentally blotted in my diary, and my sacred regard for truth forbids me to hazard a guess in a matter of this kind. Fortunately, the name of the firm doesn't matter. What does matter is a circumstance that occurred when Mr Godfrey had transacted his business. On gaining the door, he encountered a gentleman—a perfect stranger to him—who was accidentally leaving the office exactly at the same time as himself. A momentary contest of politeness ensued between them as to who should be the first to pass through the door of the bank. The stranger insisted on making Mr Godfrey precede him; Mr Godfrey said a few civil words; they bowed, and parted in the street.

Thoughtless and superficial people may say, Here is surely a very trumpery little incident related in an absurdly circumstantial manner. Oh, my young friends and fellow-sinners! beware of presuming to exercise your poor carnal reason. Oh, be morally tidy. Let your faith be as your stockings, and your stockings as your faith. Both ever spotless, and both ready to put on at a moment's notice!

I beg a thousand pardons. I have fallen insensibly into my Sunday-school style. Most inappropriate in such a record as this. Let me try to be worldly—let me say that trifles, in this case as in many others, led to terrible results. Merely premising that the polite stranger was Mr Luker, of Lambeth, we will now follow Mr Godfrey home to his residence at Kilburn.

He found waiting for him, in the hall, a poorly clad but delicate and interesting-looking little boy. The boy handed him a letter, merely mentioning that he had been entrusted with it by an old lady whom he did not know, and who had given him no instructions to wait for an answer. Such incidents as these were not uncommon in Mr Godfrey's large experience as a promoter of public charities. He let the boy go, and opened the letter.

The handwriting was entirely unfamiliar to him. It requested his attendance, within an hour's time, at a house in Northumberland-street, Strand, which he had never had occasion to enter before. The object sought was to obtain from the worthy manager certain details on the subject of the Mothers'-Small-Clothes-Conversion-Society, and the information was wanted by an elderly lady who proposed adding largely to the resources of the charity, if her questions were met by satisfactory replies. She mentioned her name, and she added that the shortness of her stay in London prevented her from giving any longer notice to the eminent philanthropist whom she addressed.

Ordinary people might have hesitated before setting aside their own engagements to suit the convenience of a stranger. The Christian Hero never hesitates where good is to be done. Mr Godfrey instantly turned back, and proceeded to the house in Northumberland Street. A most respectable though somewhat corpulent man answered the door, and, on hearing Mr Godfrey's name, immediately conducted him into an empty apartment at the back, on the drawing-room floor. He noticed two unusual things on entering the room. One of them was a faint odour of musk and camphor. The other was an ancient Oriental manuscript, richly illuminated with Indian figures and devices, that lay open to inspection on a table.

He was looking at the book, the position of which caused him to stand with his back turned towards the closed folding doors communicating with the front room, when, without the slightest previous noise to warn him, he felt himself suddenly seized round the neck from behind. He had just time to notice that the arm round his neck was naked and of a tawny-brown colour, before his eyes were bandaged, his mouth was gagged, and he was thrown helpless on the floor by (as he judged) two men. A third rifled his pockets, and—if, as a lady, I may venture to use such an expression— searched him, without ceremony, through and through to his skin.

Here I should greatly enjoy saying a few cheering words on the devout confidence which could alone have sustained Mr Godfrey in an emergency so terrible as this. Perhaps, however, the position and appearance of my admirable friend at the culminating period of the outrage (as above described) are hardly within the proper limits of female discussion. Let me pass over the next few moments, and return to Mr Godfrey at the time when the odious search of his person had been completed. The outrage had been perpetrated throughout in dead silence. At the end of it some words were exchanged, among the invisible wretches, in a language which he did not understand, but in tones which were plainly expressive (to his cultivated ear) of disappointment and rage. He was suddenly lifted from the ground, placed in a chair, and bound there hand and foot. The next moment he felt the air flowing in from the open door, listened, and concluded that he was alone again in the room.

An interval elapsed, and he heard a sound below like the rustling sound of a woman's dress. It advanced up the stairs, and stopped. A female scream rent the atmosphere of guilt. A man's voice below exclaimed 'Hullo!' A man's feet ascended the stairs. Mr Godfrey felt Christian fingers unfastening his bandage, and extracting his gag. He looked in amazement at two respectable strangers, and faintly articulated, 'What does it mean?' The two respectable strangers looked back, and said, 'Exactly the question we were going to ask *you*.'

The inevitable explanation followed. No! Let me be scrupulously particular. Sal-volatile and water followed, to compose dear Mr Godfrey's nerves. The explanation came next.

It appeared, from the statement of the landlord and landlady of the house (persons of good repute in the neighbourhood), that their first and second floor apartments had been engaged, on the previous day, for a week certain, by a most respectable-looking gentleman—the same who has been already described as answering the door to Mr Godfrey's knock. The gentleman had paid the week's rent and all the week's extras in advance, stating that the apartments were wanted for three Oriental noblemen, friends of his, who were visiting England for the first time. Early on the morning of the outrage, two of the Oriental strangers, accompanied by their respectable English friend, took possession of the apartments. The third was expected to join them shortly; and the luggage (reported as very bulky) was announced to follow when it had passed through the Custom-house, late in the afternoon. Not more than ten minutes previous to Mr Godfrey's visit, the third foreigner had arrived. Nothing out of the common had happened, to the knowledge of the landlord and landlady down-stairs, until within the last five minutes—when they had seen the three foreigners, accompanied by their respectable English friend, all leave the house together, walking quietly in the direction of the Strand. Remembering that a visitor had called, and not having seen the visitor also leave the house, the landlady had thought it rather strange that the gentleman should be left by himself up-stairs. After a short discussion with her husband, she had considered it advisable to ascertain whether anything was wrong. The result had followed, as I have already attempted to describe it; and there the explanation of the landlord and the landlady came to an end.

An investigation was next made in the room. Dear Mr Godfrey's property was found scattered in all directions. When the articles were collected, however, nothing was missing; his watch, chain, purse, keys, pocket-hand-kerchief, note-book, and all his loose papers had been closely examined, and had then been left unharmed to be resumed by the owner. In the same way, not the smallest morsel of property belonging to the proprietors of the house had been abstracted. The Oriental noblemen had removed their own illuminated manuscript, and had removed nothing else.

What did it mean? Taking the worldly point of view, it appeared to mean that Mr Godfrey had been the victim of some incomprehensible error, committed by certain unknown men. A dark conspiracy was on foot in the midst of us; and our beloved and innocent friend had been entangled in its meshes. When the Christian hero of a hundred charitable victories plunges into a pitfall that has been dug for him by mistake, oh, what a warning it is to the rest of us to be unceasingly on our guard! How soon may our own evil passions prove to be Oriental noblemen who pounce on us unawares!

I could write pages of affectionate warning on this one theme, but (alas!) I am not permitted to improve—I am condemned to narrate. My wealthy relative's cheque—henceforth, the incubus of my existence—warns me that I have not done with this record of violence yet. We must leave Mr Godfrey to recover in Northumberland Street, and must follow the proceedings of Mr Luker at a later period of the day.

After leaving the bank, Mr Luker had visited various parts of London on business errands. Returning to his own residence, he found a letter waiting for him, which was described as having been left a short time previously by a boy. In this case, as in Mr Godfrey's case, the handwriting was strange; but the name mentioned was the name of one of Mr Luker's customers. His correspondent announced (writing in the third person—apparently by the hand of a deputy) that he had been unexpectedly summoned to London. He had just established himself in lodgings in Alfred Place, Tottenham Court Road; and he desired to see Mr Luker immediately, on the subject of a purchase which he contemplated making. The gentleman was an enthusiastic collector of oriental antiquities, and had been for many years a liberal patron of the establishment in Lambeth. Oh, when shall we wean ourselves from the worship of Mammon! Mr Luker called a cab, and drove off instantly to his liberal patron.

Exactly what had happened to Mr Godfrey in Northumberland Street now happened to Mr Luker in Alfred Place. Once more the respectable man answered the door, and showed the visitor up-stairs into the back drawing-room. There, again, lay the illuminated manuscript on a table. Mr Luker's attention was absorbed, as Mr Godfrey's attention had been absorbed, by this beautiful work of Indian art. He too was aroused from his studies by a tawny naked arm round his throat, by a bandage over his eyes, and by a gag in his mouth. He too was thrown prostrate, and searched to the skin. A longer interval had then elapsed than had passed in the experience of Mr Godfrey; but it had ended as before, in the persons of the house suspecting something wrong, and going up-stairs to see what had happened. Precisely the same explanation which the landlord in Northumberland Street had given to Mr Godfrey, the landlord in Alfred Place now gave to Mr Luker. Both had been imposed on in the same way by the plausible address and well-filled purse of the respectable stranger, who introduced himself as acting for his foreign friends. The one point of difference between the two cases occurred when the scattered contents of Mr Luker's pockets were being collected from the floor. His watch and purse were safe, but (less fortunate than Mr Godfrey) one of the loose papers that he carried about him had been taken away. The paper in question acknowledged the receipt of a valuable of great price which Mr Luker had that day left in the care of his bankers. This document would be useless for purposes of fraud, inasmuch as it provided that the valuable should only be given up on the personal application of the owner. As soon as he recovered himself, Mr Luker hurried to the bank, on the chance that the thieves who had robbed him might ignorantly present themselves with the receipt. Nothing had been seen of them when he arrived at the establishment, and nothing was seen of them afterwards. Their respectable English friend had (in the opinion of the bankers) looked the receipt over before they attempted to make use of it, and had given them the necessary warning in good time.

Information of both outrages was communicated to the police, and the needful investigations were pursued, I believe, with great energy. The authorities held that a robbery had been planned, on insufficient information received by the thieves. They had been plainly not sure whether Mr Luker had, or had not, trusted the transmission of his precious gem to another person; and poor polite Mr Godfrey had paid the penalty of having been seen accidentally speaking to him. Add to this, that Mr Godfrey's absence from our Monday evening meeting had been occasioned by a consultation of the authorities, at which he was requested to assist—and all the explanations required being now given, I may proceed with the simpler story of my own little personal experiences in Montagu Square.

I was punctual to the luncheon hour on Tuesday. Reference to my diary shows this to have been a chequered day—much in it to be devoutly regretted, much in it to be devoutly thankful for.

Dear Aunt Verinder received me with her usual grace and kindness. But I noticed, after a little while, that something was wrong. Certain anxious looks escaped my aunt, all of which took the direction of her daughter. I never see Rachel myself without wondering how it can be that so insignificant-looking a person should be the child of such distinguished parents as Sir John and Lady Verinder. On this occasion, however, she not only disappointed—she really shocked me. There was an absence of all lady-like restraint in her language and manner most painful to see. She was possessed by some feverish excitement which made her distressingly loud when she laughed, and sinfully wasteful and capricious in what she ate and drank at lunch. I felt deeply for her poor mother, even before the true state of the case had been confidentially made known to me.

Luncheon over, my aunt said: 'Remember what the doctor told you, Rachel, about quieting yourself with a book after taking your meals.'

'I'll go into the library, mamma,' she answered. 'But if Godfrey calls, mind I am told of it. I am dying for more news of him, after his adventure in Northumberland Street.' She kissed her mother on the forehead, and looked my way. 'Good-bye, Clack,' she said, carelessly. Her insolence roused no angry feeling in me; I only made a private memorandum to pray for her.

When we were left by ourselves, my aunt told me the whole horrible story of the Indian Diamond, which, I am happy to know, it is not necessary to repeat here. She did not conceal from me that she would have preferred keeping silence on the subject. But when her own servants all knew of the loss of the Moonstone, and when some of the circumstances had actually found their way into the newspapers—when strangers were speculating whether there was any connection between what had happened at Lady Verinder's country-house, and what had happened in Northumberland Street and Alfred Place—concealment was not to be thought of; and perfect frankness became a necessity as well as a virtue.

Some persons, hearing what I now heard, would have been probably overwhelmed with astonishment. For my own part, knowing Rachel's spirit to have been essentially unregenerate from her childhood upwards, I was prepared for whatever my aunt could tell me on the subject of her daughter. It might have gone on from bad to worse till it ended in Murder; and I should still have said to myself, The natural result! oh, dear, dear, the natural result! The one thing that *did* shock me was the course my aunt had taken under the circumstances. Here surely was a case for a clergyman, if ever there was one yet! Lady Verinder had thought it a case for a physician. All my poor aunt's early life had been passed in her father's godless household. The natural result again! Oh, dear, dear, the natural result again!

'The doctors recommend plenty of exercise and amusement for Rachel, and strongly urge me to keep her mind as much as possible from dwelling on the past,' said Lady Verinder.

'Oh, what heathen advice!' I thought to myself. 'In this Christian country, what heathen advice!'

My aunt went on, 'I do my best to carry out my instructions. But this strange adventure of Godfrey's happens at a most unfortunate time. Rachel has been incessantly restless and excited since she first heard of it. She left me no peace till I had written and asked my nephew Ablewhite to come here. She even feels an interest in the other person who was roughly used—Mr Luker, or some such name—though the man is, of course, a total stranger to her.'

'Your knowledge of the world, dear aunt, is superior to mine,' I suggested diffidently. 'But there must be a reason surely for this extraordinary conduct on Rachel's part. She is keeping a sinful secret from you and from everybody. May there not be something in these recent events which threatens her secret with discovery?'

'Discovery?' repeated my aunt. 'What can you possibly mean? Discovery through Mr Luker? Discovery through my nephew?'

As the word passed her lips, a special providence occurred. The servant opened the door, and announced Mr Godfrey Ablewhite.

CHAPTER II

MR. GODFREY followed the announcement of his name—as Mr Godfrey does everything else—exactly at the right time. He was not so close on the servant's heels as to startle us. He was not so far behind as to cause us the double inconvenience of a pause and an open door. It is in the completeness of his daily life that the true Christian appears. This dear man was very complete.

'Go to Miss Verinder,' said my aunt, addressing the servant, 'and tell her Mr Ablewhite is here.'

We both inquired after his health. We both asked him together whether he felt like himself again, after his terrible adventure of the past week. With perfect tact, he contrived to answer us at the same moment. Lady Verinder had his reply in words. I had his charming smile.

'What,' he cried, with infinite tenderness, 'have I done to deserve all this sympathy? My dear aunt! my dear Miss Clack! I have merely been mistaken for somebody else. I have only been blindfolded; I have only been strangled; I have only been thrown flat on my back, on a very thin carpet, covering a particularly hard floor. Just think how much worse it might have been! I might have been murdered; I might have been robbed. What have I lost? Nothing but Nervous Force—which the law doesn't recognise as property; so that, strictly speaking, I have lost nothing at all. If I could have had my own way, I would have kept my adventure to myself—I shrink from all this fuss and publicity. But Mr Luker made *his* injuries public, and *my* injuries, as the necessary consequence, have been proclaimed in their turn. I have become the property of the newspapers, until the gentle reader gets sick of the subject. I am very sick indeed of it myself. May the gentle reader soon be like me! And how is dear Rachel? Still enjoying the gaieties of London? So glad to hear it! Miss Clack, I need all your indulgence. I am sadly behindhand with my Committee Work and my dear Ladies. But I really do hope to look in at the Mothers'-Small-Clothes next week. Did you make cheering progress at Monday's Committee? Was the Board hopeful about future prospects? And are we nicely off for Trousers?'

The heavenly gentleness of his smile made his apologies irresistible. The richness of his deep voice added its own indescribable charm to the interesting business question which he had just addressed to me. In truth, we were almost *too* nicely off for Trousers; we were quite overwhelmed by them. I was just about to say so, when the door opened again, and an element of worldly disturbance entered the room, in the person of Miss Verinder.

She approached dear Mr Godfrey at a most unladylike rate of speed, with her hair shockingly untidy, and her face, what *I* should call, unbecomingly flushed.

'I am charmed to see you, Godfrey,' she said, addressing him, I grieve to add, in the off-hand manner of one young man talking to another. 'I wish you had brought Mr Luker with you. You and he (as long as our present excitement lasts) are the two most interesting men in all London. It's morbid to say this; it's unhealthy; it's all that a well-regulated mind like Miss Clack's most instinctively shudders at. Never mind that. Tell me the whole of the Northumberland-street story directly. I know the newspapers have left some of it out.'

Even dear Mr Godfrey partakes of the fallen nature which we all inherit from Adam—it is a very small share of our human legacy, but, alas! he has it. I confess it grieved me to see him take Rachel's hand in both of his own hands, and lay it softly on the left side of his waistcoat. It was a direct encouragement to her reckless way of talking, and her insolent reference to me.

'Dearest Rachel,' he said, in the same voice which had thrilled me when he spoke of our prospects and our trousers, 'the newspapers have told you everything—and they have told it much better than I can.'

'Godfrey thinks we all make too much of the matter,' my aunt remarked. 'He has just been saying that he doesn't care to speak of it.'

'Why?'

She put the question with a sudden flash in her eyes, and a sudden look up into Mr Godfrey's face. On his side, he looked down at her with an indulgence so injudicious and so ill-deserved, that I really felt called on to interfere.

'Rachel, darling!' I remonstrated gently, 'true greatness and true courage are ever modest.'

'You are a very good fellow in your way, Godfrey,' she said—not taking the smallest notice, observe, of me, and still speaking to her cousin as if she was one young man addressing another. 'But I am quite sure you are not great; I don't believe you possess any extraordinary courage; and I am firmly persuaded—if you ever had any modesty—that your lady-worshippers relieved you of that virtue a good many years since. You have some private reason for not talking of your adventure in Northumberland-street; and I mean to know it.'

'My reason is the simplest imaginable, and the most easily acknowledged,' he answered, still bearing with her. 'I am tired of the subject.'

'You are tired of the subject? My dear Godfrey, I am going to make a remark.'

'What is it?'

'You live a great deal too much in the society of women. And you have contracted two very bad habits in consequence. You have learnt to talk nonsense seriously, and you have got into a way of telling fibs for the pleasure of telling them. You can't go straight with your lady-worshippers.

I mean to make you go straight with *me*. Come, and sit down. I am brimful of downright questions; and I expect you to be brimful of downright answers.'

She actually dragged him across the room to a chair by the window, where the light would fall on his face. I deeply feel being obliged to report such language, and to describe such conduct. But, hemmed in as I am, between Mr Franklin Blake's cheque on one side and my own sacred regard for truth on the other, what am I to do? I looked at my aunt. She sat unmoved; apparently in no way disposed to interfere. I had never noticed this kind of torpor in her before. It was, perhaps, the reaction after the trying time she had had in the country. Not a pleasant symptom to remark, be it what it might, at dear Lady Verinder's age, and with dear Lady Verinder's autumnal exuberance of figure.

In the meantime, Rachel had settled herself at the window with our amiable and forbearing—our too forbearing—Mr Godfrey. She began the string of questions with which she had threatened him, taking no more notice of her mother, or of myself, than if we had not been in the room.

'Have the police done anything, Godfrey?'

'Nothing whatever.'

'It is certain, I suppose, that the three men who laid the trap for you were the same three men who afterwards laid the trap for Mr Luker?'

'Humanly speaking, my dear Rachel, there can be no doubt of it.'

'And not a trace of them has been discovered?'

'Not a trace.'

'It is thought—is it not?—that these three men are the three Indians who came to our house in the country.'

'Some people think so.'

'Do you think so?'

'My dear Rachel, they blindfolded me before I could see their faces. I know nothing whatever of the matter. How can I offer an opinion on it?'

Even the angelic gentleness of Mr Godfrey was, you see, beginning to give way at last under the persecution inflicted on him. Whether unbridled curiosity, or ungovernable dread, dictated Miss Verinder's questions I do not presume to inquire. I only report that, on Mr Godfrey's attempting to rise, after giving her the answer just described, she actually took him by the two shoulders, and pushed him back into his chair.—Oh, don't say this was immodest! don't even hint that the recklessness of guilty terror could alone account for such conduct as I have described! We must not judge others. My Christian friends, indeed, indeed, indeed, we must not judge others!

She went on with her questions, unabashed. Earnest Biblical students will perhaps be reminded—as I was reminded—of the blinded children of the devil, who went on with their orgies, unabashed, in the time before the Flood.

'I want to know something about Mr Luker, Godfrey.'

'I am again unfortunate, Rachel. No man knows less of Mr Luker than I do.'

'You never saw him before you and he met accidentally at the bank?'

'Never.'

'You have seen him since?'

'Yes. We have been examined together, as well as separately, to assist the police.'

'Mr Luker was robbed of a receipt which he had got from his banker's— was he not? What was the receipt for?'

'For a valuable gem which he had placed in the safe keeping of the bank.'

'That's what the newspapers say. It may be enough for the general reader; but it is not enough for me. The banker's receipt must have mentioned what the gem was?'

'The banker's receipt, Rachel—as I have heard it described—mentioned nothing of the kind. A valuable gem, belonging to Mr Luker; deposited by Mr Luker; sealed with Mr Luker's seal; and only to be given up on Mr Luker's personal application. That was the form, and that is all I know about it.'

She waited a moment, after he had said that. She looked at her mother, and sighed. She looked back again at Mr Godfrey, and went on.

'Some of our private affairs, at home,' she said, 'seem to have got into the newspapers?'

'I grieve to say, it is so.'

'And some idle people, perfect strangers to us, are trying to trace a connection between what happened at our house in Yorkshire and what has happened since, here in London?'

'The public curiosity, in certain quarters, is, I fear, taking that turn.'

'The people who say that the three unknown men who ill-used you and Mr Luker are the three Indians, also say that the valuable gem——'

There she stopped. She had become gradually, within the last few moments, whiter and whiter in the face. The extraordinary blackness of her hair made this paleness, by contrast, so ghastly to look at, that we all thought she would faint, at the moment when she checked herself in the middle of her question. Dear Mr Godfrey made a second attempt to leave his chair. My aunt entreated her to say no more. I followed my aunt with a modest medicinal peace-offering, in the shape of a bottle of salts. We none of us produced the slightest effect on her. 'Godfrey, stay where you are. Mamma, there is not the least reason to be alarmed about me. Clack, you're dying to hear the end of it—I won't faint, expressly to oblige *you*.'

Those were the exact words she used—taken down in my diary the moment I got home. But, oh, don't let us judge! My Christian friends, don't let us judge!

She turned once more to Mr Godfrey. With an obstinacy dreadful to see, she went back again to the place where she had checked herself, and completed her question in these words:

'I spoke to you, a minute since, about what people were saying in certain quarters. Tell me plainly, Godfrey, do they any of them say that Mr Luker's valuable gem is—The Moonstone?'

As the name of the Indian Diamond passed her lips, I saw a change come over my admirable friend. His complexion deepened. He lost the genial suavity of manner which is one of his greatest charms. A noble indignation inspired his reply.

'They *do* say it,' he answered. 'There are people who don't hesitate to accuse Mr Luker of telling a falsehood to serve some private interests of his own. He has over and over again solemnly declared that, until this scandal assailed him, he had never even heard of The Moonstone. And these vile people reply, without a shadow of proof to justify them, He has his reasons for concealment; we decline to believe him on his oath. Shameful! shameful!'

Rachel looked at him very strangely—I can't well describe how—while he was speaking. When he had done, she said,

'Considering that Mr Luker is only a chance acquaintance of yours, you take up his cause, Godfrey, rather warmly.'

My gifted friend made her one of the most truly evangelical answers I ever heard in my life.

'I hope, Rachel, I take up the cause of all oppressed people rather warmly,' he said.

The tone in which those words were spoken might have melted a stone. But, oh dear, what is the hardness of stone? Nothing, compared to the hardness of the unregenerate human heart! She sneered. I blush to record it—she sneered at him to his face.

'Keep your noble sentiments for your Ladies' Committees, Godfrey. I am certain that the scandal which has assailed Mr Luker, has not spared You.'

Even my aunt's torpor was roused by those words.

'My dear Rachel,' she remonstrated, 'you have really no right to say that!'

'I mean no harm, mamma—I mean good. Have a moment's patience with me, and you will see.'

She looked back at Mr Godfrey, with what appeared to be a sudden pity for him. She went the length—the very unladylike length—of taking him by the hand.

'I am certain,' she said, 'that I have found out the true reason of your unwillingness to speak of this matter before my mother and before me. An unlucky accident has associated you in people's minds with Mr Luker. You have told me what scandal says of *him*. What does scandal say of *you*?'

Even at the eleventh hour, dear Mr Godfrey—always ready to return good for evil—tried to spare her.

'Don't ask me!' he said. 'It's better forgotten, Rachel—it is, indeed.'

'I *will* hear it!' she cried out, fiercely, at the top of her voice.

'Tell her, Godfrey!' entreated my aunt. 'Nothing can do her such harm as your silence is doing now!'

Mr Godfrey's fine eyes filled with tears. He cast one last appealing look at her—and then he spoke the fatal words:

'If you will have it, Rachel—scandal says that the Moonstone is in pledge to Mr Luker, and that I am the man who has pawned it.'

She started to her feet with a scream. She looked backwards and forwards from Mr Godfrey to my aunt, and from my aunt to Mr Godfrey, in such a frantic manner that I really thought she had gone mad.

'Don't speak to me! Don't touch me!' she exclaimed, shrinking back from all of us (I declare like some hunted animal!) into a corner of the room. 'This is my fault! I must set it right. I have sacrificed myself—I had a right to do that, if I liked. But to let an innocent man be ruined; to keep a secret which destroys his character for life—Oh, good God, it's too horrible! I can't bear it!'

My aunt half rose from her chair, then suddenly sat down again. She called to me faintly, and pointed to a little phial in her work-box.

'Quick!' she whispered. 'Six drops, in water. Don't let Rachel see.'

Under other circumstances, I should have thought this strange. There was no time now to think—there was only time to give the medicine. Dear Mr Godfrey unconsciously assisted me in concealing what I was about from Rachel, by speaking composing words to her at the other end of the room.

'Indeed, indeed, you exaggerate,' I heard him say. 'My reputation stands too high to be destroyed by a miserable passing scandal like this. It will be all forgotten in another week. Let us never speak of it again.' She was perfectly inaccessible, even to such generosity as this. She went on from bad to worse.

'I must, and will, stop it,' she said. 'Mamma! hear what I say. Miss Clack! hear what I say. I know the hand that took the Moonstone. I know——' she laid a strong emphasis on the words; she stamped her foot in the rage that possessed her—'*I know that Godfrey Ablewhite is innocent.* Take me to the magistrate, Godfrey! Take me to the magistrate, and I will swear it!'

My aunt caught me by the hand, and whispered, 'Stand between us for a minute or two. Don't let Rachel see me.' I noticed a bluish tinge in her face which alarmed me. She saw I was startled. 'The drops will put me right in a minute or two,' she said, and so closed her eyes, and waited a little.

While this was going on, I heard dear Mr Godfrey still gently remonstrating.

'You must not appear publicly in such a thing as this,' he said. '*Your* reputation, dearest Rachel, is something too pure and too sacred to be trifled with.'

'*My* reputation!' She burst out laughing. 'Why, I am accused, Godfrey, as well as you. The best detective officer in England declares that I have stolen my own Diamond. Ask him what he thinks—and he will tell you that I have pledged the Moonstone to pay my private debts!' She stopped, ran across the room—and fell on her knees at her mother's feet. 'Oh mamma! mamma! mamma! I must be mad—mustn't I?—not to own the truth *now*?' She was too vehement to notice her mother's condition—she was on her feet again, and back with Mr Godfrey, in an instant. 'I won't let you—I won't let any innocent man—be accused and disgraced through my fault. If you won't take me before the magistrate, draw out a declaration of your innocence on paper, and I will sign it. Do as I tell you, Godfrey, or I'll write it to the newspapers—I'll go out, and cry it in the streets!'

We will not say this was the language of remorse—we will say it was the language of hysterics. Indulgent Mr Godfrey pacified her by taking a sheet of paper, and drawing out the declaration. She signed it in a feverish hurry. 'Show it everywhere—don't think of *me*,' she said, as she gave it to him. 'I am afraid, Godfrey, I have not done you justice, hitherto, in my thoughts. You are more unselfish—you are a better man than I believed you to be. Come here when you can, and I will try and repair the wrong I have done you.'

She gave him her hand. Alas, for our fallen nature! Alas, for Mr Godfrey! He not only forgot himself so far as to kiss her hand—he adopted a gentleness of tone in answering her which, in such a case, was little better than a compromise with sin. 'I will come, dearest,' he said, 'on condition that we don't speak of this hateful subject again.' Never had I seen and heard our Christian Hero to less advantage than on this occasion.

Before another word could be said by anybody, a thundering knock at the street door startled us all. I looked through the window, and saw the World, the Flesh, and the Devil waiting before the house—as typified in a carriage and horses, a powdered footman, and three of the most audaciously dressed women I ever beheld in my life.

Rachel started, and composed herself. She crossed the room to her mother.

'They have come to take me to the flower-show,' she said. 'One word, mamma, before I go. I have not distressed you, have I?'

(Is the bluntness of moral feeling which could ask such a question as that, after what had just happened, to be pitied or condemned? I like to lean towards mercy. Let us pity it.)

The drops had produced their effect. My poor aunt's complexion was like itself again. 'No, no, my dear,' she said. 'Go with our friends, and enjoy yourself.'

Her daughter stooped, and kissed her. I had left the window, and was near the door, when Rachel approached it to go out. Another change had come over her—she was in tears. I looked with interest at the momentary softening of that obdurate heart. I felt inclined to say a few earnest words. Alas! my well-meant sympathy only gave offence. 'What do you mean by pitying me?' she asked in a bitter whisper, as she passed to the door. 'Don't you see how happy I am? I'm going to the flower-show, Clack; and I've got the prettiest bonnet in London.' She completed the hollow mockery of that address by blowing me a kiss—and so left the room.

I wish I could describe in words the compassion I felt for this miserable and misguided girl. But I am almost as poorly provided with words as with money. Permit me to say—my heart bled for her.

Returning to my aunt's chair, I observed dear Mr Godfrey searching for something softly, here and there, in different parts of the room. Before I could offer to assist him he had found what he wanted. He came back to my aunt and me, with his declaration of innocence in one hand, and with a box of matches in the other.

'Dear aunt, a little conspiracy!' he said. 'Dear Miss Clack, a pious fraud which even your high moral rectitude will excuse! Will you leave Rachel to suppose that I accept the generous self-sacrifice which has signed this paper? And will you kindly bear witness that I destroy it in your presence, before I leave the house?' He kindled a match, and, lighting the paper, laid it to burn in a plate on the table. 'Any trifling inconvenience that I may suffer is as nothing,' he remarked, 'compared with the importance of preserving that pure name from the contaminating contact of the world. There! We have reduced it to a little harmless heap of ashes; and our dear impulsive Rachel will never know what we have done! How do you feel? My precious friends, how do you feel? For my poor part, I am as light-hearted as a boy!'

He beamed on us with his beautiful smile; he held out a hand to my aunt, and a hand to me. I was too deeply affected by his noble conduct to speak. I closed my eyes; I put his hand, in a kind of spiritual self-forgetfulness, to my lips. He murmured a soft remonstrance. Oh the ecstasy, the pure, unearthly ecstasy of that moment! I sat—I hardly know on what—quite lost in my own exalted feelings. When I opened my eyes again, it was like descending from heaven to earth. There was nobody but my aunt in the room. He had gone.

I should like to stop here—I should like to close my narrative with the record of Mr Godfrey's noble conduct. Unhappily, there is more, much more, which the unrelenting pecuniary pressure of Mr Blake's cheque obliges me to tell. The painful disclosures which were to reveal themselves in my presence, during that Tuesday's visit to Montagu Square, were not at an end yet.

Finding myself alone with Lady Verinder, I turned naturally to the subject of her health; touching delicately on the strange anxiety which she had shown to conceal her indisposition, and the remedy applied to it, from the observation of her daughter.

My aunt's reply greatly surprised me.

'Drusilla,' she said (if I have not already mentioned that my Christian name is Drusilla, permit me to mention it now), 'you are touching—quite innocently, I know—on a very distressing subject.'

I rose immediately. Delicacy left me but one alternative—the alternative, after first making my apologies, of taking my leave. Lady Verinder stopped me, and insisted on my sitting down again.

'You have surprised a secret,' she said, 'which I had confided to my sister Mrs Ablewhite, and to my lawyer Mr Bruff, and to no one else. I can trust in their discretion; and I am sure, when I tell you the circumstances, I can trust in yours. Have you any pressing engagement, Drusilla? or is your time your own this afternoon?'

It is needless to say that my time was entirely at my aunt's disposal.

'Keep me company then,' she said, 'for another hour. I have something to tell you which I believe you will be sorry to hear. And I shall have a service to ask of you afterwards, if you don't object to assist me.'

It is again needless to say that, so far from objecting, I was all eagerness to assist her.

'You can wait here,' she went on, 'till Mr Bruff comes at five. And you can be one of the witnesses, Drusilla, when I sign my Will.'

Her Will! I thought of the drops which I had seen in her work-box. I thought of the bluish tinge which I had noticed in her complexion. A light which was not of this world—a light shining prophetically from an unmade grave—dawned on my mind. My aunt's secret was a secret no longer.

CHAPTER III

CONSIDERATION for poor Lady Verinder forbade me even to hint that I had guessed the melancholy truth, before she opened her lips. I waited her pleasure in silence; and, having privately arranged to say a few sustaining words at the first convenient opportunity, felt prepared for any duty that could claim me, no matter how painful it might be.

'I have been seriously ill, Drusilla, for some time past,' my aunt began. 'And, strange to say, without knowing it myself.'

I thought of the thousands and thousands of perishing human creatures who were all at that moment spiritually ill, without knowing it themselves. And I greatly feared that my poor aunt might be one of the number. 'Yes, dear,' I said, sadly. 'Yes.'

'I brought Rachel to London, as you know, for medical advice,' she went on. 'I thought it right to consult two doctors.'

Two doctors! And, oh me (in Rachel's state), not one clergyman! 'Yes, dear?' I said once more. 'Yes?'

'One of the two medical men,' proceeded my aunt, 'was a stranger to me. The other had been an old friend of my husband's, and had always felt a sincere interest in me for my husband's sake. After prescribing for Rachel, he said he wished to speak to me privately in another room. I expected, of course, to receive some special directions for the management of my daughter's health. To my surprise, he took me gravely by the hand, and said, "I have been looking at you, Lady Verinder, with a professional as well as a personal interest. You are, I am afraid, far more urgently in need of medical advice than your daughter." He put some questions to me, which I was at first inclined to treat lightly enough, until I observed that my answers distressed him. It ended in his making an appointment to come and see me, accompanied by a medical friend, on the next day, at an hour when Rachel would not be at home. The result of that visit—most kindly and gently conveyed to me—satisfied both the physicians that there had been precious time lost, which could never be regained, and that my case had now passed beyond the reach of their art. For more than two years I have been suffering under an insidious form of heart disease, which, without any symptoms to alarm me, has, by little and little, fatally broken me down. I may live for some months, or I may die before another day has passed over my head—the doctors cannot, and dare not, speak more positively than this. It would be vain to say, my dear, that I have not had some miserable moments since my real situation has been made known to me. But I am more resigned than I was, and I am doing my best to set my worldly affairs in order. My one great anxiety is that Rachel should be kept in ignorance of the truth. If she knew it, she would at once attribute my broken health to anxiety about the Diamond, and would reproach herself bitterly, poor child, for what is in no sense her fault. Both the doctors agree that the mischief began two, if not three years since. I am sure you will keep my secret, Drusilla—for I am sure I see sincere sorrow and sympathy for me in your face.'

Sorrow and sympathy! Oh, what Pagan emotions to expect from a Christian Englishwoman anchored firmly on her faith!

Little did my poor aunt imagine what a gush of devout thankfulness thrilled through me as she approached the close of her melancholy story. Here was a career of usefulness opened before me! Here was a beloved relative and perishing fellow-creature, on the eve of the great change, utterly unprepared; and led, providentially led, to reveal her situation to Me! How can I describe the joy with which I now remembered that the precious clerical friends on whom I could rely, were to be counted, not by ones or twos, but by tens and twenties! I took my aunt in my arms—my overflowing tenderness was not to be satisfied, *now*, with anything less than an embrace. 'Oh!' I said to her, fervently, 'the indescribable interest with which you inspire me! Oh! the good I mean to do you, dear, before we part!' After another word or two of earnest prefatory warning, I gave her her choice of three precious friends, all plying the work of mercy from morning to night in her own neighbourhood; all equally inexhaustible in exhortation; all affectionately ready to exercise their gifts at a word from *me*. Alas! the result was far from encouraging. Poor Lady Verinder looked puzzled and frightened, and met everything I could say to her with the purely worldly objection that she was not strong enough to face strangers. I yielded—for the moment only, of course. My large experience (as Reader and Visitor, under not less, first and last, than fourteen beloved clerical friends) informed me that this was another case for preparation by books. I possessed a little library of works, all suitable to the present emergency, all calculated to arouse, convince, prepare, enlighten, and fortify my aunt. 'You will read, dear, won't you?' I said, in my most winning way. 'You will read, if I bring you my own precious books? Turned down at all the right places, aunt. And marked in pencil where you are to stop and ask yourself, "Does this apply to me?"' Even that simple appeal—so absolutely heathenising is the influence of the world—appeared to startle my aunt. She said, 'I will do what I can, Drusilla, to please you,' with a look of surprise, which was at once instructive and terrible to see. Not a moment was to be lost. The clock on the mantel-piece informed me that I had just time to hurry home; to provide myself with a first series of selected readings (say a dozen only); and to return in time to meet the lawyer, and witness Lady Verinder's Will. Promising faithfully to be back by five o'clock, I left the house on my errand of mercy.

When no interests but my own are involved, I am humbly content to get from place to place by the omnibus. Permit me to give an idea of my devotion to my aunt's interests by recording that, on this occasion, I committed the prodigality of taking a cab.

I drove home, selected and marked my first series of readings, and drove back to Montagu Square, with a dozen works in a carpet-bag, the like of which, I firmly believe, are not to be found in the literature of any other country in Europe. I paid the cabman exactly his fare. He received it with an oath; upon which I instantly gave him a tract. If I had presented a pistol at his head, this abandoned wretch could hardly have exhibited greater consternation. He jumped up on his box, and, with profane exclamations of dismay, drove off furiously. Quite useless, I am happy to say! I sowed the good seed, in spite of him, by throwing a second tract in at the window of the cab.

The servant who answered the door—not the person with the capribbons, to my great relief, but the footman—informed me that the doctor had called, and was still shut up with Lady Verinder. Mr Bruff, the lawyer, had arrived a minute since and was waiting in the library. I was shown into the library to wait too.

Mr Bruff looked surprised to see me. He is the family solicitor, and we had met more than once, on previous occasions, under Lady Verinder's roof. A man, I grieve to say, grown old and grizzled in the service of the world. A man who, in his hours of business, was the chosen prophet of Law and Mammon; and who, in his hours of leisure, was equally capable of reading a novel and of tearing up a tract.

'Have you come to stay here, Miss Clack?' he asked, with a look at my carpet-bag.

To reveal the contents of my precious bag to such a person as this would have been simply to invite an outburst of profanity. I lowered myself to his own level, and mentioned my business in the house.

'My aunt has informed me that she is about to sign her Will,' I answered. 'She has been so good as to ask me to be one of the witnesses.'

'Aye? aye? Well, Miss Clack, you will do. You are over twenty-one, and you have not the slightest pecuniary interest in Lady Verinder's Will.'

Not the slightest pecuniary interest in Lady Verinder's Will. Oh, how thankful I felt when I heard that! If my aunt, possessed of thousands, had remembered poor Me, to whom five pounds is an object—if my name had appeared in the Will, with a little comforting legacy attached to it—my enemies might have doubted the motive which had loaded me with the choicest treasures of my library, and had drawn upon my failing resources for the prodigal expenses of a cab. Not the cruellest scoffer of them all could doubt now. Much better as it was! Oh, surely, surely, much better as it was!

I was aroused from these consoling reflections by the voice of Mr Bruff. My meditative silence appeared to weigh upon the spirits of this worldling, and to force him, as it were, into talking to me against his own will.

'Well, Miss Clack, what's the last news in the charitable circles? How is your friend Mr Godfrey Ablewhite, after the mauling he got from the rogues in Northumberland Street? Egad! they're telling a pretty story about that charitable gentleman at my club!'

I had passed over the manner in which this person had remarked that I was more than twenty-one, and that I had no pecuniary interest in my aunt's Will. But the tone in which he alluded to dear Mr Godfrey was too much for my forbearance. Feeling bound, after what had passed in my presence that afternoon, to assert the innocence of my admirable friend, whenever I found it called in question—I own to having also felt bound to include in the accomplishment of this righteous purpose, a stinging castigation in the case of Mr Bruff.

'I live very much out of the world,' I said; 'and I don't possess the advantage, sir, of belonging to a club. But I happen to know the story to which you allude; and I also know that a viler falsehood than that story never was told.'

'Yes, yes, Miss Clack—you believe in your friend. Natural enough. Mr Godfrey Ablewhite won't find the world in general quite so easy to convince as a committee of charitable ladies. Appearances are dead against him. He was in the house when the Diamond was lost. And he was the first person in the house to go to London afterwards. Those are ugly circumstances, ma'am, viewed by the light of later events.'

I ought, I know, to have set him right before he went any farther. I ought to have told him that he was speaking in ignorance of a testimony to Mr Godfrey's innocence, offered by the only person who was undeniably competent to speak from a positive knowledge of the subject. Alas! the temptation to lead the lawyer artfully on to his own discomfiture was too much for me. I asked what he meant by 'later events'—with an appearance of the utmost innocence.

'By later events, Miss Clack, I mean events in which the Indians are concerned,' proceeded Mr Bruff, getting more and more superior to poor Me, the longer he went on. 'What do the Indians do, the moment they are let out of the prison at Frizinghall? They go straight to London, and fix on Mr Luker. What follows? Mr Luker feels alarmed for the safety of "a valuable of great price," which he has got in the house. He lodges it privately (under a general description) in his bankers' strong-room. Wonderfully clever of him: but the Indians are just as clever on their side. They have their suspicions that the "valuable of great price" is being shifted from one place to another; and they hit on a singularly bold and complete way of clearing those suspicions up. Whom do they seize and search? Not Mr Luker only—which would be intelligible enough—but Mr Godfrey Ablewhite as well. Why? Mr Ablewhite's explanation is, that they acted on blind suspicion, after seeing him accidentally speaking to Mr Luker. Absurd! Half-a-dozen other people spoke to Mr Luker that morning. Why were they not followed home too, and decoyed into the trap? No! no! The plain inference is, that Mr Ablewhite had his private interest in the "valuable" as well as Mr Luker, and that the Indians were so uncertain as to which of the two had the disposal of it, that there was no alternative but to search them both. Public opinion says that, Miss Clack. And public opinion, on this occasion, is not easily refuted.'

He said those last words, looking so wonderfully wise in his own worldly conceit, that I really (to my shame be it spoken) could not resist leading him a little farther still, before I overwhelmed him with the truth.

'I don't presume to argue with a clever lawyer like you,' I said. 'But is it quite fair, sir, to Mr Ablewhite to pass over the opinion of the famous London police officer who investigated this case? Not the shadow of a suspicion rested upon anybody but Miss Verinder, in the mind of Sergeant Cuff.'

'Do you mean to tell me, Miss Clack, that you agree with the Sergeant?'

'I judge nobody, sir, and I offer no opinion.'

'And I commit both those enormities, ma'am. I judge the Sergeant to have been utterly wrong; and I offer the opinion that, if he had known Rachel's character as I know it, he would have suspected everybody in the house but *her*. I admit that she has her faults—she is secret, and self-willed; odd and wild, and unlike other girls of her age. But true as steel, and high-minded and generous to a fault. If the plainest evidence in the world pointed one way, and if nothing but Rachel's word of honour pointed the other, I would take her word before the evidence, lawyer as I am! Strong language, Miss Clack; but I mean it.'

'Would you object to illustrate your meaning, Mr Bruff, so that I may be sure I understand it? Suppose you found Miss Verinder quite unaccountably interested in what has happened to Mr Ablewhite and Mr Luker? Suppose she asked the strangest questions about this dreadful scandal, and displayed the most ungovernable agitation when she found out the turn it was taking?'

'Suppose anything you please, Miss Clack, it wouldn't shake my belief in Rachel Verinder by a hair's-breadth.'

'She is so absolutely to be relied on as that?'

'So absolutely to be relied on as that.'

'Then permit me to inform you, Mr Bruff, that Mr Godfrey Ablewhite was in this house not two hours since, and that his entire innocence of all concern in the disappearance of the Moonstone was proclaimed by Miss Verinder herself, in the strongest language I ever heard used by a young lady in my life.'

I enjoyed the triumph—the unholy triumph, I fear, I must admit—of seeing Mr Bruff utterly confounded and overthrown by a few plain words from Me. He started to his feet, and stared at me in silence. I kept my seat, undisturbed, and related the whole scene as it had occurred. 'And what do you say about Mr Ablewhite *now*?' I asked, with the utmost possible gentleness, as soon as I had done.

'If Rachel has testified to his innocence, Miss Clack, I don't scruple to say that I believe in his innocence as firmly as you do. I have been misled by appearances, like the rest of the world; and I will make the best atonement I can, by publicly contradicting the scandal which has assailed your friend wherever I meet with it. In the meantime, allow me to congratulate you on the masterly manner in which you have opened the full fire of your batteries on me at the moment when I least expected it. You would have done great things in my profession, ma'am, if you had happened to be a man.'

With those words he turned away from me, and began walking irritably up and down the room.

I could see plainly that the new light I had thrown on the subject had greatly surprised and disturbed him. Certain expressions dropped from his lips, as he became more and more absorbed in his own thoughts, which suggested to my mind the abominable view that he had hitherto taken of the mystery of the lost Moonstone. He had not scrupled to suspect dear Mr Godfrey of the infamy of stealing the Diamond, and to attribute Rachel's conduct to a generous resolution to conceal the crime. On Miss Verinder's own authority—a perfectly unassailable authority, as you are aware, in the estimation of Mr Bruff—that explanation of the circumstances was now shown to be utterly wrong. The perplexity into which I had plunged this high legal authority was so overwhelming that he was quite unable to conceal it from notice. 'What a case!' I heard him say to himself, stopping at the window in his walk, and drumming on the glass with his fingers. 'It not only defies explanation, it's even beyond conjecture.'

There was nothing in these words which made any reply at all needful, on my part—and yet, I answered them! It seems hardly credible that I should not have been able to let Mr Bruff alone, even now. It seems almost beyond mere mortal perversity that I should have discovered, in what he had just said, a new opportunity of making myself personally disagreeable to him. But—ah, my friends! nothing is beyond mortal perversity; and anything is credible when our fallen natures get the better of us!

'Pardon me for intruding on your reflections,' I said to the unsuspecting Mr Bruff. 'But surely there is a conjecture to make which has not occurred to us yet.'

'Maybe, Miss Clack. I own I don't know what it is.'

'Before I was so fortunate, sir, as to convince you of Mr Ablewhite's innocence, you mentioned it as one of the reasons for suspecting him, that he was in the house at the time when the Diamond was lost. Permit me to remind you that Mr Franklin Blake was also in the house at the time when the Diamond was lost.'

The old worldling left the window, took a chair exactly opposite to mine, and looked at me steadily, with a hard and vicious smile.

'You are not so good a lawyer, Miss Clack,' he remarked in a meditative manner, 'as I supposed. You don't know how to let well alone.'

'I am afraid I fail to follow you, Mr Bruff,' I said, modestly.

'It won't do, Miss Clack—it really won't do a second time. Franklin Blake is a prime favourite of mine, as you are well aware. But that doesn't matter. I'll adopt your view, on this occasion, before you have time to turn round on me. You're quite right, ma'am. I have suspected Mr Ablewhite, on grounds which abstractedly justify suspecting Mr Blake too. Very good—let's suspect them together. It's quite in his character, we will say, to be capable of stealing the Moonstone. The only question is, whether it was his interest to do so.'

'Mr Franklin Blake's debts,' I remarked, 'are matters of family notoriety.'

'And Mr Godfrey Ablewhite's debts have not arrived at that stage of development yet. Quite true. But there happen to be two difficulties in the way of your theory, Miss Clack. I manage Franklin Blake's affairs, and I beg to inform you that the vast majority of his creditors (knowing his father to be a rich man) are quite content to charge interest on their debts, and to wait for their money. There is the first difficulty—which is tough enough. You will find the second tougher still. I have it on the authority of Lady Verinder herself, that her daughter was ready to marry Franklin Blake, before that infernal Indian Diamond disappeared from the house. She had drawn him on and put him off again, with the coquetry of a young girl. But she had confessed to her mother that she loved cousin Franklin, and her mother had trusted cousin Franklin with the secret. So there he was, Miss Clack, with his creditors content to wait, and with the certain prospect before him of marrying an heiress. By all means consider him a scoundrel; but tell me, if you please, why he should steal the Moonstone?'

'The human heart is unsearchable,' I said gently. 'Who is to fathom it?'

'In other words, ma'am—though he hadn't the shadow of a reason for taking the Diamond—he might have taken it, nevertheless, through natural depravity. Very well. Say he did. Why the devil——'

'I beg your pardon, Mr Bruff. If I hear the devil referred to in that manner, I must leave the room.'

'I beg *your* pardon, Miss Clack—I'll be more careful in my choice of language for the future. All I meant to ask was this. Why—even supposing he did take the Diamond—should Franklin Blake make himself the most prominent person in the house in trying to recover it? You may tell me he cunningly did that to divert suspicion from himself. I answer that he had no need to divert suspicion—because nobody suspected him. He first steals the Moonstone (without the slightest reason) through natural depravity; and he then acts a part, in relation to the loss of the jewel, which there is not the slightest necessity to act, and which leads to his mortally offending the young lady who would otherwise have married him. That is the monstrous proposition which you are driven to assert, if you attempt to associate the disappearance of the Moonstone with Franklin Blake. No, no, Miss Clack! After what has passed here to-day, between us two, the dead-lock, in this case, is complete. Rachel's own innocence is (as her mother knows, and as I know) beyond a doubt. Mr Ablewhite's innocence is equally certain—or Rachel would never have testified to it. And Franklin Blake's innocence, as you have just seen, unanswerably asserts itself. On the one hand, we are morally certain of all these things. And, on the other hand, we are equally sure that somebody has brought the Moonstone to London, and that Mr Luker, or his banker, is in private possession of it at this moment. What is the use of my experience, what is the use of any person's experience, in such a case as that? It baffles me; it baffles you; it baffles everybody.'

No—not everybody. It had not baffled Sergeant Cuff. I was about to mention this, with all possible mildness, and with every necessary protest against being supposed to cast a slur upon Rachel—when the servant came in to say that the doctor had gone, and that my aunt was waiting to receive us.

This stopped the discussion. Mr Bruff collected his papers, looking a little exhausted by the demands which our conversation had made on him. I took up my bag-full of precious publications, feeling as if I could have gone on talking for hours. We proceeded in silence to Lady Verinder's room.

Permit me to add here, before my narrative advances to other events, that I have not described what passed between the lawyer and me, without having a definite object in view. I am ordered to include in my contribution to the shocking story of the Moonstone a plain disclosure, not only of the turn which suspicion took, but even of the names of the persons on whom suspicion rested, at the time when the Indian Diamond was believed to be in London. A report of my conversation in the library with Mr Bruff appeared to me to be exactly what was wanted to answer this purpose— while, at the same time, it possessed the great moral advantage of rendering a sacrifice of sinful self-esteem essentially necessary on my part. I have been obliged to acknowledge that my fallen nature got the better of me. In making that humiliating confession, *I* get the better of my fallen nature. The moral balance is restored; the spiritual atmosphere feels clear once more. Dear friends, we may go on again.

CHAPTER IV

THE signing of the Will was a much shorter matter than I had anticipated. It was hurried over, to my thinking, in indecent haste. Samuel, the footman, was sent for to act as second witness—and the pen was put at once into my aunt's hand. I felt strongly urged to say a few appropriate words on this solemn occasion. But Mr Bruff's manner convinced me that it was wisest to check the impulse while he was in the room. In less than two minutes it was all over—and Samuel (unbenefited by what I might have said) had gone down-stairs again.

Mr Bruff folded up the Will, and then looked my way; apparently wondering whether I did or did not mean to leave him alone with my aunt. I had my mission of mercy to fulfil, and my bag of precious publications ready on my lap. He might as well have expected to move St Paul's Cathedral by looking at it, as to move Me. There was one merit about him (due no doubt to his worldly training) which I have no wish to deny. He was quick at seeing things. I appeared to produce almost the same impression on him which I had produced on the cabman. *He* too uttered a profane expression, and withdrew in a violent hurry, and left me mistress of the field.

As soon as we were alone, my aunt reclined on the sofa, and then alluded, with some appearance of confusion, to the subject of her Will.

'I hope you won't think yourself neglected, Drusilla, she said. 'I mean to *give* you your little legacy, my dear, with my own hand.'

Here was a golden opportunity! I seized it on the spot. In other words, I instantly opened my bag, and took out the top publication. It proved to be an early edition—only the twenty-fifth—of the famous anonymous work (believed to be by precious Miss Bellows), entitled *The Serpent at Home.* The design of the book—with which the worldly reader may not be acquainted— is to show how the Evil One lies in wait for us in all the most apparently innocent actions of our daily lives. The chapters best adapted to female perusal are 'Satan in the Hair Brush'; 'Satan behind the Looking Glass'; 'Satan under the Tea Table'; 'Satan out of the Window'—and many others.

'Give your attention, dear aunt, to this precious book—and you will give me all I ask.' With those words, I handed it to her open, at a marked passage—one continuous burst of burning eloquence! Subject: Satan among the Sofa Cushions.

Poor Lady Verinder (reclining thoughtlessly on her own sofa cushions) glanced at the book, and handed it back to me looking more confused than ever.

'I'm afraid, Drusilla,' she said, 'I must wait till I am a little better, before I can read that. The doctor——'

The moment she mentioned the doctor's name, I knew what was coming. Over and over again in my past experience among my perishing fellow-creatures, the members of the notoriously infidel profession of Medicine had stepped between me and my mission of mercy—on the miserable pretence that the patient wanted quiet, and that the disturbing influence of all others which they most dreaded, was the influence of Miss Clack and her Books. Precisely the same blinded materialism (working treacherously behind my back) now sought to rob me of the only right of property that my poverty could claim—my right of spiritual property in my perishing aunt.

'The doctor tells me,' my poor misguided relative went on, 'that I am not so well to-day. He forbids me to see any strangers; and he orders me, if I read at all, only to read the lightest and the most amusing books. "Do nothing, Lady Verinder, to weary your head, or to quicken your pulse"— those were his last words, Drusilla, when he left me to-day.'

There was no help for it but to yield again—for the moment only, as before. Any open assertion of the infinitely superior importance of such a ministry as mine, compared with the ministry of the medical man, would only have provoked the doctor to practise on the human weakness of his patient, and to threaten to throw up the case. Happily, there are more ways than one of sowing the good seed, and few persons are better versed in those ways than myself.

'You might feel stronger, dear, in an hour or two,' I said. 'Or you might wake, to-morrow morning, with a sense of something wanting, and even this unpretending volume might be able to supply it. You will let me leave the book, aunt? The doctor can hardly object to that!'

I slipped it under the sofa cushions, half in, and half out, close by her handkerchief, and her smelling-bottle. Every time her hand searched for either of these, it would touch the book; and, sooner or later (who knows?), the book might touch *her*. After making this arrangement, I thought it wise to withdraw. 'Let me leave you to repose, dear aunt; I will call again to-morrow.' I looked accidentally towards the window as I said that. It was full of flowers, in boxes and pots. Lady Verinder was extravagantly fond of these perishable treasures, and had a habit of rising every now and then, and going to look at them and smell them. A new idea flashed across my mind. 'Oh! may I take a flower?' I said—and got to the window unsuspected, in that way. Instead of taking away a flower, I added one, in the shape of another book from my bag, which I left, to surprise my aunt, among the geraniums and roses. The happy thought followed, 'Why not do the same for her, poor dear, in every other room that she enters?' I immediately said good-bye; and, crossing the hall, slipped into the library. Samuel, coming up to let me out, and supposing I had gone, went down-stairs again. On the library table I noticed two of the 'amusing books' which the infidel doctor had recommended. I instantly covered them from sight with two of my own precious publications. In the breakfast-room I found my aunt's favourite canary singing in his cage. She was always in the habit of feeding the bird herself. Some groundsel was strewed on a table which stood immediately under the cage. I put a book among the groundsel. In the drawing-room I found more cheering opportunities of emptying my bag. My aunt's favourite musical pieces were on the piano. I slipped in two more books among the music. I disposed of another in the back drawing-room, under some unfinished embroidery, which I knew to be of Lady Verinder's working. A third little room opened out of the back drawing-room, from which it was shut off by curtains instead of a door. My aunt's plain old-fashioned fan was on the chimney-piece. I opened my ninth book at a very special passage, and put the fan in as a marker, to keep the place. The question then came, whether I should go higher still, and try the bed-room floor—at the risk, undoubtedly, of being insulted, if the person with the cap-ribbons happened to be in the upper regions of the house, and to find me out. But oh, what of that? It is a poor Christian that is afraid of being insulted. I went upstairs, prepared to bear anything. All was silent and solitary—it was the servants' tea-time, I suppose. My aunt's room was in front. The miniature of my late dear uncle, Sir John, hung on the wall opposite the bed. It seemed to smile at me; it seemed to say, 'Drusilla! deposit a book.' There were tables on either side of my aunt's bed. She was a bad sleeper, and wanted, or thought she wanted, many things at night. I put a book near the matches on one side, and a book under the box of chocolate drops on the other. Whether she wanted a light, or whether she wanted a drop, there was a precious publication to meet her eye, or to meet her hand, and to say with silent eloquence, in either case, 'Come, try me! try me!' But one book was now left at the bottom of my bag, and but one apartment was still unexplored—the bath-room, which opened out of the bed-room. I peeped in; and the holy inner voice that never deceives, whispered to me, 'You have met her, Drusilla, everywhere else; meet her at the bath, and the work is done.' I observed a dressing-gown thrown across a chair. It had a pocket in it, and in that pocket I put my last book. Can words express my exquisite sense of duty done, when I had slipped out of the house, unsuspected by any of them, and when I found myself in the street with my empty bag under my arm? Oh, my worldly friends, pursuing the phantom, Pleasure, through the guilty mazes of Dissipation, how easy it is to be happy, if you will only be good!

When I folded up my things that night—when I reflected on the *true* riches which I had scattered with such a lavish hand, from top to bottom of the house of my wealthy aunt—I declare I felt as free from all anxiety as if I had been a child again. I was so light-hearted that I sang a verse of the Evening Hymn. I was so light-hearted that I fell asleep before I could sing another. Quite like a child again! quite like a child again!

So I passed that blissful night. On rising the next morning, how young I felt! I might add, how young I looked, if I were capable of dwelling on the concerns of my own perishable body. But I am not capable—and I add nothing.

Towards luncheon time—not for the sake of the creature-comforts, but for the certainty of finding dear aunt—I put on my bonnet to go to Montagu Square. Just as I was ready, the maid at the lodgings in which I then lived looked in at the door, and said, 'Lady Verinder's servant, to see Miss Clack.'

I occupied the parlour-floor, at that period of my residence in London. The front parlour was my sitting-room. Very small, very low in the ceiling, very poorly furnished—but, oh, so neat! I looked into the passage to see which of Lady Verinder's servants had asked for me. It was the young footman, Samuel—a civil fresh-coloured person, with a teachable look and a very obliging manner. I had always felt a spiritual interest in Samuel, and a wish to try him with a few serious words. On this occasion, I invited him into my sitting-room.

He came in, with a large parcel under his arm. When he put the parcel down, it appeared to frighten him. 'My lady's love, Miss; and I was to say that you would find a letter inside.' Having given that message, the fresh-coloured young footman surprised me by looking as if he would have liked to run away.

I detained him to make a few kind inquiries. Could I see my aunt, if I called in Montagu Square? No; she had gone out for a drive. Miss Rachel had gone with her, and Mr Ablewhite had taken a seat in the carriage, too. Knowing how sadly dear Mr Godfrey's charitable work was in arrear, I thought it odd that he should be going out driving, like an idle man. I stopped Samuel at the door, and made a few more kind inquiries. Miss Rachel was going to a ball that night, and Mr Ablewhite had arranged to come to coffee, and go with her. There was a morning concert advertised for to-morrow, and Samuel was ordered to take places for a large party, including a place for Mr Ablewhite. 'All the tickets may be gone, Miss,' said this innocent youth, 'if I don't run and get them at once!' He ran as he said the words—and I found myself alone again, with some anxious thoughts to occupy me.

We had a special meeting of the Mothers'-Small-Clothes-Conversion Society that night, summoned expressly with a view to obtaining Mr Godfrey's advice and assistance. Instead of sustaining our sisterhood, under an overwhelming flow of Trousers which quite prostrated our little community, he had arranged to take coffee in Montagu Square, and to go to a ball afterwards! The afternoon of the next day had been selected for the Festival of the British-Ladies'-Servants'-Sunday-Sweetheart-Supervision Society. Instead of being present, the life and soul of that struggling Institution, he had engaged to make one of a party of worldlings at a morning concert! I asked myself what did it mean? Alas! it meant that our Christian Hero was to reveal himself to me in a new character, and to become associated in my mind with one of the most awful back-slidings of modern times.

To return, however, to the history of the passing day. On finding myself alone in my room, I naturally turned my attention to the parcel which appeared to have so strangely intimidated the fresh-coloured young footman. Had my aunt sent me my promised legacy? and had it taken the form of cast-off clothes, or worn-out silver spoons, or unfashionable jewellery, or anything of that sort? Prepared to accept all, and to resent nothing, I opened the parcel—and what met my view? The twelve precious publications which I had scattered through the house, on the previous day; all returned to me by the doctor's orders! Well might the youthful Samuel shrink when he brought his parcel into my room! Well might he run when he had performed his miserable errand! As to my aunt's letter, it simply amounted, poor soul, to this—that she dare not disobey her medical man.

What was to be done now? With my training and my principles, I never had a moment's doubt.

Once self-supported by conscience, once embarked on a career of manifest usefulness, the true Christian never yields. Neither public nor private influences produce the slightest effect on us, when we have once got our mission. Taxation may be the consequence of a mission; riots may be the consequence of a mission; wars may be the consequence of a mission: we go on with our work, irrespective of every human consideration which moves the world outside us. We are above reason; we are beyond ridicule; we see with nobody's eyes, we hear with nobody's ears, we feel with nobody's hearts, but our own. Glorious, glorious privilege! And how is it earned? Ah, my friends, you may spare yourselves the useless inquiry! We are the only people who can earn it—for we are the only people who are always right.

In the case of my misguided aunt, the form which pious perseverance was next to take revealed itself to me plainly enough.

Preparation by clerical friends had failed, owing to Lady Verinder's own reluctance. Preparation by books had failed, owing to the doctor's infidel obstinacy. So be it! What was the next thing to try? The next thing to try was—Preparation by Little Notes. In other words, the books themselves having been sent back, select extracts from the books, copied by different hands, and all addressed as letters to my aunt, were, some to be sent by post, and some to be distributed about the house on the plan I had adopted on the previous day. As letters they would excite no suspicion; as letters they would be opened—and, once opened, might be read. Some of them I wrote myself. 'Dear aunt, may I ask your attention to a few lines?' &c. 'Dear aunt, I was reading last night, and I chanced on the following passage,' &c. Other letters were written for me by my valued fellow-workers, the sisterhood at the Mothers'-Small-Clothes. 'Dear madam, pardon the interest taken in you by a true, though humble, friend.' 'Dear madam, may a serious person surprise you by saying a few cheering words?' Using these and other similar forms of courteous appeal, we reintroduced all my precious passages under a form which not even the doctor's watchful materialism could suspect. Before the shades of evening had closed around us, I had a dozen awakening letters for my aunt, instead of a dozen awakening books. Six I made immediate arrangements for sending through the post, and six I kept in my pocket for personal distribution in the house the next day.

Soon after two o'clock I was again on the field of pious conflict, addressing more kind inquiries to Samuel at Lady Verinder's door.

My aunt had had a bad night. She was again in the room in which I had witnessed her Will, resting on the sofa, and trying to get a little sleep.

I said I would wait in the library, on the chance of seeing her. In the fervour of my zeal to distribute the letters, it never occurred to me to inquire about Rachel. The house was quiet, and it was past the hour at which the musical performance began. I took it for granted that she and her party of pleasure-seekers (Mr Godfrey, alas! included) were all at the concert, and eagerly devoted myself to my good work, while time and opportunity were still at my own disposal.

My aunt's correspondence of the morning—including the six awakening letters which I had posted overnight—was lying unopened on the library table. She had evidently not felt herself equal to dealing with a large mass of letters—and she might be daunted by the number of them, if she entered the library later in the day. I put one of my second set of six letters on the chimney-piece by itself; leaving it to attract her curiosity, by means of its solitary position, apart from the rest. A second letter I put purposely on the floor in the breakfast-room. The first servant who went in after me would conclude that my aunt had dropped it, and would be specially careful to restore it to her. The field thus sown on the basement story, I ran lightly up-stairs to scatter my mercies next over the drawing-room floor.

Just as I entered the front room, I heard a double-knock at the street-door—a soft, fluttering, considerate little knock. Before I could think of slipping back to the library (in which I was supposed to be waiting), the active young footman was in the hall, answering the door. It mattered little, as I thought. In my aunt's state of health, visitors in general were not admitted. To my horror and amazement, the performer of the soft little knock proved to be an exception to general rules. Samuel's voice below me (after apparently answering some questions which I did not hear) said, unmistakably, 'Upstairs, if you please, sir.' The next moment I heard footsteps—a man's footsteps—approaching the drawing-room floor. Who could this favoured male visitor possibly be? Almost as soon as I asked myself the question, the answer occurred to me. Who *could* it be but the doctor?

In the case of any other visitor, I should have allowed myself to be discovered in the drawing-room. There would have been nothing out of the common in my having got tired of the library, and having gone upstairs for a change. But my own self-respect stood in the way of my meeting the person who had insulted me by sending me back my books. I slipped into the little third room, which I have mentioned as communicating with the back drawing-room, and dropped the curtains which closed the open doorway. If I only waited there for a minute or two, the usual result in such cases would take place. That is to say, the doctor would be conducted to his patient's room.

I waited a minute or two, and more than a minute or two. I heard the visitor walking restlessly backwards and forwards. I also heard him talking to himself. I even thought I recognised the voice. Had I made a mistake? Was it not the doctor, but somebody else? Mr Bruff, for instance? No! an unerring instinct told me it was not Mr Bruff. Whoever he was, he was still talking to himself. I parted the heavy curtains the least little morsel in the world, and listened.

The words I heard were, 'I'll do it to-day!' And the voice that spoke them was Mr Godfrey Ablewhite's.

CHAPTER V

MY hand dropped from the curtain. But don't suppose—oh, don't suppose—that the dreadful embarrassment of my situation was the uppermost
idea in my mind! So fervent still was the sisterly interest I felt in Mr Godfrey,
that I never stopped to ask myself why he was not at the concert. No! I
thought only of the words—the startling words—which had just fallen from
his lips. He would do it to-day. He had said, in a tone of terrible resolution,
he would do it to-day. What, oh what, would he do? Something even more
deplorably unworthy of him than what he had done already? Would he
apostatise from the faith? Would he abandon us at the Mothers' Small-
Clothes? Had we seen the last of his angelic smile in the committee-room?
Had we heard the last of his unrivalled eloquence at Exeter Hall? I was so
wrought up by the bare idea of such awful eventualities as these in
connection with such a man, that I believe I should have rushed from my
place of concealment, and implored him in the name of all the Ladies'
Committees in London to explain himself—when I suddenly heard another
voice in the room. It penetrated through the curtains; it was loud, it was
bold, it was wanting in every female charm. The voice of Rachel Verinder!

'Why have you come up here, Godfrey?' she asked. 'Why didn't you go
into the library?'

He laughed softly, and answered, 'Miss Clack is in the library.'

'Clack in the library!' She instantly seated herself on the ottoman in the
back drawing-room. 'You are quite right, Godfrey. We had much better stop
here.'

I had been in a burning fever, a moment since, and in some doubt what to
do next. I became extremely cold now, and felt no doubt whatever. To show
myself, after what I had heard, was impossible. To retreat—except into the
fire-place—was equally out of the question. A martyrdom was before me. In
justice to myself, I noiselessly arranged the curtains so that I could both see and
hear. And then I met my martyrdom, with the spirit of a primitive Christian.

'Don't sit on the ottoman,' the young lady proceeded. 'Bring a chair,
Godfrey. I like people to be opposite to me when I talk to them.'

He took the nearest seat. It was a low chair. He was very tall, and many
sizes too large for it. I never saw his legs to such disadvantage before.

'Well?' she went on. 'What did you say to them?'

'Just what you said, dear Rachel, to me.'

'That mamma was not at all well to-day? And that I didn't quite like
leaving her to go to the concert?'

'Those were the words. They were grieved to lose you at the concert, but
they quite understood. All sent their love; and all expressed a cheering belief
that Lady Verinder's indisposition would soon pass away.'

'*You* don't think it's serious, do you, Godfrey?'

'Far from it! In a few days, I feel quite sure, all will be well again.'

'I think so, too. I was a little frightened at first, but I think so too. It was very kind to go and make my excuses for me to people who are almost strangers to you. But why not have gone with them to the concert? It seems very hard that you should miss the music too.'

'Don't say that, Rachel! If you only knew how much happier I am—here, with you!'

He clasped his hands, and looked at her. In the position which he occupied, when he did that, he turned my way. Can words describe how I sickened when I noticed exactly the same pathetic expression on his face, which had charmed me when he was pleading for destitute millions of his fellow-creatures on the platform at Exeter Hall!

'It's hard to get over one's bad habits, Godfrey. But do try to get over the habit of paying compliments—do, to please me.'

'I never paid *you* a compliment, Rachel, in my life. Successful love may sometimes use the language of flattery, I admit. But hopeless love, dearest, always speaks the truth.'

He drew his chair close, and took her hand, when he said 'hopeless love.' There was a momentary silence. He, who thrilled everybody, had doubtless thrilled *her*. I thought I now understood the words which had dropped from him when he was alone in the drawing-room, 'I'll do it to-day.' Alas! the most rigid propriety could hardly have failed to discover that he was doing it now.

'Have you forgotten what we agreed on, Godfrey, when you spoke to me in the country? We agreed that we were to be cousins, and nothing more.'

'I break the agreement, Rachel, every time I see you.'

'Then don't see me.'

'Quite useless! I break the agreement every time I think of you. Oh, Rachel! how kindly you told me, only the other day, that my place in your estimation was a higher place than it had ever been yet! Am I mad to build the hopes I do on those dear words? Am I mad to dream of some future day when your heart may soften to me? Don't tell me so, if I am! Leave me my delusion, dearest! I must have *that* to cherish, and to comfort me, if I have nothing else!'

His voice trembled, and he put his white handkerchief to his eyes. Exeter Hall again! Nothing wanting to complete the parallel but the audience, the cheers, and the glass of water.

Even *her* obdurate nature was touched. I saw her lean a little nearer to him. I heard a new tone of interest in her next words.

'Are you really sure, Godfrey, that you are so fond of me as that?'

'Sure! You know what I was, Rachel. Let me tell you what I am. I have lost every interest in life, but my interest in you. A transformation has come over me which I can't account for, myself. Would you believe it? My charitable business is an unendurable nuisance to me; and when I see a Ladies' Committee now, I wish myself at the uttermost ends of the earth!'

If the annals of apostasy offer anything comparable to such a declaration as that, I can only say that the case in point is not producible from the stores of *my* reading. I thought of the Mothers' Small-Clothes. I thought of the Sunday-Sweetheart-Supervision. I thought of the other Societies, too numerous to mention, all built up on this man as on a tower of strength. I thought of the struggling Female Boards, who, so to speak, drew the breath of their business-life through the nostrils of Mr Godfrey—of that same Mr Godfrey who had just reviled our good work as a 'nuisance'—and just declared that he wished he was at the uttermost ends of the earth when he found himself in our company! My young female friends will feel encouraged to persevere, when I mention that it tried even My discipline before I could devour my own righteous indignation in silence. At the same time, it is only justice to myself to add, that I didn't lose a syllable of the conversation. Rachel was the next to speak.

'You have made your confession,' she said. 'I wonder whether it would cure you of your unhappy attachment to me, if I made mine?'

He started. I confess I started too. He thought, and I thought, that she was about to divulge the mystery of the Moonstone.

'Would you think, to look at me,' she went on, 'that I am the wretchedest girl living? It's true, Godfrey. What greater wretchedness can there be than to live degraded in your own estimation? That is my life now.'

'My dear Rachel! it's impossible you can have any reason to speak of yourself in that way!'

'How do you know I have no reason?'

'Can you ask me the question! I know it, because I know *you*. Your silence, dearest, has never lowered you in the estimation of your true friends. The disappearance of your precious birthday gift may seem strange; your unexplained connection with that event may seem stranger still——'

'Are you speaking of the Moonstone, Godfrey?'

'I certainly thought that you referred——'

'I referred to nothing of the sort. I can hear of the loss of the Moonstone, let who will speak of it, without feeling degraded in my own estimation. If the story of the Diamond ever comes to light, it will be known that I accepted a dreadful responsibility; it will be known that I involved myself in the keeping of a miserable secret—but it will be as clear as the sun at noonday that I did nothing mean! You have misunderstood me, Godfrey. It's my fault for not speaking more plainly. Cost me what it may, I will be plainer now. Suppose you were not in love with me? Suppose you were in love with some other woman?'

'Yes?'

'Suppose you discovered that woman to be utterly unworthy of you? Suppose you were quite convinced that it was a disgrace to you to waste another thought on her? Suppose the bare idea of ever marrying such a person made your face burn, only with thinking of it?'

'Yes?'

'And, suppose, in spite of all that—you couldn't tear her from your heart? Suppose the feeling she had roused in you (in the time when you believed in her) was not a feeling to be hidden? Suppose the love this wretch had inspired in you——? Oh, how can I find words to say it in! How can I make a *man* understand that a feeling which horrifies me at myself, can be a feeling that fascinates me at the same time? It's the breath of my life, Godfrey, and it's the poison that kills me—both in one! Go away! I must be out of my mind to talk as I am talking now. No! you mustn't leave me—you mustn't carry away a wrong impression. I must say what is to be said in my own defence. Mind this! *He* doesn't know—he never will know, what I have told *you*. I will never see him—I don't care what happens—I will never, never, never see him again! Don't ask me his name! Don't ask me any more! Let's change the subject. Are you doctor enough, Godfrey, to tell me why I feel as if I was stifling for want of breath? Is there a form of hysterics that bursts into words instead of tears? I dare say! What does it matter? You will get over any trouble I have caused you, easily enough now. I have dropped to my right place in your estimation, haven't I? Don't notice me! Don't pity me! For God's sake, go away!'

She turned round on a sudden, and beat her hands wildly on the back of the ottoman. Her head dropped on the cushions; and she burst out crying. Before I had time to feel shocked at this, I was horror-struck by an entirely unexpected proceeding on the part of Mr Godfrey. Will it be credited that he fell on his knees at her feet?—on *both* knees, I solemnly declare! May modesty mention that he put his arms round her next? And may reluctant admiration acknowledge that he electrified her with two words?

'Noble creature!'

No more than that! But he did it with one of the bursts which have made his fame as a public speaker. She sat, either quite thunderstruck, or quite fascinated—I don't know which—without even making an effort to put his arms back where his arms ought to have been. As for me, my sense of propriety was completely bewildered. I was so painfully uncertain whether it was my first duty to close my eyes, or to stop my ears, that I did neither. I attribute my being still able to hold the curtain in the right position for looking and listening, entirely to suppressed hysterics. In suppressed hysterics, it is admitted, even by the doctors, that one must hold something.

'Yes,' he said, with all the fascination of his evangelical voice and manner, 'you are a noble creature! A woman who can speak the truth, for the truth's own sake—a woman who will sacrifice her pride, rather than sacrifice an honest man who loves her—is the most priceless of all treasures. When such a woman marries, if her husband only wins her esteem and regard, he wins enough to ennoble his whole life. You have spoken, dearest, of your place in my estimation. Judge what that place is—when I implore you on my knees, to let the cure of your poor wounded heart be my care. Rachel! will you honour me, will you bless me, by being my wife?'

By this time I should certainly have decided on stopping my ears, if Rachel had not encouraged me to keep them open, by answering him in the first sensible words I had ever heard fall from her lips.

'Godfrey!' she said, 'you must be mad!'

'I never spoke more reasonably, dearest—in your interests, as well as in mine. Look for a moment to the future. Is your happiness to be sacrificed to a man who has never known how you feel towards him, and whom you are resolved never to see again? Is it not your duty to yourself to forget this ill-fated attachment? and is forgetfulness to be found in the life you are leading now? You have tried that life, and you are wearying of it already. Surround yourself with nobler interests than the wretched interests of the world. A heart that loves and honours you; a home whose peaceful claims and happy duties win gently on you day by day—try the consolation, Rachel, which is to be found *there*! I don't ask for your love—I will be content with your affection and regard. Let the rest be left, confidently left, to your husband's devotion, and to Time that heals even wounds as deep as yours.'

She began to yield already. Oh, what a bringing-up she must have had! Oh, how differently I should have acted in her place!

'Don't tempt me, Godfrey,' she said; 'I am wretched enough and reckless enough as it is. Don't tempt me to be more wretched and more reckless still!'

'One question, Rachel. Have you any personal objection to me?'

'I! I always liked you. After what you have just said to me, I should be insensible indeed if I didn't respect and admire you as well.'

'Do you know many wives, my dear Rachel, who respect and admire their husbands? And yet they and their husbands get on very well. How many brides go to the altar with hearts that would bear inspection by the men who take them there? And yet it doesn't end unhappily—somehow or other the nuptial establishment jogs on. The truth is, that women try marriage as a Refuge, far more numerously than they are willing to admit; and, what is more, they find that marriage has justified their confidence in it. Look at your own case once again. At your age, and with your attractions, is it possible for you to sentence yourself to a single life? Trust my knowledge of the world—nothing is less possible. It is merely a question of time. You may marry some other man, some years hence. Or you may marry the man, dearest, who is now at your feet, and who prizes your respect and admiration above the love of any other woman on the face of the earth.'

'Gently, Godfrey! you are putting something into my head which I never thought of before. You are tempting me with a new prospect, when all my other prospects are closed before me. I tell you again, I am miserable enough and desperate enough, if you say another word, to marry you on your own terms. Take the warning, and go!'

'I won't even rise from my knees, till you have said yes!'

'If I say yes you will repent, and I shall repent, when it is too late!'

'We shall both bless the day, darling, when I pressed, and when you yielded.'

'Do you feel as confidently as you speak?'

'You shall judge for yourself. I speak from what I have seen in my own family. Tell me what you think of our household at Frizinghall. Do my father and mother live unhappily together?'

'Far from it—so far as I can see.'

'When my mother was a girl, Rachel (it is no secret in the family), she had loved as you love—she had given her heart to a man who was unworthy of her. She married my father, respecting him, admiring him, but nothing more. Your own eyes have seen the result. Is there no encouragement in it for you and for me?'[1]

'You won't hurry me, Godfrey?'

'My time shall be yours.'

'You won't ask me for more than I can give?'

'My angel! I only ask you to give me yourself.'

'Take me!'

In those two words she accepted him!

He had another burst—a burst of unholy rapture this time. He drew her nearer and nearer to him till her face touched his; and then——No! I really cannot prevail upon myself to carry this shocking disclosure any farther. Let me only say, that I tried to close my eyes before it happened, and that I was just one moment too late. I had calculated, you see, on her resisting, She submitted. To every right-feeling person of my own sex, volumes could say no more.

Even my innocence in such matters began to see its way to the end of the interview now. They understood each other so thoroughly by this time, that I fully expected to see them walk off together, arm in arm, to be married. There appeared, however, judging by Mr Godfrey's next words, to be one more trifling formality which it was necessary to observe. He seated himself—unforbidden this time—on the ottoman by her side. 'Shall I speak to your dear mother?' he asked. 'Or will you?'

She declined both alternatives.

'Let my mother hear nothing from either of us, until she is better. I wish it to be kept a secret for the present, Godfrey. Go now, and come back this evening. We have been here alone together quite long enough.'

[1] See Betteredge's Narrative, chapter viii.

She rose, and in rising, looked for the first time towards the little room in which my martyrdom was going on.

'Who has drawn those curtains?' she exclaimed. 'The room is close enough, as it is, without keeping the air out of it in that way.'

She advanced to the curtains. At the moment when she laid her hand on them—at the moment when the discovery of me appeared to be quite inevitable—the voice of the fresh-coloured young footman, on the stairs, suddenly suspended any further proceedings on her side or on mine. It was unmistakably the voice of a man in great alarm.

'Miss Rachel!' he called out, 'where are you, Miss Rachel?'

She sprang back from the curtains, and ran to the door.

The footman came just inside the room. His ruddy colour was all gone. He said, 'Please to come downstairs, Miss! My lady has fainted, and we can't bring her to again.'

In a moment more I was alone, and free to go downstairs in my turn, quite unobserved.

Mr Godfrey passed me in the hall, hurrying out, to fetch the doctor. 'Go in, and help them!' he said, pointing to the room. I found Rachel on her knees by the sofa, with her mother's head on her bosom. One look at my aunt's face (knowing what I knew) was enough to warn me of the dreadful truth. I kept my thoughts to myself till the doctor came in. It was not long before he arrived. He began by sending Rachel out of the room—and then he told the rest of us that Lady Verinder was no more. Serious persons, in search of proofs of hardened scepticism, may be interested in hearing that he showed no signs of remorse when he looked at Me.

At a later hour I peeped into the breakfast-room, and the library. My aunt had died without opening one of the letters which I had addressed to her. I was so shocked at this, that it never occurred to me, until some days afterwards, that she had also died without giving me my little legacy.

CHAPTER VI

(1.) 'MISS CLACK presents her compliments to Mr Franklin Blake; and, in sending him the fifth chapter of her humble narrative, begs to say that she feels quite unequal to enlarge as she could wish on an event so awful, under the circumstances, as Lady Verinder's death. She has, therefore, attached to her own manuscript, copious Extracts from precious publications in her possession, all bearing on this terrible subject. And may those Extracts (Miss Clack fervently hopes) sound as the blast of a trumpet in the ears of her respected kinsman, Mr Franklin Blake.'

(2.) 'Mr Franklin Blake presents his compliments to Miss Clack, and begs to thank her for the fifth chapter of her narrative. In returning the extracts sent with it, he will refrain from mentioning any personal objection which he may entertain to this species of literature, and will merely say that the proposed additions to the manuscript are not necessary to the fulfilment of the purpose that he has in view.'

(3.) 'Miss Clack begs to acknowledge the return of her Extracts. She affectionately reminds Mr Franklin Blake that she is a Christian, and that it is, therefore, quite impossible for him to offend her. Miss C. persists in feeling the deepest interest in Mr Blake, and pledges herself, on the first occasion when sickness may lay him low, to offer him the use of her Extracts for the second time. In the meanwhile she would be glad to know, before beginning the final chapters of her narrative, whether she may be permitted to make her humble contribution complete, by availing herself of the light which later discoveries have thrown on the mystery of the Moonstone.'

(4.) 'Mr Franklin Blake is sorry to disappoint Miss Clack. He can only repeat the instructions which he had the honour of giving her when she began her narrative. She is requested to limit herself to her own individual experience of persons and events, as recorded in her diary. Later discoveries she will be good enough to leave to the pens of those persons who can write in the capacity of actual witnesses.'

(5.) 'Miss Clack is extremely sorry to trouble Mr Franklin Blake with another letter. Her Extracts have been returned, and the expression of her matured views on the subject of the Moonstone has been forbidden. Miss Clack is painfully conscious that she ought (in the worldly phrase) to feel herself put down. But, no—Miss C. has learnt Perserverance in the School of Adversity. Her object in writing is to know whether Mr Blake (who prohibits everything else) prohibits the appearance of the present correspondence in Miss Clack's narrative? Some explanation of the position in which Mr Blake's interference has placed her as an authoress, seems due on the ground of common justice. And Miss Clack, on her side, is most anxious that her letters should be produced to speak for themselves.'

(6.) 'Mr Franklin Blake agrees to Miss Clack's proposal, on the understanding that she will kindly consider this intimation of his consent as closing the correspondence between them.'

(7.) 'Miss Clack feels it an act of Christian duty (before the correspondence closes) to inform Mr Franklin Blake that his last letter—evidently intended to offend her—has not succeeded in accomplishing the object of the writer. She affectionately requests Mr Blake to retire to the privacy of his own room, and to consider with himself whether the training which can thus elevate a poor weak woman above the reach of insult, be not worthy of greater admiration than he is now disposed to feel for it. On being favoured with an intimation to that effect, Miss C. solemnly pledges herself to send back the complete series of her Extracts to Mr Franklin Blake.'

[To this letter no answer was received. Comment is needless.

(Signed)   DRUSILLA CLACK.]

CHAPTER VII

THE foregoing correspondence will sufficiently explain why no choice is left to me but to pass over Lady Verinder's death with the simple announcement of the fact which ends my fifth chapter.

Keeping myself for the future strictly within the limits of my own personal experience, I have next to relate that a month elapsed from the time of my aunt's decease before Rachel Verinder and I met again. That meeting was the occasion of my spending a few days under the same roof with her. In the course of my visit, something happened, relating to her marriage-engagement with Mr Godfrey Ablewhite, which is important enough to require special notice in these pages. When this last of many painful family circumstances has been disclosed, my task will be completed; for I shall then have told all that I know, as an actual (and most unwilling) witness of events.

My aunt's remains were removed from London, and were buried in the little cemetery attached to the church in her own park. I was invited to the funeral with the rest of the family. But it was impossible (with my religious views) to rouse myself in a few days only from the shock which this death had caused me. I was informed, moreover, that the rector of Frizinghall was to read the service. Having myself in past times seen this clerical castaway making one of the players at Lady Verinder's whist-table, I doubt, even if I had been fit to travel, whether I should have felt justified in attending the ceremony.

Lady Verinder's death left her daughter under the care of her brother-in-law, Mr Ablewhite the elder. He was appointed guardian by the will, until his niece married, or came of age. Under these circumstances, Mr Godfrey informed his father, I suppose, of the new relation in which he stood towards Rachel. At any rate, in ten days from my aunt's death, the secret of the marriage engagement was no secret at all within the circle of the family, and the grand question for Mr Ablewhite senior—another confirmed cast-away!—was how to make himself and his authority most agreeable to the wealthy young lady who was going to marry his son.

Rachel gave him some trouble at the outset, about the choice of a place in which she could be prevailed upon to reside. The house in Montagu Square was associated with the calamity of her mother's death. The house in Yorkshire was associated with the scandalous affair of the lost Moonstone.

Her guardian's own residence at Frizinghall was open to neither of these objections. But Rachel's presence in it, after her recent bereavement, operated as a check on the gaieties of her cousins, the Miss Ablewhites—and she herself requested that her visit might be deferred to a more favourable opportunity. It ended in a proposal, emanating from old Mr Ablewhite, to try a furnished house at Brighton. His wife, an invalid daughter, and Rachel were to inhabit it together, and were to expect him to join them later in the season. They would see no society but a few old friends, and they would have his son Godfrey, travelling backwards and forwards by the London train, always at their disposal.

I describe this aimless flitting about from one place of residence to another—this insatiate restlessness of body and appalling stagnation of soul—merely with the view to arriving at results. The event which (under Providence) proved to be the means of bringing Rachel Verinder and myself together again, was no other than the hiring of the house at Brighton.

My Aunt Ablewhite is a large, silent, fair-complexioned woman, with one noteworthy point in her character. From the hour of her birth she has never been known to do anything for herself. She has gone through life, accepting everybody's help, and adopting everybody's opinions. A more hopeless person, in a spiritual point of view, I have never met with—there is absolutely, in this perplexing case, no obstructive material to work upon. Aunt Ablewhite would listen to the Grand Lama of Thibet exactly as she listens to Me, and would reflect his views quite as readily as she reflects mine. She found the furnished house at Brighton by stopping at an hotel in London, composing herself on a sofa, and sending for her son. She discovered the necessary servants by breakfasting in bed one morning (still at the hotel), and giving her maid a holiday on condition that the girl 'would begin enjoying herself by fetching Miss Clack.' I found her placidly fanning herself in her dressing-gown at eleven o'clock. 'Drusilla, dear, I want some servants. You are so clever—please get them for me.' I looked round the untidy room. The church-bells were going for a week-day service; they suggested a word of affectionate remonstrance on my part. 'Oh, aunt!' I said sadly. 'Is *this* worthy of a Christian Englishwoman? Is the passage from time to eternity to be made in *this* manner?' My aunt answered, 'I'll put on my gown, Drusilla, if you will be kind enough to help me.' What was to be said after that? I have done wonders with murderesses—I have never advanced an inch with Aunt Ablewhite. 'Where is the list,' I asked, 'of the servants whom you require?' My aunt shook her head; she hadn't even energy enough to keep the list. 'Rachel has got it, dear,' she said, 'in the next room.' I went into the next room, and so saw Rachel again, for the first time since we had parted in Montagu Square.

She looked pitiably small and thin in her deep mourning. If I attached any serious importance to such a perishable trifle as personal appearance, I might be inclined to add that hers was one of those unfortunate complexions which always suffer when not relieved by a border of white next the skin. But what are our complexions and our looks? Hindrances and pitfalls, dear girls, which beset us on our way to higher things! Greatly to my surprise, Rachel rose when I entered the room, and came forward to meet me with outstretched hand.

'I am glad to see you,' she said. 'Drusilla, I have been in the habit of speaking very foolishly and very rudely to you, on former occasions. I beg your pardon. I hope you will forgive me.'

My face, I suppose, betrayed the astonishment I felt at this. She coloured up for a moment, and then proceeded to explain herself.

'In my poor mother's lifetime,' she went on, 'her friends were not always my friends, too. Now I have lost her, my heart turns for comfort to the people she liked. She liked you. Try to be friends with me, Drusilla, if you can.'

To any rightly-constituted mind, the motive thus acknowledged was simply shocking. Here in Christian England was a young woman in a state of bereavement, with so little idea of where to look for true comfort, that she actually expected to find it among her mother's friends! Here was a relative of mine, awakened to a sense of her shortcomings towards others, under the influence, not of conviction and duty, but of sentiment and impulse! Most deplorable to think of—but, still, suggestive of something hopeful, to a person of my experience in plying the good work. There could be no harm, I thought, in ascertaining the extent of the change which the loss of her mother had wrought in Rachel's character. I decided, as a useful test, to probe her on the subject of her marriage engagement to Mr Godfrey Ablewhite.

Having first met her advances with all possible cordiality, I sat by her on the sofa, at her own request. We discussed family affairs and future plans—always excepting that one future plan which was to end in her marriage. Try as I might to turn the conversation that way, she resolutely declined to take the hint. Any open reference to the question, on my part, would have been premature at this early stage of our reconciliation. Besides, I had discovered all I wanted to know. She was no longer the reckless, defiant creature whom I had heard and seen, on the occasion of my martyrdom in Montagu Square. This was, of itself, enough to encourage me to take her future conversion in hand—beginning with a few words of earnest warning directed against the hasty formation of the marriage tie, and so getting on to higher things. Looking at her, now, with this new interest—and calling to mind the headlong suddenness with which she had met Mr Godfrey's matrimonial views—I felt the solemn duty of interfering, with a fervour which assured me that I should achieve no common results. Rapidity of proceeding was, as I believed, of importance in this case. I went back at once to the question of the servants wanted for the furnished house.

'Where is the list, dear?'

Rachel produced it.

'Cook, kitchen-maid, housemaid, and footman,' I read. 'My dear Rachel, these servants are only wanted for a term—the term during which your guardian has taken the house. We shall have great difficulty in finding persons of character and capacity to accept a temporary engagement of that sort, if we try in London. Has the house in Brighton been found yet?'

'Yes. Godfrey has taken it; and persons in the house wanted him to hire them as servants. He thought they would hardly do for us, and came back having settled nothing.'

'And you have no experience yourself in these matters, Rachel?'

'None whatever.'

'And Aunt Ablewhite won't exert herself?'

'No, poor dear. Don't blame her, Drusilla. I think she is the only really happy woman I have ever met with.'

'There are degrees in happiness, darling. We must have a little talk, some day, on that subject. In the meantime I will undertake to meet the difficulty about the servants. Your aunt will write a letter to the people of the house——'

'She will sign a letter, if I write it for her, which comes to the same thing.'

'Quite the same thing. I shall get the letter, and I will go to Brighton to-morrow.'

'How extremely kind of you! We will join you as soon as you are ready for us. And you will stay, I hope, as *my* guest. Brighton is so lively; you are sure to enjoy it.'

In those words the invitation was given, and the glorious prospect of interference was opened before me.

It was then the middle of the week. By Saturday afternoon the house was ready for them. In that short interval I had sifted, not the characters only, but the religious views as well, of all the disengaged servants who applied to me, and had succeeded in making a selection which my conscience approved. I also discovered, and called on, two serious friends of mine, residents in the town, to whom I knew I could confide the pious object which had brought me to Brighton. One of them—a clerical friend—kindly helped me to take sittings for our little party in the church in which he himself ministered. The other—a single lady, like myself—placed the resources of her library (composed throughout of precious publications) entirely at my disposal. I borrowed half-a-dozen works, all carefully chosen with a view to Rachel. When these had been judiciously distributed in the various rooms she would be likely to occupy, I considered that my preparations were complete. Sound doctrine in the servants who waited on her; sound doctrine in the minister who preached to her; sound doctrine in the books that lay on her table—such was the treble welcome which my zeal had prepared for the motherless girl! A heavenly composure filled my mind, on that Saturday afternoon, as I sat at the window waiting the arrival of my relatives. The giddy throng passed and repassed before my eyes. Alas! how many of them felt my exquisite sense of duty done? An awful question. Let us not pursue it.

Between six and seven the travellers arrived. To my indescribable surprise, they were escorted, not by Mr Godfrey (as I had anticipated), but by the lawyer, Mr Bruff.

'How do you do, Miss Clack?' he said. 'I mean to stay this time.'

That reference to the occasion on which I had obliged him to postpone his business to mine, when we were both visiting in Montagu Square, satisfied me that the old worldling had come to Brighton with some object of his own in view. I had prepared quite a little Paradise for my beloved Rachel—and here was the Serpent already!

'Godfrey was very much vexed, Drusilla, not to be able to come with us,' said my Aunt Ablewhite. 'There was something in the way which kept him in town. Mr Bruff volunteered to take his place, and make a holiday of it till Monday morning. By-the-by, Mr Bruff, I'm ordered to take exercise, and I don't like it. That,' added Aunt Ablewhite, pointing out of window to an invalid going by in a chair on wheels, drawn by a man, 'is my idea of exercise. If it's air you want, you get it in your chair. And if it's fatigue you want, I am sure it's fatiguing enough to look at the man.'

Rachel stood silent, at a window by herself, with her eyes fixed on the sea.

'Tired, love?' I inquired.

'No. Only a little out of spirits,' she answered. 'I have often seen the sea, on our Yorkshire coast, with that light on it. And I was thinking, Drusilla, of the days that can never come again.'

Mr Bruff remained to dinner, and stayed through the evening. The more I saw of him, the more certain I felt that he had some private end to serve in coming to Brighton. I watched him carefully. He maintained the same appearance of ease, and talked the same godless gossip, hour after hour, until it was time to take leave. As he shook hands with Rachel, I caught his hard and cunning eye resting on her for a moment with a peculiar interest and attention. She was plainly concerned in the object that he had in view. He said nothing out of the common to her or to anyone on leaving. He invited himself to luncheon the next day, and then he went away to his hotel.

It was impossible the next morning to get my Aunt Ablewhite out of her dressing-gown in time for church. Her invalid daughter (suffering from nothing, in my opinion, but incurable laziness, inherited from her mother) announced that she meant to remain in bed for the day. Rachel and I went alone together to church. A magnificent sermon was preached by my gifted friend on the heathen indifference of the world to the sinfulness of little sins. For more than an hour his eloquence (assisted by his glorious voice) thundered through the sacred edifice. I said to Rachel, when we came out, 'Has it found its way to your heart, dear?' And she answered, 'No; it has only made my head ache.' This might have been discouraging to some people; but, once embarked on a career of manifest usefulness, nothing discourages Me.

We found Aunt Ablewhite and Mr Bruff at luncheon. When Rachel declined eating anything, and gave as a reason for it that she was suffering from a headache, the lawyer's cunning instantly saw, and seized, the chance that she had given him.

'There is only one remedy for a headache,' said this horrible old man. 'A walk, Miss Rachel, is the thing to cure you. I am entirely at your service, if you will honour me by accepting my arm.'

'With the greatest pleasure. A walk is the very thing I was longing for.'

'It's past two,' I gently suggested. 'And the afternoon service, Rachel, begins at three.'

'How can you expect me to go to church again,' she asked, petulantly, 'with such a headache as mine?'

Mr Bruff officiously opened the door for her. In another minute more they were both out of the house. I don't know when I have felt the solemn duty of interfering so strongly as I felt it at that moment. But what was to be done? Nothing was to be done but to interfere at the first opportunity, later in the day.

On my return from the afternoon service I found that they had just got back. One look at them told me that the lawyer had said what he wanted to say. I had never before seen Rachel so silent and so thoughtful. I had never before seen Mr Bruff pay her such devoted attention, and look at her with such marked respect. He had (or pretended that he had) an engagement to dinner that day—and he took an early leave of us all; intending to go back to London by the first train the next morning.

'Are you sure of your own resolution?' he said to Rachel at the door.

'Quite sure,' she answered—and so they parted.

The moment his back was turned, Rachel withdrew to her own room. She never appeared at dinner. Her maid (the person with the cap-ribbons) was sent downstairs to announce that her headache had returned. I ran up to her and made all sorts of sisterly offers through the door. It was locked, and she kept it locked. Plenty of obstructive material to work on here! I felt greatly cheered and stimulated by her locking the door.

When her cup of tea went up to her the next morning, I followed it in. I sat by her bedside and said a few earnest words. She listened with languid civility. I noticed my serious friend's precious publications huddled together on a table in a corner. Had she chanced to look into them?—I asked. Yes—and they had not interested her. Would she allow me to read a few passages of the deepest interest, which had probably escaped her eye? No, not now—she had other things to think of. She gave these answers, with her attention apparently absorbed in folding and refolding the frilling of her night-gown. It was plainly necessary to rouse her by some reference to those worldly interests which she still had at heart.

'Do you know, love,' I said, 'I had an odd fancy, yesterday, about Mr Bruff? I thought, when I saw you after your walk with him, that he had been telling you some bad news.'

Her fingers dropped from the frilling of her night-gown, and her fierce black eyes flashed at me.

'Quite the contrary!' she said. 'It was news I was interested in hearing— and I am deeply indebted to Mr Bruff for telling me of it.'

'Yes?' I said, in a tone of gentle interest.

Her fingers went back to the frilling, and she turned her head sullenly away from me. I had been met in this manner, in the course of plying the good work, hundreds of times. She merely stimulated me to try again. In my dauntless zeal for her welfare, I ran the great risk, and openly alluded to her marriage engagement.

'News you were interested in hearing?' I repeated. 'I suppose, my dear Rachel, that must be news of Mr Godfrey Ablewhite?'

She started up in the bed, and turned deadly pale. It was evidently on the tip of her tongue to retort on me with the unbridled insolence of former times. She checked herself—laid her head back on the pillow—considered a minute—and then answered in these remarkable words:

'*I shall never marry Mr Godfrey Ablewhite.*'

It was my turn to start at that.

'What can you possibly mean?' I exclaimed. 'The marriage is considered by the whole family as a settled thing!'

'Mr Godfrey Ablewhite is expected here to-day,' she said, doggedly. 'Wait till he comes—and you will see.'

'But, my dear Rachel——'

She rang the bell at the head of her bed. The person with the cap-ribbons appeared.

'Penelope! my bath.'

Let me give her her due. In the state of my feelings at that moment, I do sincerely believe that she had hit on the only possible way of forcing me to leave the room.

By the mere wordly mind my position towards Rachel might have been viewed as presenting difficulties of no ordinary kind. I had reckoned on leading her to higher things by means of a little earnest exhortation on the subject of her marriage. And now, if she was to be believed, no such event as her marriage was to take place at all. But ah, my friends! a working Christian of my experience (with an evangelising prospect before her) takes broader views than these. Supposing Rachel really broke off the marriage, on which the Ablewhites, father and son, counted as a settled thing, what would be the result? It could only end, if she held firm, in an exchanging of hard words and bitter accusations on both sides. And what would be the effect on Rachel when the stormy interview was over? A salutary moral depression would be the effect. Her pride would be exhausted, her stubbornness would be exhausted, by the resolute resistance which it was in her character to make under the circumstances. She would turn for sympathy to the nearest person who had sympathy to offer. And I was that nearest person—brimful of comfort, charged to overflowing with seasonable and reviving words. Never had the evangelising prospect looked brighter, to *my* eyes, than it looked now.

She came down to breakfast, but she ate nothing, and hardly uttered a word.

After breakfast she wandered listlessly from room to room—then suddenly roused herself, and opened the piano. The music she selected to play was of the most scandalously profane sort, associated with performances on the stage which it curdles one's blood to think of. It would have been premature to interfere with her at such a time as this. I privately ascertained the hour at which Mr Godfrey Ablewhite was expected, and then I escaped the music by leaving the house.

Being out alone, I took the opportunity of calling upon my two resident friends. It was an indescribable luxury to find myself indulging in earnest conversation with serious persons. Infinitely encouraged and refreshed, I turned my steps back again to the house, in excellent time to await the arrival of our expected visitor. I entered the dining-room, always empty at that hour of the day, and found myself face to face with Mr Godfrey Ablewhite!

He made no attempt to fly the place. Quite the contrary. He advanced to meet me with the utmost eagerness.

'Dear Miss Clack, I have been only waiting to see *you!* Chance set me free of my London engagements to-day sooner than I had expected, and I have got here, in consequence, earlier than my appointed time.'

Not the slightest embarrassment encumbered his explanation, though this was his first meeting with me after the scene in Montagu Square. He was not aware, it is true, of my having been a witness of that scene. But he knew, on the other hand, that my attendances at the Mothers' Small-Clothes, and my relations with friends attached to other charities, must have informed me of his shameless neglect of his Ladies and of his Poor. And yet there he was before me, in full possession of his charming voice and his irresistible smile!

'Have you seen Rachel yet?' I asked.

He sighed gently, and took me by the hand. I should certainly have snatched my hand away, if the manner in which he gave his answer had not paralysed me with astonishment.

'I have seen Rachel,' he said with perfect tranquillity. 'You are aware, dear friend, that she was engaged to me? Well, she has taken a sudden resolution to break the engagement. Reflection has convinced her that she will best consult her welfare and mine by retracting a rash promise, and leaving me free to make some happier choice elsewhere. That is the only reason she will give, and the only answer she will make to every question that I can ask of her.'

'What have you done on your side?' I inquired. 'Have you submitted.'

'Yes,' he said with the most unruffled composure, 'I have submitted.'

His conduct, under the circumstances, was so utterly inconceivable, that I stood bewildered with my hand in his. It is a piece of rudeness to stare at anybody, and it is an act of indelicacy to stare at a gentleman. I committed both those improprieties. And I said, as if in a dream, 'What does it mean?'

'Permit me to tell you,' he replied. 'And suppose we sit down?'

He led me to a chair. I have an indistinct remembrance that he was very affectionate. I don't think he put his arm round my waist to support me—but I am not sure. I was quite helpless, and his ways with ladies were very endearing. At any rate, we sat down. I can answer for that, if I can answer for nothing more.

CHAPTER VIII

'I HAVE lost a beautiful girl, an excellent social position, and a handsome income,' Mr Godfrey began; 'and I have submitted to it without a struggle. What can be the motive for such extraordinary conduct as that? My precious friend, there is no motive.'

'No motive?' I repeated.

'Let me appeal, my dear Miss Clack, to your experience of children,' he went on. 'A child pursues a certain course of conduct. You are greatly struck by it, and you attempt to get at the motive. The dear little thing is incapable of telling you its motive. You might as well ask the grass why it grows, or the birds why they sing. Well! in this matter, I am like the dear little thing—like the grass—like the birds. I don't know why I made a proposal of marriage to Miss Verinder. I don't know why I have shamefully neglected my dear Ladies. I don't know why I have apostatised from the Mothers' Small-Clothes. You say to the child, Why have you been naughty? And the little angel puts its finger into its mouth, and doesn't know. My case exactly, Miss Clack! I couldn't confess it to anybody else. I feel impelled to confess it to *you!*'

I began to recover myself. A mental problem was involved here. I am deeply interested in mental problems—and I am not, it is thought, without some skill in solving them.

'Best of friends, exert your intellect, and help me,' he proceeded. 'Tell me—why does a time come when these matrimonial proceedings of mine begin to look like something done in a dream? Why does it suddenly occur to me that my true happiness is in helping my dear Ladies, in going my modest round of useful work, in saying my few earnest words when called on by my Chairman? What do I want with a position? I have got a position. What do I want with an income? I can pay for my bread and cheese, and my nice little lodging, and my two coats a year. What do I want with Miss Verinder? She has told me with her own lips (this, dear lady, is between ourselves) that she loves another man, and that her only idea in marrying me is to try and put that other man out of her head. What a horrid union is this! Oh, dear me, what a horrid union is this! Such are my reflections, Miss Clack, on my way to Brighton. I approach Rachel with the feeling of a criminal who is going to receive his sentence. When I find that she has changed her mind too—when I hear her propose to break the engagement—I experience (there is no sort of doubt about it) a most overpowering sense of relief. A month ago I was pressing her rapturously to my bosom. An hour ago, the happiness of knowing that I shall never press her again, intoxicates me like strong liquor. The thing seems impossible—the thing can't be. And yet there are the facts, as I had the honour of stating them when we first sat down together in these two chairs. I have lost a beautiful girl, an excellent social position, and a handsome income; and I have submitted to it without a struggle. Can *you* account for it, dear friend? It's quite beyond *me*.'

His magnificent head sank on his breast, and he gave up his own mental problem in despair.

I was deeply touched. The case (if I may speak as a spiritual physician) was now quite plain to me. It is no uncommon event, in the experience of us all, to see the possessors of exalted ability occasionally humbled to the level of the most poorly-gifted people about them. The object, no doubt, in the wise economy of Providence, is to remind greatness that it is mortal, and that the power which has conferred it can also take it away. It was now—to my mind—easy to discern one of these salutary humiliations in the deplorable proceedings on dear Mr Godfrey's part, of which I had been the unseen witness. And it was equally easy to recognise the welcome reappearance of his own finer nature in the horror with which he recoiled from the idea of a marriage with Rachel, and in the charming eagerness which he showed to return to his Ladies and his Poor.

I put this view before him in a few simple and sisterly words. His joy was beautiful to see. He compared himself, as I went on, to a lost man emerging from the darkness into the light. When I answered for a loving reception of him at the Mothers' Small-Clothes, the grateful heart of our Christian Hero overflowed. He pressed my hands alternately to his lips. Overwhelmed by the exquisite triumph of having got him back among us, I let him do what he liked with my hands. I closed my eyes. I felt my head, in an ecstasy of spiritual self-forgetfulness, sinking on his shoulder. In a moment more I should certainly have swooned away in his arms, but for an interruption from the outer world, which brought me to myself again. A horrid rattling of knives and forks sounded outside the door, and the footman came in to lay the table for luncheon.

Mr Godfrey started up, and looked at the clock on the mantelpiece.

'How time flies with *you!*' he exclaimed. 'I shall barely catch the train.'

I ventured on asking why he was in such a hurry to get back to town. His answer reminded me of family difficulties that were still to be reconciled, and of family disagreements that were yet to come.

'I have heard from my father,' he said. 'Business obliges him to leave Frizinghall for London to-day, and he proposes coming on here, either this evening or to-morrow. I must tell him what has happened between Rachel and me. His heart is set on our marriage—there will be great difficulty, I fear, in reconciling him to the breaking-off of the engagement. I must stop him, for all our sakes, from coming here till he *is* reconciled. Best and dearest of friends, we shall meet again!'

With those words he hurried out. In equal haste on my side, I ran upstairs to compose myself in my own room before meeting Aunt Ablewhite and Rachel at the luncheon-table.

I am well aware—to dwell for a moment yet on the subject of Mr Godfrey—that the all-profaning opinion of the world has charged him with having his own private reasons for releasing Rachel from her engagement, at the first opportunity she gave him. It has also reached my ears, that his anxiety to recover his place in my estimation has been attributed, in certain quarters, to a mercenary eagerness to make his peace (through me) with a venerable committee-woman at the Mothers' Small-Clothes, abundantly blessed with the goods of this world, and a beloved and intimate friend of my own. I only notice these odious slanders for the sake of declaring that they never had a moment's influence on my mind. In obedience to my instructions, I have exhibited the fluctuations in my opinion of our Christian Hero, exactly as I find them recorded in my diary. In justice to myself, let me here add that, once reinstated in his place in my estimation, my gifted friend never lost that place again. I write with the tears in my eyes, burning to say more. But no—I am cruelly limited to my actual experience of persons and things. In less than a month from the time of which I am now writing, events in the money-market (which diminished even *my* miserable little income) forced me into foreign exile, and left me with nothing but a loving remembrance of Mr Godfrey which the slander of the world has assailed, and assailed in vain.

Let me dry my eyes, and return to my narrative.

I went downstairs to luncheon, naturally anxious to see how Rachel was affected by her release from her marriage engagement.

It appeared to me—but I own I am a poor authority in such matters—that the recovery of her freedom had set her thinking again of that other man whom she loved, and that she was furious with herself for not being able to control a revulsion of feeling of which she was secretly ashamed. Who was the man? I had my suspicions—but it was needless to waste time in idle speculation. When I had converted her, she would, as a matter of course, have no concealments from Me. I should hear all about the man; I should hear all about the Moonstone. If I had had no higher object in stirring her up to a sense of spiritual things, the motive of relieving her mind of its guilty secrets would have been enough of itself to encourage me to go on.

Aunt Ablewhite took her exercise in the afternoon in an invalid chair. Rachel accompanied her. 'I wish I could drag the chair,' she broke out, recklessly. 'I wish I could fatigue myself till I was ready to drop.'

She was in the same humour in the evening. I discovered in one of my friend's precious publications—the Life, Letters, and Labours of Miss Jane Ann Stamper, forty-fourth edition—passages which bore with a marvellous appropriateness on Rachel's present position. Upon my proposing to read them, she went to the piano. Conceive how little she must have known of serious people, if she supposed that my patience was to be exhausted in that way! I kept Miss Jane Ann Stamper by me, and waited for events with the most unfaltering trust in the future.

Old Mr Ablewhite never made his appearance that night. But I knew the importance which his worldly greed attached to his son's marriage with Miss Verinder—and I felt a positive conviction (do what Mr Godfrey might to prevent it) that we should see him the next day. With his interference in the matter, the storm on which I had counted would certainly come, and the salutary exhaustion of Rachel's resisting powers would as certainly follow. I am not ignorant that old Mr Ablewhite has the reputation generally (especially among his inferiors) of being a remarkably good-natured man. According to my observation of him, he deserves his reputation as long as he has his own way, and not a moment longer.

The next day, exactly as I had foreseen, Aunt Ablewhite was as near to being astonished as her nature would permit, by the sudden appearance of her husband. He had barely been a minute in the house, before he was followed, to *my* astonishment this time, by an unexpected complication, in the shape of Mr Bruff.

I never remember feeling the presence of the lawyer to be more unwelcome than I felt it at that moment. He looked ready for anything in the way of an obstructive proceeding—capable even of keeping the peace, with Rachel for one of the combatants!

'This is a pleasant surprise, sir,' said Mr Ablewhite, addressing himself with his deceptive cordiality to Mr Bruff. 'When I left your office yesterday, I didn't expect to have the honour of seeing you at Brighton to-day.'

'I turned over our conversation in my mind, after you had gone,' replied Mr Bruff. 'And it occurred to me that I might perhaps be of some use on this occasion. I was just in time to catch the train, and I had no opportunity of discovering the carriage in which you were travelling.'

Having given that explanation, he seated himself by Rachel. I retired modestly to a corner—with Miss Jane Ann Stamper on my lap, in case of emergency. My aunt sat at the window; placidly fanning herself as usual. Mr Ablewhite stood up in the middle of the room, with his bald head much pinker than I had ever seen it yet, and addressed himself in the most affectionate manner to his niece.

'Rachel, my dear,' he said, 'I have heard some very extraordinary news from Godfrey. And I am here to inquire about it. You have a sitting-room of your own in this house. Will you honour me by showing me the way to it?'

Rachel never moved. Whether she was determined to bring matters to a crisis, or whether she was prompted by some private sign from Mr Bruff, is more than I can tell. She declined doing old Mr Ablewhite the honour of conducting him into her sitting-room.

'Whatever you wish to say to me,' she answered, 'can be said here—in the presence of my relatives, and in the presence' (she looked at Mr Bruff) 'of my mother's trusted old friend.'

'Just as you please, my dear,' said the amiable Mr Ablewhite. He took a chair. The rest of them looked at his face—as if they expected it, after seventy years of worldly training, to speak the truth. *I* looked at the top of his bald head; having noticed on other occasions that the temper which was really in him had a habit of registering itself *there*.

'Some weeks ago,' pursued the old gentleman, 'my son informed me that Miss Verinder had done him the honour to engage herself to marry him. Is it possible, Rachel, that he can have misinterpreted—or presumed upon—what you really said to him?'

'Certainly not,' she replied. 'I did engage myself to marry him.'

'Very frankly answered!' said Mr Ablewhite. 'And most satisfactory, my dear, so far. In respect to what happened some weeks since, Godfrey has made no mistake. The error is evidently in what he told me yesterday. I begin to see it now. You and he have had a lovers' quarrel—and my foolish son has interpreted it seriously. Ah! I should have known better than that at his age.'

The fallen nature in Rachel—the mother Eve, so to speak—began to chafe at this.

'Pray let us understand each other, Mr Ablewhite,' she said. 'Nothing in the least like a quarrel took place yesterday between your son and me. If he told you that I proposed breaking off our marriage engagement, and that he agreed on his side—he told you the truth.'

The self-registering thermometer at the top of Mr Ablewhite's bald head began to indicate a rise of temper. His face was more amiable than ever—but *there* was the pink at the top of his face, a shade deeper already!

'Come, come, my dear!' he said, in his most soothing manner, 'now don't be angry, and don't be hard on poor Godfrey! He has evidently said some unfortunate thing. He was always clumsy from a child—but he means well, Rachel, he means well!'

'Mr Ablewhite, I have either expressed myself very badly, or you are purposely mistaking me. Once for all, it is a settled thing between your son and myself that we remain, for the rest of our lives, cousins and nothing more. Is that plain enough?'

The tone in which she said those words made it impossible, even for old Mr Ablewhite, to mistake her any longer. His thermometer went up another degree, and his voice when he next spoke, ceased to be the voice which is appropriate to a notoriously good-natured man.

'I am to understand, then,' he said, 'that your marriage engagement is broken off?'

'You are to understand that, Mr Ablewhite, if you please.'

'I am also to take it as a matter of fact that the proposal to withdraw from the engagement came, in the first instance, from *you?*'

'It came, in the first instance, from me. And it met, as I have told you, with your son's consent and approval.'

The thermometer went up to the top of the register. I mean, the pink changed suddenly to scarlet.

'My son is a mean-spirited hound!' cried this furious old worldling. 'In justice to myself as his father—not in justice to *him*—I beg to ask you, Miss Verinder, what complaint you have to make of Mr Godfrey Ablewhite?'

Here Mr Bruff interfered for the first time.

'You are not bound to answer that question,' he said to Rachel.

Old Mr Ablewhite fastened on him instantly.

'Don't forget, sir,' he said, 'that you are a self-invited guest here. Your interference would have come with a better grace if you had waited until it was asked for.'

Mr Bruff took no notice. The smooth varnish on *his* wicked old face never cracked. Rachel thanked him for the advice he had given to her, and then turned to old Mr Ablewhite—preserving her composure in a manner which (having regard to her age and her sex) was simply awful to see.

'Your son put the same question to me which you have just asked,' she said. 'I had only one answer for him, and I have only one answer for you. I proposed that we should release each other, because reflection had convinced me that I should best consult his welfare and mine by retracting a rash promise, and leaving him free to make his choice elsewhere.'

'What has my son done?' persisted Mr Ablewhite. 'I have a right to know that. What has my son done?'

She persisted just as obstinately on her side.

'You have had the only explanation which I think it necessary to give to you, or to him,' she answered.

'In plain English, it's your sovereign will and pleasure, Miss Verinder, to jilt my son?'

Rachel was silent for a moment. Sitting close behind her, I heard her sigh. Mr Bruff took her hand, and gave it a little squeeze. She recovered herself, and answered Mr Ablewhite as boldly as ever.

'I have exposed myself to worse misconstruction than that,' she said. 'And I have borne it patiently. The time has gone by, when you could mortify me by calling me a jilt.'

She spoke with a bitterness of tone which satisfied me that the scandal of the Moonstone had been in some way recalled to her mind. 'I have no more to say,' she added, wearily, not addressing the words to anyone in particular, and looking away from us all, out of the window that was nearest to her.

Mr Ablewhite got upon his feet, and pushed away his chair so violently that it toppled over and fell on the floor.

'I have something more to say on my side,' he announced, bringing down the flat of his hand on the table with a bang. 'I have to say that if my son doesn't feel this insult, I do!'

Rachel started, and looked at him in sudden surprise.

'Insult?' she repeated. 'What do you mean?'

'Insult!' reiterated Mr Ablewhite. 'I know your motive, Miss Verinder, for breaking your promise to my son! I know it as certainly as if you had confessed it in so many words. Your cursed family pride is insulting Godfrey, as it insulted *me* when I married your aunt. Her family—her beggarly family—turned their backs on her for marrying an honest man, who had made his own place and won his own fortune. I had no ancestors. I wasn't descended from a set of cutthroat scoundrels who lived by robbery and murder. I couldn't point to the time when the Ablewhites hadn't a shirt to their backs, and couldn't sign their own names. Ha! ha! I wasn't good enough for the Herncastles, when *I* married. And, now it comes to the pinch, my son isn't good enough for *you*. I suspected it, all along. You have got the Herncastle blood in you, my young lady! I suspected it all along.'

'A very unworthy suspicion,' remarked Mr Bruff. 'I am astonished that you have the courage to acknowledge it.'

Before Mr Ablewhite could find words to answer in, Rachel spoke in a tone of the most exasperating contempt.

'Surely,' she said to the lawyer, 'this is beneath notice. If he can think in *that* way, let us leave him to think as he pleases.'

From scarlet, Mr Ablewhite was now becoming purple. He gasped for breath; he looked backwards and forwards from Rachel to Mr Bruff in such a frenzy of rage with both of them that he didn't know which to attack first. His wife, who had sat impenetrably fanning herself up to this time, began to be alarmed, and attempted, quite uselessly, to quiet him. I had, throughout this distressing interview, felt more than one inward call to interfere with a few earnest words, and had controlled myself under a dread of the possible results, very unworthy of a Christian English-woman who looks, not to what is meanly prudent, but to what is morally right. At the point at which matters had now arrived, I rose superior to all considerations of mere expediency. If I had contemplated interposing any remonstrance of my own humble devising, I might possibly have still hesitated. But the distressing domestic emergency which now confronted me, was most marvellously and beautifully provided for in the Correspondence of Miss Jane Ann Stamper—Letter one thousand and one, on 'Peace in Families.' I rose in my modest corner, and I opened my precious book.

'Dear Mr Ablewhite,' I said, 'one word!'

When I first attracted the attention of the company by rising, I could see that he was on the point of saying something rude to me. My sisterly form of address checked him. He stared at me in heathen astonishment.

'As an affectionate well-wisher and friend,' I proceeded, 'and as one long accustomed to arouse, convince, prepare, enlighten, and fortify others, permit me to take the most pardonable of all liberties—the liberty of composing your mind.'

He began to recover himself; he was on the point of breaking out—he *would* have broken out, with anybody else. But my voice (habitually gentle) possesses a high note or so, in emergencies. In this emergency, I felt imperatively called upon to have the highest voice of the two.

I held up my precious book before him; I rapped the open page impressively with my forefinger. 'Not my words!' I exclaimed, in a burst of fervent interruption. 'Oh, don't suppose that I claim attention for My humble words! Manna in the wilderness, Mr Ablewhite! Dew on the parched earth! Words of comfort, words of wisdom, words of love—the blessed, blessed, blessed words of Miss Jane Ann Stamper!'

I was stopped there by a momentary impediment of the breath. Before I could recover myself, this monster in human form shouted out furiously,—

'Miss Jane Ann Stamper be——!'

It is impossible for me to write the awful word, which is here represented by a blank. I shrieked as it passed his lips; I flew to my little bag on the side table; I shook out all my tracts; I seized the one particular tract on profane swearing, entitled, 'Hush, for Heaven's Sake!'; I handed it to him with an expression of agonised entreaty. He tore it in two, and threw it back at me across the table. The rest of them rose in alarm, not knowing what might happen next. I instantly sat down again in my corner. There had once been an occasion, under somewhat similar circumstances, when Miss Jane Ann Stamper had been taken by the two shoulders and turned out of a room. I waited, inspired by *her* spirit, for a repetition of *her* martyrdom.

But no—it was not to be. His wife was the next person whom he addressed. 'Who—who—who,' he said, stammering with rage, 'asked this impudent fanatic into the house? Did you?'

Before Aunt Ablewhite could say a word, Rachel answered for her.

'Miss Clack is here,' she said, 'as my guest.'

Those words had a singular effect on Mr Ablewhite. They suddenly changed him from a man in a state of red-hot anger to a man in a state of icy-cold contempt. It was plain to everybody that Rachel had said something—short and plain as her answer had been—which gave him the upper hand of her at last.

'Oh?' he said. 'Miss Clack is here as *your* guest—in *my* house?'

It was Rachel's turn to lose her temper at that. Her colour rose, and her eyes brightened fiercely. She turned to the lawyer, and, pointing to Mr Ablewhite, asked haughtily, 'What does he mean?'

Mr Bruff interfered for the third time.

'You appear to forget,' he said, addressing Mr Ablewhite, 'that you took this house as Miss Verinder's guardian, for Miss Verinder's use.'

'Not quite so fast,' interposed Mr Ablewhite. 'I have a last word to say, which I should have said some time since, if this——' He looked my way, pondering what abominable name he should call me—'if this Rampant Spinster had not interrupted us. I beg to inform you, sir, that, if my son is not good enough to be Miss Verinder's husband, I cannot presume to consider his father good enough to be Miss Verinder's guardian. Understand, if you please, that I refuse to accept the position which is offered to me by Lady Verinder's will. In your legal phrase, I decline to act. This house has necessarily been hired in my name. I take the entire responsibility of it on my shoulders. It is my house. I can keep it, or let it, just as I please. I have no wish to hurry Miss Verinder. On the contrary, I beg her to remove her guest and her luggage, at her own entire convenience.' He made a low bow, and walked out of the room.

That was Mr Ablewhite's revenge on Rachel, for refusing to marry his son!

The instant the door closed, Aunt Ablewhite exhibited a phenomenon which silenced us all. She became endowed with energy enough to cross the room!

'My dear,' she said, taking Rachel by the hand, 'I should be ashamed of my husband, if I didn't know that it is his temper which has spoken to you, and not himself. You,' continued Aunt Ablewhite, turning on me in my corner with another endowment of energy, in her looks this time instead of her limbs—'you are the mischievous person who irritated him. I hope I shall never see you or your tracts again.' She went back to Rachel and kissed her.

'I beg your pardon, my dear,' she said, 'in my husband's name. What can I do for you?'

Consistently perverse in everything—capricious and unreasonable in all the actions of her life—Rachel melted into tears at those commonplace words, and returned her aunt's kiss in silence.

'If I may be permitted to answer for Miss Verinder,' said Mr Bruff, 'might I ask you, Mrs Ablewhite, to send Penelope down with her mistress's bonnet and shawl. Leave us ten minutes together,' he added, in a lower tone, 'and you may rely on my setting matters right, to your satisfaction as well as to Rachel's.'

The trust of the family in this man was something wonderful to see. Without a word more, on her side, Aunt Ablewhite left the room.

'Ah!' said Mr Bruff, looking after her. 'The Herncastle blood has its drawbacks, I admit. But there *is* something in good breeding after all!'

Having made that purely worldly remark, he looked hard at my corner, as if he expected me to go. My interest in Rachel—an infinitely higher interest than his—riveted me to my chair.

Mr Bruff gave it up, exactly as he had given it up at Aunt Verinder's, in Montagu Square. He led Rachel to a chair by the window, and spoke to her there.

'My dear young lady,' he said, 'Mr Ablewhite's conduct has naturally shocked you, and taken you by surprise. If it was worth while to contest the question with such a man, we might soon show him that he is not to have things all his own way. But it isn't worth while. You were quite right in what you said just now; he is beneath our notice.'

He stopped, and looked round at my corner. I sat there quite immovable, with my tracts at my elbow, and with Miss Jane Ann Stamper on my lap.

'You know,' he resumed, turning back again to Rachel, 'that it was part of your poor mother's fine nature always to see the best of the people about her, and never the worst. She named her brother-in-law your guardian because she believed in him, and because she thought it would please her sister. I had never liked Mr Ablewhite myself, and I induced your mother to let me insert a clause in the will, empowering her executors, in certain events, to consult with me about the appointment of a new guardian. One of those events has happened to-day; and I find myself in a position to end all these dry business details, I hope agreeably, with a message from my wife. Will you honour Mrs Bruff by becoming her guest? And will you remain under my roof, and be one of my family, until we wise people have laid our heads together, and have settled what is to be done next?'

At those words, I rose to interfere. Mr Bruff had done exactly what I had dreaded he would do, when he asked Mrs Ablewhite for Rachel's bonnet and shawl.

Before I could interpose a word, Rachel had accepted his invitation in the warmest terms. If I suffered the arrangement thus made between them to be carried out—if she once passed the threshold of Mr Bruff's door—farewell to the fondest hope of my life, the hope of bringing my lost sheep back to the fold! The bare idea of such a calamity as this quite overwhelmed me. I cast the miserable trammels of worldly discretion to the winds, and spoke with the fervour that filled me, in the words that came first.

'Stop!' I said—'stop! I must be heard. Mr Bruff! you are not related to her, and I am. *I* invite her—I summon the executors to appoint *me* guardian. Rachel, dearest Rachel, I offer you my modest home; come to London by the next train, love, and share it with me!'

Mr Bruff said nothing. Rachel looked at me with a cruel astonishment which she made no effort to conceal.

'You are very kind, Drusilla,' she said. 'I shall hope to visit you whenever I happen to be in London. But I have accepted Mr Bruff's invitation, and I think it will be best, for the present, if I remain under Mr Bruff's care.'

'Oh, don't say so!' I pleaded. 'I can't part with you, Rachel,—I can't part with you!'

I tried to fold her in my arms. But she drew back. My fervour did not communicate itself; it only alarmed her.

'Surely,' she said, 'this is a very unnecessary display of agitation? I don't understand it.'

'No more do I,' said Mr Bruff.

Their hardness—their hideous, worldly hardness—revolted me.

'Oh, Rachel! Rachel!' I burst out. 'Haven't you seen *yet*, that my heart yearns to make a Christian of you? Has no inner voice told you that I am trying to do for *you*, what I was trying to do for your dear mother when death snatched her out of my hands?'

Rachel advanced a step nearer, and looked at me very strangely.

'I don't understand your reference to my mother,' she said. 'Miss Clack, will you have the goodness to explain yourself?'

Before I could answer, Mr Bruff came forward, and offering his arm to Rachel, tried to lead her out of the room.

'You had better not pursue the subject, my dear,' he said. 'And Miss Clack had better not explain herself.'

If I had been a stock or a stone, such an interference as this must have roused me into testifying to the truth. I put Mr Bruff aside indignantly with my own hand, and, in solemn and suitable language, I stated the view with which sound doctrine does not scruple to regard the awful calamity of dying unprepared.

Rachel started back from me—I blush to write it—with a scream of horror.

'Come away!' she said to Mr Bruff. 'Come away, for God's sake, before that woman can say any more! Oh, think of my poor mother's harmless, useful, beautiful life! You were at the funeral, Mr Bruff; you saw how everybody loved her; you saw the poor helpless people crying at her grave over the loss of their best friend. And that wretch stands there, and tries to make me doubt that my mother, who was an angel on earth, is an angel in heaven now! Don't stop to talk about it! Come away! It stifles me to breathe the same air with her! It frightens me to feel that we are in the same room together!'

Deaf to all remonstrance, she ran to the door.

At the same moment, her maid entered with her bonnet and shawl. She huddled them on anyhow. 'Pack my things,' she said, 'and bring them to Mr Bruff's.' I attempted to approach her—I was shocked and grieved, but, it is needless to say, not offended. I only wished to say to her, 'May your hard heart be softened! I freely forgive you!' She pulled down her veil, and tore her shawl away from my hand, and, hurrying out, shut the door in my face. I bore the insult with my customary fortitude. I remember it now with my customary superiority to all feeling of offence.

Mr Bruff had his parting word of mockery for me, before he too hurried out, in his turn.

'You had better not have explained yourself, Miss Clack,' he said, and bowed, and left the room.

The person with the cap-ribbons followed.

'It's easy to see who has set them all by the ears together,' she said. 'I'm only a poor servant—but I declare I'm ashamed of you!' She too went out, and banged the door after her.

I was left alone in the room. Reviled by them all, deserted by them all, I was left alone in the room.

Is there more to be added to this plain statement of facts—to this touching picture of a Christian persecuted by the world? No! my diary reminds me that one more of the many chequered chapters in my life ends here. From that day forth, I never saw Rachel Verinder again. She had my forgiveness at the time when she insulted me. She has had my prayerful good wishes ever since. And when I die—to complete the return on my part of good for evil—she will have the *Life, Letters, and Labours of Miss Jane Ann Stamper* left her as a legacy by my will.

SECOND NARRATIVE

Contributed by Mathew Bruff, solicitor, of Gray's Inn Square.

CHAPTER I

MY fair friend, Miss Clack, having laid down the pen, there are two reasons for my taking it up next, in my turn.

In the first place, I am in a position to throw the necessary light on certain points of interest which have thus far been left in the dark. Miss Verinder had her own private reason for breaking her marriage engagement—and I was at the bottom of it. Mr Godfrey Ablewhite had his own private reason for withdrawing all claim to the hand of his charming cousin—and I discovered what it was.

In the second place, it was my good or ill fortune, I hardly know which, to find myself personally involved—at the period of which I am now writing—in the mystery of the Indian Diamond. I had the honour of an interview, at my own office, with an Oriental stranger of distinguished manners, who was no other, unquestionably, than the chief of the three Indians. Add to this, that I met with the celebrated traveller, Mr Murthwaite, the day afterwards, and that I held a conversation with him on the subject of the Moonstone, which has a very important bearing on later events. And there you have the statement of my claims to fill the position which I occupy in these pages.

The true story of the broken marriage engagement comes first in point of time, and must therefore take the first place in the present narrative. Tracing my way back along the chain of events, from one end to the other, I find it necessary to open the scene, oddly enough as you will think, at the bedside of my excellent client and friend, the late Sir John Verinder.

Sir John had his share—perhaps rather a large share—of the more harmless and amiable of the weaknesses incidental to humanity. Among these, I may mention as applicable to the matter in hand, an invincible reluctance—so long as he enjoyed his usual good health—to face the responsibility of making his will. Lady Verinder exerted her influence to rouse him to a sense of duty in this matter; and I exerted my influence. He admitted the justice of our views—but he went no further than that, until he found himself afflicted with the illness which ultimately brought him to his grave. Then, I was sent for at last, to take my client's instructions on the subject of his will. They proved to be the simplest instructions I had ever received in the whole of my professional career.

Sir John was dozing, when I entered the room. He roused himself at the sight of me.

'How do you do, Mr Bruff?' he said. 'I sha'n't be very long about this. And then I'll go to sleep again.' He looked on with great interest while I collected pens, ink, and paper. 'Are you ready?' he asked. I bowed, and took a dip of ink, and waited for my instructions.

'I leave everything to my wife,' said Sir John. 'That's all.' He turned round on his pillow, and composed himself to sleep again.

I was obliged to disturb him.

'Am I to understand,' I asked, 'that you leave the whole of the property, of every sort and description, of which you die possessed, absolutely to Lady Verinder?'

'Yes,' said Sir John. 'Only, *I* put it shorter. Why can't *you* put it shorter, and let me go to sleep again? Everything to my wife. That's my Will.'

His property was entirely at his own disposal, and was of two kinds. Property in land (I purposely abstain from using technical language), and property in money. In the majority of cases, I am afraid I should have felt it my duty to my client to ask him to reconsider his Will. In the case of Sir John, I knew Lady Verinder to be, not only worthy of the unreserved trust which her husband had placed in her (all good wives are worthy of that)—but to be also capable of properly administering a trust (which, in my experience of the fair sex, not one in a thousand of them is competent to do). In ten minutes, Sir John's Will was drawn, and executed, and Sir John himself, good man, was finishing his interrupted nap.

Lady Verinder amply justified the confidence which her husband had placed in her. In the first days of her widowhood, she sent for me, and made her Will. The view she took of her position was so thoroughly sound and sensible, that I was relieved of all necessity for advising her. My responsibility began and ended with shaping her instructions into the proper legal form. Before Sir John had been a fortnight in his grave, the future of his daughter had been most wisely and most affectionately provided for.

The Will remained in its fireproof box at my office, through more years than I like to reckon up. It was not till the summer of eighteen hundred and forty-eight that I found occasion to look at it again under very melancholy circumstances.

At the date I have mentioned, the doctors pronounced the sentence on poor Lady Verinder, which was literally a sentence of death. I was the first person whom she informed of her situation; and I found her anxious to go over her Will again with me.

It was impossible to improve the provisions relating to her daughter. But, in the lapse of time, her wishes in regard to certain minor legacies, left to different relatives, had undergone some modification; and it became necessary to add three or four Codicils to the original document. Having done this at once, for fear of accident, I obtained her ladyship's permission to embody her recent instructions in a second Will. My object was to avoid certain inevitable confusions and repetitions which now disfigured the original document, and which, to own the truth, grated sadly on my professional sense of the fitness of things.

The execution of this second Will has been described by Miss Clack, who was so obliging as to witness it. So far as regarded Rachel Verinder's pecuniary interests, it was, word for word, the exact counterpart of the first Will. The only changes introduced related to the appointment of a guardian, and to certain provisions concerning that appointment, which were made under my advice. On Lady Verinder's death, the Will was placed in the hands of my proctor to be 'proved' (as the phrase is) in the usual way.

In about three weeks from that time—as well as I can remember—the first warning reached me of something unusual going on under the surface. I happened to be looking in at my friend the proctor's office, and I observed that he received me with an appearance of greater interest than usual.

'I have some news for you,' he said. 'What do you think I heard at Doctors' Commons this morning? Lady Verinder's Will has been asked for, and examined, already!'

This was news indeed! There was absolutely nothing which could be contested in the Will; and there was nobody I could think of who had the slightest interest in examining it. (I shall perhaps do well if I explain in this place, for the benefit of the few people who don't know it already, that the law allows all Wills to be examined at Doctor's Commons by anybody who applies, on the payment of a shilling fee.)

'Did you hear who asked for the Will?' I asked.

'Yes; the clerk had no hesitation in telling *me*. Mr Smalley, of the firm of Skipp and Smalley, asked for it. The Will has not been copied yet into the great Folio Registers. So there was no alternative but to depart from the usual course, and to let him see the original document. He looked it over carefully, and made a note in his pocket-book. Have you any idea of what he wanted with it?'

I shook my head. 'I shall find out,' I answered, 'before I am a day older.' With that I went back at once to my own office.

If any other firm of solicitors had been concerned in this unaccountable examination of my deceased client's Will, I might have found some difficulty in making the necessary discovery. But I had a hold over Skipp and Smalley which made my course in this matter a comparatively easy one. My common-law clerk (a most competent and excellent man) was a brother of Mr Smalley's; and, owing to this sort of indirect connexion with me, Skipp and Smalley had, for some years past, picked up the crumbs that fell from my table, in the shape of cases brought to my office, which, for various reasons, I did not think it worth while to undertake. My professional patronage was, in this way, of some importance to the firm. I intended, if necessary, to remind them of that patronage, on the present occasion.

The moment I got back I spoke to my clerk; and, after telling him what had happened, I sent him to his brother's office, 'with Mr Bruff's compliments, and he would be glad to know why Messrs. Skipp and Smalley had found it necessary to examine Lady Verinder's Will.'

This message brought Mr Smalley back to my office, in company with his brother. He acknowledged that he had acted under instructions received from a client. And then he put it to me, whether it would not be a breach of professional confidence on his part to say more.

We had a smart discussion upon that. He was right, no doubt; and I was wrong. The truth is, I was angry and suspicious—and I insisted on knowing more. Worse still, I declined to consider any additional information offered me, as a secret placed in my keeping: I claimed perfect freedom to use my own discretion. Worse even than that, I took an unwarrantable advantage of my position. 'Choose, sir,' I said to Mr Smalley, 'between the risk of losing your client's business and the risk of losing Mine.' Quite indefensible, I admit—an act of tyranny, and nothing less. Like other tyrants, I carried my point. Mr Smalley chose his alternative, without a moment's hesitation. He smiled resignedly, and gave up the name of his client:

Mr Godfrey Ablewhite.

That was enough for me—I wanted to know no more.

Having reached this point in my narrative, it now becomes necessary to place the reader of these lines—so far as Lady Verinder's Will is concerned—on a footing of perfect equality, in respect of information, with myself.

Let me state, then, in the fewest possible words, that Rachel Verinder had nothing but a life-interest in the property. Her mother's excellent sense, and my long experience, had combined to relieve her of all responsibility, and to guard her from all danger of becoming the victim in the future of some needy and unscrupulous man. Neither she, nor her husband (if she married), could raise sixpence, either on the property in land, or on the property in money. They would have the houses in London and in Yorkshire to live in, and they would have the handsome income—and that was all.

When I came to think over what I had discovered, I was sorely perplexed what to do next.

Hardly a week had passed since I had heard (to my surprise and distress) of Miss Verinder's proposed marriage. I had the sincerest admiration and affection for her; and I had been inexpressibly grieved when I heard that she was about to throw herself away on Mr Godfrey Ablewhite. And now, here was the man—whom I had always believed to be a smooth-tongued impostor—justifying the very worst that I had thought of him, and plainly revealing the mercenary object of the marriage, on his side! And what of that?—you may reply—the thing is done every day. Granted, my dear sir. But would you think of it quite as lightly as you do, if the thing was done (let us say) with your own sister?

The first consideration which now naturally occurred to me was this. Would Mr Godfrey Ablewhite hold to his engagement, after what his lawyer had discovered for him?

It depended entirely on his pecuniary position, of which I knew nothing. If that position was not a desperate one, it would be well worth his while to marry Miss Verinder for her income alone. If, on the other hand, he stood in urgent need of realising a large sum by a given time, then Lady Verinder's Will would exactly meet the case, and would preserve her daughter from falling into a scoundrel's hands.

In the latter event, there would be no need for me to distress Miss Rachel, in the first days of her mourning for her mother, by an immediate revelation of the truth. In the former event, if I remained silent, I should be conniving at a marriage which would make her miserable for life.

My doubts ended in my calling at the hotel in London, at which I knew Mrs Ablewhite and Miss Verinder to be staying. They informed me that they were going to Brighton the next day, and that an unexpected obstacle prevented Mr Godfrey Ablewhite from accompanying them. I at once proposed to take his place. While I was only thinking of Rachel Verinder, it was possible to hesitate. When I actually saw her, my mind was made up directly, come what might of it, to tell her the truth.

I found my opportunity, when I was out walking with her, on the day after my arrival.

'May I speak to you,' I asked, 'about your marriage engagement?'

'Yes,' she said, indifferently, 'if you have nothing more interesting to talk about.'

'Will you forgive an old friend and servant of your family, Miss Rachel, if I venture on asking whether your heart is set on this marriage?'

'I am marrying in despair, Mr Bruff—on the chance of dropping into some sort of stagnant happiness which may reconcile me to my life.'

Strong language! and suggestive of something below the surface, in the shape of a romance. But I had my own object in view, and I declined (as we lawyers say) to pursue the question into its side issues.

'Mr Godfrey Ablewhite can hardly be of your way of thinking,' I said. '*His* heart must be set on the marriage at any rate?'

'He says so, and I suppose I ought to believe him. He would hardly marry me, after what I have owned to him, unless he was fond of me.'

Poor thing! the bare idea of a man marrying her for his own selfish and mercenary ends had never entered her head. The task I had set myself began to look like a harder task than I had bargained for.

'It sounds strangely,' I went on, 'in my old-fashioned ears——'

'What sounds strangely?' she asked.

'To hear you speak of your future husband as if you were not quite sure of the sincerity of his attachment. Are you conscious of any reason in your own mind for doubting him?'

Her astonishing quickness of perception detected a change in my voice, or my manner, when I put that question, which warned her that I had been speaking all along with some ulterior object in view. She stopped, and taking her arm out of mine, looked me searchingly in the face.

'Mr Bruff,' she said, 'you have something to tell me about Godfrey Ablewhite. Tell it.'

I knew her well enough to take her at her word. I told it.

She put her arm again into mine, and walked on with me slowly. I felt her hand tightening its grasp mechanically on my arm, and I saw her getting paler and paler as I went on—but not a word passed her lips while I was speaking. When I had done, she still kept silence. Her head drooped a little, and she walked by my side, unconscious of my presence, unconscious of everything about her; lost—buried, I might almost say—in her own thoughts.

I made no attempt to disturb her. My experience of her disposition warned me, on this, as on former occasions, to give her time.

The first instinct of girls in general, on being told of anything which interests them, is to ask a multitude of questions, and then to run off, and talk it all over with some favourite friend. Rachel Verinder's first instinct, under similar circumstances, was to shut herself up in her own mind, and to think it over by herself. This absolute self-dependence is a great virtue in a man. In a woman it has the serious drawback of morally separating her from the mass of her sex, and so exposing her to misconstruction by the general opinion. I strongly suspect myself of thinking as the rest of the world think in this matter—except in the case of Rachel Verinder. The self-dependence in *her* character, was one of its virtues in my estimation; partly, no doubt, because I sincerely admired and liked her; partly, because the view I took of her connexion with the loss of the Moonstone was based on my own special knowledge of her disposition. Badly as appearances might look, in the matter of the Diamond—shocking as it undoubtedly was to know that she was associated in any way with the mystery of an undiscovered theft—I was satisfied nevertheless that she had done nothing unworthy of her, because I was also satisfied that she had not stirred a step in the business, without shutting herself up in her own mind, and thinking it over first.

We had walked on, for nearly a mile I should say, before Rachel roused herself. She suddenly looked up at me with a faint reflection of her smile of happier times—the most irresistible smile I have ever seen on a woman's face.

'I owe much already to your kindness,' she said. 'And I feel more deeply indebted to it now than ever. If you hear any rumours of my marriage when you get back to London, contradict them at once, on my authority.'

'Have you resolved to break your engagement?' I asked.

'Can you doubt it?' she returned proudly, 'after what you have told me!'

'My dear Miss Rachel, you are very young—and you may find more difficulty in withdrawing from your present position than you anticipate. Have you no one—I mean a lady, of course—whom you could consult?'

'No one,' she answered.

It distressed me, it did indeed distress me, to hear her say that. She was so young and so lonely—and she bore it so well! The impulse to help her got the better of any sense of my own unfitness which I might have felt under the circumstances; and I stated such ideas on the subject as occurred to me on the spur of the moment, to the best of my ability. I have advised a prodigious number of clients, and have dealt with some exceedingly awkward difficulties, in my time. But this was the first occasion on which I had ever found myself advising a young lady how to obtain her release from a marriage engagement. The suggestion I offered amounted briefly to this. I recommended her to tell Mr Godfrey Ablewhite—at a private interview, of course—that he had, to her certain knowledge, betrayed the mercenary nature of the motive on his side. She was then to add that their marriage, after what she had discovered, was a simple impossibility—and she was to put it to him, whether he thought it wisest to secure her silence by falling in with her views, or to force her, by opposing them, to make the motive under which she was acting generally known. If he attempted to defend himself, or to deny the facts, she was, in that event, to refer him to *me*.

Miss Verinder listened attentively till I had done. She then thanked me very prettily for my advice, but informed me at the same time that it was impossible for her to follow it.

'May I ask,' I said, 'what objection you see to following it?'

She hesitated—and then met me with a question on her side.

'Suppose you were asked to express your opinion of Mr Godfrey Ablewhite's conduct?' she began.

'Yes?'

'What would you call it?'

'I should call it the conduct of a meanly deceitful man.'

'Mr Bruff! I have believed in that man. I have promised to marry that man. How can I tell him he is mean, how can I tell him he has deceived me, how can I disgrace him in the eyes of the world after that? I have degraded myself by ever thinking of him as my husband. If I say what you tell me to say to him—I am owning that I have degraded myself to his face. I can't do that. After what has passed between us, I can't do that! The shame of it would be nothing to *him*. But the shame of it would be unendurable to *me*.'

Here was another of the marked peculiarities in her character disclosing itself to me without reserve. Here was her sensitive horror of the bare contact with anything mean, blinding her to every consideration of what she owed to herself, hurrying her into a false position which might compromise her in the estimation of all her friends! Up to this time, I had been a little diffident about the propriety of the advice I had given to her. But, after what she had just said, I had no sort of doubt that it was the best advice that could have been offered; and I felt no sort of hesitation in pressing it on her again.

She only shook her head, and repeated her objection in other words.

'He has been intimate enough with me to ask me to be his wife. He has stood high enough in my estimation to obtain my consent. I can't tell him to his face that he is the most contemptible of living creatures, after that!'

'But, my dear Miss Rachel,' I remonstrated, 'it's equally impossible for you to tell him that you withdraw from your engagement without giving some reason for it.'

'I shall say that I have thought it over, and that I am satisfied it will be best for both of us if we part.'

'No more than that?'

'No more.'

'Have you thought of what he may say, on his side?

'He may say what he pleases.'

It was impossible not to admire her delicacy and her resolution, and it was equally impossible not to feel that she was putting herself in the wrong. I entreated her to consider her own position. I reminded her that she would be exposing herself to the most odious misconstruction of her motives. 'You can't brave public opinion,' I said, 'at the command of private feeling.'

'I can,' she answered. 'I have done it already.'

'What do you mean?'

'You have forgotten the Moonstone, Mr Bruff. Have I not braved public opinion, *there*, with my own private reasons for it?'

Her answer silenced me for the moment. It set me trying to trace the explanation of her conduct, at the time of the loss of the Moonstone, out of the strange avowal which had just escaped her. I might perhaps have done it when I was younger. I certainly couldn't do it now.

I tried a last remonstrance before we returned to the house. She was just as immovable as ever. My mind was in a strange conflict of feelings about her when I left her that day. She was obstinate; she was wrong. She was interesting; she was admirable; she was deeply to be pitied. I made her promise to write to me the moment she had any news to send. And I went back to my business in London, with a mind exceedingly ill at ease.

On the evening of my return, before it was possible for me to receive my promised letter, I was surprised by a visit from Mr Ablewhite the elder, and was informed that Mr Godfrey had got his dismissal—*and had accepted it*—that very day.

With the view I already took of the case, the bare fact stated in the words that I have underlined, revealed Mr Godfrey Ablewhite's motive for submission as plainly as if he had acknowledged it himself. He needed a large sum of money; and he needed it by a given time. Rachel's income, which would have helped him to anything else, would not help him here; and Rachel had accordingly released herself, without encountering a moment's serious opposition on his part. If I am told that this is a mere speculation, I ask, in my turn, What other theory will account for his giving up a marriage which would have maintained him in splendour for the rest of his life?

Any exultation I might otherwise have felt at the lucky turn which things had now taken, was effectually checked by what passed at my interview with old Mr Ablewhite.

He came, of course, to know whether I could give him any explanation of Miss Verinder's extraordinary conduct. It is needless to say that I was quite unable to afford him the information he wanted. The annoyance which I thus inflicted, following on the irritation produced by a recent interview with his son, threw Mr Ablewhite off his guard. Both his looks and his language convinced me that Miss Verinder would find him a merciless man to deal with, when he joined the ladies at Brighton the next day.

I had a restless night, considering what I ought to do next. How my reflections ended, and how thoroughly well founded my distrust of Mr Ablewhite proved to be, are items of information which (as I am told) have already been put tidily in their proper places, by that exemplary person, Miss Clack. I have only to add—in completion of her narrative—that Miss Verinder found the quiet and repose which she sadly needed, poor thing, in my house at Hampstead. She honoured us by making a long stay. My wife and daughters were charmed with her; and, when the executors decided on the appointment of a new guardian, I feel sincere pride and pleasure in recording that my guest and my family parted like old friends, on either side.

CHAPTER II

THE next thing I have to do, is to present such additional information as I possess on the subject of the Moonstone, or, to speak more correctly, on the subject of the Indian plot to steal the Diamond. The little that I have to tell is (as I think I have already said) of some importance, nevertheless, in respect of its bearing very remarkably on events which are still to come.

About a week or ten days after Miss Verinder had left us, one of my clerks entered the private room at my office, with a card in his hand, and informed me that a gentleman was below, who wanted to speak to me.

I looked at the card. There was a foreign name written on it, which has escaped my memory. It was followed by a line written in English at the bottom of the card, which I remember perfectly well:

'Recommended by Mr Septimus Luker.'

The audacity of a person in Mr Luker's position presuming to recommend anybody to *me*, took me so completely by surprise, that I sat silent for the moment, wondering whether my own eyes had not deceived me. The clerk, observing my bewilderment, favoured me with the result of his own observation of the stranger who was waiting downstairs.

'He is rather a remarkable-looking man, sir. So dark in the complexion that we all set him down in the office for an Indian, or something of that sort.'

Associating the clerk's idea with the line inscribed on the card in my hand, I thought it possible that the Moonstone might be at the bottom of Mr Luker's recommendation, and of the stranger's visit at my office. To the astonishment of my clerk, I at once decided on granting an interview to the gentleman below.

In justification of the highly unprofessional sacrifice to mere curiosity which I thus made, permit me to remind anybody who may read these lines, that no living person (in England, at any rate) can claim to have had such an intimate connexion with the romance of the Indian Diamond as mine has been. I was trusted with the secret of Colonel Herncastle's plan for escaping assassination. I received the Colonel's letters, periodically reporting himself a living man. I drew his Will, leaving the Moonstone to Miss Verinder. I persuaded his executor to act, on the chance that the jewel might prove to be a valuable acquisition to the family. And, lastly, I combated Mr Franklin Blake's scruples, and induced him to be the means of transporting the Diamond to Lady Verinder's house. If anyone can claim a prescriptive right of interest in the Moonstone, and in everything connected with it, I think it is hardly to be denied that I am the man.

The moment my mysterious client was shown in, I felt an inner conviction that I was in the presence of one of the three Indians—probably of the chief. He was carefully dressed in European costume. But his swarthy complexion, his long lithe figure, and his grave and graceful politeness of manner were enough to betray his Oriental origin to any intelligent eyes that looked at him.

I pointed to a chair, and begged to be informed of the nature of his business with me.

After first apologising—in an excellent selection of English words—for the liberty which he had taken in disturbing me, the Indian produced a small parcel the outer covering of which was of cloth of gold. Removing this and a second wrapping of some silken fabric, he placed a little box, or casket, on my table, most beautifully and richly inlaid with jewels, on an ebony ground.

'I have come, sir,' he said, 'to ask you to lend me some money. And I leave this as an assurance to you that my debt will be paid back.'

I pointed to his card. 'And you apply to me,' I rejoined, 'at Mr Luker's recommendation?'

The Indian bowed.

'May I ask how it is that Mr Luker himself did not advance the money that you require?'

'Mr Luker informed me, sir, that he had no money to lend.'

'And so he recommended you to come to me?'

The Indian, in his turn, pointed to the card. 'It is written there,' he said.

Briefly answered, and thoroughly to the purpose! If the Moonstone had been in my possession, this Oriental gentleman would have murdered me, I am well aware, without a moment's hesitation. At the same time, and barring that slight drawback, I am bound to testify that he was the perfect model of a client. He might not have respected my life. But he did what none of my own countrymen had ever done, in all my experience of them—he respected my time.

'I am sorry,' I said, 'that you should have had the trouble of coming to me. Mr Luker is quite mistaken in sending you here. I am trusted, like other men in my profession, with money to lend. But I never lend it to strangers, and I never lend it on such a security as you have produced.'

Far from attempting, as other people would have done, to induce me to relax my own rules, the Indian only made me another bow, and wrapped up his box in its two coverings without a word of protest. He rose—this admirable assassin rose to go, the moment I had answered him!

'Will your condescension towards a stranger excuse my asking one question,' he said, 'before I take my leave?'

I bowed on my side. Only one question at parting! The average in my experience was fifty.

'Supposing, sir, it had been possible (and customary) for *you* to lend me the money,' he said, 'in what space of time would it have been possible (and customary) for *me* to pay it back?'

'According to the usual course pursued in this country,' I answered, 'you would have been entitled to pay the money back (if you liked) in one year's time from the date at which it was first advanced to you.'

The Indian made me a last bow, the lowest of all—and suddenly and softly walked out of the room.

It was done in a moment, in a noiseless, supple, cat-like way, which a little startled me, I own. As soon as I was composed enough to think, I arrived at one distinct conclusion in reference to the otherwise incomprehensible visitor who had favoured me with a call.

His face, voice, and manner—while I was in his company—were under such perfect control that they set all scrutiny at defiance. But he had given me one chance of looking under the smooth outer surface of him, for all that. He had not shown the slightest sign of attempting to fix anything that I had said to him in his mind, until I mentioned the time at which it was customary to permit the earliest repayment, on the part of a debtor, of money that had been advanced as a loan. When I gave him that piece of information, he looked me straight in the face, while I was speaking, for the first time. The inference I drew from this was—that he had a special purpose in asking me his last question, and a special interest in hearing my answer to it. The more carefully I reflected on what had passed between us, the more shrewdly I suspected the production of the casket, and the application for the loan, of having been mere formalities, designed to pave the way for the parting inquiry addressed to me.

I had satisfied myself of the correctness of this conclusion—and was trying to get on a step further, and penetrate the Indian's motives next—when a letter was brought to me, which proved to be from no less a person than Mr Septimus Luker himself. He asked my pardon in terms of sickening servility, and assured me that he could explain matters to my satisfaction, if I would honour him by consenting to a personal interview.

I made another unprofessional sacrifice to mere curiosity. I honoured him by making an appointment at my office, for the next day.

Mr Luker was, in every respect, such an inferior creature to the Indian—he was so vulgar, so ugly, so cringing, and so prosy—that he is quite unworthy of being reported, at any length, in these pages. The substance of what he had to tell me may be fairly stated as follows:

The day before I had received the visit of the Indian, Mr Luker had been favoured with a call from that accomplished gentleman. In spite of his European disguise, Mr Luker had instantly identified his visitor with the chief of the three Indians, who had formerly annoyed him by loitering about his house, and who had left him no alternative but to consult a magistrate. From this startling discovery he had rushed to the conclusion (naturally enough I own) that he must certainly be in the company of one of the three men, who had blindfolded him, gagged him, and robbed him of his banker's receipt. The result was that he became quite paralysed with terror, and that he firmly believed his last hour had come.

On his side, the Indian preserved the character of a perfect stranger. He produced the little casket, and made exactly the same application which he had afterwards made to me. As the speediest way of getting rid of him, Mr Luker had at once declared that he had no money. The Indian had thereupon asked to be informed of the best and safest person to apply to for the loan he wanted. Mr Luker had answered that the best and safest person, in such cases, was usually a respectable solicitor. Asked to name some individual of that character and profession, Mr Luker had mentioned me—for the one simple reason that, in the extremity of his terror, mine was the first name which occurred to him. 'The perspiration was pouring off me like rain, sir,' the wretched creature concluded. 'I didn't know what I was talking about. And I hope you'll look over it, Mr Bruff, sir, in consideration of my having been really and truly frightened out of my wits.'

I excused the fellow graciously enough. It was the readiest way of releasing myself from the sight of him. Before he left me, I detained him to make one inquiry. Had the Indian said anything noticeable, at the moment of quitting Mr Luker's house?

Yes! The Indian had put precisely the same question to Mr Luker, at parting, which he had put to me; receiving of course, the same answer as the answer which I had given him.

What did it mean? Mr Luker's explanation gave me no assistance towards solving the problem. My own unaided ingenuity, consulted next, proved quite unequal to grapple with the difficulty. I had a dinner engagement that evening; and I went upstairs, in no very genial frame of mind, little suspecting that the way to my dressing-room and the way to discovery, meant, on this particular occasion, one and the same thing.

CHAPTER III

THE prominent personage among the guests at the dinner-party I found to be Mr Murthwaite.

On his appearance in England, after his wanderings, society had been greatly interested in the traveller, as a man who had passed through many dangerous adventures, and who had escaped to tell the tale. He had now announced his intention of returning to the scene of his exploits, and of penetrating into regions left still unexplored. This magnificent indifference to placing his safety in peril for the second time, revived the flagging interest of the worshippers in the hero. The law of chances was clearly against his escaping on this occasion. It is not every day that we can meet an eminent person at dinner, and feel that there is a reasonable prospect of the news of his murder being the news that we hear of him next.

When the gentlemen were left by themselves in the dining-room, I found myself sitting next to Mr Murthwaite. The guests present being all English, it is needless to say that, as soon as the wholesome check exercised by the presence of the ladies was removed, the conversation turned on politics as a necessary result.

In respect to this all-absorbing national topic, I happen to be one of the most un-English Englishmen living. As a general rule, political talk appears to me to be of all talk the most dreary and the most profitless. Glancing at Mr Murthwaite, when the bottles had made their first round of the table, I found that he was apparently of my way of thinking. He was doing it very dexterously—with all possible consideration for the feelings of his host—but it is not the less certain that he was composing himself for a nap. It struck me as an experiment worth attempting, to try whether a judicious allusion to the subject of the Moonstone would keep him wake, and, if it did, to see what *he* thought of the last new complication in the Indian conspiracy, as revealed in the prosaic precincts of my office.

'If I am not mistaken, Mr Murthwaite,' I began, 'you were acquainted with the late Lady Verinder, and you took some interest in the strange succession of events which ended in the loss of the Moonstone?'

The eminent traveller did me the honour of waking up in an instant, and asking me who I was.

I informed him of my professional connexion with the Herncastle family, not forgetting the curious position which I had occupied towards the Colonel and his Diamond in the bygone time.

Mr Murthwaite shifted round in his chair, so as to put the rest of the company behind him (Conservatives and Liberals alike), and concentrated his whole attention on plain Mr Bruff, of Gray's Inn Square.

'Have you heard anything, lately, of the Indians?' he asked.

'I have every reason to believe,' I answered, 'that one of them had an interview with me, in my office, yesterday.'

Mr Murthwaite was not an easy man to astonish; but that last answer of mine completely staggered him. I described what had happened to Mr Luker, and what had happened to myself, exactly as I have described it here. 'It is clear that the Indian's parting inquiry had an object,' I added. 'Why should he be so anxious to know the time at which a borrower of money is usually privileged to pay the money back?'

'Is it possible that you don't see his motive, Mr Bruff?'

'I am ashamed of my stupidity, Mr Murthwaite—but I certainly don't see it.'

The great traveller became quite interested in sounding the immense vacuity of my dulness to its lowest depths.

'Let me ask you one question,' he said. 'In what position does the conspiracy to seize the Moonstone now stand?'

'I can't say;' I answered. 'The Indian plot is a mystery to me.'

'The Indian plot, Mr Bruff, can only be a mystery to you, because you have never seriously examined it. Shall we run it over together, from the time when you drew Colonel Herncastle's Will, to the time when the Indian called at your office? In your position, it may be of very serious importance to the interests of Miss Verinder, that you should be able to take a clear view of this matter in case of need. Tell me, bearing that in mind, whether you will penetrate the Indian's motive for yourself? or whether you wish me to save you the trouble of making any inquiry into it?'

It is needless to say that I thoroughly appreciated the practical purpose which I now saw that he had in view, and that the first of the two alternatives was the alternative I chose.

'Very good,' said Mr Murthwaite. 'We will take the question of the ages of the three Indians first. I can testify that they all look much about the same age—and you can decide for yourself, whether the man whom you saw was, or was not, in the prime of life. Not forty, you think? My idea too. We will say not forty. Now look back to the time when Colonel Herncastle came to England, and when you were concerned in the plan he adopted to preserve his life. I don't want you to count the years. I will only say, it is clear that these present Indians, at their age, must be the successors of three other Indians (high caste Brahmins all of them, Mr Bruff, when they left their native country!) who followed the Colonel to these shores. Very well. These present men of ours have succeeded to the men who were here before them. If they had only done that, the matter would not have been worth inquiring into. But they have done more. They have succeeded to the organisation which their predecessors established in this country. Don't start! The organisation is a very trumpery affair, according to our ideas, I have no doubt. I should reckon it up as including the command of money; the services, when needed, of that shady sort of Englishman, who lives in the byways of foreign life in London; and, lastly, the secret sympathy of such few men of their own country, and (formerly, at least) of their own religion, as happen to be employed in ministering to some of the multitudinous wants of this great city. Nothing very formidable, as you see! But worth notice at starting, because we *may* find occasion to refer to this modest little Indian organisation as we go on. Having now cleared the ground, I am going to ask you a question; and I expect your experience to answer it. What was the event which gave the Indians their first chance of seizing the Diamond?'

I understood the allusion to my experience.

'The first chance they got,' I replied, 'was clearly offered to them by Colonel Herncastle's death. They would be aware of his death, I suppose, as a matter of course?'

'As a matter of course. And his death, as you say, gave them their first chance. Up to that time the Moonstone was safe in the strong-room of the bank. You drew the Colonel's Will leaving his jewel to his niece; and the Will was proved in the usual way. As a lawyer, you can be at no loss to know what course the Indians would take (under English advice) after *that*.'

'They would provide themselves with a copy of the Will from Doctors' Commons,' I said.

'Exactly. One or other of those shady Englishmen to whom I have alluded, would get them the copy you have described. That copy would inform them that the Moonstone was bequeathed to the daughter of Lady Verinder, and that Mr Blake the elder, or some person appointed by him, was to place it in her hands. You will agree with me that the necessary information about persons in the position of Lady Verinder and Mr Blake, would be perfectly easy information to obtain. The one difficulty for the Indians would be to decide, whether they should make their attempt on the

Diamond when it was in course of removal from the keeping of the bank, or whether they should wait until it was taken down to Yorkshire to Lady Verinder's house. The second way would be manifestly the safest way—and there you have the explanation of the appearance of the Indians at Frizinghall, disguised as jugglers, and waiting their time. In London, it is needless to say, they had their organisation at their disposal to keep them informed of events. Two men would do it. One to follow anybody who went from Mr Blake's house to the bank. And one to treat the lower men servants with beer, and to hear the news of the house. These commonplace precautions would readily inform them that Mr Franklin Blake had been to the bank, and that Mr Franklin Blake was the only person in the house who was going to visit Lady Verinder. What actually followed upon that discovery, you remember, no doubt, quite as correctly as I do.'

I remembered that Franklin Blake had detected one of the spies, in the street—that he had, in consequence, advanced the time of his arrival in Yorkshire by some hours—and that (thanks to old Betteredge's excellent advice) he had lodged the Diamond in the bank at Frizinghall, before the Indians were so much as prepared to see him in the neighbourhood. All perfectly clear so far. But, the Indians being ignorant of the precaution thus taken, how was it that they had made no attempt on Lady Verinder's house (in which they must have supposed the Diamond to be) through the whole of the interval that elapsed before Rachel's birthday?

In putting this difficulty to Mr Murthwaite, I thought it right to add that I had heard of the little boy, and the drop of ink, and the rest of it, and that any explanation based on the theory of clairvoyance was an explanation which would carry no conviction whatever with it, to *my* mind.

'Nor to mine either,' said Mr Murthwaite. 'The clairvoyance in this case is simply a development of the romantic side of the Indian character. It would be a refreshment and an encouragement to those men—quite inconceivable, I grant you, to the English mind—to surround their wearisome and perilous errand in this country with a certain halo of the marvellous and the supernatural. Their boy is unquestionably a sensitive subject to the mesmeric influence—and, under that influence, he has no doubt reflected what was already in the mind of the person mesmerising him. I have tested the theory of clairvoyance—and I have never found the manifestations get beyond that point. The Indians don't investigate the matter in this way; the Indians look upon their boy as a Seer of things invisible to their eyes—and, I repeat, in that marvel they find the source of a new interest in the purpose that unites them. I only notice this as offering a curious view of human character, which must be quite new to you. We have nothing whatever to do with clairvoyance, or with mesmerism, or with anything else that is hard of belief to a practical man, in the inquiry that we are now pursuing. My object in following the Indian plot, step by step, is to trace results back, by rational means, to natural causes. Have I succeeded to your satisfaction so far?'

'Not a doubt of it, Mr Murthwaite! I am waiting, however, with some anxiety, to hear the rational explanation of the difficulty which I have just had the honour of submitting to you.'

Mr Murthwaite smiled. 'It's the easiest difficulty to deal with of all,' he said. 'Permit me to begin by admitting your statement of the case as a perfectly correct one. The Indians were undoubtedly not aware of what Mr Franklin Blake had done with the Diamond—for we find them making their first mistake, on the first night of Mr Franklin Blake's arrival at his aunt's house.'

'Their first mistake?' I repeated.

'Certainly! The mistake of allowing themselves to be surprised, lurking about the terrace at night, by Gabriel Betteredge. However, they had the merit of seeing for themselves that they had taken a false step—for, as you say, again, with plenty of time at their disposal, they never came near the house for weeks afterwards.'

'Why, Mr Murthwaite? That's what I want to know! Why?'

'Because no Indian, Mr Bruff, ever runs an unnecessary risk. The clause you drew in Colonel Herncastle's Will, informed them (didn't it?) that the Moonstone was to pass absolutely into Miss Verinder's possession on her birthday. Very well. Tell me which was the safest course for men in their position? To make their attempt on the Diamond while it was under the control of Mr Franklin Blake, who had shown already that he could suspect and outwit them? Or to wait till the Diamond was at the disposal of a young girl, who would innocently delight in wearing the magnificent jewel at every possible opportunity? Perhaps you want a proof that my theory is correct? Take the conduct of the Indians themselves as the proof. They appeared at the house, after waiting all those weeks, on Miss Verinder's birthday; and they were rewarded for the patient accuracy of their calculations by seeing the Moonstone in the bosom of her dress! When I heard the story of the Colonel and the Diamond, later in the evening, I felt so sure about the risk Mr Franklin Blake had run (they would have certainly attacked him, if he had not happened to ride back to Lady Verinder's in the company of other people); and I was so strongly convinced of the worse risks still in store for Miss Verinder, that I recommended following the Colonel's plan, and destroying the identity of the gem by having it cut into separate stones. How its extraordinary disappearance that night made my advice useless, and utterly defeated the Hindoo plot—and how all further action on the part of the Indians was paralysed the next day by their confinement in prison as rogues and vagabonds—you know as well as I do. The first act in the conspiracy closes there. Before we go on to the second, may I ask whether I have met your difficulty, with an explanation which is satisfactory to the mind of a practical man?'

It was impossible to deny that he had met my difficulty fairly; thanks to his superior knowledge of the Indian character—and thanks to his not having had hundreds of other Wills to think of since Colonel Herncastle's time!

'So far, so good,' resumed Mr Murthwaite. 'The first chance the Indians had of seizing the Diamond was a chance lost, on the day when they were committed to the prison at Frizinghall. When did the second chance offer itself? The second chance offered itself—as I am in a condition to prove—while they were still in confinement.'

He took out his pocket-book, and opened it at a particular leaf, before he went on.

'I was staying,' he resumed, 'with some friends at Frizinghall, at the time. A day or two before the Indians were set free (on a Monday, I think), the governor of the prison came to me with a letter. It had been left for the Indians by one Mrs Macann, of whom they had hired the lodging in which they lived; and it had been delivered at Mrs Macann's door, in ordinary course of post, on the previous morning. The prison authorities had noticed that the postmark was "Lambeth," and that the address on the outside, though expressed in correct English, was, in form, oddly at variance with the customary method of directing a letter. On opening it, they had found the contents to be written in a foreign language, which they rightly guessed at as Hindustani. Their object in coming to me was, of course, to have the letter translated to them. I took a copy in my pocket-book of the original, and of my translation—and there they are at your service.'

He handed me the open pocket-book. The address on the letter was the first thing copied. It was all written in one paragraph, without any attempt at punctuation, thus: 'To the three Indian men living with the lady called Macann at Frizinghall in Yorkshire.' The Hindoo characters followed; and the English translation appeared at the end, expressed in these mysterious words:

'In the name of the Regent of the Night, whose seat is on the Antelope, whose arms embrace the four corners of the earth.

'Brothers, turn your faces to the south, and come to me in the street of many noises, which leads down to the muddy river.

'The reason is this.

'My own eyes have seen it.'

There the letter ended, without either date or signature. I handed it back to Mr Murthwaite, and owned that this curious specimen of Hindoo correspondence rather puzzled me.

'I can explain the first sentence to you,' he said; 'and the conduct of the Indians themselves will explain the rest. The god of the moon is represented, in the Hindoo mythology, as a four-armed deity, seated on an antelope; and one of his titles is the regent of the night. Here, then, to begin with, is something which looks suspiciously like an indirect reference to the Moonstone. Now, let us see what the Indians did, after the prison authorities had allowed them to receive their letter. On the very day when they were set free they went at once to the railway station, and took their places in the first train that started for London. We all thought it a pity at Frizinghall that their proceedings were not privately watched. But, after Lady Verinder had dismissed the police-officer, and had stopped all further inquiry into the loss of the Diamond, no one else could presume to stir in the matter. The Indians were free to go to London, and to London they went. What was the next news we heard of them, Mr Bruff?'

'They were annoying Mr Luker,' I answered, 'by loitering about the house at Lambeth.'

'Did you read the report of Mr Luker's application to the magistrate?'

'Yes.'

'In the course of his statement he referred, if you remember, to a foreign workman in his employment, whom he had just dismissed on suspicion of attempted theft, and whom he also distrusted as possibly acting in collusion with the Indians who had annoyed him. The inference is pretty plain, Mr Bruff, as to who wrote that letter which puzzled you just now, and as to which of Mr Luker's Oriental treasures the workman had attempted to steal.'

The inference (as I hastened to acknowledge) was too plain to need being pointed out. I had never doubted that the Moonstone had found its way into Mr Luker's hands, at the time Mr Murthwaite alluded to. My only question had been, How had the Indians discovered the circumstance? This question (the most difficult to deal with of all, as I had thought) had now received its answer, like the rest. Lawyer as I was, I began to feel that I might trust Mr Murthwaite to lead me blindfold through the last windings of the labyrinth, along which he had guided me thus far. I paid him the compliment of telling him this, and found my little concession very graciously received.

'You shall give me a piece of information in your turn before we go on,' he said. 'Somebody must have taken the Moonstone from Yorkshire to London. And somebody must have raised money on it, or it would never have been in Mr Luker's possession. Has there been any discovery made of who that person was?'

'None that I know of.'

'There was a story (was there not?) about Mr Godfrey Ablewhite. I am told he is an eminent philanthropist—which is decidedly against him, to begin with.'

I heartily agreed in this with Mr Murthwaite. At the same time, I felt bound to inform him (without, it is needless to say, mentioning Miss Verinder's name) that Mr Godfrey Ablewhite had been cleared of all suspicion, on evidence which I could answer for as entirely beyond dispute.

'Very well,' said Mr Murthwaite, quietly, 'let us leave it to time to clear the matter up. In the meantime, Mr Bruff, we must get back again to the Indians, on your account. Their journey to London simply ended in their becoming the victims of another defeat. The loss of their second chance of seizing the Diamond is mainly attributable, as I think, to the cunning and foresight of Mr Luker—who doesn't stand at the top of the prosperous and ancient profession of usury for nothing! By the prompt dismissal of the man in his employment, he deprived the Indians of the assistance which their confederate would have rendered them in getting into the house. By the prompt transport of the Moonstone to his banker's, he took the conspirators by surprise before they were prepared with a new plan for robbing him. How the Indians, in this latter case, suspected what he had done, and how they contrived to possess themselves of his bankers' receipt, are events too recent to need dwelling on. Let it be enough to say that they know the Moonstone to be once more out of their reach; deposited (under the general description of "a valuable of great price") in a banker's strong-room. Now, Mr Bruff, what is their third chance of seizing the Diamond? and when will it come?'

As the question passed his lips, I penetrated the motive of the Indian's visit to my office at last!

'I see it!' I exclaimed. 'The Indians take it for granted, as we do, that the Moonstone has been pledged; and they want to be certainly informed of the earliest period at which the pledge can be redeemed—because that will be the earliest period at which the Diamond can be removed from the safe keeping of the bank!'

'I told you you would find it out for yourself, Mr Bruff, if I only gave you a fair chance. In a year from the time when the Moonstone was pledged, the Indians will be on the watch for their third chance. Mr Luker's own lips have told them how long they will have to wait, and your respectable authority has satisfied them that Mr Luker has spoken the truth. When do we suppose, at a rough guess, that the Diamond found its way into the money-lender's hands?'

'Towards the end of last June,' I answered, 'as well as I can reckon it.'

'And we are now in the year 'forty-eight. Very good. If the unknown person who has pledged the Moonstone can redeem it in a year, the jewel will be in that person's possession again at the end of June, 'forty-nine. I shall be thousands of miles away from England and English news at that date. But it may be worth *your* while to take a note of it, and to arrange to be in London at the time.'

'You think something serious will happen?' I said.

'I think I shall be safer,' he answered, 'among the fiercest fanatics of Central Asia than I should be if I crossed the door of the bank with the Moonstone in my pocket. The Indians have been defeated twice running, Mr Bruff. It's my firm belief that they won't be defeated a third time.'

Those were the last words he said on the subject. The coffee came in; the guests rose, and dispersed themselves about the room; and we joined the ladies of the dinner-party upstairs.

I made a note of the date, and it may not be amiss if I close my narrative by repeating that note here:

June, 'forty-nine. Expect news of the Indians, towards the end of the month.

And that done, I hand the pen, which I have now no further claim to use, to the writer who follows me next.

THIRD NARRATIVE

Contributed by Franklin Blake.

CHAPTER I

IN the spring of the year eighteen hundred and forty-nine I was wandering in the East, and had then recently altered the travelling plans which I had laid out some months before, and which I had communicated to my lawyer and my banker in London.

This change made it necessary for me to send one of my servants to obtain my letters and remittances from the English consul in a certain city, which was no longer included as one of my resting-places in my new travelling scheme. The man was to join me again at an appointed place and time. An accident, for which he was not responsible, delayed him on his errand. For a week I and my people waited, encamped on the borders of a desert. At the end of that time the missing man made his appearance, with the money and the letters, at the entrance of my tent.

'I am afraid I bring you bad news, sir,' he said, and pointed to one of the letters, which had a mourning border round it, and the address on which was in the handwriting of Mr Bruff.

I know nothing, in a case of this kind, so unendurable as suspense. The letter with the mourning border was the letter that I opened first.

It informed me that my father was dead, and that I was heir to his great fortune. The wealth which had thus fallen into my hands brought its responsibilities with it, and Mr Bruff entreated me to lose no time in returning to England.

By daybreak the next morning I was on my way back to my own country.

The picture presented of me, by my old friend Betteredge, at the time of my departure from England, is (as I think) a little overdrawn. He has, in his own quaint way, interpreted seriously one of his young mistress's many satirical references to my foreign education; and has persuaded himself that he actually saw those French, German, and Italian sides to my character, which my lively cousin only professed to discover in jest, and which never had any real existence, except in our good Betteredge's own brain. But, barring this drawback, I am bound to own that he has stated no more than the truth in representing me as wounded to the heart by Rachel's treatment, and as leaving England in the first keenness of suffering caused by the bitterest disappointment of my life.

I went abroad, resolved—if change and absence could help me—to forget her. It is, I am persuaded, no true view of human nature which denies that change and absence *do* help a man under these circumstances: they force his attention away from the exclusive contemplation of his own sorrow. I never forgot her; but the pang of remembrance lost its worst bitterness, little by little, as time, distance, and novelty interposed themselves more and more effectually between Rachel and me.

On the other hand, it is no less certain that, with the act of turning homeward, the remedy which had gained its ground so steadily, began now, just as steadily, to drop back. The nearer I drew to the country which she inhabited, and to the prospect of seeing her again, the more irresistibly her influence began to recover its hold on me. On leaving England she was the last person in the world whose name I would have suffered to pass my lips. On returning to England, she was the first person I inquired after, when Mr Bruff and I met again.

I was informed, of course, of all that had happened in my absence: in other words, of all that has been related here in continuation of Betteredge's narrative—one circumstance only being excepted. Mr Bruff did not, at that time, feel himself at liberty to inform me of the motives which had privately influenced Rachel and Godfrey Ablewhite in recalling the marriage promise, on either side. I troubled him with no embarrassing questions on this delicate subject. It was relief enough to me, after the jealous disappointment caused by hearing that she had ever contemplated being Godfrey's wife, to know that reflection had convinced her of acting rashly, and that she had effected her own release from her marriage engagement.

Having heard the story of the past, my next inquiries (still inquiries after Rachel!) advanced naturally to the present time. Under whose care had she been placed after leaving Mr Bruff's house? and where was she living now?

She was living under the care of a widowed sister of the late Sir John Verinder—one Mrs Merridew—whom her mother's executors had requested to act as guardian, and who had accepted the proposal. They were reported to me as getting on together admirably well, and as being now established, for the season, in Mrs Merridew's house in Portland Place.

Half an hour after receiving this information, I was on my way to Portland Place—without having had the courage to own it to Mr Bruff!

The man who answered the door was not sure whether Miss Verinder was at home or not. I sent him upstairs with my card, as the speediest way of setting the question at rest. The man came down again with an impenetrable face, and informed me that Miss Verinder was out.

I might have suspected other people of purposely denying themselves to me. But it was impossible to suspect Rachel. I left word that I would call again at six o'clock that evening.

At six o'clock I was informed for the second time that Miss Verinder was not at home. Had any message been left for me? No message had been left for me. Had Miss Verinder not received my card? The servant begged my pardon—Miss Verinder *had* received it.

The inference was too plain to be resisted. Rachel declined to see me.

On my side, I declined to be treated in this way, without making an attempt, at least, to discover a reason for it. I sent up my name to Mrs Merridew, and requested her to favour me with a personal interview at any hour which it might be most convenient to her to name.

Mrs Merridew made no difficulty about receiving me at once. I was shown into a comfortable little sitting-room, and found myself in the presence of a comfortable little elderly lady. She was so good as to feel great regret and much surprise, entirely on my account. She was at the same time, however, not in a position to offer me any explanation, or to press Rachel on a matter which appeared to relate to a question of private feeling alone. This was said over and over again, with a polite patience that nothing could tire; and this was all I gained by applying to Mrs Merridew.

My last chance was to write to Rachel. My servant took a letter to her the next day, with strict instructions to wait for an answer.

The answer came back, literally in one sentence.

'Miss Verinder begs to decline entering into any correspondence with Mr Franklin Blake.'

Fond as I was of her, I felt indignantly the insult offered to me in that reply. Mr Bruff came in to speak to me on business, before I had recovered possession of myself. I dismissed the business on the spot, and laid the whole case before him. He proved to be as incapable of enlightening me as Mrs Merridew herself. I asked him if any slander had been spoken of me in Rachel's hearing. Mr Bruff was not aware of any slander of which I was the object. Had she referred to me in any way while she was staying under Mr Bruff's roof? Never. Had she not so much as asked, during all my long absence, whether I was living or dead? No such question had ever passed her lips. I took out of my pocket-book the letter which poor Lady Verinder had written to me from Frizinghall, on the day when I left her house in Yorkshire. And I pointed Mr Bruff's attention to these two sentences in it:

'The valuable assistance which you rendered to the inquiry after the lost jewel is still an unpardoned offence, in the present dreadful state of Rachel's mind. Moving blindfold in this matter, you have added to the burden of anxiety which she has had to bear, by innocently threatening her secret with discovery through your exertions.'

'Is it possible,' I asked, 'that the feeling towards me which is there described, is as bitter as ever against me now?'

Mr Bruff looked unaffectedly distressed.

'If you insist on an answer,' he said, 'I own I can place no other interpretation on her conduct than that.'

I rang the bell, and directed my servant to pack my portmanteau, and to send out for a railway guide. Mr Bruff asked, in astonishment, what I was going to do.

'I am going to Yorkshire,' I answered, 'by the next train.'

'May I ask for what purpose?'

'Mr Bruff, the assistance I innocently rendered to the inquiry after the Diamond was an unpardoned offence, in Rachel's mind, nearly a year since; and it remains an unpardoned offence still. I won't accept that position! I am determined to find out the secret of her silence towards her mother, and her enmity towards *me*. If time, pains, and money can do it, I will lay my hand on the thief who took the Moonstone!'

The worthy old gentleman attempted to remonstrate—to induce me to listen to reason—to do his duty towards me, in short. I was deaf to everything that he could urge. No earthly consideration would, at that moment, have shaken the resolution that was in me.

'I shall take up the inquiry again,' I went on, 'at the point where I dropped it; and I shall follow it onwards, step by step, till I come to the present time. There are missing links in the evidence, as *I* left it, which Gabriel Betteredge can supply, and to Gabriel Betteredge I go!'

Towards sunset that evening I stood again on the well-remembered terrace, and looked once more at the peaceful old country house. The gardener was the first person whom I saw in the deserted grounds. He had left Betteredge, an hour since, sunning himself in the customary corner of the back yard. I knew it well; and I said I would go and seek him myself.

I walked round by the familiar paths and passages, and looked in at the open gate of the yard.

There he was—the dear old friend of the happy days that were never to come again—there he was in the old corner, on the old beehive chair, with his pipe in his mouth, and his *Robinson Crusoe* on his lap, and his two friends, the dogs, dozing on either side of him! In the position in which I stood, my shadow was projected in front of me by the last slanting rays of the sun. Either the dogs saw it, or their keen scent informed them of my approach: they started up with a growl. Starting in his turn, the old man quieted them by a word, and then shaded his failing eyes with his hand, and looked inquiringly at the figure at the gate.

My own eyes were full of tears. I was obliged to wait for a moment before I could trust myself to speak to him.

CHAPTER II

'BETTEREDGE!' I said, pointing to the well-remembered book on his knee, 'has *Robinson Crusoe* informed you, this evening, that you might expect to see Franklin Blake?'

'By the lord Harry, Mr Franklin!' cried the old man, 'that's exactly what *Robinson Crusoe* has done!'

He struggled to his feet with my assistance, and stood for a moment, looking backwards and forwards between *Robinson Crusoe* and me, apparently at a loss to discover which of us had surprised him most. The verdict ended in favour of the book. Holding it open before him in both hands, he surveyed the wonderful volume with a stare of unutterable anticipation—as if he expected to see Robinson Crusoe himself walk out of the pages, and favour us with a personal interview.

'Here's the bit, Mr Franklin!' he said, as soon as he had recovered the use of his speech. 'As I live by bread, sir, here's the bit I was reading, the moment before you came in! Page one hundred and fifty-six as follows:—"I stood like one Thunderstruck, or as if I had seen an Apparition." If that isn't as much as to say: "Expect the sudden appearance of Mr Franklin Blake"—there's no meaning in the English language!' said Betteredge, closing the book with a bang, and getting one of his hands free at last to take the hand which I offered him.

I had expected him, naturally enough under the circumstances, to overwhelm me with questions. But no—the hospitable impulse was the uppermost impulse in the old servant's mind, when a member of the family appeared (no matter how!) as a visitor at the house.

'Walk in, Mr Franklin,' he said, opening the door behind him, with his quaint old-fashioned bow. 'I'll ask what brings you here afterwards—I must make you comfortable first. There have been sad changes, since you went away. The house is shut up, and the servants are gone. Never mind that! I'll cook your dinner; and the gardener's wife will make your bed—and if there's a bottle of our famous Latour claret left in the cellar, down your throat, Mr Franklin, that bottle shall go. I bid you welcome, sir! I bid you heartily welcome!' said the poor old fellow, fighting manfully against the gloom of the deserted house, and receiving me with the sociable and courteous attention of the bygone time.

It vexed me to disappoint him. But the house was Rachel's house, now. Could I eat in it, or sleep in it, after what had happened in London? The commonest sense of self-respect forbade me—properly forbade me—to cross the threshold.

I took Betteredge by the arm, and led him out into the garden. There was no help for it. I was obliged to tell him the truth. Between his attachment to Rachel, and his attachment to me, he was sorely puzzled and distressed at the turn things had taken. His opinion, when he expressed it, was given in his usual downright manner, and was agreeably redolent of the most positive philosophy I know—the philosophy of the Betteredge school.

'Miss Rachel has her faults—I've never denied it,' he began. 'And riding the high horse, now and then, is one of them. She has been trying to ride over *you*—and you have put up with it. Lord, Mr Franklin, don't you know women by this time better than that? You have heard me talk of the late Mrs Betteredge?'

I had heard him talk of the late Mrs Betteredge pretty often—invariably producing her as his one undeniable example of the inbred frailty and perversity of the other sex. In that capacity he exhibited her now.

'Very well, Mr Franklin. Now listen to me. Different women have different ways of riding the high horse. The late Mrs Betteredge took her exercise on that favourite female animal whenever I happened to deny her anything that she had set her heart on. So sure as I came home from my work on these occasions, so sure was my wife to call to me up the kitchen stairs, and to say that, after my brutal treatment of her, she hadn't the heart to cook me my dinner. I put up with it for some time—just as you are putting up with it now from Miss Rachel. At last my patience wore out. I went downstairs, and I took Mrs Betteredge—affectionately, you understand—up in my arms, and carried her, holus-bolus, into the best parlour where she received her company. I said "That's the right place for you, my dear," and so went back to the kitchen. I locked myself in, and took off my coat, and turned up my shirt-sleeves, and cooked my own dinner. When it was done, I served it up in my best manner, and enjoyed it most heartily. I had my pipe and my drop of grog afterwards; and then I cleared the table, and washed the crockery, and cleaned the knives and forks, and put the things away, and swept up the hearth. When things were as bright and clean again, as bright and clean could be, I opened the door and let Mrs Betteredge in. "I've had my dinner, my dear," I said; "and I hope you will find that I have left the kitchen all that your fondest wishes can desire." For the rest of that woman's life, Mr Franklin, I never had to cook my dinner again! Moral: You have put up with Miss Rachel in London; don't put up with her in Yorkshire. Come back to the house.'

Quite unanswerable! I could only assure my good friend that even *his* powers of persuasion were, in this case, thrown away on me.

'It's a lovely evening,' I said. 'I shall walk to Frizinghall, and stay at the hotel, and you must come to-morrow morning and breakfast with me. I have something to say to you.'

Betteredge shook his head gravely.

'I am heartily sorry for this,' he said. 'I had hoped, Mr Franklin, to hear that things were all smooth and pleasant again between you and Miss Rachel. If you must have your own way, sir,' he continued, after a moment's reflection, 'there is no need to go to Frizinghall to-night for a bed. It's to be had nearer than that. There's Hotherstone's Farm, barely two miles from here. You can hardly object to *that* on Miss Rachel's account,' the old man added slily. 'Hotherstone lives, Mr Franklin, on his own freehold.'

I remembered the place the moment Betteredge mentioned it. The farm-house stood in a sheltered inland valley, on the banks of the prettiest stream in that part of Yorkshire: and the farmer had a spare bedroom and parlour, which he was accustomed to let to artists, anglers, and tourists in general. A more agreeable place of abode, during my stay in the neighbourhood, I could not have wished to find.

'Are the rooms to let?' I inquired.

'Mrs Hotherstone herself, sir, asked for my good word to recommend the rooms, yesterday.'

'I'll take them, Betteredge, with the greatest pleasure.'

We went back to the yard, in which I had left my travelling-bag. After putting a stick through the handle, and swinging the bag over his shoulder, Betteredge appeared to relapse into the bewilderment which my sudden appearance had caused, when I surprised him in the beehive chair. He looked incredulously at the house, and then he wheeled about, and looked more incredulously still at me.

'I've lived a goodish long time in the world,' said this best and dearest of all old servants—'but the like of this, I never did expect to see. There stands the house, and here stands Mr Franklin Blake—and, Damme, if one of them isn't turning his back on the other, and going to sleep in a lodging!'

He led the way out, wagging his head and growling ominously. 'There's only one more miracle that *can* happen,' he said to me, over his shoulder. 'The next thing you'll do, Mr Franklin, will be to pay me back that seven-and-sixpence you borrowed of me when you were a boy.'

This stroke of sarcasm put him in a better humour with himself and with me. We left the house, and passed through the lodge gates. Once clear of the grounds, the duties of hospitality (in Betteredge's code of morals) ceased, and the privileges of curiosity began.

He dropped back, so as to let me get on a level with him. 'Fine evening for a walk, Mr Franklin,' he said, as if we had just accidentally encountered each other at that moment. 'Supposing you had gone to the hotel at Frizinghall, sir?'

'Yes?'

'I should have had the honour of breakfasting with you, to-morrow morning.'

'Come and breakfast with me at Hotherstone's Farm, instead.'

'Much obliged to you for your kindness, Mr Franklin. But it wasn't exactly breakfast that I was driving at. I think you mentioned that you had something to say to me? If it's no secret, sir,' said Betteredge, suddenly abandoning the crooked way, and taking the straight one, 'I'm burning to know what's brought you down here, if you please, in this sudden way.'

'What brought me here before?' I asked.

'The Moonstone, Mr Franklin. But what brings you now, sir?'

'The Moonstone again, Betteredge.'

The old man suddenly stood still, and looked at me in the grey twilight as if he suspected his own ears of deceiving him.

'If that's a joke, sir,' he said, 'I am afraid I'm getting a little dull in my old age. I don't take it.'

'It's no joke,' I answered. 'I have come here to take up the inquiry which was dropped when I left England. I have come here to do what nobody has done yet—to find out who took the Diamond.'

'Let the Diamond be, Mr Franklin! Take my advice, and let the Diamond be! That cursed Indian jewel has misguided everybody who has come near it. Don't waste your money and your temper—in the fine spring time of your life, sir—by meddling with the Moonstone. How can *you* hope to succeed (saving your presence), when Sergeant Cuff himself made a mess of it? Sergeant Cuff!' repeated Betteredge, shaking his forefinger at me sternly. 'The greatest policeman in England!'

'My mind is made up, my old friend. Even Sergeant Cuff doesn't daunt me. By-the-bye, I may want to speak to him, sooner or later. Have you heard anything of him lately?'

'The Sergeant won't help you, Mr Franklin.'

'Why not?'

'There has been an event, sir, in the police-circles, since you went away. The great Cuff has retired from business. He has got a little cottage at Dorking; and he's up to his eyes in the growing of roses. I have it in his own handwriting, Mr Franklin. He has grown the white moss rose, without budding it on the dog-rose first. And Mr Begbie the gardener is to go to Dorking, and own that the Sergeant has beaten him at last.'

'It doesn't much matter,' I said. 'I must do without Sergeant Cuff's help. And I must trust to you, at starting.'

It is likely enough that I spoke rather carelessly. At any rate, Betteredge seemed to be piqued by something in the reply which I had just made to him. 'You might trust to worse than me, Mr Franklin—I can tell you that,' he said a little sharply.

The tone in which he retorted, and a certain disturbance, after he had spoken, which I detected in his manner, suggested to me that he was possessed of some information which he hesitated to communicate.

'I expect you to help me,' I said, 'in picking up the fragments of evidence which Sergeant Cuff has left behind him. I know you can do that. Can you do no more?'

'What more can you expect from me, sir?' asked Betteredge, with an appearance of the utmost humility.

'I expect more—from what you said just now.'

'Mere boasting, Mr Franklin,' returned the old man obstinately. 'Some people are born boasters, and they never get over it to their dying day. I'm one of them.'

There was only one way to take with him. I appealed to his interest in Rachel, and his interest in me.

'Betteredge, would you be glad to hear that Rachel and I were good friends again?'

'I have served your family, sir, to mighty little purpose, if you doubt it!'

'Do you remember how Rachel treated me, before I left England?'

'As well as if it was yesterday! My lady herself wrote you a letter about it; and you were so good as to show the letter to me. It said that Miss Rachel was mortally offended with you, for the part you had taken in trying to recover her jewel. And neither my lady, nor you, nor anybody else could guess why.'

'Quite true, Betteredge! And I come back from my travels, and find her mortally offended with me still. I knew that the Diamond was at the bottom of it, last year, and I know that the Diamond is at the bottom of it now. I have tried to speak to her, and she won't see me. I have tried to write to her, and she won't answer me. How, in Heaven's name, am I to clear the matter up? The chance of searching into the loss of the Moonstone, is the one chance of inquiry that Rachel herself has left me.'

Those words evidently put the case before him, as he had not seen it yet. He asked a question which satisfied me that I had shaken him.

'There is no ill-feeling in this, Mr Franklin, on your side—is there?'

'There was some anger,' I answered, 'when I left London. But that is all worn out now. I want to make Rachel come to an understanding with me—and I want nothing more.'

'You don't feel any fear, sir—supposing you make any discoveries—in regard to what you may find out about Miss Rachel?'

I understood the jealous belief in his young mistress which prompted those words.

'I am as certain of her as you are,' I answered. 'The fullest disclosure of her secret will reveal nothing that can alter her place in your estimation, or in mine.'

Betteredge's last-left scruples vanished at that.

'If I am doing wrong to help you, Mr Franklin,' he exclaimed, 'all I can say is—I am as innocent of seeing it as the babe unborn! I can put you on the road to discovery, if you can only go on by yourself. You remember that poor girl of ours—Rosanna Spearman?'

'Of course!'

'You always thought she had some sort of confession, in regard to this matter of the Moonstone, which she wanted to make to you?'

'I certainly couldn't account for her strange conduct in any other way.'

'You may set that doubt at rest, Mr Franklin, whenever you please.'

It was my turn to come to a standstill now. I tried vainly, in the gathering darkness, to see his face. In the surprise of the moment, I asked a little impatiently what he meant.

'Steady, sir!' proceeded Betteredge. 'I mean what I say. Rosanna Spearman left a sealed letter behind her—a letter addressed to *you.*'

'Where is it?'

'In the possession of a friend of hers, at Cobb's Hole. You must have heard tell, when you were here last, sir, of Limping Lucy—a lame girl with a crutch.'

'The fisherman's daughter?'

'The same, Mr Franklin.'

'Why wasn't the letter forwarded to me?'

'Limping Lucy has a will of her own, sir. She wouldn't give it into any hands but yours. And you had left England before I could write to you.'

'Let's go back, Betteredge, and get it at once!'

'Too late, sir, to-night. They're great savers of candles along our coast; and they go to bed early at Cobb's Hole.'

'Nonsense! We might get there in half an hour.'

'*You* might, sir. And when you did get there, you would find the door locked.' He pointed to a light, glimmering below us; and, at the same moment, I heard through the stillness of the evening the bubbling of a stream. 'There's the Farm, Mr Franklin! Make yourself comfortable for to-night, and come to me to-morrow morning—if you'll be so kind?'

'You will go with me to the fisherman's cottage?'

'Yes, sir.'

'Early?'

'As early, Mr Franklin, as you like.'

We descended the path that led to the Farm.

CHAPTER III

I HAVE only the most indistinct recollection of what happened at Hother-stone's Farm.

I remember a hearty welcome; a prodigious supper, which would have fed a whole village in the East; a delightfully clean bedroom, with nothing in it to regret but that detestable product of the folly of our forefathers—a feather-bed; a restless night, with much kindling of matches, and many lightings of one little candle; and an immense sensation of relief when the sun rose, and there was a prospect of getting up.

It had been arranged over-night with Betteredge, that I was to call for him, on our way to Cobb's Hole, as early as I liked—which, interpreted by my impatience to get possession of the letter, meant as early as I could. Without waiting for breakfast at the Farm, I took a crust of bread in my hand, and set forth, in some doubt whether I should not surprise the excellent Betteredge in his bed. To my great relief he proved to be quite as excited about the coming event as I was. I found him ready, and waiting for me, with his stick in his hand.

'How are you this morning, Betteredge?

'Very poorly, sir.'

'Sorry to hear it. What do you complain of?'

'I complain of a new disease, Mr Franklin, of my own inventing. I don't want to alarm you, but you're certain to catch it before the morning is out.'

'The devil I am!'

'Do you feel an uncomfortable heat at the pit of your stomach, sir? and a nasty thumping at the top of your head? Ah! not yet? It will lay hold of you at Cobb's Hole, Mr Franklin. I call it the detective-fever; and *I* first caught it in the company of Sergeant Cuff.'

'Aye! aye! and the cure in this instance is to open Rosanna Spearman's letter, I suppose? Come along, and let's get it.'

Early as it was, we found the fisherman's wife astir in her kitchen. On my presentation by Betteredge, good Mrs Yolland performed a social ceremony, strictly reserved (as I afterwards learnt) for strangers of distinction. She put a bottle of Dutch gin and a couple of clean pipes on the table, and opened the conversation by saying, 'What news from London, sir?'

Before I could find an answer to this immensely comprehensive question, an apparition advanced towards me, out of a dark corner of the kitchen. A wan, wild, haggard girl, with remarkably beautiful hair, and with a fierce keenness in her eyes, came limping up on a crutch to the table at which I was sitting, and looked at me as if I was an object of mingled interest and horror, which it quite fascinated her to see.

'Mr Betteredge,' she said, without taking her eyes off me, 'mention his name again, if you please.'

'This gentleman's name,' answered Betteredge (with a strong emphasis on *gentleman*), 'is Mr Franklin Blake.'

The girl turned her back on me, and suddenly left the room. Good Mrs Yolland—as I believe—made some apologies for her daughter's odd behaviour, and Betteredge (probably) translated them into polite English. I speak of this in complete uncertainty. My attention was absorbed in following the sound of the girl's crutch. Thump-thump, up the wooden stairs; thump-thump across the room above our heads; thump-thump down the stairs again—and there stood the apparition at the open door, with a letter in its hand, beckoning me out!

I left more apologies in course of delivery behind me, and followed this strange creature—limping on before me, faster and faster—down the slope of the beach. She led me behind some boats, out of sight and hearing of the few people in the fishing-village, and then stopped, and faced me for the first time.

'Stand there,' she said, 'I want to look at you.'

There was no mistaking the expression on her face. I inspired her with the strongest emotions of abhorrence and disgust. Let me not be vain enough to say that no woman had ever looked at me in this manner before. I will only venture on the more modest assertion that no woman had ever let me perceive it yet. There is a limit to the length of the inspection which a man can endure, under certain circumstances. I attempted to direct Limping Lucy's attention to some less revolting object than my face.

'I think you have got a letter to give me,' I began. 'Is it the letter there, in your hand?'

'Say that again,' was the only answer I received.

I repeated the words, like a good child learning its lesson.

'No,' said the girl, speaking to herself, but keeping her eyes still mercilessly fixed on me. 'I can't find out what she saw in his face. I can't guess what she heard in his voice.' She suddenly looked away from me, and rested her head wearily on the top of her crutch. 'Oh, my poor dear!' she said, in the first soft tones which had fallen from her, in my hearing. 'Oh, my lost darling! what could you see in this man?' She lifted her head again fiercely, and looked at me once more. 'Can you eat and drink?' she asked.

I did my best to preserve my gravity, and answered, 'Yes.'

'Can you sleep?'

'Yes.'

'When you see a poor girl in service, do you feel no remorse?'

'Certainly not. Why should I?'

She abruptly thrust the letter (as the phrase is) into my face.

'Take it!' she exclaimed furiously. 'I never set eyes on you before. God Almighty forbid I should ever set eyes on you again.'

With those parting words she limped away from me at the top of her speed. The one interpretation that I could put on her conduct has, no doubt, been anticipated by everybody. I could only suppose that she was mad.

Having reached that inevitable conclusion, I turned to the more interesting object of investigation which was presented to me by Rosanna Spearman's letter. The address was written as follows:—'For Franklin Blake, Esq. To be given into his own hands (and not to be trusted to any one else), by Lucy Yolland.'

I broke the seal. The envelope contained a letter: and this, in its turn, contained a slip of paper. I read the letter first:—

'Sir,—If you are curious to know the meaning of my behaviour to you, whilst you were staying in the house of my mistress, Lady Verinder, do what you are told to do in the memorandum enclosed with this—and do it without any person being present to overlook you. Your humble servant,
ROSANNA SPEARMAN.'

I turned to the slip of paper next. Here is the literal copy of it, word for word:

'Memorandum:—To go to the Shivering Sand at the turn of the tide. To walk out on the South Spit, until I get the South Spit Beacon, and the flagstaff at the Coast-guard station above Cobb's Hole in a line together. To lay down on the rocks, a stick, or any straight thing to guide my hand, exactly in the line of the beacon and the flagstaff. To take care, in doing this, that one end of the stick shall be at the edge of the rocks, on the side of them which overlooks the quicksand. To feel along the stick, among the seaweed (beginning from the end of the stick which points towards the beacon), for the Chain. To run my hand along the Chain, when found, until I come to the part of it which stretches over the edge of the rocks, down into the quicksand. *And then, to pull the chain.*'

Just as I had read the last words—underlined in the original—I heard the voice of Betteredge behind me. The inventor of the detective-fever had completely succumbed to that irresistible malady. 'I can't stand it any longer, Mr Franklin. What does her letter say? For mercy's sake, sir, tell us, what does her letter say?'

I handed him the letter, and the memorandum. He read the first without appearing to be much interested in it. But the second—the memorandum—produced a strong impression on him.

'The Sergeant said it!' cried Betteredge. 'From first to last, sir, the Sergeant said she had got a memorandum of the hiding-place. And here it is! Lord save us, Mr Franklin, here is the secret that puzzled everybody, from the great Cuff downwards, ready and waiting, as one may say, to show itself to *you!* It's the ebb now, sir, as anybody may see for themselves. How long will it be till the turn of the tide?' He looked up, and observed a lad at work, at some little distance from us, mending a net. 'Tammie Bright!' he shouted at the top of his voice.

'I hear you!' Tammie shouted back.

'When 's the turn of the tide?'

'In an hour's time.'

We both looked at our watches.

'We can go round by the coast, Mr Franklin,' said Betteredge; 'and get to the quicksand in that way, with plenty of time to spare. What do you say, sir?'

'Come along!'

On our way to the Shivering Sand, I applied to Betteredge to revive my memory of events (as affecting Rosanna Spearman) at the period of Sergeant Cuff's inquiry. With my old friend's help, I soon had the succession of circumstances clearly registered in my mind. Rosanna's journey to Frizing-hall, when the whole household believed her to be ill in her own room—Rosanna's mysterious employment of the night-time, with her door locked, and her candle burning till the morning—Rosanna's suspicious purchase of the japanned tin case, and the two dog's chains from Mrs Yolland—the Sergeant's positive conviction that Rosanna had hidden something at the Shivering Sand, and the Sergeant's absolute ignorance as to what that something might be—all these strange results of the abortive inquiry into the loss of the Moonstone were clearly present to me again, when we reached the quicksand, and walked out together on the low ledge of rocks called the South Spit.

With Betteredge's help, I soon stood in the right position to see the Beacon and the Coast-guard flagstaff in a line together. Following the memorandum as our guide, we next laid my stick in the necessary direction, as neatly as we could, on the uneven surface of the rocks. And then we looked at our watches once more.

It wanted nearly twenty minutes yet of the turn of the tide. I suggested waiting through this interval on the beach, instead of on the wet and slippery surface of the rocks. Having reached the dry sand, I prepared to sit down; and, greatly to my surprise, Betteredge prepared to leave me.

'What are you going away for?' I asked.

'Look at the letter again, sir, and you will see.'

A glance at the letter reminded me that I was charged, when I made my discovery, to make it alone.

'It's hard enough for me to leave you, at such a time as this,' said Betteredge. 'But she died a dreadful death, poor soul—and I feel a kind of call on me, Mr Franklin, to humour that fancy of hers. Besides,' he added, confidentially, 'there's nothing in the letter against your letting out the secret afterwards. I'll hang about in the fir plantation, and wait till you pick me up. Don't be longer than you can help, sir. The detective-fever isn't an easy disease to deal with, under *these* circumstances.'

With that parting caution, he left me.

The interval of expectation, short as it was when reckoned by the measure of time, assumed formidable proportions when reckoned by the measure of suspense. This was one of the occasions on which the invaluable habit of smoking becomes especially precious and consolatory. I lit a cigar, and sat down on the slope of the beach.

The sunlight poured its unclouded beauty on every object that I could see. The exquisite freshness of the air made the mere act of living and breathing a luxury. Even the lonely little bay welcomed the morning with a show of cheerfulness; and the bared wet surface of the quicksand itself, glittering with a golden brightness, hid the horror of its false brown face under a passing smile. It was the finest day I had seen since my return to England.

The turn of the tide came, before my cigar was finished. I saw the preliminary heaving of the Sand, and then the awful shiver that crept over its surface—as if some spirit of terror lived and moved and shuddered in the fathomless deeps beneath. I threw away my cigar, and went back again to the rocks.

My directions in the memorandum instructed me to feel along the line traced by the stick, beginning with the end which was nearest to the beacon.

I advanced, in this manner, more than half way along the stick, without encountering anything but the edges of the rocks. An inch or two further on, however, my patience was rewarded. In a narrow little fissure, just within reach of my forefinger, I felt the chain. Attempting, next, to follow it, by touch, in the direction of the quicksand, I found my progress stopped by a thick growth of seaweed—which had fastened itself into the fissure, no doubt, in the time that had elapsed since Rosanna Spearman had chosen her hiding-place.

It was equally impossible to pull up the seaweed, or to force my hand through it. After marking the spot indicated by the end of the stick which was placed nearest to the quicksand, I determined to pursue the search for the chain on a plan of my own. My idea was to 'sound' immediately under the rocks, on the chance of recovering the lost trace of the chain at the point at which it entered the sand. I took up the stick, and knelt down on the brink of the South Spit.

In this position, my face was within a few feet of the surface of the quicksand. The sight of it so near me, still disturbed at intervals by its hideous shivering fit, shook my nerves for the moment. A horrible fancy that the dead woman might appear on the scene of her suicide, to assist my search—an unutterable dread of seeing her rise through the heaving surface of the sand, and point to the place—forced itself into my mind, and turned me cold in the warm sunlight. I own I closed my eyes at the moment when the point of the stick first entered the quicksand.

The instant afterwards, before the stick could have been submerged more than a few inches, I was free from the hold of my own superstitious terror, and was throbbing with excitement from head to foot. Sounding blindfolld, at my first attempt—at that first attempt I had sounded right! The stick struck the chain.

Taking a firm hold of the roots of the seaweed with my left hand, I laid myself down over the brink, and felt with my right hand under the overhanging edges of the rock. My right hand found the chain.

I drew it up without the slightest difficulty. And there was the japanned tin case fastened to the end of it.

The action of the water had so rusted the chain, that it was impossible for me to unfasten it from the hasp which attached it to the case. Putting the case between my knees and exerting my utmost strength, I contrived to draw off the cover. Some white substance filled the whole interior when I looked in. I put in my hand, and found it to be linen.

In drawing out the linen, I also drew out a letter crumpled up with it. After looking at the direction, and discovering that it bore my name, I put the letter in my pocket, and completely removed the linen. It came out in a thick roll, moulded, of course, to the shape of the case in which it had been so long confined, and perfectly preserved from any injury by the sea.

I carried the linen to the dry sand of the beach, and there unrolled and smoothed it out. There was no mistaking it as an article of dress. It was a nightgown.

The uppermost side, when I spread it out, presented to view innumerable folds and creases, and nothing more. I tried the undermost side, next—and instantly discovered the smear of the paint from the door of Rachel's boudoir!

My eyes remained riveted on the stain, and my mind took my back at a leap from present to past. The very words of Sergeant Cuff recurred to me, as if the man himself was at my side again, pointing to the unanswerable inference which he drew from the smear on the door.

'Find out whether there is any article of dress in this house with the stain of paint on it. Find out who that dress belongs to. Find out how the person can account for having been in the room, and smeared the paint, between midnight and three in the morning. If the person can't satisfy you, you haven't far to look for the hand that took the Diamond.'

One after another those words travelled over my memory, repeating themselves again and again with a wearisome, mechanical reiteration. I was roused from what felt like a trance of many hours—from what was really, no doubt, the pause of a few moments only—by a voice calling to me. I looked up, and saw that Betteredge's patience had failed him at last. He was just visible between the sandhills, returning to the beach.

The old man's appearance recalled me, the moment I perceived it, to my sense of present things, and reminded me that the inquiry which I had pursued thus far still remained incomplete. I had discovered the smear on the nightgown. To whom did the nightgown belong?

My first impulse was to consult the letter in my pocket—the letter which I had found in the case.

As I raised my hand to take it out, I remembered that there was a shorter way to discovery than this. The nightgown itself would reveal the truth; for, in all probability, the nightgown was marked with its owner's name.

I took it up from the sand, and looked for the mark.

I found the mark, and read—

MY OWN NAME.

There were the familiar letters which told me that the nightgown was mine. I looked up from them. There was the sun; there were the glittering waters of the bay; there was old Betteredge, advancing nearer and nearer to me. I looked back again at the letters. My own name. Plainly confronting me—my own name.

'If time, pains, and money can do it, I will lay my hand on the thief who took the Moonstone.'—I had left London, with those words on my lips. I had penetrated the secret which the quicksand had kept from every other living creature. And, on the unanswerable evidence of the paint-stain, I had discovered Myself as the Thief.

CHAPTER IV

I HAVE not a word to say about my own sensations.

My impression is, that the shock inflicted on me completely suspended my thinking and feeling power. I certainly could not have known what I was about when Betteredge joined me—for I have it on his authority that I laughed, when he asked what was the matter, and putting the nightgown into his hands, told him to read the riddle for himself.

Of what was said between us on the beach, I have not the faintest recollection. The first place in which I can now see myself again plainly is the plantation of firs. Betteredge and I are walking back together to the house; and Betteredge is telling me that I shall be able to face it, and he will be able to face it, when we have had a glass of grog.

The scene shifts from the plantation, to Betteredge's little sitting-room. My resolution not to enter Rachel's house is forgotten. I feel gratefully the coolness and shadiness and quiet of the room. I drink the grog (a perfectly new luxury to me, at that time of day), which my good old friend mixes with icy-cold water from the well. Under any other circumstances, the drink would simply stupefy me. As things are, it strings up my nerves. I begin to 'face it,' as Betteredge has predicted. And Betteredge, on his side, begins to 'face it,' too.

The picture which I am now presenting of myself, will, I suspect, be thought a very strange one, to say the least of it. Placed in a situation which may, I think, be described as entirely without parallel, what is the first proceeding to which I resort? Do I seclude myself from all human society? Do I set my mind to analyse the abominable impossibility which, neverthe- less, confronts me as an undeniable fact? Do I hurry back to London by the first train to consult the highest authorities, and to set a searching inquiry on foot immediately? No. I accept the shelter of a house which I had resolved never to degrade myself by entering again; and I sit, tippling spirits and water in the company of an old servant, at ten o'clock in the morning. Is this the conduct that might have been expected from a man placed in my horrible position? I can only answer that the sight of old Betteredge's familiar face was an inexpressible comfort to me, and that the drinking of old Betteredge's grog helped me, as I believe nothing else would have helped me, in the state of complete bodily and mental prostration into which I had fallen. I can only offer this excuse for myself; and I can only admire that invariable preservation of dignity, and that strictly logical consistency of conduct which distinguish every man and woman who may read these lines, in every emergency of their lives from the cradle to the grave.

'Now, Mr Franklin, there's one thing certain, at any rate,' said Betteredge, throwing the nightgown down on the table between us, and pointing to it as if it was a living creature that could hear him. '*He's* a liar, to begin with.'

This comforting view of the matter was not the view that presented itself to my mind.

'I am as innocent of all knowledge of having taken the Diamond as you are,' I said. 'But there is the witness against me! The paint on the nightgown, and the name on the nightgown are facts.'

Betteredge lifted my glass, and put it persuasively into my hand.

'Facts?' he repeated. 'Take a drop more grog, Mr Franklin, and you'll get over the weakness of believing in facts! Foul play, sir!' he continued, dropping his voice confidentially. 'That is how I read the riddle. Foul play somewhere—and you and I must find it out. Was there nothing else in the tin case, when you put your hand into it?'

The question instantly reminded me of the letter in my pocket. I took it out, and opened it. It was a letter of many pages, closely written. I looked impatiently for the signature at the end. 'Rosanna Spearman.'

As I read the name, a sudden remembrance illuminated my mind, and a sudden suspicion rose out of the new light.

'Stop!' I exclaimed. 'Rosanna Spearman came to my aunt out of a reformatory? Rosanna Spearman had once been a thief?'

'There's no denying that, Mr Franklin. What of it now, if you please?'

'What of it now? How do we know she may not have stolen the Diamond after all? How do we know she may not have smeared my nightgown purposely with the paint——?'

Betteredge laid his hand on my arm, and stopped me before I could say any more.

'You will be cleared of this, Mr Franklin, beyond all doubt. But I hope you won't be cleared in *that* way. See what the letter says, sir. In justice to the girl's memory, see what it says.'

I felt the earnestness with which he spoke—felt it as a friendly rebuke to me. 'You shall form your own judgement on her letter,' I said. 'I will read it out.'

I began—and read these lines:

'Sir—I have something to own to you. A confession which means much misery, may sometimes be made in very few words. This confession can be made in three words. I love you.'

The letter dropped from my hand, I looked at Betteredge. 'In the name of Heaven,' I said, 'what does it mean?'

He seemed to shrink from answering the question.

'You and Limping Lucy were alone together this morning, sir,' he said. 'Did she say nothing about Rosanna Spearman?'

'She never even mentioned Rosanna Spearman's name.'

'Please to go back to the letter, Mr Franklin. I tell you plainly, I can't find it in my heart to distress you, after what you have had to bear already. Let her speak for herself, sir. And get on with your grog. For your own sake, get on with your grog.'

I resumed the reading of the letter.

'It would be very disgraceful to me to tell you this, if I was a living woman when you read it. I shall be dead and gone, sir, when you find my letter. It is that which makes me bold. Not even my grave will be left to tell of me. I may own the truth—with the quicksand waiting to hide me when the words are written.

'Besides, you will find your nightgown in my hiding-place, with the smear of the paint on it; and you will want to know how it came to be hidden by me? and why I said nothing to you about it in my life-time? I have only one reason to give. I did these strange things, because I loved you.

'I won't trouble you with much about myself, or my life, before you came to my lady's house. Lady Verinder took me out of a reformatory. I had gone to the reformatory from the prison. I was put in the prison, because I was a thief. I was a thief, because my mother went on the streets when I was quite a little girl. My mother went on the streets, because the gentleman who was my father deserted her. There is no need to tell such a common story as this, at any length. It is told quite often enough in the newspapers.

'Lady Verinder was very kind to me, and Mr Betteredge was very kind to me. Those two, and the matron at the reformatory, are the only good people I have ever met with in all my life. I might have got on in my place—not happily—but I might have got on, if you had not come visiting. I don't blame *you*, sir. It's my fault—all my fault.

'Do you remember when you came out on us from among the sand hills, that morning, looking for Mr Betteredge? You were like a prince in a fairy-story. You were like a lover in a dream. You were the most adorable human creature I had ever seen. Something that felt like the happy life I had never led yet, leapt up in me at the instant I set eyes on you. Don't laugh at this if you can help it. Oh, if I could only make you feel how serious it is to *me!*

'I went back to the house, and wrote your name and mine in my work-box, and drew a true lovers' knot under them. Then, some devil—no, I ought to say some good angel—whispered to me, "Go and look in the glass." The glass told me—never mind what. I was too foolish to take the warning. I went on getting fonder and fonder of you, just as if I was a lady in your own rank of life, and the most beautiful creature your eyes ever rested on. I tried—oh, dear, how I tried—to get you to look at me. If you had known how I used to cry at night with the misery and the mortification of your never taking any notice of me, you would have pitied me perhaps, and have given me a look now and then to live on.

'It would have been no very kind look, perhaps, if you had known how I hated Miss Rachel. I believe I found out you were in love with her, before you knew it yourself. She used to give you roses to wear in your button-hole. Ah, Mr Franklin, you wore *my* roses oftener than either you or she thought! The only comfort I had at that time, was putting my rose secretly in your glass of water, in place of hers—and then throwing her rose away.

'If she had been really as pretty as you thought her, I might have borne it better. No; I believe I should have been more spiteful against her still. Suppose you put Miss Rachel into a servant's dress, and took her ornaments off——? I don't know what is the use of my writing in this way. It can't be denied that she had a bad figure; she was too thin. But who can tell what the men like? And young ladies may behave in a manner which would cost a servant her place. It's no business of mine. I can't expect you to read my letter, if I write it in this way. But it does stir one up to hear Miss Rachel called pretty, when one knows all the time that it's her dress does it, and her confidence in herself.

'Try not to lose patience with me, sir. I will get on as fast as I can to the time which is sure to interest you—the time when the Diamond was lost.

'But there is one thing which I have got it on my mind to tell you first.

'My life was not a very hard life to bear, while I was a thief. It was only when they had taught me at the reformatory to feel my own degradation, and to try for better things, that the days grew long and weary. Thoughts of the future forced themselves on me now. I felt the dreadful reproach that honest people—even the kindest of honest people—were to me in themselves. A heart-breaking sensation of loneliness kept with me, go where I might, and do what I might, and see what persons I might. It was my duty, I know, to try and get on with my fellow-servants in my new place. Somehow, I couldn't make friends with them. They looked (or I thought they looked) as if they suspected what I had been. I don't regret, far from it, having been roused to make the effort to be a reformed woman—but, indeed, indeed it was a weary life. You had come across it like a beam of sunshine at first—and then you too failed me. I was mad enough to love you; and I couldn't even attract your notice. There was great misery—there really was great misery in that.

'Now I am coming to what I wanted to tell you. In those days of bitterness, I went two or three times, when it was my turn to go out, to my favourite place—the beach above the Shivering Sand. And I said to myself, "I think it will end here. When I can bear it no longer, I think it will end here." You will understand, sir, that the place had laid a kind of spell on me before you came. I had always had a notion that something would happen to me at the quicksand. But I had never looked at it, with the thought of its being the means of my making away with myself, till the time came of which I am now writing. Then I did think that here was a place which would end all my troubles for me in a moment or two—and hide me for ever afterwards.

'This is all I have to say about myself, reckoning from the morning when I first saw you, to the morning when the alarm was raised in the house that the Diamond was lost.

'I was so aggravated by the foolish talk among the women servants, all wondering who was to be suspected first; and I was so angry with you (knowing no better at that time) for the pains you took in hunting for the jewel, and sending for the police, that I kept as much as possible away by myself, until later in the day, when the officer from Frizinghall came to the house.

'Mr Seegrave began, as you may remember, by setting a guard on the women's bedrooms; and the women all followed him up-stairs in a rage, to know what he meant by the insult he had put on them. I went with the rest, because if I had done anything different from the rest, Mr Seegrave was the sort of man who would have suspected me directly. We found him in Miss Rachel's room. He told us he wouldn't have a lot of women there; and he pointed to the smear on the painted door, and said some of our petticoats had done the mischief, and sent us all down-stairs again.

'After leaving Miss Rachel's room, I stopped a moment on one of the landings, by myself, to see if I had got the paint-stain by any chance on *my* gown. Penelope Betteredge (the only one of the women with whom I was on friendly terms) passed, and noticed what I was about.

' "You needn't trouble yourself, Rosanna," she said. "The paint on Miss Rachel's door has been dry for hours. If Mr Seegrave hadn't set a watch on our bedrooms, I might have told him as much. I don't know what *you* think—*I* was never so insulted before in my life!"

'Penelope was a hot-tempered girl. I quieted her, and brought her back to what she had said about the paint on the door having been dry for hours.

' "How do you know that?" I asked.

' "I was with Miss Rachel, and Mr Franklin, all yesterday morning," Penelope said, "mixing the colours, while they finished the door. I heard

Miss Rachel ask whether the door would be dry that evening, in time for the birthday company to see it. And Mr Franklin shook his head, and said it wouldn't be dry in less than twelve hours. It was long past luncheon-time—it was three o'clock before they had done. What does your arithmetic say, Rosanna? Mine says the door was dry by three this morning."

' "Did some of the ladies go up-stairs yesterday evening to see it?" I asked. "I thought I heard Miss Rachel warning them to keep clear of the door."

' "None of the ladies made the smear," Penelope answered. "I left Miss Rachel in bed at twelve last night. And I noticed the door, and there was nothing wrong with it then."

' "Oughtn't you to mention this to Mr Seegrave, Penelope?"

' "I wouldn't say a word to help Mr Seegrave for anything that could be offered to me!"

'She went to her work, and I went to mine.

'My work, sir, was to make your bed, and to put your room tidy. It was the happiest hour I had in the whole day. I used to kiss the pillow on which your head had rested all night. No matter who has done it since, you have never had your clothes folded as nicely as I folded them for you. Of all the little knick-knacks in your dressing-case, there wasn't one that had so much as a speck on it. You never noticed it, any more than you noticed me. I beg your pardon; I am forgetting myself. I will make haste, and go on again.

'Well, I went in that morning to do my work in your room. There was your nightgown tossed across the bed, just as you had thrown it off. I took it up to fold it—and I saw the stain of the paint from Miss Rachel's door!

'I was so startled by the discovery that I ran out, with the nightgown in my hand, and made for the back stairs, and locked myself into my own room, to look at it in a place where nobody could intrude and interrupt me.

'As soon as I got my breath again, I called to mind my talk with Penelope, and I said to myself, "Here's the proof that he was in Miss Rachel's sitting-room between twelve last night, and three this morning!"

'I shall not tell you in plain words what was the first suspicion that crossed my mind, when I had made that discovery. You would only be angry—and, if you were angry, you might tear my letter up and read no more of it.

'Let it be enough, if you please, to say only this. After thinking it over to the best of my ability, I made it out that the thing wasn't likely, for a reason that I will tell you. If you had been in Miss Rachel's sitting-room, at that time of night, with Miss Rachel's knowledge (and if you had been foolish enough to forget to take care of the wet door) *she* would have reminded you—*she* would never have let you carry away such a witness against her, as the witness I was looking at now! At the same time, I own I was not completely certain in my own mind that I had proved my own suspicion to be wrong. You will not have forgotten that I have owned to hating Miss Rachel. Try to think, if you can, that there was a little of that hatred in all this. It ended in my determining to keep the nightgown, and to wait, and watch, and see what use I might make of it. At that time, please to remember, not the ghost of an idea entered my head that *you* had stolen the Diamond.'

There, I broke off in the reading of the letter for the second time.

I had read those portions of the miserable woman's confession which related to myself, with unaffected surprise, and, I can honestly add, with sincere distress. I had regretted, truly regretted, the aspersion which I had thoughtlessly cast on her memory, before I had seen a line of her letter. But when I had advanced as far as the passage which is quoted above, I own I felt my mind growing bitterer and bitterer against Rosanna Spearman as I went on. 'Read the rest for yourself,' I said, handing the letter to Betteredge across the table. 'If there is anything in it that I *must* look at, you can tell me as you go on.'

'I understand you, Mr Franklin,' he answered. 'It's natural, sir, in *you*. And, God help us all!' he added in a lower tone, 'it's no less natural in *her*.'

I proceed to copy the continuation of the letter from the original, in my own possession:—

'Having determined to keep the nightgown, and to see what use my love, or my revenge (I hardly know which) could turn it to in the future, the next thing to discover was how to keep it without the risk of being found out.

'There was only one way—to make another nightgown exactly like it, before Saturday came, and brought the laundry-woman and her inventory to the house.

'I was afraid to put it off till next day (the Friday); being in doubt lest some accident might happen in the interval. I determined to make the new nightgown on that same day (the Thursday), while I could count, if I played my cards properly, on having my time to myself. The first thing to do (after locking up your nightgown in my drawer) was to go back to your bed-room—not so much to put it to rights (Penelope would have done that for me, if I had asked her) as to find out whether you had smeared off any of the paint-stain from your nightgown, on the bed, or on any piece of furniture in the room.

'I examined everything narrowly, and at last, I found a few streaks of the paint on the inside of your dressing-gown—not the linen dressing-gown you usually wore in that summer season, but a flannel dressing-gown which you had with you also. I suppose you felt chilly after walking to and fro in nothing but your nightdress, and put on the warmest thing you could find. At any rate, there were the stains, just visible, on the inside of the dressing-gown. I easily got rid of these by scraping away the stuff of the flannel. This done, the only proof left against you was the proof locked up in my drawer.

'I had just finished your room when I was sent for to be questioned by Mr Seegrave, along with the rest of the servants. Next came the examination of all our boxes. And then followed the most extraordinary event of the day—to *me*—since I had found the paint on your nightgown. This event came out of the second questioning of Penelope Betteredge by Superintendent Seegrave.

'Penelope returned to us quite beside herself with rage at the manner in which Mr Seegrave had treated her. He had hinted, beyond the possibility of mistaking him, that he suspected her of being the thief. We were all equally astonished at hearing this, and we all asked, Why?

' "Because the Diamond was in Miss Rachel's sitting-room," Penelope answered. "And because I was the last person in the sitting-room at night!"

'Almost before the words had left her lips, I remembered that another person had been in the sitting-room later than Penelope. That person was yourself. My head whirled round, and my thoughts were in dreadful confusion. In the midst of it all, something in my mind whispered to me that the smear on your nightgown might have a meaning entirely different to the meaning which I had given to it up to that time. "If the last person who was in the room is the person to be suspected," I thought to myself, "the thief is not Penelope, but Mr Franklin Blake!"

'In the case of any other gentleman, I believe I should have been ashamed of suspecting him of theft, almost as soon as the suspicion had passed through my mind.

'But the bare thought that YOU had let yourself down to my level, and that I, in possessing myself of your nightgown, had also possessed myself of the means of shielding you from being discovered, and disgraced for life—I say, sir, the bare thought of this seemed to open such a chance before me of winning your good will, that I passed blindfold, as one may say, from suspecting to believing. I made up my mind, on the spot, that you had shown yourself the busiest of anybody in fetching the police, as a blind to deceive us all; and that the hand which had taken Miss Rachel's jewel could by no possibility be any other hand than yours.

'The excitement of this new discovery of mine must, I think, have turned my head for a while. I felt such a devouring eagerness to see you—to try you with a word or two about the Diamond, and to *make* you look at me, and speak to me, in that way—that I put my hair tidy, and made myself as nice as I could, and went to you boldly in the library where I knew you were writing.

'You had left one of your rings up-stairs, which made as good an excuse for my intrusion as I could have desired. But, oh, sir! if you have ever loved, you will understand how it was that all my courage cooled, when I walked into the room, and found myself in your presence. And then, you looked up at me so coldly, and you thanked me for finding your ring in such an indifferent manner, that my knees trembled under me, and I felt as if I should drop on the floor at your feet. When you had thanked me, you looked back, if you remember, at your writing. I was so mortified at being treated in this way, that I plucked up spirit enough to speak. I said, "This is a strange thing about the Diamond, sir." And you looked up again, and said, "Yes, it is!" You spoke civilly (I can't deny that); but still you kept a distance—a cruel distance between us. Believing, as I did, that you had got the lost Diamond hidden about you, while you were speaking, your coolness so provoked me that I got bold enough, in the heat of the moment, to give you a hint. I said, "They will never find the Diamond, sir, will they? No! nor the person who took it—I'll answer for that." I nodded, and smiled at you, as much as to say, "I know!" *This* time, you looked up at me with something like interest in your eyes; and I felt that a few more words on your side and mine might bring out the truth. Just at that moment, Mr Betteredge spoilt it all by coming to the door. I knew his footstep, and I also knew that it was against his rules for me to be in the library at that time of day—let alone being there along with you. I had only just time to get out of my own accord, before he could come in and tell me to go. I was angry and disappointed; but I was not entirely without hope for all that. The ice, you see, was broken between us—and I thought I would take care, on the next occasion, that Mr Betteredge was out of the way.

'When I got back to the servants' hall, the bell was going for our dinner. Afternoon already! and the materials for making the new nightgown were still to be got! There was but one chance of getting them. I shammed ill at dinner; and so secured the whole of the interval from then till tea-time to my own use.

'What I was about, while the household believed me to be lying down in my own room; and how I spent the night, after shamming ill again at tea-time, and having been sent up to bed, there is no need to tell you. Sergeant Cuff discovered that much, if he discovered nothing more. And I can guess how. I was detected (though I kept my veil down) in the draper's shop at Frizinghall. There was a glass in front of me, at the counter where I was buying the longcloth; and—in that glass—I saw one of the shopmen point to my shoulder and whisper to another. At night again, when I was secretly at work, locked into my room, I heard the breathing of the women servants who suspected me, outside my door.

'It didn't matter then; it doesn't matter now. On the Friday morning, hours before Sergeant Cuff entered the house, there was the new night-gown—to make up your number in place of the nightgown that I had got—made, wrung out, dried, ironed, marked, and folded as the laundry woman folded all the others, safe in your drawer. There was no fear (if the linen in the house was examined) of the newness of the nightgown betraying me. All your underclothing had been renewed, when you came to our house—I suppose on your return home from foreign parts.

'The next thing was the arrival of Sergeant Cuff; and the next great surprise was the announcement of what *he* thought about the smear on the door.

'I had believed you to be guilty (as I have owned) more because I wanted you to be guilty than for any other reason. And now, the Sergeant had come round by a totally different way to the same conclusion (respecting the nightgown) as mine! And I had got the dress that was the only proof against you! And not a living creature knew it—yourself included! I am afraid to tell you how I felt when I called these things to mind—you would hate my memory for ever afterwards.'

At that place, Betteredge looked up from the letter.

'Not a glimmer of light so far, Mr Franklin,' said the old man, taking off his heavy tortoiseshell spectacles, and pushing Rosanna Spearman's confession a little away from him. 'Have you come to any conclusion, sir, in your own mind, while I have been reading?'

'Finish the letter first, Betteredge; there may be something to enlighten us at the end of it. I shall have a word or two to say to you after that.'

'Very good, sir. I'll just rest my eyes, and then I'll go on again. In the meantime, Mr Franklin—I don't want to hurry you—but would you mind telling me, in one word, whether you see your way out of this dreadful mess yet?'

'I see my way back to London,' I said, 'to consult Mr Bruff. If he can't help me——'

'Yes, sir?'

'And if the Sergeant won't leave his retirement at Dorking——'

'He won't, Mr Franklin!'

'Then, Betteredge—as far as I can see now—I am at the end of my resources. After Mr Bruff and the Sergeant, I don't know of a living creature who can be of the slightest use to me.'

As the words passed my lips, some person outside knocked at the door of the room.

Betteredge looked surprised as well as annoyed by the interruption.

'Come in,' he called out, irritably, 'whoever you are!'

The door opened, and there entered to us, quietly, the most remarkable-looking man that I had ever seen. Judging him by his figure and his movements, he was still young. Judging him by his face, and comparing him with Betteredge, he looked the elder of the two. His complexion was of a gipsy darkness; his fleshless cheeks had fallen into deep hollows, over which the bone projected like a pent-house. His nose presented the fine shape and modelling so often found among the ancient people of the East, so seldom visible among the newer races of the West. His forehead rose high and straight from the brow. His marks and wrinkles were innumerable. From this strange face, eyes, stranger still, of the softest brown—eyes dreamy and mournful, and deeply sunk in their orbits—looked out at you, and (in my case, at least) took your attention captive at their will. Add to this a quantity of thick closely-curling hair, which, by some freak of Nature, had lost its colour in the most startlingly partial and capricious manner. Over the top of his head it was still of the deep black which was its natural colour. Round the sides of his head—without the slightest gradation of grey to break the force of the extraordinary contrast—it had turned completely white. The line between the two colours preserved no sort of regularity. At one place, the white hair ran up into the black; at another, the black hair ran down into the white. I looked at the man with a curiosity which, I am ashamed to say, I found it quite impossible to control. His soft brown eyes looked back at me gently; and he met my involuntary rudeness in staring at him, with an apology which I was conscious that I had not deserved.

'I beg your pardon,' he said. 'I had no idea that Mr Betteredge was engaged.' He took a slip of paper from his pocket, and handed it to Betteredge. 'The list for next week,' he said. His eyes just rested on me again—and he left the room as quietly as he had entered it.

'Who is that?' I asked.

'Mr Candy's assistant,' said Betteredge. 'By-the-bye, Mr Franklin, you will be sorry to hear that the little doctor has never recovered that illness he caught, going home from the birthday dinner. He's pretty well in health; but he lost his memory in the fever, and he has never recovered more than the wreck of it since. The work all falls on his assistant. Not much of it now, except among the poor. *They* can't help themselves, you know. *They* must put up with the man with the piebald hair, and the gipsy complexion—or they would get no doctoring at all.'

'You don't seem to like him, Betteredge?'

'Nobody likes him, sir.'

'Why is he so unpopular?'

'Well, Mr Franklin, his appearance is against him, to begin with. And then there's a story that Mr Candy took him with a very doubtful character. Nobody knows who he is—and he hasn't a friend in the place. How can you expect one to like him, after that?'

'Quite impossible, of course! May I ask what he wanted with you, when he gave you that bit of paper?'

'Only to bring me the weekly list of the sick people about here, sir, who stand in need of a little wine. My lady always had a regular distribution of good sound port and sherry among the infirm poor; and Miss Rachel wishes the custom to be kept up. Times have changed! times have changed! I remember when Mr Candy himself brought the list to my mistress. Now it's Mr Candy's assistant who brings the list to me. I'll go on with the letter, if you will allow me, sir,' said Betteredge, drawing Rosanna Spearman's confession back to him. 'It isn't lively reading, I grant you. But, there! it keeps me from getting sour with thinking of the past.' He put on his spectacles, and wagged his head gloomily. 'There's a bottom of good sense,

Mr Franklin, in our conduct to our mothers, when they first start us on the journey of life. We are all of us more or less unwilling to be brought into the world. And we are all of us right.'

Mr Candy's assistant had produced too strong an impression on me to be immediately dismissed from my thoughts. I passed over the last unanswerable utterance of the Betteredge philosophy; and returned to the subject of the man with the piebald hair.

'What is his name?' I asked.

'As ugly a name as need be,' Betteredge answered, gruffly. 'Ezra Jennings.'

CHAPTER V

HAVING told me the name of Mr Candy's assistant, Betteredge appeared to think that we had wasted enough of our time on an insignificant subject. He resumed the perusal of Rosanna Spearman's letter.

On my side, I sat at the window, waiting until he had done. Little by little, the impression produced on me by Ezra Jennings—it seemed perfectly unaccountable, in such a situation as mine, that any human being should have produced an impression on me at all!—faded from my mind. My thoughts flowed back into their former channel. Once more, I forced myself to look my own incredible position resolutely in the face. Once more, I reviewed in my own mind the course which I had at last summoned composure enough to plan out for the future.

To go back to London that day; to put the whole case before Mr Bruff; and, last and most important, to obtain (no matter by what means or at what sacrifice) a personal interview with Rachel—this was my plan for action, so far as I was capable of forming it at the time. There was more than an hour still to spare before the train started. And there was the bare chance that Betteredge might discover something in the unread portion of Rosanna Spearman's letter, which it might be useful for me to know before I left the house in which the Diamond had been lost. For that chance I was now waiting.

The letter ended in these terms:

'You have no need to be angry, Mr Franklin, even if I did feel some little triumph at knowing that I held all your prospects in life in my own hands. Anxieties and fears soon came back to me. With the view Sergeant Cuff took of the loss of the Diamond, he would be sure to end in examining our linen and our dresses. There was no place in my room—there was no place in the house—which I could feel satisfied would be safe from him. How to hide the nightgown so that not even the Sergeant could find it? and how to do that without losing one moment of precious time?—these were not easy questions to answer. My uncertainties ended in my taking a way that may make you laugh. I undressed, and put the nightgown on me. You had worn it—and I had another little moment of pleasure in wearing it after you.

'The next news that reached us in the servants' hall showed that I had not made sure of the nightgown a moment too soon. Sergeant Cuff wanted to see the washing-book.

'I found it, and took it to him in my lady's sitting-room. The Sergeant and I had come across each other more than once in former days. I was certain he would know me again—and I was *not* certain of what he might do when he found me employed as servant in a house in which a valuable jewel had been lost. In this suspense, I felt it would be a relief to me to get the meeting between us over, and to know the worst of it at once.

'He looked at me as if I was a stranger, when I handed him the washing-book; and he was very specially polite in thanking me for bringing it. I thought those were both bad signs. There was no knowing what he might say of me behind my back; there was no knowing how soon I might not find myself taken in custody on suspicion, and searched. It was then time for your return from seeing Mr Godfrey Ablewhite off by the railway; and I went to your favourite walk in the shrubbery, to try for another chance of speaking to you—the last chance, for all I knew to the contrary, that I might have.

'You never appeared; and, what was worse still, Mr Betteredge and Sergeant Cuff passed by the place where I was hiding—and the Sergeant saw me.

'I had no choice, after that, but to return to my proper place and my proper work, before more disasters happened to me. Just as I was going to step across the path, you came back from the railway. You were making straight for the shrubbery, when you saw me—I am certain, sir, you saw me—and you turned away as if I had got the plague, and went into the house.[1]

'I made the best of my way indoors again, returning by the servants' entrance. There was nobody in the laundry-room at that time; and I sat down there alone. I have told you already of the thoughts which the Shivering Sand put into my head. Those thoughts came back to me now. I wondered in myself which it would be harder to do, if things went on in this manner—to bear Mr Franklin Blake's indifference to me, or to jump into the quicksand and end it for ever in that way?

'It's useless to ask me to account for my own conduct, at this time. I try—and I can't understand it myself.

---

[1] NOTE; by Franklin Blake.—The writer is entirely mistaken, poor creature. I never noticed her. My intention was certainly to have taken a turn in the shrubbery. But, remembering at the same moment that my aunt might wish to see me, after my return from the railway, I altered my mind, and went into the house.

'Why didn't I stop you, when you avoided me in that cruel manner? Why didn't I call out, "Mr Franklin, I have got something to say to you; it concerns yourself, and you must, and shall, hear it?" You were at my mercy—I had got the whip-hand of you, as they say. And better than that, I had the means (if I could only make you trust me) of being useful to you in the future. Of course, I never supposed that you—a gentleman—had stolen the Diamond for the mere pleasure of stealing it. No. Penelope had heard Miss Rachel, and I had heard Mr Betteredge, talk about your extravagance and your debts. It was plain enough to me that you had taken the Diamond to sell it, or pledge it, and so to get the money of which you stood in need. Well! I could have told you of a man in London who would have advanced a good large sum on the jewel, and who would have asked no awkward questions about it either.

'Why didn't I speak to you! why didn't I speak to you!

'I wonder whether the risks and difficulties of keeping the nightgown were as much as I could manage, without having other risks and difficulties added to them? This might have been the case with some women—but how could it be the case with me? In the days when I was a thief, I had run fifty times greater risks, and found my way out of difficulties to which *this* difficulty was mere child's play. I had been apprenticed, as you may say, to frauds and deceptions—some of them on such a grand scale, and managed so cleverly, that they became famous, and appeared in the newspapers. Was such a little thing as the keeping of the nightgown likely to weigh on my spirits, and to set my heart sinking within me, at the time when I ought to have spoken to you? What nonsense to ask the question! The thing couldn't be.

'Where is the use of my dwelling in this way on my own folly? The plain truth is plain enough, surely? Behind your back, I loved you with all my heart and soul. Before your face—there's no denying it—I was frightened of you; frightened of making you angry with me; frightened of what you might say to me (though you *had* taken the Diamond) if I presumed to tell you that I had found it out. I had gone as near to it as I dared when I spoke to you in the library. You had not turned your back on me then. You had not started away from me as if I had got the plague. I tried to provoke myself into feeling angry with you, and to rouse up my courage in that way. No! I couldn't feel anything but the misery and the mortification of it. "You're a plain girl; you have got a crooked shoulder; you're only a housemaid—what do you mean by attempting to speak to Me?" You never uttered a word of that, Mr Franklin; but you said it all to me, nevertheless! Is such madness as this to be accounted for? No. There is nothing to be done but to confess it, and let it be.

'I ask your pardon, once more, for this wandering of my pen. There is no fear of its happening again. I am close at the end now.

'The first person who disturbed me by coming into the empty room was Penelope. She had found out my secret long since, and she had done her best to bring me to my senses—and done it kindly too.

' "Ah!" she said, "I know why you're sitting here, and fretting, all by yourself. The best thing that can happen for your advantage, Rosanna, will be for Mr Franklin's visit here to come to an end. It's my belief that he won't be long now before he leaves the house."

'In all my thoughts of you I had never thought of your going away. I couldn't speak to Penelope. I could only look at her.

' "I've just left Miss Rachel," Penelope went on. "And a hard matter I have had of it to put up with her temper. She says the house is unbearable to her with the police in it; and she's determined to speak to my lady this evening, and to go to her Aunt Ablewhite to-morrow. If she does that, Mr Franklin will be the next to find a reason for going away, you may depend on it!"

'I recovered the use of my tongue at that. "Do you mean to say Mr Franklin will go with her?" I asked.

' "Only too gladly, if she would let him; but she won't. *He* has been made to feel her temper; *he* is in her black books too—and that after having done all he can to help her, poor fellow! No! no! If they don't make it up before to-morrow, you will see Miss Rachel go one way, and Mr Franklin another. Where he may betake himself to I can't say. But he will never stay here, Rosanna, after Miss Rachel has left us."

'I managed to master the despair I felt at the prospect of your going away. To own the truth, I saw a little glimpse of hope for myself if there was really a serious disagreement between Miss Rachel and you. "Do you know," I asked, "what the quarrel is between them?"

' "It is all on Miss Rachel's side," Penelope said. "And, for anything I know to the contrary, it's all Miss Rachel's temper, and nothing else. I am loth to distress you, Rosanna; but don't run away with the notion that Mr Franklin is ever likely to quarrel with *her*. He's a great deal too fond of her for that!"

'She had only just spoken those cruel words when there came a call to us from Mr Betteredge. All the indoor servants were to assemble in the hall. And then we were to go in, one by one, and be questioned in Mr Betteredge's room by Sergeant Cuff.

'It came to my turn to go in, after her ladyship's maid and the upper housemaid had been questioned first. Sergeant Cuff's inquiries—though he wrapped them up very cunningly—soon showed me that those two women (the bitterest enemies I had in the house) had made their discoveries outside my door, on the Tuesday afternoon, and again on the Thursday night. They had told the Sergeant enough to open his eyes to some part of the truth. He rightly believed me to have made a new nightgown secretly, but he wrongly believed the paint-stained nightgown to be mine. I felt satisfied of another thing, from what he said, which it puzzled me to understand. He suspected me, of course, of being concerned in the disappearance of the Diamond.

But, at the same time, he let me see—purposely, as I thought—that he did not consider me as the person chiefly answerable for the loss of the jewel. He appeared to think that I had been acting under the direction of somebody else. Who that person might be, I couldn't guess then, and can't guess now.

'In this uncertainty, one thing was plain—that Sergeant Cuff was miles away from knowing the whole truth. You were safe as long as the nightgown was safe—and not a moment longer.

'I quite despair of making you understand the distress and terror which pressed upon me now. It was impossible for me to risk wearing your nightgown any longer. I might find myself taken off, at a moment's notice, to the police court at Frizinghall, to be charged on suspicion, and searched accordingly. While Sergeant Cuff still left me free, I had to choose—and at once—between destroying the nightgown, or hiding it in some safe place, at some safe distance from the house.

'If I had only been a little less fond of you, I think I should have destroyed it. But oh! how could I destroy the only thing I had which proved that I had saved you from discovery? If we did come to an explanation together, and if you suspected me of having some bad motive, and denied it all, how could I win upon you to trust me, unless I had the nightgown to produce? Was it wronging you to believe, as I did, and do still, that you might hesitate to let a poor girl like me be the sharer of your secret, and your accomplice in the theft which your money-troubles had tempted you to commit? Think of your cold behaviour to me, sir, and you will hardly wonder at my unwillingness to destroy the only claim on your confidence and your gratitude which it was my fortune to possess.

'I determined to hide it; and the place I fixed on was the place I knew best—the Shivering Sand.

'As soon as the questioning was over, I made the first excuse that came into my head, and got leave to go out for a breath of fresh air. I went straight to Cobb's Hole, to Mr Yolland's cottage. His wife and daughter were the best friends I had. Don't suppose I trusted them with your secret—I have trusted nobody. All I wanted was to write this letter to you, and to have a safe opportunity of taking the nightgown off me. Suspected as I was, I could do neither of those things, with any sort of security, up at the house.

'And now I have nearly got through my long letter, writing it alone in Lucy Yolland's bedroom. When it is done, I shall go downstairs with the nightgown rolled up, and hidden under my cloak. I shall find the means I want for keeping it safe and dry in its hiding-place, among the litter of old things in Mrs Yolland's kitchen. And then I shall go to the Shivering Sand—don't be afraid of my letting my footmarks betray me!—and hide the nightgown down in the sand, where no living creature can find it without being first let into the secret by myself.

'And, when that's done, what then?

'Then, Mr Franklin, I shall have two reasons for making another attempt to say the words to you which I have not said yet. If you leave the house, as Penelope believes you will leave it, and if I haven't spoken to you before that, I shall lose my opportunity for ever. That is one reason. Then, again, there is the comforting knowledge—if my speaking does make you angry—that I have got the nightgown ready to plead my cause for me as nothing else can. That is my other reason. If these two together don't harden my heart against the coldness which has hitherto frozen it up (I mean the coldness of your treatment of me), there will be the end of my efforts—and the end of my life.

'Yes. If I miss my next opportunity—if you are as cruel as ever, and if I feel it again as I have felt it already—good-bye to the world which has grudged me the happiness that it gives to others. Good-bye to life, which nothing but a little kindness from *you* can ever make pleasurable to me again. Don't blame yourself, sir, if it ends in this way. But try—do try—to feel some forgiving sorrow for me! I shall take care that you find out what I have done for you, when I am past telling you of it myself. Will you say something kind of me then—in the same gentle way that you have when you speak to Miss Rachel? If you do that, and if there are such things as ghosts, I believe my ghost will hear it, and tremble with the pleasure of it.

'It's time I left off. I am making myself cry. How am I to see my way to the hiding-place if I let these useless tears come and blind me?

'Besides, why should I look at the gloomy side? Why not believe, while I can, that it will end well after all? I may find you in a good humour to-night—or, if not, I may succeed better to-morrow morning. I sha'n't improve my plain face by fretting—shall I? Who knows but I may have filled all these weary long pages of paper for nothing? They will go, for safety's sake (never mind now for what other reason) into the hiding-place along with the nightgown. It has been hard, hard work writing my letter. Oh! if we only end in understanding each other, how I shall enjoy tearing it up!

'I beg to remain, sir, your true lover and humble servant,

'ROSANNA SPEARMAN.'

The reading of the letter was completed by Betteredge in silence. After carefully putting it back in the envelope, he sat thinking, with his head bowed down, and his eyes on the ground.

'Betteredge,' I said, 'is there any hint to guide me at the end of the letter?'

He looked up slowly, with a heavy sigh.

'There is nothing to guide you, Mr Franklin,' he answered. 'If you take my advice you will keep the letter in the cover till these present anxieties of yours have come to an end. It will sorely distress you, whenever you read it. Don't read it now.'

I put the letter away in my pocket-book.

A glance back at the sixteenth and seventeenth chapters of Betteredge's Narrative will show that there really was a reason for my thus sparing myself, at a time when my fortitude had been already cruelly tried. Twice over, the unhappy woman had made her last attempt to speak to me. And twice over, it had been my misfortune (God knows how innocently!) to repel the advances she had made to me. On the Friday night, as Betteredge truly describes it, she had found me alone at the billiard-table. Her manner and language suggested to me—and would have suggested to any man, under the circumstances—that she was about to confess a guilty knowledge of the disappearance of the Diamond. For her own sake, I had purposely shown no special interest in what was coming; for her own sake, I had purposely looked at the billiard-balls, instead of looking at *her*—and what had been the result? I had sent her away from me, wounded to the heart! On the Saturday again—on the day when she must have foreseen, after what Penelope had told her, that my departure was close at hand—the same fatality still pursued us. She had once more attempted to meet me in the shrubbery walk, and she had found me there in company with Betteredge and Sergeant Cuff. In her hearing, the Sergeant, with his own underhand object in view, had appealed to my interest in Rosanna Spearman. Again for the poor creature's own sake, I had met the police-officer with a flat denial, and had declared—loudly declared, so that she might hear me too—that I felt 'no interest whatever in Rosanna Spearman.' At those words, solely designed to warn her against attempting to gain my private ear, she had turned away and left the place: cautioned of her danger, as I then believed; self-doomed to destruction, as I know now. From that point, I have already traced the succession of events which led me to the astounding discovery at the quicksand. The retrospect is now complete. I may leave the miserable story of Rosanna Spearman—to which, even at this distance of time, I cannot revert without a pang of distress—to suggest for itself all that is here purposely left unsaid. I may pass from the suicide at the Shivering Sand, with its strange and terrible influence on my present position and future prospects, to interests which concern the living people of this narrative, and to events which were already paving my way for the slow and toilsome journey from the darkness to the light.

CHAPTER VI

I WALKED to the railway station accompanied, it is needless to say, by Gabriel Betteredge. I had the letter in my pocket, and the nightgown safely packed in a little bag—both to be submitted, before I slept that night, to the investigation of Mr Bruff.

We left the house in silence. For the first time in my experience of him, I found old Betteredge in my company without a word to say to me. Having something to say on my side, I opened the conversation as soon as we were clear of the lodge gates.

'Before I go to London,' I began, 'I have two questions to ask you. They relate to myself, and I believe they will rather surprise you.'

'If they will put that poor creature's letter out of my head, Mr Franklin, they may do anything else they like with me. Please to begin surprising me, sir, as soon as you can.'

'My first question, Betteredge, is this. Was I drunk on the night of Rachel's Birthday?'

'*You* drunk!' exclaimed the old man. 'Why it's the great defect of your character, Mr Franklin, that you only drink with your dinner, and never touch a drop of liquor afterwards!'

'But the birthday was a special occasion. I might have abandoned my regular habits, on that night of all others.'

Betteredge considered for a moment.

'You did go out of your habits, sir,' he said. 'And I'll tell you how. You looked wretchedly ill—and we persuaded you to have a drop of brandy and water to cheer you up a little.'

'I am not used to brandy and water. It is quite possible——'

'Wait a bit, Mr Franklin. I knew you were not used, too. I poured you out half a wineglass-full of our fifty year old Cognac; and (more shame for me!) I drowned that noble liquor in nigh on a tumbler-full of cold water. A child couldn't have got drunk on it—let alone a grown man!'

I knew I could depend on his memory, in a matter of this kind. It was plainly impossible that I could have been intoxicated. I passed on to the second question.

'Before I was sent abroad, Betteredge, you saw a great deal of me when I was a boy? Now tell me plainly, do you remember anything strange of me, after I had gone to bed at night? Did you ever discover me walking in my sleep?'

Betteredge stopped, looked at me for a moment, nodded his head, and walked on again.

'I see your drift now, Mr Franklin!' he said. 'You're trying to account for how you got the paint on your nightgown, without knowing it yourself. It won't do, sir. You're miles away still from getting at the truth. Walk in your sleep? You never did such a thing in your life!'

Here again, I felt that Betteredge must be right. Neither at home nor abroad had my life ever been of the solitary sort. If I had been a sleep-walker, there were hundreds on hundreds of people who must have discovered me, and who, in the interest of my own safety, would have warned me of the habit, and have taken precautions to restrain it.

Still, admitting all this, I clung—with an obstinacy which was surely natural and excusable, under the circumstances—to one or other of the only two explanations that I could see which accounted for the unendurable position in which I then stood. Observing that I was not yet satisfied, Betteredge shrewdly adverted to certain later events in the history of the Moonstone; and scattered both my theories to the wind at once and for ever.

'Let's try it another way, sir,' he said. 'Keep your own opinion, and see how far it will take you towards finding out the truth. If we are to believe the nightgown—which I don't for one—you not only smeared off the paint from the door, without knowing it, but you also took the Diamond without knowing it. Is that right, so far?'

'Quite right. Go on.'

'Very good, sir. We'll say you were drunk, or walking in your sleep, when you took the jewel. That accounts for the night and morning, after the birthday. But how does it account for what has happened since that time? The Diamond has been taken to London, since that time. The Diamond has been pledged to Mr Luker, since that time. Did you do those two things, without knowing it, too? Were you drunk when I saw you off in the pony-chaise on that Saturday evening? And did you walk in your sleep to Mr Luker's, when the train had brought you to your journey's end? Excuse me for saying it, Mr Franklin, but this business has so upset you, that you're not fit yet to judge for yourself. The sooner you lay your head alongside of Mr Bruff's head, the sooner you will see your way out of the dead-lock that has got you now.'

We reached the station, with only a minute or two to spare.

I hurriedly gave Betteredge my address in London, so that he might write to me, if necessary; promising, on my side, to inform him of any news which I might have to communicate. This done, and just as I was bidding him farewell, I happened to glance towards the book-and-newspaper stall. There was Mr Candy's remarkable-looking assistant again, speaking to the keeper of the stall! Our eyes met at the same moment. Ezra Jennings took off his hat to me. I returned the salute, and got into a carriage just as the train started. It was a relief to my mind, I suppose, to dwell on any subject which appeared to be, personally, of no sort of importance to me. At all events, I began the momentous journey back which was to take me to Mr Bruff, wondering—absurdly enough, I admit—that I should have seen the man with the piebald hair twice in one day!

The hour at which I arrived in London precluded all hope of my finding Mr Bruff at his place of business. I drove from the railway to his private residence at Hampstead, and disturbed the old lawyer dozing alone in his dining-room, with his favourite pug-dog on his lap, and his bottle of wine at his elbow.

I shall best describe the effect which my story produced on the mind of Mr Bruff by relating his proceedings when he had heard it to the end. He ordered lights, and strong tea, to be taken into his study; and he sent a message to the ladies of his family, forbidding them to disturb us on any pretence whatever. These preliminaries disposed of, he first examined the nightgown, and then devoted himself to the reading of Rosanna Spearman's letter.

The reading completed, Mr Bruff addressed me for the first time since we had been shut up together in the seclusion of his own room.

'Franklin Blake,' said the old gentleman, 'this is a very serious matter, in more respects than one. In my opinion, it concerns Rachel quite as nearly as it concerns you. Her extraordinary conduct is no mystery *now*. She believes you have stolen the Diamond.'

I had shrunk from reasoning my own way fairly to that revolting conclusion. But it had forced itself on me, nevertheless. My resolution to obtain a personal interview with Rachel, rested really and truly on the ground just stated by Mr Bruff.

'The first step to take in this investigation,' the lawyer proceeded, 'is to appeal to Rachel. She has been silent all this time, from motives which I (who know her character) can readily understand. It is impossible, after what has happened, to submit to that silence any longer. She must be persuaded to tell us, or she must be forced to tell us, on what grounds she bases her belief that you took the Moonstone. The chances are, that the whole of this case, serious as it seems now, will tumble to pieces, if we can only break through Rachel's inveterate reserve, and prevail upon her to speak out.'

'That is a very comforting opinion for *me*,' I said. 'I own I should like to know——'

'You would like to know how I can justify it,' interposed Mr Bruff. 'I can tell you in two minutes. Understand, in the first place, that I look at this matter from a lawyer's point of view. It's a question of evidence, with me. Very well. The evidence breaks down, at the outset, on one important point.'

'On what point?'

'You shall hear. I admit that the mark of the name proves the nightgown to be yours. I admit that the mark of the paint proves the nightgown to have made the smear on Rachel's door. But what evidence is there to prove that you are the person who wore it, on the night when the Diamond was lost?'

The objection struck me, all the more forcibly that it reflected an objection which I had felt myself.

'As to this,' pursued the lawyer, taking up Rosanna Spearman's confession, 'I can understand that the letter is a distressing one to *you*. I can understand that you may hesitate to analyse it from a purely impartial point of view. But *I* am not in your position. I can bring my professional experience to bear on this document, just as I should bring it to bear on any other. Without alluding to the woman's career as a thief, I will merely remark that her letter proves her to have been an adept at deception, on her own showing; and I argue from that, that I am justified in suspecting her of not having told the whole truth. I won't start any theory, at present, as to what she may or may not have done. I will only say that, if Rachel has suspected you *on the evidence of the nightgown only*, the chances are ninety-nine to a hundred that Rosanna Spearman was the person who showed it to her. In that case, there is the woman's letter, confessing that she was jealous of Rachel, confessing that she changed the roses, confessing that she saw a glimpse of hope for herself, in the prospect of a quarrel between Rachel and you. I don't stop to ask who took the Moonstone (as a means to her end, Rosanna Spearman would have taken fifty Moonstones)—I only say that the disappearance of the jewel gave this reclaimed thief who was in love with you, an opportunity of setting you and Rachel at variance for the rest of your lives. She had not decided on destroying herself, *then*, remember; and, having the opportunity, I distinctly assert that it was in her character, and in her position at the time, to take it. What do you say to that?'

'Some such suspicion,' I answered, 'crossed my own mind, as soon as I opened the letter.'

'Exactly! And when you had read the letter, you pitied the poor creature, and couldn't find it in your heart to suspect her. Does you credit, my dear sir—does you credit!'

'But suppose it turns out that I did wear the nightgown? What then?'

'I don't see how the fact is to be proved,' said Mr Bruff. 'But assuming the proof to be possible, the vindication of your innocence would be no easy matter. We won't go into that, now. Let us wait and see whether Rachel hasn't suspected you on the evidence of the nightgown only.'

'Good God, how coolly you talk of Rachel suspecting me!' I broke out. 'What right has she to suspect Me, on any evidence, of being a thief?'

'A very sensible question, my dear sir. Rather hotly put—but well worth considering for all that. What puzzles you, puzzles me too. Search your memory, and tell me this. Did anything happen while you were staying at the house—not, of course, to shake Rachel's belief in your honour—but, let us say, to shake her belief (no matter with how little reason) in your principles generally?'

I started, in ungovernable agitation, to my feet. The lawyer's question reminded me, for the first time since I had left England, that something *had* happened.

In the eighth chapter of Betteredge's Narrative, an allusion will be found to the arrival of a foreigner and a stranger at my aunt's house, who came to see me on business. The nature of his business was this.

I had been foolish enough (being, as usual, straitened for money at the time) to accept a loan from the keeper of a small restaurant in Paris, to whom I was well known as a customer. A time was settled between us for paying the money back; and when the time came, I found it (as thousands of other honest men have found it) impossible to keep my engagement. I sent the man a bill. My name was unfortunately too well known on such documents: he failed to negotiate it. His affairs had fallen into disorder, in the interval since I had borrowed of him; bankruptcy stared him in the face; and a relative of his, a French lawyer, came to England to find me, and to insist upon the payment of my debt. He was a man of violent temper; and he took the wrong way with me. High words passed on both sides; and my aunt and Rachel were unfortunately in the next room, and heard us. Lady Verinder came in, and insisted on knowing what was the matter. The Frenchman produced his credentials, and declared me to be responsible for the ruin of a poor man, who had trusted in my honour. My aunt instantly paid him the money, and sent him off. She knew me better of course than to take the Frenchman's view of the transaction. But she was shocked at my carelessness, and justly angry with me for placing myself in a position, which, but for her interference, might have become a very disgraceful one. Either her mother told her, or Rachel heard what passed—I can't say which. She took her own romantic, high-flown view of the matter. I was 'heartless'; I was 'dishonourable'; I had 'no principle'; there was 'no knowing what I might do next'—in short, she said some of the severest things to me which I had ever heard from a young lady's lips. The breach between us lasted for the whole of the next day. The day after, I succeeded in making my peace, and thought no more of it. Had Rachel reverted to this unlucky accident, at the critical moment when my place in her estimation was again, and far more seriously, assailed? Mr Bruff, when I had mentioned the circumstances to him, answered the question at once in the affirmative.

'It would have its effect on her mind,' he said gravely. 'And I wish, for your sake, the thing had not happened. However, we have discovered that there *was* a predisposing influence against you—and there is one uncertainty cleared out of our way, at any rate. I see nothing more that we can do now. Our next step in this inquiry must be the step that takes us to Rachel.'

He rose, and began walking thoughtfully up and down the room. Twice, I was on the point of telling him that I had determined on seeing Rachel personally; and twice, having regard to his age and his character, I hesitated to take him by surprise at an unfavourable moment.

'The grand difficulty is,' he resumed, 'how to make her show her whole mind in this matter, without reserve. Have you any suggestions to offer?'

'I have made up my mind, Mr Bruff, to speak to Rachel myself.'

'You!' He suddenly stopped in his walk, and looked at me as if he thought I had taken leave of my senses. 'You, of all the people in the world!' He abruptly checked himself, and took another turn in the room. 'Wait a little,' he said. 'In cases of this extraordinary kind, the rash way is sometimes the best way.' He considered the question for a moment or two, under that new light, and ended boldly by a decision in my favour. 'Nothing venture, nothing have,' the old gentleman resumed. 'You have a chance in your favour which I don't possess—and you shall be the first to try the experiment.'

'A chance in my favour?' I repeated, in the greatest surprise.

Mr Bruff's face softened, for the first time, into a smile.

'This is how it stands,' he said. 'I tell you fairly, I don't trust your discretion, and I don't trust your temper. But I do trust in Rachel's still preserving, in some remote little corner of her heart, a certain perverse weakness for *you*. Touch that—and trust to the consequences for the fullest disclosures that can flow from a woman's lips! The question is—how are you to see her?'

'She has been a guest of yours at this house,' I answered. 'May I venture to suggest—if nothing was said about me beforehand—that I might see her here?'

'Cool!' said Mr Bruff. With that one word of comment on the reply that I had made to him, he took another turn up and down the room.

'In plain English,' he said, 'my house is to be turned into a trap to catch Rachel; with a bait to tempt her, in the shape of an invitation from my wife and daughters. If you were anybody else but Franklin Blake, and if this matter was one atom less serious than it really is, I should refuse point-blank. As things are, I firmly believe Rachel will live to thank me for turning traitor to her in my old age. Consider me your accomplice. Rachel shall be asked to spend the day here; and you shall receive due notice of it.'

'When? To-morrow?'

'To-morrow won't give us time enough to get her answer. Say the day after.'

'How shall I hear from you?'

'Stay at home all the morning and expect me to call on you.'

I thanked him for the inestimable assistance which he was rendering to me, with the gratitude that I really felt; and, declining a hospitable invitation to sleep that night at Hampstead, returned to my lodgings in London.

Of the day that followed, I have only to say that it was the longest day of my life. Innocent as I knew myself to be, certain as I was that the abominable imputation which rested on me must sooner or later be cleared off, there was nevertheless a sense of self-abasement in my mind which instinctively disinclined me to see any of my friends. We often hear (almost invariably, however, from superficial observers) that guilt can look like innocence. I believe it to be infinitely the truer axiom of the two that innocence can look like guilt. I caused myself to be denied all day, to every visitor who called; and I only ventured out under cover of the night.

The next morning, Mr Bruff surprised me at the breakfast-table. He handed me a large key, and announced that he felt ashamed of himself for the first time in his life.

'Is she coming?'

'She is coming to-day, to lunch and spend the afternoon with my wife and my girls.'

'Are Mrs Bruff, and your daughters, in the secret?'

'Inevitably. But women, as you may have observed, have no principles. My family don't feel my pangs of conscience. The end being to bring you and Rachel together again, my wife and daughters pass over the means employed to gain it, as composedly as if they were Jesuits.'

'I am infinitely obliged to them. What is this key?'

'The key of the gate in my back-garden wall. Be there at three this afternoon. Let yourself into the garden, and make your way in by the conservatory door. Cross the small drawing-room, and open the door in front of you which leads into the music-room. There, you will find Rachel—and find her, alone.'

'How can I thank you!'

'I will tell you how. Don't blame *me* for what happens afterwards.'

With those words, he went out.

I had many weary hours still to wait through. To while away the time, I looked at my letters. Among them was a letter from Betteredge.

I opened it eagerly. To my surprise and disappointment, it began with an apology warning me to expect no news of any importance. In the next sentence the everlasting Ezra Jennings appeared again! He had stopped Betteredge on the way out of the station, and had asked who I was. Informed on this point, he had mentioned having seen me to his master Mr Candy. Mr Candy hearing of this, had himself driven over to Betteredge, to express his regret at our having missed each other. He had a reason for wishing particularly to speak to me; and when I was next in the neighbour-hood of Frizinghall, he begged I would let him know. Apart from a few characteristic utterances of the Betteredge philosophy, this was the sum and substance of my correspondent's letter. The warm-hearted, faithful old man acknowledged that he had written 'mainly for the pleasure of writing to me.'

I crumpled up the letter in my pocket, and forgot it the moment after, in the all-absorbing interest of my coming interview with Rachel.

As the clock of Hampstead church struck three, I put Mr Bruff's key into the lock of the door in the wall. When I first stepped into the garden, and while I was securing the door again on the inner side, I own to having felt a certain guilty doubtfulness about what might happen next. I looked furtively on either side of me, suspicious of the presence of some unexpected witness in some unknown corner of the garden. Nothing appeared, to justify my apprehensions. The walks were, one and all, solitudes; and the birds and the bees were the only witnesses.

I passed through the garden; entered the conservatory; and crossed the small drawing-room. As I laid my hand on the door opposite, I heard a few plaintive chords struck on the piano in the room within. She had often idled over the instrument in this way, when I was staying at her mother's house. I was obliged to wait a little, to steady myself. The past and present rose side by side, at that supreme moment—and the contrast shook me.

After the lapse of a minute, I roused my manhood, and opened the door.

CHAPTER VII

AT the moment when I showed myself in the doorway, Rachel rose from the piano.

I closed the door behind me. We confronted each other in silence, with the full length of the room between us. The movement she had made in rising appeared to be the one exertion of which she was capable. All use of every other faculty, bodily or mental, seemed to be merged in the mere act of looking at me.

A fear crossed my mind that I had shown myself too suddenly. I advanced a few steps towards her. I said gently, 'Rachel!'

The sound of my voice brought the life back to her limbs, and the colour to her face. She advanced, on her side, still without speaking. Slowly, as if acting under some influence independent of her own will, she came nearer and nearer to me; the warm dusky colour flushing her cheeks, the light of reviving intelligence brightening every instant in her eyes. I forgot the object that had brought me into her presence; I forgot the vile suspicion that rested on my good name; I forgot every consideration, past, present, and future, which I was bound to remember. I saw nothing but the woman I loved coming nearer and nearer to me. She trembled; she stood irresolute. I could resist it no longer—I caught her in my arms, and covered her face with kisses.

There was a moment when I thought the kisses were returned; a moment when it seemed as if she, too, might have forgotten. Almost before the idea could shape itself in my mind, her first voluntary action made me feel that she remembered. With a cry which was like a cry of horror—with a strength which I doubt if I could have resisted if I had tried—she thrust me back from her. I saw merciless anger in her eyes; I saw merciless contempt on her lips. She looked me over, from head to foot, as she might have looked at a stranger who had insulted her.

'You coward!' she said. 'You mean, miserable, heartless coward!'

Those were her first words! The most unendurable reproach that a woman can address to a man, was the reproach that she picked out to address to Me.

'I remember the time, Rachel,' I said, 'when you could have told me that I had offended you, in a worthier way than that. I beg your pardon.'

Something of the bitterness that I felt may have communicated itself to my voice. At the first words of my reply, her eyes, which had been turned away the moment before, looked back at me unwillingly. She answered in a low tone, with a sullen submission of manner which was quite new in my experience of her.

'Perhaps there is some excuse for me,' she said. 'After what you have done, is it a manly action, on your part, to find your way to me as you have found it to-day? It seems a cowardly experiment, to try an experiment on my weakness for you. It seems a cowardly surprise, to surprise me into letting you kiss me. But that is only a woman's view. I ought to have known it couldn't be your view. I should have done better if I had controlled myself, and said nothing.'

The apology was more unendurable than the insult. The most degraded man living would have felt humiliated by it.

'If my honour was not in your hands,' I said, 'I would leave you this instant, and never see you again. You have spoken of what I have done. What have I done?'

'What have you done! *You* ask that question of *me?*'

'I ask it.'

'I have kept your infamy a secret,' she answered. 'And I have suffered the consequences of concealing it. Have I no claim to be spared the insult of your asking me what you have done? Is *all* sense of gratitude dead in you? You were once a gentleman. You were once dear to my mother, and dearer still to me——'

Her voice failed her. She dropped into a chair, and turned her back on me, and covered her face with her hands.

I waited a little before I trusted myself to say any more. In that moment of silence, I hardly know which I felt most keenly—the sting which her contempt had planted in me, or the proud resolution which shut me out from all community with her distress.

'If you will not speak first,' I said, 'I must. I have come here with something serious to say to you. Will you do me the common justice of listening while I say it?'

She neither moved, nor answered. I made no second appeal to her; I never advanced an inch nearer to her chair. With a pride which was as obstinate as her pride, I told her of my discovery at the Shivering Sand, and of all that had led to it. The narrative, of necessity, occupied some little time. From beginning to end, she never looked round at me, and she never uttered a word.

I kept my temper. My whole future depended, in all probability, on my not losing possession of myself at that moment. The time had come to put Mr Bruff's theory to the test. In the breathless interest of trying that experiment, I moved round so as to place myself in front of her.

'I have a question to ask you,' I said. 'It obliges me to refer again to a painful subject. Did Rosanna Spearman show you the nightgown? Yes, or No?'

She started to her feet; and walked close up to me of her own accord. Her eyes looked me searchingly in the face, as if to read something there which they had never read yet.

'Are you mad?' she asked.

I still restrained myself. I said quietly, 'Rachel, will you answer my question?'

She went on, without heeding me.

'Have you some object to gain which I don't understand? Some mean fear about the future, in which I am concerned? They say your father's death has made you a rich man. Have you come here to compensate me for the loss of my Diamond? And have you heart enough left to feel ashamed of your errand? Is *that* the secret of your pretence of innocence, and your story about Rosanna Spearman? Is there a motive of shame at the bottom of all the falsehood, this time?'

I stopped her there. I could control myself no longer.

'You have done me an infamous wrong!' I broke out hotly. 'You suspect me of stealing your Diamond. I have a right to know, and I *will* know, the reason why!'

'Suspect you!' she exclaimed, her anger rising with mine. '*You villain, I saw you take the Diamond with my own eyes!*'

The revelation which burst upon me in those words, the overthrow which they instantly accomplished of the whole view of the case on which Mr Bruff had relied, struck me helpless. Innocent as I was, I stood before her in silence. To her eyes, to any eyes, I must have looked like a man overwhelmed by the discovery of his own guilt.

She drew back from the spectacle of my humiliation and of her triumph. The sudden silence that had fallen upon me seemed to frighten her. 'I spared you, at the time,' she said. 'I would have spared you now, if you had not forced me to speak.' She moved away as if to leave the room—and hesitated before she got to the door. 'Why did you come here to humiliate yourself?' she asked. 'Why did you come here to humiliate me?' She went on a few steps, and paused once more. 'For God's sake, say something!' she exclaimed, passionately. 'If you have any mercy left, don't let me degrade myself in this way! Say something—and drive me out of the room!'

I advanced towards her, hardly conscious of what I was doing. I had possibly some confused idea of detaining her until she had told me more. From the moment when I knew that the evidence on which I stood condemned in Rachel's mind, was the evidence of her own eyes, nothing— not even my conviction of my own innocence—was clear to my mind. I took her by the hand; I tried to speak firmly and to the purpose. All I could say was, 'Rachel, you once loved me.'

She shuddered, and looked away from me. Her hand lay powerless and trembling in mine. 'Let go of it,' she said faintly.

My touch seemed to have the same effect on her which the sound of my voice had produced when I first entered the room. After she had said the word which called me a coward, after she had made the avowal which branded me as a thief—while her hand lay in mine I was her master still!

I drew her gently back into the middle of the room. I seated her by the side of me. 'Rachel,' I said, 'I can't explain the contradiction in what I am going to tell you, I can only speak the truth as you have spoken it. You saw me—with your own eyes, you saw me take the Diamond. Before God who hears us, I declare that I now know I took it for the first time! Do you doubt me still?'

She had neither heeded nor heard me. 'Let go of my hand,' she repeated faintly. That was her only answer. Her head sank on my shoulder; and her hand unconsciously closed on mine, at the moment when she asked me to release it.

I refrained from pressing the question. But there my forbearance stopped. My chance of ever holding up my head again among honest men depended on my chance of inducing her to make her disclosure complete. The one hope left for me was the hope that she might have overlooked something in the chain of evidence—some mere trifle, perhaps, which might nevertheless, under careful investigation, be made the means of vindicating my innocence in the end. I own I kept possession of her hand. I own I spoke to her with all that I could summon back of the sympathy and confidence of the bygone time.

'I want to ask you something,' I said. 'I want you to tell me everything that happened, from the time when we wished each other good night, to the time when you saw me take the Diamond.'

She lifted her head from my shoulder, and made an effort to release her hand. 'Oh, why go back to it!' she said. 'Why go back to it!'

'I will tell you why, Rachel. You are the victim, and I am the victim, of some monstrous delusion which has worn the mask of truth. If we look at what happened on the night of your birthday together, we may end in understanding each other yet.'

Her head dropped back on my shoulder. The tears gathered in her eyes, and fell slowly over her cheeks. 'Oh!' she said, 'have *I* never had that hope? Have *I* not tried to see it, as you are trying now?'

'You have tried by yourself,' I answered. 'You have not tried with me to help you.'

Those words seemed to awaken in her something of the hope which I felt myself when I uttered them. She replied to my questions with more than docility—she exerted her intelligence; she willingly opened her whole mind to me.

'Let us begin,' I said, 'with what happened after we had wished each other good night. Did you go to bed? or did you sit up?'

'I went to bed.'

'Did you notice the time? Was it late?'

'Not very. About twelve o'clock, I think.'

'Did you fall asleep?'

'No. I couldn't sleep that night.'

'You were restless?'

'I was thinking of you.'

The answer almost unmanned me. Something in the tone, even more than in the words, went straight to my heart. It was only after pausing a little first that I was able to go on.

'Had you any light in your room?' I asked.

'None—until I got up again, and lit my candle.'

'How long was that, after you had gone to bed?'

'About an hour after, I think. About one o'clock.'

'Did you leave your bedroom?'

'I was going to leave it. I had put on my dressing-gown; and I was going into my sitting-room to get a book——'

'Had you opened your bedroom door?'

'I had just opened it.'

'But you had not gone into the sitting-room?'

'No—I was stopped from going into it.'

'What stopped you?'

'I saw a light, under the door; and I heard footsteps approaching it.'

'Were you frightened?'

'Not then. I knew my poor mother was a bad sleeper; and I remembered that she had tried hard, that evening, to persuade me to let her take charge of my Diamond. She was unreasonably anxious about it, as I thought; and I fancied she was coming to me to see if I was in bed, and to speak to me about the Diamond again, if she found that I was up.'

'What did you do?'

'I blew out my candle, so that she might think I was in bed. I was unreasonable, on my side—I was determined to keep my Diamond in the place of my own choosing.'

'After blowing the candle out, did you go back to bed?'

'I had no time to go back. At the moment when I blew the candle out, the sitting-room door opened, and I saw——'

'You saw?'

'You.'

'Dressed as usual?'

'No.'

'In my nightgown?'

'In your nightgown—with your bedroom candle in your hand.'

'Alone?'

'Alone.'

'Could you see my face?'

'Yes.'

'Plainly?'

'Quite plainly. The candle in your hand showed it to me.'

'Were my eyes open?'

'Yes.'

'Did you notice anything strange in them? Anything like a fixed, vacant expression?'

'Nothing of the sort. Your eyes were bright—brighter than usual. You looked about in the room, as if you knew you were where you ought not to be, and as if you were afraid of being found out.'

'Did you observe one thing when I came into the room—did you observe how I walked?'

'You walked as you always do. You came in as far as the middle of the room—and then you stopped and looked about you.'

'What did you do, on first seeing me?'

'I could do nothing. I was petrified. I couldn't speak, I couldn't call out, I couldn't even move to shut my door.'

'Could I see you, where you stood?'

'You might certainly have seen me. But you never looked towards me. It's useless to ask the question. I am sure you never saw me.'

'How are you sure?'

'Would you have taken the Diamond? would you have acted as you did afterwards? would you be here now—if you had seen that I was awake and looking at you? Don't make me talk of that part of it! I want to answer you quietly. Help me to keep as calm as I can. Go on to something else.'

She was right—in every way, right. I went on to other things.

'What did I do, after I had got to the middle of the room, and had stopped there?'

'You turned away, and went straight to the corner near the window—where my Indian cabinet stands.'

'When I was at the cabinet, my back must have been turned towards you. How did you see what I was doing?'

'When you moved, I moved.'

'So as to see what I was about with my hands?'

'There are three glasses in my sitting-room. As you stood there, I saw all that you did, reflected in one of them.'

'What did you see?'

'You put your candle on the top of the cabinet. You opened, and shut, one drawer after another, until you came to the drawer in which I had put my Diamond. You looked at the open drawer for a moment. And then you put your hand in, and took the Diamond out.'

'How do you know I took the Diamond out?'

'I saw your hand go into the drawer. And I saw the gleam of the stone between your finger and thumb, when you took your hand out.'

'Did my hand approach the drawer again—to close it, for instance?'

'No. You had the Diamond in your right hand; and you took the candle from the top of the cabinet with your left hand.'

'Did I look about me again, after that?'

'No.'

'Did I leave the room immediately?'

'No. You stood quite still, for what seemed a long time. I saw your face sideways in the glass. You looked like a man thinking, and dissatisfied with his own thoughts.'

'What happened next?'

'You roused yourself on a sudden, and you went straight out of the room.'

'Did I close the door after me?'

'No. You passed out quickly into the passage, and left the door open.'

'And then?'

'Then, your light disappeared, and the sound of your steps died away, and I was left alone in the dark.'

'Did nothing happen—from that time, to the time when the whole house knew that the Diamond was lost?'

'Nothing.'

'Are you sure of that? Might you not have been asleep a part of the time?'

'I never slept. I never went back to my bed. Nothing happened until Penelope came in, at the usual time in the morning.'

I dropped her hand, and rose, and took a turn in the room. Every question that I could put had been answered. Every detail that I could desire to know had been placed before me. I had even reverted to the idea of sleep-walking, and the idea of intoxication; and, again, the worthlessness of the one theory and the other had been proved—on the authority, this time, of the witness who had seen me. What was to be said next? what was to be done next? There rose the horrible fact of the Theft—the one visible, tangible object that confronted me, in the midst of the impenetrable darkness which enveloped all besides! Not a glimpse of light to guide me, when I had possessed myself of Rosanna Spearman's secret at the Shivering Sand. And not a glimpse of light now, when I had appealed to Rachel herself, and had heard the hateful story of the night from her own lips.

She was the first, this time, to break the silence.

'Well?' she said, 'you have asked, and I have answered. You have made me hope something from all this, because *you* hoped something from it. What have you to say now?'

The tone in which she spoke warned me that my influence over her was a lost influence once more.

'We were to look at what happened on my birthday night, together,' she went on; 'and we were then to understand each other. Have we done that?'

She waited pitilessly for my reply. In answering her I committed a fatal error—I let the exasperating helplessness of my situation get the better of my self-control. Rashly and uselessly, I reproached her for the silence which had kept me until that moment in ignorance of the truth.

'If you had spoken when you ought to have spoken,' I began; 'if you had done me the common justice to explain yourself——'

She broke in on me with a cry of fury. The few words I had said seemed to have lashed her on the instant into a frenzy of rage.

'Explain myself!' she repeated. 'Oh! is there another man like this in the world? I spare him, when my heart is breaking; I screen him when my own character is at stake; and he—of all human beings, he—turns on me now, and tells me that I ought to have explained myself! After believing in him as I did, after loving him as I did, after thinking of him by day, and dreaming of him by night—he wonders I didn't charge him with his disgrace the first time we met: "My heart's darling, you are a Thief! My hero whom I love and honour, you have crept into my room under cover of the night, and stolen my Diamond!" That is what I ought to have said. You villain, you mean, mean, mean villain, I would have lost fifty diamonds, rather than see your face lying to me, as I see it lying now!'

I took up my hat. In mercy to her—yes! I can honestly say it—in mercy to her, I turned away without a word, and opened the door by which I had entered the room.

She followed, and snatched the door out of my hand; she closed it, and pointed back to the place that I had left.

'No!' she said. 'Not yet! It seems that I owe a justification of my conduct to you. You shall stay and hear it. Or you shall stoop to the lowest infamy of all, and force your way out.'

It wrung my heart to see her; it wrung my heart to hear her. I answered by a sign—it was all I could do—that I submitted myself to her will.

The crimson flush of anger began to fade out of her face, as I went back, and took my chair in silence. She waited a little, and steadied herself. When she went on, but one sign of feeling was discernible in her. She spoke without looking at me. Her hands were fast clasped in her lap, and her eyes were fixed on the ground.

'I ought to have done you the common justice to explain myself,' she said, repeating my own words. 'You shall see whether I did try to do you justice, or not. I told you just now that I never slept, and never returned to my bed, after you had left my sitting-room. It's useless to trouble you by dwelling on what I thought—you would not understand my thoughts—I will only tell you what I did, when time enough had passed to help me to recover myself. I refrained from alarming the house, and telling everybody what had happened—as I ought to have done. In spite of what I had seen, I was fond enough of you to believe—no matter what!—any impossibility, rather than admit it to my own mind that you were deliberately a thief. I thought and thought—and I ended in writing to you.'

'I never received the letter.'

'I know you never received it. Wait a little, and you shall hear why. My letter would have told you nothing openly. It would not have ruined you for life, if it had fallen into some other person's hands. It would only have said—in a manner which you yourself could not possibly have mistaken—that I had reason to know you were in debt, and that it was in my experience and in my mother's experience of you, that you were not very discreet, or very scrupulous about how you got money when you wanted it. You would have remembered the visit of the French lawyer, and you would have known what I referred to. If you had read on with some interest after that, you would have come to an offer I had to make to you—the offer, privately (not a word, mind, to be said openly about it between us!), of the loan of as large a sum of money as I could get.—And I would have got it!' she exclaimed, her colour beginning to rise again, and her eyes looking up at me once more. 'I would have pledged the Diamond myself, if I could have got the money in no other way! In those words I wrote to you. Wait! I did more than that. I arranged with Penelope to give you the letter when nobody was near. I planned to shut myself into my bedroom, and to have the sitting-room left open and empty all the morning. And I hoped—with all my heart and soul I hoped!—that you would take the opportunity, and put the Diamond back secretly in the drawer.'

I attempted to speak. She lifted her hand impatiently, and stopped me. In the rapid alternations of her temper, her anger was beginning to rise again. She got up from her chair, and approached me.

'I know what you are going to say,' she went on. 'You are going to remind me again that you never received my letter. I can tell you why. I tore it up.'

'For what reason?' I asked.

'For the best of reasons. I preferred tearing it up to throwing it away upon such a man as you! What was the first news that reached me in the morning? Just as my little plan was complete, what did I hear? I heard that you—you!!!—were the foremost person in the house in fetching the police. You were the active man; you were the leader; you were working harder than any of them to recover the jewel! You even carried your audacity far enough to ask to speak to *me* about the loss of the Diamond—the Diamond which you yourself had stolen; the Diamond which was all the time in your own hands! After that proof of your horrible falseness and cunning. I tore up my letter. But even then—even when I was maddened by the searching and questioning of the policeman, whom *you* had sent in—even then, there was some infatuation in my mind which wouldn't let me give you up. I said to myself, "He has played his vile farce before everybody else in the house. Let me try if he can play it before me." Somebody told me you were on the terrace. I went down to the terrace. I forced myself to look at you; I forced myself to speak to you. Have you forgotten what I said?'

I might have answered that I remembered every word of it. But what purpose, at that moment, would the answer have served?

How could I tell her that what she had said had astonished me, had distressed me, had suggested to me that she was in a state of dangerous nervous excitement, had even roused a moment's doubt in my mind whether the loss of the jewel was as much a mystery to her as to the rest of us—but had never once given me so much as a glimpse at the truth? Without the shadow of a proof to produce in vindication of my innocence, how could I persuade her that I knew no more than the veriest stranger could have known of what was really in her thoughts when she spoke to me on the terrace?

'It may suit your convenience to forget; it suits my convenience to remember,' she went on. 'I know what I said—for I considered it with myself, before I said it. I gave you one opportunity after another of owning the truth. I left nothing unsaid that I *could* say—short of actually telling you that I knew you had committed the theft. And all the return you made, was to look at me with your vile pretence of astonishment, and your false face of innocence—just as you have looked at me to-day; just as you are looking at me now! I left you, that morning, knowing you at last for what you were—for what you are—as base a wretch as ever walked the earth!'

'If you had spoken out at the time, you might have left me, Rachel, knowing that you had cruelly wronged an innocent man.'

'If I had spoken out before other people,' she retorted, with another burst of indignation, 'you would have been disgraced for life! If I had spoken out to no ears but yours, you would have denied it, as you are denying it now! Do you think I should have believed you? Would a man hesitate at a lie, who had done what I saw *you* do—who had behaved about it afterwards, as I saw *you* behave? I tell you again, I shrank from the horror of hearing you lie, after the horror of seeing you thieve. You talk as if this was a misunderstanding which a few words might have set right! Well! the misunderstanding is at an end. Is the thing set right? No! the thing is just where it was. I don't believe you *now!* I don't believe you found the nightgown, I don't believe in Rosanna Spearman's letter, I don't believe a word you have said. You stole it—I saw you! You affected to help the police—I saw you! You pledged the Diamond to the money-lender in London—I am sure of it! You cast the suspicion of your disgrace (thanks to my base silence!) on an innocent man! You fled to the Continent with your plunder the next morning! After all that vileness, there was but one thing more you *could* do. You could come here with a last falsehood on your lips—you could come here, and tell me that I have wronged you!'

If I had stayed a moment more, I know not what words might have escaped me which I should have remembered with vain repentance and regret. I passed by her, and opened the door for the second time. For the second time—with the frantic perversity of a roused woman—she caught me by the arm, and barred my way out.

'Let me go, Rachel,' I said. 'It will be better for both of us. Let me go.'

The hysterical passion swelled in her bosom—her quickened convulsive breathing almost beat on my face, as she held me back at the door.

'Why did you come here?' she persisted, desperately. 'I ask you again—why did you come here? Are you afraid I shall expose you? Now you are a rich man, now you have got a place in the world, now you may marry the best lady in the land—are you afraid I shall say the words which I have never said yet to anybody but you? I can't say the words! I can't expose you! I am worse, if worse can be, than you are yourself.' Sobs and tears burst from her. She struggled with them fiercely; she held me more and more firmly. 'I can't tear you out of my heart,' she said, 'even now! You may trust in the shameful, shameful weakness which can only struggle against you in this way!' She suddenly let go of me—she threw up her hands, and wrung them frantically in the air. 'Any other woman living would shrink from the disgrace of touching him!' she exclaimed. 'Oh, God! I despise myself even more heartily than I despise *him!*'

The tears were forcing their way into my eyes in spite of me—the horror of it was to be endured no longer.

'You shall know that you have wronged me, yet,' I said. 'Or you shall never see me again!'

With those words, I left her. She started up from the chair on which she had dropped the moment before: she started up—the noble creature!—and followed me across the outer room, with a last merciful word at parting.

'Franklin!' she said, 'I forgive you! Oh, Franklin, Franklin! we shall never meet again. Say you forgive *me!*'

I turned, so as to let my face show her that I was past speaking—I turned, and waved my hand, and saw her dimly, as in a vision, through the tears that had conquered me at last.

The next moment, the worst bitterness of it was over. I was out in the garden again. I saw her, and heard her, no more.

CHAPTER VIII

LATE that evening, I was surprised at my lodgings by a visit from Mr Bruff.

There was a noticeable change in the lawyer's manner. It had lost its usual confidence and spirit. He shook hands with me, for the first time in his life, in silence.

'Are you going back to Hampstead?' I asked, by way of saying something.

'I have just left Hampstead,' he answered. 'I know, Mr Franklin, that you have got at the truth at last. But, I tell you plainly, if I could have foreseen the price that was to be paid for it, I should have preferred leaving you in the dark.'

'You have seen Rachel?'

'I have come here after taking her back to Portland Place; it was impossible to let her return in the carriage by herself. I can hardly hold you responsible—considering that you saw her in my house and by my permission—for the shock that this unlucky interview has inflicted on her. All I can do is to provide against a repetition of the mischief. She is young—she has a resolute spirit—she will get over this, with time and rest to help her. I want to be assured that you will do nothing to hinder her recovery. May I depend on your making no second attempt to see her—except with my sanction and approval?'

'After what she has suffered, and after what I have suffered,' I said, 'you may rely on me.'

'I have your promise?'

'You have my promise.'

Mr Bruff looked relieved. He put down his hat, and drew his chair nearer to mine.

'That's settled!' he said. 'Now, about the future—*your* future, I mean. To my mind, the result of the extraordinary turn which the matter has now taken is briefly this. In the first place, we are sure that Rachel has told you the whole truth, as plainly as words can tell it. In the second place—though we know that there must be some dreadful mistake somewhere—we can hardly blame her for believing you to be guilty, on the evidence of her own senses; backed, as that evidence has been, by circumstances which appear, on the face of them, to tell dead against you.'

There I interposed. 'I don't blame Rachel,' I said. 'I only regret that she could not prevail on herself to speak more plainly to me at the time.'

'You might as well regret that Rachel is not somebody else,' rejoined Mr Bruff. 'And even then, I doubt if a girl of any delicacy, whose heart had been set on marrying you, could have brought herself to charge you to your face with being a thief. Anyhow, it was not in Rachel's nature to do it. In a very different matter to this matter of yours—which placed her, however, in a position not altogether unlike her position towards you—I happen to know that she was influenced by a similar motive to the motive which actuated her conduct in your case. Besides, as she told me herself, on our way to town this evening, if she *had* spoken plainly, she would no more have believed your denial then than she believes it now. What answer can you make to that? There is no answer to be made to it. Come, come, Mr Franklin! my view of the case has been proved to be all wrong, I admit—but, as things are now, my advice may be worth having for all that. I tell you plainly, we shall be wasting our time, and cudgelling our brains to no purpose, if we attempt to try back, and unravel this frightful complication from the beginning. Let us close our minds resolutely to all that happened last year at Lady Verinder's country house; and let us look to what we *can* discover in the future, instead of to what we can *not* discover in the past.'

'Surely you forget,' I said, 'that the whole thing is essentially a matter of the past—so far as I am concerned?'

'Answer me this,' retorted Mr Bruff. 'Is the Moonstone at the bottom of all the mischief—or is it not?'

'It is—of course.'

'Very good. What do we believe was done with the Moonstone, when it was taken to London?'

'It was pledged to Mr Luker.'

'We know that you are not the person who pledged it. Do we know who did?'

'No.'

'Where do we believe the Moonstone to be now?'

'Deposited in the keeping of Mr Luker's bankers.'

'Exactly. Now observe. We are already in the month of June. Towards the end of the month (I can't be particular to a day) a year will have elapsed from the time when we believe the jewel to have been pledged. There is a chance—to say the least—that the person who pawned it, may be prepared to redeem it when the year's time has expired. If he redeems it, Mr Luker must himself—according to the terms of his own arrangement—take the Diamond out of his banker's hands. Under these circumstances, I propose setting a watch at the bank, as the present month draws to an end, and discovering who the person is to whom Mr Luker restores the Moonstone. Do you see it now?'

I admitted (a little unwillingly) that the idea was a new one, at any rate.

'It's Mr Murthwaite's idea quite as much as mine,' said Mr Bruff. 'It might have never entered my head, but for a conversation we had together some time since. If Mr Murthwaite is right, the Indians are likely to be on the look-out at the bank, towards the end of the month too—and something serious may come of it. What comes of it doesn't matter to you and me—except as it may help us to lay our hands on the mysterious Somebody who pawned the Diamond. That person, you may rely on it, is responsible (I don't pretend to know how) for the position in which you stand at this moment; and that person alone can set you right in Rachel's estimation.'

'I can't deny,' I said, 'that the plan you propose meets the difficulty in a way that is very daring, and very ingenious, and very new. But——'

'But you have an objection to make?'

'Yes. My objection is, that your proposal obliges us to wait.'

'Granted. As I reckon the time, it requires you to wait about a fortnight—more or less. Is that so very long?'

'It's a lifetime, Mr Bruff, in such a situation as mine, My existence will be simply unendurable to me, unless I do something towards clearing my character at once.'

'Well, well, I understand that. Have you thought yet of what you can do?'

'I have thought of consulting Sergeant Cuff.'

'He has retired from the police. It's useless to expect the Sergeant to help you.'

'I know where to find him; and I can but try.'

'Try,' said Mr Bruff, after a moment's consideration. 'The case has assumed such an extraordinary aspect since Sergeant Cuff's time, that you *may* revive his interest in the inquiry. Try, and let me hear the result. In the meanwhile,' he continued, rising, 'if you make no discoveries between this, and the end of the month, am I free to try, on my side, what can be done by keeping a look-out at the bank?'

'Certainly,' I answered—'unless I relieve you of all necessity for trying the experiment in the interval.'

Mr Bruff smiled, and took up his hat.

'Tell Sergeant Cuff,' he rejoined, 'that *I* say the discovery of the truth depends on the discovery of the person who pawned the Diamond. And let me hear what the Sergeant's experience says to that.'

So we parted.

Early the next morning, I set forth for the little town of Dorking—the place of Sergeant Cuff's retirement, as indicated to me by Betteredge.

Inquiring at the hotel, I received the necessary directions for finding the Sergeant's cottage. It was approached by a quiet bye-road, a little way out of the town, and it stood snugly in the middle of its own plot of garden ground, protected by a good brick wall at the back and the sides, and by a high quickset hedge in front. The gate, ornamented at the upper part by smartly-painted trellis-work, was locked. After ringing at the bell, I peered through the trellis-work, and saw the great Cuff's favourite flower every-where; blooming in his garden, clustering over his door, looking in at his windows. Far from the crimes and the mysteries of the great city, the illustrious thief-taker was placidly living out the last Sybarite years of his life, smothered in roses!

A decent elderly woman opened the gate to me, and at once annihilated all the hopes I had built on securing the assistance of Sergeant Cuff. He had started, only the day before, on a journey to Ireland.

'Has he gone there on business?' I asked.

The woman smiled. 'He has only one business now, sir,' she said; 'and that's roses. Some great man's gardener in Ireland has found out something new in the growing of roses—and Mr Cuff's away to inquire into it.'

'Do you know when he will be back?'

'It's quite uncertain, sir. Mr Cuff said he should come back directly, or be away some time, just according as he found the new discovery worth nothing, or worth looking into. If you have any message to leave for him, I'll take care, sir, that he gets it.'

I gave her my card, having first written on it in pencil: 'I have something to say about the Moonstone. Let me hear from you as soon as you get back.' That done, there was nothing left but to submit to circumstances, and return to London.

In the irritable condition of my mind, at the time of which I am now writing, the abortive result of my journey to the Sergeant's cottage simply aggravated the restless impulse in me to be doing something. On the day of my return from Dorking, I determined that the next morning should find me bent on a new effort at forcing my way, through all obstacles, from the darkness to the light.

What form was my next experiment to take?

If the excellent Betteredge had been present while I was considering that question, and if he had been let into the secret of my thoughts, he would, no doubt, have declared that the German side of me was, on this occasion, my uppermost side. To speak seriously, it is perhaps possible that my German training was in some degree responsible for the labyrinth of useless speculations in which I now involved myself. For the greater part of the night, I sat smoking, and building up theories, one more profoundly improbable than another. When I did get to sleep, my waking fancies pursued me in dreams. I rose the next morning, with Objective-Subjective and Subjective-Objective inextricably entangled together in my mind; and I began the day which was to witness my next effort at practical action of some kind, by doubting whether I had any sort of right (on purely philosophical grounds) to consider any sort of thing (the Diamond included) as existing at all.

How long I might have remained lost in the mist of my own metaphysics, if I had been left to extricate myself, it is impossible for me to say. As the event proved, accident came to my rescue, and happily delivered me. I happened to wear, that morning, the same coat which I had worn on the day of my interview with Rachel. Searching for something else in one of the pockets, I came upon a crumpled piece of paper, and, taking it out, found Betteredge's forgotten letter in my hand.

It seemed hard on my good old friend to leave him without a reply. I went to my writing-table, and read his letter again.

A letter which has nothing of the slightest importance in it, is not always an easy letter to answer. Betteredge's present effort at corresponding with me came within this category. Mr Candy's assistant, otherwise Ezra Jennings, had told his master that he had seen me; and Mr Candy, in his turn, wanted to see me and say something to me, when I was next in the neighbourhood of Frizinghall. What was to be said in answer to that, which would be worth the paper it was written on? I sat idly drawing likenesses from memory of Mr Candy's remarkable-looking assistant, on the sheet of paper which I had vowed to dedicate to Betteredge—until it suddenly occurred to me that here was the irrepressible Ezra Jennings getting in my way again! I threw a dozen portraits, at least, of the man with the piebald hair (the hair in every case, remarkably like), into the waste-paper basket— and then and there, wrote my answer to Betteredge. It was a perfectly commonplace letter—but it had one excellent effect on me. The effort of writing a few sentences, in plain English, completely cleared my mind of the cloudy nonsense which had filled it since the previous day.

Devoting myself once more to the elucidation of the impenetrable puzzle which my own position presented to me, I now tried to meet the difficulty by investigating it from a plainly practical point of view. The events of the memorable night being still unintelligible to me, I looked a little farther back, and searched my memory of the earlier hours of the birthday for any incident which might prove of some assistance to me in finding the clue.

Had anything happened while Rachel and I were finishing the painted door? or, later, when I rode over to Frizinghall? or afterwards, when I went back with Godfrey Ablewhite and his sisters? or, later again, when I put the Moonstone into Rachel's hands? or, later still, when the company came, and we all assembled round the dinner-table? My memory disposed of that string of questions readily enough, until I came to the last. Looking back at the social events of the birthday dinner, I found myself brought to a standstill at the outset of the inquiry. I was not even capable of accurately remembering the number of the guests who had sat at the same table with me.

To feel myself completely at fault here, and to conclude, thereupon, that the incidents of the dinner might especially repay the trouble of investigating them, formed parts of the same mental process, in my case. I believe other people, in a similar situation, would have reasoned as I did. When the pursuit of our own interests causes us to become objects of inquiry to ourselves, we are naturally suspicious of what we don't know. Once in possession of the names of the persons who had been present at the dinner, I resolved—as a means of enriching the deficient resources of my own memory—to appeal to the memory of the rest of the guests; to write down all that they could recollect of the social events of the birthday; and to test the result, thus obtained, by the light of what had happened afterwards, when the company had left the house.

This last and newest of my many contemplated experiments in the art of inquiry—which Betteredge would probably have attributed to the clear-headed, or French, side of me being uppermost for the moment—may fairly claim record here, on its own merits. Unlikely as it may seem, I had now actually groped my way to the root of the matter at last. All I wanted was a hint to guide me in the right direction at starting. Before another day had passed over my head, that hint was given me by one of the company who had been present at the birthday feast!

With the plan of proceeding which I now had in view, it was first necessary to possess the complete list of the guests. This I could easily obtain from Gabriel Betteredge. I determined to go back to Yorkshire on that day, and to begin my contemplated investigation the next morning.

It was just too late to start by the train which left London before noon. There was no alternative but to wait, nearly three hours, for the departure of the next train. Was there anything I could do in London, which might usefully occupy this interval of time?

My thoughts went back again obstinately to the birthday dinner.

Though I had forgotten the numbers, and, in many cases, the names of the guests, I remembered readily enough that by far the larger proportion of them came from Frizinghall, or from its neighbourhood. But the larger proportion was not all. Some few of us were not regular residents in the country. I myself was one of the few. Mr Murthwaite was another. Godfrey Ablewhite was a third. Mr Bruff—no: I called to mind that business had prevented Mr Bruff from making one of the party. Had any ladies been present, whose usual residence was in London? I could only remember Miss Clack as coming within this latter category. However, here were three of the guests, at any rate, whom it was clearly advisable for me to see before I left town. I drove off at once to Mr Bruff's office; not knowing the addresses of the persons of whom I was in search, and thinking it probable that he might put me in the way of finding them.

Mr Bruff proved to be too busy to give me more than a minute of his valuable time. In that minute, however, he contrived to dispose—in the most discouraging manner—of all the questions I had to put to him.

In the first place, he considered my newly-discovered method of finding a clue to the mystery as something too purely fanciful to be seriously discussed. In the second, third, and fourth places, Mr Murthwaite was now on his way back to the scene of his past adventures; Miss Clack had suffered losses, and had settled, from motives of economy, in France; Mr Godfrey Ablewhite might, or might not, be discoverable somewhere in London. Suppose I inquired at his club? And suppose I excused Mr Bruff, if he went back to his business and wished me good morning?

The field of inquiry in London, being now so narrowed as only to include the one necessity of discovering Godfrey's address, I took the lawyer's hint, and drove to his club.

In the hall, I met with one of the members, who was an old friend of my cousin's, and who was also an acquaintance of my own. This gentleman, after enlightening me on the subject of Godfrey's address, told me of two recent events in his life, which were of some importance in themselves, and which had not previously reached my ears.

It appeared that Godfrey, far from being discouraged by Rachel's withdrawal from her engagement to him, had made matrimonial advances soon afterwards to another young lady, reputed to be a great heiress. His suit had prospered, and his marriage had been considered as a settled and certain thing. But, here again, the engagement had been suddenly and unexpectedly broken off—owing, it was said, on this occasion, to a serious difference of opinion between the bridegroom and the lady's father, on the question of settlements.

As some compensation for this second matrimonial disaster, Godfrey had soon afterwards found himself the object of fond pecuniary remembrance, on the part of one of his many admirers. A rich old lady—highly respected at the Mothers' Small-Clothes-Conversion-Society, and a great friend of Miss Clack's (to whom she had left nothing but a mourning ring)—had bequeathed to the admirable and meritorious Godfrey a legacy of five thousand pounds. After receiving this handsome addition to his own modest pecuniary resources, he had been heard to say that he felt the necessity of getting a little respite from his charitable labours, and that his doctor prescribed 'a run on the Continent, as likely to be productive of much future benefit to his health.' If I wanted to see him, it would be advisable to lose no time in paying my contemplated visit.

I went, then and there, to pay my visit.

The same fatality which had made me just one day too late in calling on Sergeant Cuff, made me again one day too late in calling on Godfrey. He had left London, on the previous morning, by the tidal train, for Dover. He was to cross to Ostend; and his servant believed he was going on to Brussels. The time of his return was rather uncertain; but I might be sure he would be away at least three months.

I went back to my lodgings a little depressed in spirits. Three of the guests at the birthday dinner—and those three all exceptionally intelligent people—were out of my reach, at the very time when it was most important to be able to communicate with them. My last hopes now rested on Betteredge, and on the friends of the late Lady Verinder whom I might still find living in the neighbourhood of Rachel's country house.

On this occasion, I travelled straight to Frizinghall—the town being now the central point in my field of inquiry. I arrived too late in the evening to be able to communicate with Betteredge. The next morning, I sent a messenger with a letter, requesting him to join me at the hotel, at his earliest convenience.

Having taken the precaution—partly to save time, partly to accommodate Betteredge—of sending my messenger in a fly, I had a reasonable prospect, if no delays occurred, of seeing the old man within less than two hours from the time when I had sent for him. During this interval, I arranged to employ myself in opening my contemplated inquiry, among the guests present at the birthday dinner who were personally known to me, and who were easily within my reach. These were my relatives, the Ablewhites, and Mr Candy. The doctor had expressed a special wish to see me, and the doctor lived in the next street. So to Mr Candy I went first.

After what Betteredge had told me, I naturally anticipated finding traces in the doctor's face of the severe illness from which he had suffered. But I was utterly unprepared for such a change as I saw in him when he entered the room and shook hands with me. His eyes were dim; his hair had turned completely grey; his face was wizen; his figure had shrunk. I looked at the once lively, rattlepated, humorous little doctor—associated in my remembrance with the perpetration of incorrigible social indiscretions and innumerable boyish jokes—and I saw nothing left of his former self, but the old tendency to vulgar smartness in his dress. The man was a wreck; but his clothes and his jewellery—in cruel mockery of the change in him—were as gay and as gaudy as ever.

'I have often thought of you, Mr Blake,' he said; 'and I am heartily glad to see you again at last. If there is anything I can do for you, pray command my services, sir—pray command my services!'

He said those few commonplace words with needless hurry and eagerness, and with a curiosity to know what had brought me to Yorkshire, which he was perfectly—I might say childishly—incapable of concealing from notice.

With the object that I had in view, I had of course foreseen the necessity of entering into some sort of personal explanation, before I could hope to interest people, mostly strangers to me, in doing their best to assist my inquiry. On the journey to Frizinghall I had arranged what my explanation was to be—and I seized the opportunity now offered to me of trying the effect of it on Mr Candy.

'I was in Yorkshire, the other day, and I am in Yorkshire again now, on rather a romantic errand,' I said. 'It is a matter, Mr Candy, in which the late Lady Verinder's friends all took some interest. You remember the mysterious loss of the Indian Diamond, now nearly a year since? Circumstances have lately happened which lead to the hope that it may yet be found—and I am interesting myself, as one of the family, in recovering it. Among the obstacles in my way, there is the necessity of collecting again all the evidence which was discovered at the time, and more if possible. There are peculiarities in this case which make it desirable to revive my recollection of everything that happened in the house, on the evening of Miss Verinder's birthday. And I venture to appeal to her late mother's friends who were present on that occasion, to lend me the assistance of their memories——'

I had got as far as that in rehearsing my explanatory phrases, when I was suddenly checked by seeing plainly in Mr Candy's face that my experiment on him was a total failure.

The little doctor sat restlessly picking at the points of his fingers all the time I was speaking. His dim watery eyes were fixed on my face with an expression of vacant and wistful inquiry very painful to see. What he was thinking of, it was impossible to divine. The one thing clearly visible was that I had failed, after the first two or three words, in fixing his attention. The only chance of recalling him to himself appeared to lie in changing the subject. I tried a new topic immediately.

'So much,' I said, gaily, 'for what brings me to Frizinghall! Now, Mr Candy, it's your turn. You sent me a message by Gabriel Betteredge——'

He left off picking at his fingers, and suddenly brightened up.

'Yes! yes! yes!' he exclaimed eagerly. 'That's it! I sent you a message!'

'And Betteredge duly communicated it by letter,' I went on. 'You had something to say to me, the next time I was in your neighbourhood. Well, Mr Candy, here I am!'

'Here you are!' echoed the doctor. 'And Betteredge was quite right. I had something to say to you. That was my message. Betteredge is a wonderful man. What a memory! At his age, what a memory!'

He dropped back into silence, and began picking at his fingers again. Recollecting what I had heard from Betteredge about the effect of the fever on his memory, I went on with the conversation, in the hope that I might help him at starting.

'It's a long time since we met,' I said. 'We last saw each other at the last birthday dinner my poor aunt was ever to give.'

'That's it!' cried Mr Candy. 'The birthday dinner!' He started impulsively to his feet, and looked at me. A deep flush suddenly overspread his faded face, and he abruptly sat down again, as if conscious of having betrayed a weakness which he would fain have concealed. It was plain, pitiably plain, that he was aware of his own defect of memory, and that he was bent on hiding it from the observation of his friends.

Thus far he had appealed to my compassion only. But the words he had just said—few as they were—roused my curiosity instantly to the highest pitch. The birthday dinner had already become the one event in the past, at which I looked back with strangely-mixed feelings of hope and distrust. And here was the birthday dinner unmistakably proclaiming itself as the subject on which Mr Candy had something important to say to me!

I attempted to help him out once more. But, this time, my own interests were at the bottom of my compassionate motive, and they hurried me on a little too abruptly, to the end I had in view.

'It's nearly a year now,' I said, 'since we sat at that pleasant table. Have you made any memorandum—in your diary, or otherwise—of what you wanted to say to me?'

Mr Candy understood the suggestion, and showed me that he understood it, as an insult.

'I require no memorandums, Mr Blake,' he said, stiffly enough. 'I am not such a very old man, yet—and my memory (thank God) is to be thoroughly depended on!'

It is needless to say that I declined to understand that he was offended with me.

'I wish I could say the same of *my* memory,' I answered. 'When *I* try to think of matters that are a year old, I seldom find my remembrance as vivid as I could wish it to be. Take the dinner at Lady Verinder's, for instance——'

Mr Candy brightened up again, the moment the allusion passed my lips.

'Ah! the dinner, the dinner at Lady Verinder's!' he exclaimed, more eagerly than ever. 'I have got something to say to you about that.'

His eyes looked at me again with the painful expression of inquiry, so wistful, so vacant, so miserably helpless to see. He was evidently trying hard, and trying in vain, to recover the lost recollection. 'It was a very pleasant dinner,' he burst out suddenly, with an air of saying exactly what he wanted to say. 'A very pleasant dinner, Mr Blake, wasn't it?' He nodded and smiled, and appeared to think, poor fellow, that he had succeeded in concealing the total failure of his memory, by a well-timed exertion of his own presence of mind.

It was so distressing that I at once shifted the talk—deeply as I was interested in his recovering the lost remembrance—to topics of local interest.

Here, he got on glibly enough. Trumpery little scandals and quarrels in the town, some of them as much as a month old, appeared to recur to his memory readily. He chattered on, with something of the smooth gossiping fluency of former times. But there were moments, even in the full flow of his talkativeness, when he suddenly hesitated—looked at me for a moment with the vacant inquiry once more in his eyes—controlled himself—and went on again. I submitted patiently to my martyrdom (it is surely nothing less than martyrdom to a man of cosmopolitan sympathies, to absorb in silent resignation the news of a country town?) until the clock on the chimney-piece told me that my visit had been prolonged beyond half an hour. Having now some right to consider the sacrifice as complete, I rose to take leave. As we shook hands, Mr Candy reverted to the birthday festival of his own accord.

'I am so glad we have met again,' he said. 'I had it on my mind—I really had it on my mind, Mr Blake, to speak to you. About the dinner at Lady Verinder's, you know? A pleasant dinner—really a pleasant dinner now, wasn't it?'

On repeating the phrase, he seemed to feel hardly as certain of having prevented me from suspecting his lapse of memory, as he had felt on the first occasion. The wistful look clouded his face again: and, after apparently designing to accompany me to the street door, he suddenly changed his mind, rang the bell for the servant, and remained in the drawing-room.

I went slowly down the doctor's stairs, feeling the disheartening conviction that he really had something to say which it was vitally important to me to hear, and that he was morally incapable of saying it. The effort of remembering that he wanted to speak to me was, but too evidently, the only effort that his enfeebled memory was now able to achieve.

Just as I reached the bottom of the stairs, and had turned a corner on my way to the outer hall, a door opened softly somewhere on the ground floor of the house, and a gentle voice said behind me:—

'I am afraid, sir, you find Mr Candy sadly changed?'

I turned round, and found myself face to face with Ezra Jennings.

CHAPTER IX

THE doctor's pretty housemaid stood waiting for me, with the street door open in her hand. Pouring brightly into the hall, the morning light fell full on the face of Mr Candy's assistant when I turned, and looked at him.

It was impossible to dispute Betteredge's assertion that the appearance of Ezra Jennings, speaking from a popular point of view, was against him. His gipsy-complexion, his fleshless cheeks, his gaunt facial bones, his dreamy eyes, his extraordinary parti-coloured hair, the puzzling contradiction between his face and figure which made him look old and young both together—were all more or less calculated to produce an unfavourable impression of him on a stranger's mind. And yet—feeling this as I certainly did—it is not to be denied that Ezra Jennings made some inscrutable appeal to my sympathies, which I found it impossible to resist. While my knowledge of the world warned me to answer the question which he had put, acknowledging that I did indeed find Mr Candy sadly changed, and then to proceed on my way out of the house—my interest in Ezra Jennings held me rooted to the place, and gave him the opportunity of speaking to me in private about his employer, for which he had been evidently on the watch.

'Are you walking my way, Mr Jennings?' I said, observing that he held his hat in his hand. 'I am going to call on my aunt, Mrs Ablewhite.'

Ezra Jennings replied that he had a patient to see, and that he was walking my way.

We left the house together. I observed that the pretty servant girl—who was all smiles and amiability, when I wished her good morning on my way out—received a modest little message from Ezra Jennings, relating to the time at which he might be expected to return, with pursed-up lips, and with eyes which ostentatiously looked anywhere rather than look in his face. The poor wretch was evidently no favourite in the house. Out of the house, I had Betteredge's word for it that he was unpopular everywhere. 'What a life!' I thought to myself, as we descended the doctor's doorsteps.

Having already referred to Mr Candy's illness on his side, Ezra Jennings now appeared determined to leave it to me to resume the subject. His silence said significantly, 'It's your turn now.' I, too, had my reasons for referring to the doctor's illness: and I readily accepted the responsibility of speaking first.

'Judging by the change I see in him,' I began, 'Mr Candy's illness must have been far more serious than I had supposed?'

'It is almost a miracle,' said Ezra Jennings, 'that he lived through it.'

'Is his memory never any better than I have found it to-day? He has been trying to speak to me——'

'Of something which happened before he was taken ill?' asked the assistant, observing that I hesitated.

'Yes.'

'His memory of events, at that past time, is hopelessly enfeebled,' said Ezra Jennings. 'It is almost to be deplored, poor fellow, that even the wreck of it remains. While he remembers dimly plans that he formed—things, here and there, that he had to say or do before his illness—he is perfectly incapable of recalling what the plans were, or what the thing was that he had to say or do. He is painfully conscious of his own deficiency, and painfully anxious, as you must have seen, to hide it from observation. If he could only have recovered in a complete state of oblivion as to the past, he would have been a happier man. Perhaps we should all be happier,' he added, with a sad smile, 'if we could but completely forget!'

'There are some events surely in all men's lives,' I replied, 'the memory of which they would be unwilling entirely to lose?'

'That is, I hope, to be said of most men, Mr Blake. I am afraid it cannot truly be said of all. Have you any reason to suppose that the lost remembrance which Mr Candy tried to recover—while you were speaking to him just now—was a remembrance which it was important to *you* that he should recall?'

In saying those words, he had touched, of his own accord, on the very point upon which I was anxious to consult him. The interest I felt in this strange man had impelled me, in the first instance, to give him the opportunity of speaking to me; reserving what I might have to say, on my side, in relation to his employer, until I was first satisfied that he was a person in whose delicacy and discretion I could trust. The little that he had said, thus far, had been sufficient to convince me that I was speaking to a gentleman. He had what I may venture to describe as the *unsought self-possession*, which is a sure sign of good breeding, not in England only, but everywhere else in the civilised world. Whatever the object which he had in view, in putting the question that he had just addressed to me, I felt no doubt that I was justified—so far—in answering him without reserve.

'I believe I have a strong interest,' I said, 'in tracing the lost remembrance which Mr Candy was unable to recall. May I ask whether you can suggest to me any method by which I might assist his memory?'

Ezra Jennings looked at me, with a sudden flash of interest in his dreamy brown eyes.

'Mr Candy's memory is beyond the reach of assistance,' he said. 'I have tried to help it often enough since his recovery, to be able to speak positively on that point.'

This disappointed me; and I owned it.

'I confess you led me to hope for a less discouraging answer than that,' I said.

Ezra Jennings smiled. 'It may not, perhaps, be a final answer, Mr Blake. It may be possible to trace Mr Candy's lost recollection, without the necessity of appealing to Mr Candy himself.'

'Indeed? Is it an indiscretion, on my part, to ask——how?'

'By no means. My only difficulty in answering your question, is the difficulty of explaining myself. May I trust to your patience, if I refer once more to Mr Candy's illness: and if I speak of it this time without sparing you certain professional details?'

'Pray go on! You have interested me already in hearing the details.'

My eagerness seemed to amuse—perhaps, I might rather say, to please him. He smiled again. We had by this time left the last houses in the town behind us. Ezra Jennings stopped for a moment, and picked some wild flowers from the hedge by the roadside. 'How beautiful they are!' he said, simply, showing his little nosegay to me. 'And how few people in England seem to admire them as they deserve!'

'You have not always been in England?' I said.

'No. I was born, and partly brought up, in one of our colonies. My father was an Englishman; but my mother——We are straying away from our subject, Mr Blake; and it is my fault. The truth is, I have associations with these modest little hedgeside flowers——It doesn't matter; we were speaking of Mr Candy. To Mr Candy let us return.'

Connecting the few words about himself which thus reluctantly escaped him, with the melancholy view of life which led him to place the conditions of human happiness in complete oblivion of the past, I felt satisfied that the story which I had read in his face was, in two particulars at least, the story that it really told. He had suffered as few men suffer; and there was the mixture of some foreign race in his English blood.

'You have heard, I dare say, of the original cause of Mr Candy's illness?' he resumed. 'The night of Lady Verinder's dinner-party was a night of heavy rain. My employer drove home through it in his gig, and reached the house, wetted to the skin. He found an urgent message from a patient, waiting for him; and he most unfortunately went at once to visit the sick person, without stopping to change his clothes. I was myself professionally detained, that night, by a case at some distance from Frizinghall. When I got back the next morning, I found Mr Candy's groom waiting in great alarm to take me to his master's room. By that time the mischief was done; the illness had set in.'

'The illness has only been described to me, in general terms, as a fever,' I said.

'I can add nothing which will make the description more accurate,' answered Ezra Jennings. 'From first to last the fever assumed no specific form. I sent at once to two of Mr Candy's medical friends in the town, both physicians, to come and give me their opinion of the case. They agreed with me that it looked serious; but they both strongly dissented from the view I took of the treatment. We differed entirely in the conclusions which we drew from the patient's pulse. The two doctors, arguing from the rapidity of the beat, declared that a lowering treatment was the only treatment to be adopted. On my side, I admitted the rapidity of the pulse, but I also pointed to its alarming feebleness as indicating an exhausted condition of the system, and as showing a plain necessity for the administration of stimulants. The two doctors were for keeping him on gruel, lemonade, barley-water, and so on. I was for giving him champagne, or brandy, ammonia, and quinine. A serious difference of opinion, as you see! a difference between two physicians of established local repute, and a stranger who was only an assistant in the house. For the first few days, I had no choice but to give way to my elders and betters: the patient steadily sinking all the time. I made a second attempt to appeal to the plain, undeniably plain, evidence of the pulse. Its rapidity was unchecked, and its feebleness had increased. The two doctors took offence at my obstinacy. They said, "Mr Jennings, either we manage this case, or you manage it. Which is it to be?" I said, "Gentlemen, give me five minutes to consider, and that plain question shall have a plain reply." When the time expired, I was ready with my answer. I said, "You positively refuse to try the stimulant treatment?" They refused in so many words. "I mean to try it at once, gentlemen."—"Try it, Mr Jennings, and we withdraw from the case." I sent down to the cellar for a bottle of champagne; and I administered half a tumbler-full of it to the patient with my own hand. The two physicians took up their hats in silence, and left the house.'

'You had assumed a serious responsibility,' I said. 'In your place, I am afraid I should have shrunk from it.'

'In my place, Mr Blake, you would have remembered that Mr Candy had taken you into his employment, under circumstances which made you his debtor for life. In my place, you would have seen him sinking, hour by hour; and you would have risked anything, rather than let the one man on earth who had befriended you, die before your eyes. Don't suppose that I had no sense of the terrible position in which I had placed myself! There were moments when I felt all the misery of my friendlessness, all the peril of my dreadful responsibility. If I had been a happy man, if I had led a prosperous life, I believe I should have sunk under the task I had imposed on myself. But *I* had no happy time to look back at, no past peace of mind to force itself into contrast with my present anxiety and suspense—and I held firm to my resolution through it all. I took an interval in the middle of the day, when my patient's condition was at its best, for the repose I needed. For the rest of the four-and-twenty hours, as long as his life was in danger, I never left his bedside. Towards sunset, as usual in such cases, the delirium incidental to the fever came on. It lasted more or less through the night; and then intermitted, at that terrible time in the early morning—from two o'clock to five—when the vital energies even of the healthiest of us are at their lowest. It is then that Death gathers in his human harvest most abundantly. It was then that Death and I fought our fight over the bed, which should have the man who lay on it. I never hesitated in pursuing the treatment on which I had staked everything. When wine failed, I tried brandy. When the other stimulants lost their influence, I doubled the dose. After an interval of suspense—the like of which I hope to God I shall never feel again—there came a day when the rapidity of the pulse slightly, but appreciably, diminished; and, better still, there came also a change in the beat—an unmistakable change to steadiness and strength. *Then*, I knew that I had saved him; and then I own I broke down. I laid the poor fellow's wasted hand back on the bed, and burst out crying. An hysterical relief, Mr Blake—nothing more! Physiology says, and says truly, that some men are born with female constitutions—and I am one of them!'

He made that bitterly professional apology for his tears, speaking quietly and unaffectedly, as he had spoken throughout. His tone and manner, from beginning to end, showed him to be especially, almost morbidly, anxious not to set himself up as an object of interest to me.

'You may well ask, why I have wearied you with all these details?' he went on. 'It is the only way I can see, Mr Blake, of properly introducing to you what I have to say next. Now you know exactly what my position was, at the time of Mr Candy's illness, you will the more readily understand the sore need I had of lightening the burden on my mind by giving it, at intervals, some sort of relief. I have had the presumption to occupy my leisure, for some years past, in writing a book, addressed to the members of my profession—a book on the intricate and delicate subject of the brain and the nervous system. My work will probably never be finished; and it will certainly never be published. It has none the less been the friend of many lonely hours; and it helped me to while away the anxious time—the time of waiting, and nothing else—at Mr Candy's bedside. I told you he was delirious, I think? And I mentioned the time at which his delirium came on?'

'Yes.'

'Well, I had reached a section of my book, at that time, which touched on this same question of delirium. I won't trouble you at any length with my theory on the subject—I will confine myself to telling you only what it is your present interest to know. It has often occurred to me in the course of my medical practice, to doubt whether we can justifiably infer—in cases of delirium—that the loss of the faculty of speaking connectedly, implies of necessity the loss of the faculty of thinking connectedly as well. Poor Mr Candy's illness gave me an opportunity of putting this doubt to the test. I understand the art of writing in shorthand; and I was able to take down the patient's "wanderings," exactly as they fell from his lips.—Do you see, Mr Blake, what I am coming to at last?'

I saw it clearly, and waited with breathless interest to hear more.

'At odds and ends of time,' Ezra Jennings went on, 'I reproduced my shorthand notes, in the ordinary form of writing—leaving large spaces between the broken phrases, and even the single words, as they had fallen disconnectedly from Mr Candy's lips. I then treated the result thus obtained, on something like the principle which one adopts in putting together a child's "puzzle." It is all confusion to begin with; but it may be all brought into order and shape, if you can only find the right way. Acting on this plan, I filled in each blank space on the paper, with what the words or phrases on either side of it suggested to me as the speaker's meaning; altering over and over again, until my additions followed naturally on the spoken words which came before them, and fitted naturally into the spoken words which came after them. The result was, that I not only occupied in this way many vacant and anxious hours, but that I arrived at something which was (as it seemed to me) a confirmation of the theory that I held. In plainer words, after putting the broken sentences together I found the superior faculty of thinking going on, more or less connectedly, in my patient's mind, while the inferior faculty of expression was in a state of almost complete incapacity and confusion.'

'One word!' I interposed eagerly. 'Did my name occur in any of his wanderings?'

'You shall hear, Mr Blake. Among my written proofs of the assertion which I have just advanced—or, I ought to say, among the written experiments, tending to put my assertion to the proof—there *is* one, in which your name occurs. For nearly the whole of one night Mr Candy's mind was occupied with *something* between himself and you. I have got the broken words, as they dropped from his lips, on one sheet of paper. And I have got the links of my own discovering which connect those words together, on another sheet of paper. The product (as the arithmeticians would say) is an intelligible statement—first, of something actually done in the past; secondly, of something which Mr Candy contemplated doing in the future, if his illness had not got in the way, and stopped him. The question is whether this does, or does not, represent the lost recollection which he vainly attempted to find when you called on him this morning?'

'Not a doubt of it!' I answered. 'Let us go back directly, and look at the papers!'

'Quite impossible, Mr Blake.'

'Why?'

'Put yourself in my position for a moment,' said Ezra Jennings. 'Would *you* disclose to another person what had dropped unconsciously from the lips of your suffering patient and your helpless friend, without first knowing that there was a necessity to justify you in opening your lips?'

I felt that he was unanswerable, here; but I tried to argue the question, nevertheless.

'My conduct in such a delicate matter as you describe,' I replied, 'would depend greatly on whether the disclosure was of a nature to compromise my friend or not.'

'I have disposed of all necessity for considering that side of the question, long since,' said Ezra Jennings. 'Wherever my notes included anything which Mr Candy might have wished to keep secret, those notes have been destroyed. My manuscript experiments at my friend's beside include nothing, now, which he would have hesitated to communicate to others, if he had recovered the use of his memory. In your case, I have every reason to suppose that my notes contain something which he actually wished to say to you——'

'And yet, you hesitate?'

'And yet, I hesitate. Remember the circumstances under which I obtained the information which I possess! Harmless as it is, I cannot prevail upon myself to give it up to you, unless you first satisfy me that there is a reason for doing so. He was so miserably ill, Mr Blake! and he was so helplessly dependent upon Me! Is it too much to ask, if I request you only to hint to me what your interest is in the lost recollection—or what you believe that lost recollection to be?'

To have answered him with the frankness which his language and his manner both claimed from me, would have been to commit myself to openly acknowledging that I was suspected of the theft of the Diamond. Strongly as Ezra Jennings had intensified the first impulsive interest which I had felt in him, he had not overcome my unconquerable reluctance to disclose the degrading position in which I stood. I took refuge once more in the explanatory phrases with which I had prepared myself to meet the curiosity of strangers.

This time I had no reason to complain of a want of attention on the part of the person to whom I addressed myself. Ezra Jennings listened patiently, even anxiously, until I had done.

'I am sorry to have raised your expectations, Mr Blake, only to disappoint them,' he said. 'Throughout the whole period of Mr Candy's illness, from first to last, not one word about the Diamond escaped his lips. The matter with which I heard him connect your name has, I can assure you, no discoverable relation whatever with the loss or the recovery of Miss Verinder's jewel.'

We arrived, as he said those words, at a place where the highway along which we had been walking branched off into two roads. One led to Mr Ablewhite's house, and the other to a moorland village some two or three miles off. Ezra Jennings stopped at the road which led to the village.

'My way lies in this direction,' he said. 'I am really and truly sorry, Mr Blake, that I can be of no use to you.'

His voice told me that he spoke sincerely. His soft brown eyes rested on me for a moment with a look of melancholy interest. He bowed, and went, without another word, on his way to the village.

For a minute or more I stood and watched him, walking farther and farther away from me; carrying farther and farther away with him what I now firmly believed to be the clue of which I was in search. He turned, after walking on a little way, and looked back. Seeing me still standing at the place where we had parted, he stopped, as if doubting whether I might not wish to speak to him again. There was no time for me to reason out my own situation—to remind myself that I was losing my opportunity, at what might be the turning point of my life, and all to flatter nothing more important than my own self-esteem! There was only time to call him back first, and to think afterwards. I suspect I am one of the rashest of existing men. I called him back—and then I said to myself, 'Now there is no help for it. I must tell him the truth!'

He retraced his steps directly. I advanced along the road to meet him.

'Mr Jennings,' I said. 'I have not treated you quite fairly. My interest in tracing Mr Candy's lost recollection is not the interest of recovering the Moonstone. A serious personal matter is at the bottom of my visit to Yorkshire. I have but one excuse for not having dealt frankly with you in this matter. It is more painful to me than I can say, to mention to anybody what my position really is.'

Ezra Jennings looked at me with the first appearance of embarrassment which I had seen in him yet.

'I have no right, Mr Blake, and no wish,' he said, 'to intrude myself into your private affairs. Allow me to ask your pardon, on my side, for having (most innocently) put you to a painful test.'

'You have a perfect right,' I rejoined, 'to fix the terms on which you feel justified in revealing what you heard at Mr Candy's bedside. I understand and respect the delicacy which influences you in this matter. How can I expect to be taken into your confidence if I decline to admit you into mine? You ought to know, and you shall know, why I am interested in discovering what Mr Candy wanted to say to me. If I turn out to be mistaken in my anticipations, and if you prove unable to help me when you are really aware of what I want, I shall trust to your honour to keep my secret—and something tells me that I shall not trust in vain.'

'Stop, Mr Blake. I have a word to say, which must be said before you go any farther.' I looked at him in astonishment. The grip of some terrible emotion seemed to have seized him, and shaken him to the soul. His gipsy complexion had altered to a livid greyish paleness; his eyes had suddenly become wild and glittering; his voice had dropped to a tone—low, stern, and resolute—which I now heard for the first time. The latent resources in the man, for good or for evil—it was hard, at that moment, to say which—leapt up in him and showed themselves to me, with the suddenness of a flash of light.

'Before you place any confidence in me,' he went on, 'you ought to know, and you *must* know, under what circumstances I have been received into Mr Candy's house. It won't take long. I don't profess, sir, to tell my story (as the phrase is) to any man. My story will die with me. All I ask, is to be permitted to tell you, what I have told Mr Candy. If you are still in the mind, when you have heard that, to say what you have proposed to say, you will command my attention and command my services. Shall we walk on?'

The suppressed misery in his face silenced me. I answered his question by a sign. We walked on.

After advancing a few hundred yards, Ezra Jennings stopped at a gap in the rough stone wall which shut off the moor from the road, at this part of it.

'Do you mind resting a little, Mr Blake?' he asked. 'I am not what I was—and some things shake me.'

I agreed of course. He led the way through the gap to a patch of turf on the heathy ground, screened by bushes and dwarf trees on the side nearest to the road, and commanding in the opposite direction a grandly desolate view over the broad brown wilderness of the moor. The clouds had gathered, within the last half hour. The light was dull; the distance was dim. The lovely face of Nature met us, soft and still colourless—met us without a smile.

We sat down in silence. Ezra Jennings laid aside his hat, and passed his hand wearily over his forehead, wearily through his startling white and black hair. He tossed his little nosegay of wild flowers away from him, as if the remembrances which it recalled were remembrances which hurt him now.

'Mr Blake!' he said, suddenly. 'You are in bad company. The cloud of a horrible accusation has rested on me for years. I tell you the worst at once. I am a man whose life is a wreck, and whose character is gone.'

I attempted to speak. He stopped me.

'No,' he said. 'Pardon me; not yet. Don't commit yourself to expressions of sympathy which you may afterwards wish to recall. I have mentioned an accusation which has rested on me for years. There are circumstances in connexion with it that tell against me. I cannot bring myself to acknowledge what the accusation is. And I am incapable, perfectly incapable, of proving my innocence. I can only assert my innocence. I assert it, sir, on my oath, as a Christian. It is useless to appeal to my honour as a man.'

He paused again. I looked round at him. He never looked at me in return. His whole being seemed to be absorbed in the agony of recollecting, and in the effort to speak.

'There is much that I might say,' he went on, 'about the merciless treatment of me by my own family, and the merciless enmity to which I have fallen a victim. But the harm is done; the wrong is beyond all remedy. I decline to weary or distress you, sir, if I can help it. At the outset of my career in this country, the vile slander to which I have referred struck me down at once and for ever. I resigned my aspirations in my profession—obscurity was the only hope left for me. I parted with the woman I loved—how could I condemn her to share my disgrace? A medical assistant's place offered itself, in a remote corner of England. I got the place. It promised me peace; it promised me obscurity, as I thought. I was wrong. Evil report, with time and chance to help it, travels patiently, and travels far. The accusation from which I had fled followed me. I got warning of its approach. I was able to leave my situation voluntarily, with the testimonials that I had earned. They got me another situation in another remote district. Time passed again; and again the slander that was death to my character found me out. On this occasion I had no warning. My employer said, "Mr Jennings, I have no complaint to make against you; but you must set yourself right, or leave me." I had but one choice—I left him. It's useless to dwell on what I suffered after that. I am only forty years old now. Look at my face, and let it tell for me the story of some miserable years. It ended in my drifting to this place, and meeting with Mr Candy. He wanted an assistant. I referred him, on the question of capacity, to my last employer. The question of character remained. I told him what I have told you—and more. I warned him that there were difficulties in the way, even if he believed me. "Here, as elsewhere," I said. "I scorn the guilty evasion of living under an assumed name: I am no safer at Frizinghall than at other places from the cloud that follows me, go where I may." He answered, "I don't do things by halves—I believe you, and I pity you. If *you* will risk what may happen, *I* will risk it too." God Almighty bless him! He has given me shelter, he has given me employment, he has given me rest of mind—and I have the certain conviction (I have had it for some months past) that nothing will happen now to make him regret it.'

'The slander has died out?' I said.

'The slander is as active as ever. But when it follows me here, it will come too late.'

'You will have left the place?'

'No, Mr Blake—I shall be dead. For ten years past I have suffered from an incurable internal complaint. I don't disguise from you that I should have let the agony of it kill me long since, but for one last interest in life, which makes my existence of some importance to me still. I want to provide for a person—very dear to me—whom I shall never see again. My own little patrimony is hardly sufficient to make her independent of the world. The hope, if I could only live long enough, of increasing it to a certain sum, has impelled me to resist the disease by such palliative means as I could devise. The one effectual palliative in my case, is—opium. To that all-potent and all-merciful drug I am indebted for a respite of many years from my sentence of death. But even the virtues of opium have their limit. The progress of the disease has gradually forced me from the use of opium to the abuse of it. I am feeling the penalty at last. My nervous system is shattered; my nights are nights of horror. The end is not far off now. Let it come—I have not lived and worked in vain. The little sum is nearly made up; and I have the means of completing it, if my last reserves of life fail me sooner than I expect. I hardly know how I have wandered into telling you this. I don't think I am mean enough to appeal to your pity. Perhaps, I fancy you may be all the readier to believe me, if you know that what I have said to you, I have said with the certain knowledge in me that I am a dying man. There is no disguising, Mr Blake, that you interest me. I have attempted to make my poor friend's loss of memory the means of bettering my acquaintance with you. I have speculated on the chance of your feeling a passing curiosity about what he wanted to say, and of my being able to satisfy it. Is there no excuse for my intruding myself on you? Perhaps there is some excuse. A man who has lived as I have lived has his bitter moments when he ponders over human destiny. You have youth, health, riches, a place in the world, a prospect before you. You, and such as you, show me the sunny side of human life, and reconcile me with the world that I am leaving, before I go. However this talk between us may end, I shall not forget that you have done me a kindness in doing that. It rests with you, sir, to say what you proposed saying, or to wish me good morning.'

I had but one answer to make to that appeal. Without a moment's hesitation I told him the truth, as unreservedly as I have told it in these pages.

He started to his feet, and looked at me with breathless eagerness as I approached the leading incident of my story.

'It is certain that I went into the room,' I said; 'it is certain that I took the Diamond. I can only meet those two plain facts by declaring that, do what I might, I did it without my own knowledge——'

Ezra Jennings caught me excitedly by the arm.

'Stop!' he said. 'You have suggested more to me than you suppose. Have *you* ever been accustomed to the use of opium?'

'I never tasted it in my life.'

'Were your nerves out of order, at this time last year? Were you unusually restless and irritable?'

'Yes.'

'Did you sleep badly?'

'Wretchedly. Many nights I never slept at all.'

'Was the birthday night an exception? Try, and remember. Did you sleep well on that one occasion?'

'I do remember! I slept soundly.'

He dropped my arm as suddenly as he had taken it—and looked at me with the air of a man whose mind was relieved of the last doubt that rested on it.

'This is a marked day in your life, and in mine,' he said, gravely. 'I am absolutely certain, Mr Blake, of one thing—I have got what Mr Candy wanted to say to you this morning, in the notes that I took at my patient's bedside. Wait! that is not all. I am firmly persuaded that I can prove you to have been unconscious of what you were about, when you entered the room and took the Diamond. Give me time to think, and time to question you. I believe the vindication of your innocence is in my hands!'

'Explain yourself, for God's sake! What do you mean?'

In the excitement of our colloquy, we had walked on a few steps, beyond the clump of dwarf trees which had hitherto screened us from view. Before Ezra Jennings could answer me, he was hailed from the high road by a man, in great agitation, who had been evidently on the look-out for him.

'I am coming,' he called back; 'I am coming as fast as I can!' He turned to me. 'There is an urgent case waiting for me at the village yonder; I ought to have been there half an hour since—I must attend to it at once. Give me two hours from this time, and call at Mr Candy's again—and I will engage to be ready for you.'

'How am I to wait!' I exclaimed, impatiently. 'Can't you quiet my mind by a word of explanation before we part?'

'This is far too serious a matter to be explained in a hurry, Mr Blake. I am not wilfully trying your patience—I should only be adding to your suspense, if I attempted to relieve it as things are now. At Frizinghall, sir, in two hours' time!'

The man on the high road hailed him again. He hurried away, and left me.

CHAPTER X

HOW the interval of suspense in which I was now condemned might have affected other men in my position, I cannot pretend to say. The influence of the two hours' probation upon *my* temperament was simply this. I felt physically incapable of remaining still in any one place, and morally incapable of speaking to any one human being, until I had first heard all that Ezra Jennings had to say to me.

In this frame of mind, I not only abandoned my contemplated visit to Mrs Ablewhite—I even shrank from encountering Gabriel Betteredge himself.

Returning to Frizinghall, I left a note for Betteredge, telling him that I had been unexpectedly called away for a few hours, but that he might certainly expect me to return towards three o'clock in the afternoon. I requested him, in the interval, to order his dinner at the usual hour, and to amuse himself as he pleased. He had, as I well knew, hosts of friends in Frizinghall; and he would be at no loss how to fill up his time until I returned to the hotel.

This done, I made the best of my way out of the town again, and roamed the lonely moorland country which surrounds Frizinghall, until my watch told me that it was time, at last, to return to Mr Candy's house.

I found Ezra Jennings ready and waiting for me.

He was sitting alone in a bare little room, which communicated by a glazed door with a surgery. Hideous coloured diagrams of the ravages of hideous diseases decorated the barren buff-coloured walls. A book-case filled with dingy medical works, and ornamented at the top with a skull, in place of the customary bust; a large deal table copiously splashed with ink; wooden chairs of the sort that are seen in kitchens and cottages; a threadbare drugget in the middle of the floor; a sink of water, with a basin and waste-pipe roughly let into the wall, horribly suggestive of its connection with surgical operations—comprised the entire furniture of the room. The bees were humming among a few flowers placed in pots outside the window; the birds were singing in the garden, and the faint intermittent jingle of a tuneless piano in some neighbouring house forced itself now and again on the ear. In any other place, these everyday sounds might have spoken pleasantly of the everyday world outside. Here, they came in as intruders on a silence which nothing but human suffering had the privilege to disturb. I looked at the mahogany instrument case, and at the huge roll of lint, occupying places of their own on the book-shelves, and shuddered inwardly as I thought of the sounds, familiar and appropriate to the everyday use of Ezra Jennings' room.

'I make no apology, Mr Blake, for the place in which I am receiving you,' he said. 'It is the only room in the house, at this hour of the day, in which we can feel quite sure of being left undisturbed. Here are my papers ready for you; and here are two books to which we may have occasion to refer, before we have done. Bring your chair to the table, and we shall be able to consult them together.'

I drew up to the table; and Ezra Jennings handed me his manuscript notes. They consisted of two large folio leaves of paper. One leaf contained writing which only covered the surface at intervals. The other presented writing, in red and black ink, which completely filled the page from top to bottom. In the irritated state of my curiosity, at that moment, I laid aside the second sheet of paper in despair.

'Have some mercy on me!' I said. 'Tell me what I am to expect, before I attempt to read this.'

'Willingly, Mr Blake! Do you mind my asking you one or two more questions?'

'Ask me anything you like!'

He looked at me with the sad smile on his lips, and the kindly interest in his soft brown eyes.

'You have already told me,' he said, 'that you have never—to your knowledge—tasted opium in your life.'

'To my knowledge,' I repeated.

'You will understand directly why I speak with that reservation. Let us go on. You are not aware of ever having taken opium. At this time, last year, you were suffering from nervous irritation, and you slept wretchedly at night. On the night of the birthday, however, there was an exception to the rule—you slept soundly. Am I right, so far?'

'Quite right!'

'Can you assign any cause for the nervous suffering, and your want of sleep?'

'I can assign no cause. Old Betteredge made a guess at the cause, I remember. But that is hardly worth mentioning.'

'Pardon me. Anything is worth mentioning in such a case as this. Betteredge attributed your sleeplessness to something. To what?'

'To my leaving off smoking.'

'Had you been an habitual smoker?'

'Yes.'

'Did you leave off the habit suddenly?'

'Yes.'

'Betteredge was perfectly right, Mr Blake. When smoking is a habit a man must have no common constitution who can leave it off suddenly without some temporary damage to his nervous system. Your sleepless nights are accounted for, to my mind. My next question refers to Mr Candy. Do you remember having entered into anything like a dispute with him—at the birthday dinner, or afterwards—on the subject of his profession?'

The question instantly awakened one of my dormant remembrances in connection with the birthday festival. The foolish wrangle which took place, on that occasion, between Mr Candy and myself, will be found described at much greater length than it deserves in the tenth chapter of Betteredge's Narrative. The details there presented of the dispute—so little had I thought of it afterwards—entirely failed to recur to my memory. All that I could now recall, and all that I could tell Ezra Jennings was, that I had attacked the art of medicine at the dinner-table with sufficient rashness and sufficient pertinacity to put even Mr Candy out of temper for the moment. I also remembered that Lady Verinder had interfered to stop the dispute, and that the little doctor and I had 'made it up again,' as the children say, and had become as good friends as ever, before we shook hands that night.

'There is one thing more,' said Ezra Jennings, 'which it is very important I should know. Had you any reason for feeling any special anxiety about the Diamond, at this time last year?'

'I had the strongest reasons for feeling anxiety about the Diamond. I knew it to be the object of a conspiracy; and I was warned to take measures for Miss Verinder's protection, as the possessor of the stone.'

'Was the safety of the Diamond the subject of conversation between you and any other person, immediately before you retired to rest on the birthday night?'

'It was the subject of a conversation between Lady Verinder and her daughter——'

'Which took place in your hearing?'

'Yes.'

Ezra Jennings took up his notes from the table, and placed them in my hands.

'Mr Blake,' he said, 'if you read those notes now, by the light which my questions and your answers have thrown on them, you will make two astounding discoveries concerning yourself. You will find:—First, that you entered Miss Verinder's sitting-room and took the Diamond, in a state of trance, produced by opium. Secondly, that the opium was given to you by Mr Candy—without your own knowledge—as a practical refutation of the opinions which you had expressed to him at the birthday dinner.'

I sat with the papers in my hand completely stupefied.

'Try and forgive poor Mr Candy,' said the assistant gently. 'He has done dreadful mischief, I own; but he has done it innocently. If you will look at the notes, you will see that—but for his illness—he would have returned to Lady Verinder's the morning after the party, and would have acknowledged the trick that he had played you. Miss Verinder would have heard of it, and Miss Verinder would have questioned him—and the truth which has laid hidden for a year would have been discovered in a day.'

I began to regain my self-possession. 'Mr Candy is beyond the reach of my resentment,' I said angrily. 'But the trick that he played me is not the less an act of treachery, for all that. I may forgive, but I shall not forget it.'

'Every medical man commits that act of treachery, Mr Blake, in the course of his practice. The ignorant distrust of opium (in England) is by no means confined to the lower and less cultivated classes. Every doctor in large practice finds himself, every now and then, obliged to deceive his patients, as Mr Candy deceived you. I don't defend the folly of playing you a trick under the circumstances. I only plead with you for a more accurate and more merciful construction of motives.'

'How was it done?' I asked. 'Who gave me the laudanum, without my knowing it myself?'

'I am not able to tell you. Nothing relating to that part of the matter dropped from Mr Candy's lips, all through his illness. Perhaps your own memory may point to the person to be suspected?'

'No.'

'It is useless, in that case, to pursue the inquiry. The laudanum was secretly given to you in some way. Let us leave it there, and go on to matters of more immediate importance. Read my notes, if you can. Familiarise your mind with what has happened in the past. I have something very bold and very startling to propose to you, which relates to the future.'

Those last words roused me.

I looked at the papers, in the order in which Ezra Jennings had placed them in my hands. The paper which contained the smaller quantity of writing was the uppermost of the two. On this, the disconnected words, and fragments of sentences, which had dropped from Mr Candy in his delirium, appeared as follows:

'. . . Mr Franklin Blake . . . and agreeable . . . down a peg . . . medicine . . . confesses . . . sleep at night . . . tell him . . . out of order . . . medicine . . . he tells me . . . and groping in the dark mean one and the same thing . . . all the company at the dinner-table . . . I say . . . groping after sleep . . . nothing but medicine . . . he says . . . leading the blind . . . know what it means . . . witty . . . a night's rest in spite of his teeth . . . wants sleep . . . Lady Verinder's medicine chest . . . five-and-twenty minims . . . without his knowing it . . . to-morrow morning . . . Well, Mr Blake . . . medicine to-day . . . never . . . without it . . . out, Mr Candy . . . excellent . . . without it . . . down on him . . . truth . . . something besides . . . excellent . . . dose of laudanum, sir . . . bed . . . what . . . medicine now.'

There, the first of the two sheets of paper came to an end. I handed it back to Ezra Jennings.

'This is what you heard at his bedside?' I said.

'Literally and exactly what I heard,' he answered—'except that the repetitions are not transferred here from my short-hand notes. He reiterated certain words and phrases a dozen times over, fifty times over, just as he attached more or less importance to the idea which they represented. The repetitions, in this sense, were of some assistance to me in putting together those fragments.

Don't suppose,' he added, pointing to the second sheet of paper, 'that I claim to have reproduced the expressions which Mr Candy himself would have used if he had been capable of speaking connectedly. I only say that I have penetrated through the obstacle of the disconnected expression, to the thought which was underlying it connectedly all the time. Judge for yourself.'

I turned to the second sheet of paper, which I now knew to be the key to the first.

Once more, Mr Candy's wanderings appeared, copied in black ink; the intervals between the phrases being filled up by Ezra Jennings in red ink. I reproduce the result here, in one plain form; the original language and the interpretation of it coming close enough together in these pages to be easily compared and verified.

'. . . Mr Franklin Blake is clever and agreeable, but he wants taking down a peg when he talks of medicine. He confesses that he has been suffering from want of sleep at night. I tell him that his nerves are out of order, and that he ought to take medicine. He tells me that taking medicine and groping in the dark mean one and the same thing. This before all the company at the dinner-table. I say to him, you are groping after sleep, and nothing but medicine can help you to find it. He says to me, I have heard of the blind leading the blind, and now I know what it means. Witty—but I can give him a night's rest in spite of his teeth. He really wants sleep; and Lady Verinder's medicine chest is at my disposal. Give him five-and-twenty minims of laudanum to-night, without his knowing it; and then call to-morrow morning. "Well, Mr Blake, will you try a little medicine to-day? You will never sleep without it."—"There you are out, Mr Candy: I have had an excellent night's rest without it." Then, come down on him with the truth! "You have had something besides an excellent night's rest; you had a dose of laudanum, sir, before you went to bed. What do you say to the art of medicine, now?" '

Admiration of the ingenuity which had woven this smooth and finished texture out of the ravelled skein was naturally the first impression that I felt, on handing the manuscript back to Ezra Jennings. He modestly interrupted the first few words in which my sense of surprise expressed itself, by asking me if the conclusion which he had drawn from his notes was also the conclusion at which my own mind had arrived.

'Do you believe as I believe,' he said, 'that you were acting under the influence of the laudanum in doing all that you did, on the night of Miss Verinder's birthday, in Lady Verinder's house?'

'I am too ignorant of the influence of laudanum to have an opinion of my own,' I answered. 'I can only follow your opinion, and feel convinced that you are right.'

'Very well. The next question is this. You are convinced; and I am convinced—how are we to carry our conviction to the minds of other people?'

I pointed to the two manuscripts, lying on the table between us. Ezra Jennings shook his head.

'Useless, Mr Blake! Quite useless, as they stand now, for three unanswerable reasons. In the first place, those notes have been taken under circumstances entirely out of the experience of the mass of mankind. Against them, to begin with! In the second place, those notes represent a medical and metaphysical theory. Against them, once more! In the third place, those notes are of *my* making; there is nothing but *my* assertion to the contrary, to guarantee that they are not fabrications. Remember what I told you on the moor—and ask yourself what my assertion is worth. No! my notes have but one value, looking to the verdict of the world outside. Your innocence is to be vindicated; and they show how it can be done. We must put our conviction to the proof—and You are the man to prove it!'

'How?' I asked.

He leaned eagerly nearer to me across the table that divided us.

'Are you willing to try a bold experiment?'

'I will do anything to clear myself of the suspicion that rests on me now.'

'Will you submit to some personal inconvenience for a time?'

'To any inconvenience, no matter what it may be.'

'Will you be guided implicitly by my advice? It may expose you to the ridicule of fools; it may subject you to the remonstrances of friends whose opinions you are bound to respect——'

'Tell me what to do!' I broke out impatiently. 'And, come what may, I'll do it.'

'You shall do this, Mr Blake,' he answered. 'You shall steal the Diamond, unconsciously, for the second time, in the presence of witnesses whose testimony is beyond dispute.'

I started to my feet. I tried to speak. I could only look at him.

'I believe it *can* be done,' he went on. 'And it *shall* be done—if you will only help me. Try to compose yourself—sit down, and hear what I have to say to you. You have resumed the habit of smoking; I have seen that for myself. How long have you resumed it?'

'For nearly a year?'

'Do you smoke more or less than you did?'

'More.'

'Will you give up the habit again? Suddenly, mind!—as you gave it up before.'

I began dimly to see his drift. 'I will give it up, from this moment,' I answered.

'If the same consequences follow, which followed last June,' said Ezra Jennings—'if you suffer once more as you suffered then, from sleepless nights, we shall have gained our first step. We shall have put you back again into something assimilating to your nervous condition on the birthday night.

If we can next revive, or nearly revive, the domestic circumstances which surrounded you; and if we can occupy your mind again with the various questions concerning the Diamond which formerly agitated it, we shall have replaced you, as nearly as possible, in the same position, physically and morally, in which the opium found you last year. In that case we may fairly hope that a repetition of the dose will lead, in a greater or lesser degree, to a repetition of the result. There is my proposal, expressed in a few hasty words. You shall now see what reasons I have to justify me in making it.'

He turned to one of the books at his side, and opened it at a place marked by a small slip of paper.

'Don't suppose that I am going to weary you with a lecture on physiology,' he said. 'I think myself bound to prove, in justice to both of us, that I am not asking you to try this experiment in deference to any theory of my own devising. Admitted principles, and recognised authorities, justify me in the view that I take. Give me five minutes of your attention; and I will undertake to show you that Science sanctions my proposal, fanciful as it may seem. Here, in the first place, is the physiological principle on which I am acting, stated by no less a person than Dr Carpenter. Read it for yourself.'

He handed me the slip of paper which had marked the place in the book. It contained a few lines of writing, as follows:—

'There seems much ground for the belief, that *every* sensory impression which has once been recognised by the perceptive consciousness, is registered (so to speak) in the brain, and may be reproduced at some subsequent time, although there may be no consciousness of its existence in the mind during the whole intermediate period.' 'Is that plain, so far?' asked Ezra Jennings.

'Perfectly plain.'

He pushed the open book across the table to me, and pointed to a passage, marked by pencil lines.

'Now,' he said, 'read that account of a case, which has—as I believe—a direct bearing on your own position, and on the experiment which I am tempting you to try. Observe, Mr Blake, before you begin, that I am now referring you to one of the greatest of English physiologists. The book in your hand is Doctor Elliotson's *Human Physiology*; and the case which the doctor cites rests on the well-known authority of Mr Combe.'

The passage pointed out to me was expressed in these terms:—

'Dr Abel informed me,' says Mr Combe, 'of an Irish porter to a warehouse, who forgot, when sober, what he had done when drunk; but, being drunk, again recollected the transactions of his former state of intoxication. On one occasion, being drunk, he had lost a parcel of some value, and in his sober moments could give no account of it. Next time he was intoxicated, he recollected that he had left the parcel at a certain house, and there being no address on it, it had remained there safely, and was got on his calling for it.'

'Plain again?' asked Ezra Jennings.

'As plain as need be.'

He put back the slip of paper in its place, and closed the book.

'Are you satisfied that I have not spoken without good authority to support me?' he asked. 'If not, I have only to go to those bookshelves, and you have only to read the passages which I can point out to you.'

'I am quite satisfied,' I said, 'without reading a word more.'

'In that case, we may return to your own personal interest in this matter. I am bound to tell you that there is something to be said against the experiment as well as for it. If we could, this year, exactly reproduce, in your case, the conditions as they existed last year, it is physiologically certain that we should arrive at exactly the same result. But this—there is no denying it—is simply impossible. We can only hope to approximate to the conditions; and if we don't succeed in getting you nearly enough back to what you were, this venture of ours will fail. If we do succeed—and I am myself hopeful of success—you may at least so far repeat your proceedings on the birthday night, as to satisfy any reasonable person that you are guiltless, morally speaking, of the theft of the Diamond. I believe, Mr Blake, I have now stated the question, on both sides of it, as fairly as I can, within the limits that I have imposed on myself. If there is anything that I have not made clear to you, tell me what it is—and if I can enlighten you, I will.'

'All that you have explained to me,' I said, 'I understand perfectly. But I own I am puzzled on one point, which you have not made clear to me yet.'

'What is the point?'

'I don't understand the effect of the laudanum on me. I don't understand my walking down-stairs, and along corridors, and my opening and shutting the drawers of a cabinet, and my going back again to my own room. All these are active proceedings. I thought the influence of opium was first to stupefy you, and then to send you to sleep.'

'The common error about opium, Mr Blake! I am, at this moment, exerting my intelligence (such as it is) in your service, under the influence of a dose of laudanum, some ten times larger than the dose Mr Candy administered to you. But don't trust to my authority—even on a question which comes within my own personal experience. I anticipated the objection you have just made: and I have again provided myself with independent testimony which will carry its due weight with it in your own mind, and in the minds of your friends.'

He handed me the second of the two books which he had by him on the table.

'There,' he said, 'are the far-famed *Confessions of an English Opium Eater!* Take the book away with you, and read it. At the passage which I have marked, you will find that when De Quincey had committed what he calls "a debauch of opium," he either went to the gallery at the Opera to enjoy the music, or he wandered about the London markets on Saturday night, and interested himself in observing all the little shifts and bargainings of the poor in providing their Sunday's dinner. So much for the capacity of a man to occupy himself actively, and to move about from place to place under the influence of opium.'

'I am answered so far,' I said; 'but I am not answered yet as to the effect produced by the opium on myself.'

'I will try to answer you in a few words,' said Ezra Jennings. 'The action of opium is comprised, in the majority of cases, in two influences—a stimulating influence first, and a sedative influence afterwards. Under the stimulating influence, the latest and most vivid impressions left on your mind—namely, the impressions relating to the Diamond—would be likely, in your morbidly sensitive nervous condition, to become intensified in your brain, and would subordinate to themselves your judgment and your will—exactly as an ordinary dream subordinates to itself your judgment and your will. Little by little, under this action, any apprehensions about the safety of the Diamond which you might have felt during the day would be liable to develop themselves from the state of doubt to the state of certainty—would impel you into practical action to preserve the jewel— would direct your steps, with that motive in view, into the room which you entered—and would guide your hand to the drawers of the cabinet, until you had found the drawer which held the stone. In the spiritualised intoxication of opium, you would do all that. Later, as the sedative action began to gain on the stimulant action, you would slowly become inert and stupefied. Later still you would fall into a deep sleep. When the morning came, and the effect of the opium had been all slept off, you would wake as absolutely ignorant of what you had done in the night as if you had been living at the Antipodes.—Have I made it tolerably clear to you so far?'

'You have made it so clear,' I said, 'that I want you to go farther. You have shown me how I entered the room, and how I came to take the Diamond. But Miss Verinder saw me leave the room again, with the jewel in my hand. Can you trace my proceedings from that moment? Can you guess what I did next?'

'That is the very point I was coming to,' he rejoined. 'It is a question with me whether the experiment which I propose as a means of vindicating your innocence, may not also be made a means of recovering the lost Diamond as well. When you left Miss Verinder's sitting-room, with the jewel in your hand, you went back in all probability to your own room——'

'Yes? and what then?'

'It is possible, Mr Blake—I dare not say more—that your idea of preserving the Diamond led, by a natural sequence, to the idea of hiding the Diamond, and that the place in which you hid it was somewhere in your bedroom. In that event, the case of the Irish porter may be your case. You may remember, under the influence of the second dose of opium, the place in which you hid the Diamond under the influence of the first.'

It was my turn, now, to enlighten Ezra Jennings. I stopped him, before he could say any more.

'You are speculating,' I said, 'on a result which cannot possibly take place. The Diamond is, at this moment, in London.'

He started, and looked at me in great surprise.

'In London?' he repeated. 'How did it get to London from Lady Verinder's house?'

'Nobody knows.'

'You removed it with your own hand from Miss Verinder's room. How was it taken out of your keeping?'

'I have no idea how it was taken out of my keeping.'

'Did you see it, when you woke in the morning?'

'No.'

'Has Miss Verinder recovered possession of it?'

'No.'

'Mr Blake! there seems to be something here which wants clearing up. May I ask how you know that the Diamond is, at this moment, in London?'

I had put precisely the same question to Mr Bruff, when I made my first inquiries about the Moonstone, on my return to England. In answering Ezra Jennings, I accordingly repeated what I had myself heard from the lawyer's own lips—and what is already familiar to the readers of these pages.

He showed plainly that he was not satisfied with my reply.

'With all deference to you,' he said, 'and with all deference to your legal adviser, I maintain the opinion which I expressed just now. It rests, I am well aware, on a mere assumption. Pardon me for reminding you, that your opinion also rests on a mere assumption as well.'

The view he took of the matter was entirely new to me. I waited anxiously to hear how he would defend it.

'*I* assume,' pursued Ezra Jennings, 'that the influence of the opium—after impelling you to possess yourself of the Diamond, with the purpose of securing its safety—might also impel you, acting under the same influence and the same motive, to hide it somewhere in your own room. *You* assume that the Hindoo conspirators could by no possibility commit a mistake. The Indians went to Mr Luker's house after the Diamond—and, therefore, in Mr Luker's possession the Diamond must be! Have you any evidence to prove that the Moonstone was taken to London at all? You can't even guess how, or by whom, it was removed from Lady Verinder's house! Have you any evidence that the jewel was pledged to Mr Luker? He declares that he never heard of the Moonstone; and his bankers' receipt acknowledges nothing but the deposit of a valuable of great price. The Indians assume that Mr Luker is lying—and you assume again that the Indians are right. All I say, in differing with you, is—that my view is possible. What more, Mr Blake, either logically or legally, can be said for yours?'

It was put strongly; but there was no denying that it was put truly as well.

'I confess you stagger me,' I replied. 'Do you object to my writing to Mr Bruff, and telling him what you have said?'

'On the contrary, I shall be glad if you will write to Mr Bruff. If we consult his experience, we may see the matter under a new light. For the present, let us return to our experiment with the opium. We have decided that you leave off the habit of smoking from this moment.'

'From this moment?'

'That is the first step. The next step is to reproduce, as nearly as we can, the domestic circumstances which surrounded you last year.'

How was this to be done? Lady Verinder was dead. Rachel and I, so long as the suspicion of theft rested on me, were parted irrevocably. Godfrey Ablewhite was away travelling on the Continent. It was simply impossible to reassemble the people who had inhabited the house, when I had slept in it last. The statement of this objection did not appear to embarrass Ezra Jennings. He attached very little importance, he said, to reassembling the same people—seeing that it would be vain to expect them to reassume the various positions which they had occupied towards me in the past times. On the other hand, he considered it essential to the success of the experiment, that I should see the same objects about me which had surrounded me when I was last in the house.

'Above all things,' he said, 'you must sleep in the room which you slept in, on the birthday night, and it must be furnished in the same way. The stairs, the corridors, and Miss Verinder's sitting-room, must also be restored to what they were when you saw them last. It is absolutely necessary, Mr Blake, to replace every article of furniture in that part of the house which may now be put away. The sacrifice of your cigars will be useless, unless we can get Miss Verinder's permission to do that.'

'Who is to apply to her for permission?' I asked.

'Is it not possible for *you* to apply?'

'Quite out of the question. After what has passed between us on the subject of the lost Diamond, I can neither see her, nor write to her, as things are now.'

Ezra Jennings paused, and considered for a moment.

'May I ask you a delicate question?' he said.

I signed to him to go on.

'Am I right, Mr Blake, in fancying (from one or two things which have dropped from you) that you felt no common interest in Miss Verinder, in former times?'

'Quite right.'

'Was the feeling returned?'

'It was.'

'Do you think Miss Verinder would be likely to feel a strong interest in the attempt to prove your innocence?'

'I am certain of it.'

'In that case, *I* will write to Miss Verinder—if you will give me leave.'

'Telling her of the proposal that you have made to me?'

'Telling her of everything that has passed between us to-day.'

It is needless to say that I eagerly accepted the service which he had offered to me.

'I shall have time to write by to-day's post,' he said, looking at his watch. 'Don't forget to lock up your cigars, when you get back to the hotel! I will call to-morrow morning and hear how you have passed the night.'

I rose to take leave of him; and attempted to express the grateful sense of his kindness which I really felt.

He pressed my hand gently. 'Remember what I told you on the moor,' he answered. 'If I can do you this little service, Mr Blake, I shall feel it like a last gleam of sunshine, falling on the evening of a long and clouded day.'

We parted. It was then the fifteenth of June. The events of the next ten days—every one of them more or less directly connected with the experiment of which I was the passive object—are all placed on record, exactly as they happened, in the Journal habitually kept by Mr Candy's assistant. In the pages of Ezra Jennings nothing is concealed, and nothing is forgotten. Let Ezra Jennings tell how the venture with the opium was tried, and how it ended.

FOURTH NARRATIVE

Extracted from the Journal of Ezra Jennings

1849.—June 15th. . . . With some interruption from patients, and some interruption from pain, I finished my letter to Miss Verinder in time for to-day's post. I failed to make it as short a letter as I could have wished. But I think I have made it plain. It leaves her entirely mistress of her own decision. If she consents to assist the experiment, she consents of her own free will, and not as a favour to Mr Franklin Blake or to me.

June 16th.—Rose late, after a dreadful night; the vengeance of yesterday's opium, pursuing me through a series of frightful dreams. At one time I was whirling through empty space with the phantoms of the dead, friends and enemies together. At another, the one beloved face which I shall never see again, rose at my bedside, hideously phosphorescent in the black darkness, and glared and grinned at me. A slight return of the old pain, at the usual time in the early morning, was welcome as a change. It dispelled the visions—and it was bearable because it did that.

My bad night made it late in the morning, before I could get to Mr Franklin Blake. I found him stretched on the sofa, breakfasting on brandy and soda-water, and a dry biscuit.

'I am beginning, as well as you could possibly wish,' he said. 'A miserable, restless night; and a total failure of appetite this morning. Exactly what happened last year, when I gave up my cigars. The sooner I am ready for my second dose of laudanum, the better I shall be pleased.'

'You shall have it on the earliest possible day,' I answered. 'In the meantime, we must be as careful of your health as we can. If we allow you to become exhausted, we shall fail in that way. You must get an appetite for your dinner. In other words, you must get a ride or a walk this morning, in the fresh air.'

'I will ride, if they can find me a horse here. By-the-by, I wrote to Mr Bruff, yesterday. Have you written to Miss Verinder?'

'Yes—by last night's post.'

'Very good. We shall have some news worth hearing, to tell each other to-morrow. Don't go yet! I have a word to say to you. You appeared to think, yesterday, that our experiment with the opium was not likely to be viewed very favourably by some of my friends. You were quite right. I call old Gabriel Betteredge one of my friends; and you will be amused to hear that he protested strongly when I saw him yesterday. "You have done a wonderful number of foolish things in the course of your life, Mr Franklin, but this tops them all!" There is Betteredge's opinion! You will make allowance for his prejudices, I am sure, if you and he happen to meet?'

I left Mr Blake, to go my rounds among my patients; feeling the better and the happier even for the short interview that I had had with him.

What is the secret of the attraction that there is for me in this man? Does it only mean that I feel the contrast between the frankly kind manner in which he has allowed me to become acquainted with him, and the merciless dislike and distrust with which I am met by other people? Or is there really something in him which answers to the yearning that I have for a little human sympathy—the yearning, which has survived the solitude and persecution of many years; which seems to grow keener and keener, as the time comes nearer and nearer when I shall endure and feel no more? How useless to ask these questions! Mr Blake has given me a new interest in life. Let that be enough, without seeking to know what the new interest is.

June 17.—Before breakfast, this morning, Mr Candy informed me that he was going away for a fortnight, on a visit to a friend in the south of England.

He gave me as many special directions, poor fellow, about the patients, as if he still had the large practice which he possessed before he was taken ill. The practice is worth little enough now! Other doctors have superseded *him*; and nobody who can help it will employ *me*.

It is perhaps fortunate that he is to be away just at this time. He would have been mortified if I had not informed him of the experiment which I am going to try with Mr Blake. And I hardly know what undesirable results might not have happened, if I had taken him into my confidence. Better as it is. Unquestionably, better as it is.

The post brought me Miss Verinder's answer, after Mr Candy had left the house.

A charming letter! It gives me the highest opinion of her. There is no attempt to conceal the interest that she feels in our proceedings. She tells me, in the prettiest manner, that my letter has satisfied her of Mr Blake's innocence, without the slightest need (so far as she is concerned) of putting my assertion to the proof. She even upbraids herself—most undeservedly, poor thing!—for not having divined at the time what the true solution of the mystery might really be. The motive underlying all this proceeds evidently from something more than a generous eagerness to make atonement for a wrong which she has innocently inflicted on another person. It is plain that she has loved him, throughout the estrangement between them. In more than one place the rapture of discovering that he has deserved to be loved, breaks its way innocently through the stoutest formalities of pen and ink, and even defies the stronger restraint still of writing to a stranger. Is it possible (I ask myself, in reading this delightful letter) that I, of all men in the world, am chosen to be the means of bringing these two young people together again? My own happiness has been trampled under foot; my own love has been torn from me. Shall I live to see a happiness of others, which is of my making—a love renewed, which is of my bringing back? Oh merciful Death, let me see it before your arms enfold me, before your voice whispers to me, 'Rest at last!'

There are two requests contained in the letter. One of them prevents me from showing it to Mr Franklin Blake. I am authorised to tell him that Miss Verinder willingly consents to place her house at our disposal; and, that said, I am desired to add no more.

So far, it is easy to comply with her wishes. But the second request embarrasses me seriously.

Not content with having written to Mr Betteredge, instructing him to carry out whatever directions I may have to give, Miss Verinder asks leave to assist me, by personally superintending the restoration of her own sitting-room. She only waits a word of reply from me to make the journey to Yorkshire, and to be present as one of the witnesses on the night when the opium is tried for the second time.

Here, again, there is a motive under the surface; and, here again, I fancy that I can find it out.

What she has forbidden me to tell Mr Franklin Blake, she is (as I interpret it) eager to tell him with her own lips, *before* he is put to the test which is to vindicate his character in the eyes of other people. I understand and admire this generous anxiety to acquit him, without waiting until his innocence may, or may not, be proved. It is the atonement that she is longing to make, poor girl, after having innocently and inevitably wronged him. But the thing cannot be done. I have no sort of doubt that the agitation which a meeting between them would produce on both sides—reviving dormant feelings, appealing to old memories, awakening new hopes—would, in their effect on the mind of Mr Blake, be almost certainly fatal to the success of our experiment. It is hard enough, as things are, to reproduce in him the conditions as they existed, or nearly as they existed, last year. With new interests and new emotions to agitate him, the attempt would be simply useless.

And yet, knowing this, I cannot find it in my heart to disappoint her. I must try if I can discover some new arrangement, before post-time, which will allow me to say Yes to Miss Verinder, without damage to the service which I have bound myself to render to Mr Franklin Blake.

Two o'clock.—I have just returned from my round of medical visits; having begun, of course, by calling at the hotel.

Mr Blake's report of the night is the same as before. He has had some intervals of broken sleep, and no more. But he feels it less to-day, having slept after yesterday's dinner. This after-dinner sleep is the result, no doubt, of the ride which I advised him to take. I fear I shall have to curtail his restorative exercise in the fresh air. He must not be too well; he must not be too ill. It is a case (as a sailor would say) of very fine steering.

He has not heard yet from Mr Bruff. I found him eager to know if I had received any answer from Miss Verinder.

I tokd him exactly what I was permitted to tell, and no more. It was quite needless to invent excuses for not showing him the letter. He told me bitterly enough, poor fellow, that he understood the delicacy which disinclined me to produce it. 'She consents, of course, as a matter of common courtesy and common justice,' he said. 'But she keeps her own opinion of me, and waits to see the result.' I was sorely tempted to hint that he was now wronging her as she had wronged him. On reflection, I shrank from forestalling her in the double luxury of surprising and forgiving him.

My visit was a very short one. After the experience of the other night, I have been compelled once more to give up my dose of opium. As a necessary result, the agony of the disease that is in me has got the upper hand again. I felt the attack coming on, and left abruptly, so as not to alarm or distress him. It only lasted a quarter of an hour this time, and it left me strength enough to go on with my work.

Five o'clock.—I have written my reply to Miss Verinder.

The arrangement I have proposed reconciles the interests on both sides, if she will only consent to it. After first stating the objections that there are to a meeting between Mr Blake and herself, before the experiment is tried, I have suggested that she should so time her journey as to arrive at the house privately, on the evening when we make the attempt. Travelling by the afternoon train from London, she would delay her arrival until nine o'clock. At that hour, I have undertaken to see Mr Blake safely into his bedchamber; and so to leave Miss Verinder free to occupy her own rooms until the time comes for administering the laudanum. When that has been done, there can be no objection to her watching the result, with the rest of us. On the next morning, she shall show Mr Blake (if she likes) her correspondence with me, and shall satisfy him in that way that he was acquitted in her estimation, before the question of his innocence was put to the proof.

In that sense, I have written to her. This is all that I can do to-day. To-morrow I must see Mr Betteredge, and give the necessary directions for re-opening the house.

June 18th.—Late again, in calling on Mr Franklin Blake. More of that horrible pain in the early morning; followed, this time, by complete prostration, for some hours. I foresee, in spite of the penalties which it exacts from me, that I shall have to return to the opium for the hundredth time. If I had only myself to think of, I should prefer the sharp pains to the frightful dreams. But the physical suffering exhausts me. If I let myself sink, it may end in my becoming useless to Mr Blake at the time when he wants me most.

It was nearly one o'clock before I could get to the hotel to-day. The visit, even in my shattered condition, proved to be a most amusing one—thanks entirely to the presence on the scene of Gabriel Betteredge.

I found him in the room, when I went in. He withdrew to the window and looked out, while I put my first customary question to my patient. Mr Blake had slept badly again, and he felt the loss of rest this morning more than he had felt it yet.

I asked next if he had heard from Mr Bruff.

A letter had reached him that morning. Mr Bruff expressed the strongest disapproval of the course which his friend and client was taking under my advice. It was mischievous—for it excited hopes that might never be realised. It was quite unintelligible to *his* mind, except that it looked like a piece of trickery, akin to the trickery of mesmerism, clairvoyance, and the like. It unsettled Miss Verinder's house, and it would end in unsettling Miss Verinder herself. He had put the case (without mentioning names) to an eminent physician; and the eminent physician had smiled, had shaken his head, and had said—nothing. On these grounds, Mr Bruff entered his protest, and left it there.

My next inquiry related to the subject of the Diamond. Had the lawyer produced any evidence to prove that the jewel was in London?

No, the lawyer had simply declined to discuss the question. He was himself satisfied that the Moonstone had been pledged to Mr Luker. His eminent absent friend, Mr Murthwaite (whose consummate knowledge of the Indian character no one could deny), was satisfied also. Under these circumstances, and with the many demands already made on him, he must decline entering into any disputes on the subject of evidence. Time would show; and Mr Bruff was willing to wait for time.

It was quite plain—even if Mr Blake had not made it plainer still by reporting the substance of the letter, instead of reading what was actually written—that distrust of *me* was at the bottom of all this. Having myself foreseen that result, I was neither mortified nor surprised. I asked Mr Blake if his friend's protest had shaken him. He answered emphatically, that it had not produced the slightest effect on his mind. I was free after that to dismiss Mr Bruff from consideration—and I did dismiss him accordingly.

A pause in the talk between us, followed—and Gabriel Betteredge came out from his retirement at the window.

'Can you favour me with your attention, sir?' he inquired addressing himself to me.

'I am quite at your service,' I answered.

Betteredge took a chair and seated himself at the table. He produced a huge old-fashioned leather pocket-book, with a pencil of dimensions to match. Having put on his spectacles, he opened the pocket-book, at a blank page, and addressed himself to me once more.

'I have lived,' said Betteredge, looking at me sternly, 'nigh on fifty years in the service of my late lady. I was page-boy before that, in the service of the old lord, her father. I am now somewhere between seventy and eighty years of age—never mind exactly where! I am reckoned to have got as pretty a knowledge and experience of the world as most men. And what does it all end in? It ends, Mr Ezra Jennings, in a conjuring trick being performed on Mr Franklin Blake, by a doctor's assistant with a bottle of laudanum—and by the living jingo, I'm appointed, in my old age, to be conjurer's boy!'

Mr Blake burst out laughing. I attempted to speak. Betteredge held up his hand, in token that he had not done yet.

'Not a word, Mr Jennings!' he said. 'it don't want a word, sir, from you. I have got my principles, thank God. If an order comes to me, which is own brother to an order come from Bedlam, it don't matter. So long as I get it from my master or mistress, as the case may be, I obey it. I may have my own opinion, which is also, you will please to remember, the opinion of Mr Bruff—the Great Mr Bruff!' said Betteredge, raising his voice, and shaking his head at me solemnly. 'It don't matter; I withdraw my opinion, for all that. My young lady says, "Do it." And I say, "Miss, it shall be done." Here

I am, with my book and my pencil—the latter not pointed so well as I could wish, but when Christians take leave of their senses, who is to expect that pencils will keep their points? Give me your orders, Mr Jennings. I'll have them in writing, sir. I'm determined not to be behind 'em, or before 'em, by so much as a hair's-breadth. I'm a blind agent—that's what I am. A blind agent!' repeated Betteredge, with infinite relish of his own description of himself.

'I am very sorry,' I began, 'that you and I don't agree——'

'Don't bring *me* into it!' interposed Betteredge. 'This is not a matter of agreement, it's a matter of obedience. Issue your directions, sir—issue your directions!'

Mr Blake made me a sign to take him at his word. I 'issued my directions' as plainly and as gravely as I could.

'I wish certain parts of the house to be reopened,' I said, 'and to be furnished, exactly as they were furnished at this time last year.'

Betteredge gave his imperfectly-pointed pencil a preliminary lick with his tongue. 'Name the parts, Mr Jennings!' he said loftily.

'First, the inner hall, leading to the chief staircase.'

' "First, the inner hall," ' Betteredge wrote. 'Impossible to furnish that, sir, as it was furnished last year—to begin with.'

'Why?'

'Because there was a stuffed buzzard, Mr Jennings, in the hall last year. When the family left, the buzzard was put away with the other things. When the buzzard was put away—he burst.'

'We will except the buzzard then.'

Betteredge took a note of the exception. ' "The inner hall to be furnished again, as furnished last year. A burst buzzard alone excepted." Please to go on, Mr Jennings.'

'The carpet to be laid down on the stairs, as before.'

' "The carpet to be laid down on the stairs, as before." Sorry to disappoint you, sir. But that can't be done either.'

'Why not?'

'Because the man who laid that carpet down is dead, Mr Jennings—and the like of him for reconciling together a carpet and a corner, is not to be found in all England, look where you may.'

'Very well. We must try the next best man in England.'

Betteredge took another note; and I went on issuing my directions.

'Miss Verinder's sitting-room to be restored exactly to what it was last year. Also, the corridor leading from the sitting-room to the first landing. Also, the second corridor, leading from the second landing to the best bedrooms. Also, the bedroom occupied last June by Mr Franklin Blake.'

Betteredge's blunt pencil followed me conscientiously, word by word. 'Go on, sir,' he said, with sardonic gravity. 'There's a deal of writing left in the point of this pencil yet.'

I told him that I had no more directions to give. 'Sir,' said Betteredge, 'in that case, I have a point or two to put on my own behalf.' He opened the pocket-book at a new page, and gave the inexhaustible pencil another preliminary lick.

'I wish to know,' he began, 'whether I may, or may not, wash my hands——'

'You may decidedly,' said Mr Blake. 'I'll ring for the waiter.'

'——of certain responsibilities,' pursued Betteredge, impenetrably declining to see anybody in the room but himself and me. 'As to Miss Verinder's sitting-room, to begin with. When we took up the carpet last year, Mr Jennings, we found a surprising quantity of pins. Am I responsible for putting back the pins?'

'Certainly not.'

Betteredge made a note of that concession, on the spot.

'As to the first corridor next,' he resumed. 'When we moved the ornaments in that part, we moved a statue of a fat naked child—profanely described in the catalogue of the house as "Cupid, god of Love." He had two wings last year, in the fleshy part of his shoulders. My eye being off him, for the moment, he lost one of them. Am I responsible for Cupid's wing?'

I made another concession, and Betteredge made another note.

'As to the second corridor,' he went on. 'There having been nothing in it, last year, but the doors of the rooms (to every one of which I can swear, if necessary), my mind is easy, I admit, respecting that part of the house only. But, as to Mr Franklin's bedroom (if *that* is to be put back to what it was before), I want to know who is responsible for keeping it in a perpetual state of litter, no matter how often it may be set right—his trousers here, his towels there, and his French novels everywhere. I say, who is responsible for untidying the tidiness of Mr Franklin's room, him or me?'

Mr Blake declared that he would assume the whole responsibility with the greatest pleasure. Betteredge obstinately declined to listen to any solution of the difficulty, without first referring it to my sanction and approval. I accepted Mr Blake's proposal; and Betteredge made a last entry in the pocket-book to that effect.

'Look in when you like, Mr Jennings, beginning from to-morrow,' he said, getting on his legs. 'You will find me at work, with the necessary persons to assist me. I respectfully beg to thank you, sir, for overlooking the case of the stuffed buzzard, and the other case of the Cupid's wing—as also for permitting me to wash my hands of all responsibility in respect of the pins on the carpet, and the litter in Mr Franklin's room. Speaking as a servant, I am deeply indebted to you. Speaking as a man, I consider you to be a person whose head is full of maggots, and I take up my testimony against your experiment as a delusion and a snare. Don't be afraid, on that account, of my feelings as a man getting in the way of my duty as a servant!

You shall be obeyed. The maggots notwithstanding, sir, you shall be obeyed. If it ends in your setting the house on fire, Damme if I send for the engines, unless you ring the bell and order them first!'

With that farewell assurance, he made me a bow, and walked out of the room.

'Do you think we can depend on him?' I asked.

'Implicitly,' answered Mr Blake. 'When we go to the house, we shall find nothing neglected, and nothing forgotten.'

June 19th.—Another protest against our contemplated proceedings! From a lady this time.

The morning's post brought me two letters. One, from Miss Verinder, consenting, in the kindest manner, to the arrangement that I have proposed. The other from the lady under whose care she is living—one Mrs Merridew.

Mrs Merridew presents her compliments, and does not pretend to understand the subject on which I have been corresponding with Miss Verinder, in its scientific bearings. Viewed in its social bearings, however, she feels free to pronounce an opinion. I am probably, Mrs Merridew thinks, not aware that Miss Verinder is barely nineteen years of age. To allow a young lady, at her time of life, to be present (without a 'chaperone') in a house full of men among whom a medical experiment is being carried on, is an outrage on propriety which Mrs Merridew cannot possibly permit. If the matter is allowed to proceed, she will feel it to be her duty—at a serious sacrifice of her own personal convenience—to accompany Miss Verinder to Yorkshire. Under these circumstances, she ventures to request that I will kindly reconsider the subject; seeing that Miss Verinder declines to be guided by any opinion but mine. Her presence cannot possibly be necessary; and a word from me, to that effect, would relieve both Mrs Merridew and myself of a very unpleasant responsibility.

Translated from polite commonplace into plain English, the meaning of this is, as I take it, that Mrs Merridew stands in mortal fear of the opinion of the world. She has unfortunately appealed to the very last man in existence who has any reason to regard that opinion with respect. I won't disappoint Miss Verinder; and I won't delay a reconciliation between two young people who love each other, and who have been parted too long already. Translated from plain English into polite commonplace, this means that Mr Jennings presents his compliments to Mrs Merridew, and regrets that he cannot feel justified in interfering any farther in the matter.

Mr Blake's report of himself, this morning, was the same as before. We determined not to disturb Betteredge by overlooking him at the house to-day. To-morrow will be time enough for our first visit of inspection.

June 20th.—Mr Blake is beginning to feel his continued restlessness at night. The sooner the rooms are refurnished, now, the better.

On our way to the house, this morning, he consulted me, with some nervous impatience and irresolution, about a letter (forwarded to him from London) which he had received from Sergeant Cuff.

The Sergeant writes from Ireland. He acknowledges the receipt (through his housekeeper) of a card and message which Mr Blake left at his residence near Dorking, and announces his return to England as likely to take place in a week or less. In the meantime, he requests to be favoured with Mr Blake's reasons for wishing to speak to him (as stated in the message) on the subject of the Moonstone. If Mr Blake can convict him of having made any serious mistake, in the course of his last year's inquiry concerning the Diamond, he will consider it a duty (after the liberal manner in which he was treated by the late Lady Verinder) to place himself at that gentleman's disposal. If not, he begs permission to remain in his retirement surrounded by the peaceful floricultural attractions of a country life.

After reading the letter, I had no hesitation in advising Mr Blake to inform Sergeant Cuff, in reply, of all that had happened since the inquiry was suspended last year, and to leave him to draw his own conclusions from the plain facts.

On second thoughts I also suggested inviting the Sergeant to be present at the experiment, in the event of his returning to England in time to join us. He would be a valuable witness to have, in any case; and, if I proved to be wrong in believing the Diamond to be hidden in Mr Blake's room, his advice might be of great importance, at a future stage of the proceedings over which I could exercise no control. This last consideration appeared to decide Mr Blake. He promised to follow my advice.

The sound of the hammer informed us that the work of refurnishing was in full progress, as we entered the drive that led to the house.

Betteredge, attired for the occasion in a fisherman's red cap, and an apron of green baize, met us in the outer hall. The moment he saw me, he pulled out the pocket-book and pencil, and obstinately insisted on taking notes of everything that I said to him. Look where we might, we found, as Mr Blake had foretold, that the work was advancing as rapidly and as intelligently as it was possible to desire. But there was still much to be done in the inner hall, and in Miss Verinder's room. It seemed doubtful whether the house would be ready for us before the end of the week.

Having congratulated Betteredge on the progress that he had made (he persisted in taking notes every time I opened my lips; declining, at the same time, to pay the slightest attention to anything said by Mr Blake); and having promised to return for a second visit of inspection in a day or two, we prepared to leave the house, going out by the back way. Before we were clear of the passages downstairs, I was stopped by Betteredge, just as I was passing the door which led into his own room.

'Could I say two words to you in private?' he asked, in a mysterious whisper.

I consented of course. Mr Blake walked on to wait for me in the garden, while I accompanied Betteredge into his room. I fully anticipated a demand for certain new concessions, following the precedent already established in the cases of the stuffed buzzard, and the Cupid's wing. To my great surprise, Betteredge laid his hand confidentially on my arm, and put this extraordinary question to me:

'Mr Jennings, do you happen to be acquainted with *Robinson Crusoe*?'

I answered that I had read *Robinson Crusoe* when I was a child.

'Not since then?' inquired Betteredge.

'Not since then.'

He fell back a few steps, and looked at me with an expression of compassionate curiosity, tempered by superstitious awe.

'He has not read *Robinson Crusoe* since he was a child,' said Betteredge, speaking to himself—not to me. 'Let's try how *Robinson Crusoe* strikes him now!'

He unlocked a cupboard in a corner, and produced a dirty and dog's-eared book, which exhaled a strong odour of stale tobacco as he turned over the leaves. Having found a passage of which he was apparently in search, he requested me to join him in the corner; still mysteriously confidential, and still speaking under his breath.

'In respect to this hocus-pocus of yours, sir, with the laudanum and Mr Franklin Blake,' he began. 'While the workpeople are in the house, my duty as a servant gets the better of my feelings as a man. When the workpeople are gone, my feelings as a man get the better of my duty as a servant. Very good. Last night, Mr Jennings, it was borne in powerfully on my mind that this new medical enterprise of yours would end badly. If I had yielded to that secret Dictate, I should have put all the furniture away again with my own hand, and have warned the workmen off the premises when they came the next morning.'

'I am glad to find, from what I have seen up-stairs,' I said, 'that you resisted the secret Dictate.'

'Resisted isn't the word,' answered Betteredge. 'Wrostled is the word. I wrostled, sir, between the silent orders in my bosom pulling me one way, and the written orders in my pocket-book pushing me the other, until (saving your presence) I was in a cold sweat. In that dreadful perturbation of mind and laxity of body, to what remedy did I apply? To the remedy, sir, which has never failed me yet for the last thirty years and more—to This Book!'

He hit the book a sounding blow with his open hand, and struck out of it a stronger smell of stale tobacco than ever.

'What did I find here,' pursued Betteredge, 'at the first page I opened? This awful bit, sir, page one hundred and seventy-eight, as follows:—"Upon these, and many like Reflections, I afterwards made it a certain rule with me, That whenever I found those secret Hints or Pressings of my Mind, to doing, or not doing any Thing that presented; or to going this Way, or that Way, I never failed to obey the secret Dictate."—As I live by bread, Mr Jennings, those were the first words that met my eye, exactly at the time when I myself was setting the secret Dictate at defiance! You don't see anything at all out of the common in that, do you, sir?'

'I see a coincidence—nothing more.'

'You don't feel at all shaken, Mr Jennings, in respect to this medical enterprise of yours?'

'Not the least in the world.'

Betteredge stared hard at me, in dead silence. He closed the book with great deliberation; he looked it up again in the cupboard with extraordinary care; he wheeled round, and stared hard at me once more. Then he spoke.

'Sir,' he said gravely, 'there are great allowances to be made for a man who has not read *Robinson Crusoe* since he was a child. I wish you good morning.'

He opened his door with a low bow, and left me at liberty to find my own way into the garden. I met Mr Blake returning to the house.

'You needn't tell me what has happened,' he said. 'Betteredge has played his last card: he has made another prophetic discovery in *Robinson Crusoe*. Have you humoured his favourite delusion? No? You have let him see that you don't believe in *Robinson Crusoe*? Mr Jennings! you have fallen to the lowest possible place in Betteredge's estimation. Say what you like, and do what you like, for the future. You will find that he won't waste another word on you now.'

June 21st.—A short entry must suffice in my journal today.

Mr Blake has had the worst night that he has passed yet. I have been obliged, greatly against my will, to prescribe for him. Men of his sensitive organisation are fortunately quick in feeling the effect of remedial measures. Otherwise, I should be inclined to fear that he will be totally unfit for the experiment when the time comes to try it.

As for myself, after some little remission of my pains for the last two days I had an attack this morning, of which I shall say nothing but that it has decided me to return to the opium. I shall close this book, and take my full dose—five hundred drops.

June 22nd.—Our prospects look better to-day. Mr Blake's nervous suffering is greatly allayed. He slept a little last night. *My* night, thanks to the opium, was the night of a man who is stunned. I can't say that I woke this morning; the fitter expression would be, that I recovered my senses.

We drove to the house to see if the refurnishing was done. It will be completed to-morrow—Saturday. As Mr Blake foretold, Betteredge raised no further obstacles. From first to last, he was ominously polite, and ominously silent.

My medical enterprise (as Betteredge calls it) must now, inevitably, be delayed until Monday next. To-morrow evening the workmen will be late in the house. On the next day, the established Sunday tyranny which is one of the institutions of this free country, so times the trains as to make it impossible to ask anybody to travel to us from London. Until Monday comes, there is nothing to be done but to watch Mr Blake carefully, and to keep him, if possible, in the same state in which I find him to-day.

In the meanwhile, I have prevailed on him to write to Mr Bruff, making a point of it that he shall be present as one of the witnesses. I especially choose the lawyer, because he is strongly prejudiced against us. If we convince *him*, we place our victory beyond the possibility of dispute.

Mr Blake has also written to Sergeant Cuff; and I have sent a line to Miss Verinder. With these, and with old Betteredge (who is really a person of importance in the family) we shall have witnesses enough for the purpose— without including Mrs Merridew, if Mrs Merridew persists in sacrificing herself to the opinion of the world.

June 23rd.—The vengeance of the opium overtook me again last night. No matter; I must go on with it now till Monday is past and gone.

Mr Blake is not so well again to-day. At two this morning, he confesses that he opened the drawer in which his cigars are put away. He only succeeded in locking it up again by a violent effort. His next proceeding, in case of temptation, was to throw the key out of window. The waiter brought it in this morning, discovered at the bottom of an empty cistern—such is Fate! I have taken possession of the key until Tuesday next.

June 24th.—Mr Blake and I took a long drive in an open carriage. We both felt beneficially the blessed influence of the soft summer air. I dined with him at the hotel. To my great relief—for I found him in an over-wrought, over-excited state this morning—he had two hours' sound sleep on the sofa after dinner. If he has another bad night, now—I am not afraid of the consequence.

June 25th, Monday.—The day of the experiment! It is five o'clock in the afternoon. We have just arrived at the house.

The first and foremost question, is the question of Mr Blake's health.

So far as it is possible for me to judge, he promises (physically speaking) to be quite as susceptible to the action of the opium to-night as he was at this time last year. He is, this afternoon, in a state of nervous sensitiveness which just stops short of nervous irritation. He changes colour readily; his hand is not quite steady; and he starts at chance noises, and at unexpected appearances of persons and things.

These results have all been produced by deprivation of sleep, which is in its turn the nervous consequence of a sudden cessation in the habit of smoking, after that habit has been carried to an extreme. Here are the same causes at work again, which operated last year; and here are, apparently, the same effects. Will the parallel still hold good, when the final test has been tried? The events of the night must decide.

While I write these lines, Mr Blake is amusing himself at the billiard table in the inner hall, practising different strokes in the game, as he was accustomed to practise them when he was a guest in this house in June last. I have brought my journal here, partly with a view to occupying the idle hours which I am sure to have on my hands between this and to-morrow morning; partly in the hope that something may happen which it may be worth my while to place on record at the time.

Have I omitted anything, thus far? A glance at yesterday's entry shows me that I have forgotten to note the arrival of the morning's post. Let me set this right before I close these leaves for the present, and join Mr Blake.

I received a few lines then, yesterday, from Miss Verinder. She has arranged to travel by the afternoon train, as I recommended. Mrs Merridew has insisted on accompanying her. The note hints that the old lady's generally excellent temper is a little ruffled, and requests all due indulgence for her, in consideration of her age and her habits. I will endeavour, in my relations with Mrs Merridew, to emulate the moderation which Betteredge displays in his relations with me. He received us to-day, portentously arrayed in his best black suit, and his stiffest white cravat. Whenever he looks my way, he remembers that I have not read *Robinson Crusoe* since I was a child, and he respectfully pities me.

Yesterday, also, Mr Blake had the lawyer's answer. Mr Bruff accepts the invitation—under protest. It is, he thinks, clearly necessary that a gentleman possessed of the average allowance of common sense, should accompany Miss Verinder to the scene of, what we will venture to call, the proposed exhibition. For want of a better escort, Mr Bruff himself will be that gentleman.—So here is poor Miss Verinder provided with two 'chaperons.' It is a relief to think that the opinion of the world must surely be satisfied with this!

Nothing has been heard of Sergeant Cuff. He is no doubt still in Ireland. We must not expect to see him to-night.

Betteredge has just come in, to say that Mr Blake has asked for me. I must lay down my pen for the present.

Seven o'clock.—We have been all over the refurnished rooms and staircases again; and we have had a pleasant stroll in the shrubbery, which was Mr Blake's favourite walk when he was here last. In this way, I hope to revive the old impressions of places and things as vividly as possible in his mind.

We are now going to dine, exactly at the hour at which the birthday dinner was given last year. My object, of course, is a purely medical one in this case. The laudanum must find the process of digestion, as nearly as may be, where the laudanum found it last year.

At a reasonable time after dinner I propose to lead the conversation back again—as inartificially as I can—to the subject of the Diamond, and of the Indian conspiracy to steal it. When I have filled his mind with these topics, I shall have done all that it is in my power to do, before the time comes for giving him the second dose.

Half-past eight.—I have only this moment found an opportunity of attending to the most important duty of all; the duty of looking in the family medicine chest, for the laudanum which Mr Candy used last year.

Ten minutes since, I caught Betteredge at an unoccupied moment, and told him what I wanted. Without a word of objection, without so much as an attempt to produce his pocket-book, he led the way (making allowances for me at every step) to the store-room in which the medicine chest is kept.

I discovered the bottle; carefully guarded by a glass stopper tied over with leather. The preparation which it contained was, as I had anticipated, the common Tincture of Opium. Finding the bottle still well filled, I have resolved to use it, in preference to employing either of the two preparations with which I had taken care to provide myself, in case of emergency.

The question of the quantity which I am to administer presents certain difficulties. I have thought it over, and have decided on increasing the dose.

My notes inform me that Mr Candy only administered twenty-five minims. This is a small dose to have produced the results which followed— even in the case of a person so sensitive as Mr Blake. I think it highly probable that Mr Candy gave more than he supposed himself to have given—knowing, as I do, that he has a keen relish of the pleasures of the table, and that he measured out the laudanum on the birthday, after dinner. In any case, I shall run the risk of enlarging the dose to forty minims. On this occasion, Mr Blake knows beforehand that he is going to take the laudanum—which is equivalent, physiologically speaking, to his having (unconsciously to himself) a certain capacity in him to resist the effects. If my view is right, a larger quantity is therefore imperatively required, this time, to repeat the results which the smaller quantity produced, last year.

Ten o'clock.—The witnesses, or the company (which shall I call them?) reached the house an hour since.

A little before nine o'clock, I prevailed on Mr Blake to accompany me to his bedroom; stating, as a reason, that I wished him to look round it, for the last time, in order to make quite sure that nothing had been forgotten in the refurnishing of the room. I had previously arranged with Betteredge, that the bedchamber prepared for Mr Bruff should be the next room to Mr Blake's, and that I should be informed of the lawyer's arrival by a knock at the door. Five minutes after the clock in the hall had struck nine, I heard the knock; and, going out immediately, met Mr Bruff in the corridor.

My personal appearance (as usual) told against me. Mr Bruff's distrust looked at me plainly enough out of Mr Bruff's eyes. Being well used to producing this effect on strangers, I did not hesitate a moment in saying what I wanted to say, before the lawyer found his way into Mr Blake's room.

'You have travelled here, I believe, in company with Mrs Merridew and Miss Verinder?' I said.

'Yes,' answered Mr Bruff, as drily as might be.

'Miss Verinder has probably told you, that I wish her presence in the house (and Mrs Merridew's presence of course) to be kept a secret from Mr Blake, until my experiment on him has been tried first?'

'I know that I am to hold my tongue, sir!' said Mr Bruff, impatiently. 'Being habitually silent on the subject of human folly, I am all the readier to keep my lips closed on this occasion. Does that satisfy you?'

I bowed, and left Betteredge to show him to his room. Betteredge gave me one look at parting, which said, as if in so many words, 'You have caught a Tartar, Mr Jennings—and the name of him is Bruff.'

It was next necessary to get the meeting over with the two ladies. I descended the stairs—a little nervously, I confess—on my way to Miss Verinder's sitting-room.

The gardener's wife (charged with looking after the accommodation of the ladies) met me in the first-floor corridor. This excellent woman treats me with an excessive civility which is plainly the offspring of downright terror. She stares, trembles, and curtseys, whenever I speak to her. On my asking for Miss Verinder, she stared, trembled, and would no doubt have curtseyed next, if Miss Verinder herself had not cut that ceremony short, by suddenly opening her sitting-room door.

'Is that Mr Jennings?' she asked.

Before I could answer, she came out eagerly to speak to me in the corridor. We met under the light of a lamp on a bracket. At the first sight of me, Miss Verinder stopped, and hesitated. She recovered herself instantly, coloured for a moment—and then, with a charming frankness, offered me her hand.

'I can't treat you like a stranger, Mr Jennings,' she said. 'Oh, if you only knew how happy your letters have made me!'

She looked at my ugly wrinkled face, with a bright gratitude so new to me in *my* experience of my fellow-creatures, that I was at a loss how to answer her. Nothing had prepared me for her kindness and her beauty. The misery of many years has not hardened my heart, thank God. I was as awkward and as shy with her, as if I had been a lad in my teens.

'Where is he now?' she asked, giving free expression to her one dominant interest—the interest in Mr Blake. 'What is he doing? Has he spoken of me?

Is he in good spirits? How does he bear the sight of the house, after what happened in it last year? When are you going to give him the laudanum? May I see you pour it out? I am so interested; I am so excited—I have ten thousand things to say to you, and they all crowd together so that I don't know what to say first. Do you wonder at the interest I take in this?'

'No,' I said. 'I venture to think that I thoroughly understand it.'

She was far above the paltry affectation of being confused. She answered me as she might have answered a brother or a father.

'You have relieved me of indescribable wretchedness; you have given me a new life. How can I be ungrateful enough to have any concealment from *you*? I love him,' she said simply, 'I have loved him from first to last—even when I was wronging him in my own thoughts; even when I was saying the hardest and the cruellest words to him. Is there any excuse for me, in that? I hope there is—I am afraid it is the only excuse I have. When tomorrow comes, and he knows that I am in the house, do you think——?'

She stopped again, and looked at me very earnestly.

'When to-morrow comes,' I said, 'I think you have only to tell him what you have just told me.'

Her face brightened; she came a step nearer to me. Her fingers trifled nervously with a flower which I had picked in the garden, and which I had put into the buttonhole of my coat.

'You have seen a great deal of him lately,' she said. 'Have you, really and truly, seen *that*?'

'Really and truly,' I answered. 'I am quite certain of what will happen to-morrow. I wish I could feel as certain of what will happen to-night.'

At that point in the conversation, we were interrupted by the appearance of Betteredge with the tea-tray. He gave me another significant look as he passed on into the sitting-room. 'Aye! aye! make your hay while the sun shines. The Tartar's upstairs, Mr Jennings—the Tartar's upstairs!'

We followed him into the room. A little old lady, in a corner, very nicely dressed, and very deeply absorbed over a smart piece of embroidery, dropped her work in her lap, and uttered a faint little scream at the first sight of my gipsy complexion and my piebald hair.

'Mrs Merridew,' said Miss Verinder, 'this is Mr Jennings.'

'I beg Mr Jennings's pardon,' said the old lady, looking at Miss Verinder, and speaking at *me*. 'Railway travelling always makes me nervous. I am endeavouring to quiet my mind by occupying myself as usual. I don't know whether my embroidery is out of place, on this extraordinary occasion. If it interferes with Mr Jennings's medical views, I shall be happy to put it away of course.'

I hastened to sanction the presence of the embroidery, exactly as I had sanctioned the absence of the burst buzzard and the Cupid's wing. Mrs Merridew made an effort—a grateful effort—to look at my hair. No! it was not to be done. Mrs Merridew looked back again at Miss Verinder.

'If Mr Jennings will permit me,' pursued the old lady, 'I should like to ask a favour. Mr Jennings is about to try a scientific experiment to-night. I used to attend scientific experiments when I was a girl at school. They invariably ended in an explosion. If Mr Jennings will be so very kind, I should like to be warned of the explosion this time. With a view to getting it over, if possible, before I go to bed.'

I attempted to assure Mrs Merridew that an explosion was not included in the programme on this occasion.

'No,' said the old lady. 'I am much obliged to Mr Jennings—I am aware that he is only deceiving me for my own good. I prefer plain dealing. I am quite resigned to the explosion—but I *do* want to get it over, if possible, before I go to bed.'

Here the door opened, and Mrs Merridew uttered another little scream. The advent of the explosion? No: only the advent of Betteredge.

'I beg your pardon, Mr Jennings,' said Betteredge, in his most elaborately confidential manner. 'Mr Franklin wishes to know where you are. Being under your orders to deceive him, in respect to the presence of my young lady in the house, I have said I don't know. That, you will please to observe, was a lie. Having one foot already in the grave, sir, the fewer lies you expect me to tell, the more I shall be indebted to you, when my conscience pricks me and my time comes.'

There was not a moment to be wasted on the purely speculative question of Betteredge's conscience. Mr Blake might make his apperance in search of me, unless I went to him at once in his own room. Miss Verinder followed me out into the corridor.

'They seem to be in a conspiracy to persecute you,' she said. 'What does it mean?'

'Only the protest of the world, Miss Verinder—on a very small scale— against anything that is new.'

'What are we to do with Mrs Merridew?'

'Tell her the explosion will take place at nine to-morrow morning.'

'So as to send her to bed?'

'Yes—so as to send her to bed.'

Miss Verinder went back to the sitting-room, and I went upstairs to Mr Blake.

To my surprise I found him alone; restlessly pacing his room, and a little irritated at being left by himself.

'Where is Mr Bruff?' I asked.

He pointed to the closed door of communication between the two rooms. Mr Bruff had looked in on him, for a moment; had attempted to renew his protest against our proceedings; and had once more failed to produce the smallest impression on Mr Blake. Upon this, the lawyer had taken refuge in a black leather bag, filled to bursting with professional papers. 'The serious business of life,' he admitted, 'was sadly out of place on such an occasion as the present. But the serious business of life must be carried on, for all that. Mr Blake would perhaps kindly make allowance for the old-fashioned habits of a practical man. Time was money—and, as for Mr Jennings, he might depend on it that Mr Bruff would be forthcoming when called upon.' With that apology, the lawyer had gone back to his own room, and had immersed himself obstinately in his black bag.

I thought of Mrs Merridew and her embroidery, and of Betteredge and his conscience. There is a wonderful sameness in the solid side of the English character—just as there is a wonderful sameness in the solid expression of the English face.

'When are you going to give me the laudanum?' asked Mr Blake impatiently.

'You must wait a little longer,' I said. 'I will stay and keep you company till the time comes.'

It was then not ten o'clock. Inquiries which I had made, at various times, of Betteredge and Mr Blake, had led me to the conclusion that the dose of laudanum given by Mr Candy could not possibly have been administered before eleven. I had accordingly determined not to try the second dose until that time.

We talked a little; but both our minds were preoccupied by the coming ordeal. The conversation soon flagged—then dropped altogether. Mr Blake idly turned over the books on his bedroom table. I had taken the precaution of looking at them, when we first entered the room. *The Guardian*; *the Tatler*; Richardson's *Pamela*; Mackenzie's *Man of Feeling*; Roscoe's *Lorenzo de' Medici*; and Robertson's *Charles the Fifth*—all classical works; all (of course) immeasurably superior to anything produced in later times; and all (from my present point of view) possessing the one great merit of enchaining nobody's interest, and exciting nobody's brain. I left Mr Blake to the composing influence of Standard Literature, and occupied myself in making this entry in my journal.

My watch informs me that it is close on eleven o'clock. I must shut up these leaves once more.

Two o'clock A.M.—The experiment has been tried. With what result, I am now to describe.

At eleven o'clock, I rang the bell for Betteredge, and told Mr Blake that he might at last prepare himself for bed.

I looked out of the window at the night. It was mild and rainy, resembling, in this respect, the night of the birthday—the twenty-first of June, last year. Without professing to believe in omens, it was at least encouraging to find no direct nervous influences—no stormy or electric perturbations—in the atmosphere. Betteredge joined me at the window, and mysteriously put a little slip of paper into my hand. It contained these lines:

'Mrs Merridew has gone to bed, on the distinct understanding that the explosion is to take place at nine tomorrow morning, and that I am not to stir out of this part of the house until she comes and sets me free. She has no idea that the chief scene of the experiment is my sitting-room—or she would have remained in it for the whole night! I am alone, and very anxious. Pray let me see you measure out the laudanum; I want to have something to do with it, even in the unimportant character of a mere looker-on.—R. V.'

I followed Betteredge out of the room, and told him to remove the medicine-chest into Miss Verinder's sitting-room.

The order appeared to take him completely by surprise. He looked as if he suspected me of some occult medical design on Miss Verinder! 'Might I presume to ask,' he said, 'what my young lady and the medicine-chest have got to do with each other?'

'Stay in the sitting-room, and you will see.'

Betteredge appeared to doubt his own unaided capacity to superintend me effectually, on an occasion when a medicine-chest was included in the proceedings.

'Is there any objection, sir,' he asked, 'to taking Mr Bruff into this part of the business?'

'Quite the contrary! I am now going to ask Mr Bruff to accompany me downstairs.'

Betteredge withdrew to fetch the medicine-chest, without another word. I went back into Mr Blake's room, and knocked at the door of communication. Mr Bruff opened it, with his papers in his hand—immersed in Law; impenetrable to Medicine.

'I am sorry to disturb you,' I said. 'But I am going to prepare the laudanum for Mr Blake; and I must request you to be present, and to see what I do.'

'Yes?' said Mr Bruff, with nine-tenths of his attention riveted on his papers, and with one-tenth unwillingly accorded to me. 'Anything else?'

'I must trouble you to return here with me, and to see me administer the dose.'

'Anything else?'

'One thing more. I must put you to the inconvenience of remaining in Mr Blake's room, and of waiting to see what happens.'

'Oh, very good!' said Mr Bruff. 'My room, or Mr Blake's room—it doesn't matter which; I can go on with my papers anywhere. Unless you object, Mr Jennings, to my importing *that* amount of common sense into the proceedings?'

Before I could answer, Mr Blake addressed himself to the lawyer, speaking from his bed.

'Do you really mean to say that you don't feel any interest in what we are going to do?' he asked. 'Mr Bruff, you have no more imagination than a cow!'

'A cow is a very useful animal, Mr Blake,' said the lawyer. With that reply he followed me out of the room, still keeping his papers in his hand.

We found Miss Verinder, pale and agitated, restlessly pacing her sitting-room from end to end. At a table in a corner stood Betteredge, on guard over the medicine-chest. Mr Bruff sat down on the first chair that he could find, and (emulating the usefulness of the cow) plunged back again into his papers on the spot.

Miss Verinder drew me aside, and reverted instantly to her one all-absorbing interest—her interest in Mr Blake.

'How is he now?' she asked. 'Is he nervous? is he out of temper? Do you think it will succeed? Are you sure it will do no harm?'

'Quite sure. Come, and see me measure it out.'

'One moment! It is past eleven now. How long will it be before anything happens?'

'It is not easy to say. An hour perhaps.'

'I suppose the room must be dark, as it was last year?'

'Certainly.'

'I shall wait in my bedroom—just as I did before. I shall keep the door a little way open. It was a little way open last year. I will watch the sitting-room door; and the moment it moves, I will blow out my light. It all happened in that way, on my birthday night. And it must all happen again in the same way, mustn't it?'

'Are you sure you can control yourself, Miss Verinder?'

'In *his* interests, I can do anything!' she answered fervently.

One look at her face told me that I could trust her. I addressed myself again to Mr Bruff.

'I must trouble you to put your papers aside for a moment,' I said.

'Oh, certainly!' He got up with a start—as if I had disturbed him at a particularly interesting place—and followed me to the medicine-chest. There, deprived of the breathless excitement incidental to the practice of his profession, he looked at Betteredge—and yawned wearily.

Miss Verinder joined me with a glass jug of cold water, which she had taken from a side-table. 'Let me pour out the water,' she whispered. 'I *must* have a hand in it!'

I measured out the forty minims from the bottle, and poured the laudanum into a medicine glass. 'Fill it till it is three parts full,' I said, and handed the glass to Miss Verinder. I then directed Betteredge to lock up the medicine chest; informing him that I had done with it now. A look of unutterable relief overspread the old servant's countenance. He had evidently suspected me of a medical design on his young lady!

After adding the water as I had directed, Miss Verinder seized a moment—while Betteredge was locking the chest, and while Mr Bruff was looking back at his papers—and slyly kissed the rim of the medicine glass.

'When you give it to him,' said the charming girl, 'give it to him on that side!'

I took the piece of crystal which was to represent the Diamond from my pocket, and gave it to her.

'You must have a hand in this, too,' I said. 'You must put it where you put the Moonstone last year.'

She led the way to the Indian cabinet, and put the mock Diamond into the drawer which the real Diamond had occupied on the birthday night. Mr Bruff witnessed this proceeding, under protest, as he had witnessed everything else. But the strong dramatic interest which the experiment was now assuming, proved (to my great amusement) to be too much for Betteredge's capacity of self-restraint. His hand trembled as he held the candle, and he whispered anxiously, 'Are you sure, miss, it's the right drawer?'

I led the way out again, with the laudanum and water in my hand. At the door, I stopped to address a last word to Miss Verinder.

'Don't be long in putting out the lights,' I said.

'I will put them out at once,' she answered. 'And I will wait in my bedroom, with only one candle alight.'

She closed the sitting-room door behind us. Followed by Mr Bruff and Betteredge, I went back to Mr Blake's room.

We found him moving restlessly from side to side of the bed, and wondering irritably whether he was to have the laudanum that night. In the presence of the two witnesses, I gave him the dose, and shook up his pillows, and told him to lie down again quietly and wait.

His bed, provided with light chintz curtains, was placed, with the head against the wall of the room, so as to leave a good open space on either side of it. On one side, I drew the curtains completely—and in the part of the room thus screened from his view, I placed Mr Bruff and Betteredge, to wait for the result. At the bottom of the bed I half drew the curtains—and placed my own chair at a little distance, so that I might let him see me or not see me, speak to me or not speak to me, just as the circumstances might direct. Having already been informed that he always slept with a light in the room, I placed one of the two lighted candles on a little table at the head of the bed, where the glare of the light would not strike on his eyes. The other candle I gave to Mr Bruff; the light, in this instance, being subdued by the screen of the chintz curtains. The window was open at the top, so as to ventilate the room. The rain fell softly, the house was quiet. It was twenty minutes past eleven, by my watch, when the preparations were completed, and I took my place on the chair set apart at the bottom of the bed.

Mr Bruff resumed his papers, with every appearance of being as deeply interested in them as ever. But looking towards him now, I saw certain signs and tokens which told me that the Law was beginning to lose its hold on him at last. The suspended interest of the situation in which we were now placed was slowly asserting its influence even on *his* unimaginative mind. As for Betteredge, consistency of principle and dignity of conduct had become, in his case, mere empty words. He forgot that I was performing a conjuring trick on Mr Franklin Blake; he forgot that I had upset the house from top to bottom; he forgot that I had not read *Robinson Crusoe* since I was a child. 'For the Lord's sake, sir,' he whispered to me, 'tell us when it will begin to work.'

'Not before midnight,' I whispered back. 'Say nothing, and sit still.'

Betteredge dropped to the lowest depth of familiarity with me, without a struggle to save himself. He answered by a wink!

Looking next towards Mr Blake, I found him as restless as ever in his bed; fretfully wondering why the influence of the laudanum had not begun to assert itself yet. To tell him, in his present humour, that the more he fidgeted and wondered, the longer he would delay the result for which we were now waiting, would have been simply useless. The wiser course to take was to dismiss the idea of the opium from his mind, by leading him insensibly to think of something else.

With this view, I encouraged him to talk to me; contriving so to direct the conversation, on my side, as to lead it back again to the subject which had engaged us earlier in the evening—the subject of the Diamond. I took care to revert to those portions of the story of the Moonstone, which related to the transport of it from London to Yorkshire; to the risk which Mr Blake had run in removing it from the bank at Frizinghall: and to the unexpected appearance of the Indians at the house, on the evening of the birthday. And I purposely assumed, in referring to these events, to have misunderstood much of what Mr Blake himself had told me a few hours since. In this way, I set him talking on the subject with which it was now vitally important to fill his mind—without allowing him to suspect that I was making him talk for a purpose. Little by little, he became so interested in putting me right that he forgot to fidget in the bed. His mind was far away from the question of the opium, at the all-important time when his eyes first told me that the opium was beginning to lay its hold on his brain.

I looked at my watch. It wanted five minutes to twelve, when the premonitory symptoms of the working of the laudanum first showed themselves to me.

At this time, no unpractised eyes would have detected any change in him. But, as the minutes of the new morning wore away, the swiftly-subtle progress of the influence began to show itself more plainly. The sublime intoxication of opium gleamed in his eyes; the dew of a stealthy perspiration began to glisten on his face. In five minutes more, the talk which he still kept up with me, failed in coherence. He held steadily to the subject of the Diamond; but he ceased to complete his sentences. A little later, the sentences dropped to single words. Then, there was an interval of silence. Then, he sat up in bed. Then, still busy with the subject of the Diamond, he began to talk again—not to me, but to himself. That change told me that the first stage in the experiment was reached. The stimulant influence of the opium had got him.

The time, now, was twenty-three minutes past twelve. The next half hour, at most, would decide the question of whether he would, or would not, get up from his bed, and leave the room.

In the breathless interest of watching him—in the unutterable triumph of seeing the first result of the experiment declare itself in the manner, and nearly at the time, which I had anticipated—I had utterly forgotten the two companions of my night vigil. Looking towards them now, I saw the Law (as represented by Mr Bruff's papers) lying unheeded on the floor. Mr Bruff himself was looking eagerly through a crevice left in the imperfectly-drawn curtains of the bed. And Betteredge, oblivious of all respect for social distinctions, was peeping over Mr Bruff's shoulder.

They both started back, on finding that I was looking at them, like two boys caught out by their schoolmaster in a fault. I signed to them to take off their boots quietly, as I was taking off mine. If Mr Blake gave us the chance of following him, it was vitally necessary to follow him without noise.

Ten minutes passed—and nothing happened. Then, he suddenly threw the bed-clothes off him. He put one leg out of bed. He waited.

'I wish I had never taken it out of the bank,' he said to himself. 'It was safe in the bank.'

My heart throbbed fast; the pulses at my temples beat furiously. The doubt about the safety of the Diamond was, once more, the dominant impression in his brain! On that one pivot, the whole success of the experiment turned. The prospect thus suddenly opened before me was too much for my shattered nerves. I was obliged to look away from him—or I should have lost my self-control.

There was another interval of silence.

When I could trust myself to look back at him he was out of his bed, standing erect at the side of it. The pupils of his eyes were now contracted; his eyeballs gleamed in the light of the candle as he moved his head slowly to and fro. He was thinking; he was doubting—he spoke again.

'How do I know?' he said. 'The Indians may be hidden in the house.'

He stopped, and walked slowly to the other end of the room. He turned—waited—came back to the bed.

'It's not even locked up,' he went on. 'It's in the drawer of her cabinet. And the drawer doesn't lock.'

He sat down on the side of the bed. 'Anybody might take it,' he said.

He rose again restlessly, and reiterated his first words.

'How do I know? The Indians may be hidden in the house.'

He waited again. I drew back behind the half curtain of the bed. He looked about the room, with a vacant glitter in his eyes. It was a breathless moment. There was a pause of some sort. A pause in the action of the opium? a pause in the action of the brain? Who could tell? Everything depended, now, on what he did next.

He laid himself down again on the bed!

A horrible doubt crossed my mind. Was it possible that the sedative action of the opium was making itself felt already? It was not in my experience that it should do this. But what is experience, where opium is concerned? There are probably no two men in existence on whom the drug acts in exactly the same manner. Was some constitutional peculiarity in him, feeling the influence in some new way? Were we to fail on the very brink of success?

No! He got up again abruptly. 'How the devil am I to sleep,' he said, 'with *this* on my mind?'

He looked at the light, burning on the table at the head of his bed. After a moment, he took the candle in his hand.

I blew out the second candle, burning behind the closed curtains. I drew back, with Mr Bruff and Betteredge, into the farthest corner by the bed. I signed to them to be silent, as if their lives had depended on it.

We waited—seeing and hearing nothing. We waited, hidden from him by the curtains.

The light which he was holding on the other side of us moved suddenly. The next moment he passed us, swift and noiseless, with the candle in his hand.

He opened the bedroom door, and went out.

We followed him along the corridor. We followed him down the stairs. We followed him along the second corridor. He never looked back; he never hesitated.

He opened the sitting-room door, and went in, leaving it open behind him.

The door was hung (like all the other doors in the house) on large old-fashioned hinges. When it was opened, a crevice was opened between the door and the post. I signed to my two companions to look through this, so as to keep them from showing themselves. I placed myself—outside the door also—on the opposite side. A recess in the wall was at my left hand, in which I could instantly hide myself, if he showed any signs of looking back into the corridor.

He advanced to the middle of the room, with the candle still in his hand: he looked about him—but he never looked back.

I saw the door of Miss Verinder's bedroom, standing ajar. She had put out her light. She controlled herself nobly. The dim white outline of her summer dress was all that I could see. Nobody who had not known it beforehand would have suspected that there was a living creature in the room. She kept back, in the dark: not a word, not a movement escaped her.

It was now ten minutes past one. I heard, through the dead silence, the soft drip of the rain and the tremulous passage of the night air through the trees.

After waiting irresolute, for a minute or more, in the middle of the room, he moved to the corner near the window, where the Indian cabinet stood.

He put his candle on the top of the cabinet. He opened, and shut, one drawer after another, until he came to the drawer in which the mock Diamond was put. He looked into the drawer for a moment. Then he took the mock Diamond out with his right hand. With the other hand, he took the candle from the top of the cabinet.

He walked back a few steps towards the middle of the room, and stood still again.

Thus far, he had exactly repeated what he had done on the birthday night. Would his next proceeding be the same as the proceeding of last year? Would he leave the room? Would he go back now, as I believed he had gone back then, to his bed-chamber? Would he show us what he had done with the Diamond, when he had returned to his own room?

His first action, when he moved once more, proved to be an action which he had *not* performed, when he was under the influence of the opium for the first time. He put the candle down on a table, and wandered on a little towards the farther end of the room. There was a sofa here. He leaned heavily on the back of it, with his left hand—then roused himself, and returned to the middle of the room. I could now see his eyes. They were getting dull and heavy; the glitter in them was fast dying out.

The suspense of the moment proved too much for Miss Verinder's self-control. She advanced a few steps—then stopped again. Mr Bruff and Betteredge looked across the open doorway at me for the first time. The prevision of a coming disappointment was impressing itself on their minds as well as on mine.

Still, so long as he stood where he was, there was hope. We waited, in unutterable expectation, to see what would happen next.

The next event was decisive. He let the mock Diamond drop out of his hand.

It fell on the floor, before the doorway—plainly visible to him, and to everyone. He made no effort to pick it up: he looked down at it vacantly, and, as he looked, his head sank on his breast. He staggered—roused himself for an instant—walked back unsteadily to the sofa—and sat down on it. He made a last effort; he tried to rise, and sank back. His head fell on the sofa cushions. It was then twenty-five minutes past one o'clock. Before I had put my watch back in my pocket, he was asleep.

It was all over now. The sedative influence had got him; the experiment was at an end.

I entered the room, telling Mr Bruff and Betteredge that they might follow me. There was no fear of disturbing him. We were free to move and speak.

'The first thing to settle,' I said, 'is the question of what we are to do with him. He will probably sleep for the next six or seven hours, at least. It is some distance to carry him back to his own room. When I was younger, I could have done it alone. But my health and strength are not what they were—I am afraid I must ask you to help me.

Before they could answer, Miss Verinder called to me softly. She met me at the door of her room, with a light shawl, and with the counterpane from her own bed.

'Do you mean to watch him while he sleeps?' she asked.

'Yes, I am not sure enough of the action of the opium in his case to be willing to leave him alone.'

She handed me the shawl and the counterpane.

'Why should you disturb him?' she whispered. 'Make his bed on the sofa. I can shut my door, and keep in my room.'

It was infinitely the simplest and the safest way of disposing of him for the night. I mentioned the suggestion to Mr Bruff and Betteredge—who both approved of my adopting it. In five minutes I had laid him comfortably on the sofa, and had covered him lightly with the counterpane and the shawl. Miss Verinder wished us good night, and closed the door. At my request, we three then drew round the table in the middle of the room, on which the candle was still burning, and on which writing materials were placed.

'Before we separate,' I began, 'I have a word to say about the experiment which has been tried to-night. Two distinct objects were to be gained by it. The first of these objects was to prove, that Mr Blake entered this room, and took the Diamond, last year, acting unconsciously and irresponsibly, under the influence of opium. After what you have both seen, are you both satisfied, so far?'

They answered me in the affirmative, without a moment's hesitation.

'The second object,' I went on, 'was to discover what he did with the Diamond, after he was seen by Miss Verinder to leave her sitting-room with the jewel in his hand, on the birthday night. The gaining of this object depended, of course, on his still continuing exactly to repeat his proceedings of last year. He has failed to do that; and the purpose of the experiment is defeated accordingly. I can't assert that I am not disappointed at the result—but I can honestly say that I am not surprised by it. I told Mr Blake from the first, that our complete success in this matter depended on our completely reproducing in him the physical and moral conditions of last year—and I warned him that this was the next thing to a downright impossibility. We have only partially reproduced the conditions, and the experiment has been only partially successful in consequence. It is also possible that I may have administered too large a dose of laudanum. But I myself look upon the first reason that I have given, as the true reason why we have to lament a failure, as well as to rejoice over a success.'

After saying those words, I put the writing materials before Mr Bruff, and asked him if he had any objection—before we separated for the night—to draw out, and sign, a plain statement of what he had seen. He at once took the pen, and produced the statement with the fluent readiness of a practised hand.

'I owe you this,' he said, signing the paper, 'as some atonement for what passed between us earlier in the evening. I beg your pardon, Mr Jennings, for having doubted you. You have done Franklin Blake an inestimable service. In our legal phrase, you have proved your case.'

Betteredge's apology was characteristic of the man.

'Mr Jennings,' he said, 'when you read *Robinson Crusoe* again (which I strongly recommend you to do), you will find that he never scruples to acknowledge it, when he turns out to have been in the wrong. Please to consider me, sir, as doing what Robinson Crusoe did, on the present occasion.' With those words he signed the paper in his turn.

Mr Bruff took me aside, as we rose from the table.

'One word about the Diamond,' he said. 'Your theory is that Franklin Blake hid the Moonstone in his room. My theory is, that the Moonstone is in the possession of Mr Luker's bankers in London. We won't dispute which of us is right. We will only ask, which of us is in a position to put his theory to the test?'

'The test, in my case,' I answered, 'has been tried tonight, and has failed.'

'The test, in my case,' rejoined Mr Bruff, 'is still in process of trial. For the last two days I have had a watch set for Mr Luker at the bank; and I shall cause that watch to be continued until the last day of the month. I know that he must take the Diamond himself out of his bankers' hands—and I am acting on the chance that the person who has pledged the Diamond may force him to do this by redeeming the pledge. In that case I may be able to lay my hand on the person. If I succeed, I clear up the mystery, exactly at the point where the mystery baffles us now! Do you admit that, so far?'

I admitted it readily.

'I am going back to town by the morning train,' pursued the lawyer. 'I may hear, when I return, that a discovery has been made—and it may be of the greatest importance that I should have Franklin Blake at hand to appeal to, if necessary. I intend to tell him, as soon as he wakes, that he must return with me to London. After all that has happened, may I trust to your influence to back me?'

'Certainly!' I said.

Mr Bruff shook hands with me, and left the room. Betteredge followed him out.

I went to the sofa to look at Mr Blake. He had not moved since I had laid him down and made his bed—he lay locked in a deep and quiet sleep.

While I was still looking at him, I heard the bedroom door softly opened. Once more, Miss Verinder appeared on the threshold, in her pretty summer dress.

'Do me a last favour?' she whispered. 'Let me watch him with you.'

I hesitated—not in the interests of propriety; only in the interest of her night's rest. She came close to me, and took my hand.

'I can't sleep; I can't even sit still, in my own room,' she said. 'Oh, Mr Jennings, if you were me, only think how you would long to sit and look at him. Say, yes! Do!'

Is it necessary to mention that I gave way? Surely not!

She drew a chair to the foot of the sofa. She looked at him in a silent ecstasy of happiness, till the tears rose in her eyes. She dried her eyes, and said she would fetch her work. She fetched her work, and never did a single stitch of it. It lay in her lap—she was not even able to look away from him long enough to thread her needle. I thought of my own youth; I thought of the gentle eyes which had once looked love at *me*. In the heaviness of my heart I turned to my Journal for relief, and wrote in it what is written here.

So we kept our watch together in silence. One of us absorbed in his writing; the other absorbed in her love.

Hour after hour he lay in his deep sleep. The light of the new day grew and grew in the room, and still he never moved.

Towards six o'clock, I felt the warning which told me that my pains were coming back. I was obliged to leave her alone with him for a little while. I said I would go upstairs, and fetch another pillow for him out of his room. It was not a long attack, this time. In a little while I was able to venture back, and let her see me again.

I found her at the head of the sofa, when I returned. She was just touching his forehead with her lips. I shook my head as soberly as I could, and pointed to her chair. She looked back at me with a bright smile, and a charming colour in her face, 'You would have done it,' she whispered, 'in my place'

It is just eight o'clock. He is beginning to move for the first time.

Miss Verinder is kneeling by the side of the sofa. She has so placed herself that when his eyes first open, they must open on her face.

Shall I leave them together?

Yes!

Eleven o'clock.—The house is empty again. They have arranged it among themselves; they have all gone to London by the ten o'clock train. My brief dream of happiness is over. I have awakened again to the realities of my friendless and lonely life.

I dare not trust myself to write down the kind words that have been said to me—especially by Miss Verinder and Mr Blake. Besides, it is needless.

Those words will come back to me in my solitary hours, and will help me through what is left of the end of my life. Mr Blake is to write, and tell me what happens in London. Miss Verinder is to return to Yorkshire in the autumn (for her marriage, no doubt); and I am to take a holiday, and be a guest in the house. Oh me, how I felt, as the grateful happiness looked at me out of her eyes, and the warm pressure of her hand said, 'This is your doing!'

My poor patients are waiting for me. Back again, this morning, to the old routine! Back again, to-night, to the dreadful alternative between the opium and the pain!

God be praised for His mercy! I have seen a little sunshine—I have had a happy time.

FIFTH NARRATIVE

The story resumed by Franklin Blake

CHAPTER I

BUT few words are needed, on my part, to complete the narrative that has been presented in the Journal of Ezra Jennings.

Of myself, I have only to say that I awoke on the morning of the twenty-sixth, perfectly ignorant of all that I had said and done under the influence of the opium—from the time when the drug first laid its hold on me, to the time when I opened my eyes, in Rachel's sitting-room.

Of what happened after my waking, I do not feel called upon to render an account in detail. Confining myself merely to results, I have to report that Rachel and I thoroughly understood each other, before a single word of explanation had passed on either side. I decline to account, and Rachel declines to account, for the extraordinary rapidity of our reconciliation. Sir and Madam, look back at the time when you were passionately attached to each other—and you will know what happened, after Ezra Jennings had shut the door of the sitting-room, as well as I know it myself.

I have, however, no objection to add, that we should have been certainly discovered by Mrs Merridew, but for Rachel's presence of mind. She heard the sound of the old lady's dress in the corridor, and instantly ran out to meet her. I heard Mrs Merridew say, 'What is the matter?' and I heard Rachel answer, 'The explosion!' Mrs Merridew instantly permitted herself to be taken by the arm, and led into the garden, out of the way of the impending shock. On her return to the house, she met me in the hall, and expressed herself as greatly struck by the vast improvement in Science, since the time when she was a girl at school. 'Explosions, Mr Blake, are infinitely milder than they were. I assure you, I barely heard Mr Jennings's explosion from the garden. And no smell afterwards, that I can detect, now we have come back to the house! I must really apologise to your medical friend. It is only due to him to say that he has managed it beautifully!'

So, after vanquishing Betteredge and Mr Bruff, Ezra Jennings vanquished Mrs Merridew herself. There is a great deal of undeveloped liberal feeling in the world, after all!

At breakfast, Mr Bruff made no secret of his reasons for wishing that I should accompany him to London by the morning train. The watch kept at the bank, and the result which might yet come of it, appealed so irresistibly to Rachel's curiosity, that she at once decided (if Mrs Merridew had no objection) on accompanying us back to town—so as to be within reach of the earliest news of our proceedings.

Mrs Merridew proved to be all pliability and indulgence, after the truly considerate manner in which the explosion had conducted itself; and Betteredge was accordingly informed that we were all four to travel back together by the morning train. I fully expected that he would have asked leave to accompany us. But Rachel had wisely provided her faithful old servant with an occupation that interested him. He was charged with completing the refurnishing of the house, and was too full of his domestic responsibilities to feel the 'detective-fever' as he might have felt it under other circumstances.

Our one subject of regret, in going to London, was the necessity of parting, more abruptly than we could have wished, with Ezra Jennings. It was impossible to persuade him to accompany us. I could only promise to write to him—and Rachel could only insist on his coming to see her when she returned to Yorkshire. There was every prospect of our meeting again in a few months—and yet there was something very sad in seeing our best and dearest friend left standing alone on the platform, as the train moved out of the station.

On our arrival in London, Mr Bruff was accosted at the terminus by a small boy, dressed in a jacket and trousers of threadbare black cloth, and personally remarkable in virtue of the extraordinary prominence of his eyes. They projected so far, and they rolled about so loosely, that you wondered uneasily why they remained in their sockets. After listening to the boy, Mr Bruff asked the ladies whether they would excuse our accompanying them back to Portland Place. I had barely time to promise Rachel that I would return, and tell her everything that had happened, before Mr Bruff seized me by the arm, and hurried me into a cab. The boy with the ill-secured eyes took his place on the box by the driver, and the driver was directed to go to Lombard Street.

'News from the bank?' I asked, as we started.

'News of Mr Luker,' said Mr Bruff. 'An hour ago, he was seen to leave his house at Lambeth, in a cab, accompanied by two men, who were recognised by *my* men as police officers in plain clothes. If Mr Luker's dread of the Indians is at the bottom of this precaution, the inference is plain enough. He is going to take the Diamond out of the bank.'

'And we are going to the bank to see what comes of it?'

'Yes—or to hear what has come of it, if it is all over by this time. Did you notice my boy—on the box, there?'

'I noticed his eyes.'

Mr Bruff laughed. 'They call the poor little wretch "Gooseberry" at the office,' he said. 'I employ him to go on errands—and I only wish my clerks who have nicknamed him were as thoroughly to be depended on as he is. Gooseberry is one of the sharpest boys in London, Mr Blake, in spite of his eyes.'

It was twenty minutes to five when we drew up before the bank in Lombard Street. Gooseberry looked longingly at his master, as he opened the cab door.

'Do you want to come in too?' asked Mr Bruff kindly. 'Come in then, and keep at my heels till further orders. He's as quick as lightning,' pursued Mr Bruff, addressing me in a whisper. 'Two words will do with Gooseberry, where twenty would be wanted with another boy.'

We entered the bank. The outer office—with the long counter, behind which the cashiers sat—was crowded with people; all waiting their turn to take money out, or to pay money in, before the bank closed at five o'clock.

Two men among the crowd approached Mr Bruff, as soon as he showed himself.

'Well,' asked the lawyer. 'Have you seen him?'

'He passed us here half an hour since, sir, and went on into the inner office.'

'Has he not come out again yet?'

'No, sir.'

Mr Bruff turned to me. 'Let us wait,' he said.

I looked round among the people about me for the three Indians. Not a sign of them was to be seen anywhere. The only person present with a noticeably dark complexion was a tall man in a pilot coat, and a round hat, who looked like a sailor. Could this be one of them in disguise? Impossible! The man was taller than any of the Indians; and his face, where it was not hidden by a bushy black beard, was twice the breadth of any of their faces at least.

'They must have their spy somewhere,' said Mr Bruff, looking at the dark sailor in his turn. 'And he may be the man.'

Before he could say more, his coat-tail was respectfully pulled by his attendant sprite with the gooseberry eyes. Mr Bruff looked where the boy was looking. 'Hush!' he said. 'Here is Mr Luker!'

The money-lender came out from the inner regions of the bank, followed by his two guardian policemen in plain clothes.

'Keep your eye on him,' whispered Mr Bruff. 'If he passes the Diamond to anybody, he will pass it here.'

Without noticing either of us, Mr Luker slowly made his way to the door—now in the thickest, now in the thinnest part of the crowd. I distinctly saw his hand move, as he passed a short, stout man, respectably dressed in a suit of sober grey. The man started a little, and looked after him. Mr Luker moved on slowly through the crowd. At the door his guard placed themselves on either side of him. They were all three followed by one of Mr Bruff's men—and I saw them no more.

I looked round at the lawyer, and then looked significantly towards the man in the suit of sober grey. 'Yes!' whispered Mr Bruff, 'I saw it too!' He turned about, in search of his second man. The second man was nowhere to be seen. He looked behind him for his attendant sprite. Gooseberry had disappeared.

'What the devil does it mean?' said Mr Bruff angrily. 'They have both left us at the very time when we want them most.'

It came to the turn of the man in the grey suit to transact his business at the counter. He paid in a cheque—received a receipt for it—and turned to go out.

'What is to be done?' asked Mr Bruff. '*We* can't degrade ourselves by following him.'

'*I* can!' I said. 'I wouldn't lose sight of that man for ten thousand pounds!'

'In that case,' rejoined Mr Bruff, 'I wouldn't lose sight of *you*, for twice the money. A nice occupation for a man in my position,' he muttered to himself, as we followed the stranger out of the bank. 'For Heaven's sake don't mention it. I should be ruined if it was known.'

The man in the grey suit got into an omnibus, going westward. We got in after him. There were latent reserves of youth still left in Mr Bruff. I assert it positively—when he took his seat in the omnibus, he blushed!

The man with the grey suit stopped the omnibus, and got out in Oxford Street. We followed him again. He went into a chemist's shop.

Mr Bruff started. 'My chemist!' he exclaimed. 'I am afraid we have made a mistake.'

We entered the shop. Mr Bruff and the proprietor exchanged a few words in private. The lawyer joined me again, with a very crestfallen face.

'It's greatly to our credit,' he said, as he took my arm, and led me out—'that's one comfort!'

'What is to our credit?' I asked.

'Mr Blake! you and I are the two worst amateur detectives that ever tried their hands at the trade. The man in the grey suit has been thirty years in the chemist's service. He was sent to the bank to pay money to his master's account—and he knows no more of the Moonstone than the babe unborn.'

I asked what was to be done next.

'Come back to my office,' said Mr Bruff. 'Gooseberry, and my second man, have evidently followed somebody else. Let us hope that *they* had their eyes about them at any rate!'

When we reached Gray's Inn Square, the second man had arrived there before us. He had been waiting for more than a quarter of an hour.

'Well!' asked Mr Bruff. 'What's your news?'

'I am sorry to say, sir,' replied the man, 'that I have made a mistake. I could have taken my oath that I saw Mr Luker pass something to an elderly gentleman, in a light-coloured paletot. The elderly gentleman turns out, sir, to be a most respectable master ironmonger in Eastcheap.'

'Where is Gooseberry?' asked Mr Bruff resignedly.

The man stared. 'I don't know, sir. I have seen nothing of him since I left the bank.'

Mr Bruff dismissed the man. 'One of two things,' he said to me. 'Either Gooseberry has run away, or he is hunting on his own account. What do you say to dining here, on the chance that the boy may come back in an hour or two? I have got some good wine in the cellar, and we can get a chop from the coffee-house.'

We dined at Mr Bruff's chambers. Before the cloth was removed, 'a person' was announced as wanting to speak to the lawyer. Was the person Gooseberry? No: only the man who had been employed to follow Mr Luker when he left the bank.

The report, in this case, presented no feature of the slightest interest. Mr Luker had gone back to his own house, and had there dismissed his guard. He had not gone out again afterwards. Towards dusk, the shutters had been put up, and the doors had been bolted. The street before the house, and the alley behind the house, had been carefully watched. No signs of the Indians had been visible. No person whatever had been seen loitering about the premises. Having stated these facts, the man waited to know whether there were any further orders. Mr Bruff dismissed him for the night.

'Do you think Mr Luker has taken the Moonstone home with him?' I asked.

'Not he,' said Mr Bruff. 'He would never have dismissed his two policemen, if he had run the risk of keeping the Diamond in his own house again.'

We waited another half-hour for the boy, and waited in vain. It was then time for Mr Bruff to go to Hampstead, and for me to return to Rachel in Portland Place. I left my card, in charge of the porter at the chambers, with a line written on it to say that I should be at my lodgings at half-past ten, that night. The card was to be given to the boy, if the boy came back.

Some men have a knack of keeping appointments; and other men have a knack of missing them. I am one of the other men. Add to this, that I passed

the evening at Portland Place, on the same seat with Rachel, in a room forty
feet long, with Mrs Merridew at the further end of it. Does anybody wonder
that I got home at half-past twelve instead of half-past ten? How thoroughly
heartless that person must be! And how earnestly I hope I may never make
that person's acquaintance!

My servant handed me a morsel of paper when he let me in.

I read, in a neat legal handwriting, these words:—'If you please, sir, I am
getting sleepy. I will come back to-morrow morning, between nine and ten.'
Inquiry proved that a boy, with very extraordinary-looking eyes, had called,
and presented my card and message, had waited an hour, had done nothing
but fall asleep and wake up again, had written a line for me, and had gone
home—after gravely informing the servant that 'he was fit for nothing unless
he got his night's rest.'

At nine, the next morning, I was ready for my visitor. At half past nine,
I heard steps outside my door. 'Come in, Gooseberry!' I called out. 'Thank
you, sir,' answered a grave and melancholy voice. The door opened. I
started to my feet, and confronted—Sergeant Cuff.

'I thought I would look in here, Mr Blake, on the chance of your being
in town, before I wrote to Yorkshire,' said the Sergeant.

He was as dreary and as lean as ever. His eyes had not lost their old trick
(so subtly noticed in Betteredge's *Narrative*) of 'looking as if they expected
something more from you than you were aware of yourself.' But, so far as
dress can alter a man, the great Cuff was changed beyond all recognition.
He wore a broad-brimmed white hat, a light shooting jacket, white trousers,
and drab gaiters. He carried a stout oak stick. His whole aim and object
seemed to be to look as if he had lived in the country all his life. When I
complimented him on his Metamorphosis, he declined to take it as a joke.
He complained, quite gravely, of the noises and the smells of London. I
declare I am far from sure that he did not speak with a slightly rustic accent!
I offered him breakfast. The innocent countryman was quite shocked. *His*
breakfast hour was half past six—and *he* went to bed with the cocks and
hens!

'I only got back from Ireland last night,' said the Sergeant, coming round
to the practical object of his visit, in his own impenetrable manner. 'Before
I went to bed, I read your letter, telling me what has happened since my
inquiry after the Diamond was suspended last year. There's only one thing
to be said about the matter on my side. I completely mistook my case. How
any man living was to have seen things in their true light, in such a situation
as mine was at the time, I don't profess to know. But that doesn't alter the
facts as they stand. I own that I made a mess of it. Not the first mess,
Mr Blake, which has distinguished my professional career! It's only in books
that the officers of the detective force are superior to the weakness of making
a mistake.'

'You have come in the nick of time to recover your reputation,' I said.

'I beg your pardon, Mr Blake,' rejoined the Sergeant. 'Now I have retired from business, I don't care a straw about my reputation. I have done with my reputation, thank God! I am here, sir, in grateful remembrance of the late Lady Verinder's liberality to me. I will go back to my old work—if you want me, and if you will trust me—on that consideration, and on no other. Not a farthing of money is to pass, if you please, from you to me. This is on honour. Now tell me, Mr Blake, how the case stands since you wrote to me last.'

I told him of the experiment with the opium, and of what had occurred afterwards at the bank in Lombard Street. He was greatly struck by the experiment—it was something entirely new in his experience. And he was particularly interested in the theory of Ezra Jennings, relating to what I had done with the Diamond, after I had left Rachel's sitting-room, on the birthday night.

'I don't hold with Mr Jennings that you hid the Moonstone,' said Sergeant Cuff. 'But I agree with him, that you must certainly have taken it back to your own room.'

'Well?' I asked. 'And what happened then?'

'Have you no suspicion yourself of what happened, sir?'

'None whatever.'

'Has Mr Bruff no suspicion?'

'No more than I have.'

Sergeant Cuff rose, and went to my writing-table. He came back with a sealed envelope. It was marked 'Private'; it was addressed to me; and it had the Sergeant's signature in the corner.

'I suspected the wrong person, last year,' he said: 'and I may be suspecting the wrong person now. Wait to open the envelope, Mr Blake, till you have got at the truth. And then compare the name of the guilty person, with the name that I have written in that sealed letter.'

I put the letter into my pocket—and then asked for the Sergeant's opinion of the measures which we had taken at the bank.

'Very well intended, sir,' he answered, 'and quite the right thing to do. But there was another person who ought to have been looked after besides Mr Luker.'

'The person named in the letter you have just given to me?'

'Yes, Mr Blake, the person named in the letter. It can't be helped now. I shall have something to propose to you and Mr Bruff, sir, when the time comes. Let's wait, first, and see if the boy has anything to tell us that is worth hearing.'

It was close on ten o'clock, and the boy had not made his appearance. Sergeant Cuff talked of other matters. He asked after his old friend Betteredge, and his old enemy the gardener. In a minute more, he would no doubt have got from this, to the subject of his favourite roses, if my servant had not interrupted us by announcing that the boy was below.

On being brought into the room, Gooseberry stopped at the threshold of the door, and looked distrustfully at the stranger who was in my company. I told the boy to come to me.

'You may speak before this gentleman,' I said. 'He is here to assist me; and he knows all that has happened. Sergeant Cuff,' I added, 'this is the boy from Mr Bruff's office.'

In our modern system of civilisation, celebrity (no matter of what kind) is the lever that will move anything. The fame of the great Cuff had even reached the ears of the small Gooseberry. The boy's ill-fixed eyes rolled, when I mentioned the illustrious name, till I thought they really must have dropped on the carpet.

'Come here, my lad,' said the Sergeant, 'and let's hear what you have got to tell us.'

The notice of the great man—the hero of many a famous story in every lawyer's office in London—appeared to fascinate the boy. He placed himself in front of Sergeant Cuff, and put his hands behind him, after the approved fashion of a neophyte who is examined in his catechism.

'What is your name?' said the Sergeant, beginning with the first question in the catechism.

'Octavius Guy,' answered the boy. 'They call me Gooseberry at the office because of my eyes.'

'Octavius Guy, otherwise Gooseberry,' pursued the Sergeant, with the utmost gravity, 'you were missed at the bank yesterday. What were you about?'

'If you please, sir, I was following a man.'

'Who was he?'

'A tall man, sir, with a big black beard, dressed like a sailor.'

'I remember the man!' I broke in. 'Mr Bruff and I thought he was a spy employed by the Indians.'

Sergeant Cuff did not appear to be much impressed by what Mr Bruff and I had thought. He went on catechising Gooseberry.

'Well?' he said—'and why did you follow the sailor?'

'If you please, sir, Mr Bruff wanted to know whether Mr Luker passed anything to anybody on his way out of the bank. I saw Mr Luker pass something to the sailor with the black beard.'

'Why didn't you tell Mr Bruff what you saw?'

'I hadn't time to tell anybody, sir, the sailor went out in such a hurry.'

'And you ran out after him—eh?'

'Yes, sir.'

'Gooseberry,' said the Sergeant, patting his head, 'you have got something in that small skull of yours—and it isn't cotton-wool. I am greatly pleased with you, so far.'

The boy blushed with pleasure. Sergeant Cuff went on.

'Well? and what did the sailor do, when he got into the street?'

'He called a cab, sir.'

'And what did you do?'

'Held on behind, and run after it.'

Before the Sergeant could put his next question, another visitor was announced—the head clerk from Mr Bruff's office.

Feeling the importance of not interrupting Sergeant Cuff's examination of the boy, I received the clerk in another room. He came with bad news of his employer. The agitation and excitement of the last two days had proved too much for Mr Bruff. He had awoke that morning with an attack of gout; he was confined to his room at Hampstead; and, in the present critical condition of our affairs, he was very uneasy at being compelled to leave me without the advice and assistance of an experienced person. The chief clerk had received orders to hold himself at my disposal, and was willing to do his best to replace Mr Bruff.

I wrote at once to quiet the old gentleman's mind, by telling him of Sergeant Cuff's visit: adding that Gooseberry was at that moment under examination; and promising to inform Mr Bruff, either personally or by letter, of whatever might occur later in the day. Having despatched the clerk to Hampstead with my note, I returned to the room which I had left, and found Sergeant Cuff at the fireplace, in the act of ringing the bell.

'I beg your pardon, Mr Blake,' said the Sergeant. 'I was just going to send word by your servant that I wanted to speak to you. There isn't a doubt on my mind that this boy—this most meritorious boy,' added the Sergeant, patting Gooseberry on the head, 'has followed the right man. Precious time has been lost, sir, through your unfortunately not being at home at half past ten last night. The only thing to do, now, is to send for a cab immediately.'

In five minutes more, Sergeant Cuff and I (with Gooseberry on the box to guide the driver) were on our way eastward, towards the City.

'One of these days,' said the Sergeant, pointing through the front window of the cab, 'that boy will do great things in my late profession. He is the brightest and cleverest little chap I have met with, for many a long year past. You shall hear the substance, Mr Blake, of what he told me while you were out of the room. You were present, I think, when he mentioned that he held on behind the cab, and ran after it?'

'Yes.'

'Well, sir, the cab went from Lombard Street to the Tower Wharf. The sailor with the black beard got out, and spoke to the steward of the Rotterdam steamboat, which was to start next morning. He asked if he could be allowed to go on board at once, and sleep in his berth over-night. The steward said, No. The cabins, and berths, and bedding were all to have a thorough cleaning that evening, and no passenger could be allowed to come on board, before the morning. The sailor turned round, and left the wharf. When he got into the street again, the boy noticed for the first time, a man dressed like a respectable mechanic, walking on the opposite side of the road, and apparently keeping the sailor in view. The sailor stopped at an eating-house in the neighbourhood, and went in. The boy—not being able to make up his mind, at the moment—hung about among some other boys, staring at the good things in the eating-house window. He noticed the mechanic waiting, as he himself was waiting—but still on the opposite side of the street. After a minute, a cab came by slowly, and stopped where the mechanic was standing. The boy could only see plainly one person in the cab, who leaned forward at the window to speak to the mechanic. He described that person, Mr Blake, without any prompting from me, as having a dark face, like the face of an Indian.'

It was plain, by this time, that Mr Bruff and I had made another mistake. The sailor with the black beard was clearly not a spy in the service of the Indian conspiracy. Was he, by any possibility, the man who had got the Diamond?

'After a little,' pursued the Sergeant, 'the cab moved on slowly down the street. The mechanic crossed the road, and went into the eating-house. The boy waited outside till he was hungry and tired—and then went into the eating-house, in his turn. He had a shilling in his pocket; and he dined sumptuously, he tells me, on a black-pudding, an eel-pie, and a bottle of ginger-beer. What can a boy *not* digest? The substance in question has never been found yet.'

'What did he see in the eating-house?' I asked.

'Well, Mr Blake, he saw the sailor reading the newspaper at one table, and the mechanic reading the newspaper at another. It was dusk before the sailor got up, and left the place. He looked about him suspiciously when he got out into the street. The boy—*being* a boy—passed unnoticed. The mechanic had not come out yet. The sailor walked on, looking about him, and apparently not very certain of where he was going next. The mechanic appeared once more, on the opposite side of the road. The sailor went on, till he got to Shore Lane, leading into Lower Thames Street. There he stopped before a public-house, under the sign of "The Wheel of Fortune," and, after examining the place outside, went in. Gooseberry went in too. There were a great many people, mostly of the decent sort, at the bar. "The Wheel of Fortune" is a very respectable house, Mr Blake; famous for its porter and pork-pies.'

The Sergeant's digressions irritated me. He saw it; and confined himself more strictly to Gooseberry's evidence when he went on.

'The sailor,' he resumed, 'asked if he could have a bed. The landlord said "No; they were full." The barmaid corrected him, and said "Number Ten was empty." A waiter was sent for to show the sailor to Number Ten. Just before that, Gooseberry had noticed the mechanic among the people at the bar. Before the waiter had answered the call, the mechanic had vanished. The sailor was taken off to his room. Not knowing what to do next, Gooseberry had the wisdom to wait and see if anything happened. Something did happen. The landlord was called for. Angry voices were heard up-stairs. The mechanic suddenly made his appearance again, collared by the landlord, and exhibiting, to Gooseberry's great surprise, all the signs and tokens of being drunk. The landlord thrust him out at the door, and threatened him with the police if he came back. From the altercation between them, while this was going on, it appeared that the man had been discovered in Number Ten, and had declared with drunken obstinacy that he had taken the room. Gooseberry was so struck by this sudden intoxication of a previously sober person, that he couldn't resist running out after the mechanic into the street. As long as he was in sight of the public-house, the man reeled about in the most disgraceful manner. The moment he turned the corner of the street, he recovered his balance instantly, and became as sober a member of society as you could wish to see. Gooseberry went back to "The Wheel of Fortune," in a very bewildered state of mind. He waited about again, on the chance of something happening. Nothing happened; and nothing more was to be heard, or seen, of the sailor. Gooseberry decided on going back to the office. Just as he came to this conclusion, who should appear, on the opposite side of the street as usual, but the mechanic again! He looked up at one particular window at the top of the public-house, which was the only one that had a light in it. The light seemed to relieve his mind. He left the place directly. The boy made his way back to Gray's Inn—got your card and message—called—and failed to find you. There you have the state of the case, Mr Blake, as it stands at the present time.'

'What is your own opinion of the case, Sergeant?'

'I think it's serious, sir. Judging by what the boy saw, the Indians are in it, to begin with.'

'Yes. And the sailor is evidently the person to whom Mr Luker passed the Diamond. It seems odd that Mr Bruff, and I, and the man in Mr Bruff's employment, should all have been mistaken about who the person was.'

'Not at all, Mr Blake. Considering the risk that person ran, it's likely enough that Mr Luker purposely misled you, by previous arrangement between them.'

'Do you understand the proceedings at the public-house?' I asked. 'The man dressed like a mechanic was acting of course in the employment of the Indians. But I am as much puzzled to account for his sudden assumption of drunkenness as Gooseberry himself.'

'I think I can give a guess at what it means, sir,' said the Sergeant. 'If you will reflect, you will see that the man must have had some pretty strict instructions from the Indians. They were far too noticeable themselves to risk being seen at the bank, or in the public-house—they were obliged to trust everything to their deputy. Very good. Their deputy hears a certain number named in the public-house, as the number of the room which the sailor is to have for the night—that being also the room (unless our notion is all wrong) which the Diamond is to have for the night, too. Under those circumstances, the Indians, you may rely on it, would insist on having a description of the room—of its position in the house, of its capability of being approached from the outside, and so on. What was the man to do, with such orders as these? Just what he did! He ran upstairs to get a look at the room, before the sailor was taken into it. He was found there, making his observations—and he shammed drunk, as the easiest way of getting out of the difficulty. That's how I read the riddle. After he was turned out of the public-house, he probably went with his report to the place where his employers were waiting for him. And his employers, no doubt, sent him back to make sure that the sailor was really settled at the public-house till the next morning. As for what happened at "The Wheel of Fortune," after the boy left—we ought to have discovered that last night. It's eleven in the morning, now. We must hope for the best, and find out what we can.'

In a quarter of an hour more, the cab stopped in Shore Lane, and Gooseberry opened the door for us to get out.

'All right?' asked the Sergeant.

'All right,' answered the boy.

The moment we entered 'The Wheel of Fortune' it was plain even to my inexperienced eyes that there was something wrong in the house.

The only person behind the counter at which the liquors were served, was a bewildered servant girl, perfectly ignorant of the business. One or two customers, waiting for their morning drink, were tapping impatiently on the counter with their money. The barmaid appeared from the inner regions of the parlour, excited and pre-occupied. She answered Sergeant Cuff's inquiry for the landlord, by telling him sharply that her master was upstairs, and was not to be bothered by anybody.

'Come along with me, sir,' said Sergeant Cuff, coolly leading the way upstairs, and beckoning to the boy to follow him.

The barmaid called to her master, and warned him that strangers were intruding themselves into the house. On the first floor we were encountered by the landlord, hurrying down, in a highly irritated state, to see what was the matter.

'Who the devil are you? and what do you want here?' he asked.

'Keep your temper,' said the Sergeant, quietly. 'I'll tell you who I am to begin with. I am Sergeant Cuff.'

The illustrious name instantly produced its effect. The angry landlord threw open the door of a sitting-room, and asked the Sergeant's pardon.

'I am annoyed and out of sorts, sir—that's the truth,' he said. 'Something unpleasant has happened in the house this morning. A man in my way of business has a deal to upset his temper, Sergeant Cuff.'

'Not a doubt of it,' said the Sergeant. 'I'll come at once, if you will allow me, to what brings us here. This gentleman and I want to trouble you with a few inquiries, on a matter of some interest to both of us.'

'Relating to what, sir?' asked the landlord.

'Relating to a dark man, dressed like a sailor, who slept here last night.'

'Good God! that's the man who is upsetting the whole house at this moment!' exclaimed the landlord. 'Do you, or does this gentleman know anything about him?'

'We can't be certain till we see him,' answered the Sergeant.

'See him?' echoed the landlord. 'That's the one thing that nobody has been able to do since seven o'clock this morning. That was the time when he left word, last night, that he was to be called. He *was* called—and there was no getting an answer from him, and no opening his door to see what was the matter. They tried again at eight, and they tried again at nine. No use! There was the door still locked—and not a sound to be heard in the room! I have been out this morning—and I only got back a quarter of an hour ago. I have hammered at the door myself—and all to no purpose. The potboy has gone to fetch a carpenter. If you can wait a few minutes, gentlemen, we will have the door opened, and see what it means.'

'Was the man drunk last night?' asked Sergeant Cuff.

'Perfectly sober, sir—or I would never have let him sleep in my house.'

'Did he pay for his bed beforehand?'

'No.'

'Could he leave the room in any way, without going out by the door?'

'The room is a garret,' said the landlord. 'But there's a trap-door in the ceiling, leading out on to the roof—and a little lower down the street, there's an empty house under repair. Do you think, Sergeant, the blackguard has got off in that way, without paying?'

'A sailor,' said Sergeant Cuff, 'might have done it—early in the morning, before the street was astir. He would be used to climbing, and his head wouldn't fail him on the roofs of the houses.'

As he spoke, the arrival of the carpenter was announced. We all went upstairs, at once, to the top story. I noticed that the Sergeant was unusually grave, even for *him*. It also struck me as odd that he told the boy (after having previously encouraged him to follow us), to wait in the room below till we came down again.

The carpenter's hammer and chisel disposed of the resistance of the door in a few minutes. But some article of furniture had been placed against it inside, as a barricade. By pushing at the door, we thrust this obstacle aside, and so got admission to the room. The landlord entered first; the Sergeant second; and I third. The other persons present followed us.

We all looked towards the bed, and all started.

The man had not left the room. He lay, dressed, on the bed—with a white pillow over his face, which completely hid it from view.

'What does that mean?' said the landlord, pointing to the pillow.

Sergeant Cuff led the way to the bed, without answering, and removed the pillow.

The man's swarthy face was placid and still; his black hair and beard were slightly, very slightly, discomposed. His eyes stared wide-open, glassy and vacant, at the ceiling. The filmy look and the fixed expression of them horrified me. I turned away, and went to the open window. The rest of them remained, where Sergeant Cuff remained, at the bed.

'He's in a fit!' I heard the landlord say.

'He's dead,' the Sergeant answered. 'Send for the nearest doctor, and send for the police.'

The waiter was despatched on both errands. Some strange fascination seemed to hold Sergeant Cuff to the bed. Some strange curiosity seemed to keep the rest of them waiting, to see what the Sergeant would do next.

I turned again to the window. The moment afterwards, I felt a soft pull at my coat-tails, and a small voice whispered, 'Look here, sir!'

Gooseberry had followed us into the room. His loose eyes rolled frightfully—not in terror, but in exultation. He had made a detective-discovery on his own account. 'Look here, sir,' he repeated—and led me to a table in the corner of the room.

On the table stood a little wooden box, open, and empty. On one side of the box lay some jewellers' cotton. On the other side, was a torn sheet of white paper, with a seal on it, partly destroyed, and with an inscription in writing, which was still perfectly legible. The inscription was in these words:

'Deposited with Messrs. Bushe, Lysaught, and Bushe, by Mr Septimus Luker, of Middlesex Place, Lambeth, a small wooden box, sealed up in this envelope, and containing a valuable of great price. The box, when claimed, to be only given up by Messrs. Bushe and Co. on the personal application of Mr Luker.'

Those lines removed all further doubt, on one point at least. The sailor had been in possession of the Moonstone, when he had left the bank on the previous day.

I felt another pull at my coat-tails. Gooseberry had not done with me yet.

'Robbery!' whispered the boy, pointing, in high delight, to the empty box.

'You were told to wait downstairs,' I said. 'Go away!'

'And Murder!' added Gooseberry, pointing, with a keener relish still, to the man on the bed.

There was something so hideous in the boy's enjoyment of the horror of the scene, that I took him by the two shoulders and put him out of the room.

At the moment when I crossed the threshold of the door, I heard Sergeant Cuff's voice, asking where I was. He met me, as I returned into the room, and forced me to go back with him to the bedside.

'Mr Blake!' he said. 'Look at the man's face. It is a face disguised—and here's a proof of it!'

He traced with his finger a thin line of livid white, running backward from the dead man's forehead, between the swarthy complexion, and the slightly-disturbed black hair. 'Let's see what is under this,' said the Sergeant, suddenly seizing the black hair, with a firm grip of his hand.

My nerves were not strong enough to bear it. I turned away again from the bed.

The first sight that met my eyes, at the other end of the room, was the irrepressible Gooseberry, perched on a chair, and looking with breathless interest, over the heads of his elders, at the Sergeant's proceedings.

'He's pulling off his wig!' whispered Gooseberry, compassionating my position, as the only person in the room who could see nothing.

There was a pause—and then a cry of astonishment among the people round the bed.

'He's pulled off his beard!' cried Gooseberry.

There was another pause—Sergeant Cuff asked for something. The landlord went to the washhand-stand, and returned to the bed with a basin of water and a towel.

Gooseberry danced with excitement on the chair. 'Come up here, along with me, sir! He's washing off his complexion now!'

The Sergeant suddenly burst his way through the people about him, and came, with horror in his face, straight to the place where I was standing.

'Come back to the bed, sir!' he began. He looked at me closer, and checked himself. 'No!' he resumed. 'Open the sealed letter first—the letter I gave you this morning.'

I opened the letter.

'Read the name, Mr Blake, that I have written inside.'

I read the name that he had written. It was—*Godfrey Ablewhite.*

'Now,' said the Sergeant, 'come with me, and look at the man on the bed.'

I went with him, and looked at the man on the bed.

GODFREY ABLEWHITE!

SIXTH NARRATIVE

Contributed by Sergeant Cuff

I

DORKING, Surrey, July 30th, 1849. To Franklin Blake, Esq. Sir,—I beg to apologise for the delay that has occurred in the production of the Report, with which I engaged to furnish you. I have waited to make it a complete Report; and I have been met, here and there, by obstacles which it was only possible to remove by some little expenditure of patience and time.

The object which I proposed to myself has now, I hope, been attained. You will find, in these pages, answers to the greater part—if not all—of the questions, concerning the late Mr Godfrey Ablewhite, which occurred to your mind when I last had the honour of seeing you.

I propose to tell you—in the first place—what is known of the manner in which your cousin met his death; appending to the statement such inferences and conclusions as we are justified (according to my opinion) in drawing from the facts.

I shall then endeavour—in the second place—to put you in possession of such discoveries as I have made, respecting the proceedings of Mr Godfrey Ablewhite, before, during, and after the time, when you and he met as guests at the late Lady Verinder's country-house.

II

As to your cousin's death, then, first.

It appears to me to be established, beyond any reasonable doubt, that he was killed (while he was asleep, or immediately on his waking) by being smothered with a pillow from his bed—that the persons guilty of murdering him are the three Indians—and that the object contemplated (and achieved) by the crime, was to obtain possession of the diamond, called The Moonstone.

The facts from which this conclusion is drawn, are derived partly from an examination of the room at the tavern; and partly from the evidence obtained at the Coroner's Inquest.

On forcing the door of the room, the deceased gentleman was discovered, dead, with the pillow of the bed over his face. The medical man who examined him, being informed of this circumstance, considered the post-mortem appearances as being perfectly compatible with murder by smother-ing—that is to say, with murder committed by some person, or persons, pressing the pillow over the nose and mouth of the deceased, until death resulted from congestion of the lungs.

Next, as to the motive for the crime.

A small box, with a sealed paper torn off from it (the paper containing an inscription) was found open, and empty, on a table in the room. Mr Luker has himself personally identified the box, the seal, and the inscription. He has declared that the box did actually contain the diamond, called the Moonstone; and he has admitted having given the box (thus sealed up) to Mr Godfrey Ablewhite (then concealed under a disguise), on the afternoon of the twenty-sixth of June last. The fair inference from all this is, that the stealing of the Moonstone was the motive of the crime.

Next, as to the manner in which the crime was committed.

On examination of the room (which is only seven feet high), a trap-door in the ceiling, leading out on to the roof of the house, was discovered open. The short ladder, used for obtaining access to the trap-door (and kept under the bed), was found placed at the opening, so as to enable any person or persons, in the room, to leave it again easily. In the trap-door itself was found a square aperture cut in the wood, apparently with some exceedingly sharp instrument, just behind the bolt which fastened the door on the inner side. In this way, any person from the outside could have drawn back the bolt, and opened the door, and have dropped (or have been noiselessly lowered by an accomplice) into the room—its height, as already observed, being only seven feet. That some person, or persons, must have got admission in this way, appears evident from the fact of the aperture being there. As to the manner in which he (or they) obtained access to the roof of the tavern, it is to be remarked that the third house, lower down in the street, was empty, and under repair—that a long ladder was left by the workmen, leading from the pavement to the top of the house—and that, on returning to their work, on the morning of the 27th, the men found the plank which they had tied to the ladder, to prevent anyone from using it in their absence, removed, and lying on the ground. As to the possibility of ascending by this ladder, passing over the roofs of the houses, passing back, and descending again, unobserved—it is discovered, on the evidence of the night policeman, that he only passes through Shore Lane twice in an hour, when out on his beat. The testimony of the inhabitants also declares, that Shore Lane, after midnight, is one of the quietest and loneliest streets in London. Here again, therefore, it seems fair to infer that—with ordinary caution, and presence of mind—any man, or men, might have ascended by the ladder, and might have descended again, unobserved. Once on the roof of the tavern, it has been proved, by experiment, that a man might cut through the trap-door, while lying down on it, and that in such a position, the parapet in front of the house would conceal him from the view of anyone passing in the street.

Lastly, as to the person, or persons, by whom the crime was committed.

It is known (1) that the Indians had an interest in possessing themselves of the Diamond. (2) It is at least probable that the man looking like an Indian, whom Octavius Guy saw at the window of the cab, speaking to the man dressed like a mechanic, was one of the three Hindoo conspirators. (3) It is certain that this same man dressed like a mechanic, was seen keeping Mr Godfrey Ablewhite in view, all through the evening of the 26th, and was found in the bedroom (before Mr Ablewhite was shown into it) under circumstances which lead to the suspicion that he was examining the room. (4) A morsel of torn gold thread was picked up in the bedroom, which persons expert in such matters, declare to be of Indian manufacture, and to be a species of gold thread not known in England. (5) On the morning of the 27th, three men, answering to the description of the three Indians, were observed in Lower Thames Street, were traced to the Tower Wharf, and were seen to leave London by the steamer bound for Rotterdam.

There is here, moral, if not legal, evidence, that the murder was committed by the Indians.

Whether the man personating a mechanic was, or was not, an accomplice in the crime, it is impossible to say. That he could have committed the murder alone, seems beyond the limits of probability. Acting by himself, he could hardly have smothered Mr Ablewhite—who was the taller and stronger man of the two—without a struggle taking place, or a cry being heard. A servant girl, sleeping in the next room, heard nothing. The landlord, sleeping in the room below, heard nothing. The whole evidence points to the interference that more than one man was concerned in this crime—and the circumstances, I repeat, morally justify the conclusion that the Indians committed it.

I have only to add, that the verdict at the Coroner's Inquest was Wilful Murder against some person, or persons, unknown. Mr Ablewhite's family have offered a reward, and no effort has been left untried to discover the guilty persons. The man dressed like a mechanic has eluded all inquiries. The Indians have been traced. As to the prospect of ultimately capturing these last, I shall have a word to say to you on that head, when I reach the end of the present Report.

In the meanwhile, having now written all that is needful on the subject of Mr Godfrey Ablewhite's death, I may pass next to the narrative of his proceedings before, during, and after the time, when you and he met at the late Lady Verinder's house.

III

With regard to the subject now in hand, I may state, at the outset, that Mr Godfrey Ablewhite's life had two sides to it.

The side turned up to the public view, presented the spectacle of a gentleman, possessed of considerable reputation as a speaker at charitable meetings, and endowed with administrative abilities, which he placed at the disposal of various Benevolent Societies, mostly of the female sort. The side kept hidden from the general notice, exhibited this same gentleman in the totally different character of a man of pleasure, with a villa in the suburbs which was not taken in his own name, and with a lady in the villa, who was not taken in his own name, either.

My investigations in the villa have shown me several fine pictures and statues; furniture tastefully selected, and admirably made; and a conservatory of the rarest flowers, the match of which it would not be easy to find in all London. My investigation of the lady has resulted in the discovery of jewels which are worthy to take rank with the flowers, and of carriages and horses which have (deservedly) produced a sensation in the Park, among persons well qualified to judge of the build of the one, and the breed of the others.

All this is, so far, common enough. The villa and the lady are such familiar objects in London life, that I ought to apologise for introducing them to notice. But what is not common and not familiar (in my experience), is that all these fine things were not only ordered, but paid for. The pictures, the statues, the flowers, the jewels, the carriages and the horses—inquiry proved, to my indescribable astonishment, that not a sixpence of debt was owing on any of them. As to the villa, it had been bought, out and out, and settled on the lady.

I might have tried to find the right reading of this riddle, and tried in vain—but for Mr Godfrey Ablewhite's death, which caused an inquiry to be made into the state of his affairs.

The inquiry elicited these facts:—

That Mr Godfrey Ablewhite was entrusted with the care of a sum of twenty thousand pounds—as one of two Trustees for a young gentleman, who was still a minor in the year eighteen hundred and forty-eight. That the Trust was to lapse, and that the young gentleman was to receive the twenty thousand pounds on the day when he came of age, in the month of February, eighteen hundred and fifty. That, pending the arrival of this period, an income of six hundred pounds was to be paid to him by his two Trustees, half-yearly—at Christmas and Midsummer Day. That this income was regularly paid by the active Trustee, Mr Godfrey Ablewhite. That the twenty thousand pounds (from which the income was supposed to be derived) had every farthing of it been sold out of the Funds, at different periods, ending with the end of the year eighteen hundred and forty-seven. That the power of attorney, authorising the bankers to sell out the stock, and the various written orders telling them what amounts to sell out, were formally signed by both the Trustees. That the signature of the second Trustee (a retired army officer, living in the country) was a signature forged, in every case, by the active Trustee—otherwise Mr Godfrey Ablewhite.

In these facts lies the explanation of Mr Godfrey's honourable conduct, in paying the debts incurred for the lady and the villa—and (as you will presently see) of more besides.

We may now advance to the date of Miss Verinder's birthday (in the year eighteen hundred and forty-eight)—the twenty-first of June.

On the day before, Mr Godfrey Ablewhite arrived at his father's house, and asked (as I know from Mr Ablewhite, senior, himself) for a loan of three hundred pounds. Mark the sum; and remember at the same time, that the half-yearly payment to the young gentleman was due on the twenty-fourth of the month. Also, that the whole of the young gentleman's fortune had been spent by his Trustee, by the end of the year 'forty-seven.

Mr Ablewhite, senior, refused to lend his son a farthing.

The next day Mr Godfrey Ablewhite rode over, with you, to Lady Verinder's house. A few hours afterwards, Mr Godfrey (as you yourself have told me) made a proposal of marriage to Miss Verinder. Here, he saw his way no doubt—if accepted—to the end of all his money anxieties, present and future. But, as events actually turned out, what happened? Miss Verinder refused him.

On the night of the birthday, therefore, Mr Godfrey Ablewhite's pecuniary position was this. He had three hundred pounds to find on the twenty-fourth of the month, and twenty thousand pounds to find in February eighteen hundred and fifty. Failing to raise these sums, at these times, he was a ruined man.

Under those circumstances, what takes place next?

You exasperate Mr Candy, the doctor, on the sore subject of his profession; and he plays you a practical joke, in return, with a dose of laudanum. He trusts the administration of the dose, prepared in a little phial, to Mr Godfrey Ablewhite—who has himself confessed the share he had in the matter, under circumstances which shall presently be related to you. Mr Godfrey is all the readier to enter into the conspiracy, having himself suffered from your sharp tongue in the course of the evening. He joins Betteredge in persuading you to drink a little brandy and water before you go to bed. He privately drops the dose of laudanum into your cold grog. And you drink the mixture.

Let us now shift the scene, if you please, to Mr Luker's house at Lambeth. And allow me to remark, by way of preface, that Mr Bruff and I, together, have found a means of forcing the money-lender to make a clean breast of it. We have carefully sifted the statement he has addressed to us; and here it is at your service.

IV

Late on the evening of Friday, the twenty-third of June ('forty-eight), Mr Luker was surprised by a visit from Mr Godfrey Ablewhite. He was more than surprised, when Mr Godfrey produced the Moonstone. No such Diamond (according to Mr Luker's experience) was in the possession of any private person in Europe.

Mr Godfrey Ablewhite had two modest proposals to make, in relation to this magnificent gem. First, Would Mr Luker be so good as to buy it? Secondly, Would Mr Luker (in default of seeing his way to the purchase) undertake to sell it on commission, and to pay a sum down, on the anticipated result?

Mr Luker tested the Diamond, weighed the Diamond, and estimated the value of the Diamond, before he answered a word. *His* estimate (allowing for the flaw in the stone) was thirty thousand pounds.

Having reached that result, Mr Luker open his lips, and put a question: 'How did you come by this?' Only six words! But what volumes of meaning in them!

Mr Godfrey Ablewhite began a story. Mr Luker opened his lips again, and only said three words, this time. 'That won't do!'

Mr Godfrey Ablewhite began another story. Mr Luker wasted no more words on him. He got up, and rang the bell for the servant to show the gentleman out.

Upon this compulsion, Mr Godfrey made an effort, and came out with a new and amended version of the affair, to the following effect.

After privately slipping the laudanum into your brandy and water, he wished you good night, and went into his own room. It was the next room to yours; and the two had a door of communication between them. On entering his own room Mr Godfrey (as he supposed) closed his door. His money troubles kept him awake. He sat, in his dressing-gown and slippers, for nearly an hour, thinking over his position. Just as he was preparing to get into bed, he heard you, talking to yourself, in your own room, and going to the door of communication, found that he had not shut it as he supposed.

He looked into your room to see what was the matter. He discovered you with the candle in your hand, just leaving your bed-chamber. He heard you say to yourself, in a voice quite unlike your own voice, 'How do I know? The Indians may be hidden in the house.'

Up to that time, he had simply supposed himself (in giving you the laudanum) to be helping to make you the victim of a harmless practical joke. It now occurred to him, that the laudanum had taken some effect on you, which had not been foreseen by the doctor, any more than by himself. In the fear of an accident happening he followed you softly to see what you would do.

He followed you to Miss Verinder's sitting-room, and saw you go in. You left the door open. He looked through the crevice thus produced, between the door and the post, before he ventured into the room himself.

In that position, he not only detected you in taking the Diamond out of the drawer—he also detected Miss Verinder, silently watching you from her bedroom, through her open door. His own eyes satisfied him that *she* saw you take the Diamond, too.

Before you left the sitting-room again, you hesitated a little. Mr Godfrey took advantage of this hesitation to get back again to his bedroom before you came out, and discovered him. He had barely got back, before you got back too. You saw him (as he supposes) just as he was passing through the door of communication. At any rate, you called to him in a strange, drowsy voice.

He came back to you. You looked at him in a dull sleepy way. You put the Diamond into his hand. You said to him, 'Take it back, Godfrey, to your father's bank. It's safe there—it's not safe here.' You turned away unsteadily, and put on your dressing-gown. You sat down in the large arm-chair in your room. You said, '*I* can't take it back to the bank. My head's like lead—and I can't feel my feet under me.' Your head sank on the back of the chair—you heaved a heavy sigh—and you fell asleep.

Mr Godfrey Ablewhite went back, with the Diamond, into his own room. His statement is, that he came to no conclusion, at that time—except that he would wait, and see what happened in the morning.

When the morning came, your language and conduct showed that you were absolutely ignorant of what you had said and done overnight. At the same time, Miss Verinder's language and conduct showed that she was resolved to say nothing (in mercy to you) on her side. If Mr Godfrey Ablewhite chose to keep the Diamond, he might do so with perfect impunity. The Moonstone stood between him and ruin. He put the Moonstone into his pocket.

V

This was the story told by your cousin (under pressure of necessity) to Mr Luker.

Mr Luker believed the story to be, as to all main essentials, true—on this ground, that Mr Godfrey Ablewhite was too great a fool to have invented it. Mr Bruff and I agree with Mr Luker, in considering this test of the truth of the story to be a perfectly reliable one.

The next question, was the question of what Mr Luker would do in the matter of the Moonstone. He proposed the following terms, as the only terms on which he would consent to mix himself up with what was (even in *his* line of business) a doubtful and dangerous transaction.

Mr Luker would consent to lend Mr Godfrey Ablewhite the sum of two thousand pounds, on condition that the Moonstone was to be deposited with him as a pledge. If, at the expiration of one year from that date, Mr Godfrey Ablewhite paid three thousand pounds to Mr Luker, he was to receive back the Diamond, as a pledge redeemed. If he failed to produce the money at the expiration of the year, the pledge (otherwise the Moonstone) was to be considered as forfeited to Mr Luker—who would, in this latter case, generously make Mr Godfrey a present of certain promissory notes of his (relating to former dealings) which were then in the money-lender's possession.

It is needless to say, that Mr Godfrey indignantly refused to listen to these monstrous terms. Mr Luker thereupon, handed him back the Diamond, and wished him good night.

Your cousin went to the door, and came back again. How was he to be sure that the conversation of that evening would be kept strictly secret between his friend and himself?

Mr Luker didn't profess to know how. If Mr Godfrey had accepted his terms, Mr Godfrey would have made him an accomplice, and might have counted on his silence as on a certainty. As things were, Mr Luker must be guided by his own interests. If awkward inquiries were made, how could he be expected to compromise himself, for the sake of a man who had declined to deal with him?

Receiving this reply, Mr Godfrey Ablewhite did, what all animals (human and otherwise) do, when they find themselves caught in a trap. He looked about him in a state of helpless despair. The day of the month, recorded on a neat little card in a box on the money-lender's chimney-piece, happened to attract his eye. It was the twenty third of June. On the twenty-fourth, he had three hundred pounds to pay to the young gentleman for whom he was trustee, and no chance of raising the money, except the chance that Mr Luker had offered to him. But for this miserable obstacle, he might have taken the Diamond to Amsterdam, and have made a marketable commodity of it, by having it cut up into separate stones. As matters stood, he had no choice but to accept Mr Luker's terms. After all, he had a year at his disposal, in which to raise the three hundred pounds—and a year is a long time.

Mr Luker drew out the necessary documents on the spot. When they were signed, he gave Mr Godfrey Ablewhite two cheques. One, dated June 23rd, for three hundred pounds. Another, dated a week on, for the remaining balance—seventeen hundred pounds.

How the Moonstone was trusted to the keeping of Mr Luker's bankers, and how the Indians treated Mr Luker and Mr Godfrey (after that had been done) you know already.

The next event in your cousin's life refers again to Miss Verinder. He proposed marriage to her for the second time—and (after having been accepted) he consented, at her request, to consider the marriage as broken off. One of his reasons for making this concession has been penetrated by Mr Bruff. Miss Verinder had only a life interest in her mother's property—and there was no raising the twenty thousand pounds on *that*.

But you will say, he might have saved the three thousand pounds, to redeem the pledged Diamond, if he had married. He might have done so certainly—supposing neither his wife, nor her guardians and trustees, objected to his anticipating more than half of the income at his disposal, for some unknown purpose, in the first year of his marriage. But even if he got over this obstacle, there was another waiting for him in the background. The lady at the Villa had heard of his contemplated marriage. A superb woman, Mr Blake, of the sort that are not to be trifled with—the sort with the light complexion and the Roman nose. She felt the utmost contempt for Mr Godfrey Ablewhite. It would be silent contempt, if he made a handsome provision for her. Otherwise, it would be contempt with a tongue to it. Miss Verinder's life interest allowed him no more hope of raising the 'provision' than of raising the twenty thousand pounds. He couldn't marry—he really couldn't marry, under all the circumstances.

How he tried his luck again with another lady, and how *that* marriage also broke down on the question of money, you know already. You also know of the legacy of five thousand pounds, left to him shortly afterwards, by one of those many admirers among the soft sex whose good graces this fascinating man had contrived to win. That legacy (as event has proved) led him to his death.

I have ascertained that when he went abroad, on getting his five thousand pounds, he went to Amsterdam. There he made all the necessary arrangements for having the Diamond cut into separate stones. He came back (in disguise), and redeemed the Moonstone, on the appointed day. A few days were allowed to elapse (as a precaution agreed to by both parties) before the jewel was actually taken out of the bank. If he had got safe with it to Amsterdam, there would have been just time between July 'forty-nine, and February 'fifty (when the young gentleman came of age) to cut the Diamond, and to make a marketable commodity (polished or unpolished) of the separate stones. Judge from this, what motives he had to run the risk which he actually ran. It was 'neck or nothing' with him—if ever it was 'neck or nothing' with a man yet.

I have only to remind you, before closing this Report, that there is a chance of laying hands on the Indians, and of recovering the Moonstone yet. They are now (there is every reason to believe) on their passage to Bombay, in an East Indiaman. The ship (barring accidents) will touch at no other port on her way out; and the authorities at Bombay (already communicated with by letter, overland) will be prepared to board the vessel, the moment she enters the harbour.

I have the honour to remain, dear sir, your obedient servant, RICHARD CUFF (late sergeant in the Detective Force, Scotland Yard, London).*

* NOTE.—Wherever the Report touches on the events of the birthday, or of the three days that followed it, compare with Betteredge's Narrative, chapters VIII to XIII.

SEVENTH NARRATIVE

In a letter from Mr Candy

FRIZINGHALL, Wednesday, September 26TH, 1849.—Dear Mr Franklin Blake, you will anticipate the sad news I have to tell you, on finding your letter to Ezra Jennings returned to you, unopened, in this enclosure. He died in my arms, at sunrise, on Wednesday last.

I am not to blame for having failed to warn you that his end was at hand. He expressly forbade me to write to you. 'I am indebted to Mr Franklin Blake,' he said, 'for having seen some happy days. Don't distress him, Mr Candy—don't distress him.'

His sufferings, up to the last six hours of his life, were terrible to see. In the intervals of remission, when his mind was clear, I entreated him to tell me of any relatives of his to whom I might write. He asked to be forgiven for refusing anything to *me*. And then he said—not bitterly—that he would die as he had lived, forgotten and unknown. He maintained that resolution to the last. There is no hope now of making any discoveries concerning him. His story is a blank.

The day before he died, he told me where to find all his papers. I brought them to him on his bed. There was a little bundle of old letters which he put aside. There was his unfinished book. There was his Diary—in many locked volumes. He opened the volume for this year, and tore out, one by one, the pages relating to the time when you and he were together. 'Give those,' he said, 'to Mr Franklin Blake. In years to come, he may feel an interest in looking back at what is written there.' Then he clasped his hands, and prayed God fervently to bless you, and those dear to you. He said he should like to see you again. But the next moment he altered his mind. 'No,' he answered, when I offered to write. 'I won't distress him! I won't distress him!'

At his request I next collected the other papers—that is to say, the bundle of letters, the unfinished book, and the volumes of the Diary—and enclosed them all in one wrapper, sealed with my own seal. 'Promise,' he said, 'that you will put this into my coffin with your own hand; and that you will see that no other hand touches it afterwards.'

I gave him my promise. And the promise has been performed.

He asked me to do one other thing for him—which it cost me a hard struggle to comply with. He said, 'Let my grave be forgotten. Give me your word of honour that you will allow no monument of any sort—not even the commonest tombstone—to mark the place of my burial. Let me sleep, nameless. Let me rest, unknown.' When I tried to plead with him to alter his resolution, he became for the first, and only time, violently agitated. I could not bear to see it; and I gave way. Nothing but a little grass mound marks the place of his rest. In time, the tombstones will rise round it. And the people who come after us will look and wonder at the name-less grave.

As I have told you, for six hours before his death his sufferings ceased. He dozed a little. I think he dreamed. Once or twice he smiled. A woman's name, as I suppose—the name of 'Ella'—was often on his lips at this time. A few minutes before the end came he asked me to lift him on his pillow, to see the sun rise through the window. He was very weak. His head fell on my shoulder. He whispered, 'It's coming!' Then he said, 'Kiss me!' I kissed his forehead. On a sudden he lifted his head. The sunlight touched his face. A beautiful expression, an angelic expression, came over it. He cried out three times, 'Peace! peace! peace!' His head sank back again on my shoulder, and the long trouble of his life was at an end.

So he has gone from us. This was, as I think, a great man—though the world never knew him. He bore a hard life bravely. He had the sweetest temper I have ever met with. The loss of him makes me feel very lonely. Perhaps I have never been quite myself again since my illness. Sometimes, I think of giving up my practice, and going away, and trying what some of the foreign baths and waters will do for me.

It is reported here, that you and Miss Verinder are to be married next month. Please to accept my best congratulations.

The pages of my poor friend's Journal are waiting for you at my house—sealed up, with your name on the wrapper. I was afraid to trust them to the post.

My best respects and good wishes attend Miss Verinder. I remain, dear Mr Franklin Blake, truly yours, THOMAS CANDY.

EIGHTH NARRATIVE

Contributed by Gabriel Betteredge

I AM the person (as you remember no doubt) who led the way in these pages, and opened the story. I am also the person who is left behind, as it were, to close the story up.

Let nobody suppose that I have any last words to say here concerning the Indian Diamond. I hold that unlucky jewel in abhorrence—and I refer you to other authority than mine, for such news of the Moonstone as you may, at the present time, be expected to receive. My purpose, in this place, is to state a fact in the history of the family, which has been passed over by everybody, and which I won't allow to be disrespectfully smothered up in that way. The fact to which I allude is—the marriage of Miss Rachel and Mr Franklin Blake. This interesting event took place at our house in

Yorkshire, on Tuesday, October ninth, eighteen hundred and forty-nine. I had a new suit of clothes on the occasion. And the married couple went to spend the honeymoon in Scotland.

Family festivals having been rare enough at our house, since my poor mistress's death, I own—on this occasion of the wedding—to having (towards the latter part of the day) taken a drop too much on the strength of it.

If you have ever done the same sort of thing yourself you will understand and feel for me. If you have not, you will very likely say, 'Disgusting old man! why does he tell us this?' The reason why is now to come.

Having, then, taken my drop (bless you! you have got your favourite vice, too; only your vice isn't mine, and mine isn't yours), I next applied the one infallible remedy—that remedy being, as you know, *Robinson Crusoe*. Where I opened that unrivalled book, I can't say. Where the lines of print at last left off running into each other, I know, however, perfectly well. It was at page three hundred and eighteen—a domestic bit concerning Robinson Crusoe's marriage, as follows:

'With those Thoughts, I considered my new Engagement, that I had a Wife'—(Observe! so had Mr Franklin!)—'one Child born'—(Observe again! that might yet be Mr Franklin's case, too!)—'and my Wife then'—What Robinson Crusoe's wife did, or did not do, 'then,' I felt no desire to discover. I scored the bit about the Child with my pencil, and put a morsel of paper for a mark to keep the place; 'Lie you there,' I said, 'till the marriage of Mr Franklin and Miss Rachel is some months older—and then we'll see!'

The months passed (more than I had bargained for), and no occasion presented itself for disturbing that mark in the book. It was not till this present month of November, eighteen hundred and fifty, that Mr Franklin came into my room, in high good spirits, and said, 'Betteredge! I have got some news for you! Something is going to happen in the house, before we are many months older.'

'Does it concern the family, sir?' I asked.

'It decidedly concerns the family,' says Mr Franklin.

'Has your good lady anything to do with it, if you please, sir?'

'She has a great deal to do with it,' says Mr Franklin, beginning to look a little surprised.

'You needn't say a word more, sir,' I answered. 'God bless you both! I'm heartily glad to hear it.'

Mr Franklin stared like a person thunderstruck. 'May I venture to inquire where you got your information?' he asked. 'I only got mine (imparted in the strictest secrecy) five minutes since.'

Here was an opportunity of producing *Robinson Crusoe*! Here was a chance of reading that domestic bit about the child which I had marked on the day of Mr Franklin's marriage! I read those miraculous words with an emphasis which did them justice, and then I looked him severely in the face. '*Now*, sir, do you believe in *Robinson Crusoe*?' I asked, with a solemnity, suitable to the occasion.

'Betteredge!' says Mr Franklin, with equal solemnity, 'I'm convinced at last.' He shook hands with me—and I felt that I had converted him.

With the relation of this extraordinary circumstance, my reappearance in these pages comes to an end. Let nobody laugh at the unique anecdote here related. You are welcome to be as merry as you please over everything else I have written. But when I write of *Robinson Crusoe*, by the Lord it's serious—and I request you to take it accordingly!

When this is said, all is said. Ladies and gentlemen, I make my bow, and shut up the story.

EPILOGUE
THE FINDING OF THE DIAMOND

====

I

The statement of Sergeant Cuff's man (1849).

ON the twenty-seventh of June last, I received instructions from Sergeant Cuff to follow three men; suspected of murder, and described as Indians. They had been seen on the Tower Wharf that morning, embarking on board the steamer bound for Rotterdam.

I left London by a steamer belonging to another company, which sailed on the morning of Thursday the twenty-eighth. Arriving at Rotterdam, I succeeded in finding the commander of the Wednesday's steamer. He informed me that the Indians had certainly been passengers on board his vessel—but as far as Gravesend only. Off that place, one of the three had inquired at what time they would reach Calais. On being informed that the steamer was bound to Rotterdam, the spokesman of the party expressed the greatest surprise and distress at the mistake which he and his two friends had made. They were all willing (he said) to sacrifice their passage money, if the commander of the steamer would only put them ashore. Commiserating their position, as foreigners in a strange land, and knowing no reason for detaining them, the commander signalled for a shore boat, and the three men left the vessel.

This proceeding of the Indians having been plainly resolved on before-hand, as a means of preventing their being traced, I lost no time in returning to England. I left the steamer at Gravesend, and discovered that the Indians had gone from that place to London. Thence, I again traced them as having left for Plymouth. Inquiries made at Plymouth proved that they had sailed, forty-eight hours previously, in the *Bewley Castle*, East Indiaman, bound direct to Bombay.

On receiving this intelligence, Sergeant Cuff caused the authorities at Bombay to be communicated with, overland—so that the vessel might be boarded by the police immediately on her entering the port. This step having been taken, my connection with the matter came to an end. I have heard nothing more of it since that time.

II

The statement of the Captain (1849).

I AM requested by Sergeant Cuff to set in writing certain facts, concerning three men (believed to be Hindoos) who were passengers, last summer, in the ship *Bewley Castle*, bound for Bombay direct, under my command.

The Hindoos joined us at Plymouth. On the passage out I heard no complaint of their conduct. They were berthed in the forward part of the vessel. I had but few occasions myself of personally noticing them.

In the latter part of the voyage, we had the misfortune to be becalmed for three days and nights, off the coast of India. I have not got the ship's journal to refer to, and I cannot now call to mind the latitude and longitude. As to our position, therefore, I am only able to state generally that the currents drifted us in towards the land, and that when the wind found us again, we reached our port in twenty-four hours afterwards.

The discipline of a ship (as all seafaring persons know) becomes relaxed in a long calm. The discipline of my ship became relaxed. Certain gentlemen among the passengers got some of the smaller boats lowered, and amused themselves by rowing about, and swimming, when the sun at evening time was cool enough to let them divert themselves in that way. The boats when done with ought to have been slung up again in their places. Instead of this they were left moored to the ship's side. What with the heat, and what with the vexation of the weather, neither officers nor men seemed to be in heart for their duty while the calm lasted.

On the third night, nothing unusual was heard or seen by the watch on deck. When the morning came, the smallest of the boats was missing—and the three Hindoos were next reported to be missing too.

If these men had stolen the boat shortly after dark (which I have no doubt they did), we were near enough to the land to make it vain to send in pursuit of them, when the discovery was made in the morning. I have no doubt they got ashore, in that calm weather (making all due allowance for fatigue and clumsy rowing), before daybreak.

On reaching our port I there learnt, for the first time, the reason these passengers had for seizing their opportunity of escaping from the ship. I could only make the same statement to the authorities which I have made here. They considered me to blame for allowing the discipline of the vessel to be relaxed. I have expressed my regret on this score to them, and to my owners. Since that time, nothing has been heard to my knowledge of the three Hindoos. I have no more to add to what is here written.

III

The statement of Mr Murthwaite (1850).
(In a letter to Mr Bruff.)

HAVE you any recollection, my dear sir, of a semi-savage person whom you met out at dinner, in London, in the autumn of 'forty-eight? Permit me to remind you that the person's name was Murthwaite, and that you and he had a long conversation together after dinner. The talk related to an Indian Diamond, called the Moonstone, and to a conspiracy then in existence to get possession of the gem.

Since that time, I have been wandering in Central Asia. Thence I have drifted back to the scene of some of my past adventures in the north and north-west of India. About a fortnight since, I found myself in a certain district or province (but little known to Europeans) called Kattiawar.

Here an adventure befel me, in which (incredible as it may appear) you are personally interested.

In the wild regions of Kattiawar (and how wild they are, you will understand, when I tell you that even the husbandmen plough the land, armed to the teeth), the population is fanatically devoted to the old Hindoo religion—to the ancient worship of Bramah and Vishnu. The few Mahometan families, thinly scattered about the villages in the interior, are afraid to taste meat of any kind. A Mahometan even suspected of killing that sacred animal, the cow, is, as a matter of course, put to death without mercy in these parts by the pious Hindoo neighbours who surround him. To strengthen the religious enthusiasm of the people, two of the most famous shrines of Hindoo pilgrimage are contained within the boundaries of Kattiawar. One of them is Dwarka, the birthplace of the god Krishna. The other is the sacred city of Somnauth—sacked, and destroyed, as long since as the eleventh century, by the Mahometan conqueror, Mahmoud of Ghizni.

Finding myself, for the second time, in these romantic regions, I resolved not to leave Kattiawar, without looking once more on the magnificent desolation of Somnauth. At the place where I planned to do this, I was (as nearly as I could calculate it) some three days distant, journeying on foot, from the sacred city.

I had not been long on the road, before I noticed that other people—by twos and threes—appeared to be travelling in the same direction as myself.

To such of these as spoke to me, I gave myself out as a Hindoo-Boodhist, from a distant province, bound on a pilgrimage. It is needless to say that my dress was of the sort to carry out this description. Add, that I know the language as well as I know my own, and that I am lean enough and brown enough to make it no easy matter to detect my European origin—and you will understand that I passed muster with the people readily: not as one of themselves, but as a stranger from a distant part of their own country.

On the second day, the number of Hindoos travelling in my direction had increased to fifties and hundreds. On the third day, the throng had swollen to thousands; all slowly converging to one point—the city of Somnauth.

A trifling service which I was able to render to one of my fellow-pilgrims, during the third day's journey, proved the means of introducing me to certain Hindoos of the higher caste. From these men I learnt that the multitude was on its way to a great religious ceremony, which was to take place on a hill at a little distance from Somnauth. The ceremony was in honour of the god of the Moon; and it was to be held at night.

The crowd detained us as we drew near to the place of celebration. By the time we reached the hill the moon was high in the heaven. My Hindoo friends possessed some special privileges which enabled them to gain access to the shrine. They kindly allowed me to accompany them. When we arrived at the place, we found the shrine hidden from our view by a curtain hung between two magnificent trees. Beneath the trees a flat projection of rock jutted out, and formed a species of natural platform. Below this, I stood, in company with my Hindoo friends.

Looking back down the hill, the view presented the grandest spectacle of Nature and Man, in combination, that I have ever seen. The lower slopes of the eminence melted imperceptibly into a grassy plain, the place of the meeting of three rivers. On one side, the graceful winding of the waters stretched away, now visible, now hidden by trees, as far as the eye could see. On the other, the waveless ocean slept in the calm of the night. People this lovely scene with tens of thousands of human creatures, all dressed in white, stretching down the sides of the hill, overflowing into the plain, and fringing the nearer banks of the winding rivers. Light this halt of the pilgrims by the wild red flames of cressets and torches, streaming up at intervals from every part of the innumerable throng. Imagine the moonlight of the East, pouring in unclouded glory over all—and you will form some idea of the view that met me when I looked forth from the summit of the hill.

A strain of plaintive music, played on stringed instruments and flutes, recalled my attention to the hidden shrine.

I turned, and saw on the rocky platform the figures of three men. In the central figure of the three I recognised the man to whom I had spoken in England, when the Indians appeared on the terrace at Lady Verinder's house. The other two who had been his companions on that occasion were no doubt his companions also on this.

One of the spectators, near whom I was standing, saw me start. In a whisper, he explained to me the apparition of the three figures on the platform of rock.

They were Brahmins (he said) who had forfeited their caste in the service of the god. The god had commanded that their purification should be the purification by pilgrimage. On that night, the three men were to part. In three separate directions, they were to set forth as pilgrims to the shrines of India. Never more were they to look on each other's faces. Never more were they to rest on their wanderings, from the day which witnessed their separation, to the day which witnessed their death.

As those words were whispered to me, the plaintive music ceased. The three men prostrated themselves on the rock, before the curtain which hid the shrine. They rose—they looked on one another—they embraced. Then they descended separately among the people. The people made way for them in dead silence. In three different directions I saw the crowd part, at one and the same moment. Slowly the grand white mass of the people closed together again. The track of the doomed men through the ranks of their fellow mortals was obliterated. We saw them no more.

A new strain of music, loud and jubilant, rose from the hidden shrine. The crowd around me shuddered, and pressed together.

The curtain between the trees was drawn aside, and the shrine was disclosed to view.

There, raised high on a throne—seated on his typical antelope, with his four arms stretching towards the four corners of the earth—there, soared above us, dark and awful in the mystic light of heaven, the god of the Moon. And there, in the forehead of the deity, gleamed the yellow Diamond, whose splendour had last shone on me in England, from the bosom of a woman's dress!

Yes! after the lapse of eight centuries, the Moonstone looks forth once more, over the walls of the sacred city in which its story first began. How it has found its way back to its wild native land—by what accident, or by what crime, the Indians regained possession of their sacred gem, may be in your knowledge, but is not in mine. You have lost sight of it in England, and (if I know anything of this people) you have lost sight of it for ever.

So the years pass, and repeat each other; so the same events revolve in the cycles of time. What will be the next adventures of the Moonstone? Who can tell?

THE END

The Law and the Lady

NOTE ADDRESSED TO THE READER

In offering this book to you, I have no Preface to write. I have only to request that you will bear in mind certain established truths, which occasionally escape your memory when you are reading a work of fiction. Be pleased, then, to remember (First): that the actions of human beings are not invariably governed by the laws of pure reason. (Secondly): that we are by no means always in the habit (especially when we happen to be women) of bestowing our love on the objects which are the most deserving of it, in the opinions of our friends. (Thirdly and Lastly): that Characters which may not have appeared, and Events which may not have taken place, within the limits of our own individual experience, may nevertheless be perfectly natural Characters and perfectly probable Events, for all that. Having said these few words, I have said all that seems to be necessary at the present time; and I bid you cordially farewell.

W.C.

London, February 1, 1875.

THE LAW AND THE LADY

CHAPTER I

The Bride's Mistake

'FOR after this manner in the old time the holy women also, who trusted in God, adorned themselves, being in subjection unto their own husbands; even as Sarah obeyed Abraham, calling him lord; whose daughters ye are, as long as ye do well, and are not afraid with any amazement.'

Concluding the Marriage Service of the Church of England in those well-known words, my Uncle Starkweather shut up his book, and looked at me across the altar rails with a hearty expression of interest on his broad red face. At the same time my aunt, Mrs Starkweather, standing by my side, tapped me smartly on the shoulder, and said,

'Valeria, you are married!'

Where were my thoughts? What had become of my attention? I was too bewildered to know. I started and looked at my new husband. He seemed to be almost as much bewildered as I was. The same thought had, as I believe, occurred to us both at the same moment. Was it really possible—in spite of his mother's opposition to our marriage—that we were Man and Wife? My Aunt Starkweather settled the question by a second tap on my shoulder.

'Take his arm!' she whispered in the tone of a woman who had lost all patience with me.

I took his arm.

'Follow your uncle.'

Holding fast by my husband's arm, I followed my uncle and the curate who had assisted him at the marriage.

The two clergymen led us into the vestry. The church was in one of the dreary quarters of London, situated between the City and the West End; the day was dull; the atmosphere was heavy and damp. We were a melancholy little wedding party, worthy of the dreary neighbourhood and the dull day. No relatives or friends of my husband's were present; his family, as I have already hinted, disapproved of his marriage. Except my uncle and my aunt, no other relations appeared on my side. I had lost both my parents, and I had but few friends. My dear father's faithful old clerk, Benjamin, attended the wedding to 'give me away,' as the phrase is. He had known me from a child, and, in my forlorn position, he was as good as a father to me.

The last ceremony left to be performed was, as usual, the signing of the marriage-register. In the confusion of the moment (and in the absence of any information to guide me) I committed a mistake—ominous, in my Aunt Starkweather's opinion, of evil to come. I signed my married instead of my maiden name.

'What!' cried my uncle, in his loudest and cheeriest tones, 'you have forgotten your own name already? Well! well! let us hope you will never repent parting with it so readily. Try again, Valeria—try again.'

With trembling fingers I struck the pen through my first effort and wrote my maiden name, very badly indeed, as follows:-

When it came to my husband's turn I noticed, with surprise, that *his* hand trembled too, and that *he* produced a very poor specimen of his customary signature:-

My aunt, on being requested to sign, complied under protest. 'A bad beginning!' she said, pointing to my first unfortunate signature with the feather-end of her pen. 'I say with my husband—I hope you may not live to regret it.'

Even then, in the days of my ignorance and my innocence, that curious outbreak of my aunt's superstition produced a certain uneasy sensation in my mind. It was a consolation to me to feel the reassuring pressure of my husband's hand. It was an indescribable relief to hear my uncle's hearty voice wishing me a happy life at parting. The good man had left his north-country Vicarage (my home since the death of my parents) expressly to read the service at my marriage; and he and my aunt had arranged to return by the mid-day train. He folded me in his great strong arms, and he gave me a kiss which must certainly have been heard by the idlers waiting for the bride and bridegroom outside the church door.

'I wish you health and happiness, my love, with all my heart. You are old enough to choose for yourself, and—no offence, Mr Woodville, you and I are new friends—and I pray God, Valeria, it may turn out that you have chosen well. Our house will be dreary enough without you; but I don't complain, my dear. On the contrary, if this change in your life makes you happier, I rejoice. Come! come! don't cry, or you will set your aunt off—and it's no joke at her time of life. Besides, crying will spoil your beauty. Dry your eyes and look in the glass there, and you will see that I am right. Good-bye, child—and God bless you!'

He tucked my aunt under his arm, and hurried out. My heart sank a little, dearly as I loved my husband, when I had seen the last of the true friend and protector of my maiden days.

The parting with old Benjamin came next. 'I wish you well, my dear; don't forget me,' was all he said. But the old days at home came back on me at those few words. Benjamin always dined with us on Sundays in my father's time, and always brought some little present with him for his master's child. I was very near to 'spoiling my beauty' (as my uncle had put it) when I offered the old man my cheek to kiss, and heard him sigh to himself, as if he too was not quite hopeful about my future life.

My husband's voice roused me, and turned my mind to happier thoughts. 'Shall we go, Valeria?' he asked.

I stopped him on our way out, to take advantage of my uncle's advice. In other words, to see how I looked in the glass over the vestry fireplace.

What does the glass show me?

The glass shows a tall and slender young woman of three-and-twenty years of age. She is not at all the sort of person who attracts attention in the street, seeing that she fails to exhibit the popular yellow hair and the popular painted cheeks. Her hair is black; dressed, in these later days (as it was dressed years since to please her father), in broad ripples drawn back from the forehead, and gathered into a simple knot behind (like the hair of the Venus de' Medici), so as to show the neck beneath. Her complexion is pale: except in moments of violent agitation there is no colour to be seen in her face. Her eyes are of so dark a blue that they are generally mistaken for black. Her eyebrows are well enough in form, but they are too dark, and too strongly marked. Her nose just inclines towards the aquiline bend, and is considered a little too large by persons difficult to please in the matter of noses. The mouth, her best feature, is very delicately shaped, and is capable of presenting great varieties of expression. As to the face in general, it is too narrow and too long at the lower part; too broad and too low in the higher regions of the eyes and the head. The whole picture, as reflected in the glass, represents a woman of some elegance, rather too pale, and rather too sedate and serious in her moments of silence and repose—in short, a person who fails to strike the ordinary observer at first sight; but who gains in general estimation, on a second, and sometimes even on a third, view. As for her dress, it studiously conceals, instead of proclaiming, that she has been married that morning. She wears a grey Cashmere tunic trimmed with grey silk, and having a skirt of the same material and colour beneath it. On her head is a bonnet to match, relieved by a quilling of white muslin, with one deep red rose, as a morsel of positive colour, to complete the effect of the whole dress.

Have I succeeded or failed in describing the picture of myself which I see in the glass? It is not for me to say. I have done my best to keep clear of the two vanities—the vanity of depreciating, and the vanity of praising, my own personal appearance. For the rest, well written or badly written, thank Heaven it is done!

And whom do I see in the glass, standing by my side?

I see a man who is not quite so tall as I am, and who has the misfortune of looking older than his years. His forehead is prematurely bald. His big chestnut-coloured beard and his long overhanging moustache are already streaked with grey. He has the colour in his face which my face wants, and the firmness in his figure which my figure wants. He looks at me with the tenderest and gentlest eyes (of a light brown) that I ever saw in the countenance of a man. His smile is rare and sweet; his manner, perfectly quiet and retiring, has yet a latent persuasiveness in it, which is (to women) irresistibly winning. He just halts a little in his walk, from the effect of an injury received in past years, when he was a soldier serving in India, and he carries a thick bamboo cane, with a curious crutch handle (an old favourite), to help himself along whenever he gets on his feet, indoors or out. With this one little drawback (if it *is* a drawback), there is nothing infirm or old or awkward about him; his slight limp when he walks has (perhaps to my partial eyes) a certain quaint grace of its own, which is pleasanter to see than the unrestrained activity of other men. And last, and best of all, I love him! I love him! I love him! And there is an end of my portrait of my husband on our wedding-day.

The glass has told me all I want to know. We leave the vestry at last.

The sky, cloudy since the morning, has darkened while we have been in the church, and the rain is beginning to fall heavily. The idlers outside stare at us grimly under their umbrellas, as we pass through their ranks, and hasten into our carriage. No cheering; no sunshine; no flowers strewn in our path; no grand breakfast; no genial speeches; no bridesmaids; no father's or mother's blessing. A dreary wedding—there is no denying it—and (if Aunt Starkweather is right) a bad beginning as well!

A *coupé* has been reserved for us at the railway station. The attentive porter, on the look-out for his fee, pulls down the blinds over the side windows of the carriage, and shuts out all prying eyes in that way. After what seems to be an interminable delay the train starts. My husband winds his arm round me. 'At last!' he whispers, with love in his eyes that no words can utter, and presses me to him gently. My arm steals round his neck; my eyes answer his eyes. Our lips meet in the first long lingering kiss of our married life.

Oh, what recollections of that journey rise in me as I write! Let me dry my eyes, and shut up my paper for the day.

CHAPTER II

The Bride's Thoughts

WE had been travelling for a little more than an hour, when a change passed insensibly over us both.

Still sitting close together, with my hand in his, with my head on his shoulder, little by little we fell insensibly into silence. Had we already exhausted the narrow yet eloquent vocabulary of love? Or had we determined by unexpressed consent, after enjoying the luxury of passion that speaks, to try the deeper and finer rapture of passion that thinks? I can hardly determine; I only know that a time came when under some strange influence our lips were closed towards each other. We travelled along, each of us absorbed in our own reverie. Was he thinking exclusively of me—as I was thinking exclusively of him? Before the journey's end I had my doubts. At a little later time I knew for certain, that his thoughts, wandering far away from his young wife, were all turned inward on his own unhappy self.

For me, the secret pleasure of filling my mind with him while I felt him by my side, was a luxury in itself.

I pictured in my thoughts our first meeting in the neighbourhood of my uncle's house.

Our famous north-country trout-stream wound its flashing and foaming way through a ravine in the rocky moorland. It was a windy, shadowy evening. A heavily clouded sunset lay low and red in the west. A solitary angler stood casting his fly, at a turn in the stream, where the backwater lay still and deep under an overhanging bank. A girl (myself) standing on the bank, invisible to the fisherman beneath, waited eagerly to see the trout rise.

The moment came; the fish took the fly.

Sometimes on the little level strip of sand at the foot of the bank; sometimes (when the stream turned again) in the shallower water rushing over its rocky bed, the angler followed the captured trout, now letting the line run out, and now winding it in again, in the difficult and delicate process of 'playing' the fish. Along the bank I followed, to watch the contest

of skill and cunning between the man and the trout. I had lived long enough
with my uncle Starkweather to catch some of his enthusiasm for field sports,
and to learn something, especially, of the angler's art. Still following the
stranger, with my eyes intently fixed on every movement of his rod and line,
and with not so much as a chance fragment of my attention to spare for the
rough path along which I was walking, I stepped by chance on the loose
overhanging earth at the edge of the bank, and fell into the stream in an
instant.

The distance was trifling; the water was shallow; the bed of the river was
(fortunately for me) of sand. Beyond the fright and the wetting I had nothing
to complain of. In a few moments I was out of the water and up again, very
much ashamed of myself, on the firm ground. Short as the interval was, it
proved long enough to favour the escape of the fish. The angler had heard
my first instinctive cry of alarm, had turned, and had thrown aside his rod
to help me. We confronted each other for the first time, I on the bank and
he in the shallow water below. Our eyes encountered, and I verily believe
our hearts encountered at the same moment. This I know for certain, we
forgot our breeding as lady and gentleman; we looked at each other in
barbarous silence.

I was the first to recover myself. What did I say to him?

I said something about my not being hurt, and then something more,
urging him to run back, and try if he might not yet recover the fish.

He went back unwillingly. He returned to me—of course, without the fish.
Knowing how bitterly disappointed my uncle would have been in his place,
I apologized very earnestly. In my eagerness to make atonement I even
offered to show him a spot where he might try again, lower down the
stream.

He would not hear of it; he entreated me to go home and change my wet
dress. I cared nothing for the wetting, but I obeyed him without knowing
why.

He walked with me. My way back to the Vicarage was his way back to
the inn. He had come to our parts, he told me, for the quiet and retirement
as much as for the fishing. He had noticed me once or twice from the
window of his room at the inn. He asked if I was not the Vicar's daughter.

I set him right. I told him that the Vicar had married my mother's sister,
and that the two had been father and mother to me since the death of my
parents. He asked if he might venture to call on Doctor Starkweather the
next day: mentioning the name of a friend of his, with whom he believed
the Vicar to be acquainted. I invited him to visit us, as if it had been my
house; I was spell-bound under his eyes and under his voice. I had fancied,
honestly fancied, myself to have been in love, often and often before this
time. Never, in any other man's company, had I felt as I now felt in the
presence of *this* man. Night seemed to fall suddenly over the evening

landscape when he left me. I leaned against the Vicarage gate. I could not breathe; I could not think; my heart fluttered as if it would fly out of my bosom—and all this for a stranger! I burned with shame; but oh, in spite of it all, I was so happy!

And now, when little more than a few weeks had passed since that first meeting, I had him by my side; he was mine for life! I lifted my head from his bosom to look at him. I was like a child with a new toy—I wanted to make sure that he was really my own.

He never moved in his corner of the carriage. Was he deep in his own thoughts? and were they thoughts of Me?

I laid down my head again softly, so as not to disturb him. My mind wandered backward once more, and showed me another picture in the golden gallery of the past.

The garden of the Vicarage formed the new scene. The time was night. We had met together in secret. We were walking slowly to and fro, out of sight of the house; now in the shadowy paths of the shrubbery, now in the lovely moonlight on the open lawn.

We had long since owned our love, and devoted our lives to each other. Already our interests were one; already we shared the pleasures and the pains of life. I had gone out to meet him that night with a heavy heart, to seek comfort in his presence, and to find encouragement in his voice. He noticed that I sighed when he first took me in his arms, and he gently turned my head towards the moonlight, to read my trouble in my face. How often he had read my happiness there in the earlier days of our love!

'You bring bad news, my angel,' he said, lifting my hair tenderly from my forehead as he spoke. 'I see the lines here which tell me of anxiety and distress. I almost wish I loved you less dearly, Valeria.'

'Why?'

'I might give you back your freedom. I have only to leave this place, and your uncle would be satisfied, and you would be relieved from all the cares that are pressing on you now.'

'Don't speak of it, Eustace! If you want me to forget my cares, say you love me more dearly than ever.'

He said it in a kiss. We had a moment of exquisite forgetfulness of the hard ways of life—a moment of delicious absorption in each other. I came back to realities, fortified and composed, rewarded for all that I had gone through, ready to go through it all over again for another kiss. Only give a woman love, and there is nothing she will not venture, suffer, and do.

'Have they been raising fresh objections to our marriage?' he asked, as we slowly walked on again.

'No; they have done with objecting. They have remembered at last that I am of age, and that I can choose for myself. They have been pleading with me, Eustace, to give you up. My aunt, whom I thought rather a hard woman, has been crying—for the first time in my experience of her. My uncle, always kind and good to me, has been kinder and better than ever. He has told me that if I persist in becoming your wife I shall not be deserted on my wedding-day. Wherever we may marry he will be there to read the service, and my aunt will go to the church with me. But he entreats me to consider seriously what I am doing—to consent to a separation from you for a time—to consult other people on my position towards you, if I am not satisfied with his opinion. Oh, my darling, they are as anxious to part us, as if you were the worst, instead of the best, of men!'

'Has anything happened since yesterday to increase their distrust of me?' he asked.

'Yes.'

'What is it?'

'You remember referring my uncle to a friend of yours and of his?'

'Yes. To Major Fitz-David.'

'My uncle has written to Major Fitz-David.'

'Why?'

He pronounced that one word in a tone so utterly unlike his natural tone that his voice sounded quite strange to me.

'You won't be angry, Eustace, if I tell you?' I said. 'My uncle, as I understood him, had several motives for writing to the Major. One of them was to inquire if he knew your mother's address.'

Eustace suddenly stood still.

I paused at the same moment, feeling that I could venture no further without the risk of offending him.

To speak the truth, his conduct, when he first mentioned our engagement to my uncle, had been (so far as appearances went) a little flighty and strange. The Vicar had naturally questioned him about his family. He had answered that his father was dead; and he had consented, though not very readily, to announce his contemplated marriage to his mother. Informing us that she too lived in the country, he had gone to see her—without more particularly mentioning her address. In two days he had returned to the Vicarage with a very startling message. His mother intended no disrespect to me or my relatives; but she disapproved so absolutely of her son's marriage that she (and the members of her family, who all agreed with her) would refuse to be present at the ceremony, if Mr Woodville persisted in keeping his engagement with Doctor Starkweather's niece. Being asked to explain this extraordinary communication, Eustace had told us that his mother and his sisters were bent on his marrying another lady, and that they were bitterly mortified and disappointed by his choosing a stranger to the family. This explanation was enough for me; it implied, so far as I was concerned, a compliment to my superior influence over Eustace, which a woman always receives with pleasure. But it failed to satisfy my uncle and my aunt. The Vicar expressed to Mr Woodville a wish to write to his mother, or to see her, on the subject of her strange message. Eustace obstinately declined to mention his mother's address, on the ground that the Vicar's interference would be utterly useless. My uncle at once drew the conclusion that the mystery about the address indicated something wrong. He refused to favour Mr Woodville's renewed proposal for my hand; and he wrote the same day to make inquiries of Mr Woodville's reference, and of his own friend—Major Fitz-David.

Under such circumstances as these, to speak of my uncle's motives was to venture on very delicate ground. Eustace relieved me from further embarrassment by asking a question to which I could easily reply.

'Has your uncle received any answer from Major Fitz-David?' he inquired.

'Yes.'

'Were you allowed to read it?' His voice sank as he said those words; his face betrayed a sudden anxiety which it pained me to see.

'I have got the answer with me to show you,' I said.

He almost snatched the letter out of my hand; he turned his back on me to read it by the light of the moon. The letter was short enough to be soon read. I could have repeated it at the time. I can repeat it now.

'DEAR VICAR,—Mr Eustace Woodville is quite correct in stating to you that he is a gentleman by birth and position, and that he inherits (under his deceased father's will) an independent fortune of two thousand a year.

'Always yours,

'LAWRENCE FITZ-DAVID.'

'Can any one wish for a plainer answer than that?' Eustace asked, handing the letter back to me.

'If *I* had written for information about you,' I answered, 'it would have been plain enough for me.'

'Is it not plain enough for your uncle?'

'No.'

'What does he say?'

'Why need you care to know, my darling?'

'I want to know, Valeria. There must be no secret between us in this matter. Did your uncle say anything when he showed you the Major's letter?'

'Yes.'

'What was it?'

'My uncle told me that his letter of inquiry filled three pages, and he bade me observe that the Major's answer contained one sentence only. He said, "I volunteered to go to Major Fitz-David and talk the matter over. You see, he takes no notice of my proposal. I asked him for the address of Mr Woodville's mother. He passes over my request, as he has passed over my proposal—he studiously confines himself to the shortest possible statement of bare facts. Use your own common sense, Valeria. Isn't this rudeness rather remarkable on the part of a man who is a gentleman by birth and breeding, and who is also a friend of mine?'

Eustace stopped me there.

'Did you answer your uncle's question?' he asked.

'No,' I replied. 'I only said that I did not understand the Major's conduct.'

'And what did your uncle say next? If you love me, Valeria, tell me the truth.'

'He used very strong language, Eustace. He is an old man; you must not be offended with him.'

'I am not offended. What did he say?'

'He said, "Mark my words! There is something under the surface in connexion with Mr Woodville, or with his family, to which Major Fitz-David is not at liberty to allude. Properly interpreted, Valeria, that letter is a warning. Show it to Mr Woodville, and tell him (if you like) what I have just told you——" '

Eustace stopped me again.

'You are sure your uncle said those words?' he asked, scanning my face attentively in the moonlight.

'Quite sure. But I don't say what my uncle says. Pray don't think that!'

He suddenly pressed me to his bosom, and fixed his eyes on mine. His look frightened me.

'Good-bye, Valeria!' he said. 'Try and think kindly of me, my darling, when you are married to some happier man.'

He attempted to leave me. I clung to him in an agony of terror that shook me from head to foot.

'What do you mean?' I asked, as soon as I could speak. 'I am yours and yours only. What have I said, what have I done, to deserve those dreadful words?'

'We must part, my angel,' he answered, sadly. 'The fault is none of yours; the misfortune is all mine. My Valeria! how can you marry a man who is an object of suspicion to your nearest and dearest friends? I have led a dreary life. I have never found in any other woman the sympathy with me, the sweet comfort and companionship, that I find in you. Oh, it is hard to lose you! it is hard to go back again to my unfriended life! I must make the sacrifice, love, for your sake. I know no more why that letter is what it is than you do. Will your uncle believe me? Will your friends believe me? One last kiss, Valeria! Forgive me for having loved you—passionately, devotedly loved you. Forgive me—and let me go!'

I held him desperately, recklessly. His eyes put me beside myself; his words filled me with a frenzy of despair.

'Go where you may,' I said, 'I go with you! Friends—reputation—I care nothing who I lose, or what I lose. Oh, Eustace, I am only a woman—don't madden me! I can't live without you. I must and will be your wife!' Those wild words were all I could say before the misery and madness in me forced their way outward in a burst of sobs and tears.

He yielded. He soothed me with his charming voice; he brought me back to myself with his tender caresses. He called the bright heaven above us to witness that he devoted his whole life to me. He vowed—oh, in such solemn, such eloquent words!—that his one thought, night and day, should be to prove himself worthy of such love as mine. And had he not nobly redeemed the pledge? Had not the betrothal of that memorable night been followed by the betrothal at the altar, by the vows before God? Ah, what a life was before me! What more than mortal happiness was mine!

Again, I lifted my head from his bosom to taste the dear delight of seeing him by my side—my life, my love, my husband, my own!

Hardly awakened yet from the absorbing memories of the past to the sweet realities of the present, I let my cheek touch his cheek, I whispered to him softly, 'Oh, how I love you! how I love you!'

The next instant I started back from him. My heart stood still. I put my hand up to my face. What did I feel on my cheek? (*I* had not been weeping—I was too happy.) What did I feel on my cheek? A tear!

His face was still averted from me. I turned it towards me, with my own hands, by main force.

I looked at him—and saw my husband, on our wedding day, with his eyes full of tears.

CHAPTER III

Ramsgate Sands

EUSTACE succeeded in quieting my alarm. But I can hardly say that he succeeded in satisfying my mind as well.

He had been thinking, he told me, of the contrast between his past and his present life. Bitter remembrances of the years that had gone had risen in his memory, and had filled him with melancholy misgivings of his capacity to make my life with him a happy one. He had asked himself if he had not met me too late? if he was not already a man soured and broken by the disappointments and disenchantments of the past? Doubts such as these, weighing more and more heavily on his mind, had filled his eyes with the tears which I had discovered—tears which he now entreated me, by my love for him, to dismiss from my memory for ever.

I forgave him, comforted him, revived him—but there were moments when the remembrance of what I had seen troubled me in secret, and when I asked myself if I really possessed my husband's full confidence as he possessed mine.

We left the train at Ramsgate.

The favourite watering-place was empty; the season was just over. Our arrangements for the wedding-tour included a cruise to the Mediterranean in a yacht lent to Eustace by a friend. We were both fond of the sea, and we were equally desirous, considering the circumstances under which we had married, of escaping the notice of friends and acquaintances. With this object in view, having celebrated our marriage privately in London, we had decided on instructing the sailing-master of the yacht to join us at Ramsgate. At this port (when the season for visitors was at an end) we could embark far more privately than at the popular yachting stations situated in the Isle of Wight.

Three days passed—days of delicious solitude, of exquisite happiness, never to be forgotten, never to be lived over again, to the end of our lives.

Early on the morning of the fourth day, just before sunrise, a trifling incident happened, which was noticeable, nevertheless, as being strange to me in my experience of myself.

I awoke, suddenly and unaccountably, from a deep and dreamless sleep, with an all-pervading sensation of nervous uneasiness, which I had never felt before. In the old days at the Vicarage, my capacity as a sound sleeper had been the subject of many a little harmless joke. From the moment when my head was on the pillow I had never known what it was to wake until the maid knocked at my door. At all seasons and times the long and uninterrupted repose of a child was the repose that I enjoyed.

And now I had awakened, without any assignable cause, hours before my usual time. I tried to compose myself to sleep again. The effort was useless. Such a restlessness possessed me that I was not even able to lie still in the bed. My husband was sleeping soundly by my side. In the fear of disturbing him I rose, and put on my dressing gown and slippers.

I went to the window. The sun was just rising over the calm grey sea. For a while, the majestic spectacle before me exercised a tranquillising influence on the irritable condition of my nerves. But, ere long, the old restlessness returned upon me. I walked slowly to and fro in the room, until I was weary of the monotony of the exercise. I took up a book and laid it aside again. My attention wandered; the author was powerless to recall it. I got on my feet once more, and looked at Eustace, and admired him and loved him in his tranquil sleep. I went back to the window, and wearied of the beautiful morning. I sat down before the glass, and looked at myself. How haggard and worn I was already, through waking before my usual time! I rose again, not knowing what to do next. The confinement to the four walls of the room began to be intolerable to me. I opened the door that led into my husband's dressing-room, and entered it, to try if the change would relieve me.

The first object that I noticed was his dressing-case, open on the toilette table.

I took out the bottles and pots and brushes and combs, the knives and scissors in one compartment, the writing materials in another. I smelt the perfumes and pomatums; I busily cleaned and dusted the bottles with my handkerchief as I took them out. Little by little I completely emptied the dressing-case. It was lined with blue velvet. In one corner I noticed a tiny strip of loose blue silk. Taking it between my finger and my thumb, and, drawing it upward, I discovered that there was a false bottom to the case, forming a secret compartment for letters and papers. In my strange condition—capricious, idle, inquisitive—it was an amusement to me to take out the papers, just as I had taken out everything else.

I found some receipted bills, which failed to interest me; some letters, which it is needless to say I laid aside, after only looking at the addresses; and, under all, a photograph, face downwards, with writing on the back of it. I looked at the writing, and saw these words:

'To my dear son, Eustace.'

His mother! the woman who had so obstinately and so mercilessly opposed herself to our marriage!

I eagerly turned the photograph, expecting to see a woman with a stern, ill-tempered, forbidding countenance. To my surprise, the face showed the remains of great beauty; the expression, though remarkably firm, was yet winning, tender, and kind. The grey hair was arranged in rows of little quaint old-fashioned curls on either side of the head, under a plain lace cap. At one corner of the mouth there was a mark, apparently a mole, which added to the characteristic peculiarity of the face. I looked and looked, fixing the portrait thoroughly in my mind. This woman, who had almost insulted me and my relatives, was, beyond all doubt or dispute, so far as appearances went, a person possessing unusual attractions—a person whom it would be a pleasure and a privilege to know.

I fell into deep thought. The discovery of the photograph quieted me as nothing had quieted me yet.

The striking of a clock downstairs in the hall warned me of the flight of time. I carefully put back all the objects in the dressing-case (beginning with the photograph) exactly as I had found them, and returned to the bedroom. As I looked at my husband still sleeping peacefully, the question forced itself into my mind, What had made that genial, gentle mother of his so sternly bent on parting us? so harshly and pitilessly resolute in asserting her disapproval of our marriage?

Could I put my question openly to Eustace when he woke? No; I was afraid to venture that length. It had been tacitly understood between us that we were not to speak of his mother—and, besides, he might be angry if he knew that I had opened the private compartment in his dressing-case.

After breakfast that morning we had news at last of the yacht. The vessel was safely moored in the inner harbour, and the sailing-master was waiting to receive my husband's orders on board.

Eustace hesitated at asking me to accompany him to the yacht. It would be necessary for him to examine the inventory of the vessel, and to decide questions, not very interesting to a woman, relating to charts and barometers, provisions and water. He asked me if I would wait for his return. The day was enticingly beautiful, and the tide was on the ebb. I pleaded for a walk on the sands; and the landlady at our lodgings, who happened to be in the room at the time, volunteered to accompany me and take care of me. It was agreed that we should walk as far as we felt inclined, in the direction of Broadstairs, and that Eustace should follow and meet us on the sands, after having completed his arrangements on board the yacht.

In half an hour more, the landlady and I were out on the beach.

The scene on that fine autumn morning was nothing less than enchanting. The brisk breeze, the brilliant sky, the flashing blue sea, the sun-bright cliffs and the tawny sands at their feet, the gliding procession of ships on the great marine highway of the English Channel—it was all so exhilarating, it was all so delightful, that I really believe if I had been by myself I could have danced for joy like a child. The one drawback to my happiness was the landlady's untiring tongue. She was a forward, good-natured, empty-headed woman, who persisted in talking, whether I listened or not; and who had a habit of perpetually addressing me as 'Mrs Woodville,' which I thought a little over-familiar as an assertion of equality from a person in her position to a person in mine.

We had been out, I should think, more than half-an-hour when we overtook a lady walking before us on the beach.

Just as we were about to pass the stranger she took her handkerchief from her pocket, and accidentally drew out with it a letter which fell, unnoticed by her, on the sand. I was nearest to the letter, and I picked it up and offered it to the lady.

The instant she turned to thank me, I stood rooted to the spot. There was the original of the photographic portrait in the dressing-case! there was my husband's mother, standing face to face with me! I recognised the quaint little grey curls, the gentle genial expression, the mole at the corner of the mouth. No mistake was possible. His mother herself!

The old lady, naturally enough, mistook my confusion for shyness. With perfect tact and kindness she entered into conversation with me. In another minute I was walking side by side with the woman who had sternly repudiated me as a member of her family; feeling, I own, terribly discomposed, and not knowing in the least whether I ought, or ought not, to assume the responsibility, in my husband's absence, of telling her who I was.

In another minute my familiar landlady, walking on the other side of my mother-in-law, decided the question for me. I happened to say that I supposed we must by that time be near the end of our walk—the little watering-place called Broadstairs. 'Oh, no, Mrs Woodville!' cried the irrepressible woman, calling me by my name, as usual; 'nothing like so near as you think!'

I looked with a beating heart at the old lady.

To my unutterable amazement, not the faintest gleam of recognition appeared in her face. Old Mrs Woodville went on talking to young Mrs Woodville just as composedly as if she had never heard her own name before in her life!

My face and manner must have betrayed something of the agitation that I was suffering. Happening to look at me at the end of her next sentence, the old lady started, and said in her kindly way,—

'I am afraid you have over-exerted yourself. You are very pale—you are looking quite exhausted. Come and sit down here; let me lend you my smelling-bottle.'

I followed her, quite helplessly, to the base of the cliff. Some fallen fragments of chalk offered us a seat. I vaguely heard the voluble landlady's expressions of sympathy and regret; I mechanically took the smelling-bottle which my husband's mother offered to me, *after hearing my name*, as an act of kindness to a stranger.

If I had only had myself to think of, I believe I should have provoked an explanation on the spot. But I had Eustace to think of. I was entirely ignorant of the relations, hostile or friendly, which existed between his mother and himself. What could I do?

In the mean time, the old lady was still speaking to me with the most considerate sympathy. She too was fatigued, she said. She had passed a weary night at the bedside of a near relative, staying at Ramsgate. Only the day before, she had received a telegram announcing that one of her sisters was seriously ill. She was herself, thank God, still active and strong; and she had thought it her duty to start at once for Ramsgate. Towards the morning the state of the patient had improved. 'The doctor assures me, ma'am, that there is no immediate danger; and I thought it might revive me, after my long night at the bedside, if I took a little walk on the beach.'

I heard the words—I understood what they meant—but I was still too bewildered and too intimidated by my extraordinary position to be able to continue the conversation. The landlady had a sensible suggestion to make; the landlady was the next person who spoke.

'Here is a gentleman coming,' she said to me, pointing in the direction of Ramsgate. 'You can never walk back. Shall we ask him to send a chaise from Broadstairs to the gap in the cliff?'

The gentleman advanced a little nearer.

The landlady and I recognised him at the same moment. It was Eustace coming to meet us, as we had arranged. The irrepressible landlady gave the freest expression to her feelings. 'Oh, Mrs Woodville, ain't it lucky? here is Mr Woodville himself!'

Once more I looked at my mother-in-law. Once more the name failed to produce the slightest effect on her. Her sight was not so keen as ours; she had not recognised her son yet. *He* had young eyes like us, and he recognised his mother. For a moment he stopped like a man thunderstruck. Then he came on—his face white with suppressed emotion, his eyes fixed on his mother.

'You here?' he said to her.

'How do you do, Eustace?' she quietly rejoined. 'Have *you* heard of your aunt's illness, too? Did you know she was staying at Ramsgate?'

He made no answer. The landlady, drawing the inevitable inference from the words she had just heard, looked from me to my mother-in-law in a state of amazement, which paralysed even *her* tongue. I waited, with my eyes on my husband, to see what he would do. If he had delayed acknowledging me another moment, the whole future course of my life might have been altered—I should have despised him.

He did *not* delay. He came to my side and took my hand.

'Do you know who this is?' he said to his mother.

She answered, looking at me with a courteous bend of her head,—

'A lady I met on the beach, Eustace, who kindly restored to me a letter that I dropped. I think I heard the name' (she turned to the landlady): 'Mrs Woodville, was it not?'

My husband's fingers unconsciously closed on my hand with a grasp that hurt me. He set his mother right, it is only just to say, without one cowardly moment of hesitation.

'Mother,' he said to her, very quietly, 'this lady is my wife.'

She had hitherto kept her seat. She now rose slowly and faced her son in silence. The first expression of surprise passed from her face. It was succeeded by the most terrible look of mingled indignation and contempt that I ever saw in a woman's eyes.

'I pity your wife,' she said.

With those words, and no more, lifting her hand she waved him back from her, and went on her way again, as we had first found her, alone.

CHAPTER IV

On the Way Home

LEFT by ourselves, there was a moment of silence amongst us. Eustace spoke first.

'Are you able to walk back?' he said to me. 'Or shall we go on to Broadstairs, and return to Ramsgate by the railway?'

He put those questions as composedly, so far as his manner was concerned, as if nothing remarkable had happened. But his eyes and his lips betrayed him. They told me that he was suffering keenly in secret. The extraordinary scene that had just passed, far from depriving me of the last remains of my courage, had strung up my nerves and restored my self-possession. I must have been more or less than woman if my self-respect had not been wounded, if my curiosity had not been wrought to the highest pitch, by the extraordinary conduct of my husband's mother when Eustace presented me to her. What was the secret of her despising him, and pitying me? Where was the explanation of her incomprehensible apathy when my name was twice pronounced in her hearing? Why had she left us, as if the bare idea of remaining in our company was abhorrent to her? The foremost interest of my life was now the interest of penetrating these mysteries. Walk? I was in such a fever of expectation that I felt as if I could have walked to the world's end, if I could only keep my husband by my side, and question him on the way!

'I am quite recovered,' I said. 'Let us go back, as we came, on foot.'

Eustace glanced at the landlady. The landlady understood him.

'I won't intrude my company on you, sir,' she said, sharply. 'I have some business to do at Broadstairs—and, now I am so near, I may as well go on. Good morning, Mrs Woodville.'

She laid a marked emphasis on my name; and she added one significant look at parting, which (in the preoccupied state of my mind at that moment) I entirely failed to comprehend. There was neither time nor opportunity to ask her what she meant. With a stiff little bow, addressed to Eustace, she left us as his mother had left us; taking the way to Broadstairs, and walking rapidly.

At last, we were alone.

I lost no time in beginning my inquiries; I wasted no words in prefatory phrases. In the plainest terms I put the question to him,—

'What does your mother's conduct mean?'

Instead of answering, he burst into a fit of laughter—loud, coarse, hard laughter, so utterly unlike any sound I had ever yet heard issue from his lips, so strangely and shockingly foreign to his character as I understood it, that I stood still on the sands, and openly remonstrated with him.

'Eustace! you are not like yourself,' I said. 'You almost frighten me.'

He took no notice. He seemed to be pursuing some pleasant train of thought just started in his mind.

'So like my mother!' he exclaimed, with the air of a man who felt irresistibly diverted by some humorous idea of his own. 'Tell me all about it, Valeria!'

'Tell *you?*' I repeated. 'After what has happened, surely it is your duty to enlighten *me.*'

'You don't see the joke?' he said.

'I not only fail to see the joke,' I rejoined, 'I see something in your mother's language and your mother's behaviour which justifies me in asking you for a serious explanation.'

'My dear Valeria! if you understood my mother as well as I do, a serious explanation of her conduct would be the last thing in the world that you would expect from me. The idea of taking my mother seriously!' He burst out laughing again. 'My darling! you don't know how you amuse me.'

It was all forced; it was all unnatural. He, the most delicate, the most refined of men—a gentleman in the highest sense of the word—was coarse and loud and vulgar! My heart sank under a sudden sense of misgiving which, with all my love for him, it was impossible to resist. In unutterable distress and alarm I asked myself: 'Is my husband beginning to deceive me? is he acting a part, and acting it badly, before we have been married a week?'

I set myself to win his confidence in a new way. He was evidently determined to force his own point of view on me. I determined, on my side, to accept his point of view.

'You tell me I don't understand your mother,' I said, gently. 'Will you help me to understand her?'

'It is not easy to help you to understand a woman who doesn't understand herself,' he answered. 'But I will try. The key to my poor dear mother's character is, in one word—Eccentricity.'

If he had picked out the most inappropriate word in the whole Dictionary to describe the lady whom I had met on the beach, 'Eccentricity' would have been that word. A child who had seen what I saw, who had heard what I heard, would have discovered that he was trifling—grossly, recklessly trifling—with the truth.

'Bear in mind what I have said,' he proceeded; 'and, if you want to understand my mother, do what I asked you to do a minute since—tell me all about it. How came you to speak to her, to begin with?'

'Your mother told you, Eustace. I was walking just behind her, when she dropped a letter by accident——'

'No accident,' he interposed. 'The letter was dropped on purpose.'

'Impossible!' I exclaimed. 'Why should your mother drop the letter on purpose?'

'Use the key to her character, my dear. Eccentricity! My mother's odd way of making acquaintance with you.'

'Making acquaintance with me? I have just told you that I was walking behind her. She could not have known of the existence of such a person as myself until I spoke to her first.'

'So you suppose, Valeria.'

'I am certain of it.'

'Pardon me—you don't know my mother as I do.'

I began to lose all patience with him.

'Do you mean to tell me,' I said, 'that your mother was out on the sands to-day for the express purpose of making acquaintance with Me?'

'I have not the slightest doubt of it,' he answered, coolly.

'Why she didn't even recognise my name!' I burst out. 'Twice over, the landlady called me Mrs Woodville in your mother's hearing—and, twice over, I declare to you on my word of honour, it failed to produce the slightest impression on her. She looked, and acted, as if she had never heard her own name before in her life.'

' "Acted" is the right word,' he said, just as composedly as before. 'The women on the stage are not the only women who can act. My mother's object was to make herself thoroughly acquainted with you, and to throw you off your guard by speaking in the character of a stranger. It is so like her to take that roundabout way of satisfying her curiosity about a daughter-in-law whom she disapproves of! If I had not joined you when I did, you would have been examined and cross-examined about yourself and about me; and you would innocently have answered under the impression that you were speaking to a chance acquaintance. There is my mother all over! She is your enemy, remember—not your friend: she is not in search of your merits but of your faults. And you wonder why no impression was produced on her when she heard you addressed by your name! Poor innocent! I can tell you this—you only discovered my mother in her own character, when I put an end to the mystification by presenting you to each other. You saw how angry she was; and now you know why.'

I let him go on without saying a word. I listened—oh, with such a heavy heart! with such a crushing sense of disenchantment and despair! The idol of my worship; the companion, guide, protector of my life—had he fallen so low? could he stoop to such shameless prevarication as this?

Was there one word of truth in all that he had said to me? Yes! If I had not discovered his mother's portrait, it was certainly true that I should not have known, not even vaguely suspected, who she really was. Apart from this, the rest was lying; clumsy lying which said one thing at least for him, that he was not accustomed to falsehood and deceit. Good Heavens—if my husband was to be believed, his mother must have tracked us to London; tracked us to the church; tracked us to the railway station; tracked us to Ramsgate! To assert that she knew me by sight as the wife of Eustace, and that she had waited on the sands, and dropped her letter for the express purpose of making acquaintance with me, was also to assert every one of these monstrous improbabilities to be facts that had actually happened!

I could say no more. I walked by his side in silence feeling the miserable conviction that there was an abyss in the shape of a family secret between my husband and me. In the spirit, if not in the body, we were separated— after a married life of barely four days!

'Valeria,' he asked, 'have you nothing to say to me?'

'Nothing.'

'Are you not satisfied with my explanation?'

I detected a slight tremor in his voice as he put that question. The tone was, for the first time since we had spoken together, a tone that my experience associated with him in certain moods of his which I had already learnt to know well. Among the hundred thousand mysterious influences which a man exercises over the woman who loves him, I doubt if there is any more irresistible to her than the influence of his voice. I am not one of those women who shed tears on the smallest provocation: it is not in my temperament, I suppose. But when I heard that little natural change in his tone, my mind went back (I can't say why) to the happy day when I first owned that I loved him. I burst out crying.

He suddenly stood still, and took me by the hand. He tried to look at me.

I kept my head down and my eyes on the ground. I was ashamed of my weakness and my want of spirit. I was determined not to look at him.

In the silence that followed, he suddenly dropped on his knees at my feet, with a cry of despair that cut through me like a knife.

'Valeria! I am vile—I am false—I am unworthy of you. Don't believe a word of what I have been saying—lies, lies, cowardly contemptible lies! You don't know what I have gone through; you don't know how I have been tortured. Oh, my darling, try not to despise me! I must have been beside myself when I spoke to you as I did. You looked hurt; you looked offended; I didn't know what to do. I wanted to spare you even a moment's pain—I wanted to hush it up, and have done with it. For God's sake don't ask me to tell you any more! My love! my angel! it's something between my mother and me; it's nothing that need disturb you, it's nothing to anybody now. I love you, I adore you; my whole heart and soul are yours. Be satisfied with that. Forget what has happened. You shall never see my mother again. We will leave this place to-morrow. We will go away in the yacht. Does it matter where we live, so long as we live for each other? Forgive and forget! Oh, Valeria, Valeria, forgive and forget!'

Unutterable misery was in his face; unutterable misery was in his voice. Remember this. And remember that I loved him.

'It is easy to forgive,' I said sadly. 'For your sake, Eustace, I will try to forget.'

I raised him gently as I spoke. He kissed my hands, with the air of a man who was too humble to venture on any more familiar expression of his gratitude than that. The sense of embarrassment between us, as we slowly walked on again, was so unendurable that I actually cast about in my mind for a subject of conversation as if I had been in the company of a stranger! In mercy to *him*, I asked him to tell me about the yacht.

He seized on the subject as a drowning man seizes on the hand that rescues him.

On that one poor little topic of the yacht, he talked, talked, talked, as if his life depended upon his not being silent for an instant on the rest of his way back. To me, it was dreadful to hear him. I could estimate what he was suffering, by the violence which he—ordinarily a silent and thoughtful man—was now doing to his true nature and to the prejudices and habits of his life. With the greatest difficulty I preserved my self-control, until we reached the door of our lodgings. There, I was obliged to plead fatigue, and ask him to let me rest for a little while in the solitude of my own room.

'Shall we sail to-morrow?' he called after me suddenly, as I ascended the stairs.

Sail with him to the Mediterranean the next day? Pass weeks and weeks absolutely alone with him, in the narrow limits of a vessel, with his horrible secret parting us in sympathy further and further from each other day by day? I shuddered at the thought of it.

'To-morrow is rather a short notice,' I said. 'Will you give me a little longer time to prepare for the voyage?'

'Oh, yes—take any time you like,' he answered, not (as I thought) very willingly. 'While you are resting—there are still one or two little things to be settled—I think I will go back to the yacht. Is there anything I can do for you, Valeria, before I go?'

'Nothing—thank you, Eustace.'

He hastened away to the harbour. Was he afraid of his own thoughts, if he were left by himself in the house? Was the company of the sailing-master and the steward better than no company at all?

It was useless to ask. What did I know about him or his thoughts? I locked myself into my room.

CHAPTER V

The Landlady's Discovery

I SAT DOWN, and tried to compose my spirits. Now, or never, was the time to decide what was my duty to my husband and my duty to myself to do next.

The effort was beyond me. Worn out in mind and body alike, I was perfectly incapable of pursuing any regular train of thought. I vaguely felt—if I left things as they were—that I could never hope to remove the shadow which now rested on the married life that had begun so brightly. We might live together, so as to save appearances. But to forget what had happened, or to feel satisfied with my position, was beyond the power of my will. My tranquillity as a woman—perhaps my dearest interests as a wife—depended absolutely on penetrating the mystery of my mother-in-law's conduct, and on discovering the true meaning of the wild words of penitence and self-reproach which my husband had addressed to me on our way home.

So far as I could advance towards realising my position—and no farther. When I asked myself what was to be done next, hopeless confusion, maddening doubt, filled my mind, and transformed me into the most listless and helpless of living women.

I gave up the struggle. In dull, stupid, obstinate despair, I threw myself on my bed, and fell, from sheer fatigue, into a broken, uneasy sleep.

I was awakened by a knock at the door of my room.

Was it my husband? I started to my feet as the idea occurred to me. Was some new trial of my patience and my fortitude at hand? Half nervously, half irritably, I asked who was there.

The landlady's voice answered me.

'Can I speak to you for a moment, if you please?'

I opened the door. There is no disguising it—though I loved him so dearly; though I had left home and friends for his sake—it was a relief to me, at that miserable time, to know that Eustace had not returned to the house.

The landlady came in, and took a seat, without waiting to be invited, close by my side. She was no longer satisfied with merely asserting herself as my equal. Ascending another step on the social ladder, she took her stand on the platform of patronage, and charitably looked down on me as an object of pity.

'I have just returned from Broadstairs,' she began. 'I hope you will do me the justice to believe that I sincerely regret what has happened?'

I bowed, and said nothing.

'As a gentlewoman myself,' proceeded the landlady—'reduced by family misfortunes to let lodgings, but still a gentlewoman—I feel sincere sympathy with you. I will even go further than that. I will take it on myself to say that I don't blame *you*. No, no. I noticed that you were as much shocked and surprised at your mother-in-law's conduct as I was; and that is saying a great deal, a great deal indeed. However, I have a duty to perform. It is disagreeable, but it is not the less a duty on that account. I am a single woman; not from want of opportunities of changing my condition—I beg you will understand that—but from choice. Situated as I am, I receive only the most respectable persons into my house. There must be no mystery about the positions of *my* lodgers. Mystery in the position of a lodger carries with it—what shall I say? I don't wish to offend you—I will say, a certain Taint. Very well. Now I put it to your own common sense. Can a person in my position be expected to expose herself to—Taint? I make these remarks in a sisterly and Christian spirit. As a lady yourself (I will even go the length of saying a cruelly-used lady) you will, I am sure, understand——'

I could endure it no longer. I stopped her there.

'I understand,' I said, 'that you wish to give us notice to quit your lodgings. When do you want us to go?'

The landlady held up a long, lean, red hand, in sorrowful and sisterly protest.

'No,' she said. 'Not that tone! not those looks! It's natural you should be annoyed; it's natural you should be angry. But do—now do please try and control yourself. I put it to your own common sense (we will say a week for the notice to quit)—why not treat me like a friend? You don't know what a sacrifice, what a cruel sacrifice I have made—entirely for your sake.'

'You!' I exclaimed. 'What sacrifice?'

'What sacrifice?' repeated the landlady. 'I have degraded myself as a gentlewoman. I have forfeited my own self-respect.' She paused for a moment, and suddenly seized me by the hand, in a perfect frenzy of friendship. 'Oh, my poor dear,' cried this intolerable person, 'I have discovered everything! A villain has deceived you. You are no more married than I am!'

I snatched my hand out of hers, and rose angrily from my chair.

'Are you mad?' I asked.

The landlady raised her eyes to the ceiling, with the air of a person who had deserved martyrdom, and who submitted to it cheerfully.

'Yes,' she said. 'I begin to think I *am* mad—mad to have devoted myself to an ungrateful woman, to a person who doesn't appreciate a sisterly and Christian sacrifice of self. Well! I won't do it again. Heaven forgive me—I won't do it again!'

'Do what again?' I asked.

'Follow your mother-in-law,' cried the landlady, suddenly dropping the character of a martyr, and assuming the character of a vixen in its place. 'I blush when I think of it. I followed that most respectable person every step of the way to her own door.'

Thus far, my pride had held me up. It sustained me no longer. I dropped back again into my chair, in undisguised dread of what was coming next.

'I gave you a look when I left you on the beach,' pursued the landlady; growing louder and louder, and redder and redder as she went on. 'A grateful woman would have understood that look. Never mind! I won't do it again. I overtook your mother-in-law at the gap in the cliff. I followed her—oh, how I feel the disgrace of it *now!*—I followed her to the station at Broadstairs. She went back by train to Ramsgate. *I* went back by train to Ramsgate. She walked to her lodgings. *I* walked to her lodgings. Behind her. Like a dog. Oh, the disgrace of it! Providentially, as I then thought—I don't know what to think of it now—the landlord of the house happened to be a friend of mine, and happened to be at home. We have no secrets from each other, where lodgers are concerned. I am in a position to tell you, madam, what your mother-in-law's name really is. She knows nothing about any such person as Mrs Woodville, for an excellent reason. Her name is *not* Woodville. Her name (and consequently her son's name) is Macallan. Mrs Macallan, widow of the late General Macallan. Yes! your husband is *not* your husband. You are neither maid, wife, nor widow. You are worse than nothing, madam—and you leave my house.'

I stopped her as she opened the door to go out. She had roused *my* temper by this time. The doubt that she had cast on my marriage was more than mortal resignation could endure.

'Give me Mrs Macallan's address,' I said.

The landlady's anger receded into the background, and the landlady's astonishment appeared in its place.

'You don't mean to tell me you are going to the old lady yourself?' she said.

'Nobody but the old lady can tell me what I want to know,' I answered. 'Your discovery (as you call it) may be enough for *you*; it is not enough for *me*. How do we know that Mrs Macallan may not have been twice married; and that her first husband's name may not have been Woodville?'

The landlady's astonishment subsided in its turn, and the landlady's curiosity succeeded as the ruling influence of the moment. Substantially, as I have already said of her, she was a good-natured woman. Her fits of temper (as is usual with good-natured people) were of the hot and the short-lived sort; easily roused and easily appeased.

'Stop a bit!' she stipulated. 'If I give you the address, will you promise to tell me everything your mother-in-law says to you when you come back?'

I gave the required promise, and received the address in return.

'No malice,' said the landlady, suddenly resuming all her old familiarity with me.

'No malice,' I answered, with all possible cordiality on my side.

In ten minutes more I was at my mother-in-law's lodgings.

CHAPTER VI

My own Discovery

FORTUNATELY for me, the landlord did not open the door when I rang. A stupid maid-of-all-work, who never thought of asking me for my name, let me in. Mrs Macallan was at home, and had no visitors with her. Giving me this information, the maid led the way upstairs, and showed me into the drawing-room without a word of announcement.

My mother-in-law was sitting alone, near a work-table, knitting. The moment I appeared in the door-way, she laid aside her work; and, rising, signed to me with a commanding gesture of her hand to let her speak first.

'I know what you have come for,' she said. 'You have come here to ask questions. Spare yourself, and spare me. I warn you beforehand that I will not answer any questions relating to my son.'

It was firmly, but not harshly, said. I spoke firmly in my turn.

'I have not come here, madam, to ask questions about your son,' I answered. 'I have come—if you will excuse me—to ask you a question about yourself.'

She started, and looked at me keenly over her spectacles. I had evidently taken her by surprise.

'What is the question?' she inquired.

'I now know for the first time, madam, that your name is Macallan,' I said. 'Your son has married me under the name of Woodville. The only honourable explanation of this circumstance, so far as I know, is that my husband is your son by a first marriage. The happiness of my life is at stake. Will you kindly consider my position? Will you let me ask if you have been twice married, and if the name of your first husband was Woodville?'

She considered a little before she replied.

'The question is a perfectly natural one, in your position,' she said. 'But I think I had better not answer it.'

'May I ask why?'

'Certainly. If I answered you, I should only lead to other questions; and I should be obliged to decline replying to them. I am sorry to disappoint you. I repeat what I said on the beach—I have no other feeling than a feeling of sympathy towards *you*. If you had consulted me before your marriage, I should willingly have admitted you to my fullest confidence. It is now too late. You are married. I recommend you to make the best of your position, and to rest satisfied with things as they are.'

'Pardon me, madam,' I remonstrated. 'As things are, I don't know that I *am* married. All I know, unless you enlighten me, is that your son has married me under a name that is not his own. How can I be sure whether I am, or am not, his lawful wife?'

'I believe there can be no doubt that you are lawfully my son's wife,' Mrs Macallan answered. 'At any rate it is easy to take a legal opinion on the subject. If the opinion is that you are *not* lawfully married, my son (whatever his faults and failings may be) is a gentleman. He is incapable of wilfully deceiving a woman who loves and trusts him; he will do you justice. On my side, I will do you justice too. If the legal opinion is adverse to your rightful claims, I will promise to answer any questions which you may choose to put to me. As it is, I believe you to be lawfully my son's wife; and I say again, make the best of your position. Be satisfied with your husband's affectionate devotion to you. If you value your peace of mind, and the happiness of your life to come, abstain from attempting to know more than you know now.'

She sat down again with the air of a woman who had said her last word.

Further remonstrance would be useless—I could see it in her face; I could hear it in her voice. I turned round to open the drawing-room door.

'You are hard on me, madam,' I said, at parting. 'I am at your mercy, and I must submit.'

She suddenly looked up, and answered me with a flush on her kind and handsome old face.

'As God is my witness, child, I pity you from the bottom of my heart!'

After that extraordinary outburst of feeling, she took up her work with one hand, and signed to me with the other to leave her.

I bowed to her in silence, and went out.

I had entered the house, far from feeling sure of the course I ought to take in the future. I left the house, positively resolved, come what might of it, to discover the secret which the mother and son were hiding from me. As to the question of the name, I saw it now in the light in which I ought to have seen it from the first. If Mrs Macallan *had* been twice married (as I had rashly chosen to suppose) she would certainly have shown some signs of recognition, when she heard me addressed by her first husband's name. Where all else was mystery, there was no mystery here. Whatever his reasons might be, Eustace had assuredly married me under an assumed name.

Approaching the door of our lodgings, I saw my husband walking backwards and forwards before it, evidently waiting for my return. If he asked me the question, I decided to tell him frankly where I had been, and what had passed between his mother and myself.

He hurried to meet me with signs of disturbance in his face and manner.

'I have a favour to ask of you, Valeria,' he said. 'Do you mind returning with me to London by the next train?'

I looked at him. In the popular phrase, I could hardly believe my own ears.

'It's a matter of business,' he went on, 'of no interest to any one but myself; and it requires my presence in London. You don't wish to sail just yet, as I understand? I can't leave you here by yourself. Have you any objection to going to London for a day or two?'

I made no objection. I too was eager to go back.

In London, I could obtain the legal opinion which would tell me whether I was lawfully married to Eustace or not. In London, I should be within reach of the help and advice of my father's faithful old clerk. I could confide in Benjamin as I could confide in no one else. Dearly as I loved my uncle Starkweather, I shrank from communicating with him in my present need. His wife had told me that I had made a bad beginning, when I signed the wrong name in the marriage register. Shall I own it? My pride shrank from acknowledging, before the honeymoon was over, that his wife was right.

In two hours more we were on the railway again. Ah, what a contrast that second journey presented to the first! On our way to Ramsgate, everybody could see that we were a newly-wedded couple. On our way to London, nobody noticed us; nobody would have doubted that we had been married for years.

We went to a private hotel in the neighbourhood of Portland Place.

After breakfast, the next morning, Eustace announced that he must leave me to attend to his business. I had previously mentioned to him that I had some purchases to make in London. He was quite willing to let me go out alone—on the condition that I should take a carriage provided by the hotel.

My heart was heavy that morning: I felt the unacknowledged estrangement that had grown up between us very keenly. My husband opened the door to go out—and came back to kiss me before he left me by myself. That little afterthought of tenderness touched me. Acting on the impulse of the moment, I put my arm round his neck, and held him to me gently.

'My darling,' I said, 'give me all your confidence. I know that you love me. Show that you can trust me too.'

He sighed bitterly, and drew back from me—in sorrow, not in anger.

'I thought we had agreed, Valeria, not to return to that subject again,' he said. 'You only distress yourself and distress me.'

He left the room abruptly, as if he dare not trust himself to say more. It is better not to dwell on what I felt after this last repulse. I ordered the carriage at once. I was eager to find a refuge from my own thoughts in movement and change.

I drove to the shops first, and made the purchases which I had mentioned to Eustace by way of giving a reason for going out. Then I devoted myself to the object which I really had at heart. I went to old Benjamin's little villa, in the by-ways of St. John's Wood.

As soon as he had got over the first surprise of seeing me, he noticed that I looked pale and careworn. I confessed at once that I was in trouble. We sat down together by the bright fireside in his little library (Benjamin, as far as his means would allow, was a great collector of books), and there I told my old friend, frankly and truly, all that I have told here.

He was too distressed to say much. He fervently pressed my hand; he fervently thanked God that my father had not lived to hear what he had heard. Then, after a pause, he repeated my mother-in-law's name to himself, in a doubting, questioning tone.

'Macallan?' he said. 'Macallan? Where have I heard that name? Why does it sound as if it wasn't strange to me?'

He gave up pursuing the lost recollection, and asked, very earnestly, what he could do for me. I answered that he could help me in the first place to put an end to the doubt—an unendurable doubt to *me*—whether I was lawfully married or not. His energy of the old days, when he had conducted my father's business, showed itself again, the moment I said those words.

'Your carriage is at the door, my dear,' he answered. 'Come with me to my own lawyer, without wasting another moment.'

We drove to Lincoln's Inn Fields.

At my request, Benjamin put my case to the lawyer, as the case of a friend in whom I was interested. The answer was given without hesitation. I had married, honestly believing my husband's name to be the name under which I had known him. The witnesses to my marriage—my uncle, my aunt, and Benjamin—had acted, as I had acted, in perfect good faith. Under those circumstances, there was no doubt about the law. I was legally married. Macallan or Woodville, I was his wife.

This decisive answer relieved me of a heavy anxiety. I accepted my old friend's invitation to return with him to St. John's Wood, and to make my luncheon at his early dinner.

On our way back I reverted to the one other subject which was now uppermost in my mind. I reiterated my resolution to discover why Eustace had not married me under the name that was really his own.

My companion shook his head, and entreated me to consider well beforehand what I proposed doing. His advice to me—so strangely do extremes meet!—was my mother-in-law's advice, repeated almost word for word. 'Leave things as they are, my dear. In the interest of your own peace of mind, be satisfied with your husband's affection. You know that you are his wife, and you know that he loves you. Surely that is enough?'

I had but one answer to this. Life, on such conditions as my good friend had just stated, would be simply unendurable to me. Nothing could alter my resolution—for this plain reason, that nothing could reconcile me to living with my husband on the terms on which we were living now. It only rested with Benjamin to say whether he would give a helping hand to his master's daughter or not.

The old man's answer was thoroughly characteristic of him.

'Mention what you want of me, my dear,' was all he said.

We were then passing a street in the neighbourhood of Portman Square. I was on the point of speaking again, when the words were suspended on my lips. I saw my husband.

He was just descending the steps of a house—as if leaving it after a visit. His eyes were on the ground: he did not look up when the carriage passed. As the servant closed the door behind him, I noticed that the number of the house was sixteen. At the next corner I saw the name of the street. It was Vivian Place.

'Do you happen to know who lives at number sixteen, Vivian Place?' I inquired of my companion.

Benjamin started. My question was certainly a strange one, after what he had just said to me.

'No,' he replied. 'Why do you ask?'

'I have just seen Eustace leaving that house.'

'Well, my dear, and what of that?'

'My mind is in a bad way, Benjamin. Everything my husband does that I don't understand, rouses my suspicion now.'

Benjamin lifted his withered old hands, and let them drop on his knees again in mute lamentation over me.

'I tell you again,' I went on, 'my life is unendurable to me. I won't answer for what I may do, if I am left much longer to live in doubt of the one man on earth whom I love. You have had experience of the world. Suppose you were shut out from Eustace's confidence, as I am? Suppose you were as fond of him as I am, and felt your position as bitterly as I feel it—what would you do?'

The question was plain. Benjamin met it with a plain answer.

'I think I should find my way, my dear, to some intimate friend of your husband's,' he said, 'and make a few discreet inquiries in that quarter first.'

Some intimate friend of my husband's? I considered with myself. There was but one friend of his whom I knew of—my uncle's correspondent, Major Fitz-David. My heart beat fast as the name recurred to my memory. Suppose I followed Benjamin's advice? Suppose I applied to Major Fitz-David? Even if he too refused to answer my questions, my position would not be more helpless than it was now. I determined to make the attempt. The only difficulty in the way, so far, was to discover the Major's address. I had given back his letter to Doctor Starkweather, at my uncle's own request; I remembered that the address from which the Major wrote was somewhere in London; and I remembered no more.

'Thank you, old friend; you have given me an idea already,' I said to Benjamin. 'Have you got a Directory in your house.'

'No, my dear,' he rejoined, looking very much puzzled. 'But I can easily send out and borrow one.'

We returned to the Villa. The servant was sent at once to the nearest stationer's to borrow a Directory. She returned with the book, just as we sat down to dinner. Searching for the Major's name, under the letter F, I was startled by a new discovery.

'Benjamin!' I said. 'This is a strange coincidence. Look here!'

He looked where I pointed. Major Fitz-David's address was Number Sixteen, Vivian Place—the very house which I had seen my husband leaving as we passed in the carriage!

CHAPTER VII

On the Way to the Major

'YES,' said Benjamin. 'It *is* a coincidence certainly. Still——'

He stopped and looked at me. He seemed a little doubtful how I might receive what he had it in his mind to say to me next.

'Go on,' I said.

'"Still, my dear, I see nothing suspicious in what has happened,' he resumed. 'To my mind, it is quite natural that your husband, being in London, should pay a visit to one of his friends. And it's equally natural that we should pass through Vivian Place, on our way back here. This seems to be the reasonable view. What do *you* say?'

'I have told you already that my mind is in a bad way about Eustace,' I answered. '*I* say there is some motive at the bottom of his visit to Major Fitz-David. It is not an ordinary call. I am firmly convinced it is not an ordinary call!'

'Suppose we get on with our dinner?' said Benjamin, resignedly. 'Here is a loin of mutton, my dear—an ordinary loin of mutton. Is there anything suspicious in *that*? Very well, then. Show me you have confidence in the mutton; please eat. There's the wine, again. No mystery, Valeria, in that claret—I'll take my oath it's nothing but innocent juice of the grape. If we can't believe in anything else, let's believe in juice of the grape. Your good health, my dear.'

I adapted myself to the old man's genial humour as readily as I could. We ate and we drank, and we talked of bygone days. For a little while I was almost happy in the company of my fatherly old friend. Why was I not old too? Why had I not done with love—with its certain miseries; its transient delights; its cruel losses; its bitterly doubtful gains? The last autumn flowers in the window basked brightly in the last of the autumn sunlight. Benjamin's little dog digested his dinner in perfect comfort on the hearth. The parrot in the next house screeched his vocal accomplishments cheerfully. I don't doubt that it is a great privilege to be a human being. But may it not be the happier destiny to be an animal or a plant?

The brief respite was soon over; all my anxieties came back. I was once more a doubting, discontented, depressed creature, when I rose to say good-bye.

'Promise, my dear, you will do nothing rash,' said Benjamin, as he opened the door for me.

'Is it rash to go to Major Fitz-David?' I asked.

'Yes—If you go by yourself. You don't know what sort of man he is; you don't know how he may receive you. Let me try first, and pave the way, as the saying is. Trust my experience, my dear. In matters of this sort there is nothing like paving the way.'

I considered a moment. It was due to my good friend to consider before I said No.

Reflection decided me on taking the responsibility, whatever it might be, upon my own shoulders. Good or bad, compassionate or cruel, the Major was a man. A woman's influence was the safest influence to trust with him—where the end to be gained was such an end as I had in view. It was not easy to say this to Benjamin, without the danger of mortifying him. I made an appointment with the old man to call on me the next morning at the hotel, and talk the matter over again. Is it very disgraceful to me to add, that I privately determined (if the thing could be accomplished) to see Major Fitz-David in the interval?

'Do nothing rash, my dear. In your own interests, do nothing rash!'

Those were Benjamin's last words, when we parted for the day.

I found Eustace waiting for me in our sitting-room at the hotel. His spirits seemed to have revived since I had seen him last. He advanced to meet me cheerfully, with an open sheet of paper in his hand.

'My business is settled, Valeria, sooner than I had expected,' he began, gaily. 'Are your purchases all completed, fair lady? Are *you* free too?'

I had learnt already (God help me!) to distrust his fits of gaiety. I asked cautiously,

'Do you mean free for to-day?'

'Free for to-day, and to-morrow and next week, and next month—and next year, too, for all I know to the contrary,' he answered, putting his arm boisterously round my waist. 'Look here!'

He lifted the open sheet of paper which I had noticed in his hand, and held it for me to read. It was a telegram to the sailing master of the yacht, informing him that we had arranged to return to Ramsgate that evening, and that we should be ready to sail for the Mediterranean with the next tide.

'I only waited for your return,' said Eustace, 'to send the telegram to the office.'

He crossed the room, as he spoke, to ring the bell. I stopped him.

'I am afraid I can't go to Ramsgate to-day,' I said.

'Why not?' he asked, suddenly changing his tone and speaking sharply.

I dare say it will seem ridiculous to some people, but it is really true that he shook my resolution to go to Major Fitz-David, when he put his arm round me. Even a mere passing caress, from *him*, stole away my heart, and softly tempted me to yield. But the ominous alteration in his tone made another woman of me. I felt once more, and felt more strongly than ever, that, in my critical position, it was useless to stand still, and worse than useless to draw back.

'I am sorry to disappoint you,' I answered. 'It is impossible for me (as I told you at Ramsgate) to be ready to sail at a moment's notice. I want time.'

'What for?'

Not only his tone, but his look, when he put that second question, jarred on every nerve in me. He roused in my mind—I can't tell how or why—an angry sense of the indignity that he had put upon his wife in marrying her under a false name. Fearing that I should answer rashly, that I should say something which my better sense might regret, if I spoke at that moment, I said nothing. Women alone can estimate what it cost me to be silent. And men alone can understand how irritating my silence must have been to my husband.

'You want time?' he repeated. 'I ask you again—what for?'

My self-control, pushed to its extremest limits, failed me. The rash reply flew out of my lips, like a bird set free from a cage.

'I want time,' I said, 'to accustom myself to my right name.'

He suddenly stepped up to me with a dark look.

'What do you mean by your "right name"?'

'Surely you know,' I answered. 'I once thought I was Mrs Woodville. I have now discovered that I am Mrs Macallan.'

He started back at the sound of his own name, as if I had struck him—he started back and turned so deadly pale that I feared he was going to drop at my feet in a swoon. Oh, my tongue! my tongue! Why had I not controlled my miserable, mischievous woman's tongue?

'I didn't mean to alarm you, Eustace,' I said. 'I spoke at random. Pray forgive me.'

He waved his hand impatiently, as if my penitent words were tangible things—ruffling, worrying things like flies in summer—which he was putting away from him.

'What else have you discovered?' he asked, in low, stern tones.

'Nothing, Eustace.'

'Nothing?' He paused as he repeated the word, and passed his hand over his forehead in a weary way. 'Nothing, of course,' he resumed, speaking to himself, 'or she would not be here.'

He paused once more, and looked at me searchingly. 'Don't say again what you said just now,' he went on. 'For your own sake, Valeria, as well as for mine.' He dropped into the nearest chair, and said no more.

I certainly heard the warning; but the only words which really produced an impression on my mind were the words preceding it, which he had spoken to himself. He had said: 'Nothing, of course, *or she would not be here.*' If I had found out some other truth besides the truth about the name, would it have prevented me from ever returning to my husband? Was that what he meant? Did the sort of discovery that he contemplated, mean something so dreadful that it would have parted us at once and for ever? I stood by his chair in silence; and tried to find the answer to those terrible questions in his face. It used to speak to me so eloquently when it spoke of his love. It told me nothing now.

He sat for some time without looking at me, lost in his own thoughts. Then he rose on a sudden, and took his hat.

'The friend who lent me the yacht is in town,' he said. 'I suppose I had better see him, and say our plans are changed.' He tore up the telegram with an air of sullen resignation as he spoke. 'You are evidently determined not to go to sea with me,' he resumed. 'We had better give it up. I don't see what else is to be done. Do you?'

His tone was almost a tone of contempt. I was too depressed about myself, too alarmed about *him*, to resent it.

'Decide as you think best, Eustace,' I said, sadly. 'Every way, the prospect seems a hopeless one. As long as I am shut out from your confidence, it matters little whether we live on land or at sea—we cannot live happily.'

'If you could control your curiosity,' he answered, sternly, 'we might live happily enough. I thought I had married a woman who was superior to the vulgar failings of her sex. A good wife should know better than to pry into affairs of her husband's with which she has no concern.'

Surely it was hard to bear this? However, I bore it.

'Is it no concern of mine,' I asked, gently, 'when I find that my husband has not married me under his family name? Is it no concern of mine when I hear your mother say, in so many words, that she pities your wife? It is hard, Eustace, to accuse me of curiosity, because I cannot accept the unendurable position in which you have placed me. Your cruel silence is a blight on my happiness, and a threat to my future. Your cruel silence is estranging us from each other, at the beginning of our married life. And you blame me for feeling this? You tell me I am prying into affairs which are yours only? They are *not* yours only: I have my interest in them too. Oh, my darling, why do you trifle with our love and our confidence in each other? Why do you keep me in the dark?'

He answered with a stern and pitiless brevity,

'For your own good.'

I turned away from him in silence. He was treating me like a child.

He followed me. Putting one hand heavily on my shoulder, he forced me to face him once more.

'Listen to this,' he said. 'What I am now going to say to you, I say for the first, and last, time. Valeria! if you ever discover what I am now keeping from your knowledge—from that moment you live a life of torture; your tranquillity is gone. Your days will be days of terror; your nights will be full of horrid dreams—through no fault of mine, mind! through no fault of mine! Every day of your life, you will feel some new distrust, some growing fear of me—and you will be doing me the vilest injustice all the time. On my faith

as a Christian, on my honour as a man, if you stir a step further in this
matter there is an end of your happiness for the rest of your life! Think
seriously of what I have said to you; you will have time to reflect. I am going
to tell my friend that our plans for the Mediterranean are given up. I shall
not be back before the evening.' He sighed, and looked at me with
unutterable sadness. 'I love you, Valeria,' he said. 'In spite of all that has
passed, as God is my witness, I love you more dearly than ever.'

So he spoke. So he left me.

I must write the truth about myself, however strange it may appear. I
don't pretend to be able to analyse my own motives; I don't pretend even
to guess how other women might have acted in my place. It is true of _me_,
that my husband's terrible warning—all the more terrible in its mystery and
its vagueness—produced no deterrent effect on my mind: it only stimulated
my resolution to discover what he was hiding from me. He had not been
gone two minutes before I rang the bell, and ordered the carriage to take
me to Major Fitz-David's house in Vivian Place.

Walking to and fro while I was waiting—I was in such a fever of
excitement that it was impossible for me to sit still—I accidentally caught
sight of myself in the glass.

My own face startled me: it was so haggard and so wild. Could I present
myself to a stranger, could I hope to produce the necessary impression in
my favour, looking as I looked at that moment? For all I knew to the
contrary, my whole future might depend upon the effect which I produced
on Major Fitz-David at first sight. I rang the bell again, and sent a message
to one of the chambermaids to follow me to my room.

I had no maid of my own with me: the stewardess of the yacht would have
acted as my attendant, if we had held to our first arrangement. It mattered
little, so long as I had a woman to help me. The chambermaid appeared. I
can give no better idea of the disordered and desperate condition of my
mind at that time, than by owning that I actually consulted this perfect
stranger on the question of my personal appearance. She was a middle-aged
woman, with a large experience of the world and its wickedness written
legibly on her manner and on her face. I put money into the woman's hand,
enough of it to surprise her. She thanked me with a cynical smile, evidently
placing her own evil interpretation on my motive for bribing her.

'What can I do for you, ma'am?' she asked, in a confidential whisper.
'Don't speak loud! There is somebody in the next room.'

'I want to look my best,' I said; 'and I have sent for you to help me.'

'I understand, ma'am.'

'What do you understand?'

She nodded her head significantly, and whispered to me again.

'Lord bless you, I'm used to this!' she said. 'There is a gentleman in the
case. Don't mind me, ma'am. It's a way I have, I mean no harm.' She

stopped and looked at me critically. 'I wouldn't change my dress, if I were you,' she went on. 'The colour becomes you.'

It was too late to resent the woman's impertinence. There was no help for it but to make use of her. Besides, she was right about the dress. It was of a delicate maize colour, prettily trimmed with lace. I could wear nothing which suited me better. My hair, however, stood in need of some skilled attention. The chambermaid rearranged it, with a ready hand which showed that she was no beginner in the art of dressing hair. She laid down the combs and brushes, and looked at me—then looked at the toilette table, searching for something which she apparently failed to find.

'Where do you keep it?' she asked.

'What do you mean?'

'Look at your complexion, ma'am. You will frighten him if he sees you like that. A touch of colour you *must* have. Where do you keep it? What! you haven't got it? you never use it? Dear, dear, dear me!'

For a moment, surprise fairly deprived her of her self-possession! Recovering herself, she begged permission to leave me for a minute. I let her go, knowing what her errand was. She came back with a box of paints and powders; and I said nothing to check her. I saw, in the glass, my skin take a false fairness, my cheeks a false colour, my eyes a false brightness—and I never shrank from it. No! I let the odious deceit go on; I even admired the extraordinary delicacy and dexterity with which it was all done. 'Anything' (I thought to myself, in the madness of that miserable time), 'so long as it helps me to win the Major's confidence! Anything so long as I discover what those last words of my husband's really mean!'

The transformation of my face was accomplished. The chambermaid pointed with her wicked forefinger in the direction of the glass.

'Bear in mind, ma'am, what you looked like when you sent for me,' she said. 'And just see for yourself how you look now. You're the prettiest woman (of your style) in London. Ah, what a thing pearl powder is, when one knows how to use it!'

CHAPTER VIII

The Friend of the Women

I FIND it impossible to describe my sensations while the carriage was taking me to Major Fitz-David's house. I doubt, indeed, if I really felt or thought at all, in the true sense of those words.

From the moment when I had resigned myself into the hands of the chambermaid, I seemed in some strange way to have lost my ordinary identity—to have stepped out of my own character. At other times, my temperament was of the nervous and anxious sort, and my tendency was to exaggerate any difficulties that might place themselves in my way. At other times, having before me the prospect of a critical interview with a stranger, I should have considered with myself what it might be wise to pass over, and what it might be wise to say. Now, I never gave my coming interview with the Major a thought; I felt an unreasoning confidence in myself, and a blind faith in *him*. Now, neither the past nor the future troubled me; I lived unreflectingly in the present. I looked at the shops as we drove by them, and at the other carriages as they passed mine. I noticed—yes! and enjoyed—the glances of admiration which chance foot-passengers on the pavement cast at me. I said to myself, 'This looks well for my prospect of making a friend of the Major!' When we drew up at the door in Vivian Place, it is no exaggeration to say that I had but one anxiety—anxiety to find the Major at home.

The door was opened by a servant out of livery, an old man who looked as if he might have been a soldier in his earlier days. He eyed me with a grave attention, which relaxed little by little into sly approval. I asked for Major Fitz-David. The answer was not altogether encouraging; the man was not sure whether his master was at home or not.

I gave him my card. My cards, being part of my wedding outfit, necessarily had the false name printed on them—*Mrs Eustace Woodville*. The servant showed me into a front room on the ground floor, and disappeared with my card in his hand.

Looking about me, I noticed a door in the wall opposite the window, communicating with some inner room. The door was not of the ordinary kind. It fitted into the thickness of the partition wall, and worked in grooves. Looking a little nearer, I saw that it had not been pulled out so as completely to close the doorway. Only the merest chink was left; but it was enough to convey to my ears all that passed in the next room.

'What did you say, Oliver, when she asked for me?' inquired a man's voice, pitched cautiously in a low key.

'I said I was not sure you were at home, sir,' answered the voice of the servant who had let me in.

There was a pause. The first speaker was evidently Major Fitz-David himself. I waited to hear more.

'I think I had better not see her, Oliver,' the Major's voice resumed.

'Very good, sir.'

'Say I have gone out, and you don't know when I shall be back again. Beg the lady to write, if she has any business with me.'

'Yes, sir.'

'Stop, Oliver!'

Oliver stopped. There was another and longer pause. Then the master resumed the examination of the man.

'Is she young, Oliver?'

'Yes, sir.'

'And—pretty?'

'Better than pretty, sir, to my thinking.'

'Aye? aye? What you call a fine woman—eh, Oliver?'

'Certainly, sir.'

'Tall?'

'Nearly as tall as I am, Major.'

'Aye? aye? aye? A good figure?'

'As slim as a sapling, sir, and as upright as a dart.'

'On second thoughts, I am at home, Oliver. Show her in! show her in!'

So far, one thing at least seemed to be clear. I had done well in sending for the chambermaid. What would Oliver's report of me have been, if I had presented myself to him with my colourless cheeks and my ill-dressed hair?

The servant reappeared, and conducted me (by way of the hall) to the inner room. Major Fitz-David advanced to welcome me. What was the Major like?

Well—he was like a finely-preserved gentleman of (say) sixty years old; little and lean, and chiefly remarkable by the extraordinary length of his nose. After this feature, I noticed, next, his beautiful brown wig; his sparkling little grey eyes; his rosy complexion; his short military whiskers, dyed to match his wig; his white teeth and his winning smile; his smart blue frock-coat, with a camellia in the button-hole; and his splendid ring—a ruby, flashing on his little finger as he courteously signed to me to take a chair.

'Dear Mrs Woodville, how very kind of you this is! I have been longing to have the happiness of knowing you. Eustace is an old friend of mine. I congratulated him when I heard of his marriage. May I make a confession?—I envy him now I have seen his wife.'

The future of my life was, perhaps, in this man's hands. I studied him attentively; I tried to read his character in his face.

The Major's sparkling little grey eyes softened as they looked at me; the Major's strong and sturdy voice dropped to its lowest and tenderest tones when he spoke to me; the Major's manner expressed, from the moment when I entered the room, a happy mixture of admiration and respect. He drew his chair close to mine, as if it was a privilege to be near me. He took my hand, and lifted my glove to his lips, as if that glove was the most delicious luxury the world could produce. 'Dear Mrs Woodville,' he said, as he softly laid my hand back on my lap, 'bear with an old fellow who worships your enchanting sex. You really brighten this dull house. It is *such* a pleasure to see you!'

There was no need for the old gentleman to make his little confession. Women, children, and dogs proverbially know by instinct who the people are who really like them. The women had a warm friend—perhaps, at one time, a dangerously warm friend—in Major Fitz-David. I knew as much of him as that before I had settled myself in my chair and opened my lips to answer him.

'Thank you, Major, for your kind reception and your pretty compliment,' I said; matching my host's easy tone as closely as the necessary restraints on my side would permit. 'You have made your confession. May I make mine?'

Major Fitz-David lifted my hand again from my lap, and drew his chair as close as possible to mine. I looked at him gravely, and tried to release my hand. Major Fitz-David declined to let go of it, and proceeded to tell me why.

'I have just heard you speak for the first time,' he said. 'I am under the charm of your voice. Dear Mrs Woodville, bear with an old fellow who is under the charm! Don't grudge me my innocent little pleasures. Lend me—I wish I could say *give* me—this pretty hand. I am such an admirer of pretty hands; I can listen so much better with a pretty hand in mine. The ladies indulge my weakness. Please indulge me too. Yes? And what were you going to say?'

'I was going to say, Major, that I felt particularly sensible of your kind welcome, because, as it happens, I have a favour to ask of you.'

I was conscious, while I spoke, that I was approaching the object of my visit a little too abruptly. But Major Fitz-David's admiration rose from one climax to another with such alarming rapidity, that I felt the importance of administering a practical check to it. I trusted to those ominous words, 'a favour to ask of you,' to administer the check—and I did not trust in vain. My aged admirer gently dropped my hand, and (with all possible politeness) changed the subject.

'The favour is granted, of course!' he said. 'And now—tell me—how is our dear Eustace?'

'Anxious and out of spirits,' I answered.

'Anxious and out of spirits!' repeated the Major. 'The enviable man who is married to You, anxious and out of spirits? Monstrous! Eustace fairly disgusts me. I shall take him off the list of my friends.'

'In that case, take me off the list with him, Major. I am in wretched spirits too. You are my husband's old friend. I may acknowledge to *you* that our married life is—just now—not quite a happy one.'

Major Fitz-David lifted his eyebrows (dyed to match his whiskers) in polite surprise.

'Already!' he exclaimed. 'What can Eustace be made of? Has he no appreciation of beauty and grace? Is he the most insensible of living beings?'

'He is the best and dearest of men,' I answered. 'But there is some dreadful mystery in his past life—'

I could get no further: Major Fitz-David deliberately stopped me. He did it with the smoothest politeness, on the surface. But I saw a look in his bright little eyes, which said plainly, 'If you *will* venture on delicate ground, madam, don't ask me to accompany you.'

'My charming friend!' he exclaimed. 'May I call you my charming friend? You have—among a thousand other delightful qualities which I can see already—a vivid imagination. Don't let it get the upper hand! Take an old fellow's advice; don't let it get the upper hand! What can I offer you, dear Mrs Woodville? A cup of tea?'

'Call me by my right name, sir,' I answered boldly. 'I have made a discovery. I know, as well as you do, that my name is Macallan.'

The Major started, and looked at me very attentively. His manner became grave, his tone changed completely, when he spoke next.

'May I ask,' he said, 'if you have communicated to your husband the discovery which you have just mentioned to me?'

'Certainly!' I answered. 'I consider that my husband owes me an explanation. I have asked him to tell me what his extraordinary conduct means—and he has refused in language that frightens me. I have appealed to his mother—and *she* has refused to explain, in language that humiliates me. Dear Major Fitz-David, I have no friends to take my part; I have nobody to come to but you! Do me the greatest of all favours—tell me why your friend Eustace has married me under a false name!'

'Do *me* the greatest of all favours,' answered the Major. 'Don't ask me to say a word about it.'

He looked, in spite of his unsatisfactory reply, as if he really felt for me. I determined to try my utmost powers of persuasion; I resolved not to be beaten at the first repulse.

'I *must* ask you,' I said. 'Think of my position. How can I live, knowing what I know—and knowing no more? I would rather hear the most horrible thing you can tell me than be condemned (as I am now) to perpetual misgiving and perpetual suspense. I love my husband with all my heart; but I cannot live with him on these terms: the misery of it would drive me mad. I am only a woman, Major. I can only throw myself on your kindness. Don't—pray, pray don't keep me in the dark!'

I could say no more. In the reckless impulse of the moment, I snatched up his hand and raised it to my lips. The gallant old gentleman started as if I had given him an electric shock.

'My dear, dear lady!' he exclaimed, 'I can't tell you how I feel for you! You charm me, you overwhelm me, you touch me to the heart. What can I say? What can I do? I can only imitate your admirable frankness, your fearless candour. You have told me what your position is. Let me tell you, in my turn, how I am placed. Compose yourself—pray compose yourself! I have a smelling-bottle here, at the service of the ladies. Permit me to offer it.'

He brought me the smelling-bottle; he put a little stool under my feet; he entreated me to take time enough to compose myself. 'Infernal fool!' I heard him say to himself, as he considerately turned away from me for a few moments. 'If *I* had been her husband—come what might of it, I would have told her the truth!'

Was he referring to Eustace? And was he going to do what he would have done in my husband's place—was he really going to tell me the truth?

The idea had barely crossed my mind, when I was startled by a loud and peremptory knocking at the street-door. The Major stopped, and listened attentively. In a few moments the door was opened, and the rustling of a woman's dress was plainly audible in the hall. The Major hurried to the door of the room, with the activity of a young man. He was too late. The door was violently opened from the outer side, just as he got to it. The lady of the rustling dress burst into the room.

CHAPTER IX

The Defeat of the Major

MAJOR FITZ-DAVID'S visitor proved to be a plump, round-eyed, over-dressed girl, with a florid complexion and straw-coloured hair. After first fixing on me a broad stare of astonishment, she pointedly addressed her apologies for intruding on us to the Major alone. The creature evidently believed me to be the last new object of the old gentleman's idolatry; and she took no pains to disguise her jealous resentment on discovering us together. Major Fitz-David set matters right in his own irresistible way. He kissed the hand of the over-dressed girl, as devotedly as he had kissed mine; he told her she was looking charmingly. Then he led her, with his happy mixture of admiration and respect, back to the door by which she had entered—a second door communicating directly with the hall.

'No apology is necessary, my dear,' he said. 'This lady is with me on a matter of business. You will find your singing-master waiting for you upstairs. Begin your lesson; and I will join you in a few minutes. *Au revoir*, my charming pupil—*au revoir*.'

The young lady answered this polite little speech in a whisper—with her round eyes fixed distrustfully on me while she spoke. The door closed on her. Major Fitz-David was at liberty to set matters right with me, in my turn.

'I call that young person one of my happy discoveries,' said the old gentleman, complacently. 'She possesses, I don't hesitate to say, the finest soprano voice in Europe. Would you believe it, I met with her at a railway station? She was behind the counter in a refreshment-room, poor innocent, rinsing wine-glasses, and singing over her work. Good heavens, such singing! Her upper notes electrified me. I said to myself, "Here is a born prima-donna—I will bring her out!" She is the third I have brought out in my time. I shall take her to Italy when her education is sufficiently advanced, and perfect her at Milan. In that unsophisticated girl, my dear lady, you see one of the future Queens of Song. Listen! she is beginning her scales. What a voice! Brava! Brava! Bravissima!'

The high soprano notes of the future Queen of Song rang through the house as he spoke. Of the loudness of the young lady's voice there could be no sort of doubt. The sweetness and the purity of it admitted, in my opinion, of considerable dispute.

Having said the polite words which the occasion rendered necessary, I ventured to recall Major Fitz-David to the subject in discussion between us when his visitor had entered the room. The Major was very unwilling to return to the perilous topic on which he had just touched when the interruption occurred. He beat time with his forefinger to the singing upstairs; he asked me about *my* voice, and whether I sang; he remarked that life would be intolerable to him without Love and Art. A man in my place would have lost all patience, and would have given up the struggle in disgust. Being a woman, and having my end in view, my resolution was invincible. I fairly wore out the Major's resistance, and compelled him to surrender at discretion. It is only justice to add that, when he did make up his mind to speak to me again of Eustace, he spoke frankly, and spoke to the point.

'I have known your husband,' he began, 'since the time when he was a boy. At a certain period of his past life, a terrible misfortune fell upon him. The secret of that misfortune is known to his friends, and is religiously kept by his friends. It is the secret that he is keeping from You. He will never tell it to you as long as he lives. And he has bound *me* not to tell it, under a promise given on my word of honour. You wished, dear Mrs Woodville, to be made acquainted with my position towards Eustace. There it is!'

'You persist in calling me Mrs Woodville,' I said.

'Your husband wishes me to persist,' the Major answered. 'He assumed the name of Woodville, fearing to give his own name, when he first called at your uncle's house. He will now acknowledge no other. Remonstrance is useless. You must do, what we do—you must give way to an unreasonable man. The best fellow in the world in other respects: in this one matter, as obstinate and self-willed as he can be. If you ask me my opinion, I tell you honestly that I think he was wrong in courting and marrying you under his false name. He trusted his honour and his happiness to your keeping, in making you his wife. Why should he not trust the story of his troubles to you as well? His mother quite shares my opinion in this matter. You must not blame her for refusing to admit you into her confidence, after your marriage: it was then too late. Before your marriage, she did all she could do—without betraying secrets which, as a good mother, she was bound to respect—to induce her son to act justly towards you. I commit no indiscretion when I tell you that she refused to sanction your marriage, mainly for the reason that Eustace declined to follow her advice, and to tell you what his position really was. On my part, I did all I could to support Mrs Macallan in the course that she took. When Eustace wrote to tell me that he had engaged himself to marry a niece of my good friend Dr Starkweather, and that he had mentioned me as his reference, I wrote back to warn him that I would have nothing to do with the affair, unless he revealed the whole truth about himself to his future wife. He refused to listen to me, as he had refused to listen to his mother; and he held me, at the same time, to my promise to keep his secret. When Starkweather wrote to me, I had no choice but to involve myself in a deception of which I thoroughly disapproved—or to answer in a tone so guarded and so brief as to stop the correspondence at the outset. I chose the last alternative; and I fear I have offended my good old friend. You now see the painful position in which I am placed. To add to the difficulties of that situation, Eustace came here, this very day, to warn me to be on my guard, in case of your addressing to me the very request which you have just made! He told me that you had met with his mother, by an unlucky accident, and that you had discovered the family name. He declared that he had travelled to London for the express purpose of speaking to me personally on this serious subject. "I know your weakness", he said, "where women are concerned. Valeria is aware that you are my old friend. She will certainly write to you; she may even be bold enough to make her way into your house. Renew your promise to keep the great calamity of my life a secret, on your honour, and on your oath." Those were his words, as nearly as I can remember them. I tried to treat the thing lightly; I ridiculed the absurdly theatrical notion of "renewing my promise," and all the rest of it. Quite useless! He refused to leave me—he reminded me of his unmerited sufferings, poor fellow, in the past time. It ended in his bursting into tears. You love him, and so do I. Can you wonder that I let him have his way? The result is that I am doubly bound to tell you nothing, by the most sacred promise that a man can give. My dear lady, I cordially side with you in this matter; I long to relieve your anxieties. But what can I do?'

He stopped, and waited—gravely waited—to hear my reply.

I had listened from beginning to end, without interrupting him. The extraordinary change in his manner, and in his way of expressing himself, while he was speaking of Eustace, alarmed me as nothing had alarmed me yet. How terrible (I thought to myself) must this untold story be, if the mere act of referring to it makes light-hearted Major Fitz-David speak seriously and sadly—never smiling; never paying me a compliment; never even noticing the singing upstairs! My heart sank in me as I drew that startling conclusion. For the first time since I had entered the house, I was at the end of my resources; I knew neither what to say nor what to do next.

And yet, I kept my seat. Never had the resolution to discover what my husband was hiding from me been more firmly rooted in my mind than it was at that moment! I cannot account for the extraordinary inconsistency in my character which this confession implies. I can only describe the facts as they really were.

The singing went on upstairs. Major Fitz-David still waited impenetrably to hear what I had to say—to know what I resolved on doing next.

Before I had decided what to say or what to do, another domestic incident happened. In plain words, another knocking announced a new visitor at the house door. On this occasion, there was no rustling of a woman's dress in the hall. On this occasion, only the old servant entered the room carrying a magnificent nosegay in his hand. 'With Lady Clarinda's kind regards. To remind Major Fitz-David of his appointment.' Another lady! This time, a lady with a title. A great lady who sent her flowers and her messages without condescending to concealment. The Major—first apologising to me—wrote a few lines of acknowledgment, and sent them out to the messenger. When the door was closed again, he carefully selected one of the choicest flowers in the nosegay. 'May I ask,' he said, presenting the flower to me with his best grace, 'whether you now understand the delicate position in which I am placed between your husband and yourself?'

The little interruption caused by the appearance of the nosegay had given a new impulse to my thoughts, and had thus helped, in some degree, to restore me to myself. I was able at last to satisfy Major Fitz-David that his considerate and courteous explanation had not been thrown away upon me.

'I thank you, most sincerely, Major,' I said. 'You have convinced me that I must not ask you to forget, on my account, the promise which you have given to my husband. It is a sacred promise which I, too, am bound to respect—I quite understand that.'

The Major drew a long breath of relief, and patted me on the shoulder in high approval of what I had said to him.

'Admirably expressed!' he rejoined, recovering his light-hearted looks and his lover-like ways all in a moment. 'My dear lady, you have the gift of sympathy; you see exactly how I am situated. Do you know, you remind me of my charming Lady Clarinda? *She* has the gift of sympathy, and sees exactly how I am situated. I should so enjoy introducing you to each other,' said the Major, plunging his long nose ecstatically into Lady Clarinda's flowers.

I had my end still to gain; and being (as you will have discovered by this time) the most obstinate of living women, I still kept that end in view.

'I shall be delighted to meet Lady Clarinda,' I replied. 'In the mean time——'

'I will get up a little dinner,' proceeded the Major, with a burst of enthusiasm. 'You and I and Lady Clarinda. Our young prima-donna shall come in the evening, and sing to us. Suppose we draw out the *menu*? My sweet friend, what is your favourite autumn soup?'

'In the mean time,' I persisted, 'to return to what we were speaking of just now——'

The Major's smile vanished, the Major's hand dropped the pen, destined to immortalise the name of my favourite autumn soup.

'*Must* we return to that?' he asked, piteously.

'Only for a moment,' I said.

'You remind me,' pursued Major Fitz-David, shaking his head sadly, 'of another charming friend of mine—a French friend—Madame Mirliflore. You are a person of prodigious tenacity of purpose. Madame Mirliflore is a person of prodigious tenacity of purpose. She happens to be in London. Shall we have her at our little dinner?' The Major brightened at the idea, and took up the pen again. 'Do tell me,' he said, 'what *is* your favourite autumn soup?'

'Pardon me,' I began; 'we were speaking just now——'

'Oh, dear me!' cried Major Fitz-David. 'Is this the other subject?'

'Yes—this is the other subject.'

The Major put down his pen for the second time, and regretfully dismissed from his mind Madame Mirliflore and the autumn soup.

'Yes?' he said with a patient bow, and a submissive smile. 'You were going to say——?'

'I was going to say,' I rejoined, 'that your promise only pledges you not to tell the secret which my husband is keeping from me. You have given no promise not to answer me, if I venture to ask you one or two questions.'

Major Fitz-David held up his hand warningly, and cast a sly look at me out of his bright little grey eyes.

'Stop!' he said. 'My sweet friend, stop there! I know where your questions will lead me, and what the result will be if I once begin to answer them. When your husband was here to-day, he took occasion to remind me that I was as weak as water in the hands of a pretty woman. He is quite right. I *am* as weak as water; I can refuse nothing to a pretty woman. Dear and admirable lady, don't abuse your influence! don't make an old soldier false to his word of honour!'

I tried to say something here in defence of my motives. The Major clasped his hands entreatingly, and looked at me with a pleading simplicity wonderful to see.

'Why press it?' he asked. 'I offer no resistance. I am a lamb—why sacrifice me? I acknowledge your power; I throw myself on your mercy. All the misfortunes of my youth and my manhood have come to me through women. I am not a bit better in my age—I am just as fond of the women, and just as ready to be misled by them as ever, with one foot in the grave. Shocking, isn't it? But how true! Look at this mark.' He lifted a curl of his beautiful brown wig, and showed me a terrible scar at the side of his head. 'That wound (supposed to be mortal at the time) was made by a pistol bullet,' he proceeded. 'Not received in the service of my country—oh, dear no! Received in the service of a much-injured lady, at the hands of her scoundrel of a husband, in a duel abroad. Well, she was worth it!' He kissed his hand affectionately to the memory of the dead, or absent, lady, and pointed to a water-colour drawing of a pretty country house, hanging on the opposite wall. 'That fine estate,' he proceeded, 'once belonged to me. It was sold years and years since. And who had the money? The women—God bless them all!—the women. I don't regret it. If I had another estate, I have no doubt it would go the same way. Your adorable sex has made its pretty playthings of my life, my time, and my money—and welcome! The one thing I have kept to myself, is my honour. And now, *that* is in danger! Yes; if you put your clever little questions, with those lovely eyes and with that gentle voice, I know what will happen! You will deprive me of the last and best of all my possessions. Have I deserved to be treated in that way—and by you, my charming friend? by you of all people in the world? Oh, fie! fie!'

He paused, and looked at me as before—the picture of artless entreaty, with his head a little on one side. I made another attempt to speak of the matter in dispute between us, from my own point of view. Major Fitz-David instantly threw himself prostrate on my mercy more innocently than ever.

'Ask of me anything else in the wide world,' he said; 'but don't ask me to be false to my friend. Spare me *that*—and there is nothing I will not do to satisfy you. I mean what I say, mind!' he went on, bending closer to me, and speaking more seriously than he had spoken yet. 'I think you are very hardly used. It is monstrous to expect that a woman placed in your situation will consent to be left for the rest of her life in the dark. No! no! if I saw you, at this moment, on the point of finding out for yourself what Eustace persists in hiding from you, I should remember that my promise, like all other promises, has its limits and reserves. I should consider myself bound in honour not to help you—but I would not lift a finger to prevent you from discovering the truth for yourself.'

At last he was speaking in good earnest; he laid a strong emphasis on his closing words. I laid a stronger emphasis on them still, by suddenly leaving my chair. The impulse to spring to my feet was irresistible. Major Fitz-David had started a new idea in my head.

'Now we understand each other!' I said. 'I will accept your own terms, Major. I will ask nothing of you but what you have just offered to me of your own accord.'

'What have I offered?' he inquired, looking a little alarmed.

'Nothing that you need repent of,' I answered; 'nothing which it is not easy for you to grant. May I ask a bold question? Suppose this house were mine instead of yours?'

'Consider it yours,' cried the gallant old gentleman. 'From the garrets to the kitchen, consider it yours!'

'A thousand thanks, Major; I will consider it mine, for the moment. You know—everybody knows—that one of a woman's many weaknesses is curiosity. Suppose my curiosity led me to examine everything in my new house?'

'Yes?'

'Suppose I went from room to room, and searched everything, and peeped in everywhere? Do you think there would be any chance——?'

The quick-witted Major anticipated the nature of my question. He followed my example; he, too, started to his feet, with a new idea in his mind.

'Would there be any chance,' I went on, 'of my finding my own way to my husband's secret, in this house? One word of reply, Major Fitz-David! Only one word—Yes, or No?'

'Don't excite yourself!' cried the Major.

'Yes, or No?' I repeated, more vehemently than ever.

'Yes,' said the Major—after a moment's consideration.

It was the reply I had asked for; but it was not explicit enough—now I had got it—to satisfy me. I felt the necessity of leading him (if possible) into details.

'Does "Yes" mean that there is some sort of clue to the mystery?' I asked. 'Something, for instance, which my eyes might see, and my hands might touch, if I could only find it?'

He considered again. I saw that I had succeeded in interesting him, in some way unknown to myself; and I waited patiently until he was prepared to answer me.

'The thing you mention,' he said; 'the clue (as you call it) might be seen and might be touched—supposing you could find it.'

'In this house?' I asked.

The Major advanced a step nearer to me, and answered,—

'In this room.'

My head began to swim; my heart throbbed violently. I tried to speak; it was in vain; the effort almost choked me. In the silence, I could hear the music lesson still going on in the room above. The future prima-donna had done practising her scales, and was trying her voice now in selections from Italian operas. At the moment when I first heard her, she was singing the lovely air from the *Sonnambula*, 'Come per me sereno.' I never hear that delicious melody, to this day, without being instantly transported in imagination to the fatal back room in Vivian Place.

The Major—strongly affected himself, by this time—was the first to break the silence.

'Sit down again,' he said; 'and pray take the easy chair. You are very much agitated; you want rest.'

He was right. I could stand no longer; I dropped into the chair. Major Fitz-David rang the bell, and spoke a few words to the servant at the door.

'I have been here a long time,' I said, faintly. 'Tell me if I am in the way.'

'In the way?' he repeated, with his irresistible smile. 'You forget that you are in your own house!'

The servant returned to us, bringing with him a tiny bottle of champagne, and a plate-full of delicate little sugared biscuits.

'I have had this wine bottled expressly for the ladies,' said the Major. 'The biscuits come to me direct from Paris. As a favour to *me* you must take some refreshment. And then——' he stopped, and looked at me very attentively. 'And then,' he resumed, 'shall I go to my young prima-donna upstairs, and leave you here alone?'

It was impossible to hint more delicately at the one request which I now had it in my mind to make to him. I took his hand and pressed it gratefully.

'The tranquillity of my whole life to come is at stake,' I said. 'When I am left here by myself, does your generous sympathy permit me to examine everything in the room?'

He signed to me to drink the champagne, and to eat a biscuit, before he gave his answer.

'This is serious,' he said. 'I wish you to be in perfect possession of yourself. Restore your strength—and then I will speak to you.'

I did as he bade me. In a minute from the time when I drank it, the delicious sparkling wine had begun to revive me.

'Is it your express wish,' he resumed, 'that I should leave you here by yourself, to search the room?'

'It is my express wish,' I answered.

'I take a heavy responsibility on myself in granting your request. But I grant it for all that, because I sincerely believe—as you believe—that the tranquillity of your life to come depends on your discovering the truth.' Saying those words, he took two keys from his pocket, 'You will naturally feel a suspicion,' he went on, 'of any locked doors that you may find here. The only locked places in the room are the doors of the cupboards under the long bookcase, and the door of the Italian cabinet in that corner. The small key opens the bookcase cupboards; the long key opens the cabinet door.'

With that explanation, he laid the keys before me on the table.

'Thus far,' he said, 'I have rigidly respected the promise which I made to your husband. I shall continue to be faithful to my promise, whatever may be the result of your examination of the room. I am bound in honour not to assist you, by word or deed. I am not even at liberty to offer you the slightest hint. Is that understood?'

'Certainly!'

'Very good. I have now a last word of warning to give you—and then I have done. If you do by any chance succeed in laying your hand on the clue, remember this—*the discovery which follows will be a terrible one.* If you have any doubt about your capacity to sustain a shock which will strike you to the soul, for God's sake give up the idea of finding out your husband's secret, at once and for ever!'

'I thank you for your warning, Major. I must face the consequences of making the discovery, whatever they may be.'

'You are positively resolved?'

'Positively.'

'Very well. Take any time you please. The house, and every person in it, is at your disposal. Ring the bell once, if you want the man servant. Ring twice, if you wish the housemaid to wait on you. From time to time, I shall just look in myself to see how you are going on. I am responsible for your comfort and security, you know, while you honour me by remaining under my roof.'

He lifted my hand to his lips, and fixed a last attentive look on me.

'I hope I am not running too great a risk,' he said—more to himself than to me. 'The women have led me into many a rash action in my time. Have *you* led me, I wonder, into the rashest action of all?'

With those ominous last words he bowed gravely, and left me alone in the room.

CHAPTER X

The Search

THE fire burning in the grate was not a very large one; and the outer air (as I had noticed on my way to the house) had something of a wintry sharpness in it that day.

Still, my first feeling when Major Fitz-David left me, was a feeling of heat and oppression—with its natural result, a difficulty of breathing freely. The nervous agitation of the time was, I suppose, answerable for these sensations. I took off my bonnet and mantle and gloves, and opened the window for a little while. Nothing was to be seen outside but a paved courtyard (with a skylight in the middle), closed at the farther end by the wall of the Major's stables. A few minutes at the window cooled and refreshed me. I shut it down again, and took my first step on the way to discovery. In other words,

I began my first examination of the four walls round me, and of all that they enclosed.

I was amazed at my own calmness. My interview with Major Fitz-David had, perhaps, exhausted my capacity for feeling any strong emotion—for the time at least. It was a relief to me to be alone; it was a relief to me to begin the search. Those were my only sensations, so far.

The shape of the room was oblong. Of the two shorter walls, one contained the door in grooves which I have already mentioned as communicating with the front room; the other was almost entirely occupied by the broad window which looked out on the courtyard.

Taking the doorway wall first, what was there, in the shape of furniture, on either side of it? There was a card-table on either side. Above each card-table stood a magnificent china bowl, placed on a gilt and carved bracket fixed to the wall.

I opened the card-tables. The drawers beneath contained nothing but cards, and the usual counters and markers. With the exception of one pack, the cards in both tables were still wrapped in their paper covers exactly as they had come from the shop. I examined the loose pack, card by card. No writing—no mark of any kind—was visible on any one of them. Assisted by a library ladder which stood against the bookcase, I looked next into the two china bowls. Both were perfectly empty. Was there anything more to examine on that side of the room? In the two corners there were two little chairs of inlaid wood, with red silk cushions. I turned them up, and looked under the cushions; and still I made no discoveries. When I had put the chairs back in their places, my search on one side of the room was complete. So far, I had found nothing.

I crossed to the opposite wall—the wall which contained the window.

The window (occupying, as I have said, almost the entire length and height of the wall) was divided into three compartments, and was adorned at either extremity by handsome curtains of dark red velvet. The ample, heavy folds of the velvet, left just room at the two corners of the wall, for two antique upright cabinets in buhl; containing rows of drawers, and supporting two fine bronze reproductions (reduced in size) of the Venus Milo and the Venus Callipyge. I had Major Fitz-David's permission to do just what I pleased. I opened the six drawers in each cabinet, and examined their contents without hesitation.

Beginning with the cabinet in the right hand corner, my investigations were soon completed. All the six drawers were alike occupied by a collection of fossils, which (judging by the curious paper inscriptions fixed on some of them) were associated with a past period of the Major's life when he had speculated, not very successfully, in mines. After satisfying myself that the drawers contained nothing but the fossils and their inscriptions, I turned to the cabinet in the left hand corner next.

Here, a variety of objects was revealed to view; and the examination accordingly occupied a much longer time.

The top drawer contained a complete collection of carpenter's tools in miniature; relics, probably, of the far distant time when the Major was a boy, and when parents or friends had made him a present of a set of toy-tools. The second drawer was filled with toys of another sort—presents made to Major Fitz-David by his fair friends. Embroidered braces, smart smoking-caps, quaint pincushions, gorgeous slippers, glittering purses, all bore witness to the popularity of the friend of the women. The contents of the third drawer were of a less interesting sort: the entire space was filled with old account books, ranging over a period of many years. After looking into each book, and opening and shaking it uselessly, in search of any loose papers which might be hidden between the leaves, I came to the fourth drawer, and found more relics of past pecuniary transactions in the shape of receipted bills, neatly tied together, and each inscribed at the back. Among the bills, I found nearly a dozen loose papers, all equally unimportant. The fifth drawer was in sad confusion. I took out first a loose bundle of ornamental cards, each containing the list of dishes at past banquets given, or attended, by the Major, in London and Paris—next, a box full of delicately tinted quill pens (evidently a lady's gift)—next, a quantity of old invitation cards—next, some dog's-eared French plays and books of the opera—next, a pocket-corkscrew, a bundle of cigarettes, and a bunch of rusty keys—lastly, a passport, a set of luggage labels, a broken silver snuff-box, two cigar-cases, and a torn map of Rome. 'Nothing anywhere to interest *me*,' I thought, as I closed the fifth, and opened the sixth, and last, drawer.

The sixth drawer was at once a surprise and a disappointment. It literally contained nothing but the fragments of a broken vase.

I was sitting, at the time, opposite to the cabinet, in a low chair. In the momentary irritation caused by my discovery of the emptiness of the last drawer, I had just lifted my foot to push it back into its place—when the door communicating with the hall opened; and Major Fitz-David stood before me.

His eyes, after first meeting mine, travelled downwards to my foot. The instant he noticed the open drawer, I saw a change in his face. It was only for a moment; but, in that moment, he looked at me with a sudden suspicion and surprise—looked as if he had caught me with my hand on the clue.

'Pray don't let me disturb you,' he said. 'I have only looked in for a moment to ask you a question.'

'What is it, Major?'

'Have you met with any letters of mine, in the course of your investigations?'

'I have found none yet,' I answered. 'If I do discover any letters, I shall of course not take the liberty of examining them.'

'I wanted to speak to you about that,' he rejoined. 'It only struck me a moment since, upstairs, that my letters might embarrass you. In your place, I should feel some distrust of anything which I was not at liberty to examine. I think I can set this matter right, however, with very little trouble to either of us. It is no violation of any promises or pledges on my part, if I simply tell you that my letters will not assist the discovery which you are trying to make. You can safely pass them over as objects that are not worth examining from your point of view. You understand me, I am sure?'

'I am much obliged to you, Major—I quite understand.'

'Are you feeling any fatigue?'

'None whatever—thank you.'

'And you still hope to succeed? You are not beginning to be discouraged already?'

'I am not in the least discouraged. With your kind leave, I mean to persevere for some time yet.'

I had not closed the drawer of the cabinet, while we were talking; and I glanced carelessly, as I answered him, at the fragments of the broken vase. By this time he had got his feelings under perfect command. He, too, glanced at the fragments of the vase, with an appearance of perfect indifference. I remembered the look of suspicion and surprise that had escaped him on entering the room; and I thought his indifference a little over-acted.

'*That* doesn't look very encouraging,' he said, with a smile, pointing to the shattered pieces of china in the drawer.

'Appearances are not always to be trusted,' I replied. 'The wisest thing I can do, in my present situation, is to suspect everything—even down to a broken vase.'

I looked hard at him as I spoke. He changed the subject.

'Does the music upstairs annoy you?' he asked.

'Not in the least, Major.'

'It will soon be over now. The singing master is going; and the Italian master has just arrived. I am sparing no pains to make my young prima-donna a most accomplished person. In learning to sing, she must also learn the language which is especially the language of music. I shall perfect her in the accent when I take her to Italy. It is the height of my ambition to have her mistaken for an Italian when she sings in public. Is there anything I can do before I leave you again? May I send you some more champagne? Please say yes!'

'A thousand thanks, Major. No more champagne for the present.'

He turned at the door to kiss his hand to me at parting. At the same moment I saw his eyes wander slily towards the bookcase. It was only for an instant. I had barely detected him before he was out of the room.

Left by myself again, I looked at the bookcase—looked at it attentively for the first time.

It was a handsome piece of furniture in ancient carved oak; and it stood against the wall which ran parallel with the hall of the house. Excepting the space occupied, in the upper corner of the room, by the second door which opened into the hall, the bookcase filled the whole length of the wall down to the window. The top was ornamented by vases, candelabra, and statuettes, in pairs, placed in a row. Looking along the row, I noticed a vacant space on the top of the bookcase, at the extremity of it which was nearest to the window. The opposite extremity, nearest to the door, was occupied by a handsome painted vase of a very peculiar pattern. Where was the corresponding vase, which ought to have been placed at the corresponding extremity of the bookcase? I returned to the open sixth drawer of the cabinet, and looked in again. There was no mistaking the pattern on the fragments, when I examined them now. The vase which had been broken was the vase which had stood in the place now vacant on the top of the bookcase, at the end nearest to the window.

Making this discovery, I took out the fragments, down to the smallest morsel of the shattered china, and examined them carefully one after another.

I was too ignorant of the subject to be able to estimate the value of the vase, or the antiquity of the vase—or even to know whether it was of British or of foreign manufacture. The ground was of a delicate cream-colour. The ornaments traced on this were wreaths of flowers and cupids, surrounding a medallion on either side of the vase. Upon the space within one of the medallions was painted with exquisite delicacy a woman's head; representing a nymph, or a goddess, or perhaps a portrait of some celebrated person—I was not learned enough to say which. The other medallion enclosed the head of a man, also treated in the classical style. Reclining shepherds and shepherdesses, in Watteau costume, with their dogs and their sheep, formed the adornments of the pedestal. Such had the vase been in the days of its prosperity, when it stood on the top of the bookcase. By what accident had it become broken? And why had Major Fitz-David's face changed when he found that I had discovered the remains of his shattered work of Art in the cabinet drawer?

The remains left those serious questions unanswered—the remains told me absolutely nothing. And yet, if my own observation of the Major was to be trusted, the way to the clue of which I was in search, lay—directly or indirectly—through the broken vase!

It was useless to pursue the question, knowing no more than I knew now. I returned to the bookcase.

Thus far, I had assumed (without any sufficient reason) that the clue of which I was in search must necessarily reveal itself through a written paper of some sort. It now occurred to me—after the movement which I had detected on the part of the Major—that the clue might quite as probably present itself in the form of a book.

I looked along the lower rows of shelves; standing just near enough to them to read the titles on the backs of the volumes. I saw Voltaire in red morocco; Shakespeare in blue; Walter Scott in green; the History of England in brown; the Annual Register in yellow calf. There I paused, wearied and discouraged already by the long rows of volumes. How (I thought to myself) am I to examine all these books? And what am I to look for, even if I do examine them all?

Major Fitz-David had spoken of a terrible misfortune which had darkened my husband's past life. In what possible way could any trace of that misfortune, or any suggestive hint of something resembling it, exist in the archives of the Annual Register, or in the pages of Voltaire? The bare idea of such a thing seemed absurd. The mere attempt to make a serious examination in this direction was surely a wanton waste of time?

And yet, the Major had certainly stolen a look at the bookcase. And again, the broken vase had once stood on the bookcase. Did these circumstances justify me in connecting the vase and the bookcase as twin landmarks on the way that led to discovery? The question was not an easy one to decide on the spur of the moment.

I looked up at the higher shelves.

Here the collection of books exhibited a greater variety. The volumes were smaller, and were not so carefully arranged as on the lower shelves. Some were bound in cloth; some were only protected by paper covers. One or two had fallen, and lay flat on the shelves. Here and there I saw empty spaces from which books had been removed and not replaced. In short, there was no discouraging uniformity in these higher regions of the bookcase. The untidy top shelves looked suggestive of some lucky accident which might unexpectedly lead the way to success. I decided, if I did examine the bookcase at all, to begin at the top.

Where was the library ladder?

I had left it against the partition wall which divided the back room from the room in front. Looking that way, I necessarily looked also towards the door that ran in grooves—the imperfectly-closed door through which I had heard Major Fitz-David question his servant on the subject of my personal appearance, when I first entered the house. No one had moved this door, during the time of my visit. Everybody entering or leaving the room had used the other door which led into the hall.

At the moment when I looked round, something stirred in the front room. The movement let the light in suddenly through the small open space left by the partially-closed door. Had somebody been watching me through the chink? I stepped softly to the door, and pushed it back until it was wide open. There was the Major, discovered in the front room! I saw it in his face—he had been watching me at the bookcase!

His hat was in his hand. He was evidently going out; and he dexterously took advantage of that circumstance to give a plausible reason for being so near the door.

'I hope I didn't frighten you,' he said.

'You startled me a little, Major.'

'I am so sorry, and so ashamed! I was just going to open the door, and tell you that I am obliged to go out. I have received a pressing message from a lady. A charming person—I should so like you to know her! She is in sad trouble, poor thing. Little bills, you know, and nasty trades people who want their money, and a husband—oh, dear me, a husband who is quite unworthy of her! A most interesting creature. You remind me of her a little—you both have the same carriage of the head. I shall not be more than half-an-hour gone. Can I do anything for you? You are looking fatigued. Pray let me send for some more champagne. No? Promise to ring when you want it. That's right! *Au revoir*, my charming friend—*au revoir!*'

I pulled the door to again, the moment his back was turned; and sat down for awhile to compose myself.

He had been watching me at the bookcase! The man who was in my husband's confidence, the man who knew where the clue was to be found, had been watching me at the bookcase! There was no doubt of it now. Major Fitz-David had shown me the hiding-place of the secret, in spite of himself!

I looked with indifference at the other pieces of furniture, ranged against the fourth wall, which I had not examined yet. I surveyed, without the slightest feeling of curiosity, all the little elegant trifles scattered on the tables and on the chimney-piece; each one of which might have been an object of suspicion to me under other circumstances. Even the water-colour drawings failed to interest me, in my present frame of mind. I observed languidly that they were most of them portraits of ladies—fair idols, no doubt, of the Major's facile adoration—and I cared to notice no more. *My* business in that room (I was certain of it now!) began and ended with the bookcase. I left my seat to fetch the library ladder; determining to begin the work of investigation on the top shelves.

On my way to the ladder I passed one of the tables, and saw the keys lying on it which Major Fitz-David had left at my disposal.

The smaller of the two keys instantly reminded me of the cupboards under the bookcase. I had strangely overlooked these. A vague distrust of the locked doors, a vague doubt of what they might be hiding from me, stole into my mind. I left the ladder in its place against the wall, and set myself to examine the contents of the cupboards first.

The cupboards were three in number. As I opened the first of them, the singing upstairs ceased. For a moment there was something almost oppressive in the sudden change from noise to silence. I suppose my nerves must have been over-wrought. The next sound in the house—nothing more remarkable than the creaking of a man's boots, descending the stairs—made me shudder all over. The man was no doubt the singing master, going away after giving his lesson. I heard the house door close on him—and started at the familiar sound as if it was something terrible which I had never heard before! Then there was silence again. I roused myself as well as I could, and began my examination of the first cupboard.

It was divided into two compartments.

The top compartment contained nothing but boxes of cigars, ranged in rows one on another. The under compartment was devoted to a collection of shells. They were all huddled together anyhow—the Major evidently setting a far higher value on his cigars than on his shells. I searched this lower compartment carefully for any object interesting to me which might be hidden in it. Nothing was to be found in any part of it, besides the shells.

As I opened the second cupboard, it struck me that the light was beginning to fail.

I looked at the window. It was hardly evening yet. The darkening of the light was produced by gathering clouds. Rain-drops pattered against the glass; the autumn wind whistled mournfully in the corners of the courtyard. I mended the fire before I renewed my search. My nerves were in fault again, I suppose. I shivered when I went back to the bookcase. My hands trembled: I wondered what was the matter with me.

The second cupboard revealed (in the upper division of it) some really beautiful cameos; not mounted, but laid on cotton wool, in neat cardboard trays. In one corner, half hidden under one of the trays, there peeped out the white leaves of a little manuscript. The manuscript proved to be a descriptive catalogue of the cameos—nothing more!

Turning to the lower division of the cupboard, I found more costly curiosities, in the shape of ivory carvings from Japan, and specimens of rare silk from China. I began to feel weary of disinterring the Major's treasures. The longer I searched, the farther I seemed to remove myself from the one object that I had it at heart to attain. After closing the door of the second cupboard, I almost doubted whether it would be worth my while to proceed farther, and open the third and last door.

A little reflection convinced me that it would be as well, now that I had begun my examination of the lower regions of the bookcase, to go on with it to the end. I opened the last cupboard.

On the upper shelf there appeared, in solitary grandeur, one object only—a gorgeously-bound book.

It was of a larger size than usual, judging of it by comparison with the dimensions of modern volumes. The binding was of blue velvet, with clasps of silver worked in beautiful arabesque patterns, and with a lock of the same precious metal to protect the book from prying eyes. When I took it up, I found that the lock was not closed.

Had I any right to take advantage of this accident, and open the book? I have put the question, since, to some of my friends, of both sexes. The women all agree that I was perfectly justified—considering the serious interests that I had at stake—in taking any advantage of any book in the Major's house. The men differ from this view, and declare that I ought to have put back the volume in blue velvet, unopened; carefully guarding myself from any after-temptation to look at it again, by locking the cupboard door. I dare say the men are right.

Being a woman, however, I opened the book, without a moment's hesitation.

The leaves were of the finest vellum, with tastefully-designed illuminations all round them. And what did these highly ornamented pages contain? To my unutterable amazement and disgust, they contained locks of hair let neatly into the centre of each page—with inscriptions beneath, which proved them to be love-tokens from various ladies, who had touched the Major's susceptible heart at different periods of his life. The inscriptions were written in other languages besides English; but they appeared to be equally devoted to the same curious purpose—namely, to reminding the Major of the dates at which his various attachments had come to an untimely end. Thus, the first page exhibited a lock of the lightest flaxen hair, with these lines beneath: 'My adored Madeline. Eternal constancy. Alas: July 22nd, 1839!' The next page was adorned by a darker shade of hair, with a French inscription under it: 'Clémence. Idole de mon âme. Toujours fidèle. Hélas: 2me Avril, 1840!' A lock of red hair followed—with a lamentation in Latin under it; a note being attached to the date of dissolution of partnership, in this case, stating that the lady was descended from the ancient Romans, and was therefore mourned appropriately in Latin by her devoted Fitz-David. More shades of hair, and more inscriptions followed, until I was weary of looking at them. I put down the book disgusted with the creatures who had assisted in filling it—and then took it up again, by an after-thought. Thus far, I had thoroughly searched everything that had presented itself to my notice. Agreeable or not agreeable, it was plainly of serious importance to my own interests to go on as I had begun, and thoroughly to search the book.

I turned over the pages until I came to the first blank leaf. Seeing that they were all blank leaves from this place to the end, I lifted the volume by the back, and, as a last measure of precaution, shook it so as to dislodge any loose papers or cards which might have escaped my notice between the leaves.

This time, my patience was rewarded by a discovery which indescribably irritated and distressed me.

A small photograph, mounted on a card, fell out of the book. A first glance showed me that it represented the portraits of two persons.

One of the persons I recognised as my husband.

The other person was a woman.

Her face was entirely unknown to me. She was not young. The picture represented her seated on a chair, with my husband standing behind, and bending over her, holding one of her hands in his. The woman's face was hard-featured and ugly, with the marking lines of strong passions and resolute self-will plainly written on it. Still, ugly as she was, I felt a pang of jealousy as I noticed the familiarly-affectionate action by which the artist (with the permission of his sitters, of course) had connected the two figures in a group. Eustace had briefly told me, in the days of our courtship, that he had more than once fancied himself to be in love, before he met with me. Could this very unattractive woman have been one of the objects of his admiration? Had she been near enough and dear enough to him, to be photographed with her hand in his? I looked and looked at the portraits, until I could endure them no longer. Women are strange creatures; mysteries even to themselves. I threw the photograph from me into a corner of the cupboard. I was savagely angry with my husband; I hated—yes, hated with all my heart and soul!—the woman who had got his hand in hers; the unknown woman with the self-willed hard-featured face.

All this time the lower shelf of the cupboard was still waiting to be looked over.

I knelt down to examine it—eager to clear my mind, if I could, of the degrading jealousy that had got possession of me.

Unfortunately the lower shelf contained nothing but relics of the Major's military life; comprising his sword and pistols, his epaulettes, his sash, and other minor accoutrements. None of these objects excited the slightest interest in me. My eyes wandered back to the upper shelf; and, like the fool I was (there is no milder word that can fitly describe me at that moment), I took the photograph out again, and enraged myself uselessly by another look at it. This time I observed, what I had not noticed before, that there were some lines of writing (in a woman's hand) at the back of the portraits. The lines ran thus:—

'To Major Fitz-David, with two vases. From his friends S. and E. M.'

Was one of those two vases the vase that had been broken? And was the change that I had noticed in Major Fitz-David's face produced by some past association in connexion with it, which in some way affected me? It might or might not be so. I was little disposed to indulge in speculation on this topic, while the far more serious question of the initials confronted me on the back of the photograph.

'S. and E. M.'? Those last two letters might stand for the initials of my husband's name—his true name—Eustace Macallan. In this case, the first letter ('S.'), in all probability, indicated *her* name. What right had she to associate herself with him in that manner? I considered a little—my memory exerted itself—I suddenly called to mind that Eustace had sisters. He had spoken of them more than once, in the time before our marriage. Had I been mad enough to torture myself with jealousy of my husband's sister? It might well be so; 'S.' might stand for his sister's Christian name. I felt heartily ashamed of myself, as this new view of the matter dawned on me. What a wrong I had done to them both, in my thoughts! I turned the photograph, sadly and penitently, to examine the portraits again with a kinder and truer appreciation of them.

I naturally looked now for a family likeness between the two faces. There was no family likeness: on the contrary, they were as unlike each other in form and expression as faces could be. *Was* she his sister after all? I looked at her hands, as represented in the portrait. Her right hand was clasped by Eustace: her left hand lay on her lap. On the third finger—distinctly visible—there was a wedding-ring. Were any of my husband's sisters married? I had myself asked him the question when he mentioned them to me; and I perfectly remembered that he had replied in the negative.

Was it possible that my first jealous instinct had led me to the right conclusion after all? If it had, what did the association of the three initial letters mean? What did the wedding-ring mean? Good Heavens! was I looking at the portrait of a rival in my husband's affections—and was that rival his Wife?

I threw the photograph from me with a cry of horror. For one terrible moment, I felt as if my reason was giving way. I don't know what would have happened—or what I should have done next—if my love for Eustace had not taken the uppermost place among the contending emotions that tortured me. That faithful love steadied my brain. That faithful love roused the reviving influences of my better and nobler sense. Was the man whom I had enshrined in my heart of hearts capable of such base wickedness as the bare idea of his marriage to another woman implied? No!—mine was the baseness, mine the wickedness, in having even for a moment thought it of him!

I picked up the detestable photograph from the floor, and put it back in the book. I hastily closed the cupboard door, fetched the library ladder, and set it against the bookcase. My one idea, now, was the idea of taking refuge in employment of any sort from my own thoughts. I felt the hateful suspicion that had degraded me coming back again in spite of my efforts to repel it. The books! the books! my only hope was to absorb myself, body and soul, in the books.

I had one foot on the ladder, when I heard the door of the room open—the door which communicated with the hall.

I looked round, expecting to see the Major. I saw instead the Major's future prima-donna, standing just inside the door, with her round eyes steadily fixed on me.

'I can stand a good deal,' the girl began, coolly; 'but I can't stand *this* any longer.'

'What is it that you can't stand any longer?' I asked.

'If you have been here a minute, you have been here two good hours,' she went on. 'All by yourself, in the Major's study. I am of a jealous disposition—*I* am. And I want to know what it means.' She advanced a few steps nearer to me, with a heightening colour and a threatening look. 'Is he going to bring *you* out on the stage?' she asked, sharply.

'Certainly not.'

'He ain't in love with you—is he?'

Under other circumstances, I might have told her to leave the room. In my position, at that critical moment, the mere presence of a human creature was a positive relief to me. Even this girl, with her coarse questions and her uncultivated manners, was a welcome intruder on my solitude: she offered me a refuge from myself.

'Your question is not very civilly put,' I said. 'However, I excuse you. You are probably not aware that I am a married woman.'

'What has that got to do with it?' she retorted. 'Married, or single, it's all one to the Major. The brazed-faced hussey who calls herself Lady Clarinda is married—and she sends him nosegays three times a week! Not that I care, mind you, about the old fool. But I've lost my situation at the railway, and I've got my own interests to look after, and I don't know what may happen if I let other women come between him and me. That's where the shoe pinches—don't you see? I'm not easy in my mind, when I see him leaving you mistress here to do just what you like. No offence! I speak out—*I* do. I want to know what you are about, all by yourself, in this room? How did you pick up with the Major? I never heard him speak of you before to-day.'

Under all the surface selfishness and coarseness of this strange girl, there was a certain frankness and freedom which pleaded in her favour—to my mind at any rate. I answered frankly and freely, on my side.

'Major Fitz-David is an old friend of my husband's,' I said; 'and he is kind to me for my husband's sake. He has given me permission to look about in this room——'

I stopped, at a loss how to describe my employment in terms which should tell her nothing, and which should at the same time successfully set her distrust of me at rest.

'To look about in this room—for what?' she asked. Her eye fell on the library ladder, beside which I was still standing. 'For a book?' she resumed.

'Yes,' I said, taking the hint. 'For a book.'

'Haven't you found it yet?'

'No.'

She looked hard at me; undisguisedly considering with herself whether I was, or was not, speaking the truth.

'You seem to be a good sort,' she said, making up her mind at last. 'There's nothing stuck-up about you. I'll help you if I can. I have rummaged

among the books here over and over again, and I know more about them
than you do. What book do you want?'

As she put that awkward question, she noticed for the first time Lady
Clarinda's nosegay lying on the side table where the Major had left it.
Instantly forgetting me and my book, this curious girl pounced like a fury
on the flowers, and actually trampled them under her feet!

'There!' she cried. 'If I had Lady Clarinda here, I'd serve her in the same
way.'

'What will the Major say?' I asked.

'What do I care? Do you suppose I'm afraid of *him*? Only last week I
broke one of his fine gimcracks up there, and all through Lady Clarinda and
her flowers!'

She pointed to the top of the bookcase—to the empty space on it, close
by the window. My heart gave a sudden bound, as my eyes took the
direction indicated by her finger. *She* had broken the vase! Was the way to
discovery about to reveal itself to me through this girl? Not a word would
pass my lips; I could only look at her.

'Yes!' she said. 'The thing stood there. He knows how I hate her flowers, and
he put her nosegay in the vase out of my way. There was a woman's face
painted on the china; and he told me it was the living image of *her* face. It was
no more like her than I am. I was in such a rage that I up with the book I was
reading at the time, and shied it at the painted face. Over the vase went, bless
your heart—crash to the floor. Stop a bit! I wonder whether *that's* the book you
have been looking after? Are you like me? Do you like reading Trials?'

Trials? Had I heard her aright? Yes: she had said, Trials.

I answered by an affirmative motion of my head. I was still speechless.
The girl sauntered in her cool way to the fireplace, and taking up the tongs,
returned with them to the bookcase.

'Here's where the book fell,' she said—'in the space between the bookcase
and the wall. I'll have it out in no time.'

I waited without moving a muscle, without uttering a word.

She approached me, with the tongs in one hand, and with a plainly-bound
volume in the other.

'Is that the book?' she said. 'Open it, and see.'

I took the book from her.

'It's tremendously interesting,' she went on. 'I've read it twice over—I
have. Mind you, *I* believe he did it, after all.'

Did it? Did what? What was she talking about? I tried to put the question
to her. I struggled—quite vainly—to say only those words: 'What are you
talking about?'

She seemed to lose all patience with me. She snatched the book out of my
hand, and opened it before me on the table by which we were standing side
by side.

'I declare you're as helpless as a baby!' she said, contemptuously. 'There! *Is* that the book?'

I read the first lines on the title-page:—

A COMPLETE REPORT OF

THE TRIAL OF

EUSTACE MACALLAN

I stopped, and looked up at her. She started back from me with a scream of terror. I looked down again at the title-page, and read the next lines:—

FOR THE ALLEGED POISONING

OF

HIS WIFE.

There, God's mercy remembered me. There, the black blank of a swoon swallowed me up.

CHAPTER XI

The Return to Life

MY FIRST remembrance, when I began to recover my senses, was the remembrance of Pain—agonising pain, as if every nerve in my body was being twisted and torn out of me. My whole being writhed and quivered under the dumb and dreadful protest of Nature against the effort to recall me to life. I would have given worlds to be able to cry out—to entreat the unseen creatures about me to give me back to death. How long that speechless agony held me, I never knew. In a longer or a shorter time there stole over me slowly, a sleepy sense of relief. I heard my own laboured breathing. I felt my hands moving feebly and mechanically like the hands of a baby. I faintly opened my eyes, and looked round me—as if I had passed through the ordeal of death, and had awakened to new senses, in a new world.

The first person I saw was a man—a stranger. He moved quietly out of my sight; beckoning, as he disappeared, to some other person in the room.

Slowly and unwillingly, the other person advanced to the sofa on which I lay. A faint cry of joy escaped me; I tried to hold out my feeble hands. The other person who was approaching me was my husband!

I looked at him eagerly. He never looked at me in return. With his eyes on the ground, with a strange appearance of confusion and distress in his face, he, too, moved away out of my sight. The unknown man whom I had first noticed, followed him out of the room. I called after him faintly,

'Eustace!' He never answered; he never returned. With an effort I moved my head on the pillow, so as to look round on the other side of the sofa. Another familiar face appeared before me as if in a dream. My good old Benjamin was sitting watching me, with the tears in his eyes.

He rose and took my hand silently, in his simple, kindly way.

'Where is Eustace?' I asked. 'Why has he gone away and left me?'

I was still miserably weak. My eyes wandered mechanically round the room as I put the question. I saw Major Fitz-David. I saw the table on which the singing-girl had opened the book to show it to me. I saw the girl herself sitting alone in a corner, with her handkerchief to her eyes as if she was crying. In one mysterious moment my memory recovered its powers. The recollection of that fatal title page came back to me in all its horror. The one feeling that it roused in me now, was a longing to see my husband—to throw myself into his arms, and tell him how firmly I believed in his innocence, how truly and dearly I loved him. I seized on Benjamin with feeble, trembling hands. 'Bring him back to me!' I cried, wildly. 'Where is he? Help me to get up.'

A strange voice answered, firmly and kindly,—

'Compose yourself, madam. Mr Woodville is waiting until you have recovered, in a room close by.'

I looked at him, and recognized the stranger who had followed my husband out of the room. Why had he returned alone? Why was Eustace not with me, like the rest of them! I tried to raise myself, and get on my feet. The stranger gently pressed me back again on the pillow. I attempted to resist him; quite uselessly of course. His firm hand held me, as gently as ever, in my place.

'You must rest a little,' he said. 'You must take some wine. If you exert yourself now, you will faint again.'

Old Benjamin stooped over me, and whispered a word of explanation.

'It's the doctor, my dear. You must do as he tells you.'

The doctor? They had called the doctor in to help them! I began dimly to understand that my fainting-fit must have presented symptoms far more serious than the fainting-fits of women in general. I appealed to the doctor, in a helpless, querulous way, to account to me for my husband's extraordinary absence.

'Why did you let him leave the room?' I asked. 'If I can't go to him, why don't you bring him here to me?'

The doctor appeared to be at a loss how to reply to me. He looked at Benjamin, and said, 'Will you speak to Mrs Woodville?'

Benjamin, in his turn, looked at Major Fitz-David, and said, 'Will *you*?' The Major signed to them both to leave us. They rose together, and went into the front room; pulling the door to after them in its grooves. As they left us, the girl who had so strangely revealed my husband's secret to me rose in her corner and approached the sofa.

'I suppose I had better go too?' she said, addressing Major Fitz-David.

'If you please,' the Major answered.

He spoke (as I thought) rather coldly. She tossed her head, and turned her back on him in high indignation. 'I must say a word for myself!' cried this strange creature, with an hysterical outbreak of energy. 'I must say a word, or I shall burst!'

With that extraordinary preface, she suddenly turned my way, and poured out a perfect torrent of words on me.

'You hear how the Major speaks to me?' she began. 'He blames me—poor Me—for everything that has happened. I am as innocent as the new-born babe. I acted for the best. I thought you wanted the book. I don't know now what made you faint dead away when I opened it. And the Major blames Me! As if it was my fault! I am not one of the fainting sort myself; but I feel it, I can tell you. Yes! I feel it, though I don't faint about it. I come of respectable parents—*I* do. My name is Hoighty—Miss Hoighty. I have my own self-respect; and it's wounded. I say my self-respect is wounded, when I find myself blamed without deserving it. You deserve it, if anybody does. Didn't you tell me you were looking for a book? And didn't I present it to you promiscuously, with the best intentions? I think you might say so yourself, now the doctor has brought you to again. I think you might speak up for a poor girl who is worked to death with singing and languages and what not—a poor girl who has nobody else to speak for her. I am as respectable as you are, if you come to that. My name is Hoighty. My parents are in business, and my mamma has seen better days, and mixed in the best of company.'

There, Miss Hoighty lifted her handkerchief again to her face, and burst modestly into tears behind it.

It was certainly hard to hold *her* responsible for what had happened. I answered as kindly as I could; and I attempted to speak to Major Fitz-David in her defence. He knew what terrible anxieties were oppressing me at that moment; and considerately refusing to hear a word, he took the task of consoling his young prima-donna entirely on himself. What he said to her I neither heard nor cared to hear; he spoke in a whisper. It ended in his pacifying Miss Hoighty, by kissing her hand, and leading her (as he might have led a duchess) out of the room.

'I hope that foolish girl has not annoyed you—at such a time as this?' he said, very earnestly, when he returned to the sofa. 'I can't tell you how grieved I am at what has happened. I was careful to warn you, as you may remember. Still, if I could only have foreseen——'

I let him proceed no farther. No human forethought could have provided against what had happened. Besides, dreadful as the discovery had been, I would rather have made it, and suffer under it, as I was suffering now, than have been kept in the dark. I told him this. And then I turned to the one subject that was now of any interest to me—the subject of my unhappy husband.

'How did he come to this house?' I asked.

'He came here with Mr Benjamin, shortly after I returned,' the Major replied.

'Long after I was taken ill?'

'No. I had just sent for the doctor—feeling seriously alarmed about you.'

'What brought him here? Did he return to the hotel, and miss me?'

'Yes. He returned earlier than he had anticipated; and he felt uneasy at not finding you at the hotel.'

'Did he suspect me of being with you? Did he come here from the hotel?'

'No. He appears to have gone first to Mr Benjamin, to inquire about you. What he heard from your old friend, I cannot say. I only know that Mr Benjamin accompanied him when he came here.'

This brief explanation was quite enough for me—I understood what had happened. Eustace would easily frighten simple old Benjamin about my absence from the hotel; and, once alarmed, Benjamin would be persuaded without difficulty to repeat the few words which had passed between us, on the subject of Major Fitz-David. My husband's presence in the Major's house was perfectly explained. But his extraordinary conduct in leaving the room, at the very time when I was just recovering my senses, still remained to be accounted for. Major Fitz-David looked seriously embarrassed when I put the question to him.

'I hardly know how to explain it to you,' he said. 'Eustace has surprised and disappointed me.'

He spoke very gravely. His looks told me more than his words: his looks alarmed me.

'Eustace has not quarrelled with you?' I said.

'Oh, no!'

'He understands that you have not broken your promise to him?'

'Certainly. My young vocalist (Miss Hoighty) told the doctor exactly what had happened; and the doctor in her presence repeated the statement to your husband.'

'Did the doctor see the "Trial"?'

'Neither the doctor nor Mr Benjamin has seen the "Trial." I have locked it up; and I have carefully kept the terrible story of your connexion with the prisoner a secret from all of them. Mr Benjamin evidently has his suspicions. But the doctor has no idea, and Miss Hoighty has no idea, of the true cause of your fainting fit. They both believe that you are subject to serious nervous attacks; and that your husband's name is really Woodville. All that the truest friend could do to spare Eustace, I have done. He persists, nevertheless, in blaming me for letting you enter my house. And worse, far worse than this, he persists in declaring that the event of to-day has fatally estranged you from him. "There is an end of our married life," he said to me, "now she knows that I am the man who was tried at Edinburgh for poisoning my wife!" '

I rose from the sofa in horror.

'Good God!' I cried; 'does Eustace suppose that I doubt his innocence?'

'He denies that it is possible for you, or for anybody, to believe in his innocence,' the Major replied.

'Help me to the door,' I said. 'Where is he? I must and will see him!'

I dropped back exhausted on the sofa as I said the words. Major Fitz-David poured out a glass of wine from the bottle on the table, and insisted on my drinking it.

'You shall see him,' said the Major. 'I promise you that. The doctor has forbidden him to leave the house, until you have seen him. Only wait a little! My poor dear lady, wait, if it is only for a few minutes, until you are stronger!'

I had no choice but to obey him. Oh, those miserable helpless minutes on the sofa! I cannot write of them without shuddering at the recollection—even at this distance of time.

'Bring him here!' I said. 'Pray, pray, bring him here!'

'Who is to persuade him to come back?' asked the Major, sadly. 'How can I, how can anybody, prevail with a man—a madman I had almost said!—who could leave you at the moment when you first opened your eyes on him? I saw Eustace alone, in the next room, while the doctor was in attendance on you. I tried to shake his obstinate distrust of your belief in his innocence, and of my belief in his innocence, by every argument and every appeal that an old friend could address to him. He had but one answer to give me. Reason as I might, and plead as I might, he still persisted in referring me to the Scotch Verdict.'

'The Scotch Verdict?' I repeated. 'What is that?'

The Major looked surprised at the question.

'Have you really never heard of the Trial?' he said.

'Never.'

'I thought it strange,' he went on, 'when you told me you had found out your husband's true name, that the discovery appeared to have suggested no painful association to your mind. It is not more than three years since all England was talking of your husband. One can hardly wonder at his taking refuge, poor fellow, in an assumed name! Where could you have been at the time?'

'Did you say it was three years ago?' I asked.

'Yes.'

I understood my strange ignorance of what appeared to be so well known to other people. Three years since, my father was alive. I was living with him, in a country house in Italy—up in the mountains, near Siena. We never saw an English newspaper, or met with an English traveller, for weeks and weeks together. There might certainly have been some reference made to the famous Scotch Trial in my father's letters from England. If there was, he never told me of it. Or, if he did mention the case, I must have forgotten it in course of time. 'Tell me,' I said to the Major, 'what has the Verdict to do with my husband's horrible doubt of us? Eustace is a free man. The verdict was Not Guilty, of course?'

Major Fitz-David shook his head sadly.

'Eustace was tried in Scotland,' he said. 'There is a verdict allowed by the Scotch law, which (so far as I know) is not permitted by the laws of any other civilized country on the face of the earth. When the jury are in doubt whether to condemn or acquit the prisoner brought before them, they are permitted, in Scotland, to express that doubt by a form of compromise. If there is not evidence enough, on the one hand, to justify them in finding a prisoner guilty, and not evidence enough, on the other hand, to thoroughly convince them that a prisoner is innocent, they extricate themselves from the difficulty by finding a verdict of Not Proven.'

'Was that the verdict when Eustace was tried?' I asked.

'Yes.'

'The jury were not quite satisfied that my husband was guilty? and not quite satisfied that my husband was innocent? Is that what the Scotch Verdict means?'

'That is what the Scotch Verdict means. For three years that doubt about him in the minds of the jury who tried him has stood on public record.'

Oh, my poor darling! my innocent martyr! I understood it at last. The false name in which he had married me; the terrible words he had spoken when he had warned me to respect his secret; the still more terrible doubt that he felt of me at that moment—it was all intelligible to my sympathies; it was all clear to my understanding, now. I got up again from the sofa, strong in a daring resolution which the Scotch Verdict had suddenly kindled in me—a resolution, at once too sacred and too desperate to be confided, in the first instance, to any other than my husband's ear.

'Take me to Eustace,' I said. 'I am strong enough to bear anything now.'

After one searching look at me, the Major silently offered me his arm. We left the room together.

CHAPTER XII

The Scotch Verdict

WE walked to the far end of the hall. Major Fitz-David opened the door of a long narrow room, built out at the back of the house as a smoking-room, and extending along one side of the courtyard as far as the stable wall.

My husband was alone in the room; seated at the farther end of it, near the fireplace. He started to his feet, and faced me in silence as I entered. The Major softly closed the door on us, and retired. Eustace never stirred a step to meet me. I ran to him, and threw my arms round his neck, and kissed him. The embrace was not returned; the kiss was not returned. He passively submitted—nothing more.

'Eustace,' I said, 'I never loved you more dearly than I love you at this moment! I never felt for you as I feel for you now!'

He released himself deliberately from my arms. He signed to me, with the mechanical courtesy of a stranger, to take a chair.

'Thank you, Valeria,' he answered, in cold measured tones. 'You could say no less to me after what has happened; and you could say no more. Thank you.'

We were standing before the fireplace. He left me, and walked away slowly with his head down; apparently intending to leave the room. I followed him—I got before him—I placed myself between him and the door.

'Why do you leave me?' I said. 'Why do you speak to me in this cruel way? Are you angry, Eustace? My darling,—you *are* angry, I ask you to forgive me.'

'It is I who ought to ask *your* pardon,' he replied. 'I beg you to forgive me, Valeria, for having made you my wife.'

He pronounced those words with a hopeless, heart-broken humility, dreadful to see. I laid my hand on his bosom. I said, 'Eustace, look at me.'

He slowly lifted his eyes to my face—eyes cold and clear and tearless, looking at me in steady resignation, in immovable despair. In the utter wretchedness of that moment, I was like him; I was as quiet and as cold as my husband. He chilled, he froze me.

'Is it possible,' I said, 'that you doubt my belief in your innocence?'

He left the question unanswered. He sighed bitterly to himself. 'Poor woman!' he said, as a stranger might have said, pitying me. 'Poor woman!'

My heart swelled in me as if it would burst. I lifted my hand from his bosom, and laid it on his shoulder to support myself.

'I don't ask you to pity me, Eustace; I ask you to do me justice. You are not doing me justice. If you had trusted me with the truth in the days when we first knew that we loved each other—if you had told me all, and more than all, that I know now—as God is my witness, I would still have married you! *Now* do you doubt that I believe you are an innocent man?'

'I don't doubt it,' he said. 'All your impulses are generous. You are speaking generously, and feeling generously. Don't blame me, my poor child, if I look on farther than you do; if I see what is to come—too surely to come—in the cruel future.'

'The cruel future!' I repeated. 'What do you mean?'

'You believe in my innocence, Valeria. The Jury who tried me doubted it—and have left that doubt on record. What reason have *you* for believing, in the face of the Verdict, that I am an innocent man?'

'I want no reason! I believe, in spite of the Verdict.'

'Will your friends agree with you? When your uncle and aunt know what has happened—and sooner or later they must know it—what will they say? They will say, "He began badly; he concealed from our niece that he had been a prisoner on his trial; he married our niece under a false name. He may say he is innocent; but we have only his word for it. When he was put on his trial, the verdict was Not Proven. Not Proven won't do for us. If the Jury have done him an injustice—if he *is* innocent—let him prove it." That is what the world thinks and says of me. That is what your friends will think and say of me. The time is coming, Valeria, when you—even You—will feel that your friends have reason to appeal to on their side, and that you have no reason on yours.'

'That time will never come!' I answered, warmly. 'You wrong me, you insult me, in thinking it possible!'

He put down my hand from him, and drew back a step, with a bitter smile.

'We have only been married a few days, Valeria. Your love for me is new and young. Time, which wears away all things, will wear away the first fervour of that love.'

'Never! never!'

He drew back from me a little farther still.

'Look at the world round you,' he said. 'The happiest husbands and wives have their occasional misunderstandings and disagreements; the brightest married life has its passing clouds. When those days come for *us*, the doubts and fears that you don't feel now, will find their way to you then. When the clouds rise on *our* married life—when I say my first harsh word, when you make your first hasty reply—then, in the solitude of your own room, in the stillness of the wakeful night, you will think of my first wife's miserable death. You will remember that I was held responsible for it, and that my innocence was never proved. You will say to yourself, "Did it begin, in *her* time, with a harsh word from him, and with a hasty reply from her? Will it one day end with me, as the Jury half feared that it ended with her?" Hideous questions for a wife to ask herself! You will stifle them; you will recoil from them, like a good woman, with horror. But, when we meet the next morning, you will be on your guard, and I shall see it, and know in my heart of hearts what it means. Embittered by that knowledge, my next harsh word may be harsher still. Your next thoughts of me may remind you, more vividly and more boldly, that your husband was once tried as a poisoner, and that the question of his first wife's death was never properly cleared up. Do you see what materials for a domestic hell are mingling for us here? Was it for nothing that I warned you, solemnly warned you, to draw back, when

I found you bent on discovering the truth? Can I ever be at your bedside now, when you are ill, and not remind you, in the most innocent things I do, of what happened at that other bedside, in the time of that other woman whom I married first? If I pour out your medicine, I commit a suspicious action—they said I poisoned *her* in her medicine. If I bring you a cup of tea, I revive the remembrance of a horrid doubt—they said I put the arsenic in *her* cup of tea. If I kiss you when I leave the room—I remind you that the prosecution accused me of kissing *her*, to save appearances and produce an effect on the nurse. Can we live together on such terms as these? No mortal creatures could support the misery of it. This very day I said to you, "If you stir a step farther in this matter, there is an end of your happiness for the rest of your life." You have taken that step—and the end has come to your happiness and to mine. The doubt that kills love has cast its blight on you and on me for the rest of our lives!'

So far I had forced myself to listen to him. At those last words, the picture of the future that he was placing before me became too hideous to be endured. I refused to hear more.

'You are talking horribly,' I said. 'At your age and at mine, have we done with love, and done with hope? It is blasphemy to love and hope to say it!'

'Wait till you have read the Trial,' he answered. 'You mean to read it, I suppose?'

'Every word of it! With a motive, Eustace, which you have yet to know.'

'No motive of yours, Valeria, no love and hope of yours can alter the inexorable facts. My first wife died poisoned; and the verdict of the Jury has not absolutely acquitted me of the guilt of causing her death. As long as you were ignorant of that, the possibilities of happiness were always within our reach. Now you know it, I say again—our married life is at an end.'

'No,' I said. 'Now I know it our married life has begun—begun with a new object for your wife's devotion, with a new reason for your wife's love!'

'What do you mean?'

I went near to him again, and took his hand.

'What did you tell me the world has said of you?' I asked. 'What did you tell me my friends would say of you? "Not Proven won't do for us. If the Jury have done him an injustice—if he *is* innocent—let him prove it." Those were the words you put into the mouths of my friends. I adopt them for mine! *I* say, Not Proven won't do for *me*. Prove your right, Eustace, to a verdict of Not Guilty. Why have you let three years pass without doing it? Shall I guess why? You have waited for your wife to help you. Here she is, my darling, ready to help you with all her heart and soul. Here she is, with one object in life—to show the world, and to show the Scotch Jury, that her husband is an innocent man!'

I had roused myself; my pulses were throbbing, my voice rang through the room. Had I roused *him?* What was his answer?

'Read the Trial.' That was his answer.

I seized his arm. In my indignation and my despair, I shook him with all my strength. God forgive me, I could almost have struck him, for the tone in which he had spoken, and the look that he had cast on me!

'I have told you that I mean to read the Trial,' I said. 'I mean to read it, line by line, with you. Some inexcusable mistake has been made. Evidence in your favour, that might have been found, has not been found. Suspicious circumstances have not been investigated. Crafty people have not been watched. Eustace! the conviction of some dreadful oversight, committed by you or by the persons who helped you, is firmly settled in my mind. The resolution to set that vile Verdict right was the first resolution that came to me, when I first heard of it in the next room. We *will* set it right! We *must* set it right—for your sake, for my sake, for the sake of our children if we are blest with children. Oh, my own love, don't look at me with those cold eyes! Don't answer me in those hard tones! Don't treat me as if I was talking ignorantly and madly of something that can never be!'

Still, I failed to rouse him. His next words were spoken compassionately rather than coldly—that was all.

'My defence was undertaken by the greatest lawyers in the land,' he said. 'After such men have done their utmost, and have failed—my poor Valeria, what can you, what can I, do? We can only submit.'

'Never!' I cried. 'The greatest lawyers are mortal men; the greatest lawyers have made mistakes before now. You can't deny that.'

'Read the Trial.' For the third time, he said those cruel words, and said no more.

In utter despair of moving him—feeling keenly, bitterly (if I must own it), his merciless superiority to all that I had said to him in the honest fervour of my devotion and my love—I thought of Major Fitz-David as a last resort. In the disordered state of my mind, at that moment, it made no difference to me that the Major had already tried to reason with him, and had failed. In the face of the facts, I had a blind belief in the influence of his old friend, if his old friend could only be prevailed upon to support my view.

'Is there no persuading you?' I said. He looked away without answering. 'At least you can wait for me a moment,' I went on. 'I want you to hear another opinion, besides mine.'

I left him, and returned to the study. Major Fitz-David was not there. I knocked at the door of communication with the front room. It was opened instantly by the Major himself. The doctor had gone away. Benjamin still remained in the room.

'Will you come and speak to Eustace?' I began. 'If you will only say what I want you to say——'

Before I could add a word more, I heard the house door opened and closed. Major Fitz-David and Benjamin heard it too. They looked at each other in silence.

I ran back, before the Major could stop me, to the room in which I had seen Eustace. It was empty. My husband had left the house.

CHAPTER XIII

The Man's Decision

MY first impulse was the reckless impulse to follow Eustace—openly, through the streets.

The Major and Benjamin both opposed this hasty resolution on my part. They appealed to my own sense of self-respect, without (so far as I remember it) producing the slightest effect on my mind. They were more successful when they entreated me next to be patient, for my husband's sake. In mercy to Eustace, they begged me to wait half an hour. If he failed to return in that time, they pledged themselves to accompany me in search of him to the hotel.

In mercy to Eustace, I consented to wait. What I suffered under the forced necessity for remaining passive at that crisis in my life, no words of mine can tell. It will be better if I go on with my narrative.

Benjamin was the first to ask me what had passed between my husband and myself.

'You may speak freely, my dear,' he said. 'I know what has happened since you have been in Major Fitz-David's house. No one has told me about it; I found it out for myself. If you remember, I was struck by the name "Macallan," when you first mentioned it to me at my cottage. I couldn't guess why, at the time. I know why, now.'

Hearing this, I told them both unreservedly what I had said to Eustace, and how he had received it. To my unspeakable disappointment, they both sided with my husband—treating my view of his position as a mere dream. They said it, as he had said it, 'You have not read the Trial.'

I was really enraged with them. 'The facts are enough for *me*,' I said. 'We know he is innocent. Why is his innocence not proved? It ought to be, it must be, it shall be! If the Trial tells me it can't be done, I refuse to believe the Trial. Where is the book, Major? Let me see for myself, if his lawyers have left nothing for his wife to do. Did they love him as I love him? Give me the book!'

Major Fitz-David looked at Benjamin.

'It will only additionally shock and distress her, if I give her the book,' he said. 'Don't you agree with me?'

I interposed before Benjamin could answer.

'If you refuse my request,' I said, 'you will oblige me, Major, to go to the nearest bookseller, and tell him to buy the Trial for me. I am determined to read it.'

This time, Benjamin sided with me.

'Nothing can make matters worse than they are, sir,' he said. 'If I may be permitted to advise, let her have her own way.'

The Major rose, and took the book out of the Italian cabinet—to which he had consigned it for safe keeping.

'My young friend tells me, that she informed you of her regrettable outbreak of temper a few days since,' he said, as he handed me the volume. 'I was not aware at the time, what book she had in her hand when she so far forgot herself as to destroy the vase. When I left you in the study, I supposed the Report of the Trial to be in its customary place, on the top shelf of the bookcase; and I own I felt some curiosity to know whether you would think of examining that shelf. The broken vase—it is needless to conceal it from you now—was one of a pair presented to me by your husband and his first wife, only a week before the poor woman's terrible death. I felt my first presentiment that you were on the brink of discovery, when I found you looking at the fragments—and I fancy I betrayed to you that something of the kind was disturbing me. You looked as if you noticed it.'

'I did notice it, Major. And I, too, had a vague idea that I was on the way to discovery. Will you look at your watch? Have we waited half-an-hour yet?'

My impatience had misled me. The ordeal of the half-hour was not yet at an end.

Slowly and more slowly, the heavy minutes followed each other—and still there were no signs of my husband's return. We tried to continue our conversation, and failed. Nothing was audible; no sounds but the ordinary sounds of the street disturbed the dreadful silence. Try as I might to repel it, there was one foreboding thought that pressed closer and closer on my mind as the interval of waiting wore its weary way on. I shuddered as I asked myself, if our married life had come to an end—if Eustace had really left me?

The Major saw—what Benjamin's slower perception had not yet discovered—that my fortitude was beginning to sink under the unrelieved oppression of suspense.

'Come!' he said. 'Let us go to the hotel.'

It then wanted nearly five minutes to the half-hour. I *looked* my gratitude to Major Fitz-David for sparing me those last five minutes: I could not speak to him, or to Benjamin. In silence we three got into a cab and drove to the hotel.

The landlady met us in the hall. Nothing had been seen or heard of Eustace. There was a letter waiting for me upstairs, on the table in our sitting-room. It had been left at the hotel by a messenger, only a few minutes since.

Trembling and breathless, I ran up the stairs; the two gentlemen following me. The writing on the address of the letter was in my husband's hand. My heart sank in me as I looked at the lines; there could be but one reason for his writing to me. That closed envelope held his farewell words. I sat with the letter on my lap, stupefied—incapable of opening it.

Kind-hearted Benjamin attempted to comfort and encourage me. The Major, with his larger experience of women, warned the old man to be silent. 'Wait!' I heard him whisper. 'Speaking to her will do no good now. Give her time.'

Acting on a sudden impulse, I held out the letter to him as he spoke. Even moments might be of importance, if Eustace had indeed left me. To give me time, might be to lose the opportunity of recalling him.

'You are his old friend,' I said. 'Open his letter, Major, and read it for me.'

Major Fitz-David opened the letter, and read it through to himself. When he had done, he threw it on the table with a gesture which was almost a gesture of contempt.

'There is but one excuse for him,' he said. 'The man is mad.'

Those words told me all. I knew the worst; and, knowing it, I could read the letter. It ran thus:—

'My beloved Valeria,—

'When you read these lines, you read my farewell words. I return to my solitary unfriended life—my life before I knew you.

'My darling, you have been cruelly treated. You have been entrapped into marrying a man who has been publicly accused of poisoning his first wife—and who has not been honourably and completely acquitted of the charge. And you know it!

'Can you live on terms of mutual confidence and mutual esteem with me, when I have committed this fraud, and when I stand towards you in this position? It was possible for you to live with me happily, while you were in ignorance of the truth. It is *not* possible, now you know all.

'No! the one atonement I can make is—to leave you. Your one chance of future happiness is to be disassociated, at once and for ever, from my dishonoured life. I love you, Valeria—truly, devotedly, passionately. But the spectre of the poisoned woman rises between us. It makes no difference that I am innocent even of the thought of harming my first wife. My innocence has not been proved. In this world my innocence can never be proved. You are young and loving, and generous and hopeful. Bless others, Valeria, with your rare attractions and your delightful gifts. They are of no avail with *me*. The poisoned woman stands between us. If you live with me now, you will see her as I see her. *That* torture shall never be yours. I love you. I leave you.

'Do you think me hard and cruel? Wait a little, and time will change that way of thinking. As the years go on, you will say to yourself, "Basely as he deceived me, there was some generosity in him. He was man enough to release me of his own free will."

'Yes, Valeria, I fully, freely release you. If it be possible to annul our marriage, let it be done. Recover your liberty by any means that you may be advised to employ; and be assured beforehand of my entire and implicit submission. My lawyers have the necessary instruction on this subject. Your uncle has only to communicate with them, and I think he will be satisfied of my resolution to do you justice. The one interest that I have now left in life, is my interest in your welfare and your happiness in the time to come. Your welfare and your happiness are no longer to be found in your union with Me.

'I can write no more. This letter will wait for you at the hotel. It will be useless to attempt to trace me. I know my own weakness. My heart is all yours; I might yield to you if I let you see me again.

'Show these lines to your uncle, and to any friends whose opinions you may value. I have only to sign my dishonoured name; and every one will understand and applaud my motive for writing as I do. The name justifies—amply justifies—the letter. Forgive me, and forget me. Farewell!

'EUSTACE MACALLAN.'

In those words, he took his leave of me. We had then been married—six days.

CHAPTER XIV

The Woman's Answer

THUS far, I have written of myself with perfect frankness and, I think I may fairly add, with some courage as well. My frankness fails me, and my courage fails me, when I look back to my husband's farewell letter, and try to recall the storm of contending passions that it roused in my mind. No! I cannot tell the truth about myself—I dare not tell the truth about myself—at that terrible time. Men! consult your observation of women, and imagine what I felt. Women! look into your own hearts, and see what I felt, for yourselves.

What I *did*, when my mind was quiet again, is an easier matter to deal with. I answered my husband's letter. My reply to him shall appear in these pages. It will show, in some degree, what effect (of the lasting sort) his desertion of me produced on my mind. It will also reveal the motives that

sustained me, the hopes that animated me, in the new and strange life which
my next chapters must describe.

I was removed from the hotel, in the care of my fatherly old friend,
Benjamin. A bedroom was prepared for me in his little villa. There, I passed
the first night of my separation from my husband. Towards the morning, my
weary brain got some rest—I slept.

At breakfast-time, Major Fitz-David called to inquire about me. He had
kindly volunteered to go and speak for me to my husband's lawyers, on the
preceding day. They had admitted that they knew where Eustace had gone;
but they declared at the same time that they were positively forbidden to
communicate his address to any one. In other respects, their 'Instructions'
in relation to the wife of their client were (as they were pleased to express
it) 'generous to a fault.' I had only to write to them, and they would furnish
me with a copy by return of post.

This was the Major's news. He refrained, with the tact that distinguished
him, from putting any questions to me beyond questions relating to the state
of my health. These answered, he took his leave of me for that day. He and
Benjamin had a long talk together afterwards, in the garden of the villa.

I retired to my room, and wrote to my uncle Starkweather; telling him
exactly what had happened, and enclosing him a copy of my husband's letter.
This done, I went out for a little while to breathe the fresh air, and to think.
I was soon weary, and went back again to my room to rest. My kind old
Benjamin left me at perfect liberty to be alone as long as I pleased. Towards
the afternoon, I began to feel a little more like my old self again. I mean by
this, that I could think of Eustace without bursting out crying, and could
speak to Benjamin without distressing and frightening the dear old man.

That night, I had a little more sleep. The next morning I was strong
enough to confront the first and foremost duty that I now owed to
myself—the duty of answering my husband's letter.

I wrote to him in these words:—

'I am still too weak and weary, Eustace, to write to you at any length. But
my mind is clear. I have formed my own opinion of you and your letter;
and I know what I mean to do now you have left me. Some women, in my
situation, might think that you had forfeited all right to their confidence. I
don't think that. So I write and tell you what is in my mind, in the plainest
and fewest words that I can use.

'You say you love me—and you leave me. I don't understand loving a
woman, and leaving her. For my part, in spite of the hard things you have
said and written to me, and in spite of the cruel manner in which you have
left me, I love you—and I won't give you up. No! As long as I live, I mean
to live your wife.

'Does this surprise you? It surprises *me*. If another woman wrote in this manner to a man who had behaved to her as you have behaved, I should be quite at a loss to account for her conduct. I am quite at a loss to account for my own conduct. I ought to hate you—and yet I can't help loving you. I am ashamed of myself; but so it is.

'You need feel no fear of my attempting to find out where you are, and of my trying to persuade you to return to me. I am not quite foolish enough to do that. You are not in a fit state of mind to return to me. You are all wrong, all over, from head to foot. When you get right again, I am vain enough to think that you will return to me of your own accord. And shall I be weak enough to forgive you? Yes, I shall certainly be weak enough to forgive you.

'But how are you to get right again?

'I have puzzled my brains over this question by night and by day—and my opinion is that you will never get right again, unless I help you.

'How am I to help you?

'The question is easily answered. What the Law has failed to do for you, your Wife must do for you. Do you remember what I said, when we were together in the back room at Major Fitz-David's house? I told you that the first thought that came to me, when I heard what the Scotch Jury had done, was the thought of setting their vile Verdict right. Well! Your letter has fixed this idea more firmly in my mind than ever. The only chance that I can see of winning you back to me, in the character of a penitent and loving husband, is to change that underhand Scotch Verdict of Not Proven, into an honest English verdict of Not Guilty.

'Are you surprised at the knowledge of the law which this way of writing betrays in an ignorant woman? I have been learning, my dear: the Law and the Lady have begun by understanding one another. In plain English, I have looked into Ogilvie's Imperial Dictionary; and Ogilvie tells me: "A verdict of Not Proven only indicates that, in the opinion of the Jury, there is a deficiency in the evidence to convict the prisoner. A verdict of Not Guilty imports the Jury's opinion that the prisoner is innocent."—Eustace! that shall be the opinion of the world in general, and of the Scotch Jury in particular, in your case. To that one object I dedicate my life to come, if God spares me!

'Who will help me, when I need help, is more than I yet know. There was a time when I had hoped that we should go hand in hand together in doing this good work. That hope is at an end. I no longer expect you, or ask you, to help me. A man who thinks as you think, can give no help to anybody—it is his miserable condition to have no hope. So be it! I will hope for two, and will work for two; and I shall find some one to help me—never fear—if I deserve it.

'I will say nothing about my plans—I have not read the Trial yet. It is quite enough for me that I know you are innocent. When a man is innocent, there *must* be a way of proving it: the one thing needful is to find the way.

Sooner or later, with or without assistance, I shall find it. Yes! before I know any single particular of the Case, I tell you positively—I shall find it!

'You may laugh over this blind confidence on my part, or you may cry over it. I don't pretend to know whether I am an object for ridicule or an object for pity. Of one thing only I am certain. I mean to win you back, a man vindicated before the world, without a stain on his character or his name—thanks to his Wife.

'Write to me sometimes, Eustace; and believe me, through all the bitterness of this bitter business, your faithful and loving

'VALERIA.'

There was my reply! Poor enough as a composition (I could write a much better letter now), it had, if I may presume to say so, one merit. It was the honest expression of what I really meant and felt.

I read it to Benjamin. He held up his hands with his customary gesture when he was thoroughly bewildered and dismayed. 'It seems the rashest letter that ever was written,' said the dear old man. 'I never heard, Valeria, of a woman doing what you propose to do. Lord help us! the new generation is beyond my fathoming. I wish your uncle Starkweather was here: I wonder what he would say? Oh, dear me, what a letter from a wife to a husband! Do you really mean to send it to him?'

I added immeasurably to my old friend's surprise, by not even employing the post-office. I wished to see the 'instructions' which my husband had left behind him. So I took the letter to his lawyers myself.

The firm consisted of two partners. They both received me together. One was a soft lean man, with a sour smile. The other was a hard fat man, with ill-tempered eyebrows. I took a great dislike to both of them. On their side, they appeared to feel a strong distrust of me. We began by disagreeing. They showed me my husband's instructions; providing, among other things, for the payment of one clear half of his income, as long as he lived, to his wife. I positively refused to touch a farthing of his money.

The lawyers were unaffectedly shocked and astonished at this decision. Nothing of the sort had ever happened before, in the whole course of their experience. They argued and remonstrated with me. The partner with the ill-tempered eyebrows wanted to know what my reasons were. The partner with the sour smile reminded his colleague satirically that I was a lady, and had therefore no reasons to give. I only answered, 'Be so good as to forward my letter, gentlemen'—and left them.

I have no wish to claim any credit to myself in these pages which I do not honestly deserve. The truth is that my pride forbade me to accept help from Eustace, now that he had left me. My own little fortune (eight hundred a year) had been settled on myself when I married. It had been more than I wanted as a single woman, and I was resolved that it should be enough for me now. Benjamin had insisted on my considering his cottage as my home. Under these circumstances, the expenses in which my determination to clear my husband's character might involve me, were the only expenses for which I had to provide. I could afford to be independent—and independent I resolved that I would be.

While I am occupied in confessing my weakness and my errors, it is only right to add that, dearly as I still loved my unhappy misguided husband, there was one little fault of his which I found it not easy to forgive.

Pardoning other things, I could not pardon his concealing from me that he had been married to a first wife. Why I should have felt this so bitterly as I did, at certain times and seasons, I am not able to explain. Jealousy was at the bottom of it, I suppose. And yet, I was not conscious of being jealous—especially when I thought of the poor creature's miserable death. Still, at odd times when I was discouraged and out of temper, I used to say to myself, 'Eustace ought not to have kept *that* secret from me.' What would *he* have said, if I had been a widow, and had never told him of it?

It was getting on towards evening when I returned to the cottage. Benjamin appeared to have been on the look-out for me. Before I could ring at the bell he opened the garden gate.

'Prepare yourself for a surprise, my dear,' he said. 'Your uncle, the Reverend Doctor Starkweather, has arrived from the North, and is waiting to see you. He received your letter this morning, and he took the first train to London as soon as he had read it.'

In another minute my uncle's strong arms were round me. In my forlorn position, I felt the good Vicar's kindness, in travelling all the way to London to see me, very gratefully. It brought the tears into my eyes—tears, without bitterness, that did me good.

'I have come, my dear child, to take you back to your old home,' he said. 'No words can tell how fervently I wish you had never left your aunt and me. Well! well! we won't talk about it. The mischief is done—and the next thing is to mend it as well as we can. If I could only get within arm's length of that husband of yours, Valeria—there! there! God forgive me, I am forgetting that I am a clergyman. What shall I forget next, I wonder? By-the-bye, your aunt sends you her dearest love. She is more superstitious than ever. This miserable business doesn't surprise her a bit. She says it all began with your making that mistake about your name in signing the church register. You remember? Was there ever such stuff? Ah, she's a foolish woman, that wife of mine! But she means well—a good soul at bottom. She would have travelled all the way here along with me, if I would have let her. I said, "No; you stop at home and look after the house and the parish; and I'll bring the child back." You shall have your old bedroom, Valeria, with the white curtains, you know, looped up with blue! We will return to the Vicarage (if you can get up in time) by the nine-forty train to-morrow morning.'

Return to the Vicarage! How could I do that? How could I hope to gain what was now the one object of my existence, if I buried myself in a remote north-country village? It was simply impossible for me to accompany Doctor Starkweather on his return to his own house.

'I thank you, uncle, with all my heart,' I said. 'But I am afraid I can't leave London for the present.'

'You can't leave London for the present?' he repeated. 'What does the girl mean, Mr Benjamin?'

Benjamin evaded a direct reply.

'She is kindly welcome here, Doctor Starkweather,' he said, 'as long as she chooses to stay with me.'

'That's no answer,' retorted my uncle, in his rough-and-ready way. He turned to me. 'What is there to keep you in London?' he asked. 'You used to hate London. I suppose there is some reason?'

It was only due to my good guardian and friend that I should take him into my confidence sooner or later. There was no help for it but to rouse my courage and tell him frankly what I had it in my mind to do. The Vicar listened in breathless dismay. He turned to Benjamin, with distress as well as surprise in his face, when I had done.

'God help her!' cried the worthy man. 'The poor thing's troubles have turned her brain!'

'I thought you would disapprove of it, sir,' said Benjamin, in his mild and moderate way. 'I confess I disapprove of it myself.'

' "Disapprove of it," isn't the word,' retorted the Vicar. 'Don't put it in that feeble way, if you please. An act of madness—that's what it is, if she really means what she says.' He turned my way, and looked as he used to look, at the afternoon service, when he was catechising an obstinate child. 'You don't mean it,' he said, 'do you?'

'I am very sorry to forfeit your good opinion, uncle,' I replied. 'But I must own that I do certainly mean it.'

'In plain English,' retorted the Vicar, 'you are conceited enough to think that you can succeed where the greatest lawyers in Scotland have failed. *They* couldn't prove this man's innocence, all working together. And *you* are going to prove it single-handed? Upon my word, you are a wonderful woman,' cried my uncle, suddenly descending from indignation to irony. 'May a plain country parson, who isn't used to lawyers in petticoats, be permitted to ask how you mean to do it?'

'I mean to begin by reading the Trial, uncle.'

'Nice reading for a young woman! You will be wanting a batch of nasty French novels next. Well, and when you have read the Trial—what then? Have you thought of that?'

'Yes, uncle. I have thought of that. I shall first try to form some conclusion (after reading the Trial) as to the guilty person who really committed the crime. Then, I shall make out a list of the witnesses who spoke in my husband's defence. I shall go to those witnesses, and tell them who I am, and what I want. I shall ask all sorts of questions which grave lawyers might think it beneath their dignity to put. I shall be guided, in what I do next, by the answers I receive. And I shall not be discouraged, no matter what difficulties are thrown in my way. Those are my plans, uncle, so far as I know them now.'

The Vicar and Benjamin looked at each other, as if they doubted the evidence of their own senses. The Vicar spoke.

'Do you mean to tell me,' he said, 'that you are going roaming about the country, to throw yourself on the mercy of strangers, and to risk whatever rough reception you may get in the course of your travels? You! A young woman! Deserted by your husband! With nobody to protect you! Mr Benjamin, do you hear her? And can you believe your ears? I declare to Heaven *I* don't know whether I am awake or dreaming. Look at her—just look at her! There she sits as cool and easy as if she had said nothing at all extraordinary, and was going to do nothing out of the common way! What am I to do with her—that's the serious question—what on earth am I to do with her?'

'Let me try my experiment, uncle, rash as it may look to you,' I said. 'Nothing else will comfort and support me; and God knows I want comfort and support. Don't think me obstinate. I am ready to admit that there are serious difficulties in my way.'

The Vicar resumed his ironical tone.

'Oh!' he said. 'You admit that, do you? Well, there is something gained, at any rate!'

'Many another woman before me,' I went on, 'has faced serious difficulties, and has conquered them—for the sake of the man she loved.'

Doctor Starkweather rose slowly to his feet, with the air of a person whose capacity of toleration had reached its last limits.

'Am I to understand that you are still in love with Mr Eustace Macallan?' he asked.

'Yes,' I answered.

'The hero of the great Poison Trial?' pursued my uncle. 'The man who has deceived and deserted you? You love him?'

'I love him more dearly than ever.'

'Mr Benjamin,' said the Vicar. 'If she recovers her senses between this and nine o'clock to-morrow morning, send her with her luggage to Loxley's Hotel, where I am now staying. Good night, Valeria. I shall consult with your aunt as to what is to be done next. I have no more to say.'

'Give me a kiss, uncle, at parting.'

'Oh, yes. I'll give you a kiss. Anything you like, Valeria. I shall be sixty-five next birthday; and I thought I knew something of women at my time of life. It seems I know nothing. Loxley's Hotel is the address, Mr Benjamin. Good night.'

Benjamin looked very grave when he returned to me, after accompanying Doctor Starkweather to the garden gate.

'Pray be advised, my dear,' he said. 'I don't ask you to consider *my* view of this matter as good for much. But your uncle's opinion is surely worth considering?'

I did not reply. It was useless to say any more. I made up my mind to be misunderstood and discouraged, and to bear it. 'Good night, my dear old friend,' was all I said to Benjamin. Then I turned away—I confess with the tears in my eyes—and took refuge in my bedroom.

The window-blind was up; and the autumn moonlight shone brilliantly into the little room.

As I stood by the window, looking out, the memory came to me of another moonlight night—when Eustace and I were walking together in the Vicarage garden before our marriage. It was the night of which I have written, many pages back, when there were obstacles to our union, and when Eustace had offered to release me from my engagement to him. I saw the dear face again, looking at me in the moonlight; I heard once more his words, and mine. 'Forgive me' (he had said) 'for having loved you—passionately, devotedly loved you. Forgive me, and let me go.'

And I had answered, 'Oh, Eustace, I am only a woman—don't madden me! I can't live without you. I must, and will, be your wife!' And now, after marriage had united us, we were parted! Parted, still loving each other as passionately as ever. And why? Because he had been accused of a crime that he had never committed, and because a Scotch jury had failed to see that he was an innocent man.

I looked at the lovely moonlight, pursuing these remembrances and these thoughts. A new ardour burnt in me. 'No!' I said to myself. 'Neither relations nor friends shall prevail on me to falter and fail in my husband's cause. The assertion of his innocence is the work of my life—I will begin it to-night!'

I drew down the blind, and lit the candles. In the quiet night—alone and unaided—I took my first step on the toilsome and terrible journey that lay before me. From the title-page to the end, without stopping to rest, and without missing a word, I read the Trial of my husband for the murder of his wife.

CHAPTER XV

The Story of the Trial. The Preliminaries

LET me confess another weakness, on my part, before I begin the story of the Trial. I cannot prevail upon myself to copy, for the second time, the horrible title-page which holds up to public ignominy my husband's name. I have copied it once in my tenth chapter. Let once be enough.

Turning to the second page of the Trial, I found a Note, assuring the reader of the absolute correctness of the Report of the proceedings. The compiler described himself as having enjoyed certain privileges. Thus, the presiding Judge had himself revised his charge to the Jury. And, again, the chief lawyers for the prosecution and the defence, following the Judge's example, had revised their speeches, for, and against, the prisoner. Lastly, particular care had been taken to secure a literally correct report of the evidence given by the various witnesses. It was some relief to me to discover this Note, and to be satisfied at the outset that the Story of the Trial was, in every particular, fully and truly told.

The next page interested me more nearly still. It enumerated the actors in the Judicial Drama—the men who held in their hands my husband's honour, and my husband's life. Here is the List:

THE LORD JUSTICE CLERK,
LORD DRUMFENNICK,   } Judges on the Bench.
LORD NOBLEKIRK,

THE LORD ADVOCATE (Mintlaw),
DONALD DREW, Esquire (Advocate-   } Counsel for
Depute),   the Crown.
Mr JAMES ARLISS, W.S., Agent for the Crown.

THE DEAN OF FACULTY   Counsel for the
(Farmichael),   } Panel (otherwise
ALEXANDER CROCKET, Esquire   the Prisoner).
(Advocate),

Mr THORNIEBANK, W.S.,   } Agents for the Panel.
Mr PLAYMORE, W.S.,

The Indictment against the Prisoner then followed. I shall not copy the uncouth language, full of needless repetitions (and, if I know anything of the subject, not guiltless of bad grammar as well), in which my innocent husband was solemnly and falsely accused of poisoning his first wife. The less there is of that false and hateful Indictment on this page, the better and the truer the page will look, to *my* eyes.

To be brief, then, Eustace Macallan was 'indicted and accused, at the instance of David Mintlaw, Esq., Her Majesty's Advocate, for Her Majesty's interest,' of the Murder of his Wife by poison, at his residence called Gleninch, in the county of Mid-Lothian. The poison was alleged to have been wickedly and feloniously given by the prisoner to his wife Sara, on two occasions, in the form of arsenic, administered in tea, medicine, 'or other article or articles of food or drink, to the prosecutor unknown, or in some other manner to the prosecutor unknown.' It was further declared that the prisoner's wife had died of the poison thus administered by her husband, on one or other, or both, of the stated occasions; and that she was thus murdered by her husband. The next paragraph asserted, that the said Eustace Macallan, taken before John Daviot, Esquire, advocate, sheriff-substitute of Mid-Lothian, did in his presence at Edinburgh (on a given date—viz:—the 29th of October), subscribe a Declaration stating his innocence of the alleged crime: this Declaration being reserved in the Indictment—together with certain Documents, papers, and articles, enumerated in an Inventory—to be used in evidence against the prisoner. The Indictment concluded by declaring that, in the event of the offence charged against the prisoner being found proven by the Verdict, he, the said Eustace Macallan, 'ought to be punished with the pains of the law, to deter others from committing the like crimes in all time coming.'

So much for the Indictment! I have done with it—and I am rejoiced to have done with it.

An Inventory of papers, documents, and articles followed at great length, on the three next pages. This, in its turn, was succeeded by the list of the witnesses, and by the names of the jurors (fifteen in number) balloted for, to try the case. And then, at last, the Report of the Trial began. It resolved itself, to my mind, into three great Questions. As it appeared to me at the time, so let me present it here.

CHAPTER XVI

First Question—Did the Woman Die Poisoned?

THE proceedings began at ten o'clock. The prisoner was placed at the Bar, before the High Court of Justiciary, at Edinburgh. He bowed respectfully to the Bench, and pleaded Not Guilty, in a low voice.

It was observed by every one present, that the prisoner's face betrayed the traces of acute mental suffering. He was deadly pale. His eyes never once wandered to the crowd in the Court. When certain witnesses appeared against him, he looked at them with a momentary attention. At other times, he kept his eyes on the ground. When the evidence touched on his wife's illness and death he was deeply affected, and covered his face with his hands. It was a subject of general remark and general surprise, that the prisoner, in this case (although a man), showed far less self-possession than the last prisoner tried in that Court for murder—a woman, who had been convicted on overwhelming evidence. There were persons present (a small minority only) who considered this want of composure on the part of the prisoner to be a sign in his favour. Self-possession, in his dreadful position, signified to their minds, the stark insensibility of a heartless and shameless criminal, and afforded in itself a presumption—not of innocence—but of guilt.

The first witness called was John Daviot, Esquire, Sheriff-Substitute of Mid-Lothian. He was examined by the Lord Advocate (as counsel for the prosecution); and said:

'The prisoner was brought before me on the present charge. He made, and subscribed, a Declaration, on the 29th of October. It was freely and voluntarily made; the prisoner having been first duly warned and admonished.'

Having identified the Declaration, the Sheriff-Substitute—being cross-examined by the Dean of Faculty (as counsel for the defence)—continued his evidence in these words:

'The charge against the prisoner was, Murder. This was communicated to him before he made the Declaration. The questions addressed to the prisoner were put, partly by me, partly by another officer, the Procurator-Fiscal. The answers were given distinctly, and, so far as I could judge, without reserve. The statements put forward in the Declaration were all made in answer to questions asked by the Procurator-Fiscal or by myself.'

A clerk in the Sheriff-Clerk's office then officially produced the Declaration, and corroborated the evidence of the witness who had preceded him.

The appearance of the next witness created a marked sensation in the Court. This was no less a person than the nurse who had attended Mrs Macallan in her last illness—by name, Christina Ormsay.

After the first formal answers, the nurse (examined by the Lord Advocate) proceeded to say:

'I was first sent for, to attend the deceased lady, on the seventh of October. She was then suffering from a severe cold, accompanied by a rheumatic affection of the left knee-joint. Previous to this, I understood that her health had been fairly good. She was not a very difficult person to nurse, when you got used to her, and understood how to manage her. The main difficulty was caused by her temper. She was not a sullen person; she was headstrong and violent—easily excited to fly into a passion, and quite reckless, in her fits of anger, as to what she said or did. At such times, I really hardly think she knew what she was about. My own idea is, that her temper was made still more irritable by unhappiness in her married life. She was far from being a reserved person. Indeed, she was disposed (as I thought) to be a little too communicative about herself and her troubles, with persons, like me, who were beneath her in station. She did not scruple, for instance, to tell me (when we had been long enough together to get used to each other) that she was very unhappy, and fretted a good deal about her husband. One night, when she was wakeful and restless, she said to me——'

The Dean of Faculty here interposed; speaking on the prisoner's behalf. He appealed to the Judges to say whether such loose and unreliable evidence as this, was evidence which could be received by the Court?

The Lord Advocate (speaking on behalf of the Crown) claimed it as his right to produce the evidence. It was of the utmost importance, in this case, to show (on the testimony of an unprejudiced witness) on what terms the husband and wife were living. The witness was a most respectable woman. She had won, and deserved, the confidence of the unhappy lady whom she attended on her deathbed.

After briefly consulting together, the Judges unanimously decided that the evidence could not be admitted. What the witness had herself seen and observed of the relations between the husband and wife, was the only evidence that they could receive.

The Lord Advocate thereupon continued his examination of the witness. Christina Ormsay resumed her evidence as follows:

'My position as nurse led necessarily to my seeing more of Mrs Macallan than any other person in the house. I am able to speak, from experience, of many things not known to others who were only in her room at intervals.

'For instance, I had more than one opportunity of personally observing that Mr and Mrs Macallan did not live together very happily. I can give you an example of this, not drawn from what others told me, but from what I noticed for myself.

'Towards the latter part of my attendance on Mrs Macallan, a young widow lady, named Mrs Beauly—a cousin of Mr Macallan's—came to stay at Gleninch. Mrs Macallan was jealous of this lady; and she showed it, in my presence, only the day before her death, when Mr Macallan came into her room to inquire how she had passed the night. "Oh," she said, "never mind how *I* have slept! What do you care whether I sleep well or ill? How has Mrs Beauly passed the night? Is she more beautiful than ever this morning? Go back to her—pray go back to her! Don't waste your time with me." Beginning in that manner, she worked herself into one of her furious rages. I was brushing her hair at the time; and, feeling that my presence was an impropriety under the circumstances, I attempted to leave the room. She forbade me to go. Mr Macallan felt, as I did, that my duty was to withdraw; and he said so in plain words. Mrs Macallan insisted on my staying, in language so insolent to her husband that he said, "If you cannot control yourself, either the nurse leaves the room or I do." She refused to yield even then. "A good excuse," she said, "for getting back to Mrs Beauly. Go!" He took her at her word, and walked out of the room. He had barely closed the door, before she began reviling him to me in the most shocking manner. She declared, among other things she said of him, that the news of all others which he would be glad to hear would be the news of her death. I ventured, quite respectfully, on remonstrating with her. She took up the hairbrush, and threw it at me—and, then and there, dismissed me from my attendance on her. I left her; and waited below until her fit of passion had worn itself out. Then I returned to my place at the bedside, and, for a while, things went on again as usual.

'It may not be amiss to add a word which may help to explain Mrs Macallan's jealousy of her husband's cousin. Mrs Macallan was a very plain woman. She had a cast in one of her eyes, and (if I may use the expression) one of the most muddy, blotchy complexions it was ever my misfortune to see in a person's face. Mrs Beauly, on the other hand, was a most attractive lady. Her eyes were universally admired; and she had a most beautifully clear and delicate colour. Poor Mrs Macallan said of her, most untruly, that she painted.

'No; the defects in the complexion of the deceased lady were not in any way attributable to her illness. I should call them born and bred defects in herself.

'Her illness, if I am asked to describe it, I should say was troublesome, nothing more. Until the last day, there were no symptoms in the least degree serious about the malady that had taken her. Her rheumatic knee was painful, of course, acutely painful if you like, when she moved it; and the confinement to bed was irksome enough, no doubt. But otherwise there was nothing in the lady's condition, before the fatal attack came, to alarm her or anybody about her. She had her books, and her writing-materials, on an invalid table which worked on a pivot, and could be arranged in any position most agreeable to her. At times, she read and wrote a great deal. At other times, she lay quiet, thinking her own thoughts, or talking with me and with one or two lady friends in the neighbourhood who came regularly to see her.

'Her writing, so far as I knew, was almost entirely of the poetical sort. She was a great hand at composing poetry. On one occasion only, she showed me some of her poems. I am no judge of such things. Her poetry was of the dismal kind; despairing about herself, and wondering why she had ever been born, and nonsense like that. Her husband came in more than once for some hard hits at his cruel heart and his ignorance of his wife's merits. In short, she vented her discontent with her pen as well as with her tongue. There were times—and pretty often too—when an angel from heaven would have failed to have satisfied Mrs Macallan.

'Throughout the period of her illness the deceased lady occupied the same room—a large bedroom situated (like all the best bedrooms) on the first floor of the house.

'Yes: the plan of the room now shown to me is quite accurately taken, according to my remembrance of it. One door led into the great passage, or corridor, on which all the doors opened. A second door, at one side (marked B on the plan), led into Mr Macallan's sleeping room. A third door, on the opposite side (marked C on the plan), communicated with a little study or book-room, used, as I was told, by Mr Macallan's mother when she was staying at Gleninch, but seldom or never entered by any one else. Mr Macallan's mother was not at Gleninch while I was there. The door between the bedroom and this study was locked, and the key was taken out. I don't know who had the key, or whether there were more keys than one in existence. The door was never opened, to my knowledge. I only got into the study, to look at it along with the housekeeper, by entering through a second door that opened on to the corridor.

'I beg to say that I can speak, from my own knowledge, positively about Mrs Macallan's illness, and about the sudden change which ended in her death. By the doctor's advice, I made notes, at the time, of dates and hours, and such like. I looked at my notes before coming here.

'From the seventh of October, when I was first called in to nurse her, to the twentieth of the same month, she slowly, but steadily, improved in health. Her knee was still painful, no doubt; but the inflammatory look of it was disappearing. As to the other symptoms, except weakness from lying in bed, and irritability of temper, there was really nothing the matter with her. She slept badly, I ought perhaps to add. But we remedied this, by means of composing-draughts, prescribed for that purpose by the doctor.

'On the morning of the twenty-first, at a few minutes past six, I got my first alarm that something was going wrong with Mrs Macallan.

'I was woke, at the time I have mentioned, by the ringing of the hand-bell which she kept on her bed-table. Let me say for myself that I had only fallen asleep on the sofa in the bedroom, at past two in the morning, from sheer fatigue. Mrs Macallan was then awake. She was in one of her bad humours with me. I had tried to prevail on her to let me remove her dressing-case from her bed-table, after she had used it in making her toilet for the night. It took up a great deal of room; and she could not possibly want it again before the morning. But no—she insisted on my letting it be. There was a glass inside the case; and, plain as she was, she never wearied of looking at herself in that glass! I saw that she was in a bad state of temper, so I gave her her way, and let the dressing-case be. Finding that she was too sullen to speak to me after that, and too obstinate to take her composing-draught from me when I offered it, I laid me down on the sofa at her bed-foot, and fell asleep, as I have said.

'The moment her bell rang, I was up and at the bedside, ready to make myself useful.

'I asked what was the matter with her. She complained of faintness and depression, and said she felt sick. I inquired if she had taken anything in the way of physic or food while I had been asleep. She answered that her husband had come in about an hour since, and, finding her still sleepless, had himself administered the composing-draught. Mr Macallan (sleeping in the next room) joined us while she was speaking. He, too, had been aroused by the bell. He heard what Mrs Macallan said to me about the composing-draught, and made no remark upon it. It seemed to me that he was alarmed at his wife's faintness. I suggested that she should take a little wine, or brandy-and-water. She answered that she could swallow nothing so strong as wine or brandy, having a burning pain in her stomach already. I put my hand on her stomach—quite lightly. She screamed when I touched her.

'This symptom alarmed us. We sent to the village for the medical man who had attended Mrs Macallan during her illness: one Mr Gale.

'The doctor seemed no better able to account for the change for the worse in his patient than we were. Hearing her complaint of thirst, he gave her some milk. Not long after taking it, she was sick. The sickness appeared to relieve her. She soon grew drowsy, and slumbered. Mr Gale left us, with strict injunctions to send for him instantly if she was taken ill again.

'Nothing of the sort happened; no change took place for the next three hours or more. She roused up towards half-past nine, and inquired about her husband. I informed her that he had returned to his own room, and asked if I should send for him. She said, "No." I asked next, if she would like anything to eat or drink. She said, "No," again, in rather a vacant, stupefied way—and then told me to go down stairs and get my breakfast. On my way down I met the housekeeper. She invited me to breakfast with her in her room, instead of in the servants' hall as usual. I remained with the housekeeper but a short time: certainly not more than half an hour.

'Going upstairs again, I met the under-housemaid, sweeping, on one of the landings.

'The girl informed me that Mrs Macallan had taken a cup of tea, during my absence in the housekeeper's room. Mr Macallan's valet had ordered the tea for his mistress, by his master's directions. The under-housemaid made it, and took it upstairs herself to Mrs Macallan's room. Her master (she said) opened the door, when she knocked, and took the teacup from her with his own hand. He opened the door widely enough for her to see into the bedroom, and to notice that nobody was with Mrs Macallan but himself.

'After a little talk with the under-housemaid, I returned to the bedroom. No one was there. Mrs Macallan was lying perfectly quiet, with her face turned away from me on the pillow. Approaching the bedside, I kicked against something on the floor. It was a broken teacup. I said to Mrs Macallan, "How comes the teacup to be broken, ma'am?" She answered, without turning towards me—in an odd, muffled kind of voice—"I dropped it." "Before you drank your tea, ma'am?" I asked. "No," she said; "in handing the cup back to Mr Macallan after I had done." I had put my question, wishing to know—in case she had spilt the tea when she dropped the cup—whether it would be necessary to get her any more. I am quite sure I remember correctly my question, and her answer. I inquired next if she had been long alone. She said, shortly, "Yes; I have been trying to sleep." I said, "Do you feel pretty comfortable?" She answered, "Yes," again. All this time she still kept her face sulkily turned from me towards the wall. Stooping over her to arrange the bed-clothes, I looked towards her table. The writing materials which were always kept on it, were disturbed; and there was wet ink on one of the pens. I said, "Surely, you haven't been writing, ma'am?" "Why not?" she said; "I couldn't sleep." "Another poem?" I asked. She laughed to herself—a bitter, short laugh. "Yes," she said; "another poem." "That's good," I said; "it looks as if you were getting quite like yourself again. We shan't want the doctor any more to-day." She made no answer to this, except an impatient sign with her hand. I didn't understand the sign. Upon that, she spoke again—and crossly enough, too! "I want to be alone; leave me."

'I had no choice but to do as I was told. To the best of my observation there was nothing the matter with her, and nothing for the nurse to do. I put the bell-rope within reach of her hand, and I went downstairs again.

'Half an hour more, as well as I can guess it, passed. I kept within hearing of the bell; but it never rang. I was not quite at my ease—without exactly knowing why. That odd muffled voice in which she had spoken to me hung on my mind, as it were. I was not quite satisfied about leaving her alone for too long a time together—and then, again, I was unwilling to risk throwing her into one of her fits of passion by going back before she rang for me. It ended in my venturing into the room on the ground floor, called the Morning Room, to consult Mr Macallan. He was usually to be found there in the forenoon of the day.

'On this occasion, however, when I looked into the Morning Room it was empty.

'At the same moment, I heard the master's voice on the terrace outside. I went out, and found him speaking to one Mr Dexter, an old friend of his, and (like Mrs Beauly) a guest staying in the house. Mr Dexter was sitting at the window of his room upstairs (he was a cripple, and could only move himself about in a chair on wheels); and Mr Macallan was speaking to him from the terrace below.

' "Dexter!" I heard Mr Macallan say; "Where is Mrs Beauly? Have you seen anything of her?"

'Mr Dexter answered, in his quick, off-hand way of speaking, "Not I! I know nothing about her."

'Then I advanced, and, begging pardon for intruding, I mentioned to Mr Macallan the difficulty I was in about going back or not to his wife's room, without waiting until she rang for me. Before he could advise me in the matter, the footman made his appearance, and informed me that Mrs Macallan's bell was then ringing—and ringing violently.

'It was close on eleven o'clock. As fast as I could mount the stairs, I hastened back to the bedroom.

'Before I opened the door, I heard Mrs Macallan groaning. She was in dreadful pain; feeling a burning heat in the stomach, and in the throat; together with the same sickness which had troubled her in the early morning. Though no doctor, I could see in her face that this second attack was of a far more serious nature than the first. After ringing the bell for a messenger to send to Mr Macallan, I ran to the door to see if any of the servants happened to be within call.

'The only person I saw in the corridor was Mrs Beauly. She was on her way from her own room, she said, to inquire after Mrs Macallan's health. I said to her, "Mrs Macallan is seriously ill again, ma'am. Would you please tell Mr Macallan, and send for the doctor?" She ran downstairs at once to do as I told her.

'I had not been long back at the bedside when Mr Macallan and Mrs Beauly both came in together. Mrs Macallan cast a strange look on them (a look I cannot at all describe), and made them leave her. Mrs Beauly, looking very much frightened, withdrew immediately. Mr Macallan advanced a step or two nearer to the bed. His wife looked at him again, in the same strange way, and cried out—half as if she was threatening him, half as if she was entreating him—"Leave me with the nurse. Go!" He only waited to say to me in a whisper, "The doctor is sent for"—and then he left the room.

'Before Mr Gale arrived, Mrs Macallan was violently sick. What came from her was muddy and frothy, and faintly streaked with blood. When Mr Gale saw it, he looked very serious; I heard him say to himself, "What does this mean?" He did his best to relieve Mrs Macallan, but with no good result that I could see. After a time, she seemed to suffer less. Then more sickness came on. Then there was another intermission. Whether she was suffering or not, I observed that her hands and feet (whenever I touched them) remained equally cold. Also, the doctor's report of her pulse was always the same—"very small and feeble." I said to Mr Gale, "What is to be done, sir?" And Mr Gale said to me, "I won't take the responsibility on myself any longer; I must have a physician from Edinburgh."

'The fastest horse in the stables at Gleninch was put into a dog-cart; and the coachman drove away full speed to Edinburgh, to fetch the famous Doctor Jerome.

'While we were waiting for the physician, Mr Macallan came into his wife's room, with Mr Gale. Exhausted as she was, she instantly lifted her hand, and signed to him to leave her. He tried by soothing words to persuade her to let him stay. No! She still insisted on sending him out of her room. He seemed to feel it—at such a time, and in the presence of the doctor. Before she was aware of him, he suddenly stepped up to the bedside, and kissed her on the forehead. She shrank from him with a scream. Mr Gale interfered, and led him out of the room.

'In the afternoon, Dr Jerome arrived.

'The great physician came just in time to see her seized with another attack of sickness. He watched her attentively, without speaking a word. In the interval when the sickness stopped, he still studied her, as it were, in perfect silence. I thought he would never have done examining her. When he was at last satisfied, he told me to leave him alone with Mr Gale. "We will ring," he said, "when we want you here again."

'It was a long time before they rang for me. The coachman was sent for, before I was summoned back to the bedroom. He was despatched to Edinburgh, for the second time, with a written message from Doctor Jerome to his head servant, saying that there was no chance of his returning to the city, and to his patients, for some hours to come. Some of us thought this looked badly for Mrs Macallan. Others said it might mean that the doctor had hopes of saving her, but expected to be a long time in doing it.

'At last I was sent for. On my presenting myself in the bedroom, Doctor Jerome went out to speak to Mr Macallan, leaving Mr Gale along with me. From that time, as long as the poor lady lived, I was never left alone with her. One of the two doctors was always in her room. Refreshments were prepared for them; but still they took it in turns to eat their meal—one relieving the other at the bedside. If they had administered remedies to their patient I should not have been surprised by this proceeding. But they were at the end of their remedies; their only business in the room seemed to be to keep watch. I was puzzled to account for this. Keeping watch was the nurse's business. I thought the conduct of the doctors very strange.

'By the time that the lamp was lit in the sick room, I could see that the end was near. Excepting an occasional feeling of cramp in her legs, she seemed to suffer less. But her eyes looked sunk in her head; her skin was cold and clammy; her lips had turned to a bluish paleness. Nothing roused her now—excepting the last attempt made by her husband to see her. He came in with Dr Jerome, looking like a man terror-struck. She was past speaking; but the moment she saw him, she feebly made signs and sounds which showed that she was just as resolved as ever not to let him come near her. He was so overwhelmed that Mr Gale was obliged to help him out of the room. No other person was allowed to see the patient. Mr Dexter and Mrs Beauly made their inquiries outside the door, and were not invited in. As the evening drew on, the doctors sat on either side of the bed, silently watching her, silently waiting for her death.

'Towards eight o'clock, she seemed to have lost the use of her hands and arms; they lay helpless outside the bed-clothes. A little later, she sank into a sort of dull sleep. Little by little, the sound of her heavy breathing grew fainter. At twenty minutes past nine, Doctor Jerome told me to bring the lamp to the bedside. He looked at her, and put his hand on her heart. Then he said to me, "You can go downstairs, nurse: it is all over." He turned to Mr Gale. "Will you inquire if Mr Macallan can see us?" he said. I opened the door for Mr Gale, and followed him out. Doctor Jerome called me back for a moment, and told me to give him the key of the door. I did so, of course—but I thought this also very strange. When I got down to the servants' hall, I found there was a general feeling that something was wrong. We were all uneasy—without knowing why.

'A little later the two doctors left the house. Mr Macallan had been quite incapable of receiving them, and hearing what they had to say. In this difficulty, they had spoken privately with Mr Dexter, as Mr Macallan's old friend, and the only gentleman then staying at Gleninch.

'Before bedtime I went upstairs, to prepare the remains of the deceased lady for the coffin. The room in which she lay was locked; the door leading into Mr Macallan's room being secured as well as the door leading into the corridor. The keys had been taken away by Mr Gale. Two of the men servants were posted outside the bedroom to keep watch. They were to be relieved at four in the morning—that was all they could tell me.

'In the absence of any explanations or directions, I took the liberty of knocking at the door of Mr Dexter's room. From his lips I first heard the startling news. Both the doctors had refused to give the usual certificate of death! There was to be a medical examination of the body the next morning.'

There the examination of the nurse, Christina Ormsay, came to an end.

Ignorant as I was of the law, I could see what impression the evidence (so far) was intended to produce on the minds of the Jury. After first showing that my husband had had two opportunities of administering the poison—once in the medicine and once in the tea—the counsel for the Crown led the Jury to infer that the prisoner had taken those opportunities to rid himself of an ugly and jealous wife whose detestable temper he could no longer endure.

Having directed his examination to the attainment of this object, the Lord Advocate had done with the witness. The Dean of Faculty—acting in the prisoner's interests—then rose to bring out the favourable side of the wife's character by cross-examining the nurse. If he succeeded in this attempt, the Jury might reconsider their conclusion that the wife was a person who had exasperated her husband beyond endurance. In that case, where (so far) was the husband's motive for poisoning her? and where was the presumption of the prisoner's guilt?

Pressed by this skilful lawyer, the nurse was obliged to exhibit my husband's first wife under an entirely new aspect. Here is the substance of what the Dean of Faculty extracted from Christina Ormsay:

'I persist in declaring that Mrs Macallan had a most violent temper. But she was certainly in the habit of making amends for the offence that she gave by her violence. When she was quiet again, she always made her excuses to me; and she made them with a good grace. Her manners were engaging at such times as these. She spoke and acted like a well-bred lady. Then again, as to her personal appearance. Plain as she was in face, she had a good figure; her hands and feet, I was told, had been modelled by a sculptor. She had a very pleasant voice; and she was reported when in health to sing beautifully. She was also (if her maid's account was to be trusted) a pattern, in the matter of dressing, for the other ladies in the neighbourhood. Then, as to Mrs Beauly, though she was certainly jealous of the beautiful young widow, she had shown at the same time that she was capable of controlling that feeling. It was through Mrs Macallan that Mrs Beauly was in the house. Mrs Beauly had wished to postpone her visit on account of the state of Mrs Macallan's health. It was Mrs Macallan herself—not her husband—who decided that Mrs Beauly should not be disappointed, and should pay her visit to Gleninch, then and there. Further, Mrs Macallan (in spite of her temper) was popular with her friends, and popular with her servants. There was hardly a dry eye in the house when it was known she was dying. And, further still, in those little domestic disagreements at which the nurse had been present, Mr Macallan had never lost his temper, and had never used harsh language; he seemed to be more sorry than angry when the quarrels took place.'—Moral for the Jury: Was this the sort of woman who would exasperate a man into poisoning her? And was this the sort of man who would be capable of poisoning his wife?

Having produced that salutary counter-impression, the Dean of Faculty sat down; and the medical witnesses were called next.

Here, the evidence was simply irresistible.

Doctor Jerome and Mr Gale positively swore that the symptoms of the illness were the symptoms of poisoning by arsenic. The surgeon who had performed the post-mortem examination followed. He positively swore that the appearance of the internal organs proved Dr Jerome and Mr Gale to be right in declaring that their patient had died poisoned. Lastly, to complete this overwhelming testimony, two analytical chemists actually produced in Court the arsenic which they had found in the body, in a quantity admittedly sufficient to have killed two persons instead of one. In the face of such evidence as this, cross-examination was a mere form. The first Question raised by the Trial—Did the Woman Die Poisoned?—was answered in the affirmative, and answered beyond the possibility of doubt.

The next witnesses called were witnesses concerned with the question that now followed—the obscure and terrible question: Who Poisoned Her?

CHAPTER XVII

Second Question—Who Poisoned her?

THE evidence of the doctors and the chemists closed the proceedings, on the first day of the Trial.

On the second day, the evidence to be produced by the prosecution was anticipated with a general feeling of curiosity and interest. The Court was now to hear what had been seen and done by the persons officially appointed to verify such cases of suspected crime as the case which had occurred at Gleninch. The Procurator-Fiscal—being the person officially appointed to direct the preliminary investigations of the Law—was the first witness called, on the second day of the Trial.

Examined by the Lord Advocate, the Fiscal gave his evidence, as follows:

'On the twenty-sixth of October, I received a communication from Doctor Jerome of Edinburgh, and from Mr Alexander Gale, medical practitioner, residing in the village or hamlet of Dingdovie, near Edinburgh. The communication related to the death, under circumstances of suspicion, of Mrs Eustace Macallan, at her husband's house, hard by Dingdovie, called Gleninch. There was also forwarded to me, enclosed in the document just mentioned, two reports. One described the results of a post-mortem examination of the deceased lady; and the other stated the discoveries made, after a chemical analysis of certain of the interior organs of her body. The result, in both instances, proved to demonstration that Mrs Eustace Macallan had died of poisoning by arsenic.

'Under these circumstances, I set in motion a search and inquiry in the house at Gleninch, and elsewhere, simply for the purpose of throwing light on the circumstances which had attended the lady's death.

'No criminal charge, in connexion with the death, was made at my office against any person, either in the communication which I received from the medical men, or in any other form. The investigations at Gleninch, and elsewhere, beginning on the twenty-sixth of October, were not completed until the twenty-eighth. Upon this latter date—acting on certain discoveries which were reported to me, and on my own examination of letters and other documents brought to my office—I made a criminal charge against the prisoner; and obtained a warrant for his apprehension. He was examined before the Sheriff, on the twenty-ninth of October, and was committed for Trial before this Court.'

The Fiscal having made his statement, and having been cross-examined (on technical matters only), the persons employed in his office were called next. These men had a story of startling interest to tell. Theirs were the fatal discoveries which had justified the Fiscal in charging my husband with the murder of his wife. The first of the witnesses was a sheriff's officer. He gave his name as Isaiah Schoolcraft.

Examined by Mr Drew—Advocate-Depute, and counsel for the Crown with the Lord Advocate—Isaiah Schoolcraft said:

'I got a warrant on the twenty-sixth of October, to go to the country house near Edinburgh, called Gleninch. I took with me Robert Lorrie, Assistant to the Fiscal. We first examined the room in which Mrs Eustace Macallan had died. On the bed, and on a movable table which was attached to it, we found books and writing materials, and a paper containing some unfinished verses in manuscript; afterwards identified as being in the handwriting of the deceased. We enclosed these articles in paper, and sealed them up.

'We next opened an Indian cabinet in the bedroom. Here we found many more verses, on many more sheets of paper, in the same handwriting. We also discovered, first, some letters—and next a crumpled piece of paper thrown aside in a corner of one of the shelves. On closer examination, a chemist's printed label was discovered on this morsel of paper. We also found in the folds of it a few scattered grains of some white powder. The paper and the letters were carefully enclosed, and sealed up as before.

'Further investigation in the room revealed nothing which could throw any light on the purpose of our inquiry. We examined the clothes, jewellery, and books of the deceased. These we left under lock and key. We also found her dressing case, which we protected by seals, and took away with us to the Fiscal's office, along with all the other articles that we had discovered in the room.

'The next day we continued our examination in the house, having received, in the interval, fresh instructions from the Fiscal. We began our work in the bedroom communicating with the room in which Mrs Macallan had died. It had been kept locked since the death. Finding nothing of any importance here, we went next to another room on the same floor, in which we were informed the prisoner was then lying, ill in bed.

'His illness was described to us as a nervous complaint, caused by the death of his wife, and by the proceedings which had followed it. He was reported to be quite incapable of exerting himself, and quite unfit to see strangers. We insisted nevertheless (in deference to our instructions) on obtaining admission to his room. He made no reply, when we inquired whether he had, or had not, removed anything from the sleeping-room next to his late wife's which he usually occupied, to the sleeping-room in which he now lay. All he did was to close his eyes, as if he was too feeble to speak to us or to notice us. Without further disturbing him, we began to examine the room and the different objects in it.

'While we were so employed, we were interrupted by a strange sound. We likened it to the rumbling of wheels in the corridor outside.

'The door opened, and there came swiftly in a gentleman—a cripple—wheeling himself along in a chair. He wheeled his chair straight up to a little table which stood by the prisoner's bedside, and said something to him in a whisper too low to be overheard. The prisoner opened his eyes, and quickly answered by a sign. We informed the crippled gentleman, quite respectfully, that we could not allow him to be in the room at this time. He appeared to think nothing of what we said. He only answered, "My name is Dexter. I am one of Mr Macallan's old friends. It is you who are intruding here; not I." We again notified to him that he must leave the room; and we pointed out particularly that he had got his chair in such a position against the bedside-table as to prevent us from examining it. He only laughed. "Can't you see for yourselves," he said; "that it is a table, and nothing more?" In reply to this, we warned him that we were acting under a legal warrant, and that he might get into trouble if he obstructed us in the execution of our duty. Finding there was no moving him by fair means, I took his chair and pulled it away, while Robert Lorrie laid hold of the table and carried it to the other end of the room. The crippled gentleman flew into a furious rage with me for presuming to touch his chair. "My chair is Me," he said: "how dare you lay hands on Me?" I first opened the door; and then, by way of accommodating him, gave the chair a good push behind with my stick, instead of my hand—and so sent It, and him, safely and swiftly out of the room.

'Having locked the door, so as to prevent any further intrusion, I joined Robert Lorrie in examining the bedside-table. It had one drawer in it, and that drawer we found secured.

'We asked the prisoner for the key.

'He flatly refused to give it to us, and said we had no right to unlock his drawers. He was so angry that he even declared it was lucky for us he was too weak to rise from his bed. I answered civilly that our duty obliged us to examine the drawer, and that, if he still declined to produce the key, he would only oblige us to take the table away and have the lock opened by a smith.

'While we were still disputing, there was a knock at the door of the room.

'I opened the door cautiously. Instead of the crippled gentleman, whom I had expected to see again, there was another stranger standing outside. The prisoner hailed him as a friend and neighbour, and eagerly called upon him for protection from us. We found this second gentleman pleasant enough to deal with. He informed us readily that he had been sent for by Mr Dexter, and that he was himself a lawyer—and he asked to see our warrant. Having looked at it, he at once informed the prisoner (evidently very much to the prisoner's surprise) that he must submit to have the drawer examined—under protest. And then, without more ado, he got the key, and opened the table drawer for us himself.

'We found inside several letters, and a large book, with a lock to it; having the words "My Diary" inscribed on it in gilt letters. As a matter of course, we took possession of the letters and the Diary, and sealed them up to be given to the Fiscal. At the same time, the gentleman wrote out a protest, on the prisoner's behalf, and handed us his card. The card informed us that he was Mr Playmore—now one of the agents for the prisoner. The card and the protest were deposited, with the other documents, in the care of the Fiscal. No other discoveries of any importance were made at Gleninch.

'Our next inquiries took us to Edinburgh—to the druggist whose label we had found on the crumpled morsel of paper and to other druggists likewise whom we were instructed to question. On the twenty-eighth of October, the Fiscal was in possession of all the information that we could collect, and our duties for the time being came to an end.'

This concluded the evidence of Schoolcraft and Lorrie. It was not shaken on cross-examination; and it was plainly unfavourable to the prisoner.

Matters grew worse still when the next witnesses were called. The druggist whose label had been found on the crumpled bit of paper now appeared on the stand, to make the position of my unhappy husband more critical than ever.

Andrew Kinlay, druggist, of Edinburgh, deposed as follows:

'I keep a special registry-book of the poisons sold by me. I produce the book. On the date therein mentioned, the prisoner at the bar, Mr Eustace Macallan, came into my shop, and said that he wished to purchase some arsenic. I asked him what it was wanted for? He told me it was wanted by his gardener, to be used, in solution, for the killing of insects in the greenhouse. At the same time he mentioned his name—Mr Macallan, of Gleninch. I at once directed my assistant to put up the arsenic (two ounces of it); and I made the necessary entry in my book. Mr Macallan signed the entry; and I signed it afterwards as witness. He paid for the arsenic, and took it away with him wrapped up in two papers—the outer wrapper being labelled with my name and address, and with the word "Poison" in large letters; exactly like the label now produced on the piece of paper found at Gleninch.'

The next witness, Peter Stockdale (also a druggist of Edinburgh), followed, and said:

'The prisoner at the bar called at my shop, on the date indicated on my register—some days later than the date indicated in the register of Mr Kinlay. He wished to purchase sixpenny-worth of arsenic. My assistant, to whom he had addressed himself, called me. It is a rule in my shop that no one sells poisons but myself. I asked the prisoner what he wanted the arsenic for. He answered that he wanted it for killing rats at his house called Gleninch. I said, "Have I the honour of speaking to Mr Macallan, of Gleninch?" He said that was his name. I sold him the arsenic—about an ounce and a half—and labelled the bottle in which I put it with the word "Poison," in my own handwriting. He signed the Register, and took the arsenic away with him, after paying for it.'

The cross-examination of these two men succeeded in asserting certain technical objections to their evidence. But the terrible fact that my husband himself had actually purchased the arsenic, in both cases, remained unshaken.

The next witnesses—the gardener, and the cook, at Gleninch—wound the chain of hostile evidence round the prisoner more mercilessly still.

On examination, the gardener said, on his oath:

'I never received any arsenic from the prisoner or from any one else, at the date to which you refer, or at any other date. I never used any such thing as a solution of arsenic, or ever allowed the men working under me to use it, in the conservatories, or in the garden, at Gleninch. I disapprove of arsenic as a means of destroying noxious insects infesting flowers and plants.'

The cook, being called next, spoke as positively as the gardener.

'Neither my master, nor any other person, gave me any arsenic to destroy rats, at any time. No such thing was wanted. I declare, on my oath, that I never saw any rats, in, or about, the house—or ever heard of any rats infesting it.'

Other household servants at Gleninch gave similar evidence. Nothing could be extracted from them on cross-examination—except that there might have been rats in the house, though they were not aware of it. The possession of the poison was traced directly to my husband, and to no one else. That he had bought it was actually proved; and that he had kept it, was the one conclusion that the evidence justified.

The witnesses who came next did their best to press the charge against the prisoner home to him. Having the arsenic in his possession, what had he done with it? The evidence led the Jury to infer what he had done with it.

The prisoner's valet deposed that his master had rung for him at twenty minutes to ten, on the morning of the day on which his mistress died, and had ordered a cup of tea for her. The man had received the order at the open door of Mrs Macallan's room, and could positively swear that no other person but his master was there at the time.

The under-housemaid, appearing next, said that she had made the tea, and had herself taken it upstairs, before ten o'clock, to Mrs Macallan's room. Her master had received it from her at the open door. She could look in, and see that he was alone in her mistress's room.

The nurse, Christina Ormsay, being recalled, repeated what Mrs Macallan had said to her, on the day when that lady was first taken ill. She had said (speaking to the nurse at six o'clock in the morning), 'Mr Macallan came in about an hour since; he found me still sleepless, and gave me my composing-draught.' This was at five o'clock in the morning, while Christina Ormsay was asleep on the sofa. The nurse further swore that she had looked at the bottle containing the composing-mixture, and had seen, by the measuring marks on the bottle, that a dose had been poured out since the dose previously given, administered by herself.

On this occasion, special interest was excited by the cross-examination. The closing questions, put to the under-housemaid and the nurse, revealed for the first time what the nature of the defence was to be.

Cross-examining the under-housemaid, the Dean of Faculty said:

'Did you ever notice, when you were setting Mrs Eustace Macallan's room to rights, whether the water left in the basin was of a blackish or bluish colour?' The witness answered, 'I never noticed anything of the sort.'

The Dean of Faculty went on:

'Did you ever find, under the pillow of the bed, or in any other hiding-place in Mrs Macallan's room, any books or pamphlets, telling of remedies used for improving a bad complexion?' The witness answered, 'No.'

The Dean of Faculty persisted:

'Did you ever hear Mrs Macallan speak of arsenic, taken as a wash, or taken as a medicine, as a good thing to improve the complexion?' The witness answered, 'Never.'

Similar questions were next put to the nurse, and were all answered, by this witness also, in the negative.

Here, then—in spite of the negative answers—was the plan of the defence made dimly visible for the first time to the Jury and to the audience. By way of preventing the possibility of a mistake in so serious a matter, the Chief Judge (the Lord Justice Clerk) put this plain question, when the witnesses had retired, to the Counsel for the defence:

'The Court and the Jury,' said his lordship, 'wish distinctly to understand the object of your cross-examination of the housemaid and the nurse. Is it the theory of the defence, that Mrs Eustace Macallan used the arsenic which her husband purchased, for the purpose of improving the defects of her complexion?'

The Dean of Faculty answered:

'That is what we say, my lord, and what we propose to prove, as the foundation of the defence. We cannot dispute the medical evidence which declares that Mrs Macallan died poisoned. But we assert that she died of an overdose of arsenic, ignorantly taken, in the privacy of her own room, as a remedy for the defects—the proved and admitted defects—of her complexion. The Prisoner's declaration before the Sheriff, expressly sets forth that he purchased the arsenic at the request of his wife.'

The Lord Justice Clerk inquired, upon this, if there was any objection, on the part of either of the learned counsel, to have the Declaration read in Court, before the Trial proceeded further.

To this, the Dean of Faculty replied that he would be glad to have the Declaration read. If he might use the expression, it would usefully pave the way, in the minds of the Jury, for the defence which he had to submit to them.

The Lord Advocate (speaking on the other side) was happy to be able to accommodate his learned brother in this matter. So long as the mere assertions which the Declaration contained were not supported by proof, he looked upon that document as evidence for the prosecution, and he, too, was quite willing to have it read.

Thereupon, the prisoner's Declaration of his innocence—on being charged before the Sheriff with the murder of his wife—was read, in the following terms:

'I bought the two packets of arsenic, on each occasion, at my wife's own request. On the first occasion, she told me the poison was wanted by the gardener, for use in the conservatories. On the second occasion, she said it was required by the cook for ridding the lower part of the house of rats.

'I handed both packets of arsenic to my wife immediately on my return home. I had nothing to do with the poison, after buying it. My wife was the person who gave orders to the gardener and the cook—not I. I never held any communication with either of them.

'I asked my wife no questions about the use of the arsenic; feeling no interest in the subject. I never entered the conservatories for months together; I care little about flowers. As for the rats, I left the killing of them to the cook and the other servants—just as I should have left any other part of the domestic business to the cook and the other servants.

'My wife never told me she wanted the arsenic to improve her complexion. Surely, I should be the last person admitted to the knowledge of such a secret of her toilet as that? I implicitly believed what she told me—viz., that the poison was wanted, for the purposes specified, by the gardener and the cook.

'I assert positively, that I lived on friendly terms with my wife; allowing, of course, for the little occasional disagreements and misunderstandings of married life. Any sense of disappointment, in connexion with my marriage, which I might have felt privately, I conceived it to be my duty, as a husband and a gentleman, to conceal from my wife. I was not only shocked and grieved by her untimely death—I was filled with fear that I had not, with all my care, behaved affectionately enough to her in her lifetime.

'Furthermore, I solemnly declare that I know no more of how she took the arsenic found in her body than the babe unborn. I am innocent even of the thought of harming that unhappy woman. I administered the composing-draught, exactly as I found it in the bottle. I afterwards gave her the cup of tea, exactly as I received it from the under-housemaid's hand. I never had access to the arsenic, after I placed the two packages in my wife's possession. I am entirely ignorant of what she did with them, or of where she kept them. I declare, before God, I am innocent of the horrible crime with which I am charged.'

With the reading of those true and touching words the proceedings on the second day of the Trial came to an end.

So far, I must own, the effect on me of reading the Report was to depress my spirits, and to lower my hopes. The whole weight of the evidence, at the close of the second day, was against my husband. Woman, as I was, and partisan, as I was, I could plainly see that.

The merciless Lord Advocate (I confess I hated him!) had proved (1) that Eustace had bought the poison; (2) that the reason which he had given to the druggists for buying the poison was not the true reason; (3) that he had had two opportunities of secretly administering the poison to his wife. On the other side, what had the Dean of Faculty proved? As yet—nothing. The assertions in the prisoner's Declaration of his innocence were still, as the Lord Advocate had remarked, assertions not supported by proof. Not one atom of evidence had been produced to show that it was the wife who had secretly used the arsenic, and used it for her complexion.

My one consolation was, that the reading of the Trial had already revealed to me the helpful figures of two friends, on whose sympathy I might surely rely. The crippled Mr Dexter had especially shown himself to be a thorough good ally of my husband's. My heart warmed to the man who had moved his chair against the bedside-table—the man who had struggled to the last to defend Eustace's papers from the wretches who had seized them! I decided, then and there, that the first person to whom I would confide my aspirations and my hopes should be Mr Dexter. If he felt any difficulty about advising me, I would then apply next to the agent, Mr Playmore—the second good friend, who had formally protested against the seizure of my husband's papers.

Fortified by this resolution, I turned the page, and read the history of the third day of the Trial.

CHAPTER XVIII

Third Question—What was his Motive?

THE first question (Did the Woman die Poisoned?) had been answered, positively. The second question (Who Poisoned Her?) had been answered, apparently. There now remained the third and final question—What Was His Motive? The first evidence called, in answer to that inquiry, was the evidence of relatives and friends of the dead wife.

Lady Brydehaven, widow of Rear Admiral Sir George Brydehaven, examined by Mr Drew (counsel for the Crown with the Lord Advocate), gave evidence as follows:—

'The deceased lady (Mrs Eustace Macallan) was my niece. She was the only child of my sister; and she lived under my roof after the time of her mother's death. I objected to her marriage—on grounds which were considered purely fanciful and sentimental by her other friends. It is extremely painful to me to state the circumstances in public; but I am ready to make the sacrifice, if the ends of justice require it.

'The prisoner at the Bar, at the time of which I am now speaking, was staying as a guest in my house. He met with an accident, while he was out riding, which caused a severe injury to one of his legs. The leg had been previously hurt, while he was serving with the army in India. This circumstance tended greatly to aggravate the injury received in the accident. He was confined to a recumbent position on a sofa for many weeks together; and the ladies in the house took it in turns to sit with him, and while away the weary time by reading to him and talking to him. My niece was foremost among these volunteer nurses. She played admirably on the piano; and the sick man happened—most unfortunately as the event proved—to be fond of music.

'The consequences of the perfectly innocent intercourse thus begun, were deplorable consequences for my niece. She became passionately attached to Mr Eustace Macallan: without awakening any corresponding affection on his side.

'I did my best to interfere, delicately and usefully, while it was still possible to interfere with advantage. Unhappily, my niece refused to place any confidence in me. She persistently denied that she was actuated by any warmer feeling towards Mr Macallan than a feeling of friendly interest. This made it impossible for me to separate them, without openly acknowledging my reason for doing so, and thus producing a scandal which might have affected my niece's reputation. My husband was alive at that time; and the one thing I could do, under the circumstances, was the thing I did. I requested him to speak privately to Mr Macallan, and to appeal to his honour to help us out of the difficulty, without prejudice to my niece.

'Mr Macallan behaved admirably. He was still helpless. But he made an excuse for leaving us which it was impossible to dispute. In two days after my husband had spoken to him, he was removed from the house.

'The remedy was well intended; but it came too late, and it utterly failed. The mischief was done. My niece pined away visibly; neither medical help nor change of air and scene did anything for her. In course of time—after Mr Macallan had recovered from the effects of his accident—I found out that she was carrying on a clandestine correspondence with him, by means of her maid. His letters, I am bound to say, were most considerately and carefully written. Nevertheless, I felt it my duty to stop the correspondence.

'My interference—what else could I do but interfere?—brought matters to a crisis. One day, my niece was missing at breakfast-time. The next day, we discovered that the poor infatuated creature had gone to Mr Macallan's chambers in London, and had been found hidden in his bedroom, by some bachelor friends who came to visit him.

'For this disaster Mr Macallan was in no respect to blame. Hearing footsteps outside, he had only time to take measures for saving her character by concealing her in the nearest room—and the nearest room happened to be his bedchamber. The matter was talked about of course, and motives were misinterpreted in the vilest manner. My husband had another private conversation with Mr Macallan. He again behaved admirably. He publicly declared that my niece had visited him as his betrothed wife. In a fortnight from that time, he silenced scandal in the one way that was possible—he married her.

'I was alone in opposing the marriage. I thought it at the time—what it has proved to be since—a fatal mistake.

'It would have been sad enough, if Mr Macallan had only married her without a particle of love on his side. But, to make the prospect more hopeless still, he was himself, at that very time, the victim of a misplaced attachment to a lady who was engaged to another man. I am well aware that he compassionately denied this—just as he compassionately affected to be in love with my niece when he married her. But his hopeless admiration of the lady whom I have mentioned, was a matter of fact notorious among his friends. It may not be amiss to add, that *her* marriage preceded *his* marriage. He had irretrievably lost the woman he really loved—he was without a hope or an aspiration in life—when he took pity on my niece.

'In conclusion, I can only repeat that no evil which could have happened (if she had remained a single woman) would have been comparable, in my opinion, to the evil of such a marriage as this. Never, I sincerely believe, were two more ill-assorted persons united in the bonds of matrimony, than the prisoner at the bar and his deceased wife.'

The evidence of this witness produced a strong sensation among the audience, and had a marked effect on the minds of the Jury. Cross-examination forced Lady Brydehaven to modify some of her opinions, and to acknowledge that the hopeless attachment of the prisoner to another woman was a matter of rumour only. But the facts in her narrative remained unshaken—and, for that one reason, they invested the crime charged against the prisoner with an appearance of possibility, which it had entirely failed to assume during the earlier part of the Trial.

Two other ladies (intimate friends of Mrs Eustace Macallan) were called next. They differed from Lady Brydehaven in their opinions on the propriety of the marriage; but on all the material points, they supported her testimony, and confirmed the serious impression which the first witness had produced on every person in Court.

The next evidence which the prosecution proposed to put in, was the silent evidence of the letters and the Diary found at Gleninch.

In answer to a question from the Bench, the Lord Advocate stated that the letters were written by friends of the prisoner and of his deceased wife, and that passages in them bore directly on the terms on which the two associated in their married life. The Diary was still more valuable as evidence. It contained the prisoner's daily record of domestic events, and of the thoughts and feelings which they aroused in him at the time.

A most painful scene followed this explanation.

Writing, as I do, long after the events took place, I still cannot prevail upon myself to describe in detail what my unhappy husband said and did, at this distressing period of the Trial. Deeply affected while Lady Bryde-haven was giving her evidence, he had with difficulty restrained himself from interrupting her. He now lost all control over his feelings. In piercing tones which rang through the Court, he protested against the contemplated violation of his own most sacred secrets and his wife's most sacred secrets. 'Hang me, innocent as I am!' he cried, 'but spare me *that!*' The effect of this terrible outbreak on the audience is reported to have been indescribable. Some of the women present were in hysterics. The Judges interfered from the Bench—but with no good result. Quiet was at length restored by the Dean of Faculty, who succeeded in soothing the prisoner—and who then addressed the Judges, pleading for indulgence to his unhappy client in most touching and eloquent language. The speech, a masterpiece of impromptu oratory, concluded with a temperate yet strongly-urged protest against the reading of the papers discovered at Gleninch.

The three Judges retired to consider the legal question submitted to them. The sitting was suspended for more than half an hour.

As usual in such cases, the excitement in the Court communicated itself to the crowd outside in the street. The general opinion here—led, as it was supposed, by one of the clerks or other inferior persons connected with the legal proceedings—was decidedly adverse to the prisoner's chance of escaping a sentence of death. 'If the letters and the Diary are read,' said the brutal spokesmen of the mob, 'the letters and the Diary will hang him.'

On the return of the Judges into Court, it was announced that they had decided, by a majority of two to one, on permitting the documents in dispute to be produced in evidence. Each of the Judges, in turn, gave his reasons for the decision at which he had arrived. This done, the Trial proceeded. The reading of the extracts from the letters and the extracts from the Diary began.

The first letters produced were the letters found in the Indian cabinet, in Mrs Eustace Macallan's room. They were addressed to the deceased lady by intimate (female) friends of hers, with whom she was accustomed to correspond. Three separate Extracts, from letters written by three different correspondents, were selected to be read in Court.

FIRST CORRESPONDENT: 'I despair, my dearest Sara, of being able to tell you how your last letter has distressed me. Pray forgive me, if I own to thinking that your very sensitive nature exaggerates or misinterprets, quite unconsciously of course, the neglect that you experience at the hands of your husband. I cannot say anything about *his* peculiarities of character, because I am not well enough acquainted with him to know what they are. But, my dear, I am much older than you, and I have had a much longer experience than yours, of what somebody calls, "the lights and shadows of married life." Speaking from that experience, I must tell you what I have observed. Young married women, like you, who are devotedly attached to their husbands, are apt to make one very serious mistake. As a rule, they all expect too much from their husbands. Men, my poor Sara, are not like *us*. Their love, even when it is quite sincere, is not like our love. It does not last, as it does with us. It is not the one hope and one thought of their lives, as it is with us. We have no alternative—even when we most truly respect and love them—but to make allowance for this difference between the man's nature and the woman's. I do not for one moment excuse your husband's coldness. He is wrong, for example, in never looking at you when he speaks to you, and in never noticing the efforts that you make to please him. He is worse than wrong—he is really cruel if you like—in never returning your kiss when you kiss him. But, my dear, are you quite sure that he is always *designedly* cold and cruel? May not his conduct be sometimes the result of troubles and anxieties which weigh on his mind, and which are troubles and anxieties that you cannot share? If you try to look at his behaviour in this light, you will understand many things which puzzle and pain you now. Be patient with him, my child. Make no complaints; and never approach him with your caresses at times when his mind is preoccupied or his temper ruffled. This may be hard advice to follow, loving him as ardently as you do. But rely on it, the secret of happiness for us women is to be found (alas, only too often!) in such exercise of restraint and resignation as your old friend now recommends. Think, my dear, over what I have written—and let me hear from you again.'

SECOND CORRESPONDENT: 'How can you be so foolish, Sara, as to waste your love on such a cold-blooded brute as your husband seems to be? To be sure, I am not married yet—or perhaps I should not be so surprised at you. But I shall be married one of these days; and if my husband ever treats me as Mr Macallan treats you, I shall insist on a separation. I declare I think I would rather be actually beaten, like the women among the lower orders, than be treated with the polite neglect and contempt which you describe. I burn with indignation when I think of it. It must be quite insufferable. Don't bear it any longer, my poor dear. Leave him, and come and stay with me. My brother is a law-student, as you know. I read to him portions of your letter; and he is of opinion that you might get, what he calls, a judicial separation. Come and consult him.'

THIRD CORRESPONDENT: 'You know, my dear Mrs Macallan, what *my* experience of men has been. Your letter does not surprise me in the least. Your husband's conduct to you points to one conclusion. He is in love with some other woman. There is Somebody in the dark, who gets from him everything that he denies to you. I have been through it all—and I know! Don't give way. Make it the business of your life to find out who the creature is. Perhaps there may be more than one of them. It doesn't matter. One, or many, if you can only discover them, you may make his existence as miserable to him as he makes your existence to you. If you want my experience to help you, say the word, and it is freely at your service. I can come and stay with you, at Gleninch, any time after the fourth of next month.'

With those abominable lines the readings from the letters of the women came to an end. The first and longest of the Extracts produced the most vivid impression in Court. Evidently the writer was, in this case, a worthy and sensible person. It was generally felt, however, that all three of the letters—no matter how widely they might differ in tone—justified the same conclusion. The wife's position at Gleninch (if the wife's account of it was to be trusted) was the position of a neglected and an unhappy woman.

The correspondence of the prisoner, which had been found, with his Diary, in the locked bed-table drawer, was produced next. The letters in this case were, with one exception, all written by men. Though the tone of them was moderation itself, as compared with the second and third of the women's letters, the conclusion still pointed the same way. The life of the husband, at Gleninch, appeared to be just as intolerable as the life of the wife.

For example, one of the prisoner's male friends wrote, inviting him to make a yacht voyage round the world. Another suggested an absence of six months on the Continent. A third recommended field sports in India. The one object aimed at by all the writers was plainly to counsel a separation, more or less plausible and more or less complete, between the married pair.

The last letter read was addressed to the prisoner in a woman's handwriting, and was signed by a woman's Christian name only.

'Ah, my poor Eustace, what a cruel destiny is ours!' (the letter began). 'When I think of your life, sacrificed to that wretched woman, my heart bleeds for you! If *we* had been man and wife—if it had been *my* unutterable happiness to love and cherish the best, the dearest of men—what a paradise of our own we might have lived in, what delicious hours we might have known! But regret is vain; we are separated, in this life—separated by ties which we both mourn, and yet which we must both respect. My Eustace, there is a world beyond this! There, our souls will fly to meet each other, and mingle in one long heavenly embrace—in a rapture forbidden to us on earth. The misery described in your letter—oh! why, why did you marry her?—has wrung this confession of feeling from me. Let it comfort you; but let no other eyes see it. Burn my rashly-written lines, and look (as I look) to the better life which you may yet share with your own HELENA.'

The reading of this outrageous letter provoked a question from the Bench. One of the Judges asked if the writer had attached any date or address to her letter.

In answer to this, the Lord Advocate stated that neither the one nor the other appeared. The envelope showed that the letter had been posted in London. 'We propose,' the learned counsel continued, 'to read certain passages from the prisoner's Diary, in which the name signed at the end of the letters occurs more than once; and we may possibly find other means of identifying the writer, to the satisfaction of your lordships, before the Trial is over.'

The promised passages from my husband's private Diary were now read. The first extract related to a period of nearly a year before the date of Mrs Eustace Macallan's death. It was expressed in these terms:

'News, by this morning's post, which has quite overwhelmed me. Helena's husband died suddenly, two days since, of heart disease. She is free—my beloved Helena is free! And I?

'I am fettered to a woman with whom I have not a single feeling in common. Helena is lost to me, by my own act. Ah! I can understand now, as I never understood before, how irresistible temptation can be, and how easily, sometimes, crime may follow it. I had better shut up these leaves for the night. It maddens me to no purpose to think of my position or to write of it.'

The next passage, dated a few days later, dwelt on the same subject:

'Of all the follies that a man can commit, the greatest is acting on impulse. I acted on impulse when I married the unfortunate creature who is now my wife.

'Helena was then lost to me, as I too hastily supposed. She had married the man to whom she rashly engaged herself, before she met with me. He was younger than I, and, to all appearances, heartier and stronger than I. So far as I could see, my fate was sealed for life. Helena had written her farewell letter, taking leave of me in this world, for good. My prospects were closed; my hopes had ended. I had not an aspiration left; I had no necessity to stimulate me to take refuge in work. A chivalrous action, an exertion of noble self-denial, seemed to be all that was left to me, all that I was fit for.

'The circumstances of the moment adapted themselves, with a fatal facility, to this idea. The ill-fated woman who had become attached to me (Heaven knows without so much as the shadow of encouragement on my part!), had, just at that time, rashly placed her reputation at the mercy of the world. It rested with me to silence the scandalous tongues that reviled her. With Helena lost to me, happiness was not to be expected. All women were equally indifferent to me. A generous action would be the salvation of *this* woman. Why not perform it? I married her on that impulse—married her, just as I might have jumped into the water and saved her, if she had been drowning; just as I might have knocked a man down, if I had seen him ill-treating her in the street!

'And now, the woman for whom I have made this sacrifice stands between me and my Helena—my Helena, free to pour out all the treasures of her love on the man who adores the earth that she touches with her foot!

'Fool! Madman! Why don't I dash out my brains against the wall that I see opposite to me while I write these lines?

'My gun is there in the corner. I have only to tie a string to the trigger, and to put the muzzle to my mouth——No! My mother is alive; my mother's love is sacred. I have no right to take the life which she gave me. I must suffer and submit. Oh, Helena! Helena!'

The third Extract—one among many similar passages—had been written about two months before the death of the prisoner's wife.

'More reproaches addressed to me! There never was such a woman for complaining; she lives in a perfect atmosphere of ill-temper and discontent.

'My new offences are two in number. I never ask her to play to me now; and, when she puts on a new dress, expressly to please me, I never notice it. Notice it! Good Heavens! The effort of my life is *not* to notice her, in anything she does or says. How could I keep my temper, unless I kept as much as possible out of the way of private interviews with her? And I do keep my temper. I am never hard on her; I never use harsh language to her. She has a double claim on my forbearance—she is a woman; and the law has made her my wife. I remember this; but I am human. The less I see of her—except when visitors are present—the more certain I can feel of preserving my self-control.

'I wonder what it is that makes her so utterly distasteful to me. She is a plain woman; but I have seen uglier women than she, whose caresses I could have endured, without the sense of shrinking that comes over me when I am obliged to submit to *her* caresses. I keep the feeling hidden from her. She loves me, poor thing!—and I pity her. I wish I could do more; I wish I could return, in the smallest degree, the feeling with which she regards me. But, no—I can only pity her. If she would be content to live on friendly terms with me, and never to exact demonstrations of tenderness, we might get on pretty well. But she wants love. Unfortunate creature, she wants love!

'Oh, my Helena! I have no love to give her. My heart is yours.

'I dreamt last night, that this unhappy wife of mine was dead. The dream was so vivid that I actually got out of my bed, and opened the door of her room, and listened.

'Her calm regular breathing was distinctly audible in the stillness of the night. She was in a deep sleep. I closed the door again, and lit my candle and read. Helena was in all my thoughts; it was hard work to fix my attention on the book. But anything was better than going to bed again, and dreaming, perhaps, for the second time, that I, too, was free.

'What a life mine is! what a life my wife's is! If the house was to take fire, I wonder whether I should make an effort to save myself, or to save her?'

The last two passages read, referred to later dates still.

'A gleam of brightness has shone over this dismal existence of mine at last.

'Helena is no longer condemned to the seclusion of widowhood. Time enough has passed to permit of her mixing again in society. She is paying visits to friends in our part of Scotland; and, as she and I are cousins, it is universally understood that she cannot leave the North without also spending a few days at my house. She writes me word that the visit, however embarrassing it may be to us privately, is nevertheless a visit that must be made, for the sake of appearances. Blessings on appearances! I shall see this angel in my purgatory—and all because Society in MidLothian would think it strange that my cousin should be visiting in my part of Scotland, and not visit Me!

'But we are to be very careful. Helena says, in so many words, "I come to see you, Eustace, as a sister. You must receive me as a brother, or not receive me at all. I shall write to your wife to propose the day for my visit. I shall not forget—do you not forget—that it is by your wife's permission that I enter your house."

'Only let me see her! I will submit to anything to obtain the unutterable happiness of seeing her!'

The last Extract followed, and consisted of these lines only:

'A new misfortune! My wife has fallen ill. She has taken to her bed, with a bad rheumatic cold, just at the time appointed for Helena's visit to Gleninch. But, on this occasion (I gladly own it!), she has behaved charmingly. She has written to Helena to say that her illness is not serious enough to render a change necessary in the arrangements, and to make it her particular request that my cousin's visit shall take place upon the day originally decided on.

'This is a great sacrifice made to me, on my wife's part. Jealous of every woman, under forty, who comes near me, she is of course jealous of Helena—and she controls herself, and trusts me!

'I am bound to show my gratitude for this, and I will show it. From this day forth, I vow to live more affectionately with my wife. I tenderly embraced her this very morning—and, I hope, poor soul, she did not discover the effort that it cost me.'

There, the readings from the Diary came to an end.

The most unpleasant pages in the whole Report of the Trial were—to me—the pages which contained the extracts from my husband's Diary. There were expressions, here and there, which not only pained me, but which almost shook Eustace's position in my estimation. I think I would have given everything I possessed to have had the power of annihilating certain lines in that Diary. As for his passionate expressions of love for Mrs Beauly, every one of them went through me like a sting! He had whispered words quite as warm into my ears, in the days of his courtship. I had no reason to doubt that he truly and dearly loved me. But the question was—Had he, just as truly and dearly, loved Mrs Beauly, before me? Had she or I won the first of his heart? He had declared to me, over and over again, that he had only fancied himself to be in love, before the day when we met. I had believed him then. I determined to believe him still. I did believe him. But I hated Mrs Beauly!

As for the painful impression produced in Court by the readings from the letters and the Diary, it seemed to be impossible to increase it. Nevertheless, it *was* perceptibly increased. In other words, it was rendered more unfavourable still towards the prisoner, by the evidence of the next, and last, witness called on the part of the prosecution.

William Enzie, under-gardener at Gleninch, was sworn, and deposed as follows:

'On the twentieth of October, at eleven o'clock in the forenoon, I was at work in the shrubbery, on the side next to the garden called the Dutch Garden. There was a summer-house in the Dutch Garden, having its back set towards the shrubbery. The day was wonderfully fine and warm for the time of year.

'Passing to my work, I passed the back of the summer-house. I heard voices inside—a man's voice and a lady's voice. The lady's voice was strange to me. The man's voice I recognized as the voice of my master. The ground in the shrubbery was soft; and my curiosity was excited. I stepped up to the back of the summer-house, without being heard; and I listened to what was going on inside.

'The first words I could distinguish were spoken in my master's voice. He said, "If I could only have foreseen that you might one day be free, what a happy man I might have been!" The lady's voice answered, "Hush! you must not talk so." My master said, upon that, "I must talk of what is in my mind; it is always in my mind that I have lost you." He stopped a bit there, and then he said on a sudden, "Do me one favour, my angel! Promise me not to marry again." The lady's voice spoke out, thereupon, sharply enough, "What do you mean?" My master said, "I wish no harm to the unhappy creature who is a burden on my life; but suppose——?" "Suppose nothing," the lady said; "come back to the house."

'She led the way into the garden, and turned round, beckoning my master to join her. In that position, I saw her face plainly; and I knew it for the face of the young widow lady who was visiting at the house. She was pointed out to me by the head-gardener, when she first arrived, for the purpose of warning me that I was not to interfere if I found her picking the flowers. The gardens at Gleninch were shown to tourists on certain days; and we made a difference, of course, in the matter of the flowers, between strangers and guests staying in the house. I am quite certain of the identity of the lady who was talking with my master. Mrs Beauly was a comely person—and there was no mistaking her for any other than herself. She and my master withdrew together on the way to the house. I heard nothing more of what passed between them.'

This witness was severely cross-examined as to the correctness of his recollection of the talk in the summer-house, and as to his capacity for identifying both the speakers. On certain minor points he was shaken. But he firmly asserted his accurate remembrance of the last words exchanged between his master and Mrs Beauly; and he personally described the lady, in terms which proved that he had correctly identified her.

With this, the answer to the third Question raised by the Trial—the question of the prisoner's Motive for poisoning his wife—came to an end.

The story for the prosecution was now a story told. The staunchest friends of the prisoner in Court were compelled to acknowledge that the evidence, thus far, pointed clearly and conclusively against him. He seemed to feel this himself. When he withdrew at the close of the third day of the Trial, he was so depressed and exhausted that he was obliged to lean on the arm of the governor of the jail.

CHAPTER XIX

The Evidence for the Defence

THE feeling of interest excited by the Trial was prodigiously increased on the fourth day. The witnesses for the defence were now to be heard; and first and foremost among them was the prisoner's mother. She looked at her son as she lifted her veil to take the oath. He burst into tears. At that moment, the sympathy felt for the mother was generally extended to the unhappy son.

Examined by the Dean of Faculty, Mrs Macallan the elder gave her answers with remarkable dignity and self-control.

Questioned as to certain private conversations which had passed between her late daughter-in-law and herself, she declared that Mrs Eustace Macallan was morbidly sensitive on the subject of her personal appearance. She was devotedly attached to her husband; the great anxiety of her life was to make herself as attractive to him as possible. The imperfections in her personal appearance—and especially in her complexion—were subjects to her of the bitterest regret. The witness had heard her say, over and over again (referring to her complexion), that there was no risk she would not run, and no pain she would not suffer, to improve it. 'Men' (she had said) 'are all caught by outward appearances: my husband might love me better, if I had a better colour.'

Being asked next if the passages from her son's Diary were to be depended on as evidence—that is to say, if they fairly represented the peculiarities in his character, and his true sentiments towards his wife—Mrs Macallan denied it in the plainest and the strongest terms.

'The extracts from my son's Diary are a libel on his character,' she said. 'And not the less a libel, because they happen to be written by himself. Speaking from a mother's experience of him, I know that he must have written the passages produced, in moments of uncontrollable depression and despair. No just person judges hastily of a man by the rash words which may escape him in his moody and miserable moments. Is my son to be so judged because he happens to have written *his* rash words, instead of speaking them? His pen has been his most deadly enemy, in this case—it has presented him at his very worst. He was not happy in his marriage—I admit that. But I say, at the same time, that he was invariably considerate towards his wife. I was implicitly trusted by both of them; I saw them in their most private moments. I declare—in the face of what she appears to have written to her friends and correspondents—that my son never gave his wife any just cause to assert that he treated her with cruelty and neglect.'

These words, firmly and clearly spoken, produced a strong impression. The Lord Advocate—evidently perceiving that any attempt to weaken that impression would not be likely to succeed—confined himself, in cross-examination, to two significant questions.

'In speaking to you of the defects in her complexion,' he said, 'did your daughter-in-law refer in any way to the use of arsenic as a remedy?'

The answer to this was, 'No.'

The Lord Advocate proceeded:

'Did you yourself ever recommend arsenic, or mention it casually, in the course of the private conversations which you have described?'

The answer to this was, 'Never.'

The Lord Advocate resumed his seat. Mrs Macallan the elder withdrew.

An interest of a new kind was excited by the appearance of the next witness. This was no less a person than Mrs Beauly herself. The Report describes her as a remarkably attractive person; modest and ladylike in her manner, and, to all appearance, feeling sensitively the public position in which she was placed.

The first portion of her evidence was almost a recapitulation of the evidence given by the prisoner's mother—with this difference, that Mrs Beauly had been actually questioned by the deceased lady on the subject of cosmetic applications to the complexion. Mrs Eustace Macallan had complimented her on the beauty of her complexion, and had asked what artificial means she used to keep it in such good order. Using no artificial means (and knowing nothing whatever of cosmetics), Mrs Beauly had resented the question; and a temporary coolness between the two ladies had been the result.

Interrogated as to her relations with the prisoner, Mrs Beauly indignantly denied that she or Mr Macallan had ever given the deceased lady the slightest cause for jealousy. It was impossible for Mrs Beauly to leave Scotland, after visiting at the houses of her cousin's neighbours, without also visiting her cousin's house. To take any other course would have been an act of downright rudeness, and would have excited remark. She did not deny that Mr Macallan had admired her in the days when they were both single people. But there was no further expression of that feeling, when she had married another man, and when he had married another woman. From that time, their intercourse was the innocent intercourse of a brother and sister. Mr Macallan was a gentleman: he knew what was due to his wife and to Mrs Beauly—she would not have entered the house if experience had not satisfied her of that. As for the evidence of the under-gardener, it was little better than pure invention. The greater part of the conversation which he had described himself as overhearing had never taken place. The little that was really said (as the man reported it) was said jestingly; and she had checked it immediately—as the witness had himself confessed. For the rest, Mr Macallan's behaviour towards his wife was invariably kind and considerate. He was constantly devising means to alleviate her sufferings from the rheumatic affection which confined her to her bed; he had spoken of her, not once but many times, in terms of the sincerest sympathy. When she ordered her husband and witness to leave the room, on the day of her death, Mr Macallan said to witness afterwards, "We must bear with her jealousy, poor soul: we know that we don't deserve it." In that patient manner he submitted to her infirmities of temper, from first to last.

The main interest in the cross-examination of Mrs Beauly centred in a question which was put at the end. After reminding her that she had given her name, on being sworn, as 'Helena Beauly,' the Lord Advocate said:

'A letter addressed to the prisoner, and signed "Helena," has been read in Court. Look at it, if you please. Are you the writer of that letter?'

Before the witness could reply, the Dean of Faculty protested against the question. The Judges allowed the protest, and refused to permit the question to be put. Mrs Beauly thereupon withdrew. She had betrayed a very perceptible agitation on hearing the letter referred to, and on having it placed in her hands. This exhibition of feeling was variously interpreted among the audience. Upon the whole, however, Mrs Beauly's evidence was considered to have aided the impression which the mother's evidence had produced in the prisoner's favour.

The next witnesses—both ladies, and both school-friends of Mrs Eustace Macallan—created a new feeling of interest in Court. They supplied the missing link in the evidence for the defence.

The first of the ladies declared that she had mentioned arsenic, as a means of improving the complexion, in conversation with Mrs Eustace Macallan. She had never used it herself, but she had read of the practice of eating arsenic, among the Styrian peasantry, for the purpose of clearing the colour, and of producing a general appearance of plumpness and good health. She positively swore that she had related this result of her reading to the deceased lady, exactly as she now related it in Court.

The second witness, present at the conversation already mentioned, corroborated the first witness in every particular: and added that she had procured the book relating to the arsenic-eating practices of the Styrian peasantry, and to their results, at Mrs Eustace Macallan's own request. This book she had herself despatched by post to Mrs Eustace Macallan at Gleninch.

There was but one assailable point in this otherwise conclusive evidence. The cross-examination discovered it.

Both the ladies were asked in turn, if Mrs Eustace Macallan had expressed to them, directly or indirectly, any intention of obtaining arsenic, with a view to the improvement of her complexion. In each case the answer to that all-important question was, 'No.' Mrs Eustace Macallan had heard of the remedy, and had received the book. But of her own intentions in the future, she had not said one word. She had begged both the ladies to consider the conversation as strictly private—and there it had ended.

It required no lawyer's eye to discern the fatal defect which was now revealed in the evidence for the defence. Every intelligent person present could see that the prisoner's chance of an honourable acquittal depended on tracing the poison to the possession of his wife—or at least on proving her expressed intention to obtain it. In either of these cases, the prisoner's Declaration of his innocence would claim the support of testimony, which—however indirect it might be—no honest and intelligent men would be likely to resist. Was that testimony forthcoming? Was the counsel for the defence not at the end of his resources yet?

The crowded audience waited, in breathless expectation, for the appearance of the next witness. A whisper went round, among certain well-instructed persons, that the Court was now to see and hear the prisoner's old friend—already often referred to in the course of the Trial, as 'Mr Dexter.'

After a brief interval of delay, there was a sudden commotion among the audience, accompanied by suppressed exclamations of curiosity and surprise. At the same moment the crier summoned the new witness by the extraordinary name of—

'MISERRIMUS DEXTER.'

CHAPTER XX

The End of the Trial

THE calling of the witness produced a burst of laughter from the public seats—due partly, no doubt, to the strange name by which he had been summoned; partly, also, to the instinctive desire of all crowded assemblies, when their interest is painfully excited, to seize on any relief in the shape of the first excuse for merriment which may present itself. A severe rebuke from the Bench restored order among the audience. The Lord Justice Clerk declared that he would 'clear the Court' if the interruption to the proceedings was renewed.

During the silence which followed this announcement, the new witness appeared.

Gliding, self-propelled in his chair on wheels, through the opening made for him among the crowd, a strange and startling creature—literally the half of a man—revealed himself to the general view. A coverlid, which had been thrown over his chair, had fallen off during his progress through the throng. The loss of it exposed to the public curiosity the head, the arms, and the trunk of a living human being: absolutely deprived of the lower limbs. To make this deformity all the more striking and all the more terrible, the victim of it was—as to his face and his body—an unusually handsome, and an unusually well-made man. His long silky hair, of a bright and beautiful chestnut colour, fell over shoulders that were the perfection of strength and grace. His face was bright with vivacity and intelligence. His large, clear blue eyes, and his long, delicate white hands, were like the eyes and hands of a beautiful woman. He would have looked effeminate, but for the manly proportions of his throat and chest: aided in their effect by his flowing beard and long moustache, of a lighter chestnut shade than the colour of his hair. Never had a magnificent head and body been more hopelessly ill-bestowed than in this instance! Never had Nature committed a more careless or a more cruel mistake than in the making of this man!

He was sworn, seated, of course, in his chair. Having given his name, he bowed to the Judges, and requested their permission to preface his evidence with a word of explanation.

'People generally laugh when they first hear my strange Christian name,' he said, in a low, clear, resonant voice, which penetrated to the remotest corners of the Court. 'I may inform the good people here that many names, still common among us, have their significations, and that mine is one of them. "Alexander," for instance, means, in the Greek, "a helper of men." "David" means, in Hebrew, "well-beloved." "Francis" means, in German, "free." My name, "Miserrimus," means, in Latin, "most unhappy." It was given to me by my father, in allusion to the deformity which you all see—the deformity with which it was my misfortune to be born. You won't laugh at "Miserrimus" again, will you?' He turned to the Dean of Faculty, waiting to examine him for the defence. 'Mr Dean, I am at your service. I apologize for delaying, even for a moment, the proceedings of the Court.'

He delivered his little address with perfect grace and good humour. Examined by the Dean, he gave his evidence clearly, without the slightest appearance of hesitation or reserve.

'I was staying at Gleninch, as a guest in the house, at the time of Mrs Eustace Macallan's death,' he began. 'Doctor Jerome and Mr Gale desired to see me, at a private interview—the prisoner being then in a state of prostration which made it impossible for him to attend to his duties as master of the house. At this interview, the two doctors astonished and horrified me, by declaring that Mrs Eustace Macallan had died poisoned. They left it to me to communicate the dreadful news to her husband; and they warned me that a post-mortem examination must be held on the body.

'If the Fiscal had seen my old friend, when I communicated the doctors' message, I doubt if he would have ventured to charge the prisoner with the murder of his wife. To my mind the charge was nothing less than an outrage. I resisted the seizure of the prisoner's Diary and letters, animated by that feeling. Now that the Diary has been produced, I agree with the prisoner's mother in denying that it is fair evidence to bring against him. A Diary (when it extends beyond a bare record of facts and dates) is, in general, nothing but an expression of the weakest side in the character of the person who keeps it. It is, in nine cases out of ten, the more or less contemptible outpouring of vanity and conceit which the writer dare not exhibit to any mortal but himself. I am the prisoner's oldest friend. I solemnly declare that I never knew he could write downright nonsense until I heard his Diary read in this Court!

'*He* kill his wife! *He* treat his wife with neglect and cruelty! I venture to say, from twenty years' experience of him, that there is no man in this

THE END OF THE TRIAL

assembly who is, constitutionally, more incapable of crime, and more incapable of cruelty, than the man who stands at that Bar. While I am about it, I go further still. I even doubt whether a man capable of crime, and capable of cruelty, could have found it in his heart to do evil to the woman whose untimely death is the subject of this inquiry.

'I have heard what the ignorant and prejudiced nurse, Christina Ormsay, has said of the deceased lady. From my own personal observation I contradict every word of it. Mrs Eustace Macallan—granting her personal defects—was nevertheless one of the most charming women I ever met with. She was highly bred, in the best sense of the word. I never saw, in any other person, so sweet a smile as hers, or such grace and beauty of movement as hers. If you liked music, she sang beautifully; and few professed musicians had such a touch on the piano as hers. If you preferred talking, I never yet met with the man (or even the woman, which is saying a great deal more) whom her conversation could not charm. To say that such a wife as this could be first cruelly neglected, and then barbarously murdered, by the man—not by the martyr—who stands there, is to tell me that the sun never shines at noonday, or that the heaven is not above the earth.

'Oh, yes! I know that the letters of her friends show that she wrote to them in bitter complaint of her husband's conduct to her. But remember what one of those friends (the wisest and the best of them) says in reply. "I own to thinking," she writes, "that your sensitive nature exaggerates or misinterprets the neglect that you experience at the hands of your husband." There, in that one sentence, is the whole truth! Mrs Eustace Macallan's nature was the imaginative, self-tormenting nature of a poet. No mortal love could ever have been refined enough for *her*. Trifles, which women of a coarser moral fibre would have passed over without notice, were causes of downright agony to that exquisitely sensitive temperament. There are persons born to be unhappy. That poor lady was one of them. When I have said this, I have said all.

'No! There is one word more still to be added.

'It may be as well to remind the prosecution that Mrs Eustace Macallan's death was, in the pecuniary sense, a serious loss to her husband. He had insisted on having the whole of her fortune settled on herself, and on her relatives after her, when he married. Her income from that fortune helped to keep in splendour the house and grounds at Gleninch. The prisoner's own resources (aided even by his mother's jointure) were quite inadequate fitly to defray the expenses of living at his splendid country seat. Knowing all the circumstances, I can positively assert that the wife's death has deprived the husband of two-thirds of his income. And the prosecution, viewing him as the basest and cruellest of men, declares that he deliberately killed her—with all his pecuniary interests pointing to the preservation of her life!

'It is useless to ask me whether I noticed anything in the conduct of the prisoner and Mrs Beauly, which might justify a wife's jealousy. I never observed Mrs Beauly with any attention; and I never encouraged the prisoner in talking to me about her. He was a general admirer of pretty women—so far as I know, in a perfectly innocent way. That he could prefer Mrs Beauly to his wife, is inconceivable to me—unless he was out of his senses. I never had any reason to believe that he was out of his senses.

'As to the question of the arsenic—I mean the question of tracing the poison to the possession of Mrs Eustace Macallan—I am able to give evidence which may perhaps be worthy of the attention of the Court.

'I was present, in the Fiscal's office, during the examination of the papers, and of the other objects discovered at Gleninch. The dressing-case belonging to the deceased lady was shown to me, after its contents had been officially investigated by the Fiscal himself. I happen to have a very sensitive sense of touch. In handling the lid of the dressing-case, on the inner side, I felt something at a certain place, which induced me to examine the whole structure of the lid very carefully. The result was the discovery of a private repository, concealed in the space between the outer wood and the lining. In that repository I found the bottle which I now produce.'

The further examination of the witness was suspended, while the hidden bottle was compared with the bottles properly belonging to the dressing-case.

These last were of the finest cut glass, and of a very elegant form—entirely unlike the bottle found in the private repository, which was of the commonest manufacture, and of the shape ordinarily in use among chemists. Not a drop of liquid, not the smallest atom of any solid substance, remained in it. No smell exhaled from it—and, more unfortunately still for the interests of the defence, no label was found attached to the bottle when it had been discovered.

The chemist who had sold the second supply of arsenic to the prisoner was recalled, and examined. He declared that the bottle was exactly like the bottle in which he placed the arsenic. It was, however, equally like hundreds of other bottles in his shop. In the absence of the label (on which he had himself written the word 'Poison') it was impossible for him to identify the bottle. The dressing-case, and the deceased lady's bed-room, had been vainly searched for the chemist's missing label—on the chance that it might have become accidentally detached from the mysterious empty bottle. In both instances the search had been without result. Morally, it was a fair conclusion that this might be really the bottle which had contained the poison. Legally, there was not the slightest proof of it.

Thus ended the last effort of the defence to trace the arsenic purchased by the prisoner to the possession of his wife. The book relating the practices of the Styrian peasantry (found in the deceased lady's room) had been produced. But could the book prove that she had asked her husband to buy arsenic for her? The crumpled paper, with the grains of powder left in it, had been identified by the chemist, and had been declared to contain grains of arsenic. But where was the proof that Mrs Eustace Macallan's hand had placed the packet in the cabinet, and had emptied it of its contents? No direct evidence anywhere! Nothing but conjecture!

The renewed examination of Miserrimus Dexter touched on matters of no general interest. The cross-examination resolved itself, in substance, into a mental trial of strength between the witness and the Lord Advocate; the struggle terminating (according to the general opinion) in favour of the witness. One question, and one answer only, I will repeat here. They appeared to me of serious importance to the object that I had in view in reading the Trial.

'I believe, Mr Dexter,' the Lord Advocate remarked, in his most ironical manner, 'that you have a theory of your own, which makes the death of Mrs Eustace Macallan no mystery to *you*?'

'I may have my own ideas on that subject, as on other subjects,' the witness replied. 'But let me ask their lordships, the Judges—Am I here to declare theories, or to state facts?'

I made a note of that answer. Mr Dexter's 'ideas' were the ideas of a true friend to my husband, and of a man of far more than average ability. They might be of inestimable value to me, in the coming time—if I could prevail on him to communicate them.

I may mention, while I am writing on the subject, that I added to this first note a second, containing an observation of my own. In alluding to Mrs Beauly, while he was giving his evidence, Mr Dexter had spoken of her so slightingly—so rudely, I might almost say—as to suggest that he had some private reasons for disliking (perhaps for distrusting) this lady. Here, again, it might be of vital importance to me to see Mr Dexter, and to clear up, if I could, what the dignity of the Court had passed over without notice.

The last witness had been now examined. The chair on wheels glided away, with the half-man in it, and was lost in a distant corner of the Court. The Lord Advocate rose to address the Jury for the prosecution.

I do not scruple to say that I never read anything so infamous as this great lawyer's speech. He was not ashamed to declare, at starting, that he firmly believed the prisoner to be guilty. What right had he to say anything of the sort? Was it for *him* to decide? Was he the Judge and Jury both, I should like to know? Having begun by condemning the prisoner, on his own authority, the Lord Advocate proceeded to pervert the most innocent actions of that unhappy man, so as to give them as vile an aspect as possible. Thus: When Eustace kissed his poor wife's forehead, on her death-bed, he did it to create a favourable impression in the minds of the doctor and the nurse! Again, when his grief under his bereavement completely overwhelmed him, he was triumphing in secret, and acting a part! If you looked into his heart, you would see there a diabolical hatred for his wife, and an infatuated passion for Mrs Beauly! In everything he had said, he had lied; in everything he had done, he had acted like a crafty and heartless wretch! So the chief counsel for the prosecution spoke of the prisoner, standing helpless before him at the Bar. In my husband's place, if I could have done nothing more, I would have thrown something at his head. As it was, I tore the pages which contained the speech for the prosecution out of the Report, and trampled them under my feet—and felt all the better, too, for having done it. At the same time, I am a little ashamed of having revenged myself on the harmless printed leaves, now.

The fifth day of the Trial opened with the speech for the defence. Ah, what a contrast to the infamies uttered by the Lord Advocate was the grand burst of eloquence by the Dean of Faculty, speaking on my husband's side!

This illustrious lawyer struck the right note at starting.

'I yield to no one,' he began, 'in the pity I feel for the wife. But I say, the martyr in this case, from first to last, is the husband. Whatever the poor woman may have endured, that unhappy man at the Bar has suffered, and is now suffering, more. If he had not been the kindest of men, the most docile and most devoted of husbands, he would never have occupied his present dreadful situation. A man of a meaner and harder nature would have felt suspicion of his wife's motives, when she asked him to buy poison—would have seen through the wretchedly commonplace excuses she made for wanting it—and would have wisely and cruelly said, "No." The prisoner is not that sort of man. He is too good to his wife, too innocent of any evil thought towards her, or towards any one, to foresee the inconveniences and the dangers to which his fatal compliance may expose him. And what is the result? He stands there, branded as a murderer, because he was too high-minded and too honourable to suspect his wife.'

Speaking thus of the husband, the Dean was just as eloquent and just as unanswerable when he came to speak of the wife.

'The Lord Advocate,' he said, 'has asked, with the bitter irony for which he is celebrated at the Scottish Bar, why we have failed entirely to prove that the prisoner placed the two packets of poison in the possession of his wife? I say, in answer, we have proved, first, that the wife was passionately attached to the husband; secondly, that she felt bitterly the defects in her personal appearance, and especially the defects in her complexion; and, thirdly, that she was informed of arsenic as a supposed remedy for these defects, taken internally. To men who know anything of human nature, there is proof enough! Does my learned friend actually suppose, that women are in the habit of mentioning the secret artifices and applications by which they improve their personal appearance? Is it in his experience of the sex, that a woman who is eagerly bent on making herself attractive to a man, would tell that man, or tell anybody else who might communicate with him, that the charm by which she hoped to win his heart—say the charm of a pretty complexion—had been artificially acquired by the perilous use of a deadly poison? The bare idea of such a thing is absurd. Of course, nobody ever heard Mrs Eustace Macallan speak of arsenic. Of course, nobody ever surprised her in the act of taking arsenic. It is in the evidence, that she would not even confide her intention to try the poison to the friends who had told her of it as a remedy, and who had got her the book. She actually begged them to consider their brief conversation on the subject as strictly private. From first to last, poor creature, she kept her secret; just as she would have kept her secret, if she had worn false hair, or if she had been indebted to the dentist for her teeth. And there you see her husband, in peril of his life, because a woman acted *like* a woman—as your wives, Gentlemen of the Jury, would, in a similar position, act towards You.'

After such glorious oratory as this (I wish I had room to quote more of it!) the next, and last, speech delivered at the Trial—that is to say the Charge of the Judge to the Jury—is dreary reading indeed.

His lordship first told the Jury that they could not expect to have direct evidence of the poisoning. Such evidence hardly ever occurred in cases of poisoning. They must be satisfied with the best circumstantial evidence. All quite true, I dare say. But having told the Jury they might accept circumstantial evidence, he turned back again on his own words, and warned them against being too ready to trust it! 'You must have evidence satisfactory and convincing to your own minds,' he said; 'in which you find no conjectures—but only irresistible and just inferences.' Who is to decide what is a just inference? And what does circumstantial evidence rest on, *but* conjecture?

After this specimen, I need give no further extracts from the summing-up. The Jury, thoroughly bewildered no doubt, took refuge in a compromise. They occupied an hour in considering and debating among themselves, in their own room. (A jury of women would not have taken a minute!) Then they returned into Court, and gave their timid and trimming Scotch Verdict in these words:

'Not Proven.'

Some slight applause followed, among the audience, which was instantly checked. The prisoner was dismissed from the Bar with the formalities observed on such occasions. He slowly retired, like a man in deep grief; his head sunk on his breast—not looking at any one, and not replying when his friends spoke to him. He knew, poor fellow, the slur that the Verdict left on him. 'We don't say you are innocent of the crime charged against you; we only say, there is not evidence enough to convict you.' In that lame and impotent conclusion the proceedings ended, at the time. And there they would have remained, for all time—but for Me.

CHAPTER XXI

I See my Way

IN the grey light of the new morning, I closed the Report of my husband's Trial for the murder of his first Wife.

No sense of fatigue overpowered me. I had no wish, after my long hours of reading and thinking, to lie down and sleep. It was strange, but it was so. I felt as if I *had* slept, and had now just awakened—a new woman, with a new mind.

I could almost understand Eustace's desertion of me. To a man of his refinement, it would have been a martyrdom to meet his wife, after she had read the things published of him to all the world, in the Report. I felt this, as he would have felt it. At the same time, I thought he might have trusted Me to make amends to him for the martyrdom, and might have come back. Perhaps, it might yet end in his coming back. In the mean while, and in that expectation, I pitied and forgave him with my whole heart.

One little matter only dwelt on my mind disagreeably, in spite of my philosophy. Did Eustace still secretly love Mrs Beauly? or had I extinguished that passion in him? To what order of beauty did this lady belong? Were we, by any chance, the least in the world like one another?

The window of my room looked to the east. I drew up the blind, and saw the sun rising grandly in a clear sky. The temptation to go out and breathe the fresh morning air was irresistible. I put on my hat and shawl, and took the Report of the Trial under my arm. The bolts of the back door were easily drawn. In another minute, I was out in Benjamin's pretty little garden.

Composed and strengthened by the inviting solitude and the delicious air, I found courage enough to face the serious question that now confronted me—the question of the future.

I had read the Trial. I had vowed to devote my life to the sacred object of vindicating my husband's innocence. A solitary, defenceless woman, I stood pledged to myself to carry that desperate resolution through to an end. How was I to begin?

The bold way of beginning was surely the wise way, in such a position as mine. I had good reasons (founded, as I have already mentioned, on the important part played by this witness at the Trial) for believing that the fittest person to advise and assist me, was—Miserrimus Dexter. He might disappoint the expectations that I had fixed on him, or he might refuse to help me, or (like my uncle Starkweather) he might think I had taken leave of my senses. All these events were possible. Nevertheless, I held to my resolution to try the experiment. If he was in the land of the living, I decided that my first step at starting should take me to the deformed man, with the strange name.

Supposing he received me, sympathized with me, understood me? What would he say? The nurse, in her evidence, had reported him as speaking in an off-hand manner. He would say, in all probability, 'What do you mean to do? And how can I help you to do it?'

Had I answers ready, if those two plain questions were put to me? Yes! if I dared own to any human creature what was, at that very moment, secretly fermenting in my mind. Yes! if I could confide to a stranger a suspicion roused in me by the Trial, which I have been thus far afraid to mention even in these pages!

It must, nevertheless, be mentioned now. My suspicion led to results, which are part of my story, and part of my life.

Let me own then, to begin with, that I closed the record of the Trial actually agreeing, in one important particular, with the opinion of my enemy and my husband's enemy—the Lord Advocate! He had characterized the explanation of Mrs Eustace Macallan's death, offered by the defence, as 'a clumsy subterfuge, in which no reasonable being could discern the smallest fragment of probability.' Without going quite so far as this, I, too, could see no reason whatever in the evidence for assuming that the poor woman had taken an over-dose of the poison, by mistake. I believed that she had the arsenic secretly in her possession, and that she had tried, or intended to try, the use of it internally, for the purpose of improving her complexion. But further than this I could not advance. The more I thought of it, the more plainly justified the lawyers for the prosecution seemed to me to be, in declaring that Mrs Eustace Macallan had died by the hand of a poisoner—although they were entirely and certainly mistaken in charging my husband with the crime.

My husband being innocent, somebody else, on my own showing, must be guilty. Who, among the persons inhabiting the house at the time, had poisoned Mrs Eustace Macallan? My suspicion, in answering that question, pointed straight to a woman. And the name of that woman was—Mrs Beauly!

Yes! To that startling conclusion I had arrived. It was, to my mind, the inevitable result of reading the evidence.

Look back for a moment to the letter produced in Court, signed 'Helena,' and addressed to Mr Macallan. No reasonable person can doubt (though the Judges excused her from answering the question) that Mrs Beauly was the writer. Very well. The letter offers, as I think, trustworthy evidence to show the state of the woman's mind when she paid her visit to Gleninch.

Writing to Mr Macallan, at a time when she was married to another man—a man to whom she had engaged herself before she met with Mr Macallan—what does she say! She says, 'When I think of your life sacrificed to that wretched woman, my heart bleeds for you.' And, again, she says, 'If it had been my unutterable happiness to love and cherish the best, the dearest of men, what a paradise of our own we might have lived in, what delicious hours we might have known!'

If this is not the language of a woman shamelessly and furiously in love with a man—not her husband—what is? She is so full of him, that even her idea of another world (see the letter) is the idea of 'embracing' Mr Macallan's 'soul.' In this condition of mind and morals, the lady one day finds herself and her embraces free, through the death of her husband. As soon as she can decently visit, she goes visiting; and, in due course of time, she becomes the guest of the man whom she adores. His wife is ill in her bed. The one other visitor at Gleninch is a cripple, who can only move in his chair on wheels. The lady has the house and the one beloved object in it, all to herself. No obstacle stands between her and 'the unutterable happiness of loving and cherishing the best, the dearest of men'—but a poor sick ugly wife, for whom Mr Macallan never has felt, and never can feel, the smallest particle of love.

Is it perfectly absurd to believe that such a woman as this, impelled by these motives, and surrounded by these circumstances, would be capable of committing a crime—if the safe opportunity offered itself?

What does her own evidence say?

She admits that she had a conversation with Mrs Eustace Macallan, in which that lady 'questioned her on the subject of cosmetic applications to the complexion.' Did nothing else take place at that interview? Did Mrs Beauly make no discoveries (afterwards turned to fatal account) of the dangerous experiment which her hostess was then trying, to improve her ugly complexion? All we know is, that Mrs Beauly said nothing about it.

What does the under-gardener say?

He heard a conversation between Mr Macallan and Mrs Beauly, which shows that the possibility of Mrs Beauly becoming Mrs Eustace Macallan had certainly presented itself to that lady's mind, and was certainly considered by her to be too dangerous a topic of discourse to be pursued. Innocent Mr Macallan would have gone on talking. Mrs Beauly is discreet, and stops him.

And what does the nurse (Christina Ormsay) tell us?

On the day of Mrs Eustace Macallan's death, the nurse is dismissed from attendance, and is sent downstairs. She leaves the sick woman, recovered from her first attack of illness, and able to amuse herself with writing. The nurse remains away for half an hour, and then gets uneasy at not hearing the invalid's bell. She goes to the Morning Room to consult Mr Macallan; and there she hears that Mrs Beauly is missing. Mr Macallan doesn't know where she is, and asks Mr Dexter if he has seen her. Mr Dexter has not set eyes on her. At what time does the disappearance of Mrs Beauly take place? At the very time when Christina Ormsay had left Mrs Eustace Macallan alone in her room!

Meanwhile, the bell rings at last, rings violently. The nurse goes back to the sick room at five minutes to eleven, or thereabouts, and finds that the bad symptoms of the morning have returned in a gravely aggravated form. A second dose of poison—larger than the dose administered in the early morning—has been given, during the absence of the nurse, and (observe) during the disappearance also of Mrs Beauly. The nurse, looking out into the corridor for help, encounters Mrs Beauly herself, innocently on her way from her own room—just up, we are to suppose, at eleven in the morning!—to inquire after the sick woman.

A little later, Mrs Beauly accompanies Mr Macallan to visit the invalid. The dying woman casts a strange look at both of them, and tells them to leave her. Mr Macallan understands this as the fretful outbreak of a person in pain, and waits in the room to tell the nurse that the doctor is sent for. What does Mrs Beauly do? She runs out panic-stricken, the instant Mrs Eustace Macallan looks at her. Even Mrs Beauly, it seems, has a conscience!

Is there nothing to justify suspicion in such circumstances as these—circumstances sworn to, on the oaths of the witnesses?

To me, the conclusion is plain. Mrs Beauly's hand gave that second dose of poison. Admit this; and the inference follows that she also gave the first dose in the early morning. How could she do it? Look again at the evidence. The nurse admits that she was asleep, from past two in the morning to six. She also speaks of a locked door of communication with the sick room, the key of which had been removed, nobody knew by whom. Some person must have stolen that key. Why not Mrs Beauly?

One word more, and all that I had in my mind at that time will be honestly revealed.

Miserrimus Dexter, under cross-examination, had indirectly admitted that he had ideas of his own on the subject of Mrs Eustace Macallan's death. At the same time, he had spoken of Mrs Beauly in a tone which plainly betrayed that he was no friend to that lady. Did *he* suspect her, too? My chief motive in deciding to ask his advice, before I applied to any one else, was to find an opportunity of putting that question to him. If he really thought of her as I did, my course was clear before me. The next step to take would be carefully to conceal my identity—and then to present myself, in the character of a harmless stranger, to Mrs Beauly.

There were difficulties, of course, in my way. The first and greatest difficulty was to obtain an introduction to Miserrimus Dexter.

The composing influence of the fresh air in the garden had, by this time, made me readier to lie down and rest than to occupy my mind in reflecting on my difficulties. Little by little, I grew too drowsy to think—then too lazy to go on walking. My bed looked wonderfully inviting, as I passed by the open window of my room.

In five minutes more I had accepted the invitation of the bed, and had said farewell to my anxieties and my troubles. In five minutes more I was fast asleep.

A discreetly gentle knock at my door was the first sound that roused me. I heard the voice of my good old Benjamin speaking outside.

'My dear! I am afraid you will be starved if I let you sleep any longer. It is half-past one o'clock; and a friend of yours has come to lunch with us.'

A friend of mine? What friends had I? My husband was far away; and my Uncle Starkweather had given me up in despair.

'Who is it?' I cried out from my bed, through the door.

'Major Fitz-David,' Benjamin answered—by the same medium.

I sprang out of bed. The very man I wanted was waiting to see me! Major Fitz-David, as the phrase is, knew everybody. Intimate with my husband, he would certainly know my husband's old friend—Miserrimus Dexter.

Shall I confess that I took particular pains with my toilet, and that I kept the luncheon waiting? The woman doesn't live who would have done otherwise—when she had a particular favour to ask of Major Fitz-David.

CHAPTER XXII

The Major makes Difficulties

As I opened the dining-room door, the Major hastened to meet me. He looked the brightest and the youngest of living elderly gentlemen—with his smart blue frock-coat, his winning smile, his ruby ring, and his ready compliment. It was quite cheering to meet the modern Don Juan once more.

'I don't ask after your health,' said the old gentleman; 'your eyes answer me, my dear lady, before I can put the question. At your age a long sleep is the true beauty-draught. Plenty of bed—there is the simple secret of keeping your good looks and living a long life—plenty of bed!'

'I have not been so long in my bed, Major, as you suppose. To tell the truth, I have been up all night, reading.'

Major Fitz-David lifted his well-painted eyebrows, in polite surprise.

'What is the happy book which has interested you so deeply?' he asked.

'The book,' I answered, 'is the Trial of my husband for the murder of his first wife.'

The Major's smile vanished. He drew back a step, with a look of dismay.

'Don't mention that horrid book!' he exclaimed. 'Don't speak of that dreadful subject! What have beauty and grace to do with Trials, Poisonings, Horrors? Why, my charming friend, profane your lips by talking of such things? Why frighten away the Loves and the Graces that lie hid in your smile? Humour an old fellow who adores the Loves and the Graces and who asks nothing better than to sun himself in your smile. Luncheon is ready. Let us be cheerful. Let us laugh, and lunch.'

He led me to the table and filled my plate and my glass, with the air of a man who considered himself to be engaged in one of the most important occupations of his life. Benjamin kept the conversation going on in the interval.

'Major Fitz-David brings you some news, my dear,' he said. 'Your mother-in-law, Mrs Macallan, is coming here to see you to-day.'

My mother-in-law coming to see me! I turned eagerly to the Major for further information.

'Has Mrs Macallan heard anything of my husband?' I asked. 'Is she coming here to tell me about him?'

'She has heard from him, I believe,' said the Major; 'and she has also heard from your uncle, the Vicar. Our excellent Starkweather has written to her—to what purpose I have not been informed. I only know that on receipt of his letter, she has decided on paying you a visit. I met the old lady last night at a party; and I tried hard to discover whether she was coming to you as your friend or your enemy. My powers of persuasion were completely thrown away on her. The fact is,' said the Major, speaking in the character of a youth of five-and-twenty, making a modest confession, 'I don't get on well with old women. Take the will for the deed, my sweet friend. I have tried to be of some use to you—and I have failed.'

Those words offered me the opportunity for which I was waiting. I determined not to lose it.

'You can be of the greatest use to me,' I said, 'if you will allow me to presume, Major, on your past kindness. I want to ask you a question; and I may have a favour to beg when you have answered me.'

Major Fitz-David set down his wine-glass on its way to his lips, and looked at me with an appearance of breathless interest.

'Command me, my dear lady—I am yours and yours only,' said the gallant old gentleman. 'What do you wish to ask me?'

'I wish to ask you if you know Miserrimus Dexter?'

'Good Heavens!' cried the Major; 'that *is* an unexpected question! Know Miserrimus Dexter? I have known him for more years than I like to reckon up. What *can* be your object——?'

'I can tell you what my object is in two words,' I interposed. 'I want you to give me an introduction to Miserrimus Dexter.'

My impression is that the Major turned pale under his paint. This, at any rate, is certain; his sparkling little grey eyes looked at me in undisguised bewilderment and alarm.

'You want to know Miserrimus Dexter?' he repeated, with the air of a man who doubted the evidence of his own senses. 'Mr Benjamin! have I taken too much of your excellent wine? Am I the victim of a delusion—or did our fair friend really ask me to give her an introduction to Miserrimus Dexter?'

Benjamin looked at me in some bewilderment on his side, and answered quite seriously—

'I think you said so, my dear.'

'I certainly said so,' I rejoined. 'What is there so very surprising in my request?'

'The man is mad!' cried the Major. 'In all England you could not have picked out a person more essentially unfit to be introduced to a lady—to a young lady especially—than Dexter. Have you heard of his horrible deformity?'

'I have heard of it—and it doesn't daunt me.'

'Doesn't daunt you! My dear lady, the man's mind is as deformed as his body. What Voltaire said satirically of the character of his countrymen in general, is literally true of Miserrimus Dexter. He is a mixture of the tiger and the monkey. At one moment, he would frighten you; and at the next, he would set you screaming with laughter. I don't deny that he is clever in some respects—brilliantly clever, I admit. And I don't say that he has ever committed any acts of violence, or ever willingly injured anybody. But, for all that, he is mad, if ever a man was mad yet. Forgive me if the inquiry is impertinent. What can your motive possibly be for wanting an introduction to Miserrimus Dexter?'

'I want to consult him.'

'May I ask on what subject?'

'On the subject of my husband's Trial.'

Major Fitz-David groaned, and sought a momentary consolation in his friend Benjamin's claret.

'That dreadful subject again!' he exclaimed. 'Mr Benjamin, why does she persist in dwelling on that dreadful subject?'

'I must dwell on what is now the one employment and the one hope of my life,' I said. 'I have reason to think that Miserrimus Dexter can help me to clear my husband's character of the stain which the Scotch Verdict has left on it. Tiger and monkey as he may be, I am ready to run the risk of being introduced to him. And I ask you again—rashly and obstinately as I fear you will think—to give me the introduction. It will put you to no inconvenience. I won't trouble you to escort me; a letter to Mr Dexter would do.'

The Major looked piteously at Benjamin, and shook his head. Benjamin looked piteously at the Major, and shook *his* head.

'She appears to insist on it,' said the Major.

'Yes,' said Benjamin. 'She appears to insist on it.'

'I won't take the responsibility, Mr Benjamin, of sending her alone to Miserrimus Dexter.'

'Shall I go with her, sir?'

The Major reflected. Benjamin, in the capacity of protector, did not appear to inspire our military friend with confidence. After a moment's consideration, a new idea seemed to strike him. He turned to me.

'My charming friend,' he said, 'be more charming than ever—consent to a compromise. Let us treat this difficulty about Dexter from a social point of view. What do you say to a little dinner?'

'A little dinner?' I repeated, not in the least understanding him.

'A little dinner,' the Major reiterated. 'At my house. You insist on my introducing you to Dexter; and I refuse to trust you alone with that crack-brained personage. The only alternative under the circumstances is to invite him to meet you, and to let you form your own opinion of him—under the protection of my roof. Who shall we have to meet you, besides?' pursued the Major, brightening with hospitable intentions. 'We want a perfect galaxy of beauty round the table, as a species of compensation, when we have got Miserrimus Dexter for one of the guests. Madame Mirliflore is still in London. You would be sure to like her—she is charming; she possesses your firmness, your extraordinary tenacity of purpose. Yes, we will have Madame Mirliflore. Who else? Shall we say Lady Clarinda? Another charming person, Mr Benjamin! You would be sure to admire her—she is so sympathetic, she resembles in so many respects our fair friend here. Yes, Lady Clarinda shall be one of us; and you shall sit next to her, Mr Benjamin, as a proof of my sincere regard for you. Shall we have my young prima donna to sing to us in the evening? I think so. She is pretty; she will assist in obscuring the deformity of Dexter. Very well; there is our party complete; I will shut myself up this evening, and approach the question of dinner with my cook. Shall we say this day week,' asked the Major, taking out his pocket-book—'at eight o'clock?'

I consented to the proposed compromise—but not very willingly. With a letter of introduction, I might have seen Miserrimus Dexter that afternoon. As it was, the 'little dinner' compelled me to wait in absolute inaction, through a whole week. However, there was no help for it but to submit. Major Fitz-David, in his polite way, could be as obstinate as I was. He had evidently made up his mind; and further opposition on my part would be of no service to me.

'Punctually at eight, Mr Benjamin,' reiterated the Major. 'Put it down in your book.'

Benjamin obeyed—with a side look at me, which I was at no loss to interpret. My good old friend did not relish meeting a man at dinner, who was described as 'half tiger, half monkey;' and the privilege of sitting next to Lady Clarinda rather daunted than delighted him. It was all my doing, and he, too, had no choice but to submit. 'Punctually at eight, sir,' said poor old Benjamin, obediently recording his formal engagement. 'Please to take another glass of wine.'

The Major looked at his watch, and rose—with fluent apologies for abruptly leaving the table.

'It is later than I thought,' he said. 'I have an appointment with a friend—a female friend; a most attractive person. You a little remind me of her, my dear lady—you resemble her in complexion; the same creamy paleness. I adore creamy paleness. As I was saying, I have an appointment with my friend; she does me the honour to ask my opinion on some very remarkable specimens of old lace. I have studied old lace. I study everything that can make me useful or agreeable to your enchanting sex. You won't forget our little dinner? I will send Dexter his invitation the moment I get home.' He took my hand, and looked at it critically, with his head a little on one side. 'A delicious hand,' he said; 'you don't mind my looking at it, you don't mind my kissing it—do you? A delicious hand is one of my weaknesses. Forgive my weaknesses. I promise to repent and amend, one of these days.'

'At your age, Major, do you think you have much time to lose?' asked a strange voice, speaking behind us.

We all three looked round towards the door. There stood my husband's mother, smiling satirically—with Benjamin's shy little maid-servant waiting to announce her.

Major Fitz-David was ready with his answer. The old soldier was not easily taken by surprise.

'Age, my dear Mrs Macallan, is a purely relative expression,' he said. 'There are some people who are never young; and there are other people who are never old. I am one of the other people. *Au revoir!*'

With that answer, the incorrigible Major kissed the tips of his fingers to us, and walked out. Benjamin, bowing with his old-fashioned courtesy, threw open the door of his little library, and, inviting Mrs Macallan and myself to pass in, left us together in the room.

CHAPTER XXIII

My Mother-in-Law Surprises me

I TOOK a chair at a respectful distance from the sofa on which Mrs Macallan seated herself. The old lady smiled, and beckoned to me to take my place by her side. Judging by appearances, she had certainly not come to see me in the character of an enemy. It remained to be discovered whether she was really disposed to be my friend.

'I have received a letter from your uncle, the Vicar,' she began. 'He asks me to visit you; and I am happy—for reasons which you shall presently hear—to comply with his request. Under other circumstances, I doubt very much, my dear child—strange as the confession may appear—whether I should have ventured into your presence. My son has behaved to you so weakly, and (in my opinion) so inexcusably, that I am really, speaking as his mother, almost ashamed to face you.'

Was she in earnest? I listened to her, and looked at her, in amazement.

'Your uncle's letter,' pursued Mrs Macallan, 'tells me how you have behaved under your hard trial, and what you propose to do, now Eustace has left you. Dr Starkweather, poor man, seems inexpressibly shocked by what you said to him when he was in London. He begs me to use my influence to induce you to abandon your present ideas, and to make you return to your old home at the Vicarage. I don't in the least agree with your uncle, my dear! Wild as I believe your plans to be—you have not the slightest chance of succeeding in carrying them out—I admire your courage; your fidelity; your unshaken faith in my unhappy son, after his unpardonable behaviour to you. You are a fine creature, Valeria! And I have come here to tell you so in plain words. Give me a kiss, child. You deserve to be the wife of a hero—and you have married one of the weakest of living mortals. God forgive me for speaking so of my own son! But it's in my mind, and it must come out!'

This way of speaking of Eustace was more than I could suffer—even from his mother. I recovered the use of my tongue, in my husband's defence.

'I am sincerely proud of your good opinion, dear Mrs Macallan,' I said. 'But you distress me—forgive me if I own it plainly—when I hear you speak so disparagingly of Eustace. I cannot agree with you that my husband is the weakest of living mortals.'

'Of course not!' retorted the old lady. 'You are like a good woman—you make a hero of the man you love, whether he deserves it or not. Your husband has hosts of good qualities, child—and perhaps I know them better than you do. But his whole conduct, from the moment when he first entered your uncle's house to the present time, has been (I say again) the conduct of an essentially weak man. What do you think he has done now by way of climax? He has joined a charitable brotherhood; and he is off to the war in Spain with a red cross on his arm, when he ought to be here on his knees asking his wife to forgive him. I say that is the conduct of a weak man. Some people might call it by a harder name.'

This news startled and distressed me. I might be resigned to his leaving me (for a time); but all my instincts as a woman revolted at his placing himself in a position of danger, during his separation from his wife. He had now deliberately added to my anxieties. I thought it cruel of him—but I would not confess what I thought to his mother. I affected to be as cool as she was; and I disputed her conclusions with all the firmness that I could summon to help me. The terrible old woman only went on abusing him more vehemently than ever.

'What I complain of in my son,' proceeded Mrs Macallan, 'is that he has entirely failed to understand you. If he had married a fool, his conduct would be intelligible enough. He would have done wisely to conceal from a fool that he had been married already, and that he had suffered the horrid public exposure of a Trial for the murder of his wife. Then, again, he would have been quite right, when this same fool had discovered the truth, to take himself off out of her way, before she could suspect him of poisoning her—for the sake of the peace and quiet of both parties. But you are not a fool. I can see that, after only a short experience of you. Why can't he see it, too? Why didn't he trust you with his secret from the first, instead of stealing his way into your affections under an assumed name? Why did he plan (as he confessed to me) to take you away to the Mediterranean, and to keep you abroad, for fear of some officious friends at home betraying him to you as the prisoner of the famous Trial? What is the plain answer to all these questions? What is the one possible explanation of this otherwise unaccountable conduct? There is only one answer, and one explanation. My poor wretched son—he takes after his father; he isn't the least like me!—is weak in his way of judging; weak in his way of acting; and, like all weak people, headstrong and unreasonable to the last degree. There is the truth! Don't get red and angry. I am as fond of him as you are. I can see his merits, too. And one of them is, that he has married a woman of spirit and resolution—so faithful, and so fond of him, that she won't even let his own mother tell her of his faults. Good child! I like you for hating me!'

'Dear madam, don't say that I hate you!' I exclaimed (feeling very much as if I did hate her, though, for all that!). 'I only presume to think that you are confusing a delicate-minded man with a weak-minded man. Our dear unhappy Eustace——'

'Is a delicate-minded man,' said the impenetrable Mrs Macallan, finishing my sentence for me. 'We will leave it there, my dear, and get on to another subject. I wonder whether we shall disagree about that, too?'

'What is the subject, madam?'

'I won't tell you, if you call me madam. Call me, mother. Say, "What is the subject, mother?" '

'What is the subject, mother?'

'Your notion of turning yourself into a Court of Appeal for a new Trial of Eustace, and forcing the world to pronounce a just verdict on him. Do you really mean to try it?'

'I do!'

Mrs Macallan considered for a moment grimly with herself.

'You know how heartily I admire your courage, and your devotion to my unfortunate son,' she said. 'You know, by this time, that *I* don't cant. But I cannot see you attempt to perform impossibilities; I cannot let you uselessly risk your reputation and your happiness, without warning you before it is too late. My child! the thing you have got it in your head to do, is not to be done by you or by anybody. Give it up.'

'I am deeply obliged to you, Mrs Macallan——'

'Mother!'

'I am deeply obliged to you, mother, for the interest that you take in me—but I cannot give it up. Right or wrong, risk or no risk, I must, and I will, try it!'

Mrs Macallan looked at me very attentively, and sighed as she looked.

'Oh, youth, youth!' she said to herself, sadly. 'What a grand thing it is to be young!' She controlled the rising regret, and turned on me suddenly, almost fiercely, with these words: 'What, in God's name, do you mean to do?'

At the instant when she put the question, the idea crossed my mind that Mrs Macallan could introduce me, if she pleased, to Miserrimus Dexter. She must know him, and know him well, as a guest at Gleninch and an old friend of her son.

'I mean to consult Miserrimus Dexter,' I answered, boldly.

Mrs Macallan started back from me, with a loud exclamation of surprise.

'Are you out of your senses?' she asked.

I told her, as I had told Major Fitz-David, that I had reason to think Mr Dexter's advice might be of real assistance to me at starting.

'And I,' rejoined Mrs Macallan, 'have reason to think that your whole project is a mad one, and that in asking Dexter's advice on it you appropriately consult a madman. You needn't start, child! There is no harm in the creature. I don't mean that he will attack you, or be rude to you. I only say that the last person whom a young woman, placed in your painful and delicate position, ought to associate herself with, is Miserrimus Dexter.'

Strange! Here was the Major's warning repeated by Mrs Macallan, almost in the Major's own words. Well! It shared the fate of most warnings. It only made me more and more eager to have my own way.

'You surprise me very much,' I said. 'Mr Dexter's evidence, given at the Trial, seems as clear and reasonable as evidence can be.'

'Of course it is!' answered Mrs Macallan. 'The shorthand writers and reporters put his evidence into presentable language, before they printed it. If you had heard what he really said, as I did, you would have been either very much disgusted with him, or very much amused by him, according to your way of looking at things. He began, fairly enough, with a modest explanation of his absurd Christian name, which at once checked the merriment of the audience. But as he went on, the mad side of him showed itself. He mixed up sense and nonsense in the strangest confusion: he was called to order over and over again; he was even threatened with fine and imprisonment for contempt of Court. In short, he was just like himself—a mixture of the strangest and the most opposite qualities; at one time, perfectly clear and reasonable, as you said just now; at another, breaking out into rhapsodies of the most outrageous kind, like a man in a state of delirium. A more entirely unfit person to advise anybody, I tell you again, never lived. You don't expect Me to introduce you to him, I hope?'

'I did think of such a thing,' I answered. 'But, after what you have said, dear Mrs Macallan, I give up the idea, of course. It is not a great sacrifice—it only obliges me to wait a week for Major Fitz-David's dinner party. He has promised to ask Miserrimus Dexter to meet me.'

'There is the Major all over!' cried the old lady. 'If you pin your faith on that man, I pity you. He is as slippery as an eel. I suppose you asked him to introduce you to Dexter?'

'Yes.'

'Exactly! Dexter despises him, my dear. He knows as well as I do that Dexter won't go to his dinner. And he takes that roundabout way of keeping you apart—instead of saying No to you plainly, like an honest man.'

This was bad news. But I was, as usual, too obstinate to own myself defeated.

'If the worst comes to the worst,' I said, 'I can but write to Mr Dexter, and beg him to grant me an interview.'

'And go to him by yourself if he does grant it?' inquired Mrs Macallan.

'Certainly. By myself.'

'You really mean it?'

'I do, indeed.'

'I won't allow you to go by yourself.'

'May I venture to ask, ma'am, how you propose to prevent me?'

'By going with you, to be sure, you obstinate hussy! Yes, yes—I can be as headstrong as you are, when I like. Mind! I don't want to know what your plans are. I don't want to be mixed up with your plans. My son is resigned to the Scotch Verdict. And I am resigned to the Scotch Verdict. It is you who won't let matters rest as they are. You are a vain and foolhardy young person. But, somehow, I have taken a liking to you; and I won't let you go to Miserrimus Dexter by yourself. Put on your bonnet!'

'Now?' I asked.

'Certainly! My carriage is at the door. And the sooner it's over, the better I shall be pleased. Get ready—and be quick about it!'

I required no second bidding. In ten minutes more, we were on our way to Miserrimus Dexter.

Such was the result of my mother-in-law's visit.

CHAPTER XXIV

Miserrimus Dexter—First View

WE had dawdled over our luncheon, before Mrs Macallan arrived at Benjamin's cottage. The ensuing conversation between the old lady and myself (of which I have only presented a brief abstract) lasted until quite late in the afternoon. The sun was setting in heavy clouds when we got into the carriage, and the dreary twilight began to fall round us while we were still on the road.

The direction in which we drove took us (as well as I could judge) towards the great northern suburb of London.

For more than an hour the carriage threaded its way through a dingy brick labyrinth of streets, growing smaller and smaller, and dirtier and dirtier, the further we went. Emerging from the labyrinth, I noticed in the gathering darkness dismal patches of waste ground which seemed to be neither town nor country. Crossing these, we passed some forlorn outlying groups of houses with dim little scattered shops among them, looking like lost country villages wandering on the way to London; disfigured and smoke-dried already by their journey! Darker and darker, and drearier and drearier the prospect grew—until the carriage stopped at last, and Mrs Macallan announced, in her sharply-satirical way, that we had reached the end of our journey. 'Prince Dexter's Palace, my dear,' she said. 'What do you think of it?'

I looked round me—not knowing what to think of it, if the truth must be told.

We had got out of the carriage, and we were standing on a rough half-made gravel path. Right and left of me, in the dim light, I saw the half-completed foundations of new houses in their first stage of existence. Boards and bricks were scattered about us. At places, gaunt scaffolding-poles rose like the branchless trees of the brick-desert. Behind us, on the other side of the high road, stretched another plot of waste ground, as yet not built on. Over the surface of this second desert, the ghastly white figures of vagrant ducks gleamed at intervals in the mystic light. In front of us, at a distance of two hundred yards or so, as well as I could calculate, rose a black mass which gradually resolved itself, as my eyes became accustomed to the twilight, into a long, low, and ancient house, with a hedge of evergreens and a pitch-black paling in front of it. The footman led the way towards the paling, through the boards and the bricks, the oyster-shells and the broken crockery, that strewed the ground. And this was 'Prince Dexter's Palace!'

There was a gate in the pitch-black paling, and a bell-handle—discovered with great difficulty. Pulling at the handle, the footman set in motion, to judge by the sound produced, a bell of prodigious size, fitter for a church than a house.

While we were waiting for admission, Mrs Macallan pointed to the low dark line of the old building.

'There is one of his madnesses!' she said. 'The speculators in this new neighbourhood have offered him, I don't know how many thousand pounds for the ground that house stands on. It was originally the manor-house of the district. Dexter purchased it, many years since, in one of his freaks of fancy. He has no old family associations with the place; the walls are all but tumbling about his ears; and the money offered would really be of use to him. But, no! He refused the proposal of the enterprising speculators, by letter, in these words: "My house is a standing monument of the picturesque and beautiful, amid the mean, dishonest, and grovelling constructions of a mean, dishonest, and grovelling age. I keep my house, gentlemen, as a useful lesson to you. Look at it, while you are building round me—and blush, if you can, for your own work." Was there ever such an absurd letter written yet? Hush! I hear footsteps in the garden. Here comes his cousin. His cousin is a woman. I may as well tell you that, or you might mistake her for a man, in the dark.'

A rough, deep voice, which I should certainly never have supposed to be the voice of a woman, hailed us from the inner side of the paling.

'Who's there?'

'Mrs Macallan,' answered my mother-in-law.

'What do you want?'

'We want to see Dexter.'

'You can't see him.'

'Why not?'

'What did you say your name was?'

'Macallan. Mrs Macallan. Eustace Macallan's mother. *Now* do you understand?'

The voice muttered and grunted behind the paling, and a key turned in the lock of the gate.

Admitted to the garden, in the deep shadow of the shrubs, I could see nothing distinctly of the woman with the rough voice, except that she wore a man's hat. Closing the gate behind us, without a word of welcome or explanation, she led the way to the house. Mrs Macallan followed her easily, knowing the place; and I walked in Mrs Macallan's footsteps as closely as I could. 'This is a nice family,' my mother-in-law whispered to me. 'Dexter's cousin is the only woman in the house, and Dexter's cousin is an idiot.'

We entered a spacious hall, with a low ceiling—dimly lit at its further end by one small oil lamp. I could see that there were pictures on the grim brown walls—but the subjects represented were invisible in the obscure and shadowy light.

Mrs Macallan addressed herself to the speechless cousin with the man's hat.

'Now tell me,' she said. 'Why can't we see Dexter?'

The cousin took a sheet of paper off the hall table, and handed it to Mrs Macallan.

'The Master's writing!' said this strange creature, in a hoarse whisper, as if the bare idea of 'the Master' terrified her. 'Read it. And stay, or go, which you please.'

She opened an invisible side-door in the wall, masked by one of the pictures—disappeared through it like a ghost—and left us together alone in the hall.

Mrs Macallan approached the oil lamp, and looked by its light at the sheet of paper which the woman had given to her. I followed, and peeped over her shoulder, without ceremony. The paper exhibited written characters, traced in a wonderfully large and firm handwriting. Had I caught the infection of madness in the air of the house? Or did I really see before me these words?

'NOTICE.—My immense imagination is at work. Visions of heroes unroll themselves before me. I re-animate in myself the spirits of the departed great. My brains are boiling in my head. Any persons who disturb me, under existing circumstances, will do it at the peril of their lives.— DEXTER.'

Mrs Macallan looked round at me quietly with her sardonic smile.

'Do you still persist in wanting to be introduced to him?' she asked.

The mockery in the tone of the question roused my pride. I determined that I would not be the first to give way.

'Not if I am putting you in peril of your life, ma'am,' I answered, pertly enough, pointing to the paper in her hand.

My mother-in-law returned to the hall-table, and put the paper back on it, without condescending to reply. She then led the way to an arched recess on our right hand, beyond which I dimly discerned a broad flight of oaken stairs.

'Follow me,' said Mrs Macallan, mounting the stairs in the dark. 'I know where to find him.'

We groped our way up the stairs to the first landing. The next flight of steps, turning in the reverse direction, was faintly illuminated, like the hall below, by one oil lamp, placed in some invisible position above us. Ascending the second flight of stairs, and crossing a short corridor, we discovered the lamp, through the open door of a quaintly-shaped circular room, burning on the mantelpiece. Its light illuminated a strip of thick tapestry, hanging loose from the ceiling to the floor, on the wall opposite to the door by which we had entered.

Mrs Macallan drew aside the strip of tapestry, and, signing to me to follow her, passed behind it.

'Listen!' she whispered.

Standing on the inner side of the tapestry, I found myself in a dark recess or passage, at the end of which a ray of light from the lamp showed me a closed door. I listened, and heard, on the other side of the door, a shouting voice, accompanied by an extraordinary rumbling and whistling sound travelling backwards and forwards, as well as I could judge, over a great space. Now the rumbling and the whistling would reach their climax of loudness, and would overcome the resonant notes of the shouting voice. Then, again, those louder sounds gradually retreated into distance, and the shouting voice made itself heard as the more audible sound of the two. The door must have been of prodigious solidity. Listen as intently as I might, I failed to catch the articulate words (if any) which the voice was pronouncing, and I was equally at a loss to penetrate the cause which produced the rumbling and whistling sounds.

'What can possibly be going on,' I whispered to Mrs Macallan, 'on the other side of that door?'

'Step softly,' my mother-in-law answered, 'and come and see.'

She arranged the tapestry behind us, so as completely to shut out the light in the circular room. Then noiselessly turning the handle, she opened the heavy door.

We kept ourselves concealed in the shadow of the recess, and looked through the open doorway.

I saw (or fancied I saw, in the obscurity,) a long room, with a low ceiling. The dying gleam of an ill-kept fire formed the only light by which I could judge of objects and distances. Redly illuminating the central portion of the room, opposite to which we were standing, the firelight left the extremities shadowed in almost total darkness. I had barely time to notice this, before I heard the rumbling and whistling sounds approaching me. A high chair on wheels moved by, through the field of red light, carrying a shadowy figure with floating hair, and arms furiously raised and lowered, working the machinery that propelled the chair at its utmost rate of speed. 'I am Napoleon, at the sunrise of Austerlitz!' shouted the man in the chair as he swept past me, on his rumbling and whistling wheels, in the red glow of the firelight. 'I give the word; and thrones rock, and kings fall, and nations tremble, and men by tens of thousands fight and bleed and die!' The chair rushed out of sight, and the shouting man in it became another hero. 'I am Nelson!' the ringing voice cried now. 'I am leading the fleet at Trafalgar. I issue my commands, prophetically conscious of victory and death. I see my own apotheosis—my public funeral, my nation's tears, my burial in the glorious church. The ages remember me, and the poets sing my praise in immortal verse!' The strident wheels turned at the far end of the room, and came back. The fantastic and frightful apparition, man and machinery blended in one—the new Centaur, half man, half chair—flew by me again in the dying light. 'I am Shakspere!' cried the frantic creature, now. 'I am writing "Lear," the tragedy of tragedies. Ancients and moderns, I am the poet who towers over them all. Light! light! the lines flow out like lava from the eruption of my volcanic mind. Light! light! for the poet of all time to write the words that live for ever!' He ground and tore his way back towards the middle of the room. As he approached the fireplace, a last morsel of unburnt coal (or wood) burst into momentary flame, and showed the open doorway. In that moment he saw us! The wheel-chair stopped with a shock that shook the crazy old floor of the room, altered its course, and flew at us with the rush of a wild animal. We drew back, just in time to escape it, against the wall of the recess. The chair passed on, and burst aside the hanging tapestry. The light of the lamp in the circular room poured in through the gap. The creature in the chair checked his furious wheels, and looked back over his shoulder with an impish curiosity horrible to see.

'Have I run over them? Have I ground them to powder for presuming to intrude on me?' he said to himself. As the expression of this amiable doubt passed his lips, his eyes lighted on us. His mind instantly veered back again to Shakspere and 'King Lear.' 'Goneril and Regan!' he cried. 'My two unnatural daughters, my she-devil children, come to mock at me!'

'Nothing of the sort,' said my mother-in-law, as quietly as if she was addressing a perfectly reasonable being. 'I am your old friend, Mrs Macallan; and I have brought Eustace Macallan's second wife to see you.'

The instant she pronounced those last words, 'Eustace Macallan's second wife,' the man in the chair sprang out of it with a shrill cry of horror, as if she had shot him. For one moment we saw a head and body in the air, absolutely deprived of the lower limbs. The moment after, the terrible creature touched the floor as lightly as a monkey, on his hands. The grotesque horror of the scene culminated in his hopping away, on his hands, at a prodigious speed, until he reached the fireplace in the long room. There he crouched over the dying embers, shuddering and shivering, and muttering, 'Oh, pity me, pity me!' dozens and dozens of times over to himself.

This was the man whose advice I had come to ask—whose assistance I had confidently counted on, in my hour of need!

CHAPTER XXV

Miserrimus Dexter—Second View

THOROUGHLY disheartened and disgusted, and (if I must honestly confess it) thoroughly frightened too, I whispered to Mrs Macallan, 'I was wrong, and you were right. Let us go.'

The ears of Miserrimus Dexter must have been as sensitive as the ears of a dog. He heard me say, 'Let us go.'

'No!' he answered. 'Bring Eustace Macallan's second wife in here. I am a gentleman—I must apologize to her. I am a student of human character—I wish to see her.'

The whole man appeared to have undergone a complete transformation. He spoke in the gentlest of voices—and he sighed hysterically when he had done, like a woman recovering from a burst of tears. Was it reviving courage or reviving curiosity? When Mrs Macallan said to me, 'The fit is over now; do you still wish to go away?' I answered, 'No; I am ready to go in.'

'Have you recovered your belief in him, already?' asked my mother-in-law, in her mercilessly satirical way.

'I have recovered from my terror of him,' I replied.

'I am sorry I terrified you,' said the soft voice at the fireplace. 'Some people think I am a little mad at times. You came, I suppose, at one of the times—if some people are right. I admit that I am a visionary. My imagination runs away with me, and I say and do strange things. On those occasions, anybody who reminds me of that horrible Trial, throws me back into the past, and causes me unutterable nervous suffering. I am a very tender-hearted man. As the necessary consequence (in such a world as this), I am a miserable wretch. Accept my excuses. Come in, both of you. Come in, and pity me.'

A child would not have been frightened of him now. A child would have gone in, and pitied him.

The room was getting darker and darker. We could just see the crouching figure of Miserrimus Dexter at the expiring fire—and that was all.

'Are we to have no light?' asked Mrs Macallan. 'And is this lady to see you, when the light comes, out of your chair?'

He lifted something bright and metallic, hanging round his neck, and blew on it a series of shrill, trilling, birdlike notes. After an interval, he was answered by a similar series of notes, sounding faintly in some distant region of the house.

'Ariel is coming,' he said. 'Compose yourself, Mama Macallan, Ariel will make me presentable to a lady's eyes.'

He hopped away on his hands into the darkness at the end of the room. 'Wait a little,' said Mrs Macallan; 'and you will have another surprise—you will see the "delicate Ariel."'

We heard heavy footsteps in the circular room.

'Ariel!' sighed Miserrimus Dexter out of the darkness, in his softest notes.

To my astonishment, the coarse masculine voice of the cousin in the man's hat—the Caliban's, rather than the Ariel's voice—answered, 'Here!'

'My chair, Ariel!'

The person thus strangely misnamed drew aside the tapestry, so as to let in more light—then entered the room, pushing the wheeled chair before her. She stooped, and lifted Miserrimus Dexter from the floor, like a child. Before she could put him into the chair, he sprang out of her arms with a little gleeful cry, and alighted on his seat, like a bird alighting on its perch!

'The lamp,' said Miserrimus Dexter. 'And the looking-glass. Pardon me,' he added, addressing us, 'for turning my back on you. You musn't see me until my hair is set to rights. Ariel! the brush, the comb, and the perfumes.'

Carrying the lamp in one hand, the looking-glass in the other, and the brush (with the comb stuck in it) between her teeth, Ariel the Second, otherwise Dexter's cousin, presented herself plainly before me for the first time. I could now see the girl's round, fleshy, inexpressive face, her rayless and colourless eyes, her coarse nose and heavy chin. A creature half alive; an imperfectly-developed animal in shapeless form, clad in a man's pilot jacket, and treading in a man's heavy laced boots: with nothing but an old red flannel petticoat, and a broken comb in her frowsy flaxen hair, to tell us that she was a woman—such was the inhospitable person who had received us in the darkness, when we first entered the house.

This wonderful valet, collecting her materials for dressing her still more wonderful master's hair, gave him the looking-glass (a hand-mirror), and addressed herself to her work.

She combed, she brushed, she oiled, she perfumed the flowing locks and the long silky beard of Miserrimus Dexter, with the strangest mixture of dulness and dexterity that I ever saw. Done in brute silence, with a lumpish look and a clumsy gait, the work was perfectly well done, nevertheless. The imp in the chair superintended the whole proceeding critically by means of his hand-mirror. He was too deeply interested in this occupation to speak, until some of the concluding touches to his beard brought the misnamed Ariel in front of him, and so turned her full face towards the part of the room in which Mrs Macallan and I were standing. Then he addressed us—taking special care, however, not to turn his head our way while his toilet was still incomplete.

'Mama Macallan,' he said, 'what is the Christian name of your son's second wife?'

'Why do you want to know?' asked my mother-in-law.

'I want to know, because I can't address her as "Mrs Eustace Macallan."'

'Why not?'

'It recalls *the other* Mrs Eustace Macallan. If I am reminded of those horrible days at Gleninch, my fortitude will give way—I shall burst out screaming again.'

Hearing this, I hastened to interpose.

'My name is Valeria,' I said.

'A Roman name,' remarked Miserrimus Dexter. 'I like it. My own name has a Roman ring in it. My bodily build would have been Roman, if I had been born with legs. I shall call you Mrs Valeria. Unless you disapprove of it?'

I hastened to say that I was far from disapproving of it.

'Very good,' said Miserrimus Dexter. 'Mrs Valeria, do you see the face of this creature in front of me?'

He pointed with the hand-mirror to his cousin, as unconcernedly as he might have pointed to a dog. His cousin, on her side, took no more notice than a dog would have taken of the contemptuous phrase by which he had designated her. She went on combing and oiling his beard as composedly as ever.

'It is the face of an idiot, isn't it?' pursued Miserrimus Dexter. 'Look at her! She is a mere vegetable. A cabbage in a garden has as much life and expression in it as that girl exhibits at the present moment. Would you believe there was latent intelligence, affection, pride, fidelity, in such a half-developed being as this?'

I was really ashamed to answer him. Quite needlessly! The impenetrable young woman went on with her master's beard. A machine could not have taken less notice of the life and the talk around it than this incomprehensible creature.

'*I* have got at that latent affection, pride, fidelity, and the rest of it,' resumed Miserrimus Dexter. '*I* hold the key to that dormant Intelligence. Grand thought! Now look at her, when I speak. (I named her, poor wretch, in one of my ironical moments. She has got to like her name, just as a dog gets to like his collar.) Now, Mrs Valeria, look and listen. Ariel!'

The girl's dull face began to brighten. The girl's mechanically-moving hand stopped, and held the comb in suspense.

'Ariel! you have learnt to dress my hair, and anoint my beard—haven't you?'

Her face still brightened. 'Yes! yes! yes!' she answered, eagerly. 'And you say I have learnt to do it well—don't you?'

'I say that. Would you like to let anybody else do it for you?'

Her eyes melted softly into light and life. Her strange unwomanly voice sank to the gentlest tones that I had heard from her yet.

'Nobody else shall do it for me,' she said, at once proudly and tenderly. 'Nobody, as long as I live, shall touch you but me.'

'Not even the lady there?' asked Miserrimus Dexter, pointing backward with his hand-mirror to the place at which I was standing.

Her eyes suddenly flashed, her hand suddenly shook the comb at me, in a burst of jealous rage.

'Let her try!' cried the poor creature, raising her voice again to its hoarsest notes. 'Let her touch you if she dares!'

Dexter laughed at the childish outbreak. 'That will do, my delicate Ariel,' he said. 'I dismiss your Intelligence for the present. Relapse into your former self. Finish my beard.'

She passively resumed her work. The new light in her eyes, the new expression in her face, faded little by little, and died out. In another minute, the face was as vacant and as lumpish as before: the hands did their work again with the lifeless dexterity which had so painfully impressed me when she first took up the brush. Miserrimus Dexter appeared to be perfectly satisfied with these results.

'I thought my little experiment might interest you,' he said. 'You see how it is? The dormant intelligence of my curious cousin is like the dormant sound in a musical instrument. I play upon it—and it answers to my touch. She likes being played upon. But her great delight is to hear me tell a story. I puzzle her to the verge of distraction; and the more I confuse her, the better she likes the story. It is the greatest fun; you really must see it some day.' He indulged himself in a last look at the mirror. 'Ah!' he said, complacently, 'now I shall do. Vanish, Ariel!'

She tramped out of the room in her heavy boots, with the mute obedience of a trained animal. I said 'Good-night' as she passed me. She neither returned the salutation nor looked at me: the words simply produced no effect on her dull senses. The one voice that could reach her was silent. She had relapsed once more into the vacant inanimate creature who had opened the gate to us—until it pleased Miserrimus Dexter to speak to her again.

'Valeria!' said my mother-in-law. 'Our modest host is waiting to see what you think of him.'

While my attention was fixed on his cousin, he had wheeled his chair round, so as to face me—with the light of the lamp falling full on him. In mentioning his appearance as a witness at the Trial, I find I have borrowed (without meaning to do so) from my experience of him at this later time. I saw plainly now the bright intelligent face, and the large clear blue eyes; the lustrous waving hair of a light chestnut colour; the long delicate white hands, and the magnificent throat and chest, which I have elsewhere described. The deformity which degraded and destroyed the manly beauty of his head and breast, was hidden from view by an Oriental robe of many colours, thrown over the chair like a coverlid. He was clothed in a jacket of black velvet, fastened loosely across his chest with large malachite buttons; and he wore lace ruffles at the ends of his sleeves, in the fashion of the last century. It may well have been due to want of perception on my part—but I could see nothing mad in him, nothing in any way repelling, as he now looked at me. The one defect that I could discover in his face was at the outer corners of his eyes, just under the temple. Here, when he laughed, and, in a lesser degree, when he smiled, the skin contracted into quaint little wrinkles and folds, which looked strangely out of harmony with the almost youthful appearance of the rest of his face. As to his other features, the mouth, so far as his beard and moustache permitted me to see it, was small and delicately formed. The nose—perfectly shaped on the straight Grecian model—was perhaps a little too thin, judged by comparison with the full cheeks and the high massive forehead. Looking at him as a whole (and speaking of him, of course, from a woman's, not a physiognomist's, point of view), I can only describe him as being an unusually handsome man. A painter would have revelled in him as a model for St John. And a young girl, ignorant of what the Oriental robe hid from view, would have said to herself the instant she looked at him, 'Here is the hero of my dreams!'

'Well, Mrs Valeria,' he said, quietly, 'do I frighten you now?'

'Certainly not, Mr Dexter.'

His blue eyes—large as the eyes of a woman, clear as the eyes of a child—rested on my face with a strangely varying play of expression, which at once interested and perplexed me.

Now, there was doubt, uneasy painful doubt, in the look: and now again it changed brightly to approval, so open and unrestrained that a vain woman might have fancied she had made a conquest of him at first sight. Suddenly, a new emotion seemed to take possession of him. His eyes sank, his head drooped; he lifted his hands with a gesture of regret. He muttered and murmured to himself; pursuing some secret and melancholy train of thought, which seemed to lead him further and further away from present objects of interest, and to plunge him deeper and deeper in troubled recollections of the past. Here and there, I caught some of the words. Little by little, I found myself trying to fathom what was darkly passing in this strange man's mind.

'A far more charming face,' I heard him say. 'But no—not a more beautiful figure. What figure was ever more beautiful than hers? Something—but not all—of her enchanting grace. Where is the resemblance which has brought her back to me? In the pose of the figure, perhaps? In the movement of the figure, perhaps? Poor martyred angel! What a life! And what a death! what a death!'

Was he comparing me with the victim of the poison—with my husband's first wife? His words seemed to justify the conclusion. If I was right, the dead woman had been evidently a favourite with him. There was no misinterpreting the broken tones of his voice when he spoke of her; he had admired her, living; he mourned her, dead. Supposing that I could prevail upon myself to admit this extraordinary person into my confidence, what would be the result? Should I be the gainer or the loser by the resemblance which he fancied he had discovered? Would the sight of me console him? or pain him? I waited eagerly to hear more on the subject of the first wife. Not a word more escaped his lips. A new change came over him. He lifted his head with a start, and looked about him, as a weary man might look if he was suddenly disturbed in a deep sleep.

'What have I done?' he said. 'Have I been letting my mind drift again?' He shuddered, and sighed. 'Oh, that house of Gleninch!' he murmured sadly to himself. 'Shall I never get away from it in my thoughts? Oh, that house of Gleninch!'

To my infinite disappointment, Mrs Macallan checked the further revelation of what was passing in his mind.

Something in the tone and manner of his allusion to her son's country house seemed to have offended her. She interposed sharply and decisively.

'Gently, my friend, gently!' she said. 'I don't think you quite know what you are talking about.'

His great blue eyes flashed at her fiercely. With one turn of his hand, he brought his chair close at her side. The next instant he caught her by the arm, and forced her to bend to him, until he could whisper in her ear. He was violently agitated. His whisper was loud enough to make itself heard where I was sitting at the time.

'I don't know what I am talking about?' he repeated—with his eyes fixed attentively, not on my mother-in-law, but on me. 'You short-sighted old woman! where are your spectacles? Look at her! Do you see no resemblance—the figure, not the face!—do you see no resemblance there to Eustace's first wife?'

'Pure fancy!' rejoined Mrs Macallan. 'I see nothing of the sort.'

He shook her impatiently.

'Not so loud,' he whispered. 'She will hear you.'

'I have heard you both,' I said. 'You need have no fear, Mr Dexter, of speaking before me. I know that my husband had a first wife; and I know how miserably she died. I have read the Trial.'

'You have read the life and death of a martyr!' cried Miserrimus Dexter. He suddenly wheeled his chair my way; he bent over me, almost tenderly; his eyes filled with tears. 'Nobody appreciated her at her true value,' he said, 'but me. Nobody but me! nobody but me!'

Mrs Macallan walked away impatiently to the end of the room.

'When you are ready, Valeria, I am,' she said. 'We cannot keep the servants and the horses waiting much longer in this bleak place.'

I was too deeply interested in leading Miserrimus Dexter to pursue the subject on which he had touched, to be willing to leave him at that moment. I pretended not to have heard Mrs Macallan. I laid my hand, as if by accident, on the wheel-chair to keep him near me.

'You showed how highly you esteemed that poor lady in your evidence at the Trial,' I said. 'I believe, Mr Dexter, you have ideas of your own about the mystery of her death?'

He had been looking at my hand, resting on the arm of his chair, until I ventured on my question. At that, he suddenly raised his eyes, and fixed them with a frowning and furtive suspicion on my face.

'How do you know I have ideas of my own?' he asked, sternly.

'I know it from reading the Trial,' I answered. 'The lawyer who cross-examined you spoke almost in the very words which I have just used. I had no intention of offending you, Mr Dexter.'

His face cleared as rapidly as it had clouded. He smiled, and laid his hand on mine. His touch struck me cold. I felt every nerve in me shivering under it—I drew my hand away quickly.

'I beg your pardon,' he said, 'if I have misunderstood you. I *have* ideas of my own, about that unhappy lady.' He paused, and looked at me in silence, very earnestly. 'Have *you* any ideas?' he asked. 'Ideas about her life? or about her death?'

I was deeply interested; I was burning to hear more. It might encourage him to speak if I was candid with him. I answered, 'Yes.'

'Ideas which you have mentioned to any one?' he went on.

'To no living creature,' I replied—'as yet.'

'This is very strange!' he said, still earnestly reading my face. 'What interest can *you* have in a dead woman whom you never knew? Why did you ask me that question, just now? Have you any motive in coming here to see me?'

I boldly acknowledged the truth. I said, 'I have a motive.'

'Is it connected with Eustace Macallan's first wife?'

'It is.'

'With anything that happened in her lifetime?'

'No.'

'With her death?'

'Yes.'

He suddenly clasped his hands, with a wild gesture of despair—and then pressed them both on his head, as if he was struck by some sudden pain.

'I can't hear it to-night!' he said; 'I would give worlds to hear it—but I daren't; I should lose all hold over myself in the state I am in now. I am not equal to raking up the horror and the mystery of the past; I have not courage enough to open the grave of the martyred dead. Did you hear me, when you came here? I have an immense imagination. It runs riot at times. It makes an actor of me. I play the parts of all the heroes that ever lived. I feel their characters. I merge myself in their individualities. For the time, I *am* the man I fancy myself to be. I can't help it. I am obliged to do it. If I restrained my imagination, when the fit is on me, I should go mad. I let myself loose. It lasts for hours. It leaves me, with my energies worn out, with my sensibilities frightfully acute. Rouse any melancholy or terrible associations in me, at such times; and I am capable of hysterics, I am capable of screaming. You heard me scream. You shall *not* see me in hysterics. No, Mrs Valeria—no, you innocent reflection of the dead and gone—I would not frighten you for the world. Will you come here to-morrow in the day-time? I have got a chaise and a pony. Ariel, my delicate Ariel, can drive. She shall call at Mama Macallan's and fetch you. We will talk to-morrow, when I am fit for it. I am dying to hear you. I will be fit for you in the morning. I will be civil, intelligent, communicative in the morning. No more of it now! Away with the subject! The too-exciting, the too-interesting subject! I must compose myself, or my brains will explode in my head. Music is the true narcotic for excitable brains. My harp! my harp!'

He rushed away in his chair to the far end of the room—passing Mrs Macallan as she returned to me, bent on hastening our departure.

'Come!' said the old lady, irritably. 'You have seen him, and he has made a good show of himself. More of him might be tiresome. Come away.'

The chair returned to us more slowly. Miserrimus Dexter was working it with one hand only. In the other, he held a harp, of a pattern which I had hitherto only seen in pictures. The strings were few in number; and the instrument was so small that I could have held it easily on my lap. It was the ancient harp of the pictured Muses and the legendary Welsh Bards.

'Good night, Dexter,' said Mrs Macallan.

He held up one hand imperatively.

'Wait!' he said. 'Let her hear me sing.' He turned to me. 'I decline to be indebted to other people for my poetry and my music,' he went on. 'I compose my own poetry, and my own music. I improvise. Give me a moment to think. I will improvise for You.'

He closed his eyes, and rested his head on the frame of the harp. His fingers gently touched the strings while he was thinking. In a few minutes he lifted his head, looked at me, and struck the first notes—the prelude to the song.

Was it good music? or bad? I cannot decide whether it was music at all. It was a wild barbaric succession of sounds; utterly unlike any modern composition. Sometimes, it suggested a slow and undulating Oriental dance. Sometimes it modulated into tones which reminded me of the severer harmonies of the old Gregorian chants. The words, when they followed the prelude, were as wild, as recklessly free from all restraint of critical rules, as the music. They were assuredly inspired by the occasion; I was the theme of the strange song. And thus—in one of the finest tenor voices I ever heard—my poet sang of me:

> Why does she come?
> She reminds me of the lost;
> She reminds me of the dead:
>   In her form like the other,
>   In her walk like the other:
> Why does she come?
>
> Does Destiny bring her?
>   Shall we range together
>   The mazes of the past?
>   Shall we search together
>   The secrets of the past?
> Shall we interchange thoughts, surmises, suspicions?
> Does Destiny bring her?
>
> The Future will show.
>   Let the night pass;
>   Let the day come.

I shall see into Her mind:
She will look into Mine.
The Future will show.

His voice sank, his fingers touched the strings more and more feebly as he approached the last lines. The overwrought brain needed, and took, its re-animating repose. At the final words, his eyes slowly closed. His head lay back on the chair. He slept with his arms round his harp, as a child sleeps, hugging its last new toy.

We stole out of the room on tiptoe, and left Miserrimus Dexter—poet, composer, and madman—in his peaceful sleep.

CHAPTER XXVI

More of my Obstinacy

ARIEL was downstairs in the shadowy hall, half asleep, half awake, waiting to see the visitors clear of the house. Without speaking to us, without looking at us, she led the way down the dark garden walk, and locked the gate behind us. 'Good night, Ariel,' I called out to her over the paling. Nothing answered me but the tramp of her heavy footsteps returning to the house, and the dull thump, a moment afterwards, of the closing door.

The footman had thoughtfully lit the carriage lamps. Carrying one of them to serve as a lantern, he lighted us over the wilds of the brick-desert, and landed us safely on the path by the high road.

'Well!' said my mother-in-law, when we were comfortably seated in the carriage again. 'You have seen Miserrimus Dexter; and I hope you are satisfied. I will do him the justice to declare that I never, in all my experience, saw him more completely crazy than he was to-night. What do *you* say?'

'I don't presume to dispute your opinion,' I answered. 'But, speaking for myself, I am not quite sure that he is mad.'

'Not mad!' cried Mrs Macallan, 'after those frantic performances in his chair? Not mad, after the exhibition he made of his unfortunate cousin? Not mad, after the song that he sang in your honour, and the falling asleep by way of conclusion? Oh, Valeria! Valeria! Well said the wisdom of our ancestors—there are none so blind as those who won't see!'

'Pardon me, dear Mrs Macallan—I saw everything that you mention; and I never felt more surprised, or more confounded, in my life. But now I have recovered from my amazement, and can think over it quietly, I must still venture to doubt whether this strange man is really mad, in the true meaning of the word. It seems to me that he openly expresses—I admit in a very reckless and boisterous way—thoughts and feelings which most of us are ashamed of as weaknesses, and which we keep to ourselves accordingly. I confess I have often fancied myself transformed into some other person, and have felt a certain pleasure in seeing myself in my new character. One of our first amusements as children (if we have any imagination at all) is to get out of our own characters, and to try the characters of other personages as a change—to be fairies, to be queens, to be anything, in short, but what we really are. Mr Dexter lets out the secret, just as the children do—and, if that is madness, he is certainly mad. But I noticed that when his imagination cooled down, he became Miserrimus Dexter again—he no more believed himself, than we believed him, to be Napoleon or Shakspere. Besides, some allowance is surely to be made for the solitary, sedentary life that he leads. I am not learned enough to trace the influence of that life in making him what he is. But I think I can see the result in an over-excited imagination; and I fancy I can trace his exhibiting his power over the poor cousin, and his singing of that wonderful song, to no more formidable cause than inordinate self-conceit. I hope the confession will not lower me seriously in your good opinion—but I must say I have enjoyed my visit; and, worse still, Miserrimus Dexter really interests me!'

'Does this learned discourse on Dexter mean that you are going to see him again?' asked Mrs Macallan.

'I don't know how I may feel about it to-morrow morning,' I said. 'But my impulse at this moment is decidedly to see him again. I had a little talk with him, while you were away at the other end of the room; and I believe he really can be of use to me——'

'Of use to you, in what?' interposed my mother-in-law.

'In the one object which I have in view—the object, dear Mrs Macallan, which, I regret to say, you do not approve.'

'And you are going to take him into your confidence? to open your whole mind to such a man as the man we have just left?'

'Yes—if I think of it to-morrow as I think of it to-night. I dare say it is a risk; but I must run risks. I know I am not prudent; but prudence won't help a woman in my position, with my end to gain.'

Mrs Macallan made no further remonstrance, in words. She opened a capacious pocket in front of the carriage, and took from it a box of matches and a railway reading-lamp.

'You provoke me,' said the old lady, 'into showing you what your husband thinks of this new whim of yours. I have got his letter with me—his last letter from Spain. You shall judge for yourself, you poor deluded young creature, whether my son is worthy of the sacrifice, the useless and hopeless sacrifice, which you are bent on making of yourself, for his sake. Strike a light!'

I willingly obeyed her. Ever since she had informed me of Eustace's departure to Spain, I had been eager for more news of him—for something to sustain my spirits, after so much that had disappointed and depressed me. Thus far, I did not even know whether my husband thought of me sometimes in his self-imposed exile. As to his regretting already the rash act which had separated us, it was still too soon to begin hoping for that.

The lamp having been lit, and fixed in its place between the two front windows of the carriage, Mrs Macallan produced her son's letter. There is no folly like the folly of love. It cost me a hard struggle to restrain myself from kissing the paper on which the dear hand had rested.

'There!' said my mother-in-law. 'Begin on the second page; the page devoted to you. Read straight down to the last line at the bottom—and, in God's name, come back to your senses, child, before it is too late!'

I followed my instructions, and read these words:

'Can I trust myself to write of Valeria? I *must* write of her! Tell me how she is, how she looks, what she is doing. I am always thinking of her. Not a day passes but I mourn the loss of her. Oh, if she had only been contented to let matters rest as they were! Oh, if she had never discovered the miserable truth!

'She spoke of reading the Trial, when I saw her last. Has she persisted in doing so? I believe—I say this seriously, mother—I believe the shame and the horror of it would have been the death of me, if I had met her face to face, when she first knew of the ignominy that I have suffered, of the infamous suspicion of which I have been publicly made the subject. Think of those pure eyes looking at a man who has been accused (and never wholly absolved) of the foulest and the vilest of all murders—and then think of what that man must feel, if he has any heart and any sense of shame left in him. I sicken as I write of it.

'Does she still meditate that hopeless project—the offspring, poor angel, of her artless, unthinking generosity? Does she still fancy that it is in *her* power to assert my innocence before the world? Oh, mother (if she does), use your utmost influence to make her give up the idea! Spare her the humiliation, the disappointment, the insult perhaps, to which she may innocently expose herself. For her sake, for my sake, leave no means untried to attain this righteous, this merciful end.

'I send her no message—I dare not do it. Say nothing when you see her, which can recall me to her memory. On the contrary, help her to forget me as soon as possible. The kindest thing I can do—the one atonement I can make to her—is to drop out of her life.'

With those wretched words it ended. I handed his letter back to his mother in silence. She said but little, on her side.

'If *this* doesn't discourage you,' she remarked, slowly folding up the letter, 'nothing will. Let us leave it there, and say no more.'

I made no answer—I was crying behind my veil. My domestic prospect looked so dreary; my unfortunate husband was so hopelessly misguided, so pitiably wrong! The one chance for both of us (and the one consolation for poor Me) was to hold by my desperate resolution more firmly than ever. If I had wanted anything to confirm me in this view, and to arm me against the remonstrances of every one of my friends, Eustace's letter would have proved more than sufficient to answer the purpose. At least, he had not forgotten me; he thought of me, and he mourned the loss of me, every day of his life. That was encouragement enough—for the present. 'If Ariel calls for me in the pony-chaise to-morrow,' I thought to myself, 'with Ariel I go.'

Mrs Macallan set me down at Benjamin's door.

I mentioned to her, at parting—I stood sufficiently in awe of her to put it off till the last moment—that Miserrimus Dexter had arranged to send his cousin and his pony-chaise to her residence, on the next day; and I inquired thereupon whether my mother-in-law would permit me to call at her house to wait for the appearance of the cousin, or whether she would prefer sending the chaise on to Benjamin's cottage. I fully expected an explosion of anger to follow this bold avowal of my plans for the next day. The old lady agreeably surprised me. She proved that she had really taken a liking to me: she kept her temper.

'If you persist in going back to Dexter, you certainly shall not go to him from my door,' she said. 'But I hope you will *not* persist. I hope you will wake a wiser woman to-morrow morning.'

The morning came. A little before noon the arrival of the pony-chaise was announced at the door, and a letter was brought in to me from Mrs Macallan.

'I have no right to control your movements,' my mother-in-law wrote. 'I send the chaise to Mr Benjamin's house; and I sincerely trust that you will not take your place in it. I wish I could persuade you, Valeria, how truly I am your friend. I have been thinking about you anxiously in the wakeful hours of the night. *How* anxiously, you will understand, when I tell you that I now reproach myself for not having done more than I did to prevent your unhappy marriage. And yet, what I could have done I don't really know. My son admitted to me that he was courting you under an assumed name—but he never told me what the name was, or who you were, or where your friends lived. Perhaps, I ought to have taken measures to find this out. Perhaps, if I had succeeded, I ought to have interfered and enlightened you, even at the sad sacrifice of making an enemy of my own son. I honestly thought I did my duty in expressing my disapproval, and in refusing to be present at the marriage. Was I too easily satisfied? It is too late to ask. Why do I trouble you with an old woman's vain misgivings and regrets? My child, if you come to any harm, I shall feel (indirectly) responsible for it. It is this uneasy state of mind which sets me writing, with nothing to say that can interest you. Don't go to Dexter! The fear has been pursuing me all night that your going to Dexter will end badly. Write him an excuse. Valeria! I firmly believe you will repent it if you return to that house.'

Was ever a woman more plainly warned, more carefully advised, than I? And yet, warning and advice were both thrown away on me!

Let me say for myself that I was really touched by the kindness of my mother-in-law's letter—though I was not shaken by it in the smallest degree. As long as I lived, moved, and thought, my one purpose now was to make Miserrimus Dexter confide to me his ideas on the subject of Mrs Eustace Macallan's death. To those ideas I looked as my guiding stars along the dark way on which I was going. I wrote back to Mrs Macallan, as I really felt, gratefully and penitently. And then I went out to the chaise.

CHAPTER XXVII

Mr Dexter at Home

I FOUND all the idle boys in the neighbourhood collected round the pony-chaise, expressing, in the occult language of slang, their high enjoyment and appreciation of the appearance of 'Ariel' in her man's jacket and hat. The pony was fidgety—*he* felt the influence of the popular uproar. His driver sat, whip in hand, magnificently impenetrable to the jibes and jests that were flying round her. I said, 'Good morning,' on getting into the chaise. Ariel only said, 'Gee up!' and started the pony.

I made up my mind to perform the journey to the distant northern suburb in silence. It was evidently useless for me to attempt to speak; and experience informed me that I need not expect to hear a word fall from the lips of my companion. Experience, however, is not always infallible. After driving for half an hour in stolid silence, Ariel astounded me by suddenly bursting into speech.

'Do you know what we are coming to?' she asked, keeping her eyes straight between the pony's ears.

'No,' I answered. 'I don't know the road. What are we coming to?'

'We are coming to a canal.'

'Well?'

'Well! I have half a mind to upset you in the canal.'

This formidable announcement appeared to me to require some explanation. I took the liberty of asking for it.

'Why should you upset me?' I inquired.

'Because I hate you,' was the cool and candid reply.

'What have I done to offend you?' I asked next.

'What do you want with The Master?' Ariel asked, in her turn.

'Do you mean Mr Dexter?'

'Yes.'

'I want to have some talk with Mr Dexter.'

'You don't! You want to take my place. You want to brush his hair and oil his beard, instead of me. You wretch!'

I now began to understand. The idea which Miserrimus Dexter had jestingly put into her head, in exhibiting her to us on the previous night, had been ripening slowly in that dull brain, and had found its way outwards into words, about fifteen hours afterwards, under the irritating influence of my presence!

'I don't want to touch his hair or his beard,' I said. 'I leave that entirely to you.'

She looked round at me; her fat face flushing, her dull eyes dilating, with the unaccustomed effort to express herself in speech, and to understand what was said to her in return.

'Say that again,' she burst out. 'And say it slower this time.'

I said it again, and I said it slower.

'Swear it!' she cried, getting more and more excited.

I preserved my gravity (the canal was just visible in the distance), and swore it.

'Are you satisfied now?' I asked.

There was no answer. Her last resources of speech were exhausted. The strange creature looked back again straight between the pony's ears, emitted hoarsely a grunt of relief; and never more looked at me, never more spoke to me, for the rest of the journey. We drove past the banks of the canal; and I escaped immersion. We rattled, in our jingling little vehicle, through the streets and across the waste patches of ground, which I dimly remembered in the darkness, and which looked more squalid and more hideous than ever in the broad daylight. The chaise turned down a lane, too narrow for the passage of any larger vehicle, and stopped at a wall and a gate that were new objects to me. Opening the gate with her key, and leading the pony, Ariel introduced me to the back garden and yard of Miserrimus Dexter's rotten and rambling old house. The pony walked off independently to his stable, with the chaise behind him. My silent companion led me through a bleak and barren kitchen, and along a stone passage. Opening a door at the end, she admitted me to the back of the hall, into which Mrs Macallan and I had penetrated by the front entrance to the house. Here, Ariel lifted a whistle which hung round her neck, and blew the shrill trilling notes, with the sound of which I was already familiar as the means of communication between Miserrimus Dexter and his slave. The whistling over, the slave's unwilling lips struggled into speech, for the last time.

'Wait till you hear The Master's whistle,' she said. 'Then go upstairs.'

So! I was to be whistled for like a dog. And worse still, there was no help for it but to submit like a dog. Had Ariel any excuses to make? Nothing of the sort! She turned her shapeless back on me, and vanished into the kitchen region of the house.

After waiting for a minute or two, and hearing no signal from the floor above, I advanced into the broader and brighter part of the hall, to look by daylight at the pictures which I had only imperfectly discovered in the darkness of the night. A painted inscription in many colours, just under the cornice of the ceiling, informed me that the works on the walls were the production of the all-accomplished Dexter himself. Not satisfied with being poet and composer, he was painter as well. On one wall the subjects were described as 'Illustrations of the Passions'; on the other, as 'Episodes in the Life of the Wandering Jew.' Chance spectators like myself were gravely warned, by means of the inscription, to view the pictures as efforts of pure imagination. 'Persons who look for mere Nature in works of Art' (the inscription announced) 'are persons to whom Mr Dexter does not address himself with the brush. He relies entirely on his imagination. Nature puts him out.'

Taking due care to dismiss all ideas of Nature from my mind, to begin with, I looked at the pictures which represented the Passions, first.

Little as I knew critically of Art, I could see that Miserrimus Dexter knew still less of the rules of drawing, colour, and composition. His pictures were, in the strictest meaning of that expressive word—Daubs. The diseased and riotous delight of the painter in representing Horrors, was (with certain exceptions to be hereafter mentioned) the one remarkable quality that I could discover in the series of his works.

The first of the Passion-pictures illustrated Revenge. A corpse, in fancy costume, lay on the bank of a foaming river, under the shade of a giant tree. An infuriated man, also in fancy costume, stood astride over the dead body, with his sword lifted to the lowering sky, and watched, with a horrid expression of delight, the blood of the man whom he had just killed, dripping slowly in a procession of big red drops down the broad blade of his weapon. The next picture illustrated Cruelty, in many compartments. In one, I saw a disembowelled horse savagely spurred on by his rider at a bull-fight. In another, an aged philosopher was dissecting a live cat, and gloating over his work. In a third, two Pagans politely congratulated each other on the torture of two saints: one saint was roasting on a gridiron; the other, hung up to a tree by his heels, had just been skinned, and was not quite dead yet. Feeling no great desire, after these specimens, to look at any more of the illustrated Passions, I turned to the opposite wall to be instructed in the career of the Wandering Jew. Here, a second inscription informed me that the painter considered the Flying Dutchman to be no other than the Wandering Jew, pursuing his interminable journey by sea.

The marine adventures of this mysterious personage were the adventures chosen for representation by Dexter's brush. The first picture showed me a harbour on a rocky coast. A vessel was at anchor, with the helmsman singing on the deck. The sea in the offing was black and rolling; thunder-clouds lay low on the horizon, split by broad flashes of lightning. In the glare of the lightning, heaving and pitching, appeared the misty form of the Phantom Ship approaching the shore. In this work, badly as it was painted, there were really signs of a powerful imagination, and even of a poetical feeling for the supernatural. The next picture showed the Phantom Ship, moored (to the horror and astonishment of the helmsman) behind the earthly vessel in the harbour. The Jew had stepped on shore. His boat was on the beach. His crew—little men with stony white faces, dressed in funereal black—sat in silent rows on the seats of the boat, with their oars in their lean long hands. The Jew, also in black, stood with his eyes and hands raised imploringly to the thunderous heaven. The wild creatures of land and sea—the tiger, the rhinoceros, the crocodile; the sea-serpent, the shark, and the devil-fish—surrounded the accursed Wanderer in a mystic circle, daunted and fascinated at the sight of him. The lightning was gone. The sky and sea had darkened to a great black blank. A faint and lurid light lit the scene, falling downward from a torch, brandished by an avenging Spirit that hovered over the Jew on outspread vulture-wings. Wild as the picture might be in its conception, there was a suggestive power in it which I confess strongly impressed me. The mysterious silence in the house, and my strange position at the moment, no doubt had their effect on my mind. While I was still looking at the ghastly composition before me, the shrill trilling sound of the whistle upstairs burst on the stillness. For the moment, my nerves were so completely upset, that I started with a cry of alarm. I felt a momentary impulse to open the door, and run out. The idea of trusting myself alone with the man who had painted those frightful pictures, actually terrified me; I was obliged to sit down on one of the hall chairs. Some minutes passed before my mind recovered its balance, and I began to feel like my ordinary self again. The whistle sounded impatiently for the second time. I rose, and ascended the broad flight of stairs which led to the ante-room. To draw back at the point which I had now reached would have utterly degraded me in my own estimation. Still, my heart did certainly beat faster than usual when I found myself on the top of the stairs; and I honestly acknowledge that I saw my own imprudence, just then, in a singularly vivid light.

There was a glass over the mantelpiece in the ante-room. I lingered for a moment (nervous as I was) to see how I looked in the glass.

The hanging tapestry over the inner door had been left partially drawn aside. Softly as I moved, the dog's ears of Miserrimus Dexter caught the sound of my dress on the floor. The fine tenor voice, which I had last heard singing, called to me gently.

'Is that Mrs Valeria? Please don't wait there. Come in!'

I entered the inner room.

The wheeled chair advanced to meet me, so slowly and so softly that I hardly knew it again. Miserrimus Dexter languidly held out his hand. His head inclined pensively to one side; his large blue eyes looked at me piteously. Not a vestige seemed to be left of the raging, shouting creature of my first visit, who was Napoleon at one moment and Shakspere at another. Mr Dexter of the morning was a mild, thoughtful, melancholy man, who only recalled Mr Dexter of the night by the inveterate oddity of his dress. His jacket, on this occasion, was of pink quilted silk. The coverlid which hid his deformity matched the jacket in pale sea-green satin; and, to complete these strange vagaries of costume, his wrists were actually adorned with massive bracelets of gold, formed on the severely-simple models which have descended to us from ancient times!

'How good of you to cheer and charm me by coming here!' he said, in his most mournful and most musical tones. 'I have dressed, expressly to receive you, in the prettiest clothes I have. Don't be surprised. Except in this ignoble and material nineteenth century, men have always worn precious stuffs and beautiful colours as well as women. A hundred years ago, a gentleman in pink silk was a gentleman properly dressed. Fifteen hundred years ago, the patricians of the classic times wore bracelets exactly like mine. I despise the brutish contempt for beauty and the mean dread of expense which degrade a gentleman's costume to black cloth, and limit a gentleman's ornaments to a finger ring, in the age I live in. I like to be bright and beautiful, especially when brightness and beauty come to see me. You don't know how precious your society is to me. This is one of my melancholy days. Tears rise unbidden to my eyes. I sigh and sorrow over myself; I languish for pity. Just think of what I am! A poor solitary creature, cursed with a frightful deformity. How pitiable! how dreadful! My affectionate heart— wasted. My extraordinary talents—useless or misapplied. Sad! sad! sad! Please pity me.'

His eyes were positively filled with tears—tears of compassion for himself. He looked at me and spoke to me with the wailing querulous entreaty of a sick child wanting to be nursed. I was quite at a loss what to do. It was perfectly ridiculous—but I was never more embarrassed in my life.

'Please pity me!' he repeated. 'Don't be cruel. I only ask a little thing. Pretty Mrs Valeria, say you pity me!'

I said I pitied him—and I felt that I blushed as I did it.

'Thank you,' said Miserrimus Dexter, humbly. 'It does me good. Go a little further. Pat my hand.'

I tried to restrain myself; but my sense of the absurdity of this last petition (quite gravely addressed to me, remember!) was too strong to be controlled. I burst out laughing.

Miserrimus Dexter looked at me with a blank astonishment which only increased my merriment. Had I offended him? Apparently not. Recovering from his astonishment, he laid his head luxuriously on the back of his chair, with the expression of a man who was listening critically to a performance of some sort. When I had quite exhausted myself, he raised his head, and clapped his shapely white hands, and honoured me with an 'encore.'

'Do it again,' he said, still in the same childish way. 'Merry Mrs Valeria, *you* have a musical laugh—*I* have a musical ear. Do it again.'

I was serious enough by this time. 'I am ashamed of myself, Mr Dexter,' I said. 'Pray forgive me.'

He made no answer to this; I doubt if he heard me. His variable temper appeared to be in course of undergoing some new change. He sat looking at my dress (as I supposed) with a steady and anxious attention, gravely forming his own conclusions, steadfastly pursuing his own train of thought.

'Mrs Valeria,' he burst out suddenly, 'you are not comfortable in that chair.'

'Pardon me,' I replied; 'I am quite comfortable.'

'Pardon *me*,' he rejoined. 'There is a chair of Indian basket-work at the end of the room, which is much better suited to you. Will you accept my apologies if I am rude enough to allow you to fetch it for yourself? I have a reason.'

He had a reason! What new piece of eccentricity was he about to exhibit? I rose and fetched the chair: it was light enough to be quite easily carried. As I returned to him, I noticed that his eyes were still strangely employed in what seemed to me to be the closest scrutiny of my dress. And stranger still, the result of this appeared to be, partly to interest and partly to distress him.

I placed the chair near him, and was about to take my seat in it, when he sent me back again, on another errand, to the end of the room.

'Oblige me indescribably,' he said. 'There is a hand-screen hanging on the wall, which matches the chair. We are rather near the fire here. You may find the screen useful. Once more forgive me for letting you fetch it for yourself. Once more let me assure you that I have a reason.'

Here was his 'reason,' reiterated, emphatically reiterated, for the second time! Curiosity made me as completely the obedient servant of his caprices as Ariel herself. I fetched the hand-screen. Returning with it, I met his eyes still fixed with the same incomprehensible attention on my perfectly plain and unpretending dress, and still expressing the same curious mixture of interest and regret.

'Thank you a thousand times,' he said. 'You have (quite innocently) wrung my heart. But you have not the less done me an inestimable kindness. Will you promise not to be offended with me, if I confess the truth?'

He was approaching his explanation! I never gave a promise more readily in my life.

'I have rudely allowed you to fetch your chair and your screen for yourself,' he went on. 'My motive will seem a very strange one, I am afraid. Did you observe that I noticed you very attentively—too attentively, perhaps?'

'Yes,' I said. 'I thought you were noticing my dress.'

He shook his head, and sighed bitterly.

'Not your dress,' he said. 'And not your face. Your dress is not pretty. Your face is still strange to me. Dear Mrs Valeria, I wanted to see you walk.'

To see me walk! What did he mean? Where was that erratic mind of his wandering to now?

'You have a rare accomplishment for an Englishwoman,' he resumed; 'you walk well. *She* walked well. I couldn't resist the temptation of seeing her again, in seeing you. It was *her* movement, *her* sweet simple unsought grace (not yours) when you walked to the end of the room and returned to me. You raised her from the dead, when you fetched the chair and the screen. Pardon me for making use of you; the idea was innocent, the motive was sacred. You have distressed, and delighted me. My heart bleeds—and thanks you.'

He paused for a moment: he let his head droop on his breast—then suddenly raised it again.

'Surely we were talking about her last night,' he said. 'What did I say? What did you say? My memory is confused; I half remember, half forget. Please remind me. You're not offended with me—are you?'

I might have been offended with another man. Not with him. I was far too anxious to find my way into his confidence—now that he had touched of his own accord on the subject of Eustace's first wife—to be offended with Miserrimus Dexter.

'We were speaking,' I answered, 'of Mrs Eustace Macallan's death; and we were saying to one another——'

He interrupted me, leaning forward eagerly in his chair.

'Yes! yes!' he exclaimed. 'And I was wondering what interest *you* could have in penetrating the mystery of her death. Tell me! Confide in me! I am dying to know!'

'Not even you have a stronger interest in that subject than the interest that I feel,' I said. 'The happiness of my whole life to come depends on my clearing up the mystery of her death.'

'Good God!—why?' he cried. 'Stop! I am exciting myself. I mustn't do that. I must have all my wits about me; I mustn't wander. The thing is too serious. Wait a minute!'

An elegant little basket was hooked on to one of the arms of his chair. He opened it, and drew out a strip of embroidery partially finished, with the necessary materials for working, all complete. We looked at each other across the embroidery. He noticed my surprise.

'Women,' he said, 'wisely compose their minds, and help themselves to think quietly, by doing needlework. Why are men such fools as to deny themselves the same admirable resource—the simple and soothing occupation which keeps the nerves steady and leaves the mind calm and free? As a man, I follow the women's wise example. Mrs Valeria, permit me to compose myself.'

Gravely arranging his embroidery, this extraordinary being began to work with the patient and nimble dexterity of an accomplished needlewoman.

'Now,' said Miserrimus Dexter, 'if you are ready, I am. You talk—I work. Please begin.'

I obeyed him, and began.

CHAPTER XXVIII

In the Dark

WITH such a man as Miserrimus Dexter, and with such a purpose I had in view, no half-confidences were possible. I must either risk the most unreserved acknowledgment of the interests that I really had at stake, or I must make the best excuse that occurred to me for abandoning my contemplated experiment at the last moment. In my present critical situation, no such refuge as a middle course lay before me—even if I had been inclined to take it. As things were, I ran all risks, and plunged headlong into my own affairs at starting.

'Thus far, you know little or nothing about me, Mr Dexter,' I said. 'You are, as I believe, quite unaware that my husband and I are not living together at the present time?'

'Is it necessary to mention your husband?' he asked, coldly, without looking up from his embroidery, and without pausing in his work.

'It is absolutely necessary,' I answered. 'I can explain myself to you in no other way.'

He bent his head, and sighed resignedly.

'You and your husband are not living together, at the present time?' he resumed. 'Does that mean that Eustace has left you?'

'He has left me, and has gone abroad.'

'Without any necessity for it?'

'Without the least necessity.'

'Has he appointed no time for his return to you?'

'If he perseveres in his present resolution, Mr Dexter, Eustace will never return to me.'

For the first time, he raised his head from his embroidery—with a sudden appearance of interest.

'Is the quarrel so serious as that?' he asked. 'Are you free of each other, pretty Mrs Valeria, by common consent of both parties?'

The tone in which he put the question was not at all to my liking. The look he fixed on me was a look which unpleasantly suggested that I had trusted myself alone with him, and that he might end in taking advantage of it. I reminded him quietly, by my manner more than by my words, of the respect which he owed to me.

'You are entirely mistaken,' I said. 'There is no anger—there is not even a misunderstanding between us. Our parting has caused bitter sorrow, Mr Dexter, to him and to me.'

He submitted to be set right with ironical resignation. 'I am all attention,' he said, threading his needle. 'Pray go on; I won't interrupt you again.' Acting on this invitation, I told him the truth about my husband and myself quite unreservedly, taking care, however, at the same time, to put Eustace's motives in the best light that they would bear. Miserrimus Dexter laid aside his embroidery on the chair, and laughed softly to himself, with an impish enjoyment of my poor little narrative, which set every nerve in me on edge as I looked at him.

'I see nothing to laugh at,' I said, sharply.

His beautiful blue eyes rested on me with a look of innocent surprise.

'Nothing to laugh at,' he repeated, 'in such an exhibition of human folly as you have described!' His expression suddenly changed; his face darkened and hardened very strangely. 'Stop!' he cried, before I could answer him. 'There can be only one reason for your taking it as seriously as you do. Mrs Valeria, you are fond of your husband.'

'Fond of him isn't strong enough to express it,' I retorted. 'I love him with my whole heart.'

Miserrimus Dexter stroked his magnificent beard, and contemplatively repeated my words. 'You love him with your whole heart? Do you know why?'

'Because I can't help it,' I answered, doggedly.

He smiled satirically, and went on with his embroidery. 'Curious!' he said to himself; 'Eustace's first wife loved him, too. There are some men whom the women all like; and there are other men whom the women never care for. Without the least reason for it in either case. The one man is just as good as the other; just as handsome, as agreeable, as honourable, and as high in rank as the other. And yet, for Number One, they will go through fire and water; and for Number Two, they won't so much as turn their heads to look at him. Why? They don't know themselves—as Mrs Valeria has just said! Is there a physical reason for it? Is there some potent magnetic emanation from Number One, which Number Two doesn't possess? I must investigate this when I have the time, and when I find myself in the humour.' Having so far settled the question to his own entire satisfaction, he looked up at me again. 'I am still in the dark about you and your motives,' he said. 'I am still as far as ever from understanding what your interest is in investigating that hideous tragedy at Gleninch. Clever Mrs Valeria, please take me by the hand, and lead me into the light. You're not offended with me—are you? Make it up; and I will give you this pretty piece of embroidery when I have done it. I am only a poor, solitary, deformed wretch, with a quaint turn of mind; I mean no harm. Forgive me! indulge me! enlighten me!'

He resumed his childish ways; he recovered his innocent smile, with the odd little puckers and wrinkles accompanying it at the corners of his eyes. I began to doubt whether I might not have been unreasonably hard on him. I penitently resolved to be more considerate towards his infirmities of mind and body, during the remainder of my visit.

'Let me go back for a moment, Mr Dexter, to past times at Gleninch,' I said. 'You agree with me in believing Eustace to be absolutely innocent of the crime for which he was tried. Your evidence at the Trial tells me that.'

He paused over his work, and looked at me with a grave and stern attention which presented his face in quite a new light.

'That is *our* opinion,' I resumed. 'But it was not the opinion of the Jury. Their verdict, you remember, was Not Proven. In plain English, the Jury who tried my husband declined to express their opinion, positively and publicly, that he was innocent. Am I right?'

Instead of answering, he suddenly put his embroidery back in the basket, and moved the machinery of his chair, so as to bring it close by mine.

'Who told you this?' he asked.

'I found it for myself, in a book.'

Thus far, his face had expressed steady attention—and no more. Now, for the first time, I thought I saw something darkly passing over him which betrayed itself to my mind as rising distrust.

'Ladies are not generally in the habit of troubling their heads about dry questions of law,' he said. 'Mrs Eustace Macallan the Second, you must have some very powerful motive for turning your studies that way.'

'I have a very powerful motive, Mr Dexter. My husband is resigned to the Scotch Verdict. His mother is resigned to it. His friends (so far as I know) are resigned to it——'

'Well?'

'Well! I don't agree with my husband, or his mother, or his friends. I refuse to submit to the Scotch Verdict.'

The instant I said those words, the madness in him, which I had hitherto denied, seemed to break out. He suddenly stretched himself over his chair: he pounced on me, with a hand on each of my shoulders; his wild eyes questioned me fiercely, frantically, within a few inches of my face.

'What do you mean?' he shouted, at the utmost pitch of his ringing and resonant voice.

A deadly fear of him shook me. I did my best to hide the outward betrayal of it. By look and word, I showed him, as firmly as I could, that I resented the liberty he had taken with me.

'Remove your hands, sir,' I said. 'And retire to your proper place.'

He obeyed me mechanically. He apologised to me mechanically. His whole mind was evidently still filled with the words that I had spoken to him, and still bent on discovering what those words meant.

'I beg your pardon,' he said; 'I humbly beg your pardon. The subject excites me, frightens me, maddens me. You don't know what a difficulty I have in controlling myself. Never mind. Don't take me seriously. Don't be frightened at me. I am so ashamed of myself—I feel so small and so miserable at having offended you. Make me suffer for it. Take a stick and beat me. Tie me down in my chair. Call up Ariel, who is as strong as a horse, and tell her to hold me. Dear Mrs Valeria! Injured Mrs Valeria! I'll endure anything in the way of punishment, if you will only tell me what you mean by not submitting to the Scotch Verdict?' He backed his chair penitently, as he made that entreaty. 'Am I far enough away yet?' he asked, with a rueful look. 'Do I still frighten you? I'll drop out of sight, if you prefer it, in the bottom of the chair.'

He lifted the sea-green coverlid. In another moment he would have disappeared, like a puppet in a show, if I had not stopped him.

'Say nothing more, and do nothing more; I accept your apologies,' I said. 'When I tell you that I refuse to submit to the opinion of the Scotch Jury, I mean exactly what my words express. That Verdict has left a stain on my husband's character. He feels the stain bitterly. How bitterly no one knows so well as I do. His sense of his degradation is the sense that has parted him from me. It is not enough for *him* that I am persuaded of his innocence. Nothing will bring him back to me—nothing will persuade Eustace that I think him worthy to be the guide and companion of my life—but the proof of his innocence, set before the Jury which doubts it, and the public which doubts it, to this day. He, and his friends, and his lawyers all despair of ever finding that proof, now. But I am his wife; and none of you love him as I love him. I alone refuse to despair; I alone refuse to listen to reason. If God spares me, Mr Dexter, I dedicate my life to the vindication of my husband's innocence. You are his old friend—I am here to ask you to help me.'

It appeared to be now my turn to frighten *him*. The colour left his face. He passed his hand restlessly over his forehead, as if he was trying to brush some delusion out of his brain.

'Is this one of my dreams?' he asked, faintly. 'Are you a vision of the night?'

'I am only a friendless woman,' I said, 'who has lost all that she loved and prized, and who is trying to win it back again.'

He began to move in his chair nearer to me once more. I lifted my hand. He stopped the chair directly. There was a moment of silence. We sat watching one another. I saw his hands tremble as he laid them on the coverlid; I saw his face grow paler and paler, and his under lip drop. What dead and buried remembrances had I brought to life in him, in all their olden horror?

He was the first to speak again.

'So this is your interest,' he said, 'in clearing up the mystery of Mrs Eustace Macallan's death?'

'Yes.'

'And you believe that I can help you?'

'I do.'

He slowly lifted one of his hands, and pointed at me with his long forefinger.

'You suspect somebody,' he said.

The tone in which he spoke was low and threatening: it warned me to be careful. At the same time, if I now shut him out of my confidence, I should lose the reward that might yet be to come, for all that I had suffered and risked at that perilous interview.

'You suspect somebody,' he repeated.

'Perhaps!' was all I said in return.

'Is the person within your reach?'

'Not yet.'

'Do you know where the person is?'

'No.'

He laid his head languidly on the back of his chair, with a trembling long-drawn sigh. Was he disappointed? Or was he relieved? or was he simply exhausted in mind and body alike? Who could fathom him? Who could say?

'Will you give me five minutes?' he asked, feebly and wearily, without raising his head. 'You know already how any reference to events at Gleninch excites and shakes me. I shall be fit for it again, if you will kindly give me a few minutes to myself. There are books in the next room. Please excuse me.'

I at once retired to the circular ante-chamber. He followed me in his chair, and closed the door between us.

CHAPTER XXIX

In the Light

A LITTLE interval of solitude was a relief to me, as well as to Miserrimus Dexter.

Startling doubts beset me as I walked restlessly backwards and forwards, now in the ante-room, and now in the corridor outside. It was plain that I had (quite innocently) disturbed the repose of some formidable secrets in Miserrimus Dexter's mind. I confused and wearied my poor brains in trying to guess what the secrets might be. All my ingenuity—as after events showed me—was wasted on speculations not one of which even approached the truth. I was on surer ground, when I arrived at the conclusion that Dexter had really kept every mortal creature out of his confidence. He could never have betrayed such serious signs of disturbance as I had noticed in him, if he had publicly acknowledged at the Trial, or if he had privately communicated to any chosen friend, all that he knew of the tragic and terrible drama acted in the bed-chamber at Gleninch. What powerful influence had induced him to close his lips? Had he been silent in mercy to others? or in dread of consequences to himself? Impossible to tell! Could I hope that he would confide to Me what he had kept secret from Justice and Friendship alike? When he knew what I really wanted of him, would he arm me, out of his own stores of knowledge, with the weapon that would win me victory in the struggle to come? The chances were all against it—there was no denying that. Still, the end was worth trying for. The caprice of the moment might yet stand my friend, with such a wayward being as Miserrimus Dexter. My plans and projects were sufficiently strange, sufficiently wide of the ordinary limits of a woman's thoughts and actions, to attract his sympathies. 'Who knows' (I thought to myself) 'if I may not take his confidence by surprise, by simply telling him the truth!'

The interval expired; the door was thrown open; the voice of my host summoned me again to the inner room.

'Welcome back!' said Miserrimus Dexter. 'Dear Mrs Valeria, I am quite myself again. How are you?'

He looked and spoke with the easy cordiality of an old friend. During the period of my absence, short as it was, another change had passed over this most multiform of living beings. His eyes sparkled with good humour; his cheeks were flushing under a new excitement of some sort. Even his dress had undergone alteration since I had seen it last. He now wore an extemporised cap of white paper; his ruffles were tucked up; a clean apron was thrown over the seagreen coverlid. He backed his chair before me, bowing and smiling; and waved me to a seat with the grace of a dancing-master, chastened by the dignity of a lord in waiting.

'I am going to cook,' he announced, with the most engaging simplicity. 'We both stand in need of refreshment, before we return to the serious business of our interview. You see me in my cook's dress—forgive it. There is a form in these things; I am a great stickler for forms. I have been taking some wine. Please sanction that proceeding by taking some wine too.'

He filled a goblet of ancient Venetian glass with a purple red liquor, beautiful to see.

'Burgundy!' he said. 'The King of Wines. And this is the King of Burgundies—Clos Vougeot. I drink to your health and happiness!'

He filled a second goblet for himself, and honoured the toast by draining it to the bottom. I now understood the sparkle in his eyes and the flush in his cheeks! It was my interest not to offend him. I drank a little of his wine—and I quite agreed with him; I thought it delicious.

'What shall we eat?' he asked. 'It must be something worthy of our Clos Vougeot. Ariel is good at roasting and boiling joints, poor wretch! But I don't insult your taste by offering you Ariel's cookery. Plain joints!' he exclaimed, with an expression of refined disgust. 'Bah! A man who eats a plain joint is only one remove from a cannibal—or a butcher. Will you leave it to me to discover something more worthy of us? Let us go to the kitchen.'

He wheeled his chair round; and invited me to accompany him with a courteous wave of his hand.

I followed the chair to some closed curtains at one end of the room, which I had not hitherto noticed. Drawing aside the curtains, he revealed to view an alcove, in which stood a neat little gas stove for cooking. Drawers and cupboards, plates, dishes, and saucepans were ranged round the alcove—all on a miniature scale, all scrupulously bright and clean. 'Welcome to the kitchen!' said Miserrimus Dexter. He drew out of a recess in the wall a marble slab which served as a table, and reflected profoundly with his hand to his head. 'I have it!' he cried—and opening one of the cupboards next, took from it a black bottle of a form that was new to me. Sounding this bottle with a spike, he pierced and produced to view some little irregularly formed black objects, which might have been familiar enough to a woman accustomed to the luxurious tables of the rich; but which were a new revelation to a person like myself, who had led a simple country life in the house of a clergyman with small means. When I saw my host carefully lay out these occult substances, of uninviting appearance, on a clean napkin, and then plunge once more into profound reflection at the sight of them, my curiosity could be no longer restrained. I ventured to say, 'What are those things, Mr Dexter? and are we really going to eat them?'

He started at the rash question, and looked at me, with hands outspread in irrepressible astonishment.

'Where is our boasted progress?' he cried. 'What is education but a name? Here is a cultivated person who doesn't know Truffles when she sees them!'

'I have heard of truffles,' I answered humbly. 'But I never saw them before. We had no such foreign luxuries as those, Mr Dexter, at home in the North.'

Miserrimus Dexter lifted one of the truffles tenderly on his spike, and held it up to me in a favourable light.

'Make the most of one of the few first sensations in this life, which has no ingredient of disappointment lurking under the surface,' he said. 'Look at it; meditate over it. You shall eat it, Mrs Valeria, stewed in Burgundy!'

He lit the gas for cooking, with the air of a man who was about to offer me an inestimable proof of his good will.

'Forgive me if I observe the most absolute silence,' he said, 'dating from the moment when I take this in my hand.' He produced a bright little stew-pan from his collection of culinary utensils as he spoke. 'Properly pursued, the Art of Cookery allows of no divided attention,' he continued gravely. 'In that observation you will find the reason why no woman ever has reached, or ever will reach, the highest distinction as a cook. As a rule, women are incapable of absolutely concentrating their attention on any one occupation, for any given time. Their minds will run on something else—say typically, for the sake of illustration, their sweetheart, or their new bonnet. The one obstacle, Mrs Valeria, to your rising equal to the men in the various industrial processes of life is not raised, as the women vainly suppose, by the defective institutions of the age they live in. No! the obstacle is in themselves. No institutions that can be devised to encourage them will ever be strong enough to contend successfully with the sweetheart and the new bonnet. A little while ago, for instance, I was instrumental in getting women employed in our local post-office here. The other day I took the trouble—a serious business to me—of getting downstairs, and wheeling myself away to the office to see how they were getting on. I took a letter with me to register. It had an unusually long address. The registering-women began copying the address on the receipt-form, in a business-like manner cheering and delightful to see. Half-way through, a little child, sister of one of the other women employed, trotted into the office, and popped under the counter to go and speak to her relative. The registering-woman's mind instantly gave way. Her pencil stopped; her eyes wandered off to the child, with a charming expression of interest. "Well, Lucy!" she said, "how-d'ye-do?" Then she remembered business again, and returned to her receipt. When I took it across the counter, an important line in the address of my letter was left out in the copy. Thanks to Lucy. Now a man in the same position would not have seen Lucy—he would have been too closely occupied with what he was about at the moment. There is the whole difference between the mental constitution of the sexes, which no legislation will ever alter as long as the world lasts! What does it matter? Women are infinitely superior to men in the moral qualities which are the true adornments of humanity. Be content—oh, my mistaken sisters, be content with that!'

He twisted his chair round towards the stove. It was useless to dispute the question with him, even if I had felt inclined to do so. He absorbed himself in his stew-pan.

I looked about me in the room.

The same insatiable relish for horrors exhibited downstairs by the pictures in the hall, was displayed again here. The photographs hanging on the wall, represented the various forms of madness taken from the life. The plaster casts ranged on the shelf opposite, were casts (after death) of the heads of famous murderers. A frightful little skeleton of a woman hung in a cupboard, behind a glazed door, with this cynical inscription placed above the skull—'Behold the scaffolding on which beauty is built!' In a corresponding cupboard, with the door wide open, there hung in loose folds a shirt (as I took it to be) of chamois leather. Touching it (and finding it to be far softer than any chamois leather that my fingers had ever felt before), I disarranged the folds, and disclosed a ticket pinned among them, describing the thing in these horrid lines:—'Skin of a French Marquis, tanned in the Revolution of Ninety Three. Who says the nobility are not good for something? They make good leather.'

After this last specimen of my host's taste in curiosities, I pursued my investigation no farther. I returned to my chair, and waited for the Truffles.

After a brief interval, the voice of the poet-painter-composer-and-cook summoned me back to the alcove.

The gas was out. The stew-pan and its accompaniments had vanished. On the marble slab were two plates, two napkins, two rolls of bread—and a dish, with another napkin in it, on which reposed two quaint little black balls. Miserrimus Dexter, regarding me with a smile of benevolent interest, put one of the balls on my plate, and took the other himself. 'Compose yourself, Mrs Valeria,' he said. 'This is an epoch in your life. Your first Truffle! Don't touch it with the knife. Use the fork alone. And—pardon me; this is most important—eat slowly.'

I followed my instructions, and assumed an enthusiasm which I honestly confess I did not feel. I privately thought the new vegetable a great deal too rich, and, in other respects, quite unworthy of the fuss that had been made about it. Miserrimus Dexter lingered and languished over his truffles, and sipped his wonderful Burgundy, and sang his own praises as a cook—until I was really almost mad with impatience to return to the real object of my visit. In the reckless state of mind which this feeling produced, I abruptly reminded my host that he was wasting our time, by the most dangerous question that I could possibly put to him.

'Mr Dexter,' I said, 'have you heard anything lately of Mrs Beauly?'

The easy sense of enjoyment expressed in his face left it at those rash words, and went out like a suddenly-extinguished light. That furtive distrust of me which I had already noticed, instantly made itself felt again in his manner and in his voice.

'Do you know Mrs Beauly?' he asked.

'I only know her,' I answered, 'by what I have read of her in the Trial.'

He was not satisfied with that reply.

'You must have an interest of some sort in Mrs Beauly,' he said, 'or you would not have asked me about her. Is it the interest of a friend? or the interest of an enemy?'

Rash as I might be, I was not quite reckless enough yet, to meet that plain question by an equally plain reply. I saw enough in his face to warn me to be careful with him before it was too late.

'I can only answer you in one way,' I rejoined. 'I must return to a subject which is very painful to you—the subject of the Trial.'

'Go on!' he said with one of his grim outbursts of humour. 'Here I am at your mercy—a martyr at the stake. Poke the fire! poke the fire!'

'I am only an ignorant woman,' I resumed; 'and I daresay I am quite wrong. But there is one part of my husband's trial which doesn't at all satisfy me. The defence set up for him seems to me to have been a complete mistake.'

'A complete mistake?' he repeated. 'Strange language, Mrs Valeria, to say the least of it!' He tried to speak lightly; he took up his goblet of wine. But I could see that I had produced an effect on him. His hand trembled as it carried the wine to his lips.

'I don't doubt that Eustace's first wife really asked him to buy the arsenic,' I continued. 'I don't doubt that she used it secretly to improve her complexion. But what I do *not* believe is—that she died of an overdose of the poison, taken by mistake.'

He put back the goblet of wine on the table near him, so unsteadily that he spilt the greater part of it. For a moment his eyes met mine; then looked down again.

'How do you believe she died?' he inquired, in tones so low that I could hardly hear them.

'By the hand of a poisoner,' I answered.

He made a movement as if he was about to start up in the chair, and sank back again, seized apparently with a sudden faintness.

'Not my husband!' I hastened to add. 'You know that I am satisfied of *his* innocence.'

I saw him shudder. I saw his hands fasten their hold convulsively on the arms of his chair.

'Who poisoned her?' he asked—still lying helplessly back in the chair.

At the critical moment, my courage failed me. I was afraid to tell him in what direction my suspicions pointed.

'Can't you guess?' I said.

There was a pause. I supposed him to be secretly following his own train of thought. It was not for long. On a sudden, he started up in his chair. The prostration which had possessed him appeared to vanish in an instant. His eyes recovered their wild light; his hands were steady again; his colour was brighter than ever. Had he been pondering over the secret of my interest in Mrs Beauly, and had he guessed? He had!

'Answer me on your word of honour!' he cried. 'Don't attempt to deceive me. Is it a woman?'

'It is.'

'What is the first letter of her name? Is it one of the first three letters of the alphabet?'

'Yes.'

'B?'

'Yes.'

'Beauly?'

'Beauly.'

He threw his hands up above his head, and burst into a frantic fit of laughter.

'I have lived long enough!' he broke out wildly. 'At last I have discovered one other person in the world who sees it as plainly as I do. Cruel Mrs Valeria! why did you torture me? Why didn't you own it before?'

'What!' I exclaimed, catching the infection of his excitement. 'Are *your* ideas, *my* ideas? Is it possible that *you* suspect Mrs Beauly, too?'

He made this remarkable reply:

'Suspect?' he repeated, contemptuously. 'There isn't the shadow of a doubt about it. Mrs Beauly poisoned her.'

CHAPTER XXX

The Indictment of Mrs Beauly

I STARTED to my feet, and looked at Miserrimus Dexter. I was too much agitated to be able to speak to him.

My utmost expectations had not prepared me for the tone of absolute conviction in which he had spoken. At the best, I had anticipated that he might, by the barest chance, agree with me in suspecting Mrs Beauly. And now, his own lips had said it, without hesitation or reserve! 'There isn't the shadow of a doubt; Mrs Beauly poisoned her.'

'Sit down,' he said, quietly. 'There's nothing to be afraid of. Nobody can hear us in this room.'

I sat down again, and recovered myself a little.

'Have you never told any one else what you have told me?' was the first question I put to him.

'Never. No one else suspected her.'

'Not even the lawyers?'

'Not even the lawyers. There is no legal evidence against Mrs Beauly. There is nothing but moral certainty.'

'Surely you might have found the evidence, if you had tried?'

He laughed at the idea.

'Look at me!' he said. 'How is a man to hunt up evidence who is tied to this chair? Besides, there were other difficulties in my way. I am not generally in the habit of needlessly betraying myself—I am a cautious man, though you may not have noticed it. But my immeasurable hatred of Mrs Beauly was not to be concealed. If eyes can tell secrets, she must have discovered, in my eyes, that I hungered and thirsted to see her in the hangman's hands. From first to last, I tell you, Mrs Borgia-Beauly was on her guard against me. Can I describe her cunning? All my resources of language are not equal to the task. Take the degrees of comparison to give you a faint idea of it. I am positively cunning; the devil is comparatively cunning; Mrs Beauly is superlatively cunning. No! no! If she is ever discovered, at this distance of time, it will not be done by a man—it will be done by a woman, a woman whom she doesn't suspect; a woman who can watch her with the patience of a tigress in a state of starvation——'

'Say a woman like Me!' I broke out. 'I am ready to try.'

His eyes glittered; his teeth showed themselves viciously under his moustache; he drummed fiercely with both hands on the arms of his chair.

'Do you really mean it?' he asked.

'Put me in your position,' I answered. 'Enlighten me with your moral certainty (as you call it)—and you shall see.'

'I'll do it!' he said. 'Tell me one thing first. How did an outside stranger, like you, come to suspect her?'

I set before him, to the best of my ability, the various elements of suspicion which I had collected from the evidence at the Trial; and I laid especial stress on the fact (sworn to by the nurse) that Mrs Beauly was missing, exactly at the time when Christina Ormsay had left Mrs Eustace Macallan alone in her room.

'You have hit it!' cried Miserrimus Dexter. 'You are a wonderful woman! What was she doing on the morning of the day when Mrs Eustace Macallan died poisoned? And where was she, during the dark hours of the night? I can tell you where she was *not*—she was not in her own room.'

'Not in her own room?' I repeated. 'Are you really sure of that?'

'I am sure of everything that I say, when I am speaking of Mrs Beauly. Mind that; and now listen! This is a drama; and I excel in dramatic narrative. You shall judge for yourself. Date, the twentieth of October. Scene, The Corridor, called The Guests' Corridor, at Gleninch. On one side, a row of windows looking out into the garden. On the other, a row of four bedrooms, with dressing-rooms attached. First bedroom (beginning from the staircase), occupied by Mrs Beauly. Second bedroom, empty. Third bedroom, occupied by Miserrimus Dexter. Fourth bedroom, empty. So much for the Scene! The time comes next—the time is eleven at night. Dexter discovered in his bedroom, reading. Enter to him Eustace Macallan. Eustace speaks:—"My dear fellow, be particularly careful not to make any noise; don't bowl your chair up and down the corridor to-night." Dexter inquires, "Why?" Eustace answers, "Mrs Beauly has been dining with some friends in Edinburgh, and has come back terribly fatigued; she has gone up to her room to rest." Dexter makes another inquiry (satirical inquiry, this time):—"How does she look when she is terribly fatigued? As beautiful as ever?" Answer:—"I don't know; I have not seen her; she slipped upstairs, without speaking to anybody." Third inquiry by Dexter (logical inquiry, on this occasion):—"If she spoke to nobody, how do you know she is fatigued?" Eustace hands me a morsel of paper, and answers, "Don't be a fool! I found this on the hall table. Remember what I have told you about keeping quiet; good night!" Eustace retires. Dexter looks at the paper, and reads these lines in pencil:—"Just returned. Please forgive me for going to bed without saying good night. I have over-exerted myself; I am dreadfully fatigued. (Signed) HELENA." Dexter is by nature suspicious; Dexter suspects Mrs Beauly. Never mind his reasons; there is no time to enter into his reasons now. He puts the case to himself thus:—"A weary woman would never have given herself the trouble to write this. She would have found it much less fatiguing to knock at the drawing-room door as she passed, and to make her apologies by word of mouth. I see something here out of the ordinary way: I shall make a night of it in my chair." Very good. Dexter proceeds to make a night of it. He opens his door; wheels himself softly into the corridor; locks the doors of the two empty bedrooms, and returns (with the keys in his pocket) to his own room. "Now," says D. to himself, "if I hear a door softly opened in this part of the house, I shall know for certain it is Mrs Beauly's door!" Upon that, he closes his own door, leaving the tiniest little chink to look through; puts out his light; and waits and watches at his tiny little chink, like a cat at a mousehole. The corridor is the only place he wants to see; and a lamp burns there all night. Twelve o'clock strikes; he hears the doors below bolted and locked, and nothing happens. Half-past twelve—and nothing still. The house is as silent as the grave. One o'clock; two o'clock—same silence. Half-past two—and something happens at last. Dexter hears a sound close by, in the corridor. It is the sound of a handle turning very softly in a door—in the only door that can be opened, the door of Mrs Beauly's room. Dexter drops noiselessly from his chair, on to his hands; lies flat on the floor at his chink; and listens. He hears the handle closed again; he sees a dark object flit by him; he pops his head out of his door, down on the floor where nobody would think of looking for him. And, what does he see? Mrs Beauly! There she goes, with the long brown cloak over her shoulders which she wears when she is driving, floating behind her. In a moment more, she disappears, past the fourth bedroom, and turns at a right angle, into a second corridor, called the South Corridor. What rooms are in the South Corridor? There are three rooms. First room, the little study, mentioned in the nurse's evidence. Second room, Mrs Eustace Macallan's bedchamber.

Third room, her husband's bedchamber. What does Mrs Beauly (supposed to be worn out by fatigue) want in that part of the house, at half-past two in the morning? Dexter decides on running his risk of being seen—and sets forth on a voyage of discovery. Do you know how he gets from place to place, without his chair? Have you seen the poor deformed creature hop on his hands? Shall he show you how he does it, before he goes on with his story?'

I hastened to stop the proposed exhibition.

'I saw you hop last night,' I said. 'Go on! pray go on with your story!'

'Do you like my dramatic style of narrative?' he asked. 'Am I interesting?'

'Indescribably interesting, Mr Dexter. I am eager to hear more.'

He smiled in high approval of his own abilities.

'I am equally good at the autobiographical style,' he said. 'Shall we try that next, by way of variety?'

'Anything you like,' I cried, losing all patience with him, 'if you will only go on!'

'Part Two: Autobiographical Style,' he announced, with a wave of his hand. 'I hopped along the Guests' Corridor, and turned into the South Corridor. I stopped at the little study. Door open; nobody there. I crossed the study to the second door, communicating with Mrs Macallan's bedchamber. Locked! I looked through the keyhole. Was there something hanging over it, on the other side? I can't say—I only know there was nothing to be seen, but blank darkness. I listened. Nothing to be heard. Same blank darkness, same absolute silence, inside the locked second door of Mrs Eustace's room, opening on the corridor. I went on to her husband's bedchamber. I had the worst possible opinion of Mrs Beauly—I should not have been in the least surprised if I had caught her in Eustace's room. I looked through the keyhole. In this case, the key was out of it—or was turned the right way for me—I don't know which. Eustace's bed was opposite the door. No discovery. I could see him, by his nightlight, innocently asleep. I reflected a little. The back staircase was at the end of the corridor, beyond me. I slid down the stairs, and looked about me on the lower floor, by the light of the night-lamp. Doors all fast locked, and keys outside, so that I could try them myself. House door barred and bolted. Door leading into the servants' offices barred and bolted. I got back to my own room, and thought it out quietly. Where could she be? Certainly *in* the house, somewhere. Where? I had made sure of the other rooms; the field of search was exhausted. She could only be in Mrs Macallan's room—the *one* room which had baffled my investigations; the *only* room which had not lent itself to examination. Add to this, that the key of the door in the study, communicating with Mrs Macallan's room, was stated in the nurse's evidence to be missing; and don't forget that the dearest object of Mrs Beauly's life (on the showing of her own letter, read at the Trial) was to be

Eustace Macallan's happy wife. Put these things together in your own mind, and you will know what my thoughts were, as I sat waiting for events in my chair, without my telling you. Towards four o'clock, strong as I am, fatigue got the better of me. I fell asleep. Not for long. I woke with a start and looked at my watch. Twenty-five minutes past four. Had she got back to her room while I was asleep? I hopped to her door, and listened. Not a sound. I softly opened the door. The room was empty. I went back again to my own room to wait and watch. It was hard work to keep my eyes open. I drew up the window to let the cool air refresh me; I fought hard with exhausted nature; and exhausted nature won. I fell asleep again. This time it was eight in the morning when I woke. I have goodish ears, as you may have noticed. I heard women's voices talking under my open window. I peeped out. Mrs Beauly and her maid, in close confabulation! Mrs Beauly and her maid, looking guiltily about them to make sure that they were neither seen nor heard! "Take care, ma'am," I heard the maid say; "that horrid deformed monster is as sly as a fox. Mind he doesn't discover you." Mrs Beauly answered, "You go first, and look out in front; I will follow you; and make sure there is nobody behind us." With that, they disappeared round the corner of the house. In five minutes more I heard the door of Mrs Beauly's room softly opened and closed again. Three hours later, the nurse met her in the corridor, innocently on her way to make inquiries at Mrs Eustace Macallan's door. What do you think of these circumstances? What do you think of Mrs Beauly and her maid having something to say to each other, which they didn't dare say in the house—for fear of my being behind some door listening to them? What do you think of these discoveries of mine being made, on the very morning when Mrs Eustace was taken ill—on the very day when she died by a poisoner's hand? Do you see your way to the guilty person? And has mad Miserrimus Dexter been of some assistance to you, so far?'

I was too violently excited to answer him. The way to the vindication of my husband's innocence was opened to me at last!

'Where is she?' I cried. 'And where is that servant who is in her confidence?'

'I can't tell you,' he said. 'I don't know.'

'Where can I inquire? Can you tell me that?'

He considered a little.

'There is one man who must know where she is—or who could find it out for you,' he said.

'Who is he? What is his name?'

'He is a friend of Eustace's. Major Fitz-David.'

'I know him! I am going to dine with him next week. He has asked you to dine too.'

Miserrimus Dexter laughed contemptuously.

'Major Fitz-David may do very well for the ladies,' he said. 'The ladies can treat him as a species of elderly human lap-dog. I don't dine with lap-dogs; I have said, No. You go. He, or some of his ladies, may be of use to you. Who are the guests? Did he tell you?'

'There was a French lady whose name I forget,' I said, 'and Lady Clarinda——'

'That will do! She is a friend of Mrs Beauly's. She is sure to know where Mrs Beauly is. Come to me, the moment you have got your information. Find out if the maid is with her: she is the easiest to deal with of the two. Only make the maid open her lips; and we have got Mrs Beauly. We crush her,' he cried, bringing his hand down like lightning on the last languid fly of the season, crawling over the arm of his chair, 'we crush her as I crush this fly. Stop! A question; a most important question in dealing with the maid. Have you got any money?'

'Plenty of money.'

He snapped his fingers joyously.

'The maid is ours!' he cried. 'It's a matter of pounds, shillings, and pence, with the maid. Wait! Another question. About your name? If you approach Mrs Beauly in your own character as Eustace's wife, you approach her as the woman who has taken her place—you make a mortal enemy of her at starting. Beware of that!'

My jealousy of Mrs Beauly, smouldering in me all through the interview, burst into flame at those words. I could resist it no longer—I was obliged to ask him if my husband had ever loved her.

'Tell me the truth,' I said. 'Did Eustace really——?'

He burst out laughing maliciously; he penetrated my jealousy, and guessed my question almost before it had passed my lips.

'Yes,' he said, 'Eustace did really love her—and no mistake about it. She had every reason to believe (before the Trial) that the wife's death would put her in the wife's place. But the Trial made another man of Eustace. Mrs Beauly had been a witness of the public degradation of him. That was enough to prevent his marrying Mrs Beauly. He broke off with her at once and for ever—for the same reason precisely which has led him to separate himself from you. Existence with a woman who knew that he had been tried for his life as a murderer, was an existence that he was not hero enough to face. You wanted the truth. There it is! You have need to be cautious of Mrs Beauly—you have no need to be jealous of her. Take the safe course. Arrange with the Major, when you meet Lady Clarinda at his dinner, that you meet her under an assumed name.'

'I can go to the dinner,' I said, 'under the name in which Eustace married me. I can go as "Mrs Woodville."'

'The very thing!' he exclaimed. 'What would I not give to be present when Lady Clarinda introduces you to Mrs Beauly! Think of the situation. A woman with a hideous secret, hidden in her inmost soul: and another woman who knows of it—another woman who is bent, by fair means or foul, on dragging that secret into the light of day. What a struggle! What a plot for a novel! I am in a fever when I think of it. I am beside myself when I look into the future, and see Mrs Borgia-Beauly brought to her knees at last. Don't be alarmed!' he cried, with the wild light flashing once more in his eyes. 'My brains are beginning to boil again in my head. I must take refuge in physical exercise. I must blow off the steam, or I shall explode in my pink jacket on the spot!'

The old madness seized on him again. I made for the door, to secure my retreat in case of necessity—and then ventured to look round at him.

He was off on his furious wheels—half man, half chair—flying like a whirlwind to the other end of the room. Even this exercise was not violent enough for him, in his present mood. In an instant he was down on the floor; poised on his hands, and looking in the distance like a monstrous frog. Hopping down the room, he overthrew, one after another, all the smaller and lighter chairs as he passed them. Arrived at the end, he turned, surveyed the prostrate chairs, encouraged himself with a scream of triumph, and leapt rapidly over chair after chair, on his hands—his limbless body, now thrown back from the shoulders, and now thrown forward to keep the balance, in a manner at once wonderful and horrible to behold. 'Dexter's Leapfrog!' he cried, cheerfully, perching himself, with his bird-like lightness, on the last of the prostrate chairs, when he had reached the further end of the room. 'I'm pretty active, Mrs Valeria, considering I'm a cripple. Let us drink to the hanging of Mrs Beauly, in another bottle of Burgundy!'

I seized desperately on the first excuse that occurred to me for getting away from him.

'You forget,' I said—'I must go at once to the Major. If I don't warn him in time, he may speak of me to Lady Clarinda by the wrong name.'

Ideas of hurry and movement were just the ideas to take his fancy, in his present state. He blew furiously on the whistle that summoned Ariel from the kitchen regions, and danced up and down on his hands in the full frenzy of his delight.

'Ariel shall get you a cab!' he cried. 'Drive at a gallop to the Major's. Set the trap for her without losing a moment. Oh, what a day of days this has been! Oh, what a relief to get rid of my dreadful secret, and share it with You! I am suffocating with happiness—I am like the Spirit of the Earth in Shelley's poem.' He broke out with the magnificent lines in 'Prometheus Unbound,' in which the Earth feels the Spirit of Love, and bursts into speech. ' "The joy, the triumph, the delight, the madness! The boundless, overflowing, bursting gladness, The vaporous exultation not to be confined! Ha! ha! the animation of delight, Which wraps me like an atmosphere of light, And bears me as a cloud is borne by its own wind." That's how I feel, Valeria! that's how I feel!'

I crossed the threshold while he was still speaking. The last I saw of him, he was pouring out that glorious flood of words—his deformed body, poised on the overthrown chair, his face lifted in rapture to some fantastic Heaven of his own making. I slipped out softly into the antechamber. Even as I crossed the room, he changed once more. I heard his ringing cry; I heard the soft thump-thump of his hands on the floor. He was going down the room again, in 'Dexter's Leapfrog,' flying over the prostrate chairs!

In the hall, Ariel was on the watch for me.

As I approached her, I happened to be putting on my gloves. She stopped me; and taking my right arm, lifted my hand towards her face. Was she going to kiss it? or to bite it? Neither. She smelt it like a dog—and dropped it again with a hoarse chuckling laugh.

'You don't smell of his perfumes,' she said. 'You *haven't* touched his beard. *Now* I believe you. Want a cab?'

'Thank you. I'll walk till I meet a cab.'

She was bent on being polite to me—now I had *not* touched his beard.

'I say!' she burst out, in her deepest notes.

'Yes?'

'I'm glad I didn't upset you in the canal. There now!'

She gave me a friendly smack on the shoulder which nearly knocked me down—relapsed, the instant after, into her leaden stolidity of look and manner—and led the way out by the front door. I heard her hoarse chuckling laugh as she locked the gate behind me. My star was at last in the ascendant! In one and the same day, I had found my way into the confidence of Ariel, and Ariel's Master!

CHAPTER XXXI

The Defence of Mrs Beauly

THE days that elapsed before Major Fitz-David's dinner-party were precious days to me.

My long interview with Miserrimus Dexter had disturbed me far more seriously than I suspected at the time. It was not until some hours after I had left him, that I really began to feel how my nerves had been tried by all that I had seen and heard, during my visit at his house. I started at the slightest noises; I dreamed of dreadful things; I was ready to cry without reason, at one moment, and to fly into a passion without reason, at another. Absolute rest was what I wanted, and (thanks to my good Benjamin) was what I got.

The dear old man controlled his anxieties on my account, and spared me the questions which his fatherly interest in my welfare made him eager to ask. It was tacitly understood between us that all conversation on the subject of my visit to Miserrimus Dexter (of which, it is needless to say, he strongly disapproved), should be deferred until repose had restored my energies of body and mind. I saw no visitors. Mrs Macallan came to the cottage, and Major Fitz-David came to the cottage—one of them to hear what had passed between Miserrimus Dexter and myself: the other to amuse me with the latest gossip about the guests at the forthcoming dinner. Benjamin took it on himself to make my apologies, and to spare me the exertion of receiving my visitors. We hired a little open carriage, and took long drives in the pretty country lanes, still left flourishing within a few miles of the northern suburb of London. At home, we sat and talked quietly of old times, or played at backgammon and dominoes—and so, for a few happy days, led the peaceful, unadventurous life which was good for me. When the day of the dinner arrived, I felt restored to my customary health. I was ready again, and eager again, for the introduction to Lady Clarinda, and the discovery of Mrs Beauly.

Benjamin looked a little sadly at my flushed face, as we drove to Major Fitz-David's house.

'Ah, my dear,' he said, in his simple way, 'I see you are well again! You have had enough of our quiet life already.'

My recollection of events and persons, in general, at the dinner-party, is singularly indistinct. I remember that we were very merry, and as easy and familiar with one another as if we had been old friends. I remember that Madame Mirliflore was unapproachably superior to the other women present, in the perfect beauty of her dress, and in the ample justice which she did to the luxurious dinner set before us. I remember the Major's young prima-donna, more round-eyed, more over-dressed, more shrill and strident as the coming 'Queen of Song,' than ever. I remember the Major himself, always kissing our hands, always luring us to indulge in dainty dishes and drinks, always making love, always detecting resemblances between us, always 'under the charm,' and never once out of his character as elderly Don Juan, from the beginning of the evening to the end. I remember dear old Benjamin completely bewildered, shrinking into corners, blushing when he was personally drawn into the conversation, frightened at Madame Mirliflore, bashful with Lady Clarinda, submissive to the Major, suffering under the music, and, from the bottom of his honest old heart, wishing himself home again. And there, as to the members of that cheerful little gathering, my memory finds its limits—with one exception. The appearance of Lady Clarinda is as present to me as if I had met her yesterday; and of the memorable conversation which we two held together privately, towards the close of the evening, it is no exaggeration to say that I can still call to mind almost every word.

I see her dress, I hear her voice again, while I write.

She was attired, I remember, with that extreme assumption of simplicity which always defeats its own end, by irresistibly suggesting art. She wore plain white muslin, over white silk, without trimming or ornament of any kind. Her rich brown hair, dressed in defiance of the prevailing fashion, was thrown back from her forehead, and gathered into a simple knot behind, without adornment of any sort. A little white ribbon encircled her neck, fastened by the only article of jewellery that she wore—a tiny diamond brooch. She was unquestionably handsome; but her beauty was of the somewhat hard and angular type which is so often seen in English women of her race: the nose and chin too prominent and too firmly shaped; the well-opened grey eyes full of spirit and dignity, but wanting in tenderness and mobility of expression. Her manner had all the charm which fine breeding can confer—exquisitely polite, easily cordial; showing that perfect yet unobtrusive confidence in herself, which (in England) seems to be the natural outgrowth of pre-eminent social rank. If you had accepted her for what she was, on the surface, you would have said, Here is the model of a noble woman who is perfectly free from pride. And if you had taken a liberty with her, on the strength of that conviction, she would have made you remember it to the end of your life.

We got on together admirably. I was introduced as 'Mrs Woodville,' by previous arrangement with the Major, effected through Benjamin. Before the dinner was over, we had promised to exchange visits. Nothing but the opportunity was wanting to lead Lady Clarinda into talking, as I wanted her to talk, of Mrs Beauly.

Late in the evening, the opportunity came.

I had taken refuge from the terrible bravura singing of the Major's strident prima-donna, in the back drawing-room. As I had hoped and anticipated, after a while, Lady Clarinda (missing me from the group round the piano) came in search of me. She seated herself by my side, out of sight and out of hearing of our friends in the front room; and, to my infinite relief and delight, touched on the subject of Miserrimus Dexter, of her own accord. Something I had said of him, when his name had been accidentally mentioned at dinner, remained in her memory, and led us, by perfectly natural gradations, into speaking of Mrs Beauly. 'At last,' I thought to myself, 'the Major's little dinner will bring me my reward!'

And what a reward it was, when it came! My heart sinks in me again—as it sank on that never-to-be-forgotten evening—while I sit at my desk, thinking of it.

'So Dexter really spoke to you of Mrs Beauly!' exclaimed Lady Clarinda. 'You have no idea how you surprise me.'

'May I ask why?'

'He hates her! The last time I saw him, he wouldn't allow me to mention her name. It is one of his innumerable oddities. If any such feeling as sympathy is a possible feeling in such a nature as his, he ought to like Helena Beauly. She is the most completely unconventional person I know. When she does break out, poor dear, she says things and does things, which are almost reckless enough to be worthy of Dexter himself. I wonder whether you would like her?'

'You have kindly asked me to visit you, Lady Clarinda. Perhaps I may meet her at your house?'

Lady Clarinda laughed as if the idea amused her.

'I hope you will not wait until *that* is likely to happen,' she said. 'Helena's last whim is to fancy that she has got—the gout, of all the maladies in the world! She is away at some wonderful baths in Hungary, or Bohemia (I don't remember which)—and where she will go, or what she will do, next, it is perfectly impossible to say. Dear Mrs Woodville! is the heat of the fire too much for you? You are looking quite pale.'

I *felt* that I was looking pale. The discovery of Mrs Beauly's absence from England was a shock for which I was quite unprepared. For the moment, it unnerved me.

'Shall we go into the other room?' asked Lady Clarinda.

To go into the other room would be to drop the conversation. I was determined not to let that catastrophe happen. It was just possible that Mrs Beauly's maid might have quitted her service, or might have been left behind in England. My information would not be complete, until I knew what had become of the maid. I pushed my chair back a little from the fire-place, and took a hand-screen from a table near me. It might be made useful in hiding my face, if any more disappointments were in store for me.

'Thank you, Lady Clarinda: I was only a little too near the fire. I shall do admirably here. You surprise me about Mrs Beauly. From what Mr Dexter said to me, I had imagined——'

'Oh, you must not believe anything Dexter tells you!' interposed Lady Clarinda. 'He delights in mystifying people; and he purposely misled you, I have no doubt. If all that I hear is true, *he* ought to know more of Helena Beauly's strange freaks and fancies than most people. He all but discovered her, in one of her adventures (down in Scotland), which reminds me of the story in Auber's charming opera—what is it called? I shall forget my own name next! I mean the opera in which the two nuns slip out of the convent, and go to the ball. Listen! how very odd! That vulgar girl is singing the castanet song in the second act, at this moment. Major! what opera is the young lady singing from?'

The Major was scandalised at the interruption. He bustled into the back room—whispered 'Hush! hush! my dear lady. The *Domino Noir*'—and bustled back again to the piano.

'Of course!' said Lady Clarinda. 'How stupid of me! The *Domino Noir*. And how strange that you should forget it too!'

I had remembered it perfectly; but I could not trust myself to speak. If, as I believed, the 'adventure' mentioned by Lady Clarinda was connected, in some way, with Mrs Beauly's mysterious proceedings on the morning of the twenty-first of October, I was on the brink of the very discovery which it was the one interest of my life to make! I held the screen so as to hide my face; and I said, in the steadiest voice that I could command at the moment,—

'Pray go on! Pray tell me what the adventure was!'

Lady Clarinda was quite flattered by my eager desire to hear the coming narrative.

'I hope my story will be worthy of the interest which you are so good as to feel in it,' she said. 'If you only knew Helena—it is *so* like her! I have it, you must know, from her maid. She has taken a woman who speaks foreign languages with her to Hungary, and she has left the maid with me. A perfect treasure! I should only be too glad if I could keep her in my service: she has but one defect, a name I hate—Phœbe. Well! Phœbe and her mistress were staying at a place near Edinburgh, called (I think) Gleninch. The house belonged to that Mr Macallan, who was afterwards tried—you remember it, of course?—for poisoning his wife. A dreadful case; but don't be alarmed—my story has nothing to do with it; my story has to do with Helena Beauly. One evening (while she was staying at Gleninch) she was engaged to dine with some English friends visiting Edinburgh. The same night—also in Edinburgh—there was a masked ball, given by somebody whose name I forget. The ball (almost an unparalleled event in Scotland!) was reported to be not at all a reputable affair. All sorts of amusing people were to be there. Ladies of doubtful virtue, you know; and gentlemen on the outlying limits of society, and so on. Helena's friends had contrived to get cards, and were going, in spite of the objections—in the strictest incognito, of course; trusting to their masks. And Helena herself was bent on going with them, if she could only manage it without being discovered at Gleninch. Mr Macallan was one of the strait-laced people who disapproved of the ball. No lady, he said, could show herself at such an entertainment without compromising her reputation. What stuff! Well, Helena, in one of her wildest moments, hit on a way of going to the ball without discovery, which was really as ingenious as a plot in a French play. She went to the dinner in the carriage from Gleninch, having sent Phœbe to Edinburgh before her. It was not a grand dinner—a little friendly gathering; no evening dress. When the time came for going back to Gleninch, what do you think Helena did? She sent her maid back in the carriage, instead of herself! Phœbe was dressed in her mistress's cloak and bonnet and veil. She was instructed to run upstairs the moment she got to the house; leaving on the hall-table a little note of apology (written by Helena of course!) pleading fatigue as an excuse for not saying good night to her host. The mistress and the maid were about the same height; and the servants naturally never discovered the trick. Phœbe got up to her mistress's room, safely enough. There, her instructions were to wait until the house was quiet for the night, and then to steal up to her own room. While she was waiting, the girl fell asleep. She only woke at two in the morning, or later. It didn't much matter, as she thought. She stole out on tip-toe, and closed the door behind her. Before she was at the end of the corridor, she fancied she heard something. She waited till she was safe on the upper storey, and then she looked over the banisters. There was Dexter—so like him!—hopping about on his hands (did you ever see it? the most grotesquely-horrible exhibition you can imagine!)—there was Dexter, hopping about, and looking through keyholes—evidently in search of the person who had left her room at two in the morning; and no doubt taking Phœbe for her mistress, seeing that she had forgotten to take her mistress's cloak off her shoulders. The next morning early, Helena came back in a hired carriage from Edinburgh, with a hat and mantle borrowed from her English friends. She left the carriage in the road; and got into the house by way of the garden—without being discovered, this time, by Dexter, or by anybody. Clever and daring, wasn't it? And, as I said just now, quite a new version of the *Domino Noir*. You will wonder, as I did, how it was that Dexter didn't make mischief in the morning? He would have done it no doubt. But even *he* was silenced (as Phœbe told me) by the dreadful event that happened in the house on the same day.——My dear Mrs Woodville! the heat of this room is certainly too much for you. Take my smelling-bottle. Let me open the window.'

I was just able to answer, 'Pray say nothing! Let me slip out into the air!'

I made my way unobserved to the landing, and sat down on the stairs to compose myself, where nobody could see me. In a moment more, I felt a hand laid gently on my shoulder, and discovered good Benjamin looking at me in dismay. Lady Clarinda had considerately spoken to him, and had assisted him in quietly making his retreat from the room, while his host's attention was still absorbed by the music.

'My dear child!' he whispered, 'what is the matter?'

'Take me home, and I will tell you,' was all that I could say.

CHAPTER XXXII

A Specimen of my Wisdom

THE scene must follow my erratic movements—the scene must close on London for a while, and open in Edinburgh.

Two days had passed since Major Fitz-David's dinner-party. I was able to breathe again freely, after the utter destruction of all my plans for the future, and of all the hopes that I had founded on them. I could now see that I had been trebly in the wrong—wrong in hastily and cruelly suspecting an innocent woman; wrong in communicating my suspicions (without an attempt to verify them previously) to another person; wrong in accepting the flighty inferences and conclusions of Miserrimus Dexter as if they had been solid truths. I was so ashamed of my folly, when I thought of the past; so completely discouraged, so rudely shaken in my confidence in myself, when I thought of the future, that, for once in a way, I accepted sensible advice when it was offered to me. 'My dear,' said good old Benjamin, after we had thoroughly talked over my discomfiture on our return from the dinner-party, 'judging by what you tell me of him, I don't fancy Mr Dexter. Promise me that you will not go back to him, until you have first consulted some person who is fitter to guide you through this dangerous business than I am.'

I gave him my promise, on one condition. 'If I fail to find the person,' I said, 'will you undertake to help me?'

Benjamin pledged himself to help me, cheerfully.

The next morning, when I was brushing my hair, and thinking over my affairs, I called to mind a forgotten resolution of mine, at the time when I first read the Report of my husband's Trial. I mean the resolution—if Miserrimus Dexter failed me—to apply to one of the two agents (or solicitors, as we should term them) who had prepared Eustace's defence, namely, Mr Playmore. This gentleman, it may be remembered, had especially recommended himself to my confidence by his friendly interference, when the sheriff's officers were in search of my husband's papers. Referring back to the evidence of 'Isaiah Schoolcraft,' I found that Mr Playmore had been called in to assist and advise Eustace, by Miserrimus Dexter. He was therefore not only a friend on whom I might rely, but a friend who was personally acquainted with Dexter as well. Could there be a fitter man to apply to for enlightenment in the darkness that had now gathered round me? Benjamin, when I put the question to him, acknowledged that I had made a sensible choice on this occasion, and at once exerted himself to help me. He discovered (through his own lawyer) the address of Mr Playmore's London agents; and from these gentlemen he obtained for me a letter of introduction to Mr Playmore himself. I had nothing to conceal from my new adviser; and I was properly described in the letter as Eustace Macallan's second wife.

The same evening, we two set forth (Benjamin refused to let me travel alone) by the night mail for Edinburgh.

I had previously written to Miserrimus Dexter (by my old friend's advice), merely saying that I had been unexpectedly called away from London for a few days, and that I would report to him the result of my interview with Lady Clarinda on my return. A characteristic answer was brought back to the cottage by Ariel. 'Mrs Valeria, I happen to be a man of quick perceptions; and I can read the *unwritten* part of your letter. Lady Clarinda has shaken your confidence in me. Very good. I pledge myself to shake your confidence in Lady Clarinda. In the mean time, I am not offended. In serene composure I wait the honour and the happiness of your visit. Send me word by telegraph, whether you would like Truffles again, or whether you would prefer something simpler and lighter—say that incomparable French dish, Pig's Eyelids and Tamarinds. Believe me always your ally and admirer, your poet and cook—DEXTER.'

Arrived in Edinburgh, Benjamin and I had a little discussion. The question in dispute between us was, whether I should go with him, or go alone, to Mr Playmore. I was all for going alone.

'My experience of the world is not a very large one,' I said. 'But I have observed that, in nine cases out of ten, a man will make concessions to a woman, if she approaches him by herself, which he would hesitate even to consider, if another man was within hearing. I don't know how it is—I only know that it is so. If I find that I get on badly with Mr Playmore, I will ask him for a second appointment, and, in that case, you shall accompany me. Don't think me self-willed. Let me try my luck alone, and let us see what comes of it.'

Benjamin yielded, with his customary consideration for me. I sent my letter of introduction to Mr Playmore's office—his private house being in the neighbourhood of Gleninch. My messenger brought back a polite answer, inviting me to visit him at an early hour in the afternoon. At the appointed time to the moment, I rang the bell at the office door.

CHAPTER XXXIII

A Specimen of my Folly

THE incomprehensible submission of Scotchmen to the ecclesiastical tyranny of their Established Church, has produced—not unnaturally as I think—a very mistaken impression of the national character in the popular mind.

Public opinion looks at the institution of 'The Sabbath' in Scotland; finds it unparalleled in Christendom for its senseless and savage austerity; sees a nation content to be deprived by its priesthood of every social privilege on one day in every week—forbidden to travel; forbidden to telegraph; forbidden to eat a hot dinner; forbidden to read a newspaper; in short, allowed the use of two liberties only, the liberty of exhibiting oneself at the Church, and the liberty of secluding oneself over the bottle—public opinion sees this, and arrives at the not unreasonable conclusion that the people who submit to such social laws as these are the most stolid, stern, and joyless people on the face of the earth. Such are Scotchmen supposed to be, when viewed at a distance. But how do Scotchmen appear when they are seen under a closer light, and judged by the test of personal experience? There are no people more cheerful, more companionable, more hospitable, more liberal in their ideas, to be found on the face of the civilized globe than the very people who submit to the Scotch Sunday! On the six days of the week, there is an atmosphere of quiet humour, a radiation of genial common sense, about Scotchmen in general, which is simply delightful to feel. But on the seventh day, these same men will hear one of their ministers seriously tell them that he views taking a walk on the Sabbath in the light of an act of profanity, and will be the only people in existence who can let a man talk downright nonsense without laughing at him.

I am not clever enough to be able to account for this anomaly in the national character; I can only notice it by way of necessary preparation for the appearance in my little narrative of a personage not frequently seen, in writing—a cheerful Scotchman.

In all other respects I found Mr Playmore only negatively remarkable. He was neither old nor young, neither handsome nor ugly; he was personally not in the least like the popular idea of a lawyer; and he spoke perfectly good English, touched with only the slightest possible flavour of a Scotch accent.

'I have the honour to be an old friend of Mr Macallan,' he said, cordially shaking hands with me; 'and I am honestly happy to become acquainted with Mr Macallan's wife. Where will you sit? Near the light? You are young enough not to be afraid of the daylight, just yet. Is this your first visit to Edinburgh? Pray let me make it as pleasant to you as I can. I shall be delighted to present Mrs Playmore to you. We are staying in Edinburgh for a little while. The Italian opera is here; and we have a box for to-night. Will you kindly waive all ceremony, and dine with us and go to the music afterwards?'

'You are very kind,' I answered. 'But I have some anxieties just now which will make me a very poor companion for Mrs Playmore at the opera. My letter to you mentions, I think, that I have to ask your advice on matters which are of very serious importance to me.'

'Does it?' he rejoined. 'To tell you the truth, I have not read the letter through. I observed your name in it, and I gathered from your message that you wished to see me here. I sent my note to your hotel—and then went on with something else. Pray pardon me. Is this a professional consultation? For your own sake, I sincerely hope not.'

'It is hardly a professional consultation, Mr Playmore. I find myself in a very painful position; and I come to you to advise me, under very unusual circumstances. I shall greatly surprise you when you hear what I have to say; and I am afraid I shall occupy more than my fair share of your time.'

'I, and my time, are entirely at your disposal,' he said. 'Tell me what I can do for you—and tell it in your own way.'

The kindness of his language was more than matched by the kindness of his manner. I spoke to him freely and fully—I told him my strange story, exaggerating nothing, and suppressing nothing.

He showed the varying impressions that I produced on his mind, without the slightest concealment. My separation from Eustace distressed him. My resolution to dispute the Scotch Verdict, and my unjust suspicions of Mrs Beauly, first amused, then surprised him. It was not, however, until I had described my extraordinary interview with Miserrimus Dexter, and my hardly less remarkable conversation with Lady Clarinda, that I produced the greatest effect on the lawyer's mind. I saw him change colour for the first time. He started, and muttered to himself, as if he had completely forgotten me. 'Good God!' I heard him say—'Can it be possible? Does the truth lie *that* way, after all?'

I took the liberty of interrupting him. I had no idea of allowing him to keep his thoughts to himself.

'I seem to have surprised you?' I said.

He started at the sound of my voice.

'I beg ten thousand pardons!' he exclaimed. 'You have not only surprised me—you have opened an entirely new view to my mind. I see a possibility, a really startling possibility, in connexion with the poisoning at Gleninch, which never occurred to me until the present moment. This is a nice state of things,' he added, falling back again into his ordinary humour. 'Here is the client leading the lawyer. My dear Mrs Eustace, which is it—do you want my advice? or do I want yours?'

'May I hear the new idea?' I asked.

'Not just yet, if you will excuse me,' he answered. 'Make allowances for my professional caution. I don't want to be professional with You—my great anxiety is to avoid it. But the lawyer gets the better of the man, and refuses to be suppressed. I really hesitate to realize what is passing in my own mind, without some further inquiry. Do me a great favour. Let us go over a part of the ground again, and let me ask you some questions as we proceed. Do you feel any objection to obliging me in this matter?'

'Certainly not, Mr Playmore. How far shall we go back?'

'To your visit to Dexter, with your mother-in-law. When you first asked him if he had any ideas of his own, on the subject of Mrs Macallan's death, did I understand you to say that he looked at you suspiciously?'

'Very suspiciously.'

'And his face cleared up again, when you told him that your question was only suggested by what you had read in the Report of the Trial?'

'Yes.'

He drew a slip of paper out of the drawer in his desk, dipped his pen in the ink, considered a little, and placed a chair for me close at his side.

'The lawyer disappears,' he said, 'and the man resumes his proper place. There shall be no professional mysteries between you and me. As your husband's old friend, Mrs Eustace, I feel no common interest in you. I see a serious necessity for warning you before it is too late; and I can only do so to any good purpose, by running a risk on which few men in my place would venture. Personally and professionally, I am going to trust you—though I *am* a Scotchman and a lawyer! Sit here and look over my shoulder while I make my notes. You will see what is passing in my mind, if you see what I write.'

I sat down by him and looked over his shoulder, without the smallest pretence of hesitation.

He began to write as follows:—

'The poisoning at Gleninch. Queries: In what position does Miserrimus Dexter stand towards the poisoning? And what does he (presumably) know about that matter?

'He has ideas which are secrets. He suspects that he has betrayed them, or that they have been discovered in some way, inconceivable to himself. He is palpably relieved when he finds that this is not the case.'

The pen stopped; and the question went on.

'Let us advance to your second visit,' said Mr Playmore, 'when you saw Dexter alone. Tell me again what he did, and how he looked, when you informed him that you were not satisfied with the Scotch Verdict.'

I repeated what I have already written. The pen went back to the paper again, and added these lines:—

'He hears nothing more remarkable than that a person visiting him, who is interested in the case, refuses to accept the verdict at the Macallan Trial, as a final verdict, and proposes to re-open the inquiry. What does he do upon that?

'He exhibits all the symptoms of a panic of terror; he sees himself in some incomprehensible danger; he is frantic at one moment, and servile at the next; he must and will know what this disturbing person really means. And when he is informed on that point, he first turns pale and doubts the evidence of his own senses; and next, with nothing said to justify it, gratuitously accuses his visitor of suspecting somebody. Query here: When a small sum of money is missing in a household, and the servants in general are called together to be informed of the circumstance, what do we think of the one servant, in particular, who speaks first, and who says, "Do you suspect *me?*" '

He laid down the pen again.

'Is that right?' he asked.

I began to see the end to which the notes were drifting. Instead of answering his question, I entreated him to enter into the explanations that were still wanting to convince my own mind. He held up a warning forefinger and stopped me.

'Not yet,' he said. 'Once again, am I right—so far?'

'Quite right.'

'Very well. Now tell me what Dexter did next. Don't mind repeating yourself. Give me all the details, one after another to the end.'

I gave him all the details, exactly as I remembered them. Mr Playmore returned to his writing for the third and last time. Thus the notes ended:—

'He is indirectly assured that *he* at least is not the person suspected. He sinks back in his chair; he draws a long breath; he asks to be left awhile by himself, under the pretence that the subject excites him. When the visitor returns, Dexter has been drinking in the interval. The visitor resumes the subject—not Dexter. The visitor is convinced that Mrs Eustace Macallan died by the hand of a poisoner, and openly says so. Dexter sinks back in his chair like a man fainting. What is the horror that has got possession of him? It is easy to understand, if we call it guilty horror. It is beyond all understanding, if we call it anything else. And how does it leave him? He flies from one extreme to another; he is indescribably delighted when he discovers that the visitor's suspicions are all fixed on an absent person. And then, and then only, he takes refuge in the declaration that he has been of one mind with his guest, in the matter of suspicion, from the first! These are facts. To what plain conclusion do they point?'

He shut up his notes, and, steadily watching my face waited for me to speak first.

'I understand you, Mr Playmore,' I began, impetuously. 'You believe that Mr Dexter——'

His warning forefinger stopped me there.

'Tell me,' he interposed, 'what Dexter said to you when he was so good as to confirm your opinion of poor Mrs Beauly?'

'He said, "There isn't a doubt about it. Mrs Beauly poisoned her." '

'I can't do better than follow so good an example—with one trifling difference. I say too, There isn't a doubt about it! Dexter poisoned her.'

'Are you joking, Mr Playmore?'

'I never was more in earnest in my life. Your rash visit to Dexter, and your extraordinary imprudence in taking him into your confidence, have led to astonishing results. The light which the whole machinery of the Law was unable to throw on the poisoning case at Gleninch, has been accidentally let in on it, by a Lady who refuses to listen to reason and who insists on having her own way. Quite incredible, and nevertheless quite true!'

'Impossible!' I exclaimed.

'What is impossible!' he asked, coolly.

'That Dexter poisoned my husband's first wife.'

'And why is that impossible, if you please?'

I began to be almost enraged with Mr Playmore.

'Can you ask the question?' I replied, indignantly, 'I have told you that I heard him speak of her, in terms of respect and affection of which any woman might be proud. He lives in the memory of her. I owe his friendly reception of me to some resemblance which he fancies he sees between my figure and hers. I have seen tears in his eyes, I have heard his voice falter and fail him, when he spoke of her. He may be the falsest of men in all besides; but he is true to *her*—he has not misled me in that one thing. There are signs that never deceive a woman, when a man is talking to her of what is really near his heart. I saw those signs. It is as true that I poisoned her, as that he did. I am ashamed to set my opinion against yours, Mr Playmore; but I really cannot help it. I declare I am almost angry with you!'

He seemed to be pleased, instead of offended, by the bold manner in which I expressed myself.

'My dear Mrs Eustace, you have no reason to be angry with me! In one respect, I entirely share your view—with this difference, that I go a little further than you do.'

'I don't understand you.'

'You will understand me directly. You describe Dexter's feeling for the late Mrs Eustace, as a happy mixture of respect and affection. I can tell you, it was a much warmer feeling towards her than that. I have my information from the poor lady herself—who honoured me with her confidence and friendship for the best part of her life. Before she married Mr Macallan—she kept it a secret from him, and you had better keep it a secret too—Miserrimus Dexter was in love with her. Miserrimus Dexter asked her—deformed as he was, seriously asked her—to be his wife.'

'And in the face of that,' I cried, 'you say that he poisoned her!'

'I do. I see no other conclusion possible, after what happened during your visit to him. You all but frightened him into a fainting-fit. What was he afraid of?'

I tried hard to find an answer to that. I even embarked on an answer, without quite knowing where my own words might lead me.

'Mr Dexter is an old and true friend of my husband's,' I began. 'When he heard me say I was not satisfied with the Verdict, he might have felt alarmed——'

'He might have felt alarmed at the possible consequences to your husband of re-opening the inquiry,' said Mr Playmore, ironically finishing the sentence for me. 'Rather far-fetched, Mrs Eustace! and not very consistent with your faith in your husband's innocence! Clear your mind of one mistake,' he continued, seriously, 'which may fatally mislead you, if you persist in pursuing your present course. Miserrimus Dexter, you may take my word for it, ceased to be your husband's friend on the day when your husband married his first wife. Dexter has kept up appearances, I grant you—both in public and in private. His evidence in his friend's favour at the Trial, was given with the deep feeling which everybody expected from him.

Nevertheless I firmly believe, looking under the surface, that Mr Macallan has no bitterer enemy living than Miserrimus Dexter.'

He turned me cold. I felt that here, at least, he was right. My husband had wooed and won the woman who had refused Dexter's offer of marriage. Was Dexter the man to forgive that? My own experience answered me—and said, No.

'Bear in mind what I have told you,' Mr Playmore proceeded. 'And now let us get on to your own position in this matter, and to the interests that you have at stake. Try to adopt my point of view for the moment; and let us inquire what chance we have of making any further advance towards a discovery of the truth. It is one thing to be morally convinced (as I am) that Miserrimus Dexter is the man who ought to have been tried for the murder at Gleninch; and it is another thing, at this distance of time, to lay our hands on the plain evidence which can alone justify anything like a public assertion of his guilt. There, as I see it, is the insuperable difficulty in the case. Unless I am completely mistaken, the question is now narrowed to this plain issue: The public assertion of your husband's innocence depends entirely on the public assertion of Dexter's guilt. How are you to arrive at that result? There is not a particle of evidence against him. You can only convict Dexter on Dexter's own confession. Are you listening to me?'

I was listening, most unwillingly. If he was right, things had indeed come to that terrible pass. But I could not—with all my respect for his superior knowledge and experience—I could not persuade myself that he *was* right. And I owned it, with the humility which I really felt.

He smiled good-humouredly.

'At any rate,' he said, 'you will admit that Dexter has not freely opened his mind to you, thus far? He is still keeping something from your knowledge, which you are interested in discovering?'

'Yes. I admit that.'

'Very good. What applies to your view of the case, applies to mine. I say, he is keeping from you the confession of his guilt. You say, he is keeping from you information which may fasten the guilt on some other person. Let us start from that point. Confession, or information, how are you to get at what he is now withholding from you? What influence can you bring to bear on him, when you see him again?'

'Surely, I might persuade him?'

'Certainly. And if persuasion fails—what then? Do you think you can entrap him into speaking out? or terrify him into speaking out?'

'If you will look at your notes, Mr Playmore, you will see that I have already succeeded in terrifying him—though I am only a woman, and though I didn't mean to do it.'

'Very well answered! You mark the trick. What you have done once, you think you can do again. Well! as you are determined to try the experiment, it can do you no harm to know a little more of Dexter than you know now. Before you go back to London, suppose we apply for information to somebody who can help us?'

I started, and looked round the room. He made me do it: he spoke as if the person who was to help us was close at our elbows.

'Don't be alarmed,' he said. 'The oracle is silent; and the oracle is here.'

He unlocked one of the drawers of his desk; produced a bundle of letters; and picked out one.

'When we were arranging your husband's defence,' he said, 'we felt some difficulty about including Miserrimus Dexter among our witnesses. We had not the slightest suspicion of him—I need hardly tell you. But we were all afraid of his eccentricity; and some among us even feared that the excitement of appearing at the Trial might drive him completely out of his mind. In this emergency we applied to a doctor to help us. Under some pretext, which I forget now, we introduced him to Dexter. And in due course of time we received his report. Here it is.'

He opened the letter; and, marking a certain passage in it with a pencil, handed it to me.

'Read the lines which I have marked,' he said; 'they will be quite sufficient for our purpose.'

I read these words:—

'Summing up the results of my observation, I may give it as my opinion that there is undoubtedly latent insanity in this case; but that no active symptoms of madness have presented themselves as yet. You may, I think, produce him at the Trial, without fear of consequences. He may say and do all sorts of odd things; but he has his mind under the control of his will, and you may trust his self-esteem to exhibit him in the character of a substantially intelligent witness.

'As to the future, I am, of course, not able to speak positively. I can only state my views.

'That he will end in madness (if he lives), I entertain little or no doubt. The question of *when* the madness will show itself, depends entirely on the state of his health. His nervous system is highly sensitive; and there are signs that his way of life has already damaged it. If he conquers the bad habits to which I have alluded in an earlier part of my report, and if he passes many hours of every day quietly in the open air, he may last as a sane man for years to come. If he persists in his present way of life—or, in other words, if further mischief occurs to that sensitive nervous system—his lapse into insanity must infallibly take place when the mischief has reached its culminating point. Without warning to himself or to others, the whole mental structure will give way; and, at a moment's notice, while he is acting as quietly or speaking as intelligently as at his best time, the man will drop (if I may use the expression) into madness or idiocy. In either case, when the catastrophe has happened, it is only due to his friends to add, that they can (as I believe) entertain no hope of his cure. The balance once lost, will be lost for life.'

There it ended. Mr Playmore put the letter back in his drawer.

'You have just read the opinion of one of our highest living authorities,' he said. 'Does Dexter strike you as a likely man to give his nervous system a chance of recovery? Do you see no obstacles and no perils in your way?'

My silence answered him.

'Suppose you go back to Dexter,' he proceeded. 'And suppose that the doctor's opinion exaggerates the peril, in his case. What are you to do? The last time you saw him, you had the immense advantage of taking him by surprise. Those sensitive nerves of his gave way; and he betrayed the fear that you roused in him. Can you take him by surprise again? Not you! He is prepared for you now; and he will be on his guard. If you encounter nothing worse, you will have his cunning to deal with, next. Are you his match at that? But for Lady Clarinda he would have hopelessly misled you on the subject of Mrs Beauly.'

There was no answering this, either. I was foolish enough to try to answer it, for all that.

'He told me the truth, so far as he knew it,' I rejoined. 'He really saw, what he said he saw, in the corridor at Gleninch.'

'He told you the truth,' returned Mr Playmore, 'because he was cunning enough to see that the truth would help him in irritating your suspicions. You don't really believe that he shared your suspicions?'

'Why not?' I said. 'He was as ignorant of what Mrs Beauly was really doing on that night, as I was—until I met Lady Clarinda. It remains to be seen whether he will not be as much astonished as I was, when I tell him what Lady Clarinda told me.'

This smart reply produced an effect which I had not anticipated.

To my surprise, Mr Playmore abruptly dropped all further discussion on his side. He appeared to despair of convincing me, and he owned it indirectly in his next words.

'Will nothing that I can say to you,' he asked, 'induce you to think as I think in this matter?'

'I have not your ability, or your experience,' I answered. 'I am sorry to say, I can't think as you think.'

'And are you really determined to see Miserrimus Dexter again?'

'I have engaged myself to see him again.'

He waited a little, and thought over it.

'You have honoured me by asking for my advice,' he said. 'I earnestly advise you, Mrs Eustace, to break your engagement. I go even further than that. I *entreat* you not to see Dexter again.'

Just what my mother-in-law had said! just what Benjamin and Major Fitz-David had said! They were all against me. And still I held out. I wonder, when I look back at it, at my own obstinacy. I am almost ashamed to relate that I made Mr Playmore no reply. He waited, still looking at me. I felt irritated by that fixed look. I rose, and stood before him with my eyes on the floor.

He rose in his turn. He understood that the conference was over.

'Well! well!' he said, with a kind of sad good-humour, 'I suppose it is unreasonable of me to expect that a young woman like you should share any opinion with an old lawyer like me. Let me only remind you that our conversation must remain strictly confidential, for the present—and then let us change the subject. Is there anything that I can do for you? Are you alone in Edinburgh?'

'No. I am travelling with an old friend of mine, who has known me from childhood.'

'And do you stay here to-morrow?'

'I think so.'

'Will you do me one favour? Will you think over what has passed between us, and will you come back to me in the morning?'

'Willingly, Mr Playmore, if it is only to thank you again for your kindness.'

On that understanding we parted. He sighed—the cheerful man sighed—as he opened the door for me. Women are contradictory creatures. That sigh affected me more than all his arguments. I felt myself blush for my own headstrong resistance to him, as I took my leave and turned away into the street.

CHAPTER XXXIV

Gleninch

I FOUND Benjamin at the hotel, poring over a cheap periodical; absorbed in guessing one of the weekly 'Enigmas' which the Editor presented to his readers. My old friend was a great admirer of these verbal 'puzzles,' and had won all sorts of cheap prizes by his ingenuity in arriving at the right solution of the problems submitted to him. On ordinary occasions, it was useless to attempt to attract his attention, while he was occupied with his favourite amusement. But his interest in hearing the result of my interview with the lawyer proved to be even keener than his interest in solving the problem before him. He shut up his journal the moment I entered the room, and asked, eagerly, 'What news, Valeria? What news?'

In telling him what had happened, I of course respected Mr Playmore's confidence in me. Not a word relating to the lawyer's horrible suspicion of Miserrimus Dexter passed my lips.

'Aha!' said Benjamin, complacently. 'So the lawyer thinks as I do. You will listen to Mr Playmore (won't you?), though you wouldn't listen to me?'

'You must forgive me, my old friend,' I replied. 'I am afraid it has come to this—try as I may, I can listen to nobody who advises me. On our way here, I honestly meant to be guided by Mr Playmore—we should never have taken this long journey, if I had *not* honestly meant it. I have tried, tried hard, to be a teachable, reasonable woman. But there is something in me that won't be taught. I am afraid I shall go back to Dexter.'

Even Benjamin lost all patience with me, this time.

'What is bred in the bone,' he said, quoting the old proverb, 'will never come out of the flesh. In years gone by, you were the most obstinate child that ever made a mess in a nursery. Oh, dear me, we might as well have stayed in London!'

'No,' I replied, 'now we have travelled to Edinburgh, we will see something (interesting to *me* at any rate), which we should never have seen if we had not left London. My husband's country house is within a few miles of us, here. To-morrow we will go to Gleninch.'

'Where the poor lady was poisoned?' asked Benjamin, with a look of dismay. 'You mean that place?'

'Yes. I want to see the room in which she died; I want to go all over the house.'

Benjamin crossed his hands resignedly on his lap. 'I try to understand the new generation,' said the old man, sadly. 'But I can't manage it. The new generation beats me.'

I sat down to write to Mr Playmore about the visit to Gleninch. The house in which the tragedy had occurred that had blighted my husband's life, was, to my mind, the most interesting house on the habitable globe. The prospect of visiting Gleninch had, indeed (to tell the truth), strongly influenced my resolution to consult the Edinburgh lawyer. I sent my note to Mr Playmore by a messenger, and received the kindest reply in return. If I would wait until the afternoon, he would get the day's business done, and would take us to Gleninch in his own carriage.

Benjamin's obstinacy—in its own quiet way, and on certain occasions only—was quite a match for mine. He had privately determined, as one of the old generation, to have nothing to do with Gleninch. Not a word on the subject escaped him, until Mr Playmore's carriage was at the hotel door. At that appropriate moment, Benjamin remembered an old friend of his in Edinburgh. 'Will you please to excuse me, Valeria? My friend's name is Saunders—and he will take it unkindly of me if I don't dine with him to-day.'

Apart from the associations that I connected with it, there was nothing to interest a traveller at Gleninch.

The country round was pretty and well cultivated, and nothing more. The park was, to an English eye, wild and badly kept. The house had been built within the last seventy or eighty years. Outside, it was as bare of all ornament as a factory, and as gloomily heavy in effect as a prison. Inside, the deadly dreariness, the close oppressive solitude, of a deserted dwelling wearied the eye and weighed on the mind, from the roof to the basement. The house had been shut up since the time of the Trial. A lonely old couple, man and wife, had the keys, and the charge of it. The man shook his head in silent and sorrowful disapproval of our intrusion, when Mr Playmore ordered him to open the doors and shutters, and let the light in on the dark, deserted place. Fires were burning in the library and the picture gallery, to preserve the treasures which they contained from the damp. It was not easy, at first, to look at the cheerful blaze, without fancying that the inhabitants of the house must surely come in and warm themselves! Ascending to the upper floor, I saw the rooms made familiar to me by the Report of the Trial. I entered the little study, with the old books on the shelves, and the key still missing from the locked door of communication with the bedchamber. I looked into the room in which the unhappy mistress of Gleninch had suffered and died. The bed was left in its place; the sofa on which the nurse had snatched her intervals of repose was at its foot; the Indian cabinet, in which the crumpled paper with the grains of arsenic had been found, still held its little collection of curiosities. I moved on its pivot the invalid table on which she had taken her meals, and written her poems, poor soul. The place was dreary and dreadful; the heavy air felt as if it was still burdened with its horrid load of misery and distrust. I was glad to get out (after a passing glance at the room which Eustace had occupied, in those days) into the Guests' Corridor. There was the bedroom, at the door of which Miserrimus Dexter had waited and watched! There was the oaken floor along which he had hopped, in his horrible way, following the footsteps of the servant disguised in her mistress's clothes! Go where I might, the ghosts of the dead and the absent went with me, step by step. Go where I might, the lonely horror of the house had its still and awful voice for Me:—'*I* keep the secret of the Poison! *I* hide the mystery of the death!'

The oppression of the place became unendurable. I longed for the pure sky, and the free air. My companion noticed and understood me.

'Come!' he said. 'We have had enough of the house. Let us look at the grounds.'

In the grey quiet of the evening, we roamed about the lonely gardens, and threaded our way through the rank, neglected shrubberies. Wandering here and wandering there, we drifted into the kitchen garden—with one little patch still sparely cultivated by the old man and his wife, and all the rest a wilderness of weeds. Beyond the far end of the garden, divided from it by a low paling of wood, there stretched a piece of waste ground, sheltered on three sides by trees. In one lost corner of the ground, an object, common enough elsewhere, attracted my attention here. The object was a dust-heap.

The great size of it, and the curious situation in which it was placed, roused a moment's languid curiosity in me. I stopped, and looked at the dust and ashes, at the broken crockery and the old iron. Here, there was a torn hat; and there, some fragments of rotten old boots; and, scattered round, a small attendant litter of waste paper and frowsy rags.

'What are you looking at?' asked Mr Playmore.

'At nothing more remarkable than the dust-heap,' I answered.

'In tidy England, I suppose you would have all that carted away, out of sight,' said the lawyer. 'We don't mind in Scotland, as long as the dust-heap is far enough away not to be smelt at the house. Besides, some of it, sifted, comes in usefully as manure for the garden. Here, the place is deserted, and the rubbish in consequence has not been disturbed. Everything at Gleninch, Mrs Eustace (the big dust-heap included), is waiting for the new mistress to set it to rights. One of these days, you may be queen here—who knows!'

'I have done with Gleninch, Mr Playmore, when I leave it to-day!'

'Don't be too sure of that,' returned my companion. 'Time has its surprises in store for all of us.'

We turned away, and walked back in silence to the park gate, at which the carriage was waiting.

On the return to Edinburgh, Mr Playmore directed the conversation to topics entirely unconnected with my visit to Gleninch. He saw that my mind stood in need of relief; and he most goodnaturedly, and successfully, exerted himself to amuse me. It was not until we were close to the city that he touched on the subject of my return to London.

'Have you decided yet on the day when you leave Edinburgh?' he asked.

'We leave Edinburgh,' I replied, 'by the train of to-morrow morning.'

'Do you still see no reason to alter the opinions which you expressed yesterday? Does your speedy departure mean that?'

'I am afraid it does, Mr Playmore. When I am an older woman, I may be a wiser woman. In the mean time, I can only trust to your indulgence if I still blindly blunder on, in my own way.'

He smiled pleasantly, and patted my hand—then changed on a sudden, and looked at me gravely and attentively, before he opened his lips again.

'This is my last opportunity of speaking to you before you go,' he said. 'May I speak freely?'

'As freely as you please, Mr Playmore! Whatever you may say to me, will only add to my grateful sense of your kindness.'

'I have very little to say, Mrs Eustace—and that little begins with a word of caution. You told me yesterday that, when you paid your last visit to Miserrimus Dexter, you went to him alone. Don't do that again. Take somebody with you.'

'Do you think I am in any danger, then?'

'Not in the ordinary sense of the word. I only think that a friend may be useful in keeping Dexter's audacity (he is one of the most impudent men living) within proper limits. Then, again, in case anything worth remembering and acting on *should* fall from him in his talk, a friend may be valuable as witness. In your place, I should have a witness with me who could take notes—but then I am a lawyer, and my business is to make a fuss about trifles. Let me only say—go with a companion, when you next visit Dexter; and be on your guard against yourself, when the talk turns on Mrs Beauly.'

'On my guard against myself? What do you mean?'

'Practice, my dear Mrs Eustace, has given me an eye for the little weaknesses of human nature. You are (quite naturally) disposed to be jealous of Mrs Beauly; and you are, in consequence, not in full possession of your excellent common sense, when Dexter uses that lady as a means of blindfolding you. Am I speaking too freely?'

'Certainly not! It is very degrading to me to be jealous of Mrs Beauly. My vanity suffers dreadfully when I think of it. But my common sense yields to conviction. I dare say you are right.'

'I am delighted to find that we agree on one point,' he rejoined, drily. 'I don't despair yet of convincing you, in that far more serious matter which is still in dispute between us. And, what is more, if you will throw no obstacles in the way, I look to Dexter himself to help me.'

This roused my curiosity. How Miserrimus Dexter could help him, in that or in any other way, was a riddle beyond my reading.

'You propose to repeat to Dexter all that Lady Clarinda told you about Mrs Beauly,' he went on. 'And you think it is likely that Dexter will be overwhelmed, as you were overwhelmed, when he hears the story. I am going to venture on a prophecy. I say that Dexter will disappoint you. Far from showing any astonishment, he will boldly tell you that you have been duped by a deliberately false statement of facts, invented and set afloat, in her own guilty interests, by Mrs Beauly. Now tell me—if he really tries, in that way, to renew your unfounded suspicion of an innocent woman, will *that* shake your confidence in your own opinion?'

'It will entirely destroy my confidence in my own opinion, Mr Playmore.'

'Very good. I shall expect you to write to me, in any case; and I believe we shall be of one mind, before the week is out. Keep strictly secret all that I said to you yesterday about Dexter. Don't even mention my name, when you see him. Thinking of him as I think now, I would as soon touch the hand of the hangman as the hand of that monster! God bless you! Good bye.'

So he said his farewell words at the door of the hotel. Kind, genial, clever—but oh, how easily prejudiced, how shockingly obstinate in holding to his own opinion! And *what* an opinion! I shuddered as I thought of it.

CHAPTER XXXV

Mr Playmore's Prophecy

WE reached London between eight and nine in the evening. Strictly methodical in all his habits, Benjamin had telegraphed to his housekeeper, from Edinburgh, to have supper ready for us by ten o'clock, and to send the cabman whom he always employed to meet us at the station.

Arriving at the villa, we were obliged to wait for a moment to let a pony-chaise get by us before we could draw up at Benjamin's door. The chaise passed very slowly, driven by a rough-looking man, with a pipe in his mouth. But for the man, I might have doubted whether the pony was quite a stranger to me. As things were, I thought no more of the matter.

Benjamin's respectable old housekeeper opened the garden gate, and startled me by bursting into a devout ejaculation of gratitude at the sight of her master. 'The Lord be praised, Sir!' she cried. 'I thought you would never come back!'

'Anything wrong?' asked Benjamin, in his own impenetrably quiet way.

The housekeeper trembled at the question, and answered in these enigmatical words:—

'My mind's upset, Sir; and whether things are wrong or whether things are right, is more than I can say. Hours ago, a strange man came in and asked'—she stopped as if she was completely bewildered—looked for a moment vacantly at her master—and suddenly addressed herself to me. 'And asked,' she proceeded, 'when *you* was expected back, ma'am. I told him what my master had telegraphed, and the man says upon that, "Wait a bit" (he says); "I'm coming back." He came back in a minute or less; and he carried a Thing in his arms which curdled my blood—it did!—and set me shaking from the crown of my head to the sole of my foot. I know I ought to have stopped it; but I couldn't stand upon my legs—much less put the man out of the house. In he went, without *with* your leave, or *by* your leave, Mr Benjamin, Sir—in he went with the Thing in his arms, straight through to your library. And there It has been all these hours. And there It is now. I've spoken to the Police; but they wouldn't interfere—and what to do next, is more than my poor head can tell. Don't you go in by yourself, ma'am! You'll be frightened out of your wits—you will!'

I persisted in entering the house, for all that. Aided by the pony, I easily solved the mystery of the housekeeper's otherwise unintelligible narrative. Passing through the dining-room (where the supper table was already laid for us), I looked through the half-opened library door.

Yes; there was Miserrimus Dexter, arrayed in his pink jacket, fast asleep in Benjamin's favourite arm-chair! No coverlid hid his horrible deformity.

Nothing was sacrificed to conventional ideas of propriety, in his extraordinary dress. I could hardly wonder that the poor old housekeeper trembled from head to foot when she spoke of him!

'Valeria!' said Benjamin, pointing to the Portent in the chair. 'Which is it—an Indian idol? or a man?'

I have already described Miserrimus Dexter as possessing the sensitive ear of a dog. He now showed that he also slept the light sleep of a dog. Quietly as Benjamin had spoken, the strange voice roused him on the instant. He rubbed his eyes, and smiled as innocently as a waking child.

'How do you do, Mrs Valeria?' he said. 'I have had a nice little sleep. You don't know how happy I am to see you again. Who is this?'

He rubbed his eyes once more, and looked at Benjamin. Not knowing what else to do in this extraordinary emergency, I presented my visitor to the master of the house.

'Excuse my getting up, Sir,' said Miserrimus Dexter. 'I can't get up—I have got no legs. You look as if you thought I was occupying your chair? If I am committing an intrusion, be so good as to put your umbrella under me, and give me a jerk. I shall fall on my hands, and I shan't be offended with you. I will submit to a tumble and a scolding—but please don't break my heart by sending me away. That beautiful woman, there, can be very cruel sometimes, Sir, when the fit takes her. She went away when I stood in the sorest need of a little talk with her—she went away, and left me to my loneliness and my suspense. I am a poor deformed wretch, with a warm heart, and (perhaps) an insatiable curiosity as well. Insatiable curiosity (have you ever felt it?) is a curse. I bore it till my brains began to boil in my head; and then I sent for my gardener, and made him drive me here. I like being here. The air of your library soothes me; the sight of Mrs Valeria is balm to my wounded heart. She has something to tell me—something that I am dying to hear. If she is not too tired after her journey, and if you will let her tell it, I promise to have myself taken away when she has done. Dear Mr Benjamin, you look like the refuge of the afflicted. I am afflicted. Shake hands like a good Christian, and take me in.'

He held out his hand. His soft blue eyes melted into an expression of piteous entreaty. Completely stupefied by the amazing harangue of which he had been made the object, Benjamin took the offered hand, with the air of a man in a dream. 'I hope I see you well, Sir,' he said, mechanically—and then looked round at me to know what he was to do next.

'I understand Mr Dexter,' I whispered. 'Leave him to me.'

Benjamin stole a last bewildered look at the Object in the chair; bowed to it, with the instinct of politeness which never failed him; and (still with the air of a man in a dream) withdrew into the next room.

Left together, we looked at each other, for the first moment, in silence.

Whether I unconsciously drew on that inexhaustible store of indulgence which a woman always keeps in reserve for a man who owns that he has need of her—or whether, resenting as I did Mr Playmore's horrible suspicion of him, my heart was especially accessible to feelings of compassion, in his unhappy case—I cannot tell. I only know that I pitied Miserrimus Dexter, at that moment, as I had never pitied him yet; and that I spared him the reproof which I should certainly have administered to any other man, who had taken the liberty of establishing himself, uninvited, in Benjamin's house.

He was the first to speak.

'Lady Clarinda has destroyed your confidence in me!' he began, wildly.

'Lady Clarinda has done nothing of the sort,' I replied. 'She has not attempted to influence my opinion. I was really obliged to leave London, as I told you.'

He sighed, and closed his eyes contentedly, as if I had relieved him of a heavy weight of anxiety.

'Be merciful to me,' he said; 'and tell me something more. I have been so miserable in your absence.' He suddenly opened his eyes again, and looked at me with an appearance of the greatest interest. 'Are you very much fatigued with travelling?' he proceeded. 'I am hungry for news of what happened at the Major's dinner-party. Is it cruel of me to tell you so, when you have not rested after your journey? Only one question to-night! and I will leave the rest till to-morrow. What did Lady Clarinda say about Mrs Beauly? All that you wanted to hear?'

'All, and more,' I answered.

'What? what? what?' he cried, wild with impatience in a moment.

Mr Playmore's last prophetic words were vividly present to my mind. He had declared, in the most positive manner, that Dexter would persist in misleading me, and would show no signs of astonishment when I repeated what Lady Clarinda had told me of Mrs Beauly. I resolved to put the lawyer's prophecy—so far as the question of astonishment was concerned—to the sharpest attainable test. I said not a word to Miserrimus Dexter, in the way of preface or preparation; I burst on him with my news as abruptly as possible.

'The person you saw in the corridor was *not* Mrs Beauly,' I said. 'It was the maid, dressed in her mistress's cloak and hat. Mrs Beauly herself was not in the house at all. Mrs Beauly herself was dancing at a masked ball in Edinburgh. There is what the maid told Lady Clarinda; and there is what Lady Clarinda told *me*.'

In the absorbing interest of the moment, I poured out those words one after another as fast as they could pass my lips. Miserrimus Dexter completely falsified the lawyer's prediction. He shuddered under the shock. His eyes opened wide with amazement. 'Say it again!' he cried. 'I can't take it all in at once. You stun me.'

I was more than contented with this result—I triumphed in my victory. For once, I had really some reason to feel satisfied with myself. I had taken the Christian and merciful side in my discussion with Mr Playmore; and I had won my reward. I could sit in the same room with Miserrimus Dexter, and feel the blessed conviction that I was not breathing the same air with a poisoner. Was it not worth the visit to Edinburgh to have made sure of that?

In repeating, at his own desire, what I had already said to him, I took care to add the details which made Lady Clarinda's narrative coherent and credible. He listened throughout with breathless attention—here and there repeating the words after me to impress them the more surely and the more deeply on his mind.

'What is to be said? what is to be done?' he asked, with a look of blank despair. 'I can't disbelieve it. From first to last, strange as it is, it sounds true.'

(How would Mr Playmore have felt, if he had heard those words? I did him the justice to believe that he would have felt heartily ashamed of himself!)

'There is nothing to be said,' I rejoined; 'except that Mrs Beauly is innocent, and that you and I have done her a grievous wrong. Don't you agree with me?'

'I entirely agree with you,' he answered, without an instant's hesitation. 'Mrs Beauly is an innocent woman. The defence at the Trial was the right defence after all.'

He folded his arms complacently; he looked perfectly satisfied to leave the matter there.

I was not of his mind. To my own amazement, I now found myself the least reasonable person of the two!

Miserrimus Dexter (to use the popular phrase) had given me more than I had bargained for. He had not only done all that I had anticipated, in the way of falsifying Mr Playmore's prediction—he had actually advanced beyond my limits. I could go the length of recognising Mrs Beauly's innocence; but at that point I stopped. If the Defence at the Trial was the right defence—farewell to all hope of asserting my husband's innocence! I held to that hope, as I held to my love and my life.

'Speak for yourself,' I said. 'My opinion of the Defence remains unchanged.'

He started and knit his brows, as if I had disappointed and displeased him.

'Does that mean that you are determined to go on?'

'It does.'

He was downright angry with me. He cast his customary politeness to the winds.

'Absurd! Impossible!' he cried, contemptuously. 'You have yourself declared that we wronged an innocent woman, when we suspected Mrs

Beauly. Is there any one else whom we can suspect? It is ridiculous to ask the question! There is no alternative left but to accept the facts as they are, and to stir no further in the matter of the poisoning at Gleninch. It is childish to dispute plain conclusions. You *must* give up.'

'You may be angry with me, if you will, Mr Dexter. Neither your anger nor your arguments will make me give up.'

He controlled himself by an effort—he was quiet and polite again, when he next spoke to me.

'Very well. Pardon me for a moment, if I absorb myself in my own thoughts. I want to do something which I have not done yet.'

'What may that be, Mr Dexter?'

'I am going to put myself into Mrs Beauly's skin, and to think with Mrs Beauly's mind. Give me a minute. Thank you.'

What did he mean? What new transformation of him was passing before my eyes? Was there ever such a puzzle of a man as this? Who that saw him now, intently pursuing his new train of thought, would have recognised him as the childish creature who had woke up so innocently, and who had amazed Benjamin by the infantine nonsense which he talked? It is said, and said truly, that there are many sides to every human character. Dexter's many sides were developing themselves at such a rapid rate of progress, that they were already beyond my counting!

He lifted his head, and fixed a look of keen inquiry on me.

'I have come out of Mrs Beauly's skin,' he announced. 'And I have arrived at this result:—We are two impetuous people; and we have been a little hasty in rushing at a conclusion.'

He stopped. I said nothing. Was the shadow of a doubt of him beginning to rise in my mind? I waited, and listened.

'I am as fully satisfied as ever of the truth of what Lady Clarinda told you,' he proceeded. 'But I see, on consideration, what I failed to see at the time. The story admits of two interpretations. One on the surface, and another under the surface. I look under the surface, in your interests; and I say, it is just possible that Mrs Beauly may have been cunning enough to forestall suspicion, and to set up an Alibi.'

I am ashamed to own that I did not understand what he meant by the last word—Alibi. He saw that I was not following him, and he spoke out more plainly.

'Was the maid something more than her mistress's passive accomplice?' he said. 'Was she the Hand that her mistress used? Was she on her way to give the first dose of poison, when she passed me in the corridor? Did Mrs Beauly spend the night in Edinburgh—so as to have her defence ready, if suspicion fell upon her?'

My shadowy doubt of him became substantial doubt, when I heard that. Had I absolved him a little too readily? Was he really trying to renew my suspicions of Mrs Beauly, as Mr Playmore had foretold? This time I was obliged to answer him. In doing so, I unconsciously employed one of the phrases which the lawyer had used to me, during my first interview with him.

'That sounds rather far-fetched, Mr Dexter,' I said.

To my relief, he made no attempt to defend the new view that he had advanced.

'It *is* far-fetched,' he admitted. 'When I said it was just possible—though I didn't claim much for my idea—I said more for it perhaps than it deserved. Dismiss my view as ridiculous; what are you to do next? If Mrs Beauly is not the poisoner (either by herself or by her maid), who is? She is innocent, and Eustace is innocent. Where is the other person whom you can suspect? Have *I* poisoned her?' he cried, with eyes flashing, and his voice rising to its highest notes. 'Do you, does anybody, suspect Me? I loved her; I adored her; I have never been the same man since her death. Hush! I will trust you with a secret. (Don't tell your husband; it might be the destruction of our friendship.) I would have married her, before she met with Eustace, if she would have taken me. When the doctors told me she had died poisoned—ask Doctor Jerome what I suffered! *he* can tell you! All through that horrible night, I was awake: watching my opportunity until I found my way to her! I got into the room, and took my last leave of the cold remains of the angel whom I loved. I cried over her. I kissed her, for the first and last time. I stole one little lock of her hair. I have worn it ever since; I have kissed it night and day. Oh, God! the room comes back to me! the dead face comes back to me! Look! look!'

He tore from its place of concealment in his bosom a little locket, fastened by a ribbon round his neck. He threw it to me where I sat; and burst into a passion of tears.

A man in my place might have known what to do. Being only a woman, I yielded to the compassionate impulse of the moment.

I got up and crossed the room to him. I gave him back his locket, and put my hand, without knowing what I was about, on the poor wretch's shoulder. 'I am incapable of suspecting you, Mr Dexter,' I said, gently. 'No such idea ever entered my head. I pity you from the bottom of my heart.'

He caught my hand in his, and devoured it with kisses. His lips burnt me like fire. He twisted himself suddenly in the chair, and wound his arm round my waist. In the terror and indignation of the moment, vainly struggling with him, I cried out for help.

The door opened, and Benjamin appeared on the threshold. Dexter let go his hold of me.

I ran to Benjamin and prevented him from advancing into the room. In all my long experience of my fatherly old friend, I had never seen him really angry yet. I saw him more than angry now. He was pale—the patient, gentle old man was pale with rage! I held him at the door with all my strength.

'You can't lay your hand on a cripple,' I said. 'Send for his servant outside to take him away.'

I drew Benjamin out of the room, and closed and locked the library door. The housekeeper was in the dining-room. I sent her out to call the driver of the pony-chaise into the house.

The man came in—the rough man whom I had noticed when we were approaching the garden gate. Benjamin opened the library door in stern silence. It was perhaps unworthy of me—but I could *not* resist the temptation to look in.

Miserrimus Dexter had sunk down in the chair. The rough man lifted his master with a gentleness that surprised me. 'Hide my face,' I heard Dexter say to him, in broken tones. He opened his coarse pilot jacket, and hid his master's head under it, and so went silently out—with the deformed creature held to his bosom, like a woman sheltering her child.

CHAPTER XXXVI

Ariel

I PASSED a sleepless night.

The outrage that had been offered to me was bad enough in itself. But consequences were associated with it which might affect me more seriously still. In so far as the attainment of the one object of my life might yet depend on my personal association with Miserrimus Dexter, an insurmountable obstacle appeared to be now placed in my way. Even in my husband's interests, ought I to permit a man who had grossly insulted me, to approach me again? Although I was no prude, I recoiled from the thought of it.

I rose late, and sat down at my desk, trying to summon energy enough to write to Mr Playmore—and trying in vain.

Towards noon (while Benjamin happened to be out for a little while), the housekeeper announced the arrival of another strange visitor at the gate of the villa.

'It's a woman this time, ma'am—or something like one,' said this worthy person, confidentially. 'A great, stout, awkward, stupid creature, with a man's hat on, and a man's stick in her hand. She says she has got a note for you, and she won't give it to anybody *but* you. I'd better not let her in—had I?'

Recognising the original of the picture, I astonished the housekeeper by consenting to receive the messenger immediately.

Ariel entered the room—in stolid silence, as usual. But I noticed a change in her which puzzled me. Her dull eyes were red and bloodshot. Traces of tears (as I fancied) were visible on her fat, shapeless cheeks. She crossed the room, on her way to my chair, with a less determined tread than was customary with her. Could Ariel (I asked myself) be woman enough to cry? Was it within the limits of possibility that Ariel should approach me in sorrow and in fear?

'I hear you have brought something for me?' I said. 'Won't you sit down?'

She handed me a letter—without answering, and without taking a chair. I opened the envelope. The letter inside was written by Miserrimus Dexter. It contained these lines:—

'Try to pity me, if you have any pity left for a miserable man; I have bitterly expiated the madness of a moment. If you could see me—even you would own that my punishment has been heavy enough. For God's sake, don't abandon me! I was beside myself when I let the feeling that you have awakened in me get the better of my control. It shall never show itself again; it shall be a secret that dies with me. Can I expect you to believe this? No. I won't ask you to believe me; I won't ask you to trust me in the future. If you ever consent to see me again, let it be in the presence of any third person whom you may appoint to protect you. I deserve that—I will submit to it; I will wait till time has composed your angry feeling against me. All I ask now, is leave to hope. Say to Ariel, "I forgive him; and one day I will let him see me again." She will remember it, for love of me. If you send her back without a message, you send me to the madhouse. Ask her, if you don't believe me.—MISERRIMUS DEXTER.'

I finished the strange letter, and looked at Ariel.

She stood with her eyes on the floor, and held out to me the thick walking-stick which she carried in her hand.

'Take the stick'—were the first words she said to me.

'Why am I to take it?' I asked.

She struggled a little with her sluggishly-working mind, and slowly put her thoughts into words.

'You're angry with the Master,' she said. 'Take it out on Me. Here's the stick. Beat me.'

'Beat you!' I exclaimed.

'My back's broad,' said the poor creature. 'I won't make a row. I'll bear it. Drat you, take the stick! Don't vex *him*. Whack it out on my back. Beat *me*.'

She roughly forced the stick into my hand; she turned her poor shapeless shoulders to me, waiting for the blow. It was at once dreadful and touching to see her. The tears rose in my eyes. I tried, gently and patiently, to reason with her. Quite useless! The idea of taking the Master's punishment on herself was the one idea in her mind. 'Don't vex *him*,' she repeated. 'Beat *me*.'

'What do you mean by "vexing him"?' I asked.

She tried to explain, and failed to find the words. She showed me by imitation, as a savage might have shown me, what she meant. Striding to the fireplace, she crouched on the rug, and looked into the fire with a horrible vacant stare. Then she clasped her hands over her forehead, and rocked slowly to and fro, still staring into the fire. 'There's how he sits!' she said, with a sudden burst of speech. 'Hours on hours, there's how he sits! Notices nobody. Cries about *you*.'

The picture she presented recalled to my memory the Report of Dexter's health, and the doctor's plain warning of peril waiting for him in the future. Even if I could have resisted Ariel, I must have yielded to the vague dread of consequences which now shook me in secret.

'Don't do that!' I cried. She was still rocking herself in imitation of the 'Master,' and still staring into the fire with her hands to her head. 'Get up, pray! I am not angry with him now. I forgive him.'

She rose on her hands and knees, and waited, looking up intently into my face. In that attitude—more like a dog than a human being—she repeated her customary petition, when she wanted to fix words that interested her in her mind.

'Say it again!'

I did as she bade me. She was not satisfied.

'Say it as it is in the letter,' she went on. 'Say it as the Master said it to Me.'

I looked back at the letter, and repeated the form of message contained in the latter part of it, word for word: 'I forgive him; and one day I will let him see me again.'

She sprang to her feet at a bound. For the first time since she had entered the room, her dull face began to break slowly into light and life.

'That's it!' she cried. 'Hear if I can say it, too! Hear if I've got it by heart.'

Teaching her, exactly as I should have taught a child, I slowly fastened the message, word by word, on her mind.

'Now rest yourself,' I said; 'and let me give you something to eat and drink, after your long walk.'

I might as well have spoken to one of the chairs! She snatched up her stick from the floor, and burst out with a hoarse shout of joy. 'I've got it by heart!' she cried. 'This will cool the Master's head! Hooray!' She dashed out into the passage, like a wild animal escaping from its cage. I was just in time to see her tear open the garden gate, and set forth on her walk back, at a pace which made it hopeless to attempt to follow and stop her.

I returned to the sitting-room, pondering on a question which has perplexed wiser heads than mine. Could a man who was hopelessly and entirely wicked, have inspired such devoted attachment to him as Dexter had inspired in the faithful woman who had just left me—in the rough gardener, who had carried him out so gently on the previous night? Who can decide? The greatest scoundrel living always has a friend—in a woman, or a dog.

I sat down again at the desk, and made another attempt to write to Mr Playmore.

Recalling, for the purpose of my letter, all that Miserrimus Dexter had said to me, my memory dwelt, with special interest, on the strange outbreak of feeling which had led him to betray the secret of his infatuation for Eustace's first wife. I saw again the ghastly scene in the death-chamber—the deformed creature crying over the corpse, in the stillness of the first dark hours of the new day. The horrible picture took a strange hold on my mind. I rose, and walked up and down, and tried to turn my thoughts some other way. It was not to be done: the scene was too familiar to be easily dismissed. I had myself walked in the corridor which Dexter had crossed, on his way to take his last leave of her.

The corridor? I stopped. My thoughts suddenly took a new direction, uninfluenced by any effort of my will.

What other association, besides the associations with Dexter, did I connect with the corridor? Was it something I had seen, during my visit to Gleninch? No. Was it something I had read? I snatched up the Report of the Trial to see. It opened at a page which contained the nurse's evidence. I read the evidence through again, without recovering the lost remembrance, until I came to these lines close at the end:—

'Before bedtime I went upstairs to prepare the remains of the deceased lady for the coffin. The room in which she lay was locked; the door leading into Mr Macallan's room being secured, as well as the door leading into the corridor. The keys had been taken away by Mr Gale. Two of the men-servants were posted outside the bedroom to keep watch. They were to be relieved at four in the morning—that was all they could tell me.'

There was my lost association with the corridor! There was what I ought to have remembered when Miserrimus Dexter was telling me of his visit to the dead!

How had he got into the bedroom—the doors being locked, and the keys being taken away by Mr Gale? There was but one of the locked doors, of which Mr Gale had not got the key: the door of communication between the study and the bedroom. The key was missing from this. Had it been stolen? And was Dexter the thief? He might have passed by the men on the watch, while they were asleep; or he might have crossed the corridor, in an unguarded interval while the men were being relieved. But how could he have got into the bedchamber, except by way of the locked study door? He *must* have had the key! And he *must* have secreted it, weeks before Mrs Eustace Macallan's death! When the nurse first arrived at Gleninch, on the seventh of the month, her evidence declared the key of the door of communication to be then missing.

To what conclusion did these considerations and discoveries point? Had Miserrimus Dexter, in a moment of ungovernable agitation, unconsciously placed the clue in my hands? Was the pivot on which turned the whole mystery of the poisoning at Gleninch, the missing key?

I went back for the third time to my desk. The one person who might be trusted to find the answer to those questions was Mr Playmore. I wrote him a full and careful account of all that had happened; I begged him to forgive and forget my ungracious reception of the advice which he had so kindly offered to me; and I promised beforehand to do nothing, without first consulting his opinion, in the new emergency which now confronted me.

The day was fine, for the time of year; and by way of getting a little wholesome exercise, after the surprises and occupations of the morning, I took my letter to Mr Playmore to the post.

Returning to the villa, I was informed that another visitor was waiting to see me; a civilized visitor this time, who had given her name. My mother-in-law—Mrs Macallan.

CHAPTER XXXVII

At the Bedside

BEFORE she had uttered a word, I saw in my mother-in-law's face that she brought bad news.

'Eustace?' I said.

She answered me by a look.

'Let me hear it at once!' I cried. 'I can bear anything but suspense.'

Mrs Macallan lifted her hand, and showed me a telegraphic despatch which she had hitherto kept concealed in the folds of her dress.

'I can trust your courage,' she said. 'There is no need, my child, to prevaricate with you. Read that.'

I read the telegram. It was sent by the chief surgeon of a field-hospital; and it was dated from a village in the north of Spain.

'Mr Eustace severely wounded in a skirmish, by a stray shot. Not in danger, so far. Every care taken of him. Wait for another telegram.'

I turned away my face, and bore as best I might the pang that wrung me when I read those words. I thought I knew how dearly I loved him. I had never known it till that moment.

My mother-in-law put her arm round me, and held me to her tenderly. She knew me well enough not to speak to me at that moment.

I rallied my courage, and pointed to the last sentence in the telegram.

'Do you mean to wait?' I asked.

'Not a day!' she answered. 'I am going to the Foreign Office about my passport—I have some interest there: they can give me letters; they can advise and assist me. I leave to-night by the mail train to Calais!'

'*You* leave?' I said. 'Do you suppose I will let you go without me? Get my passport when you get yours. At seven this evening, I will be at your house.'

She attempted to remonstrate; she spoke of the perils of the journey. At the first words, I stopped her. 'Don't you know yet, mother, how obstinate I am? They may keep you waiting at the Foreign Office. Why do you waste the precious hours here?'

She yielded with a gentleness that was not in her everyday character. 'Will my poor Eustace ever know what a wife he has got!' That was all she said. She kissed me, and went away in her carriage.

My remembrances of our journey are strangely vague and imperfect.

As I try to recall them, the memory of those more recent and more interesting events which occurred after my return to England, gets between me and my adventures in Spain, and seems to force these last into a shadowy background, until they look like adventures that happened many years since. I confusedly recollect delays and alarms that tried our patience and our courage. I remember our finding friends (thanks to our letters of recommendation) in a Secretary to the Embassy, and in a Queen's Messenger, who assisted and protected us at a critical point in the journey. I recall to mind a long succession of men, in our employment as travellers, all equally remarkable for their dirty cloaks and their clean linen, for their highly-civilised courtesy to women, and their utterly-barbarous cruelty to horses. Last, and most important of all, I see again, more clearly than I can see anything else, the one wretched bedroom of a squalid village inn, in which we found our poor darling, prostrate between life and death, insensible to everything that passed in the narrow little world that lay round his bedside.

There was nothing romantic or interesting in the accident which had put my husband's life in peril.

He had ventured too near the scene of the conflict (a miserable affair) to rescue a poor lad who lay wounded on the field—mortally wounded as the event proved. A rifle-bullet had struck him in the body. His brethren of the field-hospital had carried him back to their quarters, at the risk of their lives. He was a great favourite with all of them; patient, and gentle, and brave; only wanting a little more judgment to be the most valuable recruit who had joined the brotherhood.

In telling me this, the surgeon kindly and delicately added a word of warning as well.

The fever caused by the wound had brought with it delirium as usual. My poor husband's mind, in so far as his wandering words might interpret it, was filled by the one image of his wife. The medical attendant had heard enough, in the course of his ministrations at the bedside, to satisfy him that any sudden recognition of me by Eustace (if he recovered) might be attended by the most lamentable results. As things were at that sad time, I might take my turn at nursing him, without the slightest chance of his discovering me, perhaps for weeks and weeks to come. But on the day when he was declared out of danger—if that happy day ever arrived—I must resign my place at his bedside, and must wait to show myself until the surgeon gave me leave.

My mother-in-law and I relieved each other regularly, day and night, in the sick room.

In the hours of his delirium—hours that recurred with a pitiless regularity—my name was always on my poor darling's fevered lips. The ruling idea in him was the one dreadful idea which I had vainly combated at our last interview. In the face of the verdict pronounced at the Trial, it was impossible even for his wife to be really and truly persuaded that he was an innocent man. All the wild pictures which his distempered imagination drew, were equally inspired by that one obstinate conviction. He fancied himself to be still living with me, under those dreaded conditions. Do what he might, I was always recalling to him the terrible ordeal through which he had passed. He acted his part, and he acted mine. He gave me a cup of tea; and I said to him, 'We quarrelled yesterday, Eustace. Is it poisoned?' He kissed me, in token of our reconciliation; and I laughed and said, 'It's morning now, my dear. Shall I die by nine o'clock to-night?' I was ill in bed, and he gave me my medicine. I looked at him with a doubting eye. I said to him, 'You are in love with another woman. Is there anything in the medicine that the doctor doesn't know of?' Such was the horrible drama which now perpetually acted itself in his mind. Hundreds and hundreds of times I heard him repeat it, almost always in the same words. On other occasions, his thoughts wandered away to my desperate project of proving him to be an innocent man. Sometimes, he laughed at it. Sometimes, he mourned over it. Sometimes, he devised cunning schemes for placing unsuspected obstacles in my way. He was especially hard on me when he was inventing his preventive stratagems—he cheerfully instructed the visionary people who assisted him, not to hesitate at offending or distressing me. 'Never mind if you make her angry; never mind if you make her cry. It's all for her good; it's all to save the poor fool from dangers she doesn't dream of. You mustn't pity her when she says she does it for my sake. See! she is going to be insulted; she is going to be deceived; she is going to disgrace herself without knowing it. Stop her! stop her!' It was weak of me I know; I ought to have kept the plain fact that he was out of his senses always present to my mind. Still, it is true that my hours passed at my husband's pillow were, many of them, hours of mortification and misery of which he, poor dear, was the innocent and only cause.

The weeks passed; and he still hovered between life and death.

I kept no record of the time, and I cannot now recall the exact date on which the first favourable change took place. I only remember that it was towards sunrise on a fine winter morning, when we were relieved at last of our heavy burden of suspense. The surgeon happened to be by the bedside, when his patient woke. The first thing he did, after looking at Eustace, was to caution me by a sign to be silent, and to keep out of sight. My mother-in-law and I both knew what this meant. With full hearts we thanked God together for giving us back the husband and the son.

The same evening, being alone, we ventured to speak of the future—for the first time since we had left home.

'The surgeon tells me,' said Mrs Macallan, 'that Eustace is too weak to be capable of bearing anything in the nature of a surprise, for some days to come. We have time to consider whether he is, or is not, to be told that he owes his life as much to your care as to mine. Can you find it in your heart to leave him, Valeria, now that God's mercy has restored him to you and to me?'

'If I only consulted my own heart,' I answered, 'I should never leave him again.'

Mrs Macallan looked at me in grave surprise.

'What else have you to consult?' she asked.

'If we both live,' I replied, 'I have to think of the happiness of his life, and the happiness of mine, in the years that are to come. I can bear a great deal mother, but I cannot endure the misery of his leaving me for the second time.'

'You wrong him, Valeria—I firmly believe you wrong him—in thinking it possible that he can leave you again!'

'Dear Mrs Macallan, have you forgotten what we have both heard him say of me, while we have been sitting by his bedside?'

'We have heard the ravings of a man in delirium. It is surely hard to hold Eustace responsible for what he said when he was out of his senses?'

'It is harder still,' I said, 'to resist his mother when she is pleading for him. Dearest and best of friends! I don't hold Eustace responsible for what he said in the fever—but I *do* take warning by it. The wildest words that fell from him were, one and all, the faithful echo of what he said to me in the best days of his health and his strength. What hope have I that he will recover with an altered mind towards me? Absence has not changed it; suffering has not changed it. In the delirium of fever, and in the full possession of his reason, he has the same dreadful doubt of me. I see but one way of winning him back. I must destroy at its root his motive for leaving me. It is hopeless to persuade him that I believe in his innocence: I must show him that belief is no longer necessary; I must prove to him that his position towards me has become the position of an innocent man.'

'Valeria! Valeria! you are wasting time and words. You have tried the experiment; and you know as well as I do, the thing is not to be done.'

I had no answer to that. I could say no more than I had said already.

'Suppose you go back to Dexter, out of sheer compassion for a mad and miserable wretch who has already insulted you,' proceeded my mother-in-law. 'You can only go back, accompanied by me, or by some other trustworthy person. You can only stay long enough to humour the creature's wayward fancy, and to keep his crazy brain quiet for a time. That done, all is done—you leave him. Even supposing Dexter to be still capable of helping you, how can you make use of him but by admitting him to terms of confidence and familiarity—by treating him, in short, on the footing of an intimate friend? Answer me honestly: can you bring yourself to do that, after what happened at Mr Benjamin's house?'

I had told her of my last interview with Miserrimus Dexter, in the natural confidence that she inspired in me as relative and fellow-traveller; and this was the use to which she turned her information! I suppose I had no right to blame her; I suppose the motive sanctioned everything. At any rate, I had no choice but to give offence, or to give an answer. I gave it. I acknowledged that I could never again permit Miserrimus Dexter to treat me on terms of familiarity, as a trusted and intimate friend.

Mrs Macallan pitilessly pressed the advantage that she had won.

'Very well,' she said, 'that resource being no longer open to you, what hope is left? Which way are you to turn next?'

There was no meeting those questions, in my present situation, by any adequate reply. I felt strangely unlike myself—I submitted in silence. Mrs Macallan struck the last blow that completed her victory.

'My poor Eustace is weak and wayward,' she said; 'but he is not an ungrateful man. My child! you have returned him good for evil—you have proved how faithfully and how devotedly you love him, by suffering hardships and by risking dangers for his sake. Trust me, and trust him! He cannot resist you. Let him see the dear face that he has been dreaming of, looking at him again with all the old love in it; and he is yours once more, my daughter—yours for life.' She rose and touched my forehead with her lips; her voice sank to tones of tenderness which I had never heard from her yet. 'Say yes, Valeria,' she whispered; 'and be dearer to me and dearer to him than ever!'

My heart sided with her. My energies were worn out. No letter had arrived from Mr Playmore, to guide and to encourage me. I had resisted so long and so vainly; I had tried and suffered so much; I had met with such cruel disasters and such reiterated disappointments—and *he* was in the room beneath me, feebly finding his way back to consciousness and to life—how could I resist? It was all over! In saying Yes (if Eustace confirmed his mother's confidence in him), I was saying adieu to the one cherished ambition, the one dear and noble hope of my life. I knew it—and I said Yes.

And so good-bye to the grand struggle! And so welcome to the new resignation which owned that I had failed!

My mother-in-law and I slept together under the only shelter that the inn could offer to us—a sort of loft at the top of the house. The night that followed our conversation was bitterly cold. We felt the chilly temperature, in spite of the protection of our dressing gowns and our travelling wrappers. My mother-in-law slept; but no rest came to me. I was too anxious and too wretched, thinking over my changed position, and doubting how my husband would receive me, to be able to sleep.

Some hours, as I suppose, must have passed, and I was still absorbed in my own melancholy thoughts—when I suddenly became conscious of a new and strange sensation which astonished and alarmed me. I started up in the bed, breathless and bewildered. The movement awakened Mrs Macallan. 'Are you ill?' she asked. 'What is the matter with you?' I tried to tell her, as well as I could. She seemed to understand me before I had done; she took me tenderly in her arms, and pressed me to her bosom. 'My poor innocent child,' she said, 'is it possible you don't know? Must I really tell you?' She whispered her next words. Shall I ever forget the tumult of feelings which the whisper aroused in me—the strange medley of joy and fear, and wonder and relief, and pride and humility, which filled my whole being, and made a new woman of me from that moment? Now, for the first time, I knew it! If God spared me for a few months more, the most enduring and the most sacred of all human joys might be mine—the joy of being a mother.

I don't know how the rest of the night passed. I only found my memory again, when the morning came, and when I went out by myself to breathe the crisp wintry air on the open moor behind the inn.

I have said that I felt like a new woman. The morning found me with a new resolution and a new courage. When I thought of the future, I had not only my husband to consider now. His good name was no longer his own and mine—it might soon become the most precious inheritance that he could leave to his child. What had I done, while I was in ignorance of this? I had resigned the hope of cleansing his name from the stain that had rested on it—a stain still, no matter how little it might look in the eye of the Law. Our child might live to hear malicious tongues say, 'Your father was tried for the vilest of all murders, and was never absolutely acquitted of the charge.' Could I face the glorious perils of childbirth, with that possibility present to my mind? No! not until I had made one more effort to lay the conscience of Miserrimus Dexter bare to my view! not until I had once again renewed the struggle, and brought the truth that vindicated the husband and the father to the light of day!

I went back to the house, with my new courage to sustain me. I opened my heart to my friend and mother, and told her frankly of the change that had come over me, since we had last spoken of Eustace.

She was more than disappointed, she was almost offended with me. The one thing needful had happened, she said. The happiness that was coming to us would form a new tie between my husband and me. Every other consideration but this, she treated as purely fanciful. If I left Eustace now, I did a heartless thing and a foolish thing. I should regret, to the end of my days, having thrown away the one golden opportunity of my married life.

It cost me a hard struggle, it oppressed me with many a painful doubt; but I held firm, this time. The honour of the father, the inheritance of the child—I kept those thoughts as constantly as possible before my mind. Sometimes they failed me, and left me nothing better than a poor fool who had some fitful bursts of crying, and was ashamed of herself afterwards. But my native obstinacy (as Mrs Macallan said) carried me through. Now and then, I had a peep at Eustace, while he was asleep, and that helped me too. Though they made my heart ache and shook me sadly at the time, those furtive visits to my husband fortified me afterwards. I cannot explain how this happened (it seems so contradictory); I can only repeat it as one of my experiences at that troubled time.

I made one concession to Mrs Macallan—I consented to wait for two days, before I took any steps for returning to England, on the chance that my mind might change in the interval.

It was well for me that I yielded so far. On the second day, the director of the field-hospital sent to the post-office, at our nearest town, for letters addressed to him or to his care. The messenger brought back a letter for me. I thought I recognized the handwriting, and I was right. Mr Playmore's answer had reached me at last!

If I had been in any danger of changing my mind, the good lawyer would have saved me in the nick of time. The extract that follows contains the pith of his letter; and shows how he encouraged me, when I stood in sore need of a few cheering and friendly words.

'Let me now tell you' (he wrote) 'what I have done towards verifying the conclusion to which your letter points.

'I have traced one of the servants who was appointed to keep watch in the corridor, on the night when the first Mrs Eustace died at Gleninch. The man perfectly remembers that Miserrimus Dexter appeared before him and his fellow-servant (in his chair), after the house was quiet for the night. Dexter said to them, "I suppose there is no harm in my going into the study to read? I can't sleep after what has happened; I must relieve my mind somehow." The men had no orders to keep any one out of the study. They knew that the door of communication with the bedchamber was locked, and that the keys of the two other doors of communication were in the possession of Mr Gale. They accordingly permitted Dexter to go into the study. He closed the door (the door that opened on the corridor), and remained absent for some time—in the study as the men supposed; in the bedchamber as *we* know, from what he let out at his interview with you. Now, he could enter that room, as you rightly imagine, in but one way—by being in possession of the missing key. How long he remained there, I cannot discover. The point is of little consequence. The servant remembers that he came out of the study again "as pale as death," and that he passed on without a word, on his way back to his own room.

'These are facts. The conclusion to which they lead is serious in the last degree. It justifies everything that I confided to you in my office at Edinburgh. You remember what passed between us. I say no more.

'As to yourself next. You have innocently aroused in Miserrimus Dexter a feeling towards you, which I need not attempt to characterize. There is a certain something—I saw it myself—in your figure, and in some of your movements, which does recall the late Mrs Eustace to those who knew her well, and which has evidently had its effect on Dexter's morbid mind. Without dwelling further on this subject, let me only remind you that he has shown himself (as a consequence of your influence over him) to be incapable, in his moments of agitation, of thinking before he speaks, while he is in your presence. It is not merely possible, it is highly probable, that he may betray himself far more seriously than he has betrayed himself yet, if you give him the opportunity. I owe it to you (knowing what your interests are) to express myself plainly on this point. I have no sort of doubt that you have advanced one step nearer to the end which you have in view, in the brief interval since you left Edinburgh. I see in your letter (and in my discoveries) irresistible evidence that Dexter must have been in secret communication with the deceased lady (innocent communication, I am certain, so far as *she* was concerned), not only at the time of her death, but probably for weeks before it. I cannot disguise from myself, or from you, my own strong persuasion that, if you succeed in discovering the nature of this communication, in all human likelihood you prove your husband's innocence by the discovery of the truth. As an honest man, I am bound not to conceal this. And, as an honest man also, I am equally bound to add that, not even with your reward in view, can I find it in my conscience to advise you to risk what you must risk, if you see Miserrimus Dexter again. In this difficult and delicate matter, I cannot, and will not, take the responsibility. The final decision must rest with yourself. One favour only I entreat you to grant—let me hear what you resolve to do as soon as you know it yourself.'

The difficulties which my worthy correspondent felt were no difficulties to me. I did not possess Mr Playmore's judicial mind. My resolution (come what might of it) to see Miserrimus Dexter again, was settled before I had read his letter to the end.

The mail to France crossed the frontier the next day. There was a place for me under the protection of the conductor, if I chose to take it. Without consulting a living creature—rash as usual, headlong as usual—I took it.

CHAPTER XXXVIII

On the Journey Back

IF I had been travelling homeward in my own carriage, the remaining chapters of this narrative would never have been written. Before we had been an hour on the road, I should have called to the driver, and should have told him to turn back.

Who can be always resolute?

In asking that question, I speak of the women, not of the men. I had been resolute in turning a deaf ear to Mr Playmore's doubts and cautions; resolute in holding out against my mother-in-law; resolute in taking my place by the French mail. Until ten minutes after we had driven away from the inn my courage held out—and then it failed me; then I said to myself, 'You wretch, you have deserted your husband!' For hours afterwards, if I could have stopped the mail, I would have done it. I hated the conductor, the kindest of men. I hated the Spanish ponies that drew us, the cheeriest animals that ever jingled a string of bells. I hated the bright day that *would* make things pleasant, and the bracing air that forced me to feel the luxury of breathing, whether I liked it or not. Never was a journey more miserable than my safe and easy journey to the frontier! But one little comfort helped me to bear my heart-ache resignedly—a stolen morsel of Eustace's hair. We had started at an hour of the morning when he was still sound asleep. I could creep into his room, and kiss him, and cry over him softly, and cut off a stray lock of his hair, without danger of discovery. How I summoned resolution enough to leave him is, to this hour, not clear to my mind. I think my mother-in-law must have helped me, without meaning to do it. She came into the room with an erect head, and a cold eye: she said, with an unmerciful emphasis on the word, 'If you *mean* to go, Valeria, the carriage is here.' Any woman with a spark of spirit in her would have 'meant' it under those circumstances. I meant it—and did it.

And then I was sorry for it. Poor humanity!

Time has got all the credit of being the great consoler of afflicted mortals. In my opinion, Time has been over-rated in this matter. Distance does the same beneficent work, far more speedily, and (when assisted by Change) far more effectually as well. On the railroad to Paris, I became capable of taking a sensible view of my position. I could now remind myself that my husband's reception of me—after the first surprise and the first happiness had passed away—might not have justified his mother's confidence in him. Admitting that I ran a risk in going back to Miserrimus Dexter, should I not have been equally rash, in another way, if I had returned, uninvited, to a husband who had declared that our conjugal happiness was impossible, and that our married life was at an end? Besides, who could say that the events of the future might not yet justify me—not only to myself, but to him? I might yet hear him say, 'She was inquisitive when she had no business to inquire; she was obstinate when she ought to have listened to reason; she left my bedside when other women would have remained: but in the end she atoned for it all—she turned out to be right!'

I rested a day at Paris, and wrote three letters.

One to Benjamin, telling him to expect me the next evening. One to Mr Playmore, warning him in good time, that I meant to make a last effort to penetrate the mystery at Gleninch. One to Eustace (of a few lines only), owning that I had helped to nurse him through the dangerous part of his illness; confessing the one reason which had prevailed with me to leave him; and entreating him to suspend his opinion of me, until time had proved that I loved him more dearly than ever. This last letter I enclosed to my mother-in-law; leaving it to her discretion to choose the right time for giving it to her son. I positively forbade Mrs Macallan, however, to tell Eustace of the new tie between us. Although he *had* separated himself from me, I was determined that he should not hear of it from other lips than mine. Never mind why! There are certain little matters which I must keep to myself; and this is one of them.

My letters being written, my duty was done. I was free to play my last card in the game—the darkly-doubtful game which was neither quite for me, nor quite against me, as the chances now stood.

CHAPTER XXXIX

On the Way to Dexter

'I DECLARE to Heaven, Valeria, I believe that monster's madness is infectious—and you have caught it!'

This was Benjamin's opinion of me (on my arrival at the villa); after I had announced my intention of returning Miserrimus Dexter's visit, in his company.

Being determined to carry my point, I could afford to try the influence of mild persuasion. I begged my good friend to have a little patience with me. 'And do remember what I have already told you,' I added. 'It is of serious importance to me to see Dexter again.'

I only heaped fuel on the fire. 'See him again?' Benjamin repeated, indignantly. 'See him, after he grossly insulted you, under my roof, in this very room? I can't be awake; I must be asleep and dreaming.'

It was wrong of me, I know. But Benjamin's virtuous indignation was so very virtuous that it let the spirit of mischief loose in me. I really could not resist the temptation to outrage his sense of propriety, by taking an audaciously liberal view of the whole matter.

'Gently, my good friend, gently!' I said. 'We must make allowances for a man who suffers under Dexter's infirmities, and lives Dexter's life. And really we must not let our modesty lead us beyond reasonable limits. I begin to think that I took rather a prudish view of the thing myself, at the time. A woman who respects herself, and whose whole heart is with her husband, is not so very seriously injured when a wretched crippled creature is rude enough to put his arm round her waist. Virtuous indignation (if I may venture to say so) is sometimes very cheap indignation. Besides, I have forgiven him—and you must forgive him, too. There is no fear of his forgetting himself again, while you are with me. His house is quite a curiosity; it is sure to interest you; the pictures alone are worth the journey. I will write to him to-day, and we will go and see him together to-morrow. We owe it to ourselves (if we don't owe it to Mr Dexter) to pay this visit. If you will look about you, Benjamin, you will see that benevolence towards everybody is the great virtue of the time we live in. Poor Mr Dexter must have the benefit of the prevailing fashion. Come, come, march with the age! Open your mind to the new ideas!'

Instead of accepting this polite invitation, worthy old Benjamin flew at the age we lived in, like a bull at a red cloth.

'Oh, the new ideas! the new ideas! By all manner of means, Valeria, let us have the new ideas! The old morality's all wrong, the old ways are all worn out. Let's march with the age we live in. Nothing comes amiss to the age we live in. The wife in England and the husband in Spain, married or not married, living together or not living together—it's all one to the new ideas. I'll go with you, Valeria; I'll be worthy of the generation I live in. When we have done with Dexter, don't let's do things by halves. Let's go and get crammed with ready-made science at a lecture—let's hear the last new professor, the man who has been behind the scenes at Creation, and knows to a T how the world was made, and how long it took to make it. There's the other fellow, too: mind we don't forget the modern Solomon who has left his proverbs behind him—the bran-new philosopher who considers the consolations of religion in the light of harmless playthings, and who is kind enough to say that he might have been all the happier if he could only have been childish enough to play with them himself. Oh, the new ideas, the new ideas, what consoling, elevating, beautiful discoveries have been made by the new ideas! We were all monkeys before we were men, and molecules before we were monkeys! And what does it matter? And what does anything matter to anybody? I'm with you, Valeria—I'm ready! The sooner the better. Come to Dexter! Come to Dexter!'

'I am so glad you agree with me,' I said. 'But let us do nothing in a hurry. Three o'clock to-morrow will be time enough for Mr Dexter. I will write at once and tell him to expect us. Where are you going?'

'I am going to clear my mind of cant,' said Benjamin, sternly. 'I am going into the library.'

'What are you going to read?'

'I am going to read——"Puss in Boots," and "Jack and the Bean-Stalk," and anything else I can find that doesn't march with the age we live in.'

With that parting shot at the new ideas, my old friend left me for a time.

Having despatched my note, I found myself beginning to revert, with a certain feeling of anxiety, to the subject of Miserrimus Dexter's health. How had he passed through the interval of my absence from England? Could anybody, within my reach, tell me news of him? To inquire of Benjamin would only be to provoke a new outbreak. While I was still considering, the housekeeper entered the room on some domestic errand. I asked, at a venture, if she had heard anything more, while I had been away, of the extraordinary person who had so seriously alarmed her on a former occasion.

The housekeeper shook her head, and looked as if she thought it in bad taste to mention the subject at all.

'About a week after you had gone away, ma'am,' she said, with extreme severity of manner, and with excessive carefulness in her choice of words, 'the Person you mention had the impudence to send a letter to you. The messenger was informed, by my master's orders, that you had gone abroad, and he and his letter were both sent about their business together. Not long afterwards, ma'am, I happened, while drinking tea with Mrs Macallan's housekeeper, to hear of the Person again. He himself called in his chaise, at Mrs Macallan's, to inquire about you there. How he can contrive to sit, without legs to balance him, is beyond my understanding—but that is neither here nor there. Legs or no legs, the housekeeper saw him, and she says, as I say, she will never forget him to her dying day. She told him (as soon as she recovered herself) of Mr Eustace's illness, and of you and Mrs Macallan being in foreign parts nursing him. He went away, so the housekeeper told me, with tears in his eyes, and oaths and curses on his lips—a sight shocking to see. That's all I know about the Person, ma'am, and I hope to be excused if I venture to say that the subject is (for good reasons) extremely disagreeable to me.'

She made a formal curtsey, and quitted the room.

Left by myself, I felt more anxious and more uncertain than ever, when I thought of the experiment that was to be tried on the next day. Making due allowance for exaggeration, the description of Miserrimus Dexter, on his departure from Mrs Macallan's house, suggested that he had not endured my long absence very patiently, and that he was still as far as ever from giving his shattered nervous system its fair chance of repose.

The next morning brought me Mr Playmore's reply to the letter which I had addressed to him from Paris.

He wrote very briefly, neither approving nor blaming my decision, but strongly reiterating his opinion that I should do well to choose a competent witness as my companion at my coming interview with Dexter. The most interesting part of the letter was at the end. 'You must be prepared,' Mr Playmore wrote, 'to see a change for the worse in Dexter. A friend of mine was with him on a matter of business a few days since, and was struck by the alteration in him. Your presence is sure to have its effect one way or another. I can give you no instructions for managing him—you must be guided by the circumstances. Your own tact will tell you whether it is wise, or not, to encourage him to speak of the late Mrs Eustace. The chances of his betraying himself all revolve (as I think) round that one topic: keep him to it if you can.' To this was added, in a postscript: 'Ask Mr Benjamin if he was near enough to the library door to hear Dexter tell you of his entering the bedchamber, on the night of Mrs Eustace Macallan's death.'

I put the question to Benjamin when we met at the luncheon-table, before setting forth for the distant suburb in which Miserrimus Dexter lived. My old friend disapproved of the contemplated expedition as strongly as ever. He was unusually grave and unusually sparing of words, when he answered me.

'I am no listener,' he said. 'But some people have voices which insist on being heard. Mr Dexter is one of them.'

'Does that mean that you heard him?' I asked.

'The door couldn't muffle him, and the wall couldn't muffle him,' Benjamin rejoined. 'I heard him—and I thought it infamous. There!'

'I may want you to do more than hear him, this time,' I ventured to say. 'I may want you to make notes of our conversation, while Mr Dexter is speaking to me. You used to write down what my father said, when he was dictating his letters to you. Have you got one of your little note-books to spare?'

Benjamin looked up from his plate with an aspect of stern surprise.

'It is one thing,' he said, 'to write under the dictation of a great merchant, conducting a vast correspondence by which thousands of pounds change hands in due course of post. And it's another thing to take down the gibberish of a maundering mad monster who ought to be kept in a cage. Your good father, Valeria, would never have asked me to do that.'

'Forgive me, Benjamin: I must really ask you to do it. It is Mr Playmore's idea, mind!—not mine. Come! give way this once, dear, for my sake.'

Benjamin looked down again at his plate, with a rueful resignation which told me that I had carried my point.

'I have been tied to her apron-string all my life,' I heard him grumble to himself. 'And it's too late in the day to get loose from her now.' He looked up again at me. 'I thought I had retired from business,' he said. 'But it seems I must turn clerk again. Well? What is the new stroke of work that's expected from me, this time?'

The cab was announced to be waiting for us at the gate, as he asked the question. I rose and took his arm, and gave him a grateful kiss on his rosy old cheek.

'Only two things,' I said. 'Sit down behind Mr Dexter's chair, so that he can't see you. But take care to place yourself, at the same time, so that you can see me.'

'The less I see of Mr Dexter, the better I shall be pleased,' growled Benjamin. 'What am I to do, after I have taken my place behind him?'

'You are to wait until I make you a sign; and when you see it you are to begin writing down in your note-book what Mr Dexter is saying—and you are to go on, until I make another sign which means, Leave off!'

'Well?' said Benjamin, 'What's the sign for, Begin? and what's the sign for, Leave off?'

I was not quite prepared with an answer to this. I asked him to help me with a hint. No! Benjamin would take no active part in the matter. He was resigned to be employed in the capacity of passive instrument—and there all concession ended, so far as he was concerned.

Left to my own resources, I found it no easy matter to invent a telegraphic system which should sufficiently inform Benjamin, without awakening Dexter's quick suspicion. I looked into the glass to see if I could find the necessary suggestion in anything that I wore. My earrings supplied me with the idea of which I was in search.

'I shall take care to sit in an arm-chair,' I said. 'When you see me rest my elbow on the chair, and lift my hand to my earring, as if I was playing with it—write down what he says; and go on until—well, suppose we say, until you hear me move my chair. At that sound, stop. You understand me?'

'I understand you.'

We started for Dexter's house.

CHAPTER XL

Nemesis at Last!

THE gardener opened the gate to us on this occasion. He had evidently received his orders, in anticipation of my arrival.

'Mrs Valeria?' he asked.

'Yes.'

'And friend?'

'And friend.'

'Please to step upstairs. You know the house.'

Crossing the hall, I stopped for a moment, and looked at a favourite walking-cane which Benjamin still kept in his hand.

'Your cane will only be in your way,' I said. 'Had you not better leave it here?'

'My cane may be useful upstairs,' retorted Benjamin gruffly. '*I* haven't forgotten what happened in the library.'

It was no time to contend with him. I led the way up the stairs.

Arriving at the upper flight of steps, I was startled by hearing a sudden cry from the room above. It was like the cry of a person in pain; and it was twice repeated, before we entered the circular ante-chamber. I was the first to approach the inner room, and to see the many-sided Miserrimus Dexter in another new aspect of his character.

The unfortunate Ariel was standing before a table, with a dish of little cakes placed in front of her. Round each of her wrists was tied a string, the free end of which (at a distance of a few yards) was held in Miserrimus Dexter's hands. 'Try again, my beauty!' I heard him say, as I stopped on the threshold of the door. 'Take a cake.' At the word of command, Ariel submissively stretched out one arm towards the dish. Just as she touched a cake with the tips of her fingers, her hand was jerked away by a pull at the string, so savagely cruel in the nimble and devilish violence of it, that I felt inclined to snatch Benjamin's cane out of his hand, and break it over Miserrimus Dexter's back. Ariel suffered the pain this time in Spartan silence. The position in which she stood enabled her to be the first to see me at the door. She had discovered me. Her teeth were set; her face was flushed under the struggle to restrain herself. Not even a sigh escaped her in my presence.

'Drop the strings!' I called out, indignantly. 'Release her, Mr Dexter, or I shall leave the house.'

At the sound of my voice he burst out with a shrill cry of welcome. His eyes fastened on me with a fierce, devouring delight.

'Come in! come in!' he cried. 'See what I am reduced to, in the maddening suspense of waiting for you. See how I kill the time when the time parts us. Come in! come in! I am in one of my malicious humours this morning, caused entirely, Mrs Valeria, by my anxiety to see you. When I am in my malicious humours I must tease something. I am teasing Ariel. Look at her! She has had nothing to eat all day, and she hasn't been quick enough to snatch a morsel of cake yet. You needn't pity her. Ariel has no nerves—I don't hurt her.'

'Ariel has no nerves,' echoed the poor creature, frowning at me for interfering between her master and herself. 'He doesn't hurt me.'

I heard Benjamin beginning to swing his cane behind me.

'Drop the strings!' I reiterated, more vehemently than ever. 'Drop them—or I shall instantly leave you.'

Miserrimus Dexter's delicate nerves shuddered at my violence. 'What a glorious voice!' he exclaimed—and dropped the strings. 'Take the cakes,' he added, addressing Ariel in his most imperial manner.

She passed me, with the strings hanging from her swollen wrists, and the dish of cakes in her hand. She nodded her head at me defiantly.

'Ariel has got no nerves,' she repeated, proudly. 'He doesn't hurt me.'

'You see,' said Miserrimus Dexter, 'there is no harm done—and I dropped the strings when you told me. Don't *begin* by being hard on me, Mrs Valeria, after your long, long absence.' He paused. Benjamin, standing silent in the doorway, attracted his attention for the first time. 'Who is this?' he asked; and wheeled his chair suspiciously nearer to the door. 'I know!' he cried, before I could answer. 'This is the benevolent gentleman who looked like the refuge of the afflicted, when I saw him last. You have altered for the worse since then, Sir. You have stepped into quite a new character—you personify Retributive Justice, now. Your new protector, Mrs Valeria—I understand!' He bowed low to Benjamin, with ferocious irony. 'Your humble servant, Mr Retributive Justice! I have deserved you—and I submit to you. Walk in, Sir! I will take care that your new office shall be a sinecure. This lady is the Light of my Life. Catch me failing in respect towards her, if you can!' He backed his chair before Benjamin (who listened to him in contemptuous silence) until he reached the part of the room in which I was standing. 'Your hand, Light of my Life!' he murmured, in his gentlest tones. 'Your hand—only to show you have forgiven me!' I gave him my hand. 'One?' he whispered, entreatingly. 'Only one?' He kissed my hand once, respectfully—and dropped it with a heavy sigh. 'Ah, poor Dexter!' he said, pitying himself with the whole sincerity of his egotism. 'A warm heart, wasted in solitude, mocked by deformity. Sad! sad! Ah, poor Dexter!' He looked round again at Benjamin, with another flash of his ferocious irony. 'A beautiful day, Sir,' he said, with mock-conventional courtesy. 'Seasonable weather indeed after the late long-continued rains. Can I offer you any refreshment? Won't you sit down? Retributive Justice, when it is no taller than you are, looks best in a chair.'

'And a monkey looks best in a cage,' rejoined Benjamin, enraged at the satirical reference to his shortness of stature. 'I was waiting, Sir, to see you get into your swing.'

The retort produced no effect on Miserrimus Dexter: it appeared to have passed by him unheard. He had changed again; he was thoughtful, he was subdued; his eyes were fixed on me with a sad and rapt attention. I took the nearest arm-chair; first casting a glance at Benjamin, which he immediately understood. He placed himself behind Dexter, at an angle which commanded a view of my chair. Ariel, silently devouring her cakes, crouched on a stool at 'the Master's' feet, and looked up at him like a faithful dog. There was an interval of quiet and repose. I was able to observe Miserrimus Dexter uninterruptedly, for the first time since I had entered the room.

I was not surprised—I was nothing less than alarmed by the change for the worse in him, since we had last met. Mr Playmore's letter had not prepared me for the serious deterioration in him which I could now discern.

His features were pinched and worn; the whole face seemed to have wasted strangely in substance and size, since I had last seen it. The softness in his eyes was gone. Blood-red veins were intertwined all over them now; they were set in a piteous and vacant stare. His once firm hands looked withered; they trembled as they lay on the coverlid. The paleness of his face (exaggerated, perhaps, by the black velvet jacket that he wore) had a sodden and sickly look—the fine outline was gone. The multitudinous little wrinkles at the corners of his eyes had deepened. His head sank into his shoulders when he leaned forward in his chair. Years appeared to have passed over him, instead of months, while I had been absent from England. Remembering the medical report which Mr Playmore had given me to read—recalling the doctor's positively-declared opinion that the preservation of Dexter's sanity depended on the healthy condition of his nerves—I could not but feel that I had done wisely (if I might still hope for success) in hastening my return from Spain. Knowing what I knew, fearing what I feared, I believed that his time was near. I felt, when our eyes met by accident, that I was looking at a doomed man.

I pitied him.

Yes! yes! I know that compassion for him was utterly inconsistent with the motive which had taken me to his house—utterly inconsistent with the doubt, still present to my mind whether Mr Playmore had really wronged him in believing that his was the guilt which had compassed the first Mrs Eustace's death. I felt this: I knew him to be cruel; I believed him to be false. And yet, I pitied him! Is there a common fund of wickedness in us all? Is the suppression or the development of that wickedness a mere question of training and temptation? And is there something in our deeper sympathies which mutely acknowledges this, when we feel for the wicked; when we crowd to a criminal trial; when we shake hands at parting (if we happen to be present officially) with the vilest monster that ever swung on a gallows? It is not for me to decide. I can only say that I pitied Miserrimus Dexter—and that he found it out.

'Thank you,' he said, suddenly. 'You see I am ill, and you feel for me. Dear and good Valeria!'

'This lady's name, Sir, is Mrs Eustace Macallan,' interposed Benjamin, speaking sternly behind him. 'The next time you address her, remember, if you please, that you have no business with her Christian name.'

Benjamin's rebuke passed, like Benjamin's retort, unheeded and unheard. To all appearance, Miserrimus Dexter had completely forgotten that there was such a person in the room.

'You have delighted me with the sight of you,' he went on. 'Add to the pleasure by letting me hear your voice. Talk to me of yourself. Tell me what you have been doing since you left England.'

It was necessary to my object to set the conversation afloat; and this was as good a way of doing it as any other. I told him plainly how I had been employed during my absence.

'So you are still fond of Eustace?' he said, bitterly.

'I love him more dearly than ever.'

He lifted his hands, and hid his face. After waiting awhile, he went on; speaking in an odd, muffled manner, still under cover of his hands.

'And you leave Eustace in Spain?' he said; 'and you return to England by yourself! What made you do that?'

'What made me first come here, and ask you to help me, Mr Dexter?'

He dropped his hands, and looked at me. I saw in his eyes, not amazement only, but alarm.

'Is it possible,' he exclaimed, 'that you won't let that miserable matter rest even yet? Are you still determined to meddle with the mystery at Gleninch!'

'I am still determined, Mr Dexter; and I still hope that you may be able to help me.'

The old distrust that I remembered so well, darkened again over his face the moment I said those words.

'How can I help you?' he asked. 'Can I alter facts?' He stopped. His face brightened again, as if some sudden sense of relief had come to him. 'I *did* try to help you,' he went on. 'I told you that Mrs Beauly's absence was a device to screen herself from suspicion; I told you that the poison might have been given by Mrs Beauly's maid. Has reflection convinced you? Do you see something in the idea?'

This return to Mrs Beauly gave me my first chance of leading the talk to the right topic.

'I see nothing in the idea,' I answered. 'I see no motive. Had the maid any reason to be an enemy to the late Mrs Eustace?'

'Nobody had any reason to be an enemy to the late Mrs Eustace!' he broke out, loudly and vehemently. 'She was all goodness, all kindness; she never injured any human creature in thought or deed. She was a saint upon earth. Respect her memory! Let the martyr rest in her grave!' He covered his face again with his hands, and shook and shuddered under the paroxysm of emotion that I had roused in him.

Ariel suddenly and softly left her stool and approached me.

'Do you see my ten claws?' she whispered, holding out her hands. 'Vex the Master again—and you will feel my ten claws on your throat!'

Benjamin rose from his seat: he had seen the action, without hearing the words. I signed to him to keep his place. Ariel returned to her stool, and looked up again at the Master.

'Don't cry,' she said. 'Come on. Here are the strings. Tease me again. Make me screech with the smart of it.'

He never answered and never moved.

Ariel bent her slow mind to meet the difficulty of attracting his attention. I saw it in her frowning brows, in her colourless eyes looking at me vacantly. On a sudden, she joyfully struck the open palm of one of her hands with the fist of the other. She had triumphed. She had got an idea.

'Master!' she cried. 'Master! You haven't told me a story for ever so long. Puzzle my thick head. Make my flesh creep. Come on. A good long story. All blood and crimes.'

Had she accidentally hit on the right suggestion to strike his wayward fancy? I knew his high opinion of his own skill in 'dramatic narrative.' I knew that one of his favourite amusements was to puzzle Ariel by telling her stories that she could not understand. Would he wander away into the region of wild romance? Or would he remember that my obstinacy still threatened him with re-opening the inquiry into the tragedy at Gleninch? and would he set his cunning at work to mislead me by some new stratagem? This latter course was the course which my past experience of him suggested that he would take. But, to my surprise and alarm, I found my past experience at fault. Ariel succeeded in diverting his mind from the subject which had been in full possession of it the moment before she spoke! He showed his face again. It was overspread by a broad smile of gratified self-esteem. He was weak enough now to let even Ariel find her way to his vanity! I saw it, with a sense of misgiving, with a doubt whether I had not delayed my visit until too late, which turned me cold, from head to foot.

Miserrimus Dexter spoke—to Ariel, not to me.

'Poor devil!' he said, patting her head complacently. 'You don't understand a word of my stories, do you? And yet I can make the flesh creep on your great clumsy body—and yet I can stir your stagnant mind, and make you like it! Poor devil!' He leaned back serenely in his chair, and looked my way again. Would the sight of me remind him of the words that had passed between us, not a minute since? No! There was the pleasantly-tickled self-conceit smiling at me exactly as it had smiled at Ariel. 'I excel in dramatic narrative, Mrs Valeria,' he said. 'And this creature here on the stool, is a remarkable proof of it. She is quite a psychological study, when I tell her one of my stories. It is really amusing to see the half-witted wretch's desperate efforts to understand me. You shall have a specimen. I have been out of spirits, while you were away—I haven't told her a story for weeks past; I will tell her one now. Don't suppose it's any effort to me! My invention is inexhaustible. You are sure to be amused—you are naturally serious—but you are sure to be amused. I am naturally serious, too: and I always laugh at her.'

Ariel clapped her great shapeless hands. 'He always laughs at me!' she said, with a proud look of superiority, directed straight at Me.

I was at a loss, seriously at a loss, what to do. The outbreak which I had provoked in leading him to speak of the late Mrs Eustace warned me to be careful, and to wait for my opportunity, before I reverted to *that* subject. How else could I turn the conversation, so as to lead him, little by little, towards the betrayal of the secrets which he was keeping from me? In this uncertainty, one thing only seemed to be plain. To let him tell his story, would be simply to let him waste the precious minutes. With a vivid remembrance of Ariel's 'ten claws,' I decided nevertheless on discouraging Dexter's new whim, at every opportunity and by every means in my power.

'Now, Mrs Valeria!' he began, loudly and loftily. 'Listen. Now, Ariel! Bring your brains to a focus. I improvise poetry; I improvise fiction. We will begin with the good old formula of the fairy stories. Once upon a time——'

I was waiting for my opportunity to interrupt him, when he interrupted himself. He stopped, with a bewildered look. He put his hand to his head, and passed it backwards and forwards over his forehead. He laughed feebly.

'I seem to want rousing,' he said.

Was his mind gone? There had been no signs of it, until I had unhappily stirred his memory of the dead mistress of Gleninch. Was the weakness which I had already noticed, was the bewilderment which I now saw, attributable to the influence of a passing disturbance only? In other words, had I witnessed nothing more serious than a first warning to him, and to us? Would he soon recover himself, if we were patient, and gave him time? Even Benjamin was interested at last; I saw him trying to look at Dexter round the corner of the chair. Even Ariel was surprised and uneasy. She had no dark glances to cast at me now.

We all waited to see what he would do, to hear what he would say, next.

'My harp!' he cried. 'Music will rouse me.'

Ariel brought him his harp.

'Master!' she said, wonderingly. 'What's come to you?' He waved his hand, commanding her to be silent.

'Ode to Invention,' he announced loftily, addressing himself to me. 'Poetry and music improvised by Dexter. Silence! Attention!'

His fingers wandered feebly over the harp-strings; awakening no melody, suggesting no words. In a little while, his hand dropped; his head sank forward gently, and rested on the frame of the harp. I started to my feet and approached him. Was it a sleep? or was it a swoon?

I touched his arm, and called to him by his name.

Ariel instantly stepped between us, with a threatening look at me. At the same moment, Miserrimus Dexter raised his head. My voice had reached him. He looked at me with a curious contemplative quietness in his eyes, which I had never seen in them before.

'Take away the harp,' he said to Ariel, speaking in languid tones, like a man who was very weary.

The mischievous half witted creature—in sheer stupidity, or in downright malice towards me, I am not sure which—irritated him once more.

'Why, Master?' she asked, staring at him with the harp hugged in her arms. 'What has come to you? Where is the story?'

'We don't want the story,' I interposed. 'I have many things to say to Mr Dexter which I have not said yet.'

Ariel lifted her heavy hand. 'You *will* have it!' she said, and advanced towards me. At the same moment the Master's voice stopped her.

'Put away the harp, you fool!' he repeated sternly. 'And wait for the story until I choose to tell it.'

She took the harp submissively back to its place at the end of the room. Miserrimus Dexter moved his chair a little closer to mine. 'I know what will rouse me,' he said, confidentially. 'Exercise will do it. I have had no exercise lately. Wait a little, and you will see.'

He put his hands on the machinery of the chair, and started on his customary course down the room. Here again, the ominous change in him showed itself under a new form. The pace at which he travelled was not the furious pace that I remembered; the chair no longer rushed under him on rumbling and whistling wheels. It went, but it went slowly. Up the room, and down the room, he painfully urged it—and then he stopped, for want of breath.

We followed him. Ariel was first, and Benjamin was by my side. He motioned impatiently to both of them to stand back, and to let me approach him alone.

'I'm out of practice,' he said, faintly. 'I hadn't the heart to make the wheels roar, and the floor tremble, while you were away.'

Who would not have pitied him? Who would have remembered his misdeeds at that moment? Even Ariel felt it. I heard her beginning to whine and whimper behind me. The magician who alone could rouse the dormant sensibilities in her nature had awakened them now by his neglect. Her fatal cry was heard again, in mournful, moaning tones.

'What's come to you, Master? Have you forgot me? Where's the story?'

'Never mind her,' I whispered to him. 'You want the fresh air. Send for the gardener. Let us take a drive in your pony-chaise.'

It was useless. Ariel would be noticed. The mournful cry came once more. 'Where's the story? Where's the story?'

The sinking spirit leapt up in Dexter again.

'You wretch! you fiend!' he cried, whirling his chair round, and facing her. 'The story is coming. I *can* tell it! I *will* tell it! Wine! You whimpering idiot, get me the wine. Why didn't I think of it before? The kingly Burgundy! that's what I want, Valeria, to set my invention alight and flaming in my head. Glasses for everybody! Honour to the King of the Vintages—the Royal Clos Vougeot!'

Ariel opened the cupboard in the alcove, and produced the wine and the high Venetian glasses. Dexter drained his goblet full of Burgundy at a draught; he forced us to drink (or at least pretend to drink) with him. Even Ariel had her share, this time, and emptied her glass in rivalry with her master. The powerful wine mounted almost instantly to her weak head. She began to sing hoarsely a song of her own devising, in imitation of Dexter. It was nothing but the repetition, the endless mechanical repetition, of her demand for the story. 'Tell us the story. Master! master! tell us the story!' Absorbed over his wine, the Master silently filled his goblet for the second time. Benjamin whispered to me, while his eye was off us, 'Take my advice, Valeria, for once; let us go.'

'One last effort,' I whispered back. 'Only one!'

Ariel went drowsily on with her song.

'Tell us the story. Master! master! tell us the story.'

Miserrimus Dexter looked up from his glass. The generous stimulant was beginning to do its work. I saw the colour rising in his face. I saw the bright intelligence flashing again in his eyes. The Burgundy *had* roused him! The good wine offered me a last chance!

'Now for the story!' he cried.

'No story!' I said. 'I want to talk to you, Mr Dexter. I am not in the humour for a story.'

'Not in the humour!' he repeated, with a gleam of the old impish irony showing itself again in his face. 'That's an excuse. I see what it is! You think my invention is gone—and you are not frank enough to confess it. I'll show you you're wrong. I'll show you that Dexter is himself again. Silence, you Ariel, or you shall leave the room! I have got it, Mrs Valeria, all laid out here, with scenes and characters complete.' He touched his forehead, and looked at me with a furtive and smiling cunning, before he added his next words. 'It's the very thing to interest *you*, my fair friend. It's the Story of a Mistress and a Maid. Come back to the fire and hear it.'

The Story of a Mistress and a Maid? If that meant anything, it meant the story of Mrs Beauly and her maid, told in disguise!

The title, and the look which had escaped him when he announced it, revived the hope that was well-nigh dead in me. He had rallied at last. He was again in possession of his natural foresight and his natural cunning. Under pretence of telling Ariel her story, he was evidently about to make the attempt to mislead me, for the second time. The conclusion was irresistible. To use his own words—Dexter was himself again.

I took Benjamin's arm as we followed him back to the fireplace in the middle of the room. 'There is a chance for me yet,' I whispered. 'Don't forget the signals.'

We returned to the places which we had already occupied. Ariel cast another threatening look at me. She had just sense enough left, after emptying her goblet of wine, to be on the watch for a new interruption on my part. I took care, of course, that nothing of the sort should happen. I was now as eager as Ariel to hear the story. The subject was full of snares for the narrator. At any moment, in the excitement of speaking, Dexter's memory of the true events might show itself reflected in the circumstances of the fiction. At any moment, he might betray himself.

He looked round him, and began.

'My public, are you seated? My public, are you ready?' he asked, gaily. 'Your face a little more this way,' he added, in his softest and tenderest tones, motioning to me to turn my full face towards him. 'Surely I am not asking too much? You look at the meanest creature that crawls—look at Me. Let me find my inspiration in your eyes. Let me feed my hungry admiration on your form. Come! have one little pitying smile left for the man whose happiness you have wrecked. Thank you. Light of my Life, thank you!' He kissed his hand to me, and threw himself back luxuriously in his chair. 'The story,' he resumed. 'The story at last! In what form shall I cast it? In the dramatic form—the oldest way, the truest way, the shortest way of telling a story! Title, first. A short title, a taking title: "Mistress and Maid." Scene, the land of romance—Italy. Time, the age of romance—the fifteenth century. Ha! look at Ariel. She knows no more about the fifteenth century than the cat in the kitchen, and yet she is interested already. Happy Ariel!'

Ariel looked at me again, in the double intoxication of the wine and the triumph.

'I know no more than the cat in the kitchen,' she repeated, with a broad grin of gratified vanity. 'I am "happy Ariel!" What are You?'

Miserrimus Dexter laughed uproariously.

'Didn't I tell you?' he said. 'Isn't she fun? Persons of the Drama,' he resumed:—'Three in number. Women only. Angelica, a noble lady; noble alike in spirit and in birth. Cunegonda, a beautiful devil, in woman's form. Damoride, her unfortunate maid. First scene. A dark vaulted chamber in a castle. Time, evening. The owls are hooting in the wood; the frogs are croaking in the marsh. Look at Ariel! Her flesh creeps; she shudders audibly. Admirable Ariel!'

My rival in the Master's favour eyed me defiantly. 'Admirable Ariel!' she repeated, in drowsy accents. Miserrimus Dexter paused to take up his goblet of Burgundy—placed close at hand on a little sliding table attached to his chair. I watched him narrowly, as he sipped the wine. The flush was still mounting in his face; the light was still brightening in his eyes. He set down his glass again, with a jovial smack of his lips—and went on.

'Persons present in the vaulted chamber:—Cunegonda and Damoride. Cunegonda speaks. "Damoride!" "Madam?" "Who lies ill in the chamber above us?" "Madam, the noble lady, Angelica." (A pause. Cunegonda speaks again.) "Damoride!" "Madam?" "How does Angelica like you?" "Madam, the noble lady, sweet and good to all who approach her, is sweet and good to me." "Have you attended on her, Damoride?" "Sometimes, madam, when the nurse was weary." "Has she taken her healing medicine from your hand?" "Once or twice, madam, when I happened to be by." "Damoride, take this key, and open the casket on the table there." (Damoride obeys.) "Do you see a green vial in the casket?" "I see it, madam." "Take it out." (Damoride obeys.) "Do you see a liquid in the green vial? can you guess what it is?" "No, madam." "Shall I tell you?" (Damoride bows respectfully.) "Poison is in the vial." (Damoride starts; she shrinks from the poison; she would fain put it aside. Her mistress signs to her to keep it in her hand; her mistress speaks.) "Damoride, I have told you one of my secrets; shall I tell you another?" (Damoride waits, fearing what is to come. Her mistress speaks.) "I hate the Lady Angelica. Her life stands between me and the joy of my heart. You hold her life in your hand." (Damoride drops on her knees; she is a devout person; she crosses herself, and then she speaks.) "Mistress, you terrify me. Mistress, what do I hear?" (Cunegonda advances, stands over her, looks down on her with terrible eyes, whispers the next words.) "Damoride, the Lady Angelica must die—and I must not be suspected. The Lady Angelica must die—and by your hand." '

He paused again. To sip the wine once more? No; to drink a deep draught of it, this time.

Was the stimulant beginning to fail him already?

I looked at him attentively, as he laid himself back again in his chair, to consider for a moment before he went on.

The flush on his face was as deep as ever; but the brightness in his eyes was beginning to fade already. I had noticed that he spoke more and more slowly as he advanced to the later dialogue of the scene. Was he feeling the effort of invention already? Had the time come when the wine had done all that the wine could do for him?

We waited. Ariel sat watching him, with vacantly-staring eyes and vacantly-open mouth. Benjamin, impenetrably expecting the signal, kept his open note-book on his knee, covered by his hand.

Miserrimus Dexter went on.

'Damoride hears those terrible words; Damoride clasps her hands in entreaty. "Oh, madam! madam! how can I kill the dear and noble lady? What motive have I for harming her?" Cunegonda answers, "You have the motive of obeying Me." Damoride falls with her face on the floor, at her mistress's feet. "Madam, I cannot do it! Madam, I dare not do it!" Cunegonda answers, "You run no risk: I have my plan for diverting discovery from myself, and my plan for diverting discovery from you." Damoride repeats, "I cannot do it! I dare not do it!" Cunegonda's eyes flash lightnings of rage. She takes from its place of concealment in her bosom——'

He stopped in the middle of the sentence, and put his hand to his head. Not like a man in pain, but like a man who had lost his idea.

Would it be well if I tried to help him to recover his idea? or would it be wiser (if I could only do it) to keep silence?

I could see the drift of his story plainly enough. His object, under the thin disguise of the Italian romance, was to meet my unanswerable objection to suspecting Mrs Beauly's maid—the objection that the woman had no motive for committing herself to an act of murder. If he could practically contradict this, by discovering a perfectly reasonable and perfectly probable motive, his end would be gained. Those enquiries which I had pledged myself to pursue—those inquiries which might, at any moment, take a turn that directly concerned him—would, in that case, be successfully diverted from the right to the wrong person. The innocent maid would set my strictest scrutiny at defiance; and Dexter would be safely shielded behind her.

I determined to give him time. Not a word passed my lips.

The minutes followed each other. I waited in the deepest anxiety. It was a trying and a critical moment. If he succeeded in inventing a probable motive, and in shaping it neatly to suit the purpose of his story, he would prove, by that act alone, that there were reserves of mental power still left in him, which the practised eye of the Scotch doctor had failed to see. But the question was—would he do it?

He did it! Not in a new way; not in a convincing way; not without a painfully-evident effort. Still, well done, or ill done, he found a motive for the maid.

'Cunegonda,' he resumed, 'takes from its place of concealment in her bosom a written paper, and unfolds it. "Look at this," she says. Damoride looks at the paper, and sinks again at her mistress's feet in a paroxysm of horror and despair. Cunegonda is in possession of a shameful secret in the maid's past life. Cunegonda can say to her, "Choose your alternative. Either submit to an exposure which disgraces you, and disgraces your parents, for ever—or make up your mind to obey Me." Damoride might submit to the disgrace if it only affected herself. But her parents are honest people; she cannot disgrace her parents. She is driven to her last refuge—there is no hope of melting the hard heart of Cunegonda. Her only resource is to raise difficulties; she tries to show that there are obstacles between her and the crime. "Madam! madam!" she cries, "how can I do it, when the nurse is there to see me?" Cunegonda answers, "Sometimes the nurse sleeps; sometimes the nurse is away." Damoride still persists. "Madam! madam! the door is kept locked, and the nurse has got the key." '

The key! I instantly thought of the missing key at Gleninch. Had *he* thought of it too? He certainly checked himself as the word escaped him. I resolved to make the signal! I rested my elbow on the arm of my chair, and played with my earring. Benjamin took out his pencil, and arranged his

note-book, so that Ariel could not see what he was about, if she happened
to look his way.

We waited, until it pleased Miserrimus Dexter to proceed. The interval
was a long one. His hand went up again to his forehead. A duller and duller
look was palpable stealing over his eyes. When he did speak, it was not to
go on with the narrative, but to put a question.

'Where did I leave off?' he asked.

My hopes sank again as rapidly as they had risen. I managed to answer
him, however, without showing any change in my manner.

'You left off,' I said, 'where Damoride was speaking to Cunegonda——'

'Yes! yes!' he interposed. 'And what did she say?'

'She said, "The door is kept locked, and the nurse has got the key." '

He instantly leaned forward in his chair.

'No!' he answered, vehemently. 'You're wrong. "Key?" Nonsense! I never
said "Key." '

'I thought you did, Mr. Dexter.'

'I never did! I said something else; and you have forgotten it.'

I refrained from disputing with him, in fear of what might follow. We
waited again. Benjamin, sullenly submitting to my caprices, had taken down
the questions and answers that had passed between Dexter and myself. He
still mechanically kept his page open, and still held his pencil in readiness
to go on. Ariel, quietly submitting to the drowsy influence of the wine while
Dexter's voice was in her ears, felt uneasily the change to silence. She
glanced round her restlessly; she lifted her eyes to 'the Master.'

There he sat, silent, with his hand to his head, still struggling to marshal
his wandering thoughts; still trying to see light through the darkness that was
closing round him.

'Master!' cried Ariel, piteously, 'what's become of the story?'

He started as if she had awakened him out of a sleep: he shook his head
impatiently, as though he wanted to throw off some oppression that weighed
upon it.

'Patience! patience!' he said. 'The story is going on again.'

He dashed at it desperately: he picked up the first lost thread that fell in
his way, reckless whether it was the right thread or the wrong one.

'Damoride fell on her knees. She burst into tears. She said——'

He stopped, and looked about him with vacant eyes.

'What name did I give the other woman?' he asked; not putting the
question to me, or to either of my companions: asking it of himself, or asking
it of the empty air.

'You called the other woman, Cunegonda,' I said.

At the sound of my voice, his eyes turned slowly—turned on me, and yet
failed to look at me. Dull and absent, still and changeless, they were eyes
that seemed to be fixed on something far away. Even his voice was altered

when he spoke next. It had dropped to a quiet, vacant, monotonous tone. I had heard something like it while I was watching by my husband's bedside, at the time of his delirium—when Eustace's mind appeared to be too weary to follow his speech. Was the end so near as this?

'I called her Cunegonda,' he repeated. 'And I called the other——'

He stopped once more.

'And you called the other Damoride,' I said.

Ariel looked up at him with a broad stare of bewilderment. She pulled impatiently at the sleeve of his jacket, to attract his notice.

'Is this the story, Master?' she asked.

He answered without looking at her; his changeless eyes still fixed, as it seemed, on something far away.

'This is the story,' he said, absently. 'But why Cunegonda? why Damoride? Why not Mistress and Maid? It's easier to remember Mistress and Maid——'

He hesitated; he shivered as he tried to raise himself in his chair. Then he seemed to rally. 'What did the Maid say to the Mistress?' he muttered. 'What? what? what?' He hesitated again. Then, something seemed to dawn upon him, unexpectedly. Was it some new thought that had struck him? Or some lost thought that he had recovered? Impossible to say! He went on, suddenly and rapidly went on, in these strange words.

' "The letter." The Maid said, "The letter." Oh, my heart! Every word a dagger. A dagger in my heart. Oh, you letter. Horrible, horrible, horrible letter.'

What, in God's name, was he talking about? What did those words mean?

Was he unconsciously pursuing his faint and fragmentary recollections of a past time at Gleninch, under the delusion that he was going on with the story? In the wreck of the other faculties, was memory the last to sink? Was the truth, the dreadful truth, glimmering on me dimly, through the awful shadow cast before it by the advancing eclipse of the brain? My breath failed me; a nameless horror crept through my whole being.

Benjamin, with his pencil in his hand, cast one warning look at me. Ariel was quiet and satisfied. 'Go on, Master,' was all she said. 'I like it! I like it! Go on with the story.'

He went on—like a man sleeping with his eyes open, and talking in his sleep.

'The Maid said to the Mistress. No: the Mistress said to the Maid. The Mistress said, "Show him the letter. Must, must, must do it." The Maid said, "No. Mustn't do it, Shan't show it. Stuff. Nonsense. Let him suffer. We can get him off. Show it? No. Let the worst come to the worst. Show it then." The Mistress said——' He paused, and waved his hand rapidly to and fro before his eyes, as if he was brushing away some visionary confusion or entanglement. 'Which was it last?' he said, 'Mistress or Maid? Mistress? No.

Maid speaks, of course. Loud. Positive. "You scoundrels. Keep away from that table. The Diary's there. Number Nine, Caldershaws. Ask for Dandie. You shan't have the Diary. A secret in your ear. The Diary will hang him. I won't have him hanged. How dare you touch my chair? My chair is Me? How dare you touch Me?'

The last words burst on me like a gleam of light! I had read them in the Report of the Trial—in the evidence of the sheriff's officer. Miserrimus Dexter had spoken in those very terms, when he had tried vainly to prevent the men from seizing my husband's papers, and when the men had pushed his chair out of the room. There was no doubt now of what his memory was busy with. The mystery at Gleninch! His last backward flight of thought circled, feebly and more feebly, nearer and nearer to the mystery at Gleninch!

Ariel roused him again. She had no mercy on him; she insisted on hearing the whole story.

'Why do you stop, Master? Get along with it! get along with it! Tell us quick—what did the Missus say to the Maid?'

He laughed feebly, and tried to imitate her.

'What did the Missus say to the Maid?' he repeated. His laugh died away. He went on speaking, more and more vacantly, more and more rapidly. 'The Mistress said to the Maid, "We've got him off. What about the letter? Burn it now. No fire in the grate. No matches in the box. House topsy-turvy. Servants all gone. Tear it up. Shake it up in the basket. Along with the rest. Shake it up. Waste paper. Throw it away. Gone for ever. Oh, Sara, Sara, Sara. Gone for ever." '

Ariel clapped her hands, and mimicked him, in her turn.

' "Oh, Sara, Sara, Sara," ' she repeated. ' "Gone for ever." That's prime, Master! Tell us—who was Sara?'

His lips moved. But his voice sank so low that I could barely hear him. He began again, with the old melancholy refrain.

'The Maid said to the Mistress. No: the Mistress said to the Maid——' He stopped abruptly, and raised himself erect in the chair; he threw up both his hands above his head; and burst into a frightful screaming laugh. 'Aha-ha-ha-ha! How funny! Why don't you laugh? Funny, funny, funny, funny. Aha-ha-ha-ha-ha——'

He fell back in the chair. The shrill and dreadful laugh died away into a low sob. Then there was one long, deep, wearily-drawn breath. Then, nothing but a mute vacant face turned up to the ceiling, with eyes that looked blindly, with lips parted in a senseless, changeless grin. Nemesis at last! The foretold doom had fallen on him. The night had come.

But one feeling animated me, when the first shock was over. Even the horror of that fearful sight seemed only to increase the pity that I felt for the stricken wretch. I started impulsively to my feet. Seeing nothing, thinking of nothing, but the helpless figure in the chair, I sprang forward to raise him; to revive him; to recall him (if such a thing might be possible) to himself. At the first step that I took, I felt hands on me—I was violently drawn back. 'Are you blind?' cried Benjamin, dragging me nearer and nearer to the door.

'Look there!'

He pointed; and I looked.

Ariel had been beforehand with me. She had raised her master in the chair; she had got one arm round him. In her free hand she brandished an Indian club, torn from a 'trophy' of Oriental weapons that ornamented the wall over the fireplace. The creature was transfigured! Her dull eyes glared like the eyes of a wild animal. She gnashed her teeth in the frenzy that possessed her. 'You have done this!' she shouted to me, waving the club furiously round and round over her head. 'Come near him; and I'll dash your brains out! I'll mash you till there's not a whole bone left in your skin!' Benjamin, still holding me with one hand, opened the door with the other. I let him do with me as he would; Ariel fascinated me; I could look at nothing but Ariel. Her frenzy vanished as she saw us retreating. She dropped the club: she threw both arms round him, and nestled her head on his bosom, and sobbed and wept over him. 'Master! Master! They shan't vex you any more. Look up again. Laugh at me as you used to do. Say, "Ariel; you're a fool." Be like yourself again!' I was forced into the next room. I heard a long, low, wailing cry of misery from a poor creature who loved him with a dog's fidelity and a woman's devotion. The heavy door was closed between us. I was in the quiet antechamber; crying over that piteous sight; clinging to my kind old friend, as helpless and as useless as a child.

Benjamin turned the key in the lock.

'There's no use in crying about it,' he said quietly. 'It would be more to the purpose, Valeria, if you thanked God that you have got out of that room, safe and sound. Come with me.'

He took the key out of the lock, and led me downstairs into the hall. After a little consideration, he opened the front door of the house. The gardener was still quietly at work in the grounds.

'Your master is taken ill,' Benjamin said; 'and the woman who attends upon him has lost her head—if she ever had a head to lose. Where does the nearest doctor live?'

The man's devotion to Dexter showed itself as the woman's devotion had shown itself—in the man's rough way. He threw down the spade, with an oath.

'The Master taken bad?' he said. 'I'll fetch the doctor. I shall find him sooner than you will.'

'Tell the doctor to bring a man with him,' Benjamin added. 'He may want help.'

The gardener turned round sternly.

'*I'm* the man,' he said. 'Nobody shall help but me.'

He left us. I sat down on one of the chairs in the hall, and did my best to compose myself. Benjamin walked to and fro, deep in thought. 'Both of them fond of him,' I heard my old friend say to himself. 'Half monkey, half man—and both of them fond of him. *That* beats me.'

The gardener returned with the doctor—a quiet, dark, resolute man. Benjamin advanced to meet them. 'I have got the key,' he said. 'Shall I go upstairs with you?'

Without answering, the doctor drew Benjamin aside into a corner of the hall. The two talked together in low voices. At the end of it, the doctor said, 'Give me the key. You can be of no use; you will only irritate her.'

With those words, he beckoned to the gardener. He was about to lead the way up the stairs, when I ventured to stop him.

'May I stay in the hall, Sir?' I said. 'I am very anxious to hear how it ends.'

He looked at me for a moment before he replied.

'You had better go home, Madam,' he said. 'Is the gardener acquainted with your address?'

'Yes, Sir.'

'Very well. I will let you know how it ends, by means of the gardener. Take my advice. Go home.'

Benjamin placed my arm in his. I looked back, and saw the doctor and the gardener ascending the stairs together, on their way to the locked-up room.

'Never mind the doctor!' I whispered. 'Let's wait in the garden.'

Benjamin would not hear of deceiving the doctor. 'I mean to take you home,' he said. I looked at him in amazement. My old friend, who was all meekness and submission, so long as there was no emergency to try him, now showed the dormant reserve of manly spirit and decision in his nature, as he had never (in my experience) shown it yet. He led me into the garden. We had kept our cab: it was waiting for us at the gate.

On our way home, Benjamin produced his note-book.

'What's to be done, my dear, with the gibberish that I have written here?' he said.

'Have you written it all down?' I asked, in surprise.

'When I undertake a duty I do it,' he answered. 'You never gave me the signal to leave off—you never moved your chair. I have written every word of it. What shall I do? Throw it out of the cab-window?'

'Give it to me!'

'What are you going to do with it?'

'I don't know yet. I will ask Mr Playmore.'

CHAPTER XLI

Mr Playmore in a New Character

BY that night's post—although I was far from being fit to make the exertion—I wrote to Mr Playmore, to tell him what had taken place, and to beg for his earliest assistance and advice.

The notes in Benjamin's book were partly written in shorthand, and were, on that account, of no use to me in their existing condition. At my request, he made two fair copies. One of the copies I enclosed in my letter to Mr Playmore. The other I laid by me, on my bedside table when I went to rest.

Over and over again, through the long hours of the wakeful night, I read and re-read the last words which had dropped from Miserrimus Dexter's lips. Was it possible to interpret them to any useful purpose? At the very outset, they seemed to set interpretation at defiance. After trying vainly to solve the hopeless problem, I did at last what I might as well have done at first—I threw down the paper in despair. Where were my bright visions of discovery and success now? Scattered to the winds! Was there the faintest chance of the stricken man's return to reason? I remembered too well what I had seen to hope for it. The closing lines of the medical report which I had read in Mr Playmore's office recurred to my memory, in the stillness of the night. 'When the catastrophe has happened, his friends can entertain no hope of his cure: the balance once lost, will be lost for life.'

The confirmation of that terrible sentence was not long in reaching me. The next morning the gardener brought a note, containing the information which the doctor had promised to give me on the previous day.

Miserrimus Dexter and Ariel were still where Benjamin and I had left them together—in the long room. They were watched by skilled attendants; waiting the decision of Dexter's nearest relative (a younger brother), who lived in the country, and who had been communicated with by telegraph. It had been found impossible to part the faithful Ariel from her Master, without using the bodily restraints adopted in cases of raging insanity. The doctor and the gardener (both unusually strong men) had failed to hold the poor creature, when they first attempted to remove her on entering the room. Directly they permitted her to return to her Master, the frenzy vanished: she was perfectly quiet and contented, so long as they let her sit at his feet and look at him.

Sad as this was, the report of Miserrimus Dexter's condition was more melancholy still.

'My patient is in a state of absolute imbecility'—those were the words in the doctor's letter; and the gardener's simple narrative confirmed them as the truest words that could have been used. Dexter was unconscious of poor

Ariel's devotion to him—he did not even appear to know that she was present in the room. For hours together, he remained in a state of utter lethargy in his chair. He showed an animal interest in his meals, and a greedy animal enjoyment of eating and drinking as much as he could get—and that was all. 'This morning,' the honest gardener said to me, at parting, 'we thought he seemed to wake up a bit. Looked about him, you know, and made queer signs with his hands. I couldn't make out what he meant; no more could the doctor. She knew, poor thing—she did. Went and got him his harp, and put his hand up to it. Lord bless you, no use! He couldn't play, no more than I can. Twanged at it anyhow, and grinned and gabbled to himself. No: he'll never come right again. Any person can see that, without the doctor to help 'em. Enjoys his meals, as I told you; and that's all. It would be the best thing that could happen, if it would please God to take him. There's no more to be said. I wish you good morning, Ma'am.'

He went away with the tears in his eyes; and left me, I own it, with the tears in mine.

An hour later, there came some news which revived me. I received a telegram from Mr Playmore, expressed in these welcome words: 'Obliged to go to London by to-night's mail train. Expect me to breakfast to-morrow morning.'

The appearance of the lawyer at our breakfast-table duly followed the appearance of his telegram. His first words cheered me. To my infinite surprise and relief, he was far from sharing the despondent view which I took of my position.

'I don't deny,' he said, 'that there are some serious obstacles in your way. But I should never have called here before I attend to my professional business in London, if Mr Benjamin's notes had not produced a very strong impression on my mind. For the first time, as *I* think—you really have a prospect of success. For the first time, I feel justified in offering (under certain restrictions) to help you. That miserable wretch, in the collapse of his intelligence, has done what he would never have done in the possession of his sense and cunning—he has let us see the first precious glimmerings of the light of truth.'

'Are you sure it *is* the truth?' I asked.

'In two important particulars,' he answered, 'I know it to be the truth. Your idea about him is the right one. His memory (as you suppose) was the least injured of his faculties, and was the last to give way, under the strain of trying to tell that story. I believe his memory to have been speaking to you (unconsciously to himself) in all that he said—from the moment when the first reference to "the letter" escaped him, to the end.'

'But what does the reference to the letter mean?' I asked. 'For my part, I am entirely in the dark about it.'

'So am I,' he answered, frankly. 'The chief one among the obstacles which I mentioned just now, is the obstacle presented by that same "letter." The late Mrs Eustace must have been connected with it in some way—or Dexter would never have spoken of it as "a dagger in his heart"; Dexter would never have coupled her name with the words which describe the tearing up of the letter, and the throwing of it away. I can arrive with some certainty at this result, and I can get no further. I have no more idea than you have of who wrote the letter, or of what was written in it. If we are ever to make that discovery—probably the most important discovery of all—we must despatch our first inquiries a distance of three thousand miles. In plain English, my dear lady, we must send to America.'

This naturally enough, took me completely by surprise. I waited eagerly to hear why we were to send to America.

'It rests with you,' he proceeded, 'when you hear what I have to tell you, to say whether you will go to the expense of sending a man to New York, or not. I can find the right man for the purpose; and I estimate the expense (including a telegram)——'

'Never mind the expense!' I interposed, losing all patience with the eminently Scotch view of the case which put my purse in the first place of importance. 'I don't care for the expense; I want to know what you have discovered.'

He smiled. 'She doesn't care for the expense,' he said to himself, pleasantly. 'How like a woman!'

I might have retorted, 'He thinks of the expense, before he thinks of anything else. How like a Scotchman!' As it was, I was too anxious to be witty. I only drummed impatiently with my fingers on the table; and said, 'Tell me! tell me!'

He took out the fair copy from Benjamin's note-book, which I had sent to him, and showed me these among Dexter's closing words:—'What about the letter? Burn it now. No fire in the grate. No matches in the box. House topsy-turvy. Servants all gone.'

'Do you really understand what those words mean?' I asked.

'I look back into my own experience,' he answered; 'and I understand perfectly what the words mean.'

'And can you make me understand them too?'

'Easily. In those incomprehensible sentences, Dexter's memory has correctly recalled certain facts. I have only to tell you the facts; and you will be as wise as I am. At the time of the Trial, your husband surprised and distressed me by insisting on the instant dismissal of all the household servants at Gleninch. I was instructed to pay them a quarter's wages in advance; to give them the excellent written characters which their good conduct thoroughly deserved, and to see the house clear of them at an hour's notice. Eustace's motive for this summary proceeding was much the same motive which animated his conduct towards you. "If I am ever to return to Gleninch," he said, "I cannot face my honest servants, after the infamy of having stood my trial for murder." There was his reason! Nothing that I could say to him, poor fellow, shook his resolution. I dismissed the servants accordingly. At an hour's notice, they quitted the house, leaving their work for the day all undone. The only persons placed in charge of Gleninch were persons who lived on the outskirts of the park—that is to say, the lodge-keeper and his wife and daughter. On the last day of the Trial, I instructed the daughter to do her best to make the rooms tidy. She was a good girl enough; but she had no experience as a housemaid: it would never enter her head to lay the bedroom fires ready for lighting, or to replenish the empty match-boxes. Those chance words that dropped from Dexter would, no doubt, exactly describe the state of his room, when he returned to Gleninch, with the prisoner and his mother, from Edinburgh. That he tore up the mysterious letter in his bedroom, and (finding no means immediately at hand for burning it) that he threw the fragments into the empty grate, or into the waste-paper basket, seems to be the most reasonable conclusion that we can draw from what we know. In any case, he would not have much time to think about it. Everything was done in a hurry on that day. Eustace and his mother, accompanied by Dexter, left for England the same evening by the night-train. I myself locked up the house, and gave the keys to the lodge-keeper. It was understood that he was to look after the preservation of the reception-rooms on the ground floor; and that his wife and daughter were to perform the same service, between them, in the rooms upstairs. On receiving your letter, I drove at once to Gleninch, to question the old woman on the subject of the bedrooms, and of Dexter's room especially. She remembered the time when the house was shut up, by associating it with the time when she was confined to her bed by an attack of sciatica. She had not crossed the lodge-door, she was sure, for at least a week (if not longer) after Gleninch had been left in charge of her husband and herself. Whatever was done in the way of keeping the bedrooms aired and tidy, during her illness, was done by her daughter. She, and she only, must have disposed of any litter which might have been lying about in Dexter's room. Not a vestige of torn paper, as I can myself certify, is to be discovered in any part of the room, now. Where did the girl find the fragments of the letter? and what did she do with them? Those are the questions (if you approve of it) which we must send three thousand miles away to ask—for this sufficient reason, that the lodge-keeper's daughter was married more than a year since, and that she is settled with her husband in business at New York. It rests with you to decide what is to be done. Don't let me mislead you with false hopes! Don't let me tempt you to throw away your money! Even if this woman does remember what she did with the torn paper, the chances, at this distance of time, are enormously against our ever recovering a single morsel of it. Be in no haste to decide. I have my work to do in the City—I can give you the whole day to think it over.'

'Send the man to New York by the next steamer,' I said. 'There is my decision, Mr Playmore, without keeping you waiting for it!'

He shook his head, in grave disapproval of my impetuosity. In my former interview with him, we had never once touched on the question of money. I was now, for the first time, to make acquaintance with Mr Playmore on the purely Scotch side of his character!

'Why, you don't even know what it will cost you!' he exclaimed, taking out his pocket-book with the air of a man who was equally startled and scandalised. 'Wait till I tot it up,' he said, 'in English and American money.'

'I can't wait! I want to make more discoveries!'

He took no notice of my interruption: he went on impenetrably with his calculations.

'The man will go second-class and will take a return-ticket. Very well. His ticket includes his food; and (being, thank God, a teetotaller) he won't waste your money in buying liquor on board. Arrived at New York, he will go to a cheap German house, where he will, as I am credibly informed, be boarded and lodged at the rate——'

By this time (my patience being completely worn out) I had taken my cheque-book from the table-drawer; had signed my name; and had handed the blank cheque across the table to my legal adviser.

'Fill it in with whatever the man wants,' I said. 'And for Heaven's sake let us get back to Dexter!'

Mr Playmore fell back in his chair, and lifted his hands and eyes to the ceiling. I was not in the least impressed by that solemn appeal to the unseen powers of arithmetic and money. I insisted positively on being fed with more information.

'Listen to this,' I went on; reading from Benjamin's notes. 'What did Dexter mean, when he said, "Number Nine, Caldershaws. Ask for Dandie. You shan't have the Diary. A secret in your ear. The Diary will hang him?" How came Dexter to know what was in my husband's Diary? And what does he mean by "Number Nine, Caldershaws," and the rest of it? Facts again?'

'Facts again!' Mr Playmore answered, 'muddled up together, as you may say—but positive facts for all that. Caldershaws, you must know, is one of the most disreputable districts in Edinburgh. One of my clerks (whom I am in the habit of employing confidentially) volunteered to inquire for "Dandie," at "Number nine." It was a ticklish business, in every way; and my man wisely took a person with him who was known in the neighbourhood. "Number nine" turned out to be (ostensibly) a shop for the sale of rags and old iron; and "Dandie" was suspected of trading now and then, additionally, as a receiver of stolen goods. Thanks to the influence of his companion, backed by a bank-note (which can be repaid, by the way, out of the fund for the American expenses), my clerk succeeded in making the fellow speak. Not to trouble you with needless details, the result in substance was this. A fortnight or more before the date of Mrs Eustace's death, "Dandie" made two keys from wax models supplied to him by a new customer. The mystery observed in the matter by the agent who managed it, excited Dandie's distrust. He had the man privately watched before he delivered the keys; and he ended in discovering that his customer was—Miserrimus Dexter. Wait a little! I have not done yet. Add to this information Dexter's incomprehensible knowledge of the contents of your husband's Diary; and the product is—that the wax models sent to the old iron shop in Caldershaws, were models taken by the theft from the key of the Diary and the key of the table-drawer in which it was kept. I have my own idea of the revelations that are still to come, if this matter is properly followed up. Never mind going into that, at present. Dexter (I tell you again) is answerable for the late Mrs Eustace's death. *How* he is answerable, I believe you are in a fair way of finding out. And, more than that, I say now, what I could not venture to say before—it is a duty towards Justice, as well as a duty towards your husband, to bring the truth to light. As for the difficulties to be encountered, I don't think they need daunt you. The greatest difficulties give way in the end, when they are attacked by the united alliance of patience, resolution,—*and* economy.'

With a strong emphasis on the last words, my worthy adviser, mindful of the flight of time and the claims of business, rose to take his leave.

'One word more,' I said, as he held out his hand. 'Can you manage to see Miserrimus Dexter before you go back to Edinburgh? From what the gardener told me, his brother must be with him by this time. It would be a relief to me to hear the latest news of him, and to hear it from you.'

'It is part of my business in London to see him,' said Mr Playmore. 'But, mind! I have no hope of his recovery: I only wish to satisfy myself that his brother is able and willing to take care of him. So far as *we* are concerned, Mrs Eustace, that unhappy man has said his last words.'

He opened the door—stopped—considered—and came back to me.

'With regard to that matter of sending the agent to America,' he resumed. 'I propose to have the honour of submitting to you a brief abstract——'

'Oh, Mr Playmore!'

'A brief abstract in writing, Mrs Eustace, of the estimated expenses of the whole proceeding. You will be good enough maturely to consider the same; making any remarks on it, tending to economy, which may suggest themselves to your mind at the time. And you will further oblige me, if you approve of the abstract, by yourself filling in the blank space on your cheque with the needful amount in words and figures. No, Madam! I really cannot justify it to my conscience to carry about my person any such loose and reckless document as a blank cheque. There's a total disregard of the first claims of prudence and economy implied in this small slip of paper, which is nothing less than a flat contradiction of the principles that have governed my whole life. I can't submit to flat contradiction. Good morning, Mrs Eustace—good morning.'

He laid my cheque on the table with a low bow, and left me. Among the curious developments of human stupidity which occasionally present themselves to view, surely the least excusable is the stupidity which, to this day, persists in wondering why the Scotch succeed so well in life!

CHAPTER XLII

More Surprises

THE same evening I received my 'abstract' by the hands of a clerk.

It was an intensely characteristic document. My expenses were remorselessly calculated down to shillings and even to pence; and our unfortunate messenger's instructions, in respect of his expenditure, were reduced to a nicety which must have made his life in America nothing less than a burden to him. In mercy to the man, I took the liberty, when I wrote back to Mr Playmore, of slightly increasing the indicated amount of the figures which were to appear on the cheque. I ought to have better known the correspondent whom I had to deal with. Mr Playmore's reply (informing me that our emissary had started on his voyage) returned a receipt in due form—and the whole of the surplus money, to the last farthing!

A few hurried lines accompanied the 'abstract,' and stated the result of the lawyer's visit to Miserrimus Dexter.

There was no change for the better—there was no change at all. Mr Dexter (the brother) had arrived at the house, accompanied by a medical man accustomed to the charge of the insane. The new doctor declined to give any definite opinion on the case until he had studied it carefully with plenty of time at his disposal. It had been accordingly arranged that he should remove Miserrimus Dexter to the asylum of which he was the proprietor, as soon as the preparations for receiving the patient could be completed. The one difficulty that still remained to be met, related to the disposal of the faithful creature who had never left her master, night or day, since the catastrophe had happened. Ariel had no friends, and no money. The proprietor of the asylum could not be expected to receive her without the customary payment; and Mr Dexter's brother 'regretted to say that he was not rich enough to find the money.' A forcible separation from the one human being whom she loved, and a removal in the character of a pauper to a public asylum—such was the prospect which awaited the unfortunate creature, unless some one interfered in her favour before the end of the week.

Under these sad circumstances, good Mr Playmore—passing over the claims of economy in favour of the claims of humanity—suggested that we should privately start a Subscription, and offered to head the list liberally himself.

I must have written all these pages to very little purpose, if it is necessary for me to add that I instantly sent a letter to Mr Dexter (the brother) undertaking to be answerable for whatever money was required, while the subscriptions were being collected, and only stipulating that when Miserrimus Dexter was removed to the asylum, Ariel should accompany him. This was readily conceded. But serious objections were raised, when I further requested that she might be permitted to attend on her master in the asylum, as she had attended on him in the house. The rules of the establishment forbade it, and the universal practice in such cases forbade it, and so on, and so on. However, by dint of perseverance and persuasion, I so far carried my point as to gain a reasonable concession. During certain hours in the day, and under certain wise restrictions, Ariel was to be allowed the privilege of waiting on the Master in his room, as well as of accompanying him when he was brought out in his chair to take the air in the garden. For the honour of humanity, let me add, that the liability which I had undertaken made no very serious demands on my resources. Placed in Benjamin's charge, our subscription list prospered. Friends, and even strangers sometimes, opened their hearts and their purses when they heard Ariel's melancholy story.

The day which followed the day of Mr Playmore's visit brought me news from Spain, in a letter from my mother-in-law. To describe what I felt, when I broke the seal, and read the first lines, is simply impossible. Let Mrs Macallan be heard on this occasion in my place.

Thus she wrote:—

'Prepare yourself, my dearest Valeria, for a delightful surprise. Eustace has justified my confidence in him. When he returns to England, he returns—if you will let him—to his wife.

'This resolution, let me hasten to assure you, has not been brought about by any persuasions of mine. It is the natural outgrowth of your husband's gratitude and your husband's love. The first words he said to me, when he was able to speak, were these: "If I live to return to England, and if I go to Valeria, do you think she will forgive me?" We can only leave it to you, my dear, to give the answer. If you love us, answer us by return of post.

'Having now told you what he said, when I first informed him that you had been his nurse—and remember, if it seems very little, that he is still too weak to speak, except with difficulty—I shall purposely keep my letter back for a few days. My object is to give him time to think, and to frankly tell you of it, if the interval produces any change in his resolution.

'Three days have passed; and there is no change. He has but one feeling now—he longs for the day which is to unite him again to his wife.

'But there is something else connected with Eustace, that you ought to know, and that I ought to tell you.

'Greatly as time and suffering have altered him, in many respects, there is no change, Valeria, in the aversion—the horror I may even say—with which he views your design of inquiring anew into the circumstances which attended the lamentable death of his first wife. I dare not give him your letter: if I touch on the subject, I irritate and distress him. "Has she given up that idea? Can you positively say she has given up that idea?" Over and over again, he has put those questions to me. I have answered—what else could I do, in the miserably feeble state in which he still lies?—I have answered in such a manner as to soothe and satisfy him. I have said, "Relieve your mind of all anxiety on that subject: Valeria has no choice but to give up the idea; the obstacles in her way have proved to be insurmountable—the obstacles have conquered her." This, if you remember, was what I really believed would happen when you and I spoke of that painful topic; and I have heard nothing from you since which has tended to shake my opinion in the smallest degree. If I am right (as I pray God I may be) in the view that I take, you have only to confirm me in your reply, and all will be well. In the other event—that is to say, if you are still determined to persevere in your hopeless project—then make up your mind to face the result. Set Eustace's prejudices at defiance in this particular; and you lose your hold on his gratitude, his penitence, and his love—you will in my belief, never see him again.

'I express myself strongly, in your own interests, my dear, and for your own sake. When you reply, write a few lines to Eustace, enclosed in your letter to me.

'As for the date of our departure, it is still impossible for me to give you any definite information. Eustace recovers very slowly: the doctor has not yet allowed him to leave his bed. And when we do travel, we must journey by easy stages. It will be at least six weeks, at the earliest, before we can hope to be back again in dear Old England.

'Affectionately yours,
CATHERINE MACALLAN.'

I laid down the letter, and did my best (vainly enough for some time) to compose my spirits. To understand the position in which I now found myself, it is only necessary to remember one circumstance. The messenger to whom we had committed our inquiries was, at that moment, crossing the Atlantic on his way to New York.

What was to be done?

I hesitated. Shocking as it may seem to some people, I hesitated. There was really no need to hurry my decision. I had the whole day before me.

I went out, and took a wretched lonely walk, and turned the matter over in my mind. I came home again, and turned the matter over once more, by the fireside. To offend and repel my darling when he was returning to me, penitently returning of his own free will, was what no woman in my position, and feeling as I did, could under any earthly circumstances have brought herself to do. And yet, on the other hand, how, in Heaven's name, could I give up my grand enterprise, at the very time when even wise and prudent Mr Playmore saw such a prospect of succeeding in it that he had actually volunteered to help me! Placed between those two cruel alternatives, which could I choose? Think of your own frailties; and have some mercy on mine. I turned my back on both the alternatives. Those two agreeable fiends, Prevarication and Deceit, took me as it were softly by the hand: 'Don't commit yourself either way, my dear,' they said, in their most persuasive manner. 'Write just enough to compose your mother-in-law, and to satisfy your husband. You have got time before you. Wait and see if Time doesn't stand your friend, and get you out of the difficulty.'

Infamous advice! And yet, I took it—I, who had been well brought up, and who ought to have known better. You who read this shameful confession, would have known better, I am sure. *You* are not included, in the Prayer Book category, among the 'miserable sinners.'

Well! well! let me have virtue enough to tell the truth. In writing to my mother-in-law, I informed her that it had been found necessary to remove Miserrimus Dexter to an asylum—and I left her to draw her own conclusions from that fact, unenlightened by so much as one word of additional information. In the same way, I told my husband a part of the truth, and no more. I said I forgave him with all my heart—and I did! I said he had only to come to me, and I would receive him with open arms—and so I would! As for the rest, let me say with Hamlet: 'The rest is silence.'

Having despatched my unworthy letters, I found myself growing restless, and feeling the want of a change. It would be necessary to wait at least eight or nine days before we could hope to hear by telegraph from New York. I bade farewell for a time to my dear and admirable Benjamin, and betook myself to my old home in the North, at the vicarage of my Uncle Starkweather. My journey to Spain to nurse Eustace had made my peace with my worthy relatives; we had exchanged friendly letters; and I had promised to be their guest as soon as it was possible for me to leave London.

I passed a quiet, and (all things considered) a happy time, among the old scenes. I visited once more the bank by the river side, where Eustace and I had first met. I walked again on the lawn, and loitered through the shrubbery—those favourite haunts in which we had so often talked over our troubles, and so often forgotten them in a kiss. How sadly and strangely had our lives been parted since that time! How uncertain still was the fortune which the future had in store for us!

The associations amid which I was now living, had their softening effect on my heart, their elevating influence over my mind. I reproached myself, bitterly reproached myself, for not having written more fully and frankly to Eustace. Why had I hesitated to sacrifice to him my hopes and my interests in the coming investigation? *He* had not hesitated, poor fellow—*his* first thought was the thought of his wife!

I had passed a fortnight with my uncle and aunt, before I heard again from Mr Playmore. When a letter from him arrived at last, it disappointed me indescribably. A telegram from our messenger informed us that the lodge-keeper's daughter and her husband had left New York, and that he was still in search of a trace of them.

There was nothing to be done but to wait as patiently as we could, on the chance of hearing better news. I remained in the North, by Mr Playmore's advice, so as to be within an easy journey to Edinburgh—in case it might be necessary for me to consult him personally. Three more weeks of weary expectation passed, before a second letter reached me. This time it was impossible to say whether the news was good or bad. It might have been either—it was simply bewildering. Even Mr Playmore himself was taken by surprise. These were the last wonderful words—limited of course by considerations of economy—which reached us (by telegram) from our agent in America:—

> '*Open the dust-heap at Gleninch.*'

CHAPTER XLIII

At Last!

MY letter from Mr Playmore, enclosing the agent's extraordinary telegram, was not inspired by the sanguine view of our prospects which he had expressed to me when we met at Benjamin's house.

'If the telegram means anything,' he wrote, 'it means that the fragments of the torn letter have been cast into the housemaid's bucket (along with the dust, the ashes, and the rest of the litter in the room), and have been emptied on the dust-heap at Gleninch. Since this was done, the accumulated refuse collected from the periodical cleansings of the house, during a term of nearly three years—including, of course, the ashes from the fires kept burning, for the greater part of the year, in the library and picture gallery—have been poured upon the heap, and have buried the precious morsels of paper deeper and deeper, day by day. Even if we have a fair chance of finding these fragments, what hope can we feel, at this distance of time, of recovering them with the writing in a state of preservation? I shall be glad to hear, by return of post, if possible, how the matter strikes you. If you could make it convenient to consult with me personally in Edinburgh, we should save time, when time may be of serious importance to us. While you are at Doctor Starkweather's, you are within easy reach of this place. Please think of it.'

I thought of it seriously enough. The foremost question which I had to consider was the question of my husband.

The departure of the mother and son from Spain had been so long delayed, by the surgeon's orders, that the travellers had only advanced on their homeward journey as far as Bordeaux, when I had last heard from Mrs Macallan three or four days since. Allowing for an interval of repose at Bordeaux, and for the slow rate at which they would be compelled to move afterwards, I might still expect them to arrive in England some time before a letter from the agent in America could reach Mr Playmore. How, in this position of affairs, I could contrive to join the lawyer in Edinburgh, after meeting my husband in London, it was not easy to see. The wise way and the right way, as I thought, was to tell Mr Playmore frankly that I was not mistress of my own movements, and that he had better address his next letter to me at Benjamin's house.

Writing to my legal adviser in this sense, I had a word of my own to add, about the dust-heap and the torn letter.

In the last years of my father's life I had travelled with him in Italy; and I had seen in the Museum at Naples the wonderful relics of a bygone time discovered among the ruins of Pompeii. By way of encouraging Mr Playmore, I now reminded him that the eruption which had overwhelmed the town had preserved, for more than sixteen hundred years, such perishable things as the straw in which pottery had been packed; the paintings on house walls; the dresses worn by the inhabitants; and (most noticeable of all, in our case) a piece of ancient paper, still attached to the volcanic ashes which had fallen over it. If these discoveries had been made after a lapse of sixteen centuries, under a layer of dust and ashes on a large scale, surely we might hope to meet with similar cases of preservation, after a lapse of three or four years only, under a layer of dust and ashes on a small scale? Taking for granted (what was perhaps doubtful enough) that the fragments of the letter could be recovered, my own conviction was that the writing on them, though it might be faded, would certainly still be legible. The very accumulations which Mr Playmore deplored would be the means of preserving them from the rain and the damp. With these modest hints I closed my letter; and thus for once, thanks to my Continental experience, I was able to instruct my lawyer!

Another day passed; and I heard nothing of the travellers.

I began to feel anxious. I made my preparations for the journey southward, over night; and I resolved to start for London the next day—unless I heard of some change in Mrs Macallan's travelling arrangements in the interval.

The post of the next morning decided my course of action. It brought me a letter from my mother-in-law, which added one more to the memorable dates in my domestic calendar.

Eustace and his mother had advanced as far as Paris on their homeward journey, when a cruel disaster had befallen them. The fatigues of travelling, and the excitement of his anticipated meeting with me, had proved together to be too much for my husband. He had held out as far as Paris with the greatest difficulty; and he was now confined to his bed again, struck down by a relapse. The doctors, this time, had no fear for his life; provided that his patience would support him through a lengthened period of the most absolute repose.

'It now rests with you, Valeria,' Mrs Macallan wrote, 'to fortify and comfort Eustace under this new calamity. Do not suppose that he has ever blamed, or thought of blaming, you, for leaving him in Spain, when the surgeon had pronounced him to be out of danger. "It was *I* who left *her*," he said to me, when we first talked about it; "and it is my wife's right to expect that I should go back to her." Those were his words, my dear; and he has done all he can to abide by them. Helpless in his bed, he now asks you to take the will for the deed, and to join him in Paris. I think I know you well enough, my child, to be sure that you will do this; and I need only add one word of caution, before I close my letter. Avoid all reference, not only to the Trial (you will do that of your own accord), but even to our house at Gleninch. You will understand how he feels, in his present state of nervous depression, when I tell you that I should never have ventured on asking you to join him here, if your letter had not informed me that your visits to Dexter were at an end. Would you believe it?—his horror of anything which recalls our past troubles is still so vivid, that he has actually asked me to give my consent to selling Gleninch!'

So Eustace's mother wrote of him. But she had not trusted entirely to her own powers of persuasion. A slip of paper was enclosed in her letter, containing these two lines, traced in pencil—oh, so feebly and so wearily!— by my poor darling himself:—'I am too weak to travel any farther, Valeria. Will you come to me and forgive me?' A few pencil-marks followed; but they were illegible. The writing of those two short sentences had exhausted him.

It is not saying much for myself I know—but, having confessed it when I was wrong, let me at least record it when I did what was right—I decided instantly on giving up all further connexion with the recovery of the torn letter. If Eustace asked me the question, I was resolved to be able to answer truly:—'I have made the sacrifice that assures your tranquillity. When resignation was hardest, I have given way for my husband's sake.'

The motive which had determined me on returning to England, when I first knew that I was mother as well as wife, was still present to my mind when I arrived at this resolution. The one change in me was, that I now treated my husband's tranquillity as the first and foremost consideration. In making this concession, I was not without hope to sustain me. Eustace might yet see the duty of asserting his innocence, in a new light—he might see it as a duty which the father owed to the child.

That morning, I wrote again to Mr Playmore; telling him what my position was, and withdrawing, definitely, from all share in investigating the mystery which lay hidden under the dust-heap at Gleninch.

CHAPTER XLIV

Our New Honeymoon

IT is not to be disguised or denied that my spirits were depressed, on my journey to London.

To resign the one cherished purpose of my life, when I had suffered so much in pursuing it, and when I had (to all appearance) so nearly reached the realisation of my hopes, was putting to a hard trial a woman's fortitude, and a woman's sense of duty. Still, even if the opportunity had been offered to me, I would not have recalled my letter to Mr Playmore. 'It is done, and well done,' I said to myself; 'and I have only to wait a day to be reconciled to it—when I give my husband my first kiss.'

I had planned and hoped to reach London, in time to start for Paris by the night-mail. But the train was twice delayed on the long journey from the North; and there was no help for it but to sleep at Benjamin's villa, and to defer my departure until the morning.

It was, of course, impossible for me to warn my old friend of the change in my plans. My arrival took him by surprise. I found him alone in his library, with a wonderful illumination of lamps and candles; absorbed over some morsels of torn paper scattered on the table before him.

'What in the world are you about?' I asked.

Benjamin blushed—I was going to say, like a young girl. But young girls have given up blushing in these latter days of the age we live in.

'Oh, nothing, nothing!' he said, confusedly. 'Don't notice it.'

He stretched out his hand to brush the morsels of paper off the table. Those morsels raised a sudden suspicion in my mind. I stopped him.

'You have heard from Mr Playmore!' I said. 'Tell me the truth, Benjamin. Yes, or No?'

Benjamin blushed a shade deeper, and answered 'Yes.'

'Where is the letter?'

'I mustn't show it to you, Valeria.'

This (need I say it?) made me determined to see the letter. My best way of persuading Benjamin to show it to me was to tell him of the sacrifice that I had made to my husband's wishes. 'I have no further voice in the matter,' I added, when I had done. 'It now rests entirely with Mr Playmore to go on or to give up; and this is my last opportunity of discovering what he really thinks about it. Don't I deserve some little indulgence? Have I no claim to look at the letter?'

Benjamin was too much surprised, and too much pleased with me, when he heard what had happened, to be able to resist my entreaties. He gave me the letter.

Mr Playmore wrote, to appeal confidentially to Benjamin as a commercial man. In the long course of his occupation in business, it was just possible that he might have heard of cases in which documents had been put together again, after having been torn up, by design or by accident. Even if his experience failed in this particular, he might be able to refer to some authority in London who would be capable of giving an opinion on the subject. By way of explaining his strange request, Mr Playmore reverted to the notes which Benjamin had taken at Miserrimus Dexter's house, and informed him of the serious importance of 'the gibberish' which he had reported under protest. The letter closed by recommending that any correspondence which ensued should be kept a secret from me—on the ground that it might excite false hopes in my mind if I was informed of it.

I now understood the tone which my worthy adviser had adopted in writing to me. His interest in the recovery of the letter was evidently so overpowering that common prudence compelled him to conceal it from me, in case of ultimate failure. This did not look as if Mr Playmore was likely to give up the investigation, on my withdrawal from it. I glanced again at the fragments of paper on Benjamin's table, with an interest in them which I had not felt yet.

'Has anything been found in Gleninch?' I asked.

'No,' said Benjamin. 'I have only been trying experiments with a little note of my own, before I wrote to Mr Playmore.'

'Oh, you have torn up your little note yourself, then?'

'Yes. And, to make it all the more difficult to put them together again, I shook up the pieces in a basket. It's a childish thing to do, my dear, at my age——'

He stopped, looking very much ashamed of himself.

'Well,' I went on; 'and have you succeeded in putting the pieces together again?'

'It's not very easy, Valeria. But I have made a beginning. It's the same principle as the principle in the "Puzzles" which we used to put together when I was a boy. Only get one central bit of it right, and the rest of the Puzzle falls into its place in a longer or a shorter time. Please don't tell anybody, my dear. People might say I was in my dotage.'

People might have said that, who did not know Benjamin as I knew him. I remembered my old friend's delight in guessing riddles in the columns of the cheap periodicals—and I perfectly understood the strong hold that the new 'Puzzle' had taken on his fancy. 'It's almost as interesting as solving Enigmas—isn't it?' I said slyly.

'Enigmas!' Benjamin repeated, contemptuously. 'It's better than any Enigma I ever guessed yet. To think of that gibberish in my note-book having a meaning in it, after all! I only got Mr Playmore's letter this morning; and—I am really almost ashamed to mention it—I have been trying experiments, off and on, ever since. You won't tell upon me, will you?'

I answered the dear old man by a hearty embrace. Now that he had lost his steady moral balance, and had caught the infection of my enthusiasm, I loved him better than ever!

But I was not quite happy, though I tried to appear so. Struggle against it as I might, I felt a little mortified, when I remembered that I had resigned all further connexion with the search for the letter at such a time as this. My one comfort was to think of Eustace. My one encouragement was to keep my mind fixed as constantly as possible on the bright change for the better that now appeared in the domestic prospect. Here, at least, there was no disaster to fear; here I could honestly feel that I had triumphed. My husband had come back to me of his own free will; he had not given way, under the hard weight of evidence—he had yielded to the nobler influences of his gratitude and his love. And I had taken him to my heart again—not because I had made discoveries which left him no other alternative than to live with me, but because I believed in the better mind that had come to him, and loved and trusted him without reserve. Was it not worth some sacrifice to have arrived at this result! True—most true! And yet I was a little out of spirits. Ah, well! well! the remedy was within a day's journey. The sooner I was with Eustace the better.

Early the next morning, I left London for Paris, by the tidal-train. Benjamin accompanied me to the Terminus.

'I shall write to Edinburgh by to-day's post,' he said, in the interval before the train moved out of the station. 'I think I can find the man Mr Playmore wants to help him, if he decides to go on. Have you any message to send, Valeria?'

'No. I have done with it, Benjamin; I have nothing more to say.'

'Shall I write and tell you how it ends, if Mr Playmore does really try the experiment at Gleninch?'

I answered, as I felt, a little bitterly.

'Yes,' I said. 'Write and tell me, if the experiment fails.'

My old friend smiled. He knew me better than I knew myself.

'All right!' he said, resignedly. 'I have got the address of your banker's correspondent in Paris. You will have to go there for money, my dear; and you *may* find a letter waiting for you in the office, when you least expect it. Let me hear how your husband goes on. Good-bye—and God bless you!'

That evening, I was restored to Eustace.

He was too weak, poor fellow, even to raise his head from the pillow. I knelt down at the bedside and kissed him. His languid weary eyes kindled with a new life, as my lips touched his. 'I must try to live now,' he whispered, 'for your sake.'

My mother-in-law had delicately left us together. When he said those words, the temptation to tell him of the new hope that had come to brighten our lives was more than I could resist.

'You must try to live now, Eustace,' I said, 'for some one else, besides me.'

His eyes looked wonderingly into mine.

'Do you mean my mother?' he asked.

I laid my head on his bosom, and whispered back,

'I mean your child.'

I had all my reward for all that I had given up! I forgot Mr Playmore; I forgot Gleninch. Our new honeymoon dates, in my remembrance, from that day.

The quiet time passed, in the bye street in which we lived. The outer stir and tumult of Parisian life ran its daily course around us, unnoticed and unheard. Steadily, though slowly, Eustace gained strength. The doctors, with a word or two of caution, left him almost entirely to me. 'You are his physician,' they said; 'the happier you make him, the sooner he will recover.' The quiet monotonous round of my new life was far from wearying me. I, too, wanted repose—I had no interests, no pleasures, out of my husband's room.

Once, and only once, the placid surface of our lives was just gently ruffled by an allusion to the past. Something that I accidentally said, reminded Eustace of our last interview at Major Fitz-David's house. He referred, very delicately, to what I had then said of the Verdict pronounced on him at the Trial; and he left me to infer that a word from my lips, confirming what his mother had already told him, would quiet his mind at once and for ever.

My answer involved no embarrassments or difficulties: I could, and did, honestly tell him that I had made his wishes my law. But it was hardly in womanhood, I am afraid, to be satisfied with merely replying, and to leave it there. I thought it due to me that Eustace too should concede something, in the way of an assurance which might quiet *my* mind. As usual with me, the words followed the impulse to speak them. 'Eustace,' I asked, 'are you quite cured of those cruel doubts which once made you leave me?'

His answer (as he afterwards said) made me blush with pleasure. 'Ah, Valeria, I should never have gone away, if I had known you then as well as I know you now!'

So the last shadows of distrust melted away out of our lives.

The very remembrance of the turmoil and the trouble of my past days in London seemed now to fade from my memory. We were lovers again; we were absorbed again in each other; we could almost fancy that our marriage dated back once more to only a day or two since. But one last victory over myself was wanting to make my happiness complete. I still felt secret longings, in those dangerous moments when I was left to myself, to know whether the search for the torn letter had, or had not, taken place. What wayward creatures we are! With everything that a woman could want to make her happy, I was ready to put that happiness in peril, rather than remain ignorant of what was going on at Gleninch! I actually hailed the day when my empty purse gave me an excuse for going to my banker's correspondent on business, and so receiving any letters waiting for me which might be placed in my hands.

I applied for my money without knowing what I was about; wondering all the time whether Benjamin had written to me or not. My eyes wandered over the desks and tables in the office, looking for letters furtively. Nothing of the sort was visible. But a man appeared from an inner office: an ugly man, who was yet beautiful to my eyes, for this sufficient reason—he had a letter in his hand, and he said, 'Is this for you, ma'am?'

A glance at the address showed me Benjamin's handwriting.

Had they tried the experiment of recovering the letter? and had they failed?

Somebody put my money in my bag, and politely led me out to the little hired carriage which was waiting for me at the door. I remember nothing distinctly, until I looked at my news from Benjamin on my way home. His first words told me that the dust-heap had been examined, and that the fragments of the torn letter had been found!

CHAPTER XLV

The Dust-Heap Disturbed

MY head turned giddy. I was obliged to wait and let my overpowering agitation subside, before I could read any more.

Looking at the letter again, after an interval, my eyes fell accidentally on a sentence near the end, which surprised and startled me.

I stopped the driver of the carriage, at the entrance to the street in which our lodgings were situated, and told him to take me to the beautiful Park of

Paris—the famous Bois de Boulogne. My object was to gain time enough, in this way, to read the letter carefully through by myself, and to ascertain whether I ought, or ought not, to keep the receipt of it a secret, before I confronted my husband and his mother at home.

This precaution taken, I read the narrative which my good Benjamin had so wisely and so thoughtfully written for me. Treating the various incidents methodically, he began with the Report which had arrived, in due course of mail, from our agent in America.

Our man had successfully traced the lodge-keeper's daughter and her husband to a small town in one of the Western States. Mr Playmore's letter of introduction at once secured him a cordial reception from the married pair, and a patient hearing when he stated the object of his voyage across the Atlantic.

His first questions led to no very encouraging results. The woman was confused and surprised, and was apparently quite unable to exert her memory to any useful purpose. Fortunately, her husband proved to be a very intelligent man. He took the agent privately aside, and said to him, 'I understand my wife, and you don't. Tell me exactly what it is you want to know, and leave it to me to discover how much she remembers, and how much she forgets.'

This sensible suggestion was readily accepted. The agent waited for events, a day and a night.

Early the next morning, the husband said to him,—'Talk to my wife now, and you will find she has something to tell you. Only mind this! Don't laugh at her when she speaks of trifles. She is half ashamed to speak of trifles, even to me. Thinks men are above such matters, you know. Listen quietly, and let her talk—and you will get at it all in that way.'

The agent followed his instructions, and 'got at it' as follows:—

The woman remembered, perfectly well, being sent to clean the bedrooms and put them tidy, after the gentlefolks had all left Gleninch. Her mother had a bad hip at the time, and could not go with her and help her. She did not much fancy being alone in the great house, after what had happened in it. On her way to her work, she passed two of the cottagers' children in the neighbourhood, at play in the park. Mr Macallan was always kind to his poor tenants, and never objected to the young ones round about having a run on the grass. The two children idly followed her to the house. She took them inside, along with her; not liking the place, as already mentioned, and feeling that they would be company in the solitary rooms.

She began her work in the Guests' Corridor—leaving the room in the other Corridor, in which the death had happened, to the last.

There was very little to do in the two first rooms. There was not litter enough, when she had swept the floors and cleaned the grates, to even half fill the housemaid's bucket which she carried with her. The children followed her about; and, all things considered, were 'very good company,' in the lonely place.

The third room (that is to say, the bedchamber which had been occupied by Miserrimus Dexter) was in a much worse state than the other two, and wanted a great deal of tidying. She did not much notice the children here, being occupied with her work. The litter was swept up from the carpet, and the cinders and ashes were taken out of the grate, and the whole of it was in the bucket, when her attention was recalled to the children by hearing one of them cry.

She looked about the room without at first discovering them.

A fresh outburst of crying led her in the right direction, and showed her the children under a table in a corner of the room. The youngest of the two had got into a waste-paper basket. The eldest had found an old bottle of gum, with a brush fixed in the cork, and was gravely painting the face of the smaller child with what little remained of the contents of the bottle. Some natural struggles, on the part of the little creature, had ended in the overthrow of the basket and the usual outburst of crying had followed as a matter of course.

In this state of things the remedy was soon applied. The woman took the bottle away from the eldest child, and gave it a 'box on the ear.' The younger one she set on its legs again, and she put the two 'in the corner' to keep them quiet. This done, she swept up such fragments of the torn paper in the basket as had fallen on the floor; threw them back again into the basket, along with the gum-bottle; fetched the bucket, and emptied the basket into it; and then proceeded to the fourth and last room in the corridor, where she finished her work for that day.

Leaving the house, with the children after her, she took the filled bucket to the dust-heap, and emptied it in a hollow place among the rubbish, about half-way up the mound. Then she took the children home; and there was an end of it, for the day.

Such was the result of the appeal made to the woman's memory of domestic events at Gleninch.

The conclusion at which Mr Playmore arrived, from the facts submitted to him, was, that we might now hope to recover the letter. Thrown on the refuse ashes in the housemaid's bucket, and afterwards covered by litter from the fourth room, the torn morsels would be protected above as well as below, when they were emptied on the dust-heap.

Succeeding weeks and months would add to that protection, by adding to the accumulated refuse. In the neglected condition of the grounds, the dust-heap had not been disturbed in search of manure. There it stood, untouched, from the time when the family left Gleninch to the present day. And there, hidden deep somewhere in the mound, the fragments of the letter must be!

Such were the lawyer's conclusions. He had written immediately to communicate them to Benjamin. And, thereupon, what had Benjamin done?

After having tried his powers of reconstruction on his own correspondence, the prospect of experimenting on the mysterious letter itself had proved to be a temptation too powerful for the old man to resist. 'I almost fancy, my dear, this business of yours has bewitched me,' he wrote. 'You see I have the misfortune to be an idle man. I have time to spare and money to spare. And the end of it is, that I am here at Gleninch, engaged on my own responsibility (with good Mr Playmore's permission), in searching the dust-heap!'

Benjamin's description of his first view of the field of action at Gleninch followed these characteristic lines of apology.

I passed over the description, without ceremony. My remembrance of the scene was too vivid to require any prompting of that sort. I saw again, in the dim evening light, the unsightly mound which had so strangely attracted my attention at Gleninch. I heard again the words in which Mr Playmore had explained to me the custom of the dust-heap in Scotch country-houses. What had Benjamin and Mr Playmore done? What had Benjamin and Mr Playmore found? For me, the true interest in the narrative was there—and to that portion of it I eagerly turned next.

They had proceeded methodically, of course, with one eye on the pounds, shillings, and pence, and the other on the object in view. In Benjamin, the lawyer had found what he had not met with in me—a sympathetic mind, alive to the value of 'an abstract of the expenses,' and conscious of that most remunerative of human virtues, the virtue of economy.

At so much a week, they had engaged men to dig into the mound and to sift the ashes. At so much a week, they had hired a tent to shelter the open dust-heap from wind and weather. At so much a week, they had engaged the services of a young man (personally known to Benjamin), who was employed in a laboratory under a professor of chemistry, and who had distinguished himself by his skilful manipulation of paper in a recent case of forgery on a well-known London firm. Armed with these preparations, they had begun the work; Benjamin and the young chemist living at Gleninch, and taking it in turns to superintend the proceedings.

Three days of labour with the spade and the sieve produced no results of the slightest importance. However, the matter was in the hands of two quietly-determined men. They declined to be discouraged. They went on.

On the fourth day, the first morsels of paper were found.

Upon examination, they proved to be the fragments of a tradesman's prospectus. Nothing dismayed, Benjamin and the young chemist still persevered. At the end of the day's work, more pieces of paper were turned up. These proved to be covered with written characters. Mr Playmore (arriving at Gleninch, as usual, every evening on the conclusion of his labours in the law) was consulted as to the handwriting. After careful examination, he declared that the mutilated portions of sentences submitted to him had been written, beyond all doubt, by Eustace Macallan's first wife!

This discovery roused the enthusiasm of the searchers to fever height.

Spades and sieves were from that moment forbidden utensils. However unpleasant the task might be, hands alone were used in the farther examination of the mound. The first and foremost necessity was to place the morsels of paper (in flat cardboard boxes prepared for the purpose), in their order as they were found. Night came; the labourers were dismissed; Benjamin and his two colleagues worked on by lamplight. The morsels of paper were turned up by dozens, instead of by ones and twos. For awhile the search prospered in this way; and then the morsels appeared no more. Had they all been recovered? or would renewed hand digging yield more yet? The next light layers of rubbish were carefully removed—and the grand discovery of the day followed. There (upside down) was the gum-bottle, which the lodge-keeper's daughter had spoken of! And, more precious still, under it, were more fragments of written paper, all stuck together in a little lump, by the last drippings from the gum-bottle dropping upon them as they lay in the dust-heap!

The scene now shifted to the interior of the house. When the searchers next assembled, they met at the great table in the library at Gleninch.

Benjamin's experience with the 'Puzzles' which he had put together in the days of his boyhood proved to be of some use to his companions. The fragments accidentally stuck together, would, in all probability, be found to fit each other, and would certainly (in any case) be the easiest fragments to reconstruct, as a centre to start from.

The delicate business of separating these pieces of paper, and of preserving them in the order in which they had adhered to each other, was assigned to the practised fingers of the chemist. But the difficulties of his task did not end here. The writing was (as usual in letters) traced on both sides of the paper, and it could only be preserved for the purpose of reconstruction by splitting each morsel into two—so as artificially to make a blank side, on which could be spread the fine cement used for reuniting the fragments in their original form.

To Mr Playmore and Benjamin, the prospect of successfully putting the letter together, under these disadvantages, seemed to be almost hopeless. Their skilled colleague soon satisfied them that they were wrong.

He drew their attention to the thickness of the paper—note-paper of the strongest and best quality—on which the writing was traced. It was of more than twice the substance of the last paper on which he had operated, when he was engaged in the forgery case; and it was, on that account, comparatively easy for him (aided by the mechanical appliances which he had brought from London) to split the morsels of the torn paper, within a given space of time which might permit them to begin the reconstruction of the letter that night.

With these explanations, he quietly devoted himself to his work. While Benjamin and the lawyer were still poring over the scattered morsels of the letter which had been first discovered, and trying to piece them together again, the chemist had divided the greater part of the fragments specially confided to him into two halves each; and had correctly put together some five or six sentences of the letter, on the smooth sheet of cardboard prepared for that purpose.

They looked eagerly at the reconstructed writing, so far.

It was correctly done: the sense was perfect. The first result gained by examination was remarkable enough to reward them for all their exertions. The language used, plainly identified the person to whom the late Mrs Eustace had addressed her letter.

That person was—my husband.

And the letter thus addressed—if the plainest circumstantial evidence could be trusted—was identical with the letter which Miserrimus Dexter had suppressed until the Trial was over, and had then destroyed by tearing it up.

These were the discoveries that had been made, at the time when Benjamin wrote to me. He had been on the point of posting his letter, when Mr Playmore had suggested that he should keep it by him for a few days longer, on the chance of having more still to tell me.

'We are indebted to her for these results,' the lawyer had said. 'But for her resolution, and her influence over Miserrimus Dexter, we should never have discovered what the dust-heap was hiding from us—we should never have seen so much as a glimmering of the truth. She has the first claim to the fullest information. Let her have it.'

The letter had been accordingly kept back for three days. That interval being at an end, it was hurriedly resumed, and concluded in terms which indescribably alarmed me.

'The chemist is advancing rapidly with his part of the work' (Benjamin wrote); 'and I have succeeded in putting together a separate portion of the torn writing which makes sense. Comparison of what he has accomplished with what I have accomplished has led to startling conclusions. Unless Mr Playmore and I are entirely wrong (and God grant we may be so!) there is a serious necessity for your keeping the reconstruction of the letter strictly secret from everybody about you. The disclosures suggested by what has come to light are so heart-rending and so dreadful, that I cannot bring myself to write about them, until I am absolutely obliged to do so. Please forgive me for disturbing you with this news. We are bound, sooner or later, to consult with you in the matter; and we think it right to prepare your mind for what may be to come.'

To this there was added a postscript in Mr Playmore's handwriting.

'Pray observe strictly the caution which Mr Benjamin impresses on you. And bear this in mind, as a warning from *me*. If we succeed in reconstructing the entire letter, the last person living who ought (in my opinion) to be allowed to see it, is—your husband.'

I read those startling words; and I asked myself what I was to do next.

As matters now stood, my husband's tranquillity was, so to speak, committed to my charge. It was surely due to *himself*, that I should not receive Benjamin's letter and Mr Playmore's postscript in silence. At the same time, it was due to myself that I should honestly tell Eustace I was in correspondence with Gleninch—only waiting to speak until I knew more than I knew now.

Thus I reasoned with myself. And, to this day, I am not quite sure whether I was right or wrong.

CHAPTER XLVI
The Crisis Deferred

'TAKE care, Valeria!' said Mrs Macallan. 'I ask you no questions; I only caution you, for your own sake. Eustace has noticed, what I have noticed—Eustace has seen a change in you. Take care!'

So my mother-in-law spoke to me, later in the day, when we happened to be alone. I had done my best to conceal all traces of the effect produced on me by the strange and terrible news from Gleninch. But who could read what I had read—who could feel what I now felt—and still maintain an undisturbed serenity of look and manner? If I had been the vilest hypocrite living, I doubt, even then, if my face could have kept my secret, while my mind was full of Benjamin's letter.

Having spoken her word of caution, Mrs Macallan made no further advance to me. I dare say she was right. Still, it seemed hard to be left, without a word of advice or of sympathy, to decide for myself what it was my duty to my husband to do next.

To show him Benjamin's narrative, in his state of health, and in the face of the warning addressed to me, was simply out of the question. At the same time, it was equally impossible, after I had already betrayed myself, to keep him entirely in the dark. I thought over it anxiously in the night. When the morning came, I decided to appeal to my husband's confidence in me.

I went straight to the point, in these terms:

'Eustace, your mother said yesterday that you noticed a change in me, when I came back from my drive. Is she right?'

'Quite right, Valeria,' he answered—speaking in lower tones than usual, and not looking at me.

'We have no concealments from each other, now,' I answered. 'I ought to tell you, and I do tell you, that I found a letter from England waiting at the banker's, which has caused me some agitation and alarm. Will you leave it to me to choose my own time for speaking more plainly? And will you believe, love, that I am really doing my duty towards you, as a good wife, in making this request?'

I paused. He made no answer: I could see that he was secretly struggling with himself. Had I ventured too far? Had I over-estimated the strength of my influence? My heart beat fast, my voice faltered—but I summoned courage enough to take his hand, and to make a last appeal to him. 'Eustace!' I said. 'Don't you know me, yet, well enough to trust me?'

He turned towards me for the first time. I saw a last vanishing trace of doubt in his eyes as they looked into mine.

'You promise, sooner or later, to tell me the whole truth?' he said.

'I promise with all my heart!'

'I trust you, Valeria!'

His brightening eyes told me that he really meant what he said. We sealed our compact with a kiss. Pardon me for mentioning these trifles—I am still writing (if you will kindly remember it) of our new honeymoon.

By that day's post I answered Benjamin's letter, telling him what I had done, and entreating him, if he and Mr Playmore approved of my conduct, to keep me informed of any future discoveries which they might make at Gleninch.

After an interval—an endless interval, as it seemed to me—of ten days more, I received a second letter from my old friend; with another postscript added by Mr Playmore.

'We are advancing steadily and successfully with the putting together of the letter,' Benjamin wrote. 'The one new discovery which we have made is of serious importance to your husband. We have reconstructed certain sentences, declaring, in the plainest words, that the arsenic which Eustace procured was purchased at the request of his wife, and was in her possession at Gleninch. This, remember, is in the handwriting of the wife, and is signed by the wife—as we have also found out. Unfortunately, I am obliged to add, that the objection to taking your husband into our confidence, mentioned when I last wrote, still remains in force—in greater force, I may say, than ever. The more we make out of the letter, the more inclined we are (if we only studied our own feelings) to throw it back into the dust-heap, in mercy to the memory of the unhappy writer. I shall keep this open for a day or two. If there is more news to tell you, by that time, you will hear of it from Mr Playmore.'

Mr Playmore's postscript followed, dated three days later.

'The concluding part of the late Mrs Macallan's letter to her husband,' the lawyer wrote, 'has proved accidentally to be the first part which we have succeeded in piecing together. With the exception of a few gaps still left, here and there, the writing of the closing paragraphs has been perfectly reconstructed. I have neither the time nor the inclination to write to you on this sad subject, in any detail. In a fortnight more, at the longest, we shall, I hope, send you a copy of the letter, complete from the first line to the last. Meanwhile, it is my duty to tell you that there is one bright side to this otherwise deplorable and shocking document. Legally speaking, as well as morally speaking, it absolutely vindicates your husband's innocence. And it may be lawfully used for this purpose—if he can reconcile it to his conscience, and to the mercy due to the memory of the dead, to permit the public exposure of the letter in Court. Understand me, he cannot be tried again on what we call the criminal charge—for certain technical reasons with which I need not trouble you. But, if the facts which were involved at the criminal trial can also be shown to be involved in a civil case (and, in this case, they can), the entire matter may be made the subject of a new legal inquiry; and the verdict of a second jury, completely vindicating your husband, may be thus obtained. Keep this information to yourself for the present. Preserve the position which you have so sensibly adopted towards Eustace, until you have read the restored letter. When you have done this, my own idea is that you will shrink, in pity to *him*, from letting him see it. How he is to be kept in ignorance of what we have discovered is another question, the discussion of which must be deferred until we can consult together. Until that time comes, I can only repeat my advice,—Wait till the next news reaches you from Gleninch.'

I waited. What I suffered, what Eustace thought of me, does not matter. Nothing matters now but the facts.

In less than a fortnight more, the task of restoring the letter was completed. Excepting certain instances, in which the morsels of the torn paper had been irretrievably lost—and in which it had been necessary to complete the sense, in harmony with the writer's intention—the whole letter had been put together; and the promised copy of it was forwarded to me in Paris.

Before you, too, read that dreadful letter, do me one favour. Let me briefly remind you of the circumstances under which Eustace Macallan married his first wife.

Remember that the poor creature fell in love with him, without awakening any corresponding affection on his side. Remember that he separated himself from her, and did all he could to avoid her, when he found this out. Remember that she presented herself at his residence in London, without a word of warning; that he did his best to save her reputation; that he failed, through no fault of his own; and that he ended, rashly ended, in a moment of despair, by marrying her, to silence the scandal that must otherwise have blighted her life as a woman for the rest of her days. Bear all this in mind (it is the sworn testimony of respectable witnesses); and pray do not forget—however foolishly and blameably he may have written about her in the secret pages of his Diary—that he was proved to have done his best to conceal from his wife the aversion which the poor soul inspired in him; and that he was (in the opinion of those who could best judge him) at least a courteous and a considerate husband, if he could be no more.

And now take the letter. It asks but one favour of you; it asks to be read by the light of Christ's teaching:—'Judge not, that ye be not judged.'

CHAPTER XLVII

The Wife's Confession

'Gleninch, October 19, 18——.

'MY HUSBAND:—

I HAVE something very painful to tell you, about one of your oldest friends.

'You have never encouraged me to come to you with any confidences of mine. If you had allowed me to be as familiar with you as some wives are with their husbands, I should have spoken to you personally, instead of writing. As it is, I don't know how you might receive what I have to say to you, if I said it by word of mouth. So I write.

'The man against whom I warn you is still a guest in this house—Miserrimus Dexter. No falser or wickeder creature walks the earth. Don't throw my letter aside! I have waited to say this until I could find proof that might satisfy you. I have got the proof.

'You may remember that I ventured to express some disapproval, when you first told me you had asked this man to visit us. If you had allowed me time to explain myself, I might have been bold enough to give you a good reason for the aversion I felt towards your friend. But you would not wait. You hastily (and most unjustly) accused me of feeling prejudiced against the miserable creature on account of his deformity. No other feeling than compassion for deformed persons has ever entered my mind. I have, indeed, almost a fellow-feeling for them; being that next worst thing myself to a deformity—a plain woman. I objected to Mr Dexter as your guest, because he had asked me to be his wife in past days, and because I had reason to fear that he still regarded me (after my marriage) with a guilty and a horrible love. Was it not my duty, as a good wife, to object to his being your guest at Gleninch? And was it not your duty, as a good husband, to encourage me to say more?

'Well! Mr Dexter has been your guest for many weeks; and Mr Dexter has dared to speak to me again of his love. He has insulted me, and insulted you, by declaring that *he* adores me, and that *you* hate me. He has promised me a life of unalloyed happiness, in a foreign country with my lover. And he has prophesied for me a life of unendurable misery, at home with my husband.

'Why did I not make my complaint to you, and have this monster dismissed from the house at once and for ever?

'Are you sure you would have believed me, if I had complained, and if your bosom friend had denied all intention of insulting me? I heard you once say (when you were not aware that I was within hearing) that the vainest women were always the ugly women. You might have accused *me* of vanity. Who knows?

'But I have no desire to shelter myself under this excuse. I am a jealous unhappy creature; always doubtful of your affection for me; always fearing that another woman has got my place in your heart. Miserrimus Dexter has practised on this weakness of mine. He has declared he can prove to me (if I will permit him) that I am, in your secret heart, an object of loathing to you; that you shrink from touching me; that you curse the hour when you were foolish enough to make me your wife. For two nights and days I struggled against the temptation to let him produce his proofs. It was a terrible temptation, to a woman who was far from feeling sure of the sincerity of your affection for her; and it ended in getting the better of my resistance. I wickedly concealed the disgust which the wretch inspired in me; I wickedly gave him leave to explain himself; I wickedly permitted this enemy of yours and of mine to take me into his confidence. And why? Because I loved you and you only; and because Miserrimus Dexter's proposal did, after all, echo a doubt of you that had long been gnawing secretly at my heart.

'Forgive me, Eustace! This is my first sin against you. It shall be my last.

'I will not spare myself; I will write a full confession of what I said to him and of what he said to me. You may make me suffer for it, when you know what I have done; but you will at least be warned in time; you will see your false friend in his true light.

'I said to him, "How can you prove to me that my husband hates me in secret?"

'He answered, "I can prove it, under his own handwriting; you shall see it in his Diary."

'I said, "His Diary has a lock; and the drawer in which he keeps it has a lock. How can you get at the Diary and the drawer?"

'He answered, "I have my own way of getting at both of them, without the slightest risk of being discovered by your husband. All you have to do is to give me the opportunity of seeing you privately. I will engage, in return, to bring the open Diary with me to your room."

'I said, "How can I give you the opportunity? What do you mean?"'

'He pointed to the key, in the door of communication between my room and the little study.'

'He said, "With my infirmity, I may not be able to profit by the first opportunity of visiting you here, unobserved: I must be able to choose my own time and my own way of getting to you secretly. Let me take the key; leaving the door locked. When the key is missed, if *you* say it doesn't matter—if *you* point out that the door is locked, and tell the servants not to trouble themselves about finding the key—there will be no disturbance in the house; and I shall be in secure possession of a means of communication with you which no one will suspect. Will you do this?"'

'I have done it.'

'Yes! I have become the accomplice of this double-faced villain. I have degraded myself, and outraged you, by making an appointment to pry into your Diary. I know how base my conduct is. I can make no excuse. I can only repeat that I love you, and that I am sorely afraid you don't love me. And Miserrimus Dexter offers to end my doubts by showing me the most secret thoughts of your heart, in your own writing.'

'He is to be with me, for this purpose (while you are out), some time in the course of the next two hours. I shall decline to be satisfied with only once looking at your Diary; and I shall make an appointment with him to bring it to me again, at the same time to-morrow. Before then, you will receive these lines, by the hand of my nurse. Go out as usual, after reading them. But return privately, and unlock the table drawer in which you keep your book. You will find it gone. Post yourself quietly in the little study; and you will discover the Diary (when Miserrimus Dexter leaves me), in the hands of your friend.[1]

'October 20.

'I have read your Diary.

'At last I know what you really think of me. I have read what Miserrimus Dexter promised I should read—the confession of your loathing for me, in your own handwriting.'

'You will not receive what I wrote to you yesterday, at the time, or in the manner, which I had proposed. Long as my letter is, I have still (after reading your Diary) some more words to add. After I have closed and sealed the envelope, and addressed it to you, I shall put it under my pillow. It will

---

[1] Note by Mr Playmore:—The greatest difficulties of reconstruction occurred in this first portion of the torn letter. In the fourth paragraph from the beginning, we have been obliged to supply lost words in no less than three places. In the ninth, tenth, and seventeenth paragraphs the same proceeding was, in a greater or less degree, found to be necessary. In all these cases, the utmost pains have been taken to supply the deficiency in exact accordance with what appeared to be the meaning of the writer, as indicated in the existing pieces of the manuscript.

be found there when I am laid out for the grave—and then, Eustace (when it is too late for hope or help), my letter will be given to you.

'Yes: I have had enough of my life. Yes: I mean to die.

'I have already sacrificed everything but my life to my love for you. Now I know that my love is not returned, the last sacrifice left is easy. My death will set you free to marry Mrs Beauly.

'You don't know what it cost me to control my hatred of her, and to beg her to pay her visit here, without minding my illness. I could never have done it if I had not been so fond of you, and so fearful of irritating you against me by showing my jealousy. And how did you reward me? Let your Diary answer! "I tenderly embraced her, this very morning; and I hope, poor soul, she did not discover the effort that it cost me."

'Well, I have discovered it now. I know that you privately think your life with me "a purgatory." I know that you have compassionately hidden from me the "sense of shrinking that comes over you when you are obliged to submit to my caresses." I am nothing but an obstacle—an "utterly distasteful" obstacle—between you and the woman whom you love so dearly that you "adore the earth which she touches with her foot." Be it so! I will stand in your way no longer. It is no sacrifice and no merit on my part. Life is unendurable to me, now I know that the man whom I love with all my heart and soul, secretly shrinks from me whenever I touch him.

'I have got the means of death close at hand.

'The arsenic that I twice asked you to buy for me is in my dressing-case. I deceived you when I mentioned some common-place reasons for wanting it. My true reason was to try if I could not improve my ugly complexion— not from any vain feeling of mine: only to make myself look better and more lovable in your eyes. I have taken some of it for that purpose; but I have got plenty left to kill myself with. The poison will have its use at last. It might have failed to improve my complexion. It will not fail to relieve you of your ugly wife.

'Don't let me be examined after death. Show this letter to the doctor who attends me. It will tell him that I have committed suicide; it will prevent any innocent person from being suspected of poisoning me. I want nobody to be blamed or punished. I shall remove the chemist's label, and carefully empty the bottle containing the poison, so that he may not suffer on my account.

'I must wait here, and rest a little while—then take up my letter again. It is far too long already. But these are my farewell words. I may surely dwell a little on my last talk with you!

'October 21. Two o'clock in the morning.

'I sent you out of the room yesterday, when you came in to ask how I had passed the night. And I spoke of you shamefully, Eustace, after you had gone, to the hired nurse who attends on me. Forgive me. I am almost beside myself now. You know why.

'Half-past three.

'Oh, my husband, I have done the deed which will relieve you of the wife whom you hate! I have taken the poison—all of it that was left in the paper packet, which was the first that I found. If this is not enough to kill me, I have more left in the bottle.

'Ten minutes past five.

'You have just gone, after giving me my composing draught. My courage failed me at the sight of you. I thought to myself, "If he looks at me kindly, I will confess what I have done, and let him save my life." You never looked at me at all. You only looked at the medicine. I let you go, without saying a word.

'Half-past five.

'I begin to feel the first effects of the poison. The nurse is asleep at the foot of my bed. I won't call for assistance; I won't wake her. I will die.

'Half-past nine.

'The agony was beyond my endurance—I woke the nurse. I have seen the doctor.

'Nobody suspects anything. Strange to say, the pain has left me; I have evidently taken too little of the poison. I must open the bottle which contains the larger quantity. Fortunately, you are not near me—my resolution to die, or rather, my loathing of life, remains as bitterly unaltered as ever. To make sure of my courage, I have forbidden the nurse to send for you. She has just gone downstairs by my orders. I am free to get the poison out of my dressing case.

'Ten minutes to ten.

'I had just time to hide the bottle (after the nurse had left me), when you came into my room.

'I had another moment of weakness when I saw you. I determined to give myself a last chance of life. That is to say, I determined to offer you a last opportunity of treating me kindly. I asked you to get me a cup of tea. If, in paying me this little attention, you only encouraged me by one fond word or one fond look, I resolved not to take the second dose of poison.

'You obeyed my wishes, but you were not kind. You gave me my tea, Eustace, as if you were giving a drink to your dog. And then you wondered, in a languid way (thinking, I suppose, of Mrs Beauly all the time), at my dropping the cup in handing it back to you. I really could not help it; my hand *would* tremble. In my place, your hand might have trembled, too—with the arsenic under the bedclothes. You politely hoped, before you went away, that the tea would do me good—and, oh God, you could not even look at me when you said that! You looked at the broken bits of the tea-cup.

'The instant you were out of the room I took the poison—a double dose this time.

'I have a little request to make here, while I think of it.

'After removing the label from the bottle, and putting it back, clean, in my dressing-case, it struck me that I had failed to take the same precaution (in the early morning) with the empty paper packet, bearing on it the name of the other chemist. I threw it aside on the counterpane of the bed, among some other loose papers. My ill-tempered nurse complained of the litter, and crumpled them all up, and put them away somewhere. I hope the chemist will not suffer through my carelessness. Pray bear it mind to say that he is not to blame.

'Dexter—something reminds me of Miserrimus Dexter. He has put your Diary back again in the drawer, and he presses me for an answer to his proposals. Has this false wretch any conscience? If he has, even *he* will suffer—when my death answers him.

'The nurse has been in my room again. I have sent her away. I have told her I want to be alone.

'How is the time going? I cannot find my watch. Is the pain coming back again, and paralysing me? I don't feel it keenly yet.

'It may come back, though, at any moment. I have still to close my letter, and to address it to you. And, besides, I must save up my strength to hide it under the pillow, so that nobody may find it until after my death.

'Farewell, my dear. I wish I had been a prettier woman. A more loving woman (towards you) I could not be. Even now, I dread the sight of your dear face. Even now, if I allowed myself the luxury of looking at you, I don't know that you might not charm me into confessing what I have done—before it is too late to save me.

'But you are not here. Better as it is! better as it is!

'Once more, farewell! Be happier than you have been with me. I love you, Eustace—I forgive you. When you have nothing else to think about, think sometimes, as kindly as you can, of your poor ugly.

'SARA MACALLAN.'[1]

---

[1] Note by Mr Playmore:—The lost words and phrases supplied in this concluding portion of the letter are so few in number that it is needless to mention them. The fragments which were found accidentally stuck together by the gum, and which represent the part of the letter first completely reconstructed, begin at the phrase, 'I spoke of you shamefully, Euustace'; and end with the broken sentence, 'If, in paying me this little attention, you only encouraged me by one fond word or one fond look, I resolved not to take——' With the assistance thus afforded to us, the labour of putting together the concluding half of the letter (dated 'October 20th') was trifling, compared with the almost insurmountable difficulties which we encountered in dealing with the scattered wreck of the preceding pages.

CHAPTER XLVIII

What else could I do?

As soon as I could dry my eyes and compose my spirits, after reading the wife's pitiable and dreadful farewell, my first thought was of Eustace—my first anxiety was to prevent him from ever reading what I had read.

Yes! to this end it had come. I had devoted my life to the attainment of one object; and that object I had gained. There, on the table before me, lay the triumphant vindication of my husband's innocence; and, in mercy to him, in mercy to the memory of his dear wife, my one hope was that he might never see it! My one desire was to hide it from the public view!

I looked back at the strange circumstances under which the letter had been discovered.

It was all my doing—as the lawyer had said. And yet, what I had done, I had, so to speak, done blindfold. The merest accident might have altered the whole course of later events. I had over and over again interfered to check Ariel, when she entreated the Master to 'tell her a story.' If she had not succeeded, in spite of my opposition, Miserrimus Dexter's last effort of memory might never have been directed to the tragedy at Gleninch. And again, if I had only remembered to move my chair, and so to give Benjamin the signal to leave off, he would never have written down the apparently senseless words which have led us to the discovery of the truth.

Looking back at events in this frame of mind, the very sight of the letter sickened and horrified me. I cursed the day which had disinterred the fragments of it from their foul tomb. Just at the time when Eustace had found his weary way back to health and strength; just at the time when we were united again and happy again—when a month or two more might make us father and mother, as well as husband and wife—that frightful record of suffering and sin had risen against us like an avenging spirit. There it faced me on the table, threatening my husband's tranquillity; nay, for all I knew (if he read it at the present critical stage of his recovery), even threatening his life!

The hour struck from the clock on the mantel-piece. It was Eustace's time for paying me his morning visit, in my own little room. He might come in at any moment; he might see the letter; he might snatch the letter out of my hand. In a frenzy of terror and loathing, I caught up the vile sheets of paper, and threw them into the fire.

It was a fortunate thing that a copy only had been sent to me. If the original letter had been in its place, I believe I should have burnt the original at that moment.

The last morsel of paper had been barely consumed by the flames when the door opened, and Eustace came in.

He glanced at the fire. The black cinders of the burnt paper were still floating at the back of the grate. He had seen the letter brought to me at the breakfast-table. Did he suspect what I had done? He said nothing—he stood gravely looking into the fire. Then he advanced and fixed his eyes on me. I suppose I was very pale. The first words he spoke were words which asked me if I felt ill.

I was determined not to deceive him, even in the merest trifle.

'I am feeling a little nervous, Eustace,' I answered. 'That is all!'

He looked at me again, as if he expected me to say something more. I remained silent. He took a letter out of the breast-pocket of his coat, and laid it on the table before me—just where the Confession had lain before I destroyed it!

'I have had a letter, too, this morning,' he said. 'And *I*, Valeria, have no secrets from *you*.'

I understood the reproach which my husband's last words conveyed; but I made no attempt to answer him.

'Do you wish me to read it?' was all I said, pointing to the envelope which he had laid on the table.

'I have already said that I have no secrets from you,' he repeated. 'The envelope is open. See for yourself what is enclosed in it.'

I took it out—not a letter, but a printed paragraph, cut from a Scotch newspaper.

'Read it,' said Eustace.

I read, as follows:—

'STRANGE DOINGS AT GLENINCH.—A romance in real life seems to be in course of progress at Mr Macallan's country-house. Private excavations are taking place—if our readers will pardon us the unsavoury allusion?—at the dust-heap, of all places in the world! Something has assuredly been discovered; but nobody knows what. This alone is certain:— For weeks past, two strangers from London (superintended by our respected fellow-citizen, Mr Playmore) have been at work night and day in the library at Gleninch, with the door locked. Will the secret ever be revealed? And will it throw any light on a mysterious and shocking event which our readers have learnt to associate with the past history of Gleninch? Perhaps when Mr Macallan returns, he may be able to answer these questions. In the mean time, we can only await events.'

I laid the newspaper slip on the table, in no very Christian frame of mind towards the persons concerned in producing it. Some reporter in search of news had evidently been prying about the grounds at Gleninch, and some busybody in the neighbourhood had in all probability sent the published paragraph to Eustace. Entirely at a loss what to do, I waited for my husband to speak. He did not keep me in suspense—he questioned me instantly.

'Do you understand what it means, Valeria?'

I answered honestly—I owned that I understood what it meant.

He waited again, as if he expected me to say more. I still kept the only refuge left to me—the refuge of silence.

'Am I to know no more than I know now?' he proceeded, after an interval. 'Are you not bound to tell me what is going on in my own house?'

It is a common remark that people, if they can think at all, think quickly in emergencies. There was but one way out of the embarrassing position in which my husband's last words had placed me. My instincts showed me the way, I suppose. At any rate, I took it.

'You have promised to trust me,' I began.

He admitted that he had promised.

'I must ask you, for your own sake, Eustace, to trust me for a little while longer. I will satisfy you, if you will only give me time.'

His face darkened. 'How much longer must I wait?' he asked.

I saw that the time had come for trying some stronger form of persuasion than words.

'Kiss me,' I said, 'before I tell you!'

He hesitated (so like a husband!). And I persisted (so like a wife!). There was no choice for him but to yield. Having given me my kiss (not over-graciously), he insisted once more on knowing how much longer I wanted him to wait.

'I want you to wait,' I answered, 'until our child is born.'

He started. My condition took him by surprise. I gently pressed his hand, and gave him a look. He returned the look (warmly enough, this time, to satisfy me). 'Say you consent,' I whispered.

He consented.

So I put off the day of reckoning once more. So I gained time to consult again with Benjamin and Mr Playmore.

While Eustace remained with me in the room, I was composed, and capable of talking to him. But, when he left me, after a time, to think over what had passed between us, and to remember how kindly he had given way to me, my heart turned pityingly to those other wives (better women, some of them, than I am); whose husbands, under similar circumstances, would have spoken hard words to them, would perhaps even have acted more cruelly still. The contrast thus suggested between their fate and mine quite overcame me. What had I done to deserve my happiness? What had *they* done, poor souls, to deserve their misery? My nerves were overwrought, I dare say, after reading the dreadful confession of Eustace's first wife. I burst out crying—and I was all the better for it afterwards!

CHAPTER XLIX

Past and Future

I WRITE from memory, unassisted by notes or diaries; and I have no distinct recollection of the length of our residence abroad. It certainly extended over a period of some months. Long after Eustace was strong enough to take the journey to London, the doctors persisted in keeping him in Paris. He had shown symptoms of weakness in one of his lungs, and his medical advisers, seeing that he prospered in the dry atmosphere of France, warned him to be careful of breathing too soon the moist air of his own country.

Thus it happened that we were still in Paris, when I received my next news from Gleninch.

This time, no letters passed on either side. To my surprise and delight, Benjamin quietly made his appearance, one morning, in our pretty French drawing-room. He was so preternaturally smart in his dress, and so incomprehensibly anxious (while my husband was in the way) to make us understand that his reasons for visiting Paris were holiday reasons only, that I at once suspected him of having crossed the Channel in a double character—say, as tourist in search of pleasure, when third persons were present: as ambassador from Mr Playmore, when he and I had the room to ourselves.

Later in the day I contrived that we should be left together, and I soon found that my anticipations had not misled me. Benjamin had set out for Paris, at Mr Playmore's express request, to consult with me as to the future, and to enlighten me as to the past. He presented me with his credentials, in the shape of a little note from the lawyer.

'There are some few points' (Mr Playmore wrote) 'which the recovery of the letter does not seem to clear up. I have done my best, with Mr Benjamin's assistance, to find the right explanation of these debatable matters, and I have treated the subject, for the sake of brevity, in the form of Questions and Answers. Will you accept me as interpreter, after the mistakes I made when you consulted me in Edinburgh? Events, I admit, have proved that I was entirely wrong in trying to prevent you from returning to Dexter—and partially wrong in suspecting Dexter of being directly, instead of indirectly, answerable for the first Mrs Eustace's death! I frankly make my confession, and leave you to tell Mr Benjamin whether you think my new Catechism worthy of examination or not.'

I thought his 'new Catechism' (as he called it) decidedly worthy of examination. If you don't agree with this view, and if you are dying to be done with me and my narrative, pass on to the next chapter by all means!

Benjamin produced the Questions and Answers, and read them to me, at my request, in these terms:—

'Questions suggested by the letter discovered at Gleninch. First Group: Questions relating to the Diary. First Question:—In obtaining access to Mr Macallan's private journal, was Miserrimus Dexter guided by any previous knowledge of its contents?

'Answer:—It is doubtful if he had any such knowledge. The probabilities are that he noticed how carefully Mr Macallan secured his Diary from observation; that he inferred therefrom the existence of dangerous domestic secrets in the locked-up pages; and that he speculated on using those secrets for his own purpose, when he caused the false keys to be made.

'Second question:—To what motive are we to attribute Miserrimus Dexter's interference with the sheriff's officers, on the day when they seized Mr Macallan's Diary, along with his other papers?

'Answer:—In replying to this question, we must first do justice to Dexter himself. Infamously as we now know him to have acted, the man was not a downright fiend. That he secretly hated Mr Macallan, as his successful rival in the affections of the woman whom he loved—and that he did all he could to induce the unhappy lady to desert her husband—are, in this case, facts not to be denied. On the other hand, it is fairly to be doubted whether he was additionally capable of permitting the friend who trusted him to be tried for murder, through his fault, without making an effort to save the innocent man. It had naturally never occurred to Mr Macallan (being guiltless of his wife's death) to destroy his Diary and his letters, in the fear that they might be used against him. Until the prompt and secret action of the Fiscal took him by surprise, the idea of his being charged with the murder of his wife was an idea which we know, from his own statement, had never even entered his mind. But Dexter must have looked at the matter from another point of view. In his last wandering words (spoken when his mind broke down) he refers to the Diary in these terms, "The Diary will hang him; I won't have him hanged." If he could have found his opportunity of getting at it in time—or if the sheriff's officers had not been too quick for him—there can be no reasonable doubt that Dexter would have himself destroyed the Diary, foreseeing the consequences of its production in Court. So strongly does he appear to have felt these considerations, that he even resisted the officers in the execution of their duty. His agitation when he sent for Mr Playmore to interfere was witnessed by that gentleman, and (it may not be amiss to add) was genuine agitation beyond dispute.

'Questions of the Second Group: relating to the Wife's Confession. First Question:—What prevented Dexter from destroying the letter, when he first discovered it under the dead woman's pillow?

'Answer:—The same motives which led him to resist the seizure of the Diary, and to give his evidence in the prisoner's favour at the Trial, induced him to preserve the letter, until the verdict was known. Looking back once more at his last words (as taken down by Mr Benjamin), we may infer that if the verdict had been Guilty, he would not have hesitated to save the innocent husband by producing the wife's confession. There are degrees in all wickedness. Dexter was wicked enough to suppress the letter, which wounded his vanity by revealing him as an object for loathing and contempt—but he was not wicked enough deliberately to let an innocent man perish on the scaffold. He was capable of exposing the rival whom he hated to the infamy and torture of a public accusation of murder; but, in the event of an adverse verdict, he shrank before the direr cruelty of letting him be hanged. Reflect, in this connexion, on what he must have suffered, villain as he was, when he first read the wife's confession. He had calculated on undermining her affection for her husband—and whither had his calculations led him? He had driven the woman whom he loved to the last dreadful refuge of death by suicide! Give these considerations their due weight; and you will understand that some little redeeming virtue might show itself, as the result even of *this* man's remorse.

'Second Question:—What motive influenced Miserrimus Dexter's conduct, when Mrs (Valeria) Macallan informed him that she proposed re-opening the inquiry into the poisoning at Gleninch?

'Answer:—In all probability, Dexter's guilty fears suggested to him that he might have been watched, on the morning when he secretly entered the chamber in which the first Mrs Eustace lay dead. Feeling no scruples himself, to restrain him from listening at doors and looking through keyholes, he would be all the more ready to suspect other people of the same practices. With this dread in him, it would naturally occur to his mind that Mrs Valeria might meet with the person who had watched him, and might hear all that the person had discovered—unless he led her astray at the outset of her investigations. Her own jealous suspicions of Mrs Beauly offered him the chance of easily doing this. And he was all the readier to profit by the chance, being himself animated by the most hostile feeling towards that lady. He knew her, as the enemy who destroyed the domestic peace of the mistress of the house; he loved the mistress of the house—and he hated her enemy, accordingly. The preservation of his guilty secret, and the persecution of Mrs Beauly: there you have the greater and the lesser motive of his conduct, in his relations with Mrs Eustace the second!'[1]

Benjamin laid down his notes, and took off his spectacles.

---

[1] Note by the writer of the narrative:—Look back for a further illustration of this point of view to the scene at Benjamin's house (Chapter XXXV), where Dexter, in a moment of ungovernable agitation, betrays his own secret to Valeria.

'We have not thought it necessary to go farther than this,' he said. 'Is there any point you can think of that is still left unexplained?'

I reflected. There was no point of any importance left unexplained that I could remember. But there was one little matter (suggested by the recent allusions to Mrs Beauly) which I wished (if possible) to have thoroughly cleared up.

'Have you and Mr Playmore ever spoken together on the subject of my husband's former attachment to Mrs Beauly?' I asked. 'Has Mr Playmore ever told you why Eustace did not marry her, after the Trial?'

'I put that question to Mr Playmore myself,' said Benjamin. 'He answered it easily enough. Being your husband's confidential friend and adviser, he was consulted when Mr Eustace wrote to Mrs Beauly, after the Trial; and he repeated the substance of the letter, at my request. Would you like to hear what I remember of it, in my turn?'

I owned that I should like to hear it. What Benjamin thereupon told me, exactly coincided with what Miserrimus Dexter had told me—as related in the thirtieth chapter of my narrative. Mrs Beauly had been a witness of the public degradation of my husband. That was enough in itself to prevent him from marrying her. He broke off with *her* for the same reason which had led him to separate himself from *me*. Existence with a woman who knew that he had been tried for his life as a murderer, was an existence which he had not resolution enough to face. The two accounts agreed in every particular. At last my jealous curiosity was pacified; and Benjamin was free to dismiss the past from further consideration, and to approach the more critical and more interesting topic of the future.

His first inquiries related to Eustace. He asked if my husband had any suspicion of the proceedings which had taken place at Gleninch.

I told him what had happened, and how I had contrived to put off the inevitable disclosure for a time.

My old friend's face cleared up as he listened to me.

'This will be good news for Mr Playmore,' he said. 'Our excellent friend, the lawyer, is sorely afraid that our discoveries may compromise your position with your husband. On the one hand, he is naturally anxious to spare Mr Eustace the distress which he must certainly feel, if he reads his first wife's confession. On the other hand, it is impossible, in justice (as Mr Playmore puts it) to the unborn children of your marriage, to suppress a document which vindicates the memory of their father from the aspersion that the Scotch Verdict might otherwise cast on it.'

I listened attentively. In referring to our future, Benjamin had touched on a trouble which was still secretly preying on my mind.

'How does Mr Playmore propose to meet the difficulty?' I asked.

'He can only meet it in one way,' Benjamin replied. 'He proposes to seal up the original manuscript of the letter, and to add to it a plain statement of the circumstances under which it was discovered; supported by your signed attestation and mine, as witnesses to the facts. This done, he must leave it to you to take your husband into your confidence, at your own time. It will then be for Mr Eustace to decide whether he will open the enclosure—or whether he will leave it, with the seal unbroken, as an heirloom to his children, to be made public or not, at their discretion, when they are of an age to think for themselves. Do you consent to this, my dear? or would you prefer that Mr Playmore should see your husband, and act for you in the matter?'

I decided, without hesitation, to take the responsibility on myself. Where the question of guiding Eustace's decision was concerned, I considered my influence to be decidedly superior to the influence of Mr Playmore. My choice met with Benjamin's full approval. He arranged to write to Edinburgh, and relieve the lawyer's anxieties, by that day's post.

The one last thing now left to be settled, related to our plans for returning to England. The doctors were the authorities on this subject. I promised to consult them about it, at their next visit to Eustace.

'Have you anything more to say to me?' Benjamin inquired, as he opened his writing-case.

I thought of Miserrimus Dexter and Ariel; and I inquired if he had heard any news of them lately. My old friend sighed, and warned me that I had touched on a painful subject.

'The best thing that can happen to that unhappy man, is likely to happen,' he said. 'The one change in him is a change that threatens paralysis. You may hear of his death before you get back to England.'

'And Ariel?' I asked.

'Quite unaltered,' Benjamin answered. 'Perfectly happy so long as she is with "the Master." From all I can hear of her, poor soul, she doesn't reckon Dexter among mortal beings. She laughs at the idea of his dying; and she waits patiently, in the firm persuasion that he will recognise her again.'

Benjamin's news saddened and silenced me. I left him to his letter.

CHAPTER L

The Last of the Story

IN ten days more we returned to England, accompanied by Benjamin.

Mrs Macallan's house in London offered us ample accommodation. We gladly availed ourselves of her proposal, when she invited us to stay with her until our child was born, and our plans for the future were arranged.

keep it out of my mind. At last, an odd fancy strikes me.
the baby's hands, and put the letter under it—and so
dreadful record of sin and misery with something innocent
seems to hallow and to purify it.

pass; the half-hour longer strikes from the clock on the
and at last I hear him! He knocks softly, and opens the door.
pale: I fancy I can detect traces of tears on his cheeks. But
signs of agitation escape him, as he takes his seat by my side. I
he has waited until he could control himself—for my sake.
my hand, and kisses me tenderly.

he says. 'Let me once more ask you to forgive what I said, and
byegone time. If I understand nothing else, my love, I understand
proof of my innocence has been found; and I owe it entirely to
ge and the devotion of my wife!'

I a little, to enjoy the full luxury of hearing him say those words—to
ever the love and the gratitude that moisten his dear eyes as they look at
me. Then, I rouse my resolution, and put the momentous question on which
our future depends.

'Do you wish to see the letter, Eustace?'

Instead of answering directly, he questions me in his turn.

'Have you got the letter here?'

'Yes.'

'Sealed up?'

'Sealed up.'

He waits a little, considering what he is going to say next, before he
says it.

'Let me be sure that I know exactly what it is I have to decide,' he
proceeds. 'Suppose I insist on reading the letter——?'

There I interrupt him. I know it is my duty to restrain myself. But I
cannot do my duty.

'Darling, don't talk of reading the letter! Pray, pray spare yourself——'

holds up his hand for silence.

not thinking of myself,' he says. 'I am thinking of my dead wife. If
the public vindication of my innocence, in my own lifetime—if I
seal of the letter unbroken—do you say, as Mr Playmore says, that
acting mercifully and tenderly towards the memory of my wife?'

stace, there cannot be the shadow of a doubt of it!'

be making some little atonement for any pain that I may have
ly caused her to suffer in her lifetime?'

ria—shall I please You?'

, you will enchant me!'

e letter?'

The sad news from the asylum (for which Benjamin had prepared my
mind at Paris) reached me soon after our return to England. Miserrimus
Dexter's release from the burden of life had come to him, by slow degrees.
A few hours before he breathed his last, he rallied for a while, and
recognised Ariel at his bedside. He feebly pronounced her name, and looked
at her, and asked for me. They thought of sending for me, but it was too
late. Before the messenger could be despatched, he said, with a touch of his
old self-importance, 'Silence all of you! my brains are weary; I am going to
sleep.' He closed his eyes in slumber, and never woke again. So for this man
too the end came mercifully, without grief or pain! So that strange and
many-sided life—with its guilt and its misery, its fitful flashes of poetry
and humour, its fantastic gaiety, cruelty, and vanity—ran its destined course,
and faded out like a dream!

Alas for Ariel! She had lived for the Master—what more could she do,
now the Master was gone? She could die for him.

They had mercifully allowed her to attend the funeral of Miserrimus
Dexter—in the hope that the ceremony might avail to convince her of his
death. The anticipation was not realized; she still persisted in denying that
'the Master' had left her. They were obliged to restrain the poor creature
by force, when the coffin was lowered into the grave; and they could only
remove her from the cemetery, by the same means, when the burial service
was over. From that time, her life alternated, for a few weeks, between fits
of raving delirium, and intervals of lethargic repose. At the annual ball given
in the asylum, when the strict superintendence of the patients was in some
degree relaxed, the alarm was raised, a little before midnight, that Ariel was
missing. The nurse in charge had left her asleep, and had yielded to the
temptation of going downstairs to look at the dancing. When the woman
returned to her post, Ariel was gone. The presence of strangers, and the
confusion incidental to the festival, offered her facilities for escaping which
would not have presented themselves at any other time. That night the
search for her proved to be useless. The next morning brought with it
the last touching and terrible tidings of her. She had strayed back to the
burial-ground; and she had been found towards sunrise, dead of cold and
exposure, on Miserrimus Dexter's grave. Faithful to the last, Ariel had
followed the Master! Faithful to the last, Ariel had died on the Master's
grave!

Having written these sad words, I turn willingly to a less painful theme.

Events had separated me from Major Fitz-David, after the date of the
dinner-party which had witnessed my memorable meeting with Lady
Clarinda. From that time, I heard little or nothing of the Major; and I am
ashamed to say I had almost entirely forgotten him—when I was reminded
of the modern Don Juan, by the amazing appearance of wedding-cards,

addressed to me at my mother-in-law's house. The Major had settled in life at last. And, more wonderful still, the Major had chosen as the lawful ruler of his household and himself—'the future Queen of Song;' the round-eyed over-dressed young lady with the strident soprano voice!

We paid our visit of congratulation in due form; and we really did feel for Major Fitz-David.

The ordeal of marriage had so changed my gay and gallant admirer of former times, that I hardly knew him again. He had lost all his pretensions to youth; he had become, hopelessly and undisguisedly, an old man. Standing behind the chair on which his imperious young wife sat enthroned, he looked at her submissively between every two words that he addressed to me, as if he waited for her permission to open his lips and speak. Whenever she interrupted him—and she did it, over and over again, without ceremony—he submitted with a senile docility and admiration, at once absurd and shocking to see.

'Isn't she beautiful?' he said to me (in his wife's hearing!). 'What a figure, and what a voice! You remember her voice? It's a loss, my dear lady, an irretrievable loss, to the operatic stage! Do you know, when I think what that grand creature might have done, I sometimes ask myself if I really had any right to marry her. I feel, upon my honour I feel, as if I had committed a fraud on the public!'

As for the favoured object of this quaint mixture of admiration and regret, she was pleased to receive me graciously, as an old friend. While Eustace was talking to the Major, the bride drew me aside out of their hearing, and explained her motives for marrying, with a candour which was positively shameless.

'You see we are a large family at home, quite unprovided for!' this odious young woman whispered in my ear. 'It's all very well to talk about my being a "Queen of Song" and the rest of it. Lord bless you, I have been often enough to the opera, and I have learnt enough of my music-master, to know what it takes to make a fine singer. I haven't the patience to work at it as those foreign women do: a parcel of brazen-faced Jezebels—I hate them. No! no! between you and me, it was a great deal easier to get the money by marrying the old gentleman. Here I am, provided for—and there's all my family provided for, too,—and nothing to do but to spend the money. I am fond of my family; I'm a good daughter and sister—I am! See how I'm dressed; look at the furniture: I haven't played my cards badly, have I? It's a great advantage to marry an old man—you can twist him round your little finger. Happy? Oh, yes! I'm quite happy; and I hope you are, too. Where are you living now? I shall call soon, and have a long gossip with you. I always had a sort of liking for you, and (now I'm as good as you are) I want to be friends.'

I made a short and civil reply to this; determining inwardly that when she did visit me, she should get no farther than the house door. I don't scruple

to say that I was thoroughly disgust
to a man, that vile bargain is n
it happens to be made unde

As I sit at the desk thinking, the
from my memory—and the last sce

The place is my bedroom. The pe
excuse them), are myself and my son.
he is now lying fast asleep by his mother's s
is coming to London to baptise him. Mrs Ma
and his godfathers will be Benjamin and Mr P
my christening will pass off more merrily than my

The doctor has just left the house, in some little pe
has found me reclining as usual (latterly) in my arm
particular day, he has detected symptoms of exhaustion, w
unaccountable under the circumstances, and which warn hi
authority by sending me back to my bed.

The truth is that I have not taken the doctor into my confiden
are two causes for those signs of exhaustion which have surpa
medical attendant—and the names of them are: Anxiety and Suspens

On this day, I have at last summoned courage enough to perform t
promise which I made to my husband in Paris. He is informed, by this ti
how his wife's confession was discovered. He knows (on Mr Playm
authority) that the letter may be made the means, if he so wills it, of pub
vindicating his innocence in a Court of Law. And, last and most imp
of all, he is now aware that the Confession itself has been kept a sealed
from him, out of compassionate regard for his own peace of mind,
as for the memory of the unhappy woman who was once his wif

These necessary disclosures I have communicated to my hu
word of mouth; when the time came, I shrank from
personally of his first wife—but by a written statement of
taken mainly out of my letters received in Paris, fro
Playmore. He has now had ample time to read al
him, and to reflect on it in the retirement of his
with the fatal letter in my hand—and my mo
next room to me—to hear from his own lips
the seal or not.

The minutes pass; and still we fail to he
doubts as to which way his decision ma
uneasily the longer I wait. The very po
excited state of my nerves, oppresses a
it, or looking at it. I move it about r

and still I cannot
I lift up one of
associat that dr
and tty that
To minutes
chimy-piece
H deadl
no ard s
canhat
Es

did
th

I
lene
I'd be
Oh, Eu
'Shall I
oughtless
'Yes! yes!
'And, Va
'My darlin
'Where is t

'In your son's hand, Eustace.'

He goes round to the other side of the bed, and lifts the baby's little pink hand to his lips. For a while, he waits so, in sad and secret communion with himself. I see his mother softly open the door, and watch him as I am watching him. In a moment more, our suspense is at an end. With a heavy sigh, he lays the child's hand back again on the sealed letter; and, by that one little action, says (as if in words) to his son:—'I leave it to You!'

And so it ended! Not as I thought it would end; not perhaps as you thought it would end. What do we know of our own lives? What do we know of the fulfilment of our dearest wishes? God knows—and that is best.

Must I shut up the paper? Yes. There is nothing more for you to read, or for me to say.

Except this—as a postscript. Don't bear hardly, good people, on the follies and the errors of my husband's life. Abuse *me* as much as you please. But pray think kindly of Eustace, for my sake.

THE END

SC   Collins, Wilkie
COL   The woman in white.